ZANE GREY

FOUR COMPLETE NOVELS

SECOND SERIES

ABOUT THE AUTHOR

ZANE GREY was born in Zanesville, Ohio. Originally a dentist, his love and knowledge of Western lore, history, and geography led him to become a writer of Western novels. He was enormously successful, publishing more than sixty books, which sold more than thirteen million copies. His dramatic tales emphasize the toughness and chivalry of his cowboy heroes, and many have been made into popular movies. He also wrote many books on deep-sea and fresh-water game fishing.

ZANE GREY

FOUR COMPLETE NOVELS

SECOND SERIES

The Rainbow Trail

The Lone Star Ranger

Under the Tonto Rim

Wyoming

AVENEL BOOKS
New York

This Omnibus edition was previously published in separate volumes
under the titles:
The Rainbow Trail copyright MCMXV by Zane Grey, copyright
MCMXLIII by Lina Elise Grey.
The Lone Star Ranger copyright MCMXV by Zane Grey, copyright
MCMXLIII by Lina Elise Grey.
Under the Tonto Rim copyright MCMXXV by Curtis Publishing
Company, copyright MCMXXVI by Zane Grey, copyright MCMLIII,
© MCMLIV by Lina Elise Grey.
Wyoming copyright MCMXXXII by Pictorial Review Co.

Under the Tonto Rim appeared serially under another title, *The Bee Hunter.*
Wyoming was published serially under the title of *Young Runaway.*

This 1982 edition is published by Avenel Books,
distributed by Crown Publishers, Inc., by arrangement with
Harper & Row, Publishers, Inc.

Manufactured in the United States of America

h g f e d c b a

Library of Congress Cataloging in Publication Data

Grey, Zane, 1872–1939.
Four complete novels series II.

Contents: The lone star ranger—Under the Tonto Rim—Wyoming—[etc.]
1. Western stories.   I. Title.
PS3513.R6545A6   1982   813'.52   82-13726
ISBN: 0-517-39457X

CONTENTS

CONTENTS

THE RAINBOW TRAIL

Foreword

The spell of the desert comes back to me, as it always will come. I see the veils, like purple smoke, in the cañons, and I feel the silence. And it seems that again I must try to pierce both and to get at the strange wild life of the last American wilderness—wild still, almost, as it ever was.

While this romance is an independent story, yet readers of *Riders of the Purple Sage* will find in it an answer to a question often asked.

I wish to say also that this story has appeared serially in a different form in one of the monthly magazines under the title of "The Desert Crucible."

Zane Grey

1
Red Lake

SHEFFORD halted his tired horse and gazed with slowly realizing eyes.

A league-long slope of sage rolled and billowed down to Red Lake, a dry red basin, denuded and glistening, a hollow in the desert, a lonely and desolate door to the vast, wild, and broken upland beyond.

All day Shefford had plodded onward with the clear horizon-line a thing unattainable; and for days before that he had ridden the wild bare flats and climbed the rocky desert benches. The great colored reaches and steps had led endlessly onward and upward through dim and deceiving distance.

A hundred miles of desert travel, with its mistakes and lessons and intimations, had not prepared him for what he now saw. He beheld what seemed a world that knew only magnitude. Wonder and awe fixed his gaze, and thought remained aloof. Then that dark and unknown northland flung a menace at him. An irresistible call had drawn him to this seamed and peaked border of Arizona, this broken battlemented wilderness of Utah upland; and at first sight they frowned upon him, as if to warn him not to search for what lay hidden beyond the ranges. But Shefford thrilled with both fear and exultation. That was the country which had been described to him. Far across the red valley, far beyond the ragged line of black mesa and yellow range, lay the wild cañon with its haunting secret.

Red Lake must be his Rubicon. Either he must enter the unknown to seek, to strive, to find, or turn back and fail and never know and be always haunted. A friend's strange story had prompted his singular journey; a beautiful rainbow with its mystery and promise had decided him. Once in his life he had answered a wild call to the kingdom of adventure within him, and once in his life he had been happy. But here in the horizon-wide face of that up-flung and cloven desert he grew cold; he faltered even while he felt more fatally drawn.

As if impelled Shefford started his horse down the sandy trail, but he checked his former far-reaching gaze. It was the month of April, and the waning sun lost heat and brightness. Long shadows crept down the slope ahead of him and the scant sage deepened its gray. He watched the lizards shoot like brown streaks across the sand, leaving their slender tracks; he heard the rustle of pack-rats as they darted into their brushy homes; the whir of a low-sailing hawk startled his horse.

Like ocean waves the slope rose and fell, its hollows choked with sand, its ridge-tops showing scantier growth of sage and grass and weed. The last ridge was a sand-dune, beautifully ribbed and scalloped and lined by the wind, and from its knife-sharp crest a thin wavering sheet of sand blew, almost like smoke. Shefford wondered why the sand looked red at a distance, for here it seemed almost white. It rippled everywhere, clean and glistening, always leading down.

Suddenly Shefford became aware of a house looming out of the bareness of the slope. It dominated that long white incline. Grim, lonely, forbidding, how strangely it harmonized with the surroundings! The structure was octagon-shaped, built of uncut stone, and resembled a fort. There was no door on the sides exposed to Shefford's gaze, but small apertures two-thirds the way up probably served as windows and port-holes. The roof appeared to be made of poles covered with red earth.

Like a huge cold rock on a wide plain this house stood there on the windy slope. It was an outpost of the trader Presbrey, of whom Shefford had heard at Flagstaff and Tuba. No living thing appeared in the limit of Shefford's vision. He gazed shudderingly at the unwelcoming habitation, at the dark eyelike windows, at the sweep of barren slope merging into the vast red valley, at the bold, bleak bluffs. Could any one live here? The nature of that sinister valley forbade a home there, and the spirit of the place hovered in the silence and space. Shefford thought irresistibly of how his enemies would have consigned him to just such a hell. He thought bitterly and mockingly of the narrow congregation that had proved him a failure in the ministry, that had repudiated his ideas of religion and immortality and God, that had driven him, at the age of twenty-four, from the calling forced upon him by his people. As a boy he had yearned to make himself an artist; his family had made him a clergyman; fate had made him a failure. A failure only so far in his life, something urged him to add—for in the lonely days and silent nights of the desert he had experienced a strange birth of hope. Adventure had called him, but it was a vague and spiritual hope, a dream of promise, a nameless attainment that fortified his wilder impulse.

As he rode around a corner of the stone house his horse snorted and stopped. A lean, shaggy pony jumped at sight of him, almost displacing a red long-haired blanket that covered an Indian saddle. Quick thuds of hoofs in sand drew Shefford's attention to a corral made of peeled poles, and here he saw another pony.

Shefford heard subdued voices. He dismounted and walked to an open door. In the dark interior he dimly descried a high counter, a stairway, a pile of bags of flour, blankets, and silver-ornamented objects, but the persons he had heard were not in that part of the house. Around another corner of the octagon-shaped wall he found another open door, and through it saw goat-skins and a mound of dirty sheep-wool, black and brown and white. It was light in this part of the building. When he crossed the threshold he was astounded to see a man struggling with a girl—an Indian girl. She was straining back from him, panting, and uttering low guttural sounds. The man's face was corded and dark with passion. This scene affected Shefford strangely. Primitive emotions were new to him.

Before Shefford could speak the girl broke loose and turned to flee. She was an Indian and this place was the uncivilized desert, but Shefford knew terror when he saw it. Like a dog the man rushed after her. It was instinct that made Shefford strike, and his blow laid the man flat. He lay stunned a moment, then raised himself to a sitting posture, his hand to his face, and the gaze he fixed upon Shefford seemed to combine astonishment and rage.

"I hope you're not Presbrey," said Shefford, slowly. He felt awkward, not sure of himself.

The man appeared about to burst into speech, but repressed it. There was blood on his mouth and his hand. Hastily he scrambled to his feet. Shefford saw this man's amaze and rage change to shame. He was tall and rather stout; he had a smooth tanned face, soft of outline, with a weak chin; his eyes were dark. The look of him and his corduroys and his soft shoes gave Shefford an impression that he was not a man who worked hard. By contrast with the few other worn and rugged desert men Shefford had met, this stranger stood out strikingly. He stooped to pick up a soft felt hat and, jamming it on his head, he hurried out. Shefford followed him and watched him from the door. He went directly to the corral, mounted the pony, and rode out, to turn down the slope toward the south. When he reached the level of the basin, where evidently the sand was hard, he put the pony to a lope and gradually drew away.

"Well!" ejaculated Shefford. He did not know what to make of this adventure. Presently he became aware that the Indian girl was sitting on a roll of blankets near the wall. With curious interest Shefford studied her appearance. She had long, raven-black hair, tangled and disheveled, and she wore a soiled white band of cord above her brow. The color of her face struck him; it was dark, but not red nor bronzed; it almost had a tinge of gold. Her profile was clear-cut, bold, almost stern. Long black eyelashes hid her eyes. She wore a tight-fitting waist garment of material resembling velveteen. It was ripped along her side, exposing a skin still more richly gold than that of her face. A string of silver ornaments

and turquoise-and-white beads encircled her neck, and it moved gently up and
down with the heaving of her full bosom. Her skirt was some gaudy print goods,
torn and stained and dusty. She had little feet, encased in brown moccasins,
fitting like gloves and buttoning over the ankles with silver coins.

"Who was that man? Did he hurt you?" inquired Shefford, turning to gaze
down the valley where a moving black object showed on the bare sand.

"No savvy," replied the Indian girl.

"Where's the trader Presbrey?" asked Shefford.

She pointed straight down into the red valley.

"Toh," she said.

In the center of the basin lay a small pool of water shining brightly in the
sunset glow. Small objects moved around it, so small that Shefford thought he
saw several dogs led by a child. But it was the distance that deceived him. There
was a man down there watering his horses. That reminded Shefford of the duty
owing to his own tired and thirsty beast. Whereupon he untied his pack, took
off the saddle, and was about ready to start down when the Indian girl grasped
the bridle from his hand.

"Me go," she said.

He saw her eyes then, and they made her look different. They were as black
as her hair. He was puzzled to decide whether or not he thought her handsome.

"Thanks, but I'll go," he replied, and, taking the bridle again, he started
down the slope. At every step he sank into the deep, soft sand. Down a little
way he came upon a pile of tin cans; they were everywhere, buried, half buried,
and lying loose; and these gave evidence of how the trader lived. Presently
Shefford discovered that the Indian girl was following him with her own pony.
Looking upward at her against the light, he thought her slender, lithe, picturesque.
At a distance he liked her.

He plodded on, at length glad to get out of the drifts of sand to the hard level
floor of the valley. This, too, was sand, but dried and baked hard, and red in
color. At some season of the year this immense flat must be covered with water.
How wide it was, and empty! Shefford experienced again a feeling that had been
novel to him—and it was that he was loose, free, unanchored, ready to veer
with the wind. From the foot of the slope the water hole had appeared to be a
few hundred rods out in the valley. But the small size of the figures made
Shefford doubt; and he had to travel many times a few hundred rods before those
figures began to grow. Then Shefford made out that they were approaching him.

Thereafter they rapidly increased to normal proportions of man and beast.
When Shefford met them he saw a powerful, heavily built young man leading
two ponies.

"You're Mr. Presbrey, the trader?" inquired Shefford.

"Yes, I'm Presbrey, without the Mister," he replied.

"My name's Shefford. I'm knocking about on the desert. Rode from beyond Tuba to-day."

"Glad to see you," said Presbrey. He offered his hand. He was a stalwart man, clad in gray shirt, overalls, and boots. A shock of tumbled light hair covered his massive head; he was tanned, but not darkly, and there was red in his cheeks; under his shaggy eyebrows were deep, keen eyes; his lips were hard and set, as if occasion for smiles or words was rare; and his big, strong jaw seemed locked.

"Wish more travelers came knocking around Red Lake," he added. "Reckon here's the jumping-off place."

"It's pretty—lonesome," said Shefford, hesitating as if at a loss for words.

Then the Indian girl came up. Presbrey addressed her in her own language, which Shefford did not understand. She seemed shy and would not answer; she stood with downcast face and eyes. Presbrey spoke again, at which she pointed down the valley, and then moved on with her pony toward the water-hole.

Presbrey's keen eyes fixed on the receding black dot far down that oval expanse.

"That fellow left—rather abruptly," said Shefford, constrainedly. "Who was he?"

"His name's Willetts. He's a missionary. He rode in to-day with this Navajo girl. He was taking her to Blue Cañon, where he lives and teaches the Indians. I've met him only a few times. You see, not many white men ride in here. He's the first white man I've seen in six months, and you're the second. Both the same day! . . . Red Lake's getting popular! It's queer, though, his leaving. He expected to stay all night. There's no other place to stay. Blue Cañon is fifty miles away."

"I'm sorry to say—no, I'm not sorry, either—but I must tell you I was the cause of Mr. Willetts leaving," replied Shefford.

"How so?" inquired the other.

Then Shefford related the incident following his arrival.

"Perhaps my action was hasty," he concluded, apologetically. "I didn't think. Indeed, I'm surprised at myself."

Presbrey made no comment and his face was as hard to read as one of the distant bluffs.

"But what did the man mean?" asked Shefford, conscious of a little heat. "I'm a stranger out here. I'm ignorant of Indians—how they're controlled. Still I'm no fool. . . . If Willetts didn't mean evil, at least he was brutal."

"He was teaching her religion," replied Presbrey. His tone held faint scorn and implied a joke, but his face did not change in the slightest.

Without understanding just why, Shefford felt his conviction justified and his action approved. Then he was sensible of a slight shock of wonder and disgust.

"I am—I was a minister of the Gospel," he said to Presbrey. "What you hint seems impossible. I can't believe it."

"I didn't hint," replied Presbrey, bluntly, and it was evident that he was a sincere, but close-mouthed, man. "Shefford, so you're a preacher? . . . Did you come out here to try to convert the Indians?"

"No. I said I *was* a minister. I am no longer. I'm just a—a wanderer."

"I see. Well, the desert's no place for missionaries, but it's good for wanderers. . . . Go water your horse and take him up to the corral. You'll find some hay for him. I'll get grub ready."

Shefford went on with his horse to the pool. The water appeared thick, green, murky, and there was a line of salty crust extending around the margin of the pool. The thirsty horse splashed in and eagerly bent his head. But he did not like the taste. Many times he refused to drink, yet always lowered his nose again. Finally he drank, though not his fill. Shefford saw the Indian girl drink from her hand. He scooped up a handful and found it too sour to swallow. When he turned to retrace his steps she mounted her pony and followed him.

A golden flare lit up the western sky, and silhouetted dark and lonely against it stood the trading-post. Upon his return Shefford found the wind rising, and it chilled him. When he reached the slope thin gray sheets of sand were blowing low, rising, whipping, falling, sweeping along with soft silken rustle. Sometimes the gray veils hid his boots. It was a long, toilsome climb up that yielding, dragging ascent, and he had already been lame and tired. By the time he had put his horse away twilight was everywhere except in the west. The Indian girl left her pony in the corral and came like a shadow toward the house.

Shefford had difficulty in finding the foot of the stairway. He climbed to enter a large loft, lighted by two lamps. Presbrey was there, kneading biscuit dough in a pan.

"Make yourself comfortable," he said.

The huge loft was the shape of a half-octagon. A door opened upon the valley side, and here, too, there were windows. How attractive the place was in comparison with the impressions gained from the outside! The furnishings consisted of Indian blankets on the floor, two beds, a desk and table, several chairs and a couch, a gun-rack full of rifles, innumerable silver-ornamented belts, bridles, and other Indian articles upon the walls, and in one corner a wood-burning stove with teakettle steaming, and a great cupboard with shelves packed full of canned foods.

Shefford leaned in the doorway and looked out. Beneath him on a roll of blankets sat the Indian girl, silent and motionless. He wondered what was in her mind, what she would do, how the trader would treat her. The slope now was a long slant of sheeted moving shadows of sand. Dusk had gathered in the valley. The bluffs loomed black beyond. A pale star twinkled above. Shefford suddenly became aware of the intense nature of the stillness about him. Yet, as he listened to this silence, he heard an intermittent and immeasurably low moan, a fitful, mournful murmur. Assuredly it was only the wind. Nevertheless, it made his blood run cold. It was a different wind from that which had made music under the eaves of his Illinois home. This was a lonely, haunting wind, with desert hunger in it, and more which he could not name. Shefford listened to this spirit-brooding sound while he watched night envelop the valley. How black, how thick the mantle! Yet it brought no comforting sense of close-folded protection, of walls of soft sleep, of a home. Instead there was the feeling of space, of emptiness, of an infinite hall down which a mournful wind swept streams of murmuring sand.

"Well, grub's about ready," said Presbrey.

"Got any water?" asked Shefford.

"Sure. There in the bucket. It's rain-water. I have a tank here."

Shefford's sore and blistered face felt better after he had washed off the sand and alkali dust.

"Better not wash your face often while you're in the desert. Bad plan," went on Presbrey, noting how gingerly his visitor had gone about his ablutions. "Well, come and eat."

Shefford marked that if the trader did live a lonely life he fared well. There was more on the table than twice two men could have eaten. It was the first time in four days that Shefford had sat at a table, and he made up for lost opportunity. His host's actions indicated pleasure, yet the strange, hard face never relaxed, never changed. When the meal was finished Presbrey declined assistance, had a generous thought of the Indian girl, who, he said, could have a place to eat and sleep down-stairs, and then with the skill and despatch of an accomplished housewife cleared the table, after which work he filled a pipe and evidently prepared to listen.

It took only one question for Shefford to find that the trader was starved for news of the outside world; and for an hour Shefford fed that appetite, even as he had been done by. But when he had talked himself out there seemed indication of Presbrey being more than a good listener.

"How'd you come in?" he asked, presently.

"By Flagstaff—across the Little Colorado—and through Moencopie."

"Did you stop at Moen Ave?"

"No. What place is that?"

"A missionary lives there. Did you stop at Tuba?"

"Only long enough to drink and water my horse. That was a wonderful spring for the desert."

"You said you were a wanderer. . . . Do you want a job? I'll give you one."

"No, thank you, Presbrey."

"I saw your pack. That's no pack to travel with in this country. Your horse won't last, either. Have you any money?"

"Yes, plenty of money."

"Well, that's good. Not that a white man out here would ever take a dollar from you. But you can buy from the Indians as you go. Where are you making for, anyhow?"

Shefford hesitated, debating in mind whether to tell his purpose or not. His host did not press the question.

"I see. Just foot-loose and wandering around," went on Presbrey. "I can understand how the desert appeals to you. Preachers lead easy, safe, crowded, bound lives. They're shut up in a church with a Bible and good people. When once in a lifetime they get loose—they break out."

"Yes, I've broken out—beyond all bounds," replied Shefford, sadly. He seemed retrospective for a moment, unaware of the trader's keen and sympathetic glance, and then he caught himself. "I want to see some wild life. Do you know the country north of here?"

"Only what the Navajos tell me. And they're not much to talk. There's a trail goes north, but I've never traveled it. It's a new trail every time an Indian goes that way, for here the sand blows and covers old tracks. But few Navajos ride in from the north. My trade is mostly with Indians up and down the valley."

"How about water and grass?"

"We've had rain and snow. There's sure to be water. Can't say about grass, though the sheep and ponies from the north are always fat. . . . But, say, Shefford, if you'll excuse me for advising you—don't go north."

"Why?" asked Shefford, and it was certain that he thrilled.

"It's unknown country, terribly broken, as you can see from here, and there are bad Indians hiding in the cañons. I've never met a man who had been over the pass between here and Kayenta. The trip's been made, so there must be a trail. But it's a dangerous trip for any man, let alone a tenderfoot. You're not even packing a gun."

"What's this place Kayenta?" asked Shefford.

"It's a spring. Kayenta means Bottomless Spring. There's a little trading-post, the last and the wildest in northern Arizona. Withers, the trader who keeps it, hauls his supplies in from Colorado and New Mexico. He's never come down this way. I never saw him. Know nothing of him except hearsay. Reckon he's a nervy and strong man to hold that post. If you want to go there, better go by way of Keams Cañon, and then around the foot of Black Mesa. It 'll be a long ride—maybe two hundred miles."

"How far straight north over the pass?"

"Can't say. Upward of seventy-five miles over rough trails, if there are trails at all. . . . I've heard rumors of a fine tribe of Navajos living in there, rich in sheep and horses. It may be true and it may not. But I do know there are bad Indians, half-breeds and outcasts, hiding in there. Some of them have visited me here. Bad customers! More than that, you'll be going close to the Utah line, and the Mormons over there are unfriendly these days."

"Why?" queried Shefford, again with that curious thrill.

"They are being persecuted by the government."

Shefford asked no more questions and his host vouchsafed no more information on that score. The conversation lagged. Then Shefford inquired about the Indian girl and learned that she lived up the valley somewhere. Presbrey had never seen her before Willetts came with her to Red Lake. And this query brought out the fact that Presbrey was comparatively new to Red Lake and vicinity. Shefford wondered why a lonely six months there had not made the trader old in experience. Probably the desert did not readily give up its secrets. Moreover, this Red Lake house was only an occasionally used branch of Presbrey's main trading-post, which was situated at Willow Springs, fifty miles westward over the mesa.

"I'm closing up here soon for a spell," said Presbrey, and now his face lost its set hardness and seemed singularly changed. It was a difference of light and softness. "Won't be so lonesome over at Willow Springs. . . . I'm being married soon."

"That's fine," replied Shefford, warmly. He was glad for the sake of this lonely desert man. What good a wife would bring into a trader's life!

Presbrey's naïve admission, however, appeared to detach him from his present surroundings, and with his massive head enveloped by a cloud of smoke he lived in dreams.

Shefford respected his host's serene abstraction. Indeed, he was grateful for silence. Not for many nights had the past impinged so closely upon the present. The wound in his soul had not healed, and to speak of himself made it bleed anew. Memory was too poignant; the past was too close; he wanted to forget until he had toiled into the heart of this forbidding wilderness—until time had gone by and he dared to face his unquiet soul. Then he listened to the steadily rising roar of the wind. How strange and hollow! That wind was freighted with heavy sand, and he heard it sweep, sweep, sweep by in gusts, and then blow with dull, steady blast against the walls. The sound was provocative of thought. This moan and rush of wind was no dream—this presence of his in a night-enshrouded and sand-besieged house of the lonely desert was a reality—this adventure was not one of fancy. True indeed, then, must be the wild, strange story that had led him hither. He was going on to seek, to strive, to find. Somewhere northward in the broken fastnesses lay hidden a valley walled in from the world. Would they be there, those lost fugitives whose story had thrilled him? After twelve years would she be alive, a child grown to womanhood in the solitude of a beautiful cañon? Incredible! Yet he believed his friend's story and he indeed knew how strange and tragic life was. He fancied he heard her voice on the sweeping wind. She called to him, haunted him. He admitted the improbability of her existence, but lost nothing of the persistent intangible hope that drove him. He believed himself a man stricken in soul, unworthy, through doubt of God, to minister to the people who had banished him. Perhaps a labor of Hercules, a mighty and perilous work of rescue, the saving of this lost and imprisoned girl, would help him in his trouble. She might be his salvation. Who could tell? Always as a boy and as a man he had fared forth to find the treasure at the foot of the rainbow.

2
The Sagi

NEXT morning the Indian girl was gone and the tracks of her pony led north. Shefford's first thought was to wonder if he would overtake her on the trail; and this surprised him with the proof of how unconsciously his resolve to go on had formed.

Presbrey made no further attempt to turn Shefford back. But he insisted on replenishing the pack, and that Shefford take weapons. Finally Shefford was persuaded to accept a revolver. The trader bade him good-by and stood in the door while Shefford led his horse down the slope toward the water-hole. Perhaps the trader believed he was watching the departure of a man who would never return. He was still standing at the door of the post when Shefford halted at the pool.

Upon the level floor of the valley lay thin patches of snow which had fallen during the night. The air was biting cold, yet stimulated Shefford while it stung him. His horse drank rather slowly and disgustedly. Then Shefford mounted and reluctantly turned his back upon the trading-post.

As he rode away from the pool he saw a large flock of sheep approaching. They were very closely, even densely, packed, in a solid slow-moving mass, and coming with a precision almost like a march. This fact surprised Shefford, for there was not an Indian in sight. Presently he saw that a dog was leading the flock, and a little later he discovered another dog in the rear of the sheep. They were splendid, long-haired dogs, of a wild-looking shepherd breed. He halted his horse to watch the procession pass by. The flock covered fully an acre of ground and the sheep were black, white, and brown. They passed him, making a little pattering roar on the hard-caked sand. The dogs were taking the sheep in to water.

Shefford went on and was drawing close to the other side of the basin, where the flat red level was broken by rising dunes and ridges, when he espied a bunch of ponies. A shrill whistle told him that they had seen him. They were wild, shaggy, with long manes and tails. They stopped, threw up their heads, and watched him. Shefford certainly returned the attention. There was no Indian with them. Presently, with a snort, the leader, which appeared to be a stallion, trotted behind the others, seemed to be driving them, and went clear round the band to get in the lead again. He was taking them in to water, the same as the dogs had taken the sheep.

These incidents were new and pleasing to Shefford. How ignorant he had been of life in the wilderness! Once more he received subtle intimations of what he might learn out in the open; and it was with a less weighted heart that he faced the gateway between the huge yellow bluffs on his left and the slow rise of ground to the black mesa on his right. He looked back in time to see the trading-post, bleak and lonely on the bare slope, pass out of sight behind the bluffs. Shefford felt no fear—he really had little experience of physical fear—but it was certain that he gritted his teeth and welcomed whatever was to come to him. He had lived a narrow, insulated life with his mind on spiritual things; his family and his congregation and his friends—except that one new friend whose story had enthralled him—were people of quiet religious habit; the man deep down in him had never had a chance. He breathed hard as he tried to imagine the world opening to him, and almost dared to be glad for the doubt that had sent him adrift.

The tracks of the Indian girl's pony were plain in the sand. Also there were other tracks, not so plain, and these Shefford decided had been made by Willetts and the girl the day before. He climbed a ridge, half soft sand and half hard, and saw right before him, rising in striking form, two great yellow buttes, like elephant legs. He rode between them, amazed at their height. Then before him stretched a slowly ascending valley, walled on one side by the black mesa and on the other by low bluffs. For miles a dark-green growth of greasewood covered the valley, and Shefford could see where the green thinned and failed, to give place to sand. He trotted his horse and made good time on this stretch.

The day contrasted greatly with any he had yet experienced. Gray clouds obscured the walls of rock a few miles to the west, and Shefford saw squalls of snow like huge veils dropping down and spreading out. The wind cut with the keenness of a knife. Soon he was chilled to the bone. A squall swooped and roared down upon him, and the wind that bore the driving white pellets of snow, almost like hail, was so freezing bitter cold that the former wind seemed warm

in comparison. The squall passed as swiftly as it had come, and it left Shefford
so benumbed he could not hold the bridle. He tumbled off his horse and walked.
By and by the sun came out and soon warmed him and melted the thin layer of
snow on the sand. He was still on the trail of the Indian girl, but hers were now
the only tracks he could see.

All morning he gradually climbed, with limited view, until at last he mounted
to a point where the country lay open to his sight on all sides except where the
endless black mesa ranged on into the north. A rugged yellow peak dominated
the landscape to the fore, but it was far away. Red and ragged country extended
westward to a huge flat-topped wall of gray rock. Lowering swift clouds swept
across the sky, like drooping mantles, and they darkened the sun. Shefford built
a little fire out of dead greasewood sticks, and with his blanket round his shoulders
he hung over the blaze, scorching his clothes and hands. He had been cold before
in his life, but he had never before appreciated fire. This desert blast pierced
him. The squall enveloped him, thicker and colder and windier than the other,
but, being better fortified, he did not suffer so much. It howled away, hiding
the mesa and leaving a white desert behind. Shefford walked on, leading his
horse, until the exercise and the sun had once more warmed him.

This last squall had rendered the Indian girl's trail difficult to follow. The
snow did not quickly melt, and, besides, sheep tracks and the tracks of horses
gave him trouble, until at last he was compelled to admit that he could not follow
her any longer. A faint path or trail led north, however, and, following that, he
soon forgot the girl. Every surmounted ridge held a surprise for him. The desert
seemed never to change in the vast whole that encompassed him, yet near him
it was always changing. From Red Lake he had seen a peaked, walled, and
cañoned country, as rough as a stormy sea; but when he rode into that country
the sharp and broken features held to the distance.

He was glad to get out of the sand. Long narrow flats, gray with grass and
dotted with patches of greasewood, and lined by low bare ridges of yellow rock,
stretched away from him, leading toward the yellow peak that seemed never to
be gained upon.

Shefford had pictures in his mind, pictures of stone walls and wild valleys
and domed buttes, all of which had been painted in colorful and vivid words by
his friend Venters. He believed he would recognize the distinctive and remarkable
landmarks Venters had portrayed, and he was certain that he had not yet come
upon one of them. This was his second lonely day of travel and he had grown
more and more susceptible to the influence of horizon and the different prominent
points. He attributed a gradual change in his feelings to the loneliness and the
increasing wildness. Between Tuba and Flagstaff he had met Indians and an
occasional prospector and teamster. Here he was alone, and though he felt some
strange gladness, he could not help but see the difference.

He rode on during the gray, lowering, chilly day, and toward evening the clouds broke in the west, and a setting sun shone through the rift, burnishing the desert to red and gold. Shefford's instinctive but deadened love of the beautiful in nature stirred into life, and the moment of its rebirth was a melancholy and sweet one. Too late for the artist's work, but not too late for his soul!

For a place to make camp he halted near a low area of rock that lay like an island in a sea of grass. There was an abundance of dead greasewood for a camp-fire, and, after searching over the rock, he found little pools of melted snow in the depressions. He took off the saddle and pack, watered his horse, and, hobbling him as well as his inexperience permitted, he turned him loose on the grass.

Then while he built a fire and prepared a meal the night came down upon him. In the lee of the rock he was well sheltered from the wind, but the air was bitter cold. He gathered all the dead greasewood in the vicinity, replenished the fire, and rolled in his blanket, back to the blaze. The loneliness and the coyotes did not bother him this night. He was too tired and cold. He went to sleep at once and did not awaken until the fire died out. Then he rebuilt it and went to sleep again. Every half-hour all night long he repeated this, and was glad indeed when the dawn broke.

The day began with misfortune. His horse was gone; it had been stolen, or had walked out of sight, or had broken the hobbles and made off. From a high stone ridge Shefford searched the grassy flats and slopes, all to no purpose. Then he tried to track the horse, but this was equally futile. He had expected disasters, and the first one did not daunt him. He tied most of his pack in the blanket, threw the canteen across his shoulder, and set forth, sure at least of one thing— that he was a very much better traveler on foot than on horseback.

Walking did not afford him the leisure to study the surrounding country; however, from time to time, when he surmounted a bench he scanned the different landmarks that had grown familiar. It took hours of steady walking to reach and pass the yellow peak that had been a kind of goal. He saw many sheep trails and horse tracks in the vicinity of this mountain, and once he was sure he espied an Indian watching him from a bold ridge-top.

The day was bright and warm, with air so clear it magnified objects he knew to be far away. The ascent was gradual; there were many narrow flats connected by steps; and the grass grew thicker and longer. At noon Shefford halted under the first cedar-tree, a lonely, dwarfed shrub that seemed to have had a hard life. From this point the rise of ground was more perceptible, and straggling cedars led the eye on to a purple slope that merged into green of piñon and pine. Could that purple be the sage Venters had so feelingly described, or was it merely the purple of deceiving distance? Whatever it might be, it gave Shefford a thrill and made him think of the strange, shy, and lovely woman Venters had won out here in this purple-sage country.

He calculated that he had ridden thirty miles the day before and had already traveled ten miles today, and therefore could hope to be in the pass before night. Shefford resumed his journey with too much energy and enthusiasm to think of being tired. And he discovered presently that the straggling cedars and the slope beyond were much closer than he had judged them to be. He reached the sage to find it gray instead of purple. Yet it was always purple a little way ahead, and if he half shut his eyes it was purple near at hand. He was surprised to find that he could not breathe freely, or it seemed so, and soon made the discovery that the sweet, pungent, penetrating fragrance of sage and cedar had this strange effect upon him. This was an exceedingly dry and odorous forest, where every open space between the clumps of cedars was choked with luxuriant sage. The piñons were higher up on the mesa, and the pines still higher. Shefford appeared to lose himself. There were no trails; the black mesa on the right and the wall of stone on the left could not be seen; but he pushed on with what was either singular confidence or rash impulse. And he did not know whether that slope was long or short.

Once at the summit he saw with surprise that it broke abruptly and the descent was very steep and short on that side. Through the trees he once more saw the black mesa, rising to the dignity of a mountain; and he had glimpses of another flat, narrow valley, this time with a red wall running parallel with the mesa. He could not help but hurry down to get an unobstructed view. His eagerness was rewarded by a splendid scene, yet to his regret he could not force himself to believe it had any relation to the pictured scenes in his mind. The valley was half a mile wide, perhaps several miles long, and it extended in a curve between the cedar-sloped mesa and a looming wall of red stone. There was not a bird or a beast in sight. He found a well-defined trail, but it had not been recently used. He passed a low structure made of peeled logs and mud, with a dark opening like a door. It did not take him many minutes to learn that the valley was longer than he had calculated. He walked swiftly and steadily, in spite of the fact that the pack had become burdensome. What lay beyond the jutting corner of the mesa had increasing fascination for him and acted as a spur. At last he turned the corner, only to be disappointed at sight of another cedar slope. He had a glimpse of a single black shaft of rock rising far in the distance, and it disappeared as his striding forward made the crest of the slope rise toward the sky.

Again his view became restricted, and he lost the sense of a slow and gradual uplift of rock and an increase in the scale of proportion. Half-way up this ascent he was compelled to rest; and again the sun was slanting low when he entered the cedar forest. Soon he was descending, and he suddenly came into the open to face a scene that made his heart beat thick and fast.

He saw lofty crags and cathedral spires, and a wonderful cañon winding between huge beetling red walls. He heard the murmur of flowing water. The trail led down to the cañon floor, which appeared to be level and green and cut by deep washes in red earth. Could this cañon be the mouth of Deception Pass? It bore no resemblance to any place Shefford had heard described, yet somehow he felt rather than saw that it was the portal to the wild fastness he had traveled so far to enter.

Not till he had descended the trail and had dropped his pack did he realize how weary and footsore he was. Then he rested. But his eyes roved to and fro, and his mind was active. What a wild and lonesome spot! The low murmur of shallow water came up to him from a deep, narrow cleft. Shadows were already making the cañon seem full of blue haze. He saw a bare slope of stone out of which cedar-trees were growing. And as he looked about him he became aware of a singular and very perceptible change in the lights and shades. The sun was setting; the crags were gold-tipped; the shadows crept upward; the sky seemed to darken swiftly; then the gold changed to red, slowly dulled, and the grays and purples stood out. Shefford was entranced with the beautiful changing effects, and watched till the walls turned black and the sky grew steely and a faint star peeped out. Then he set about the necessary camp tasks.

Dead cedars right at hand assured him a comfortable night with steady fire; and when he had satisfied his hunger he arranged an easy seat before the blazing logs, and gave his mind over to thought of his weird, lonely environment.

The murmur of running water mingled in harmonious accompaniment with the moan of the wind in the cedars—wild, sweet sounds that were balm to his wounded spirit! They seemed a part of the silence, rather than a break in it or a hindrance to the feeling of it. But suddenly that silence did break to the rattle of a rock. Shefford listened, thinking some wild animal was prowling around. He felt no alarm. Presently he heard the sound again, and again. Then he recognized the crack of unshod hoofs upon rock. A horse was coming down the trail. Shefford rather resented the interruption, though he still had no alarm. He believed he was perfectly safe. As a matter of fact, he had never in his life been anything but safe and padded around with wool, hence, never having experienced peril, he did not know what fear was.

Presently he saw a horse and rider come into dark prominence on the ridge just above his camp. They were silhouetted against the starry sky. The horseman stopped and he and his steed made a magnificent black statue, somehow wild and strange, in Shefford's sight. Then he came on, vanished in the darkness under the ridge, presently to emerge into the circle of camp-fire light.

He rode to within twenty feet of Shefford and the fire. The horse was dark, wild-looking, and seemed ready to run. The rider appeared to be an Indian, and yet had something about him suggesting the cowboy. At once Shefford remem-

bered what Presbrey had said about half-breeds. A little shock, inexplicable to
Shefford, rippled over him.

He greeted his visitor, but received no answer. Shefford saw a dark, squat
figure bending forward in the saddle. The man was tense. All about him was
dark except the glint of a rifle across the saddle. The face under the sombrero
was only a shadow. Shefford kicked the fire-logs and a brighter blaze lightened
the scene. Then he saw this stranger a little more clearly, and made out an
unusually large head, broad dark face, a sinister tight-shut mouth, and gleaming
black eyes.

Those eyes were unmistakably hostile. They roved searchingly over Shefford's
pack and then over his person. Shefford felt for the gun that Presbrey had given
him. But it was gone. He had left it back where he had lost his horse, and had
not thought of it since. Then a strange, slow-coming cold agitation possessed
Shefford. Something gripped his throat.

Suddenly Shefford was stricken at a menacing movement on the part of the
horseman. He had drawn a gun. Shefford saw it shine darkly in the firelight.
The Indian meant to murder him. Shefford saw the grim, dark face in a kind of
horrible amaze. He felt the meaning of that drawn weapon as he had never felt
anything before in his life. And he collapsed back into his seat with an icy,
sickening terror. In a second he was dripping wet with cold sweat. Lightning-
swift thoughts flashed through his mind. It had been one of his platitudes that
he was not afraid of death. Yet here he was a shaking, helpless coward. What
had he learned about either life or death? Would this dark savage plunge him
into the unknown? It was then that Shefford realized his hollow philosophy and
the bitter-sweetness of life. He had a brain and a soul, and between them he
might have worked out his salvation. But what were they to this ruthless night-
wanderer, this raw and horrible wildness of the desert?

Incapable of voluntary movement, with tongue cleaving to the roof of his
mouth, Shefford watched the horseman and the half-poised gun. It was not yet
leveled. Then it dawned upon Shefford that the stranger's head was turned a
little, his ear to the wind. He was listening. His horse was listening. Suddenly
he straightened up, wheeled his horse, and trotted away into the darkness. But
he did not climb the ridge down which he had come.

Shefford heard the click of hoofs upon the stony trail. Other horses and riders
were descending into the cañon. They had been the cause of his deliverance,
and in the relaxation of feeling he almost fainted. Then he sat there, slowly
recovering, slowly ceasing to tremble, divining that this situation was somehow
to change his attitude toward life.

Three horses, two with riders, moved in dark shapes across the sky-line above
the ridge, disappeared as had Shefford's first visitor, and then rode into the light.
Shefford saw two Indians—a man and a woman; then with surprise recognized

the latter to be the Indian girl he had met at Red Lake. He was still more surprised to recognize in the third horse the one he had lost at the last camp. Shefford rose, a little shaky on his legs, to thank these Indians for a double service. The man slipped from his saddle and his moccasined feet thudded lightly. He was tall, lithe, erect, a singularly graceful figure, and as he advanced Shefford saw a dark face and sharp, dark eyes. The Indian was bareheaded, with his hair bound in a band. He resembled the girl, but appeared to have a finer face.

"How do?" he said, in a voice low and distinct. He extended his hand, and Shefford felt a grip of steel. He returned the greeting. Then the Indian gave Shefford the bridle of the horse, and made signs that appeared to indicate the horse had broken his hobbles and strayed. Shefford thanked him. Thereupon the Indian unsaddled and led the horses away, evidently to water them. The girl remained behind. Shefford addressed her, but she was shy and did not respond. He then set about cooking a meal for his visitors, and was busily engaged at this when the Indian returned without the horses. Presently Shefford resumed his seat by the fire and watched the two eat what he had prepared. They certainly were hungry and soon had the pans and cups empty. Then the girl drew back a little into the shadow, while the man sat with his legs crossed and his feet tucked under him.

His dark face was smooth, yet it seemed to have lines under the surface. Shefford was impressed. He had never seen an Indian who interested him as this one. Looked at superficially, he appeared young, wild, silent, locked in his primeval apathy, just a healthy savage; but looked at more attentively, he appeared matured, even old, a strange, sad, brooding figure, with a burden on his shoulders. Shefford found himself growing curious.

"What place?" asked Shefford, waving his hand toward the dark opening between the black cliffs.

"Sagi," replied the Indian.

That did not mean anything to Shefford, and he asked if the Sagi was the pass, but the Indian shook his head.

"Wife?" asked Shefford, pointing to the girl.

The Indian shook his head again. "*Bi-la,*" he said.

"What you mean?" asked Shefford. "What *bi-la*?"

"Sister," replied the Indian. He spoke the word reluctantly, as if the white man's language did not please him, but the clearness and correct pronunciation surprised Shefford.

"What name—what call her?" he went on.

"Glen Naspa."

"What your name?" inquired Shefford, indicating the Indian.

"Nas Ta Bega," answered the Indian.

"Navajo?"

The Indian bowed with what seemed pride and stately dignity.

"My name John Shefford. Come far 'way back toward rising sun. Come stay here long."

Nas Ta Bega's dark eyes were fixed steadily upon Shefford. He reflected that he could not remember having felt so penetrating a gaze. But neither the Indian's eyes nor face gave any clue to his thoughts.

"Navajo no savvy Jesus Christ," said the Indian, and his voice rolled out low and deep.

Shefford felt both amaze and pain. The Indian had taken him for a missionary.

"No! . . . Me no missionary," cried Shefford, and he flung up a passionately repudiating hand.

A singular flash shot from the Indian's dark eyes. It struck Shefford even at this stinging moment when the past came back.

"Trade—buy wool—blanket?" queried Nas Ta Bega.

"No," replied Shefford. "Me want ride—walk far." He waved his hand to indicate a wide sweep of territory. "Me sick."

Nas Ta Bega laid a significant finger upon his lungs.

"No," replied Shefford. "Me strong. Sick here." And with motions of his hands he tried to show that his was a trouble of the heart.

Shefford received instant impression of this Indian's intelligent comprehension, but he could not tell just what had given him the feeling. Nas Ta Bega rose then and walked away into the shadow. Shefford heard him working around the dead cedar-tree, where he had probably gone to get fire-wood. Then Shefford heard a splintering crash, which was followed by a crunching, bumping sound. Presently he was astounded to see the Indian enter the lighted circle dragging the whole cedar-tree, trunk first. Shefford would have doubted the ability of two men to drag that tree, and here came Nas Ta Bega, managing it easily. He laid the trunk on the fire, and then proceeded to break off small branches, to place them advantageously where the red coals kindled them into a blaze.

The Indian's next move was to place his saddle, which he evidently meant to use for a pillow. There he spread a goat-skin on the ground, lay down upon it, with his back to the fire, and, pulling a long-haired saddle-blanket over his shoulders, he relaxed and became motionless. His sister, Glen Naspa, did likewise, except that she stayed farther away from the fire, and she had a larger blanket, which covered her well. It appeared to Shefford that they went to sleep at once.

Shefford felt as tired as he had ever been, but he did not think he could soon drop into slumber, and in fact he did not want to.

There was something in the companionship of these Indians that he had not experienced before. He still had a strange and weak feeling—the aftermath of that fear which had sickened him with its horrible icy grip. Nas Ta Bega's arrival had frightened away that dark and silent prowler of the night; and Shefford was convinced the Indian had saved his life. The measure of his gratitude was a source of wonder to him. Had he cared so much for life? Yes—he had, when face to face with death. That was something to know. It helped him. And he gathered from his strange feelings that the romantic quest which had brought him into the wilderness might turn out to be an antidote for the morbid bitterness of heart.

With new sensations had come new thoughts. Right then it was very pleasant to sit in the warmth and light of the roaring cedar fire. There was a deep-seated ache of fatigue in his bones. What joy it was to rest! He had felt the dry scorch of desert thirst and the pang of hunger. How wonderful to learn the real meaning of water and food! He had just finished the longest, hardest day's work of his life! Had that anything to do with a something almost like peace which seemed to hover near in the shadows, trying to come to him? He had befriended an Indian girl, and now her brother had paid back the service. Both the giving and receiving were somehow sweet to Shefford. They opened up hitherto vague channels of thought. For years he had imagined he was serving people, when he had never lifted a hand. A blow given in the defense of an Indian girl had somehow operated to make a change in John Shefford's existence. It had liberated a spirit in him. Moreover, it had worked its influence outside his mind. The Indian girl and her brother had followed his trail to return his horse, perhaps to guide him safely, but, unknowingly perhaps, they had done infinitely more than that for him. As Shefford's eye wandered over the dark, still figures of the sleepers he had a strange, dreamy premonition, or perhaps only a fancy, that there was to be more come of this fortunate meeting.

For the rest, it was good to be there in the speaking silence, to feel the heat on his outstretched palms and the cold wind on his cheek, to see the black wall lifting its bold outline and the crags reaching for the white stars.

3

Kayenta

THE stamping of horses awoke Shefford. He saw a towering crag, rosy in the morning light, like a huge red spear splitting the clear blue of sky. He got up, feeling cramped and sore, yet with unfamiliar exhilaration. The whipping air

made him stretch his hands to the fire. An odor of coffee and broiled meat
mingled with the fragrance of wood smoke. Glen Naspa was on her knees broiling
a rabbit on a stick over the red coals. Nas Ta Bega was saddling the ponies. The
cañon appeared to be full of purple shadows under one side of dark cliffs and
golden streaks of mist on the other where the sun struck high up on the walls.

"Good morning," said Shefford.

Glen Naspa shyly replied in Navajo.

"How," was Nas Ta Bega's greeting.

In daylight the Indian lost some of the dark somberness of face that had
impressed Shefford. He had a noble head, in poise like that of an eagle, a bold,
clean-cut profile, and stern, close-shut lips. His eyes were the most striking and
attractive feature about him; they were coal-black and piercing; the intent look
out of them seemed to come from a keen and inquisitive mind.

Shefford ate breakfast with the Indians, and then helped with the few preparations for departure. Before they mounted, Nas Ta Bega pointed to horse tracks
in the dust. They were those that had been made by Shefford's threatening visitor
of the night before. Shefford explained by word and sign, and succeeded at least
in showing that he had been in danger. Nas Ta Bega followed the tracks a little
way and presently returned.

"Shadd," he said, with an ominous shake of his head. Shefford did not
understand whether he meant the name of his visitor or something else, but the
menace connected with the word was clear enough.

Glen Naspa mounted her pony, and it was a graceful action that pleased
Shefford. He climbed a little stiffly into his own saddle. Then Nas Ta Bega got
up and pointed northward.

"Kayenta?" he inquired.

Shefford nodded and then they were off, with Glen Naspa in the lead. They
did not climb the trail which they had descended, but took one leading to the
right along the base of the slope. Shefford saw down into the red wash that
bisected the cañon floor. It was a sheer wall of red clay or loam, a hundred feet
high, and at the bottom ran a swift, shallow stream of reddish water. Then for
a time a high growth of greasewood hid the surroundings from Shefford's sight.
Presently the trail led out into the open, and Shefford saw that he was at the
neck of a wonderful valley that gradually widened with great jagged red peaks
on the left and the black mesa, now a mountain, running away to the right. He
turned to find that the opening of the Sagi could no longer be seen, and he was
conscious of a strong desire to return and explore that cañon.

Soon Glen Naspa put her pony to a long, easy, swinging canter and her
followers did likewise. As they got outward into the valley Shefford lost the
sense of being overshadowed and crowded by the nearness of the huge walls
and crags. The trail appeared level underfoot, but at a distance it was seen to

climb. Shefford found where it disappeared over the foot of a slope that formed a graceful rising line up to the cedared flank of the mesa. The valley floor, widening away to the north, remained level and green. Beyond rose the jagged range of red peaks, all strangely cut and slanting. These distant deceiving features of the country held Shefford's gaze until the Indian drew his attention to things near at hand. Then Shefford saw flocks of sheep dotting the gray-green valley, and bands of beautiful long-maned, long-tailed ponies.

For several miles the scene did not change except that Shefford imagined he came to see where the upland plain ended or at least broke its level. He was right, for presently the Indian pointed, and Shefford went on to halt upon the edge of a steep slope leading down into a valley vast in its barren gray reaches.

"Kayenta," said Nas Ta Bega.

Shefford at first saw nothing except the monotonous gray valley reaching far to the strange, grotesque monuments of yellow cliff. Then close under the foot of the slope he espied two squat stone houses with red roofs, and a corral with a pool of water shining in the sun.

The trail leading down was steep and sandy, but it was not long. Shefford's sweeping eyes appeared to take in everything at once—the crude stone structures with their earthen roofs, the piles of dirty wool, the Indians lolling around, the tents, and wagons, and horses, little lazy burros and dogs, and scattered everywhere saddles, blankets, guns, and packs.

Then a white man came out of the door. He waved a hand and shouted. Dust and wool and flour were thick upon him. He was muscular and weather-beaten, and appeared young in activity rather than face. A gun swung at his hip and a row of brass-tipped cartridges showed in his belt. Shefford looked into a face that he thought he had seen before, until he realized the similarity was only the bronze and hard line and rugged cast common to desert men. The gray searching eyes went right through him.

"Glad to see you. Get down and come in. Just heard from an Indian that you were coming. I'm the trader Withers," he said to Shefford. His voice was welcoming and the grip of his hand made Shefford's ache.

Shefford told his name and said he was as glad as he was lucky to arrive at Kayenta.

"Hello! Nas Ta Bega!" exclaimed Withers. His tone expressed a surprise his face did not show. "Did this Indian bring you in?"

Withers shook hands with the Navajo while Shefford briefly related what he owed to him. Then Withers looked at Nas Ta Bega and spoke to him in the Indian tongue.

"Shadd," said Nas Ta Bega.

Withers let out a dry little laugh and his strong hand tugged at his mustache.

"Who's Shadd?" asked Shefford.

"He's a half-breed Ute—bad Indian, outlaw, murderer. He's in with a gang of outlaws who hide in the San Juan country. . . . Reckon you're lucky. How'd you come to be there in the Sagi alone?"

"I traveled from Red Lake. Presbrey, the trader there, advised against it, but I came anyway."

"Well." Withers's gray glance was kind, if it did express the foolhardiness of Shefford's act. "Come into the house. . . . Never mind the horse. My wife will sure be glad to see you."

Withers led Shefford by the first stone house, which evidently was the trading-store, into the second. The room Shefford entered was large, with logs smoldering in a huge open fireplace, blankets covering every foot of floor space, and Indian baskets and silver ornaments everywhere, and strange Indian designs painted upon the whitewashed walls. Withers called his wife and made her acquainted with Shefford. She was a slight, comely little woman, with keen, earnest, dark eyes. She seemed to be serious and quiet, but she made Shefford feel at home immediately. He refused, however, to accept the room offered him, saying that he meant to sleep out under the open sky. Withers laughed at this and said he understood. Shefford, remembering Presbrey's hunger for news of the outside world, told this trader and his wife all he could think of; and he was listened to with that close attention a traveler always gained in the remote places.

"Sure am glad you rode in," said Withers, for the fourth time. "Now you make yourself at home. Stay here—come over to the store—do what you like. I've got to work. To-night we'll talk."

Shefford went out with his host. The store was as interesting as Presbrey's, though much smaller and more primitive. It was full of everything, and smelled strongly of sheep and goats. There was a narrow aisle between sacks of flour and blankets on one side and a high counter on the other. Behind this counter Withers stood to wait upon the buying Indians. They sold blankets and skins and bags of wool, and in exchange took silver money. Then they lingered and with slow, staid reluctance bought one thing and then another—flour, sugar, canned goods, coffee, tobacco, ammunition. The counter was never without two or three Indians leaning on their dark, silver-braceleted arms. But as they were slow to sell and buy and go, so were others slow to come in. Their voices were soft and low and it seemed to Shefford they were whispering. He liked to hear them and to look at the banded heads, the long, twisted rolls of black hair tied with white cords, the still dark faces and watchful eyes, the silver ear-rings, the slender, shapely brown hands, the lean and sinewy shapes, the corduroys with a belt and gun, and the small, close-fitting buckskin moccasins buttoned with coins. These Indians all appeared young, and under the quiet, slow demeanor there was fierce blood and fire.

By and by two women came in, evidently squaw and daughter. The former was a huge, stout Indian with a face that was certainly pleasant if not jolly. She had the corners of a blanket tied under her chin and in the folds behind on her broad back was a naked Indian baby, round and black of head, brown-skinned, with eyes as bright as beads. When the youngster caught sight of Shefford he made a startled dive into the sack of the blanket. Manifestly, however, curiosity got the better of fear, for presently Shefford caught a pair of wondering dark eyes peeping at him.

"They're good spenders, but slow," said Withers. "The Navajos are careful and cautious. That's why they're rich. This squaw, Yan As Pa, has flocks of sheep and more mustangs than she knows about."

"Mustangs. So that's what you call the ponies?" replied Shefford.

"Yep. They're mustangs, and mostly wild as jack-rabbits."

Shefford strolled outside and made the acquaintance of Withers's helper, a Mormon named Whisner. He was a stockily built man past maturity, and his sun-blistered face and watery eyes told of the open desert. He was engaged in weighing sacks of wool brought in by the Indians. Near by stood a framework of poles from which an immense bag was suspended. From the top of this bag protruded the head and shoulders of an Indian who appeared to be stamping and packing wool with his feet. He grinned at the curious Shefford. But Shefford was more interested in the Mormon. So far as he knew, Whisner was the first man of that creed he had ever met, and he could scarcely hide his eagerness. Venters's stories had been of a long-past generation of Mormons, fanatical, ruthless, and unchangeable. Shefford did not expect to meet Mormons of this kind. But any man of that religion would have interested him. Besides this, Whisner seemed to bring him closer to that wild secret cañon he had come West to find. Shefford was somewhat amazed and discomfited to have his polite and friendly overtures repulsed. Whisner might have been an Indian. He was cold, incommunicative, aloof; and there was something about him that made the sensitive Shefford feel his presence was resented.

Presently Shefford strolled on to the corral, which was full of shaggy mustangs. They snorted and kicked at him. He had a half-formed wish that he would never be called upon to ride one of those wild brutes, and then he found himself thinking that he would ride one of them, and after a while any of them. Shefford did not understand himself, but he fought his natural instinctive reluctance to meet obstacles, peril, suffering.

He traced the white-bordered little stream that made the pool in the corral, and when he came to where it oozed out of the sand under the bluff he decided that was not the spring which had made Kayenta famous. Presently down below the trading-post he saw a trough from which burros were drinking. Here he found the spring, a deep well of eddying water walled in by stones, and the overflow made a shallow stream meandering away between its borders of alkali, like a crust of salt. Shefford tasted the water. It bit, but it was good.

Shefford had no trouble in making friends with the lazy sleepy-eyed burros. They let him pull their long ears and rub their noses, but the mustangs standing around were unapproachable. They had wild eyes; they raised long ears and looked vicious. He let them alone.

Evidently this trading-post was a great deal busier than Red Lake. Shefford counted a dozen Indians lounging outside, and there were others riding away. Big wagons told how the bags of wool were transported out of the wilds and how supplies were brought in. A wide, hard-packed road led off to the east, and another, not so clearly defined, wound away to the north. And Indian trails streaked off in all directions.

Shefford discovered, however, when he had walked off a mile or so across the valley to lose sight of the post, that the feeling of wildness and loneliness returned to him. It was a wonderful country. It held something for him besides the possible rescue of an imprisoned girl from a wild cañon.

That night after supper, when Withers and Shefford sat alone before the blazing logs in the huge fireplace, the trader laid his hand on Shefford's and said, with directness and force:

"I've lived my life in the desert. I've met many men and have been a friend to most. . . . You're no prospector or trader or missionary?"

"No," replied Shefford.

"You've had trouble?"

"Yes."

"Have you come in here to hide? Don't be afraid to tell me. I won't give you away."

"I didn't come to hide."

"Then no one is after you? You've done no wrong?"

"Perhaps I wronged myself, but no one else," replied Shefford, steadily.

"I reckoned so. Well, tell me, or keep your secret——it's all one to me."

Shefford felt a desire to unburden himself. This man was strong, persuasive, kindly. He drew Shefford.

"You're welcome in Kayenta," went on Withers. "Stay as long as you like. I take no pay from a white man. If you want work I have it aplenty."

"Thank you. That is good. I need to work. We'll talk of it later. . . . But just yet I can't tell you why I came to Kayenta, what I want to do, how long I shall stay. My thoughts put in words would seem so like dreams. Maybe they are dreams. Perhaps I'm only chasing a phantom—perhaps I'm only hunting the treasure at the foot of the rainbow."

"Well, this is the country for rainbows," laughed Withers. "In summer from

June to August when it storms we have rainbows that'll make you think you're in another world. The Navajos have rainbow mountains, rainbow cañons, rainbow bridges of stone, rainbow trails. It sure is rainbow country.''

That deep and mystic chord in Shefford thrilled. Here it was again—something tangible at the bottom of his dream.

Withers did not wait for Shefford to say any more, and almost as if he read his visitor's mind he began to talk about the wild country he called home.

He had lived at Kayenta for several years—hard and profitless years by reason of marauding outlaws. He could not have lived there at all but for the protection of the Indians. His father-in-law had been friendly with the Navajos and Piutes for many years, and his wife had been brought up among them. She was held in peculiar reverence and affection by both tribes in that part of the country. Probably she knew more of the Indians' habits, religion, and life than any white person in the West. Both tribes were friendly and peaceable, but there were bad Indians, half-breeds, and outlaws that made the trading-post a venture Withers had long considered precarious, and he wanted to move and intended to some day. His nearest neighbors in New Mexico and Colorado were a hundred miles distant and at some seasons the roads were impassable. To the north, however, twenty miles or so, was situated a Mormon Village named Stonebridge. It lay across the Utah line. Withers did some business with this village, but scarcely enough to warrant the risks he had to run. During the last year he had lost several pack-trains, one of which he had never heard of after it left Stonebridge.

"Stonebridge!" exclaimed Shefford, and he trembled. He had heard that name. In his memory it had a place beside the name of another village Shefford longed to speak of to this trader.

"Yes—Stonebridge," replied Withers. "Ever heard the name?"

"I think so. Are there other villages in—in that part of the country?"

"A few, but not close. Glaze is now only a waterhole. Bluff and Monticello are far north across the San Juan. . . . There used to be another village— but that wouldn't interest you."

"Maybe it would," replied Shefford, quietly.

But his hint was not taken by the trader. Withers suddenly showed a semblance to the aloofness Shefford had observed in Whisner.

"Withers, pardon an impertinence—I am deeply serious. . . . Are you a Mormon?"

"Indeed I'm not," replied the trader, instantly.

"Are you for the Mormons or against them?"

"Neither. I get along with them. I know them. I believe they are a misunderstood people."

"That's for them."

"No. I'm only fair-minded."

Shefford paused, trying to curb his thrilling impulse, but it was too strong.

"You said there used to be another village. . . . Was the name of it—Cottonwoods?"

Withers gave a start and faced round to stare at Shefford in blank astonishment.

"Say, did you give me a straight story about yourself?" he queried, sharply.

"So far as I went," replied Shefford.

"You're no spy on the lookout for sealed wives?"

"Absolutely not. I don't even know what you mean by sealed wives."

"Well, it's damn strange that you'd know the name Cottonwoods. . . . Yes, that's the name of the village I meant—the one that used to be. It's gone now, all except a few stone walls."

"What became of it?"

"Torn down by Mormons years ago. They destroyed it and moved away. I've heard Indians talk about a grand spring that was there once. It's gone, too. It's name was—let me see—"

"Amber Spring," interrupted Shefford.

"By George, you're right!" rejoined the trader, again amazed. "Shefford, this beats me. I haven't heard that name for ten years. I can't help seeing what a tenderfoot—stranger—you are to the desert. Yet, here you are—speaking of what you should know nothing of. . . . And there's more behind this."

Shefford rose, unable to conceal his agitation.

"Did you ever hear of a rider named Venters?"

"Rider? You mean a cowboy? Venters. No, I never heard that name."

"Did you ever hear of a gunman named Lassiter?" queried Shefford, with increasing emotion.

"No."

"Did you ever hear of a Mormon woman named—Jane Withersteen?"

"No."

Shefford drew his breath sharply. He had followed a gleam—he had caught a fleeting glimpse of it.

"Did you every hear of a child—a girl—a woman—called Fay Larkin?"

Withers rose slowly with a paling face.

"If you're a spy it'll go hard with you—though I'm no Mormon," he said, grimly.

Shefford lifted a shaking hand.

"I *was* a clergyman. Now I'm nothing—a wanderer—least of all a spy."

Withers leaned closer to see into the other man's eyes; he looked long and then appeared satisfied.

"I've heard the name Fay Larkin," he said, slowly. "I reckon that's all I'll say till you tell your story."

Shefford stood with his back to the fire and he turned the palms of his hands to catch the warmth. He felt cold. Withers had affected him strangely. What was the meaning of the trader's somber gravity? Why was the very mention of Mormons attended by something austere and secret?

"My name is John Shefford. I am twenty-four," began Shefford. "My family—"

Here a knock on the door interrupted Shefford.

"Come in," called Withers.

The door opened and like a shadow Nas Ta Bega slipped in. He said something in Navajo to the trader.

"How," he said to Shefford, and extended his hand. He was stately, but there was no mistaking his friendliness. Then he sat down before the fire, doubled his legs under him after the Indian fashion, and with dark eyes on the blazing logs seemed to lose himself in meditation.

"He likes the fire," explained Withers. "Whenever he comes to Kayenta he always visits with me like this. . . . Don't mind him. Go on with your story."

"My family were plain people, well-to-do, and very religious," went on Shefford. "When I was a boy we moved from the country to a town called Beaumont, Illinois. There was a college in Beaumont and eventually I was sent to it to study for the ministry. I wanted to be— But never mind that. . . . By the time I was twenty-two I was ready for my career as a clergyman. I preached for a year around at different places and then got a church in my home town of Beaumont. I became exceedingly good friends with a man named Venters, who had recently come to Beaumont. He was a singular man. His wife was a strange, beautiful woman, very reserved, and she had wonderful dark eyes. They had money and were devoted to each other, and perfectly happy. They owned the finest horses ever seen in Illinois, and their particular enjoyment seemed to be riding. They were always taking long rides. It was something worth going far for to see Mrs. Venters on a horse.

"It was through my own love of horses that I became friendly with Venters. He and his wife attended my church, and as I got to see more of them, gradually we grew intimate. And it was not until I did get intimate with them that I realized that both seemed to be haunted by the past. They were sometimes sad even in their happiness. They drifted off into dreams. They lived back in another world. They seemed to be listening. Indeed, they were a singularly interesting couple, and I grew genuinely fond of them. By and by they had a little girl whom they named Jane. The coming of the baby made a change in my friends. They were happier, and I observed that the haunting shadow did not so often return.

"Venters had spoken of a journey west that he and his wife meant to take some time. But after the baby came he never mentioned his wife in connection with the trip. I gathered that he felt compelled to go to clear up a mystery or to find something—I did not make out just what. But eventually, and it was about a year ago, he told me his story—the strangest, wildest, and most tragic I ever heard.

"I can't tell it all now. It is enough to say that fifteen years before he had been a rider for a rich Mormon woman named Jane Withersteen, of this village Cottonwoods. She had adopted a beautiful Gentile child named Fay Larkin. Her interest in Gentiles earned the displeasure of her churchmen, and as she was proud there came a breach. Venters and a gunman named Lassiter became involved in her quarrel. Finally Venters took to the cañons. Here in the wilds he found the strange girl he eventually married. For a long time they lived in a wonderful hidden valley, the entrance to which was guarded by a hugh balancing rock. Venters got away with the girl. But Lassiter and Jane Withersteen and the child Fay Larkin were driven into the cañon. They escaped to the valley where Venters had lived. Lassiter rolled the balancing rock, and, crashing down the narrow trail, it loosened the weathered walls and closed the narrow outlet for ever."

4

New Friends

SHEFFORD ended his narrative out of breath, pale, and dripping with sweat. Withers sat leaning forward with an expression of intense interest. Nas Ta Bega's easy, graceful pose had succeeded to one of strained rigidity. He seemed a statue of bronze. Could a few intelligible words, Shefford wondered, have created that strange, listening posture?

"Venters got out of Utah, of course, as you know," went on Shefford. "He got out, knowing—as I feel I would have known—that Jane, Lassiter, and little Fay Larkin were shut up, walled up in Surprise Valley. For years Venters considered it would not have been safe for him to venture to rescue them. He had no fears for their lives. They could live in Surprise Valley. But Venters always intended to come back with Bess and find the valley and his friends. No wonder he and Bess were haunted. However, when his wife had the baby that made a difference. It meant he had to go alone. And he was thinking seriously of starting when I—when there were developments that made it desirable for me to leave Beaumont. Venters's story haunted me as he had been haunted. I dreamed of that wild valley—of little Fay Larkin grown to womanhood—such a woman as Bess Venters was. And the longing to come was great. . . . And, Withers—here I am."

The trader reached out and gave Shefford the grip of a man in whom emotion was powerful, but deep and difficult to express.

"Listen to this. . . . I wish I could help you. Life is a queer deal. . . . Shefford, I've got to trust you. Over here in the wild cañon country there's a village of Mormons' sealed wives. It's in Arizona, perhaps twenty miles from here, and near the Utah line. When the United States government began to persecute, or prosecute, the Mormons for polygamy, the Mormons over here in Stonebridge took their sealed wives and moved them out of Utah, just across the line. They built houses, established a village there. I'm the only Gentile who knows about it. And I pack supplies every few weeks in to these women. There are perhaps fifty women, mostly young—second or third or fourth wives of Mormons—sealed wives. And I want you to understand that sealed means *sealed* in all that religion or loyalty can get out of the word. There are also some old women and old men in the village, but they hardly count. And there's a flock of the finest children you ever saw in your life.

"The idea of the Mormons must have been to escape prosecution. The law of the government is one wife for each man—no more. All over Utah polygamists have been arrested. The Mormons are deeply concerned. I believe they are a good, law abiding people. But this law is a direct blow at their religion. In my opinion they can't obey both. And therefore they have not altogether given up plural wives. Perhaps they will some day. I have no proof, but I believe the Mormons of Stonebridge pay secret night visits to their sealed wives across the line in the lonely, hidden village.

"Now once over in Stonebridge I overheard some Mormons talking about a girl who was named Fay Larkin. I never forgot the name. Later I heard the name in this sealed-wife village. But, as I told you, I never heard of Lassiter or Jane Withersteen. Still if Mormons had found them I would never have heard of it. And Deception Pass—that might be the Sagi. . . . I'm not surprised at your rainbow-chasing adventure. It's a great story. . . . This Fay Larkin I've heard of *might* be your Fay Larkin—I almost believe so. Shefford, I'll help you find out."

"Yes, yes—I must know," replied Shefford. "Oh, I hope, I pray we can find her! But—I'd rather she was dead—if she's not still hidden in the valley."

"Naturally. You've dreamed yourself into rescuing this lost Fay Larkin. . . . But, Shefford, you're old enough to know life doesn't work out as you want it to. One way or another I fear you're in for a bitter disappointment."

"Withers, take me to the village."

"Shefford, you're liable to get in bad out here," said the trader, gravely.

"I couldn't be any more ruined than I am now," replied Shefford, passionately.

"But there's risk in this—risk such as you never had," persisted Withers.

"I'll risk anything."

"Reckon this's a funny deal for a sheep-trader to have on his hands," continued Withers. "Shefford, I like you. I've a mind to see you through this. It's a damn strange story. . . . I'll tell you what—I will help you. I'll give you a job packing supplies in to the village. I meant to turn that over to a Mormon cowboy—Joe Lake. The job shall be yours, and I'll go with you first trip. Here's my hand on it. . . . Now, Shefford, I'm more curious about you than I was before you told your story. What ruined you? As we're to be partners, you can tell me now. I'll keep your secret. Maybe I can do you good."

Shefford wanted to confess, yet it was hard. Perhaps, had he not been so agitated, he would not have answered to impulse. But this trader was a man— a man of the desert—he would understand.

"I told you I was a clergyman," said Shefford in low voice. "I didn't want to be one, but they made me one. I did my best. I failed. . . . I had doubts of religion—of the Bible—of God, as my Church believed in them. As I grew older thought and study convinced me of the narrowness of religion as my congregation lived it. I preached what I believed. I alienated them. They put me out, took my calling from me, disgraced me, ruined me."

"So that's all!" exclaimed Withers, slowly. "You didn't believe in the God of the Bible. . . . Well, I've been in the desert long enough to know there *is* a God, but probably not the one your Church worships. . . . Shefford, go to the Navajo for a faith!"

Shefford had forgotten the presence of Nas Ta Bega, and perhaps Withers had likewise. At this juncture the Indian rose to his full height, and he folded his arms to stand with the somber pride of a chieftain while his dark, inscrutable eyes were riveted upon Shefford. At that moment he seemed magnificent. How infinitely more he seemed than just a common Indian who had chanced to befriend a white man! The difference was obscure to Shefford. But he felt that it was there in the Navajo's mind. Nas Ta Bega's strange look was not to be interpreted. Presently he turned and passed from the room.

"By George!" cried Withers, suddenly, and he pounded his knee with his fist. "I'd forgotten."

"What?" ejaculated Shefford.

"Why, that Indian understood every word we said. He knows English. He's educated. Well, if this doesn't beat me. . . . Let me tell you about Nas Ta Bega."

Withers appeared to be recalling something half forgotten.

"Years ago, in fifty-seven, I think, Kit Carson with his soldiers chased the

Navajo tribes and rounded them up to be put on reservations. But he failed to catch all the members of one tribe. They escaped up into wild cañons like the Sagi. The descendants of these fugitives live there now and are the finest Indians on earth—the finest because unspoiled by the white man. Well, as I got the story, years after Carson's round-up one of his soldiers guided some interested travelers in here. When they left they took an Indian boy with them to educate. From what I know of Navajos I'm inclined to think the boy was taken against his parents' wish. Anyway, he was taken. That boy was Nas Ta Bega. The story goes that he was educated somewhere. Years afterward, and perhaps not long before I came in here, he returned to his people. There have been missionaries and other interested fools who have given Indians a white man's education. In all the instances I know of, these educated Indians returned to their tribes, repudiating the white man's knowledge, habits, life, and religion. I have heard that Nas Ta Bega came back, laid down the white man's clothes along with the education, and never again showed that he had known either.

"You have just seen how strangely he acted. It's almost certain he heard our conversation. Well, it doesn't matter. He won't tell. He can hardly be made to use an English word. Besides, he's a noble red man, if there ever was one. He has been a friend in need to me. If you stay long out here you'll learn something from the Indians. Nas Ta Bega has befriended you, too, it seems. I thought he showed unusual interest in you."

"Perhaps that was because I saved his sister—well, to be charitable, from the rather rude advances of a white man," said Shefford, and he proceeded to tell of the incident that occurred at Red Lake.

"Willetts!" exclaimed Withers, with much the same expression that Presbrey had used. "I never met him. But I know about him. He's—well, the Indians don't like him much. Most of the missionaries are good men—good for the Indians, in a way, but sometimes one drifts out here who is bad. A bad missionary teaching religion to savages! Queer, isn't it? The queerest part is the white people's blindness—the blindness of those who send the missionaries. Well, I dare say Willetts isn't very good. When Presbrey said that was Willetts's way of teaching religion he meant just what he said. If Willetts drifts over here he'll be risking much. . . . This you told me explains Nas Ta Bega's friendliness toward you, and also his bringing his sister Glen Naspa to live with relatives up in the pass. She had been living near Red Lake."

"Do you mean Nas Ta Bega wants to keep his sister far removed from Willetts?" inquired Shefford.

"I mean that," replied Withers, "and I hope he's not too late."

Later Shefford went outdoors to walk and think. There was no moon, but the stars made light enough to cast his shadow on the ground. The dark, illimitable expanse of blue sky seemed to be glittering with numberless points of fire. The air was cold and still. A dreaming silence lay over the land. Shefford saw and felt all these things, and their effect was continuous and remained with him and helped calm him. He was conscious of a burden removed from his mind. Confession of his secret had been like tearing a thorn from his flesh, but, once done, it afforded him relief and a singular realization that out here it did not matter much. In a crowd of men all looking at him and judging him by their standards he had been made to suffer. Here, if he were judged at all, it would be by what he could do, how he sustained himself and helped others.

He walked far across the valley toward the low bluffs, but they did not seem to get any closer. And, finally, he stopped beside a stone and looked around at the strange horizon and up at the heavens. He did not feel utterly aloof from them, nor alone in a waste, nor a useless atom amid incomprehensible forces. Something like a loosened mantle fell from about him, dropping down at his feet; and all at once he was conscious of freedom. He did not understand in the least why abasement left him, but it was so. He had come a long way, in bitterness, in despair, believing himself to be what men had called him. The desert and the stars and the wind, the silence of the night, the loneliness of this vast country where there was room for a thousand cities—these somehow vaguely, yet surely, bade him lift his head. They withheld their secret, but they made a promise. The thing which he had been feeling every day and every night was a strange enveloping comfort. And it was at this moment that Shefford, divining whence his help was to come, embraced all that wild and speaking nature around and above him and surrendered himself utterly.

"I am young. I am free. I have my life to live," he said. "I'll be a man. I'll take what comes. Let me learn here!"

When he had spoken out, settled once and for ever his attitude toward his future, he seemed to be born again, wonderfully alive to the influences around him, ready to trust what yet remained a mystery.

Then his thoughts reverted to Fay Larkin. Could this girl be known to the Mormons? It was possible. Fay Larkin was an unusual name. Deep into Shefford's heart had sunk the story Venters had told. Shefford found that he had unconsciously created a like romance—he had been loving a wild and strange and lonely girl, like beautiful Bess Venters. It was a shock to learn the truth, but, as it had been only a dream, it could hardly be vital.

Shefford retraced his steps toward the post. Halfway back he espied a tall, dark figure moving toward him, and presently the shape and the step seemed familiar. Then he recognized Nas Ta Bega. Soon they were face to face. Shefford felt that the Indian had been trailing him over the sand, and that this was to be a significant meeting. Remembering Withers's revelation about the Navajo, Shefford scarcely knew how to approach him now. There was no difference to be made out in Nas Ta Bega's dark face and inscrutable eyes, yet there was a difference to be felt in his presence. But the Indian did not speak, and turned to walk by Shefford's side. Shefford could not long be silent.

"Nas Ta Bega, were you looking for me?" he asked.

"You had no gun," replied the Indian.

But for his very low voice, his slow speaking of the words, Shefford would have thought him a white man. For Shefford there was indeed an instinct in this meeting, and he turned to face the Navajo.

"Withers told me you had been educated, that you came back to the desert, that you never showed your training. . . . Nas Ta Bega, did you understand all I told Withers?"

"Yes," replied the Indian.

"You won't betray me?"

"I am a Navajo."

"Nas Ta Bega, you trail me—you say I had no gun." Shefford wanted to ask this Indian if he cared to be the white man's friend, but the question was not easy to put, and, besides, seemed unnecessary. "I am alone and strange in this wild country. I must learn."

"Nas Ta Bega will show you the trails and the water-holes and how to hide from Shadd."

"For money—for silver you will do this?" inquired Shefford.

Shefford felt that the Indian's silence was a rebuke. He remembered Withers's singular praise of this red man. He realized he must change his idea of Indians.

"Nas Ta Bega, I know nothing. I feel like a child in the wilderness. When I speak it is out of the mouths of those who have taught me. I must find a new voice and a new life. . . . You heard my story to Withers. I am an outcast from my own people. If you will be my friend—be so."

The Indian clasped Shefford's hand and held it in a response that was more beautiful for its silence. So they stood for a moment in the starlight.

"Nas Ta Bega, what did Withers mean when he said go to the Navajo for a faith?" asked Shefford.

"He meant the desert is my mother. . . . Will you go with Nas Ta Bega into the cañons and the mountains?"

"Indeed I will."

They unclasped hands and turned toward the trading-post.

"Nas Ta Bega, have you spoken my tongue to any other white man since you returned to your home?" asked Shefford.

"No."

"Why do you—why are you different for me?"

The Indian maintained silence.

"Is it because of—of Glen Naspa?" inquired Shefford.

Nas Ta Bega stalked on, still silent, but Shefford divined that, although his service to Glen Naspa would never be forgotten, still it was not wholly responsible for the Indian's subtle sympathy.

"Bi Nai! The Navajo will call his white friend Bi Nai—brother," said Nas Ta Bega, and he spoke haltingly, not as if words were hard to find, but strange to speak. "I was stolen from my mother's hogan and taken to California. They kept me ten years in a mission at San Bernardino and four years in a school. They said my color and my hair were all that was left of the Indian in me. But they could not see my heart. They took fourteen years of my life. They wanted to make me a missionary among my own people. But the white man's ways and his life and his God are not the Indian's. They never can be."

How strangely productive of thought for Shefford to hear the Indian talk! What fatality in this meeting and friendship! Upon Nas Ta Bega had been forced education, training, religion, that had made him something more and something less than an Indian. It was something assimilated from the white man which made the Indian unhappy and alien in his own home—something meant to be good for him and his kind that had ruined him. For Shefford felt the passion and the tragedy of this Navajo.

"Bi Nai, the Indian is dying!" Nas Ta Bega's low voice was deep and wonderful with its intensity of feeling. "The white man robbed the Indian of lands and homes, drove him into the deserts, made him a gaunt and sleepless spiller of blood. . . . The blood is all spilled now, for the Indian is broken. But the white man sells him rum and seduces his daughters. . . . He will not leave the Indian in peace with his own God! . . . Bi Nai, the Indian is dying!"

That night Shefford lay in his blankets out under the open sky and the stars. The earth had never meant much to him, and now it was a bed. He had preached of the heavens, but until now had never studied them. An Indian slept beside him. And not until the gray of morning had blotted out the starlight did Shefford close his eyes.

With break of the next day came full, varied, and stirring incidents to Shefford. He was strong, though unskilled at most kinds of outdoor tasks. Withers had work for ten men, if they could have been found. Shefford dug and packed and lifted till he was so sore and tired that rest was a blessing.

He never succeeded in getting on a friendly footing with the Mormon Whisner, though he kept up his agreeable and kindly advances. He listened to the trader's wife as she told him about the Indians, and what he learned he did not forget. And his wonder and respect increased in proportion to his knowledge.

One day there rode into Kayenta the Mormon for whom Withers had been waiting. His name was Joe Lake. He appeared young, and slipped off his superb bay with a grace and activity that were astounding in one of his huge bulk. He had a still, smooth face, with the color of red bronze and the expression of a cherub; big, soft, dark eyes; and a winning smile. He was surprisingly different from Whisner or any Mormon character that Shefford had naturally conceived. His costume was that of the cowboy on active service; and he packed a gun at his hip. The hand-shake he gave Shefford was an ordeal for that young man and left him with his whole right side momentarily benumbed.

"I sure am glad to meet you," he said in a lazy, mild voice. And he was taking friendly stock of Shefford when the bay mustang reached with vicious muzzle to bite at him. Lake gave a jerk on the bridle that almost brought the mustang to his knees. He reared then, snorted, and came down to plant his forefeet wide apart, and watched his master with defiant eyes. This mustang was the finest horse Shefford had ever seen. He appeared quite large for his species, was almost red in color, had a racy and powerful build, and a fine thoroughbred head with dark, fiery eyes. He did not look mean, but he had spirit.

"Navvy, you've sure got bad manners," said Lake, shaking the mustang's bridle. He spoke as if he were chiding a refractory little boy. "Didn't I break you better 'n that? What's this gentleman goin' to think of you? Tryin' to bite my ear off!"

Lake had arrived about the middle of the forenoon, and Withers announced his intention of packing at once for the trip. Indians were sent out on the ranges to drive in burros and mustangs. Shefford had his thrilling expectancy somewhat chilled by what he considered must have been Lake's reception of the trader's plan. Lake seemed to oppose him, and evidently it took vehemence and argument on Withers's part to make the Mormon tractable. But Withers won him over, and then he called Shefford to his side.

"You fellows got to be good friends," he said. "You'll have charge of my pack-trains. Nas Ta Bega wants to go with you. I'll feel safer about my supplies and stock than I've ever been. . . . Joe, I'll back this stranger for all I'm worth. He's square. . . . And, Shefford, Joe Lake is a Mormon of the younger generation. I want to start you right. You can trust him as you trust me. He's white clean through. And he's the best horse-wrangler in Utah."

It was Lake who first offered his hand, and Shefford made haste to meet it with his own. Neither of them spoke. Shefford intuitively felt an alteration in Lake's regard, or at least a singular increase of interest. Lake had been told that Shefford had been a clergyman, was now a wanderer, without any religion. Again it seemed to Shefford that he owed a forming of friendship to this singular fact. And it hurt him. But strangely it came to him that he had taken a liking to a Mormon.

About one o'clock the pack-train left Kayenta. Nas Ta Bega led the way up the slope. Following him climbed half a dozen patient, plodding, heavily laden burros. Withers came next, and he turned in his saddle to wave good-by to his wife. Joe Lake appeared to be busy keeping a red mule and a wild gray mustang and a couple of restive blacks in the trail. Shefford brought up in the rear.

His mount was a beautiful black mustang with three white feet, a white spot on his nose, and a mane that swept to his knees. "His name's Nack-yal," Withers had said. "It means two bits, or twenty-five cents. He ain't worth more." To look at Nack-yal had pleased Shefford very much indeed, but, once upon his back, he grew dubious. The mustang acted queer. He actually looked back at Shefford, and it was a look of speculation and disdain. Shefford took exception to Nack-yal's manner and to his reluctance to go, and especially to a habit the mustang had of turning off the trail to the left. Shefford had managed some rather spirited horses back in Illinois; and though he was willing and eager to learn all over again, he did not enjoy the prospect of Lake and Withers seeing this black mustang make a novice of him. And he guessed that was just what Nack-yal intended to do. However, once up over the hill, with Kayenta out of sight, Nack-yal trotted along fairly well, needing only now and then to be pulled back from his strange swinging to the left of the trail.

The pack-train traveled steadily and soon crossed the upland plain to descend into the valley again. Shefford saw the jagged red peaks with an emotion he could not name. The cañons between them were purple in the shadows, the great walls and slopes brightened to red, and the tips were gold in the sun. Shefford forgot all about his mustang and the trail.

Suddenly with a pound of hoofs Nack-yal seemed to rise. He leaped sidewise out of the trail, came down stiff-legged. Then Shefford shot out of the saddle. He landed so hard that he was stunned for an instant. Sitting up, he saw the mustang bent down, eyes and ears showing fight, and his fore-feet spread. He appeared to be looking at something in the trail. Shefford got up and soon saw what had been the trouble. A long, crooked stick, rather thick and black and yellow, lay in the trail, and any mustang looking for an excuse to jump might have mistaken it for a rattlesnake. Nack-yal appeared disposed to be satisfied, and gave Shefford no trouble in mounting. The incident increased Shefford's dubiousness. These Arizona mustangs were unknown quantities.

Thereafter Shefford had an eye for the trail rather than the scenery, and this continued till the pack-train entered the mouth of the Sagi. Then those wonderful lofty cliffs, with their peaks and towers and spires, loomed so close and so beautiful that he did not care if Nack-yal did throw him. Along here, however, the mustang behaved well, and presently Shefford decided that if it had been otherwise he would have walked. The trail suddenly stood on end and led down into the deep wash, where some days before he had seen the stream of reddish water. This day there appeared to be less water and it was not so red. Nack-yal sank deep as he took short and careful steps down. The burros and other mustangs were drinking, and Nack-yal followed suit. The Indian, with a hand clutching his mustang's mane, rode up a steep, sandy slope on the other side that Shefford would not have believed any horse could climb. The burros plodded up and over the rim, with Withers calling to them. Joe Lake swung his rope and cracked the flanks of the gray mare and the red mule; and the way the two kicked was a revelation and a warning to Shefford. When his turn came to climb the trail he got off and walked, an action that Nack-yal appeared fully to appreciate.

From the head of this wash the trail wound away up the widening cañon, through greasewood flats and over greasy levels and across sandy stretches. The looming walls made the valley look narrow, yet it must have been half a mile wide. The slopes under the cliffs were dotted with hugh stones and cedar-trees. There were deep indentations in the walls, running back to form box cañons, choked with green of cedar and spruce and piñon. These notches haunted Shefford, and he was ever on the lookout for more of them.

Withers came back to ride just in advance and began to talk.

"Reckon this Sagi Cañon is your Deception Pass," he said. "It's sure a queer hole. I've been lost more than once, hunting mustangs in here. I've an idea Nas Ta Bega knows all this country. He just pointed out a cliff-dwelling to me. See it?. . . . There 'way up in that cave of the wall."

Shefford saw a steep, rough slope leading up to a bulge of the cliff, and finally he made out strange little houses with dark, eyelike windows. He wanted to climb up there. Withers called his attention to more caves with what he believed were the ruins of cliff-dwellings. And as they rode along the trader showed him remarkable formations of rock where the elements were slowly hollowing out a bridge. They came presently to a region of intersecting cañons, and here the breaking of the trail up and down the deep washes took Withers back to his task with the burros and gave Shefford more concern than he liked with Nack-yal. The mustang grew unruly and was continually turning to the left. Sometimes he tried to climb the steep slope. He had to be pulled hard away from the opening cañons on the left. It seemed strange to Shefford that the mustang never swerved to the right. This habit of Nack-yal's and the increasing caution needed on the trail took all of Shefford's attention. When he dismounted, however, he had a chance to look around, and more and more he was amazed at the increasing proportions and wildness of the Sagi.

He came at length to a place where a fallen tree blocked the trail. All of the rest of the pack-train had jumped the log. But Nack-yal balked. Shefford dismounted, pulled the bridle over the mustang's head, and tried to lead him. Nack-yal, however, refused to budge. Whereupon Shefford got a stick and, remounting, he gave the balky mustang a cut across the flank. Then something violent happened. Shefford received a sudden propelling jolt, and then he was rising into the air, and then falling. Before he alighted he had a clear image of Nack-yal in the air above him, bent double, and seemingly possessed of devils. Then

Shefford hit the ground with no light thud. He was thoroughly angry when he got dizzily upon his feet, but he was not quick enough to catch the mustang. Nack-yal leaped easily over the log and went on ahead, dragging his bridle. Shefford hurried after him, and the faster he went just by so much the cunning Nack-yal accelerated his gait. As the pack-train was out of sight somewhere ahead, Shefford could not call to his companions to halt his mount, so he gave up trying, and walked on now with free and growing appreciation of his surroundings.

The afternoon had waned. The sun blazed low in the west in a notch of the cañon ramparts, and one wall was darkening into purple shadow while the other shone through a golden haze. It was a weird, wild world to Shefford, and every few strides he caught his breath and tried to realize actuality was not a dream.

Nack-yal kept about a hundred paces to the fore and ever and anon he looked back to see how his new master was progressing. He varied these occasions by reaching down and nipping a tuft of grass. Evidently he was too intelligent to go on fast enough to be caught by Withers. Also he kept continually looking up the slope to the left as if seeking a way to climb out of the valley in that direction. Shefford thought it was well the trail lay at the foot of a steep slope that ran up to unbroken bluffs.

The sun set and the cañon lost its red and its gold and deepened its purple. Shefford calculated he had walked five miles, and though he did not mind the effort, he would rather have ridden Nack-yal into camp. He mounted a cedar ridge, crossed some sandy washes, turned a corner of bold wall to enter a wide, green level. The mustangs were rolling and snorting. He heard the bray of a burro. A bright blaze of camp-fire greeted him, and the dark figure of the Indian approached to intercept and catch Nack-yal. When he stalked into camp Withers wore a beaming smile, and Joe Lake, who was on his knees making biscuit dough in a pan, stopped proceedings and drawled:

"Reckon Nack-yal bucked you off."

"Bucked! Was that it? Well, he separated himself from me in a new and somewhat painful manner—to me."

"Sure, I saw that in his eye," replied Lake; and Withers laughed with him.

"Nack-yal never was well broke," he said. "But he's a good mustang, nothing like Joe's Navvy or that gray mare Dynamite. All this Indian stock will buck on a man once in a while."

"I'll take the bucking along with the rest," said Shefford.

Both men liked his reply, and the Indian smiled for the first time.

Soon they all sat round a spread tarpaulin and ate like wolves. After supper came the rest and talk before the camp-fire. Joe Lake was droll, he said the most serious things in a way to make Shefford wonder if he was not joking. Withers talked about the cañon, the Indians, the mustangs, the scorpions running out of the heated sand; and to Shefford it was all like a fascinating book. Nas Ta Bega smoked in silence, his brooding eyes upon the fire.

5
On the Trail

SHEFFORD was awakened next morning by a sound he had never heard before— the plunging of hobbled horses on soft turf. It was clear daylight, with a ruddy color in the sky and a tinge of red along the cañon rim. He saw Withers, Lake, and the Indian driving the mustangs toward camp.

The burros appeared lazy, yet willing. But the mustangs and the mule Withers called Red and the gray mare Dynamite were determined not to be driven into camp. It was astonishing how much action they had, how much ground they could cover with their forefeet hobbled together. They were exceedingly skillful; they lifted both forefeet at once, and then plunged. And they all went in different directions. Nas Ta Bega darted in here and there to head off escape.

Shefford pulled on his boots and went out to help. He got too close to the gray mare and, warned by a yell from Withers, he jumped back just in time to avoid her vicious heels. Then Shefford turned his attention to Nack-yal and chased him all over the flat in a futile effort to catch him. Nas Ta Bega came to Shefford's assistance and put a rope over Nack-yal's head.

"Don't ever get behind one of these mustangs," said Withers, warningly, as Shefford came up. "You might be killed. . . . Eat your bite now. We'll soon be out of here."

Shefford had been late in awakening. The others had breakfasted. He found eating somewhat difficult in the excitement that ensued. Nas Ta Bega held ropes which were round the necks of Red and Dynamite. The mule showed his cunning and always appeared to present his heels to Withers, who tried to approach him with a pack-saddle. The patience of the trader was a revelation to Shefford. And at length Red was cornered by the three men, the pack-saddle was strapped on, and then the packs. Red promptly bucked the packs off, and the work had to be done over again. Then Red dropped his long ears and seemed ready to be tractable.

When Shefford turned his attention to Dynamite he decided that this was his first sight of a wild horse. The gray mare had fiery eyes that rolled and showed

the white. She jumped straight up, screamed, pawed, bit, and then plunged down
to shoot her hind hoofs into the air as high as her head had been. She was
amazingly agile and she seemed mad to kill something. She dragged the Indian
about, and when Joe Lake got a rope on her hind foot she dragged them both.
They lashed her with the ends of the lassoes, which action only made her kick
harder. She plunged into camp, drove Shefford flying for his life, knocked down
two of the burros, and played havoc with the unstrapped packs. Withers ran to
the assistance of Lake, and the two of them hauled back with all their strength
and weight. They were both powerful and heavy men. Dynamite circled round
and finally, after kicking the camp-fire to bits, fell down on her haunches in the
hot embers. "Let—her—set—there!" panted Withers. And Joe Lake shouted,
"Burn up, you durn coyote!" Both men appeared delighted that she had brought
upon herself just punishment. Dynamite sat in the remains of the fire long enough
to get burnt, and then she got up and meekly allowed Withers to throw a tarpaulin
and a roll of blankets over her and tie them fast.

Lake and Withers were sweating freely when this job was finished.

"Say, is that a usual morning's task with the pack-animals?" asked Shefford.

"They're all pretty decent to-day, except Dynamite," replied Withers. "She's
got to be worked out."

Shefford felt both amusement and consternation. The sun was just rising over
the ramparts of the cañon, and he had already seen more difficult and dangerous
work accomplished than half a dozen men of his type could do in a whole day.
He liked the outlook of his new duty as Withers's assistant, but he felt helplessly
inefficient. Still, all he needed was experience. He passed over what he anticipated would be pain and peril—the cost was of no moment.

Soon the pack-train was on the move, with the Indian leading. This morning
Nack-yal began his strange swinging off to the left, precisely as he had done the
day before. It got to be annoying to Shefford, and he lost patience with the
mustang and jerked him sharply round. This, however, had no great effect upon
Nack-yal.

As the train headed straight up the cañon Joe Lake dropped back to ride beside
Shefford. The Mormon had been amiable and friendly.

"Flock of deer up that draw," he said, pointing up a narrow side cañon.

Shefford gazed to see a half-dozen small, brown, long-eared objects, very like
burros, watching the pack-train pass.

"Are they deer?" he asked, delightedly.

"Sure are," replied Joe, sincerely. "Get down and shoot one. There's a rifle
in your saddle-sheath."

Shefford had already discovered that he had been armed this morning, a matter
which had caused him reflection. These animals certainly looked like deer; he
had seen a few deer, though not in their native wild haunts; and he experienced

the thrill of the hunter. Dismounting, he drew the rifle out of the sheath and started toward the little cañon.

"Hyar! Where you going with that gun?" yelled Withers. "That's a bunch of burros. . . . Joe's up to his old tricks. Shefford, look out for Joe!"

Rather sheepishly Shefford returned to his mustang and sheathed the rifle, and then took a long look at the animals up the draw. They resembled deer, but upon second glance they surely were burros.

"Durn me! Now if I didn't think they sure were deer!" exclaimed Joe. He appeared absolutely sincere and innocent. Shefford hardly knew how to take this likable Mormon, but vowed he would be on his guard in the future.

Nas Ta Bega soon led the pack-train toward the left wall of the cañon, and evidently intended to scale it. Shefford could not see any trail, and the wall appeared steep and insurmountable. But upon nearing the cliff he saw a narrow broken trail leading zigzag up over smooth rock, weathered slope, and through cracks.

"Spread out, and careful now!" yelled Withers.

The need of both advices soon became manifest to Shefford. The burros started stones rolling, making danger for those below. Shefford dismounted and led Nack-yal and turned aside many a rolling rock. The Indian and the burros, with the red mule leading, climbed steadily. But the mustangs had trouble. Joe's spirited bay had to be coaxed to face the ascent; Nack-yal balked at every difficult step; and Dynamite slipped on a flat slant of rock and slid down forty feet. Withers and Lake with ropes hauled the mare out of the dangerous position. Shefford, who brought up the rear, saw all the action, and it was exciting, but his pleasure in the climb was spoiled by sight of blood and hair on the stones. The ascent was crooked, steep, and long, and when Shefford reached the top of the wall he was glad to rest. It made him gasp to look down and see what he had surmounted. The cañon floor, green and level, lay a thousand feet below; and the wild burros which had followed on the trail looked like rabbits.

Shefford mounted presently, and rode out upon a wide, smooth trail leading into a cedar forest. There were bunches of gray sage in the open places. The air was cool and crisp, laden with a sweet fragrance. He saw Lake and Withers bobbing along, now on one side of the trail, and they kept to a steady trot. Occasionally the Indian and his bright-red saddle-blanket showed in an opening of the cedars.

It was level country, and there was nothing for Shefford to see except cedar and sage, an outcropping of red rock in places, and the winding trail. Mocking-birds made melody everywhere. Shefford seemed full of a strange pleasure, and the hours flew by. Nack-yal still wanted to be everlastingly turning off the trail, and, moreover, now he wanted to go faster. He was eager, restless, dissatisfied.

At noon the pack-train descended into a deep draw, well covered with cedar and sage. There was plenty of grass and shade, but no water. Shefford was surprised to see that every pack was removed; however, the roll of blankets was left on Dynamite.

The men made a fire and began to cook a noonday meal. Shefford, tired and warm, sat in a shady spot and watched. He had become all eyes. He had almost forgotten Fay Larkin; he had forgotten his trouble; and the present seemed sweet and full. Presently his ears were filled by a pattering roar and, looking up the draw, he saw two streams of sheep and goats coming down. Soon an Indian shepherd appeared, riding a fine mustang. A cream-colored colt bounded along behind, and presently a shaggy dog came in sight. The Indian dismounted at the camp, and his flock spread by in two white and black streams. The dog went with them. Withers and Joe shook hands with the Indian, whom Joe called "Navvy," and Shefford lost no time in doing likewise. Then Nas Ta Bega came in, and he and the Navajo talked. When the meal was ready all of them sat down round the canvas. The shepherd did not tie his horse.

Presently Shefford noticed that Nack-yal had returned to camp and was acting strangely. Evidently he was attracted by the Indian's mustang or the cream-colored colt. At any rate, Nack-yal hung around, tossed his head, whinnied in a low, nervous manner, and looked strangely eager and wild. Shefford was at first amused, then curious. Nack-yal approached too close to the mother of the colt, and she gave him a sounding kick in the ribs. Nack-yal uttered a plaintive snort and backed away, to stand, crestfallen, with all his eagerness and fire vanished.

Nas Ta Bega pointed to the mustang and said something in his own tongue. Then Withers addressed the visiting Indian, and they exchanged some words, whereupon the trader turned to Shefford.

"I bought Nack-yal from this Indian three years ago. This mare is Nack-yal's mother. He was born over here to the south. That's why he always swung left off the trail. He wanted to go home. Just now he recognized his mother and she whaled away and gave him a whack for his pains. She's got a colt now and probably didn't recognize Nack-yal. But he's broken-hearted."

The trader laughed, and Joe said, "You can't tell what these durn mustangs will do." Shefford felt sorry for Nack-yal, and when it came time to saddle him again found him easier to handle than ever before. Nack-yal stood with head down, broken-spirited.

Shefford was the first to ride up out of the draw, and once upon the top of the ridge he halted to gaze, wide-eyed and entranced. A rolling, endless plain sloped down beneath him, and led him on to a distant round-topped mountain. To the right a red cañon opened its jagged jaws, and away to the north rose a whorled and strange sea of curved ridges, crags, and domes.

Nas Ta Bega rode up then, leading the pack-train.

"Bi Nai, that is Na-tsis-an," he said, pointing to the mountain. "Navajo

Mountain. And there in the north are the cañons.''

Shefford followed the Indian down the trail and soon lost sight of that wide green-and-red wilderness. Nas Ta Bega turned at an intersecting trail, rode down into the cañon, and climbed out on the other side. Shefford got a glimpse now and then of the black dome of the mountain, but for the most part the distant points of the country were hidden. They crossed many trails, and went up and down the sides of many shallow cañons. Troops of wild mustangs whistled at them, stood on ridge-tops to watch, and then dashed away with manes and tails flying.

Withers rode forward presently and halted the pack-train. He had some conversation with Nas Ta Bega, whereupon the Indian turned his horse and trotted back, to disappear in the cedars.

''I'm some worried,'' explained Withers. ''Joe thinks he saw a bunch of horsemen trailing us. My eyes are bad and I can't see far. The Indian will find out. I took a roundabout way to reach the village because I'm always dodging Shadd.''

This communication lent an added zest to the journey. Shefford could hardly believe the truth that his eyes and his ears brought to his consciousness. He turned in behind Withers and rode down the rough trail, helping the mustang all in his power. It occurred to him that Nack-yal had been entirely different since that meeting with his mother in the draw. He turned no more off the trail; he answered readily to the rein; he did not look afar from every ridge. Shefford conceived a liking for the mustang.

Withers turned sidewise in his saddle and let his mustang pick the way.

''Another time we'll go up round the base of the mountain, where you can look down on the grandest scene in the world,'' said he. ''Two hundred miles of wind-worn rock, all smooth and bare, without a single straight line—cañons, caves, bridges—the most wonderful country in the world! Even the Indians haven't explored it. It's haunted, for them, and they have strange gods. The Navajos will hunt on this side of the mountain, but not on the other. That north side is consecrated ground. My wife has long been trying to get the Navajos to tell her the secret of Nonnezoshe. Nonnezoshe means Rainbow Bridge. The Indians worship it, but as far as she can find out only a few have ever seen it. I imagine it'd be worth some trouble.''

''Maybe that's the bridge Venters talked about—the one overarching the entrance to Surprise Valley,'' said Shefford.

''It might be,'' replied the trader. ''You've got a good chance of finding out. Nas Ta Bega is the man. You stick to that Indian. . . . Well, we start down here into this cañon, and we go down some, I reckon. In half an hour you'll see sago-lilies and Indian paint-brush and vermillion cactus.''

About the middle of the afternoon the pack-train and its drivers arrived at the hidden Mormon village. Nas Ta Bega had not returned from his scout back along the trail.

Shefford's sensibilities had all been overstrained, but he had left in him enthusiasm and appreciation that made the situation of this village a fairyland. It was a valley, a cañon floor, so long that he could not see the end, and perhaps a quarter of a mile wide. The air was hot, still, and sweetly odorous of unfamiliar flowers. Piñon and cedar trees surrounded the little log and stone houses, and along the walls of the cañon stood sharp-pointed, dark-green spruce-trees. These walls were singular of shape and color. They were not imposing in height, but they waved like the long, undulating swell of a sea. Every foot of surface was perfectly smooth, and the long curved lines of darker tinge that streaked the red followed the rounded line of the slope at the top. Far above, yet overhanging, were great yellow crags and peaks, and between these, still higher, showed the pine-fringed slope of Navajo Mountain with snow in the sheltered places, and glistening streams, like silver threads, running down.

All this Shefford noticed as he entered the valley from round a corner of wall. Upon nearer view he saw and heard a host of children, who, looking up to see the intruders, scattered like frightened quail. Long gray grass covered the ground, and here and there wide, smooth paths had been worn. A swift and murmuring brook ran through the middle of the valley, and its banks were bordered with flowers.

Withers led the way to one side near the wall, where a clump of cedar-trees and a dark, swift spring boiling out of the rocks and banks of amber moss with purple blossoms made a beautiful camp site. Here the mustangs were unsaddled and turned loose without hobbles. It was certainly unlikely that they would leave such a spot. Some of the burros were unpacked, and the others Withers drove off into the village.

"Sure's pretty nice," said Joe, wiping his sweaty face. "I'll never want to leave. It suits me to lie on this moss. . . . Take a drink of that spring."

Shefford complied with alacrity and found the water cool and sweet, and he seemed to feel it all through him. Then he returned to the mossy bank. He did not reply to Joe. In fact, all his faculties were absorbed in watching and feeling, and he lay there long after Joe went off to the village. The murmur of water, the hum of bees, the songs of strange birds, the sweet, warm air, the dreamy summer somnolence of the valley—all these added drowsiness to Shefford's weary lassitude, and he fell asleep. When he awoke Nas Ta Bega was sitting near him and Joe was busy near a camp-fire.

"Hello, Nas Ta Bega!" said Shefford. "Was there any one trailing us?"
The Navajo nodded.
Joe raised his head and with forceful brevity said, "Shadd."

"Shadd!" echoed Shefford, remembering the dark, sinister face of his visitor that night in the Sagi. "Joe, is it serious—his trailing us?"

"Well, I don't know how durn serious it is, but I'm scared to death," replied Lake. "He and his gang will hold us up somewhere on the way home."

Shefford regarded Joe with both concern and doubt. Joe's words were at variance with his looks.

"Say, pard, can you shoot a rifle?" queried Joe.

"Yes. I'm a fair shot at targets."

The Mormon nodded his head as if pleased. "That's good. These outlaws are all poor shots with a rifle. So'm I. But I can handle a six-shooter. I reckon we'll make Shadd sweat if he pushes us."

Withers returned, driving the burros, all of which had been unpacked down to the saddles. Two gray-bearded men accompanied him. One of them appeared to be very old and venerable, and walked with a stick. The other had a sad-lined face and kind, mild blue eyes. Shefford observed that Lake seemed unusually respectful. Withers intoduced these Mormons merely as Smith and Henninger. They were very cordial and pleasant in their greetings to Shefford. Presently another, somewhat younger, man joined the group, a stalwart, jovial fellow with ruddy face. There was certainly no mistaking his kindly welcome as he shook Shefford's hand. His name was Beal. The three stood round the camp-fire for a while, evidently glad of the presence of fellow-men and to hear news from the outside. Finally they went away, taking Joe with them. Withers took up the task of getting supper where Joe had been made to leave it.

"Shefford, listen," he said, presently, as he knelt before the fire. "I told them right out that you'd been a Gentile clergyman—that you'd gone back on your religion. It impressed them and you've been well received. I'll tell the same thing over at Stonebridge. You'll get in right. Of course I don't expect they'll make a Mormon of you. But they'll try to. Meanwhile you can be square and friendly all the time you're trying to find your Fay Larkin. To-morrow you'll meet some of the women. They're good souls, but, like any women, crazy for news. Think what it is to be shut up in here between these walls!"

"Withers, I'm intensely interested," replied Shefford, "and excited, too. Shall we stay here long?"

"I'll stay a couple of days, then go to Stonebridge with Joe. He'll come back here, and when you both feel like leaving, and if Nas Ta Bega thinks it safe, you'll take a trail over to some Indian hogans and pack me out a load of skins and blankets. . . . My boy, you've all the time there is, and I wish you luck. This isn't a bad place to loaf. I always get sentimental over here. Maybe it's the women. Some of them are pretty, and one of them—Shefford, they call her the Sago Lily. Her first name is Mary, I'm told. Don't know her last name. She's lovely. And I'll bet you forget Fay Larkin in a flash. Only—be careful. You drop in here with rather peculiar credentials, so to speak—as my helper and as a man with no religion! You'll not only be fully trusted, but you'll be welcome to these lonely women. So be careful. Remember it's my secret belief they are sealed wives and are visited occasionally at night by their husbands. I don't *know* this, but I believe it. And you're not supposed to dream of that."

"How many men in the village?" asked Shefford.

"Three. You met them."

"Have they wives?" asked Shefford, curiously.

"Wives! Well, I guess. But only one each that I know of. Joe Lake is the only unmarried Mormon I've met."

"And no men-strangers, cowboys, outlaws—ever come to this village?"

"Except to Indians, it seems to be a secret so far," replied the trader, earnestly. "But it can't be kept secret. I've said that time after time over in Stonebridge. With Mormons it's 'sufficient unto the day is the evil thereof.' "

"What'll happen when outsiders do learn and ride in here?"

"There'll be trouble—maybe bloodshed. Mormon women are absolutely good, but they're human, and want and need a little life. And, strange to say, Mormon men are pig-headedly jealous. . . . Why, if some of the cowboys I knew in Durango would ride over here there'd simply be hell. But that's a long way, and probably this village will be deserted before news of it ever reaches Colorado. There's more danger of Shadd and his gang coming in. Shadd's half Piute. He must know of this place. And he's got some white outlaws in his gang. . . . Come on. Grub's ready, and I'm too hungry to talk."

Later, when shadows began to gather in the valley and the lofty peaks above were gold in the sunset glow, Withers left camp to look after the straying mustangs, and Shefford strolled to and fro under the cedars. The lights and shades in the Sagi that first night had moved him to enthusiastic watchfulness, but here they were so weird and beautiful that he was enraptured. He actually saw great shafts of gold and shadows of purple streaming from the peaks down into the valley. It was day on the heights and twilight in the valley. The swiftly changing colors were like rainbows.

While he strolled up and down several women came to the spring and filled their buckets. They wore shawls or hoods and their garments were somber, but, nevertheless, they appeared to have youth and comeliness. They saw him, looked at him curiously, and then, without speaking, went back on the well-trodden path. Presently down the path appeared a woman—a girl in lighter garb. It was almost white. She was shapely and walked with free, graceful step, reminding him of the Indian girl, Glen Naspa. This one wore a hood shaped like a huge sunbonnet and it concealed her face. She carried a bucket. When she reached the spring and went down the few stone steps Shefford saw that she did not have on shoes. As she braced herself to lift the bucket her bare foot clung to the mossy stone. It was a strong, sinewy, beautiful foot, instinct with youth. He was curious enough, he thought, but the awakening artist in him made him more so. She dragged at the full bucket and had difficulty in lifting it out of the hole. Shefford strode forward and took the bucket-handle from her.

"Won't you let me help you?" he said, lifting the bucket. "Indeed—it's very heavy."

"Oh—thank you," she said, without raising her head. Her voice seemed singularly young and sweet. He had not heard a voice like it. She moved down the path and he walked beside her. He felt embarrassed, yet more curious than ever; he wanted to say something, to turn and look at her, but he kept on for a dozen paces without making up his mind.

Finally he said: "Do you really carry this heavy bucket? Why, it makes my arm ache."

"Twice every day—morning and evening," she replied. "I'm very strong."

Then he stole a look out of the corner of his eye, and, seeing that her face was hidden from his by the hood, he turned to observe her at better advantage. A long braid of hair hung down her back. In the twilight it gleamed dull gold. She came up to his shoulder. The sleeve nearest him was rolled up to her elbow, revealing a fine round arm. Her hand, like her foot, was brown, strong, and well shaped. It was a hand that had been developed by labor. She was full-bosomed, yet slender, and she walked with a free stride that made Shefford admire and wonder.

They passed several of the little stone and log houses, and women greeted them as they went by, and children peered shyly from the doors. He kept trying to think of something to say, and, failing in that, determined to have one good look under the hood before he left her.

"You walk lame," she said, solicitously. "Let me carry the bucket now— please. My house is near."

"Am I lame? . . . Guess so, a little," he replied. "It was a hard ride for me. But I'll carry the bucket just the same."

They went on under some piñon-trees, down a path to a little house identical with the others, except that it had a stone porch. Shefford smelled fragrant wood-smoke and saw a column curling from the low, flat, stone chimney. Then he set the bucket down on the porch.

"Thank you, Mr. Shefford," she said.

"You know my name?" he asked.

"Yes. Mr. Withers spoke to my nearest neighbor and she told me."

"Oh, I see. And you—"

He did not go on and she did not reply. When she stepped upon the porch and turned he was able to see under the hood. The face there was in shadow, and for that very reason he answered to ungovernable impulse and took a step closer to her. Dark, grave, sad eyes looked down at him, and he felt as if he could never draw his own glance away. He seemed not to see the rest of her face, and yet felt that it was lovely. Then a downward movement of the hood hid from him the strange eyes and the shadowy loveliness.

"I—I beg your pardon," he said, quickly, drawing back. "I'm rude. . . . Withers told me about a girl he called—he said looked like a sago-lily. That's no excuse to stare under your hood. But I—I was curious. I wondered if—"

He hesitated, realizing how foolish his talk was. She stood a moment, probably watching him, but he could not be sure, for her face was hidden.

"They call me that," she said. "But my name is Mary."

"Mary—what?" he asked.

"Just Mary," she said, simply. "Good night."

He did not say good night and could not have told why. She took up the bucket and went into the dark house. Shefford hurried away into the gathering darkness.

6

In the Hidden Valley

SHEFFORD had hardly seen her face, yet he was more interested in a woman than he had ever been before. Still, he reflected, as he returned to camp, he had been under a long strain, he was unduly excited by this new and adventurous life, and these, with the mystery of this village, were perhaps accountable for a state of mind that could not last.

He rolled in his blankets on the soft bed of moss and he saw the stars through the needle-like fringe of the piñons. It seemed impossible to fall asleep. The two domed peaks split the sky, and back of them, looming dark and shadowy, rose the mountain. There was something cold, austere, and majestic in their lofty presence, and they made him feel alone, yet not alone. He raised himself to see the quiet forms of Withers and Nas Ta Bega prone in the starlight, and their slow, deep breathing was that of tired men. A bell on a mustang rang somewhere off in the valley and gave out a low, strange, reverberating echo from wall to wall. When it ceased a silence set in that was deader than any silence he had ever felt, but gradually he became aware of the low murmur of the brook. For the rest there was no sound of wind, no bark of dog or yelp of coyote, no sound of voice in the village.

He tried to sleep, but instead thought of this girl who was called Sago Lily. He recalled everything incident to their meeting and the walk to her home. Her swift, free step, her graceful poise, her shapely form—the long braid of hair, dull gold in the twilight, the beautiful bare foot and the strong round arm—these he thought of and recalled vividly. But of her face he had no idea except the shadowy, haunting loveliness, and that grew more and more difficult to remember. The tone of her voice and what she had said—how the one had thrilled him and the other mystified! It was her voice that had most attracted him. There was something in it besides music—what, he could not tell—sadness, depth, something like that in Nas Ta Bega's—a beauty springing from disuse. But this seemed absurd. Why should he imagine her voice one that had not been used as freely as any other woman's? She was a Mormon; very likely, almost surely, she was a sealed wife. His interest, too, was absurd, and he tried to throw it off, or imagine it one he might have felt in any other of these strange women of the hidden village.

But Shefford's intelligence and his good sense, which became operative when he was fully roused and set the situation clearly before his eyes, had no effect upon his deeper, mystic, and primitive feelings. He saw the truth and he felt something that he could not name. He would not be a fool, but there was no harm in dreaming. And unquestionably, beyond all doubt, the dream and the romance that had lured him to the wilderness were here, hanging over him like the shadows of the great peaks. His heart swelled with emotion when he thought of how the black and incessant despair of the past was gone. So he embraced any attraction that made him forget and think and feel; some instinct stronger than intelligence bade him drift.

Joe's rolling voice awoke him next morning and he rose with a singular zest. When or where in his life had he awakened in such a beautiful place? Almost he understood why Venters and Bess had been haunted by memories of Surprise Valley. The morning was clear, cool, sweet; the peaks were dim and soft in rosy cloud; shafts of golden sunlight shot down into the purple shadows. Mocking-birds were singing. His body was sore and tired from the unaccustomed travel, but his heart was full, happy. His spirit wanted to run, and he knew there was something out there waiting to meet it. The Indian and the trader and the Mormon all meant more to him this morning. He had grown a little overnight. Nas Ta Bega's deep "Bi Nai" rang in his ears, and the smiles of Withers and Joe were greetings. He had friends; he had work; and there was rich, strange, and helpful life to live. There was even a difference in the mustang Nack-yal. He came readily; he did not look wild; he had a friendly eye; and Shefford liked him more.

"What is there to do?" asked Shefford, feeling equal to a hundred tasks.

"No work," replied the trader, with a laugh, and he drew Shefford aside. "I'm in no hurry. I like it here. And Joe never wants to leave. To-day you can meet the women. Make yourself popular. I've already made you that. These women are most all young and lonesome. Talk to them. Make them like you. Then some day you may be safe to ask questions. Last night I wanted to ask old Mother Smith if she ever heard the name Fay Larkin. But I thought better of it. If there's a girl here or at Stonebridge of that name we'll learn it. If there's mystery we'd better go slow. Mormons are hell on secret and mystery, and to pry into their affairs is to queer yourself. My advice is—just be as nice as you can be, and let things happen."

Fay Larkin! All in a night Shefford had forgotten her. Why? He pondered over the matter, and then the old thrill, the old desire, came back.

"Shefford, what do you think Nas Ta Bega said to me last night?" asked Withers in lower voice.

"Haven't any idea," replied Shefford, curiously.

"We were sitting beside the fire. I saw you walking under the cedars. You seemed thoughtful. That keen Indian watched you, and he said to me in Navajo, 'Bi Nai has lost his God. He has come far to find a wife. Nas Ta Bega is his brother.' . . . He meant he'll find both God and wife for you. I don't know about that, but I say take the Indian as he thinks he is—your brother. Long before I knew Nas Ta Bega well my wife used to tell me about him. He's a sage and a poet—the very spirit of this desert. He's worth cultivating for his own sake. But more—remember, if Fay Larkin is still shut in that valley the Navajo will find her for you."

"I shall take Nas Ta Bega as my brother—and be proud," replied Shefford.

"There's another thing. Do you intend to confide in Joe?"

"I hadn't thought of that."

"Well, it might be a good plan. But wait until you know him better and he knows you. He's ready to fight for you now. He's taken your trouble to heart. You wouldn't think Joe is deeply religious. Yet he is. He may never breathe a word about religion to you. . . . Now, Shefford, go ahead. You've struck a trail. It's rough, but it'll make a man of you. It 'll lead somewhere."

"I'm singularly fortunate—I—who had lost all friends. Withers, I am grateful. I'll prove it. I'll show—"

Withers's upheld hand checked further speech, and Shefford realized that beneath the rough exterior of this desert trader there was fine feeling. These men of crude toil and wild surroundings were beginning to loom up large in Shefford's mind.

The day began leisurely. The men were yet at breakfast when the women of the village began to come one by one to the spring. Joe Lake made friendly and joking remarks to each. And as each one passed on down the path he poised a biscuit in one hand and a cup of coffee in the other, and with his head cocked sidewise like an owl he said, "Reckon I've got to get me a woman like her."

Shefford saw and heard, yet he was all the time half unconsciously watching with strange eagerness for a white figure to appear. At last he saw her—the same girl with the hood, the same swift step. A little shock or quiver passed over him, and at the moment all that was explicable about it was something associated with regret.

Joe Lake whistled and stared.

"I haven't met her," he muttered.

"That's the Sago Lily," said Withers.

"Reckon I'm going to carry that bucket," went on Joe.

"And queer yourself with all the other women who've been to the spring? Don't do it, Joe," advised the trader.

"But her bucket's bigger," protested Joe, weakly.

"That's true. But you ought to know Mormons. If she'd come first, all right. As she didn't—why, don't single her out."

Joe kept his seat. The girl came to the spring. A low "good morning" came from under the hood. Then she filled her bucket and started home. Shefford observed that this time she wore moccasins and she carried the heavy bucket with ease. When she disappeared he had again the vague, inexplicable sensation of regret.

Joe Lake breathed heavily. "Reckon I've got to get me a woman like her," he said. But the former jocose tone was lacking and he appeared thoughtful.

Withers first took Shefford to the building used for a school. It was somewhat larger than the other houses, had only one room with two doors and several windows. It was full of children of all sizes and ages, sitting on rude board benches.

There were half a hundred of them, sturdy, healthy, rosy boys and girls, clad in home-made garments. The young woman teacher was as embarrassed as her pupils were shy, and the visitors withdrew without having heard a word of lessons.

Withers then called upon Smith, Henninger, and Beal, and their wives. Shefford found himself cordially received, and what little he did say showed him how he would be listened to when he cared to talk. These folk were plain and kindly, and he found that there was nothing about them to dislike. The men appeared mild and quiet, and when not conversing seemed austere. The repose of the women was only on the surface; underneath he felt their intensity. Especially in many of the younger women, whom he met in the succeeding hour, did he feel this power of restrained emotion. This surprised him, as did also the fact that almost every one of them was attractive and some of them were ex-

ceedingly pretty. He became so interested in them all as a whole that he could
not individualize one. They were as widely different in appearance and temperament as women of any other class, but it seemed to Shefford that one
common trait united them—and it was a strange, checked yearning for something
that he could not discover. Was it happiness? They certainly seemed to be happy,
far more so than those millions of women who were chasing phantoms. Were
they really sealed wives, as Withers believed, and was this unnatural wifehood
responsible for the strange intensity? At any rate he returned to camp with the
conviction that he had stumbled upon a remarkable situation.

He had been told the last names of only three women, and their husbands
were in the village. The names of the others were Ruth, Rebecca, Joan—he
could not recall them all. They were the mothers of these beautiful children.
The fathers, as far as he was concerned, were as intangible as myths. Shefford
was an educated clergyman, a man of the world, and, as such, knew women in
his way. Mormons might be strange and different, yet the fundamental truth was
that all over the world mothers of children were wives; there was a relation
between wife and mother that did not need to be named to be felt; and he divined
from this that, whatever the situation of these lonely and hidden women, they
knew themselves to be wives. Shefford absolutely satisfied himself on that score.
If they were miserable they certainly did not show it, and the question came to
him how just was the criticism of uninformed men? His judgment of Mormons
had been established by what he had heard and read, rather than what he knew.
He wanted now to have an open mind. He had studied the totemism and exogamy
of the primitive races, and here was his opportunity to understand polygamy.
One wife for one man—that was the law. Mormons broke it openly; Gentiles
broke it secretly. Mormons acknowledged all their wives and protected their
children; Gentiles acknowledged one wife only. Unquestionably the Mormons
were wrong, but were not the Gentiles still more wrong?

The following day Joe Lake appeared reluctant to start for Stonebridge with
Withers.

"Joe, you'd better come along," said the trader, dryly. "I reckon you've seen
a little too much of the Sago Lily."

Lake offered no reply, but it was evident from his sober face that Withers had
not hit short of the mark. Withers rode off, with a parting word to Shefford, and
finally Joe somberly mounted his bay and trotted down the valley. As Nas Ta
Bega had gone off somewhere to visit Indians, Shefford was left alone.

He went into the village and made himself useful and agreeable. He made
friends with the children and he talked to the women until he was hoarse. Their
ignorance of the world was a spur to him, and never in his life had he had such
an attentive audience. And as he showed no curiosity, asked no difficult ques-

tions, gradually what reserve he had noted wore away, and the end of the day saw him on a footing with them that Withers had predicted.

By the time several like days had passed it seemed from the interest and friendliness of these women that he might have lived long among them. He was possessed of wit and eloquence and information, which he freely gave, and not with selfish motive. He liked these women; he liked to see the somber shade pass from their faces, to see them brighten. He had met the girl Mary at the spring and along the path, but he had not yet seen her face. He was always looking for her, hoping to meet her, and confessed to himself that the best of the day for him were the morning and evening visits she made to the spring. Nevertheless, for some reason hard to divine, he was reluctant to seek her deliberately. Always while he had listened to her neighbors' talk, he had hoped they might let fall something about her. But they did not. He received an impression that she was not so intimate with the others as he had supposed. They all made one big family. Still, she seemed a little outside. He could bring no proofs to strengthen this idea. He merely felt it, and many of his feelings were independent of intelligent reason. Something had been added to curiosity, that was sure.

It was his habit to call upon Mother Smith in the afternoons. From the first her talk to him hinted of a leaning toward thought of making him a Mormon. Her husband and the other men took up her cue and spoke of their religion, casually at first, but gradually opening their minds to free and simple discussion of their faith. Shefford lent respectful attention. He would rather have been a Mormon than an atheist, and apparently they considered him the latter, and were earnest to save his soul. Shefford knew that he could never be one any more than the other. He was just at sea. But he listened, and he found them simple in faith, blind, perhaps, but loyal and good. It was noteworthy that Mother Smith happened to be the only woman in the village who had ever mentioned religion to him. She was old, of a past generation; the young women belonged to the present. Shefford pondered the significant difference.

Every day made more steadfast his impression of the great mystery that was like a twining shadow round these women, yet in the same time many little ideas shifted and many new characteristics became manifest. This last was of course the result of acquaintance; he was learning more about the villagers. He gathered from keen interpretation of subtle words and looks that here in this lonely village, the same as in all the rest of the world where women were together, there were cliques, quarrels, dislikes, loves, and jealousies. The truth, once known to him, made him feel natural and fortified his confidence to meet the demands of an increasingly interesting position. He discovered, with a somewhat grim amusement, that a clergyman's experience in a church full of women had not been entirely useless.

One afternoon he let fall a careless remark that was a subtle question in regard to the girl Mary, whom Withers called the Sago Lily. In response he received an answer couched in the sweet poisoned honey of woman's jealousy. He said no more. Certain ideas of his were strengthened, and straight-way he became thoughtful.

That afternoon late, as he did his camp chores, he watched for her. But she did not come. Then he decided to go to see her. But even the decision and the strange thrill it imparted did not change his reluctance.

Twilight was darkening the valley when he reached her house, and the shadows were thick under the piñons. There was no light in the door or window. He saw a white shape on the porch, and as he came down the path it rose. It was the girl Mary, and she appeared startled.

"Good evening," he said. "It's Shefford. May I stay and talk a little while?"

She was silent for so long that he began to feel awkward.

"I'd be glad to have you," she replied, finally.

There was a bench on the porch, but he preferred to sit upon a blanket on the step.

"I've been getting acquainted with everybody—except you," he went on.

"I have been here," she replied.

That might have been a woman's speech, but it certainly had been made in a girl's voice. She was neither shy nor embarrassed nor self-conscious. As she stood back from him he could not see her face in the dense twilight.

"I've been wanting to call on you."

She made some slight movement. Shefford felt a strange calm, yet he knew the moment was big and potent.

"Won't you sit here?" he asked.

She complied with his wish, and then he saw her face, though dimly, in the twilight. And it struck him mute. But he had no glimpse such as had flashed upon him from under the hood that other night. He thought of a white flower in shadow, and received his first impression of the rare and perfect lily Withers had said graced the wild cañons. She was only a girl. She sat very still, looking straight before her, and seemed to be waiting, listening. Shefford saw the quick rise and fall of her bosom.

"I want to talk," he began, swiftly, hoping to put her at her ease. "Every one here has been good to me and I've talked—oh, for hours and hours. But the thing in my mind I haven't spoken of. I've never asked any questions. That makes my part so strange. I want to tell why I came out here. I need some one who will keep my secret, and perhaps help me. . . . Would you?"

"Yes, if I could," she replied.

"You see I've got to trust you, or one of these other women. You're all Mormons. I don't mean that's anything against you. I believe you're all good and noble. But the fact makes—well, makes a liberty of speech impossible. What can I do?''

Her silence probably meant that she did not know. Shefford sensed less strain in her and more excitement. He believed he was on the right track and did not regret his impulse. Even had he regretted it he would have gone on, for opposed to caution and intelligence was his driving mystic force.

Then he told her the truth about his boyhood, his ambition to be an artist, his renunciation to his father's hope, his career as a clergyman, his failure in religion, and the disgrace that had made him a wanderer.

''Oh—I'm sorry!'' she said. The faint starlight shone on her face, in her eyes, and if he ever saw beauty and soul he saw them then. She seemed deeply moved. She had forgotten herself. She betrayed girlhood then—all the quick sympathy, the wonder, the sweetness of a heart innocent and untutored. She looked at him with great, starry, questioning eyes, as if they had just become aware of his presence, as if a man had been strange to her.

''Thank you. It's good of you to be sorry,'' he said. ''My instinct guided me right. Perhaps you'll be my friend.''

''I will be—if I can,'' she said.

''But can you be?''

''I don't know. I never had a friend. I . . . But, sir, I mustn't talk of myself. . . . Oh, I'm afraid I can't help you.''

How strange the pathos of her voice! Almost he believed she was in need of help or sympathy or love. But he could not wholly trust a judgment formed from observation of a class different from hers.

''Maybe you can help me. Let's see,'' he said. ''I don't seek to make you talk of yourself. But—you're a human being—a girl—almost a woman. You're not dumb. But even a nun can talk.''

''A nun? What is that?''

''Well—a nun is a sister of mercy—a woman consecrated to God—who has renounced the world. In some ways you Mormon women here resemble nuns. It is sacrifice that nails you in this lonely valley. . . . You see—how I talk! One word, one thought brings another, and I speak what perhaps should be unsaid. And it's hard, because I feel I could unburden myself to you.''

''Tell me what you want,'' she said.

Shefford hesitated, and became aware of the rapid pound of his heart. More than anything he wanted to be fair to this girl. He saw that she was warming to his influence. Her shadowy eyes were fixed upon him. The starlight, growing brighter, shone on her golden hair and white face.

''I'll tell you presently,'' he said. ''I've trusted you. I'll trust you with all. . . . But let me have my own time. This is so strange a thing, my wanting to confide in you. It's selfish, perhaps. I have my own ax to grind. I hope I won't wrong you. That's why I'm going to be perfectly frank. I might wait for days to get better acquainted. But the impulse is on me. I've been so interested in all you Mormon women. The fact—the meaning of this hidden village is so—so terrible to me. But that's none of my business. I have spent my afternoons and evenings with these women at the different cottages. You do not mingle with them. They are lonely, but have not such loneliness as yours. I have passed here every night. No light—no sound. I can't help thinking. Don't censure me or be afraid to draw within yourself just because I must think. I may be all wrong. But I'm curious. I wonder about you. Who are you? Mary—Mary what? Maybe I really don't want to know. I came with selfish motive and now I'd like to— to—what shall I say? Make your life a little less lonely for the while I'm here. That's all. It needn't offend. And if you accept it, how much easier I can tell you my secret. You are a Mormon and I—well, I am only a wanderer in these wilds. But—we might help each other. . . . Have I made a mistake?''

"No—no," she cried, almost wildly.

"We can be friends then. You will trust me, help me?"

"Yes, if I dare."

"Surely you may dare what the other women would?"

She was silent.

And the wistfulness of her silence touched him. He felt contrition. He did not stop to analyze his own emotions, but he had an inkling that once this strange situation was ended he would have food for reflection. What struck him most now was the girl's blanched face, the strong, nervous clasp of her hands, the visible tumult of her bosom. Excitement alone could not be accountable for this. He had not divined the cause for such agitation. He was puzzled, troubled, and drawn irresistibly. He had not said what he had planned to say. The moment had given birth to his speech, and it had flowed. What was guiding him?

"Mary," he said, earnestly, "tell me—have you mother, father, sister, brother? Something prompts me to ask that."

"All dead—gone—years ago," she answered.

"How old are you?"

"Eighteen, I think. I'm not sure."

"You *are* lonely."

His words were gentle and divining.

"O God!" she cried. "Lonely!"

Then as a man in a dream he beheld her weeping. There was in her the unconsciousness of a child and the passion of a woman. He gazed out into the dark shadows and up at the white stars, and then at the bowed head with its mass of glinting hair. But her agitation was no longer strange to him. A few gentle and kind words have proved her undoing. He knew then that whatever her life was, no kindness or sympathy entered it. Presently she recovered, and sat as before, only whiter of face it seemed, and with something tragic in her dark eyes. She was growing cold and still again, aloof, more like those other Mormon women.

"I understand," he said. "I'm sorry I spoke. I felt your trouble, whatever it is. . . . Do not retreat into your cold shell, I beg of you. . . . Let me trust you with my secret."

He saw her shake out of the cold apathy. She wavered. He felt an inexplicable sweetness in the power his voice seemed to have upon her. She bowed her head in acquiescence. And Shefford began his story. Did she grow still, like stone, or was that only his vivid imagination? He told her of Venters and Bess—of Lassiter and Jane—of little Fay Larkin—of the romance, and then the tragedy of Surprise Valley.

"So, when my Church disowned me," he concluded, "I conceived the idea of wandering into the wilds of Utah to save Fay Larkin from that cañon prison. It grew to be the best and strongest desire of my life. I think if I could save her that it would save me. I never loved any girl. I can't say that I love Fay Larkin. How could I when I've never seen her—when she's only a dream girl? But I believe if she were to become a reality—a flesh-and-blood girl—that I would love her."

That was more than Shefford had ever confessed to any one, and it stirred him to his depths. Mary bent her head on her hands in strange, stonelike rigidity.

"So here I am in the cañon country," he continued. "Withers tells me it is a country of rainbows, both in the evanescent air and in the changeless stone. Always as a boy there had been for me some haunting promise, some treasure at the foot of the rainbow. I shall expect the curve of a rainbow to lead me down into Surprise Valley. A dreamer, you will call me. But I have had strange dreams come true. . . . Mary, do you think *this* dream will come true?"

She was silent so long that he repeated his question.

"Only—in heaven," she whispered.

He took her reply strangely and a chill crept over him.

"You think my plan to seek to strive, to find—you think that idle, vain?"

"I think it noble. . . . Thank God I've met a man like you!"

"Don't praise me!" he exclaimed, hastily. "Only help me. . . . Mary, will you answer a few little questions, if I swear by my honor I'll never reveal what you tell me?"

"I'll try."

He moistened his lips. Why did she seem so strange, so far away? The hovering shadows made him nervous. Always he had been afraid of the dark. His mood now admitted of unreal fancies.

"Have you ever heard of Fay Larkin?" he asked, very low.

"Yes."

"Was there only one Fay Larkin?"

"Only one."

"Did you—ever see her?"

"Yes," came the faint reply.

He was grateful. How she might be breaking faith with creed or duty! He had not dared to hope so much. All his inner being trembled at the portent of his next query. He had not dreamed it would be so hard to put, or would affect him so powerfully. A warmth, a glow, a happiness pervaded his spirit; and the chill, the gloom were as if they had never been.

"Where is Fay Larkin now?" he asked, huskily.

He bent over her, touched her, leaned close to catch her whisper.

"She is—dead!"

Slowly Shefford rose, with a sickening shock, and then in bitter pain he strode away into the starlight.

7

Sago-Lilies

THE Indian returned to camp that night, and early the next day, which was Sunday, Withers rode in, accompanied by a stout, gray-bearded personage wearing a long black coat.

"Bishop Kane, this is my new man, John Shefford," said the trader.

Shefford acknowledged the introduction with the respectful courtesy evidently in order, and found himself being studied intently by clear blue eyes. The bishop appeared old, dry, and absorbed in thought; he spoke quaintly, using in every speech some Biblical word or phrase; and he had an air of authority. He asked Shefford to hear him preach at the morning service, and then he went off into the village.

"Guess he liked your looks," remarked Withers.

"He certainly sized me up," replied Shefford.

"Well, what could you expect? Sure I never heard of a deal like this—a handsome young fellow left alone with a lot of pretty Mormon women! You'll understand when you learn to know Mormons. Bishop Kane's a square old chap. Crazy on religion, maybe, but otherwise he's a good fellow. I made the best stand I could for you. The Mormons over at Stonebridge were huffy because I hadn't consulted them before fetching you over here. If I had, of course you'd never have gotten here. It was Joe Lake who made it all right with them. Joe's well thought of, and he certainly stood up for you.''

"I owe him something, then," replied Shefford. "Hope my obligations don't grow beyond me. Did you leave Joe at Stonebridge?''

"Yes. He wanted to stay, and I had work there that'll keep him awhile. Shefford, we got news of Shadd—bad news. The half-breed's cutting up rough. His gang shot up some Piutes over here across the line. Then he got run out of Durango a few weeks ago for murder. A posse of cowboys trailed him. But he slipped them. He's a fox. You know he was trailing us here. He left the trail, Nas Ta Bega said. I learned at Stonebridge that Shadd is well disposed toward Mormons. It takes the Mormons to handle Indians. Shadd knows of this village and that's why he shunted off our trail. But he might hang down in the pass and wait for us. I think I'd better go back to Kayenta alone, across country. You stay here till Joe and the Indian think it safe to leave. You'll be going up on the slope of Navajo to load a pack-train, and from there it may be well to go down West Cañon to Red Lake, and home over the divide, the way you came. Joe'll decide what's best. And you might as well buckle on a gun and get used to it. Sooner or later you'll have to shoot your way through."

Shefford did not respond with his usual enthusiasm, and the omission caused the trader to scrutinize him closely.

"What's the matter?" he queried. "There's no light in your eye to-day. You look a little shady."

"I didn't rest well last night," replied Shefford. "I'm depressed this morning. But I'll cheer up directly."

"Did you get along with the women?"

"Very well indeed. And I've enjoyed myself. It's a strange, beautiful place."

"Do you like the women?"

"Yes."

"Have you seen much of the Sago Lily?"

"No. I carried her bucket one night—and saw her only once again. I've been with the other women most of the time."

"It's just as well you didn't run often into Mary. Joe's sick over her. I never saw a girl with a face and form to equal hers. There's danger here for any man, Shefford. Even for you who think you've turned your back on the world! Any of these Mormon women may fall in love with you. They can't love their husbands. That's how I figure it. Religion holds them, not love. And the peculiar thing is this: they're second, third, or fourth wives, all sealed. That means their husbands are old, have picked them out for youth and physical charms, have chosen the very opposite to their first wives, and then have hidden them here in this lonely hole. . . . Did you ever imagine so terrible a thing?''

"No, Withers, I did not."

"Maybe that's what depressed you. Anyway, my hunch is worth taking. Be as nice as you can, Shefford. Lord knows it would be good for these poor women if every last one of them fell in love with you. That won't hurt them so long as you keep your head. Savvy? Perhaps I seem rough and coarse to a man of your class. Well, that may be. But human nature is human nature. And in this strange and beautiful place you might love an Indian girl, let alone the Sago Lily. That's all. I sure feel better with that load off my conscience. Hope I don't offend."

"No indeed. I thank you, Withers," replied Shefford, with his hand on the trader's shoulder. "You are right to caution me. I seem to be wild—thirsting for adventure—chasing a gleam. In these unstable days I can't answer for my heart. But I can for my honor. These unfortunate women are as safe with me as—as they are with you and Joe."

Withers uttered a blunt laugh.

"See here, son, look things square in the eye. Men of violent, lonely, toilsome lives store up hunger for the love of woman. Love of a strange woman, if you want to put it that way. It's nature. It seems all the beautiful young women in Utah are corralled in this valley. When I come over here I feel natural, but I'm not happy. I'd like to make love to—to that flower-faced girl. And I'm not ashamed to own it. I've told Molly, my wife, and she understands. As for Joe, it's much harder for him. Joe never has had a wife or sweetheart. I tell you he's sick, and if I'd stay here a month I'd be sick."

Withers had spoken with fire in his eyes, with grim humor on his lips, with uncompromising brutal truth. What he admitted was astounding to Shefford, but, once spoken, not at all strange. The trader was a man who spoke his inmost thought. And what he said suddenly focused Shefford's mental vision clear and whole upon the appalling significance of the tragedy of those women, especially of the girl whose life was lonelier, sadder, darker than that of the others.

"Withers, trust me," replied Shefford.

"All right. Make the best of a bad job," said the trader, and went off about his tasks.

Shefford and Withers attended the morning service, which was held in the school-house. Exclusive of the children every inhabitant of the village was there. The women, except the few eldest, were dressed in white and looked exceedingly well. Manifestly they had bestowed care upon this Sabbath morning's toilet. One thing surely this dress occasion brought out, and it was evidence that the Mormon women were not poor, whatever their misfortunes might be. Jewelry was not wanting, nor fine lace. And they all wore beautiful wild flowers of a kind unknown to Shefford. He received many a bright smile. He looked for Mary, hoping to see her face for the first time in the daylight, but she sat far forward and did not turn. He saw her graceful white neck, the fine lines of her throat, and her colorless cheek. He recognized her, yet in the light she seemed a stranger.

The service began with a short prayer and was followed by the singing of a hymn. Nowhere had Shefford heard better music or sweeter voices. How deeply they affected him! Had any man ever fallen into a stranger adventure than this? He had only to shut his eyes to believe it all a creation of his fancy—the square log cabin with its red mud between the chinks and a roof like an Indian hogan— the old bishop in his black coat, standing solemnly, his hand beating time to the tune—the many young women, fresh and handsome, lifting their voices.

Shefford listened intently to the bishop's sermon. In some respects it was impossible for an intelligent man to regard seriously. It was very long, lasting an hour and a half, and the parts that were helpful to Shefford came from the experience and wisdom of a man who had grown old in the desert. The physical things that had molded characters of iron, the obstacles that only strong, patient men could have overcome, the making of homes in a wilderness, showed the greatness of this alien band of Mormons. Shefford conceded greatness to them. But the strange religion—the narrowing down of the world to the soil of Utah, the intimations of prophets on earth who had direct converse with God, the austere self-conscious omnipotence of this old bishop—these were matters that Shefford felt he must understand better, and see more favorably, if he were not to consider them impossible.

Immediately after the service, forgetting that his intention had been to get the long-waited-for look at Mary in the light of the sun, Shefford hurried back to camp and to a secluded spot among the cedars. Strikingly it had come to him that the fault he had found in Gentile religion he now found in the Mormon religion. An old question returned to haunt him—were all religions the same in blindness? As far as he could see, religion existed to uphold the founders of a Church, a creed. The Church of his own kind was a place where narrow men and women went to think of their own salvation. They did not go there to think of others. And now Shefford's keen mind saw something of Mormonism and found it wanting. Bishop Kane was a sincere, good, mistaken man. He believed what he preached, but that would not stand logic. He taught blindness and mostly it appeared to be directed at the women. Was there no religion divorced from power, no religion as good for one man as another, no religion in the spirit of brotherly love? Nas Ta Bega's "Bi Nai" (brother)—that was love, if not religion, and perhaps the one and the other were the same. Shefford kept in mind an intention to ask Nas Ta Bega what he thought of the Mormons.

Later, when opportunity afforded, he did speak to the Indian. Nas Ta Bega threw away his cigarette and made an impressive gesture that conveyed as much sorrow as scorn.

"The first Mormon said God spoke to him and told him to go to a certain place and dig. He went there and found the Book of Mormon. It said follow me, marry many wives, go into the desert and multiply, send your sons out into the world and bring us young women, many young women. And when the first Mormon became strong with many followers he said again: Give to me part of your labor—of your cattle and sheep—of your silver—that I may build me great cathedrals for you to worship in. And I will commune with God and make it right and good that you have more wives. That is what the bishop preached. That is Mormonism."

"Nas Ta Bega, you mean the Mormons are a great and good people blindly following a leader?"

"Yes. And the leader builds for himself—not for them."

"They have no God. They are blind like the Mokis who have the creeping growths on their eyes. They have no God they can see and hear and feel, who is with them day and night."

It was late in the afternoon when Bishop Kane rode through the camp and halted on his way to speak to Shefford. He was kind and fatherly.

"Young man, are you open to faith?" he questioned, gravely.

"I think I am," replied Shefford, thankful he could answer readily.

"Then come into the fold. You are a lost sheep. 'Away on the desert I heard its cry.' . . . God bless you. Visit me when you ride to Stonebridge."

He flicked his horse with a cedar branch and trotted away beside the trader, and presently the green-choked neck of the valley hid them from view. Shefford could not have said that he was glad to be left behind, and yet neither was he sorry.

That Sabbath evening as he sat quietly with Nas Ta Bega, watching the sunset gilding the peaks, he was visited by three of the young Mormon women—Ruth, Joan, and Hester. They deliberately sought him and merrily led him off to the village and to the evening service of singing and prayer. Afterward he was surrounded and made much of. He had been popular before, but this was different. When he thoughtfully wended his way campward under the quiet stars he realized that the coming of Bishop Kane had made a subtle change in the women. That change was at first hard to define, but from every point by which he approached it he came to the same conclusion—the bishop had not objected to his presence in the village. The women became natural, free, and unrestrained. A dozen or twenty young and attractive women thrown much into companionship with one man. He might become a Mormon. The idea made him laugh. But upon reflection it was not funny; it sobered him. What a situation! He felt instinctively that he ought to fly from this hidden valley. But he could not have done it, even had he not been in the trader's employ. The thing was provokingly seductive. It was like an Arabian Nights' tale. What would these strange, fatally bound women do? Would any one of them become involved in sweet toils such as were possible to him? He was no fool. Already eyes had flashed and lips had smiled.

A thousand like thoughts whirled through his mind. And when he had calmed down somewhat two things were not lost upon him—an intricate and fascinating situation, with no end to its possibilities, threatened and attracted him—and the certainty that, whatever change the bishop had inaugurated, it had made these poor women happier. The latter fact weighed more with Shefford than fears for himself. His word was given to Withers. He would have felt just the same without having bound himself. Still, in the light of the trader's blunt philosophy, and of his own assurance that he was no fool, Shefford felt it incumbent upon him to accept a belief that there were situations no man could resist without an anchor. The ingenuity of man could not have devised a stranger, a more enticing, a more overpoweringly fatal situation. Fatal in that it could not be left untried! Shefford gave in and clicked his teeth as he let himself go. And suddenly he thought of her whom these bitter women called the Sago Lily.

The regret that had been his returned with thought of her. The saddest disillusion of his life, the keenest disappointment, the strangest pain, would always be associated with her. He had meant to see her face once, clear in the sunlight, so that he could always remember it, and then never go near her again. And now it came to him that if he did see much of her these other women would find him like the stone wall in the valley. Folly! Perhaps it was, but she would be safe, maybe happier. When he decided, it was certain that he trembled.

Then he buried the memory of Fay Larkin.

Next day Shefford threw himself with all the boy left in him into the work and play of the village. He helped the women and made games for the children. And he talked or listened. In the early evening he called on Ruth, chatted awhile, and went on to see Joan, and from her to another. When the valley became shrouded in darkness he went unseen down the path to Mary's lonely home.

She was there, a white shadow against the black. When she replied to his greeting her voice seemed full, broken, eager to express something that would not come. She was happier to see him than she should have been, Shefford thought. He talked, swiftly, eloquently, about whatever he believed would interest her. He stayed long, and finally left, not having seen her face except in pale starlight and shadow; and the strong clasp of her hand remained with him as he went away under the piñons.

Days passed swiftly. Joe Lake did not return. The Indian rode in and out of camp, watered and guarded the pack-burros and the mustangs. Shefford grew strong and active. He made a garden for the women; he cut cords of fire-wood; he dammed the brook and made an irrigation ditch; he learned to love these fatherless children, and they loved him.

In the afternoons there was leisure for him and for the women. He had no favorites, and let the occasion decide what he should do and with whom he should be. They had little parties at the cottages and picnics under the cedars. He rode up and down the valley with Ruth, who could ride a horse as no other girl he had ever seen. He climbed with Hester. He walked with Joan. Mostly he contrived to include several at once in the little excursions, though it was not rare for him to be out alone with one.

It was not a game he was playing. More and more, as he learned to know these young women, he liked them better, he pitied them, he was good for them. It shamed him, hurt him, somehow, to see how they tried to forget something when they were with him. Not improbably a little of it was coquetry, as natural as a laugh to any pretty woman. But that was not what hurt him. It was to see Ruth or Rebecca, as the case might be, full of life and fun, thoroughly enjoying some jest or play, all of a sudden be strangely recalled from the wholesome pleasure of a girl to become a deep and somber woman. The crimes in the name of religion! How he thought of the blood and the ruin laid at the door of religion! He wondered if that were so with Nas Ta Bega's religion, and he meant to find out some day. The women he liked best he imagined the least religious, and they made less effort to attract him.

Every night in the dark he went to Mary's home and sat with her on the porch. He never went inside. For all he knew, his visits were unknown to her neighbors. Still, it did not matter to him if they found out. To her he could talk as he had never talked to any one. She liberated all his thought and fancy. He filled her mind.

As there had been a change in the other women, so was there in Mary; however, it had no relation to the bishop's visit. The time came when Shefford could not but see that she lived and dragged through the long day for the sake of those few hours in the shadow of the stars with him. She seldom spoke. She listened. Wonderful to him—sometimes she laughed—and it seemed the sound was a ghost of childhood pleasure. When he stopped to consider that she might fall in love with him he drove the thought from him. When he realized that his folly had become sweet and that the sweetness imperiously drew him, he likewise cast off that thought. The present was enough. And if he had any treasures of mind and heart he gave them to her.

She never asked him to stay, but she showed that she wanted him to. That made it hard to go. Still, he never stayed late. The moment of parting was like a break. Her good-by was sweet, low music; it lingered on his ear; it bade him come to-morrow night; and it sent him away into the valley to walk under the stars, a man fighting against himself.

One night at parting, as he tried to see her face in the wan glow of a clouded moon, he said:

"I've been trying to find a sago-lily."

"Have you never seen one?" she asked.

"No." He meant to say something with a double meaning, in reference to her face and the name of the flower, but her unconsciousness made him hold his tongue. She was wholly unlike the other women.

"I'll show you where the lilies grow," she said.

"When?"

"To-morrow. Early in the afternoon I'll come to the spring. Then I'll take you."

Next morning Joe Lake returned and imparted news that was perturbing to Shefford. Reports of Shadd had come in to Stonebridge from different Indian villages; Joe was not inclined to linger long at the camp, and favored taking the trail with the pack-train.

Shefford discovered that he did not want to leave the valley, and the knowledge made him reflective. That morning he did not go into the village, and stayed in camp alone. A depression weighed upon him. It was dispelled, however, early in the afternoon by the sight of a slender figure in white swiftly coming down the path to the spring. He had an appointment with Mary to go to see the sago-lilies; everything else slipped his mind.

Mary wore the long black hood that effectually concealed her face. It made of her a woman, a Mormon woman, and strangely belied the lithe form and the braid of gold hair.

"Good day," she said, putting down her bucket. "Do you still want to go— to see the lilies?"

"Yes," replied Shefford, with a short laugh.

"Can you climb?"

"I'll go where you go."

Then she set off under the cedars and Shefford stalked at her side. He was aware that Nas Ta Bega watched them walk away. This day, so far, at least, Shefford did not feel talkative; and Mary had always been one who mostly listened. They came at length to a place where the wall rose in low, smooth swells, not steep, but certainly at an angle Shefford would not of his own accord have attempted to scale.

Light, quick, and sure as a mountain-sheep Mary went up the first swell to an offset above. Shefford, in amaze and admiration, watched the little moccasins as they flashed and held on to the smooth rock.

When he essayed to follow her he slipped and came to grief. A second attempt resulted in like failure. Then he backed away from the wall, to run forward fast and up the slope, only to slip, halfway up, and fall again.

He made light of the incident, but she was solicitous. When he assured her he was unhurt she said he had agreed to go where she went.

"But I'm not a—a bird," he protested.

"Take off your boots. Then you can climb. When we get over the wall it'll be easy," she said.

In his stocking-feet he had no great difficulty walking up the first bulge of the walls. And from there she led him up the strange waves of wind-worn rock. He could not attend to anything save the red, polished rock under him, and so saw little. The ascent was longer than he would have imagined, and steep enough to make him pant, but at last a huge round summit was reached.

From here he saw down into the valley where the village lay. But for the lazy columns of blue smoke curling up from the piñons the place would have seemed uninhabited. The wall on the other side was about level with the one upon which he stood. Beyond rose other walls and cliffs, up and up to the great towering peaks between which the green-and-black mountain loomed. Facing the other way, Shefford had only a restricted view. There were low crags and smooth stone ridges, between which were aisles green with cedar and piñon. Shefford's companion headed toward one of these, and when he had followed her a few steps he could no longer see down into the valley. The Mormon village where she lived was as if it were lost, and when it vanished Shefford felt a difference. Scarcely had the thought passed when Mary removed the dark hood. Her small head glistened like gold in the sunlight.

Shefford caught up with her and walked at her side, but could not bring himself at once deliberately to look at her. They entered a narrow, low-walled lane where cedars and piñons grew thickly, their fragrance heavy in the warm air, and flowers began to show in the grassy patches.

"This is Indian paint-brush," she said, pointing to little, low scarlet flowers. A gray sage-bush with beautiful purple blossoms she called purple sage, another brush with yellow flowers she named buck-brush, and there were vermilion cacti and low, flat mounds of lavender daisies which she said had no name. A whole mossy bank was covered with lace like green leaves and tiny blossoms the color of violets, which she called loco.

"Loco? Is this what makes the horses go crazy when they eat it?" he said.

"It is, indeed," she said, laughing.

When she laughed it was impossible not to look at her. She walked a little in advance. Her white cheek and temple seemed framed in the gold of her hair. How white her skin! But it was like pearl, faintly veined and flushed. The profile, clear-cut and pure, appeared cold, almost stern. He knew now that she was singularly beautiful, though he had yet to see her full face.

They walked on. Quite suddenly the lane opened out between two rounded bluffs, and Shefford looked down upon a grander and more awe-inspiring scene than ever he had viewed in his dreams.

What appeared to be a green mountainside sloped endlessly down to a plain, and that rolled and billowed away to a boundless region of strangely carved rock. The greatness of the scene could not be grasped in a glance. The slope was long; the plain not as level as it seemed to be on first sight; here and there round, red rocks, isolated and strange, like lonely castles, rose out of the green. Beyond the green all the earth seemed naked, showing smooth, glistening bones. It was a formidable wall of rock that flung itself up in the distance, carved into a thousand cañons and walls and domes and peaks, and there was not a straight nor a broken nor a jagged line in all that wildness. The color low down was red, dark blue, and purple in the clefts, yellow upon the heights, and in the distance rainbow-hued. A land of curves and color!

Shefford uttered an exclamation.

"That's Utah," said Mary. "I come often to sit here. You see that winding blue line. There. . . . That's San Juan Cañon. And the other dark line, that's Escalante Cañon. They wind down into this great purple chasm—'way over here to the left—and that's the Grand Cañon. They say not even the Indians have been in there."

Shefford had nothing to say. The moment was one of subtle and vital assimilation. Such places as this to be unknown to men! What strength, what wonder, what help, what glory, just to sit there an hour, slowly and appallingly to realize! Something came to Shefford from the distance, out of the purple cañons and from those dim, wind-worn peaks. He resolved to come here to this promontory again and again, alone and in humble spirit, and learn to know why he had been silenced, why peace pervaded his soul.

It was with this emotion upon him that he turned to find his companion watching him. Then for the first time he saw her face fully, and was thrilled that chance had reserved the privilege for this moment. It was a girl's face he saw, flower-like, lovely and pure as a Madonna's, and strangely, tragically sad. The eyes were large, dark gray, the color of the sage. They were as clear as the air which made distant things close, and yet they seemed full of shadows, like a ruffled pool under midnight stars. They disturbed him. Her mouth had the sweet curves and redness of youth, but it showed bitterness, pain, and repression.

"Where are the sago-lilies?" he asked, suddenly.

"Farther down. It's too cold up here for them. Come," she said.

He followed her down a winding trail—down and down till the green plain rose to blot out the scrawled wall of rock, down into a verdant cañon where a brook made swift music over stones, where the air was sultry and hot, laden with the fragrant breath of flower and leaf. This was a cañon of summer, and it bloomed.

The girl bent and plucked something from the grass.

"Here's a white lily," she said. "There are three colors. The yellow and pink ones are deeper down in the cañons."

Shefford took the flower and regarded it with great interest. He had never seen such an exquisite thing. It had three large petals, curving cuplike, of a whiteness purer than new-fallen snow, and a heart of rich, warm gold. Its fragrance was so faint as to be almost indistinguishable, yet of a haunting, unforgettable sweetness. And even while he looked at it the petals drooped and their whiteness shaded and the gold paled. In a moment the flower was wilted.

"I don't like to pluck the lilies," said Mary. "They die so swiftly."

Shefford saw the white flowers everywhere in the open, sunny places along the brook. They swayed with stately grace in the slow, warm wind. They seemed like three-pointed stars shining out of the green. He bent over one with a particularly lofty stem, and after a close survey of it he rose to look at her face. His action was plainly one of comparison. She laughed and said it was foolish for the women to call her the Sago Lily. She had no coquetry; she spoke as she would have spoken of the stones at her feet; she did not know that she was beautiful. Shefford imagined there was some resemblance in her to the lily—the same whiteness, the same rich gold, and, more striking than either, a strange, rare quality of beauty, of life, intangible as something fleeting, the spirit that had swiftly faded from the plucked flower. Where had the girl been born—what had her life been? Shefford was intensely curious about her. She seemed as different from any other women he had known as this rare cañon lily was different from the tame flowers at home.

On the return up the slope she outstripped him. She climbed lightly and tirelessly. When he reached her upon the promontory there was a stain of red in her cheeks and her expression had changed.

"Let's go back up over the rocks," she said. "I've not climbed for—for so long."

"I'll go where you go," he replied.

Then she was off, and he followed. She took to the curves of the bare rocks and climbed. He sensed a spirit released in her. It was so strange, so keen, so wonderful to be with her, and when he did catch her he feared to speak lest he break this mood. Her eyes grew dark and daring, and often she stopped to look away across the wavy sea of stones to something beyond the great walls. When they got high the wind blew her hair loose and it flew out, a golden stream, with the sun bright upon it. He saw that she changed her direction, which had been in line with the two peaks, and now she climbed toward the heights. They came to more difficult ascent, where the stone still held to the smooth curves, yet was marked by steep bulges and slants and crevices. Here she became a wild thing.

She ran, she leaped, she would have left him far behind had he not called. Then she appeared to remember him and waited.

Her face had now lost its whiteness; it was flushed, rosy, warm.

"Where—did you—ever learn—to run over rocks—this way?" he panted.

"All my life I've climbed," she said. "Ah! it's so good to be up on the walls again—to feel the wind—to see!"

Thereafter he kept close to her, no matter what the effort. He would not miss a moment of her, if he could help it. She was wonderful. He imagined she must be like an Indian girl, or a savage who loved the lofty places and the silence. When she leaped she uttered a strange, low, sweet cry of wildness and exultation. Shefford guessed she was a girl freed from her prison, forgetting herself, living again youthful hours. Still she did not forget him. She waited for him at the bad places, lent him a strong hand, and sometimes let it stay long in his clasp. Tireless and agile, sure-footed as a goat, fleet and wild she leaped and climbed and ran until Shefford marveled at her. This adventure was indeed fulfillment of a dream. Perhaps she might lead him to the treasure at the foot of the rainbow. But that thought, sad with memory daring forth from its grave, was irrevocably linked with a girl who was dead. He could not remember her, in the presence of this wonderful creature who was as strange as she was beautiful. When Shefford reached for the brown hand stretched forth to help him in a leap, when he felt its strong clasp, the youth and vitality and life of it, he had the fear of a man who was running toward a precipice and who could not draw back. This was a climb, a lark, a wild race to the Mormon girl, bound now in the village, and by the very freedom of it she betrayed her bonds. To Shefford it was also a wild race, but toward one sure goal he dared not name.

They went on, and at length, hand in hand, even where no steep step or wide fissure gave reason for the clasp. But she seemed unconscious. They were nearing the last height, a bare eminence, when she broke from him and ran up the smooth stone. When he surmounted it she was standing on the very summit, her arms wide, her full breast heaving, her slender body straight as an Indian's, her hair flying in the wind and blazing in the sun. She seemed to embrace the west, to reach for something afar, to offer herself to the wind and distance. Her face was scarlet from the exertion of the climb, and her broad brow was moist. Her eyes had the piercing light of an eagle's, though now they were dark. Shefford instinctively grasped the essence of this strange spirit, primitive and wild. She was not the woman who had met him at the spring. She had dropped some side of her with that Mormon hood, and now she stood totally strange.

She belonged up here, he divined. She was a part of that wildness. She must have been born and brought up in loneliness, where the wind blew and the peaks loomed and silence held dominion. The sinking sun touched the rim of the distant wall, and as if in parting regret shone with renewed golden fire. And the girl was crowned as with a glory.

Shefford loved her then. Realizing it, he thought he might have loved her before, but that did not matter when he was certain of it now. He trembled a little, fearfully, though without regret. Everything pertaining to his desert experience had been strange—this the strangest of all.

The sun sank swiftly, and instantly there was a change in the golden light. Quickly it died out. The girl changed as swiftly. She seemed to remember herself, and sat down as if suddenly weary. Shefford went closer and seated himself beside her.

"The sun has set. We must go," she said. But she made no movement.

"Whenever you are ready," replied he.

Just as the blaze had died out of her eyes, so the flush faded out of her face. The whiteness stole back, and with it the sadness. He had to bite his tongue to keep from telling her what he felt, to keep from pouring out a thousand questions. But the privilege of having seen her, of having been with her when she had forgotten herself—that he believed was enough. It had been wonderful; it had made him love her. But it need not add to the tragedy of her life, whatever that was. He tried to eliminate himself. And he watched her.

Her eyes were fixed upon the gold-rimmed ramparts of the distant wall in the west. Plain it was how she loved that wild upland. And there seemed to be some haunting memory of the past in her gaze—some happy part of life, agonizing to think of now.

"We must go," she said, and rose.

Shefford rose to accompany her. She looked at him, and her haunting eyes seemed to want him to know that he had helped her to forget the present, to remember girlhood, and that somehow she would always associate a wonderful happy afternoon with him. He divined that her silence then was a Mormon seal on lips.

"Mary, this has been the happiest, the best, the most revealing day of my life," he said, simply.

Swiftly, as if startled, she turned and faced down the slope. At the top of the wall above the village she put on the dark hood, and with it that somber something which was Mormon.

Twilight had descended into the valley, and shadows were so thick Shefford had difficulty in finding Mary's bucket. He filled it at the spring and made offer to carry it home for her, which she declined.

"You'll come to-night—late?" she asked.

"Yes," he replied, hurriedly promising. Then he watched her white form slowly glide down the path to disappear in the shadows.

Nas Ta Bega and Joe were busy at the camp-fire. Shefford joined them. This night he was uncommunicative. Joe peered curiously at him in the flare of the blaze. Later, after the meal, when Shefford appeared restless and strode to and fro, Joe spoke up gruffly:

"Better hang round camp to-night."

Shefford heard, but did not heed. Nevertheless, the purport of the remark, which was either jealousy or admonition, haunted him with the possibility of its meaning.

He walked away from the camp-fire, under the dark piñons, out into the starry open; and every step was hard to take, unless it pointed toward the home of the girl whose beauty and sadness and mystery had bewitched him. After what seemed hours he took the well-known path toward her cabin, and then every step seemed lighter. He divined he was rushing to some fate—he knew not what.

The porch was in shadow. He peered in vain for the white form against the dark background. In the silence he seemed to hear his heart-beats thick and muffled.

Some distance down the path he heard the sound of hoofs. Withdrawing into the gloom of a cedar, he watched. Soon he made out moving horses with riders. They filed past him to the number of half a score. Like a flash of fire the truth burned him. Mormons come for one of those mysterious night visits to sealed wives!

Shefford stalked far down the valley, into the lonely silence and the night shadows under the walls.

8

The Hogan of Nas Ta Bega

THE home of Nas Ta Bega lay far up the cedared slope, with the craggy yellow cliffs and the black cañons and the pine-fringed top of Navajo Mountain behind, and to the fore the vast, rolling descent of cedar groves and sage flats and sandy washes. No dim, dark range made bold outline along the horizon; the stretch of gray and purple and green extended to the blue line of sky.

Down the length of one sage level Shefford saw a long land where the brush and the grass had been beaten flat. This, the Navajo said, was a track where the young braves had raced their mustangs and had striven for supremacy before the eyes of maidens and the old people of the tribe.

"Nas Ta Bega, did you ever race here?" asked Shefford.

"I am a chief by birth. But I was stolen from my home, and now I cannot ride well enough to race the braves of my tribe," the Indian replied, bitterly.

In another place Joe Lake halted his horse and called Shefford's attention to a big yellow rock lying along the trail. And then he spoke in Navajo to the Indian.

"I've heard of this stone—Isende Aha," said Joe, after Nas Ta Bega had spoken. "Get down, and let's see."

Shefford dismounted, but the Indian kept his seat in the saddle.

Joe placed a big hand on the stone and tried to move it. According to Shefford's eye measurement the stone was nearly oval, perhaps three feet high, by a little over two in width. Joe threw off his sombrero, took a deep breath, and, bending over, clasped the stone in his arms. He was an exceedingly heavy and powerful man, and it was plain to Shefford that he meant to lift the stone if that were possible. Joe's broad shoulders strained, flattened; his arms bulged, his joints cracked, his neck corded, and his face turned black. By gigantic effort he lifted the stone and moved it about six inches. Then as he released his hold he fell, and when he sat up his face was wet with sweat.

"Try it," he said to Shefford, with his lazy smile. "See if you can heave it."

Shefford was strong, and there had been a time when he took pride in his strength. Something in Joe's supreme effort and in the gloom of the Indian's eyes made Shefford curious about this stone. He bent over and grasped it as Joe had done. He braced himself and lifted with all his power, until a red blur obscured his sight and shooting stars seemed to explode in his head. But he could not even stir the stone.

"Shefford, maybe you'll be able to heft it some day," observed Joe. Then he pointed to the stone and addressed Nas Ta Bega.

The Indian shook his head and spoke for a moment.

"This is the Isende Aha of the Navajos," explained Joe. "The young braves are always trying to carry this stone. As soon as one of them can carry it he is a man. He who carries it farthest is the biggest man. And just so soon as any Indian can no longer lift it he is old. Nas Ta Bega says the stone has been carried two miles in his lifetime. His own father carried it the length of six steps."

"Well! It's plain to me that I am not a man," said Shefford, "or else I am old."

Joe Lake drawled his lazy laugh and mounting, rode up the trail. But Shefford lingered beside the Indian.

"Bi Nai," said Nas Ta Bega, "I am a chief of my tribe, but I have never been a man. I never lifted that stone. See what the pale-face education has done for the Indian!"

The Navajo's bitterness made Shefford thoughtful. Could greater injury be done to man than this—to rob him of his heritage of strength?

Joe drove the bobbing pack-train of burros into the cedars where the smoke of the hogans curled upward, and soon the whistling of mustangs, the barking of dogs, the bleating of sheep, told of his reception. And presently Shefford was in the midst of an animated scene. Great, wooly, fierce dogs, like wolves, ran out to meet the visitors. Sheep and goats were everywhere, and little lambs scarcely able to walk, with others frisky and frolicsome. There were pure-white lambs, and some that appeared to be painted, and some so beautiful with their fleecy white all except black faces or ears or tails or feet. They ran right under Nack-yal's legs and bumped against Shefford, and kept bleating their thin-piped welcome. Under the cedars surrounding the several hogans were mustangs that took Shefford's eye. He saw an iron-gray with white mane and tail sweeping to the ground; and a fiery black, wilder than any other beast he had ever seen; and a pinto as wonderfully painted as the little lambs; and, most striking of all, a pure, cream-colored mustang with grace and fine lines and beautiful mane and tail, and, strange to see, eyes as blue as azure. This albino mustang came right up to Shefford, an action in singular contrast with that of the others, and showed a tame and friendly spirit toward him and Nack-yal. Indeed, Shefford had reason to feel ashamed of Nack-yal's temper or jealousy.

The first Indians to put in an appearance were a flock of children, half naked, with tangled manes of raven-black hair and skin like gold bronze. They appeared bold and shy by turns. Then a little, sinewy man, old and beaten and gray, came out of the principal hogan. He wore a blanket round his bent shoulders. His name was Hosteen Doetin, and it meant gentle man. His fine, old wrinkled face lighted with a smile of kindly interest. His squaw followed him, and she was as venerable as he. Shefford caught a glimpse of the shy, dark Glen Naspa, Nas Ta Bega's sister, but she did not come out. Other Indians appeared, coming from adjacent hogans.

Nas Ta Bega turned the mustangs loose among those Shefford had noticed, and presently there rose a snorting, whistling, kicking, plunging mêlée. A cloud of dust hid them, and then a thudding of swift hoofs told of a run through the cedars. Joe Lake began picking over stacks of goat-skins and bags of wool that were piled against the hogan.

"Reckon we'll have one grand job packing out this load," he growled. "It's not so heavy, but awkward to pack."

It developed, presently, from talk with the old Navajo, that this pile was only a half of the load to be packed to Kayenta, and the other half was round the corner of the mountain in the camp of Piutes. Hosteen Doetin said he would send to the camp and have the Piutes bring their share over. The suggestion suited Joe, who wanted to save his burros as much as possible. Accordingly, a messenger was despatched to the Piute camp. And Shefford, with time on his hands and poignant memory to combat, decided to recall his keen interest in the Navajo, and learn, if possible, what the Indian's life was like. What would a day of his natural life be?

In the gray of dawn, when the hush of the desert night still lay deep over the land, the Navajo stirred in his blanket and began to chant to the morning light. It began very soft and low, a strange, broken murmur, like the music of a brook, and as it swelled that weird and mournful tone was slowly lost in one of hope and joy. The Indian's soul was coming out of night, blackness, the sleep that resembled death, into the day, the light that was life.

Then he stood in the door of his hogan, his blanket around him, and faced the east.

Night was lifting out of the clefts and ravines; the rolling cedar ridges and the sage flats were softly gray, with thin veils like smoke mysteriously rising and vanishing; the colorless rocks were changing. A long, horizon-wide gleam of light, rosiest in the center, lay low down in the east and momentarily brightened. One by one the stars in the deep-blue sky paled and went out and the blue dome changed and lightened. Night had vanished on invisible wings and silence broke to the music of a mockingbird. The rose in the east deepened; a wisp of cloud turned gold; dim distant mountains showed dark against the red; and low down in a notch a rim of fire appeared. Over the soft ridges and valleys crept a wondrous transfiguration. It was as if every blade of grass, every leaf of sage, every twig of cedar, the flowers, the trees, the rocks came to life at sight of the sun. The red disk rose, and a golden fire burned over the glowing face of that lonely waste.

The Navajo, dark, stately, inscrutable, faced the sun—his god. This was his Great Spirit. The desert was his mother, but the sun was his life. To the keeper of the winds and rains, to the master of light, to the maker of fire, to the giver of life the Navajo sent up his prayer:

> Of all the good things of the Earth let me always
>   have plenty.
> Of all the beautiful of the Earth let me always have
>   plenty.
> Peacefully let my horses go and peacefully let my
>   sheep go.
> God of the Heavens, give me many sheep and
>   horses.
> God of the Heavens, help me to talk straight.

Goddess of the Earth, my Mother, let me walk
straight.
Now all is well, now all is well, now all is well,
now all is well.

Hope and faith were his.

A chief would be born to save the vanishing tribe of Navajos. A bride would rise from a wind—kiss of the lilies in the moonlight.

He drank from the clear, cold spring bubbling from under mossy rocks. He went into the cedars, and the tracks in the trails told him of the visitors of night. His mustangs whistled to him from the ridge-tops, standing clear with heads up and manes flying, and then trooped down through the sage. The shepherd-dogs, guardians of the flocks, barked him a welcome, and the sheep bleated and the lambs pattered round him.

In the hogan by the warm, red fire his women baked his bread and cooked his meat. And he satisfied his hunger. Then he took choice meat to the hogan of a sick relative, and joined in the song and the dance and the prayer that drove away the evil spirit of illness. Down in the valley, in a sandy, sunny place, was his corn-field, and here he turned in the water from the ditch, and worked awhile, and went his contented way.

He loved his people, his women, and his children. To his son he said: "Be bold and brave. Grow like the pine. Work and ride and play that you may be strong. Talk straight. Love your brother. Give half to your friend. Honor your mother that you may honor your wife. Pray and listen to your gods."

Then with his gun and his mustang he climbed the slope of the mountain. He loved the solitude, but he was never alone. There were voices on the wind and steps on his trail. The lofty pine, the lichened rock, the tiny bluebell, the seared crag—all whispered their secrets. For him their spirits spoke. In the morning light Old Stone Face, the mountain, was a red god calling him to the chase. He was a brother of the eagle, at home on the height where the winds swept and the earth lay revealed below.

In the golden afternoon, with the warm sun on his back and the blue cañons at his feet, he knew the joy of doing nothing. He did not need rest, for he was never tired. The sage-sweet breath of the open was thick in his nostrils, the silence that had so many whisperings was all about him, the loneliness of the wild was his. His falcon eye saw mustang and sheep, the puff of dust down on the cedar level, the Indian riding on a distant ridge, the gray walls, and the blue clefts. Here was home, still free, still wild, still untainted. He saw with the eyes of his ancestors. He felt them around him. They had gone into the elements from which their voices came on the wind. They were the watchers on his trails.

At sunset he faced the west, and this was his prayer:

> *Great Spirit, God of my Fathers,*
> *Keep my horses in the night.*
> *Keep my sheep in the night.*
> *Keep my family in the night.*
> *Let me wake to the day.*
> *Let me be worthy of the light.*
> *Now all is well, now all is well.*
> *Now all is well, now all is well.*

And he watched the sun go down and the gold sink from the peaks and the red die out of the west and the gray shadows creep out of the cañons to meet the twilight and the slow, silent, mysterious approach of night with its gift of stars.

Night fell. The white stars blinked. The wind sighed in the cedars. The sheep bleated. The shepherd-dogs bayed the mourning coyotes. And the Indian lay down in his blankets with his dark face tranquil in the starlight. All was well in his lonely world. Phantoms hovered, illness lingered, injury and pain and death were there, the shadow of a strange white hand flitted across the face of the moon—but now all was well—the Navajo had prayed to the god of his Fathers. Now all was well!

And this, thought Shefford in revolt, was what the white man had killed in the Indian tribes, was reaching out now to kill in this wild remnant of the Navajos. The padre, the trapper, the trader, the prospector, and the missionary— so the white man had come, some of him good, no doubt, but more of him evil; and the young brave learned a thirst that could never be quenched at the cold, sweet spring of his forefathers, and the young maiden burned with a fever in her blood, and lost the sweet, strange, wild fancies of her tribe.

Joe Lake came to Shefford and said, "Withers told me you had a mix-up with a missionary at Red Lake."

"Yes, I regret to say," replied Shefford.

"About Glen Naspa?"

"Yes, Nas Ta Bega's sister."

"Withers just mentioned it. Who was the missionary?"

"Willetts, so Presbrey, the trader, said."

"What'd he look like?"

Shefford recalled the smooth, brown face, the dark eyes, the weak chin, the mild expression, and the soft, lax figure of the missionary.

"Can't tell by what you said," went on Joe. "But I'll bet a peso to a horse-hair that's the fellow who's been here. Old Hosteen Doetin just told me. First visits he ever had from the priest with the long gown. That's what he called the missionary. These old fellows will never forget what's come down from father to son about the Spanish padres. Well, anyway, Willetts has been here twice after Glen Naspa. The old chap is impressed, but he doesn't want to let the girl go. I'm inclined to think Glen Naspa would as lief go as stay. She may be Navajo, but she's a girl. She won't talk much.''

"Where's Nas Ta Bega?" asked Shefford.

"He rode off somewhere yesterday. Perhaps to the Piute camp. These Indians are slow. They may take a week to pack that load over here. But if Nas Ta Bega or someone doesn't come with a message to-day I'll ride over there myself.''

"Joe, what do you think about this missionary?" queried Shefford, bluntly.

"Reckon there's not much to think, unless you see him or find out something. I heard of Willetts before Withers spoke of him. He's friendly with Mormons. I understand he's worked for Mormon interests, someway or another. That's on the quiet. Savvy? This matter of him coming after Glen Naspa, reckon that's all right. The missionaries all go after the young people. What'd be the use to try to convert the old Indians? No, the missionary's work is to educate the Indian, and, of course, the younger he is the better.''

"You approve of the missionary?"

"Shefford, if you understood a Mormon you wouldn't ask that. Did you ever read or hear of Jacob Hamblin? . . . Well, he was a Mormon missionary among the Navajos. The Navajos were as fierce as Apaches till Hamblin worked among them. He made them friendly to the white man.''

"That doesn't prove he made converts of them," replied Shefford, still bluntly.

"No. For the matter of that, Hamblin let religion alone. He made presents, then traded with them, then taught them useful knowledge. Mormon or not, Shefford, I'll admit this: a good man, strong with his body, and learned in ways with his hands, with some knowledge of medicine, can better the condition of these Indians. But just as soon as he begins to preach his religion, then his influence wanes. That's natural. These heathen have the ideals, their gods.''

"Which the white man should leave them!" replied Shefford, feelingly.

"That's a matter of opinion. But don't let's argue. . . . Willetts is after Glen Naspa. And if I know Indian girls he'll persuade her to go to his school.''

"Persuade her!" Then Shefford broke off and related the incident that had occurred at Red Lake.

"Reckon any means justifies the end," replied Joe, imperturbably. "Let him talk love to her or rope her or beat her, so long as he makes a Christian of her.''

Shefford felt a hot flush and had difficulty in controlling himself. From this single point of view the Mormon was impossible to reason with.

"That, too, is a matter of opinion. We won't discuss it," continued Shefford.

"But—if old Hosteen Doetin objects to the girl leaving, and if Nas Ta Bega does the same, won't that end the matter?"

"Reckon not. The end of the matter is Glen Naspa. If she wants to go she'll go."

Shefford thought best to drop the discussion. For the first time he had occasion to be repelled by something in this kind and genial Mormon, and he wanted to forget it. Just as he had never talked about men to the sealed wives in the hidden valley, so he could not talk of women to Joe Lake.

Nas Ta Bega did not return that day, but next morning a messenger came calling Lake to the Piute camp. Shefford spent the morning high on the slope learning more with every hour in the silence and loneliness, that he was stronger of soul than he had dared to hope, and that the added pain which had come to him could be borne.

Upon his return toward camp, in the cedar grove, he caught sight of Glen Naspa with a white man. They did not see him. When Shefford recognized Willetts an embarrassment as well as an instinct made him halt and step into a bushy, low-branched cedar. It was not his intention to spy on them. He merely wanted to avoid a meeting. But the missionary's hand on the girl's arm, and her uplifted head, her pretty face, strange, intent, troubled, struck Shefford with an unusual and irresistible curiosity. Willetts was talking earnestly; Glen Naspa was listening intently. Shefford watched long enough to see that the girl loved the missionary, and that he reciprocated or was pretending. His manner scarcely savored of pretense, Shefford concluded, as he slipped away under the trees.

He did not go at once into camp. He felt troubled, and wished that he had not encountered the two. His duty in the matter, of course, was to tell Nas Ta Bega what he had seen. Upon reflection Shefford decided to give the missionary the benefit of a doubt; and if he really cared for the Indian girl, and admitted or betrayed it, to think all the better of him for the fact. Glen Naspa was certainly pretty enough, and probably lovable enough, to please any lonely man in this desert. The pain and the yearning in Shefford's heart made him lenient. He had to fight himself—not to forget, for that was impossible—but to keep rational and sane when a white flower-like face haunted him and a voice called.

The cracking of hard hoofs on stones caused him to turn toward camp, and as he emerged from the cedar grove he saw three Indian horsemen ride into the cleared space before the hogans. They were superbly mounted and well armed, and impressed him as being different from Navajos. Perhaps they were Piutes. They dismounted and led the mustangs down to the pool below the spring. Shefford saw another mustang, standing bridle down and carrying a pack behind the saddle. Some squaws with children hanging behind their skirts were standing at the door of Hosteen Doetin's hogan. Shefford glanced in to see Glen Naspa, pale, quiet, almost sullen. Willetts stood with his hands spread. The old Navajo's seamed face worked convulsively as he tried to lift his bent form to some semblance of dignity, and his voice rolled out, sonorously: "Me no savvy Jesus Christ! Me hungry! . . . Me no eat Jesus Christ!"

Shefford drew back as if he had received a blow. That had been Hosteen Doetin's reply to the importunities of the missionary. The old Navajo could work no longer. His sons were gone. His squaw was worn out. He had no one save Glen Naspa to help him. She was young, strong. He was hungry. What was the white man's religion to him?

With long, swift stride Shefford entered the hogan. Willetts, seeing him, did not look so mild as Shefford had him pictured in memory, nor did he appear surprised. Shefford touched Hosteen Doetin's shoulder and said, "Tell me."

The aged Navajo lifted a shaking hand.

"Me no savvy Jesus Christ! Me hungry! . . . Me no eat Jesus Christ!"

Shefford then made signs that indicated the missionary's intention to take the girl away.

"Him come—big talk—Jesus—all Jesus. . . . Me no want Glen Naspa go," replied the Indian.

Shefford turned to the missionary.

"Willetts, is he a relative of the girl?"

"There's some blood tie, I don't know what. But it's not close," replied Willetts.

"Then don't you think you'd better wait till Nas Ta Bega returns? He's her brother."

"What for?" demanded Willetts. "That Indian may be gone a week. She's willing to go."

Shefford looked at the girl.

"Glen Naspa, do you want to go?"

She was shy, ashamed, and silent, but manifestly willing to accompany the missionary. Shefford pondered a moment. How he hoped Nas Ta Bega would come back! It was thought of the Indian that made Shefford stubborn. What his stand ought to be was hard to define, unless he answered to impulse; and here in the wilds he had become imbued with the idea that his impulses and instincts were no longer false.

"Willetts, what do you want with the girl?" queried Shefford, coolly, and at the question he seemed to find himself. He peered deliberately and searchingly into the other's face. The missionary's gaze shifted and a tinge of red crept up from under his collar.

"Absurd thing to ask a missionary!" he burst out, impatiently.

"Do you care for Glen Naspa?"

"I care as God's disciple—who cares to save the soul of heathen," he replied, with the lofty tone of prayer.

"Has Glen Naspa no—no other interest in you—except to be taught religion?"

The missionary's face flamed, and his violent tremor showed that under his exterior there was a different man.

"What right have you to question me?" he demanded. "You're an adventurer—an outcast. I've my duty here. I'm a missionary with Church and state and government behind me."

"Yes, I'm an outcast," replied Shefford, bitterly. "And you may be all you say. But we're alone now out here on the desert. And this girl's brother is absent. You haven't answered me yet. . . . Is there anything between you and Glen Naspa except religion?"

"No, you insulting beggar!"

Shefford had forced the reply that he had expected and which damned the missionary beyond any consideration.

"Willetts, you are a liar!" said Shefford, steadily.

"And what are you?" cried Willetts, in shrill fury. "I've heard all about you. Heretic! Atheist! Driven from your Church! Hated and scorned for your blasphemy!"

Then he gave way to ungovernable rage, and cursed Shefford as a religious fanatic might have cursed the most debased of sinners. Shefford heard with the blood beating, strangling the pulse in his ears. Somehow this missionary had learned his secret—most likely from the Mormons in Stonebridge. And the terms of disgrace were coals of fire upon Shefford's head. Strangely, however, he did not bow to them, as had been his humble act in the past, when his calumniators had arraigned and flayed him. Passion burned in him now, and hate, for the first time in his life, made a tiger of him. And these raw emotions, new to him, were difficult to control.

"You can't take the girl," he replied, when the other had ceased. "Not without her brother's consent."

"I will take her!"

Shefford threw him out of the hogan and strode after him. Willetts had stumbled. When he straightened up he was white and shaken. He groped for the bridle of his horse while keeping his eyes upon Shefford, and when he found it he whirled quickly, mounted, and rode off. Shefford saw him halt a moment under the cedars to speak with the three strange Indians, and then he galloped away. It came to Shefford then that he had been unconscious of the last strained moment of that encounter. He seemed all cold, tight, locked, and was amazed to find his hand on his gun. Verily the wild environment had liberated strange instincts and impulses, which he had answered. That he had no regrets proved how he had changed.

Shefford heard the old woman scolding. Peering into the hogan, he saw Glen

Naspa flounce sullenly down, for all the world like any other thwarted girl. Hosteen Doetin came out and pointed down the slope at the departing missionary.

"Heap talk Jesus—all talk—all Jesus!" he exclaimed, contemptuously. Then he gave Shefford a hard rap on the chest. "Small talk—heap man!"

The matter appeared to be adjusted for the present. But Shefford felt that he had made a bitter enemy, and perhaps a powerful one.

He prepared and ate his supper alone that evening, for Joe Lake and Nas Ta Bega did not put in an appearance. He observed that the three strange Indians, whom he took for Piutes, kept to themselves, and, so far as he knew, had no intercourse with any one at the camp. This would not have seemed unusual, considering the taciturn habit of Indians, had he not remembered seeing Willetts speak to the trio. What had he to do with them? Shefford was considering the situation with vague doubts when, to his relief, the three strangers rode off into the twilight. Then he went to bed.

He was awakened by violence. It was the gray hour before dawn. Dark forms knelt over him. A cloth pressed down hard over his mouth. Strong hands bound it while other strong hands held him. He could not cry out. He could not struggle. A heavy weight, evidently a man, held down his feet. Then he was rolled over, securely bound, and carried, to be thrown like a sack over the back of a horse.

All this happened so swiftly as to be bewildering. He was too astounded to be frightened. As he hung head downward he saw the legs of a horse and a dim trail. A stirrup swung to and fro, hitting him in the face. He began to feel exceedingly uncomfortable, with a rush of blood to his head, and cramps in his arms and legs. This kept on and grew worse for what seemed a long time. Then the horse was stopped and a rude hand tumbled him to the ground. Again he was rolled over on his face. Strong fingers plucked at his clothes, and he believed he was being searched. His captors were as silent as if they had been dumb. He felt when they took his pocketbook and knife and all that he had. Then they cut, tore, and stripped off all his clothing. He was lifted, carried a few steps, and dropped upon what seemed a soft, low mound, and left lying there, still tied and naked. Shefford heard the rustle of sage and the dull thud of hoofs as his assailants went away.

His first sensation was one of immeasurable relief. He had not been murdered. Robbery was nothing. And though roughly handled, he had not been hurt. He associated the assault with the three strange visitors of the preceding day. Still, he had no proof of that. Not the slightest clue remained to help him ascertain who had attacked him.

It might have been a short while or a long one, his mind was so filled with growing conjectures, but a time came when he felt cold. As he lay face down, only his back felt cold at first. He was grateful that he had not been thrown upon the rocks. The ground under him appeared soft, spongy, and gave somewhat as he breathed. He had really sunk down a little in this pile of soft earth. The day was not far off, as he could tell by the brightening of the gray. He began to suffer with the cold, and then slowly he seemed to freeze and grow numb. In an effort to roll over upon his back he discovered that his position, or his being bound, or the numbness of his muscles was responsible for the fact that he could not move. Here was a predicament. It began to look serious. What would a few hours of the powerful sun do to his uncovered skin? Somebody would trail and find him; still, he might not be found soon.

He saw the sky lighten, turn rosy and then gold. The sun shone upon him, but some time elapsed before he felt its warmth. All of a sudden a pain, like a sting, shot through his shoulder. He could not see what caused it; probably a bee. Then he felt another upon his leg, and about simultaneously with it a tiny, fiery stab in his side. A sickening sensation pervaded his body, slowly moving, as if poison had entered the blood of his veins. Then a puncture, as from a hot wire, entered the skin of his breast. Unmistakably it was a bite. By dint of great effort he twisted his head to see a big red ant on his breast. Then he heard a faint sound, so exceedingly faint that he could not tell what it was like. But presently his strained ears detected a low, swift, rustling, creeping sound, like the slipping rattle of an infinite number of tiny bits of moving gravel. Then it was a sound like the seeping of wind-blown sand. Several hot bites occurred at once. And then with his head twisted he saw a red stream of ants pour out of the mound and spill over his quivering flesh.

In an instant he realized his position. He had been dropped intentionally upon an ant-heap, which had sunk with his weight, wedging him between the crust. At the mercy of those terrible desert ants! A frantic effort to roll out proved futile, as did another and another. His violent muscular contractions infuriated the ants, and in an instant he was writhing in pain so horrible and so unendurable that he nearly fainted. But he was too strong to faint suddenly. A bath of vitriol, a stripping of his skin and red embers of fire thrown upon raw flesh, could not have equaled this. There was fury in the bites and poison in the fangs of these ants. Was this an Indian's brutal trick or was it the missionary's revenge? Shefford realized that it would kill him soon. He sweat what seemed blood, although perhaps the blood came from the bites. A strange, hollow, buzzing roar filled his ears, and it must have been the pouring of the angry ants from their mound.

Then followed a time that was hell—worse than fire, for fire would have given merciful death—agony under which his physical being began spasmodically to jerk and retch—and his eyeballs turned and his breast caved in.

A cry rang through the roar in his ears. "Bi Nai! Bi Nai!"

His fading sight seemed to shade round the dark face of Nas Ta Bega.

Then powerful hands dragged him from the mound, through the grass and sage, rolled him over and over, and brushed his burning skin with strong, swift sweep.

9

In the Desert Crucible

THAT hard experience was but the beginning of many cruel trials for John Shefford.

He never knew who his assailants were, nor their motive other than robbery; and they had gotten little, for they had not found the large sum of money sewed in the lining of his coat. Joe Lake declared it was Shadd's work, and the Mormon showed the stern nature that lay hidden under his habitual mild manner. Nas Ta Bega shook his head and would not tell what he thought. But a somber fire burned in his eyes.

The three started with a heavily laden pack-train and went down the mountain slope into West Cañon. The second day they were shot at from the rim walls. Lake was wounded, hindering the swift flight necessary to escape deeper into the cañon. Here they hid for days, while the Mormon recovered and the Indian took stealthy trips to try to locate the enemy. Lack of water and grass for the burros drove them on. They climbed out of a side cañon, losing several burros on a rough trail, and had proceeded to within half a day's journey of Red Lake when they were attacked while making camp in a cedar grove. Shefford sustained an exceedingly painful injury to his leg, but, fortunately, the bullet went through without breaking a bone. With that burning pain there came to Shefford the meaning of fight, and his rifle grew hot in his hands. Night alone saved the trio from certain fatality. Under the cover of darkness the Indian helped Shefford to escape. Joe Lake looked out for himself. The pack-train was lost, and the mustangs, except Nack-yal.

Shefford learned what it meant to lie out at night, listening for pursuit, cold to his marrow, sick with dread, and enduring frightful pain from a ragged bullet-hole. Next day the Indian led him down into the red basin, where the sun shone hot and the sand reflected the heat. They had no water. A wind arose and the valley became a place of flying sand. Through a heavy, stifling pall Nas Ta Bega somehow got Shefford to the trading-post at Red Lake. Presbrey attended to Shefford's injury and made him comfortable. Next day Joe Lake limped in, surly

and somber, with the news that Shadd and eight or ten of his outlaw gang had
gotten away with the pack-train.

In short time Shefford was able to ride, and with his companions went over
the pass to Kayenta. Withers already knew of his loss, and all he said was that
he hoped to meet Shadd some day.

Shefford showed a reluctance to go again to the hidden village in the silent
cañon with the rounded walls. The trader appeared surprised, but did not press
the point. And Shefford meant sooner or later to tell him, yet never quite reached
the point. The early summer brought more work for the little post, and Shefford
toiled with the others. He liked the outdoor tasks, and at night was grateful that
he was too tired to think. Then followed trips to Durango and Bluff and Monticello. He rode fifty miles a day for many days. He knew how a man fares who
packs light and rides far and fast. When the Indian was with him he got along
well, but Nas Ta Bega would not go near the towns. Thus many mishaps were
Shefford's fortune.

Many and many a mile he trailed his mustang, for Nack-yal never forgot the
Sagi, and always headed for it when he broke his hobbles. Shefford accompanied
an Indian teamster into Durango with a wagon and four wild mustangs. Upon
the return, with a heavy load of supplies, accident put Shefford in charge of the
outfit. In despair he had to face the hardest task that could have been given
him—to take care of a crippled Indian, catch, water, feed, harness, and drive
four wild mustangs that did not know him and tried to kill him at every turn,
and to get that precious load of supplies home to Kayenta. That he accomplished
it proved to him the possibilities of a man, for both endurance and patience.
From that time he never gave up in the front of any duty.

In the absence of an available Indian he rode to Durango and back in record
time. Upon one occasion he was lost in a cañon for days, with no food and little
water. Upon another he went through a sand-storm in the open desert, facing
it for forty miles and keeping to the trail. When he rode in to Kayenta that night
the trader, in grim praise, said there was no worse to endure. At Monticello
Shefford stood off a band of desperadoes, and this time Shefford experienced
a strange, sickening shock in the wounding of a man. Later he had other fights,
but in none of them did he know whether or not he had shed blood.

The heat of midsummer came, when the blistering sun shone, and a hot blast
blew across the sand, and the furious storms made floods in the washes. Day
and night Shefford was always in the open, and any one who had ever known
him in the past would have failed to recognize him now.

In the early fall, with Nas Ta Bega as companion, he set out to the south of
Kayenta upon long-neglected business of the trader. They visited Red Lake,
Blue Cañon, Keams Cañon, Oribi, the Moki villages, Tuba, Moencopie, and
Moen Ave. This trip took many weeks and gave Shefford all the opportunity he

wanted to study the Indians, and the conditions nearer to the border of civilization. He learned the truth about the Indians and the missionaries.

Upon the return trip he rode over the trail he had followed alone to Red Lake and thence on to the Sagi, and it seemed that years had passed since he first entered this wild region which had come to be home, years that had molded him in the stern and fiery crucible of the desert.

10

Stonebridge

IN October Shefford arranged for a hunt in the Cresaw Mountains with Joe Lake and Nas Ta Bega. The Indian had gone home for a short visit, and upon his return the party expected to start. But Nas Ta Bega did not come back. Then the arrival of a Piute with news that excited Withers and greatly perturbed Lake convinced Shefford that something was wrong.

The little trading-post seldom saw such disorder; certainly Shefford had never known the trader to neglect work. Joe Lake threw a saddle on a mustang he would have scorned to notice in an ordinary moment, and without a word of explanation or farewell rode hard to the north on the Stonebridge trail.

Shefford had long since acquired patience. He was curious, but he did not care particularly what was in the wind. However, when Withers came out and sent an Indian to drive up the horses Shefford could not refrain from a query.

"I hate to tell you," replied the trader.

"Go on," added Shefford, quickly.

"Did I tell you about the government sending a Supreme Court judge out to Utah to prosecute the polygamists?"

"No," replied Shefford.

"I forgot to, I reckon. You've been away a lot. Well, there's been hell up in Utah for six months. Lately this judge and his men have worked down into southern Utah. He visited Bluff and Monticello a few weeks ago. . . . Now what do you think?"

"Withers! Is he coming to Stonebridge?"

"He's there now. Some one betrayed the where-abouts of the hidden village over in the canõn. All the women have been arrested and taken to Stonebridge. The trial begins to-day."

"Arrested!" echoed Shefford blankly. "Those poor, lonely good women? What on earth for?"

"Sealed wives!" exclaimed Withers, tersely. "This judge is after the polygamists. They say he's absolutely relentless."

"But—women can't be polygamists. Their husbands are the ones wanted."

"Sure. But the prosecutors have got to find the sealed wives—the second wives—to find the law-breaking husbands. That'll be a job, or I don't know Mormons. . . . Are you going to ride over to Stonebridge with me?"

Shefford shrank at the idea. Months of toil and pain and travail had not been enough to make him forget the strange girl he had loved. But he had remembered only at poignant intervals, and the lapse of time had made thought of her a dream like that sad dream which had lured him into the desert. With the query of the trader came a bitter-sweet regret.

"Better come with me," said Withers. "Have you forgotten the Sago Lily? She'll be put on trial. . . . That girl—that child! . . . Shefford, you know she hasn't any friends. And now no Mormon man dare protect her, for fear of prosecution."

"I'll go," replied Shefford, shortly.

The Indian brought up the horses. Nack-yal was thin from his long travel during the hot summer, but he was as hard as iron, and the way he pointed his keen nose toward the Sagi showed how he wanted to make for the upland country, with its clear springs and valleys of grass. Withers mounted his bay and with a hurried farewell to his wife spurred the mustang into the trail. Shefford took time to get his weapons and the light pack he always carried, and then rode out after the trader.

The pace Withers set was the long, steady lope to which these Indian mustangs had been trained all their lives. In an hour they reached the mouth of the Sagi, and at sight of it it seemed to Shefford that the hard half-year of suffering since he had been there had disappeared. Withers, to Shefford's regret, did not enter the Sagi. He turned off to the north and took a wild trail into a split of the red wall, and wound in and out, and climbed a crack so narrow that the light was obscured and the cliffs could be reached from both sides of a horse.

Once up on the wild plateau, Shefford felt again in a different world from the barren desert he had lately known. The desert had crucified him and had left him to die or survive, according to his spirit and his strength. If he had loved the glare, the endless level, the deceiving distance, the shifting sand, it had certainly not been as he loved this softer, wilder, more intimate upland. With the red peaks shining up into the blue, and the fragrance of cedar and piñon, and the purple sage and flowers and grass and splash of water over stones—with these there came back to him something that he had lost and which had haunted him.

It seemed he had returned to this wild upland of color and cañons and lofty crags and green valleys and silent places with a spirit gained from victory over himself in the harsher and sterner desert below. And, strange to him, he found his old self, the dreamer, the artist, the lover of beauty, the searcher for he knew not what, come to meet him on the fragrant wind.

He felt this, saw the old wildness with glad eyes, yet the greater part of his mind was given over to the thought of the unfortunate women he expected to see in Stonebridge.

Withers was harder to follow, to keep up with, than an Indian. For one thing he was a steady and tireless rider, and for another there were times when he had no mercy on a horse. Then an Indian always found easier steps in a trail and shorter cuts. Withers put his mount to some bad slopes, and Shefford had no choice but to follow. But they crossed the great broken bench of upland without mishap, and came out upon a promontory of a plateau from which Shefford saw a wide valley and the dark-green alfalfa fields of Stonebridge.

Stonebridge lay in the center of a fertile valley surrounded by pink cliffs. It must have been a very old town, certainly far older than Bluff or Monticello, though smaller, and evidently it had been built to last. There was one main street, very wide, that divided the town and was crossed at right angles by a stream spanned by a small natural stone bridge. A line of poplar-trees shaded each foot-path. The little log cabins and stone houses and cottages were half hidden in foliage now tinted with autumn colors. Toward the center of the town the houses and stores and shops fronted upon the street and along one side of a green square, or plaza. Here were situated several edifices, the most prominent of which was a church built of wood, white-washed, and remarkable, according to Withers, for the fact that not a nail had been used in its construction. Beyond the church was a large, low structure of stone, with a split-shingle roof, and evidently this was the town hall.

Shefford saw, before he reached the square, that this day in Stonebridge was one of singular action and excitement for a Mormon village. The town was full of people and, judging from the horses hitched everywhere and the big canvas-covered wagons, many of the people were visitors. A crowd surrounded the hall—a dusty, booted, spurred, shirt-sleeved and sombreroed assemblage that did not wear the hall-mark Shefford had come to associate with Mormons. They were riders, cowboys, horse-wranglers, and some of them Shefford had seen in Durango. Navajos and Piutes were present, also, but they loitered in the background.

Withers drew Shefford off to the side where, under a tree, they hitched their horses.

"Never saw Stonebridge full of a riffraff gang like this to-day," said Withers. "I'll bet the Mormons are wild. There's a tough outfit from Durango. If they

can get anything to drink—or if they've got it—Stonebridge will see smoke to-
day! . . . Come on. I'll get in that hall."

But before Withers reached the hall he started violently and pulled up short,
then, with apparent unconcern, turned to lay a hand upon Shefford. The trader's
face had blanched and his eyes grew hard and shiny, like flint. He gripped
Shefford's arm.

"Look! Over to your left!" he whispered. "See that gang of Indians there—
by the big wagon. See the short Indian with the chaps. He's got a face big as
a ham, dark, fierce. That's Shadd! . . . You ought to know him. Shadd and his
outfit here! How's that for nerve? But he pulls a rein with the Mormons."

Shefford's keen eye took in a lounging group of ten or twelve Indians and
several white men. They did not present any great contrast to the other groups
except that they were isolated, appeared quiet and watchful, and were all armed.
A bunch of lean, racy mustangs, restive and spirited, stood near by in charge
of an Indian. Shefford had to take a second and closer glance to distinguish the
half-breed. At once he recognized in Shadd the broad-faced squat Indian who
had paid him a threatening visit that night long ago in the mouth of the Sagi.
A fire ran along Shefford's veins and seemed to concentrate in his breast. Shadd's
dark, piercing eyes alighted upon Shefford and rested there. Then the half-breed
spoke to one of his white outlaws and pointed at Shefford. His action attracted
the attention of others in the gang and for a moment Shefford and Withers were
treated to a keen-eyed stare.

The trader cursed low. "Maybe I wouldn't like to mix it with that damned
breed," he said. "But what chance have we with that gang? Besides, we're here
on other and more important business. All the same, before I forget, let me
remind you that Shadd has had you spotted ever since you came out here. A
friendly Piute told me only lately. Shefford, did any Indian between here and
Flagstaff ever see that bunch of money you persist in carrying?"

"Why, yes, I suppose so—'way back in Tuba, when I first came out," replied
Shefford.

"Huh! Well, Shadd's after that. . . . Come on now, let's get inside the hall."

The crowd opened for the trader, who appeared to be known to everybody.
A huge man with a bushy beard blocked the way to shut the door.

"Hello, Meade!" said Withers. "Let us in."

The man opened the door, permitted Withers and Shefford to enter, and then
closed it.

Shefford, coming out of the bright glare of sun into the hall, could not see
distinctly at first. His eyes blurred. He heard a subdued murmur of many voices.
Withers appeared to be affected with the same kind of blindness, for he stood
bewildered a moment. But he recovered sooner than Shefford. Gradually the
darkness shrouding many obscure forms lifted. Withers drew him through a

crowd of men and women to one side of the hall, and squeezed along a wall to a railing where progress was stopped. Then Shefford raised his head to look with bated breath and strange curiosity.

The hall was large and had many windows. Men were in consultation upon a platform. Women to the number of twenty sat close together upon benches. Back of them stood another crowd. But the women on the benches held Shefford's gaze. They were prisoners. They made a somber group. Some were hooded, some veiled, all clad in dark garments except one on the front bench, and she was dressed in white. She wore a long hood that concealed her face. Shefford recognized the hood and then the slender shape. She was Mary—she whom her jealous neighbors had named the Sago Lily. At sight of her a sharp pain pierced Shefford's breast. His eyes were blurred when he forced them away from her, and it took a moment for him to see clearly.

Withers was whispering to him or to some one near at hand, but Shefford did not catch the meaning of what was said. He paid more attention; however, Withers ceased speaking. Shefford gazed upon the crowd back of him. The women were hooded and it was not possible to see what they looked like. There were many stalwart, clean-cut young Mormons of Joe Lake's type, and these appeared troubled, even distressed and at a loss. There was little about them resembling the stern, quiet, somber austerity of the more matured men, and nothing at all of the strange, aloof, serene impassiveness of the gray-bearded old patriarchs. These venerable men were the Mormons of the old school, the sons of the pioneers, the ruthless fanatics. Instinctively Shefford felt that it was in them that polygamy was embodied; they were the husbands of the sealed wives. He conceived an absorbing curiosity to learn if his instinct was correct; and hard upon that followed a hot, hateful eagerness to see which one was the husband of Mary.

"There's Bishop Kane," whispered Withers, nudging Shefford. "And there's Waggoner with him."

Shefford saw the bishop, and then beside him a man of striking presence.

"Who's Waggoner?" asked Shefford, as he looked.

"He owns more than any Mormon in southern Utah," replied the trader. "He's the biggest man in Stonebridge, that's sure. But I don't know his relation to the Church. They don't call him elder or bishop. But I'll bet he's some pumpkins. He never had any use for me or any Gentile. A close-fisted, tight-lipped Mormon—a skinflint if I ever saw one! Just look him over."

Shefford had been looking, and considered it unlikely that he would ever forget this individual called Waggoner. He seemed old, sixty at least, yet at that only in the prime of a wonderful physical life. Unlike most of the others, he wore his grizzled beard close-cropped, so close that it showed the lean, wolfish line of his jaw. All his features were of striking sharpness. His eyes, of a

singularly brilliant blue, were yet cold and pale. The brow had a serious, thoughtful cast; long furrows sloped down the cheeks. It was a strange, secretive face,
full of a power that Shefford had not seen in another man's, full of intelligence
and thought that had not been used as Shefford had known them used among
men. The face mystified him. It had so much more than the strange aloofness
so characteristic of his fellows.

"Waggoner had five wives and fifty-five children before the law went into
effect," whispered Withers. "Nobody knows and nobody will ever know how
many he's got now. That's my private opinion."

Somehow, after Withers told that, Shefford seemed to understand the strange
power in Waggoner's face. Absolutely it was not the force, the strength given
to a man from his years of control of men. Shefford, long schooled now in his
fair-mindedness, fought down the feelings of other years, and waited with patience. Who was he to judge Waggoner or any other Mormon? But whenever
his glance strayed back to the quiet, slender form in white, when he realized
again and again the appalling nature of this court, his heart beat heavy and
labored within his breast.

Then a bustle among the men upon the platform appeared to indicate that
proceedings were about to begin. Some men left the platform; several sat down
at the table upon which were books and papers, and others remained standing.
These last were all roughly garbed, in riding-boots and spurs, and Shefford's
keen eye detected the bulge of hidden weapons. They looked like deputy-marshals
upon duty.

Somebody whispered that the judge's name was Stone. The name fitted him.
He was not young, and looked a man suited to the prosecution of these secret
Mormons. He had a ponderous brow, a deep, cavernous eye that emitted gleams
but betrayed no color or expression. His mouth was the saving human feature
of his stony face.

Shefford took the man upon the judge's right to be a lawyer, and the one on
his left an officer of court, perhaps a prosecuting attorney. Presently this fellow
pounded upon the table and stood up as if to address a court-room. Certainly
he silenced that hallful of people. Then he perfunctorily and briefly stated that
certain women had been arrested upon suspicion of being sealed wives of Mormon
polygamists, and were to be herewith tried by a judge of the United States Court.
Shefford felt how the impressive words affected that silent hall of listeners, but
he gathered from the brief preliminaries that the trial could not be otherwise than
a crude, rapid investigation, and perhaps for that the more sinister.

The first woman on the foremost bench was led forward by a deputy to a
vacant chair on the platform just in front of the judge's table. She was told to
sit down, and showed no sign that she had heard. Then the judge courteously
asked her to take the chair. She refused. And Stone nodded his head as if he had

experienced that sort of thing before. He stroked his chin wearily, and Shefford conceived an idea that he was a kind man, if he was a relentless judge.

"Please remove your veil," requested the prosecutor.

The woman did so, and proved to be young and handsome. Shefford had a thrill as he recognized her. She was Ruth, who had been one of his best known acquaintances in the hidden village. She was pale, angry, almost sullen, and her breast heaved. She had no shame, but she seemed to be outraged. Her dark eyes, scornful and blazing, passed over the judge and his assistants, and on to the crowd behind the railing. Shefford, keen as a blade, with all his faculties absorbed, fancied he saw Ruth stiffen and change slightly as her glance encountered some one in that crowd. Then the prosecutor in deliberate and chosen words enjoined her to kiss the Bible handed to her and swear to tell the truth. How strange for Shefford to see her kiss the book which he had studied for so many years! Stranger still to hear the low murmur from the listening audience as she took the oath!

"What is your name?" asked Judge Stone, leaning back and fixing the cavernous eyes upon her.

"Ruth Jones," was the cool reply.

"How old are you?"

"Twenty."

"Where were you born?" went on the judge. He allowed time for the clerk to record her answers.

"Panguitch, Utah."

"Were your parents Mormons?"

"Yes."

"Are you a Mormon?"

"Yes."

"Are you a married woman?"

"No."

The answer was instant, cold, final. It seemed to the truth. Almost Shefford believed she spoke truth. The judge stroked his chin and waited a moment, and then hesitatingly he went on.

"Have you—any children?"

"No." And the blazing eyes met the cavernous ones.

That about the children was true enough, Shefford thought, and he could have testified to it.

"You live in the hidden village near this town?"

"Yes."

"What is the name of this village?"

"It has none."

"Did you ever hear of Fre-donia, another village far west of here?"

"Yes."

"It is in Arizona, near the Utah line. There are few men there. It is the same kind of village as this one in which you live?"

"Yes."

"What does Fre-donia mean? The name—has it any meaning?"

"It means free women."

The judge maintained silence for a moment, turned to whisper to his assistants, and presently, without glancing up, said to the woman:

"That will do."

Ruth was led back to the bench, and the woman next to her brought forward. This was a heavier person, with the figure and step of a matured woman. Upon removing her bonnet she showed the plain face of a woman of forty, and it was striking only in that strange, stony aloofness noted in the older men. Here, Shefford thought, was the real Mormon, different in a way he could not define from Ruth. This woman seated herself in the chair and calmly faced her prosecutors. She manifested no emotion whatever. Shefford remembered her and could not see any change in her deportment. This trial appeared to be of little moment to her and she took the oath as if doing so had been a habit all her life.

"What is your name?" asked Judge Stone, glancing up from a paper he held.

"Mary Danton."

"Family or married name?"

"My husband's name was Danton."

"Was. Is he living?"

"No."

"Where did you live when you were married to him?"

"In St. George, and later here in Stonebridge."

"You were both Mormons?"

"Yes."

"Did you have any children by him?"

"Yes."

"How many?"

"Two."

"Are they living?"

"One of them is living."

Judge Stone bent over his paper and then slowly raised his eyes to her face.

"Are you married now?"

"No."

Again the judge consulted his notes, and held a whispered colloquy with the two men at his table.

"Mrs. Danton, when you were arrested there were five children found in your home. To whom do they belong?"

"Me."

"Are you their mother?"

"Yes."

"Your husband Danton is the father of only one, the eldest, according to your former statement. Is that correct?"

"Yes."

"Who, then, is the father—or who are the fathers, of your other children?"

"I do not know."

She said it with the most stony-faced calmness, with utter disregard of what significance her words had. A strong, mystic wall of cold flint insulated her. Strangely it came to Shefford how impossible either to doubt or believe her. Yet he did both! Judge Stone showed a little heat.

"You don't know the father of one of all of these children?" he queried, with sharp rising inflection of voice.

"I do not."

"Madam, I beg to remind you that you are under oath."

The woman did not reply.

"These children are nameless, then—illegitimate?"

"They are."

"You swear you are not the sealed wife of some Mormon?"

"I swear."

"How do you live—maintain yourself?"

"I work."

"What at?"

"I weave, sew, bake, and work in my garden."

"My men made note of your large and comfortable cabin, even luxurious, considering this country. How is that?"

"My husband left me comfortable."

Judge Stone shook a warning finger at the defendant.

"Suppose I were to sentence you to jail for perjury? For a year? Far from your home and children! Would you speak—tell the truth?"

"I am telling the truth. I can't speak what I don't know. . . . Send me to jail."

Baffled, with despairing, angry impatience, Judge Stone waved the woman away.

"That will do for her. Fetch the next one," he said.

One after another he examined three more women, and arrived, by various questions and answers different in tone and temper, at precisely the same point as had been made in the case of Mrs. Danton. Thereupon the proceedings rested a few moments while the judge consulted with his assistants.

Shefford was grateful for his respite. He had been worked up to an unusual degree of interest, and now, as the next Mormon woman to be examined was she whom he had loved and loved still, he felt rise in him emotion that threatened to make him conspicuous unless it could be hidden. The answers of these Mormon women had been not altogether unexpected by him, but once spoken in cold blood under oath, how tragic, how appallingly significant of the shadow, the mystery, the yoke that bound them! He was amazed, saddened. He felt bewildered. He needed to think out the meaning of the falsehoods of women he knew to be good and noble. Surely religion, instead of fear and loyalty, was the foundation and the strength of this disgrace, this sacrifice. Absolutely, shame was not in these women, though they swore to shameful facts. They had been coached to give these baffling answers, every one of which seemed to brand them, not the brazen mothers of illegitimate offspring, but faithful, unfortunate sealed wives. To Shefford the truth was not in their words, but it sat upon their somber brows.

Was it only his heightened imagination, or did the silence and the suspense grow more intense when a deputy led that dark-hooded, white-clad, slender woman to the defendant's chair? She did not walk with the poise that had been manifest in the other women, and she sank into the chair as if she could no longer stand.

"Please remove your hood," requested the prosecutor.

How well Shefford remembered the strong, shapely hands! He saw them tremble at the knot of ribbon, and that tremor was communicated to him in a sympathy which made his pulses beat. He held his breath while she removed the hood. And then there was revealed, he thought, the loveliest and the most tragic face that ever was seen in a court-room.

A low, whispering murmur that swelled like a wave ran through the hall. And by it Shefford divined, as clearly as if the fact had been blazoned on the walls, that Mary's face had been unknown to these villagers. But the name Sago Lily had not been unknown; Shefford heard it whispered on all sides.

The murmuring subsided. The judge and his assistants stared at Mary. As for Shefford, there was no need of his personal feeling to make the situation dramatic. Not improbably Judge Stone had tried many Mormon women. But manifestly this one was different. Unhooded, Mary appeared to be only a young girl, and a court, confronted suddenly with her youth and the suspicion attached to her, could not but have been shocked. Then her beauty made her seem, in that somber company, indeed the white flower for which she had been named. But, more likely, it was her agony that bound the court into silence which grew painful. Perhaps the thought that flashed into Shefford's mind was telepathic; it seemed to him that every watcher there realized that in this defendant the judge had a girl of softer mold, of different spirit, and from her the bitter truth could be wrung.

Mary faced the court and the crowd on that side of the platform. Unlike the other women, she did not look at or seem to see any one behind the railing. Shefford was absolutely sure there was not a man or a woman who caught her glance. She gazed afar, with eyes strained, humid, fearful.

When the prosecutor swore her to the oath her lips were seen to move, but no one heard her speak.

"What is your name?" asked the judge.

"Mary." Her voice was low with slight tremor.

"What's your other name?"

"I won't tell."

Her singular reply, the tones of her voice, her manner before the judge, marked her with strange simplicity. It was evident that she was not accustomed to questions.

"What were your parents' names?"

"I won't tell," she replied, very low.

Judge Stone did not press the point. Perhaps he wanted to make the examination as easy as possible for her or to wait till she showed more composure.

"Were your parents Mormons?" he went on.

"No, sir." She added the sir with a quaint respect, contrasting markedly with the short replies of the women before her.

"Then you were not born a Mormon?"

"No, sir."

"How old are you?"

"Seventeen or eighteen. I'm not sure."

"You don't know your exact age?"

"No."

"Where were you born?"

"I won't tell."

"Was it in Utah?"

"Yes, sir."

"How long have you lived in this state?"

"Always—except last year."

"And that's been over in the hidden village where you were arrested?"

"Yes."

"But you often visited here—this town Stonebridge?"

"I never was here—till yesterday."

Judge Stone regarded her as if his interest as a man was running counter to his duty as an officer. Suddenly he leaned forward.

"Are you a Mormon *now?*" he queried, forcibly.

"No, sir," she replied, and here her voice rose a little clearer.

It was an unexpected reply. Judge Stone stared at her. The low buzz ran

through the listening crowd. And as for Shefford, he was astounded. When his
wits flashed back and he weighed her words and saw in her face truth as clear
as light, he had the strangest sensation of joy. Almost it flooded away the gloom
and pain that attended this ordeal.

The judge bent his head to his assistants as if for counsel. All of them were
eager where formerly they had been weary. Shefford glanced around at the dark
and somber faces, and slow wrath grew within him. Then he caught a glimpse
of Waggoner. The steel-blue, piercing intensity of the Mormon's gaze impressed
him at a moment when all that older generation of Mormons looked as hard and
immutable as iron. Either Shefford was over-excited and mistaken or the hour
had become fraught with greater suspense. The secret, the mystery, the power,
the hate, the religion of people were thick and tangible in that hall. For Shefford
the feeling of the presence of Withers on his left was entirely different from that
of the Mormon on his other side. If there was not a shadow there, then the sun
did not shine so brightly as it had shone when he entered. The air seemed clogged
with nameless passion.

"I gather that you've lived mostly in the country—away from people?" the
judge began.

"Yes, sir," replied the girl.

"Do you know anything about the government of the United States?"

"No, sir."

He pondered again, evidently weighing his queries, leading up to the fatal
and inevitable question. Still his interest in this particular defendant had become
visible.

"Have you any idea of the consequences of perjury?"

"No, sir."

"Do you understand what perjury is?"

"It's to lie."

"Do you tell lies?"

"No, sir."

"Have you ever told a single lie?"

"Not—yet," she replied, almost whispering.

It was the answer of a child and affected the judge. He fussed with his papers.
Perhaps his task was not easy; certainly it was not pleasant. Then he leaned
forward again and fixed those deep cavernous eyes upon the sad face.

"Do you understand what a sealed wife is?"

"I've never been told."

"But you know there *are* sealed wives in Utah?"

"Yes, sir; I've been told that."

Judge Stone halted there, watching her. The hall was silent except for faint
rustlings and here and there deep breaths drawn guardedly. The vital question

hung like a sword over the white-faced girl. Perhaps she divined its impending stroke, for she sat like a stone with dilating, appealing eyes upon her executioner.

"Are you a sealed wife?" he flung at her.

She could not answer at once. She made effort, but the words would not come. He flung the question again, sternly.

"No!" she cried.

And then there was silence. That poignant word quivered in Shefford's heart. He believed it was a lie. It seemed he would have known it if this hour was the first in which he had ever seen the girl. He heard, he felt, he sensed the fatal thing. The beautiful voice had lacked some quality before present. And the thing wanting was something subtle, an essence, a beautiful ring—the truth. What a hellish thing to make that pure girl a liar—a perjurer! The heat deep within Shefford kindled to fire.

"You are not married?" went on Judge Stone.

"No, sir," she answered, faintly.

"Have you ever been married?"

"No, sir."

"Do you expect ever to be married?"

"Oh! No, sir."

She was ashen pale now, quivering all over, with her strong hands clasping the black hood, and she could no longer meet the judge's glance.

"Have you—any—any—children?" the judge asked haltingly. It was a hard question to get out.

"No."

Judge Stone leaned far over the table, and that his face was purple showed Shefford he was a man. His big fist clenched.

"Girl, you're not going to swear you, too, were visited—over there by men. . . . You're not going to swear that?"

"Oh—no, sir!"

Judge Stone settled back in his chair, and while he wiped his moist face that same foreboding murmur, almost a menace, moaned through the hall.

Shefford was sick in his soul and afraid of himself. He did not know this spirit that flamed up in him. His helplessness was a most hateful fact.

"Come—confess you are a sealed wife," called her interrogator.

She maintained silence but shook her head.

Suddenly he seemed to leap forward.

"Unfortunate child! Confess."

That forced her to lift her head and face him, yet still she did not speak. It was the strength of despair. She could not endure much more.

"Who is your husband?" he thundered at her.

She rose wildly, terror-stricken. It was terror that dominated her, not of the stern judge, for she took a faltering step toward him, lifting a shaking hand, but of some one or of some thing far more terrible than any punishment she could have received in the sentence of a court. Still she was not proof against the judge's will. She had weakened, and the terror must have been because of that weakening.

"Who is the Mormon who visits you?" he thundered, relentlessly.

"I—never—knew—his—name."

"But you'd know his face. I'll arrest every Mormon in this country and bring him before you. You'd know his face?"

"Oh, I wouldn't. I *couldn't* tell! . . . I—*never—saw his face—in the light!*"

The tragic beauty of her, the certainty of some monstrous crime to youth and innocence, the presence of an agony and terror that unfathomably seemed not to be for herself—these transfixed the court and the audience, and held them silenced, till she reached out blindly and then sank in a heap to the floor.

11
After the Trial

SHEFFORD might have leaped over the railing but for Withers's restraining hand, and when there appeared to be some kindness in those other women for the unconscious girl Shefford squeezed through the crowd and got out of the hall.

The gang outside that had been denied admittance pressed upon Shefford, with jest and curious query, and a good nature that jarred upon him. He was far from gentle as he jostled off the first importuning fellows; the others, gaping at him, opened a lane for him to pass through.

Then there was a hand laid on his shoulder that he did not shake off. Nas Ta Bega loomed dark and tall beside him. Neither the trader nor Joe Lake nor any white man Shefford had met influenced him as this Navajo.

"Nas Ta Bega! you here, too. I guess the whole country is here. We waited at Kayenta. What kept you so long?"

The Indian, always slow to answer, did not open his lips till he drew Shefford apart from the noisy crowd.

"Bi Nai, there is sorrow in the hogan of Hosteen Doetin," he said.

"Glen Naspa!" exclaimed Shefford.

"My sister is gone from the home of her brother. She went away alone in the summer."

"Blue Cañon! She went to the missionary. Nas Ta Bega, I thought I saw her there. But I wasn't sure. I didn't want to make sure. I was afraid it might be true."

"A brave who loved my sister trailed her there."

"Nas Ta Bega, will you—will we go find her, take her home?"

"No. She will come home some day."

What bitter sadness and wisdom in his words!

"But, my friend, that damned missionary—" began Shefford, passionately. The Indian had met him at a bad hour.

"Willetts is here. I saw him go in there," interrupted Nas Ta Bega, and he pointed to the hall.

"Here! He gets around a good deal," declared Shefford. "Nas Ta Bega, what are you going to do to him?"

The Indian held his peace and there was no telling from his inscrutable face what might be in his mind. He was dark, impassive. He seemed a wise and bitter Indian, beyond savagery of his tribe and the suffering Shefford divined was deep.

"He'd better keep out of my sight," muttered Shefford, more to himself than to his companion.

"The half-breed is here," said Nas Ta Bega.

"Shadd? Yes, we saw him. There! He's still with his gang. Nas Ta Bega, what are they up to?"

"They will steal what they can."

"Withers says Shadd is friendly with the Mormons."

"Yes, and with the missionary, too."

"With Willetts?"

"I saw them talk together—strong talk."

"Strange. But maybe it's not so strange. Shadd is known well in Monticello and Bluff. He spends money there. They are afraid of him, but he's welcome just the same. Perhaps everybody knows him. It'd be like him to ride into Kayenta. But, Nas Ta Bega, I've got to look out for him, because Withers says he's after me."

"Bi Nai wears a scar that is proof," said the Indian.

"Then it must be he found out long ago I had a little money."

"It might be. But, Bi Nai, the half-breed has a strange step on your trail."

"What do you mean?" demanded Shefford.

"Nas Ta Bega cannot tell what he does not know," replied the Navajo. "Let that be. We shall know some day. Bi Nai, there is sorrow to tell that is not the Indian's. . . . Sorrow for my brother!"

Shefford lifted his eyes to the Indian's, and if he did not see sadness there he was much deceived.

"Bi Nai, long ago you told a story to the trader. Nas Ta Bega sat before the fire that night. You did not know he could understand your language. He listened. And he learned what brought you to the country of the Indian. That night he made you his brother. . . . All his lonely rides into the cañons have been to find the little golden-haired child, the lost girl—Fay Larkin. . . . Bi Nai, I have found the girl you wanted for your sweetheart."

Shefford was bereft of speech. He could not see steadily, and the last solemn words of the Indian seemed far away.

"Bi Nai, I have found Fay Larkin," repeated Nas Ta Bega.

"Fay Larkin!" gasped Shefford, shaking his head. "But—she's dead."

"It would be less sorrow for Bi Nai if she were dead."

Shefford clutched at the Indian. There was something terrible to be revealed. Like an aspen-leaf in the wind he shook all over. He divined the revelation— divined the coming blow—but that was as far as his mind got.

"She's in there," said the Indian, pointing toward the hall.

"Fay Larkin?" whispered Shefford.

"Yes, Bi Nai."

"My God! *How* do you know? Oh, I could have seen. I've been blind. . . . Tell me, Indian. Which one?"

"Fay Larkin is the Sago Lily."

Shefford strode away into a secluded corner of the square, where in the shade and quiet of the trees he suffered a storm of heart and mind. During that short or long time—he had no idea how long—the Indian remained with him. He never lost the feeling of Nas Ta Bega close beside him. When the period of acute pain left him and some order began to replace the tumult in his mind he felt in Nas Ta Bega the same quality—silence or strength or help—that he had learned to feel in the deep cañons and the lofty crags. He realized then that the Indian was indeed a brother. And Shefford needed him. What he had to fight was more fatal than suffering and love—it was hate rising out of the unsuspected dark gulf of his heart—the instinct to kill—the murder in his soul. Only now did he come to understand Jane Withersteen's tragic story and the passion of Venters and what had made Lassiter a gun-man.

The desert had transformed Shefford. The elements had entered into his muscle and bone, into the very fiber of his heart. Sun, wind, sand, cold, storm, space, stone, the poison cactus, the racking toil, the terrible loneliness—the iron of the desert man, the cruelty of the desert savage, the wildness of the mustang, the ferocity of hawk and wolf, the bitter struggle of every surviving thing—these were as if they had been melted and merged together and now made a dark and passionate stream that was his throbbing blood. He realized what he had become and glorified in it, yet there, looking on with grave and earnest eyes, was his old self, the man of reason, of intellect, of culture, who had been a good man despite the failure and shame of his life. And he gave heed to the voice of warning, of conscience. Not by revengefully seeking the Mormon who had ruined Fay Larkin and blindly dealing a wild justice could he help this unfortunate girl. This fierce, newborn strength and passion must be tempered by reason, lest he become merely elemental, a man answering wholly to primitive impulses. In the darkness of that hour he mined deep into his heart, understood himself, trembled at the thing he faced, and won his victory. He would go forth from that hour a man. He might fight, and perhaps there was death in the balance, but hate would never overthrow him.

Then when he looked at future action he felt a strange, unalterable purpose to save Fay Larkin. She was very young—seventeen or eighteen, she said—and there could be, there must be some happiness before her. It had been his dream to chase a rainbow—it had been his determination to find her in the lost Surprise Valley. Well, he had found her. It never occurred to him to ask Nas Ta Bega how he had discovered that the Sago Lily was Fay Larkin. The wonder was, Shefford thought, that he had so long been blind himself. How simply everything worked out now! Every thought, every recollection of her was proof. Her strange beauty like that of the sweet and rare lily, her low voice that showed the habit of silence, her shapely hands with the clasp strong as a man's, her lithe form, her swift step, her wonderful agility upon the smooth, steep walls, and the wildness of her upon the heights, and the haunting, brooding shadow of her eyes when she gazed across the cañons—all these fitted so harmoniously the conception of a child lost in a beautiful Surprise Valley and growing up in its wildness and silence, tutored by the sad love of broken Jane and Lassiter. Yes, to save her had been Shefford's dream, and he had loved the child. The secret of her hiding-place as revealed by the story told him and his slow growth from dream to action—these had strangely given Fay Larkin to him. Then had come the bitter knowledge that she was dead. In the light of this subsequent revelation how easy to account for his loving Mary, too. Never would she be Mary again to him! Fay Larkin and the Sago Lily were one and the same. She was here, near him, and he was powerless for the present to help her or to reveal himself. She was held back there in that gloomy hall among those somber Mormons, alien to the women, bound in some fatal way to one of the men, and now, by reason of her weakness in the trial, surely to be hated. Thinking of her past and her present, of the future, and that secret Mormon whose face she had never seen, Shefford felt a sinking of his heart, a terrible cold pang in his breast, a fainting of his spirit. She had sworn she was no sealed wife. But had she not lied? So, then, how utterly powerless he was!

But here to save him, to uplift him, came that strange mystic insight which had been the gift of the desert to him. She was not dead. He had found her. What mattered obstacles, even that implacable creed to which she had been sacrificed, in the face of this blessed and overwhelming truth? It was as mighty as the love suddenly dawning upon him. A strong and terrible and deathly sweet wind seemed to fill his soul with the love of her. It was her fate that had drawn him; and now it was her agony, her innocence, her beauty, that bound him for all time. Patience and cunning and toil, passion and blood, the unquenchable spirit of a man to save—these were nothing to give—life itself were little, could he but free her.

Patience and cunning! His sharpening mind cut these out of his greatest assets for the present. And his thoughts flashed like light through his brain. . . . Judge Stone and his court would fail to convict any Mormon in Stonebridge, just the same as they had failed in the northern towns. They would go away, and Stone-bridge would fall to the slow, sleepy tenor of its former way. The hidden village must become known to all men, honest and outlawed, in that country, but this fact would hardly make any quick change in the plans of the Mormons. They did not soon change. They would send the sealed wives back to the cañon and, after the excitement had died down, visit them as usual. Nothing, perhaps, would ever change these old Mormons but death.

Shefford resolved to remain in Stonebridge and ingratiate himself deeper into the regard of the Mormons. He would find work there, if the sealed wives were not returned to the hidden village. In case the women went back to the valley Shefford meant to resume his old duty of driving Withers's pack-trains. Wanting that opportunity, he would find some other work, some excuse to take him there.

In due time he would reveal to Fay Larkin that he knew her. How the thought thrilled him! She might deny, might persist in fear, might fight to keep her secret. But he would learn it—hear her story—hear what had become of Jane Withersteen and Lassiter—and if they were alive, which now he believed he would find them—and he would take them and Fay out of the country.

The duty, the great task, held a grim fascination for him. He had a foreboding of cost; he had a dark realization of the force he meant to oppose. There were duty here and pity and unselfish love, but these alone did not actuate Shefford. Mystically fate seemed again to come like a gleam and bid him follow.

When Shefford and Nas Ta Bega returned to the town hall the trial had been ended, the hall was closed, and only a few Indians and cowboys remained in the square, and they were about to depart. On the street, however, and the paths and in the doorways of stores were knots of people, talking earnestly. Shefford walked up and down, hoping to meet Withers or Joe Lake. Nas Ta Bega said he would take the horses to water and feed and then return.

There were indications that Stonebridge might experience some of the excitement and perhaps violence common to towns like Monticello and Durango. There was only one saloon in Stonebridge, and it was full of roystering cowboys and horse-wranglers. Shefford saw the bunch of mustangs, in charge of the same Indian, that belonged to Shadd and his gang. The men were inside, drinking. Next door was a tavern called Hopewell House, a stone structure of some pretensions. There were Indians lounging outside. Shefford entered through a wide door and found himself in a large bare room, boarded like a loft, with no ceiling except the roof. The place was full of men and noise. Here he encountered Joe Lake talking to Bishop Kane and other Mormons. Shefford got a friendly greeting from the bishop, and then was well received by the strangers, to whom Joe introduced him.

"Have you seen Withers?" asked Shefford.

"Reckon he's around somewhere," replied Joe.

"Better hang up here, for he'll drop in sooner or later."

"When are you going back to Kayenta?" went on Shefford.

"Hard to say. We'll have to call off our hunt. Nas Ta Bega is here, too."

"Yes, I've been with him."

The older Mormons drew aside, and then Joe mentioned the fact that he was half starved. Shefford went with him into another clapboard room, which was evidently a dining-room. There were half a dozen men at the long table. The seat at the end was a box, and scarcely large enough or safe enough for Joe and Shefford, but they risked it.

"Saw you in the hall," said Joe. "Hell—wasn't it?"

"Joe, I never knew how much I dared say to you, so I don't talk much. But, it was hell," replied Shefford.

"You needn't be so scared of me," spoke up Joe, testily.

That was the first time Shefford had heard the Mormon speak that way.

"I'm not scared, Joe. But I like you—respect you. I can't say so much of— of your people."

"Did you stick out the whole mix?" asked Joe.

"No. I had enough when—when they got through with Mary." Shefford spoke low and dropped his head. He heard the Mormon grind his teeth. There was silence for a little space while neither man looked at the other.

"Reckon the judge was pretty decent," presently said Joe.

"Yes, I thought so. He might have—" But Shefford did not finish that sentence. "How'd the thing end?"

"It ended all right."

"Was there no conviction—no sentence?" Shefford felt a curious eagerness.

"Naw," he snorted. "That court might have saved its breath."

"I suppose. Well, Joe, between you and me, as old friends now, that trial established one fact, even if it couldn't be proved. . . . Those woman *are* sealed wives.''

Joe had no reply for that. He looked gloomy, and there was a stern line in his lips. To-day he seemed more like a Mormon.

''Judge Stone knew that as well as I knew,'' went on Shefford. ''Any man of penetration could have seen it. What an ordeal that was for good women to go through! I know they're good. And there they were swearing to—''

''Didn't it make me sick?'' interrupted Joe in a kind of growl. ''Reckon it made Judge Stone sick, too. After Mary went under he conducted that trial like a man cuttin' out steers at a round-up. He wanted to get it over. He never forced any question. . . . Bad job to ride down Stonebridge way! It's out of creation. There's only six men in the party, with a poor lot of horses. Really, government officers or not, they're not safe. And they've taken a hunch.''

''Have they left already?'' inquired Shefford.

''Were packed an hour ago. I didn't see them go, but somebody said they went. Took the trail for Bluff, which sure is the only trail they could take, unless they wanted to go to Colorado by the way of Kayenta. That might have been the safest trail.''

''Joe, what might happen to them?'' asked Shefford, quietly, with eyes on the Mormon.

''Aw, you know that rough trail. Bad on horses. Weathered slopes—slipping ledges—a rock might fall on you any time. Then Shadd's here with his gang. And bad Piutes.''

''What became of the women?'' Shefford asked, presently.

''They're around among friends.''

''Where are their children?''

''Left over there with the old women. Couldn't be fetched over. But there are some pretty young babies in that bunch—need their mothers.''

''I should—think so,'' replied Shefford, constrainedly. ''When will their mothers get back to them?''

''To-night, maybe, if this mob of cow-punchers and wranglers get out of town. . . . It's a bad mix, Shefford, here's a hunch on that. These fellows will get full of whisky. And trouble might come if they—approach the women.''

''You mean they might get drunk enough to take the oaths of those poor women—take the meaning literally—pretend to believe the women what they swore they were?''

''Reckon you've got the hunch,'' replied Joe, gloomily.

''My God! man, that would be horrible!'' exclaimed Shefford.

''Horrible or not, it's liable to happen. The women can be kept here yet awhile. Reckon there won't be any trouble here. It'll be over there in the valley. Shefford, getting the women over there safe is a job that's been put to me. I've got a bunch of fellows already. Can I count on you? I'm glad to say you're well thought of. Bishop Kane liked you, and what he says goes.''

"Yes, Joe, you can count on me," replied Shefford.

They finished their meal then and repaired to the big office-room of the house. Several groups of men were there and loud talk was going on outside. Shefford saw Withers talking to Bishop Kane and two other Mormons, both strangers to Shefford. The trader appeared to be speaking with unwonted force, emphasizing his words with energetic movements of his hands.

"Reckon something's up," whispered Joe, hoarsely. "It's been in the air all day."

Withers must have been watching for Shefford.

"Here's Shefford now," he said to the trio of Mormons, as Joe and Shefford reached for the group. "I want you to hear him speak for himself."

"What's the matter?" asked Shefford.

"Give me a hunch and I'll put in my say-so," said Joe Lake.

"Shefford, it's the matter of a good name more than a job," replied the trader. "A little while back I told the bishop I meant to put you on the pack job over to the valley—same as when you first came to me. Well, the bishop was pleased and said he might put something in your way. Just now I ran in here to find you—not wanted. When I kicked I got the straight hunch. Willetts has said things about you. One of them—the one that sticks in my craw—was that you'd do anything even pretend to be inclined toward Mormonism, just to be among those Mormon women over there. Willetts is your enemy. And he's worse than I thought. Now I want you to tell Bishop Kane *why* this missionary is bitter toward you."

"Gentlemen, I knocked him down," replied Shefford, simply.

"What for?" inquired the bishop, in surprise and curiosity.

Shefford related the incident which had occurred at Red Lake and that now seemed again to come forward fatefully.

"You insinuate he had evil intent toward the Indian girl?" queried Kane.

"I insinuate nothing. I merely state what led to my acting as I did."

"Principles of religion, sir?"

"No. A man's principles."

Withers interposed in his blunt way, "Bishop, did you ever see Glen Naspa?"

"No."

"She's the prettiest Navajo in the country. Willetts was after her, that's all."

"My dear man, I can't believe that of a Christian missionary. We've known Willetts for years. He's a man of influence. He has money back of him. He's doing a good work. You hint of a love relation."

"No, I don't hint," replied Withers, impatiently. "I know. It's not the first time I've known a missionary to do this sort of thing. Nor is it the first time for

Willetts. Bishop Kane, I live among the Indians. I see a lot I never speak of.
My work is to trade with the Indians, that's all. But I'll not have Willetts or any
other damned hypocrite run down my friend here. John Shefford is the finest
young man that ever came to me in the desert. And he's got to be put right
before you all or I'll not set foot in Stonebridge again. . . . Willetts was after
Glen Naspa. Shefford punched him. And later threw him out of the old Indian's
hogan up on the mountain. That explains Willetts's enmity. He was after the
girl.''

"What's more, gentlemen, he *got* her," added Shefford. "Glen Naspa has
not been home for six months. I saw her at Blue Cañon. . . . I would like to
face this Willetts before you all.''

"Easy enough," replied Withers, with a grim chuckle. "He's just outside.''

The trader went out; Joe Lake followed at his heels and the three Mormons
were next; Shefford brought up the rear and lingered in the door while his eye
swept the crowd of men and Indians. His feeling was in direct contrast to his
movements. He felt the throbbing of fierce anger. But it seemed a face came
between him and his passion—a sweet and tragic face that would have had power
to check him in a vastly more critical moment than this. And in an instant he
had himself in hind, and, strangely, suddenly felt the strength that had come to
him.

Willetts stood in earnest colloquy with a short, squat Indian—the half-breed
Shadd. They leaned against a hitching-rail. Other Indians were there, and outlaws. It was a mixed group, rough and hard-looking.

"Hey, Willetts!" called the trader, and his loud, ringing voice, not pleasant,
stilled the movement and sound.

When Willetts turned, Shefford was half-way across the wide walk. The
missionary not only saw him, but also Nas Ta Bega, who was striding forward.
Joe Lake was ahead of the trader, the Mormons followed with decision, and
they all confronted Willetts. He turned pale. Shadd had cautiously moved along
the rail, nearer to his gang, and then they, with the others of the curious crowd,
drew closer.

"Willetts, here's Shefford. Now say it to his face!" declared the trader. He
was angry and evidently wanted the fact known, as well as the situation.

Willetts had paled, but he showed boldness. For an instant Shefford studied
the smooth face, with its sloping lines, the dark, wine-colored eyes.

"Willetts, I understand you've maligned me to Bishop Kane and others,"
began Shefford, curtly.

"I called you an atheist," returned the missionary, harshly.

"Yes, and more than that. And I told these men *why* you vented your spite
on me.''

Willetts uttered a half-laugh, an uneasy, contemptuous expression of scorn and repudiation.

"The charges of such a man as you are can't hurt me," he said.

The man did not show fear so much as disgust at the meeting. He seemed to be absorbed in thought, yet no serious consideration of the situation made itself manifest. Shefford felt puzzled. Perhaps there was no fire to strike from this man. The desert had certainly not made him flint. He had not toiled or suffered or fought.

"But *I* can hurt you," thundered Shefford, with startling suddenness. "Here! Look at this Indian! Do you know him? Glen Naspa's brother. Look at him. Let us see you face him while I accuse you. . . . You made love to Glen Naspa— took her from her home!"

"Harping infidel!" replied Willetts, hoarsely. "So that's your game. Well, Glen Naspa came to my school of her own accord and she will say so."

"Why will she? Because you blinded the simple Indian girl. . . . Willetts, I'll waste little more time on you."

And swift and light as a panther Shefford leaped upon the man and, fastening powerful hands round the thick neck, bore him to his knees and bent back his head over the rail. There was a convulsive struggle, a hard flinging of arms, a straining wrestle, and then Willetts was in a dreadful position. Shefford held him in iron grasp.

"You damned, white-livered hypocrite—I'm liable to kill you!" cried Shefford. "I watched you and Glen Naspa that day up on the mountain. I saw you embrace her. I saw that she loved you. Tell *that*, you liar! That 'll be enough."

The face of the missionary turned purple as Shefford forced his head back over the rail.

"I'll *kill* you, man," repeated Shefford, piercingly. "Do you want to go to your God unprepared? Say you made love to Glen Naspa—tell that you persuaded her to leave her home. Quick!"

Willetts raised a shaking hand and then Shefford relaxed the paralyzing grip and let his head come forward. The half-strangled man gasped out a few incoherent words that his livid, guilty face made unnecessary.

Shefford gave him a shove and he fell into the dust at the feet of the Navajo.

"Gentlemen, I leave him to Nas Ta Bega," said Shefford, with a strange change from passion to calmness.

Late that night, when the roystering visitors had gone or were deep in drunken slumber, a melancholy and strange procession filed out of Stonebridge. Joe Lake and his armed comrades were escorting the Mormon women back to the hidden valley. They were mounted on burros and mustangs, and in all that dark and somber line there was only one figure which shone white under the pale moon.

At the starting, until that white-clad figure had appeared, Shefford's heart had seemed to be in his throat; and thereafter its beat was muffled and painful in his breast. Yet there was some sad sweetness in the knowledge that he could see her now, be near her, watch over her.

By and by the overcast clouds drifted and the moon shone bright. The night was still; the great dark mountain loomed to the stars; the numberless waves of rounded rock that must be crossed and circled lay deep in shadow. There was only a steady pattering of light hoofs.

Shefford's place was near the end of the line, and he kept well back, riding close to one woman and then another. No word was spoken. These sealed wives rode where their mounts were led or driven, as blind in their hoods as veiled Arab women in palanquins. And their heads drooped wearily and their shoulders bent, as if under a burden. It took an hour of steady riding to reach the ascent to the plateau, and here, with the beginning of rough and smooth and shadowed trail, the work of the escort began. The line lengthened out and each man kept to the several women assigned to him. Shefford had three, and one of them was the girl he loved. She rode as if the world and time and life were naught to her. As soon as he dared trust his voice and his control he meant to let her know the man whom perhaps she had not forgotten was there with her, a friend. Six months! It had been a lifetime to him. Surely eternity to her! Had she forgotten? He felt like a coward who had basely deserted her. Oh—had he only known!

She rode a burro that was slow, continually blocking the passage for those behind, and eventually it became lame. Thus the other women forged ahead. Shefford dismounted and stopped her burro. It was a moment before she noted the halt, and twice in that time Shefford tried to speak and failed. What poignant pain, regret, love made his utterance fail!

"Ride my horse," he finally said, and his voice was not like his own.

Obediently and wearily she dismounted from the burro and got up on Nackyal. The stirrups were long for her and he had to change them. His fingers were all thumbs as he fumbled with the buckles.

Suddenly he became aware that there had been a subtle change in her. He knew it without looking up and he seemed to be unable to go on with his task. If his life had depended upon keeping his head lowered he could not have done it. The listlessness of her drooping form was no longer manifest. The peak of the dark hood pointed toward him. He knew then that she was gazing at him.

Never so long as he lived would that moment be forgotten! They were alone. The others had gotten so far ahead that no sound came back. The stillness was so deep it could be felt. The moon shone with white, cold radiance and the shining slopes of smooth stone waved away, crossed by shadows of piñons.

Then she leaned a little toward him. One swift hand flew up to tear the black hood back so that she could see. In its place flashed her white face. And her eyes were like the night.

"*You!*" she whispered.

His blood came leaping to sting neck and cheek and temple. What dared he interpret from that single word? Could any other word have meant so much?

"No—one—else," he replied, unsteadily.

Her white hand flashed again to him, and he met it with his own. He felt himself standing cold and motionless in the moonlight. He saw her, wonderful, with the deep, shadowy eyes, and a silver sheen on her hair. And as he looked she released her hand and lifted it, with the other, to her hood. He saw the shiny hair darken and disappear—and then the lovely face with its sad eyes and tragic lips.

He drew Nack-yal's bridle forward, and led him up the moonlit trail.

12
The Revelation

THE following afternoon cowboys and horse-wranglers, keen-eyed as Indians for tracks and trails, began to arrive in the quiet valley to which the Mormon women had been returned.

Under every cedar clump there were hobbled horses, packs, and rolled bedding in tarpaulins. Shefford and Joe Lake had pitched camp in the old site near the spring. The other men of Joe's escort went to the homes of the women; and that afternoon, as the curious visitors began to arrive, these homes became barred and dark and quiet, as if they had been closed and deserted for the winter. Not a woman showed herself.

Shefford and Joe, by reason of the location of their camp and their alertness, met all the new-comers. The ride from Stonebridge was a long and hard one, calculated to wear off the effects of the whisky imbibed by the adventure-seekers. This fact alone saved the situation. Nevertheless, Joe expected trouble. Most of the visitors were decent, good-natured fellows, merely curious, and simple enough to believe that this really was what the Mormons had claimed—a village of free women. But there were those among them who were coarse, evil-minded, and dangerous.

By supper-time there were two dozen or more of these men in the valley, camped along the west wall. Fires were lighted, smoke curled up over the cedars, gay songs disturbed the usual serenity of the place. Later in the early twilight the curious visitors, by twos and threes, walked about the village, peering at the dark cabins and jesting among themselves. Joe had informed Shefford that all the women had been put in a limited number of cabins, so that they could be protected. So far as Shefford saw or heard there was no unpleasant incident in the village; however, as the sauntering visitors returned toward their camps they loitered at the spring, and here developments threatened.

In spite of the fact that the majority of these cowboys and their comrades were decent-minded and beginning to see the real relation of things, they were not disposed to be civil to Shefford. They were certainly not Mormons. And his position, apparently as a Gentile, among these Mormons was one open to crit- icism. They might have been jealous, too; at any rate, remarks were passed in his hearing, meant for his ears, that made it exceedingly trying for him not to resent. Moreover, Joe Lake's increasing impatience rendered the situation more difficult. Shefford welcomed the arrival of Nas Ta Bega. The Indian listened to the loud talk of several loungers round the camp-fire; and thereafter he was like Shefford's shadow, silent, somber, watchful.

Nevertheless, it did not happen to be one of the friendly and sarcastic cowboys that precipitated the crisis. A horse-wrangler named Hurley, a man of bad repute, as much outlaw as anything, took up the bantering.

"Say, Shefford, what in the hell's your job here, anyway?" he queried as he kicked a cedar branch into the camp-fire. The brightening blaze showed him swarthy, unshaven, a large-featured, ugly man.

"I've been doing odd jobs for Withers," replied Shefford. "Except to drive pack-trains in here for a while."

"You must stand strong with these Mormons. Must be a Mormon yerself?"

"No," replied Shefford, briefly.

"Wal, I'm stuck on your job. Do you need a packer? I can throw a diamond- hitch better 'n any feller in this country."

"I don't need help."

"Mebbe you'll take me over to see the ladies" he went on, with a coarse laugh.

Shefford did not show that he had heard. Hurley waited, leering as he looked from the keen listeners to Shefford.

"Want to have them all yerself, eh?" he jeered.

Shefford struck him—sent him tumbling heavily, like a log. Hurley, cursing as he half rose, jerked his gun out. Nas Ta Bega, swift as light, kicked the gun out of his hand. And Joe Lake picked it up.

Deliberately the Mormon cocked the weapon and stood over Hurley.

"Get up!" he ordered, and Shefford heard the ruthless Mormon in him then.

Hurley rose slowly. Then Joe prodded him in the middle with the cocked gun. Shefford, startled, expected the gun to go off. So did the others, especially Hurley, who shrank in panic from the dark Mormon.

"Rustle!" said Joe, and gave the man a harder prod. Assuredly the gun did not have a hairtrigger.

"Joe, mebbe it's loaded!" protested one of the cowboys.

Hurley shrank back, and turned to hurry away, with Joe close after him. They disappeared in the darkness. A constrained silence was maintained around the camp-fire for a while. Presently some of the men walked off and others began to converse. Everybody heard the sound of hoofs passing down the trail. The patter ceased, and in a few moments Lake returned. He still carried Hurley's gun.

The crowd dispersed then. There was no indication of further trouble. However, Shefford and Joe and Nas Ta Bega divided the night in watches, so that some one would be wide awake.

Early next morning there was an exodus from the village of the better element among the visitors. "No fun hangin' round hyar," one of them expressed it, and as good-naturedly as they had come they rode away. Six or seven of the desperado class remained behind, bent on mischief; and they were reinforced by more arrivals from Stonebridge. They avoided the camp by the spring, and when Shefford and Lake attempted to go to them they gave them a wide berth. This caused Joe to assert that they were up to some dirty work. All morning they lounged around under the cedars, keeping out of sight, and evidently the reinforcement from Stonebridge had brought liquor. When they gathered together at their camp, half drunk, all noisy, some wanting to swagger off into the village and others trying to hold them back, Joe Lake said, grimly, that somebody was going to get shot. Indeed, Shefford saw that there was every likelihood of bloodshed.

"Reckon we'd better take to one of the cabins," said Joe.

Thereupon the three repaired to the nearest cabin, and, entering, kept watch from the windows. During a couple of hours, however, they did not see or hear anything of the ruffians. Then came a shot from over in the village, a single yell, and, after that, a scattering volley. The silence and suspense which followed were finally broken by hoof-beats. Nas Ta Bega called Joe and Shefford to the window he had been stationed at. From here they saw the unwelcome visitors ride down the trail, to disappear in the cedars toward the outlet of the valley. Joe, who had numbered them, said that all but one of them had gone.

"Reckon he got it," added Joe.

So indeed it turned out; one of the men, a well-known rustler named Harker, had been killed, by whom no one seemed to know. He had brazenly tried to force his way into one of the houses, and the act had cost him his life. Naturally

Shefford, never free from his civilized habit of thought, remarked apprehensively that he hoped this affair would not cause the poor women to be arrested again and haled before some rude court.

"Law!" grunted Joe. "There ain't any. The nearest sheriff is in Durango. That's Colorado. And he'd give us a medal for killing Harker. It was a good job, for it'll teach these rowdies a lesson."

The Mormons, notwithstanding their indifference to the killing of the desperado, gave him decent burial and prayed for his soul.

Next day the old order of life was resumed in the village. And the arrival of a heavily laden pack-train, under the guidance of Withers, attested to the fact that the Mormons meant not only to continue to live in the valley, but also to build and plant and enlarge. This was good news to Shefford. At least the village could be made less lonely. And there was plenty of work to give him excuse for staying there. Furthermore, Withers brought a message from Bishop Kane to the effect that the young man was offered a place as teacher in the school, in co-operation with the Mormon teachers. Shefford experienced no twinge of conscience when he accepted.

It was the fourth evening after the never-to-be-forgotten moonlight ride to the valley that Shefford passed under the dark piñon-tree on his way to Fay Larkin's cottage. He paused in the gloom and memory beset him. The six months were annihilated, and it was the night he had fled. But now all was silent. He seemed to be trying to drag himself back. A beginning must be made. Only how to meet her—what to say—what to conceal!

He tapped on the door and she came out. After all, it was a meeting vastly different from what his feeling made him imagine it might have been. She was nervous, frightened, as were all the other women, for that matter. She was alone in the cottage. He made haste to reassure her about the improbability of any further trouble such as had befallen the last week. As he had always done on those former visits to her, he talked rapidly, using all his wit, and here his emotion made him eloquent; he avoided personalities, except to tell about his prospects of work in the village, and he sought above all to lead her mind from thought of herself and her condition. Before he left her he had the gladness of knowing he had succeeded.

When he said good night he felt the strange falsity of his position. He did not expect to be able to keep up the deception for long. That roused him, and half the night he lay awake, thinking. Next day he was the life of the work and study and play in that village. Kindness and good-will did not need inspiration, but it was keen, deep passion that made him a plotter for influence and friendship. Was there a woman in the village whom he might trust, in case he needed one? And his instinct guided him to her whom he had liked well—Ruth. Ruth Jones she had called herself at the trial, and when Shefford used the name she laughed mockingly. Ruth was not very religious, and sometimes she was bitter and hard. She wanted life, and here she was a prisoner in a lonely valley. She welcomed Shefford's visits. He imagined that she had slightly changed, and whether it was the added six months with its trouble and pain or a growing revolt he could not tell. After a time he divined that the inevitable retrogression had set in: she had not enough faith to uphold the burden she had accepted, nor the courage to cast it off. She was ready to love him. That did not frighten Shefford, and if she did love him he was not so sure it would not be an anchor for her. He saw her danger, and then he became what he had never really been in all the days of his ministry—the real helper. Unselfishly, for her sake, he found power to influence her; and selfishly, for the sake of Fay Larkin, he began slowly to win her to a possible need.

The days passed swiftly. Mormons came and went, though in the open day, as laborers; new cabins went up, and a store, and other improvements. Some part of every evening Shefford spent with Fay, and these visits were no longer unknown to the village. Women gossiped, in a friendly way about Shefford, but with jealous tongues about the girl. Joe Lake told Shefford the run of the village talk. Anything concerning the Sago Lily the droll Mormon took to heart. He had been hard hit, and admitted it. Sometimes he went with Shefford to call upon her, but he talked little and never remained long. Shefford had anticipated antagonism on the part of Joe; however, he did not find it.

Shefford really lived through the busy day for that hour with Fay in the twilight. And every evening seemed the same. He would find her in the dark, alone, silent, brooding, hopeless. Her mood did not puzzle him, but how to keep from plunging her deeper into despair baffled him. He exhausted all his powers trying to do for her what he had been able to do for Ruth. Yet he failed. Something had blunted her. The shadow of that baneful trail hovered over her, and he came to sense a strange terror in her. It was mostly always present. Was she thinking of Jane Withersteen and Lassiter, left dead or imprisoned in the valley from which she had been brought so mysteriously? Shefford wearied his brain revolving these questions. The fate of her friends, and the cross she bore— of these was tragedy born, but the terror—that Shefford divined came of waiting for the visit of the Mormon whose face she had never seen. Shefford prayed that he might never meet this man. Finally he grew desperate. When he first arrived at the girl's home she would speak, she showed gladness, relief, and then straightway she dropped back into the shadow of her gloom. When he got up to go then there was a wistfulness, an unspoken need, an unconscious reliance, in her reluctant good night.

Then the hour came when he reached his limit. He must begin his revelation.

"You never ask me anything—let alone about myself," he said.

"I'd like to hear," she replied, timidly.

"Do I strike you as an unhappy man?"

"No, indeed,"

"Well, how *do* I strike you?"

This was an entirely new tack he had veered to.

"Very good and kind to us women," she said.

"I don't know about that. If I am so, it doesn't bring me happiness. . . . Do you remember what I told you once, about my being a preacher—disgrace, ruin, and all that—and my rainbow-chasing dream out here after a—a lost girl?"

"I—remember all—you said," she replied, very low.

"Listen." His voice was a little husky, but behind it there seemed a tide of resistless utterance. "Loss of faith and name did not send me to this wilderness. But I had love—love for that lost girl, Fay Larkin. I dreamed about her till I loved her. I dreamed that I would find her—my treasure—at the foot of a rainbow. Dreams! . . . When you told me she was dead I accepted your reticence. But something died in me then. I lost myself, the best of me, the good that might have uplifted me. I went away, down upon the barren desert, and there I rode and slept and grew into another and a harder man. Yet, strange to say, I never forgot her, though my dreams were done. As I toiled and suffered and changed I loved her—if not her, the thought of her—more and more. Now I have come back to these walled valleys—to the smell of piñon, to the flowers in the nooks, to the wind on the heights, to the silence and loneliness and beauty. And here the dreams come back and *she* is *with* me always. Her spirit is all that keeps me kind and good, as you say I am. But I suffer, I long for her alive. If I love her dead, how could I love her living! Always I torture myself with the vain dream that—that she *might* not be dead. I have never been anything but a dreamer. And here I go about my work by day and lie awake at night with that lost girl in my mind. . . . I love her. Does that seem strange to you? But it would not if you understood. Think. I had lost faith, hope. I set myself a great work—to find Fay Larkin. And by the fire and the iron and the blood that I felt it would cost to save her some faith must come to me again. . . . My work is undone— I've never saved her. But listen, how strange it is to feel—now—as I let myself go—that just the loving her and the living here in the wildness that holds her somewhere have brought me hope again. Some faith must come, too. It was through her that I met this Indian, Nas Ta Bega. He has saved my life—taught me much. What would I ever have learned of the naked and vast earth, of the sublimity of the wild uplands, of the storm and night and sun, if I had not followed a gleam she inspired? In my hunt for a lost girl perhaps I wandered into a place where I shall find a God and my salvation. Do you marvel that I love Fay Larkin—that she is not dead to me? Do you marvel that I love her, when I *know,* were she alive, chained in a cañon, or bound, or lost in any way, my destiny would lead me to her, and she should be saved?"

Shefford ended, overcome with emotion. In the dusk he could not see the girl's face, but the white form that had drooped so listlessly seemed now charged by some vitalizing current. He knew he had spoken irrationally; still he held it no dishonor to have told her he loved her as one dead. If she took that love to the secret heart of living Fay Larkin, then perhaps a spirit might light in her darkened soul. He had no thought yet that Fay Larkin might ever belong to him. He divined a crime—he had seen her agony. And this avowal of his was only one step toward her deliverance.

Softly she rose, retreating into the shadow.

"Forgive me if I—I disturb you, distress you," he said. "I wanted to tell you. She was—somehow known to you. I am not happy. And are *you* happy? . . . Let her memory be a bond between us. . . . Good night."

"Good night."

Faintly as the faintest whisper breathed her reply, and, though it came from a child forced into womanhood, it whispered of girlhood not dead, of sweet incredulity, of amazed tumult, of a wondering, frantic desire to run and hide, of the bewilderment incident to a first hint of love.

Shefford walked away into the darkness. The whisper filled his soul. Had a word of love ever been spoken to that girl? Never—not the love which had been on his lips. Fay Larkin's lonely life spoke clearly in her whisper.

Next morning as the sun gilded the looming peaks and shafts of gold slanted into the valley she came swiftly down the path to the spring.

Shefford paused in his task of chopping wood. Joe Lake, on his knees, with his big hands in a pan of dough, lifted his head to stare. She had left off the somber black hood, and, although that made a vast difference in her, still it was not enough to account for what struck both men.

"Good morning," she called, brightly.

They both answered, but not spontaneously. She stopped at the spring and with one sweep of her strong arm filled the bucket and lifted it. Then she started back down the path and, pausing opposite the camp, set the bucket down.

"Joe, do you still pride yourself on your sour dough?" she asked.

"Reckon I do," replied Joe, with a grin.

"I've heard your boasts, but never tasted your bread," she went on.

"I'll ask you to eat with us some day."

"Don't forget," she replied.

And then shyly she looked at Shefford. She was like the fresh dawn, and the gold of the sun shone on her head.

"Have you chopped all that wood—so early?" she asked.

"Sure," replied Shefford, laughing. "I have to get up early to keep Joe from doing all the camp chores."

She smiled, and then to Shefford she seemed to gleam, to be radiant.

"It 'd be a lovely morning to climb—'way high."

"Why—yes—it would," replied Shefford, awkwardly. "I wish I didn't have my work."

"Joe, will *you* climb with me some day?"

"I should smile I will," declared Joe.

"But I can run right up the walls."

"I reckon. Mary, it wouldn't surprise me to see you fly."

"Do you mean I'm like a cañon swallow or an angel?"

Then, as Joe stared speechlessly, she said good-by and, taking up the bucket, went on with her swift, graceful step.

"She's perked up," said the Mormon, staring after her. "Never heard her say more'n yes or no till now."

"She did seem—bright," replied Shefford.

He was stunned. What had happened to her? To-day this girl had not been Mary, the sealed wife, or the Sago Lily, alien among Mormon women. Then it flashed upon him—she was Fay Larkin. She who had regarded herself as dead had come back to life. In one short night what had transformed her—what had taken place in her heart? Shefford dared not accept, nor allow lodgment in his mind, a thrilling idea that he had made her forget her misery.

"Shefford, did you ever see her like that?" asked Joe.

"Never."

"Haven't you—something to do with it?"

"Maybe I have. I—I hope so."

"Reckon you've seen how she's faded—since the trial?"

"No," replied Shefford, swiftly. "But I've not seen her face in daylight since then."

"Well, take my hunch," said Joe, soberly. "She's begun to fade like the cañon lily when it's broken. And she's going to die unless—"

"Why, man!" ejaculated Shefford. "Didn't you see—"

"Sure I see," interrupted the Mormon. "I see a lot you don't. She's so white you can look through her. She's grown thin, all in a week. She doesn't eat. Oh, I know, because I've made it my business to find out. It's no news to the women. But they'd like to see her die. And she will die unless—"

"My God!" exclaimed Shefford, huskily. "I never noticed—I never thought. . . . Joe, hasn't she any friends?"

"Sure. You and Ruth—and me. Maybe Nas Ta Bega, too. He watches her a good deal."

"We can do so little, when she needs so much."

"Nobody can help her, unless it's you," went on the Mormon. "That's plain talk. She seemed different this morning. Why, she was alive—she talked—she smiled. . . . Shefford, if you cheer her up I'll go to hell for you!''

The big Mormon, on his knees, with his hands in a pan of dough, and his shirt all covered with flour, presented an incongruous figure of a man actuated by pathos and passion. Yet the contrast made his emotion all the simpler and stronger. Shefford grew closer to Joe in that moment.

"Why do you think *I* can cheer her, help her?" queried Shefford.

"I don't know. But she's different with you. It's not that you're a Gentile, though, for all the women are crazy about you. You talk to her. You have power over her, Shefford. I feel that. She's only a kid.''

"Who is she, Joe? Where did she come from?" asked Shefford, very low, with his eyes cast down.

"I don't know. I can't find out. Nobody knows. It's a mystery—to all the younger Mormons, anyway.''

Shefford burned to ask questions about the Mormon whose sealed wife the girl was, but he respected Joe too much to take advantage of him in a poignant moment like this. Besides, it was only jealousy that made him burn to know the Mormon's identity, and jealousy had become a creeping, insidious, growing fire. He would be wise not to add fuel to it. He rejected many things before he thought of one that he could voice to his friend.

"Joe, it's only her body that belongs to—to . . . Her soul is lost to—''

"John Shefford, let that go. My mind's tired. I've been taught so and so, and I'm not bright. But, after all, men are much alike. The thing with you and me is this—we don't want to see *her* grave!''

Love spoke there. The Mormon had seized upon the single elemental point that concerned him and his friend in their relation to this unfortunate girl. His simple, powerful statement united them; it gave the lie to his hint of denseness; it stripped the truth naked. It was such a wonderful thought-provoking statement that Shefford needed time to ponder how deep the Mormon was. To what limit would he go? Did he mean that here, between two men who loved the same girl, class, duty, honor, creed were nothing if they stood in the way of her deliverance and her life?

"Joe Lake, you Mormons are impossible," said Shefford, deliberately. "You don't want to see her grave. So long as she lives—remains on the earth—white and gold like the flower you call her, that's enough for you. It's her body you think of. And that's the great and horrible error in your religion. . . . But death of the soul is infinitely worse than death of the body. I have been thinking of her soul. . . . So here we stand, you and I. You to save her life—I to save her soul! What will you do?''

"Why, John, I'd turn Gentile," he said, with terrible softness. It was a softness that scorned Shefford for asking, and likewise it flung defiance at his creed and into the face of hell.

Shefford felt the sting and the exaltation.

"And I'd be a Mormon," he said.

"All right. We understand each other. Reckon there won't be any call for such extremes. I haven't an idea what you mean—what can be done. But I say, go slow, so we won't all find graves. First cheer her up somehow. Make her want to live. But go slow, John. *And don't be with her late!*"

That night Shefford found her waiting for him in the moonlight—a girl who was as transparent as crystal-clear water, who had left off the somber gloom with the black hood, who tremulously embraced happiness without knowing it, who was one moment timid and wild like a half-frightened fawn, and the next, exquisitely half-conscious of what it meant to be thought dead, but to be alive, to be awakening, wondering, palpitating, and to be loved.

Shefford lived the hour as a dream and went back to the quiet darkness under the cedars to lie wide-eyed, trying to recall all that she had said. For she had talked as if utterance had long been dammed behind a barrier of silence.

There followed other hours like that one, indescribable hours, so sweet they stung, and in which, keeping pace with his love, was the nobler stride of a spirit that more every day lightened her burden.

The thing he had to do, sooner or later, was to tell her he knew she was Fay Larkin, not dead, but alive, and that, not love nor religion, but sacrifice, nailed her down to her martyrdom. Many and many a time he had tried to force himself to tell her, only to fail. He hated to risk ending this sweet, strange, thoughtless, girlish mood of hers. It might not be soon won back—perhaps never. How could he tell what chains bound her? And so as he vacillated between Joe's cautious advice to go slow and his own pity the days and weeks slipped by.

One haunting fear kept him sleepless half the nights and sick even in his dreams, and it was that the Mormon whose sealed wife she was might come, surely would come, some night. Shefford could bear it. But what would that visit do to Fay Larkin? Shefford instinctively feared the awakening in the girl of womanhood, of deeper insight, of a spiritual realization of what she was, of a physical dawn.

He might have spared himself needless torture. One day Joe Lake eyed him with penetrating glance.

"Reckon you don't have to sleep right on that Stonebridge trail," said the Mormon, significantly.

Shefford felt the blood burn his neck and face. He had pulled his tarpaulin closer to the trail, and his motive was as an open page to the keen Mormon.

"Why?" asked Shefford.

"There won't be any Mormons riding in here soon—by night—to visit the women," replied Joe, bluntly. "Haven't you figured there might be government spies watching the trails?"

"No, I haven't."

"Well, take a hunch, then," added the Mormon, gruffly, and Shefford divined, as well as if he had been told, that warning word had gone to Stonebridge. Gone despite the fact that Nas Ta Bega had reported every trail free of watchers! There was no sign of any spies, cowboys, outlaws, or Indians in the vicinity of the valley. A passionate gratitude to the Mormon overcame Shefford; and the un-reasonableness of it, the nature of it, perturbed him greatly. But, something hammered into his brain, if he loved one of these sealed wives, how could he help being jealous?

The result of Joe's hint was that Shefford put off the hour of revelation, lived in his dream, helped the girl grow farther and farther away from her trouble, until that inevitable hour arrived when he was driven by accumulated emotion as much as the exigency of the case.

He had not often walked with her beyond the dark shade of the piñons round the cottage, but this night, when he knew he must tell her, he led her away down the path, through the cedar grove to the west end of the valley where it was wild and lonely and sad and silent.

The moon was full and the great peaks were crowned as with snow. A coyote uttered his cutting cry. There were a few melancholy notes from a night bird of the stone walls. The air was clear and cold, with a tang of frost in it. Shefford gazed about him at the vast, uplifted, insulating walls, and that feeling of his which was more than a sense told him how walls like these and the silence and shadow and mystery had been nearly all of Fay Larkin's life. He felt them all in her.

He stopped out in the open, near the line where dark shadow of the wall met the silver moonlight on the grass, and here, by a huge flat stone where he had come often alone and sometimes with Ruth, he faced Fay Larkin in the spirit to tell her gently that he knew her, and sternly to force her secret from her.

"Am I your friend?" he began.

"Ah!—my only friend," she said.

"Do you trust me, believe I mean well by you, want to help you?"

"Yes, indeed."

"Well, then, let me speak of you. You know one topic we've never touched upon. You!"

She was silent, and looked wonderingly, a little fearfully, at him, as if vague, disturbing thoughts were entering the fringe of her mind.

"Our friendship is a strange one, is it not?" he went on.

"How do I know? I never had any other friendship. What do you mean by strange?"

"Well, I'm a young man. You're a—a married woman. We are together a good deal—and like to be."

"Why is that strange?" she asked.

Suddenly Shefford realized that there was nothing strange in what was natural. A remnant of sophistication clung to him and that had spoken. He needed to speak to her in a way which in her simplicity she would understand.

"Never mind strange. Say that I am interested in you, and, as you're not happy, I want to help you. And say that your neighbors are curious and oppose my idea. Why do they?"

"They're jealous and want you themselves," she replied, with sweet directness. "They've said things I don't understand. But I felt they—they hated in me what would be all right in themselves."

Here to simplicity she added truth and wisdom, as an Indian might have expressed them. But shame was unknown to her, and she had as yet only vague perceptions of love and passion. Shefford began to realize the quickness of her mind, that she was indeed awakening.

"They are jealous—were jealous before I ever came here. That's only human nature. I was trying to get to a point. Your neighbors are curious. They oppose me. They hate you. It's all bound up in the—the fact of your difference from them, your youth, beauty, that you're not a Mormon, that you nearly betrayed their secret at the trial in Stonebridge."

"Please—please don't—speak of that!" she faltered.

"But I must," he replied, swiftly. "That trial was a torture to you. It revealed so much to me. . . . I know you are a sealed wife. I know there has been a crime. I know you've sacrificed yourself. I know that love and religion have nothing to do with—what you are. . . . Now, is not all that true?"

"I must not tell," she whispered.

"But I shall *make* you tell," he replied, and his voice rang.

"Oh no, you cannot," she said.

"I can—with just one word!"

Her eyes were great, starry, shadowy gulfs, dark in the white beauty of her face. She was calm now. She had strength. She invited him to speak the word, and the wistful, tremulous quiver of her lips was for his earnest thought of her.

"Wait—a—little," said Shefford, unsteadily. "I'll come to that presently. Tell me this—have you ever thought of being free?"

"Free!" she echoed, and there was singular depth and richness in her voice. That was the first spark of fire he had struck from her. "Long ago, the minute I was unwatched, I'd have leaped from a wall had I dared. Oh, I wasn't afraid. I'd love to die that way. But I never dared."

"Why?" queried Shefford, piercingly.

She was silent then.

"Suppose I offered to give you freedom that meant life?"

"I—couldn't—take it."

"Why?"

"Oh, my friend, don't ask me any more."

"I know, I can see—you want to tell me—you need to tell."

"But I daren't."

"Won't you trust me?"

"I do—I do."

"Then tell me."

"No—no—oh no!"

The moment had come. How sad, tragic, yet glorious for him! It would be like a magic touch upon this lovely, cold, white ghost of Fay Larkin, transforming her into a living, breathing girl. He held his love as a thing aloof, and, as such, intangible because of the living death she believed she lived, it had no warmth and intimacy for them. What might it not become with a lightning flash of revelation? He dreaded, yet he was driven to speak. He waited, swallowing hard, fighting the tumultuous storm of emotion, and his eyes dimmed.

"What did I come to this country for?" he asked, suddenly, in ringing, powerful voice.

"To find a girl," she whispered.

"I've found her!"

She began to shake. He saw a white hand go to her breast.

"Where is Surprise Valley? . . . How were you taken from Jane Withersteen and Lassiter? . . . I know they're alive. But where?"

She seemed to turn to stone.

"Fay!—*Fay Larkin!* . . . I KNOW YOU!" he cried, brokenly.

She slipped off the stone to her knees, swayed forward blindly with her hands reaching out, her head falling back to let the moon fall full upon the beautiful, snow-white, tragically convulsed face.

13

The Story of Surprise Valley

". . .Oh, I remember so well! Even now I dream of it sometimes. I hear the roll and crash of falling rock—like thunder. . . . We rode and rode. Then the horses fell. Uncle Jim took me in his arms and started up the cliff. Mother Jane climbed close after us. They kept looking back. Down there in the gray valley came the Mormons. I see the first one now. He rode a white horse. That was Tull. Oh, I remember so well! And I was five or six years old.

"We climbed up and up and into dark cañons and wound in and out. Then there was the narrow white trail, straight up, with the little cut steps and the great, red, ruined walls. I looked down over Uncle Jim's shoulder. I saw Mother Jane dragging herself up. Uncle Jim's blood spotted the trail. He reached a flat place at the top and fell with me. Mother Jane crawled up to us.

"Then she cried out and pointed. Tull was 'way below, climbing the trail. His men came behind him. Uncle Jim went to a great, tall rock and leaned against it. There was a bloody hole in his hand. He pushed the rock. It rolled down banging the loose walls. They crashed and crashed—then all was terrible thunder and red smoke. I couldn't hear—I couldn't see.

"Uncle Jim carried me down and down out of the dark and dust into a beautiful valley all red and gold, with a wonderful arch of stone over the entrance.

"I don't remember well what happened then for what seemed a long, long time. I can feel how the place looked, but not so clear as it is now in my dreams. I seem to see myself with the dogs, and with Mother Jane, learning my letters, marking with red stone on the walls.

"But I remember now how I felt when I first understood we were shut in for ever. Shut in Surprise Valley where Venters had lived so long. I was glad. The Mormons would never get me. I was seven or eight years old then. From that time all is clear in my mind.

"Venters had left supplies and tools and grain and cattle and burros, so we had a good start to begin life there. He had killed off the wildcats and kept the coyotes out, so the rabbits and quail multiplied till there were thousands of them. We raised corn and fruit, and stored what we didn't use. Mother Jane taught me to read and write with the soft red stone that marked well on the walls.

"The years passed. We kept track of time pretty well. Uncle Jim's hair turned white and Mother Jane grew gray. Every day was like the one before. Mother Jane cried sometimes and Uncle Jim was sad because they could never be able to get me out of the valley. It was long before they stopped looking and listening for some one. Venters would come back, Uncle Jim always said. But Mother Jane did not think so.

"I loved Surprise Valley. I wanted to stay there always. I remembered Cottonwoods, how the children there hated me, and I didn't want to go back. The only unhappy times I ever had in the valley were when Ring and Whitie, my dogs, grew old and died. I roamed the valley. I climbed to every nook upon the mossy ledges. I learned to run up the steep cliffs. I could almost stick on the straight walls. Mother Jane called me a wild girl. We had put away the clothes we wore when we got there, to save them, and we made clothes of skins. I always laughed when I thought of my little dress—how I grew out of it. I think Uncle Jim and Mother Jane talked less as the years went by. And after I'd learned all she could teach me we didn't talk much. I used to scream into the caves just to hear my voice, and the echoes would frighten me.

"The older I grew the more I was alone. I was always running round the valley. I would climb to a high place and sit there for hours, doing nothing. I just watched and listened. I used to stay in the cliff-dwellers' caves and wonder about them. I loved to be out in the wind. And my happiest time was in the summer storms with the thunder echoes under the walls. At evening it was such a quiet place—after the night bird's cry, no sound. The quiet made me sad, but I loved it. I loved to watch the stars as I lay awake.

"So it was beautiful and happy for me there till . . .

"Two years or more ago there was a bad storm, and one of the great walls caved. The walls were always weathering, slipping. Many and many a time have I heard the rumble of an avalanche, but most of them were in other cañons. This slide in the valley made it possible, Uncle Jim said, for men to get down into the valley. But we could not climb out unless helped from above. Uncle Jim never rested well after that. But it never worried me.

"One day, over a year ago, while I was across the valley, I heard strange shouts, and then screams. I ran to our camp. I came upon men with ropes and guns. Uncle Jim was tied, and a rope was round his neck. Mother Jane was lying on the ground. I thought she was dead until I heard her moan. I was not afraid. I screamed and flew at Uncle Jim to tear the ropes off him. The men held me back. They called me a pretty cat. Then they talked together, and some were for hanging Lassiter—that was the first time I ever knew any name for him but Uncle Jim—and some were for leaving him in the valley. Finally they decided to hang him. But Mother Jane pleaded so and I screamed and fought so that they left off. Then they went away and we saw them climb out of the valley.

"Uncle Jim said they were Mormons, and some among them had been born in Cottonwoods. I was not told why they had such a terrible hate for him. He said they would come back and kill him. Uncle Jim had no guns to fight with.

"We watched and watched. In five days they did come back, with more men, and some of them wore black masks. They came to our cave with ropes and guns. One was tall. He had a cruel voice. The others ran to obey him. I could see white hair and sharp eyes behind the mask. The men caught me and brought me before him.

"He said Lassiter had killed many Mormons. He said Lassiter had killed his father and should be hanged. But Lassiter would be let live and Mother Jane could stay with him, both prisoners there in the valley, if I would marry the Mormon. I must marry him, accept the Mormon faith, and bring up my children as Mormons. If I refused they would hang Lassiter, leave the heretic Jane Withersteen alone in the valley, and take me and break me to their rule.

"I agreed. But Mother Jane absolutely forbade me to marry him. Then the Mormons took me away. It nearly killed me to leave Uncle Jim and Mother Jane. I was carried and lifted out of the valley, and rode a long way on a horse. They brought me here, to the cabin where I live, and I have never been away except that—that time—to—Stonebridge. Only little by little did I learn my position. Bishop Kane was kind, but stern, because I could not be quick to learn the faith.

"I am not a sealed wife. But they're trying to make me one. The master Mormon—he visited me often—at night—till lately. He threatened me. He never told me a name—except Saint George. I don't—know him—except his voice. I never—saw his face—in the light!"

Fay Larkin ended her story. Toward its close Shefford had grown involuntarily restless, and when her last tragic whisper ceased all his body seemed shaken with a terrible violence of his joy. He strode to and fro in the dark shadow of the stone. The receding blood left him cold, with a pricking, sickening sensation over his body, but there seemed to be an overwhelming tide accumulating deep in his breast—a tide of passion and pain. He dominated the passion, but the ache remained. And he returned to the quiet figure on the stone.

"Fay Larkin!" he exclaimed, with a deep breath of relief that the secret was disclosed. "So you're not a wife! . . . You're free! Thank Heaven! But I felt it was sacrifice. I knew there had been a crime. For crime it is. You child! You can't understand what crime. Oh, almost I wish you and Jane and Lassiter had never been found. But that's wrong of me. One year of agony—that shall not ruin your life. Fay, I will take you away."

"Where?" she whispered.

"Away from this Mormon country—to the East," he replied, and he spoke of what he had known, of travel, of cities, of people, of happiness possible for a young girl who had spent all her life hidden between the narrow walls of a silent, lonely valley—he spoke swiftly and eloquently till he lost his breath.

There was an instant of flashing wonder and joy on her white face, and then the radiance paled, the glow died. Her soul was the darker for that one strange, leaping glimpse of a glory not for such as she.

"I must stay here," she said, shudderingly.

"Fay!—How strange to *say* Fay aloud to *you!*—Fay, do you know the way to Surprise Valley?"

"I don't know where it is, but I could go straight to it," she replied.

"Take me there. Show me your beautiful valley. Let me see where you ran and climbed and spent so many lonely years."

"Ah, how I'd love to! But I dare not. And why should you want me to take you? We can run and climb here."

"I want to—I mean to save Jane Withersteen and Lassiter," he declared.

She uttered a little cry of pain. "Save them?"

"Yes, save them. Get them out of the valley, take them out of the country, far away where they and *you*—"

"But I can't go," she wailed. "I'm afraid. I'm bound. It *can't* be broken. If I dared—if I tried to go they would catch me. They would hang Uncle Jim and leave Mother Jane alone there to starve."

"Fay, Lassiter and Jane both will starve—at least they will die there if we do not save them. You have been terribly wronged. You're a slave. You're not a wife."

"They—said I'll be burned in hell if I don't marry him. . . . Mother Jane never taught me about God. I don't know. But *he*—he said God was there. I dare not break it."

"Fay, you have been deceived by old men. Let them have their creed. But *you* mustn't accept it."

"John, what is God to you?"

"Dear child, I—I am not sure of that myself," he replied, huskily. "When all this trouble is behind us, surely I can help you to understand and you can help me. The fact that you are alive—that Lassiter and Jane are alive—that I shall save you all—that lifts me up. I tell you—Fay Larkin will be my salvation."

"Your words trouble me. Oh, I shall be torn one way and another. . . . But, John, I daren't run away. I will not tell you where to find Lassiter and Mother Jane."

"I shall find them. I have the Indian. He found you for me. Nas Ta Bega will find Surprise Valley."

"Nas Ta Bega! . . . Oh, I remember. There was an Indian with the Mormons who found us. But he was a Piute."

"Nas Ta Bega never told me how he learned about you. That he learned was enough. And, Fay, he will find Surprise Valley. He will save Uncle Jim and Mother Jane.''

Fay's hands clasped Shefford's in strong, trembling pressure; the tears streamed down her white cheeks; a tragic and eloquent joy convulsed her face.

"Him! Fay—he shall not harm you,'' replied Shefford in passionate earnestness.

She caught the hand he had struck out with.

"You talk—you look like Uncle Jim when he spoke of the Mormons,'' she said. "Then I used to be afraid of him. He was so different. John, you must not do anything about me. Let me be. It's too late. He—and his men—they would hang you. And I couldn't bear that. I've enough to bear without losing my friend. Say you won't watch and wait—for—for him.''

Shefford had to promise her. Like an Indian she gave expression to primitive feeling, for it certainly never occurred to her that, whatever Shefford might do, he was not the kind of man to wait in hiding for an enemy. Fay had faltered through her last speech and was now weak and nervous and frightened. Shefford took her back to the cabin.

"Fay, don't be distressed,'' he said. "I won't do anything right away. You can trust me. I won't be rash. I'll consult you before I make a move. I haven't any idea what I could do, anyway. . . . You must bear up. Why, it looks as if you're sorry I found you.''

"Oh! I'm glad!'' she whispered.

"Then if you're glad you mustn't break down this way again. Suppose some of the women happened to run into us.''

"I won't again. It's only you—you surprised me so. I used to think how I'd like you to know—I wasn't really dead. But now—it's different. It hurts me here. Yet I'm glad—if my being alive makes you—a little happier.''

Shefford felt that he had to go then. He could not trust himself any further.

"Good night, Fay,'' he said.

"Good night, John,'' she whispered. "I promise—to be good to-morrow.''

She was crying softly when he left her. Twice he turned to see the dim, white slender form against the gloom of the cabin. Then he went on under the piñons, blindly down the path, with his heart as heavy as lead. That night as he rolled in his blanket and stretched wearily he felt that he would never be able to sleep. The wind in the cedars made him shiver. The great stars seemed relentless, passionless, white eyes, mocking his little destiny and his pain. The huge shadow of the mountain resembled the shadow of the insurmountable barrier between Fay and him.

Her pitiful, childish promise to be good was in his mind when he went to her home on the next night. He wondered how she would be, and he realized a desperate need of self-control.

But that night Fay Larkin was a different girl. In the dark, before she spoke, he felt a difference that afforded him surprise and relief. He greeted her as usual. And then it seemed, though not at all clearly, that he was listening to a girl, strangely and unconsciously glad to see him, who spoke with deeper note in her voice, who talked where always she had listened, whose sadness was there under an eagerness, a subdued gaiety as new to her, as sweet as it was bewildering. And he responded with emotion, so that the hour passed swiftly, and he found himself back in camp, in a kind of dream, unable to remember much of what she had said, sure only of this strange sweetness suddenly come to her.

Upon the following night, however, he discovered what had wrought this singular change in Fay Larkin. She loved him and she did not know it. How passionately sweet and sad and painful was that realization for Shefford! The hour spent with her then was only a moment.

He walked under the stars that night and they shed a glorious light upon him. He tried to think, to plan, but the sweetness of remembered word or look made mental effort almost impossible. He got as far as the thought that he would do well to drift, to wait till she learned she loved him, and then, perhaps, she could be persuaded to let him take her and Lassiter and Jane away together.

And from that night he went at his work and the part he played in the village with a zeal and a cunning that left him free to seek Fay when he chose.

Sometimes in the afternoon, always for a while in the evening, he was with her. They climbed the walls, and sat upon a lonely height to look afar; they walked under the stars, and the cedars, and the shadows of the great cliffs. She had a beautiful mind. Listening to her, he imagined he saw down into beautiful Surprise Valley with all its weird shadows, its colored walls and painted caves, its golden shafts of morning light and the red haze at sunset; and he felt the silence that must have been there, and the singing of the wind in the cliffs, and the sweetness and fragrance of the flowers, and the wildness of it all. Love had worked a marvelous transformation in this girl who had lived her life in a cañon. The burden upon her did not weigh heavily. She could not have an unhappy thought. She spoke of the village, of her Mormon companions, of daily happenings, of Stonebridge, of many things in a matter-of-fact way that showed how little they occupied her mind. She even spoke of sealed wives in a kind of dreamy abstraction. Something had possession of her, something as strong as the nature which had developed her, and in its power she, in her simplicity, was utterly unconscious, a watching and feeling girl. A strange, witching, radiant beauty lurked in her smile. And Shefford heard her laugh in his dreams.

The weeks slipped by. The black mountain took on a white cap of snow; in the early mornings there was ice in the crevices on the heights and frost in the

valley. In the sheltered cañons where sunshine seemed to linger it was warm
and pleasant, so that winter did not kill the flowers.

Shefford waited so long for Fay's awakening that he believed it would never
come, and, believing, had not the heart to force it upon her. Then there was a
growing fear with him. What would Fay Larkin do when she awakened to the
truth? Fay was indeed like that white and fragile lily which bloomed in the silent,
lonely cañons, but the same nature that had created it had created her. Would
she droop as the lily would in a furnace blast? More than that, he feared a sudden
flashing into life of strength, power, passion, hate. She did not hate yet because
she did not yet realize love. She was utterly innocent of any wrong having been
done her. More and more he began to fear, and a foreboding grew upon him.
He made up his mind to broach the subject of Surprise Valley and of escaping
with Lassiter and Jane; still, every time he was with Fay the girl and her beauty
and her love were so wonderful that he put off the ordeal till the next night. As
time flew by he excused his vacillation on the score that winter was not a good
time to try to cross the desert. There was no grass for the mustangs, except in
well-known valleys, and these he must shun. Spring would soon come. So the
days passed, and he loved Fay more all the time, desperately living out to its
limit the sweetness of every moment with her, and paying for his bliss in the
increasing trouble that beset him when once away from her charm.

One starry night, about ten o'clock, he went, as was his custom, to drink at
the spring. Upon his return to the cedars Nas Ta Bega, who slept under the same
tree with him, had arisen, with his blanket hanging half off his shoulder.

"Listen," said the Indian.

Shefford took one glance at the dark, somber face, with its inscrutable eyes,
now so strange and piercing, and then, with a kind of cold excitement, he faced
the way the Indian looked, and listened. But he heard only the soft moan of the
night wind in the cedars.

Nas Ta Bega kept the rigidity of his position for a moment, and then he
relaxed, and stood at ease. Shefford knew the Indian had made a certainty of
what must have been a doubtful sound. And Shefford leaned his ear to the wind
and strained his hearing.

Then the soft night breeze brought a faint patter—the slow trot of horses on
a hard trail. Some one was coming into the village at a late hour. Shefford
thought of Joe Lake. But Joe lay right behind him, asleep in his blankets. It
could not be Withers, for the trader was in Durango at that time. Shefford thought
of Willetts and Shadd.

"Who's coming?" he asked low of the Indian.

Nas Ta Bega pointed down the trail without speaking.

Shefford peered through the white dim haze of starlight and presently he made out moving figures. Horses, with riders—a string of them—one—two—three—four—five—and he counted up to eleven. Eleven horsemen riding into the village! He was amazed, and suddenly keenly anxious. This visit might be one of Shadd's raids.

"Shadd's gang!" he whispered.

"No, Bi Nai," replied Nas Ta Bega, and he drew Shefford farther into the shade of the cedars. His voice, his action, the way he kept a hand on Shefford's shoulder, all this told much to the young man.

Mormons come on a night visit! Shefford realized it with a slight shock. Then swift as a lightning flash he was rent by another shock—one that brought cold moisture to his brow and to his heart a flame of hell.

He was shaking when he sank down to find the support of a log. Like a shadow the Indian silently moved away. Shefford watched the eleven horses pass the camp, go down the road, to disappear in the village. They vanished, and the soft clip-clops of hoofs died away. There was nothing left to prove he had not dreamed.

Nothing to prove it except this sudden terrible demoralization of his physical and spiritual being! While he peered out into the valley, toward the black patch of cedars and piñons that hid the cabins, moments and moments passed, and in them he was gripped with cold and fire.

Was the Mormon who had abducted Fay—the man with the cruel voice—was he among those eleven horsemen? He might not have been. What a torturing hope! But vain—vain, for inevitably he must be among them. He was there in the cabin already. He had dismounted, tied his horse, had knocked on her door. Did he need to knock? No, he would go in, he would call her in that cruel voice, and then . . .

Shefford pulled a blanket from his bed and covered his cold and trembling body. He had sunk down off the log, was leaning back upon it. The stars were pale, far off, and the valley seemed unreal. He found himself listening—listening with sick and terrible earnestness, trying to hear against the thrum and beat of his heart, straining to catch a sound in all that cold, star-blanched, silent valley. But he could hear no sound. It was as if death held the valley in its perfect silence. How he hated that silence! There ought to have been a million horrible, bellowing demons making the night hideous. Did the stars serenely look down upon the lonely cabins of these exiles? Was there no thunderbolt to drop down from that dark and looming mountain upon the silent cabin where tragedy had entered? In all the world, under the sea, in the abysmal caves, in the vast spaces of the air, there was no such terrible silence as this. A scream, a long cry, a moan—these were natural to a woman, and why did not one of these sealed wives, why did not Fay Larkin, damn this everlasting acquiescent silence? Perhaps she would fly out of her cabin, come running along the path. Shefford peered into the bright patches of starlight and into the shadows of the cedars. But he saw no moving form in the open, no dim white shape against the gloom. And he heard no sound—not even a whisper of wind in the branches overhead.

Nas Ta Bega returned to the shade of the cedars and, lying down on his blankets, covered himself and went to sleep. The fact seemed to bring bitter reality to Shefford. Nothing was going to happen. The valley was to be the same this night as any other night. Shefford accepted the truth. He experienced a kind of self-pity. The night he had thought so much about, prepared for, and had forgotten had now arrived. Then he threw another blanket round him, and, cold, dark, grim, he faced that lonely vigil, meaning to sit there, wide-eyed, to endure and to wait.

Jealousy and pain, following his frenzy, abided with him long hours, and when they passed he divined that selfishness passed with them. What he suffered then was for Fay Larkin and for her sisters in misfortune. He grew big enough to pity these fanatics. The fiery, racing tide of blood that had made of him only an animal had cooled with thought of others. Still he feared that stultifying thing which must have been hate. What a tempest had raged within him! This blood of his, that had received a stronger strain from his desert life, might in a single moment flood out reason and intellect and make him a vengeful man. So in those starlit hours that dragged interminably he looked deep into his heart and tried to fortify himself against a dark and evil moment to come.

Midnight—and the valley seemed a tomb! Did he alone keep wakeful? The sky was a darker blue, the stars burned a whiter fire, the peaks stood looming and vast, tranquil sentinels of that valley, and the wind rose to sigh, to breathe, to mourn through the cedars. It was a sad music. The Indian lay prone, dark face to the stars. Joe Lake lay prone, sleeping as quietly, with his dark face exposed to the starlight. The gentle movement of the cedar branches changed the shape of the bright patches on the grass where shadow and light met. The walls of the valley waved upward, dark below and growing paler, to shine faintly at the rounded rims. And there was a tiny, silvery tinkle of running water over stones.

Here was a little nook of the vast world. Here were tranquillity, beauty, music, loneliness, life. Shefford wondered—did he alone keep watchful? Did he feel that he could see dark, wide eyes peering into the gloom? And it came to him after a time that he was not alone in his vigil, nor was Fay Larkin alone in her agony. There was some one else in the valley, a great and breathing and watchful spirit. It entered into Shefford's soul and he trembled. What had come to him? And he answered—only added pain and new love, and a strange strength from the firmament and the peaks and the silence and the shadows.

The bright belt with its three radiant stars sank behind the western wall and there was a paler gloom upon the valley.

Then a few lights twinkled in the darkness that enveloped the cabins; a woman's laugh strangely broke the silence, profaning it, giving the lie to that somber yoke which seemed to consist of the very shadows; the voices of men were heard, and then the slow clip-clop of trotting horses on the hard trail.

Shefford saw the Mormons file out into the paling starlight, ride down the valley, and vanish in the gray gloom. He was aware that the Indian sat up to watch the procession ride by, and that Joe turned over, as if disturbed.

One by one the stars went out. The valley became a place of gray shadows. In the east a light glowed. Shefford sat there, haggard and worn, watching the coming of the dawn, the kindling of the light; and had the power been his the dawn would never have broken and the rose and gold never have tipped the lofty peaks.

Shefford attended to his camp chores as usual. Several times he was aware of Joe's close scrutiny, and finally, without looking at him, Shefford told of the visit of the Mormons. A violent expulsion of breath was Joe's answer and it might have been a curse. Straightway Joe ceased his cheery whistling and became as somber as the Indian. The camp was silent; the men did not look at one another. While they sat at breakfast Shefford's back was turned toward the village; he had not looked in that direction since dawn.

"Ugh!" suddenly exclaimed Nas Ta Bega.

Joe Lake muttered low and deep, and this time there was no mistake about the nature of his speech. Shefford did not have the courage to turn to see what had caused these exclamations. He knew since today had dawned that there was calamity in the air.

"Shefford, I reckon if I know women there's a little hell coming to you," said the Mormon, significantly.

Shefford wheeled as if a powerful force had turned him on a pivot. He saw Fay Larkin. She seemed to be almost running. She was unhooded and her bright hair streamed down. Her swift, lithe action was without its usual grace. She looked wild, and she almost fell crossing the stepping-stones of the brook.

Joe hurried to meet her, took hold of her arm and spoke, but she did not seem to hear him. She drew him along with her, up the little bench under the cedars straight toward Shefford. Her face held a white, mute agony, as if in the hour of strife it had hardened into marble. But her eyes were dark-purple fire— windows of an extraordinarily intense and vital life. In one night the girl had become a women. But the blight Shefford had dreaded to see—the withering of the exquisite soul and spirit and purity he had considered inevitable, just as inevitable as the death of something similar in the flower she resembled, when it was broken and defiled—nothing of this was manifest in her. Straight and swiftly she came to him back in the shade of the cedars and took hold of his hands.

"Last night—*he came!*" she said.

"Yes—Fay—I—I know," replied Shefford, haltingly.

He was tremblingly conscious of amaze at her—of something wonderful in her. She did not heed Joe, who stepped aside a little; she did not see Nas Ta Bega, who sat motionless on a log, apparently oblivious to her presence.

"You knew he came?"

"Yes, Fay. I was awake when—they rode in. I watched them. I sat up all night. I saw them ride away."

"If you knew when he came why didn't you run to me—to get to me before he did?"

Her question was unanswerable. It had the force of a blow. It stunned him. Its sharp, frank directness sprang from a simplicity and a strength that had not been nurtured in the life he had lived. So far men had wandered from truth and nature!

"I came to you as soon as I was able," she went on. "I must have fainted. I just had to drag myself around. . . . And now I can tell you."

He was powerless to reply, as if she had put another unanswerable question. What did she mean to tell him? What might she not tell him? She loosed her hands from his and lifted them to his shoulders, and that was the first conscious action of feeling, of intimacy, which she had ever shown. It quite robbed Shefford of strength, and in spite of his sorrow there was an indefinable thrill in her touch. He looked at her, saw the white-and-gold beauty that was hers yesterday and seemed changed to-day, and he recognized Fay Larkin in a woman he did not know.

"Listen! He came—"

"Fay, don't—tell me," interrupted Shefford.

"I *will* tell you," she said.

Did the instinct of love teach her how to mitigate his pain? Shefford felt that, as he felt the new-born strength in her.

"Listen," she went on. "He came when I was undressing for bed. I heard the horse. He knocked on the door. Something terrible happened to me then. I felt sick and my head wasn't clear. I remember next—his being in the room— the lamp was out—I couldn't see very well. He thought I was sick and he gave me a drink and let the air blow in on me through the window. I remember I lay back in the chair and I thought. And I listened. When would you come? I didn't feel that you could leave me there alone with him. For his coming was different this time. That pain like a blade in my side! . . . When it came I was not the same. I loved you. I understood then. I belonged to you. I couldn't let him touch me. I had never been his wife. When I realized this—that he was there, that you might suffer for it—I cried right out.

"He thought I was sick. He worked over me. He gave me medicine. And then he prayed. I saw him, in the dark, on his knees, praying for me. That seemed strange. Yet he was kind, so kind that I begged him to let me go. I was not a Mormon. I couldn't marry him. I begged him to let me go.

"Then he thought I had been deceiving him. He fell into a fury. He talked for a long time. He called upon God to visit my sins upon me. He tried to make me pray. But I wouldn't. And then—I fought him. I'd have screamed for you had he not smothered me. I got weak. . . . And you never came. I know I thought you would come. But you didn't. Then I—I gave out. And after—some time—I must have fainted."

"Fay! For Heaven's sake, how could I come to you?" burst out Shefford, hoarse and white with remorse, passion, pain.

"If I'm any man's wife I'm yours. It's a thing you *feel,* isn't it? I know that now. . . . But I want to know what to do?"

"Fay!" he cried, huskily.

"I'm sick of it all. If it weren't for you I'd climb the wall and throw myself off. That would be easy for me. I'd love to die that way. All my life I've been high up on the walls. To fall would be nothing!"

"Oh you mustn't talk like that!"

"Do you love me?" she asked, with a low and deathless sweetness.

"Love you? With all my heart! Nothing can change that!"

"Do you want me—as you used to want the Fay Larkin lost in Surprise Valley? Do you love me that way? I understand things better than before, but still—not all. I *am* Fay Larkin. I think I must have dreamed of you all my life. I was glad when you came here. I've been happy lately. I forgot—till last night. Maybe it needed that to make me see I've loved you all the time. . . . And I fought him like a wildcat! . . . Tell me the truth. I *feel* I'm yours. Is that true? If I'm not—I'll not live another hour. Something holds me up. I am the same. . . . Do you want me?"

"Yes, Fay Larkin, I want you," replied Shefford, steadily, with his grip on her arms.

"Then take me away. I don't want to live here another hour."

"Fay, I'll take you. But it can't be done at once. We must plan. I need help. There are Lassiter and Jane to get out of Surprise Valley. Give me time, dear— give me time. It 'll be a hard job. And we must plan so we can positively get away. Give me time, Fay."

"Suppose *he* comes back?" she queried, with a singular depth of voice.

"We'll have to risk that," replied Shefford, miserably. "But—he won't come soon."

"He said he would," she flashed.

Shefford seemed to freeze inwardly with her words. Love had made her a woman and now the woman in her was speaking. She saw the truth as he could not see it. And the truth was nature. She had been hidden all her life from the world, from knowledge as he had it, yet when love betrayed her womanhood to her she acquired all its subtlety.

"If I wait and he *does* come will you keep me from him?" she asked.

"How can I? I'm staking all on the chance of his not coming soon. . . . But, Fay, if he does come and I don't give up our secret—how on earth can I keep you from him?" demanded Shefford.

"If you love me you will do it," she said, as simply as if she were fate.

"But how?" cried Shefford, almost beside himself.

"You are a man. Any man would save the woman who loves him from— from— Oh, from a beast! . . . How would Lassiter do it?"

"Lassiter!"

"You can kill him!"

It was there, deep and full in her voice, the strength of the elemental forces that had surrounded her, primitive passion and hate and love, as they were in woman in the beginning.

"My God!" Shefford cried aloud with his spirit when all that was red in him sprang again into a flame of hell. That was what had been wrong with him last night. He could kill this stealthy nightrider, and now, face to face with Fay, who had never been so beautiful and wonderful as in this hour when she made love the only and the sacred thing of life, now he had it in him to kill. Yet, murder—even to kill a brute—that was not for John Shefford, not the way for him to save a woman. Reason and wisdom still fought the passion in him. If he could but cling to them—have them with him in the dark and contending hour!

She leaned against him now, exhausted, her soul in her eyes, and they saw only him. Shefford was all but powerless to resist the longing to take her into his arms, to hold her to his heart, to let himself go. Did not her love give her to him? Shefford gazed helplessly at the stricken Joe Lake, at the somber Indian, as if from them he expected help.

"I know him now," said Fay, breaking the silence with startling suddenness.

"What!"

"I've seen him in the light. I flashed a candle in his face. I saw it. I know him now. He was there at Stonebridge with us, and I never knew him. But I know him now. His name is—"

"For God's sake don't tell me who he is!" implored Shefford.

Ignorance was Shefford's safeguard against himself. To make a name of this heretofore intangible man, to give him an identity apart from the crowd, to be able to recognize him—that for Shefford would be fatal.

"Fay—tell me—no more," he said, brokenly. "I love you and I will give you my life. Trust me. I swear I'll save you."

"Will you take me away soon?"

"Yes."

She appeared satisfied with that and dropped her hands and moved back from him. A light flitted over her white face, and her eyes grew dark and humid, losing their fire in changing, shadowing thought of submission, of trust, of hope.

"I can lead you to Surprise Valley," she said. "I feel the way. It's there!" And she pointed to the west.

"Fay, we'll go—soon. I must plan. I'll see you to-night. Then we'll talk. Run home now, before some of the women see you here."

She said good-by and started away under the cedars, out into the open where her hair shone like gold in the sunlight, and she took the stepping-stones with her old free grace, and strode down the path swift and lithe as an Indian. Once she turned to wave a hand.

Shefford watched her with a torture of pride, love, hope, and fear contending within him.

14

The Navajo

THAT morning a Piute rode into the valley. Shefford recognized him as the brave who had been in love with Glen Naspa. The moment Nas Ta Bega saw this visitor he made a singular motion with his hands—a motion that somehow to Shefford suggested despair—and then he waited, somber and statuesque, for the messenger to come to him. It was the Piute who did all the talking, and that was brief. Then the Navajo stood motionless, with his hands crossed over his breast. Shefford drew near and waited.

"Bi Nai," said the Navajo, "Nas Ta Bega said his sister would come home some day. . . . Glen Naspa is in the hogan of her grandfather."

He spoke in his usual slow, guttural voice, and he might have been bronze for all the emotion he expressed; yet Shefford instinctively felt the despair that had been hinted to him, and he put his hand on the Indian's shoulder.

"If I am the Navajo's brother, then I am brother to Glen Naspa," he said. "I will go with you to the hogan of Hosteen Doetin."

Nas Ta Bega went away into the valley for the horses. Shefford hurried to the village, made his excuses at the school, and then called to explain to Fay that trouble of some kind had come to the Indian.

Soon afterward he was riding Nack-yal on the rough and winding trail up through the broken country of cliffs and cañons to the great league-long sage and cedar slope of the mountain. It was weeks since he had ridden the mustang. Nack-yal was fat and lazy. He loved his master, but he did not like the climb, and so fell far behind the lean and wiry pony that carried Nas Ta Bega. The sage levels were as purple as the haze of the distance, and there was a bitter-sweet tang on the strong, cool wind. The sun was gold behind the dark line of fringe on the mountain-top. A flock of sheep swept down one of the sage levels, looking like a narrow stream of white and black and brown. It was always amazing for Shefford to see how swiftly these Navajo sheep grazed along. Wild mustangs plunged out of the cedar clumps and stood upon the ridges, whistling defiance or curiosity, and their manes and tails waved in the wind.

Shefford mounted slowly to the cedar bench in the midst of which were hidden the few hogans. And he halted at the edge to dismount and take a look at the downward-sweeping world of color, of wide space, at the wild desert upland which from there unrolled its magnificent panorama.

Then he passed on into the cedars. How strange to hear the lambs bleating again! Lambing-time had come early, but still spring was there in the new green of grass, in the bright upland flower. He led his mustang out of the cedars into the cleared circle. It was full of colts and lambs, and there were the shepherd-dogs and a few old rams and ewes. But the circle was a quiet place this day. There were no Indians in sight. Shefford loosened the saddlegirths on Nack-yal and, leaving him to graze, went toward the hogan of Hosteen Doetin. A blanket was hung across the door. Shefford heard a low chanting. He waited beside the door till the covering was pulled in, then he entered.

Hosteen Doetin met him, clasped his hand. The old Navajo could not speak; his fine face was working in grief; tears streamed from his dim old eyes and rolled down his wrinkled cheeks. His sorrow was no different from a white man's sorrow. Beyond him Shefford saw Nas Ta Bega standing with folded arms, somehow terrible in his somber impassiveness. At his feet crouched the old woman, Hosteen Doetin's wife, and beside her, prone and quiet, half covered with a blanket, lay Glen Naspa.

She was dead. To Shefford she seemed older than when he had last seen her. And she was beautiful. Calm, cold, dark, with only bitter lips to give the lie to peace! There was a story in those lips.

At her side, half hidden under the fold of blanket, lay a tiny bundle. Its human shape startled Shefford. Then he did not need to be told the tragedy. When he looked again at Glen Naspa's face he seemed to understand all that had made her older, to feel the pain that had lined and set her lips.

She was dead, and she was the last of Nas Ta Bega's family. In the old grandfather's agony, in the wild chant of the stricken grandmother, in the brother's stern and terrible calmness Shefford felt more than the death of a loved one. The shadow of ruin, of doom, of death hovered over the girl and her family and her tribe and her race. There was no consolation to offer these relatives of Glen Naspa. Shefford took one more fascinated gaze at her dark, eloquent, prophetic face, at the tragic tiny shape by her side, and then with bowed head he left the hogan.

Outside he paced to and fro, with an aching heart for Nas Ta Bega, with something of the white man's burden of crime toward the Indian weighing upon his soul.

Old Hosteen Doetin came to him with shaking hands and words memorable of the time Glen Naspa left his hogan.

"Me no savvy Jesus Christ. Me hungry. Me no eat Jesus Christ!"

That seemed to be all of his trouble that he could express to Shefford. He could not understand the religion of the missionary, this Jesus Christ who had called his granddaughter away. And the great fear of an old Indian was not death, but hunger. Shefford remembered a custom of the Navajos, a thing barbarous looked at with a white man's mind. If an old Indian failed on a long march he was inclosed by a wall of stones, given plenty to eat and drink, and left there to die in the desert. Not death did he fear, but hunger! Old Hosteen Doetin expected to starve, now that the young and strong squaw of his family was gone.

Shefford spoke in his halting Navajo and assured the old Indian that Nas Ta Bega would never let him starve.

At sunset Shefford stood with Nas Ta Bega facing the west. The Indian was magnificent in repose. He watched the sun go down upon the day that had seen the burial of the last of his family. He resembled an impassive destiny, upon which no shocks fell. He had the light of that flaring golden sky in his face, the majesty of the mountain in his mien, the silence of the great gulf below on his lips. This educated Navajo, who had reverted to the life of his ancestors, found in the wildness and loneliness of his environment a strength no white teaching could ever have given him. Shefford sensed in him a measureless grief, an impenetrable gloom, a tragic acceptance of the meaning of Glen Naspa's ruin and death—the vanishing of his race from the earth. Death had written the law of such bitter truth round Glen Naspa's lips, and the same truth was here in the grandeur and gloom of the Navajo.

"Bi Nai," he said, with the beautiful sonorous roll in his voice, "Glen Naspa is in her grave and there are no paths to the place of her sleep. Glen Naspa is gone.''

"Gone! Where? Nas Ta Bega, remember I lost my own faith, and I have not yet learned yours.''

"The Navajo has one mother—the earth. Her body has gone to the earth and it will become dust. But her spirit is in the air. It shall whisper to me from the wind. I shall hear it on running waters. It will hide in the morning music of a mocking-bird and in the lonely night cry of the cañon hawk. Her blood will go to make the red of the Indian flowers and her soul will rest at midnight in the lily that opens only to the moon. She will wait in the shadow for me, and live in the great mountain that is my home, and for ever step behind me on the trail.''

"You will kill Willetts?'' demanded Shefford.

"The Navajo will not seek the missionary.''

"But if you meet him you'll kill him?''

"Bi Nai, would Nas Ta Bega kill after it is too late? What good could come? The Navajo is above revenge.''

"If he crosses my trail I think I couldn't help but kill him,'' muttered Shefford in a passion that wrung the threat from him.

The Indian put his arm around the white man's shoulders.

"Bi Nai, long ago I made you my brother. And now you make me your brother. Is it not so? Glen Naspa's spirit calls for wisdom, not revenge. Willetts must be a bad man. But we'll let him live. Life will punish him. Who knows if he was all to blame? Glen Naspa was only one pretty Indian girl. There are many white men in the desert. She loved a white man when she was a baby. The thing was a curse. . . . Listen, Bi Nai, and the Navajo will talk.

"Many years ago the Spanish padres, the first white men, came into the land of the Indian. Their search was for gold. But they were not wicked men. They did not steal and kill. They taught the Indian many useful things. They brought him horses. But when they went away they left him unsatisfied with his life and his god.

"Then came the pioneers. They crossed the great river and took the pasture-lands and the hunting-grounds of the Indian. They drove him backward, and the Indian grew sullen. He began to fight. The white man's government made treaties with the Indian, and these were broken. Then war came—fierce and bloody war. The Indian was driven to the waste places. The stream of pioneers, like a march of ants, spread on into the desert. Every valley where grass grew, every river, became a place for farms and towns. Cattle choked the waterholes where the buffalo and deer had once gone to drink. The forests in the hills were cut and the springs dried up. And the pioneers followed to the edge of the desert.

"Then came the prospectors, mad, like the padres for the gleam of gold. The day was not long enough for them to dig in the creeks and the cañons; they worked in the night. And they brought weapons and rum to the Indian, to buy from him the secret of the places where the shining gold lay hidden.

"Then came the traders. And they traded with the Indian. They gave him little for much, and that little changed his life. He learned a taste for the sweet foods of the white man. Because he could trade for a sack of flour he worked less in the field. And the very fiber of his bones softened.

"Then came the missionaries. They were proselytizers for converts to their religion. The missionaries are good men. There may be a bad missionary, like Willetts, the same as there are bad men in other callings, or bad Indians. They say Shadd is a half-breed. But the Piutes can tell you he is a full-blood, and he, like me, was sent to a white man's school. In the beginning the missionaries did well for the Indian. They taught him cleaner ways of living, better farming, useful work with tools—many good things. But the wrong to the Indian was the undermining of his faith. It was not humanity that sent the missionary to the Indian. Humanity would have helped the Indian in his ignorance of sickness and work, and left him his god. For to trouble the Indian about his god worked at the roots of his nature.

"The beauty of the Indian's life is in his love of the open, of all that is nature, of silence, freedom, wildness. It is a beauty of mind and soul. The Indian would have been content to watch and feel. To a white man he might be dirty and lazy—content to dream life away without trouble or what the white man calls evolution. The Indian might seem cruel because he leaves his old father out in the desert to die. But the old man wants to die that way, alone with his spirits and the sunset. And the white man's medicine keeps his old father alive days and days after he ought to be dead. Which is more cruel? The Navajos used to fight with other tribes. And then they were stronger men than they are to-day.

"But leaving religion, greed, and war out of the question, contact with the white man would alone have ruined the Indian. The Indian and the white man cannot mix. The Indian brave learns the habits of the white man, acquires his diseases, and has not the mind or body to withstand them. The Indian girl learns to love the white man—and that is death of her Indian soul, if not of life.

"So the red man is passing. Tribes once powerful have died in the life of Nas Ta Bega. The curse of the white man is already heavy upon my race in the south. Here in the north, in the wildest corner of the desert, chased here by the great soldier, Carson, the Navajo has made his last stand.

"Bi Nai, you have seen the shadow in the hogan of Hosteen Doetin. Glen Naspa has gone to her grave, and no sisters, no children, will make paths to the place of her sleep. Nas Ta Bega will never have a wife—a child. He sees the end. It is the sunset of the Navajo. . . . Bi Nai, the Navajo is dying—dying—dying!"

15
Wild Justice

A CRESCENT moon hung above the lofty peak over the valley and a train of white
stars ran along the bold rim of the western wall. A few young frogs peeped
plaintively. The night was cool, yet had a touch of balmy spring, and a sweeter
fragrance, as if the cedars and piñons had freshened in the warm sun of that
day.

Shefford and Fay were walking in the aisles of moonlight and the patches of
shade, and Nas Ta Bega, more than ever a shadow of his white brother, followed
them silently.

"Fay, it's growing late. Feel the dew?" said Shefford. "Come, I must take
you back."

"But the time's so short. I have said nothing that I wanted to say," she
replied.

"Say it quickly, then, as we go."

"After all, it's only—will you take me away soon?"

"Yes, very soon. The Indian and I have talked. But we've made no plan yet.
There are only three ways to get out of this country. By Stonebridge, by Kayenta
and Durango, and by Red Lake. We must choose one. All are dangerous. We
must lose time finding Surprise Valley. I hoped the Indian could find it. Then
we'd bring Lassiter and Jane here and hide them near till dark, then take you
and go. That would give us a night's start. But you must help us to Surprise
Valley."

"I can go right to it, blindfolded, or in the dark. . . . Oh, John, hurry! I dread
the wait. *He* might come again."

"Joe says—they won't come very soon."

"Is it far—where we're going—out of the country?"

"Ten days' hard riding."

"Oh! that night ride to and from Stonebridge nearly killed me. But I could
walk very far, and climb for ever."

"Fay, we'll get out of the country if I have to carry you."

When they arrived at the cabin Fay turned on the porch step and, with her
face nearer a level with his, white and sweet in the moonlight, with her eyes
shining and unfathomable, she was more than beautiful.

"You've never been inside my house," she said. "Come in. I've something for you."

"But it's late," he remonstrated. "I suppose you've got me a cake or pie—something to eat. You women all think Joe and I have to be fed."

"No. You'd never guess. Come in," she said and the rare smile on her face was something Shefford would have gone far to see.

"Well, then, for a minute."

He crossed the porch, the threshold, and entered her home. Her dim, white shape moved in the darkness. And he followed into a room where the moon shone through the open window, giving soft, mellow, shadowy light. He discerned objects, but not clearly, for his senses seemed absorbed in the strange warmth and intimacy of being for the first time with her in her home.

"No, it's not good to eat," she said, and her laugh was happy. "Here—"

Suddenly she abruptly ceased speaking. Shefford saw her plainly, and the slender form had stiffened, alert and strained. She was listening.

"What was that?" she whispered.

"I didn't hear anything," he whispered back.

He stepped softly nearer the open window and listened.

Clip-clop! clip-clop! clip-clop! Hard hoofs on the hard path outside!

A strong and rippling thrill went over Shefford. In the soft light her eyes seemed unnaturally large and black and fearful.

Clip-clop! clip-clop!

The horse stopped outside. Then followed a metallic clink of spur against stirrup—thud of boots on hard ground—heavy footsteps upon the porch.

A swift, cold contraction of throat, of breast, convulsed Shefford. His only thought was that he could not think.

"Ho—Mary!"

A voice liberated both Shefford's muscle and mind—a voice of strange, vibrant power. Authority of religion and cruelty of will—these Mormon attributes constituted that power. And Shefford suffered a transformation which must have been ordered by demons. That sudden flame seemed to curl and twine and shoot along his veins with blasting force. A rancorous and terrible cry leaped to his lips.

"Ho—Mary!" Then came a heavy tread across the threshold of the outer room.

Shefford dared not look at Fay. Yet, dimly, from the corner of his eye, he saw her, a pale shadow, turned to stone, with her arms out. If he looked, if he made sure of that, he was lost. When had he drawn his gun? It was there, a dark and glinting thing in his hand. He must fly—not through cowardice and fear, but because in one more moment he would kill a man. Swift as the thought he dove through the open window. And, leaping up, he ran under the dark piñons toward camp.

Joe Lake had been out late himself. He sat by the fire, smoking his pipe. He must have seen or heard Shefford coming, for he rose with unwonted alacrity, and he kicked the smoldering logs into a flickering blaze.

Shefford, realizing his deliverance, came panting, staggering into the light. The Mormon uttered an exclamation. Then he spoke, anxiously, but what he said was not clear in Shefford's thick and throbbing ears. He dropped his pipe, a sign of perturbation, and he stared.

But Shefford, without a word, lunged swiftly away into the shadow of the cedars. He found relief in action. He began a steep ascent of the east wall, a dangerous slant he had never dared even in daylight, and he climbed it without a slip. Danger, steep walls, perilous heights, night, and black cañon the same— these he never thought of. But something drove him to desperate effort, that the hours might seem short.

The red sun was tipping the eastern wall when he returned to camp, and he was neither calm nor sure of himself nor ready for sleep or food. Only he had put the night behind him.

The Indian showed no surprise. But Joe Lake's jaw dropped and his eyes rolled. Moreover, Joe bore a singular aspect, the exact nature of which did not at once dawn upon Shefford.

"By God! you've got nerve—or you're crazy!" he ejaculated, hoarsely.

Then it was Shefford's turn to stare. The Mormon was haggard, grieved, frightened, and utterly amazed. He appeared to be trying to make certain of Shefford's being there in the flesh and then to find reason for it.

"I've no nerve and I am crazy," replied Shefford. "But, Joe—what do you mean? Why do you look at me like that?"

"I reckon if I get your horse that'll square us. Did you come back for him? You'd better hit the trail quick."

"It's you now who're crazy," burst out Shefford.

"Wish to God I was," replied Joe.

It was then Shefford realized catastrophe, and cold fear gnawed at his vitals, so that he was sick.

"Joe, what has happened?" he asked, with the blood thick in his heart.

"Hadn't you better tell me?" demanded the Mormon, and a red wave blotted out the haggard shade of his face.

"You talk like a fool," said Shefford, sharply, and he strode right up to Joe.

"See here, Shefford, we've been pards. You're making it hard for me. Reckon you ain't square."

Shefford shot out a long arm and his hand clutched the Mormon's burly shoulder.

"Why am I not square? What do you mean?"

Joe swallowed hard and gave himself a shake. Then he eyed his comrade steadily.

"I was afraid you'd kill him. I reckon I can't blame you. I'll help you get away. . . . And I'm a Mormon! Do you take the hunch? . . . But don't deny you killed him!"

"Killed whom?" gasped Shefford.

"Her husband!"

Shefford seemed stricken by a slow, paralyzing horror. The Mormon's changing face grew huge and indistinct and awful in his sight. He was clutched and shaken in Joe's rude hands, yet scarcely felt them. Joe seemed to be bellowing at him, but the voice was far off. Then Shefford began to see, to hear through some cold and terrible deadness that had come between him and everything.

"Say *you* killed him!" hoarsely supplicated the Mormon.

Shefford had not yet control of speech. Something in his gaze appeared to drive Joe frantic.

"Damn you! Tell me quick. Say *you* killed him! . . . If you want to know my stand, why, I'm glad! . . . Shefford, don't look so stony! . . . For *her* sake, say you killed him!"

Shefford stood with a face as gray and still as stone. With a groan the Mormon drew away from him and sank upon a log. He bowed his head; his broad shoulders heaved; husky sounds came from him. Then with a violent wrench he plunged to his feet and shook himself like a huge, savage dog.

"Reckon it's no time to weaken," he said, huskily, and with the words a dark, hard, somber bitterness came to his face.

"Where—is—she?" whispered Shefford.

"Shut up in the school-house," he replied.

"Did she—did she—"

"She neither denied nor confessed."

"Have you—seen her?"

"Yes."

"How did—she look?"

"Cool and quiet as the Indian there. . . . Game as hell! She always had stuff in her."

"Oh, Joe! . . . It's unbelievable!" cried Shefford. "That lovely, innocent girl! She couldn't—she couldn't."

"She's fixed him. Don't think of that. It's too late. We ought to have saved her."

"God! . . . She begged me to hurry—to take her away."

"Think what we can do *now* to save her," cut in the Mormon.

Shefford sustained a vivifying shock. "To save her?" he echoed.

"Think, man!"

"Joe, I can hit the trail and let you tell them I killed him," burst out Shefford in panting excitement.

"Reckon I can."

"So help me God I'll do it!"

The Mormon turned a dark and austere glance upon Shefford.

"You mustn't leave her. She killed him for your sake. . . . You must fight for her now—save her—take her away."

"But the law!"

"Law!" scoffed Joe. "In these wilds men get killed and there's no law. But if she's taken back to Stonebridge those iron-jawed old Mormons will make law enough to—to . . . Shefford, the thing is—get her away. Once out of the country, she's safe. Mormons keep their secrets."

"I'll take her. Joe, will you help me?"

Shefford, even in his agitation, felt the Mormon's silence to be a consent that need not have been asked. And Shefford had a passionate gratefulness toward his comrade. That stultifying and blinding prejudice which had always seemed to remove a Mormon outside the pale of certain virtue suffered final eclipse; and Joe Lake stood out a man, strange and crude, but with a heart and a soul.

"Joe, tell me what to do," said Shefford, with a simplicity that meant he needed only to be directed.

"Pull yourself together. Get your nerve back," replied Joe. "Reckon you'd better show yourself over there. No one saw you come in this morning—your absence from camp isn't known. It's better you seem curious and shocked like the rest of us. Come on. We'll go over. And afterward we'll get the Indian, and plan."

They left camp and, crossing the brook, took the shaded path toward the village. Hope of saving Fay, the need of all his strength and nerve and cunning to effect that end, gave Shefford the supreme courage to overcome his horror and fear. On that short walk under the piñons to Fay's cabin he had suffered many changes of emotion, but never anything like this change which made him fierce and strong to fight, deep and crafty to plan, hard as iron to endure.

The village appeared very quiet, though groups of women stood at the doors of cabins. If they talked, it was very low. Henninger and Smith, two of the three Mormon men living in the village, were standing before the closed door of the school-house. A tigerish feeling thrilled Shefford when he saw them on guard there. Shefford purposely avoided looking at Fay's cabin as long as he could keep from it. When he had to look he saw several hooded, whispering women in the yard, and Beal, the other Mormon man, standing in the cabin door. Upon the porch lay the long shape of a man, covered with blankets.

Shefford experienced a horrible curiosity.

"Say, Beal, I've fetched Shefford over," said Lake. "He's pretty much cut up."

Beal wagged a solemn head, but said nothing. His mind seemed absent or steeped in gloom, and he looked up as one silently praying.

Joe Lake strode upon the little porch and, reaching down, he stripped the blanket from the shrouded form.

Shefford saw sharp, cold, ghastly face. "*Waggonner!*" he whispered.

"Yes," replied Lake.

Waggoner! Shefford remembered the strange power in his face, and, now that life had gone, that power was stripped of all disguise. Death, in Shefford's years of ministry, had lain under his gaze many times and in a multiplicity of aspects, but never before had he seen it stamped so strangely. Shefford did not need to be told that here was a man who believed he had conversed with God on earth, who believed he had a divine right to rule women, who had a will that would not yield itself to death utterly. Waggoner, then, was the devil who had come masked to Surprise Valley, had forced a martyrdom upon Fay Larkin. And this was the Mormon who had made Fay Larkin a murderess. Shefford had hated him living, and now he hated him dead. Death here was robbed of all nobility, of pathos, of majesty. It was only retribution. Wild justice! But alas! that it had to be meted out by a white-souled girl whose innocence was as great as the unconscious savagery which she had assimilated from her lonely and wild environment. Shefford laid a despairing curse upon his own head, and a terrible remorse knocked at his heart. He had left her alone, this girl in whom love had made the great change—like a coward he had left her alone. That curse he visited upon himself because he had been the spirit and the motive of this wild justice, and his should have been the deed.

Joe Lake touched Shefford's arm and pointed at the haft of a knife protruding from Waggoner's breast. It was a wooden haft. Shefford had seen it before somewhere.

Then he was struck with what perhaps Joe meant him to see—the singular impression the haft gave of one sweeping, accurate, powerful stroke. A strong arm had driven that blade home. The haft was sunk deep; there was a little depression in the cloth; no blood showed; and the weapon looked as if it could not be pulled out. Shefford's thought went fatally and irresistibly to Fay Larkin's strong arm. He saw her flash that white arm and lift the heavy bucket from the spring with an ease he wondered at. He felt the strong clasp of her hand as she had given it to him in a flying leap across a crevice upon the walls. Yes, her fine hand and the round, strong arm possessed the strength to have given that

blade its singular directness and force. The marvel was not in the physical action.
It hid inscrutably in the mystery of deadly passion rising out of a gentle and sad
heart.

Joe Lake drew up the blanket and shut from Shefford's fascinated gaze that
spare form, that accusing knife, that face of strange, cruel power.

"Anybody been sent for?" asked Lake of Beal.

"Yes. An Indian boy went for the Piute. We'll send him to Stonebridge,"
replied the Mormon.

"How soon do you expect any one here from Stonebridge?"

"To-morrow, mebbe by noon."

"Meantime what's to be done with—this?"

"Elder Smith thinks the body should stay right here where it fell till they come
from Stonebridge."

"Waggoner was found here, then?"

"Right here."

"Who found him?"

"Mother Smith. She came over early. An' the sight made her scream. The
women all came runnin'. Mother Smith had to be put to bed."

"Who found—Mary?"

"See here, Joe, I told you all I knowed once before," replied the Mormon,
testily.

"I've forgotten. Was sort of bewildered. Tell me again. . . . Who found—
her?"

"The women folks. She laid right inside the door, in a dead faint. She hadn't
undressed. There was blood on her hands an' a cut or scratch. The women
fetched her to. But she wouldn't talk. Then Elder Smith come an' took her.
They've got her locked up."

Then Joe led Shefford away from the cabin farther on into the village. When
they were halted by the somber, grieving women it was Joe who did the talking.
They passed the school-house, and here Shefford quickened his step. He could
scarcely bear the feeling that rushed over him. And the Mormon gripped his
arm as if he understood.

"Shefford, which one of these younger women do you reckon your best
friend? Ruth?" asked Lake, earnestly.

"Ruth, by all means. Just lately I haven't seen her often. But we've been
close friends. I think she'd do much for me."

"Maybe there'll be a chance to find out. Maybe we'll need Ruth. Let's have
a word with her. I haven't seen her out among the women."

They stopped at the door of Ruth's cabin. It was closed. When Joe knocked
there came a sound of footsteps inside, a hand drew aside the window-blind,
and presently the door opened. Ruth stood there, dressed in somber hue. She

was a pretty, slender, blue-eyed, brown-haired young woman. Shefford imagined from her pallor and the set look of shock upon her face, that the tragedy had affected her more powerfully that it had the other women. When he remembered that she had been more friendly with Fay Larkin than any other neighbor, he made sure he was right in his conjecture.

"Come in," was Ruth's greeting.

"No. We just wanted to say a word. I noticed you've not been out. Do you know—all about it?"

She gave them a strange glance.

"Any of the women folks been in?" added Joe.

"Hester ran over. She told me through the window. Then I barred my door to keep the other women out."

"What for?" asked Joe, curiously.

"Please come in," she said, in reply.

They entered, and she closed the door after them. The change that came over her then was the loosing of restraint.

"Joe—what will they do with Mary?" she queried tensely.

The Mormon studied her with dark, speculative eyes. "Hang her!" he rejoined in brutal harshness.

"O Mother of Saints!" she cried, and her hands went up.

"You're sorry for Mary, then?" asked Joe, bluntly.

"My heart is breaking for her."

"Well, so's Shefford's," said the Mormon, huskily. "And mine's kind of damn shaky."

Ruth glided to Shefford with a woman's swift softness.

"You've been my good—my best friend. You were hers, too. Oh, I know! . . . Can't you do something for her?"

"I hope to God I can," replied Shefford.

Then the three stood looking from one to the other, in a strong and subtly realizing moment, drawn together.

"Ruth," whispered Joe, hoarsely, and then he glanced fearfully around, at the window and door, as if listeners were there. It was certain that his dark face had paled. He tried to whisper more, only to fail. Shefford divined the weight of Mormonism that burdened Joe Lake then. Joe was faithful to a love for Fay Larkin, noble in friendship to Shefford, desperate in a bitter strait with his own manliness, but the power of that creed by which he had been raised struck his lips mute. For to speak on meant to be false to that creed. Already in his heart he had decided, yet he could not voice the thing.

"Ruth"—Shefford took up the Mormon's unfinished whisper—"if we plan to save her—if we need you—will you help?"

Ruth turned white, but an instant and splendid fire shone in her eyes.

"Try me," she whispered back. "I'll change places with her—so you can get her away. They can't do much to me."

Shefford wrung her hands. Joe licked his lips and found his voice: "We'll come back later." Then he led the way out and Shefford followed. They were silent all the way back to camp.

Nas Ta Bega sat in repose where they had left him, a thoughtful, somber figure. Shefford went directly to the Indian, and Joe tarried at the campfire, where he raked out some red embers and put one upon the bowl of his pipe. He puffed clouds of white smoke, then found a seat beside the others.

"Shefford, go ahead. Talk. It'll take a deal of talk. I'll listen. Then I'll talk. It'll be Nas Ta Bega who makes the plan out of it all."

Shefford launched himself so swiftly that he scarcely talked coherently. But he made clear the points that he must save Fay, get her away from the village, let her lead him to Surprise Valley, rescue Lassiter and Jane Withersteen, and take them all out of the country.

Joe Lake dubiously shook his head. Manifestly the Surprise Valley part of the situation presented a new and serious obstacle. It changed the whole thing. To try to take the three out by way of Kayenta and Durango was not to be thought of, for reasons he briefly stated. The Red Lake trail was the only one left, and if that were taken the chances were against Shefford. It was five days over sand to Red Lake—impossible to hide a trail—and even with a day's start Shefford could not escape the hard-riding men who would come from Stonebridge. Besides, after reaching Red Lake, there were days and days of desert-travel needful to avoid places like Blue Cañon, Tuba, Moencopie, and the Indian villages.

"We'll have to risk all that," declared Shefford, desperately.

"It's a fool risk," retorted Joe. "Listen. By tomorrow noon all of Stonebridge, more or less, will be riding in here. You've got to get away to-night with the girl—or never! And to-morrow you've got to find that Lassiter and the woman in Surprise Valley. This valley must be back, deep in the cañon country. Well, you've got to come out this way again. No trail through here would be safe. Why, you'd put all your heads in a rope! . . . You mustn't come through this way. It'll have to be tried across country, off the trails, and that means hell— day-and-night travel, no camp, no feed for horses—maybe no water. Then you'll have the best trackers in Utah like hounds on your trail."

When the Mormon ceased his forceful speech there was a silence fraught with hopeless meaning. He bowed his head in gloom. Shefford, growing sick again to his marrow, fought a cold, hateful sense of despair.

"Bi Nai!" In his extremity he called to the Indian.

"The Navajo has heard," replied Nas Ta Bega, strangely speaking in his own language.

With a long, slow heave of breast Shefford felt his despair leave him. In the

Shefford approached Ruth's cabin in a roundabout way; nevertheless, she saw him coming before he got there and, opening the door, stood pale, composed, and quietly bade him enter. Briefly, in low and earnest voice, Shefford acquainted her with the plan.

"You love her so much," she said, wistfully, wonderingly.

"Indeed I do. Is it too much to ask of you to do this thing?" he asked.

"Do it?" she queried, with a flash of spirit. "Of course I'll do it."

"Ruth, I can't thank you. I can't. I've only a faint idea what you're risking. That distresses me. I'm afraid of what may happen to you."

She gave him another of the strange glances. "I don't risk so much as you think," she said, significantly.

"Why?"

She came close to him, and her hands clasped his arms and she looked up at him, her eyes darkening and her face growing paler. "Will you swear to keep my secret?" she asked, very low.

"Yes, I swear."

"I was one of Waggoner's sealed wives!"

"God Almighty!" broke out Shefford, utterly overwhelmed.

"Yes. That's why I say I don't risk so much. I will make up a story to tell the bishop and everybody. I'll tell that Waggoner was jealous, that he was brutal to Mary, that I believed she was goaded to her mad deed, that I thought she ought to be free. They'll be terrible. But what can they do to me? My husband is dead . . . and if I have to go to hell to keep from marrying another married Mormon, I'll go!"

In that low, passionate utterance Shefford read the death-blow to the old Mormon polygamous creed. In the uplift of his spirit, in the joy at this revelation, he almost forgot the stern matter at hand. Ruth and Joe Lake belonged to a younger generation of Mormons. Their nobility in this instance was in part a revolt at the conditions of their lives. Doubt was knocking at Joe Lake's heart, and conviction had come to this young sealed wife, bitter and hopeless while she had been fettered, strong and mounting now that she was free. In a flash of inspiration Shefford saw the old order changing. The Mormon creed might survive, but that part of it which was an affront to nature, a horrible yoke on women's necks, was doomed. It could not live. It could never have survived more than a generation or two of religious fanatics. Shefford had marked a different force and religious fervor in the younger Mormons, and now he understood them.

"Ruth, you talk wildly," he said. "But I understand. I see. You are free and you're going to stay free. . . . It stuns me to think of that man of many wives. What did you feel when you were told he was dead?"

"I dare not think of that. It makes me wicked. And he was good to me.

. . . Listen. Last night about midnight he came to my window and woke me.
I got up and let him in. He was in a terrible state. I thought he was crazy. He
walked the floor and called on his saints and prayed. When I wanted to light a
lamp he wouldn't let me. He was afraid I'd see his face. But I saw well enough
in the moonlight. And I knew something had happened. So I soothed and coaxed
him. He had been a man as close-mouthed as a stone. Yet then I got him to talk.
. . . He had gone to Mary's, and upon entering, thought he heard some one with
her. She didn't answer him at first. When he found her in her bedroom she was
like a ghost. He accused her. Her silence made him furious. Then he berated
her, brought down the wrath of God upon her, threatened her with damnation.
All of which she never seemed to hear. But when he tried to touch her she flew
at him like a she-panther. That's what he called her. She said she'd kill him!
And she drove him out of her house. . . . He was all weak and unstrung, and
I believe scared, too, when he came to me. She must have been a fury. Those
quiet, gentle women are furies when they're once roused. Well, I was hours up
with him and finally he got over it. He didn't pray any more. He paced the room.
It was just daybreak when he said the wrath of God had come to him. I tried
to keep him from going back to Mary. But he went. . . . An hour later the
women ran to tell me he had been found dead at Mary's door.''

"Ruth—she was mad—driven—she didn't know what she—was doing,'' said
Shefford, brokenly.

"She was always a strange girl, more like an Indian than any one I ever knew.
We called her the Sago Lily. I gave her the name. She was so sweet, lovely,
white and gold, like those flowers. . . . And to think! Oh, it's horrible for her!
You must save her. If you get her away there never will be anything come of
it. The Mormons will hush it up.''

"Ruth, time is flying,'' rejoined Shefford, hurriedly. "I must go back to Joe.
You be ready for us when we come. Wear something loose, easily thrown off,
and don't forget the long hood.''

"I'll be ready and watching,'' she said. "The sooner the better, I'd say.''

He left her and returned toward camp in the same circling route by which he
had come. The Indian had disappeared and so had his mustang. This significant
fact augmented Shefford's hurried, thrilling excitement. But one glance at Joe's
face changed all that to a sudden numbness, a sinking of his heart.

"What is it?'' he queried.

"Look there!'' exclaimed the Mormon.

Shefford's quick eye caught sight of horses and men down the valley. He saw
several Indians and three or four white men. They were making camp.

"Who are they?'' demanded Shefford.

"Shadd and some of his gang. Reckon that Piute told the news. By to-morrow
the valley will be full as a horse-wrangler's corral. . . . Lucky Nas Ta Bega got

away before that gang rode in. Now things won't look as queer as they might have looked. The Indian took a pack of grub, six mustangs, and my guns. Then there was your rifle in your saddle-sheath. So you'll be well heeled in case you come to close quarters. Reckon you can look for a running fight. For now, as soon as your flight is discovered, Shadd will hit your trail. He's in with the Mormons. You know him—what you'll have to deal with. But the advantage will all be yours. You can ambush the trail.''

"We're in for it. And the sooner we're off the better,'' replied Shefford, grimly.

"Reckon that's gospel. Well—come on!''

The Mormon strode off, and Shefford, catching up with him, kept at his side. Shefford's mind was full, but Joe's dark and gloomy face did not invite communication. They entered the piñon grove and passed the cabin where the tragedy had been enacted. A tarpaulin had been stretched across the front porch. Beal was not in sight, nor were any of the women.

"I forgot,'' said Shefford, suddenly. "Where am I to meet the Indian?''

"Climb the west wall, back of camp,'' replied Joe. "Nas Ta Bega took the Stonebridge trail. But he'll leave that, climb the rocks, then hide the outfit and come back to watch for you. Reckon he'll see you when you top the wall.''

They passed on into the heart of the village. Joe tarried at the window of a cabin, and passed a few remarks to a woman there, and then he inquired for Mother Smith at her house. When they left here the Mormon gave Shefford a nudge. Then they separated, Joe going toward the school-house, while Shefford bent his steps in the direction of Ruth's home.

Her door opened before he had a chance to knock. He entered. Ruth, white and resolute, greeted him with a wistful smile.

"All ready?'' she asked.

"Yes. Are you?'' he replied, low-voiced.

"I've only to put on my hood. I think luck favors you. Hester was here and she said Elder Smith told some one that Mary hadn't been offered anything to eat yet. So I'm taking her a little. It'll be a good excuse for me to get in the school-house to see her. I can throw off this dress and she can put it on in a minute. Then the hood. I mustn't forget to hide her golden hair. You know how it flies. But this is a big hood. . . . Well, I'm ready now. And—this's our last time together.''

"Ruth, what can I say—how can I thank you?''

"I don't want any thanks. It'll be something to think of always—to make me happy. . . . Only I'd like to feel you—you cared a little.''

The wistful smile was there, a tremor on the sad lips, and a shadow of soul-hunger in her eyes. Shefford did not misunderstand her. She did not mean love, although it was a yearning for real love that she mutely expressed.

"Care! I shall care all my life," he said, with strong feeling. "I shall never forget you."

"It's not likely I'll forget you. . . . Good-by, John!"

Shefford took her in his arms and held her close. "Ruth—good-by!" he said, huskily.

Then he released her. She adjusted the hood and, taking up a little tray which held food covered with a napkin, she turned to the door. He opened it and they went out.

They did not speak another word.

It was not a long walk from Ruth's home to the school-house, yet if it were to be measured by Shefford's emotion the distance would have been unending. The sacrifice offered by Ruth and Joe would have been noble under any circumstances had they been Gentiles or persons with no particular religion, but, considering that they were Mormons, that Ruth had been a sealed wife, that Joe had been brought up under the strange, secret, and binding creed, their action was no less than tremendous in its import. Shefford took it to mean vastly more than loyalty to him and pity for Fay Larkin. As Ruth and Joe had arisen to this height, so perhaps would other young Mormons have arisen. It needed only the situation, the climax, to focus these long-insulated, slow-developing and inquiring minds upon the truth—that one wife, one mother of children, for one man at one time was a law of nature, love, and righteousness. Shefford felt as if he were marching with the whole younger generation of Mormons, as if somehow he had been a humble instrument in the working out of their destiny, in the awakening that was to eliminate from their religion the only thing which kept it from being as good for man, and perhaps as true, as any other religion.

And then suddenly he turned the corner of the school-house to encounter Joe talking with the Mormon Henninger. Elder Smith was not present.

"Why, hello, Ruth!" greeted Joe. "You've fetched Mary some dinner. Now that's good of you."

"May I go in?" asked Ruth.

"Reckon so," replied Henninger, scratching his head. He appeared to be tractable, and probably was good-natured under pleasant conditions. "She ought to have somethin' to eat. An' nobody 'pears to have remembered thet—we're so set up."

He unbarred the huge, clumsy door and allowed Ruth to pass in.

"Joe, you can go in if you want," he said. "But hurry out before Elder Smith comes back from his dinner."

Joe mumbled something, gave a husky cough, and then went in.

Shefford experienced great difficulty in presenting to this mild Mormon a natural and unagitated front. When all his internal structure seemed to be in a state of turmoil he did not see how it was possible to keep the fact from showing in his face. So he turned away and took aimless steps here and there.

"'Pears like we'd hev rain," observed Henninger. "It's right warm an' them clouds are onseasonable."

"Yes," replied Shefford. "Hope so. A little rain would be good for the grass."

"Joe tells me Shadd rode in, an' some of his fellers."

"So I see. About eight in the party."

Shefford was gritting his teeth and preparing to endure the ordeal of controlling his mind and expression when the door opened and Joe stalked out. He had his sombrero pulled down so that it hid the upper half of his face. His lips were a shade off healthy color. He stood there with his back to the door.

"Say, what Mary needs is quiet—to be left alone," he said. "Ruth says if she rests, sleeps a little, she won't get fever. . . . Henninger, don't let anybody disturb her till night."

"All right, Joe," replied the Mormon. "An' I take it good of Ruth an' you to concern yourselves."

A slight tap on the inside of the door sent Shefford's pulses to throbbing. Joe opened it with a strong and vigorous sweep that meant more than the mere action.

"Ruth—reckon you didn't stay long," he said, and his voice rang clear. "Sure you feel sick and weak. Why, seeing her flustered even me!"

A slender, dark-garbed woman wearing a long black hood stepped uncertainly out. She appeared to be Ruth. Shefford's heart stood still because she looked so like Ruth. But she did not step steadily, she seemed dazed, she did not raise the hooded head.

"Go home," said Joe, and his voice rang a little louder. "Take her home, Shefford. Or, better, walk her round some. She's faintish. . . . And see here, Henninger—"

Shefford led the girl away with a hand in apparent carelessness on her arm. After a few rods she walked with a freer step and then a swifter. He found it necessary to make that hold on her arm a real one, so as to keep her from walking too fast. No one, however, appeared to observe them. When they passed Ruth's house then Shefford began to lose his fear that this was not Fay Larkin. He was far from being calm or clear-sighted. He thought he recognized that free step; nevertheless, he could not make sure. When they passed under the trees, crossed the brook, and turned down along the west wall, then doubt ceased in Shefford's mind. He knew this was not Ruth. Still, so strange was his agitation, so keen his suspense, that he needed confirmation of ear, of eye. He wanted to hear her voice, to see her face. Yet just as strangely there was a twist of feeling, a reluctance, a sadness that kept off the moment.

They reached the low, slow-swelling slant of wall and started to ascend. How impossible not to recognize Fay Larkin now in that swift grace and skill on the steep wall! Still, though he knew her, he perversely clung to the unreality of the moment. But when a long braid of dead-gold hair tumbled from under the hood, then his heart leaped. That identified Fay Larkin. He had freed her. He was taking her away. Then a sadness embittered his joy.

As always before, she distanced him in the ascent to the top. She went on without looking back. But Shefford had an irresistible desire to look again and the last time at this valley where he had suffered and loved so much.

16
Surprise Valley

FROM the summit of the wall the plateau waved away in red and yellow ridges, with here and there little valleys green with cedar and piñon.

Upon one of these ridges, silhouetted against the sky, appeared the stalking figure of the Indian. He had espied the fugitives. He disappeared in a niche, and presently came again into view round a corner of cliff. Here he waited, and soon Shefford and Fay joined him.

"Bi Nai, it is well," he said.

Shefford eagerly asked for the horses, and Nas Ta Bega silently pointed down the niche, which was evidently an opening into one of the shallow cañons. Then he led the way, walking swiftly. It was Shefford, and not Fay, who had difficulty in keeping close to him. This speed caused Shefford to become more alive to the business, instead of the feeling, of the flight. The Indian entered a crack between low cliffs—a very narrow cañon full of rocks and clumps of cedars— and in a half-hour or less he came to where the mustangs were halted among some cedars. Three of the mustangs, including Nack-yal, were saddled; one bore a small pack, and the remaining two had blankets strapped on their backs.

"Fay, can you ride in that long skirt?" asked Shefford. How strange it seemed that his first words to her were practical when all his impassioned thought had been only mute! But the instant he spoke he experienced a relief, a relaxation.

"I'll take it off," replied Fay, just as practically. And in a twinkling she slipped out of both waist and skirt. She had worn them over the short white-flannel dress with which Shefford had grown familiar.

As Nack-yal appeared to be the safest mustang for her to ride, Shefford helped her upon him and then attended to the stirrups. When he had adjusted them to the proper length he drew the bridle over Nack-yal's head and, upon handing it to her, found himself suddenly looking into her face. She had taken off the hood, too. The instant their eyes met he realized that she was strangely afraid to meet his glance, as he was to meet hers. That seemed natural. But her face was flushed and there were unmistakable signs upon it of growing excitement, of mounting happiness. Save for that fugitive glance she would have been the Fay Larkin of yesterday. How he had expected her to look he did not know, but it was not like this. And never had he felt her strange quality of simplicity so powerfully.

"Have you ever been here—through this little cañon?" he asked.

"Oh yes, lots of times."

"You'll be able to lead us to Surprise Valley, you think?"

"I know it. I shall see Uncle Jim and Mother Jane before sunset!"

"I hope—you do," he replied, a little shakily. "Perhaps we'd better not tell them of the—the—about what happened last night."

Her beautiful, grave, and troubled glance returned to meet his, and he received a shock that he considered was amaze. And after more swift consideration he believed he was amazed because that look, instead of betraying fear or gloom or any haunting shadow of darkness, betrayed apprehension for him—grave, sweet, troubled love for him. She was not thinking of herself at all—of what he might think of her, of a possible gulf between them, of a vast and terrible change in the relation of soul to soul. He experienced a profound gladness. Though he could not understand her, he was happy that the horror of Waggoner's death had escaped her. He loved her, he meant to give his life to her, and right then and there he accepted the burden of her deed and meant to bear it without ever letting her know of the shadow between them.

"Fay, we'll forget—what's behind us," he said. "Now to find Surprise Valley. Lead on. Nack-yal is gentle. Pull him the way you want to go. We'll follow."

Shefford mounted the other saddled mustang, and they set off, Fay in advance. Presently they rode out of this cañon up to level cedar-patched, solid rock, and here Fay turned straight west. Evidently she had been over the ground before. The heights to which he had climbed with her were up to the left, great slopes and looming promontories. And the course she chose was as level and easy as any he could have picked out in that direction.

When a mile or more of this up-and-down travel had been traversed Fay halted and appeared to be at fault. The plateau was losing its rounded, smooth, wavy characteristics, and to the west grew bolder, more rugged, more cut up into low crags and buttes. After a long, sweeping glance Fay headed straight for this rougher country. Thereafter from time to time she repeated this action.

"Fay, how do you know you're going in the right direction?" asked Shefford, anxiously.

"I never forget any ground I've been over. I keep my eyes close ahead. All that seems strange to me is the wrong way. What I've seen before must be the right way, because I saw it when they brought me from Surprise Valley."

Shefford had to acknowledge that she was following an Indian's instinct for ground he had once covered.

Still Shefford began to worry, and finally dropped back to question Nas Ta Bega.

"Bi Nai, she has the eye of a Navajo," replied the Indian. "Look! Iron-shod horses have passed here. See the marks in the stone?"

Shefford indeed made out faint cut tracks that would have escaped his own sight. They had been made long ago, but they were unmistakable.

"She's following the trail by memory—she must remember the stones, trees, sage, cactus," said Shefford in surprise.

"Pictures in her mind," replied the Indian.

Thereafter the farther she progressed the less at fault she appeared and the faster she traveled. She made several miles an hour, and about the middle of the afternoon entered upon the more broken region of the plateau. View became restricted. Low walls, and ruined cliffs of red rock with cedars at their base, and gullies growing into cañons and cañons opening into larger ones—these were passed and crossed and climbed and rimmed in travel that grew more difficult as the going became wilder. Then there was a steady ascent, up and up all the time, though not steep, until another level, green with cedar and piñon, was reached.

It reminded Shefford of the forest near the mouth of the Sagi. It was so dense he could not see far ahead of Fay, and often he lost sight of her entirely. Presently he rode out of the forest into a strip of purple sage. It ended abruptly, and above that abrupt line, seemingly far away, rose a long, red wall. Instantly he recognized that to be the opposite wall of a cañon which as yet he could not see.

Fay was acting strangely and he hurried forward. She slipped off Nack-yal and fell, sprang up and ran wildly, to stand upon a promontory, her arms uplifted, her hair a mass of moving gold in the wind, her attitude one of wild and eloquent significance.

Shefford ran, too, and as he ran the red wall in his eager sight seemed to enlarge downward, deeper and deeper, and then it merged into a strip of green.

Suddenly beneath him yawned a red-walled gulf, a deceiving gulf seen through transparent haze, a softly shining green-and-white valley, strange, wild, beautiful, like a picture in his memory.

"Surprise Valley!" he cried, in wondering recognition.

Fay Larkin waved her arms as if they were wings to carry her swiftly downward, and her plaintive cry fitted the wildness of her manner and the lonely height where she leaned.

Shefford drew her back from the rim.

"Fay, we are here," he said. "I recognize the valley. I miss only one thing—the arch of stone."

His words seemed to recall her to reality.

"The arch? That fell when the wall slipped, in the great avalanche. See! There is the place. We can get down there. Oh, let us hurry!"

The Indian reached the rim and his falcon gaze swept the valley. "Ugh!" he exclaimed. He, too, recognized the valley that he had vainly sought for half a year.

"Bring the lassos," said Shefford.

With Fay leading, they followed the rim toward the head of the valley. Here the wall had caved in, and there was a slope of jumbled rock a thousand feet wide and more than that in depth. It was easy to descend because there were so many rocks waist-high that afforded a handhold. Shefford marked, however, that Fay never took advantage of these. More than once he paused to watch her. Swiftly she went down; she stepped from rock to rock; lightly she crossed cracks and pits; she ran along the sharp and broken edge of a long ledge; she poised on a pointed stone and, sure-footed as a mountain-sheep, she sprang to another that had scarce surface for a foothold; her moccasins flashed, seemed to hold wondrously on any angle; and when a rock tipped or slipped with her she leaped to a surer stand. Shefford watched her performance, so swift, agile, so perfectly balanced, showing such wonderful accord between eye and foot; and then when he swept his gaze down upon that wild valley where she had roamed alone for twelve years he marveled no more.

The farther down he got the greater became the size of rocks, until he found himself amid huge pieces of cliff as large as houses. He lost sight of Fay entirely, and he anxiously threaded a narrow, winding, descending way between the broken masses. Finally he came out upon flat rock again. Fay stood on another rim, looking down. He saw that the slide had moved far out into the valley, and the lower part of it consisted of great sections of wall. In fact, the base of the great wall had just moved out with the avalanche, and this much of it held its vertical position. Looking upward, Shefford was astounded and thrilled to see how far he had descended, how the walls leaned like a great, wide, curving, continuous rim of mountain.

"Here! Here!" called Fay. "Here's where they got down—where they brought me up. Here are the sticks they used. They stuck them in this crack, down to that ledge."

Shefford ran to her side and looked down. There was a narrow split in this section of wall and it was perhaps sixty feet in depth. The floor of rock below led out in a ledge, with a sheer drop to the valley level.

As Shefford gazed, pondering on a way to descend lower, the Indian reached his side. He had no sooner looked than he proceeded to act. Selecting one of the sticks, which were strong pieces of cedar, well hewn and trimmed, he jammed it between the walls of the crack till it stuck fast. Then sitting astride this one he jammed in another some three feet below. When he got down upon that one it was necessary for Shefford to drop him a third stick. In a comparatively short time the Indian reached the ledge below. Then he called for the lassos. Shefford threw them down. His next move was an attempt to assist Fay, but she slipped out of his grasp and descended the ladder with a swiftness that made him hold his breath. Still, when his turn came, her spirit so governed him that he went down as swiftly, and even leaped sheer the last ten feet.

Nas Ta Bega and Fay were leaning over the ledge.

"Here's the place," she said, excitedly. "Let me down on the rope."

It took two thirty-foot lassos tied together to reach the floor of the valley. Shefford folded his vest, put it round Fay, and slipped a loop of the lasso under her arms. Then he and Nas Ta Bega lowered her to the grass below. Fay, throwing off the loop, bounded away like a wild creature, uttering the strangest cries he had ever heard, and she disappeared along the wall.

"I'll go down," said Shefford to the Indian. "You stay here to help pull us up."

Hand over hand Shefford descended, and when his feet touched the grass he experienced a shock of the most singular exultation.

"In Surprise Valley!" he breathed, softly. The dream that had come to him with his friend's story, the years of waiting, wondering, and then the long, fruitless, hopeless search in the desert uplands—these were in his mind as he turned along the wall where Fay had disappeared. He faced a wide terrace, green with grass and moss and starry with strange white flowers, and dark-foliaged, spear-pointed spruce-trees. Below the terrace sloped a bench covered with thick copse; and this merged into a forest of dwarf oaks, and beyond that was a beautiful strip of white aspens, their leaves quivering in the stillness. The air was close, sweet, warm, fragrant, and remarkably dry. It reminded him of the air he had smelled in dry caves under cliffs. He reached a point from where he saw a meadow dotted with red-and-white-spotted cattle and little black burros. There were many of them. And he remembered with a start the agony of toil and peril Venters had endured bringing the progenitors of this stock into the valley. What a strange, wild, beautiful story it all was! But a story connected with this valley could not have been otherwise.

Beyond the meadow, on the other side of the valley, extended the forest, and that ended in the rising bench of thicket, which gave place to green slope and mossy terrace of sharp-tipped spruces—and all this led the eye irresistibly up to the red wall where a vast, dark, wonderful cavern yawned, with its rust-colored streaks of stain on the wall, and the queer little houses of the cliff-dwellers, with their black, vacant, silent windows speaking so weirdly of the unknown past.

Shefford passed a place where the ground had been cultivated, but not as recently as the last six months. There was a scant shock of corn and many meager standing stalks. He became aware of a low, whining hum and a fragrance overpowering in its sweetness. And there round another corner of wall he came upon an orchard all pink and white in blossom and melodious with the buzz and hum of innumerable bees.

He crossed a little stream that had been dammed, went along a pond, down beside an irrigation-ditch that furnished water to orchard and vineyard, and from there he strode into a beautiful cove between two jutting corners of red wall. It was level and green and the spruces stood gracefully everywhere. Beyond their dark trunks he saw caves in the wall.

Suddenly the fragrance of blossom was overwhelmed by the stronger fragrance of smoke from a wood fire. Swiftly he strode under the spruces. Quail fluttered before him as tame as chickens. Big gray rabbits scarcely moved out of his way. The branches above him were full of mockingbirds. And then—there before him stood three figures.

Fay Larkin was held close to the side of a magnificent woman, barbarously clad in garments made of skins and pieces of blanket. Her face worked in noble emotion. Shefford seemed to see the ghost of that fair beauty Venters had said was Jane Withersteen's. Her hair was gray. Near her stood a lean, stoop-shouldered man whose long hair was perfectly white. His gaunt face was bare of beard. It had strange, sloping, sad lines. And he was staring with mild, surprised eyes.

The moment held Shefford mute till sight of Fay Larkin's tear-wet face broke the spell. He leaped forward and his strong hands reached for the woman and the man.

"Jane Withersteen! . . . Lassiter! I have found you!"

"Oh, sir, who are you?" she cried, with rich and deep and quivering voice. "This child came running—screaming. She could not speak. We thought she had gone mad—and escaped to come back to us."

"I am John Shefford," he replied, swiftly. "I am a friend of Bern Venters—of his wife Bess. I learned your story. I came west. I've searched a year. I found Fay. And we've come to take you away."

"You found Fay? But that masked Mormon who forced her to sacrifice herself to save us! . . . What of him? It's not been so many long years—I remember what my father was—and Dyer and Tull—all those cruel churchmen.''

"Waggoner is dead," replied Shefford.

"Dead? She is free! Oh, what—how did he die?''

"He was killed.''

"Who did it?''

"That's no matter," replied Shefford, stonily, and he met her gaze with steady eyes. "He's out of the way. Fay was never his wife. Fay's free. We've come to take you out of the country. We must hurry. We'll be tracked—pursued. But we've horses and an Indian guide. We'll get away . . . I think it better to leave here at once. There's no telling how soon we'll be hunted. Get what things you want to take with you.''

"Oh—yes—Mother Jane, let us hurry!" cried Fay. "I'm so full—I can't talk—my heart hurts so!''

Jane Withersteen's face shone with an exceedingly radiant light, and a glory blended with a terrible fear in her eyes.

"Fay! my little Fay!''

Lassiter had stood there with his mild, clear blue eyes upon Shefford.

"I shore am glad to see you-all," he drawled, and extended his hand as if the meeting were casual. "What'd you say your name was?''

Shefford repeated it as he met the proffered hand.

"How's Bern an' Bess?" Lassiter inquired.

"They were well, prosperous, happy when last I saw them. . . . They had a baby.''

"Now ain't thet fine? . . . Jane, did you hear? Bess has a baby. An', Jane, didn't I always say Bern would come back to get us out? Shore it's just the same.''

How cool, easy, slow, and mild this Lassiter seemed! Had the man grown old, Shefford wondered? The past to him manifestly was only yesterday, and the danger of the present was as nothing. Looking in Lassiter's face, Shefford was baffled. If he had not remembered the greatness of this old gun-man he might have believed that the lonely years in the valley had unbalanced his mind. In an hour like this coolness seemed inexplicable—assuredly would have been impossible in an ordinary man. Yet what hid behind that drawling coolness? What was the meaning of those long, sloping, shadowy lines of the face? What spirit lay in the deep, mild, clear eyes? Shefford experienced a sudden check to what had been his first growing impression of a drifting, broken old man.

"Lassiter, pack what little you can carry—mustn't be much—and we'll get out of here," said Shefford.

"I shore will. Reckon I ain't a-goin' to need a pack-train. We saved the clothes we wore in here. Jane never thought it no use. But I figgered we might need them some day. They won't be stylish, but I reckon they'll do better 'n these skins. An' there's an old coat thet was Venters's.''

The mild, dreamy look became intensified in Lassiter's eyes.

"Did Venters have any hosses when you knowed him?'' he asked.

"He had a farm full of horses,'' replied Shefford, with a smile. "And there were two blacks—the grandest horses I ever saw. Black Star and Night! You remember, Lassiter?''

"Shore. I was wonderin' if he got the blacks out. They must be growin' old by now. . . . Grand hosses, they was. But Jane had another hoss, a big devil of a sorrel. His name was Wrangle. Did Venters ever tell you about him—an' thet race with Jerry Card?''

"A hundred times!'' replied Shefford.

"Wrangle run the blacks off their legs. But Jane never would believe thet. An' I couldn't change her all these years. . . . Reckon mebbe we'll get to see them blacks?''

"Indeed, I hope—I believe you will,'' replied Shefford, feelingly.

"Shore won't thet be fine. Jane, did you hear? Black Star an' Night are livin' an' we'll get to see them.''

But Jane Withersteen only clasped Fay in her arms, and looked at Lassiter with wet and glistening eyes.

Shefford told them to hurry and come to the cliff where the ascent from the valley was to be made. He thought best to leave them alone to make their preparations and bid farewell to the cavern home they had known for so long.

Then he strolled back along the wall, loitering here to gaze into a cave, and there to study crude red paintings in the nooks. And sometimes he halted thoughtfully and did not see anything. At length he rounded a corner of cliff to espy Nas Ta Bega sitting upon the ledge, reposeful and watchful as usual. Shefford told the Indian they would be climbing out soon, and then he sat down to wait and let his gaze rove over the valley.

He might have sat there a long while, so sad and reflective and wondering was his thought, but it seemed a very short time till Fay came in sight with her free, swift grace, and Lassiter and Jane some distance behind. Jane carried a small bundle and Lassiter had a sack over his shoulder that appeared no inconsiderable burden.

"Them beans shore is heavy,'' he drawled, as he deposited the sack upon the ground.

Shefford curiously took hold of the sack and was amazed to find that a second and hard muscular effort was required to lift it.

"Beans?'' he queried.

"Shore,'' replied Lassiter.

"That's the heaviest sack of beans I ever saw. Why—it's not possible it can be . . . Lassiter, we've a long, rough trail. We've got to pack light."

"Wal, I ain't a-goin' to leave this here sack behind. Reckon I've been all of twelve years in fillin' it," he declared, mildly.

Shefford could only stare at him.

"Fay may need them beans," went on Lassiter.

"Why?"

"Because they're gold."

"Gold!" ejaculated Shefford.

"Shore. An' they represent some work. Twelve years of diggin' an' washin'!"

Shefford laughed constrainedly. "Well, Lassiter, that alters the case considerably. A sack of gold nuggets or grains, or beans, as you call them, certainly must not be left behind. . . . Come, now, we'll tackle this climbing job."

He called up to the Indian and, grasping the rope, began to walk up the first slant, and then by dint of hand-over-hand effort and climbing with knees and feet he succeeded, with Nas Ta Bega's help, in making the ledge. Then he let down the rope to haul up the sack and bundle. That done, he directed Fay to fasten the noose round her as he had fixed it before. When she had complied he called to her to hold herself out from the wall while he and Nas Ta Bega hauled her up.

"Hold the rope tight," replied Fay. "I'll walk up."

And to Shefford's amaze and admiration, she virtually walked up that almost perpendicular wall by slipping her hands along the rope and stepping as she pulled herself up. There, if never before, he saw the fruit of her years of experience on steep slopes. Only such experience could have made the feat possible.

Jane had to be hauled up, and the task was a painful one for her. Lassiter's turn came then, and he showed more strength and agility than Shefford had supposed him capable of. From the ledge they turned their attention to the narrow crack with its ladder of sticks. Fay had already ascended and now hung over the rim, her white face and golden hair framed vividly in the narrow stream of blue sky above.

"Mother Jane! Uncle Jim! You are so slow," she called.

"Wal, Fay, we haven't been second cousins to a cañon squirrel all these years," replied Lassiter.

This upper half of the climb bid fair to be as difficult for Jane, if not so painful, as the lower. It was necessary for the Indian to go up and drop the rope, which was looped around her, and then, with him pulling from above and Shefford assisting Jane as she climbed, she was finally gotten up without mishap. When Lassiter reached the level they rested a little while and then faced the great slide of jumbled rocks. Fay led the way, light, supple, tireless, and Shefford never ceased looking at her. At last they surmounted the long slope and, winding along the rim, reached the point where Fay had led out of the cedars.

Nas Ta Bega, then, was the one to whom Shefford looked for every decision or action of the immediate future. The Indian said he had seen a pool of water in a rocky hole, that the day was spent, that here was a little grass for the mustangs, and it would be well to camp right there. So while Nas Ta Bega attended to the mustangs Shefford set about such preparations for camp and supper as their light pack afforded. The question of beds was easily answered, for the mats of soft needles under piñon and cedar would be comfortable places to sleep.

When Shefford felt free again the sun was setting. Lassiter and Jane were walking under the trees. The Indian had returned to camp. But Fay was missing. Shefford imagined he knew where to find her, and upon going to the edge of the forest he saw her sitting on the promontory. He approached her, drawn in spite of a feeling that perhaps he ought to stay away.

"Fay, would you rather be alone?" he asked.

His voice startled her.

"I want you," she replied, and held out her hand.

Taking it in his own, he sat beside her.

The red sun was at their backs. Surprise Valley lay hazy, dusky, shadowy beneath them. The opposite wall seemed fired by crimson flame, save far down at its base, which the sun no longer touched. And the dark line of red slowly rose, encroaching upon the bright crimson. Changing, transparent, yet dusky veils seemed to float between the walls; long, red rays, where the sun shone through notch or crack in the rim, split the darker spaces; deep down at the floor the forest darkened, the strip of aspen paled, the meadow turned gray; and all under the shelves and in the great caverns a purple gloom deepened. Then the sun set. And swiftly twilight was there below while day lingered above. On the opposite wall the fire died and the stone grew cold.

A cañon night-hawk voiced his lonely, weird, and melancholy cry, and it seemed to pierce and mark the silence.

A pale star, peering out of a sky that had begun to turn blue, marked the end of twilight. And all the purple shadows moved and hovered and changed till, softly and mysteriously, they embraced black night.

Beautiful, wild, strange, silent Surprise Valley! Shefford saw it before and beneath him, a dark abyss now, the abode of loneliness. He imagined faintly what was in Fay Larkin's heart. For the last time she had seen the sun set there and night come with its dead silence and sweet mystery and phantom shadows, its velvet blue sky and white trains of stars.

He, who had dreamed and longed and searched, found that the hour had been incalculable for him in its import.

17
The Trail to Nonnezoshe

WHEN Shefford awoke next morning and sat up on his bed of piñon boughs the dawn had broken cold with a ruddy gold brightness under the trees. Nas Ta Bega and Lassiter were busy around a camp-fire; the mustangs were haltered near by; Jane Withersteen combed out her long, tangled tresses with a crude wooden comb; and Fay Larkin was not in sight. As she had been missing from the group at sunset, so she was now at sunrise. Shefford went out to take his last look at Surprise Valley.

On the evening before the valley had been a place of dusky red veils and purple shadows, and now it was pink-walled, clear and rosy and green and white, with wonderful shafts of gold slanting down from the notched eastern rim. Fay stood on the promontory, and Shefford did not break the spell of her silent farewell to her wild home. A strange emotion abided with him and he knew he would always, all his life, regret leaving Surprise Valley.

Then the Indian called.

"Come, Fay," said Shefford, gently.

And she turned away with dark, haunted eyes and a white, still face.

The somber Indian gave a silent gesture for Shefford to make haste. While they had breakfast the mustangs were saddled and packed. And soon all was in readiness for the flight. Fay was given Nack-yal, Jane the saddled horse Shefford had ridden, and Lassiter the Indian's roan. Shefford and Nas Ta Bega were to ride the blanketed mustangs, and the sixth and last one bore the pack. Nas Ta Bega set off, leading this horse; the others of the party lined in behind with Shefford at the rear.

Nas Ta Bega led at a brisk trot, and sometimes, on level stretches of ground, at an easy canter; and Shefford had a grim realization of what this flight was going to be for these three fugitives, now so unaccustomed to riding. Jane and Lassiter, however, needed no watching, and showed they had never forgotten how to manage a horse. The Indian back-trailed yesterday's path for an hour, then headed west to the left, and entered a low pass. All parts of this plateau country looked alike, and Shefford was at some pains to tell the difference of this strange ground from that which he had been over. In another hour they got out of the rugged, broken rock to the wind-worn and smooth, shallow cañon.

Shefford calculated that they were coming to the end of the plateau. The low walls slanted lower; the cañon made a turn; Nas Ta Bega disappeared; and then the others of the party. When Shefford turned the corner of wall he saw a short strip of bare, rocky ground with only sky beyond. The Indian and his followers had halted in a group. Shefford rode to them, halted himself, and in one sweeping glance realized the meaning of their silent gaze. But immediately Nas Ta Bega started down, and the mustangs, without word or touch, followed him. Shefford, however, lingered on the promontory.

His gaze seemed impelled and held by things afar—the great yellow-and-purple corrugated world of distance, now on a level with his eyes. He was drawn by the beauty and the grandeur of that scene and transfixed by the realization that he had dared to venture to find a way through this vast, wild, and unflung fastness. He kept looking afar, sweeping the three-quartered circle of horizon till his judgment of distance was confounded and his sense of proportion dwarfed one moment and magnified the next. Then he withdrew his fascinated gaze to adopt the Indian's method of studying unlimited spaces in the desert—to look with slow, contracted eyes from near to far.

His companions had begun to zigzag down a long slope, bare of rock, with yellow gravel patches showing between the scant strips of green, and here and there a scrub-cedar. Half a mile down, the slope merged into green level. But close, keen gaze made out this level to be a rolling plain, growing darker green, with blue lines of ravines, and thin, undefined spaces that might be mirage. Miles and miles it swept and rolled and heaved to lose its waves in apparent darker level. A round, red rock stood isolated, marking the end of the barren plain, and farther on were other round rocks, all isolated, all of different shape. They resembled huge grazing cattle. But as Shefford gazed, and his sight gained strength from steadily holding it to separate features, these rocks were strangely magnified. They grew and grew into mounds, castles, domes, crags—great, red, wind-carved buttes. One by one they drew his gaze to the wall of upflung rock. He seemed to see a thousand domes of a thousand shapes and colors, and among them a thousand blue clefts, each one a little mark in his sight, yet which he knew was a cañon.

So far he gained some idea of what he saw. But beyond this wide area of curved lines rose another wall, dwarfing the lower, dark red, horizon-long, magnificent in frowning boldness, and because of its limitless deceiving surfaces, breaks, and lines, incomprehensible to the sight of man. Away to the eastward began a winding, ragged, blue line, looping back upon itself, and then winding away again, growing wider and bluer. This line was the San Juan Cañon. Where was Joe Lake at that moment? Had he embarked yet on the river—did that blue line, so faint, so deceiving, hold him and the boat? Almost it was impossible to believe. Shefford followed the blue line all its length, a hundred miles, he fancied, down toward the west where it joined a dark, purple, shadowy cleft. And this was the Grand Cañon of the Colorado. Shefford's eye swept along with that winding mark, farther and farther to the west, round to the left, until the cleft, growing larger and coming closer, losing its deception, was seen to be a wild and winding cañon. Still farther to the left, as he swung in fascinated gaze, it split the wonderful wall—a vast plateau now with great red peaks and yellow mesas. The cañon was full of purple smoke. It turned, it closed, it gaped, it lost itself and showed again in that chaos of a million cliffs. And then farther on it became again a cleft, a purple line, at last to fail entirely in deceiving distance.

Shefford imagined there was no scene in all the world to equal that. The tranquillity of lesser spaces was not here to manifest. Sound, movement, life, seemed to have no fitness here. Ruin was there and desolation and decay. The meaning of the ages was flung at him, and a man became nothing. When he had gazed at the San Juan Cañon he had been appalled at the nature of Joe Lake's Herculean task. He had lost hope, faith. The thing was not possible. But when Shefford gazed at that sublime and majestic wilderness, in which the Grand Cañon was only a dim line, he strangely lost his terror and something else came to him from across the shining spaces. If Nas Ta Bega led them safely down to the river, if Joe Lake met them at the mouth of Nonnezoshe Boco, if they survived the rapids of that terrible gorge, then Shefford would have to face his soul and the meaning of this spirit that breathed on the wind.

He urged his mustang to the descent of the slope, and as he went down, slowly drawing nearer to the other fugitives, his mind alternated between this strange intimation of faith, this subtle uplift of his spirit, and the growing gloom and shadow in his love for Fay Larkin. Not that he loved her less but more! A possible God hovering near him, like the Indian's spirit-step on the trail, made his soul the darker for Fay's crime, and he saw the clearer sight, with deeper sadness, with sterner truth.

More than once the Indian turned on his mustang to look up the slope and the light flashed from his dark, somber face. Shefford instinctively looked back himself, and then realized the unconscious motive of the action. Deep within him there had been a premonition of certain pursuit, and the Indian's reiterated backward glance had at length brought the feeling upward. Thereafter, as they descended, Shefford gradually added to his already wrought emotions a mounting anxiety.

No sign of a trail showed where the base of the slope rolled out to meet the green plain. The earth was gravelly, with dark patches of heavy silt, almost like cinders; and round, black rocks, flinty and glassy, cracked away from the hoofs of the mustangs. There was a level bench a mile wide, then a ravine, and then an ascent, and after that, rounded ridge and ravine, one after the other, like huge swells of a monstrous sea. Indian paint-brush vied in its scarlet hue with the deep magenta of cactus. There was no sage. Soapweed and meager grass and a bunch of cactus here and there lent the green to that barren; and it was green only at a distance. Nas Ta Bega kept on a steady, even trot. The sun climbed. The wind rose and whipped dust from under the mustangs.

Shefford looked back often, and the farther out in the plain he reached the higher loomed the plateau they had descended; and as he faced ahead again the lower sank the red-domed and castled horizon to the fore. The ravines became deeper, with dry rock bottoms, and the ridge-tops sharper, with outcroppings of yellow, crumbling ledges. Once across the central depression of that wide plain a gradual ascent became evident, and the red, round rocks grew clearer in sight, began to rise and shine and grow. And thereafter every slope brought them nearer.

The sun was straight overhead and hot when Nas Ta Bega halted the party under the first lonely scrub-cedar. They all dismounted to stretch their limbs and rest the horses. It was not a talkative group. Lassiter's comments on the never-ending green plain elicited no response. Jane Withersteen looked afar with the past in her eyes. Shefford felt Fay's wistful glance and could not meet it; indeed, he seemed to want to hide something from her. The Indian bent a falcon gaze on the distant slope, and Shefford did not like that intent, searching, steadfast watchfulness. Suddenly Nas Ta Bega stiffened and whipped the halter he held.

"Ugh!" he exclaimed.

All eyes followed the direction of his dark hand. Puffs of dust rose from the base of the long slope they had descended; tiny dark specks moved with the pace of a snail.

"Shadd!" added the Indian.

"I expected it," said Shefford, darkly as he rose.

"An' who's Shadd?" drawled Lassiter in his cool, slow speech.

Briefly Shefford explained, and then, looking at Nas Ta Bega, he added:

"The hardest-riding outfit in the country! We can't get away from them."

Jane Withersteen was silent, but Fay uttered a low cry. Shefford did not look at either of them. The Indian began swiftly to tighten the saddle-cinches of his roan, and Shefford did likewise for Nack-yal. Then Shefford drew his rifle out of the saddle-sheath and Joe Lake's big guns from the saddle-bag.

"Here, Lassiter, maybe you haven't forgotten how to use these," he said.

The old gun-man started as if he had seen ghosts. His hands grew clawlike as he reached for the guns. He threw open the cylinders, spilled out the shells, snapped back the cylinders. Then he went through motions too swift for Shefford to follow. But Shefford heard the hammers falling so swiftly they blended their clicks almost in one sound. Lassiter reloaded the guns with speed comparable with the other actions. A remarkable transformation had come over him. He did not seem the same man. The mild eyes had changed; the long, shadowy, sloping lines were tense cords; and there was a cold, ashy shade on his face.

"Twelve years!" he muttered to himself. "I dropped them old guns back there where I rolled the rock. . . . Twelve years!"

Shefford realized the twelve years were as if they had never been. And he would rather have had this old gun-man with him than a dozen ordinary men.

The Indian spoke rapidly in Navajo, saying that once in the rocks they were safe. Then, after another look at the distant dust-puffs, he wheeled his mustang.

It was doubtful if the party could have kept near him had they been responsible for the gait of their mounts. The fact was that the way the Indian called to his mustang or some leadership in the one he rode drew the others to like trot or climb or canter. For a long time Shefford did not turn round; he knew what to expect. And when he did turn he was startled at the gain made by the pursuers. But he was encouraged as well by the looming, red, rounded peaks seemingly now so close. He could see the dark splits between the sloping curved walls, the piñon patches in the amphitheater under the circled walls. That was a wild place they were approaching, and once in there, he believed pursuit would be useless. However, there were miles to go still, and those hard-riding devils behind made alarming decrease in the intervening distance. Shefford could see the horses plainly now. How they made the dust fly! He counted up to six—and then the dust and moving line caused the others to be indistinguishable.

At last only a long, gently rising slope separated the fugitives from that labyrinthine network of wildly carved rock. But it was the clear air that made the distance seem short. Mile after mile the mustangs climbed, and when they were perhaps half-way across that last slope to the rocks the first horse of the pursuers mounted to the level behind. In a few moments the whole band was strung out in sight. Nas Ta Bega kept his mustang at a steady walk, in spite of the gaining pursuers. There came a point, however, when the Indian, reaching comparatively level ground, put his mount to a swinging canter. The other mustangs broke into the same gait.

It became a race then, with the couple of miles between fugitives and pursuers only imperceptibly lessened. Nas Ta Bega had saved his mustangs and Shadd had ridden his to the limit. Shefford kept looking back, gripping his rifle, hoping it would not come to a fight, yet slowly losing that reluctance.

Sage began to show on the slope, and other kinds of brush and cedars straggled everywhere. The great rocks loomed closer, the red color mixed with yellow, and the slopes lengthening out, not so steep, yet infinitely longer than they had seemed at a distance.

Shefford ceased to feel the dry wind in his face. They were already in the lee of the wall. He could see the rock-squirrels scampering to their holes. The mustangs valiantly held to the gait, and at last the Indian disappeared between two rounded corners of cliff. The others were close behind. Shefford wheeled once more. Shadd and his gang were a mile in the rear, but coming fast, despite winded horses.

Shefford rode around the wall into a widening space thick with cedars. It ended in a bare slope of smooth rock. Here the Indian dismounted. When the others came up with him he told them to lead their horses and follow. Then he began the ascent of the rock.

It was smooth and hard, though not slippery. There was not a crack. Shefford did not see a broken piece of stone. Nas Ta Bega climbed straight up for a while, and then wound around a swell, to turn this way and that, always going up. Shefford began to see similar mounds of rock all around him, of every shape that could be called a curve. There were yellow domes far above, and small red domes far below. Ridges ran from one hill of rock to another. There were no abrupt breaks, but holes and pits and caves were everywhere, and occasionally, deep down, an amphitheater green with cedar and piñon. The Indian appeared to have a clear idea of where he wanted to go, though there was no vestige of a trail on those bare slopes. At length Shefford was high enough to see back upon the plain, but the pursuers were no longer in sight.

Nas Ta Bega led to the top of that wall, only to disclose to his followers another and a higher wall beyond, with a ridged, bare, wild, and scalloped depression between. Here footing began to be precarious for both man and beast. When the ascent of the second wall began it was necessary to zigzag up, slowly and carefully, taking advantage of every level bulge or depression. They must have consumed half an hour mounting this slope to the summit. Once there, Shefford drew a sharp breath with both backward and forward glances. Shadd and his gang, in single file, showed dark upon the bare stone ridge behind. And to the fore there twisted and dropped and curved the most dangerous slopes Shefford had ever seen. The fugitives had reached the height of stone wall, of the divide, and many of the drops upon this side were perpendicular and too steep to see the bottom.

Nas Ta Bega led along the ridge-top and then started down, following the waves in the rock. He came out upon a round promontory from which there could not have been any turning of a horse. The long slant leading down was at an angle Shefford declared impossible for the animals. Yet the Indian started down. His mustang needed urging, but at last edged upon the steep descent. Shefford and the others had to hold back and wait. It was thrilling to see the intelligent mustang. He did not step. He slid his fore hoofs a few inches at a time and kept directly behind the Indian. If he fell he would knock Nas Ta Bega off his feet and they would both roll down together. There was no doubt in Shefford's mind that the mustang knew this as well as the Indian. Foot by foot they worked down to a swelling bulge, and here Nas Ta Bega left his mustang and came back for the pack-horse. It was even more difficult to get this beast down. Then the Indian called for Lassiter and Jane and Fay to come down. Shefford began to keep a sharp lookout behind and above, and did not see how the three fared on the slope, but evidently there was no mishap. Nas Ta Bega mounted the slope again, and at the moment sight of Shadd's dark bays silhouetted against the sky caused Shefford to call out:

"We've got to hurry!"

The Indian led one mustang and called to the others. Shefford stepped close behind. They went down in single file, inch by inch, foot by foot, and safely reached the comparative level below.

"Shadd's gang are riding their horses up and down these walls!" exclaimed Shefford.

"Shore," replied Lassiter.

Both the women were silent.

Nas Ta Bega led the way swiftly to the right. He rounded a huge dome, climbed a low, rolling ridge, descended and ascended, and came out upon the rim of a steep-walled amphitheater. Along the rim was a yard-wide level, with the chasm to the left and steep slope to the right. There was no time to flinch at the danger, when an even greater danger menaced from the rear. Nas Ta Bega led, and his mustang kept at his heels. One misstep would have plunged the animal to his death. But he was surefooted and his confidence helped the others. At the apex of the curve the only course led away from the rim, and here there was no level. Four of the mustangs slipped and slid down the smooth rock until they stopped in a shallow depression. It cost time to get them out, to straighten pack and saddles. Shefford thought he heard a yell in the rear, but he could not see anything of the gang.

They rounded this precipice only to face a worse one. Shefford's nerve was sorely tried when he saw steep slants everywhere, all apparently leading down into chasms, and no place a man, let alone a horse, could put a foot with safety. Nevertheless the imperturbable Indian never slacked his pace. Always he appeared to find a way, and he never had to turn back. His winding course, however, did not now cover much distance in a straight line, and herein lay the greatest peril. Any moment Shadd and his men might come within range.

Upon a particularly tedious and dangerous side of rocky hill the fugitives lost so much time that Shefford grew exceedingly alarmed. Still, they accomplished it without accident, and their pursuers did not heave in sight. Perhaps they were having trouble in a bad place.

The afternoon was waning. The red sun hung low above the yellow mesa to the left, and there was a perceptible shading of light.

At last Nas Ta Bega came to a place that halted him. It did not look so bad as places they had successfully passed. Yet upon closer study Shefford did not see how they were to get around the neck of the gully at their feet. Presently the Indian put the bridle over the head of his mustang and left him free. He did likewise for two more mustangs, while Lassiter and Shefford rendered a like service to theirs. Then the Indian started down, with his mustang following him. The pack-animal came next, then Fay and Nack-yal, then Lassiter and his mount, with Jane and hers next, and Shefford last. They followed the Indian, picking their steps swiftly, looking nowhere except at the stone under their feet. The right side of the chasm was rimmed, the curve at the head crossed, and then the real peril of this trap had to be faced. It was a narrow slant of ledge, doubling back parallel with the course already traversed.

A sharp warning cry from Nas Ta Bega scarcely prepared Shefford for hoarse yells, and then a rattling rifle-volley from the top of the slope opposite. Bullets thudded on the cliff, whipped up red dust, and spanged and droned away.

Fay Larkin screamed and staggered back against the wall. Nack-yal was hit, and with frightened snort he reared, pawed the air, and came down, pounding the stone. The mustang behind him went to his knees, sank with his head over the rim, and, slipping off, plunged into the depths. In an instant a dull crash came up.

For a moment there was imminent peril for the horses, more in the yawning hole than in the spanging of badly aimed bullets. Lassiter drew Jane up a little slope out of the way of the frightened mustangs, and Shefford, risking his neck, rushed to Fay. She was holding her arm, which was bleeding. Unheeding the rain of bullets, he half carried, half dragged her along the slope of the low bluff, where he hid behind a corner till the Indian drove the mustangs round it. Shefford's swift fingers were wet and red with the blood from Fay's arm when he had bound the wound with his scarf. Lassiter had gotten around with Jane and was calling Shefford to hurry.

It had been Shefford's idea to halt there and fight. But he did not want to send Fay on alone, so he hurried ahead with her. The Indian had the horses going fast on a long level, overhung by bulging wall. Lassiter and Jane were looking back. Shefford, becoming aware of a steep slope to his left, looked down to see a narrow chasm and great crevices in the cliffs, with bunches of cedars here and there.

Presently Nas Ta Bega disappeared with the mustangs. He had evidently turned off to go down behind the split cliffs. Shefford and Fay caught up with Lassiter and Jane, and, panting, hurrying, looking backward and then forward, they kept on, as best they could, in the Indian's course. Shefford made sure they had lost him, when he appeared down to the left. Then they all ran to catch up with him. They went around the chasm, and then through one of the narrow cracks to come out upon the rim, among cedars. Here the Indian waited for them. He pointed down another long swell of naked stone to a narrow green split which was

evidently different from all these curved pits and holes and abysses, for this one
had straight walls and wound away out of sight. It was the head of a cañon.

"Nonnezoshe Boco!" said the Indian.

"Nas Ta Bega, go on!" replied Shefford. "When Shadd comes out on that
slope above he can't see you—where you go down. Hurry on with the horses
and women. Lassiter, you go with them. And if Shadd passes me and comes
up with you—do your best . . . I'm going to ambush that Piute and his gang!"

"Shore you've picked out a good place," replied Lassiter.

In another moment Shefford was alone. He heard the light, soft pat and slide
of the hoofs of the mustangs as they went down. Presently that sound ceased.

He looked at the red stain on his hands—from the blood of the girl he loved.
And he had to stifle a terrible wrath that shook his frame. In regard to Shadd's
pursuit, it had not been blood that he had feared, but capture for Fay. He and
Nas Ta Bega might have expected a shot if they resisted, but to wound that
unfortunate girl—it made a tiger out of him. When he had stilled the emotions
that weakened and shook him and reached cold and implacable control of himself,
he crawled under the cedars to the rim and, well hidden, he watched and waited.

Shadd appeared to be slow for the first time since he had been sighted. With
keen eyes Shefford watched the corner where he and the others had escaped from
that murderous volley. But Shadd did not come.

The sun had lost its warmth and was tipping the lofty mesa to his right. Soon
twilight would make travel on those walls more perilous and darkness would
make it impossible. Shadd must hurry or abandon the pursuit for that day.
Shefford found himself grimly hopeful.

Suddenly he heard the click of hoofs. It came, faint yet clear, on the still air.
He glued his sight upon that corner where he expected the pursuers to appear.
More cracks of hoofs pierced his ear, clearer and sharper this time. Presently
he gathered that they could not possibly come from beyond the corner he was
watching. So he looked far to the left of that place, seeing no one, then far to
the right. Out over a bulge of stone he caught sight of the bobbing head of a
horse—then another—and still another.

He was astounded. Shadd had gone below that place where the attack had
been made and he had come up this steep slope. More horses appeared—to the
number of eight. Shefford easily recognized a low, broad, squat rider to be
Shadd. Assuredly the Piute did not know this country. Possibly, however, he
had feared an ambush. But Shefford grew convinced that Shadd had not expected
an ambush, or at least did not fear it, and had mistaken the Indian's course.
Moreover, if he led his gang a few rods farther up that slope he would do worse
than make a mistake—he would be facing a double peril.

What fearless horsemen these Indians were! Shadd was mounted, as were
three others of his gang. Evidently the white men, the outlaws, were the ones

on foot. Shefford thrilled and his veins stung when he saw these pursuers come passing what he considered the danger mark. But manifestly they could not see their danger. Assuredly they were aware of the chasm; however, the level upon which they were advancing narrowed gradually, and they could not tell that very soon they could not go any farther nor could they turn back. The alternative was to climb the slope, and that was a desperate chance.

They came up, now about on a level with Shefford, and perhaps three hundred yards distant. He gripped his rifle with a fatal assurance that he could kill one of them now. Still he waited. Curiosity consumed him because every foot they advanced heightened their peril. Shefford wondered if Shadd would have chosen that course if he had not supposed the Navajo had chosen it first. It was plain that one of the walking Piutes stooped now and then to examine the rock. He was looking for some faint sign of a horse track.

Shadd halted within two hundred yards of where Shefford lay hidden. His keen eye had caught the significance of the narrowing level before he had reached the end. He pointed and spoke. Shefford heard his voice. The others replied. They all looked up at the steep slope, down into the chasm right below them, and across into the cedars. The Piute in the rear succeeded in turning his horse, went back, and began to circle up the slope. The others entered into an argument and they became more closely grouped upon the narrow bench. Their mustangs were lean, wiry, wild, vicious, and Shefford calculated grimly upon what a stampede might mean in that position.

Then Shadd turned his mustang up the slope. Like a goat he climbed. Another Indian in the rear succeeded in pivoting his steed and started back, apparently to circle round and up. The others of the gang appeared uncertain. They yelled hoarsely at Shadd, who halted on the steep slant some twenty paces above them. He spoke and made motions that evidently meant the climb was easy enough. It looked easy for him. His dark face flashed red in the rays of the sun.

At this critical moment Shefford decided to fire. He meant to kill Shadd, hoping if the leader was gone the others would abandon the pursuit. The rifle wavered a little as he aimed, then grew still. He fired. Shadd never flinched. But the fiery mustang, perhaps wounded, certainly terrified, plunged down with piercing, horrid scream. Shadd fell under him. Shrill yells rent the air. Like a thunderbolt the sliding horse was upon men and animals below.

A heavy shock, wild snorts, upflinging heads and hoofs, a terrible tramping, thudding, shrieking mêlée, then a brown, twisting, tangled mass shot down the slant over the rim!

Shefford dazedly thought he saw men running. He did see plunging horses. One slipped, fell, rolled, and went into the chasm.

Then up from the depths came a crash, a long, slipping roar. In another instant there was a lighter crash and a lighter sliding roar.

Two horses, shaking, paralyzed with fear, were left upon the narrow level. Beyond them a couple of men were crawling along the stone. Up on the level stood the two Indians, holding down frightened horses, and staring at the fatal slope.

And Shefford lay there under the cedar, in the ghastly grip of the moment, hardly comprehending that his ill-aimed shot had been a thunderbolt.

He did not think of shooting at the Piutes; they, however, recovering from their shock, evidently feared the ambush, for they swiftly drew up the slope and passed out of sight. The frightened horses below whistled and tramped along the lower level, finally vanishing. There was nothing left on the bare wall to prove to Shefford that it had been the scene of swift and tragic death. He leaned from his covert and peered over the rim. Hundreds of feet below he saw dark growths of piñons. There was no sign of a pile of horses and men, and then he realized that he could not tell the number that had perished. The swift finale had been as stunning to him as if lightning had struck near him.

Suddenly it flashed over him what state of suspense and torture Fay and Jane must be in at that very moment. And, leaping up, he ran out of the cedars to the slope behind and hurried down at risk of limb. The sun had set by this time. He hoped he could catch up with the party before dark. He went straight down, and the end of the slope was a smooth, low wall. The Indian must have descended with the horses at some other point. The cañon was about fifty yards wide and it headed under the great slope of Navajo Mountain. These smooth, rounded walls appeared to end at its low rim.

Shefford slid down upon a grassy bank, and finding the tracks of the horses, he followed them. They led along the wall. As soon as he had assured himself that Nas Ta Bega had gone down the cañon he abandoned the tracks and pushed ahead swiftly. He heard the soft rush of running water. In the center of the cañon wound heavy lines of bright-green foliage, bordering a rocky brook. The air was close, warm, and sweet with perfume of flowers. The walls were low and shelving, and soon lost that rounded appearance peculiar to the wind-worn slopes above. Shefford came to where the horses had plowed down a gravelly bank into the clear, swift water of the brook. The little pools of water were still muddy. Shefford drank, finding the water cold and sweet, without the bitter bite of alkali. He crossed and pushed on, running on the grassy levels. Flowers were everywhere, but he did not notice them particularly. The cañon made many leisurely turns, and its size, if it enlarged at all, was not perceptible to him yet. The rims above him were perhaps fifty feet high. Cottonwood-trees began to appear along the brook, and blossoming buck-brush in the corners of wall.

He had traveled perhaps a mile when Nas Ta Bega, appearing to come out of the thicket, confronted him.

"Hello!" called Shefford. "Where're Fay—and the others?"

The Indian made a gesture that signified the rest of the party were beyond a little way. Shefford took Nas Ta Bega's arm, and as they walked, and he panted for breath, he told what had happened back on the slopes.

The Indian made one of his singular speaking sweeps of hand, and he scrutinized Shefford's face, but he received the news in silence. They turned a corner of wall, crossed a wide, shallow, boulder-strewn place in the brook, and mounted the bank to a thicket. Beyond this, from a clump of cottonwoods, Lassiter strode out with a gun in each hand. He had been hiding.

"Shore I'm glad to see you," he said, and the eyes that piercingly fixed on Shefford were now as keen as formerly they had been mild.

"Gone! Lassiter—they're gone," broke out Shefford. "Where's Fay—and Jane?"

Lassiter called, and presently the women came out of the thick brake, and Fay bounded forward with her swift stride, while Jane followed with eager step and anxious face. Then they all surrounded Shefford.

"It was Shadd—and his gang," panted Shefford. "Eight in all. Three or four Piutes—the others outlaws. They lost track of us. Went below the place—where they shot at us. And they came up—on a bad slope."

Shefford described the slope and the deep chasm and how Shadd led up to the point where he saw his mistake and then how the catastrophe fell.

"I shot—and missed," repeated Shefford, with the sweat in beads on his pale face. "I missed Shadd. Maybe I hit the horse. He plunged—reared—fell back— a terrible fall—right upon that bunch of horses and men below. . . . In a horrible, wrestling, screaming tangle they slid over the rim! I don't know how many. I saw some men running along. I saw three other horses plunging. One slipped and went over . . . I have no idea how many, but Shadd and some of his gang went to destruction."

"Shore thet's fine!" said Lassiter. "But mebbe I won't get to use them guns, after all."

"Hardly on that gang," laughed Shefford. "The two Piutes and what others escaped turned back. Maybe they'll meet a posse of Mormons—for of course the Mormons will track us, too—and come back to where Shadd lost his life. That's an awful place. Even the Piute got lost—couldn't follow Nas Ta Bega. It would take any pursuers some time to find how we got in here. I believe we need not fear further pursuit. Certainly not to-night or to-morrow. Then we'll be far down the cañon."

When Shefford concluded his earnest remarks the faces of Fay and Jane had lost the signs of suppressed dread.

"Nas Ta Bega, make camp here," said Shefford. "Water—wood—grass— why, this's something like. . . . Fay, how's your arm?"

"It hurts," she replied, simply.

"Come with me down to the brook and let me wash and bind it properly."

They went, and she sat upon a stone while he knelt beside her and untied his scarf from her arm. As the blood had hardened, it was necessary to slit her sleeve to the shoulder. Using his scarf, he washed the blood from the wound, and found it to be merely a cut, a groove, on the surface.

"That's nothing," Shefford said, lightly. "It'll heal in a day. But there'll always be a scar. And when we—we get back to civilization, and you wear a pretty gown without sleeves, people will wonder what made this mark on your beautiful arm."

Fay looked at him with wonderful eyes. "Do women wear gowns without sleeves?" she asked.

"They do."

"Have I a—beautiful arm?"

She stretched it out, white, blue-veined, the skin fine as satin, the lines graceful and flowing, a round, firm, strong arm.

"The most beautiful I ever saw," he replied.

But the pleasure his compliment gave her was not communicated to him. His last impression of that right arm had been of its strength, and his mind flashed with lightning swiftness to a picture that haunted him—Waggoner lying dead on the porch with that powerfully driven knife in his breast. Shefford shuddered through all his being. Would this phantom come often to him like that? Hurriedly he bound up her arm with the scarf and did not look at her, and was conscious that she felt a subtle change in him.

The short twilight ended with the fugitives comfortable in a camp that for natural features could not have been improved upon. Darkness found Fay and Jane asleep on a soft mossy bed, a blanket tucked around them, and their faces still and beautiful in the flickering camp-fire light. Lassiter did not linger long awake. Nas Ta Bega, seeing Shefford's excessive fatigue, urged him to sleep. Shefford demurred, insisting that he share the night-watch. But Nas Ta Bega, by agreeing that Shefford might have the following night's duty, prevailed upon him.

Shefford seemed to shut his eyes upon darkness and to open them immediately to the light. The stream of blue sky above, the gold tints on the western rim, the rosy, brightening colors down in the cañon, were proofs of the sunrise. This morning Nas Ta Bega proceeded leisurely, and his manner was comforting. When all was in readiness for a start he gave the mustang he had ridden to Shefford, and walked, leading the pack-animal.

The mode of travel here was a selection of the best levels, the best places to cross the brook, the best banks to climb, and it was a process of continual repetition. As the Indian picked out the course and the mustangs followed his lead there was nothing for Shefford to do but take his choice between reflection that seemed predisposed toward gloom and an absorption in the beauty, color, wildness, and changing character of Nonnezoshe Boco.

Assuredly his experience in the desert did not count in it a trip down into a strange, beautiful, lost cañon such as this. It did not widen, though the walls grew higher. They began to lean and bulge, and the narrow strip of sky above resembled a flowing blue river. Huge caverns had been hollowed out by some work of nature, what, he could not tell, though he was sure it could not have been wind. And when the brook ran close under one of these overhanging places the running water made a singular, indescribable sound. A crack from a hoof on a stone rang like a hollow bell and echoed from wall to wall. And the croak of a frog—the only living creature he had so far noted in the cañon—was a weird and melancholy thing.

Fay rode close to him, and his heart seemed to rejoice when she spoke, when she showed how she wanted to be near him, yet, try as he might, he could not respond. His speech to her—what little there was—did not come spontaneously. And he suffered a remorse that he could not be honestly natural to her. Then he would drive away the encroaching gloom, trusting that a little time would dispel it.

"We are deeper down than Surprise Valley," said Fay.

"How do you know?" he asked.

"Here are the pink and yellow sago-lilies. You remember we went once to find the white ones? I have found white lilies in Surprise Valley, but never any pink or yellow."

Shefford had seen flowers all along the green banks, but he had not marked the lilies. Here he dismounted and gathered several. They were larger than the white ones of higher altitudes, of the same exquisite beauty and fragility, of such rare pink and yellow hues as he had never seen. He gave the flowers to Fay.

"They bloom only where it's always summer," she said.

That expressed their nature. They were the orchids of the summer cañons. They stood up everywhere starlike out of the green. It was impossible to prevent the mustangs treading them under hoof. And as the cañon deepened, and many little springs added their tiny volume to the brook, every grassy bench was dotted with lilies, like a green sky star-spangled. And this increasing luxuriance manifested itself in the banks of purple moss and clumps of lavender daisies and great clusters of yellow violets. The brook was lined by blossoming buck-rush; the rocky corners showed the crimson and magenta of cactus; ledges were green with shining moss that sparkled with little white flowers. The hum of bees filled the air.

But by and by this green and colorful and verdant beauty, the almost level floor of the cañon, the banks of soft earth, the thickets and the clumps of cottonwoods, the shelving caverns and the bulging walls—these features gradually

were lost, and Nonnezoshe Boco began to deepen in bare red and white stone
steps, the walls sheered away from one another, breaking into sections and
ledges, and rising higher and higher, and there began to be manifested a dark
and solemn concordance with the nature that had created this rent in the earth.

There was a stretch of miles where steep steps in hard red rock alternated with
long levels of round boulders. Here one by one the mustangs went lame. And
the fugitives, dismounting to spare the faithful beasts, slipped and stumbled over
these loose and treacherous stones. Fay was the only one who did not show
distress. She was glad to be on foot again and the rolling boulders were as stable
as solid rock for her.

The hours passed; the toil increased; the progress diminished; one of the
mustangs failed entirely and was left; and all the while the dimensions of Nonnezoshe Boco magnified and its character changed. It became a thousand-foot
walled cañon, leaning, broken, threatening, with great yellow slides blocking
passage, with huge sections split off from the main wall, with immense dark
and gloomy caverns. Strangely, it had no intersecting cañons. It jealously guarded
its secret. Its unusual formations of cavern and pillar and half-arch led the mind
to expect any monstrous stone-shape left by an avalanche or cataclysm.

Down and down the fugitives toiled. And now the stream-bed was bare of
boulders, and the banks of earth. The floods that had rolled down that cañon
had here borne away every loose thing. All the floor was bare red and white
stone, polished, glistening, slippery, affording treacherous foothold. And the
time came when Nas Ta Bega abandoned the stream-bed to take to the rock-
strewn and cactus-covered ledges above.

Jane gave out and had to be assisted upon the weary mustang. Fay was
persuaded to mount Nack-yal again. Lassiter plodded along. The Indian bent
tired steps far in front. And Shefford traveled on after him, footsore and hot.

The cañon widened ahead into a great, ragged, iron-hued amphitheater, and
from there apparently turned abruptly at right angles. Sunset rimmed the walls.
Shefford wondered dully when the Indian would halt to camp. And he dragged
himself onward with eyes down on the rough ground.

When he raised them again the Indian stood on a point of slope with folded
arms, gazing down where the cañon veered. Something in Nas Ta Bega's pose
quickened Shefford's pulse and then his steps. He reached the Indian and the
point where he, too, could see beyond that vast jutting wall that had obstructed
his view.

A mile beyond all was bright with the colors of sunset, and spanning the
cañon in the graceful shape and beautiful hues of a rainbow was a magnificent
stone bridge.

"Nonnezoshe!" exclaimed the Navajo, with a deep and sonorous roll in his
voice.

18

At the Foot of the Rainbow

THE rainbow bridge was the one great natural phenomenon, the one grand spectacle, which Shefford had ever seen that did not at first give vague disappointment, a confounding of reality, a disenchantment of contrast with what the mind had conceived.

But this thing was glorious. It silenced him, yet did not awe or stun. His body and brain, weary and dull from the toil of travel, received a singular and revivifying freshness. He had a strange, mystic perception of this rosy-hued stupendous arch of stone, as if in a former life it had been a goal he could not reach. This wonder of nature, though all-satisfying, all-fulfilling to his artist's soul, could not be a resting-place for him, a destination where something awaited him, a height he must scale to find peace, the end of his strife. But it seemed all these. He could not understand his perception or his emotion. Still, here at last, apparently, was the rainbow of his boyish dreams and of his manhood—a rainbow magnified even beyond those dreams, no longer transparent and ethereal, but solidified, a thing of ages, sweeping up majestically from the red walls, its iris-hued arch against the blue sky.

Nas Ta Bega led on down the ledge and Shefford plodded thoughtfully after him. The others followed. A jutting corner of wall again hid the cañon. The Indian was working round to circle the huge amphitheater. It was slow, irritating, strenuous toil, for the way was on a steep slant, rough and loose and dragging. The rocks were as hard and jagged as lava. And the cactus further hindered progress. When at last the long half-circle had been accomplished the golden and rosy lights had faded.

Again the cañon opened to view. All the walls were pale and steely and the stone bridge loomed dark. Nas Ta Bega said camp would be made at the bridge, which was now close. Just before they reached it the Navajo halted with one of his singular actions. Then he stood motionless. Shefford realized that Nas Ta Bega was saying his prayer to this great stone god. Presently the Indian motioned for Shefford to lead the others and the horses on under the bridge. Shefford did so, and, upon turning, was amazed to see the Indian climbing the steep and difficult slope on the other side. All the party watched him until he disappeared behind the huge base of cliff that supported the arch. Shefford selected a level place for camp, some few rods away, and here, with Lassiter, unsaddled and unpacked the lame, drooping mustangs. When this was done twilight had fallen. Nas Ta Bega appeared, coming down the steep slope on this side of the bridge. Then Shefford divined why the Navajo had made that arduous climb. He would not go under the bridge. Nonnezoshe was a Navajo god. And Nas Ta Bega, though educated as a white man, was true to the superstition of his ancestors.

Nas Ta Bega turned the mustangs loose to fare for what scant grass grew on bench and slope. Firewood was even harder to find than grass. When the camp duties had been performed and the simple meal eaten, there was gloom gathering in the cañon and the stars had begun to blink in the pale strip of blue above the lofty walls. The place was oppressive and the fugitives mostly silent. Shefford spread a bed of blankets for the women, and Jane at once lay wearily down. Fay stood beside the flickering fire, and Shefford felt her watching him. He was conscious of a desire to get away from her haunting gaze. To the gentle good-night he bade her she made no response.

Shefford moved away into a strange dark shadow cast by the bridge against the pale starlight. It was a weird, black belt, where he imagined he was invisible, but out of which he could see. There was a slab of rock near the foot of the bridge, and here Shefford composed himself to watch, to feel, to think the unknown thing that seemed to be inevitably coming to him.

A slight stiffening of his neck made him aware that he had been continually looking up at the looming arch. And he found that insensibly it had changed and grown. It had never seemed the same any two moments, but that was not what he meant. Near at hand it was too vast a thing for immediate comprehension. He wanted to ponder on what had formed it—to reflect upon its meaning as to age and force of nature, yet all he could do at each moment was to see. White stars hung along the dark curved line. The rim of the arch seemed to shine. The moon must be up there somewhere. The far side of the cañon was now a blank, black wall. Over its towering rim showed a pale glow. It brightened. The shades in the cañon lightened, then a white disk of moon peered over the dark line. The bridge turned to silver, and the gloomy, shadowy belt it had cast blanched and vanished.

Shefford became aware of the presence of Nas Ta Bega. Dark, silent, statu-esque, with inscrutable eyes uplifted, with all that was spiritual of the Indian suggested by a somber and tranquil knowledge of his place there, he represented the same to Shefford as a solitary figure of human life brought out the greatness of a great picture. Nonnezoshe Boco needed life, wild life, life of its millions of years—and here stood the dark and silent Indian.

There was a surge in Shefford's heart and in his mind a perception of a moment of incalculable change to his soul. And at that moment Fay Larkin stole like a phantom to his side and stood there with her uncovered head shining and her white face lovely in the moonlight.

"May I stay with you—a little?" she asked, wistfully. "I can't sleep."

"Surely you may," he replied. "Does your arm hurt too badly, or are you too tired to sleep?"

"No—it's this place. I—I—can't tell you how I feel."

But the feeling was there in her eyes for Shefford to read. Had he too great an emotion—did he read too much—did he add from his soul? For him the wild, starry, haunted eyes mirrored all that he had seen and felt under Nonnezoshe. And for herself they shone eloquently of courage and love.

"I need to talk—and I don't know how," she said.

He was silent, but he took her hands and drew her closer.

"Why are you so—so different?" she asked, bravely.

"Different?" he echoed.

"Yes. You are kind—you speak the same to me as you used to. But since we started you've been different, somehow."

"Fay, think how hard and dangerous the trip's been! I've been worried—and sick with dread—with— Oh, you can't imagine the strain I'm under! How could I be my old self?"

"It isn't worry I mean."

He was too miserable to try to find out what she did mean; besides, he believed, if he let himself think about it, he would know what troubled her.

"I—I am almost happy," she said, softly.

"Fay! . . . Aren't you at all afraid?"

"No. You'll take care of me. . . . Do—do you love me—like you did before?"

"Why, child! Of course—I love you," he replied, brokenly, and he drew her closer. He had never embraced her, never kissed her. But there was a whiteness about her then—a wraith—a something from her soul, and he could only gaze at her.

"I love you," she whispered. "I thought I knew it that—that night. But I'm only finding it out now. . . . And somehow I had to tell you here."

"Fay, I haven't said much to you," he said, hurriedly, huskily. "I haven't had a chance. I love you. I—I ask you—will you be my wife?"

"Of course," she said, simply, but the white, moon-blanched face colored with a dark and leaping blush.

"We'll be married as soon as we get out of the desert," he went on. "And we'll forget—all—all that's happened. You're so young. You'll forget."

"I'd forgotten already, till this difference came in you. And pretty soon—when I can say something more to you—I'll forget all except Surprise Valley—and my evenings in the starlight with you."

"Say it then—quick!"

She was leaning against him, holding his hands in her strong clasp, soulful, tender, almost passionate.

"You couldn't help it. . . . I'm to blame. . . . I remember what I said."

"What?" he queried in amaze.

" *'You can kill him!'* . . . I said that. I made you kill him."

"Kill—whom?" cried Shefford.

"Waggoner. I'm to blame. . . . That must be what's made you different. And, oh, I've wanted you to know it's all my fault. . . . But I wouldn't be sorry if you weren't. . . . I'm glad he's dead."

"*You—think—I—*" Shefford's gasping whisper failed in the shock of the revelation that Fay believed he had killed Waggoner. Then with the inference came the staggering truth—her guiltlessness; and a paralyzing joy held him stricken.

A powerful hand fell upon Shefford's shoulder, startling him. Nas Ta Bega stood there, looking down upon him and Fay. Never had the Indian seemed so dark, inscrutable of face. But in his magnificent bearing, in the spirit that Shefford sensed in him, there were nobility and power and a strange pride.

The Indian kept one hand on Shefford's shoulder, and with the other he struck himself on the breast. The action was that of an Indian, impressive and stern, significant of an Indian's prowess.

"My God!" breathed Shefford, very low.

"Oh, what does he mean?" cried Fay.

Shefford held her with shaking hands, trying to speak, to fight a way out of these stultifying emotions.

"Nas Ta Bega—you heard. She thinks—I killed Waggoner!"

All about the Navajo then was dark and solemn disproof of her belief. He did not need to speak. His repetition of that savage, almost boastful blow on his breast added only to the dignity, and not to the denial, of a warrior.

"Fay, he means he killed the Mormon," said Shefford. "He must have, for *I* did not!"

"Ah!" murmured Fay, and she leaned to him with passionate, quivering gladness. It was the woman—the human—the soul born in her that came uppermost then; now, when there was no direct call to the wild and elemental in her nature, she showed a heart above revenge, the instinct of a saving right, of truth as Shefford knew them. He took her into his arms and never had he loved her so well.

"Nas Ta Bega, you killed the Mormon," declared Shefford, with a voice that had gained strength. No silent Indian suggestion of a deed would suffice in that moment. Shefford needed to hear the Navajo speak—to have Fay hear him speak. "Nas Ta Bega, I know—I understand. But tell her. Speak so she will know. Tell it as a white man would!"

"I heard her cry out," replied the Indian, in his slow English. "I waited. When he came I killed him."

A poignant why was wrenched from Shefford. Nas Ta Bega stood silent.

"*Bi Nai!*" And when that sonorous Indian name rolled in dignity from his lips he silently stalked away into the gloom. That was his answer to the white man.

Shefford bent over Fay, and as the strain on him broke he held her closer and closer and his tears streamed down and his voice broke in exclamations of tenderness and thanksgiving. It did not matter what she had thought, but she must never know what he had thought. He clasped her as something precious he had lost and regained. He was shaken with a passion of remorse. How could he have believed Fay Larkin guilty of murder? Women less wild and less justified than she had been driven to such a deed, yet how could he have believed it of her, when for two days he had been with her, had seen her face, and deep into her eyes? There was a mystery in his very blindness. He cast the whole thought from him for ever. There was no shadow between Fay and him. He had found her. He had saved her. She was free. She was innocent. And suddenly, as he seemed delivered from contending tumults within, he became aware that it was no unresponsive creature he had folded to his breast.

He became suddenly alive to the warm, throbbing contact of her bosom, to her strong arms clinging round his neck, to her closed eyes, to the rapt whiteness of her face. And he bent to cold lips that seemed to receive his first kisses as new and strange; but tremulously changed, at last to meet his own, and then to burn with sweet and thrilling fire.

"My darling, my dream's come true," he said. "You are my treasure. I found you here at the foot of the rainbow! . . . What if it is a stone rainbow—if all is not as I had dreamed? I followed a gleam. And it's led me to love and faith!"

Hours afterward Shefford walked alone to and fro under the bridge. His trouble had given place to serenity. But this night of nights he must live out wide-eyed to its end.

The moon had long since crossed the streak of star-fired blue above and the cañon was black in shadow. At times a current of wind, with all the strangeness of that strange country in its hollow moan, rushed through the great stone arch. At other times there was silence such as Shefford imagined dwelt deep under this rocky world. At still other times an owl hooted, and the sound was nameless. But it had a mocking echo that never ended. An echo of light, silence, gloom, melancholy death, age, eternity!

The Indian lay asleep with his dark face upturned, and the other sleepers lay calm and white in the starlight.

Shefford saw in them the meaning of life and the past—the illimitable train

of faces that had shone under the stars. There was a spirit in the cañon, and
whether or not it was what the Navajo embodied in the great Nonnezoshe, or
the life of the present, or the death of the ages, or the nature so magnificently
manifested in those silent, dreaming, waiting walls—the truth for Shefford was
that this spirit was God.

Life was eternal. Man's immortality lay in himself. Love of a woman was
hope—happiness. Brotherhood—that mystic and grand "Bi Nai!" of the Navajo—that was religion.

19
The Grand Cañon of the Colorado

THE night passed, the gloom turned gray, the dawn stole cool and pale into the
cañon. When Nas Ta Bega drove the mustangs into camp the lofty ramparts of
the walls were rimmed with gold and the dark arch of Nonnezoshe began to lose
its steely gray.

The women had rested well and were in better condition to travel. Jane was
cheerful and Fay radiant one moment and in a dream the next. She was beginning
to live in that wonderful future. They talked more than usual at breakfast, and
Lassiter made droll remarks. Shefford, with his great and haunting trouble ended
for ever, with now only danger to face ahead, was a different man, but thoughtful
and quiet.

This morning the Indian leisurely made preparations for the start. For all the
concern he showed he might have known every foot of the cañon below Nonnezoshe. But, for Shefford, with the dawn had returned anxiety, a restless feeling
of the need of hurry. What obstacles, what impassable gorges, might lie between
this bridge and the river! The Indian's inscrutable serenity and Fay's trust, her
radiance, the exquisite glow upon her face, sustained Shefford and gave him
patience to endure and conceal his dread.

At length the flight was resumed, with Nas Ta Bega leading on foot, and
Shefford walking in the rear. A quarter of a mile below camp the Indian led
down a declivity into the bottom of the narrow gorge, where the stream ran. He
did not gaze backward for a last glance at Nonnezoshe; nor did Jane or Lassiter.
Fay, however, checked Nack-yal at the rim of the descent and turned to look
behind. Shefford contrasted her tremulous smile, her half-happy good-by to this

place, with the white stillness of her face when she had bade farewell to Surprise Valley. Then she rode Nack-yal down into the gorge.

Shefford knew that this would be his last look at the rainbow bridge. As he gazed the tip of the great arch lost its cold, dark stone color and began to shine. The sun had just arisen high enough over some low break in the wall to reach the bridge. Shefford watched. Slowly, in wondrous transformation, the gold and blue and rose and pink and purple blended their hues, softly, mistily, cloudily, until once again the arch was a rainbow.

Ages before life had evolved upon the earth it had spread its grand arch from wall to wall, black and mystic at night, transparent and rosy in the sunrise, at sunset a flaming curve limned against the heavens. When the race of man had passed it would, perhaps, stand there still. It was not for many eyes to see. Only by toil, sweat, endurance, blood, could any man ever look at Nonnezoshe. So it would always be alone, grand, silent, beautiful, unintelligible.

Shefford bade Nonnezoshe a mute, reverent farewell. Then plunging down the weathered slope of the gorge to the stream below, he hurried forward to join the others. They had progressed much farther than he imagined they would have, and this was owing to the fact that the floor of the gorge afforded easy travel. It was gravel on rock bottom, tortuous, but open, with infrequent and shallow downward steps. The stream did not now rush and boil along and tumble over rock-encumbered ledges. In corners the water collected in round, green, eddying pools. There were patches of grass and willows and mounds of moss. Shefford's surprise equaled his relief, for he believed that the violent descent of Nonnezoshe Boco had been passed. Any turn now, he imagined, might bring the party out upon the river. When he caught up with them he imparted this conviction, which was received with cheer. The hopes of all, except the Indian, seemed mounting; and if he ever hoped or despaired it was never manifest.

Shefford's anticipation, however, was not soon realized. The fugitives traveled miles farther down Nonnezoshe Boco, and the only changes were that the walls of the lower gorge heightened and merged into those above and that these upper ones towered ever loftier. Shefford had to throw his head straight back to look up at the rims, and the narrow strip of sky was now indeed a flowing stream of blue.

Difficult steps were met, too, yet nothing compared to those of the upper cañon. Shefford calculated that this day's travel had advanced several hours; and more than ever now he was anticipating the mouth of Nonnezoshe Boco. Still another hour went by. And then came striking changes. The cañon narrowed till the walls were scarcely twenty paces apart; the color of stone grew dark red above and black down low; the light of day became shadowed, and the floor was a level, gravelly, winding lane, with the stream meandering slowly and silently.

Suddenly the Indian halted. He turned his ear down the cañon lane. He had heard something. The others grouped round him, but did not hear a sound except the soft flow of water and the heave of the mustangs. Then the Indian went on. Presently he halted again. And again he listened. This time he threw up his head and upon his dark face shone a light which might have been pride.

"Tse Ko-n-tsa-igi," he said.

The others could not understand but they were impressed.

"Shore he means somethin' big," drawled Lassiter.

"Oh, what did he say?" queried Fay in eagerness.

"Nas Ta Bega, tell us," said Shefford. "We are full of hope."

"Grand Cañon," replied the Indian.

"How do you know?" asked Shefford.

"I hear the roar of the river."

But Shefford, listen as he might, could not hear it. They traveled on, winding down the wonderful lane. Every once in a while Shefford lagged behind, let the others pass out of hearing, and then he listened. At last he was rewarded. Low and deep, dull and strange, with some quality to incite dread, came a roar. Thereafter, at intervals, usually at turns in the cañon, and when a faint stir of warm air fanned his cheeks, he heard the sound, growing clearer and louder.

He rounded an abrupt corner to have the roar suddenly fill his ears, to see the lane extend straight to a ragged vent, and beyond that, at some distance, a dark, ragged, bulging wall, like iron. As he hurried forward he was surprised to find that the noise did not increase. Here it kept a strange uniformity of tone and volume. The others of the party passed out of the mouth of Nonnezoshe Boco in advance of Shefford, and when he reached it they were grouped upon a bank of sand. A dark-red cañon yawned before them, and through it slid the strangest river Shefford had ever seen. At first glance he imagined the strangeness consisted of the dark-red color of the water, but at the second he was not so sure. All the others, except Nas Ta Bega, eyed the river blankly, as if they did not know what to think. The roar came from round a huge bulging wall downstream. Up the cañon, half a mile, at another turn, there was a leaping rapid of dirty red-white waves, and the sound of this, probably, was drowned in the unseen but nearer rapid.

"This is the Grand Cañon of the Colorado," said Shefford. "We've come out at the mouth of Nonnezoshe Boco. . . . And now to wait for Joe Lake!"

They made camp on a dry, level sand-bar under a shelving wall. Nas Ta Bega collected a pile of driftwood to be used for fire, and then he took the mustangs back up the side cañon to find grass for them. Lassiter appeared unusually quiet, and soon passed from weary rest on the sand to deep slumber. Fay and Jane succumbed to an exhaustion that manifested itself the moment relaxation set in, and they, too, fell asleep. Shefford patrolled the long strip of sand under the wall, and watched up the river for Joe Lake. The Indian returned and went along the river, climbed over the jutting, sharp slopes that reached into the water, and passed out of sight upstream toward the rapid.

Shefford had a sense that the river and the cañon were too magnificent to be compared with others. Still, all his emotions and sensations had been so wrought upon, he seemed not to have any left by which he might judge of what constituted the difference. He would wait. He had a grim conviction that before he was safely out of this earth-riven crack he would know. One thing, however, struck him, and it was that up the cañon, high over the lower walls, hazy and blue, stood other walls, and beyond and above them, dim in purple distance, upreared still other walls. The haze and the blue and the purple meant great distance, and, likewise, the height seemed incomparable.

The red river attracted him most. Since this was the medium by which he must escape with his party, it was natural that it absorbed him, to the neglect of the gigantic cliffs. And the more he watched the river, studied it, listened to it, imagined its nature, its power, its relentlessness, the more he dreaded it. As the hours of the afternoon wore away, and he strolled along and rested on the banks, his first impressions, and what he realized might be his truest ones, were gradually lost. He could not bring them back. The river was changing, deceitful. It worked upon his mind. The low, hollow roar filled his ears and seemed to mock him. Then he endeavored to stop thinking about it, to confine his attention to the gap up-stream where sooner or later he prayed that Joe Lake and his boat would appear. But, though he controlled his gaze, he could not his thought, and his strange, impondering dread of the river augmented.

The afternoon waned. Nas Ta Bega came back to camp and said any likelihood of Joe's arrival was past for that day. Shefford could not get over an impression of strangeness—of the impossibility of the reality presented to his naked eyes. These lonely fugitives in the huge-walled cañon waiting for a boatman to come down that river! Strange and wild—those were the words which, inadequately at best, suited this country and the situations it produced.

After supper he and Fay walked along the bars of smooth, red sand. There were a few moments when the distant peaks and domes and turrets were glorified in changing sunset hues. But the beauty was fleeting. Fay still showed lassitude. She was quiet, yet cheerful, and the sweetness of her smile, her absolute trust in him, stirred and strengthened anew his spirit. Yet he suffered torture when he thought of trusting Fay's life, her soul, and her beauty to this strange red river.

Night brought him relief. He could not see the river; only the low roar made its presence known out there in the shadows. And, there being no need to stay awake, he dropped at once into heavy slumber. He was roused by hands dragging at him. Nas Ta Bega bent over him. It was broad daylight. The yellow wall high above was glistening. A fire was crackling and pleasant odors were wafted to him. Fay and Jane and Lassiter sat around the tarpaulin at breakfast. After the meal suspense and strain were manifested in all the fugitives, even the imperturbable Indian being more than usually watchful. His eyes scarcely ever left the black gap where the river slid round the turn above. Soon, as on the preceding day, he disappeared up the ragged, iron-bound shore. There was scarcely an attempt at conversation. A controlling thought bound that group into silence— if Joe Lake was ever going to come he would come to-day.

Shefford asked himself a hundred times if it were possible, and his answer seemed to be in the low, sullen, muffled roar of the river. And as the morning wore on toward noon his dread deepened until all chance appeared hopeless. Already he had begun to have vague and unformed and disquieting ideas of the only avenue of escape left—to return up Nonnezoshe Boco—and that would be to enter a trap.

Suddenly a piercing cry pealed down the cañon. It was followed by echoes, weird and strange, that clapped from wall to wall in mocking concatenation. Nas Ta Bega appeared high on the ragged slope. The cry had been the Indian's. He swept an arm out, pointing up-stream, and stood like a statue on the iron rocks.

Shefford's keen gaze sighted a moving something in the bend of the river. It was long, low, dark, and flat, with a lighter object upright in the middle. A boat and a man!

"Joe! It's Joe!" yelled Shefford madly. "There! . . . Look!"

Jane and Fay were on their knees in the sand, clasping each other, pale faces toward that bend in the river.

Shefford ran up the shore toward the Indian. He climbed the jutting slant of rock. The boat was now full in the turn—it moved faster—it was nearing the smooth incline above the rapid. There! it glided down—heaved darkly up— settled back—and disappeared in the frothy, muddy roughness of water. Shefford held his breath and watched. A dark, bobbing object showed, vanished, showed again to enlarge—to take the shape of a big flatboat—and then it rode the swift, choppy current out of the lower end of the rapid.

Nas Ta Bega began to make violent motions, and Shefford, taking his cue, frantically waved his red scarf. There was a five-mile-an-hour current right before them, and Joe must needs see them so that he might sheer the huge and clumsy craft into the shore before it drifted too far down.

Presently Joe did see them. He appeared to be half-naked; he raised aloft both arms, and bellowed down the cañon. The echoes boomed from wall to wall, every one stronger with the deep, hoarse triumph in the Mormon's voice, till they passed on, growing weaker, to die away in the roar of the river below. Then Joe bent to a long oar that appeared to be fastened to the stern of the boat, and the craft drifted out of the swifter current toward the shore. It reached a point opposite to where Shefford and the Indian waited, and, though Joe made prodigious efforts, it slid on. Still, it also drifted shoreward, and half-way down to the mouth of Nonnezoshe Boco Joe threw the end of a rope to the Indian.

"Ho! Ho!" yelled the Mormon, again setting into motion the fiendish echoes. He was naked to the waist; he had lost flesh; he was haggard, worn, dirty, wet. While he pulled on a shirt Nas Ta Bega made the rope fast to a snag of a log of driftwood embedded in the sand, and the boat swung to shore. It was perhaps thirty feet long by half as many wide, crudely built of rough-hewn boards. The steering-gear was a long pole with a plank nailed to the end. The craft was empty save for another pole and plank, Joe's coat, and a broken-handled shovel. There were water and sand on the flooring.

Joe stepped ashore and he was gripped first by Shefford and then by the Indian. He was an unkempt and gaunt giant, yet how steadfast and reliable, how grimly strong to inspire hope!

"Reckon most of me's here," he said in reply to greetings. "I've had water aplenty. My God! I've had *water!*" He rolled out a grim laugh. "But no grub for three days. . . . Forgot to fetch some!"

How practical he was! He told Fay she looked good for sore eyes, but he needed a biscuit most of all. There was just a second of singular hestitation when he faced Lassiter, and then the big, strong hand of the young Mormon went out to meet the old gunman's. While they fed him and he ate like a starved man Shefford told of the flight from the village, the rescuing of Jane and Lassiter from Surprise Valley, the descent from the plateau, the catastrophe to Shadd's gang—and, concluding, Shefford, without any explanation, told that Nas Ta Bega had killed the Mormon Waggoner.

"Reckon I had that figured," replied Joe. "First off I didn't think so. . . . So Shadd went over the cliff. That's good riddance. It beats me, though. Never knew that Piute's like with a horse. And he had some grand horses in his outfit. Pity about them."

Later when Joe had a moment alone with Shefford he explained that during his ride to Kayenta he had realized Fay's innocence and who had been responsible for the tragedy. He took Withers, the trader, into his confidence, and they planned a story, which Withers was to carry to Stonebridge, that would exculpate Fay and Shefford of anything more serious than flight. If Shefford got Fay safely out of the country at once that would end the matter for all concerned.

"Reckon I'm some ferry-boatman, too—a *fairy* boatman. Haw! Haw!" he added. "And we're going through. . . . Now I want you to help me rig this tarpaulin up over the bow of the boat. If we can fix it up strong it'll keep the waves from curling over. They filled her four times for me."

They folded the tarpaulin three times, and with stout pieces of split plank and horsehoe nails from Shefford's saddle-bags and pieces of rope they rigged up a screen around bow and front corners.

Nas Ta Bega put the saddles in the boat. The mustangs were far up Nonnezoshe Boco and would work their way back to green and luxuriant cañons. The Indian said they would soon become wild and would never be found. Shefford regretted Nack-yal, but was glad the faithful little mustang would be free in one of those beautiful cañons.

"Reckon we'd better be off," called Joe. "All aboard!" He placed Fay and Jane in a corner of the bow, where they would be spared sight of the rapids. Shefford loosed the rope and sprang aboard. "Pard," said Joe, "it's one hell of a river! And now with the snow melting up in the mountains it's twenty feet above normal and rising fast. But that's well for us. It covers the stones in the rapids. If it hadn't been in flood Joe would be an angel now!"

The boat cleared the sand, lazily wheeled in the eddying water, and suddenly seemed caught by some powerful gliding force. When it swept out beyond the jutting wall Shefford saw a quarter of a mile of sliding water that appeared to end abruptly. Beyond lengthened out the gigantic gap between the black and frowning cliffs.

"Wow!" ejaculated Joe. "Drops out of sight there. But that one ain't much. I can tell by the roar. When you see my hair stand up straight—then watch out! . . . Lassiter, you look after the women. Shefford, you stand ready to bail out with the shovel, for we'll sure ship water. Nas Ta Bega, you help here with the oar."

The roar became a heavy, continuous rumble; the current quickened; little streaks and ridges seemed to race along the boat; strange gurglings rose from under the bow. Shefford stood on tiptoe to see the break in the river below. Swiftly it came into sight—a wonderful, long, smooth red slant of water, a swelling mound, a huge back-curling wave, another and another, a sea of frothy, uplifting crests, leaping and tumbling and diminishing down to the narrowing apex of the rapid. It was a frightful sight, yet it thrilled Shefford. Joe worked the steering-oar back and forth and headed the boat straight for the middle of the incline. The boat reached the round rim, gracefully dipped with a heavy sop, and went shooting down. The wind blew wet in Shefford's face. He stood erect, thrilling, fascinated, frightened. Then he seemed to feel himself lifted; the curling wave leaped at the boat; there was a shock that laid him flat; and when he rose to his knees all about him was roar and spray and leaping, muddy waves. Shock after shock jarred the boat. Splashes of water stung his face. And then the jar and the motion, the confusion and roar, gradually lessened until presently Shefford rose to see smooth water ahead and the long, trembling rapid behind.

"Get busy, bailer," yelled Joe. "Pretty soon you'll be glad you have to bail— so you *can't* see!"

There were several inches of water in the bottom of the boat and Shefford learned for the first time the expediency of a shovel in the art of bailing.

"That tarpaulin worked powerful good," went on Joe. "And it saves the women. Now if it just don't bust on a big wave! That one back there was little."

When Shefford had scooped out all the water he went forward to see how Fay and Jane and Lassiter had fared. The women were pale, but composed. They had covered their heads.

"But the dreadful roar!" exclaimed Fay.

Lassiter looked shaken for once.

"Shore I'd rather taken a chance meetin' them Mormons on the way out," he said.

Shefford spoke with an encouraging assurance which he did not himself feel. Almost at the moment he marked a silence that had fallen into the cañon; then it broke to a low, dull, strange roar.

"Aha! Hear that?" The Mormon shook his shaggy head. "Reckon we're in Cataract Cañon. We'll be standing on end from now on. Hang on to her, boys!"

Danger of this unusual kind had brought out a peculiar levity in the somber Mormon—a kind of wild, gay excitement. His eyes rolled as he watched the river ahead and he puffed out his cheek with his tongue.

The rugged, overhanging walls of the cañon grew sinister in Shefford's sight. They were jaws. And the river—that made him shudder to look down into it. The little whirling pits were eyes peering into his, and they raced on with the boat, disappeared, and came again, always with the little, hollow gurgles.

The craft drifted swiftly and the roar increased. Another rapid seemed to move up into view. It came at a bend in the cañon. When the breeze struck Shefford's cheeks he did not this time experience exhilaration. The current accelerated its sliding motion and bore the flatboat straight for the middle of the curve. Shefford saw the bend, a long, dark, narrow, gloomy cañon, and a stretch of contending waters, then, crouching low, he waited for the dip, the race, the shock. They came—the last stopping the boat—throwing it aloft—letting it drop—and crests of angry waves curled over the side. Shefford, kneeling, felt the water slap around him, and in his ears was a deafening roar. There were endless moments of strife and hell and flying darkness of spray all about him, and under him the rocking boat. When they lessened—ceased in violence—he stood ankle-deep in water, and then madly began to bail.

Another roar deadened his ears, but he did not look up from his toil. And when he had to get down to avoid the pitch he closed his eyes. That rapid passed and with more water to bail, he resumed his share in the manning of the crude craft. It was more than a share—a tremendous responsibility to which he bent with all his might. He heard Joe yell—and again—and again. He heard the increasing roars one after another till they seemed one continuous bellow. He felt the shock, the pitch, the beating waves, and then the lessening power of sound and current. That set him to his task. Always in these long intervals of toil he seemed to see, without looking up, the growing proportions of the cañon. And the river had become a living, terrible thing. The intervals of his tireless effort when he scooped the water overboard were fleeting, and the rides through rapid after rapid were endless periods of waiting terror. His spirit and his hope were overwhelmed by the rush and roar and fury.

Then, as he worked, there came a change—a rest to deafened ears—a stretch of river that seemed quiet after chaos—and here for the first time he bailed the boat clear of water.

Jane and Fay were huddled in a corner, with the flapping tarpaulin now half fallen over them. They were wet and muddy. Lassiter crouched like a man dazed by a bad dream, and his white hair hung, stained and bedraggled, over his face. The Indian and the Mormon, grim, hard, worn, stood silent at the oar.

The afternoon was far advanced and the sun had already descended below the western ramparts. A cool breeze blew up the cañon, laden with a sound that was the same, yet not the same, as those low, dull roars which Shefford dreaded more and more.

Joe Lake turned his ear to the breeze. A stronger puff brought a heavy, quivering rumble. This time he did not vent his gay and wild defiance to the river. He bent lower—listened. Then as the rumble became a strange, deep, reverberating roll, as if the monstrous river were rolling huge stones down a subterranean cañon, Shefford saw with dilating eyes that the Mormon's hair was rising stiff upon his head.

"Hear that!" said Joe, turning an ashen face to Shefford. "We'll drop off the earth now. Hang on to the girl, so if we go you can go together. . . . And, pard, if you've a God—*pray!*"

Nas Ta Bega faced the bend from whence that rumble came, and he was the same dark, inscrutable, impassive Indian as of old. What was death to him?

Shefford felt the strong, rushing love of life surge in him, and it was not for himself he thought, but for Fay and the happiness she merited. He went to her, patted the covered head, and tried with words choking in his throat to give hope. And he leaned with hands gripping the gunwale, with eyes wide open, ready for the unknown.

The river made a quick turn and from round the bend rumbled a terrible uproar. The current racing that way was divided or uncertain, and it gave strange motion to the boat. Joe and Nas Ta Bega shoved desperately upon the oar, all to no purpose. The currents had their will. The bow of the boat took the place of the stern. Then swift at the head of a curved incline it shot beyond the bulging wall.

And Shefford saw an awful place before them. The cañon had narrowed to half its width, and turned almost at right angles. The huge clamor of appalling sound came from under the cliff where the swollen river had to pass and where there was not space. The rapid rushed in gigantic swells right upon the wall, boomed against it, climbed and spread and fell away, to recede and gather new impetus, to leap madly on down the cañon.

Shefford went to his knees, clasped Fay, and Jane, too. But facing this appalling thing he had to look. Courage and despair came to him at the last. This must be the end. With long, buoyant swing the boat sailed down, shot over the first waves, was caught and lifted upon the great swell and impelled straight toward the cliff. Huge whirlpools raced alongside, and from them came a horrible, engulfing roar. Monstrous bulges rose on the other side. All the stupendous power of that mighty river of downward-rushing silt swung the boat aloft, up and up, as the swell climbed the wall. Shefford, with transfixed eyes and harrowed soul, watched the wet black wall. It loomed down upon him. The stern of the boat went high. Then when the crash that meant doom seemed imminent the swell spread and fell back from the wall and the boat never struck at all. By some miraculous chance it had been favored by a strange and momentary receding of the huge spent swell. Then it slid back, was caught and whirled by the current into a red, frothy, upflung rapids below. Shefford bowed his head over Fay and saw no more, nor felt nor heard. What seemed a long time after that the broken voice of the Mormon recalled him to his labors.

The boat was half full of water. Nas Ta Bega scooped out great sheets of it with his hands. Shefford sprang to aid him, found the shovel, and plunged into the task. Slowly but surely they emptied that boat. And then Shefford saw that twilight had fallen. Joe was working the craft toward a narrow bank of sand, to which, presently, they came, and the Indian sprang out to moor to a rock.

The fugitives went ashore and, weary and silent and drenched, they dropped in the warm sand.

But Shefford could not sleep. The river kept him awake. In the distance it rumbled, low, deep, reverberating, and near at hand it was a thing of mutable mood. It moaned, whined, mocked, and laughed. It had the soul of a devil. It was a river that had cut its way to the bowels of the earth, and its nature was destructive. It harbored no life. Fighting its way through those dead walls, cutting and tearing and wearing, its heavy burden of silt was death, destruction, and decay. A silent river, a murmuring, strange, fierce, terrible, thundering river of the desert! Even in the dark it seemed to wear the hue of blood.

All night long Shefford heard it, and toward the dark hours before dawn, when a restless, broken sleep came to him, his dreams were dreams of a river of sounds.

All the beautiful sounds he knew and loved he heard—the sigh of the wind in the pines, the mourn of the wolf, the cry of the laughing-gull, the murmur of running brooks, the song of a child, the whisper of a woman. And there were the boom of the surf, the roar of the north wind in the forest, the roll of thunder. And there were the sounds not of earth—a river of the universe rolling the planets, engulfing the stars, pouring the sea of blue into infinite space.

Night with its fitful dreams passed. Dawn lifted the ebony gloom out of the cañon and sunlight far up on the ramparts renewed Shefford's spirit. He rose and awoke the others. Fay's wistful smile still held its faith. They ate of the gritty, water-soaked food. Then they embarked. The current carried them swiftly down and out of hearing of the last rapid. The character of the river and the cañon changed. The current lessened to a slow, smooth, silent, eddying flow. The walls grew straight, sheer, gloomy, and vast. Shefford noted these features, but he was listening so hard for the roar of the next rapid that he scarcely appreciated them. All the fugitives were listening. Every bend in the cañon— and now the turns were numerous—might hold a rapid. Shefford strained his ears. He imagined the low, dull, strange rumble. He had it in his ears, yet there was the growing sensation of silence.

"Shore this 's a dead place," muttered Lassiter.

"She's only slowed up for a bigger plunge," replied Joe. "Listen! Hear that?"

But there was no true sound. Joe only imagined what he expected and hated and dreaded to hear.

Mile after mile they drifted through the silent gloom between those vast and magnificent walls. After the speed, the turmoil, the whirling, shrieking, thundering, the never-ceasing sound and change and motion of the rapids above, this slow, quiet drifting, this utter, absolute silence, these eddying stretches of still water below, worked strangely upon Shefford's mind and he feared he was going mad.

There was no change to the silence, no help for the slow drift, no lessening of the strain. And the hours of the day passed as moments, the sun crossed the blue gap above, the golden lights hung on the upper walls, the gloom returned, and still there was only the dead, vast, insupportable silence.

There came bends where the current quickened, ripples widened, long lanes of little waves roughened the surface, but they made no sound.

And then the fugitives turned through a V-shaped vent in the cañon. The ponderous walls sheered away from the river. There was space and sunshine, and far beyond this, league-wide open rose vermilion-colored cliffs. A mile below the river disappeared in a dark, boxlike passage from which came a rumble that made Shefford's flesh creep.

The Mormon flung high his arms and let out the stentorian yell that had rolled down to the fugitives as they waited at the mouth of Nonnezoshe Boco. But now it had a wilder, more exultant note. Strange how he shifted his gaze to Fay Larkin!

"Girl! Get up and look!" he called. "The Ferry! The Ferry!"

Then he bent his brawny back over the steering-oar, and the clumsy craft slowly turned toward the left-hand shore, where a long, low bank of green willows and cottonwoods gave welcome relief to the eyes. Upon the opposite side of the river Shefford saw a boat, similar to the one he was in, moored to the bank.

"Shore, if I ain't losin' my eyes, I seen an Injun with a red blanket," said Lassiter.

"Yes, Lassiter," cried Shefford. "Look, Fay! Look, Jane! See! Indians—hogans—mustangs—there above the green bank!"

The boat glided slowly shoreward. And the deep, hungry, terrible rumble of the remorseless river became something no more to dread.

20

Willow Springs

Two days' travel from the river, along the saw-toothed range of Echo Cliffs, stood Presbrey's trading-post, a little red-stone square house in a green and pretty valley called Willow Springs.

It was nearing the time of sunset—that gorgeous hour of color in the Painted Desert—when Shefford and his party rode down upon the post.

The scene lacked the wildness characteristic of Kayenta or Red Lake. There were wagons and teams, white men and Indians, burros, sheep, lambs, mustangs saddled and unsaddled, dogs, and chickens. A young, sweet-faced woman stood in the door of the post and she it was who first sighted the fugitives. Presbrey was weighing bags of wool on a scale, and when she called he lazily turned, as if to wonder at her eagerness.

Then he flung up his head, with its shock of heavy hair, in a start of surprise, and his florid face lost its lazy indolence to become wreathed in a huge smile.

"Haven't seen a white person in six months!" was his extraordinary greeting.

An hour later Shefford, clean-shaven, comfortably clothed once more, found himself a different man; and when he saw Fay in white again, with a new and definable light shining through that old, haunting shadow in her eyes, then the world changed and he embraced perfect happiness.

There was a dinner such as Shefford had not seen for many a day, and such as Fay had never seen, and that brought to Jane Withersteen's eyes the dreamy memory of the bountiful feasts which, long years ago, had been her pride. And there was a story told to the curious trader and his kind wife—a story with its beginning back in those past years, of riders of the purple sage, of Fay Larkin as a child and then as a wild girl in Surprise Valley, of the flight down Nonnezoshe Boco and the cañon, of a great Mormon and a noble Indian.

Presbrey stared with his deep-set eyes and wagged his tousled head and stared again; then with the quick perception of the practical desert man he said:

"I'm sending teamsters in to Flagstaff to-morrow. Wife and I will go along with you. We've light wagons. Three days, maybe—or four—and we'll be there. . . . Shefford, I'm going to see you marry Fay Larkin!"

Fay and Jane and Lassiter showed strangely against this background of approaching civilization. And Shefford realized more than ever the loneliness and isolation and wildness of so many years for them.

When the women had retired Shefford and the men talked awhile. Then Joe Lake rose to stretch his big frame.

"Friends, reckon I'm all in," he said. "Good night." In passing he laid a heavy hand on Shefford's shoulder. "Well, you got out. I've only a queer notion how. But *Some One* besides an Indian and a Mormon guided you out! . . . Be good to the girl. . . . Good-by, pard!"

Shefford grasped the big hand and in the emotion of the moment did not catch the significance of Joe's last words.

Later Shefford stepped outside into the starlight for a few moments' quiet walk and thought before he went to bed. It was a white night. The coyotes were yelping. The stars shone steadfast, bright, cold. Nas Ta Bega stalked out of the shadow of the house and joined Shefford. They walked in silence. Shefford's heart was too full for utterance and the Indian seldom spoke at any time. When Shefford was ready to go in Nas Ta Bega extended his hand.

"Good-by—Bi Nai!" he said, strangely, using English and Navajo in what Shefford supposed to be merely good night. The starlight shone full upon the dark, inscrutable face of the Indian. Shefford bade him good night and then watched him stride away in the silver gloom.

But next morning Shefford understood. Nas Ta Bega and Joe Lake were gone. It was a shock to Shefford. Yet what could he have said to either? Joe had shirked saying good-by to him and Fay. And the Indian had gone out of Shefford's life as he had come into it.

What these two men represented in Shefford's uplift was too great for the present to define, but they and the desert that had developed them had taught him the meaning of life. He might fail often, since failure was the lot of his kind, but could he ever fail again in faith in man or God while he had mind to remember the Indian and the Mormon?

Still, though he placed them on a noble height and loved them well, there would always abide with him a sorrow for the Mormon and a sleepless and eternal regret for that Indian on his lonely cedar slope with the spirits of his vanishing race calling him.

Willow Springs appeared to be a lively place that morning. Presbrey was gay and his sweet-faced wife was excited. The teamsters were a jolly, whistling lot. And the lean mustangs kicked and bit at one another. The trader had brought out two light wagons for the trip, and after the manner of desert men, desired to start at sunrise.

Far across the Painted Desert towered the San Francisco peaks, black-timbered, blue-cañoned, purple-hazed, with white snow, like the clouds, around their summits.

Jane Withersteen looked at the radiant Fay and lived again in her happiness. And at last excitement had been communicated to the old gun-man.

"Shore we're goin' to live with Fay an' John, an' be near Venters an' Bess, an' see the blacks again, Jane. . . . An' Venters will tell you, as he did me, how Wrangle run Black Star off his legs!"

All connected with that early start was sweet, sad, hopeful.

And so they rode away from Willow Springs through the green fields of alfalfa and cottonwood, down the valley with its smoking hogans and whistling mustangs and scarlet-blanketed Indians, and out upon the bare, ridgy, colorful desert toward the rosy sunrise.

Epilogue

ON the outskirts of a little town in Illinois there was a farm of rolling pasture-land. And here a beautiful meadow, green and red in clover, merged upon an orchard in the midst of which a brown-tiled roof showed above the trees.

One afternoon in May a group of people, strangely agitated, walked down a shady lane toward the meadow.

"Wal, Jane, I always knew we'd get a look at them hosses again—I shore knew," Lassiter was saying in the same old, cool, careless drawl. But his clawlike hands shook a little.

"Oh! will they know me?" asked Jane Withersteen, turning to a stalwart man—no other than the dark-faced Venters, her rider of other days.

"Know you? I'll bet they will," replied Venters. "What do you say, Bess?"

The shadow brightened in Bess's somber blue eyes, as if his words had recalled her from a sad and memorable past.

"Black Star will know her, surely," replied Bess. "Sometimes he points his nose toward the west and watches as if he saw the purple slopes and smelt the sage of Utah! He has never forgotten. But Night has grown deaf and partly blind of late. I doubt if he'll remember."

Shefford and Fay walked arm in arm in the background.

Out in the meadow two horses were grazing. They were sleek, shiny, long-maned, long-tailed, black as coal, and, though old, still splendid in every line.

"Do you remember them?" whispered Shefford.

"Oh, I only needed to see Black Star," murmured Fay, her voice quivering. "I can remember being lifted on his back. . . . How strange! It seems so long ago. . . . Look! Mother Jane is going out to them."

Jane Withersteen advanced alone through the clover, and it was with unsteady steps. Presently she halted. What glorious and bitter memories were expressed in her strange, poignant call!

Black Star started and swept up his noble head and looked. But Night went on calmly grazing. Then Jane called again—the same strange call, only louder, and this time broken. Black Star raised his head higher and he whistled a piercing blast. He saw Jane; he knew her as he had remembered the call; and he came pounding toward her. She met him, encircled his neck with her arms, and buried her face in his mane.

"Shore I reckon I'd better never say any more about Wrangle runnin' the blacks off their legs thet time," muttered Lassiter, as if to himself.

"Lassiter, you only dreamed that race," replied Venters, with a smile.

"Oh, Bern, isn't it good that Black Star remembered her—that she'll have him—something left of her old home?" asked Bess, wistfully.

"Indeed it is good. But, Bess, Jane Withersteen will find a new spirit and new happiness here."

Jane came toward them, leading both horses. "Dear friends, I am happy. To-day I bury all regrets. Of the past I shall remember only—my rider of the purple sage."

Venters smiled his gladness. "And you—Lassiter—what shall you remember?" he queried.

The old gun-man looked at Jane and then at his clawlike hands and then at Fay. His eyes lost their shadow and began to twinkle.

"Wal, I rolled a stone once, but I reckon now thet time Wrangle—"

"Lassiter, I said you dreamed that race. Wrangle never beat the blacks," interrupted Venters. . . . "And you, Fay, what shall you remember?"

"Surprise Valley," replied Fay, dreamily.

"And you—Shefford?"

Shefford shook his head. For him there could never be one memory only. In his heart there would never change or die memories of the wild uplands, of the great towers and walls, of the golden sunsets on the cañon ramparts, of the silent, fragrant valleys where the cedars and the sago-lilies grew, of those starlit nights when his love and faith awoke, of grand and lonely Nonnezoshe, of that red, sullen, thundering, mysterious Colorado River, of a wonderful Indian and a noble Mormon—of all that was embodied for him in the meaning of the rainbow trail.

THE LONE STAR RANGER

I⊤ may seem strange to you that out of all the stories I heard on the Rio Grande I should choose as the first that of Buck Duane—outlaw and gunman.

But, indeed, Ranger Coffee's story of the last of the Duanes has haunted me, and I have given full rein to imagination and have retold it in my own way. It deals with the old law—the old border days—therefore it is better first. Soon, perchance, I shall have the pleasure of writing of the border of to-day, which in Joe Sitter's laconic speech, "Shore is 'most as bad an' wild as ever!"

In the North and East there is a popular idea that the frontier of the West is a thing long past, and remembered now only in stories. As I think of this I remember Ranger Sitter when he made that remark, while he grimly stroked an unhealed bullet wound. And I remember the giant Vaughn, that typical son of stalwart Texas, sitting there quietly with bandaged head, his thoughtful eye boding ill to the outlaw who had ambushed him. Only a few months have passed since then—when I had my memorable sojourn with you—and yet, in that short time, Russell and Moore have crossed the Divide, like Rangers.

Gentlemen,—I have the honor to dedicate this book to you, and the hope that it shall fall to my lot to tell the world the truth about a strange, unique, and misunderstood body of men—the Texas Rangers—who made the great Lone Star State habitable, who never know peaceful rest and sleep, who are passing, who surely will not be forgotten and will some day come into their own.

ZANE GREY

Book I
The Outlaw

1

So it was in him, then—an inherited fighting instinct, a driving intensity to kill. He was the last of the Duanes, that old fighting stock of Texas. But not the memory of his dead father, nor the pleading of his soft-voiced mother, nor the warning of this uncle who stood before him now, had brought to Buck Duane so much realization of the dark passionate strain in his blood. It was the recurrence, a hundredfold increased in power, of a strange emotion that for the last three years had arisen in him.

"Yes, Cal Bain's in town, full of bad whiskey an' huntin' for you," repeated the elder man, gravely.

"It's the second time," muttered Duane, as if to himself.

"Son, you can't avoid a meetin'. Leave town till Cal sobers up. He ain't got it in for you when he's not drinkin'."

"But what's he want me for?" demanded Duane. "To insult me again? I won't stand that twice."

"He's got a fever that's rampant in Texas these days, my boy. He wants gunplay. If he meets you he'll try to kill you."

Here it stirred in Duane again,, that bursting gush of blood, like a wind of flame shaking all his inner being, and subsiding to leave him strangely chilled.

"Kill me! What for?" he asked.

"Lord knows there ain't any reason. But what's that to do with most of the shootin' these days? Didn't five cowboys over to Everall's kill one another dead all because they got to jerkin' at a quirt among themselves? An' Cal has no reason to love you. His girl was sweet on you."

"I quit when I found out she was his girl."

"I reckon she ain't quit. But never mind her or reasons. Cal's here, just drunk enough to be ugly. He's achin' to kill somebody. He's one of them four-flush

211

gun-fighters. He'd like to be thought bad. There's a lot of wild cowboys who 're ambitious for a reputation. They talk about how quick they are on the draw. They ape Bland an' King Fisher an' Hardin an' all the big outlaws. They make threats about joinin' the gangs along the Rio Grande. They laugh at the sheriffs an' brag about how they'd fix the rangers. Cal's sure not much for you to bother with, if you only keep out of his way.''

"You mean for me to run?" asked Duane, in scorn.

"I reckon I wouldn't put it that way. Just avoid him. Buck, I'm not afraid Cal would get you if you met down there in town. You've your father's eye an' his slick hand with a gun. What I'm most afraid of is that you'll kill Bain.''

Duane was silent, letting his uncle's earnest words sink in, trying to realize their significance.

"If Texas ever recovers from that fool war an' kills off these outlaws, why, a young man will have a lookout," went on the uncle. "You're twenty-three now, an' a powerful sight of a fine fellow, barrin' your temper. You've a chance in life. But if you go gun-fightin', if you kill a man, you're ruined. Then you'll kill another. It'll be the same old story. An' the rangers would make you an outlaw. The rangers mean law an' order for Texas. This even-break business doesn't work with them. If you resist arrest they'll kill you. If you submit to arrest, then you go to jail, an' mebbe you hang.''

"I'd never hang," muttered Duane, darkly.

"I reckon you wouldn't," replied the old man. "You'd be like your father. He was ever ready to draw—too ready. In times like these, with the Texas rangers enforcin' the law, your Dad would have been driven to the river. An', son, I'm afraid you're a chip off the old block. Can't you hold in—keep your temper—run away from trouble? Because it'll only result in you gettin' the worst of it in the end. Your father was killed in a street-fight. An' it was told of him that he shot twice after a bullet had passed through his heart. Think of the terrible nature of a man to be able to do that. If you have any such blood in you, never give it a chance.''

"What you say is all very well, uncle," returned Duane, "but the only way out for me is to run, and I won't do it. Cal Bain and his outfit have already made me look like a coward. He says I'm afraid to come out and face him. A man simply can't stand that in this country. Besides, Cal would shoot me in the back some day if I didn't face him.''

"Well, then, what 're you goin' to do?" inquired the elder man.

"I haven't decided—yet.''

"No, but you're comin' to it mighty fast. That damned spell is workin' in you. You're different to-day. I remember how you used to be moody an' lose your temper an' talk wild. Never was much afraid of you then. But now you're gettin' cool an' quiet, an' you think deep, an' I don't like the light in your eye. It reminds me of your father.''

''I wonder what Dad would say to me to-day if he were alive and here,'' said Duane.

''What do you think? What could you expect of a man who never wore a glove on his right hand for twenty years?''

''Well, he'd hardly have said much. Dad never talked. But he would have done a lot. And I guess I'll go down-town and let Cal Bain find me.''

Then followed a long silence, during which Duane sat with downcast eyes, and the uncle appeared lost in sad thought of the future. Presently he turned to Duane with an expression that denoted resignation, and yet a spirit which showed wherein they were of the same blood.

''You've got a fast horse—the fastest I know of in this country. After you meet Bain hurry back home. I'll have a saddle-bag packed for you and the horse ready.''

With that he turned on his heel and went into the house, leaving Duane to revolve in his mind his singular speech. Buck wondered presently if he shared his uncle's opinion of the result of a meeting between himelf and Bain. His thoughts were vague. But on the instant of final decision, when he had settled with himself that he would meet Bain, such a storm of passion assailed him that he felt as if he was being shaken with ague. Yet it was all internal, inside his breast, for his hand was like a rock and, for all he could see, not a muscle about him quivered. He had no fear of Bain or of any other man; but a vague fear of himself, of this strange force in him, made him ponder and shake his head. It was as if he had not all to say in this matter. There appeared to have been in him a reluctance to let himself go, and some voice, some spirit from a distance, something he was not accountable for, had compelled him. That hour of Duane's life was like years of actual living, and in it he became a thoughtful man.

He went into the house and buckled on his belt and gun. The gun was a Colt .45, six-shot, and heavy, with an ivory handle. He had packed it, on and off, for five years. Before that it had been used by his father. There were a number of notches filed in the bulge of the ivory handle. This gun was the one his father had fired twice after being shot through the heart, and his hand had stiffened so tightly upon it in the death-grip that his fingers had to be pried open. It had never been drawn upon any man since it had come into Duane's possession. But the cold, bright polish of the weapon showed how it had been used. Duane could draw it with inconceivable rapidity, and at twenty feet he could split a card pointing edgewise toward him.

Duane wished to avoid meeting his mother. Fortunately, as he thought, she was away from home. He went out and down the path toward the gate. The air was full of the fragrance of blossoms and the melody of birds. Outside in the road a neighbor woman stood talking to a countryman in a wagon; they spoke to him; and he heard, but did not reply. Then he began to stride down the road toward the town.

Wellston was a small town, but important in that unsettled part of the great state because it was the trading-center of several hundred miles of territory. On the main street there were perhaps fifty buildings, some brick, some frame, mostly adobe, and one-third of the lot, and by far the most prosperous, were saloons. From the road Duane turned into this street. It was a wide thoroughfare lined by hitching-rails and saddled horses and vehicles of various kinds. Duane's eye ranged down the street, taking in all at a glance, particularly persons moving leisurely up and down. Not a cowboy was in sight. Duane slackened his stride, and by the time he reached Sol White's place, which was the first saloon, he was walking slowly. Several people spoke to him and turned to look back after they had passed. He paused at the door of White's saloon, took a sharp survey of the interior, then stepped inside.

The saloon was large and cool, full of men and noise and smoke. The noise ceased upon his entrance, and the silence ensuing presently broke to the clink of Mexican silver dollars at a *monte* table. Sol White, who was behind the bar, straightened up when he saw Duane; then, without speaking, he bent over to rinse a glass. All eyes except those of the Mexican gamblers were turned upon Duane; and these glances were keen, speculative, questioning. These men knew Bain was looking for trouble; they probably had heard his boasts. But what did Duane intend to do? Several of the cowboys and ranchers present exchanged glances. Duane had been weighed by unerring Texas instinct, by men who all packed guns. The boy was the son of his father. Whereupon they greeted him and returned to their drinks and cards. Sol White stood with his big red hands out upon the bar; he was a tall, raw-boned Texan with a long mustache waxed to sharp points.

"Howdy, Buck," was his greeting to Duane. He spoke carelessly and averted his dark gaze for an instant.

"Howdy, Sol," replied Duane, slowly. "Say, Sol, I hear there's a gent in town looking for me bad."

"Reckon there is, Buck," replied White. "He came in heah aboot an hour ago. Shore he was some riled an' a-roarin' for gore. Told me confidential a certain party had given you a white silk scarf, an' he was hell-bent on wearin' it home spotted red."

"Anybody with him?" queried Duane.

"Burt an' Sam Outcalt an' a little cowpuncher I never seen before. They-all was coaxin' him to leave town. But he's looked on the flowin' glass, Buck, an' he's heah for keeps."

"Why doesn't Sheriff Oaks lock him up if he's that bad?"

"Oaks went away with the rangers. There's been another raid at Flesher's ranch. The King Fisher gang, likely. An' so the town's shore wide open."

Duane stalked outdoors and faced down the street. He walked the whole length of the long block, meeting many people—farmers, ranchers, clerks, merchants, Mexicans, cowboys, and women. It was a singular fact that when he turned to retrace his steps the street was almost empty. He had not returned a hundred yards on his way when the street was wholly deserted. A few heads protruded from doors and around corners. That main street of Wellston saw some such situation every few days. If it was an instinct for Texans to fight, it was also instinctive for them to sense with remarkable quickness the signs of a coming gun-play. Rumor could not fly so swiftly. In less than ten minutes everybody who had been on the street or in the shops knew that Buck Duane had come forth to meet his enemy.

Duane walked on. When he came to within fifty paces of a saloon he swerved out into the middle of the street, stood there for a moment, then went ahead and back to the sidewalk. He passed on in this way the length of the block. Sol White was standing in the door of his saloon.

"Buck, I'm a-tippin' you off," he said, quick and low-voiced. "Cal Bain's over at Everall's. If he's a-huntin' you bad, as he brags, he'll show there."

Duane crossed the street and started down. Notwithstanding White's statement Duane was wary and slow at every door. Nothing happened, and he traversed almost the whole length of the block without seeing a person. Everall's place was on the corner.

Duane knew himself to be cold, steady. He was conscious of a strange fury that made him want to leap ahead. He seemed to long for this encounter more than anything he had ever wanted. But, vivid as were his sensations, he felt as if in a dream.

Before he reached Everall's he heard loud voices, one of which was raised high. Then the short door swung outward as if impelled by a vigorous hand. A bow-legged cowboy wearing wooley chaps burst out upon the sidewalk. At sight of Duane he seemed to bound into the air, and he uttered a savage roar.

Duane stopped in his tracks at the outer edge of the sidewalk, perhaps a dozen rods from Everall's door.

If Bain was drunk he did not show it in his movement. He swaggered forward, rapidly closing up the gap. Red, sweaty, disheveled, and hatless, his face distorted and expressive of the most malignant intent, he was a wild and sinister figure. He had already killed a man, and this showed in his demeanor. His hands were extended before him, the right hand a little lower than the left. At every step he bellowed his rancor in speech mostly curses. Gradually he slowed his walk, then halted. A good twenty-five paces separated the men.

"Won't nothin' make you draw, you—!" he shouted, fiercely.

"I'm waitin' on you, Cal," replied Duane.

Bain's right hand stiffened—moved. Duane threw his gun as a boy throws a ball underhand—a draw his father had taught him. He pulled twice, his shots almost as one. Bain's big Colt boomed while it was pointed downward and he was falling. His bullet scattered dust and gravel at Duane's feet. He fell loosely, without contortion.

In a flash all was reality for Duane. He went forward and held his gun ready for the slightest movement on the part of Bain. But Bain lay upon his back, and all that moved were his breast and his eyes. How strangely the red had left his face—and also the distortion! The devil that had showed in Bain was gone. He was sober and conscious. He tried to speak, but failed. His eyes expressed something pitifully human. They changed—rolled—set blankly.

Duane drew a deep breath and sheathed his gun. He felt calm and cool, glad the fray was over. One violent expression burst from him. "The fool!"

When he looked up there were men around him.

"Plumb center," said one.

Another, a cowboy who evidently had just left the gaming-table, leaned down and pulled open Bain's shirt. He had the ace of spades in his hand. He laid it on Bain's breast, and the black figure on the card covered the two bullet-holes just over Bain's heart.

Duane wheeled and hurried away. He heard another man say:

"Reckon Cal got what he deserved. Buck Duane's first gun-play. Like father like son!"

2

A THOUGHT kept repeating itself to Duane, and it was that he might have spared himself concern through his imagining how awful it would be to kill a man. He had no such feeling now. He had rid the community of a drunken, bragging, quarrelsome cowboy.

When he came to the gate of his home and saw his uncle there with a mettlesome horse, saddled, with canteen, rope, and bags all in place, a subtle shock pervaded his spirit. It had slipped his mind—the consequence of his act. But sight of the horse and the look of his uncle recalled the fact that he must now become a fugitive. An unreasonable anger took hold of him.

"The d——d fool!" he exclaimed, hotly. "Meeting Bain wasn't much, Uncle Jim. He dusted my boots, that's all. And for that I've got to go on the dodge."

"Son, you killed him—then?" asked the uncle, huskily.

"Yes. I stood over him—watched him die. I did as I would have been done by."

"I knew it. Long ago I saw it comin'. But now we can't stop to cry over spilt blood. You've got to leave town an' this part of the country."

"Mother!" exclaimed Duane.

"She's away from home. You can't wait. I'll break it to her—what she always feared."

Suddenly Duane sat down and covered his face with his hands.

"My God! Uncle, what have I done?" His broad shoulders shook.

"Listen, son, an' remember what I say," replied the elder man, earnestly. "Don't ever forget. You're not to blame. I'm glad to see you take it this way, because maybe you'll never grow hard an' callous. You're not to blame. This is Texas. You're your father's son. These are wild times. The law as the rangers are laying it down now can't change life all in a minute. Even your mother, who's a good, true woman, has had her share in making you what you are this moment. For she was one of the pioneers—the fightin' pioneers of this state. Those years of wild times, before you was born, developed in her instinct to fight, to save her life, her children, an' that instinct has cropped out in you. It will be many years before it dies out of the boys born in Texas."

"I'm a murderer," said Duane, shuddering.

"No, son, you're not. An' you never will be. But you've got to be an outlaw till time makes it safe for you to come home."

"An outlaw?"

"I said it. If we had money an' influence we'd risk a trial. But we've neither. An' I reckon the scaffold or jail is no place for Buckley Duane. Strike for the wild country, an' wherever you go an' whatever you do—be a man. Live honestly, if that's possible. If it isn't, be as honest as you can. If you have to herd with outlaws try not to become bad. There are outlaws who're not all bad— many who have been driven to the river by such a deal as this you had. When you get among these men avoid brawls. Don't drink; don't gamble. I needn't tell you what to do if it comes to gun-play, as likely it will. You can't come home. When this thing is lived down, if that time ever comes, I'll get word into the unsettled country. It'll reach you some day. That's all. Remember, be a man. Goodby."

Duane, with blurred sight and contracting throat, gripped his uncle's hand and bade him a wordless farewell. Then he leaped astride the black and rode out of town.

As swiftly as was consistent with a care for his steed, Duane put a distance

of fifteen or eighteen miles behind him. With that he slowed up, and the matter
of riding did not require all his faculties. He passed several ranches and was
seen by men. This did not suit him, and he took an old trail across country. It
was a flat region with a poor growth of mesquite and prickly-pear cactus. Occasionally he caught a glimpse of low hills in the distance. He had hunted often
in that section, and knew where to find grass and water. When he reached this
higher ground he did not, however, halt at the first favorable camping-spot, but
went on and on. Once he came out upon the brow of a hill and saw a considerable
stretch of country beneath him. It had the gray sameness characterizing all that
he had traversed. He seemed to want to see wide spaces—to get a glimpse of
the great wilderness lying somewhere beyond to the southwest. It was sunset
when he decided to camp at a likely spot he came across. He led the horse to
water, and then began searching through the shallow valley for a suitable place
to camp. He passed by old camp-sites that he well remembered. These, however,
did not strike his fancy this time, and the significance of the change in him did
not occur at the moment. At last he found a secluded spot, under cover of thick
mesquites and oaks, at a goodly distance from the old trail. He took saddle and
pack off the horse. He looked among his effects for a hobble, and, finding that
his uncle had failed to put one in, he suddenly remembered that he seldom used
a hobble, and never on this horse. He cut a few feet off the end of his lasso and
used that. The horse, unused to such hampering of his free movements, had to
be driven out upon the grass.

Duane made a small fire, prepared and ate his supper. This done, ending the
work of that day, he sat down and filled his pipe. Twilight had waned into dusk.
A few wan stars had just begun to show and brighten. Above the low continuous
hum of insects sounded the evening carol of robins. Presently the birds ceased
their singing, and then the quiet was more noticeable. When night set in and the
place seemed all the more isolated and lonely for that Duane had a sense of
relief.

It dawned upon him all at once that he was nervous, watchful, sleepless. The
fact caused him surprise, and he began to think back, to take note of his late
actions and their motives. The change one day had wrought amazed him. He
who had always been free, easy, happy, especially when out alone in the open,
had become in a few short hours bound, serious, preoccupied. The silence that
had once been sweet now meant nothing to him except a medium whereby he
might the better hear the sounds of pursuit. The loneliness, the night, the wild,
that had always been beautiful to him, now only conveyed a sense of safety for
the present. He watched, he listened, he thought. He felt tired, yet had no
inclination to rest. He intended to be off by dawn, heading toward the southwest.
Had he a destination? It was vague as his knowledge of that great waste of

mesquite and rock bordering the Rio Grande. Somewhere out there was a refuge. For he was a fugitive from justice, an outlaw.

This being an outlaw then meant eternal vigilance. No home, no rest, no sleep, no content, no life worth the living! He must be a lone wolf or he must herd among men obnoxious to him. If he worked for an honest living he still must hide his identity and take risks of detection. If he did not work on some distant outlying ranch, how was he to live? The idea of stealing was repugnant to him. The future seemed gray and somber enough. And he was twenty-three years old.

Why had this hard life been imposed upon him?

The bitter question seemed to start a strange iciness that stole along his veins. What was wrong with him? He stirred the few sticks of mesquite into a last flickering blaze. He was cold, and for some reason he wanted some light. The black circle of darkness weighted down upon him, closed in around him. Suddenly he sat bolt upright and then froze in that position. He had heard a step. It was behind him—no—on the side. Some one was there. He forced his hand down to his gun, and the touch of cold steel was another icy shock. Then he waited. But all was silent—silent as only a wilderness arroyo can be, with its low murmuring of wind in the mesquite. Had he heard a step? He began to breathe again.

But what was the matter with the light of his camp-fire? It had taken on a strange green luster and seemed to be waving off into the outer shadows. Duane heard no step, saw no movement; nevertheless, there was another present at that camp-fire vigil. Duane saw him. He lay there in the middle of the green brightness, prostrate, motionless, dying. Cal Bain! His features were wonderfully distinct, clearer than any cameo, more sharply outlined than those of any picture. It was a hard face softening at the threshold of eternity. The red tan of sun, the coarse signs of drunkenness, the ferocity and hate so characteristic of Bain were no longer there. This face represented a different Bain, showed all that was human in him fading, fading as swiftly as it blanched white. The lips wanted to speak, but had not the power. The eyes held an agony of thought. They revealed what might have been possible for this man if he lived—that he saw his mistake too late. Then they rolled, set blankly, and closed in death.

That haunting visitation left Duane sitting there in a cold sweat, a remorse gnawing at his vitals, realizing the curse that was on him. He divined that never would he be able to keep off that phantom. He remembered how his father had been eternally pursued by the furies of accusing guilt, how he had never been able to forget in work or in sleep those men he had killed.

The hour was late when Duane's mind let him sleep, and then dreams troubled him. In the morning he bestirred himself so early that in the gray gloom he had difficulty in finding his horse. Day had just broken when he struck the old trail again.

He rode hard all morning and halted in a shady spot to rest and graze his horse. In the afternoon he took to the trail at an easy trot. The country grew wilder. Bald, rugged mountains broke the level of the monotonous horizon. About three in the afternoon he came to a little river which marked the boundary line of his hunting territory.

The decision he made to travel up-stream for a while was owing to two facts: the river was high with quicksand bars on each side, and he felt reluctant to cross into that region where his presence alone meant that he was a marked man. The bottom-lands through which the river wound to the southwest were more inviting than the barrens he had traversed. The rest of that day he rode leisurely up-stream. At sunset he penetrated the brakes of willow and cottonwood to spend the night. It seemed to him that in this lonely cover he would feel easy and content. But he did not. Every feeling, every imagining he had experienced the previous night returned somewhat more vividly and accentuated by newer ones of the same intensity and color.

In this kind of travel and camping he spent three more days, during which he crossed a number of trails, and one road where cattle—stolen cattle, probably—had recently passed. Thus time exhausted his supply of food, except salt, pepper, coffee, and sugar, of which he had a quantity. There were deer in the brakes; but, as he could not get close enough to kill them with a revolver, he had to satisfy himself with a rabbit. He knew he might as well content himself with the hard fare that assuredly would be his lot.

Somewhere up this river there was a village called Huntsville. It was distant about a hundred miles from Wellston, and had a reputation throughout southwestern Texas. He had never been there. The fact was this reputation was such that honest travelers gave the town a wide berth. Duane had considerable money for him in his possession, and he concluded to visit Huntsville, if he could find it, and buy a stock of provisions.

The following day, toward evening, he happened upon a road which he believed might lead to the village. There were a good many fresh horse-tracks in the sand, and these made him thoughtful. Nevertheless, he followed the road, proceeding cautiously. He had not gone very far when the sound of rapid hoof-beats caught his ears. They came from his rear. In the darkening twilight he could not see any great distance back along the road. Voices, however, warned him that these riders, whoever they were, had approached closer than he liked. To go farther down the road was not to be thought of, so he turned a little way in among the mesquites and halted, hoping to escape being seen or heard. As he was now a fugitive, it seemed every man was his enemy and pursuer.

The horsemen were fast approaching. Presently they were abreast of Duane's position, so near that he could hear the creak of saddles, the clink of spurs.

"Shore he crossed the river below," said one man.

"I reckon you're right, Bill. He's slipped us," replied another.

Rangers or a posse of ranchers in pursuit of a fugitive! The knowledge gave Duane a strange thrill. Certainly they could not have been hunting him. But the feeling their proximity gave him was identical to what it would have been had he been this particular hunted man. He held his breath; he clenched his teeth; he pressed a quieting hand upon his horse. Suddenly he became aware that these horsemen had halted. They were whispering. He could just make out a dark group closely massed. What had made them halt so suspiciously?

"You're wrong, Bill," said a man, in a low but distinct voice. "The idea of hearin' a hoss heave. You're wuss'n a ranger. An' you're hell-bent on killin' that rustler. Now I say let's go home an' eat."

"Wal, I'll just take a look at the sand," replied the man called Bill.

Duane heard the clink of spurs on steel stirrup and the thud of boots on the ground. There followed a short silence which was broken by a sharply breathed exclamation.

Duane waited for no more. They had found his trail. He spurred his horse straight into the brush. At the second crashing bound there came yells from the road, and then shots. Duane heard the hiss of a bullet close by his ear, and as it struck a branch it made a peculiar singing sound. These shots and the proximity of that lead missile roused in Duane a quick, hot resentment which mounted into a passion almost ungovernable. He must escape, yet it seemed that he did not care whether he did or not. Something grim kept urging him to halt and return the fire of these men. After running a couple of hundred yards he raised himself from over the pommel, where he had bent to avoid the stinging branches, and tried to guide his horse. In the dark shadows under mesquites and cotton-woods he was hard put to it to find open passage; however, he succeeded so well and made such little noise that gradually he drew away from his pursuers. The sound of their horses crashing through the thickets died away. Duane reined in and listened. He had distanced them. Probably they would go into camp till daylight, then follow his tracks. He started on again, walking his horse, and peered sharply at the ground, so that he might take advantage of the first trail he crossed. It seemed a long while until he came upon one. He followed it until a late hour, when, striking the willow brakes again and hence the neighborhood of the river, he picketed his horse and lay down to rest. But he did not sleep. His mind bitterly revolved the fate that had come upon him. He made efforts to think of other things, but in vain. Every moment he expected the chill, the sense of loneliness that yet was ominous of a strange visitation, the peculiarly imagined lights and shades of the night—these things that presaged the coming of Cal Bain. Doggedly Duane fought against the insidious phantom. He kept telling himself that it was just imagination, that it would wear off in time. Still in his heart he did not believe what he hoped. But he would not give up; he would not accept the ghost of his victim as a reality.

Gray dawn found him in the saddle again headed for the river. Half an hour of riding brought him to the dense chaparral and willow thickets. These he threaded to come at length to the ford. It was a gravel bottom, and therefore an easy crossing. Once upon the opposite shore he reined in his horse and looked darkly back. This action marked his acknowledgment of his situation: he had voluntarily sought the refuge of the outlaws; he was beyond the pale. A bitter and passionate curse passed his lips as he spurred his horse into the brakes on that alien shore.

He rode perhaps twenty miles, not sparing his horse nor caring whether or not he left a plain trail.

"Let them hunt me!" he muttered.

When the heat of the day began to be oppressive, and hunger and thirst made themselves manifest, Duane began to look about him for a place to halt for the noon-hours. The trail led into a road which was hard packed and smooth from the tracks of cattle. He doubted not that he had come across one of the roads used by border raiders. He headed into it, and had scarcely traveled a mile when, turning a curve, he came point-blank upon a single horseman riding toward him. Both riders wheeled their mounts sharply and were ready to run and shoot back. Not more than a hundred paces separated them. They stood then for a moment watching each other.

"Mawnin', stranger," called the man, dropping his hand from his hip.

"Howdy," replied Duane, shortly.

They rode toward each other, closing half the gap, then they halted again.

"I seen you ain't no ranger," called the rider, "an' shore I ain't none."

He laughed loudly, as if he had made a joke.

"How'd you know I wasn't a ranger?" asked Duane, curiously. Somehow he had instantly divined that his horseman was no officer, or even a rancher trailing stolen stock.

"Wal," said the fellow, starting his horse forward at a walk, "a ranger'd never git ready to run the other way from one man."

He laughed again. He was small and wiry, slouchy of attire, and armed to the teeth, and he bestrode a fine bay horse. He had quick, dancing brown eyes, at once frank and bold, and a coarse, bronzed face. Evidently he was a good-natured ruffian.

Duane acknowledged the truth of the assertion, and turned over in his mind how shrewdly the fellow had guessed him to be a hunted man.

"My name's Luke Stevens, an' I hail from the river. Who're you?" said this stranger.

Duane was silent.

"I reckon you're Buck Duane," went on Stevens. "I heerd you was a damn bad man with a gun."

This time Duane laughed, not at the doubtful compliment, but at the idea that the first outlaw he met should know him. Here was proof of how swiftly facts about gun-play traveled on the Texas border.

"Wal, Buck," said Stevens, in a friendly manner, "I ain't presumin' on your time or company. I see you're headin' fer the river. But will you stop long enough to stake a feller to a bite of grub?"

"I'm out of grub, and pretty hungry myself," admitted Duane.

"Been pushin' your hoss, I see. Wal, I reckon you'd better stock up before you hit thet stretch of country."

He made a wide sweep of his right arm, indicating the southwest, and there was that in his action which seemed significant of a vast and barren region.

"Stock up?" queried Duane, thoughtfully.

"Shore. A feller has jest got to eat. I can rustle along without whisky, but not without grub. Thet's what makes it so embarrassin' travelin' these parts dodgin' your shadow. Now, I'm on my way to Mercer. It's a little two-bit town up the river a ways. I'm goin' to pack out some grub."

Stevens's tone was inviting. Evidently he would welcome Duane's companionship, but he did not openly say so. Duane kept silence, however, and then Stevens went on.

"Stranger, in this here country two's a crowd. It's safer. I never was much on this lone-wolf dodgin', though I've done it of necessity. It takes a damn good man to travel alone any length of time. Why, I've been thet sick I was jest achin' fer some ranger to come along an' plug me. Give me a pardner any day. Now, mebbe you're not thet kind of a feller, an' I'm shore not presumin' to ask. But I just declares myself sufficient."

"You mean you'd like me to go with you?" asked Duane.

Stevens grinned. "Wal, I should smile. I'd be particular proud to be braced with a man of your reputation."

"See here, my good fellow, that's all nonsence," declared Duane, in some haste.

"Shore I think modesty becomin' to a youngster," replied Stevens. "I hate a brag. An' I've no use fer these four-flush cowboys thet 're always lookin' fer trouble an' talkin' gun-play. Buck, I don't know much about you. But every man who's lived along the Texas border remembers a lot about your Dad. It was expected of you, I reckon, an' much of your rep was established before you throwed your gun. I jest heerd thet you was lightnin' on the draw, an' when you cut loose with a gun, why the figger on the ace of spades would cover your cluster of bullet-holes. Thet's the word thet's gone down the border. It's the kind of reputation most sure to fly far an' swift ahead of a man in this country.

An' the safest, too; I'll gamble on thet. It's the land of the draw. I see now you're only a boy, though you're shore a strappin' husky one. Now, Buck, I'm not a spring chicken, an' I've been long on the dodge. Mebbe a little of my society won't hurt you none. You'll need to learn the country."

There was something sincere and likable about this outlaw.

"I dare say you're right," replied Duane, quietly. "And I'll go to Mercer with you."

Next moment he was riding down the road with Stevens. Duane had never been much of a talker, and now he found speech difficult. But his companion did not seem to mind that. He was a jocose, voluble fellow, probably glad now to hear the sound of his own voice. Duane listened, and sometimes he thought with a pang of the distinction of name and heritage of blood his father had left to him.

3

LATE that day, a couple of hours before sunset, Duane and Stevens, having rested their horses in the shade of some mesquites near the town of Mercer, saddled up and prepared to move.

"Buck, as we're lookin' fer grub, an' not trouble, I reckon you'd better hang up out here," Stevens was saying, as he mounted. "You see, towns an' sheriffs an' rangers are always lookin' fer new fellers gone bad. They sort of forget most of the old boys, except those as are plumb bad. Now, nobody in Mercer will take notice of me. Reckon there's been a thousand men run into the river country to become outlaws since yours truly. You jest wait here an' be ready to ride hard. Mebbe my besettin' sin will go operatin' in spite of my good intentions. In which case there'll be—"

His pause was significant. He grinned, and his brown eyes danced with a kind of wild humor.

"Stevens, have you got any money?" asked Duane.

"Money!" exclaimed Luke, blankly. "Say, I haven't owned a two-bit piece since—wal, fer some time."

"I'll furnish money for grub," returned Duane. "And for whisky, too, providing you hurry back here—without making trouble."

"Shore you're a downright good pard," declared Stevens, in admiration, as he took the money. "I give my word, Buck, an' I'm here to say I never broke it yet. Lay low, an' look fer me back quick."

With that he spurred his horse and rode out of the mesquites toward the town. At that distance, about a quarter of a mile, Mercer appeared to be a cluster of low adobe houses set in a grove of cottonwoods. Pastures of alfalfa were dotted by horses and cattle. Duane saw a sheep-herder driving in a meager flock.

Presently Stevens rode out of sight into the town. Duane waited, hoping the outlaw would make good his word. Probably not a quarter of an hour had elapsed when Duane heard the clear reports of a Winchester rifle, the clatter of rapid hoof-beats, and yells unmistakably the kind to mean danger for a man like Stevens. Duane mounted and rode to the edge of the mesquites.

He saw a cloud of dust down the road and a bay horse running fast. Stevens apparently had not been wounded by any of the shots, for he had a steady seat in his saddle and his riding, even at that moment, struck Duane as admirable. He carried a large pack over the pommel, and he kept looking back. The shots had ceased, but the yells increased. Duane saw several men running and waving their arms. Then he spurred his horse and got into a swift stride, so Stevens would not pass him. Presently the outlaw caught up with him. Stevens was grinning, but there was now no fun in the dancing eyes. It was a devil that danced in them. His face seemed a shade paler.

"Was jest comin' out of the store," yelled Stevens. "Run plumb into a rancher—who knowed me. He opened up with a rifle. Think they'll chase us."

They covered several miles before there were any signs of pursuit, and when horsemen did move into sight out of the cottonwoods Duane and his companion steadily drew farther away.

"No hosses in thet bunch to worry us," called out Stevens.

Duane had the same conviction, and he did not look back again. He rode somewhat to the fore, and was constantly aware of the rapid thudding of hoofs behind, as Stevens kept close to him. At sunset they reached the willow brakes and the river. Duane's horse was winded and lashed with sweat and lather. It was not until the crossing had been accomplished that Duane halted to rest his animal. Stevens was riding up the low, sandy bank. He reeled in the saddle. With an exclamation of surprise Duane leaped off and ran to the outlaw's side.

Stevens was pale, and his face bore beads of sweat. The whole front of his shirt was soaked with blood.

"You're shot!" cried Duane.

"Wal, who 'n hell said I wasn't? Would you mind givin' me a lift—on this here pack?"

Duane lifted the heavy pack down and then helped Stevens to dismount. The outlaw had a bloody foam on his lips, and he was spitting blood.

"Oh, why didn't you *say* so!" cried Duane. "I never thought. You seemed all right."

"Wal, Luke Stevens may be as gabby as an old woman, but sometimes he doesn't say anythin'. It wouldn't have done no good."

Duane bade him sit down, removed his shirt, and washed the blood from his breast and back. Stevens had been shot in the breast, fairly low down, and the bullet had gone clear through him. His ride, holding himself and that heavy pack in the saddle, had been a feat little short of marvelous, Duane did not see how it had been possible, and he felt no hope for the outlaw. But he plugged the wounds and bound them tightly.

"Feller's name was Brown," Stevens said. "Me an' him fell out over a hoss I stole from him over in Huntsville. We had a shootin'-scrape then. Wal, as I was straddlin' my hoss back there in Mercer I seen this Brown, an' seen him before he seen me. Could have killed him, too. But I wasn't breakin' my word to you. I kind of hoped he wouldn't spot me. But he did—an' fust shot he got me here. What do you think of this hole?"

"It's pretty bad," replied Duane; and he could not look the cheerful outlaw in the eyes.

"I reckon it is. Wal, I've had some bad wounds I lived over. Guess mebbe I can stand this one. Now, Buck, get me some place in the brakes, leave me some grub an' water at my hand, an' then you clear out."

"Leave you here alone?" asked Duane, sharply.

"Shore. You see, I can't keep up with you. Brown an' his friends will foller us acrost the river a ways. You've got to think of number one in this game."

"What would you do in my case?" asked Duane, curiously.

"Wal, I reckon I'd clear out an' save my hide," replied Stevens.

Duane felt inclined to doubt the outlaw's assertion. For his own part he decided his conduct without further speech. First he watered the horses, filled canteens and water-bag, and then tied the pack upon his own horse. That done, he lifted Stevens upon his horse, and, holding him in the saddle, turned into the brakes, being careful to pick out hard or grassy ground that left little signs of tracks. Just about dark he ran across a trail that Stevens said was a good one to take into the wild country.

"Reckon we'd better keep right on in the dark—till I drop," concluded Stevens, with a laugh.

All that night Duane, gloomy and thoughtful, attentive to the wounded outlaw, walked the trail and never halted till daybreak. He was tired then and very hungry. Stevens seemed in bad shape, although he was spirited and cheerful. Duane made camp. The outlaw refused food, but asked for both whisky and water. Then he stretched out.

"Buck, will you take off my boots?" he asked, with a faint smile on his pallid face.

Duane removed them, wondering if the outlaw had the thought that he did not want to die with his boots on. Stevens seemed to read his mind.

"Buck, my old daddy used to say thet I was born to be hanged. But I wasn't—an' dyin' with your boots on is the next wust way to croak."

"You've a chance to—to get over this," said Duane.

"Shore. But I want to be correct about the boots—an' say, pard, if I do go over, jest you remember thet I was appreciatin' of your kindness."

Then he closed his eyes and seemed to sleep.

Duane could not find water for the horses, but there was an abundance of dew-wet grass upon which he hobbled them. After that was done he prepared himself a much-needed meal. The sun was getting warm when he lay down to sleep, and when he awoke it was sinking in the west. Stevens was still alive, for he breathed heavily. The horses were in sight. All was quiet except the hum of insects in the brush. Duane listened awhile, then rose and went for the horses.

When he returned with them he found Stevens awake, bright-eyed, cheerful as usual, and apparently stronger.

"Wal, Buck, I'm still with you an' good fer another night's ride," he said. "Guess about all I need now is a big pull on thet bottle. Help me, will you? There! thet was bully. I ain't swallowin' my blood this evenin'. Mebbe I've bled all there was in me."

While Duane got a hurried meal for himself, packed up the little outfit, and saddled the horses Stevens kept on talking. He seemed to be in a hurry to tell Duane all about the country. Another night ride would put them beyond fear of pursuit, within striking distance of the Rio Grande and the hiding-places of the outlaws.

When it came time for mounting the horses Stevens said, "Reckon you can pull on my boots once more." In spite of the laugh accompanying the words Duane detected a subtle change in the outlaw's spirit.

On this night travel was facilitated by the fact that the trail was broad enough for two horses abreast, enabling Duane to ride while upholding Stevens in the saddle.

The difficulty most persistent was in keeping the horses in a walk. They were used to a trot, and that kind of gait would not do for Stevens. The red died out of the west; a pale afterglow prevailed for a while; darkness set in; then the broad expanse of blue darkened and the stars brightened. After a while Stevens ceased talking and drooped in his saddle. Duane kept the horses going, however, and the slow hours wore away. Duane thought the quiet night would never break to dawn, that there was no end to the melancholy, brooding plain. But at length a grayness blotted out the stars and mantled the level of mesquite and cactus.

Dawn caught the fugitives at a green camping-site on the bank of a rocky little stream. Stevens fell a dead weight into Duane's arms, and one look at the haggard face showed Duane that the outlaw had taken his last ride. He knew it, too. Yet that cheerfulness prevailed.

"Buck, my feet are orful tired packin' them heavy boots," he said, and seemed immensely relieved when Duane had removed them.

This matter of the outlaw's boots was strange, Duane thought. He made Stevens as comfortable as possible, then attended to his own needs. And the outlaw took up the thread of his conversation where he had left off the night before.

"This trail splits up a ways from here, an' every branch of it leads to a hole where you'll find men—a few, mebbe, like yourself—some like me—an' gangs of no-good hoss-thieves, rustlers, an' such. It's easy livin', Buck. I reckon, though, that you'll not find it easy. You'll never mix in. You'll be a lone wolf. I seen that right off. Wal, if a man can stand the loneliness, an' if he's quick on the draw, mebbe lone-wolfin' it is the best. Shore I don't know. But these fellers in here will be suspicious of a man who goes it alone. If they get a chance they'll kill you."

Stevens asked for water several times. He had forgotten or he did not want the whisky. His voice grew perceptibly weaker.

"Be quiet," said Duane. "Talking uses up your strength."

"Aw, I'll talk till—I'm done," he replied, doggedly. "See here, pard, you can gamble on what I'm tellin' you. An' it'll be useful. From this camp we'll— you'll meet men right along. An' none of them will be honest men. All the same, some are better'n others. I've lived along the river fer twelve years. There's three big gangs of outlaws. King Fisher—you know him, I reckon, fer he's half the time livin' among respectable folks. King is a pretty good feller. It'll do to tie up with him an' his gang. Now, there's Cheseldine, who hangs out in the Rim Rock way up the river. He's an outlaw chief. I never seen him, though I stayed once right in his camp. Late years he's got rich an' keeps back pretty well hid. But Bland—I knowed Bland fer years. An' I haven't any use fer him. Bland has the biggest gang. You ain't likely to miss strikin' his place sometime or other. He's got a regular town, I might say. Shore there's some gamblin' an' gun-fightin' goin' on at Bland's camp all the time. Bland has killed some twenty men, an' thet's not countin' greasers."

Here Stevens took another drink and then rested for a while.

"You ain't likely to get on with Bland," he resumed, presently. "You're too strappin' big an' good-lookin' to please the chief. Fer he's got women in his camp. Then he'd be jealous of your possibilities with a gun. Shore I reckon he'd be careful, though. Bland's no fool, an' he loves his hide. I reckon any of the other gangs would be better fer you when you ain't goin' it alone."

Apparently that exhausted the fund of information and advice Stevens had been eager to impart. He lapsed into silence and lay with closed eyes. Meanwhile the sun rose warm; the breeze waved the mesquites; the birds came down to splash in the shallow stream; Duane dozed in a comfortable seat. By and by something roused him. Stevens was once more talking, but with a changed tone.

"Feller's name—was Brown," he rambled. "We fell out—over a hoss I stole from him—in Huntsville. He stole it fust. Brown's one of them sneaks—afraid of the open—he steals an' pretends to be honest. Say, Buck, mebbe you'll meet Brown some day—You an' me are pards now."

"I'll remember, if I ever meet him," said Duane.

That seemed to satisfy the outlaw. Presently he tried to lift his head, but had not the strength. A strange shade was creeping across the bronzed rough face.

"My feet are pretty heavy. Shore you got my boots off?"

Duane held them up, but was not certain that Stevens could see them. The outlaw closed his eyes again and muttered incoherently. Then he fell asleep. Duane believed that sleep was final. The day passed, with Duane watching and waiting. Toward sundown Stevens awoke, and his eyes seemed clearer. Duane went to get some fresh water, thinking his comrade would surely want some. When he returned Stevens made no sign that he wanted anything. There was something bright about him, and suddenly Duane realized what it meant.

"Pard, you—stuck—to me!" the outlaw whispered.

Duane caught a hint of gladness in the voice; he traced a faint surprise in the haggard face. Stevens seemed like a little child.

To Duane the moment was sad, elemental, big, with a burden of mystery he could not understand.

Duane buried him in a shallow arroyo and heaped up a pile of stones to mark the grave. That done, he saddled his comrade's horse, hung the weapons over the pommel; and, mounting his own steed, he rode down the trail in the gathering twilight.

4

Two days later, about the middle of the forenoon, Duane dragged the two horses up the last ascent of an exceedingly rough trail and found himself on top of the Rim Rock, with a beautiful green valley at his feet, the yellow, sluggish Rio

Grande shining in the sun, and the great, wild, mountainous barren of Mexico stretching to the south.

Duane had not fallen in with any travelers. He had taken the likeliest-looking trail he had come across. Where it had led him he had not the slightest idea, except that here was the river, and probably the inclosed valley was the retreat of some famous outlaw.

No wonder outlaws were safe in that wild refuge! Duane had spent the last two days climbing the roughest and most difficult trail he had ever seen. From the looks of the descent he imagined the worst part of his travel was yet to come. Not improbably it was two thousand feet down to the river. The wedge-shaped valley, green with alfalfa and cottonwood, and nestling down amid the bare walls of yellow rock, was a delight and a relief to his tired eyes. Eager to get down to a level and to find a place to rest, Duane began the descent.

The trail proved to be the kind that could not be descended slowly. He kept dodging rocks which his horses loosed behind him. And in a short time he reached the valley, entering at the apex of the wedge. A stream of clear water tumbled out of the rocks here, and most of it ran into irrigation-ditches. His horses drank thirstily. And he drank with that fullness and gratefulness common to the desert traveler finding sweet water. Then he mounted and rode down the valley wondering what would be his reception.

The valley was much larger than it had appeared from the high elevation. Well watered, green with grass and tree, and farmed evidently by good hands, it gave Duane a considerable surprise. Horses and cattle were everywhere. Every clump of cottonwoods surrounded a small adobe house. Duane saw Mexicans working in the fields and horsemen going to and fro. Presently he passed a house bigger than the others with a porch attached. A woman, young and pretty he thought, watched him from a door. No one else appeared to notice hm.

Presently the trail widened into a road, and that into a kind of square lined by a number of adobe and log buildings of rudest structure. Within sight were horses, dogs, a couple of steers, Mexican women with children, and white men, all of whom appeared to be doing nothing. His advent created no interest until he rode up to the white men, who were lolling in the shade of a house. This place evidently was a store and saloon, and from the inside came a lazy hum of voices.

As Duane reined to a halt one of the loungers in the shade rose with a loud exclamation:

"Bust me if thet ain't Luke's hoss!"

The others accorded their interest, if not assent, by rising to advance toward Duane.

"How about it, Euchre? Ain't thet Luke's bay?" queried the first man.

"Plain as your nose," replied the fellow called Euchre.

"There ain't no doubt about thet, then," laughed another, "fer Bosomer's nose is shore plain on the landscape."

These men lined up before Duane, and as he coolly regarded them he thought they could have been recognized anywhere as desperadoes. The man called Bosomer, who had stepped forward, had a forbidding face which showed yellow eyes, an enormous nose, and a skin the color of dust, with a thatch of sandy hair.

"Stranger, who are you an' where in the hell did you git thet bay hoss?" he demanded. His yellow eyes took in Stevens's horse, then the weapons hung on the saddle, and finally turned their glinting, hard light upward to Duane.

Duane did not like the tone in which he had been addressed, and he remained silent. At least half his mind seemed busy with curious interest in regard to something that leaped inside him and made his breast feel tight. He recognized it as that strange emotion which had shot through him often of late, and which had decided him to go out to the meeting with Bain. Only now it was different, more powerful.

"Stranger, who are you?" asked another man, somewhat more civilly.

"My name's Duane," replied Duane, curtly.

"An' how'd you come by the hoss?"

Duane answered briefly, and his words were followed by a short silence, during which the men looked at him. Bosomer began to twist the ends of his beard.

"Reckon he's dead, all right, or nobody'd hev his hoss an' guns," presently said Euchre.

"Mister Duane," began Bosomer, in low, stinging tones, "I happen to be Luke Stevens's side-pardner."

Duane looked him over, from dusty, worn-out boots to his slouchy sombrero. That look seemed to inflame Bosomer.

"An' I want the hoss an' them guns," he shouted.

"You or anybody else can have them, for all I care. I just fetched them in. But the pack is mine," replied Duane. "And say, I befriended your pard. If you can't use a civil tongue you'd better cinch it."

"Civil? Haw, haw!" rejoined the outlaw. "I don't know you. How do we know you didn't plug Stevens, an' stole his hoss, an' jest happened to stumble down here?"

"You'll have to take my word, that's all," replied Duane, sharply.

"____ ____! I ain't takin' your word! Savvy thet? An' I was Luke's pard!"

With that Bosomer wheeled and, pushing his companions aside, he stamped into the saloon, where his voice broke out in a roar.

Duane dismounted and threw his bridle.

"Stranger, Bosomer is shore hot-headed," said the man Euchre. He did not appear unfriendly, nor were the others hostile.

At this juncture several more outlaws crowded out of the door, and the one in the lead was a tall man of stalwart physique. His manner proclaimed him a leader. He had a long face, a flaming red beard, and clear, cold blue eyes that fixed in close scrutiny upon Duane. He was not a Texan; in truth, Duane did not recognize one of these outlaws as native to his state.

"I'm Bland," said the tall man, authoritatively. "Who're you and what're you doing here?"

Duane looked at Bland as he had at the others. This outlaw chief appeared to be reasonable, if he was not courteous. Duane told his story again, this time a little more in detail.

"I believe you," replied Bland, at once. "Think I know when a fellow is lying."

"I reckon you're on the right trail," put in Euchre. "Thet about Luke wantin' his boots took off–thet satisfies me. Luke hed a mortal dread of dyin' with his boots on."

At this sally the chief and his men laughed.

"You said Duane—Buck Duane?" queried Bland. "Are you a son of that Duane who was a gunfighter some years back?"

"Yes," replied Duane.

"Never met him, and glad I didn't," said Bland, with a grim humor. "So you got in trouble and had to go on the dodge? What kind of trouble?"

"Had a fight."

"Fight? Do you mean gun-play?" questioned Bland. He seemed eager, curious, speculative.

"Yes. It ended in gun-play, I'm sorry to say," answered Duane.

"Guess I needn't ask the son of Duane if he killed his man," went on Bland, ironically. "Well, I'm sorry you bucked against trouble in my camp. But as it is, I guess you'd be wise to make yourself scarce."

"Do you mean I'm politely told to move on?" asked Duane, quietly.

"Not exactly that," said Bland, as if irritated. "If this isn't a free place there isn't one on earth. Every man is equal here. Do you want to join my band?"

"No, I don't."

"Well, even if you did I imagine that wouldn't stop Bosomer. He's an ugly fellow. He's one of the few gunmen I've met who wants to kill somebody all the time. Most men like that are four-flushes. But Bosomer is all one color, and that's red. Merely for your own sake I advise you to hit the trail."

"Thanks. But if that's all I'll stay," returned Duane. Even as he spoke he felt that he did not know himself.

Bosomer appeared at the door, pushing men who tried to detain him, and as he jumped clear of a last reaching hand he uttered a snarl like an angry dog. Manifestly the short while he had spent inside the saloon had been devoted to drinking and talking himself into a frenzy. Bland and the other outlaws quickly moved aside, letting Duane stand alone. When Bosomer saw Duane standing motionless and watchful a strange change passed quickly in him. He halted in his tracks, and as he did that the men who had followed him out piled over one another in their hurry to get to one side.

Duane saw all the swift action, felt intuitively the meaning of it, and in Bosomer's sudden change of front. The outlaw was keen, and he had expected a shrinking, or at least a frightened antagonist. Duane knew he was neither. He felt like iron, and yet thrill after thrill ran through him. It was almost as if this situation had been one long familiar to him. Somehow he understood this yellow-eyed Bosomer. The outlaw had come out to kill him. And now, though somewhat checked by the stand of a stranger, he still meant to kill. Like so many desperadoes of his ilk, he was victim of a passion to kill for the sake of killing. Duane divined that no sudden animosity was driving Bosomer. It was just his chance. In that moment murder whould have been joy to him. Very likely he had forgotten his pretext for a quarrel. Very probably his faculties were absorbed in conjecture as to Duane's possibilities.

But he did not speak a word. He remained motionless for a long moment, his eyes pale and steady, his right hand like a claw.

That instant gave Duane a power to read in his enemy's eyes the thought that preceded action. But Duane did not want to kill another man. Still he would have to fight, and he decided to cripple Bosomer. When Bosomer's hand moved Duane's gun was spouting fire. Two shots only—both from Duane's gun—and the outlaw fell with his right arm shattered. Bosomer cursed harshly and floundered in the dust, trying to reach the gun with his left hand. His comrades, however, seeing that Duane would not kill unless forced, closed in upon Bosomer and prevented any further madness on his part.

5

OF the outlaws present Euchre appeared to be the one most inclined to lend friendliness to curiosity; and he led Duane and the horses away to a small adobe shack. He tied the horses in an open shed and removed their saddles. Then, gathering up Stevens's weapons, he invited his visitor to enter the house.

It had two rooms—windows without coverings—bare floors. One room contained blankets, weapons, saddles, and bridles; the other a stone fireplace, rude table and bench, two bunks, a box cupboard, and various blackened utensils.

"Make yourself to home as long as you want to stay," said Euchre. "I ain't rich in this world's goods, but I own what's here, an' you're welcome."

"Thanks. I'll stay awhile and rest. I'm pretty well played out," replied Duane. Euchre gave him a keen glance.

"Go ahead an' rest. I'll take your horses to grass."

Euchre left Duane alone in the house. Duane relaxed then, and mechanically he wiped the sweat from his face. He was laboring under some kind of a spell or shock which did not pass off quickly. When it had worn away he took off his coat and belt and made himself comfortable on the blankets. And he had a thought that if he rested or slept what difference would it make on the morrow? No rest, no sleep could change the gray outlook of the future. He felt glad when Euchre came bustling in, and for the first time he took notice of the outlaw.

Euchre was old in years. What little hair he had was gray, his face clean-shaven and full of wrinkles; his eyes were half shut from long gazing through the sun and dust. He stooped. But his thin frame denoted strength and endurance still unimpaired.

"Hev a drink or a smoke?" he asked.

Duane shook his head. He had not been unfamiliar with whisky, and he had used tobacco moderately since he was sixteen. But now, strangely, he felt a disgust at the idea of stimulants. He did not understand clearly what he felt. There was that vague idea of something wild in his blood, something that made him fear himself.

Euchre wagged his old head sympathetically. "Reckon you feel a little sick. When it comes to shootin' I run. What's your age?"

"I'm twenty-three," replied Duane.

Euchre showed surprise. "You're only a boy! I thought you thirty anyways. Buck, I heard what you told Bland, an' puttin' thet with my own figgerin', I reckon you're no criminal yet. Throwin' a gun in self-defense—thet ain't no crime!"

Duane, finding relief in talking, told more about himself.

"Huh," replied the old man. "I've been on this river fer years, an' I've seen hundreds of boys come in on the dodge. Most of them, though, was no good. An' thet kind don't last long. This river country has been an' is the refuge fer criminals from all over the states. I've bunked with bank cashiers, forgers, plain thieves, an' out-an'-out murderers, all of which had no bizness on the Texas border. Fellers like Bland are exceptions. He's no Texan—you seen thet. The gang he rules here come from all over, an' they're tough cusses, you can bet on thet. They live fat an' easy. If it wasn't fer the fightin' among themselves they'd shore grow populous. The Rim Rock is no place for a peaceable, decent feller. I heard you tell Bland you wouldn't join his gang. Thet'll not make him take a likin' to you. Have you any money?''

"Not much," replied Duane.

"Could you live by gamblin'? Are you any good at cards?"

"No."

"You wouldn't steal hosses or rustle cattle?"

"No."

"When your money's gone how'n hell will you live? There ain't any work a decent feller could do. You can't herd with greasers. Why, Bland's men would shoot at you in the fields. What'll you do, son?"

"God knows," replied Duane, hopelessly. "I'll make my money last as long as possible—then starve."

"Wal, I'm pretty pore, but you'll never starve while I got anythin'."

Here it struck Duane again—that something human and kind and eager which he had seen in Stevens. Duane's estimate of outlaws had lacked this quality. He had not accorded them any virtues. To him, as to the outside world, they had been merely vicious men without one redeeming feature.

"I'm much obliged to you, Euchre," replied Duane. "But of course I won't live with any one unless I can pay my share."

"Have it any way you like, my son," said Euchre, good-humoredly. "You make a fire, an' I'll set about gettin' grub. I'm a sourdough, Buck. Thet man doesn't live who can beat my bread."

"How do you ever pack supplies in here?" asked Duane, thinking of the almost inaccessible nature of the valley.

"Some comes across from Mexico, an' the rest down the river. Thet river trip is a bird. It's more'n five hundred miles to any supply point. Bland has *mozos*, greaser boatmen. Sometimes, too, he gets supplies in from down-river. You see, Bland sells thousands of cattle in Cuba. An' all this stock has to go down by boat to meet the ships."

"Where on earth are the cattle driven down to the river?" asked Duane.

"Thet's not my secret," replied Euchre, shortly. "Fact is, I don't know. I've rustled cattle for Bland, but he never sent me through the Rim Rock with them."

Duane experienced a sort of pleasure in the realization that interest had been stirred in him. He was curious about Bland and his gang, and glad to have something to think about. For every once in a while he had a sensation that was almost like a pang. He wanted to forget. In the next hour he did forget, and enjoyed helping in the preparation and eating of the meal. Euchre, after washing and hanging up the several utensils, put on his hat and turned to go out.

"Come along or stay here, as you want," he said to Duane.

"I'll stay," rejoined Duane, slowly.

The old outlaw left the room and trudged away, whistling cheerfully.

Duane looked around him for a book or paper, anything to read; but all the printed matter he could find consisted of a few words on cartridge-boxes and an advertisement on the back of a tobacco-pouch. There seemed to be nothing for him to do. He had rested; he did not want to lie down any more. He began to walk to and fro, from one end of the room to the other. And as he walked he fell into the lately acquired habit of brooding over his misfortune.

Suddenly he straightened up with a jerk. Unconsciously he had drawn his gun. Standing there with the bright cold weapon in his hand, he looked at it in consternation. How had he come to draw it? With difficulty he traced his thoughts backward, but could not find any that was accountable for his act. He discovered, however, that he had a remarkable tendency to drop his hand to his gun. That might have come from the habit long practice in drawing had given him. Likewise, it might have come from a subtle sense, scarcely thought of at all, of the late, close, and inevitable relation between that weapon and himself. He was amazed to find that, bitter as he had grown at fate, the desire to live burned strong in him. If he had been as unfortunately situated, but with the difference that no man wanted to put him in jail or take his life, he felt that this burning passion to be free, to save himself, might not have been so powerful. Life certainly held no bright prospects for him. Already he had begun to despair of ever getting back to his home. But to give up like a white-hearted coward, to let himself be handcuffed and jailed, to run from a drunken, bragging cowboy, or be shot in cold blood by some border brute who merely wanted to add another notch to his gun—these things were impossible for Duane because there was in him the temper to fight. In that hour he yielded only to fate and the spirit inborn in him. Hereafter this gun must be a living part of him. Right then and there he returned to a practice he had long discontinued—the draw. It was now a stern, bitter, deadly business with him. He did not need to fire the gun, for accuracy was a gift and had become assured. Swiftness on the draw, however, could be improved, and he set himself to acquire the limit of speed possible to any man. He stood still in his tracks; he paced the room; he sat down, lay down, put himself in awkward positions; and from every position he practised throwing his gun—practised it till he was hot and tired and his arm ached and his hand burned. That practice he determined to keep up every day. It was one thing, at least, that would help pass the weary hours.

Later he went outdoors to the cooler shade of the cottonwoods. From this point he could see a good deal of the valley. Under different circumstances Duane felt that he would have enjoyed such a beautiful spot. Euchre's shack sat against the first rise of the slope of the wall, and Duane, by climbing a few rods, got a view of the whole valley. Assuredly it was an outlaw settlement. He saw a good many Mexicans, who, of course, were hand and glove with Bland. Also he saw enormous flat-boats, crude of structure, moored along the banks of the river. The Rio Grande rolled away between high bluffs. A cable, sagging deep in the middle, was stretched over the wide yellow stream, and an old scow, evidently used as a ferry, lay anchored on the far shore.

The valley was an ideal retreat for an outlaw band operating on a big scale. Pursuit scarcely need be feared over the broken trails of the Rim Rock. And the open end of the valley could be defended against almost any number of men coming down the river. Access to Mexico was easy and quick. What puzzled Duane was how Bland got cattle down to the river, and he wondered if the rustler really did get rid of his stolen stock by use of boats.

Duane must have idled considerable time up on the hill, for when he returned to the shack Euchre was busily engaged around the camp-fire.

"Wal, glad to see you ain't so pale about the gills as you was," he said, by way of greeting. "Pitch in an' we'll soon have grub ready. There's shore one consolin' fact round this here camp."

"What's that?" asked Duane.

"Plenty of good juicy beef to eat. An' it doesn't cost a short bit."

"But it costs hard rides and trouble, bad conscience, and life, too, doesn't it?"

"I ain't shore about the bad conscience. Mine never bothered me none. An' as for life, why, thet's cheap in Texas."

"Who is Bland?" asked Duane, quickly changing the subject. "What do you know about him?"

"We don't know who he is or where he hails from," replied Euchre. "Thet's always been somethin' to interest the gang. He must have been a young man when he struck Texas. Now he's middle-aged. I remember how years ago he was softspoken an' not rough in talk or act like he is now. Bland ain't likely his right name. He knows a lot. He can doctor you, an' he's shore a knowin' feller with tools. He's the kind thet rules men. Outlaws are always ridin' in here to join his gang, an' if it hadn't been fer the gamblin' an' gun-play he'd have a thousand men around him."

"How many in his gang now?"

"I reckon there's short of a hundred now. The number varies. Then Bland has several small camps up an' down the river. Also he has men back on the cattle-ranges."

"How does he control such a big force?" asked Duane. "Especially when his band's composed of bad men. Luke Stevens said he had no use for Bland. And I heard once somewhere that Bland was a devil."

"Thet's it. He is a devil. He's as hard as flint, violent in temper, never made any friends except his right-hand men, Dave Rugg an' Chess Alloway. Bland'll shoot at a wink. He's killed a lot of fellers, an' some fer nothin'. The reason

thet outlaws gather round him an' stick is because he's a safe refuge, an' then
he's well heeled. Bland is rich. They say he has a hundred thousand *pesos* hid
somewhere, an' lots of gold. But he's free with money. He gambles when he's
not off with a shipment of cattle. He throws money around. An' the fact is
there's always plenty of money where he is. Thet's what holds the gang. Dirty,
bloody money!''

"It's a wonder he hasn't been killed. All these years on the border!" exclaimed
Duane.

"Wal," replied Euchre, dryly, "he's been quicker on the draw than the other
fellers who hankered to kill him, thet's all.''

Euchre's reply rather chilled Duane's interest for the moment. Such remarks
always made his mind revolve round facts pertaining to himself.

"Speakin' of this here swift wrist game," went on Euchre, 'there's been
considerable talk in camp about your throwin' of a gun. You know, Buck, thet
among us fellers—us hunted men—there ain't anythin' calculated to rouse respect
like a slick hand with a gun. I heard Bland say this afternoon—an' he said it
serious-like an' speculative—thet he'd never seen your equal. He was watchin'
of you close, he said, an' just couldn't follow your hand when you drawed. All
the fellers who seen you meet Bosomer had somethin' to say. Bo was about as
handy with a gun as any man in this camp, barrin' Chess Alloway an' mebbe
Bland himself. Chess is the captain with a Colt—or he was. An' he shore didn't
like the references made about your speed. Bland was honest in acknowledgin'
it, but he didn't like it, neither. Some of the fellers allowed your draw might
have been just accident. But most of them figgered different. An' they all shut
up when Bland told who an' what your Dad was. 'Pears to me I once seen your
Dad in a gunscrape over at Santone, years ago. Wal, I put my oar in to-day
among the fellers, an' I says: 'What ails you locoed gents? Did young Duane
budge an inch when Bo came roarin' out, blood in his eye? Wasn't he cool an'
quiet, steady of lips, an' weren't his eyes readin' Bo's mind? An' thet lightnin'
draw—can't you-all see thet's a family gift?' ''

Euchre's narrow eyes twinkled, and he gave the dough he was rolling a slap
with his flour-whitened hand. Manifestly he had proclaimed himself a champion
and partner of Duane's, with all the pride an old man could feel in a young one
whom he admired.

"Wal," he resumed, presently, "thet's your introduction to the border, Buck.
An' your card was a high trump. You'll be let severely alone by real gun-fighters
an' men like Bland, Alloway, Rugg, an' the bosses of the other gangs. After
all, these real men *are* men, you know, an' onless you cross them they're no
more likely to interfere with you than you are with them. But there's a sight of
fellers like Bosomer in the river country. They'll all want your game. An' every
town you ride into will scare up some cowpuncher full of booze or a long-haired

four-flush gunman or a sheriff—an' these men will be playin' to the crowd an' yellin' for your blood. Thet's the Texas of it. You'll have to hide fer ever in the brakes or you'll have to *kill* such men. Buck, I reckon this ain't cheerful news to a decent chap like you. I'm only tellin' you because I've taken a likin' to you, an' I seen right off thet you ain't border-wise. Let's eat now, an' afterward we'll go out so the gang can see you're not hidin'.''

When Duane went out with Euchre the sun was setting behind a blue range of mountains across the river in Mexico. The valley appeared to open to the southwest. It was a tranquil, beautiful scene. Somewhere in a house near at hand a woman was singing. And in the road Duane saw a little Mexican boy driving home some cows, one of which wore a bell. The sweet, happy voice of a woman and a whistling barefoot boy—these seemed utterly out of place here.

Euchre presently led to the square and the row of rough houses Duane remembered. He almost stepped on a wide imprint in the dust where Bosomer had confronted him. And a sudden fury beset him that he should be affected strangely by the sight of it.

"Let's have a look in here," said Euchre.

Duane had to bend his head to enter the door. He found himself in a very large room inclosed by adobe walls and roofed with brush. It was full of rude benches, tables, seats. At one corner a number of kegs and barrels lay side by side in a rack. A Mexican boy was lighting lamps hung on posts that sustained the log rafters of the roof.

"The only feller who's goin' to put a close eye on you is Benson," said Euchre. "He runs the place an' sells drinks. The gang calls him Jackrabbit Benson, because he's always got his eye peeled an' his ear cocked. Don't notice him if he looks you over, Buck. Benson is scared to death of every new-comer who rustles into Bland's camp. An' the reason, I take it, is because he's done somebody dirt. He's hidin'. Not from a sheriff or ranger! Men who hide from them don't act like Jackrabbit Benson. He's hidin' from some guy who's huntin' him to kill him. Wal, I'm always expectin' to see some feller ride in here an' throw a gun on Benson. Can't say I'd be grieved.''

Duane casually glanced in the direction indicated, and he saw a spare, gaunt man with a face strikingly white beside the red and bronze and dark skins of the men around him. It was a cadaverous face. The black mustache hung down; a heavy lock of black hair dropped down over the brow; deep-set, hollow, staring eyes looked out piercingly. The man had a restless, alert, nervous manner. He put his hands on the board that served as a bar and stared at Duane. But when he met Duane's glance he turned hurriedly to go on serving out liquor.

"What have you got against him?" inquired Duane, as he sat down beside

Euchre. He asked more for something to say than from real interest. What did he care about a mean, haunted, cravenfaced criminal?

"Wal, mebbe I'm cross-grained," replied Euchre, apologetically. "Shore an outlaw an' rustler such as me can't be touchy. But I never stole nothin' but cattle from some rancher who never missed 'em anyway. Thet sneak Benson—he was the means of puttin' a little girl in Bland's way."

"Girl?" queried Duane, now with real attention.

"Shore. Bland's great on women. I'll tell you about this girl when we get out of here. Some of the gang are goin' to be sociable, an' I can't talk about the chief."

During the ensuing half-hour a number of outlaws passed by Duane and Euchre, halted for a greeting or sat down for a moment. They were all gruff, loud-voiced, merry, and good-natured. Duane replied civilly and agreeably when he was personally addressed; but he refused all invitations to drink and gamble. Evidently he had been accepted, in a way, as one of their clan. No one made any hint of an allusion to his affair with Bosomer. Duane saw readily that Euchre was well liked. One outlaw borrowed money from him; another asked for tobacco.

By the time it was dark the big room was full of outlaws and Mexicans, most of whom were engaged at *monte*. These gamblers, especially the Mexicans, were intense and quiet. The noise in the place came from the drinkers, the loungers. Duane had seen gambling-resorts—some of the famous ones in San Antonio and El Paso, a few in border towns where license went unchecked. But this place of Jackrabbit Benson's impressed him as one where guns and knives were accessories to the game. To his perhaps rather distinguishing eye the most prominent thing about the gamesters appeared to be their weapons. On several of the tables were piles of silver—Mexican *pesos*—as large and high as the crown of his hat. There were also piles of gold and silver in United States coin. Duane needed no experienced eyes to see that betting was heavy and that heavy sums exchanged hands. The Mexicans showed a sterner obsession, an intenser passion. Some of the Americans staked freely, nonchalantly, as befitted men to whom money was nothing. These latter were manifestly winning, for there were brother outlaws there who wagered coin with grudging, sullen, greedy eyes. Boisterous talk and laughter among the drinking men drowned, except at intervals, the low, brief talk of the gamblers. The clink of coin sounded incessantly; sometimes just low, steady musical rings; and again, when a pile was tumbled quickly, there was a silvery crash. Here an outlaw pounded on a table with the butt of his gun; there another noisily palmed a roll of dollars while he studied his opponent's face. The noises, however, in Benson's den did not contribute to any extent to the sinister aspect of the place. That seemed to come from the grim and reckless faces, from the bent, intent heads, from the dark lights and shades. There were bright lights, but these served only to make the shadows. And in the shadows lurked unrestrained lust of gain, a spirit ruthless and reckless, a something at once suggesting lawlessness, theft, murder, and hell.

"Bland's not here to-night," Euchre was saying. "He left today on one of his trips, takin' Alloway an' some others. But his other man, Rugg, he's here. See him standin' with them three fellers, all close to Benson. Rugg's the little bow-legged man with the half of his face shot off. He's one-eyed. But he can shore see out of the one he's got. An', darn me! there's Hardin. You know him? He's got an outlaw gang as big as Bland's. Hardin is standin' next to Benson. See how quiet an' unassumin' he looks. Yes, thet's Hardin. He comes here once in a while to see Bland. They're friends, which's shore strange. Do you see thet greaser there—the one with gold an' lace on his sombrero? Thet's Manuel, a Mexican bandit. He's a great gambler. Comes here often to drop his coin. Next to him is Bill Marr—the feller with the bandana round his head. Bill rode in the other day with some fresh bullet-holes. He's been shot more'n any feller I ever heard of. He's full of lead. Funny, because Bill's no trouble-hunter, an', like me, he'd rather run than shoot. But he's the best rustler Bland's got—a grand rider, an' a wonder with cattle. An' see the tow-headed youngster. Thet's Kid Fuller, the kid of Bland's gang. Fuller has hit the pace hard, an' he won't last the year out on the border. He killed his sweetheart's father, got run out of Staceytown, took to stealin' hosses. An' next he's here with Bland. Another boy gone wrong, an' now shore a hard nut."

Euchre went on calling Duane's attention to other men, just as he happened to glance over them. Any one of them would have been a marked man in a respectable crowd. Here each took his place with more or less distinction, according to the record of his past wild prowess and his present possibilities. Duane, realizing that he was tolerated there, received in careless friendly spirit by this terrible class of outcasts, experienced a feeling of revulsion that amounted almost to horror. Was his being there not an ugly dream? What had he in common with such ruffians? Then in a flash of memory came the painful proof—he was a criminal in sight of Texas law; he, too, was an outcast.

For the moment Duane was wrapped up in painful reflections; but Euchre's heavy hand, clapping with a warning hold on his arm, brought him back to outside things.

The hum of voices, the clink of coin, the loud laughter had ceased. There was a silence that manifestly had followed some unusual word or action sufficient to still the room. It was broken by a harsh curse and the scrape of a bench on the floor. Some man had risen.

"You stacked the cards, you—!"

"Say that twice," another voice replied, so different in its cool, ominous tone from the other.

"I'll say it twice," returned the first gamester, in hot haste. "I'll say it three times. I'll whistle it. Are you deaf? You light-fingered gent! You stacked the cards!"

Silence ensued, deeper than before, pregnant with meaning. For all that Duane saw, not an outlaw moved for a full moment. Then suddenly the room was full of disorder as men rose and ran and dived everywhere.

"Run or duck!" yelled Euchre, close to Duane's ear. With that he dashed for the door. Duane leaped after him. They ran into a jostling mob. Heavy gun-shots and hoarse yells hurried the crowd Duane was with pell-mell out into the darkness. There they all halted, and several peeped in at the door.

"Who was the Kid callin'?" asked one outlaw.

"Bud Marsh," replied another.

"I reckon them fust shots was Bud's. *Adios* Kid. It was comin' to him," went on yet another.

"How many shots?"

"Three or four, I counted."

"Three heavy an' one light. Thet light one was the Kid's .38. Listen! There's the Kid hollerin' now. He ain't cashed, anyway."

At this juncture most of the outlaws began to file back into the room. Duane thought he had seen and heard enough in Benson's den for one night and he started slowly down the walk. Presently Euchre caught up with him.

"Nobody hurt much, which's shore some strange," he said. "The Kid—young Fuller thet I was tellin' you about—he was drinkin' an' losin'. Lost his nut, too, callin' Bud Marsh thet way. Bud's as straight at cards as any of 'em. Somebody grabbed Bud, who shot into the roof. An' Fuller's arm was knocked up. He only hit a greaser."

6

NEXT morning Duane found that a moody and despondent spell had fastened on him. Wishing to be alone, he went out and walked a trail leading round the river bluff. He thought and thought. After a while he made out that the trouble with him probably was that he could not resign himself to his fate. He abhorred the possibility chance seemed to hold in store for him. He could not believe there was no hope. But what to do appeared beyond his power to tell.

Duane had intelligence and keenness enough to see his peril—the danger threatening his character as a man, just as much as that which threatened his life. He cared vastly more, he discovered, for what he considered honor and integrity than he did for life. He saw that it was bad for him to be alone. But, it appeared, lonely months and perhaps years inevitably must be his. Another thing puzzled him. In the bright light of day he could not recall the state of mind that was his at twilight or dusk or in the dark night. By day these visitations became to him what they really were—phantoms of his conscience. He could dismiss the thought of them then. He could scarcely remember or believe that this strange feat of fancy or imagination had troubled him, pained him, made him sleepless and sick.

That morning Duane spent an unhappy hour wrestling decision out of the unstable condition of his mind. But at length he determined to create interest in all that he came across and so forget himself as much as possible. He had an opportunity now to see just what the outlaw's life really was. He meant to force himself to be curious, sympathetic, clear-sighted. And he would stay there in the valley until its possibilities had been exhausted or until circumstances sent him out upon his uncertain way.

When he returned to the shack Euchre was cooking dinner.

"Say, Buck, I've news for you," he said; and his tone conveyed either pride in his possession of such news or pride in Duane. "Feller named Bradley rode in this mornin'. He's heard some about you. Told about the ace of spades they put over the bullet-holes in thet cowpuncher Bain you plugged. Then there was a rancher shot at a water-hole twenty miles south of Wellston. Reckon you didn't do it?"

"No, I certainly did not," replied Duane.

"Wal, you get the blame. It ain't nothin' for a feller to be saddled with gun-plays he never made. An', Buck, if you ever get famous, as seems likely, you'll be blamed for many a crime. The border'll make an outlaw an' murderer out of you. Wal, thet's enough of thet. I've more news. You're goin' to be popular."

"Popular? What do you mean?"

"I met Bland's wife this mornin'. She seen you the other day when you rode in. She shore wants to meet you, an' so do some of the other women in camp. They always want to meet the new fellers who've just come in. It's lonesome for women here, an' they like to hear news from the towns."

"Well, Euchre, I don't want to be impolite, but I'd rather not meet any women," rejoined Duane.

"I was afraid you wouldn't. Don't blame you much. Women are hell. I was hopin', though, you might talk a little to thet poor lonesome kid."

"What kid?" inquired Duane, in surprise.

"Didn't I tell you about Jennie—the girl Bland's holdin' here—the one Jack-rabbit Benson had a hand in stealin'?"

"You mentioned a girl. That's all. Tell me now," replied Duane, abruptly.

"Wal, I got it this way. Mebbe it's straight, an' mebbe it ain't. Some years ago Benson made a trip over the river to buy mescal an' other drinks. He'll sneak over there once in a while. An' as I get it he run across a gang of greasers with some gringo prisoners. I don't know, but I reckon there was some barterin', perhaps murderin'. Anyway, Benson fetched the girl back. She was more dead than alive. But it turned out she was only starved an' scared half to death. She hadn't been harmed. I reckon she was then about fourteen years old. Benson's idee, he said, was to use her in his den sellin' drinks an' the like. But I never went much on Jackrabbit's word. Bland seen the kid right off and took her— bought her from Benson. You can gamble Bland didn't do thet from notions of chivalry. I ain't gainsayin', however, but thet Jennie was better off with Kate Bland. She's been hard on Jennie, but she's kept Bland an' the other men from treatin' the kid shameful. Late Jennie has growed into an all-fired pretty girl, an' Kate is powerful jealous of her. I can see hell brewin' over there in Bland's cabin. Thet's why I wish you'd come over with me. Bland's hardly ever home. His wife's invited you. Shore, if she gets sweet on you, as she has on— Wal, thet 'd complicate matters. But you'd get to see Jennie, an' mebbe you could help her. Mind, I ain't hintin' nothin'. I'm just wantin' to put her in your way. You're a man an' can think fer yourself. I had a baby girl once, an' if she'd lived she be as big as Jennie now, an', by Gawd, I wouldn't want her here in Bland's camp."

"I'll go, Euchre. Take me over," replied Duane. He felt Euchre's eyes upon him. The old outlaw, however, had no more to say.

In the afternoon Euchre set off with Duane, and soon they reached Bland's cabin. Duane remembered it as the one where he had seen the pretty woman watching him ride by. He could not recall what she looked like. The cabin was the same as the other adobe structures in the valley, but it was larger and pleasantly located rather high up in a grove of cottonwoods. In the windows and upon the porch were evidences of a woman's hand. Through the open door Duane caught a glimpse of bright Mexican blankets and rugs.

Euchre knocked upon the side of the door.

"Is that you, Euchre?" asked a girl's voice, low, hesitatingly. The tone of it, rather deep and with a note of fear, struck Duane. He wondered what she would be like.

"Yes, it's me, Jennie. Where's Mrs. Bland?" answered Euchre.

"She went over to Deger's. There's somebody sick," replied the girl.

Euchre turned and whispered something about luck. The snap of the outlaw's eyes was added significance to Duane.

"Jennie, come out or let us come in. Here's the young man I was tellin' you about," Euchre said.

"Oh, I can't! I look so—so— "

"Never mind how you look," interrupted the outlaw, in a whisper. "It ain't no time to care fer thet. Here's young Duane. Jennie, he's no rustler, no thief. He's different. Come out, Jennie, an' mebbe he'll—"

Euchre did not complete his sentence. He had spoken low, with his glance shifting from side to side.

But what he said was sufficient to bring the girl quickly. She appeared in the doorway with downcast eyes and a stain of red in her white cheek. She had a pretty, sad face and bright hair.

"Don't be bashful, Jennie," said Euchre. "You an' Duane have a chance to talk a little. Now I'll go fetch Mrs. Bland, but I won't be hurryin'."

With that Euchre went away through the cottonwoods.

"I'm glad to meet you, Miss—Miss Jennie," said Duane. "Euchre didn't mention your last name. He asked me to come over to—"

Duane's attempt at pleasantry halted short when Jennie lifted her lashes to look at him. Some kind of a shock went through Duane. Her gray eyes were beautiful, but it had not been beauty that cut short his speech. He seemed to see a tragic struggle between hope and doubt that shone in her piercing gaze. She kept looking, and Duane could not break the silence. It was no ordinary moment.

"What did you come here for?" she asked, at last.

"To see you," replied Duane, glad to speak.

"Why?"

"Well—Euchre thought—he wanted me to talk to you, cheer you up a bit," replied Duane, somewhat lamely. The earnest eyes embarrassed him.

"Euchre's good. He's the only person in this awful place who's been good to me. But he's afraid of Bland. He said you were different. Who are you?"

Duane told her.

"You're not a robber or rustler or murderer or some bad man come here to hide?"

"No, I'm not," replied Duane, trying to smile.

"Then why are you here?"

"I'm on the dodge. You know what that means. I got in a shooting-scrape at home and had to run off. When it blows over I hope to go back."

"But you can't be honest here?"

"Yes, I can."

"Oh, I know what these outlaws are. Yes, you're different." She kept the strained gaze upon him, but hope was kindling, and the hard lines of her youthful face were softening.

Something sweet and warm stirred deep in Duane as he realized the unfortunate girl was experiencing a birth of trust in him.

"O God! Maybe you're the man to save me—to take me away before it's too late!"

Duane's spirit leaped.

"Maybe I am," he replied, instantly.

She seemed to check a blind impulse to run into his arms. Her cheek flamed, her lips quivered, her bosom swelled under her ragged dress. Then the glow began to fade; doubt once more assailed her.

"It can't be. You're only—after me, too, like Bland—like all of them."

Duane's long arms went out and his hands clasped her shoulders. He shook her.

"Look at me—straight in the eye. There are decent men. Haven't you a father—a brother?"

"They're dead—killed by raiders. We lived in Dimmit County. I was carried away," Jennie replied, hurriedly. She put up an appealing hand to him. "Forgive me. I believe—I know you're good. It was only—I live so much in fear—I'm half crazy—I've almost forgotten what good men are like, Mister Duane, you'll help me?"

"Yes, Jennie, I will. Tell me how. What must I do? Have you any plan?"

"Oh no. But take me away."

"I'll try," said Duane, simply. "That won't be easy, though. I must have time to think. You must help me. There are many things to consider. Horses, food, trails, and then the best time to make the attempt. Are you watched—kept prisoner?"

"No. I could have run off lots of times. But I was afraid. I'd only have fallen into worse hands. Euchre has told me that. Mrs. Bland beats me, half starves me, but she has kept me from her husband and these other dogs. She's been as good as that, and I'm grateful. She hasn't done it for love of me, though. She always hated me. And lately she's growing jealous. There was a man came here by the name of Spence—so he called himself. He tried to be kind to me. But she wouldn't let him. She was in love with him. She's a bad woman. Bland finally shot Spence, and that ended that. She's been jealous ever since. I hear her fighting with Bland about me. She swears she'll kill me before he gets me. And Bland laughs in her face. Then I've heard Chess Alloway try to persuade Bland to give me to him. But Bland doesn't laugh then. Just lately before Bland went away things almost came to a head. I couldn't sleep. I wished Mrs. Bland would kill me. I'll certainly kill myself if they ruin me. Duane, you must be quick if you'd save me."

"I realize that," replied he, thoughtfully. "I think my difficulty will be to fool Mrs. Bland. If she suspected me she'd have the whole gang of outlaws on me at once."

"She would that. You've got to be careful—and quick."

"What kind of woman is she?" inquired Duane.

"She's—she's brazen. I've heard her with her lovers. They get drunk sometimes when Bland's away. She's got a terrible temper. She's vain. She likes flattery. Oh, you could fool her easy enough if you'd lower yourself to—to—"

"To make love to her?" interrupted Duane.

Jennie bravely turned shamed eyes to meet his.

"My girl, I'd do worse than that to get you away from here," he said, bluntly.

"But—Duane," she faltered, and again she put out the appealing hand. "Bland will kill you."

Duane made no reply to this. He was trying to still a rising strange tumult in his breast. The old emotion—the rush of an instinct to kill! He turned cold all over.

"Chess Alloway will kill you if Bland doesn't," went on Jennie, with her tragic eyes on Duane's.

"Maybe he will," replied Duane. It was difficult for him to force a smile. But he achieved one.

"Oh, better take me off at once," she said. "Save me without risking so much—without making love to Mrs. Bland!"

"Surely, if I can. There! I see Euchre coming with a woman."

"That's her. Oh, she mustn't see me with you."

"Wait—a moment," whispered Duane, as Jennie slipped indoors. "We've settled it. Don't forget. I'll find some way to get word to you, perhaps through Euchre. Meanwhile keep up your courage. Remember I'll save you somehow. We'll try strategy first. Whatever you see or hear me do, don't think less of me—"

Jennie checked him with a gesture and a wonderful gray flash of eyes.

"I'll bless you with every drop of blood in my heart," she whispered, passionately.

It was only as she turned away into the room that Duane saw she was lame and that she wore Mexican sandals over bare feet.

He sat down upon a bench on the porch and directed his attention to the approaching couple. The trees of the grove were thick enough for him to make reasonably sure that Mrs. Bland had not seen him talking to Jennie. When the outlaw's wife drew near Duane saw that she was a tall, strong, fullbodied woman, rather good-looking with a fullblown, bold attractiveness. Duane was more concerned with her expression than with her good looks; and as she appeared unsuspicious he felt relieved. The situation then took on a singular zest.

Euchre came up on the porch and awkwardly introduced Duane to Mrs. Bland. She was young, probably not over twenty-five, and not quite so prepossessing at close range. Her eyes were large, rather prominent, and brown in color. Her mouth, too, was large, with the lips full, and she had white teeth.

Duane took her proffered hand and remarked frankly that he was glad to meet her.

Mrs. Bland appeared pleased; and her laugh, which followed, was loud and rather musical.

"Mr. Duane—Buck Duane, Euchre said, didn't he?" she asked.

"Buckley," corrected Duane. "The nickname's not of my choosing."

"I'm certainly glad to meet you, Buckley Duane," she said, as she took the seat Duane offered her. "Sorry to have been out. Kid Fuller's lying over at Deger's. You know he was shot last night. He's got fever to-day. When Bland's away I have to nurse all these shot-up boys, and it sure takes my time. Have you been waiting here alone? Didn't see that slattern girl of mine?"

She gave him a sharp glance. The woman had an extraordinary play of feature, Duane thought, and unless she was smiling was not pretty at all.

"I've been alone," replied Duane. "Haven't seen anybody but a sick-looking girl with a bucket. And she ran when she saw me."

"That was Jen," said Mrs. Bland. "She's the kid we keep here, and she sure hardly pays her keep. Did Euchre tell you about her?"

"Now that I think of it, he did say something or other."

"What did he tell you about me?" bluntly asked Mrs. Bland.

"Wal, Kate," replied Euchre speaking for himself, "you needn't worry none, for I told Buck nothin' but compliments."

Evidently the outlaw's wife liked Euchre, for her keen glance rested with amusement upon him.

"As for Jen, I'll tell you her story some day," went on the woman. "It's a common enough story along this river. Euchre here is a tender-hearted old fool, and Jen has taken him in."

"Wal, seein' as you've got me figgered correct," replied Euchre, dryly, "I'll go in an' talk to Jennie if I may."

"Certainly. Go ahead. Jen calls you her best friend," said Mrs. Bland, amiably. "You're always fetching some Mexican stuff, and that's why, I guess."

When Euchre had shuffled into the house Mrs. Bland turned to Duane with curiosity and interest in her gaze.

"Bland told me about you."

"What did he say?" queried Duane, in pretended alarm.

"Oh, you needn't think he's done you dirt Bland's not that kind of a man. He said: 'Kate, there's a young fellow in camp—rode in here on the dodge. He's no criminal, and he refused to join my band. Wish he would. Slickest hand with a gun I've seen for many a day! I'd like to see him and Chess meet out there in the road.' Then Bland went on to tell how you and Bosomer came together.''

"What did you say?'' inquired Duane, as she paused.

"Me? Why, I asked him what you looked like,'' she replied, gayly.

"Well?'' went on Duane.

"Magnificent chap, Bland said. Bigger than any man in the valley. Just a great blue-eyed sunburned boy!''

"Humph!'' exclaimed Duane. "I'm sorry he led you to expect somebody worth seeing.''

"But I'm not disappointed,'' she returned, archly. "Duane, are you going to stay long here in camp?''

"Yes, till I run out of money and have to move. Why?''

Mrs. Bland's face underwent one of the singular changes. The smiles and flushes and glances, all that had been coquettish about her, had lent her a certain attractiveness, almost beauty and youth. But with some powerful emotion she changed and instantly became a woman of discontent, Duane imagined, of deep, violent nature.

"I'll tell you, Duane,'' she said, earnestly, "I'm sure glad if you mean to bide here awhile. I'm a miserable woman, Duane. I'm an outlaw's wife, and I hate him and the life I have to lead. I come of a good family in Brownsville. I never knew Bland was an outlaw till long after he married me. We were separated at times, and I imagined he was away on business. But the truth came out. Bland shot my own cousin, who told me. My family cast me off, and I had to flee with Bland. I was only eighteen then. I've lived here since. I never see a decent woman or man. I never hear anything about my old home or folks or friends. I'm buried here—buried alive with a lot of thieves and murderers. Can you blame me for being glad to see a young fellow—a gentleman—like the boys I used to go with? I tell you it makes me feel full—I want to cry. I'm sick for somebody to talk to. I have no children, thank God! If I had I'd not stay here. I'm sick of this hole. I'm lonely—''

There appeared to be no doubt about the truth of all this. Genuine emotion checked, then halted the hurried speech. She broke down and cried. It seemed strange to Duane that an outlaw's wife—and a woman who fitted her consort and the wild nature of their surroundings—should have weakness enough to weep. Duane believed and pitied her.

"I'm sorry for you,'' he said.

"Don't be *sorry* for me,'' she said. "That only makes me see the—the difference between you and me. And don't pay any attention to what these outlaws say about me. They're ignorant. They couldn't understand me. You'll hear that Bland killed men who ran after me. But that's a lie. Bland, like all the other outlaws along this river, is always looking for somebody to kill. He *swears* not, but I don't believe him. He explains that gunplay gravitates to men who are the real thing—that it is provoked by the four-flushes, the bad men. I don't know. All I know is that somebody is being killed every other day. He hated Spence before Spence ever saw me.''

"Would Bland object if I called on you occasionally?'' inquired Duane.

"No, he wouldn't. He likes me to have friends. Ask him yourself when he comes back. The trouble has been that two or three of his men fell in love with me, and when half drunk got to fighting. You're not going to do that.''

"I'm not going to get half drunk, that's certain,'' replied Duane.

He was surprised to see her eyes dilate, then glow with fire. Before she could reply Euchre returned to the porch, and that put an end to the conversation.

Duane was content to let the matter rest there, and had little more to say. Euchre and Mrs. Bland talked and joked, while Duane listened. He tried to form some estimate of her character. Manifestly she had suffered a wrong, if not worse, at Bland's hands. She was bitter, morbid, overemotional. If she was a liar, which seemed likely enough, she was a frank one, and believed herself. She had no cunning. The thing which struck Duane so forcibly was that she thirsted for respect. In that, better than in her weakness of vanity, he thought he had discovered a trait through which he could manage her.

Once, while he was revolving these thoughts, he happened to glance into the house, and deep in the shadow of a corner he caught a pale gleam of Jennie's face with great, staring eyes on him. She had been watching him, listening to what he said. He saw from her expression that she had realized what had been so hard for her to believe. Watching his chance, he flashed a look at her; and then it seemed to him the change in her face was wonderful.

Later, after he had left Mrs. Bland with a meaning "Adios—mañana," and was walking along beside the old outlaw, he found himself thinking of the girl instead of the woman, and of how he had seen her face blaze with hope and gratitude.

7

THAT night Duane was not troubled by ghosts haunting his waking and sleeping hours. He awoke feeling bright and eager, and grateful to Euchre for having put something worth while into his mind. During breakfast, however, he was unusually thoughtful, working over the idea of how much or how little he would confide in the outlaw. He was aware of Euchre's scrutiny.

"Wal," began the old man, at last, "how'd you make out with the kid?"

"Kid?" inquired Duane, tentatively.

"Jennie, I mean. What'd you an' she talk about?"

"We had a little chat. You know you wanted me to cheer her up."

Euchre sat with coffee-cup poised and narrow eyes studying Duane.

"Reckon you cheered her, all right. What I'm afeared of is mebbe you done the job too well."

"How so?"

"Wal, when I went in to Jen last night I thought she was half crazy. She was burstin' with excitement, an' the look in her eyes hurt me. She wouldn't tell me a darn word you said. But she hung onto my hands, an' showed every way without speakin' how she wanted to thank me fer bringin' you over. Buck, it was plain to me thet you'd either gone the limit or else you'd been kinder prodigal of cheer an' hope. I'd hate to think you'd led Jennie to hope more'n ever would come true."

Euchre paused, and, as there seemed no reply forthcoming, he went on:

"Buck, I've seen some outlaws whose word was good. Mine is. You can trust me. I trusted you, didn't I, takin' you over there an' puttin' you wise to my tryin' to help the poor kid?"

Thus enjoined by Euchre, Duane began to tell the conversations with Jennie and Mrs. Bland word for word. Long before he had reached an end Euchre set down the coffe-cup and began to stare, and at the conclusion of the story his face lost some of its red color and beads of sweat stood out thickly on his brow.

"Wal, if thet doesn't floor me!" he ejaculated, blinking at Duane. "Young man, I figgered you was some swift, an' sure to make your mark on this river; but I reckon I missed your real caliber. So thet's what it means to be a man! I guess I'd forgot. Wal, I'm old, an' even if my heart was in the right place I never was built fer big stunts. Do you know what it'll take to do all you promised Jen?"

"I haven't any idea," replied Duane, gravely.

"You'll have to pull the wool over Kate Bland's eyes, an' even if she falls in love with you, which 's shore likely, thet won't be easy. An' she'd kill you in a minnit, Buck, if she ever got wise. You ain't mistaken her none, are you?"

"Not me, Euchre. She's a woman. I'd fear her more than any man."

"Wal, you'll have to kill Bland an' Chess Alloway an' Rugg, an' mebbe some others, before you can ride off into the hills with thet girl."

"Why? Can't we plan to be nice to Mrs. Bland and then at an opportune time sneak off without any gun-play?"

"Don't see how on earth," returned Euchre, earnestly. "When Bland's away he leaves all kinds of spies an' scouts watchin' the valley trails. They've all got rifles. You couldn't git by them. But when the boss is home there's a difference. Only, of course, him an' Chess keep their eyes peeled. They both stay to home pretty much, except when they're playin' *monte* or poker over at Benson's. So I say the best is to pick out a good time in the afternoon, drift over careless-like with a couple of hosses, choke Mrs. Bland or knock her on the head, take Jennie with you, an' make a rush to git out of the valley. If you had luck you might pull thet stunt without throwin' a gun. But I reckon the best figgerin' would include dodgin' some lead an' leavin' at least Bland or Alloway dead behind you. I'm figgerin', of course, thet when they come home an' find out you're visitin' Kate frequent they'll jest naturally look fer results. Chess don't like you, fer no reason except you're swift on the draw—mebbe swifter 'n him. Thet's the hell of this gun-play business. No one can ever tell who's the swifter of two gunmen till they meet. Thet fact holds a fascination mebbe you'll learn some day. Bland would treat you civil onless there was reason not to, an' then I don't believe he'd invite himself to a meetin' with you. He'd set Chess or Rugg to put you out of the way. Still Bland's no coward, an' if you came across him at a bad moment you'd have to be quicker'n you was with Bosomer.''

"All right. I'll meet what comes," said Duane, quickly. "The great point is to have horses ready and pick the right moment, then rush the trick through.''

"Thet's the *only* chance fer success. An' you can't do it alone.''

"I'll have to. I wouldn't ask you to help me. Leave you behind!''

"Wal, I'll take my chances," replied Euchre, gruffly. "I'm goin' to help Jennie, you can gamble your last peso on thet. There's only four men in this camp who would shoot me—Bland, an' his right-hand pards, an' thet rabbit-faced Benson. If you happened to put out Bland and Chess, I'd stand a good show with the other two. Anyway, I'm old an' tired—what's the difference if I do git plugged? I can risk as much as you, Buck, even if I am afraid of gun-play. You said correct, 'hosses ready, the right minnit, then rush the trick.' Thet much 's settled. Now let's figger all the little details.''

They talked and planned, though in truth it was Euchre who planned, Duane who listened and agreed. While awaiting the return of Bland and his lieutenants it would be well for Duane to grow friendly with the other outlaws, to sit in a few games of *monte,* or show a willingness to spend a little money. The two schemers were to call upon Mrs. Bland every day—Euchre to carry messages of cheer and warning to Jennie, Duane to blind the elder woman at any cost. These preliminaries decided upon, they proceeded to put them into action.

No hard task was it to win the friendship of the most of those good-natured outlaws. They were used to men of a better order than theirs coming to the hidden camps and sooner or later sinking to their lower level. Besides, with them everything was easy come, easy go. That was why life itself went on so carelessly and usually ended so cheaply. There were men among them, however, that made Duane feel that terrible inexplicable wrath rise in his breast. He could not bear to be near them. He could not trust himself. He felt that any instant a word, a deed, something might call too deeply to that instinct he could no longer control. Jackrabbit Benson was one of these men. Because of him and other outlaws of his ilk Duane could scarcely ever forget the reality of things. This was a hidden valley, a robbers' den, a rendezvous for murderers, a wild place stained red by deeds of wild men. And because of that there was always a charged atmosphere. The merriest, idlest, most careless moment might in the flash of an eye end in ruthless and tragic action. In an assemblage of desperate characters it could not be otherwise. The terrible thing that Duane sensed was this. The valley was beautiful, sunny, fragrant, a place to dream in; the mountaintops were always blue or gold rimmed, the yellow river slid slowly and majestically by, the birds sang in the cottonwoods, the horses grazed and pranced, children played and women longed for love, freedom, happiness; the outlaws rode in and out, free with money and speech; they lived comfortably in their adobe homes, smoked, gambled, talked, laughed, whiled away the idle hours—and all the time life there was wrong, and the simplest moment might be precipitated by that evil into the most awful of contrasts. Duane felt rather than saw a dark, brooding shadow over the valley.

Then, without any solicitation or encouragement from Duane, the Bland woman fell passionately in love with him. His conscience was never troubled about the beginning of that affair. She launched herself. It took no great perspicuity on his part to see that. And the thing which evidently held her in check was the newness, the strangeness, and for the moment the all-satisfying fact of his respect for her. Duane exerted himself to please, to amuse, to interest, to fascinate her, and always with deference. That was his strong point, and it had made his part easy so far. He believed he could carry the whole scheme through without involving himself any deeper.

He was playing at a game of love—playing with life and death! Sometimes he trembled, not that he feared Bland or Alloway or any other man, but at the deeps of life he had come to see into. He was carried out of his old mood. Not once since this daring motive had stirred him had he been haunted by the phantom of Bain beside his bed. Rather had he been haunted by Jennie's sad face, her wistful smile, her eyes. He never was able to speak a word to her. What little communication he had with her was through Euchre, who carried short messages. But he caught glimpses of her every time he went to the Bland house. She contrived somehow to pass door or window, to give him a look when chance afforded. And Duane discovered with surprise that these moments were more thrilling to him than any with Mrs. Bland. Often Duane knew Jennie was sitting just inside the window, and then he felt inspired in his talk, and it was all made for her. So at least she came to know him while as yet she was almost a stranger. Jennie had been instructed by Euchre to listen, to understand that this was Duane's only chance to help keep her mind from constant worry, to gather the import of every word which had a double meaning.

Euchre said that the girl had begun to wither under the strain, to burn up with intense hope which had flamed within her. But all the difference Duane could see was a paler face and darker, more wonderful eyes. The eyes seemed to be entreating him to hurry, that time was flying, that soon it might be too late. Then there was another meaning in them, a light, a strange fire wholly inexplicable to Duane. It was only a flash gone in an instant. But he remembered it because he had never seen it in any other woman's eyes. And all through those waiting days he knew that Jennie's face, and especially the warm, fleeting glance she gave him, was responsible for a subtle and gradual change in him. This change he fancied, was only that through remembrance of her he got rid of his pale, sickening ghosts.

One day a careless Mexican threw a lighted cigarette up into the brush matting that served as a ceiling for Benson's den, and there was a fire which left little more than the adobe walls standing. The result was that while repairs were being made there was no gambling and drinking. Time hung very heavily on the hands of some twoscore outlaws. Days passed by without a brawl, and Bland's valley saw more successive hours of peace than ever before. Duane, however, found the hours anything but empty. He spent more time at Mrs. Bland's; he walked miles on all the trails leading out of the valley; he had a care for the condition of his two horses.

Upon his return from the latest of these tramps Euchre suggested that they go down to the river to the boat-landing.

"Ferry couldn't run ashore this mornin'," said Euchre. "River gettin' low an' sand-bars makin' it hard fer hosses. There's a greaser freight-wagon stuck in the mud. I reckon we might hear news from the freighters. Bland's supposed to be in Mexico."

Nearly all the outlaws in camp were assembled on the riverbank, lolling in the shade of the cottonwoods. The heat was oppressive. Not an outlaw offered to help the freighters, who were trying to dig a heavily freighted wagon out of the quicksand. Few outlaws would work for themselves, let alone for the despised Mexicans.

Duane and Euchre joined the lazy group and sat down with them. Euchre lighted a black pipe, and, drawing his hat over his eyes, lay back in comfort after the manner of the majority of the outlaws. But Duane was alert, observing, thoughtful. He never missed anything. It was his belief that any moment an idle word might be of benefit to him. Moreover, these rough men were always interesting.

"Bland's been chased acrost the river," said one.

"Naw, he's deliverin' cattle to thet Cuban ship," replied another.

"Big deal on, hey?"

"Some big. Rugg says the boss hed an order fer fifteen thousand."

"Say, that order 'll take a year to fill."

"Naw. Hardin is in cahoots with Bland. Between 'em they'll fill orders bigger'n thet."

"Wondered what Hardin was rustlin' in here fer."

Duane could not possibly attend to all the conversation among the outlaws. He endeavored to get the drift of talk nearest to him.

"Kid Fuller's goin' to cash," said a sandy-whiskered little outlaw.

"So Jim was tellin' me. Blood-poison, ain't it? Thet hole wasn't bad. But he took the fever," rejoined a comrade.

"Deger says the Kid might pull through if he hed nursin'."

"Wal, Kate Bland ain't nursin' any shot-up boys these days. She hasn't got time."

A laugh followed this sally; then came a penetrating silence. Some of the outlaws glanced good-naturedly at Duane. They bore him no ill will. Manifestly they were aware of Mrs. Bland's infatuation.

"Pete, 'pears to me you've said thet before."

"Shore. Wal, it's happened before."

This remark drew louder laughter and more significant glances at Duane. He did not choose to ignore them any longer.

"Boys, poke all the fun you like at me, but don't mention any lady's name again. My hand is nervous and itchy these days."

He smiled as he spoke, and his speech was drawled; but the good humor in no wise weakened it. Then his latter remark was significant to a class of men who from inclination and necessity practised at gun-drawing until they wore callous and sore places on their thumbs and inculcated in the very deeps of their nervous organization a habit that made even the simplest and most innocent motion of the hand end at or near the hip. There was something remarkable about a gun-fighter's hand. It never seemed to be gloved, never to be injured, never out of sight or in an awkward position.

There were grizzled outlaws in that group, some of whom had many notches on their gun-handles, and they, with their comrades, accorded Duane silence that carried conviction of the regard in which he was held.

Duane could not recall any other instance where he had let fall a familiar speech to these men, and certainly he had never before hinted of his possibilities. He saw instantly that he could not have done better.

"Orful hot, ain't it?" remarked Bill Black, presently. Bill could not keep quiet for long. He was a typical Texas desperado, had never been anything else. He was stoop-shouldered and bow-legged from much riding; a wiry little man, all muscle, with a square head, a hard face partly black from scrubby beard and red from sun, and a bright, roving, cruel eye. His shirt was open at the neck, showing a grizzled breast.

"Is there any guy in this heah outfit sport enough to go swimmin'?" he asked.

"My Gawd, Bill, you ain't agoin' to wash!" exclaimed a comrade.

This raised a laugh in which Black joined. But no one seemed eager to join him in a bath.

"Laziest outfit I ever rustled with," went on Bill, discontentedly. "Nuthin' to do! Say, if nobody wants to swim maybe some of you'll gamble?"

He produced a dirty pack of cards and waved them at the motionless crowd.

"Bill, you're too good at cards," replied a lanky outlaw.

"Now, Jasper, you say thet powerful sweet, an' you look sweet, er I might take it to heart," replied Black, with a sudden change of tone.

Here it was again—that upflashing passion. What Jasper saw fit to reply would mollify the outlaw or it would not. There was an even balance.

"No offense, Bill," said Jasper, placidly, without moving.

Bill grunted and forgot Jasper. But he seemed restless and dissatisfied. Duane knew him to be an inveterate gambler. And as Benson's place was out of running-order, Black was like a fish on dry land.

"Wal, if you-all are afraid of the cairds, what will you bet on?" he asked, in disgust.

"Bill, I'll play you a game of mumbly peg fer two bits." replied one.

Black eagerly accepted. Betting to him was a serious matter. The game obsessed him, not the stakes. He entered into the mumbly-peg contest with a thoughtful mien and a corded brow. He won. Other comrades tried their luck with him and lost. Finally, when Bill had exhausted their supply of two-bit pieces or their desire for that particular game, he offered to bet on anything.

"See thet turtle-dove there?" he said, pointing. "I'll bet he'll scare at one stone or he won't. Five pesos he'll fly or he won't fly when some one chucks a stone. Who'll take me up?"

That appeared to be more than the gambling spirit of several outlaws could withstand.

"Take thet. Easy money," said one.

"Who's goin' to chuck the stone?" asked another.

"Anybody," replied Bill.

"Wal, I'll bet you I can scare him with one stone," said the first outlaw.

"We're in on thet, Jim to fire the darnick," chimed in the others.

The money was put up, the stone thrown. The turtle-dove took flight, to the great joy of all the outlaws except Bill.

"I'll bet you-all he'll come back to thet tree inside of five minnits," he offered, imperturbably.

Hereupon the outlaws did not show any laziness in their alacrity to cover Bill's money as it lay on the grass. Somebody had a watch, and they all sat down, dividing attention between the timepiece and the tree. The minutes dragged by to the accompaniment of various jocular remarks anent a fool and his money. When four and three-quarter minutes had passed a turtle-dove alighted in the cottonwood. Then ensued an impressive silence while Bill calmly pocketed the fifty dollars.

"But it hain't the same dove!" exclaimed one outlaw, excitedly. "This 'n' is smaller, dustier, not so purple."

Bill eyed the speaker loftily.

"Wal, you'll have to ketch the other one to prove thet. *Sabe,* pard? Now I'll bet any gent heah the fifty I won thet I can scare thet dove with one stone."

No one offered to take his wager.

"Wal, then, I'll bet any of you even money thet you *can't* scare him with one stone."

Not proof against this chance, the outlaws made up a purse, in no wise disconcerted by Bill's contemptuous allusions to their banding together. The stone was thrown. The dove did not fly. Thereafter, in regard to that bird, Bill was unable to coax or scorn his comrades into any kind of wager.

He tried them with a multiplicity of offers, and in vain. Then he appeared at a loss for some unusual and seductive wager. Presently a little ragged Mexican boy came along the river trail, a particularly starved and poor-looking little fellow. Bill called to him and gave him a handful of silver coins. Speechless, dazed, he went his way hugging the money.

"I'll bet he drops some before he gits to the road," declared Bill. "I'll bet he runs. Hurry, you four-flush gamblers."

Bill failed to interest any of his companions, and forthwith became sullen and silent. Strangely his good humor departed in spite of the fact that he had won considerable.

Duane, watching the disgruntled outlaw, marveled at him and wondered what was in his mind. These men were more variable than children, as unstable as water, as dangerous as dynamite.

"Bill, I'll bet you ten you can't spill whatever's in the bucket thet peon's packin'," said the outlaw called Jim.

Black's head came up with the action of a hawk about to swoop.

Duane glanced from Black to the road, where he saw a crippled peon carrying a tin bucket toward the river. This peon was a half-witted Indian who lived in a shack and did odd jobs for the Mexicans. Duane had met him often.

"Jim, I'll take you up," replied Black.

Something, perhaps a harshness in his voice, caused Duane to whirl. He caught a leaping gleam in the outlaw's eye.

"Aw, Bill, thet's too fur a shot," said Jasper, as Black rested an elbow on his knee and sighted over the long, heavy Colt. The distance to the peon was about fifty paces, too far for even the most expert shot to hit a moving object so small as a bucket.

Duane, marvelously keen in the alignment of sights, was positive that Black held too high. Another look at the hard face, now tense and dark with blood, confirmed Duane's suspicion that the outlaw was not aiming at the bucket at all. Duane leaped and struck the leveled gun out of his hand. Another outlaw picked it up.

Black fell back astounded. Deprived of his weapon, he did not seem the same man, or else he was cowed by Duane's significant and formidable front. Sullenly he turned away without even asking for his gun.

8

WHAT a contrast, Duane thought, the evening of that day presented to the state of his soul!

The sunset lingered in golden glory over the distant Mexican mountains; twilight came slowly; a faint breeze blew from the river cool and sweet; the late cooing of a dove and the tinkle of a cowbell were the only sounds; a serene and tranquil peace lay over the valley.

Inside Duane's body there was strife. This third facing of a desperate man had thrown him off his balance. It had not been fatal, but it threatened so much. The better side of his nature seemed to urge him to die rather than to go on fighting or opposing ignorant, unfortunate, savage men. But the perversity of him was so great that it dwarfed reason, conscience. He could not resist it. He felt something dying in him. He suffered. Hope seemed far away. Despair had seized upon him and was driving him into a reckless mood when he thought of Jennie.

He had forgotten her. He had forgotten that he had promised to save her. He had forgotten that he meant to snuff out as many lives as might stand between her and freedom. The very remembrance sheered off his morbid introspection. She made a difference. How strange for him to realize that! He felt grateful to her. He had been forced into outlawry; she had been stolen from her people and carried into captivity. They had met in the river fastness, he to instil hope into her despairing life, she to be the means, perhaps, of keeping him from sinking to the level of her captors. He became conscious of a strong and beating desire to see her, talk with her.

These thoughts had run through his mind while on his way to Mrs. Bland's house. He had let Euchre go on ahead because he wanted more time to compose himself. Darkness had about set in when he reached his destination. There was no light in the house. Mrs. Bland was waiting for him on the porch.

She embraced him, and the sudden, violent, unfamiliar contact sent such a shock through him that he all but forgot the deep game he was playing. She, however, in her agitation did not notice his shrinking. From her embrace and the tender, incoherent words that flowed with it he gathered that Euchre had acquainted her of his action with Black.

"He might have killed you!" she whispered, more clearly; and if Duane had ever heard love in a voice he heard it then. It softened him. After all, she was a woman, weak, fated through her nature, unfortunate in her experience of life, doomed to unhappiness and tragedy. He met her advance so far that he returned the embrace and kissed her. Emotion such as she showed would have made any woman sweet, and she had a certain charm. It was easy, even pleasant, to kiss her; but Duane resolved that, whatever her abandonment might become, he would not go further than the lie she made him act.

"Buck, you love me?" she whispered.

"Yes—yes," he burst out, eager to get it over, and even as he spoke he caught the pale gleam of Jennie's face through the window. He felt a shame he was glad she could not see. Did she remember that she had promised not to misunderstand any action of his? What did she think of him, seeing him out there in the dusk with this bold woman in his arms? Somehow that dim sight of Jennie's pale face, the big dark eyes, thrilled him, inspired him to his hard task of the present.

"Listen, dear," he said to the woman, and he meant his words for the girl. "I'm going to take you away from this outlaw den if I have to kill Bland, Alloway, Rugg—anybody who stands in my path. You were dragged here. You are good—I know it. There's happiness for you somewhere—a home among good people who will care for you. Just wait till—"

His voice trailed off and failed from excess of emotion. Kate Bland closed her eyes and leaned her head on his breast. Duane felt her heart beat against his, and conscience smote him a keen blow. If she loved him so much! But memory and understanding of her character hardened him again, and he gave her such commiseration as was due her sex, and no more.

"Boy, that's good of you," she whispered, "but it's too late. I'm done for. I can't leave Bland. All I ask is that you love me a little and stop your gun-throwing."

The moon had risen over the eastern bulge of dark mountain, and now the valley was flooded with mellow light, and shadows of cottonwoods wavered against the silver.

Suddenly the clip-clop, clip-clop of hoofs caused Duane to raise his head and listen. Horses were coming down the road from the head of the valley. The hour was unusual for riders to come in. Presently the narrow, moonlit lane was crossed at its far end by black moving objects. Two horses Duane discerned.

"It's Bland!" whispered the woman, grasping Duane with shaking hands. "You must run! No, he'd see you. That 'd be worse. It's Bland! I know his horse's trot."

"But you said he wouldn't mind my calling here," protested Duane. "Euchre's with me. It'll be all right."

"Maybe so," she replied, with visible effort at self-control. Manifestly she had a great fear of Bland. "If I could only think!"

Then she dragged Duane to the door, pushed him in.

"Euchre, come out with me! Duane, you stay with the girl! I'll tell Bland you're in love with her. Jen, if you give us away I'll wring your neck."

The swift action and fierce whisper told Duane that Mrs. Bland was herself again. Duane stepped close to Jennie, who stood near the window. Neither spoke, but her hands were outstretched to meet his own. They were small, trembling hands, cold as ice. He held them close, trying to convey what he felt—that he would protect her. She leaned against him, and they looked out of the window. Duane felt calm and sure of himself. His most pronounced feeling besides that for the frightened girl was a curiosity as to how Mrs. Bland would rise to the occasion. He saw the riders dismount down the lane and wearily come forward. A boy led away the horses. Enchre, the old fox, was talking loud and with remarkable ease, considering what he claimed was his natural cowardice.

"—that was way back in the sixties, about the time of the war," he was saying. "Rustlin' cattle wasn't nuthin' then to what it is now. An' times is rougher these days. This gun-throwin' has come to be a disease. Men have an itch for the draw same as they used to have fer poker. The only real gambler outside of greasers we ever had here was Bill, an' I presume Bill is burnin' now."

The approaching outlaws, hearing voices, halted a rod or so from the porch. Then Mrs. Bland uttered an exclamation, ostensibly meant to express surprise, and hurried out to meet them. She greeted her husband warmly and gave welcome to the other man. Duane could not see well enough in the shadow to recognize Bland's companion, but he believed it was Alloway.

"Dog-tired we are and starved," said Bland, heavily. "Who's here with you?"

"That's Euchre on the porch. Duane is inside at the window with Jen," replied Mrs. Bland.

"Duane!" He exclaimed. Then he whispered low—something Duane could not catch.

"Why, I asked him to come," said the chief's wife. She spoke easily and naturally and made no change in tone. "Jen has been ailing. She gets thinner and whiter every day. Duane came here one day with Euchre, saw Jen, and went loony over her pretty face, same as all you men. So I let him come."

Bland cursed low and deep under his breath. The other man made a violent action of some kind and apparently was quieted by a restraining hand.

"Kate, you let Duane make love to Jennie?" queried Bland, incredulously.

"Yes, I did," replied the wife, stubbornly. "Why not? Jen's in love with him. If he takes her away and marries her she can be a decent woman."

Bland kept silent a moment, then his laugh pealed out loud and harsh.

"Chess, did you get that? Well, by God! what do you think of my wife?"

"She's lyin' or she's crazy," replied Alloway, and his voice carried an unpleasant ring.

Mrs. Bland promptly and indignantly told her husband's lieutenant to keep his mouth shut.

"Ho, ho, ho!" rolled out Bland's laugh.

Then he led the way to the porch, his spurs clinking, the weapons he was carrying rattling, and he flopped down on a bench.

"How are you, boss?" asked Euchre.

"Hello, old man. I'm well, but all in."

Alloway slowly walked on to the porch and leaned against the rail. He answered Euchre's greeting with a nod. Then he stood there a dark, silent figure.

Mrs. Bland's full voice in eager questioning had a tendency to ease the situation. Bland replied briefly to her, reporting a remarkably successful trip.

Duane thought it time to show himself. He had a feeling that Bland and Alloway would let him go for the moment. They were plainly non-plussed, and Alloway seemed sullen, brooding.

"Jennie," whispered Duane, "that was clever of Mrs. Bland. We'll keep up the deception. Any day now be ready!"

She pressed close to him, and a barely audible "Hurry!" came breathing into his ear.

"Good night, Jennie," he said, aloud. "Hope you feel better to-morrow."

Then he stepped out into the moonlight and spoke. Bland returned the greeting, and, though he was not amiable, he did not show resentment.

"Met Jasper as I rode in," said Bland, presently. "He told me you made Bill Black mad, and there's liable to be a fight. What did you go off the handle about?"

Duane explained the incident. "I'm sorry I happened to be there," he went on. "It wasn't my business."

"Scurvy trick that 'd been," muttered Bland. "You did right. All the same, Duane, I want you to stop quarreling with my men. If you were one of us—that'd be different. I can't keep my men from fighting. But I'm not called on to let an outsider hang around my camp and plug my rustlers."

"I guess I'll have to be hitting the trail for somewhere," said Duane.

"Why not join my band? You've got a bad start already, Duane, and if I know this border you'll never be a respectable citizen again. You're a born killer. I know every bad man on this frontier. More than one of them have told me that something exploded in their brain, and when sense came back there lay another dead man. It's not so with me. I've done a little shooting, too, but I never wanted to kill another man just to rid myself of the last one. My dead men don't sit on my chest at night. That's the gun-fighter's trouble. He's crazy. He has to kill a new man—he's driven to it to forget the last one."

"But I'm no gun-fighter," protested Duane. "Circumstances made me—"

"No doubt," interrupted Bland, with a laugh. "Circumstances made me a rustler. You don't know yourself. You're young; you've got a temper; your father was one of the most dangerous men Texas ever had. I don't see any other career for you. Instead of going it alone—a lone wolf, as the Texans say—why not make friends with other outlaws? You'll live longer."

Euchre squirmed in his seat.

"Boss, I've been givin' the boy egzactly thet same line of talk. Thet's why I took him in to bunk with me. If he makes pards among us there won't be any more trouble. An' he'd be a grand feller fer the gang. I've seen Wild Bill Hickok throw a gun, an' Billy the Kid, an' Hardin, an' Chess here—all the fastest men on the border. An' with apologies to present company, I'm here to say Duane has them all skinned. His draw is different. You can't see how he does it."

Euchre's admiring praise served to create an effective little silence. Alloway shifted uneasily on his feet, his spurs jangling faintly, and did not lift his head. Bland seemed thoughtful.

"That's about the only qualification I have to make me eligible for your band," said Duane, easily.

"It's good enough," replied Bland, shortly. "Will you consider the idea?"

"I'll think it over. Good night."

He left the group, followed by Euchre. When they reached the end of the lane, and before they had exchanged a word, Bland called Euchre back. Duane proceeded slowly along the moonlit road to the cabin and sat down under the cottonwoods to wait for Euchre. The night was intense and quiet, a low hum of insects giving the effect of a congestion of life. The beauty of the soaring moon, the ebony cañons of shadow under the mountain, the melancholy serenity of the perfect night, made Duane shudder in the realization of how far aloof he now was from enjoyment of these things. Never again so long as he lived could he be natural. His mind was clouded. His eye and ear henceforth must register impressions of nature, but the joy of them had fled.

Still, as he sat there with a foreboding of more and darker work ahead of him there was yet a strange sweetness left to him, and it lay in thought of Jennie. The pressure of her cold little hands lingered in his. He did not think of her as a woman, and he did not analyze his feelings. He just had vague, dreamy thoughts and imaginations that were interspersed in the constant and stern revolving of plans to save her.

A shuffling step roused him. Euchre's dark figure came crossing the moonlit grass under the cottonwoods. The moment the outlaw reached him Duane saw that he was laboring under great excitement. It scarcely affected Duane. He seemed to be acquiring patience, calmness, strength.

"Bland kept you pretty long," he said.

"Wait til I git my breath," replied Euchre. He sat silent a little while, fanning himself with a sombrero, though the night was cool, and then he went into the cabin to return presently with a lighted pipe.

"Fine night," he said; and his tone further acquainted Duane with Euchre's quaint humor. "Fine night for love-affairs, by gum!"

"I'd noticed that," rejoined Duane, dryly.

"Wal, I'm a son of a gun if I didn't stand an' watch Bland choke his wife till her tongue stuck out an' she got black in the face."

"No!" ejaculated Duane.

"Hope to die if I didn't. Buck, listen to this here yarn. When I got back to the porch I seen Bland was wakin' up. He'd been too fagged out to figger much. Alloway an' Kate had gone in the house, where they lit up the lamps. I heard Kate's high voice, but Alloway never chirped. He's not the talkin' kind, an' he's damn dangerous when he's thet way. Bland asked me some questions right from the shoulder. I was ready for them, an' I swore the moon was green cheese. He was satisfied. Bland always trusted me, an' liked me, too, I reckon. I hated to lie black thet way. But he's a hard man with bad intentions toward Jennie, an' I'd double-cross him any day.

"Then we went into the house. Jennie had gone to her little room, an' Bland called her to come out. She said she was undressin'. An' he ordered her to put her clothes back on. Then, Buck, his next move was some surprisin'. He deliberately throwed a gun on Kate. Yes sir, he pointed his big blue Colt right at her, an' he says:

" 'I've a mind to blow out your brains.'

" 'Go ahead,' says Kate, cool as could be.

" 'You lied to me,' he roars.

"Kate laughed in his face. Bland slammed the gun down an' made a grab fer her. She fought him, but wasn't a match fer him, an' he got her by the throat. He choked her till I thought she was strangled. Alloway made him stop. She flopped down on the bed an' gasped fer a while. When she come to them hard-shelled cusses went after her, trying to make her give herself away. I think Bland was jealous. He suspected she'd got thick with you an' was foolin' him. I reckon thet's a sore feelin' fer a man to have——to guess pretty nice, but not to *be* sure. Bland gave it up after a while. An' then he cussed an' raved at her. One sayin' of his is worth pinnin' in your sombrero: 'It ain't nuthin' to kill a man. I don't need much fer thet. But I want to *know,* you hussy!'

"Then he went in an' dragged poor Jen out. She'd had time to dress. He was so mad he hurt her sore leg. You know Jen got thet injury fightin' off one of them devils in the dark. An' when I seen Bland twist her—hurt her—I had a queer hot feelin' deep down in me, an' fer the only time in my life I wished I was a gun-fighter.

"Wal, Jen amazed me. She was whiter'n a sheet, an' her eyes were big and stary, but she had nerve. Fust time I ever seen her show any.

" 'Jennie,' he said, 'my wife said Duane came here to see you. I believe she's lyin'. I think she's been carryin' on with him, an' I want to *know.* If she's been an' you tell me the truth I'll let you go. I'll send you out to Huntsville, where you can communicate with your friends. I'll give you money.'

"Thet must hev been a hell of a minnit fer Kate Bland. If ever I seen death in a man's eye I seen it in Bland's. He loves her. Thet's the strange part of it.

" 'Has Duane been comin' here to see my wife?' Bland asked, fierce-like.

" 'No,' said Jennie.

" 'He's been after you?'

" 'Yes.'

" 'He has fallen in love with you? Kate said thet.'

" 'I—I'm not—I don't know—he hasn't told me.'

" 'But you're in love with him?'

" 'Yes,' she said; an', Buck, if you only could have seen her! She throwed up her head, an' her eyes were full of fire. Bland seemed dazed at sight of her. An' Alloway, why, thet little skunk of an outlaw cried right out. He was hit plumb center. He's in love with Jen. An' the look of her then was enough to make any feller quit. He jest slunk out of the room. I told you, mebbe, thet he'd been tryin' to git Bland to marry Jen to him. So even a tough like Alloway can love a woman!

"Bland stamped up an' down the room. He sure was dyin' hard.

" 'Jennie,' he said, once more turnin' to her. 'You swear in fear of your life thet you're tellin' truth. Kate's not in love with Duane? She's let him come to see *you*? There's been nuthin' between them?'

" 'No. I swear,' answered Jennie; an' Bland sat down like a man licked.

" 'Go to bed, you white-faced—' Bland choked on some word or other—a bad one, I reckon—an' he positively shook in his chair.

"Jennie went then, an' Kate began to have hysterics. An' your Uncle Euchre ducked his nut out of the door an' come home.''

Duane did not have a word to say at the end of Euchre's long harangue. He experienced relief. As a matter of fact, he had expected a good deal worse. He thrilled at the thought of Jennie perjuring herself to save that abandoned woman. What mysteries these feminine creatures were!

"Wal, there's where our little deal stands now," resumed Euchre, meditatively. "You know, Buck, as well as me thet if you'd been some feller who hadn't shown he was a wonder with a gun you'd now be full of lead. If you'd happen to kill Bland an' Alloway, I reckon you'd be as safe on this here border as you would in Santone. Such is gun fame in this land of the draw.''

9

BOTH men were awake early, silent with the premonition of trouble ahead, thoughtful of the fact that the time for the long-planned action was at hand. It was remarkable that a man as loquacious as Euchre could hold his tongue so long; and this was significant of the deadly nature of the intended deed. During breakfast he said a few words customary in the service of food. At the conclusion of the meal he seemed to come to an end of deliberation.

"Buck, the sooner the better now," he declared, with a glint in his eye. "The more time we use up now the less surprised Bland 'll be.''

"I'm ready when you are," replied Duane, quietly, and he rose from the table.

"Wal, saddle up, then," went on Euchre, gruffly. "Tie on them two packs I made, one fer each saddle. You can't tell—mebbe either hoss will be carryin' double. It's good they're both big, strong hosses. Guess thet wasn't a wise move of your Uncle Euchre's—bringin' in your hosses an' havin' them ready?''

"Euchre, I hope you're not going to get in bad here. I'm afraid you are. Let me do the rest now," said Duane.

The old outlaw eyed him sarcastically.

"Thet 'd be turrible now wouldn't it? If you want to know, why, I'm in bad already. I didn't tell you thet Alloway called me last night. He's gettin' wise pretty quick."

"Euchre, you're going with me?" queried Duane, suddenly divining the truth.

"Wal, I reckon. Either to hell or safe over the mountain! I wisht I was a gunfighter. I hate to leave here without takin' a peg at Jackrabbit Benson. Now, Buck, you do some hard figgerin' while I go nosin' round. It's pretty early, which 's all the better."

Euchre put on his sombrero, and as he went out Duane saw that he wore a gun-and-cartridge belt. It was the first time Duane had ever seen the outlaw armed.

Duane packed his few belongings into his saddlebags, and then carried the saddles out to the corral. An abundance of alfalfa in the corral showed that the horses had fared well. They had gotten almost fat during his stay in the valley. He watered them, put on the saddles loosely cinched, and then the bridles. His next move was to fill the two canvas water-bottles. That done, he returned to the cabin to wait.

At the moment he felt no excitement or agitation of any kind. There was no more thinking and planning to do. The hour had arrived, and he was ready. He understood perfectly the desperate chances he must take. His thoughts became confined to Euchre and the surprising loyalty and goodness in the hardened old outlaw. Time passed slowly. Duane kept glancing at his watch. He hoped to start the thing and get away before the outlaws were out of their beds. Finally he heard the shuffle of Euchre's boots on the hard path. The sound was quicker than usual.

When Euchre came around the corner of the cabin Duane was not so astounded as he was concerned to see the outlaw white and shaking. Sweat dripped from him. He had a wild look.

"Luck ours—so—fur, Buck!" he panted.

"You don't look it," replied Duane.

"I'm turrible sick. Jest killed a man. Fust one I ever killed!"

"Who?" asked Duane, startled.

"Jackrabbit Benson. An' sick as I am, I'm gloryin' in it. I went nosin' round up the road. Saw Alloway goin' into Deger's. He's thick with the Degers. Reckon he's askin' questions. Anyway, I was sure glad to see him away from Bland's. An' he didn't see me. When I dropped into Benson's there wasn't nobody there but Jackrabbit an' some greasers he was startin' to work. Benson never had no use fer me. An' he up an' said he wouldn't give a two-bit piece fer my life. I asked him why.

" 'You're double-crossin' the boss an' Chess,' he said.

" 'Jack, what 'd you give fer your own life?' I asked him.

"He straightened up surprised an' mean-lookin'. An' I let him have it, plumb center! He wilted, an' the greasers run. I reckon I'll never sleep again. But I had to do it."

Duane asked if the shot had attracted any attention outside.

"I didn't see anybody but the greasers, an' I sure looked sharp. Comin' back I cut across through the cottonwoods past Bland's cabin. I meant to keep out of sight, but somehow I had an idee I might find out if Bland was awake yet. Sure enough I run plumb into Beppo, the boy who tends Bland's hosses. Beppo likes me. An' when I inquired of his boss he said Bland had been up all night fightin' with the Señora. An', Buck, here's how I figger. Bland couldn't let up last night. He was sore, an' he went after Kate again, tryin' to wear her down. Jest as likely he might have went after Jennie, with wuss intentions. Anyway, he an' Kate must have had it hot an' heavy. We're pretty lucky."

"It seems so. Well, I'm going," said Duane, tersely.

"Lucky! I should smile! Bland's been up all night after a most draggin' ride home. He'll be fagged out this mornin', sleepy, sore, an' he won't be expectin' hell before breakfast. Now, you walk over to his house. Meet him how you like. Thet's your game. But I'm suggestin', if he comes out an' you want to parley, you can jest say you'd thought over his proposition an' was ready to join his band, or you ain't. You'll have to kill him, an' it'd save time to go fer your gun on sight. Might be wise, too, fer it's likely he'll do thet same."

"How about the horses?"

"I'll fetch them an' come along about two minnits behind you. 'Pears to me you ought to have the job done an' Jennie outside by the time I git there. Once on them hosses, we can ride out of camp before Alloway or anybody else gits into action. Jennie ain't much heavier 'n a rabbit. Thet big black will carry you both."

"All right. But once more let me persuade you to stay—not to mix any more in this," said Duane, earnestly.

"Nope. I'm goin'. You heard what Benson told me. Alloway wouldn't give me the benefit of any doubts. Buck, a last word—look out fer thet Bland woman!"

Duane merely nodded, and then, saying that the horses were ready, he strode away through the grove. Accounting for the short cut across grove and field, it was about five minutes' walk up to Bland's house. To Duane it seemed long in time and distance, and he had difficulty in restraining his pace. As he walked there came a gradual and subtle change in his feelings. Again he was going out to meet a man in conflict. He could have avoided this meeting. But despite the fact of his courting the encounter he had not as yet felt that hot, inexplicable rush of blood. The motive of this deadly action was not personal, and somehow that made a difference.

No outlaws were in sight. He saw several Mexican herders with cattle. Blue columns of smoke curled up over some of the cabins. The fragrant smell of it reminded Duane of his home and cutting wood for the stove. He noted a cloud of creamy mist rising above the river, dissolving in the sunlight.

Then he entered Bland's lane.

While yet some distance from the cabin he heard loud, angry voices of man and woman. Bland and Kate still quarreling! He took a quick survey of the surroundings. There was now not even a Mexican in sight. Then he hurried a little. Halfway down the lane he turned his head to peer through the cottonwoods. This time he saw Euchre coming with the horses. There was no indication that the old outlaw might lose his nerve at the end. Duane had feared this.

Duane now changed his walk to a leisurely saunter. He reached the porch and then distinguished what was said inside the cabin.

"If you do, Bland, by Heaven I'll fix you and her!" That was panted out in Kate Bland's full voice.

"Let me loose! I'm going in there, I tell you!" replied Bland, hoarsely.

"What for?"

"I want to make a little love to her. Ha! ha! It'll be fun to have the laugh on her new lover."

"You lie!" cried Kate Bland.

"I'm not saying what I'll do to her *afterward!*" His voice grew hoarser with passion. "Let me go now!"

"No! no! I won't let you go. You'll choke the—the truth out of her—you'll kill her."

"The *truth!*" hissed Bland.

"Yes. I lied. Jen lied. But she lied to save me. You needn't—murder her—for that."

Bland cursed horribly. Then followed a wrestling sound of bodies in violent straining contact—the scrape of feet—the jangle of spurs—a crash of sliding table or chair, and then the cry of a woman in pain.

Duane stepped into the open door, inside the room. Kate Bland lay half across a table where she had been flung, and she was trying to get to her feet. Bland's back was turned. He had opened the door into Jennie's room and had one foot across the threshold. Duane caught the girl's low, shuddering cry. Then he called out loud and clear.

With cat-like swiftness Bland wheeled, then froze on the threshold. His sight, quick as his action, caught Duane's menacing unmistakable position.

Bland's big frame filled the door. He was in a bad place to reach for his gun. But he would not have time for a step. Duane read in his eyes the desperate calculation of chances. For a fleeting instant Bland shifted his glance to his wife. Then his whole body seemed to vibrate with the swing of his arm.

Duane shot him. He fell forward, his gun exploding as it hit into the floor, and dropped loose from stretching fingers. Duane stood over him, stooped to turn him on his back. Bland looked up with clouded gaze, then gasped his last.

"Duane, you've killed him!" cried Kate Bland, huskily. "I knew you'd have to!"

She staggered against the wall, her eyes dilating, her strong hands clenching, her face slowly whitening. She appeared shocked, half stunned, but showed no grief.

"Jennie!" called Duane, sharply.

"Oh—Duane!" came a halting reply.

"Yes. Come out. Hurry!"

She came out with uneven steps, seeing only him, and she stumbled over Bland's body. Duane caught her arm, swung her behind him. He feared the woman when she realized how she had been duped. His action was protective, and his movement toward the door equally as significant.

"Duane!" cried Mrs. Bland.

It was no time for talk. Duane edged on, keeping Jennie behind him. At that moment there was a pounding of iron-shod hoofs out in the lane. Kate Bland bounded to the door. When she turned back her amazement was changing to realization.

"Where're you taking Jen?" she cried, her voice like a man's.

"Get out of my way," replied Duane. His look perhaps, without speech, was enough for her. In an instant she was transformed into a fury.

"You hound! All the time you were fooling me! You made love to me! You let me believe—you swore you loved me! Now I see what was queer about you. All for that girl! But you can't have her. You'll never leave here alive. Give me that girl! Let me—get at her! She'll never win any more men in this camp."

She was a powerful woman, and it took all Duane's strength to ward off her onslaughts. She clawed at Jennie over his upheld arm. Every second her fury increased.

"Help! help! help!" she shrieked, in a voice that must have penetrated to the remotest cabin in the valley.

"Let go! Let go!" cried Duane, low and sharp. He still held his gun in his right hand, and it began to be hard for him to ward the woman off. His coolness had gone with her shriek for help. "Let go!" he repeated, and he shoved her fiercely.

Suddenly she snatched a rifle off the wall and backed away, her strong hands fumbling at the lever. As she jerked it down, throwing a shell into the chamber and cocking the weapon, Duane leaped upon her. He struck up the rifle as it went off, the powder burning his face.

"Jennie, run out! Get on a horse!" he said.

Jennie flashed out of the door.

With an iron grasp Duane held to the rifle-barrel. He had grasped it with his left hand, and he gave such a pull that he swung the crazed woman off the floor. But he could not loose her grip. She was as strong as he.

"Kate! Let go!"

He tried to intimidate her. She did not see his gun thrust in her face, or reason had given way to such an extent to passion that she did not care. She curse. Her husband had used the same curses, and from her lips they seemed strange, unsexed, more deadly. Like a tigress she fought him; her face no longer resembled a woman's. The evil of that outlaw life, the wildness and rage, the meaning to kill, was even in such a moment terribly impressed upon Duane.

He heard a cry from outside—a man's cry, hoarse and alarming.

It made him think of loss of time. This demon of a woman might yet block his plan.

"Let go!" he whispered, and felt his lips stiff. In the grimness of that instant he relaxed his hold on the rifle-barrel.

With sudden, redoubled, irresistible strength she wrenched the rifle down and discharged it. Duane felt a blow—a shock—a burning agony tearing through his breast. Then in a frenzy he jerked so powerfully upon the rifle that he threw the woman against the wall. She fell and seemed stunned.

Duane leaped back, whirled, flew out of the door to the porch. The sharp cracking of a gun halted him. He saw Jennie holding to the bridle of his bay horse. Euchre was astride the other, and he had a Colt leveled, and he was firing down the lane. Then came a single shot, heavier, and Euchre's ceased. He fell from the horse.

A swift glance back showed to Duane a man coming down the lane. Chess Alloway! His gun was smoking. He broke into a run. Then in an instant he saw Duane, and tried to check his pace as he swung up his arm. But that slight pause was fatal. Duane shot, and Alloway was falling when his gun went off. His bullet whistled close to Duane and thudded into the cabin.

Duane bounded down to the horses. Jennie was trying to hold the plunging bay. Euchre lay flat on his back, dead, a bullet-hole in his shirt, his face set hard, and his hands twisted round gun and bridle.

"Jennie, you've nerve, all right!" cried Duane, as he dragged down the horse she was holding. "Up with you now! There! Never mind—long stirrups! Hang on somehow!"

He caught his bridle out of Euchre's clutching grip and leaped astride. The frightened horses jumped into a run and thundered down the lane into the road. Duane saw men running from cabins. He heard shouts. But there were no shots fired. Jennie seemed able to stay on her horse, but without stirrups she was thrown about so much that Duane rode closer and reached out to grasp her arm.

Thus they rode through the valley to the trail that led up over the steep and broken Rim Rock. As they began to climb Duane looked back. No pursuers were in sight.

"Jennie, we're going to get away!" he cried, exultation for her in his voice.

She was gazing horror-stricken at his breast, as in turning to look back he faced her.

"Oh, Duane, your shirt's all bloody!" she faltered, pointing with trembling fingers.

With her words Duane became aware of two things—the hand he instinctively placed to his breast still held his gun, and he had sustained a terrible wound.

Duane had been shot through the breast far enough down to give him grave apprehension of his life. The clean-cut hole made by the bullet bled freely both at its entrance and where it had come out, but with no signs of hemorrhage. He did not bleed at the mouth; however, he began to cough up a reddish-tinged foam.

As they rode on, Jennie, with pale face and mute lips, looked at him.

"I'm badly hurt, Jennie," he said, "but I guess I'll stick it out."

"The woman—did she shoot you?"

"Yes. She was a devil. Euchre told me to look out for her. I wasn't quick enough."

"You didn't have to—to—" shivered the girl.

"No! no!" he replied.

They did not stop climbing while Duane tore a scarf and made compresses, which he bound tightly over his wounds. The fresh horses made fast time up the rough trail. From open places Duane looked down. When they surmounted the steep ascent and stood on top of the Rim Rock, with no signs of pursuit down in the valley, and with the wild, broken fastnesses before them, Duane turned to the girl and assured her that they now had every chance of escape.

"But—your—wound!" she faltered, with dark, troubled eyes. "I see—the blood—dripping from your back!"

"Jennie, I'll take a lot of killing," he said.

Then he became silent and attended to the uneven trail. He was aware presently that he had not come into Bland's camp by this route. But that did not matter; any trail leading out beyond the Rim Rock was safe enough. What he wanted was to get far away into some wild retreat where he could hide till he recovered from his wound. He seemed to feel a fire inside his breast, and his throat burned so that it was necessary for him to take a swallow of water every little while. He began to suffer considerable pain, which increased as the hours went by and then gave way to a numbness. From that time on he had need of his great strength and endurance. Gradually he lost his steadiness and his keen sight; and he realized that if he were to meet foes, or if pursuing outlaws should come up with him, he could make only a poor stand. So he turned off on a trail that appeared seldom traveled.

Soon after this move he became conscious of a further thickening of his senses. He felt able to hold on to his saddle for a while longer, but he was failing. Then he thought he ought to advise Jennie, so in case she was left alone she would have some idea of what to do.

"Jennie, I'll give out soon," he said. "No—I don't mean—what you think. But I'll drop soon. My strength's going. If I die—you ride back to the main trail. Hide and rest by day. Ride at night. That trail goes to water. I believe you could get across the Nueces, where some rancher will take you in."

Duane could not get the meaning of her incoherent reply. He rode on, and soon he could not see the trail or hear his horse. He did not know whether they traveled a mile or many times that far. But he was conscious when the horse stopped, and had a vague sense of falling and feeling Jennie's arms before all became dark to him.

When consciousness returned he found himself lying in a little hut of mesquite branches. It was well built and evidently some years old. There were two doors or openings, one in front and the other at the back. Duane imagined it had been built by a fugitive—one who meant to keep an eye both ways and not to be surprised. Duane felt weak and had no desire to move. Where was he, anyway? A strange, intangible sense of time, distance, of something far behind weighed upon him. Sight of the two packs Euchre had made brought his thought to Jennie. What had become of her? There was evidence of her work in a smoldering fire and a little blackened coffee-pot. Probably she was outside looking after the horses or getting water. He thought he heard a step and listened, but he felt tired, and presently his eyes closed and he fell into a doze.

Awakening from this, he saw Jennie sitting beside him. In some way she seemed to have changed. When he spoke she gave a start and turned eagerly to him.

"Duane!" she cried.

"Hello. How're you, Jennie, and how am I?" he said, finding it a little difficult to talk.

"Oh, I'm all right," she replied. "And you've come to—your wound's healed; but you've been sick. Fever, I guess. I did all I could."

Duane saw now that the difference in her was a whiteness and tightness of skin, a hollowness of eye, a look of strain.

"Fever? How long have we been here?" he asked.

She took some pebbles from the crown of his sombrero and counted them.

"Nine. Nine days," she answered.

"Nine days!" he exclaimed, incredulously. But another look at her assured him that she meant what she said. "I've been sick all the time? You nursed me?"

"Yes."

"Bland's men didn't come along here?"

"No."

"Where are the horses?"

"I keep them grazing down in a gorge back of here. There's good grass and water."

"Have you slept any?"

"A little. Lately I couldn't keep awake."

"Good Lord! I should think not. You've had a time of it sitting here day and night nursing me, watching for the outlaws. Come, tell me all about it."

"There's nothing much to tell."

"I want to know, anyway, just what you did—how you felt."

"I can't remember very well," she replied, simply. "We must have ridden forty miles that day we got away. You bled all the time. Toward evening you lay on your horse's neck. When we came to this place you fell out of the saddle. I dragged you in here and stopped your bleeding. I thought you'd die that night. But in the morning I had a little hope. I had forgotten the horses. But luckily they didn't stray far. I caught them and kept them down in the gorge. When your wounds closed and you began to breathe stronger I thought you'd get well quick. It was fever that put you back. You raved a lot, and that worried me, because I couldn't stop you. Anybody trailing us could have heard you a good ways. I don't know whether I was scared most then or when you were quiet, and it was so dark and lonely and still all around. Every day I put a stone in your hat."

"Jennie, you saved my life," said Duane.

"I don't know. Maybe. I did all I knew how to do," she replied. "You saved mine—more than my life."

Their eyes met in a long gaze, and then their hands in a close clasp.

"Jennie, we're going to get away," he said, with gladness. "I'll be well in a few days. You don't know how strong I am. We'll hide by day and travel by night. I can get you across the river."

"And then?" she asked.

"We'll find some honest rancher."

"And then?" she persisted.

"Why," he began, slowly, "that's as far as my thoughts ever got. It was pretty hard, I tell you, to assure myself of so much. It means your safety. You'll tell your story. You'll be sent to some village or town and taken care of until a relative or friend is notified."

"And you?" she inquired, in a strange voice.

Duane kept silence.

"What will you do?" she went on.

"Jennie, I'll go back to the brakes. I daren't show my face among respectable people. I'm an outlaw."

"You're no criminal!" she declared, with deep passion.

"Jennie, on this border the little difference between an outlaw and a criminal doesn't count for much."

"You won't go back among those terrible men? You, with your gentleness and sweetness—all that's good about you? Oh, Duane, don't—don't go!"

"I can't go back to the outlaws, at least not Bland's band. No, I'll go alone. I'll lone-wolf it, as they say on the border. What else can I do, Jennie?"

"Oh, I don't know. Couldn't you hide? Couldn't you slip out of Texas—go far away?"

"I could never get out of Texas without being arrested. I could hide, but a man must live. Never mind about me, Jennie."

In three days Duane was able with great difficulty to mount his horse. During daylight, by short relays, he and Jennie rode back to the main trail, where they hid again till he had rested. Then in the dark they rode out of the cañons and gullies of the Rim Rock, and early in the morning halted at the first water to camp.

From that point they traveled after nightfall and went into hiding during the day. Once across the Nueces River, Duane was assured of safety for her and great danger for himself. They had crossed into a country he did not know. Somewhere east of the river there were scattered ranches. But he was as liable to find the rancher in touch with the outlaws as he was likely to find him honest. Duane hoped his good fortune would not desert him in this last service to Jennie. Next to the worry of that was realization of his condition. He had gotten up too soon; he had ridden too far and hard, and now he felt that any moment he might fall from his saddle. At last, far ahead over a barren mesquite-dotted stretch of dusty ground, he espied a patch of green and a little flat, red ranch-house. He headed his horse for it and turned a face he tried to make cheerful for Jennie's sake. She seemed both happy and sorry.

When near at hand he saw that the rancher was a thrifty farmer. And thrift spoke for honesty. There were fields of alfalfa, fruit-trees, corrals, windmill pumps, irrigation-ditches, all surrounding a neat little adobe house. Some children were playing in the yard. The way they ran at sight of Duane hinted of both the loneliness and the fear of their isolated lives. Duane saw a woman come to the door, then a man. The latter looked keenly, then stepped outside. He was a sandy-haired, freckled Texan.

"Howdy, stranger," he called, as Duane halted. "Get down, you an' your woman. Say, now, air you sick or shot or what? Let me—"

Duane, reeling in his saddle, bent searching eyes upon the rancher. He thought he saw good will, kindness, honesty. He risked all on that one sharp glance. Then he almost plunged from the saddle.

The rancher caught him, helped him to a bench.

"Martha, come out here!" he called. "This man's sick. No; he's shot, or I don't know blood-stains."

Jennie had slipped off her horse and to Duane's side. Duane appeared about to faint.

"Air you his wife?" asked the rancher.

"No. I'm only a girl he saved from outlaws. Oh, he's so pale! Duane, Duane!"

"Buck Duane!" exclaimed the rancher, excitedly. "The man who killed Bland an' Alloway? Say, I owe him a good turn, an' I'll pay it, young woman."

The rancher's wife came out, and with a manner at once kind and practical essayed to make Duane drink from a flask. He was not so far gone that he could not recognize its contents, which he refused, and weakly asked for water. When that was given him he found his voice.

"Yes, I'm Duane. I've only overdone myself—just all in. The wounds I got at Bland's are healing. Will you take this girl in—hide her awhile till the excitement's over among the outlaws?"

"I shore will," replied the Texan.

"Thanks. I'll remember you—I'll square it."

"What're you goin' to do?"

"I'll rest a bit—then go back to the brakes."

"Young man, you ain't in any shape to travel. See here—any rustlers on your trail?"

"I think we gave Bland's gang the slip."

"Good. I'll tell you what. I'll take you in along with the girl, an' hide both of you till you get well. It'll be safe. My nearest neighbor is five miles off. We don't have much company."

"You risk a great deal. Both outlaws and rangers are hunting me," said Duane.

"Never seen a ranger yet in these parts. An' have always got along with outlaws, mebbe exceptin' Bland. I tell you I owe you a good turn."

"My horses might betray you," added Duane.

"I'll hide them in a place where there's water an' grass. Nobody goes to it. Come now, let me help you indoors."

Duane's last fading sensations of that hard day were the strange feel of a bed, a relief at the removal of his heavy boots, and of Jennie's soft, cool hands on his hot face.

He lay ill for three weeks before he began to mend, and it was another week then before he could walk out a little in the dusk of the evenings. After that his strength returned rapidly. And it was only at the end of this long siege that he recovered his spirits. During most of his illness he had been silent, moody.

"Jennie, I'll be riding off soon," he said, one evening. "I can't impose on this good man Andrews much longer. I'll never forget his kindness. His wife, too—she's been so good to us. Yes, Jennie, you and I will have to say good-by very soon."

"Don't hurry away," she replied.

Lately Jennie had appeared strange to him. She had changed from the girl he use to see at Mrs. Bland's house. He took her reluctance to say good-by as another indication of her regret that he must go back to the brakes. Yet somehow it made him observe her more closely. She wore a plain, white dress made from material Mrs. Andrews had given her. Sleep and good food had improved her. If she had been pretty out there in the outlaw den now she was more than that. But she had the same paleness, the same strained look, the same dark eyes full of haunting shadows. After Duane's realization of the change in her he watched her more, with a growing certainty that he would be sorry not to see her again.

"It's likely we won't ever see each other again," he said. "That's strange to think of. We've been through some hard days, and I seem to have known you a long time."

Jennie appeared shy, almost sad, so Duane changed the subject to something less personal.

Andrews returned one evening from a several days' trip to Huntsville.

"Duane, everybody's talking' about how you cleaned up the Bland outfit," he said, important and full of news. "It's some exaggerated, accordin' to what you told me; but you've shore made friends on this side of the Nueces. I reckon there ain't a town where you wouldn't find people to welcome you. Huntsville, you know, is some divided in its ideas. Half the people are crooked. Likely enough, all them who was so loud in praise of you are the crookedest. For instance, I met King Fisher, the boss outlaw of these parts. Well, King thinks he's a decent citizen. He was tellin' me what a grand job yours was for the border an' honest cattlemen. Now that Bland and Alloway are done for, King Fisher will find rustlin' easier. There's talk of Hardin movin' his camp over to

Bland's. But I don't know how true it is. I reckon there ain't much to it. In the past when a big outlaw chief went under, his band almost always broke up an' scattered. There's no one left who could run thet outfit.''

"Did you hear of any outlaws hunting me?" asked Duane.

"Nobody from Bland's outfit is huntin' you, thet's shore," replied Andrews. "Fisher said there never was a hoss straddled to go on your trail. Nobody had any use for Bland. Anyhow, his men would be afraid to trail you. An' you could go right in to Huntsville, where you'd be some popular. Reckon you'd be safe, too, except when some of them fool saloon loafers or bad cowpunchers would try to shoot you for the glory in it. Them kind of men will bob up everywhere you go, Duane.''

"I'll be able to ride and take care of myself in a day or two," went on Duane. "Then I'll go—I'd like to talk to you about Jennie."

"She's welcome to a home here with us."

"Thank you, Andrews. You're a kind man. But I want Jennie to get farther away from the Rio Grande. She'd never be safe here. Besides, she may be able to find relatives. She has some, though she doesn't know where they are."

"All right, Duane. Whatever you think best. I reckon now you'd better take her to some town. Go north an' strike for Shelbyville or Crockett. Them's both good towns. I'll tell Jennie the names of men who'll help her. You needn't ride into town at all.''

"Which place is nearer, and how far is it?"

"Shelbyville. I reckon about two days' ride. Poor stock country, so you ain't liable to meet rustlers. All the same, better hit the trail at night an' go careful.''

At sunset two days later Duane and Jennie mounted their horses and said good-by to the rancher and his wife. Andrews would not listen to Duane's thanks.

"I tell you I'm beholden to you yet," he declared.

"Well, what can I do for you?" asked Duane. "I may come along here again some day."

"Get down an' come in, then, or you're no friend of mine. I reckon there ain't nothin' I can think of— I just happen to remember— '' Here he led Duane out of earshot of the women and went on in a whisper. "Buck, I used to be well-to-do. Got skinned by a man named Brown—Rodney Brown. He lives in Huntsville, an' he's my enemy. I never was much on fightin', or I'd fixed him. Brown ruined me—stole all I had. He's a hoss an' cattle thief, an' he has pull enough at home to protect him. I reckon I needn't say any more.''

"Is this Brown a man who shot an outlaw named Stevens?" queried Duane, curiously.

"Shore, he's the same. I heard thet story. Brown swears he plugged Stevens through the middle. But the outlaw rode off, an' nobody ever knew for shore.''

"Luke Stevens died of that shot. I buried him," said Duane.

Andrews made no further comment, and the two men returned to the women.
"The main road for about three miles, then where it forks take the left-hand
road and keep on straight. That what you said, Andrews?"

"Shore. An' good luck to you both!"

Duane and Jennie trotted away into the gathering twilight. At the moment an
insistent thought bothered Duane. Both Luke Stevens and rancher Andrews had
hinted to Duane to kill a man named Brown. Duane wished with all his heart
that they had not mentioned it, let alone taken for granted the execution of the
deed. What a bloody place Texas was! Men who robbed and men who were
robbed both wanted murder. It was in the spirit of the country. Duane certainly
meant to avoid ever meeting this Rodney Brown. And that very determination
showed Duane how dangerous he really was—to men and to himself. Sometimes
he had a feeling how little stood between his sane and better self and a self
utterly wild and terrible. He reasoned that only intelligence could save him—
only a thoughtful understanding of his danger and a hold upon some ideal.

Then he fell into low conversation with Jennie, holding out hopeful views of
her future, and presently darkness set in. The sky was overcast with heavy
clouds; there was no air moving; the heat and oppression threatened storm. By
and by Duane could not see a rod in front of him, though his horse had no
difficulty in keeping to the road. Duane was bothered by the blackness of the
night. Traveling fast was impossible, and any moment he might miss the road
that led off to the left. So he was compelled to give all his attention to peering
into the thick shadows ahead. As good luck would have it, he came to higher
ground where there was less mesquite, and therefore not such impenetrable
darkness; and at this point he came to where the road split.

Once headed in the right direction, he felt easier in mind. To his annoyance,
however, a fine, misty rain set in. Jennie was not well dressed for wet weather;
and, for that matter, neither was he. His coat, which in that dry warm climate
he seldom needed, was tied behind his saddle, and he put it on Jennie.

They traveled on. The rain fell steadily; if anything, growing thicker. Duane
grew uncomfortably wet and chilly. Jennie, however, fared somewhat better by
reason of the heavy coat. The night passed quickly despite the discomfort, and
soon a gray, dismal, rainy dawn greeted the travelers.

Jennie insisted that he find some shelter where a fire could be built to dry his
clothes. He was not in a fit condition to risk catching cold. In fact, Duane's
teeth were chattering. To find a shelter in that barren waste seemed a futile task.
Quite unexpectedly, however, they happened upon a deserted adobe cabin situated a little off the road. Not only did it prove to have a dry interior, but also
there was firewood. Water was available in pools everywhere; however, there
was no grass for the horses.

A good fire and hot food and drink changed the aspect of their condition as far as comfort went. And Jennie lay down to sleep. For Duane, however, there must be vigilance. This cabin was no hiding-place. The rain fell harder all the time, and the wind changed to the north. "It's a norther, all right," muttered Duane. "Two or three days." And he felt that his extraordinary luck had not held out. Still one point favored him, and it was that travelers were not likely to come along during the storm.

Jennie slept while Duane watched. The saving of this girl meant more to him than any task he had ever assumed. First it had been partly from a human feeling to succor an unfortunate woman, and partly a motive to establish clearly to himself that he was no outlaw. Lately, however, had come a different sense, a strange one, with something personal and warm and protective in it.

As he looked down upon her, a slight, slender girl with bedraggled dress and disheveled hair, her face, pale and quiet, a little stern in sleep, and her long, dark lashes lying on her cheek, he seemed to see her fragility, her prettiness, her femininity as never before. But for him she might at that very moment have been a broken, ruined girl lying back in that cabin of the Blands'. The fact gave him a feeling of his importance in this shifting of her destiny. She was unharmed, still young; she would forget and be happy; she would live to be a good wife and mother. Somehow the thought swelled his heart. His act, death-dealing as it had been, was a noble one, and helped him to hold on to his drifting hopes. Hardly once since Jennie had entered into his thought had those ghosts returned to torment him.

To-morrow she would be gone among good, kind people with a possibility of finding her relatives. He thanked God for that; nevertheless, he felt a pang.

She slept more than half the day. Duane kept guard, always alert, whether he was sitting, standing, or walking. The rain pattered steadily on the roof and sometimes came in gusty flurries through the door. The horses were outside in a shed that afforded poor shelter, and they stamped restlessly. Duane kept them saddled and bridled.

About the middle of the afternoon Jennie awoke. They cooked a meal and afterward sat beside the little fire. She had never been, in his observation of her, anything but a tragic figure, an unhappy girl, the farthest removed from serenity and poise. That characteristic capacity for agitation struck him as stronger in her this day. He attributed it, however, to the long strain, the suspense nearing an end. Yet sometimes when her eyes were on him she did not seem to be thinking of her freedom, of her future.

"This time to-morrow you'll be in Shelbyville," he said.

"Where will you be?" she asked, quickly.

"Me? Oh, I'll be making tracks for some lonesome place," he replied.

The girl shuddered.

"I've been brought up in Texas. I remember what a hard lot the men of my family had. But poor as they were, they had a roof over their heads, a hearth with a fire, a warm bed—somebody to love them. And you, Duane—oh, my God! What must your life be? You must ride and hide and watch eternally. No decent food, no pillow, no friendly word, no clean clothes, no woman's hand! Horses, guns, trails, rocks, holes—these must be the important things in your life. You must go on riding, hiding, killing until you meet—''

She ended with a sob and dropped her head on her knees. Duane was amazed, deeply touched.

''My girl, thank you for that thought of me,'' he said, with a tremor in his voice. ''You don't know how much that means to me.''

She raised her face, and it was tear-stained, eloquent, beautiful.

''I've heard tell—the best of men go to the bad out there. You won't. Promise me you won't. I never—knew any man—like you. I—I—we may never see each other again—after to-day. I'll never forget you. I'll pray for you, and I'll never give up trying to—to do something. Don't despair. It's never too late. It was my hope that kept me alive—out there at Bland's—before you came. I was only a poor weak girl. But if I could hope—so can you. Stay away from men. Be a lone wolf. Fight for you life. Stick out your exile—and maybe—some day—''

Then she lost her voice. Duane clasped her hand and with feeling as deep as hers promised to remember her words. In her despair for him she had spoken wisdom—pointed out the only course.

Duane's vigilance, momentarily broken by emotion, had no sooner reasserted itself than he discovered the bay horse, the one Jennie rode, had broken his halter and gone off. The soft wet earth had deadened the sound of his hoofs. His tracks were plain in the mud. There were clumps of mesquite in sight, among which the horse might have strayed. It turned out, however, that he had not done so.

Duane did not want to leave Jennie alone in the cabin so near the road. So he put her up on his horse and bade her follow. The rain had ceased for the time being, though evidently the storm was not yet over. The tracks led up a wash to a wide flat where mesquite, prickly pear, and thorn-bush grew so thickly that Jennie could not ride into it. Duane was thoroughly concerned. He must have her horse. Time was flying. It would soon be night. He could not expect her to scramble quickly through that brake on foot. Therefore he decided to risk leaving her at the end of the thicket and go in alone.

As he went in a sound startled him. Was it the breaking of a branch he had stepped on or thrust aside? He heard the impatient pound of his horse's hoofs. Then all was quiet. Still he listened, not wholly satisfied. He was never satisfied in regard to safety; he knew too well that there never could be safety for him in this country.

The bay horse had threaded the aisles of the thicket. Duane wondered what had drawn him there. Certainly it had not been grass, for there was none. Presently he heard the horse tramping along, and then he ran. The mud was deep, and the sharp thorns made going difficult. He came up with the horse, and at the same moment crossed a multitude of fresh horse-tracks.

He bent lower to examine them, and was alarmed to find that they had been made very recently, even since it had ceased raining. They were tracks of well-shod horse. Duane straightened up with a cautious glance all around. His instant decision was to hurry back to Jennie. But he had come a goodly way through the thicket, and it was impossible to rush back. Once or twice he imagined he heard crashings in the brush, but did not halt to make sure. Certain he was now that some kind of danger threatened.

Suddenly there came an unmistakable thump of horses' hoofs off somewhere to the fore. Then a scream sent the air. It ended abruptly. Duane leaped forward, tore his way through the thorny brake. He heard Jennie cry again—an appealing call quickly hushed. It seemed more to his right, and he plunged that way. He burst into a glade where a smoldering fire and ground covered with footprints and tracks showed that campers had lately been. Rushing across this, he broke his passage out to the open. But he was too late. His horse had disappeared. Jennie was gone. There were no riders in sight. There was no sound. There was a heavy trail of horses going north. Jennie had been carried off—probably by outlaws. Duane realized that pursuit was out of the question—that Jennie was lost.

10

A hundred miles from the haunts most familiar with Duane's deeds, far up where the Nueces ran a trickling clear stream between yellow cliffs, stood a small deserted shack of covered mesquite poles. It had been made long ago, but was well preserved. A door faced the overgrown trail, and another faced down into a gorge of dense thickets. On the border fugitives from law and men who hid in fear of some one they had wronged never lived in houses with only one door.

It was a wild spot, lonely, not fit for human habitaion except for the outcast. He, perhaps, might have found it hard to leave for most of the other wild nooks in that barren country. Down in the gorge there was never-failing sweet water, grass all the year round, cool, shady retreats, deer, rabbits, turkeys, fruit, and miles and miles of narrow-twisting, deep cañon full of broken rocks and impenetrable thickets. The scream of the panther was heard there, the squall of the wildcat, the cough of the jaguar. Innumerable bees buzzed in the spring blossoms, and, it seemed, scattered honey to the winds. All day there was continuous song of birds, that of the mocking-bird loud and sweet and mocking above the rest.

On clear days—and rare indeed were cloudy days—with the subsiding of the wind at sunset a hush seemed to fall around the little hut. Far-distant dim-blue mountains stood gold-rimmed gradually to fade with the shading of light.

At this quiet hour a man climbed up out of the gorge and sat in the westward door of the hut. This lonely watcher of the west and listener to the silence was Duane. And this hut was the one where, three years before, Jennie had nursed him back to life.

The killing of a man named Sellers, and the combination of circumstances that had made the tragedy a memorable regret, had marked, if not a change, at least a cessation in Duane's activities. He had trailed Sellers to kill him for the supposed abducting of Jennie. He had trailed him long after he had learned Sellers traveled alone. Duane wanted absolute assurance of Jennie's death. Vague rumors, a few words here and there, unauthenticated stories, were all Duane had gathered in years to substantiate his belief—that Jennie died shortly after the beginning of her second captivity. But Duane did not know surely. Sellers might have told him. Duane expected, if not to force it from him at the end, to read it in his eyes. But the bullet went too unerringly; it locked his lips and fixed his eyes.

After that meeting Duane lay long at the ranchhouse of a friend, and when he recovered from the wound Sellers had given him he started with two horses and a pack for the lonely gorge on the Nueces. There he had been hidden for months, a prey to remorse, a dreamer, a victim of phantoms.

It took work for him to find subsistence in that rocky fastness. And work, action, helped to pass the hours. But he could not work all the time, even if he had found it to do. Then in his idle moments and at night his task was to live with the hell in his mind.

The sunset and the twilight hour made all the rest bearable. The little hut on the rim of the gorge seemed to hold Jennie's presence. It was not as if he felt her spirit. If it had been he would have been sure of her death. He hoped Jennie had not survived her second misfortune; and that intense hope had burned into belief, if not surety. Upon his return to that locality, on the occasion of his first visit to the hut, he had found things just as they had left them, and a poor, faded piece of ribbon Jennie had used to tie around her bright hair. No wandering outlaw or traveler had happened upon the lonely spot, which further endeared it to Duane.

A strange feature of this memory of Jennie was the freshness of it—the failure of years, toil, strife, death-dealing to dim it—to deaden the thought of what might have been. He had a marvelous gift of visualization. He could shut his eyes and see Jennie before him just as clearly as if she had stood there in the flesh. For hours he did that, dreaming, dreaming of life he had never tasted and now never would taste. He saw Jennie's slender, graceful figure, the old brown ragged dress in which he had seen her first at Bland's, her little feet in Mexican sandals, her fine hands coarsened by work, her round arms and swelling throat, and her pale, sad, beautiful face with its staring dark eyes. He remembered every look she had given him, every word she had spoken to him, every time she had touched him. He thought of her beauty and sweetness, of the few things which had come to mean to him that she must have loved him; and he trained himself to think of these in preference to her life at Bland's, the escape with him, and then her recapture, because such memories led to bitter, fruitless pain. He had to fight suffering because it was eating out his heart.

Sitting there, eyes wide open, he dreamed of the old homestead and his white-haired mother. He saw the old home life, sweetened and filled by dear new faces and added joys, go on before his eyes with him a part of it.

Then in the inevitable reaction, in the reflux of bitter reality, he would send out a voiceless cry no poignant because it was silent: "Poor fool! No, I shall never see mother again—never go home—never have a home. I am Duane, the Lone Wolf! Oh, God! I wish it were over! These dreams torture me! What have I to do with a mother, a home, a wife? No bright-haired boy, no dark-eyed girl will ever love me. I am an outlaw, an outcast, dead to the good and decent world. I am alone—alone. Better be a callous brute or better dead! I shall go mad thinking! Man, what is left to you? A hiding-place like a wolf's—lonely silent days, lonely nights with phantoms! Or the trail and the road with their bloody tracks, and then the hard ride, the sleepless, hungry ride to some hole in rocks or brakes. What hellish thing drives me? Why can't I end it all? What is left? Only that damned unquenchable spirit of the gun-fighter to live—to hang on to miserable life—to have no fear of death, yet to cling like a leach—to die as gun-fighters seldom die, with boots off! Bain, you were first, and you're long avenged. I'd change with you. And Sellers, you were last, and you're avenged. And you others—you're avenged. Lie quiet in your graves and give me peace!"

But they did not lie quiet in their graves and give him peace.

A group of specters trooped out of the shadows of dusk and, gathering round him, escorted him to his bed.

When Duane had been riding the trails passion-bent to escape pursuers, or passion-bent in his search, the constant action and toil and exhaustion made him sleep. But when in hiding, as time passed, gradually he required less rest and sleep, and his mind became more active. Little by little his phantoms gained hold on him, and at length, but for the saving power of his dreams, they would have claimed him utterly.

How many times he had said to himself: "I am an intelligent man. I'm not crazy. I'm in full possession of my faculties. All this is fancy—imagination—conscience. I've no work, no duty, no ideal, no hope—and my mind is obsessed, thronged with images. And these images naturally are of the men with whom I have dealt. I can't forget them. They come back to me, hour after hour; and when my tortured mind grows weak, then maybe I'm not just right till the mood wears out and lets me sleep."

So he reasoned as he lay down in his comfortable camp. The night was star-bright above the cañon-walls, darkly shadowing down between them. The insects hummed and chirped and thrummed a continuous thick song, low and monotonous. Slow-running water splashed softly over stones in the stream-bed. From far down the cañon came the mournful hoot of an owl. The moment he lay down, thereby giving up action for the day, all these things weighed upon him like a great heavy mantle of loneliness. In truth, they did not constitute loneliness.

And he could no more have dispelled thought than he could have reached out to touch a cold, bright star.

He wondered how many outcasts like him lay under this star-studded, velvety sky across the fifteen hundred miles of wild country between El Paso and the mouth of the river. A vast wild territory—a refuge for outlaws! Somewhere he had heard or read that the Texas Rangers kept a book with names and records of outlaws—three thousand known outlaws! Yet these could scarcely be half of that unfortunate horde which had been recruited from all over the states. Duane had traveled from camp to camp, den to den, hiding-place to hiding-place, and he knew these men. Most of them were hopeless criminals; some were avengers; a few were wronged wanderers; and among them occasionally was a man, human in his way, honest as he could be, not yet lost to good.

But all of them were akin in one sense—their outlawry; and that starry night they lay with their dark faces up, some in packs like wolves, others alone like the gray wolf who knew no mate. It did not make much difference in Duane's thought of them that the majority were steeped in crime and brutality, more often than not stupid from rum, incapable of a fine feeling, just lost wild dogs.

Duane doubted that there was a man among them who did not realize his moral wreck and ruin. He had met poor, half-witted wretches who knew it. He believed he could enter into their minds and feel the truth of all their lives—the hardened outlaw, coarse, ignorant, bestial, who murdered as Bill Black had murdered, who stole for the sake of stealing, who craved money to gamble and drink, defiantly ready for death, and, like that terrible outlaw, Helm, who cried out on the scaffold, "Let her rip!"

The wild youngsters seeking notoriety and reckless adventure; the cowboys with a notch on their guns, with boastful pride in the knowledge that they were marked by rangers; the crooked men from the North, defaulters, forgers, murderers, all pale-faced, flat-chested men not fit for that wilderness and not surviving; the dishonest cattlemen, hand and glove with outlaws, driven from their homes; the old grizzled, bow-legged genuine rustlers—all these Duane had come in contact with, had watched and known, and as he felt with them he seemed to see that as their lives were bad, sooner or later to end dismally or tragically, so they must pay some kind of earthly penalty—if not of conscience, then of fear; if not of fear, then of that most terrible of all things to restless, active men—pain, the pang of flesh and bone.

Duane knew, for he had seen them pay. Best of all, moreover, he knew the internal life of the gun-fighter of that select but by no means small class of which he was representative. The world that judged him and his kind judged him as a machine, a killing-machine, with only mind enough to hunt, to meet, to slay another man. It had taken three endless years for Duane to understand his own father. Duane knew beyond all doubt that the gun-fighters like Bland, like Alloway, like Sellers, men who were evil and had no remorse, no spiritual accusing Nemesis, had something far more torturing to mind, more haunting, more murderous of rest and sleep and peace; and that something was abnormal fear of death. Duane knew this, for he had shot these men; he had seen the quick, dark shadow in eyes, the presentiment that the will could not control, and then the horrible certainty. These men must have been in agony at every meeting with a possible or certain foe—more agony than the hot rend of a bullet. They were haunted, too, haunted by this fear, by every victim calling from the grave that nothing was so inevitable as death, which lurked behind every corner, hid in every shadow, lay deep in the dark tube of every gun. These men could not have a friend; they could not love or trust a woman. They knew their one chance of holding on to life lay in their own distrust, watchfulness, dexterity, and that hope, by the very nature of their lives, could not be lasting. They had doomed themselves. What, then, could possibly have dwelt in the depths of their minds as they went to their beds on a starry night like this, with mystery in silence and shadow, with time passing surely, and the dark future and its secret approaching every hour—what, then, but hell?

The hell in Duane's mind was not fear of man or fear of death. He would have been glad to lay down the burden of life, providing death came naturally. Many times he had prayed for it. But that overdeveloped, superhuman spirit of defense in him precluded suicide or the inviting of an enemy's bullet. Sometimes he had a vague, scarcely analyzed idea that this spirit was what had made the Southwest habitable for the white man.

Every one of his victims, singly and collectively, returned to him for ever, it seemed, in cold, passionless, accusing domination of these haunted hours.

They did not accuse him of dishonor or cowardice or brutality or murder; they only accused him of Death. It was as if they knew more than when they were alive, had learned that life was a divine mysterious gift not to be taken. They thronged about him with their voiceless clamoring, drifted around him with their fading eyes.

11

AFTER nearly six months in the Nueces gorge the loneliness and inaction of his life drove Duane out upon the trails seeking anything rather than to hide longer alone, a prey to the scourge of his thoughts. The moment he rode into sight of men a remarkable transformation occurred in him. A strange warmth stirred in him—a longing to see the faces of people, to hear their voices—a pleasurable emotion sad and strange. But it was only a precursor of his old bitter, sleepless, and eternal vigilance. When he hid alone in the brakes he was safe from all except his deeper, better self; when he escaped from this into the haunts of men his force and will went to the preservation of his life.

Mercer was the first village he rode into. He had many friends there. Mercer claimed to owe Duane a debt. On the outskirts of the village there was a grave overgrown by brush so that the rude-lettered post which marked it was scarcely visible to Duane as he rode by. He had never read the inscription. But he thought now of Hardin, no other than the erstwhile ally of Bland. For many years Hardin had harassed the stockmen and ranchers in and around Mercer. On an evil day for him he or his outlaws had beaten and robbed a man who once succored Duane when sore in need. Duane met Hardin in the little plaza of the village, called him every name known to border men, taunted him to draw, and killed him in the act.

Duane went to the house of one Jones, a Texan who had known his father, and there he was warmly received. The feel of an honest hand, the voice of a friend, the prattle of children who were not afraid of him or his gun, good wholesome food, and change of clothes—these things for the time being made a changed man of Duane. To be sure, he did not often speak. The price of his head and the weight of his burden made him silent. But eagerly he drank in all the news that was told him. In the years of his absence from home he had never heard a word about his mother or uncle. Those who were his real friends on the border would have been the last to make inquiries, to write or receive letters that might give a clue to Duane's whereabouts.

Duane remained all day with this hospitable Jones, and as twilight fell was loath to go and yielded to a pressing invitation to remain overnight. It was seldom indeed that Duane slept under a roof. Early in the evening, while Duane sat on the porch with two awed and hero-worshiping sons of the house, Jones returned from a quick visit down to the postoffice. Summarily he sent the boys off. He labored under intense excitement.

"Duane, there's rangers in town," he whispered. "It's all over town, too, that you're here. You rode in long after sunup. Lots of people saw you. I don't believe there's a man or boy that'd squeal on you. But the women might. They gossip, and these rangers are handsome fellows—devils with the women."

"What company of rangers?" asked Duane, quickly.

"Company A, under Captain MacNelly, that new ranger. He made a big name in the war. And since he's been in the ranger service he's done wonders. He's cleaned up some bad places south, and he's working north."

"MacNelly. I've heard of him. Describe him to me."

"Slight-built chap, but wiry and tough. Clean face, black mustache and hair. Sharp black eyes. He's got a look of authority. MacNelly's a fine man, Duane. Belongs to a good Southern family. I'd hate to have him look you up."

Duane did not speak.

"MacNelly's got nerve, and his rangers are all experienced men. If they find out you're here they'll come after you. MacNelly's no gun-fighter, but he wouldn't hesitate to do his duty, even if he faced sure death. Which he would in this case. Duane, you mustn't meet Captain MacNelly. Your record is clean, if it is terrible. You never met a ranger or any officer except a rotten sheriff now and then, like Rod Brown."

Still Duane kept silence. He was not thinking of danger, but of the fact of how fleeting must be his stay among friends.

"I've already fixed up a pack of grub," went on Jones. "I'll slip out to saddle your horse. You watch here."

He had scarcely uttered the last word when soft, swift footsteps sounded on the hard path. A man turned in at the gate. The light was dim, yet clean enough to disclose an unusually tall figure. When it appeared nearer he was seen to be walking with both arms raised, hands high. He slowed his stride.

"Does Burt Jones live here?" he asked, in a low, hurried voice.

"I reckon. I'm Burt. What can I do for you?" replied Jones.

The stranger peered around, stealthily came closer, still with his hands up.

"It is known that Buck Duane is here. Captain MacNelly's camping on the river just out of town. He sends word to Duane to come out there after dark."

The stranger wheeled and departed as swifty and strangely as he had come.

"Bust me! Duane, whatever do you make of that?" exclaimed Jones.

"A new one on me." replied Duane, thoughtfully.

"First fool thing I ever heard of MacNelly doing. Can't make head nor tails of it. I'd have said offhand that MacNelly wouldn't double-cross anybody. He struck me as a square man, sand all through. But, hell! he must mean treachery. I can't see anything else in that deal."

"Maybe the Captain wants to give me a fair chance to surrender without bloodshed," observed Duane. "Pretty decent of him, if he meant that."

"He *invites* you out to his camp *after dark*. Something strange about this, Duane. But MacNelly's a new man out here. He does some queer things. Perhaps he's getting a swelled head. Well, whatever his intentions, his presence around Mercer is enough for us. Duane, you hit the road and put some miles between you and the amiable Captain before daylight. To-morrow I'll go out there and ask him what in the devil he meant."

"That messenger he sent—he was a ranger," said Duane.

"Sure he was, and a nervy one! It must have taken sand to come bracing you that way. Duane, the fellow didn't pack a gun. I'll swear to that. Pretty odd, this trick. But you can't trust it. Hit the road, Duane."

A little later a black horse with muffled hoofs, bearing a tall, dark rider who peered keenly into every shadow, trotted down a pasture lane back of Jones's house, turned into the road, and then, breaking into swifter gait, rapidly left Mercer behind.

Fifteen or twenty miles out Duane drew rein in a forest of mesquite, dismounted, and searched about for a glade with a little grass. Here he staked his horse on a long lariat; and, using his saddle for a pillow, his saddle-blanket for covering, he went to sleep.

Next morning he was off again, working south. During the next few days he paid brief visits to several villages that lay in his path. And in each some one particular friend had a piece of news to impart that made Duane profoundly thoughtful. A ranger had made a quiet, unobtrusive call upon these friends and left this message, "Tell Buck Duane to ride into Captain MacNelly's camp some time after night."

Duane concluded, and his friends all agreed with him, that the new ranger's main purpose in the Nueces country was to capture or kill Buck Duane, and that this message was simply an original and striking ruse, the daring of which might appeal to certain outlaws.

But it did not appeal to Duane. His curiosity was aroused; it did not, however, tempt him to any foolhardy act. He turned southwest and rode a hundred miles until he again reached the sparsely settled country. Here he heard no more of rangers. It was a barren region he had never but once ridden through, and that ride had cost him dear. He had been compelled to shoot his way out. Outlaws were not in accord with the few ranchers and their cowboys who ranged there. He learned that both outlaws and Mexican raiders had long been at bitter enmity with these ranchers. Being unfamiliar with roads and trails, Duane had pushed on into the heart of this district, when all the time he really believed he was traveling around it. A rifle-shot from a ranch-house, a deliberate attempt to kill him because he was an unknown rider in those parts, discovered to Duane his mistake; and a hard ride to get away persuaded him to return to his old methods of hiding by day and traveling by night.

He got into rough country, rode for three days without covering much ground, but believed that he was getting on safer territory. Twice he came to a wide bottom-land green with willow and cottonwood and thick as chaparral, somewhere through the middle of which ran a river he decided must be the lower Nueces.

One evening, as he stole out from a covert where he had camped, he saw the lights of a village. He tried to pass it on the left, but was unable to because the brakes of this bottom-land extended in almost to the outskirts of the village, and he had to retrace his steps and go round to the right. Wire fences and horses in pasture made this a task, so it was well after midnight before he accomplished it. He made ten miles or more then by daylight, and after that proceeded cautiously along a road which appeared to be well worn from travel. He passed several thickets where he would have halted to hide during the day but for the fact that he had to find water.

He was a long while in coming to it, and then there was no thicket or clump of mesquite near the waterhole that would afford him covert. So he kept on.

The country before him was ridgy and began to show cottonwoods here and there in the hollows and yucca and mesquite on the higher ground. As he mounted a ridge he noted that the road made a sharp turn, and he could not see what was beyond it. He slowed up and was making the turn, which was down-hill between high banks of yellow clay, when his mettlesome horse heard something to frighten him or shied at something and bolted.

The few bounds he took before Duane's iron arm checked him were enough to reach the curve. One flashing glance showed Duane the open once more, a little valley below with a wide, shallow, rocky stream, a clump of cottonwoods beyond, a somber group of men facing him, and two dark, limp, strangely grotesque figures hanging from branches.

The sight was common enough in southwest Texas, but Duane had never before found himself so unpleasantly close.

A hoarse voice pealed out: "By hell! there's another one!"

"Stranger, ride down an' account fer yourself!" yelled another.

"Hands up!"

"Thet's right, Jack; don't take no chances. Plug him!"

These remarks were so swiftly uttered as almost to be continuous. Duane was wheeling his horse when a rifle cracked. The bullet struck his left forearm and he thought broke it, for he dropped the rein. The frightened horse leaped. Another bullet whistled past Duane. Then the bend in the road saved him probably from certain death. Like the wind his fleet steed went down the long hill.

Duane was in no hurry to look back. He knew what to expect. His chief concern of the moment was for his injured arm. He found that the bones were still intact; but the wound, having been made by a soft bullet, was an exceedingly bad one. Blood poured from it. Giving the horse his head, Duane wound his scarf tightly round the holes, and with teeth and hand tied it tightly. That done, he looked back over his shoulder.

Riders were making the dust fly on the hillside road. There were more coming round the cut where the road curved. The leader was perhaps a quarter of a mile back, and the others strung out behind him. Duane needed only one glance to tell him that they were fast and hard-riding cowboys in a land where all riders were good. They would not have owned any but strong, swift horses. Moreover, it was a district where ranchers had suffered beyond all endurance the greed and brutality of outlaws. Duane had simply been so unfortunate as to run right into a lynching party at a time of all times when any stranger would be in danger and any outlaw put to his limit to escape with his life.

Duane did not look back again till he had crossed the ridgy piece of ground and had gotten to the level road. He had gained upon his pursuers. When he ascertained this he tried to save his horse, to check a little that killing gait. This horse was a magnificent animal, big, strong, fast; but his endurance had never been put to a grueling test. And that worried Duane. His life had made it impossible to keep one horse very long at a time, and this one was an unknown quantity.

Duane had only one plan—the only plan possible in this case—and that was to make the river-bottoms, where he might elude his pursuers in the willow brakes. Fifteen miles or so would bring him to the river, and this was not a hopeless distance for any good horse if not too closely pressed. Duane concluded presently that the cowboys behind were losing a little in the chase because they were not extending their horses. It was decidedly unusual for such riders to save their mounts. Duane pondered over this, looking backward several times to see if their horses were stretched out. They were not, and the fact was disturbing. Only one reason presented itself to Duane's conjecturing, and it was that with him headed straight on that road his pursuers were satisfied not to force the running. He began to hope and look for a trail or a road turning off to right or left. There was none. A rough, mesquite-dotted and yucca-spired country extended away on either side. Duane believed that he would be compelled to take to this hard going. One thing was certain—he had to go round the village. The river, however, was on the outskirts of the village; and once in the willows, he would be safe.

Dust-clouds far ahead caused his alarm to grow. He watched with his eyes strained; he hoped to see a wagon, a few stray cattle. But no, he soon descried several horsemen. Shots and yells behind him attested to the fact that his pursuers likewise had seen these new-comers on the scene. More than a mile separated these two parties, yet that distance did not keep them from soon understanding each other. Duane waited only to see this new factor show signs of sudden quick action, and then, with a muttered curse, he spurred his horse off the road into the brush.

He chose the right side, because the river lay nearer that way. There were patches of open sandy ground between clumps of cactus and mesquite, and he found that despite a zigzag course he made better time. It was impossible for him to locate his pursuers. They would come together, he decided, and take to his tracks.

What, then, was his surprise and dismay to run out of a thicket right into a low ridge of rough, broken rock, impossible to get a horse over. He wheeled to the left along its base. The sandy ground gave place to a harder soil, where his horse did not labor so. Here the growths of mesquite and cactus became scanter, affording better travel but poor cover. He kept sharp eyes ahead, and, as he had expected, soon saw moving dust-clouds and the dark figures of horses. They were half a mile away, and swinging obliquely across the flat, which fact proved that they had entertained a fair idea of the country and the fugitive's difficulty.

Without an instant's hesitation Duane put his horse to his best efforts, straight ahead. He had to pass those men. When this was seemingly made impossible by a deep wash from which he had to turn, Duane began to feel cold and sick. Was this the end? Always there had to be an end to an outlaw's career. He wanted then to ride straight at these pursuers. But reason outweighed instinct. He ws fleeing for his life; nevertheless, the strongest instinct at the time was his desire to fight.

He knew when these three horsemen saw him and a moment afterward he lost sight of them as he got into the mesquite again. He meant now to try to reach the road, and pushed his mount severely, though still saving him for a final burst. Rocks, thickets, bunches of cactus, washes—all operated against his following a straight line. Almost he lost his bearings, and finally would have ridden toward his enemies had not good fortune favored him in the matter of an open burned-over stretch of ground.

Here he saw both groups of pursuers, one on each side and almost within gunshot. Their sharp yells, as much as his cruel spurs, drove his horse into that pace which now meant life or death for him. And never had Duane bestrode a gamer, swifter, stancher beast. He seemed about to accomplish the impossible. In the dragging sand he was far superior to any horse in pursuit, and on this sandy open stretch he gained enough to spare a little in the brush beyond. Heated now and thoroughly terrorized, he kept the pace through thickets that almost tore Duane from his saddle. Something weighty and grim eased off Duane. He was going to get out in front! The horse had speed, fire, stamina.

Duane dashed out into another open place dotted by few trees, and here, right in his path, within pistol-range, stood horsemen waiting. They yelled, they spurred toward him, but did not fire at him. He turned his horse—faced to the right. Only one thing kept him from standing his ground to fight it out. He remembered those dangling limp figures hanging from the cottonwoods. These ranchers would rather hang an outlaw than do anything. They might draw all his fire and then capture him. His horror of hanging was so great as to be all out of proportion compared to his gun-fighter's instinct of self-preservation.

A race began then, a dusty, crashing drive through gray mesquite. Duane could scarcely see, he was so blinded by stinging branches across his eyes. The hollow wind roared in his ears. He lost his sense of the nearness of his pursuers. But they must have been close. Did they shoot at him? He imagined he heard shots. But that might have been the cracking of dead snags. His left arm hung limp, almost useless; he handled the rein with his right; and most of the time he hung low over the pommel. The gray walls flashing by him, the whip of twigs, the rush of wind, the heavy, rapid pound of hoofs, the violent motion of his horse—these vied in sensation with the smart of sweat in his eyes, the rack of his wound, the cold, sick cramp in his stomach. With these also was dull, raging fury. He had to run when he wanted to fight. It took all his mind to force back that bitter hate of himself, of his pursuers, of this race for his useless life.

Suddenly he burst out of a line of mesquite into the road. A long stretch of lonely road! How fiercely, with hot, strange joy, he wheeled his horse upon it! Then he was sweeping along, sure now that he was out in front. His horse still had strength and speed, but showed signs of breaking. Presently Duane looked back. Pursuers—he could not count how many—were loping along in his rear. He paid no more attention to them, and with teeth set he faced ahead, grimmer now in his determination to foil them.

He passed a few scattered ranch-houses where horses whistled from corrals, and men curiously watched him fly past. He saw one rancher running, and he felt intuitively that this fellow was going to join in the chase. Duane's steed pounded on, not noticeably slower, but with a lack of former smoothness, with a strained, convulsive, jerking stride which showed he was almost done.

Sight of the village ahead surprised Duane. He had reached it sooner than he expected. Then he made a discovery—he had entered the zone of wire fences. As he dared not turn back now, he kept on, intending to ride through the village.

Looking backward, he saw that his pursuers were half a mile distant, too far to alarm any villagers in time to intercept him in his flight. As he rode by the first houses his horse broke and began to labor. Duane did not believe he would last long enough to go through the village.

Saddled horses in front of a store gave Duane an idea, not by any means new, and one he had carried out successfully before. As he pulled in his heaving mount and leaped off, a couple of ranchers came out of the place, and one of them stepped to a clean-limbed, fiery bay. He was about to get into his saddle when he saw Duane, and then he halted, a foot in the stirrup.

Duane strode forward, grasped the bridle of this man's horse.

"Mine's done—but not killed," he panted. "Trade with me."

"Wal, stranger, I'm shore always ready to trade," drawled the man. "But ain't you a little swift?"

Duane glanced back up the road. His pursuers were entering the village.

"I'm Duane—Buck Duane," he cried, menacingly. "Will you trade? Hurry!"

The rancher, turning white, dropped his foot from the stirrup and fell back.

"I reckon I'll trade," he said.

Bounding up, Duane dug spurs into the bay's flanks. The horse snorted in fright, plunged into a run. He was fresh, swift, half wild. Duane flashed by the remaining houses on the street out into the open. But the road ended at that village or else led out from some other quarter, for he had ridden straight into the fields and from them into rough desert. When he reached the cover of mesquite once more he looked back to find six horsemen within rifle-shot of him, and more coming behind them.

His new horse had not had time to get warm before Duane reached a high sandy bluff below which lay the willow brakes. As far as he could see extended an immense flat strip of red-tinged willow. How welcome it was to his eye! He felt like a hunted wolf that, weary and lame, had reached his hole in the rocks. Zigzagging down the soft slope, he put the bay to the dense wall of leaf and branch. But the horse balked.

There was little time to lose. Dismounting, he dragged the stubborn beast into the thicket. This was harder and slower work than Duane cared to risk. If he had not been rushed he might have had better success. So he had to abandon the horse—a circumstance that only such sore straits could have driven him to. Then he went slipping swiftly through the narrow aisles.

He had not gotten under cover any too soon. For he heard his pursuers piling over the bluff, loud-voiced, confident, brutal. They crashed into the willows.

"Hi, Sid! Heah's your hoss!" called one, evidently to the man Duane had forced into a trade.

"Say, if you locoed gents 'll hold up a little I'll tell you somethin'," replied a voice from the bluff.

"Come on, Sid! We got him corralled," said the first speaker.

"Wal, mebbe, an' if you hev it's liable to be damn hot. *Thet feller was Buck Duane!*"

Absolute silence followed that statement. Presently it was broken by a rattling of loose gravel and then low voices.

"He can't git acrost the river, I tell you," came to Duane's ears. "He's corralled in the brake. I know thet hole."

Then Duane, gliding silently and swifty through the willows, heard no more from his pursuers. He headed straight for the river. Threading a passage through a willow brake was an old task for him. Many days and nights had gone to the acquiring of a skill that might have been envied by an Indian.

The Rio Grande and its tributaries for the most of their length in Texas ran between wide, low, flat lands covered by a dense growth of willow. Cottonwood, mesquite, prickly pear, and other growths mingled with the willow, and altogether they made a matted, tangled copse, a thicket that an inexperienced man would have considered impenetrable. From above, these wild brakes looked green and red; from the inside they were gray and yellow—a striped wall. Trails and glades were scarce. There were a few deer-runways and sometimes little paths made by peccaries—the *jabali,* or wild pigs, of Mexico. The ground was clay and unusually dry, sometimes baked so hard that it left no imprint of a track. Where a growth of cottonwood had held back the encroachment of the willows there usually was thick grass and underbrush. The willows were short, slender poles with stems so close together that they almost touched, and with the leafy foliage forming a thick covering.

The depths of this brake Duane had penetrated was a silent, dreamy, strange place. In the middle of the day the light was weird and dim. When a breeze fluttered the foliage, then slender shafts and spears of sunshine pierced the green mantle and danced like gold on the ground.

Duane had always felt the strangeness of this kind of place, and likewise he had felt a protecting, harboring something which always seemed to him to be the sympathy of the brake for a hunted creature. Any unwounded creature, strong and resourceful, was safe when he had glided under the low, rustling green roof of this wild covert. It was not hard to conceal tracks; the springy soil gave forth no sound; and men could hunt each other for weeks, pass within a few yards of each other and never know it. The problem of sustaining life was difficult; but, then, hunted men and animals survived on very little.

Duane wanted to cross the river if that was possible, and, keeping in the brake, work his way upstream till he had reached country more hospitable. Remembering what the man had said in regard to the river, Duane had his doubts about crossing. But he would take any chance to put the river between him and his hunters. He pushed on. His left arm had to be favored, as he could scarcely move it. Using his right to spread the willows, he slipped sideways between them and made fast time. There were narrow aisles and washes and holes low down and paths brushed by animals, all of which he took advantage of, running, walking, crawling, stooping any way to get along. To keep in a straight line was not easy—he did it by marking some bright sunlit stem or tree ahead, and when he reached it looked straight on to mark another. His progress necessarily grew slower, for as he advanced the brake became wilder, denser, darker. Mosquitoes began to whine about his head. He kept on without pause. Deepening shadows under the willows told him that the afternoon was far advanced. He began to fear he had wandered in a wrong direction. Finally a strip of light ahead relieved his anxiety, and after a toilsome penetration of still denser brush he broke through to the bank of the river.

He faced a wide, shallow, muddy stream with brakes on the opposite bank extending like a green and yellow wall. Duane perceived at a glance the futility of his trying to cross at this point. Everywhere the sluggish water laved quicksand bars. In fact, the bed of the river was all quicksand, and very likely there was not a foot of water anywhere. He could not swim; he could not crawl; he could not push a log across. Any solid thing touching that smooth yellow sand would be grasped and sucked down. To prove this he seized a long pole and, reaching down from the high bank, thrust it into the stream. Right there near shore there apparently was no bottom to the treacherous quicksand. He abandoned any hope of crossing the river. Probably for miles up and down it would be just the same as here. Before leaving the bank he tied his hat upon the pole and lifted enough water to quench his thirst. Then he worked his way back to where thinner growth made advancement easier, and kept on up-stream till the shadows were so deep he could not see. Feeling around for a place big enough to stretch out on, he lay down. For the time being he was as safe there as he would have been beyond in the Rim Rock. He was tired, though not exhausted, and in spite of the throbbing pain in his arm he dropped at once into sleep.

12

SOME time during the night Duane awoke. A stillness seemingly so thick and heavy as to have substance blanketed the black willow brake. He could not see a star or a branch or tree-trunk or even his hand before his eyes. He lay there waiting, listening, sure that he had been awakened by an unusual sound. Ordinary noises of the night in the wilderness never disturbed his rest. His faculties, like those of old fugitives and hunted creatures, had become trained to a marvelous keenness. A long low breath of slow wind moaned through the willows, passed away; some stealthy, softfooted beast trotted by him in the darkness; there was a rustling among dry leaves; a fox barked lonesomely in the distance. But none of these sounds had broken his slumber.

Suddenly, piercing the stillness, came a bay of a bloodhound. Quickly Duane sat up, chilled to his marrow. The action made him aware of his crippled arm. Then came other bays, lower, more distant. Silence enfolded him again, all the more oppressive and menacing in his suspense. Bloodhounds had been put on his trail, and the leader was not far away. All his life Duane had been familiar with bloodhounds; and he knew that if the pack surrounded him in this impenetrable darkness he would be held at bay or dragged down as wolves dragged a stag. Rising to his feet, prepared to flee as best he could, he waited to be sure of the direction he should take.

The leader of the hounds broke into cry again, a deep, full-toned, ringing bay, strange, ominous, terribly significant in its power. It caused a cold sweat to ooze out all over Duane's body. He turned from it, and with his uninjured arm outstretched to feel for the willows he groped his way along. As it was impossible to pick out the narrow passages, he had to slip and squeeze and plunge between the yielding stems. He made such a crashing that he no longer heard the baying of the hounds. He had no hope to elude them. He meant to climb the first cottonwood that he stumbled upon in his blind flight. But it appeared he never was going to be lucky enough to run against one. Often he fell, sometimes flat, at others upheld by the willows. What made the work so hard was the fact that he had only one arm to open a clump of close-growing stems and his feet would catch or tangle in the narrow crotches, holding him fast. He had to struggle desperately. It was as if the willows were clutching hands, his enemies, fiendishly impeding his progress. He tore his clothes on sharp branches and his flesh suffered many a prick. But in a terrible earnestness he kept on until he brought up hard against a cottonwood tree.

There he leaned and rested. He found himself as nearly exhausted as he had ever been, wet with sweat, his hands torn and burning, his breast laboring, his legs stinging from innumerable bruises. While he leaned there to catch his breath he listened for the pursuing hounds. For a long time there was no sound from them. This, however, did not deceive him into any hopefulness. There were bloodhounds that bayed often on a trail, and others that ran mostly silent. The former were more valuable to their owner and the latter more dangerous to the fugitive. Presently Duane's ears were filled by a chorus of short ringing yelps. The pack had found where he had slept, and now the trail was hot. Satisfied that they would soon overtake him, Duane set about climbing the cottonwood, which in his condition was difficult of ascent.

It happened to be a fairly large tree with a fork about fifteen feet up, and branches thereafter in succession. Duane climbed until he got above the enshrouding belt of blackness. A pale gray mist hung above the brake, and through it shone a line of dim lights. Duane decided these were bonfires made along the bluff to render his escape more difficult on that side. Away round in the direction he thought was north he imagined he saw more fires, but, as the mist was thick, he could not be sure. While he sat there pondering the matter, listening for the hounds, the mist and the gloom on one side lightened; and this side he concluded was east and meant that dawn was near. Satisfying himself on this score, he descended to the first branch of the tree.

His situation now, though still critical, did not appear to be so hopeless as it had been. The hounds would soon close in on him, and he would kill them or drive them away. It was beyond the bounds of possibility that any men could have followed running hounds through that brake in the night. The thing that worried Duane was the fact of the bonfires. He had gathered from the words of one of his pursuers that the brake was a kind of trap, and he began to believe there was only one way out of it, and that was along the bank where he had entered, and where obviously all night long his pursuers had kept fires burning. Further conjecture on this point, however, was interrupted by a crashing in the willows and the rapid patter of feet.

Underneath Duane lay a gray, foggy obscurity. He could not see the ground, nor any object but the black trunk of the tree. Sight would not be needed to tell him when the pack arrived. With a pattering rush through the willows the hounds reached the tree; and then high above crash of brush and thud of heavy paws rose a hideous clamor. Duane's pursuers far off to the south would hear that and know what it meant. And at daybreak, perhaps before, they would take a short cut across the brake, guided by the baying of hounds that had treed their quarry.

It wanted only a few moments, however, till Duane could distinguish the vague forms of the hounds in the gray shadow below. Still he waited. He had no shots to spare. And he knew how to treat bloodhounds. Gradually the obscurity lightened, and at length Duane had good enough sight of the hounds for his purpose. His first shot killed the huge brute leader of the pack. Then, with unerring shots, he crippled several others. That stopped the baying. Piercing howls arose. The pack took fright and fled, its course easily marked by the howls of the crippled members. Duane reloaded his gun, and, making certain all the hounds had gone, he descended to the ground and set off at a rapid pace to the northward.

The mist had dissolved under a rising sun when Duane made his first halt some miles north of the scene where he had waited for the hounds. A barrier to further progress, in shape of a precipitous rocky bluff, rose sheer from the willow brake. He skirted the base of the cliff, where walking was comparatively easy, around in the direction of the river. He reached the end finally to see there was absolutely no chance to escape from the brake at that corner. It took extreme labor, attended by some hazard and considerable pain to his arm, to get down where he could fill his sombrero with water. After quenching his thirst he had a look at his wound. It was caked over with blood and dirt. When washed off the arm was seen to be inflamed and swollen around the bullet-hole. He bathed it, experiencing a soothing relief in the cool water. Then he bandaged it as best he could and arranged a sling round his neck. This mitigated the pain of the injured member and held it in a quiet and restful position, where it had a chance to begin mending.

As Duane turned away from the river he felt refreshed. His great strength and endurance had always made fatigue something almost unknown to him. However, tramping on foot day and night was as unusual to him as to any other riders of the Southwest, and it had begun to tell on him. Retracing his steps, he reached the point where he had abruptly come upon the bluff, and here he determined to follow along its base in the other direction until he found a way out or discovered the futility of such effort.

Duane covered ground rapidly. From time to time he paused to listen. But he was always listening, and his eyes were ever roving. This alertness had become second nature with him, so that except in extreme cases of caution he performed it while he pondered his gloomy and fateful situation. Such habit of alertness and thought made time fly swiftly.

By noon he had rounded the wide curve of the brake and was facing south. The bluff had petered out from a high, mountainous wall to a low abutment of rock, but it still held to its steep, rough nature and afforded no crack or slope where quick ascent could have been possible. He pushed on, growing warier as he approached the danger-zone, finding that as he neared the river on this side it was imperative to go deeper into the willows. In the afternoon he reached a point where he could see men pacing to and fro on the bluff. This assured him that whatever place was guarded was one by which he might escape. He headed toward these men and approached to within a hundred paces of the bluff where they were. There were several men and several boys, all armed and, after the manner of Texans, taking their task leisurely. Farther down Duane made out black dots on the horizon of the bluff-line, and these he concluded were more guards stationed at another outlet. Probably all the available men in the district were on duty. Texans took a grim pleasure in such work. Duane remembered that upon several occasions he had served such duty himself.

Duane peered through the branches and studied the lay of the land. For several hundred yards the bluff could be climbed. He took stock of those careless guards. They had rifles, and that made vain any attempt to pass them in daylight. He believed an attempt by night might be successful; and he was swiftly coming to a determination to hide there till dark and then try it, when the sudden yelping of a dog betrayed him to the guards on the bluff.

The dog had likely been placed there to give an alarm, and he was lustily true to his trust. Duane saw the men run together and begin to talk excitedly and peer into the brake, which was a signal for him to slip away under the willows. He made no noise, and he assured himself he must be invisible. Nevertheless, he heard shouts, then the cracking of rifles, and bullets began to zip and swish through the leafy covert. The day was hot and windless, and Duane concluded that whenever he touched a willow stem, even ever so slightly, it vibrated to the top and sent a quiver among the leaves. Through this the guards had located his position. Once a bullet hissed by him; another thudded into the ground before him. This shooting loosed a rage in Duane. He had to fly from these men, and he hated them and himself because of it. Always in the fury of such moments he wanted to give back shot for shot. But he slipped on through the willows, and at length the rifles ceased to crack.

He sheered to the left again, in line with the rocky barrier, and kept on, wondering what the next mile would bring.

It brought worse, for he was seen by sharp-eyed scouts, and a hot fusillade drove him to run for his life, luckily to escape with no more than a bullet-creased shoulder.

Later that day, still undaunted, he sheered again toward the trap-wall, and found that the nearer he approached to the place where he had come down into the brake the greater his danger. To attempt to run the blockade of that trail by day would be fatal. He waited for night, and after the brightness of the fires had somewhat lessened he assayed to creep out of the brake. He succeeded in reaching the foot of the bluff, here only a bank, and had begun to crawl stealthily up under cover of a shadow when a hound again betrayed his position. Retreating to the willows was as perilous a task as had ever confronted Duane, and when he had accomplished it, right under what seemed a hundred blazing rifles, he felt that he had indeed been favored by Providence. This time men followed him a goodly ways into the brake, and the ripping of lead through the willows sounded on all sides of him.

When the noise of pursuit ceased Duane sat down in the darkness, his mind clamped between two things—whether to try again to escape or wait for possible opportunity. He seemed incapable of decision. His intelligence told him that every hour lessened his chances for escape. He had little enough chance in any case, and that was what made another attempt so desperately hard. Still it was not love of life that bound him. There would come an hour, sooner or later, when he would wrench decision out of this chaos of emotion and thought. But that time was not yet.

When he had remained quiet long enough to cool off and recover from his run he found that he was tired. He stretched out to rest. But the swarms of vicious mosquitoes prevented sleep. This corner of the brake was low and near the river, a breeding-ground for the blood-suckers. They sang and hummed and whined around him in an ever-increasing horde. He covered his head and hands with his coat and lay there patiently. That was a long and wretched night. Morning found him still strong physically, but in a dreadful state of mind.

First he hurried for the river. He could withstand the pangs of hunger, but it was imperative to quench thirst. His wound made him feverish, and therefore more than usually hot and thirsty. Again he was refreshed. That morning he was hard put to it to hold himself back from attempting to cross the river. If he could find a light log it was within the bounds of possibility that he might ford the shallow water and bars of quicksand. But not yet! Wearily, doggedly he faced about toward the bluff.

All that day and all that night, all the next day and all the next night, he stole like a hunted savage from river to bluff; and every hour forced upon him the bitter certainty that he was trapped.

Duane lost track of days, of events. He had come to an evil pass. There arrived an hour when, closely pressed by pursuers at the extreme southern corner of the brake, he took to a dense thicket of willows, driven to what he believed was his last stand.

If only these human bloodhounds would swiftly close in on him! Let him fight to the last bitter gasp and have it over! But these hunters, eager as they were to get him, had care of their own skins. They took few risks. They had him cornered.

It was the middle of the day, hot, dusty, oppressive, threatening storm. Like a snake Duane crawled into a little space in the darkest part of the thicket and lay still. Men had cut him off from the bluff, from the river, seemingly from all sides. But he heard voices only from in front and toward his left. Even if his passage to the river had not been blocked, it might just as well have been.

"Come on fellers—down hyar," called one man from the bluff.

"Got him corralled at last," shouted another.

"Reckon ye needn't be too shore. We thought thet more'n once," taunted another.

"I seen him, I tell you."

"Aw, thet was a deer."

"But Bill found fresh tracks an' blood on the willows."

"If he's winged we needn't hurry."

"Hold on thar, you boys," came a shout in authoritative tones from farther up the bluff. "Go slow. You-all air gittin' foolish at the end of a long chase."

"Thet's right, Colonel. Hold 'em back. There's nothin' shorer than somebody 'll be stoppin' lead pretty quick. He'll be huntin' us soon!"

"Let's surround this corner an' starve him out."

"Fire the brake."

How clearly all this talk pierced Duane's ears! In it he seemed to hear his doom. This, then, was the end he had always expected, which had been close to him before, yet never like now.

"By God!" whispered Duane, "The thing for me to do now—is go out— meet them!"

That was prompted by the fighting, the killing instinct in him. In that moment it had almost superhuman power. If he must die, that was the way for him to die. What else could be expected of Buck Duane? He got to his knees and drew his gun. With his swollen and almost useless hand he held what spare ammunition he had left. He ought to creep out noiselessly to the edge of the willows, suddenly face his pursuers, then, while there was a beat left in his heart, kill, kill, kill. These men all had rifles. The fight would be short. But the marksmen did not live on earth who could make such a fight go wholly against him. Confronting them suddenly he could kill a man for every shot in his gun.

Thus Duane reasoned. So he hoped to accept his fate—to meet this end. But when he tried to step forward something checked him. He forced himself; yet he could not go. The obstruction that opposed his will was as insurmountable as it had been physically impossible for him to climb the bluff.

Slowly he fell back, crouched low, and then lay flat. The grim and ghastly dignity that had been his a moment before fell away from him. He lay there stripped of his last shred of self-respect. He wondered was he afraid; had he, the last of the Duanes—had he come to feel fear? No! Never in all his wild life had he so longed to go out and meet men face to face. It was not fear that held him back. He hated this hiding, this eternal vigilance, this hopeless life. The damnable paradox of the situation was that if he went out to met these men there was absolutely no doubt of his doom. If he clung to his covert there was a chance, a merest chance, for his life. These pursuers, dogged and unflagging as they had been, were mortally afraid of him. It was his fame that made them cowards. Duane's keenness told him that at the very darkest and most perilous moment there was still a chance for him. And the blood in him, the temper of his father, the years of his outlawry, the pride of his unsought and hated career, the nameless, inexplicable something in him made him accept that slim chance.

Waiting then became a physical and mental agony. He lay under the burning sun, parched by thirst, laboring to breathe, sweating and bleeding. his uncared-for wound was like a red-hot prong in his flesh. Blotched and swollen from the never-ending attack of flies and mosquitoes his face seemed twice its natural size, and it ached and stung.

On one side, then, was this physical torture; on the other the old hell, terribly augmented at this crisis, in his mind. It seemed that thought and imagination had never been so swift. If death found him presently, how would it come? Would he get decent burial or be left for the peccaries and the coyotes? Would his people ever know where he had fallen? How wretched, how miserable his state! It was cowardly, it was monstrous for him to cling longer to this doomed life. Then the hate in his heart, the hellish hate of these men on this trail—that was like a scourge. He felt no longer human. He had degenerated into an animal that could think. His heart pounded, his pulse beat, his breast heaved; and this internal strife seemed to thunder into his ears. He was now enacting the tragedy of all crippled, starved, hunted wolves at bay in their dens. Only his tragedy was infinitely more terrible because he had mind enough to see his plight, his resemblance to a lonely wolf, bloody-fanged, dripping, snarling, fire-eyed in a last instinctive defiance.

Mounted upon the horror of Duane's thought was a watching, listening intensity so supreme that it registered impressions which were creations of his imagination. He heard stealthy steps that were not there; he saw shadowy moving figures that were only leaves. A hundred times when he was about to pull trigger he discovered his error. Yet voices came from a distance, and steps and crackings in the willows, and other sounds real enough. But Duane could not distinguish the real from the false. There were times when the wind which had arisen sent a hot, pattering breath down the willow aisles, and Duane heard it as an approaching army.

This straining of Duane's faculties brought on a reaction which in itself was a respite. He saw the sun darkened by thick slow spreading clouds. A storm appeared to be coming. How slowly it moved! The air was like steam. If there broke one of those dark, violent storms common though rare to the country, Duane believed he might slip away in the fury of wind and rain. Hope, that seemed unquenchable in him, resurged again. He hailed it with a bitterness that was sickening.

Then at a rustling step he froze into the old strained attention. He heard a slow patter of soft feet. A tawny shape crossed a little opening in the thicket. It was that of a dog. The moment while that beast came into full view was an age. The dog was not a bloodhound, and if he had a trail or a scent he seemed to be at fault on it. Duane waited for the inevitable discovery. Any kind of a hunting-dog could have found him in that thicket. Voices from outside could be heard urging on the dog. Rover they called him. Duane sat up at the moment the dog entered the little shaded covert. Duane expected a yelping, a baying, or at least a bark that would tell of his hiding-place. A strange relief swiftly swayed over Duane. The end was near now. He had no further choice. Let them come—a quick fierce exchange of shots—and then this torture past! He waited for the dog to give the alarm.

But the dog looked at him and trotted by into the thicket without a yelp. Duance could not believe the evidence of his senses. He thought he had suddenly gone deaf. He saw the dog disappear, heard him running to and fro among the willows, getting farther and farther away, till all sound from him ceased.

"Thar's Rover," called a voice from the bluffside. "He's been through thet black patch."

"Nary a rabbit in there," replied another.

"Bah! Thet pup's no good," scornfully growled another man. "Put a hound at thet clump of villows."

"Fire's the game. Burn the brake before the rain comes."

The voices droned off as their owners evidently walked up the ridge.

Then upon Duane fell the crushing burden of the old waiting, watching, listening spell. After all, it was not to end just now. His chance still persisted—looked a little brighter—led him on, perhaps, to forlorn hope.

All at once twilight settled quickly down upon the willow brake, or else Duane noted it suddenly. He imagined it to be caused by the approaching storm. But there was little movement of air or cloud, and thunder still muttered and rumbled at a distance. The fact was the sun had set, and at this time of overcast sky night was at hand.

Duane realized it with the awakening of all his old force. He would yet elude his pursuers. That was the moment when he seized the significance of all these fortunate circumstances which had aided him. Without haste and without sound he began to crawl in the direction of the river. It was not far, and he reached the bank before darkness set in. There were men up on the bluff carrying wood to build a bonfire. For a moment he half yielded to a temptation to try to slip along the river-shore, close in under the willows. But when he raised himself to peer out he saw that an attempt of this kind would be liable to failure. At the same moment he saw a rough-hewn plank lying beneath him, lodged against some willows. The end of the plank extended in almost to a point beneath him. Quick as a flash he saw where a desperate chance invited him. Then he tied his gun in an oilskin bag and put it in his pocket.

The bank was steep and crumbly. He must not break off any earth to splash into the water. There was a willow growing back some few feet from the edge of the bank. Cautiously he pulled it down, bent it over the water so that when he released it there would be no springing back. Then he trusted his weight to it, with his feet sliding carefully down the bank. He went into the water almost up to his knees, felt the quicksand grip his feet, then, leaning forward till he reached the plank, he pulled it toward him and lay upon it.

Without a sound one end went slowly under water and the farther end appeared lightly braced against the overhanging willows. Very carefully then Duane began to extricate his right foot from the sucking sand. It seemed as if his foot was incased in solid rock. But there was a movement upward, and he pulled with all the power he dared use. It came slowly and at length was free. The left one he released with less difficulty. The next few moments he put all his attention on the plank to ascertain if his weight would sink it into the sand. The far end slipped off the willows with a little splash and gradually settled to rest upon the bottom. But it sank no farther, and Duane's greatest concern was relieved. However, as it was manifestly impossible for him to keep his head up for long he carefully crawled out upon the plank until he could rest an arm and shoulder upon the willows.

When he looked up it was to find the night strangely luminous with fires. There was a bonfire on the extreme end of the bluff, another a hundred paces beyond. A great flare extended over the brake in that direction. Duane heard a roaring on the wind, and he knew his pursuers had fired the willows. He did not believe that would help them much. The brake was dry enough, but too green to burn readily. And as for the bonfires he discovered that the men, probably having run out of wood, were keeping up the light with oil and stuff from the village. A dozen men kept watch on the bluff scarcely fifty paces from where Duane lay concealed by the willows. They talked, cracked jokes, sang songs, and manifestly considered this outlaw-hunting a great lark. As long as the bright light lasted Duane dared not move. He had the patience and the endurance to wait for the breaking of the storm, and if that did not come, then the early hour before dawn when the gray fog and gloom were over the river.

Escape was now in his grasp. He felt it. And with that in his mind he waited, strong as steel in his conviction, capable of withstanding any strain endurable by the human frame.

The wind blew in puffs, grew wilder, and roared through the willows, carrying bright sparks upward. Thunder rolled down over the river, and lightning began to flash. Then the rain fell in heavy sheets, but not steadily. The flashes of lightning and the broad flares played so incessantly that Duane could not trust himself out on the open river. Certainly the storm rather increased the watchfulness of the men on the bluff. He knew how to wait, and he waited, grimly standing pain and cramp and chill. The storm wore away as desultorily as it had come, and the long night set in. There were times when Duane thought he was paralyzed, others when he grew sick, giddy, weak from the strained posture. The first paling of the stars quickened him with a kind of wild joy. He watched them grow paler, dimmer, disappear one by one. A shadow hovered down, rested upon the river, and gradually thickened. The bonfire on the bluff showed as through a foggy veil. The watchers were mere groping dark figures.

Duane, aware of how cramped he had become from long inaction, began to move his legs and uninjured arm and body, and at length overcame a paralyzing stiffness. Then, digging his hand in the sand and holding the plank with his knees, he edged it out into the river. Inch by inch he advanced until clear of the willows. Looking upward, he saw the shadowy figures of the men on the bluff. He realized they ought to see him, feared that they would. But he kept on, cautiously, noiselessly, with a heart-numbing slowness. From time to time his elbow made a little gurgle and splash in the water. Try as he might, he could not prevent this. It got to be like the hollow roar of a rapid filling his ears with mocking sound. There was a perceptible current out in the river, and it hindered straight advancement. Inch by inch he crept on, expecting to hear the bang of rifles, the spattering of bullets. He tried not to look backward, but failed. The fire appeared a little dimmer, the moving shadows a little darker.

Once the plank stuck in the sand and felt as if it were settling. Bringing feet to aid his hand, he shoved it over the treacherous place. This way he made faster progress. The obscurity of the river seemed to be enveloping him. When he looked back again the figures of the men were coalescing with the surrounding gloom, the fires were streaky, blurred patches of light. But the sky above was brighter. Dawn was not far off.

To the west all was dark. With infinite care and implacable spirit and waning strength Duane shoved the plank along, and when at last he discerned the black border of bank it came in time, he thought, to save him. He crawled out, rested till the gray dawn broke, and then headed north through the willows.

13

How long Duane was traveling out of that region he never knew. But he reached familiar country and found a rancher who had before befriended him. Here his arm was attended to; he had food and sleep; and in a couple of weeks he was himself again.

When the time came for Duane to ride away on his endless trail his friend reluctantly imparted the information that some thirty miles south, near the village of Shirley, there was posted at a certain cross-road a reward for Buck Duane dead or alive. Duane had heard of such notices, but he had never seen one. His friend's reluctance and refusal to state for what particular deed this reward was offered roused Duane's curiosity. He had never been any closer to Shirley than this rancher's home. Doubtless some post-office burglary, some gun-shooting scrape had been attributed to him. And he had been accused of worse deeds. Abruptly Duane decided to ride over there and find out who wanted him dead or alive, and why.

As he started south on the road he reflected that this was the first time he had ever deliberately hunted trouble. Introspection awarded him this knowledge; during that last terrible flight on the lower Nueces and while he lay abed recuperating he had changed. A fixed, immutable, hopeless bitterness abided with him. He had reached the end of his rope. All the power of his mind and soul were unavailable to turn him back from his fate. That fate was to become an outlaw in every sense of the term, to be what he was credited with being—that is to say, to embrace evil. He had never committed a crime. He wondered now was crime close to him? He reasoned finally that the desperation of crime had been forced upon him, if not its motive; and that if driven, there was no limit to his possibilities. He understood now many of the hitherto inexplicable actions of certain noted outlaws—why they had returned to the scene of the crime that had outlawed them; why they took such strangely fatal chances; why life was no more to them than a breath of wind; why they rode straight into the jaws of death to confront wronged men or hunting rangers, vigilantes, to laugh in their very faces. It was such bitterness as this that drove these men.

Toward afternoon, from the top of a long hill, Duane saw the green fields and trees and shining roofs of a town he considered must be Shirley. And at the bottom of the hill he came upon an intersecting road. There was a placard nailed on the crossroad sign-post. Duane drew rein near it and leaned close to read the faded print. $1000 REWARD FOR BUCK DUANE DEAD OR ALIVE. Peering closer to read the finer, more faded print, Duane learned that he was wanted for the murder of Mrs. Jeff Aiken at her ranch near Shirley. The month September was named, but the date was illegible. The reward was offered by the woman's husband, whose name appeared with that of a sheriff's at the bottom of the placard.

Duane read the thing twice. When he straightened he was sick with the horror of his fate, wild with passion at those misguided fools who could believe that he had harmed a woman. Then he remembered Kate Bland, and, as always when she returned to him, he quaked inwardly. Years before word had gone abroad that he had killed her, and so it was easy for men wanting to fix a crime to name him. Perhaps it had been done often. Probably he bore on his shoulders a burden of numberless crimes.

A dark, passionate fury possessed him. It shook him like a storm shakes the oak. When it passed, leaving him cold, with clouded brow and piercing eye, his mind was set. Spurring his horse, he rode straight toward the village.

Shirley appeared to be a large, pretentious country town. A branch of some railroad terminated there. The main street was wide, bordered by trees and commodious houses, and many of the stores were of brick. A large plaza shaded by giant cottonwood trees occupied a central location.

Duane pulled his running horse and halted him, plunging and snorting, before a group of idle men who lounged on benches in the shade of a spreading cottonwood. How many times had Duane seen just that kind of lazy shirt-sleeved Texas group! Not often, however, had he seen such placid, lolling, good-natured men change their expression, their attitude so swiftly. His advent apparently was momentous. They evidently took him for an unusual visitor. So far as Duane could tell, not one of them recognized him, had a hint of his identity.

He slid off his horse and threw the bridle.

"I'm Buck Duane," he said. "I saw that placard—out there on a sign-post. It's a damn lie! Somebody find this man Jeff Aiken. I want to see him."

His announcement was taken in absolute silence. That was the only effect he noted, for he avoided looking at these villagers. The reason was simple enough; Duane felt himself overcome with emotion. There were tears in his eyes. He sat down on a bench, put his elbows on his knees and his hands to his face. For once he had absolutely no concern for his fate. This ignominy was the last straw.

Presently, however, he became aware of some kind of commotion among these villagers. He heard whisperings, low, hoarse voices, then the shuffle of rapid feet moving away. All at once a violent hand jerked his gun from its holster. When Duane rose a gaunt man, livid of face, shaking like a leaf, confronted him with his own gun.

"Hands up, thar, you Buck Duane!" he roared, waving the gun.

That appeared to be the cue for pandemonium to break loose. Duane opened his lips to speak, but if he had yelled at the top of his lungs he could not have made himself heard. In weary disgust he looked at the gaunt man, and then at the others, who were working themselves into a frenzy. He made no move, however, to hold up his hands. The villagers surrounded him, emboldened by finding him now unarmed. Then several men lay hold of his arms and pinioned them behind his back. Resistance was useless even if Duane had had the spirit. Some one of them fetched his halter from his saddle, and with this they bound him helpless.

People were running now from the street, the stores, the houses. Old men, cowboys, clerks, boys, ranchers came on the trot. The crowd grew. The increasing clamor began to attract women as well as men. A group of girls ran up, then hung back in fright and pity.

The presence of cowboys made a difference. They split up the crowd, got to Duane, and lay hold of him with rough, businesslike hands. One of them lifted his fists and roared at the frenzied mob to fall back, to stop the racket. He beat them back into a circle; but it was some little time before the hubbub quieted down so a voice could be heard.

"——shut up, will you-all?" he was yelling. "Give us a chance to hear somethin'. Easy now—soho. There ain't nobody goin' to be hurt. Thet's right; everybody quiet now. Let's see what's come off."

This cowboy, evidently one of authority, or at least one of strong personality, turned to the gaunt man, who still waved Duane's gun.

"Abe, put the gun down," he said. "It might go off. Here, give it to me. Now, what's wrong? Who's this roped gent, an' what's he done?"

The gaunt fellow, who appeared now about to collapse, lifted a shaking hand and pointed.

"Thet thar feller—he's Buck Duane!" he panted.

An angry murmur ran through the surrounding crowd.

"The rope! The rope! Throw it over a branch! String him up!" cried an excited villager.

"Buck Duane! Buck Duane!"

"Hang him!"

The cowboy silenced these cries.

"Abe, how do you know this fellow is Buck Duane?" he asked, sharply.

"Why—he said so," replied the man called Abe.

"What!" came the exclamation, incredulously.

"It's a tarnal fact," panted Abe, waving his hands importantly. He was an old man and appeared to be carried away with the significance of his deed. "He like to rid' his hoss right over us-all. Then he jumped off, says he was Buck Duane, an' he wanted to see Jeff Aiken bad."

This speech caused a second commotion as noisy though not so enduring as the first. When the cowboy, assisted by a couple of his mates, had restored order again some one had slipped the noose-end of Duane's rope over his head.

"Up with him!" screeched a wild-eyed youth.

The mob surged closer, was shoved back by the cowboys.

"Abe, if you ain't drunk or crazy tell thet over," ordered Abe's interlocutor.

With some show of resentment and more of dignity Abe reiterated his former statement.

"If he's Buck Duane how'n hell did you get hold of his gun?" bluntly queried the cowboy.

"Why—he set down thar—an' he kind of hid his face on his hand. An' I grabbed his gun an' got the drop on him."

What the cowboy thought of this was expressed in a laugh. His mates likewise grinned broadly. Then the leader turned to Duane.

"Stranger, I reckon you'd better speak up for yourself," he said.

That stilled the crowd as no command had done.

"I'm Buck Duane, all right." said Duane, quietly. "It was this way—"

The big cowboy seemed to vibrate with a shock. All the ruddy warmth left his face; his jaw began to bulge; the corded veins in his neck stood out in knots. In an instant he had a hard, stern, strange look. He shot out a powerful hand that fastened in the front of Duane's blouse.

"Somethin' queer here. But if you're Duane you're sure in bad. Any fool ought to know that. You mean it, then?"

"Yes."

"Rode in to shoot up the town, eh? Same old stunt of you gunfighters? Meant to kill the man who offered a reward? Wanted to see Jeff Aiken bad, huh?"

"No," replied Duane. "Your citizen here misrepresented things. He seems a little off his head."

"Reckon he is. Somebody is, that's sure. You claim Buck Duane, then, an' all his doings?"

"I'm Duane; yes. But I won't stand for the blame of things I never did. That's why I'm here. I saw that placard out there offering the reward. Until now I never was within half a day's ride of this town. I'm blamed for what I never did. I rode in here, told who I was, asked somebody to send for Jeff Aiken."

"An' then you set down an' let this old guy throw your own gun on you?" queried the cowboy in amazement.

"I guess that's it," replied Duane.

"Well, it's powerful strange, if you're really Buck Duane."

A man elbowed his way into the circle.

"It's Duane. I recognize him. I seen him in more'n one place," he said. "Sibert, you can rely on what I tell you. I don't know if he's locoed or what. But I do know he's the genuine Buck Duane. Any one who'd ever seen him onct would never forget him."

"What do you want to see Aiken for?" asked the cowboy Sibert.

"I want to face him, and tell him I never harmed his wife."

"Why?"

"Because I'm innocent, that's all."

"Suppose we send for Aiken an' he hears you an' doesn't believe you; what then?"

"If he won't believe me—why, then my case's so bad—I'd be better off dead."

A momentary silence was broken by Sibert.

"If this isn't a queer deal! Boys, reckon we'd better send for Jeff."

"Somebody went fer him. He'll be comin' soon," replied a man.

Duane stood a head taller than that circle of curious faces. He gazed out above and beyond them. It was in this way that he chanced to see a number of women on the outskirts of the crowd. Some were old, with hard faces, like the men.

Some were young and comely, and most of these seemed agitated by excitement or distress. They cast fearful, pitying glances upon Duane as he stood there with that noose round his neck. Women were more human than men, Duane thought. He met eyes that dilated, seemed fascinated at his gaze, but were not averted. It was the old women who were voluble, loud in expression of their feelings.

Near the trunk of the cottonwood stood a slender woman in white. Duane's wandering glance rested upon her. Her eyes were riveted upon him. A soft-hearted woman, probably, who did not want to see him hanged!

"Thar comes Jeff Aiken now," called a man, loudly.

The crowd shifted and trampled in eagerness.

Duane saw two men coming fast, one of whom, in the lead, was of stalwart build. He had a gun in his hand, and his manner was that of fierce energy.

The cowboy Sibert thrust open the jostling circle of men.

"Hold on, Jeff," he called, and he blocked the man with the gun. He spoke so low Duane ould not hear what he said, and his form hid Aiken's face. At that juncture the crowd spread out, closed in, and Aiken and Sibert were caught in the circle. There was a pushing forward, a pressing of many bodies, hoarse cries and flinging hands—again the insane tumult was about to break out—the demand for an outlaw's blood, the call for a wild justice executed a thousand times before on Texas's bloody soil.

Sibert bellowed at the dark encroaching mass. The cowboys with him beat and cuffed in vain.

"Jeff, will you listen?" broke in Sibert, hurriedly, his hand on the other man's arm.

Aiken nodded coolly. Duane, who had seen many men in perfect control of themselves under circumstances like these, recognized the spirit that dominated Aiken. He was white, cold, passionless. There were lines of bitter grief deep round his lips. If Duane ever felt the meaning of death he felt it then.

"Sure this 's your game, Aiken," said Sibert. "But hear me a minute. Reckon there's no doubt about this man bein' Buck Duane. He seen the placard out at the cross-roads. He rides in to Shirley. He says he's Buck Duane an' he's lookin' for Jeff Aiken. That's all clear enough. You know how these gunfighters go lookin' for trouble. But here's what stumps me. Duane sits down there on the bench and lets old Abe Strickland grab his gun an' get the drop on him. More'n that, he gives me some strange talk about how, if he couldn't make you believe he's innocent, he'd better be dead. You see for yourself Duane ain't drunk or crazy or locoed. He doesn't strike me as a man who rode in here huntin' blood. So I reckon you'd better hold on till you hear what he has to say."

Then for the first time the drawn-faced, hungry-eyed giant turned his gaze upon Duane. He had intelligence which was not yet subservient to passion.

Moreover, he seemed the kind of man Duane would care to have judge him in a critical moment like this.

"Listen," said Duane, gravely, with his eyes steady on Aiken's, "I'm Buck Duane. I never lied to any man in my life. I was forced into outlawry. I've never had a chance to leave the country. I've killed men to save my own life. I never intentionally harmed any woman. I rode thirty miles to-day—deliberately to see what this reward was, who made it, what for. When I read the placard I went sick to the bottom of my soul. So I rode in here to find you—to tell you this: I never saw Shirley before to-day. It was impossible for me to have—killed your wife. Last September I was two hundred miles north of here on the upper Nueces. I can prove that. Men who know me will tell you I couldn't murder a woman. I haven't any idea why such a deed should be laid at my hands. It's just that wild border gossip. I have no idea what reasons you have for holding me responsible. I only know—you're wrong. You've been deceived. And see here, Aiken. You understand I'm a miserable man. I'm about broken, I guess. I don't care any more for life, for anything. If you can't look me in the eyes, man to man, and believe what I say—why, by God! you can kill me!"

Aiken heaved a great breath.

"Buck Duane, whether I'm impressed or not by what you say needn't matter. You've had accusers, justly or unjustly, as will soon appear. The thing is we can prove you innocent or guilty. My girl Lucy saw my wife's assailant."

He motioned for the crowd of men to open up.

"Somebody—you, Sibert—go for Lucy. That'll settle this thing."

Duane heard as a man in an ugly dream. The faces around him, the hum of voices, all seemed far off. His life hung by the merest thread. Yet he did not think of that so much as of the brand of a woman-murderer which might be soon sealed upon him by a frightened, imaginative child.

The crowd trooped apart and closed again. Duane caught a blurred image of a slight girl clinging to Sibert's hand. He could not see distinctly. Aiken lifted the child, whispered soothingly to her not to be afraid. Then he fetched her closer to Duane.

"Lucy, tell me. Did you ever see this man before?" asked Aiken, huskily and low. "Is he the one—who came in the house that day—struck you down—and dragged mama—?"

Aiken's voice failed.

A lightning flash seemed to clear Duane's blurred sight. He saw a pale, sad face and violet eyes fixed in gloom and horror upon his. No terrible moment in Duane's life ever equaled this one of silence—of suspense.

"It's ain't him!" cried the child.

Then Sibert was flinging the noose off Duane's neck and unwinding the bonds round his arms. The spellbound crowd awoke to hoarse exclamations.

"See there, my locoed gents, how easy you'd hang the wrong man," burst out the cowboy, as he made the rope-end hiss. "You-all are a lot of wise rangers. Haw! haw!"

He freed Duane and thrust the bone-handled gun back in Duane's holster.

"You Abe, there. Reckon you pulled a stunt! But don't try the like again. And, men, I'll gamble there's a hell of a lot of bad work Buck Duane's named for—which all he never done. Clear away there. Where's his hoss? Duane, the road's open out of Shirley."

Sibert swept the gaping watchers aside and pressed Duane toward the horse, which another cowboy held. Mechanically Duane mounted, felt a lift as he went up. Then the cowboy's hard face softened in a smile.

"I reckon it ain't uncivil of me to say—hit the road quick!" he said, frankly.

He led the horse out of the crowd. Aiken joined him, and between them they escorted Duane across the plaza. The crowd appeared irresistibly drawn to follow.

Aiken paused with his big hand on Duane's knee. In it, unconsciously, probably, he still held the gun.

"Duane, a word with you," he said. "I believe you're not so black as you've been painted. I wish there was time to say more. Tell me this anyway. Do you know the Ranger Captain MacNelly?"

"I do not," replied Duane, in surprise.

"I met him only a week ago over in Fairfield," went on Aiken, hurriedly. "He declared you never killed my wife. I didn't believe him—argued with him. We almost had hard words over it. Now—I'm sorry. The last thing he said was: 'If you ever see Duane don't kill him. Send him into my camp after dark!' He meant something strange. What—I can't say. But he was right, and I was wrong. If Lucy had batted an eye I'd have killed you. Still, I wouldn't advise you to hunt up MacNelly's camp. He's clever. Maybe he believes there's no treachery in his new ideas of ranger tactics. I tell you for all it's worth. Good-by. May God help you further as he did this day!"

Duane said good-by and touched the horse with his spurs.

"So long, Buck!" called Sibert, with that frank smile breaking warm over his brown face; and he held his sombrero high.

14

WHEN Duane reached the crossing of the roads the name Fairfield on the sign-post seemed to be the thing that tipped the oscillating balance of decision in favor of that direction.

He answered here to unfathomable impulse. If he had been driven to hunt up Jeff Aiken, now he was called to find this unknown ranger captain. In Duane's state of mind clear reasoning, common sense, or keenness were out of the question. He went because he felt he was compelled.

Dusk had fallen when he rode into a town which inquiry discovered to be Fairfield. Captain MacNelly's camp was stationed just out of the village limits on the other side.

No one except the boy Duane questioned appeared to notice his arrival. Like Shirley, the town of Fairfield was large and prosperous, compared to the innumerable hamlets dotting the vast extent of southwestern Texas. As Duane rode through, being careful to get off the main street, he heard the tolling of a church-bell that was a melancholy reminder of his old home.

There did not appear to be any camp on the outskirts of the town. But as Duane sat his horse, peering around and undecided what further move to make, he caught the glint of flickering lights through the darkness. Heading toward them, he rode perhaps a quarter of a mile to come upon a grove of mesquite. The brightness of several fires made the surrounding darkness all the blacker. Duane saw the moving forms of men and heard horses. He advanced naturally, expecting any moment to be halted.

"Who goes there?" came the sharp call out of the gloom.

Duane pulled his horse. The gloom was impenetrable.

"One man—alone," replied Duane.

"A stranger?"

"Yes."

"What do you want?"

"I'm trying to find the ranger camp."

"You've struck it. What's your errand?"

"I want to see Captain MacNelly."

"Get down and advance. Slow. Don't move your hands. It's dark, but I can see."

Duane dismounted, and, leading his horse, slowly advanced a few paces. He saw a dully bright object—a gun—before he discovered the man who held it. A few more steps showed a dark figure blocking the trail. Here Duane halted.

"Come closer, stranger. Let's have a look at you," the guard ordered, curtly.

Duane advanced again until he stood before the man. Here the rays of light from the fires flickered upon Duane's face.

"Reckon you're a stranger, all right. What's your name and your business with the Captain?"

Duane hesitated, pondering what best to say.

"Tell Captain MacNelly I'm the man he's been asking to ride into his camp—after dark," finally said Duane.

The ranger bent forward to peer hard at this night visitor. His manner had been alert, and now it became tense.

"Come here, one of you men, quick," he called, without turning in the least toward the camp-fire.

"Hello! What's up, Pickens?" came the swift reply. It was followed by a rapid thud of boots on soft ground. A dark form crossed the gleams from the fire-light. Then a ranger loomed up to reach the side of the guard. Duane heard whispering, the purport of which he could not catch. The second ranger swore under his breath. Then he turned away and started back.

"Here, ranger, before you go, understand this. My visit is peaceful—friendly if you'll let it be. Mind, I was asked to come here—after dark."

Duane's clear, penetrating voice carried far. The listening rangers at the camp-fire heard what he said.

"Ho, Pickens! Tell that fellow to wait," replied an authoritative voice. Then a slim figure detached itself from the dark, moving group at the camp-fire and hurried out.

"Better be foxy, Cap," shouted a ranger, in warning.

"Shut up—all of you," was the reply.

This officer, obviously Captain MacNelly, soon joined the two rangers who were confronting Duane. He had no fear. He strode straight up to Duane.

"I'm MacNelly," he said. "If you're my man, don't mention your name—yet."

All this seemed so strange to Duane, in keeping with much that had happened lately.

"I met Jeff Aiken to-day," said Duane. "He sent me—"

"You've met Aiken!" exclaimed MacNelly, sharp, eager, low. "By all that's bully!" Then he appeared to catch himself, to grow restrained.

"Men, fall back, leave us alone a moment."

The rangers slowly withdrew.

"Buck Duane! It's you?" he whispered, eagerly.

"Yes."

"If I give my word you'll not be arrested—you'll be treated fairly—will you come into camp and consult with me?"

"Certainly."

"Duane, I'm sure glad to meet you," went on MacNelly; and he extended his hand.

Amazed and touched, scarcely realizing this actuality, Duane gave his hand and felt no unmistakable grip of warmth.

"It doesn't seem natural, Captain MacNelly, but I believe I'm glad to meet you," said Duane, soberly.

"You will be. Now we'll go back to camp. Keep your identity mum for the present."

He led Duane in the direction of the camp-fire.

"Pickens, go back on duty," he ordered, "and, Beeson, you look after this horse."

When Duane got beyond the line of mesquite, which had hid a good view of the camp-site, he saw a group of perhaps fifteen rangers sitting around the fires, near a long low shed where horses were feeding, and a small adobe house at one side.

"We've just had grub, but I'll see you get some. Then we'll talk," said MacNelly. "I've taken up temporary quarters here. Have a rustler job on hand. Now, when you've eaten, come right into the house."

Duane was hungry, but he hurried through the ample supper that was set before him, urged on by curiosity and astonishment. The only way he could account for his presence there in a ranger's camp was that MacNelly hoped to get useful information out of him. Still that would hardly have made this captain so eager. There was a mystery here, and Duane could scarcely wait for it to be solved. While eating he had bent keen eyes around him. After a first quiet scrutiny the rangers apparently paid no more attention to him. They were all veterans in service—Duane saw that—and rugged, powerful men of iron constitution. Despite the occasional joke and sally of the more youthful members, and a general conversation of camp-fire nature, Duane was not deceived about the fact that his advent had been an unusual and striking one, which had caused an undercurrent of conjecture and even consternation among them. These rangers were too well trained to appear openly curious about their captain's guest. If they had not deliberately attempted to be oblivious of his presence Duane would have concluded they thought him an ordinary visitor, somehow of use to MacNelly. As it was, Duane felt a suspense that must have been due to a hint of his identity.

He was not long in presenting himself at the door of the house.

"Come in and have a chair," said MacNelly, motioning for the one other occupant of the room to rise. "Leave us, Russell, and close the door. I'll be through these reports right off."

MacNelly sat at a table upon which was a lamp and various papers. Seen in the light he was a fine-looking, soldierly man of about forty years, dark-haired and dark-eyed, with a bronzed face, shrewd, stern, strong, yet not wanting in kindliness. He scanned hastily over some papers, fussed with them, and finally put them in envelopes. Without looking up he pushed a cigar-case toward Duane, and upon Duane's refusal to smoke he took a cigar, rose to light it at the lamp-chimney, and then, settling back in his chair, he faced Duane, making a vain attempt to hide what must have been the fulfilment of a long-nourished curiosity.

"Duane, I've been hoping for this for two years," be began.

Duane smiled a little—a smile that felt strange on his face. He had never been much of a talker. And speech here seemed more than ordinarily difficult.

MacNelly must have felt that.

He looked long and earnestly at Duane, and his quick nervous manner changed to grave thoughtfulness.

"I've lots to say, but where to begin," he mused. "Duane, you've had a hard life since you went on the dodge. I never met you before, don't know what you looked like as a boy. But I can see what—well, even ranger life isn't all roses."

He rolled his cigar between his lips and puffed clouds of smoke.

"Ever hear from home since you left Wellston?" he asked, abruptly.

"No."

"Never a word?"

"Not one," replied Duane, sadly.

"That's tough. I'm glad to be able to tell you that up to just lately your mother, sister, uncle—all your folks, I believe—were well. I've kept posted. But haven't heard lately."

Duane averted his face a moment, hesitated till the swelling left his throat, and then said, "It's worth what I went through to-day to hear that."

"I can imagine how you feel about it. When I was in the war—but let's get down to the business of this meeting."

He pulled his chair close to Duane's.

"You've had word more than once in the last two years that I wanted to see you?"

"Three times, I remember," replied Duane.

"Why didn't you hunt me up?"

"I supposed you imagined me one of those gun-fighters who couldn't take a dare and expected me to ride up to your camp and be arrested."

"That was natural, I suppose," went on MacNelly. "You didn't know me, otherwise you would have come. I've been a long time getting to you. But the nature of my job, as far as you're concerned, made me cautious. Duane, you're aware of the hard name you bear all over the Southwest?"

"Once in a while I'm jarred into realizing," replied Duane.

"It's the hardest, barring Murrell and Cheseldine, on the Texas border. But there's this difference. Murrell in his day was known to deserve his infamous name. Cheseldine in his day also. But I've found hundreds of men in southwest Texas who 're your friends, who swear you never committed a crime. The farther south I get the clearer this becomes. What I want to know is the truth. Have you ever done anything criminal? Tell me the truth, Duane. It won't make any difference in my plan. And when I say crime I mean what *I* would call crime, or any reasonable Texan."

"That way my hands are clean," replied Duane.

"You never held up a man, robbed a store for grub, stole a horse when you needed him bad—never anything like that?"

"Somehow I always kept out of that, just when pressed the hardest."

"Duane, I'm damn glad!" MacNelly exclaimed, gripping Duane's hand. "Glad for your mother's sake! But, all the same, in spite of this, you are a Texas outlaw accountable to the state. You're perfectly aware that under existing circumstances, if you fell into the hands of the law, you'd probably hang, at least go to jail for a long term."

"That's what kept me on the dodge all these years," replied Duane.

"Certainly." MacNelly removed his cigar. His eyes narrowed and glittered. The muscles along his brown cheeks set hard and tense. He leaned closer to Duane, laid sinewy, pressing fingers upon Duane's knee.

"Listen to this," he whispered, hoarsely. "If I place a pardon in your hand— make you a free, honest citizen once more, clear your name of infamy, make your mother, your sister proud of you—will you swear yourself to a service, *any* service I demand of you?"

Duane sat stock still, stunned.

Slowly, more persuasively, with show of earnest agitation, Captain MacNelly reiterated his startling query.

"My God!" burst from Duane. "What's this? MacNelly, you *can't* be in earnest!"

"Never more so in my life. I've a deep game. I'm playing it square. What do you say?"

He rose to his feet. Duane, as if impelled, rose with him. Ranger and outlaw then locked eyes that searched each other's souls. In MacNelly's Duane read truth, strong, fiery purpose, hope, even gladness, and a fugitive mounting assurance of victory.

Twice Duane endeavored to speak, failed of all save a hoarse, incoherent sound, until, forcing back a flood of speech, he found a voice.

"Any service? Every service! MacNelly, I give my word," said Duane.

A light played over MacNelly's face, warming out all the grim darkness. He held out his hand. Duane met it with his in a clasp that men unconsciously give in moments of stress.

When they unclasped and Duane stepped back to drop into a chair MacNelly fumbled for another cigar—he had bitten the other into shreds—and, lighting it as before, he turned to his visitor, now calm and cool. He had the look of a man who had justly won something at considerable cost. His next move was to take a long leather case from his pocket and extract from it several folded papers.

"Here's your pardon from the Governor," he said, quietly. "You'll see, when

you look it over, that it's conditional. When you sign this paper I have here the
condition will be met."

He smoothed out the paper, handed Duane a pen, ran his forefinger along a
dotted line.

Duane's hand was shaky. Years had passed since he had held a pen. It was
with difficulty that he achieved his signature. Buckley Duane—how strange the
name looked!

"Right here ends the career of Buck Duane, outlaw and gunfighter," said
MacNelly; and, seating himself, he took the pen from Duane's fingers and wrote
several lines in several places upon the paper. Then with a smile he handed it
to Duane.

"That makes you a member of Company A, Texas Rangers."

"So that's it!" burst out Duane, a light breaking in upon his bewilderment.
"You want me for ranger service?"

"Sure. That's it," replied the Captain, dryly. "Now to hear what that service
is to be. I've been a busy man since I took this job, and, as you may have heard,
I've done a few things. I don't mind telling you that political influence put me
in here and that up Austin way there's a good deal of friction in the Department
of State in regard to whether or not the ranger service is any good—whether it
should be discontinued or not. I'm on the party side who's defending the ranger
service. I contend that it's made Texas habitable. Well, it's been up to me to
produce results. So far I have been successful. My great ambition is to break
up the outlaw gangs along the river. I have never ventured in there yet because
I've been waiting to get the lieutenant I needed. You, of course, are the man
I had in mind. It's my idea to start way up the Rio Grande and begin with
Cheseldine. He's the strongest, the worst outlaw of the times. He's more than
rustler. It's Cheseldine and his gang who are operating on the banks. They're
doing bank-robbing. That's my private opinion, but it's not been backed up by
any evidence. Cheseldine doesn't leave evidences. He's intelligent, cunning. No
one seems to have seen him—to know what he looks like. I assume, of course,
that you are a stranger to the country he dominates. It's five hundred miles west
of your ground. There's a little town over there called Fairdale. It's the nest of
a rustler gang. They rustle and murder at will. Nobody knows who the leader
is. I want you to find out. Well, whatever way you decide is best you will
proceed to act upon. You are your own boss. You know such men and how they
can be approached. You will take all the time needed, if it's months. It will be
necessary for you to communicate with me, and that will be a difficult matter.
For Cheseldine dominates several whole counties. You must find some way to
let me know when I and my rangers are needed. The plan is to break up
Cheseldine's gang. It's the toughest job on the border. Arresting him alone isn't
to be heard of. He couldn't be brought out. Killing him isn't much better, for

his select men, the ones he operates with, are as dangerous to the community as he is. We want to kill or jail this choice selection of robbers and break up the rest of the gang. To find them, to get among them somehow, to learn their movements, to lay your trap for us rangers to spring—that, Duane, is your service to me, and God knows it's a great one!''

"I have accepted it," replied Duane.

"Your work will be secret. You are now a ranger in my service. But no one except the few I choose to tell will know of it until we pull off the job. You will simply be Buck Duane till it suits our purpose to acquaint Texas with the fact that you're a ranger. You'll see there's no date on that paper. No one will ever know just when you entered the service. Perhaps we can make it appear that all or most of your outlawry has really been good service to the state. At that, I'll believe it'll turn out so."

MacNelly paused a moment in his rapid talk, chewed his cigar, drew his brows together in a dark frown, and went on. "No man on the border knows so well as you the deadly nature of this service. It's a thousand to one that you'll be killed. I'd say there was no chance at all for any other man beside you. Your reputation will go far among the outlaws. Maybe that and your nerve and your gun-play will pull you through. I'm hoping so. But it's a long, long chance against your ever coming back."

"That's not the point," said Duane. "But in case I get killed out there— what—"

"Leave that to me," interrupted Captain MacNelly. "Your folks will know at once of your pardon and your ranger duty. If you lose your life out there I'll see your name cleared—the service you render known. You can rest assured of that."

"I am satisfied," replied Duane. "That's so much more than I've dared to hope."

"Well, it's settled, then. I'll give you money for expenses. You'll start as soon as you like—the sooner the better. I hope to think of other suggestions, especially about communicating with me."

Long after the lights were out and the low hum of voices had ceased round the camp-fire Duane lay wide awake, eyes staring into the blackness, marveling over the strange events of the day. He was humble, grateful to the depths of his soul. A huge and crushing burden had been lifted from his heart. He welcomed this hazardous service to the man who had saved him. Thought of his mother and sister and Uncle Jim, of his home, of old friends came rushing over him the first time in years that he had happiness in the memory. The disgrace he had put upon them would now be removed; and in the light of that, his wasted life of the past, and its probable tragic end in future service as atonement changed their aspects. And as he lay there, with the approach of sleep finally dimming the vividness of his thought, so full of mystery, shadowy faces floated in the blackness around him, haunting him as he had always been haunted.

It was broad daylight when he awakened. MacNelly was calling him to breakfast. Outside sounded voices of men, crackling of fires, snorting and stamping of horses, the barking of dogs. Duane rolled out of his blankets and made good use of the soap and towel and razor and brush near by on a bench—things of rare luxury to an outlaw on the ride. The face he saw in the mirror was as strange as the past he had tried so hard to recall. Then he stepped to the door and went out.

The rangers were eating in a circle round a tarpaulin spread upon the ground.

"Fellows," said MacNelly, "shake hands with Buck Duane. He's on secret ranger service for me. Service that'll likely make you all hump soon! Mind you, keep mum about it."

The rangers surprised Duane with a roaring greeting, the warmth of which he soon divined was divided between pride of his acquisition to their ranks and eagerness to meet that violent service of which their captain hinted. They were jolly wild fellows, with just enough gravity in their welcome to show Duane their respect and appreciation, while not forgetting his lone-wolf record. When he had seated himself in that circle, now one of them, a feeling subtle and uplifting pervaded him.

After the meal Captain MacNelly drew Duane aside.

"Here's the money. Make it go as far as you can. Better strike straight for El Paso, snook around there and hear things. Then go to Valentine. That's near the river and within fifty miles or so of the edge of the Rim Rock. Somewhere up there Cheseldine holds fort. Somewhere to the north is the town Fairdale. But he doesn't hide all the time in the rocks. Only after some daring raid or hold-up. Cheseldine's got border towns on his staff, or scared of him, and these places we want to know about, especially Fairdale. Write me care of the adjutant at Austin. I don't have to warn you to be careful where you mail letters. Ride a hundred, two hundred miles, if necessary, or go clear to El Paso."

MacNelly stopped with an air of finality, and then Duane slowly rose.

"I'll start at once," he said, extending his hand to the Captain. "I wish—I'd like to thank you!"

"Hell, man! Don't thank me!" replied MacNelly, crushing the proffered hand. "I've sent a lot of good men to their deaths, and maybe you're another. But, as I've said, you've one chance in a thousand. And, by Heaven! I'd hate to be Cheseldine or any other man you were trailing. No, not good-by—*Adios,* Duane! May we meet again!"

Book II
The Ranger

15

WEST of the Pecos River Texas extended a vast wild region, barren in the north where the Llano Estacado spread its shifting sands, fertile in the south along the Rio Grande. A railroad marked an undeviating course across five hundred miles of this country, and the only villages and towns lay on or near this line of steel. Unsettled as was this western Texas, and despite the acknowledged dominance of the outlaw bands, the pioneers pushed steadily into it. First had come the lone rancher; then his neighbors in near and far valleys; then the hamlets; at last the railroad and the towns. And still the pioneers came, spreading deeper into the valleys, farther and wider over the plains. It was mesquite-dotted, cactus-covered desert, but rich soil upon which water acted like magic. There was little grass to an acre, but there were millions of acres. The climate was wonderful. Cattle flourished and ranchers prospered.

The Rio Grande flowed almost due south along the western boundary for a thousand miles, and then, weary of its course, turned abruptly north, to make what was called the Big Bend. The railroad, running west, cut across this bend, and all that country bounded on the north by the railroad and on the south by the river was as wild as the Staked Plains. It contained not one settlement. Across the face of this Big Bend, as if to isolate it, stretched the Ord mountain range, of which Mount Ord, Cathedral Mount, and Elephant Mount raised bleak peaks above their fellows, In the valleys of the foothills and out across the plains were ranches, and farther north villages, and the towns of Alpine and Marfa.

Like other parts of the great Lone Star State, this section of Texas was a world in itself—a world where the riches of the rancher were ever enriching the outlaw. The village closest to the gateway of this outlaw-infested region was a little place called Ord, named after the dark peak that loomed some miles to the south. It had been settled originally by Mexicans—there were still the ruins of adobe

321

missions—but with the advent of the rustler and outlaw many inhabitants were shot or driven away, so that at the height of Ord's prosperity and evil sway there were but few Mexicans living there, and these had their choice between holding hand-and-glove with the outlaws or furnishing target practice for that wild element.

Toward the close of a day in September a stranger rode into Ord, and in a community where all men were remarkable for one reason or another he excited interest. His horse, perhaps, received the first and most engaging attention— horses in that region being apparently more important than men. This particular horse did not attract with beauty. At first glance he seemed ugly. But he was a giant, black as coal, rough despite the care manifestly bestowed upon him, long of body, ponderous of limb, huge in every way. A bystander remarked that he had a grand head. True, if only his head had been seen he would have been a beautiful horse. Like men, horses show what they are in the shape, the size, the line, the character of the head. This one denoted fire, speed, blood, loyalty, and his eyes were as soft and dark as a woman's. His face was solid black, except in the middle of his forehead, where there was a round spot of white.

"Say mister, mind tellin' me his name?" asked a ragged urchin, with born love of a horse in his eyes.

"Bullet," replied the rider.

"Thet there's fer the white mark, ain't it?" whispered the youngster to another. "Say, ain't he a whopper? Biggest hoss I ever seen."

Bullet carried a huge black silver-ornamented saddle of Mexican make, a lariat and canteen, and a small pack rolled into a tarpaulin.

This rider apparently put all care of appearances upon his horse. His apparel was the ordinary jeans of the cowboy without vanity, and it was torn and travel-stained. His boots showed evidence of an intimate acquaintance with cactus. Like his horse, this man was a giant in stature, but rangier, not so heavily built. Otherwise the only striking thing about him was his somber face with its piercing eyes, and hair white over the temples. He packed two guns, both low down— but that was too common a thing to attract notice in the Big Bend. A close observer, however, would have noted a singular fact—this rider's right hand was more bronzed, more weather-beaten than his left. He never wore a glove on that right hand!

He had dismounted before a ramshackle structure that bore upon its wide, high-boarded front the sign, "Hotel." There were horsemen coming and going down the wide street between its rows of old stores, saloons, and houses. Ord certainly did not look enterprising. Americans had manifestly assimilated much of the leisure of the Mexicans. The hotel had a wide platform in front, and this did duty as porch and sidewalk. Upon it, and leaning against a hitching-rail, were men of varying ages, most of them slovenly in old jeans and slouched sombreros. Some were booted, belted, and spurred. No man there wore a coat, but all wore vests. The guns in that group would have outnumbered the men.

It was a crowd seemingly too lazy to be curious. Good nature did not appear to be wanting, but it was not the frank and boisterous kind natural to the cowboy or rancher in town for a day. These men were idlers; what else, perhaps, was easy to conjecture. Certainly to this arriving stranger, who flashed a keen eye over them, they wore an atmosphere never associated with work.

Presently a tall man, with a drooping, sandy mustache, leisurely detached himself from the crowd.

"Howdy, stranger," he said.

The stranger had bent over to loosen the cinches; he straightened up and nodded. Then: "I'm thirsty!"

That brought a broad smile to faces. It was characteristic greeting. One and all trooped after the stranger into the hotel. It was a dark, ill-smelling barn of a place, with a bar as high as a short man's head. A bartender with a scarred face was serving drinks.

"Line up, gents," said the stranger.

They piled over one another to get to the bar, with coarse jests and oaths and laughter. None of them noted that the stranger did not appear so thirsty as he had claimed to be. In fact, though he went through the motions, he did not drink at all.

"My name's Jim Fletcher," said the tall man with the drooping, sandy mustache. He spoke laconically, nevertheless there was a tone that showed he expected to be known. Something went with that name. The stranger did not appear to be impressed.

"My name might be Blazes, but it ain't," he replied. "What do you call this burg?"

"Stranger, this heah me-tropoles bears the handle Ord. Is thet new to you?"

He leaned back against the bar, and now his little yellow eyes, clear as crystal, flawless as a hawk's, fixed on the stranger. Other men crowded close, forming a circle, curious, ready to be friendly or otherwise, according to how the tall interrogator marked the new-comer.

"Sure, Ord's a little strange to me. Off the railroad some, ain't it? Funny trails hereabouts."

"How fur was you goin'?"

"I reckon I was goin' as far as I could," replied the stranger, with a hard laugh.

His reply had subtle reaction on that listening circle. Some of the men exchanged glances. Fletcher stroked his drooping mustache, seemed thoughtful, but lost something of that piercing scrutiny.

"Wal, Ord's the jumpin'-off place," he said, presently. "Sure you've heerd of the Big Bend country?"

"I sure have, an' was makin' tracks fer it," replied the stranger.

Fletcher turned toward a man in the outer edge of the group. "Knell, come in heah."

This individual elbowed his way in and was seen to be scarcely more than a boy, almost pale beside those bronzed men, with a long, expressionless face, thin and sharp.

"Knell, this heah's—" Fletcher wheeled to the stranger. "What'd you call yourself?"

"I'd hate to mention what I've been callin' myself lately."

This sally fetched another laugh. The stranger appeared cool, careless, indifferent. Perhaps he knew, as the others present knew, that this show of Fletcher's, this pretense of introduction, was merely talk while he was looked over.

Knell stepped up, and it was easy to see, from the way Fletcher relinquished his part in the situation, that a man greater than he had appeared upon the scene.

"Any business here?" he queried, curtly. When he spoke his expressionless face was in strange contrast with the ring, the quality, the cruelty of his voice. This voice betrayed an absence of humor, of friendliness, of heart.

"Nope," replied the stranger.

"Know anybody hereabouts?"

"Nary one."

"Jest ridin' through?"

"Yep."

"Slopin' fer back country, eh?"

There came a pause. The stranger appeared to grow a little resentful and drew himself up disdainfully.

"Wal, considerin' you-all seem so damn friendly an' oncurious down here in this Big Bend country, I don't mind sayin' yes—I am in on the dodge," he replied, with deliberate sarcasm.

"From west of Ord—out El Paso way, mebbe?"

"Sure."

"A-huh! Thet so?" Knell's words cut the air, stilled the room. "You're from way down the river. Thet's what they say down there—'on the dodge.' . . . Stranger, you're a liar!"

With swift clink of spur and thump of boot the crowd split, leaving Knell and the stranger in the center.

Wild breed of that ilk never made a mistake in judging a man's nerve. Knell had cut out with the trenchant call, and stood ready. The stranger suddenly lost his every semblance to the rough and easy character before manifest in him. He became bronze. That situation seemed familiar to him. His eyes held a singular piercing light that danced like a compass-needle.

"Sure I lied," he said; "so I ain't takin' offense at the way you called me. I'm lookin' to make friends, not enemies. You don't strike me as one of them four-flushes, achin' to kill somebody. But if you are—go ahead an' open the ball. . . . You see, I never throw a gun on them fellers till they go fer theirs."

Knell coolly eyed his antagonist, his strange face not changing in the least. Yet somehow it was evident in his look that here was metal which rang differently from what he had expected. Invited to start a fight or withdraw, as he chose, Knell proved himself big in the manner characteristic of only the genuine gunman.

"Stranger, I pass," he said, and turning to the bar, he ordered liquor.

The tension relaxed, the silence broke, the men filled up the gap; the incident seemed closed. Jim Fletcher attached himself to the stranger, and now both respect and friendliness tempered his asperity.

"Wal, fer want of a better handle I'll call you Dodge," he said.

"Dodge's as good as any. . . . Gents, line up again—an' if you can't be friendly, be careful!"

Such was Buck Duane's debut in the little outlaw hamlet of Ord.

Duane had been three months out of the Nueces country. At El Paso he bought the finest horse he could find, and, armed and otherwise outfitted to suit him, he had taken to unknown trails. Leisurely he rode from town to town, village to village, ranch to ranch, fitting his talk and his occupation to the impression he wanted to make upon different people whom he met. He was in turn a cowboy, a rancher, a cattleman, a stockbuyer, a boomer, a land-hunter; and long before he reached the wild and inhospitable Ord he had acted the part of an outlaw, drifting into new territory. He passed on leisurely because he wanted to learn the lay of the country, the location of villages and ranches, the work, habit, gossip, pleasures, and fears of the people with whom he came in contact. The one subject most impelling to him—outlaws—he never mentioned; but by talking all around it, sifting the old ranch and cattle story, he acquired a knowledge calculated to aid his plot. In this game time was of no moment; if necessary he would take years to accomplish his task. The stupendous and perilous nature of it showed in the slow, wary preparation. When he heard Fletcher's name and faced Knell he knew he had reached the place he sought. Ord was a hamlet on the fringe of the grazing country, of doubtful honesty, from which, surely, winding trails led down into that free and never-disturbed paradise of outlaws— the Big Bend.

Duane made himself agreeable, yet not too much so, to Fletcher and several other men disposed to talk and drink and eat; and then, after having a care for his horse, he rode out of town a couple of miles to a grove he had marked, and there, well hidden, he prepared to spend the night. This proceeding served a double purpose—he was safer, and the habit would look well in the eyes of outlaws, who would be more inclined to see in him the lone-wolf fugitive.

Long since Duane had fought out a battle with himself, won a hard-earned victory. His outer life, the action, was much the same as it had been; but the inner life had tremendously changed. He could never become a happy man, he could never shake utterly those haunting phantoms that had once been his despair and madness; but he had assumed a task impossible for any man save one like him, he had felt the meaning of it grow strangely and wonderfully, and through that flourished up consciousness of how passionately he now clung to this thing which would blot out his former infamy. The iron fetters no more threatened his hands; the iron door no more haunted his dreams. He never forgot that he was free. Strangely, too, along with this feeling of new manhood there gathered the force of imperious desire to run these chief outlaws to their dooms. He never called them outlaws—but rustlers, thieves, robbers, murderers, criminals. He sensed the growth of a relentless driving passion, and sometimes he feared that, more than the newly acquired zeal and pride in this ranger service, it was the old, terrible inherited killing instinct lifting its hydra-head in new guise. But of that he could not be sure. He dreaded the thought. He could only wait.

Another aspect of the change in Duane, neither passionate nor driving, yet not improbably even more potent of new significance to life, was the imperceptible return of an old love of nature dead during his outlaw days.

For years a horse had been only a machine of locomotion, to carry him from place to place, to beat and spur and goad mercilessly in flight; now this giant black, with his splendid head, was a companion, a friend, a brother, a loved thing, guarded jealously, fed and trained and ridden with an intense appreciation of his great speed and endurance. For years the daytime, with its birth of sunrise on through long hours to the ruddy close, had been used for sleep or rest in some rocky hole or willow brake or deserted hut, had been hated because it augmented danger of pursuit, because it drove the fugitive to lonely, wretched hiding; now the dawn was a greeting, a promise of another day to ride, to plan, to remember, and sun, wind, cloud, rain, sky—all were joys to him, somehow speaking his freedom. For years the night had been a black space, during which he had to ride unseen along the endless trails, to peer with cat-eyes through gloom for the moving shape that ever pursued him; now the twilight and the dusk and the shadows of grove and cañon darkened into night with its train of stars, and brought him calm reflection of the day's happenings, of the morrow's possibilities, perhaps a sad, brief procession of the old phantoms, then sleep. For years cañons and valleys and mountains had been looked at as retreats that might be dark and wild enough to hide even an outlaw; now he saw these features of the great desert with something of the eyes of the boy who had once burned for adventure and life among them.

This night a wonderful afterglow lingered long in the west, and against the golden-red of clear sky the bold, black head of Mount Ord reared itself aloft, beautiful but aloof, sinister yet calling. Small wonder that Duane gazed in fascination upon the peak! Somewhere deep in its corrugated sides or lost in a rugged cañon was hidden the secret stronghold of the master outlaw Cheseldine. All down along the ride from El Paso Duane had heard of Cheseldine, of his band, his fearful deeds, his cunning, his widely separated raids, of his flitting here and there like a Jack-o'-lantern; but never a word of his den, never a word of his appearance.

Next morning Duane did not return to Ord. He struck off to the north, riding down a rough, slow-descending road that appeared to have been used occasionally for cattle-driving. As he had ridden in from the west, this northern direction led him into totally unfamiliar country. While he passed on, however, he exercised such keen observation that in the future he would know whatever might be of service to him if he chanced that way again.

The rough, wild, brush-covered slope down from the foothills gradually leveled out into plain, a magnificent grazing country, upon which till noon of that day Duane did not see a herd of cattle or a ranch. About that time he made out smoke from the railroad, and after a couple of hours' riding he entered a town which inquiry discovered to be Bradford. It was the largest town he had visited since Marfa, and he calculated must have a thousand or fifteen hundred inhabitants, not including Mexicans. He decided this would be a good place for him to hold up for a while, being the nearest town to Ord, only forty miles away. So he hitched his horse in front of a store and leisurely set about studying Bradford.

It was after dark, however, that Duane verified his suspicions concerning Bradford. The town was awake after dark, and there was one long row of saloons, dance-halls, gambling-resorts in full blast. Duane visited them all, and was surprised to see wildness and license equal to that of the old river camp of Bland's in its palmiest days. Here it was forced upon him that the farther west one traveled along the river the sparser the respectable settlements, the more numerous the hard characters, and in consequence the greater the element of lawlessness. Duane returned to his lodging-house with the conviction that MacNelly's task of cleaning up the Big Bend country was a stupendous one. Yet, he reflected, a company of intrepid and quick-shooting rangers could have soon cleaned up this Bradford.

The innkeeper had one other guest that night, a long black-coated and wide-sombreroed Texan who reminded Duane of his grandfather. This man had penetrating eyes, a courtly manner, and an unmistakable leaning toward companionship and mintjuleps. The gentleman introduced himself as Colonel Webb, of

Marfa, and took it as a matter of course that Duane made no comment about himself.

"Sir, it's all one to me," he said, blandly, waving his hand. "I have traveled. Texas is free, and this frontier is one where it's healthier and just as friendly for a man to have no curiosity about his companion. You might be Cheseldine, of the Big Bend, or you might be Judge Little, of El Paso—it's all one to me. I enjoy drinking with you anyway."

Duane thanked him, conscious of a reserve and dignity that he could not have felt or pretended three months before. And then, as always, he was a good listener. Colonel Webb told, among other things, that he had come out to the Big Bend to look over the affairs of a deceased brother who had been a rancher and a sheriff of one of the towns, Fairdale by name.

"Found no affairs, no ranch, not even his grave," said Colonel Webb. "And I tell you, sir, if hell's any tougher than this Fairdale I don't want to expiate my sins there."

"Fairdale. . . . I imagine sheriffs have a hard row to hoe out here," replied Duane, trying not to appear curious.

The Colonel swore lustily.

"My brother was the only honest sheriff Fairdale ever had. It was wonderful how long he lasted. But he had nerve, he could throw a gun, and he was on the square. Then he was wise enough to confine his work to offenders of his own town and neighborhood. He let the riding outlaws alone, else he wouldn't have lasted at all. . . . What this frontier needs, sir, is about six companies of Texas Rangers."

Duane was aware of the Colonel's close scrutiny.

"Do you know anything about the service?" he asked.

"I used to. Ten years ago when I lived in San Antonio. A fine body of men, sir, and the salvation of Texas."

"Governor Stone doesn't entertain that opinion," said Duane.

Here Colonel Webb exploded. Manifestly the governor was not his choice for a chief executive of the great state. He talked politics for a while, and of the vast territory west of the Pecos that seemed never to get a benefit from Austin. He talked enough for Duane to realize that here was just the kind of intelligent, well-informed, honest citizen that he had been trying to meet. He exerted himself thereafter to be agreeable and interesting; and he saw presently that here was an opportunity to make a valuable acquaintance, if not a friend.

"I'm a stranger in these parts," said Duane, finally. "What is this outlaw situation you speak of?"

"It's damnable, sir and unbelievable. Not rustling any more, but just wholesale herd-stealing, in which some big cattlemen, supposed to be honest, are equally guilty with the outlaws. On this border, you know, the rustler has always been able to steal cattle in any numbers. But to get rid of big bunches—that's the hard job. The gang operating between here and Valentine evidently have not this trouble. Nobody knows where the stolen stock goes. But I'm not alone in my opinion that most of it goes to several big stockmen. They ship to San Antonio, Austin, New Orleans, also to El Paso. If you travel the stock-road between here and Marfa and Valentine you'll see dead cattle all along the line and stray cattle out in the scrub. The herds have been driven fast and far, and stragglers are not rounded up.''

"Wholesale business, eh?'' remarked Duane. "Who are these—er—big stock-buyers?''

Colonel Webb seemed a little startled at the abrupt query. He bent his penetrating gaze upon Duane and thoughtfully stroked his pointed beard.

"Names, of course, I'll not mention. Opinions are one thing, direct accusation another. This is not a healthy country for the informer.''

When it came to the outlaws themselves Colonel Webb was disposed to talk freely. Duane could not judge whether the Colonel had a hobby of that subject or the outlaws were so striking in personality and deed that any man would know all about them. The great name along the river was Cheseldine, but it seemed to be a name detached from an individual. No person of veracity known to Colonel Webb had ever seen Cheseldine, and those who claimed that doubtful honor varied so diversely in descriptions of the chief that they confused the reality and lent to the outlaw only further mystery. Strange to say of an outlaw leader, as there was no one who could identify him, so there was no one who could prove he had actually killed a man. Blood flowed like water over the Big Bend country, and it was Cheseldine who spilled it. Yet the fact remained there were no eye-witnesses to connect any individual called Cheseldine with these deeds of violence. But in striking contrast to this mystery was the person, character, and cold-blooded action of Poggin and Knell, the chief's lieutenants. They were familiar figures in all the towns within two hundred miles of Bradford. Knell had a record, but as gunman with an incredible list of victims Poggin was supreme. If Poggin had a friend no one ever heard of him. There were a hundred stories of his nerve, his wonderful speed with a gun, his passion for gambling, his love of a horse—his cold, implacable, inhuman wiping out of his path any man that crossed it.

"Cheseldine is a name, a terrible name,'' said Colonel Webb. "Sometimes I wonder if he's not only a name. In that case where does the brains of this gang come from? No; there must be a master craftsman behind this border pillage; a master capable of handling those terrors Poggin and Knell. Of all the thousands of outlaws developed by western Texas in the last twenty years these three are the greatest. In southern Texas, down between the Pecos and the Nueces, there have been and are still many bad men. But I doubt if any outlaw there, possibly excepting Buck Duane, ever equaled Poggin. You've heard of this Duane?''

"Yes, a little," replied Duane, quietly. "I'm from southern Texas. Buck Duane then is known out here?''

"Why, man, where isn't his name known?" returned Colonel Webb. "I've kept tract of his record as I have all the others. Of course, Duane, being a lone outlaw, is somewhat of a mystery also, but not like Cheseldine. Out here there have drifted many stories of Duane, horrible some of them. But despite them a sort of romance clings to that Nueces outlaw. He's killed three great outlaw leaders, I believe—Bland, Hardin, and the other I forgot. Hardin was known in the Big Bend, had friends there. Bland had a hard name at Del Rio.''

"Then this man Duane enjoys rather an unusual repute west of the Pecos?'' inquired Duane.

"He's considered more of an enemy to his kind than to honest men. I understand Duane had many friends, that whole counties swear by him—secretly, of course, for he's a hunted outlaw with rewards on his head. His fame in this country appears to hang on his matchless gun-play and his enmity toward outlaw chiefs. I've heard many a rancher say: 'I wish to God that Buck Duane would drift out here! I'd give a hundred pesos to see him and Poggin meet.' It's a singular thing, stranger, how jealous these great outlaws are of each other.''

"Yes, indeed, all about them is singular," replied Duane. "Has Cheseldine's gang been busy lately?''

"No. This section has been free of rustling for months, though there's unexplained movements of stock. Probably all the stock that's being shipped now was rustled long ago. Cheseldine works over a wide section, too wide for news to travel inside of weeks. Then sometimes he's not heard of at all for a spell. These lulls are pretty surely indicative of a big storm sooner or later. And Cheseldine's deals, as they grow fewer and farther between, certainly get bigger, more daring. There are some people who think Cheseldine had nothing to do with the bank-robberies and train-holdups during the last few years in this country. But that's poor reasoning. The jobs have been too well done, too surely covered, to be the work of greasers or ordinary outlaws.''

"What's your view of the outlook? How's all this going to wind up? Will the outlaw ever be driven out?'' asked Duane.

"Never. There will always be outlaws along the Rio Grande. All the armies in the world couldn't comb the wild brakes of that fifteen hundred miles of river. But the sway of the outlaw, such as is enjoyed by these great leaders, will sooner or later be past. The criminal element flock to the Southwest. But not so thick and fast as the pioneers. Besides, the outlaws kill themselves, and the ranchers are slowly rising in wrath, if not in action. That will come soon. If they only had a leader to start the fight! But that will come. There's talk of Vigilantes, the same that were organized in California and are now in force in Idaho. So far it's only talk. But the time will come. And the days of Cheseldine and Poggin are numbered.''

Duane went to bed that night exceedingly thoughtful. The long trail was growing hot. This voluble colonel had given him new ideas. It came to Duane in surprise that he was famous along the upper Rio Grande. Assuredly he would not long be able to conceal his identity. He had no doubt that he would soon meet the chiefs of this clever and bold rustling gang. He could not decide whether he would be safer unknown or known. In the latter case his one chance lay in the fatality connected with his name, in his power to look it and act it. Duane had never dreamed of any sleuth-hound tendency in his nature, but now he felt something like one. Above all others his mind fixed on Poggin—Poggin the brute, the executor of Cheseldine's will, but mostly upon Poggin the gunman. This in itself was a warning to Duane. He felt terrible forces at work within him. There was the stern and indomitable resolve to make MacNelly's boast good to the governor of the state—to break up Cheseldine's gang. Yet this was not in Duane's mind before a strange grim and deadly instinct—which he had to drive away for fear he would find in it a passion to kill Poggin, not for the state, nor for his word to MacNelly, but for himself. Had his father's blood and the hard years made Duane the kind of man who instinctively wanted to meet Poggin? He was sworn to MacNelly's service, and he fought himself to keep that, and that only, in his mind.

Duane ascertained that Fairdale was situated two days' ride from Bradford toward the north. There was a stage which made the journey twice a week.

Next morning Duane mounted his horse and headed for Fairdale. He rode leisurely, as he wanted to learn all he could about the country. There were few ranches. The farther he traveled the better grazing he encountered, and, strange to note, the fewer herds of cattle.

It was just sunset when he made out a cluster of adobe houses that marked the half-way point between Bradford and Fairdale. Here, Duane had learned, was stationed a comfortable inn for wayfarers.

When he drew up before the inn the landlord and his family and a number of loungers greeted him laconically.

''Beat the stage in, hey?'' remarked one.

''There she comes now,'' said another. ''Joel shore is drivin' to-night.''

Far down the road Duane saw a cloud of dust and horses and a lumbering coach. When he had looked after the needs of his horse he returned to the group before the inn. They awaited the stage with that interest common to isolated people. Presently it rolled up, a large mud-bespattered and dusty vehicle, littered with baggage on top and tied on behind. A number of passengers alighted, three of whom excited Duane's interest. One was a tall, dark, striking-looking man, and the other two were ladies, wearing long gray ulsters and veils. Duane heard the proprietor of the inn address the man as Colonel Longstreth, and as the party entered the inn Duane's quick ears caught a few words which acquainted him with the fact that Longstreth was the Mayor of Fairdale.

Duane passed inside himself to learn that supper would soon be ready. At table he found himself opposite the three who had attracted his attention.

"Ruth, I envy the lucky cowboys," Longstreth was saying.

Ruth was a curly-headed girl with gray or hazel eyes.

"I'm crazy to ride bronchos," she said.

Duane gather she was on a visit to western Texas. The other girl's deep voice, sweet like a bell, made Duane regard her closer. She had beauty as he had never seen it in another woman. She was slender, but the development of her figure gave Duane the impression she was twenty years old or more. She had the most exquisite hands Duane had ever seen. She did not resemble the Colonel, who was evidently her father. She looked tired, quiet, even melancholy. A finely chiseled oval face; clear, olive-tinted skin, long eyes set wide apart and black as coal, beautiful to look into; a slender, straight nose that had something nervous and delicate about it which made Duane think of a thoroughbred; and a mouth by no means small, but perfectly curved; and hair like jet—all these features proclaimed her beauty to Duane. Duane believed her a descendant of one of the old French families of eastern Texas. He was sure of it when she looked at him, drawn by his rather persistent gaze. There were pride, fire, and passion in her eyes. Duane felt himself blushing in confusion. His stare at her had been rude, perhaps, but unconscious. How many years had passed since he had seen a girl like her! Thereafter he kept his eyes upon his plate, yet he seemed to be aware that he had aroused the interest of both girls.

After supper the guests assembled in a big sitting-room where an open fire place with blazing mesquite sticks gave out warmth and cheery glow. Duane took a seat by a table in the corner, and, finding a paper, began to read. Presently when he glanced up he saw two dark-faced men, strangers who had not appeared before, and were peering in from a doorway. When they saw Duane had observed them they stepped back out of sight.

It flashed over Duane that the strangers acted suspiciously. In Texas in the seventies it was always bad policy to let strangers go unheeded. Duane pondered a moment. Then he went out to look over these two men. The doorway opened into a patio, and across that was a little dingy, dim-lighted bar-room. Here Duane found the innkeeper dispensing drinks to the two strangers. They glanced up when he entered, and one of them whispered. He imagined he had seen one of them before. In Texas, where outdoor men were so rough, bronzed, bold, and sometimes grim of aspect, it was no easy task to pick out the crooked ones. But

Duane's years on the border had augmented a natural instinct or gift to read character, or at least to sense the evil in men; and he knew at once that these strangers were dishonest.

"Hev somethin'?" one of them asked, leering. Both looked Duane up and down.

"No thanks, I don't drink," Duane replied, and returned their scrutiny with interest. "How's tricks in the Big Bend?"

Both men stared. It had taken only a close glance for Duane to recognize a type of ruffian most frequently met along the river. These strangers had that stamp, and their surprise proved he was right. Here the innkeeper showed signs of uneasiness, and seconded the surprise of his customers. No more was said at the instant, and the two rather hurriedly went out.

"Say, boss, do you know those fellows?" Duane asked the innkeeper.

"Nope."

"Which way did they come?"

"Now I think of it, them fellers rid in from both corners to-day," he replied, and he put both hands on the bar and looked at Duane. "They nooned heah, comin' from Bradford, they said, an' trailed in after the stage."

When Duane returned to the sitting-room Colonel Longstreth was absent, also several of the other passengers. Miss Ruth sat in the chair he had vacated, and across the table from her sat Miss Longstreth. Duane went directly to them.

"Excuse me," said Duane, addressing them. "I want to tell you there are a couple of rough-looking men here. I've just seen them. They mean evil. Tell your father to be careful. Lock your doors—bar your windows to-night."

"Oh!" cried Ruth, very low. "Ray, do you hear?"

"Thank you; we'll be careful," said Miss Longstreth, gracefully. The rich color had faded in her cheek. "I saw those men watching you from that door. They had such bright black eyes. Is there really danger—here?"

"I think so," was Duane's reply.

Soft swift steps behind him preceded a harsh voice: "Hands up!"

No man quicker than Duane to recognize the intent in those words! His hands shot up. Miss Ruth uttered a little frightened cry and sank into her chair. Miss Longstreth turned white, her eyes dilated. Both girls were staring at some one behind Duane.

"Turn around!" ordered the harsh voice.

The big, dark stranger, the bearded one who had whispered to his comrade in the bar-room and asked Duane to drink, had him covered with a cocked gun. He strode forward, his eyes gleaming, pressed the gun against him, and with his other hand dove into his pocket and tore out his roll of bills. Then he reached low at Duane's hip, felt his gun, and took it. Then he slapped the other hip, evidently in search of another weapon. That done, he backed away, wearing an expression of fiendish satisfaction that made Duane think he was only a common thief, a novice at this kind of game.

His comrade stood in the door with a gun leveled at two other men, who stood there frightened, speechless.

"Git a move on, Bill," called this fellow; and he took a hasty glance backward. A stamp of hoofs came from outside. Of course the robbers had horses waiting. The one called Bill strode across the room, and with brutal, careless haste began to prod the two men with his weapon and to search them. The robber in the doorway called "Rustle!" and disappeared.

Duane wondered where the innkeeper was, and Colonel Longstreth and the other two passengers. The bearded robber quickly got through with his searching, and from his growls Duane gathered he had not been well remunerated. Then he wheeled once more. Duane had not moved a muscle, stood perfectly calm with his arms high. The robber strode back with his bloodshot eyes fastened upon the girls. Miss Longstreth never flinched, but the little girl appeared about to faint.

"Don't yap, there!" he said, low and hard. He thrust the gun close to Ruth. Then Duane knew for sure that he was no knight of the road, but a plain cutthroat robber. Danger always made Daune exult in a kind of cold glow. But now something hot worked within him. He had a little gun in his pocket. The robber had missed it. And he began to calculate chances.

"Any money, jewelry, diamonds!" ordered the ruffian, fiercely.

Miss Ruth collapsed. Then he made at Miss Longstreth. She stood with her hands at her breast. Evidently the robber took this position to mean that she had valuables concealed there. But Duane fancied she had instinctively pressed her hands against a throbbing heart.

"Come out with it!" he said, harshly, reaching for her.

"Don't dare touch me!" she cried, her eyes ablaze. She did not move. She had nerve.

It made Duane thrill. He saw he was going to get a chance. Waiting had been a science with him. But here it was hard. Miss Ruth had fainted, and that was well. Miss Longstreth had fight in her, which fact helped Duane, yet made injury possible to her. She eluded two lunges the man made at her. Then his rough hand caught her waist, and with one pull ripped it asunder, exposing her beautiful shoulder, white as snow.

She cried out. The prospect of being robbed or even killed had not shaken Miss Longstreth's nerve as had this brutal tearing off of half her waist.

The ruffian was only turned partially away from Duane. For himself he could have waited no longer. But for her! That gun was still held dangerously upward close to her. Duane watched only that. Then a bellow made him jerk his head.

Colonel Longstreth stood in the doorway in a magnificent rage. He had no weapon. Strange how he showed no fear! He bellowed something again.

Duane's shifting glance caught the robber's sudden movement. It was a kind of start. He seemed stricken. Duane expected him to shoot Longstreth. Instead the hand that clutched Miss Longstreth's torn waist loosened its hold. The other hand with its cocked weapon slowly dropped till it pointed to the floor. That was Duane's chance.

Swift as a flash he drew his gun and fired. Thud! went his bullet, and he could not tell on the instant whether it hit the robber or went into the ceiling. Then the robber's gun boomed harmlessly. He fell with blood spurting over his face. Duane realized he had hit him, but the small bullet had glanced.

Miss Longstreth reeled and might have fallen had Duane not supported her. It was only a few steps to a couch, to which he half led, half carried her. Then he rushed out of the room, across the patio, through the bar to the yard. Nevertheless, he was cautious. In the gloom stood a saddled horse, probably the one belonging to the fellow he had shot. His comrade had escaped. Returning to the sitting-room, Duane found a condition approaching pandemonium.

The innkeeper rushed in, pitchfork in hands. Evidently he had been out at the barn. He was now shouting to find out what had happened. Joel, the stage-driver, was trying to quiet the men who had been robbed. The woman, wife of one of the men, had come in, and she had hysterics. The girls were still and white. The robber Bill lay where he had fallen, and Duane guessed he had made a fair shot, after all. And, lastly, the thing that struck Duane most of all was Longstreth's rage. He never saw such passion. Like a caged lion Longstreth stalked and roared. There came a quieter moment in which the innkeeper shrilly protested:

"Man, what're you ravin' aboot? Nobody's hurt, an' thet's lucky. I swear to God I hadn't nothin' to do with them fellers!"

"I ought to kill you anyhow!" replied Longstreth. And his voice now astounded Duane, it was so full of power.

Upon examination Duane found that his bullet had furrowed the robber's temple, torn a great piece out of his scalp, and, as Duane had guessed, had glanced. He was not seriously injured, and already showed signs of returning consciousness.

"Drag him out of here!" ordered Longstreth; and he turned to his daughter.

Before the innkeeper reached the robber Duane had secured the money and gun taken from him; and presently recovered the property of the other men. Joel helped the innkeeper carry the injured man somewhere outside.

Miss Longstreth was sitting white but composed upon the couch, where lay Miss Ruth, who evidently had been carried there by the Colonel. Duane did not think she had wholly lost consciousness, and now she lay very still, with eyes dark and shadowy, her face pallid and wet. The Colonel, now that he finally remembered his women-folk, seemed to be gentle and kind. He talked soothingly to Miss Ruth, made light of the adventure, said she must learn to have nerve out here where things happened.

"Can I be of any service?" asked Duane, solicitously.

"Thanks; I guess there's nothing you can do. Talk to these frightened girls while I go see what's to be done with that thick-skulled robber," he replied, and, telling the girls that there was no more danger, he went out.

Miss Longstreth sat with one hand holding her torn waist in place; the other she extended to Duane. He took it awkwardly, and he felt a strange thrill.

"You saved my life," she said, in grave, sweet seriousness.

"No, no!" Duane exclaimed. "He might have struck you, hurt you, but no more."

"I saw murder in his eyes. He thought I had jewels under my dress. I couldn't bear his touch. The beast! I'd have fought. Surely my life was in peril."

"Did you kill him?" asked Miss Ruth, who lay listening.

"Oh no. He's not badly hurt."

"I'm very glad he's alive," said Miss Longstreth, shuddering.

"My intention was bad enough," Duane went on. "It was a ticklish place for me. You see, he was half drunk, and I was afraid his gun might go off. Fool careless he was!"

"Yet you say you didn't save me," Miss Longstreth returned, quickly.

"Well, let it go at that," Duane responded. "I saved you something."

"Tell me about it?" asked Miss Ruth, who was fast recovering.

Rather embarrassed, Duane briefly told the incident from his point of view.

"Then you stood there all the time with your hands up thinking of nothing—watching for nothing except a little moment when you might draw your gun?" asked Miss Ruth.

"I guess that's about it," he replied.

"Cousin," said Miss Longstreth, thoughtfully, "it was fortunate for us that this gentlemen happened to be here. Papa scouts—laughs at danger. He seemed to think there was no danger. Yet he raved after it came."

"Go with us all the way to Fairdale—please?" asked Miss Ruth, sweetly offering her hand. "I am Ruth Herbert. And this is my cousin, Ray Longstreth."

"I'm traveling that way," replied Duane, in great confusion. He did not know how to meet the situation.

Colonel Longstreth returned then, and after bidding Duane a good night, which seemed rather curt by contrast to the graciousness of the girls, he led them away.

Before going to bed Duane went outside to take a look at the injured robber and perhaps to ask him a few questions. To Duane's surprise, he was gone, and so was his horse. The innkeeper was dumfounded. He said that he left the fellow on the floor in the bar-room.

"Had he come to?" inquired Duane.

"Sure. He asked for whisky."

"Did he say anything else?"

"Not to me. I heard him talkin' to the father of them girls."

"You mean Colonel Longstreth?"

"I reckon. He sure was some riled, wasn't he? Jest as if I was to blame fer that two-bit of a hold-up!"

"What did you make of the old gent's rage?" asked Duane, watching the innkeeper. He scratched his head dubiously. He was sincere, and Duane believed in his honesty.

"Wal, I'm doggoned if I know what to make of it. But I reckon he's either crazy or got more nerve than most Texans."

"More nerve, maybe," Duane replied. "Show me a bed now, innkeeper."

Once in bed in the dark, Duane composed himself to think over the several events of the evening. He called up the details of the holdup and carefully revolved them in mind. The Colonel's wrath, under circumstances where almost any Texan would have been cool, nonplussed Duane, and he put it down to a choleric temperament. He pondered long on the action of the robber when Longstreth's bellow of rage burst in upon him. This ruffian, as bold and mean a type as Duane had ever encountered, had, from some cause or other, been startled. From whatever point Duane viewed the man's strange indecision he could come to only one conclusion—his start, his check, his fear had been that of recognition. Duane compared this effect with the suddenly acquired sense he had gotten of Colonel Longstreth's powerful personality. Why had that desperate robber lowered his gun and stood paralyzed at sight and sound of the Mayor of Fairdale? This was not answerable. There might have been a number of reasons, all to Colonel Longstreth's credit, but Duane could not understand. Longstreth had not appeared to see danger for his daughter, even though she had been roughly handled, and had advanced in front of a cocked gun. Duane probed deep into this singular fact, and he brought to bear on the thing all his knowledge and experience of violent Texas life. And he found that the instant Colonel Longstreth had appeared on the scene there *was* no further danger threatening his daughter. Why? That likewise Duane could not answer. Then his rage, Duane concluded, had been solely at the idea of *his* daughter being assaulted by a robber. This deduction was indeed a thought-disturber, but Duane put it aside to crystallize and for more careful consideration.

Next morning Duane found that the little town was called Sanderson. It was larger than he had at first supposed. He walked up the main street and back again. Just as he arrived some horsemen rode up to the inn and dismounted. And at this juncture the Longstreth party came out. Duane heard Colonel Longstreth utter an exclamation. Then he saw him shake hands with a tall man.

Longstreth looked surpised and angry, and he spoke with force; but Duane could
not hear what it was he said. The fellow laughed, yet somehow he struck Duane
as sullen, until suddenly he espied Miss Longstreth. Then his face changed, and
he removed his sombrero. Duane went closer.

"Floyd, did you come with the teams?" asked Longstreth, sharply.

"Not me. I rode a horse, good and hard," was the reply.

"Humph! I'll have a word to say to you later." Then Longstreth turned to
his daughter. "Ray, here's the cousin I've told you about. You used to play
with him ten years ago—Floyd Lawson. Floyd, my daughter—and my niece,
Ruth Herbert."

Duane always scrutinized every one he met, and now with a dangerous game
to play, with a consciousness of Longstreth's unusual and significant personality,
he bent a keen and searching glance upon this Floyd Lawson.

He was under thirty, yet gray at his temples—dark, smooth-shaven, with lines
left by wildness, dissipation, shadows under dark eyes, a mouth strong and
bitter, and a square chin—a reckless, careless, handsome, sinister face strangely
losing the hardness when he smiled. The grace of a gentleman clung round him,
seemed like an echo in his mellow voice. Duane doubted not that he, like many
a young man, had drifted out to the frontier, where rough and wild life had
wrought sternly but had not quite effaced the mark of good family.

Colonel Longstreth apparently did not share the pleasure of his daughter and
his niece in the advent of this cousin. Something hinged on this meeting. Duane
grew intensely curious, but, as the stage appeared ready for the journey, he had
no further opportunity to gratify it.

16

DUANE followed the stage through the town, out into the open, on to a wide,
hard-packed road showing years of travel. It headed northwest. To the left rose
a range of low, bleak mountains he had noted yesterday, and to the right sloped
the mesquite-patched sweep of ridge and flat. The driver pushed his team to a
fast trot, which gait surely covered ground rapidly.

The stage made three stops in the forenoon, one at a place where the horses
could be watered, the second at a chuck-wagon belonging to cowboys who were
riding after stock, and the third at a small cluster of adobe and stone houses
constituting a hamlet the driver called Longstreth, named after the Colonel. From

that point on to Fairdale there were only a few ranches, each one controlling great acreage.

Early in the afternoon from a ridge-top Duane sighted Fairdale, a green patch in the mass of gray. For the barrens of Texas it was indeed a fair sight. But he was more concerned with its remoteness from civilization than its beauty. At that time, in the early seventies, when the vast western third of Texas was a wilderness, the pioneer had done wonders to settle there and establish places like Fairdale.

It needed only a glance for Duane to pick out Colonel Longstreth's ranch. The house was situated on the only elevation around Fairdale, and it was not high, nor more than a few minutes' walk from the edge of the town. It was a low flat-roofed structure made of red adobe bricks, and covered what appeared to be fully an acre of ground. All was green about it, except where the fenced corrals and numerous barns or sheds showed gray and red.

Duane soon reached the shady outskirts of Fairdale, and entered the town with mingled feelings of curiosity, eagerness, and expectation. The street he rode down was a main one, and on both sides of the street was a solid row of saloons, resorts, hotels. Saddled horses stood hitched all along the sidewalk in two long lines, with a buckboard and team here and there breaking the continuity. This block was busy and noisy.

From all outside appearances Fairdale was no different from other frontier towns, and Duane's expectations were scarcely realized. As the afternoon was waning he halted at a little inn. A boy took charge of his horse. Duane questioned the lad about Fairdale and gradually drew to the subject most in mind.

"Colonel Longstreth has a big outfit, eh?"

"Reckon he has," replied the lad. "Doan know how many cowboys. They're always comin' and goin'. I ain't acquainted with half of them."

"Much movement of stock these days?"

"Stock's always movin'," he replied, with a queer look.

"Rustlers?"

But he did not follow up that look with the affirmative Duane expected.

"Lively place, I hear—Fairdale is?"

"Ain't so lively as Sanderson, but it's bigger."

"Yes, I heard it was. Fellow down there was talking about two cowboys who were arrested."

"Sure. I heered all about that. Joe Bean an' Brick Higgins—they belong heah, but they ain't heah much. Longstreth's boys."

Duane did not want to appear over-inquisitive, so he turned the talk into other channels.

After getting supper Duane strolled up and down the main street. When darkness set in he went into a hotel, bought cigars, sat around, and watched.

Then he passed out and went into the next place. This was of rough crude exterior, but the inside was comparatively pretentious and ablaze with lights. It was full of men coming and going—a dusty-booted crowd that smelled of horses and smoke. Duane sat down for a while, with wide eyes and open ears. Then he hunted up the bar, where most of the guests had been or were going. He found a great square room lighted by six huge lamps, a bar at one side, and all the floorspace taken up by tables and chairs. This was the only gambling-place of any size in southern Texas in which he had noted the absence of Mexicans. There was some card-playing going on at this moment. Duane stayed in there for a while, and knew that strangers were too common in Fairdale to be conspicuous. Then he returned to the inn where he had engaged a room.

Duane sat down on the steps of the dingy little restaurant. Two men were conversing inside, and they had not noticed Duane.

"Laramie, what's the stranger's name?" asked one.

"He didn't say," replied the other.

"Sure was a strappin' big man. Struck me a little odd, he did. No cattleman, him. How'd you size him?"

"Well, like one of them cool, easy, quiet Texans who's been lookin' for a man for years—to kill him when he found him."

"Right you are, Laramie; and between you an' me, I hope he's lookin' for Long—"

"'S-sh!" interrupted Laramie. "You must be half drunk, to go talkin' that way."

Thereafter they conversed in too low a tone for Duane to hear, and presently Laramie's visitor left. Duane went inside, and, making himself agreeable, began to ask casual questions about Fairdale. Laramie was not communicative.

Duane went to his room in a thoughtful frame of mind. Had Laramie's visitor meant he hoped some one had come to kill Longstreth? Duane inferred just that from the interrupted remark. There was something wrong about the Mayor of Fairdale. Duane felt it. And he felt also, if there was a crooked and dangerous man, it was this Floyd Lawson. The innkeeper Laramie would be worth cultivating. And last in Duane's thoughts that night was Miss Longstreth. He could not help thinking of her—how strangely the meeting with her had affected him. It made him remember tha long-past time when girls had been a part of his life. What a sad and dark and endless void lay between that past and the present! He had no right even to dream of a beautiful woman like Ray Longstreth. That conviction, however, did not dispel her; indeed, it seemed perversely to make her grow more fascinating. Duane grew conscious of a strange, unaccountable hunger, a something that was like a pang in his breast.

Next day he lounged about the inn. He did not make any overtures to the taciturn proprietor. Duane had no need of hurry now. He contented himself with watching and listening. And at the close of that day he decided Fairdale was what MacNelly had claimed it to be, and that he was on the track of an unusual adventure. The following day he spent in much the same way, though on one occasion he told Laramie he was looking for a man. The innkeeper grew a little less furtive and reticent after that. He would answer casual queries, and it did not take Duane long to learn that Laramie had seen better days—that he was now broken, bitter, and hard. Some one had wronged him.

Several days passed. Duane did not succeed in getting any closer to Laramie, but he found the idlers on the corners and in front of the stores unsuspicious and willing to talk. It did not take him long to find out that Fairdale stood parallel with Huntsville for gambling, drinking, and fighting. The street was always lined with dusty, saddled horses, the town full of strangers. Money appeared more abundant than in any place Duane had ever visited; and it was spent with the abandon that spoke forcibly of easy and crooked acquirement. Duane decided that Sanderson, Bradford, and Ord were but notorious outposts to this Fairdale, which was a secret center of rustlers and outlaws. And what struck Duane strangest of all was the fact that Longstreth was mayor here and held court daily. Duane knew intuitively, before a chance remark gave him proof, that this court was a sham, a farce. And he wondered if it were not a blind. This wonder of his was equivalent to suspicion of Colonel Longstreth, and Duane reproached himself. Then he realized that the reproach was because of the daughter. Inquiry had brought him the fact that Ray Longstreth had just come to live with her father. Longstreth had originally been a planter in Louisiana, where his family had remained after his advent in the West. He was a rich rancher; he owned half of Fairdale; he was a cattle-buyer on a large scale. Floyd Lawson was his lieutenant and associate in deals.

On the afternoon of the fifth day of Duane's stay in Fairdale he returned to the inn from his usual stroll, and upon entering was amazed to have a rough-looking young fellow rush by him out of the door. Inside Laramie was lying on the floor, with a bloody bruise on his face. He did not appear to be dangerously hurt.

"Bo Snecker! He hit me and went after the cash-drawer," said Laramie, laboring to his feet.

"Are you hurt much?" queried Duane.

"I guess not. But Bo needn't to have soaked me. I've been robbed before without that."

"Well, I'll take a look after Bo," replied Duane.

He went out and glanced down the street toward the center of the town. He did not see any one he could take for the inkeeper's assailant. Then he looked up the street, and he saw the young fellow about a block away, hurrying along and gazing back.

Duane yelled for him to stop and started to go after him. Snecker broke into a run. Then Duane set out to overhaul him. There were two motives in Duane's action—one of anger, and the other a desire to make a friend of this man Laramie, whom Duane believed could tell him much.

Duane was light on his feet, and he had a giant stride. He gained rapidly upon Snecker, who, turning this way and that, could not get out of sight. Then he took to the open country and ran straight for the green hill where Longstreth's house stood. Duane had almost caught Snecker when he reached the shrubbery and trees and there eluded him. But Duane kept him in sight, in the shade, on the paths, and up the road into the courtyard, and he saw Snecker go straight for Longstreth's house.

Duane was not to be turned back by that, singular as it was. He did not stop to consider. It seemed enough to know that fate had directed him to the path of this rancher Longstreth. Duane entered the first open door on that side of the court. It opened into a corridor which led into a plaza. It had wide, smooth stone porches, and flowers and shrubbery in the center. Duane hurried through to burst into the presence of Miss Longstreth and a number of young people. Evidently she was giving a little party.

Lawson stood leaning against one of the pillars that supported the porch roof; at sight of Duane his face changed remarkably, expressing amazement, consternation, then fear.

In the quick ensuing silence Miss Longstreth rose white as her dress. The young women present stared in astonishment, if they were not equally perturbed. There were cowboys present who suddenly grew intent and still. By these things Duane gathered that his appearance must be disconcerting. He was panting. He wore no hat or coat. His big gun-sheath showed plainly at his hip.

Sight of Miss Longstreth had an unaccountable effect upon Duane. He was plunged into confusion. For the moment he saw no one but her.

"Miss Longstreth—I came—to search—your house," panted Duane.

He hardly knew what he was saying, yet the instant he spoke he realized that that should have been the last thing for him to say. He had blundered. But he was not used to women, and this dark-eyed girl made him thrill and his heart beat thickly and his wits go scattering.

"Search my house!" exclaimed Miss Longstreth; and red succeeded the white in her cheeks. She appeared astonished and angry. "What for? Why, how dare you! This is unwarrantable!"

"A man—Bo Snecker—assaulted and robbed Jim Laramie," replied Duane, hurriedly. "I chased Snecker here—saw him run into the house."

"Here? Oh, sir, you must be mistaken. We have seen no one. In the absence of my father I'm mistress here. I'll not permit you to search."

Lawson appeared to come out of his astonishment. He stepped forward.

"Ray, don't be bothered now," he said, to his cousin. "This fellow's making a bluff. I'll settle him. See here, Mister, you clear out!"

"I want Snecker. He's here, and I'm going to get him," replied Duane, quietly.

"Bah! That's all a bluff," sneered Lawson. "I'm on to your game. You just wanted an excuse to break in here—to see my cousin again. When you saw the company you invented that excuse. Now, be off, or it'll be the worse for you."

Duane felt his face burn with a tide of hot blood. Almost he felt that he was guilty of such motive. Had he not been unable to put this Ray Longstreth out of his mind? There seemed to be scorn in her eyes now. And somehow that checked his embarrassment.

"Miss Longstreth, will you let me search the house?" he asked.

"No."

"Then—I regret to say—I'll do so without your permission."

"You'll not dare!" she flashed. She stood erect, her bosom swelling.

"Pardon me—yes, I will."

"Who are you?" she demanded, suddenly.

"I'm a Texas Ranger," replied Duane.

"*A Texas Ranger!*" she echoed.

Floyd Lawson's dark face turned pale.

"Miss Longstreth, I don't need warrants to search houses," said Duane. "I'm sorry to annoy you. I'd prefer to have your permission. A ruffian has taken refuge here—in your father's house. He's hidden somewhere. May I look for him?"

"If you are indeed a ranger."

Duane produced his papers. Miss Longstreth haughtily refused to look at them.

"Miss Longstreth, I've come to make Fairdale a safer, cleaner, better place for women and children. I don't wonder at your resentment. But to doubt me—insult me. Some day you may be sorry."

Floyd Lawson made a violent motion with his hands.

"All stuff! Colusin, go on with your party. I'll take a couple of cowboys and go with this—this Texas Ranger."

"Thanks," said Duane, coolly, as he eyed Lawson. "Perhaps you'll be able to find Snecker quicker than I could."

"What do you mean?" demanded Lawson, and now he grew livid. Evidently he was a man of fierce quick passions.

"Don't quarrel," said Miss Longstreth. "Floyd, you go with him. Please hurry. I'll be nervous till—the man's found or you're sure there's not one."

They started with several cowboys to search the house. They went through the rooms searching, calling out, peering into dark places. It struck Duane more than forcibly that Lawson did all the calling. He was hurried, too, tried to keep in the lead. Duane wondered if he knew his voice would be recognized by the hiding man. Be that as it might, it was Duane who peered into a dark corner and then, with a gun leveled, said "Come out!"

He came forth into the flare—a tall, slim, dark-faced youth, wearing sombrero, blouse and trousers, Duane collared him before any of the others could move and held the gun close enough to make him shrink. But he did not impress Duane as being frightened just then; nevertheless, he had a clammy face, the pallid look of a man who had just gotten over a shock. He peered into Duane's face, then into that of the cowboy next to him, then into Lawson's, and if ever in Duane's life he beheld relief it was then. That was all Duane needed to know, but he meant to find out more if he could.

"Who're you?" asked Duane, quietly.

"Bo Snecker," he said.

"What'd you hide here for?"

He appeared to grow sullen.

"Reckoned I'd be as safe in Longstreth's as anywheres."

"Ranger, what'll you do with him?" Lawson queried, as if uncertain, now the capture was made.

"I'll see to that," replied Duane, and he pushed Snecker in front of him out into the court.

Duane had suddenly conceived the idea of taking Snecker before Mayor Longstreth in the court.

When Duane arrived at the hall where court was held there were other men there, a dozen or more, and all seemed excited; evidently, news of Duane had preceded him. Longstreth sat at a table up on a platform. Near him sat a thick-set grizzled man, with deep eyes, and this was Hanford Owens, county judge. To the right stood a tall, angular, yellow-faced fellow with a drooping sandy mustache. Conspicuous on his vest was a huge silver shield. This was Gorsech, one of Longstreth's sheriffs. There were four other men whom Duane knew by sight, several whose faces were familiar, and half a dozen strangers, all dusty horsemen.

Longstreth pounded hard on the table to be heard. Mayor or not, he was unable at once to quell the excitement. Gradually, however, it subsided, and from the last few utterances before quiet was restored Duane gathered that he had intruded upon some kind of a meeting in the hall.

"What'd you break in here for," demanded Longstreth.

"Isn't this the court? Aren't you the Mayor of Fairdale?" interrogated Duane. His voice was clear and loud, almost piercing.

"Yes," replied Longstreth. Like flint he seemed, yet Duane felt his intense interest.

"I've arrested a criminal," said Duane.

"Arrested a criminal!" ejaculated Longstreth. *"You? Who're you?"*

"I'm a ranger," replied Duane.

A significant silence ensued.

"I charge Snecker with assault on Laramie and attempted robbery—if not murder. He's had a shady past here, as this court will know if it keeps a record."

"What's this I hear about you, Bo? Get up and speak for yourself," said Longstreth, gruffly.

Snecker got up, not without a furtive glance at Duane, and he had shuffled forward a few steps toward the Mayor. He had an evil front, but not the boldness even of a rustler.

"It ain't so, Longstreth," he began, loudly. "I went in Laramie's place fer grub. Some feller I never seen before come in from the hall an' hit Laramie an' wrastled him on the floor. I went out. Then this big ranger chased me an' fetched me here. I didn't do nothin'. This ranger's hankerin' to arrest somebody. Thet's my hunch, Longstreth."

Longstreth said something in an undertone to Judge Owens, and that worthy nodded his great bushy head.

"Bo, you're discharged," said Longstreth, bluntly. "Now the rest of you clear out of here."

He absolutely ignored the ranger. That was his rebuff to Duane—his slap in the face to an interfering ranger service. If Longstreth was crooked he certainly had magnificent nerve. Duane almost decided he was above suspicion. But his nonchalance, his air of finality, his authoritative assurance—these to Duane's keen and practised eyes were in significant contrast to a certain tenseness of line about his mouth and a slow paling of his olive skin. In that momentary lull Duane's scrutiny of Longstreth gathered an impression of the man's intense curiosity.

Then the prisoner, Snecker, with a cough that broke the spell of silence, shuffled a couple of steps toward the door.

"Hold on!" called Duane. The call halted Snecker, as if it had been a bullet.

"Longstreth, I saw Snecker attack Laramie," said Duane, his voice still ringing. "What has the court to say to that?"

"The court has this to say. West of the Pecos we'll not aid any ranger service. We don't want you out here. Fairdale doesn't need you."

"That's a lie, Longstreth," retorted Duane. "I've letters from Fairdale citizens all begging for ranger service."

Longstreth turned white. The veins corded at his temples. He appeared about to burst into rage. He was at a loss for quick reply.

Floyd Lawson rushed in and up to the table. The blood showed black and thick in his face; his utterance was incoherent, his uncontrollable outbreak of temper seemed out of all proportion to any cause he should reasonably have had for anger. Longstreth shoved him back with a curse and a warning glare.

"Where's your warrant to arrest Snecker?" shouted Longstreth.

"I don't need warrants to make arrests. Longstreth, you're ignorant of the power of Texas Rangers."

"You'll come none of your damned ranger stunts out here. I'll block you."

That passionate reply of Longstreth's was the signal Duane had been waiting for. He had helped on the crisis. He wanted to force Longstreth's hand and show the town his stand.

Duane backed clear of everybody.

"Men! I call on you all!" cried Duane, piercingly. "I call on you to witness the arrest of a criminal prevented by Longstreth, Mayor of Fairdale. It will be recorded in the report to the Adjutant-General at Austin. Longstreth, you'll never prevent another arrest."

Longstreth sat white with working jaw.

"Longstreth, you've shown your hand," said Duane, in a voice that carried far and held those who heard. "Any honest citizen of Fairdale can now see what's plain—yours is a damn poor hand! You're going to hear me call a spade a spade. In the two years you've been Mayor you've never arrested one rustler. Strange, when Fairdale's a nest for rustlers! You've never sent a prisoner to Del Rio, let alone to Austin. You have no jail. There have been nine murders during your office—innumerable street-fights and holdups. Not one arrest! But you have ordered arrests for trivial offenses, and have punished these out of all proportion. There have been lawsuits in your court—suits over water-rights, cattle deals, property lines. Strange how in these lawsuits you or Lawson or other men close to you were always involved! Strange how it seems the law was stretched to favor your interest!"

Duane paused in his cold, ringing speech. In the silence, both outside and inside the hall, could be heard the deep breathing of agitated men. Longstreth was indeed a study. Yet did he betray anything but rage at this interloper?

"Longstreth, here's plain talk for you and Fairdale," went on Duane. "I don't accuse you and your court of dishonesty. I say *strange!* Law here has been a farce. The motive behind all this laxity isn't plain to me—yet. But I call your hand!"

17

DUANE left the hall, elbowed his way through the crowd, and went down the street. He was certain that on the faces of some men he had seen ill-concealed wonder and satisfaction. He had struck some kind of a hot trail, and he meant to see where it led. It was by no means unlikely that Cheseldine might be at the other end. Duane controlled a mounting eagerness. But ever and anon it was shot through with a remembrance of Ray Longstreth. He suspected her father of being not what he pretended. He might, very probably would, bring sorrow and shame to this young woman. The thought made him smart with pain. She began to haunt him, and then he was thinking more of her beauty and sweetness than of the disgrace he might bring upon her. Some strange emotion, long locked inside Duane's heart, knocked to be heard, to be let out. He was troubled.

Upon returning to the inn he found Laramie there, apparently none the worse for his injury.

"How are you, Laramie?" he asked.

"Reckon I'm feelin' as well as could be expected," replied Laramie. His head was circled by a bandage that did not conceal the lump where he had been struck. He looked pale, but was bright enough.

"That was a good crack Snecker gave you," remarked Duane.

"I ain't accusin' Bo," remonstrated Laramie, with eyes that made Duane thoughtful.

"Well, I accuse him. I caught him—took him to Longstreth's court. But they let him go."

Laramie appeared to be agitated by this intimation of friendship.

"See here, Laramie," went on Duane, "in some parts of Texas it's policy to be close-mouthed. Policy and health-preserving! Between ourselves, I want you to know I lean on your side of the fence."

Laramie gave a quick start. Presently Duane turned and frankly met his gaze. He had startled Laramie out of his habitual set taciturnity; but even as he looked the light that might have been amaze and joy faded out of his face, leaving it the same old mask. Still Duane had seen enough. Like a bloodhound he had a scent.

"Talking about work, Laramie, who'd you say Snecker worked for?"

"I didn't say."

"Well, say so now, can't you? Laramie, you're powerful peevish to-day. It's that bump on your head. Who does Snecker work for?"

"When he works at all, which sure ain't often, he rides for Longstreth."

"Humph! Seems to me that Longstreth's the whole circus round Fairdale. I was some sore the other day to find I was losing good money at Longstreth's faro game. Sure if I'd won I wouldn't have been sore—ha, ha! But I was surprised to hear some one say Longstreth owned the Hope So joint."

"He owns considerable property hereabouts," replied Laramie, constrainedly.

"Humph again! Laramie, like every other fellow I meet in this town, you're afraid to open your trap about Longstreth. Get me straight, Laramie. I don't care a damn for Colonel Mayor Longstreth. And for cause I'd throw a gun on him just as quick as on any rustler in Pecos."

"Talk's cheap," replied Laramie, making light of his bluster, but the red was deeper in his face.

"Sure, I know that," Duane said. "And usually I don't talk. Then it's not well known that Longstreth owns the Hope So?"

"Reckon it's known in Pecos, all right. But Longstreth's name isn't connected with the Hope So. Blandy runs the place."

"That Blandy. His faro game's crooked, or I'm a locoed bronch. Not that we don't have lots of crooked faro-dealers. A fellow can stand for them. But Blandy's mean, back-handed, nerver looks you in the eyes. That Hope So place ought to be run by a good fellow like you, Laramie."

"Thanks," replied he; and Duane imagined his voice a little husky. "Didn't you hear I used to—run it?"

"No. Did you?" Duane said, quickly.

"I reckon. I built the place, made additions twice, owned it for eleven years."

"Well, I'll be doggoned." It was indeed Duane's turn to be surprised, and with the surprise came a glimmering. "I'm sorry you're not there now. Did you sell out?"

"No. Just lost the place."

Laramie was bursting for relief now—to talk, to tell. Sympathy had made him soft.

"It was two years ago—two years last March," he went on. "I was in a big cattle deal with Longstreth. We got the stock—an' my share, eighteen hundred head, was rustled off. I owed Longstreth. He pressed me. It come to a lawsuit—an' I—was ruined."

It hurt Duane to look at Laramie. He was white, and tears rolled down his cheeks. Duane saw the bitterness, the defeat, the agony of the man. He had failed to meet his obligations; nevertheless, he had been swindled. All that he suppressed, all that would have been passion had the man's spirit not been broken, lay bare for Duane to see. He had now the secret of his bitterness. But the reason he did not openly accuse Longstreth, the secret of his reticence and fear—these Duane thought best to try to learn at some later time.

"Hard luck! It certainly was tough," Duane said. "But you're a good loser. And the wheel turns! Now, Laramie, here's what. I need your advice. I've got a little money. But before I lose it I want to invest some. Buy some stock, or buy an interest in some rancher's herd. What I want you to steer me on is a good square rancher. Or maybe a couple of ranchers, if there happen to be two honest ones. Ha, ha! No deals with ranchers who ride in the dark with rustlers! I've a hunch Fairdale is full of them. Now, Laramie, you've been here for years. Sure you must know a couple of men above suspicion."

"Thank God I do," he replied, feelingly. "Frank Morton an' Si Zimmer, my friends an' neighbors all my prosperous days, an' friends still. You can gamble on Frank and Si. But if you want advice from me—don't invest money in stock now."

"Why?"

"Because any new feller buyin' stock these days will be rustled quicker 'n he can say Jack Robinson. The pioneers, the new cattlemen—these are easy pickin' for the rustlers. Lord knows all the ranchers are easy enough pickin'. But the new fellers have to learn the ropes. They don't know anythin' or anybody. An' the old ranchers are wise an' sore. They'd fight if they—"

"What?" Duane put in, as he paused. "If they knew who was rustling the stock?"

"Nope."

"If they had the nerve?"

"Not thet so much."

"What then? What'd make them fight?"

"A leader!"

"Howdy thar, Jim," boomed a big voice.

A man of great bulk, with a ruddy, merry face, entered the room.

"Hello, Morton," replied Laramie. "I'd introduce you to my guest here, but I don't know his name."

"Haw! Haw! Thet's all right. Few men out hyar go by their right names."

"Say, Morton," put in Duane, "Laramie gave me a hunch you'd be a good man to tie to. Now, I've a little money and before I lose it I'd like to invest it in stock."

Morton smiled broadly.

"I'm on the square," Duane said, bluntly, "If you fellows never size up your neighbors any better than you have sized me—well, you won't get any richer."

It was enjoyment for Duane to make his remarks to these men pregnant with meaning. Morton showed his pleasure, his interest, but his faith held aloof.

"I've got some money. Will you let me in on some kind of deal? Will you start me up as a stockman with a little herd all my own?"

"Wal, stranger, to come out flat-footed, you'd be foolish to buy cattle now. I don't want to take your money an' see you lose out. Better go back across the Pecos where the rustlers ain't so strong. I haven't had more'n twenty-five hundred herd of stock for ten years. The rustlers let me hang on to a breedin' herd. Kind of them, ain't it?"

"Sort of kind. All I hear is rustlers, Morton," replied Duane, with impatience. "You see, I haven't ever lived long in a rustler-run county. Who heads the gang, anyway?"

Morton looked at Duane with a curiously amused smile, then snapped his big jaw as if to shut in impulsive words.

"Look here, Morton. It stands to reason, no matter how strong these rustlers are, how hidden their work, however involved with supposedly honest men— they *can't* last."

"They come with the pioneers, an' they'll last till thar's a single steer left," he declared.

"Well, if you take that view of circumstances I just figure you as one of the rustlers!"

Morton looked as if he were about to brain Duane with the butt of his whip. His anger flashed by then, evidently as unworthy of him, and, something striking him as funny, he boomed out a laugh.

"It's not so funny," Duane went on. "If you're going to pretend a yellow streak, what else will I think?"

"Pretend?" he repeated.

"Sure. I know men of nerve. And here they're not any different from those in other places. I say if you show anything like a lack of sand it's all bluff. By nature you've got nerve. There are a lot of men around Fairdale who're afraid of their shadows—afraid to be out after dark—afraid to open their mouths. But you're not one. So I say if you claim these rustlers will last you're pretending lack of nerve just to help the popular idea along. For they *can't* last. What you need out here is some new blood. Savvy what I mean?"

"Wal, I reckon I do," he replied, looking as if a storm had blown over him. "Stranger, I'll look you up the next time I come to town."

Then he went out.

Laramie had eyes like flint striking fire.

He breathed a deep breath and looked around the room before his gaze fixed again on Duane.

"Wal," he replied, speaking low. "You've picked the right men. Now, who in the hell are you?"

Reaching into the inside pocket of his buckskin vest, Duane turned the lining out. A star-shaped bright silver object flashed as he shoved it, pocket and all, under Jim's hard eyes.

"*Ranger!*" he whispered, cracking the table with his fist. "You sure rung true to me."

"Laramie, do you know who's boss of this secret gang of rustlers hereabouts?" asked Duane, bluntly. It was characteristic of him to come sharp to the point. His voice—something deep, easy, cool about him—seemed to steady Laramie.

"No," replied Laramie.

"Does anybody know?" went on Duane.

"Wal, I reckon there's not one honest native who *knows*."

"But you have your suspicions?"

"We have."

"Give me your idea about this crowd that hangs round the saloons—the regulars."

"Jest a bad lot," replied Laramie, with the quick assurance of knowledge. "Most of them have been here years. Others have drifted in. Some of them work, odd times. They rustle a few steers, steal, rob, anythin' for a little money to drink an' gamble. Jest a bad lot!"

"Have you any idea whether Cheseldine and his gang are associated with this gang here?"

"Lord knows. I've always suspected them the same gang. None of us ever seen Cheseldine—an' thet's strange, whjen Knell, Poggin, Panhandle Smith, Blossom Kane, and Fletcher, they all ride here often. No, Poggin doesn't come often. But the others do. For thet matter, they're around all over west of the Pecos."

"Now I'm puzzled over this," said Duane. "Why do men—apparently honest men—seem to be so close-mouthed here? Is that a fact, or only my impression?"

"It's a sure fact," replied Laramie, darkly. "Men have lost cattle an' property in Fairdale—lost them honestly or otherwise, as hasn't been proved. An' in some cases when they talked—hinted a little—they was found dead. Apparently held up an' robbed. But dead. Dead men don't talk! Thet's why we're close-mouthed."

Duane felt a dark, somber sternness. Rustling cattle was not intolerable. Western Texas had gone on prospering, growing in spite of the hordes of rustlers ranging its vast stretches; but a cold, secret, murderous hold on a little struggling community was something too strange, too terrible for men to stand long.

The ranger was about to speak again when the clatter of hoofs interrupted him. Horses halted out in front, and one rider got down. Floyd Lawson entered. He called for tobacco.

If his visit surprised Laramie he did not show any evidence. But Lawson showed rage as he saw the ranger, and then a dark glint flitted from the eyes that shifted from Duane to Laramie and back again. Duane leaned easily against the counter.

"Say, that was a bad break of yours," Lawson said. "If you come fooling round the ranch again there'll be hell."

It seemed strange that a man who had lived west of the Pecos for ten years could not see in Duane something which forbade that kind of talk. It certainly was not nerve Lawson showed; men of courage were seldom intolerant. With the matchless nerve that characterized the great gunmen of the day there was a cool, unobtrusive manner, a speech brief, almost gentle, certainly courteous. Lawson was a hot-headed Louisianian of French extraction; a man, evidently, who had never been crossed in anything, and who was strong, brutal, passionate, which qualities in the face of a situation like this made him simply a fool.

"I'm saying again, you used your ranger bluff just to get near Ray Longstreth," Lawson sneered. "Mind you, if you come up there again there'll be hell."

"You're right. But not the kind you think," Duane retorted, his voice sharp and cold.

"Ray Longstreth wouldn't stoop to know a dirty blood-tracker like you," said Lawson, hotly. He did not seem to have a deliberate intention to rouse Duane; the man was simply rancorous, jealous. "I'll call you right, You cheap bluffer! You four-flushed! You damned interfering, conceited ranger!"

"Lawson, I'll not take offense, because you seem to be championing your beautiful cousin," replied Duane, in slow speech. "But let me return your compliment. You're a fine Southerner! Why, you're only a cheap four-flush— damned, bullheaded *rustler!*"

Duane hissed the last word. Then for him there was the truth in Lawson's working passion-blackened face.

Lawson jerked, moved, meant to draw. But how slow! Duane lunged forward. His long arm swept up. And Lawson staggered backward, knocking table and chairs, to fall hard, in a half-sitting posture against the wall.

"Don't draw!" warned Duane.

"Lawson, git away from your gun!" yelled Laramie.

But Lawson was crazed with fury. He tugged at his hip, his face corded with purple welts, malignant, murderous. Duane kicked the gun out of his hand. Lawson got up, raging, and rushed out.

Laramie lifted his shaking hands.

"What'd you wing him for?" he wailed. "He was drawin' on you. Kickin' men like him won't do out here."

"That bull-headed fool will roar and butt himself with all his gang right into our hands. He's just the man I've needed to meet. Besides, shooting him would have been murder."

"Murder!" exclaimed Laramie.

"Yes, for me," replied Duane.

"That may be true—whoever you are—but if Lawson's the man you think he is he'll begin thet secret underground bizness. Why, Lawson won't sleep of nights now. He an' Longstreth have always been after me."

"Laramie, what are your eyes for?" demanded Duane. "Watch out. And now here. See your friend Morton. Tell him this game grows hot. Together you approach four or five men you know well and can absolutely trust. I may need your help."

Then Duane went from place to place, corner to corner, bar to bar, watching, listening, recording. The excitement had preceded him, and speculation was rife. He thought best to keep out of it. After dark he stole up to Longstreth's ranch. The evening was warm; the doors were open; and in the twilight the only lamps that had been lit were in Longstreth's big sitting-room, at the far end of the house. When a buckboard drove up and Longstreth and Lawson alighted, Duane was well hidden in the bushes, so well screened that he could get but a fleeting glimpse of Longstreth as he went in. For all Duane could see, he appeared to be a calm and quiet man, intense beneath the surface, with an air of dignity under insult. Duane's chance to observe Lawson was lost. They went into the house without speaking and closed the door.

At the other end of the porch, close under a window, was an offset between step and wall, and there in the shadow Duane hid. So Duane waited there in the darkness with patience born of many hours of hiding.

Presently a lamp was lit; and Duane heard the swish of skirts.

"Something's happened surely, Ruth," he heard Miss Longstreth say, anxiously. "Papa just met me in the hall and didn't speak. He seemed pale, worried."

"Cousin Floyd looked like a thunder-cloud," said Ruth. "For once he didn't try to kiss me. Something's happened. Well, Ray, this had been a bad day."

"Oh, dear! Ruth, what can we do? These are wild men. Floyd makes life miserable for me. And he teases you unmer—"

"I don't call it teasing. Floyd wants to spoon," declared Ruth, emphatically. "He'd run after any woman."

"A fine compliment to me, Cousin Ruth," laughed Ray.

"I don't care," replied Ruth, stubbornly. "It's so. He's mushy. And when he's been drinking and tries to kiss me—I hate him!"

There were steps on the hall floor.

"Hello, girls!" sounded out Lawson's voice, minus its usual gaiety.

"Floyd, what's the matter?" asked Ray, presently. "I never saw papa as he is to-night, nor you so—so worried. Tell me, what has happened?"

"Well, Ray, we had a jar to-day," replied Lawson, with a blunt, expressive laugh.

"Jar?" echoed both the girls, curiously.

"We had to submit to a damnable outrage," added Lawson, passionately, as if the sound of his voice augmented his feeling. "Listen, girls; I'll tell you all about it." He coughed, cleared his throat in a way that betrayed he had been drinking.

Duane sunk deeper into the shadow of his covert, and, stiffening his muscles for a protracted spell of rigidity, prepared to listen with all acuteness and intensity. Just one word from this Lawson, inadvertently uttered in a moment of passion, might be the word Duane needed for his clue.

"It happened at the town hall," began Lawson, rapidly. "Your father and Judge Owens and I were there in consultation with three ranchers from out of town. Then that damned ranger stalked in dragging Snecker, the fellow who hid here in the house. He had arrested Snecker for alleged assault on a restaurant-keeper named Laramie. Snecker being obviously innocent, he was discharged. Then this ranger began shouting his insults. Law was a farce in Fairdale. The court was a farce. There was no law. Your father's office as mayor should be impeached. He made arrests only for petty offenses. He was afraid of the rustlers, highwaymen, murderers. He was afraid or—he just let them alone. He used his office to cheat ranchers and cattlemen in lawsuits. All this the ranger yelled for every one to hear. A damnable outrage. Your father, Ray, insulted in his own court by a rowdy ranger!"

"Oh!" cried Ray Longstreth, in mingled distress and anger.

"The ranger service wants to rule western Texas," went on Lawson. "These rangers are all a low set, many of them worse then the outlaws they hunt. Some of them were outlaws and gun-fighters before they became rangers. This is one of the worst of the lot. He's keen, intelligent, smooth, and that makes him more to be feared. For he is to be feared. He wanted to kill. He would kill. If your father had made the least move he would have shot him. He's a cold-nerved devil—the born gunman. My God, any instant I expected to see your father fall dead at my feet!"

"Oh, Floyd! The unspeakable ruffian!" cried Ray Longstreth, passionately.

"You see, Ray, this fellow, like all rangers, seeks notoriety. He made that play with Snecker just for a chance to rant against your father. He tried to inflame all Fairdale against him. That about the lawsuits was the worst! Damn him! He'll make us enemies."

"What do you care for the insinuations of such a man?" said Ray Longstreth, her voice now deep and rich with feeling. "After a moment's thought no one will be influenced by them. Do not worry, Floyd. Tell papa not to worry. Surely after all these years he can't be injured in reputation by—by an adventurer."

"Yes, he can be injured," replied Floyd, quickly. "The frontier is a queer place. There are many bitter men here—men who have failed at ranching. And your father has been wonderfully successful. The ranger has dropped poison, and it'll spread.''

18

STRANGERS rode into Fairdale; and other hard-looking customers, new to Duane if not to Fairdale, helped to create a charged and waiting atmosphere. The saloons did unusual business and were never closed. Respectable citizens of the town were awakened in the early dawn by rowdies carousing in the streets.

Duane kept pretty close under cover during the day. He did not entertain the opinion that the first time he walked down-street he would be a target for guns. Things seldom happened that way; and when they did happen so, it was more accident than design. But at night he was not idle. He met Laramie, Morton, Zimmer, and others of like character; a secret club had been formed; and all the members were ready for action. Duane spent hours at night watching the house where Floyd Lawson stayed when he was not up at Longstreth's. At night he was visited, or at least the house was, by strange men who were swift, stealthy, mysterious—all that kindly disposed friends or neighbors would not have been. Duane had not been able to recognize any of these night visitors; and he did not think the time was ripe for a bold holding-up of one of them. Nevertheless, he was sure such an event would discover Lawson, or some one in that house, to be in touch with crooked men.

Laramie was right. Not twenty-four hours after his last talk with Duane, in which he advised quick action, he was found behind the little bar of his restaurant with a bullet-hole in his breast, dead. No one could be found who had heard a shot. It had been deliberate murder, for upon the bar had been left a piece of paper rudely scrawled with a pencil: ''All friends of rangers look for the same.''

This roused Duane. His first move, however, was to bury Laramie. None of Laramie's neighbors evinced any interest in the dead man or the unfortunate family he had left. Duane saw that these neighbors were held in check by fear. Mrs. Laramie was ill; the shock of her husband's death was hard on her; and she had been left almost destitute with five children. Duane rented a small adobe house on the outskirts of town and moved the family into it. Then he played the part of provider and nurse and friend.

After several days Duane went boldly into town and showed that he meant business. It was his opinion that there were men in Fairdale secretly glad of a ranger's presence. What he intended to do was food for great speculation. A company of militia could not have had the effect upon the wild element of Fairdale that Duane's presence had. It got out that he was a gunman lightning swift on the draw. It was death to face him. He had killed thirty men—wildest rumor of all. It was actually said of him he had the gun-skill of Buck Duane or of Poggin.

At first there had not only been great conjecture among the vicious element, but also a very decided checking of all kinds of action calculated to be conspicuous to a keen-eyed ranger. At the tables, at the bars and lounging-places Duane heard the remarks: "Who's thet ranger after? What'll he do fust off? Is he waitin' fer somebody? Who's goin' to draw on him fust—an' go to hell? Jest about how soon will he be found somewheres full of lead?"

When it came out somewhere that Duane was openly cultivating the honest stay-at-home citizens to array them in time against the other element, then Fairdale showed its wolf teeth. Several times Duane was shot at in the dark and once slightly injured. Rumor had it that Poggin, the gunman, was coming to meet him. But the lawless element did not rise up in a mass to slay Duane on sight. It was not so much that the enemies of the law awaited his next move, but just a slowness peculiar to the frontier. The ranger was in their midst. He was interesting, if formidable. He would have been welcomed at card-tables, at the bars, to play and drink with the men who knew they were under suspicion. There was a rude kind of good humor even in their open hostility.

Besides, one ranger or a company of rangers could not have held the undivided attention of these men from their games and drinks and quarrels except by some decided move. Excitement, greed, appetite were rife in them. Duane marked, however, a striking exception to the usual run of strangers he had been in the habit of seeing. Snecker had gone or was under cover. Again Duane caught a vague rumor of the coming of Poggin, yet he never seemed to arrive. Moreover, the goings-on among the habitués of the resorts and the cowboys who came in to drink and gamble were unusually mild in comparison with former conduct. This lull, however, did not deceive Duane. It could not last. The wonder was that it had lasted so long.

Duane went often to see Mrs. Laramie and her children. One afternoon while he was there he saw Miss Longstreth and Ruth ride up to the door. They carried a basket. Evidently they had heard of Mrs. Laramie's trouble. Duane felt strangely glad, but he went into an adjoining room rather than meet them.

"Mrs. Laramie, I've come to see you," said Miss Longstreth, cheerfully.

The little room was not very light, there being only one window and the doors, but Duane could see plainly enough. Mrs. Laramie lay, hollow-cheeked and haggard, on a bed. Once she had evidently been a woman of some comeliness.

The ravages of trouble and grief were there to read in her worn face; it had not, however, any of the hard and bitter lines that had characterized her husband's.

Duane wondered, considering that Longstreth had ruined Laramie, how Mrs. Laramie was going to regard the daughter of an enemy.

"So you're Granger Longstreth's girl?" queried the woman, with her bright, black eyes fixed on her visitor.

"Yes," replied Miss Longstreth, simply. "This is my cousin, Ruth Herbert. We've come to nurse you, take care of the children, help you in any way you'll let us."

There was a long silence.

"Well, you look a little like Longstreth," finally said Mrs. Laramie, "but you're not at all like him. You must take after your mother. Miss Longstreth, I don't know if I can—if I ought accept anything from you. Your father ruined my husband."

"Yes, I know," replied the girl, sadly. "That's all the more reason you should let me help you. Pray don't refuse. It will—mean so much to me."

If this poor, stricken woman had any resentment it speedily melted in the warmth and sweetness of Miss Longstreth's manner. Duane's idea was that the impression of Ray Longstreth's beauty was always swiftly succeeded by that of her generosity and nobility. At any rate, she had started well with Mrs. Laramie, and no sooner had she begun to talk to the children than both they and the mother were won. The opening of that big basket was an event. Poor, starved little beggars! Duane's feelings seemed too easily roused. Hard indeed would it have gone with Jim Laramie's slayer if he could have laid eyes on him then. However, Miss Longstreth and Ruth, after the nature of tender and practical girls, did not appear to take the sad situation to heart. The havoc was wrought in that household. The needs now were cheerfulness, kindness, help, action—and these the girls furnished with a spirit that did Duane good.

"Mrs. Laramie, who dressed this baby?" presently asked Miss Longstreth. Duane peeped in to see a dilapidated youngster on her knee. The sight, if any other was needed, completed his full and splendid estimate of Ray Longstreth and wrought strangely upon his heart.

"The ranger," replied Mrs. Laramie.

"The ranger!" exclaimed Miss Longstreth.

"Yes, he's taken care of us all since—since—" Mrs. Laramie choked.

"Oh! So you've had no help but his," replied Miss Longstreth, hastily. "No women. Too bad! I'll send some one, Mrs. Laramie, and I'll come myself."

"It'll be good of you," went on the older woman. "You see, Jim had few friends—that is, right in town. And they've been afraid to help us—afraid they'd get what poor Jim—"

"That's awful!" burst out Miss Longstreth, passionately. "A brave lot of friends! Mrs. Laramie, don't you worry any more. We'll take care of you. Here, Ruth, help me. Whatever is the matter with baby's dress?''

Manifestly Miss Longstreth had some difficulty in subduing her emotion.

"Why, it's on hind side before," declared Ruth. "I guess Mr. Ranger hasn't dressed many babies.''

"He did the best he could," said Mrs. Laramie. "Lord only knows what would have become of us!''

"Then he is—is something more than a ranger?'' queried Miss Longstreth, with a little break in her voice.

"He's more than I can tell," replied Mrs. Laramie. "He buried Jim. He paid our debts. He fetched us here. He bought food for us. He cooked for us and fed us. He washed and dressed the baby. He sat with me the first two nights after Jim's death, when I thought I'd die myself. He's so kind, so gentle, so patient. He has kept me up just by being near. Sometimes I'd wake from a doze, an', seeing him there, I'd know how false were all these tales Jim heard about him and believed at first. Why, he plays with the children just—just like any good man might. When he has the baby up I just can't believe he's a bloody gunman, as they say. He's good, but he isn't happy. He has such sad eyes. He looks far off sometimes when the children climb round him. They love him. His life is sad. Nobody need tell me—he sees the good in things. Once he said somebody had to be a ranger. Well, I say, 'Thank God for a ranger like him!' ''

Duane did not want to hear more, so he walked into the room.

"It was thoughful of you," Duane said. "Womankind are needed here. I could do so little. Mrs. Laramie, you look better already. I'm glad. And here's baby, all clean and white. Baby, what a time I had trying to puzzle out the way your clothes went on! Well, Mrs. Laramie, didn't I tell you—friends would come? So will the brighter side.''

"Yes, I've more faith than I had," replied Mrs. Laramie. "Granger Longstreth's daughter has come to me. There for a while after Jim's death I thought I'd sink. We have nothing. How could I ever take care of my little ones? But I'm gaining courage to—''

"Mrs. Laramie, do not distress yourself any more," said Miss Longstreth. "I shall see you are well cared for. I promise you.''

"Miss Longstreth, that's fine!" exclaimed Duane. "It's what I'd have—expected of you.''

It must have been sweet praise to her, for the whiteness of her face burned out in a beautiful blush.

"And it's good of you, too, Miss Herbert, to come," added Duane. "Let me thank you both. I'm glad I have you girls as allies in part of my lonely task here. More than glad for the sake of this good woman and the little ones. But both of you be careful about coming here alone. There's risk. And now I'll be going. Good-by, Mrs. Laramie. I'll drop in again to-night. Good-by."

"Mr. Ranger, wait!" called Miss Longstreth, as he went out. She was white and wonderful. She stepped out of the door close to him.

"I have wronged you!" she said, impulsively.

"Miss Longstreth! How can you say that?" he returned.

"I believed what my father and Floyd Lawson said about you. Now I see— I wronged you."

"You make me very glad. But, Miss Longstreth, please don't speak of wronging me. I have been a—a gunman, I *am* a ranger—and much said of me is true. My duty is hard on others—sometimes on those who are innocent, alas! But God knows that duty is hard, too, on me."

"I did wrong you. If you entered my home again I would think it an honor. I—"

"Please—please don't, Miss Longstreth," interrupted Duane.

"But, sir, my conscience flays me," she went on. There was no other sound like her voice. "Will you take my hand? Will you forgive me?"

She gave it royally, while the other was there pressing at her breast. Duane took the proffered hand. He did not know what else to do.

Then it seemed to dawn upon him that there was more behind this white, sweet, noble intensity of her than just the making amends for a fancied or real wrong. Duane thought the man did not live on earth who could have resisted her then.

"I honor you for your goodness to this unfortunate woman," she said, and now her speech came swiftly. "When she was all alone and helpless you were her friend. It was the deed of a man. But Mrs. Laramie isn't the only unfortunate woman in the world. I, too, am unfortunate. Ah, how *I* may soon need a friend! Will *you* be my friend? I'm so alone. I'm terribly worried. I fear—I fear— Oh, surely I'll need a friend soon—soon. Oh, I'm afraid of what you'll find out sooner or later. I want to help you. Let us save life if not honor. Must I stand alone—all alone? Will you—will you be—" Her voice failed.

It seemed to Duane that she must have discovered what he had begun to suspect—that her father and Lawson were not the honest ranchers they pretended to be. Perhaps she knew more! Her appeal to Duane shook him deeply. He wanted to help her more than he had ever wanted anything. And with the meaning of the tumultuous sweetness she stirred in him there came realization of a dangerous situation.

"I must be true to my duty," he said, hoarsely.

"If you knew me you'd know I could never ask you to be false to it."

"Well, then—I'll do anything for you."

"Oh, thank you! I'm ashamed that I believed my cousin Floyd! He lied—he lied. I'm all in the dark, strangely distressed. My father wants me to go back home. Floyd is trying to keep me here. They've quarreled. Oh, I know something dreadful will happen. I know I'll need you if—if—Will you help me?''

"Yes," replied Duane, and his look brought the blood to her face.

19

AFTER supper Duane stole out for his usual evening's spying. The night was dark, without starlight, and a stiff wind rustled the leaves. Duane bent his steps toward the Longstreth's ranchhouse. He had so much to think about that he never knew where the time went. This night when he reached the edge of the shrubbery he heard Lawson's well-known footsteps and saw Longstreth's door open, flashing a broad bar of light in the darkness. Lawson crossed the threshold, the door closed, and all was dark again outside. Not a ray of light escaped from the window.

Little doubt there was that his talk with Longstreth would be interesting to Duane. He tiptoed to the door and listened, but could hear only a murmur of voices. Besides, that position was too risky. He went round the corner of the house.

This side of the big adobe house was of much older construction than the back and larger part. There was a narrow passage between the houses, leading from the outside through to the patio.

This passage now afforded Duane an opportunity, and he decided to avail himself of it in spite of the very great danger. Crawling on very stealthily, he got under the shrubbery to the entrance of the passage. In the blackness a faint streak of light showed the location of a crack in the wall. He had to slip in sidewise. It was a tight squeeze, but he entered without the slightest noise. As he progressed the passage grew a very little wider in that direction, and that fact gave rise to the thought that in case of a necessary and hurried exit he would do best by working toward the patio. It seemed a good deal of time was consumed in reaching a vantage-point. When he did get there the crack he had marked was a foot over his head. There was nothing to do but find toe-holes in the crumbling walls, and by bracing knees on one side, back against the other, hold himself up. Once with his eye there he did not care what risk he ran. Longstreth appeared disturbed; he sat stroking his mustache; his brow was clouded. Lawson's face seemed darker, more sullen, yet lighted by some indomitable resolve.

"We'll settle both deals to-night," Lawson was saying. "That's what I came for."

"But suppose I don't choose to talk here?" protested Longstreth, impatiently. "I never before made my house a place to—"

"We've waited long enough. This place's as good as any. You've lost your nerve since that ranger hit the town. First now, will you give Ray to me?"

"Floyd, you talk like a spoiled boy. Give Ray to you! Why, she's a woman, and I'm finding out that she's got a mind of her own. I told you I was willing for her to marry you. I tried to persuade her. But Ray hasn't any use for you now. She liked you at first. But now she doesn't. So what can I do?"

"You can make her marry me," replied Lawson.

"Make that girl do what she doesn't want to? It couldn't be done even if I tried. And I don't believe I'll try. I haven't the highest opinion of you as a prospective son-in-law, Floyd. But if Ray loved you I would consent. We'd all go away together before this damned miserable business is out. Then she'd never know. And maybe you might be more like you used to be before the West ruined you. But as matters stand, you fight your own game with her. And I'll tell you now you'll lose."

"What'd you want to let her come out here for?" demanded Lawson, hotly. "It was a dead mistake. I've lost my head over her. I'll have her or die. Don't you think if she was my wife I'd soon pull myself together? Since she came we've none of us been right. And the gang has put up a holler. No, Longstreth, we've got to settle things to-night."

"Well, we can settle what Ray's concerned in, right now," replied Longstreth, rising. "Come on; we'll ask her. See where you stand."

They went out, leaving the door open. Duane dropped down to rest himself and to wait. He would have liked to hear Miss Longstreth's answer. But he could guess what it would be. Lawson appeared to be all Duane had thought him, and he believed he was going to find out presently that he was worse.

The men seemed to be absent a good while, though that feeling might have been occasioned by Duane's thrilling interest and anxiety. Finally he heard heavy steps. Lawson came in alone. He was leaden-faced, humiliated. Then something abject in him gave place to rage. He strode the room; he cursed. Then Longstreth returned, now appreciably calmer. Duane could not but decide that he felt relief at the evident rejection of Lawson's proposal.

"Don't fuss about it, Floyd," he said. "You see I can't help it. We're pretty wild out here, but I can't rope my daughter and give her to you as I would an unruly steer."

"Longstreth, I can *make* her marry me," declared Lawson, thickly.

"How?"

"You know the hold I got on you—the deal that made you boss of this rustler gang?"

"It isn't likely I'd forget," replied Lonstreth, grimly.

"I can go to Ray, tell her that, make her believe I'd tell it broadcast—tell this ranger—unless she'd marry me."

Lawson spoke breathlessly, with haggard face and shadowed eyes. He had no shame. He was simply in the grip of passion.

Longstreth gazed with dark, controlled fury at this relative. In that look Duane saw a strong, unscrupulous man fallen into evil ways, but still a man. It betrayed Lawson to be the wild and passionate weakling. Duane seemed to see also how during all the years of association this strong man had upheld the weak one. But that time had gone for ever, both in intent on Longstreth's part and in possibility. Lawson, like the great majority of evil and unrestrained men on the border, had reached a point where influence was futile. Reason had degenerated. He saw only himself.

"But, Floyd, Ray's the one person on earth who must never know I'm a rustler, a thief, a red-handed ruler of the worst gang on the border," replied Longstreth, impressively.

Floyd bowed his head at that, as if the significance had just occurred to him. But he was not long at a loss.

"She's going to find it out sooner or later. I tell you she knows now there's something wrong out here. She's got eyes. Mark what I say."

"Ray has changed, I know. But she hasn't any idea yet that her daddy's a boss rustler. Ray's concerned about what she calls my duty as mayor. Also I think she's not satisfied with my explanations in regard to certain property."

Lawson halted in his restless walk and leaned against the stone mantelpiece. He had his hands in his pockets. He squared himself as if this was his last stand. He looked desperate, but on the moment showed an absence of his usual nervous excitement.

"Longstreth, that may well be true," he said. "No doubt all you say is true. But it doesn't help me. I want the girl. If I don't get her—I reckon we'll all go to hell!"

He might have meant anything, probably meant the worst. He certainly had something more in mind. Longstreth gave a slight start, barely perceptible, like the switch of an awakening tiger. He sat there, head down, stroking his mustache. Almost Duane saw his thought. He had long experience in reading men under stress of such emotion. He had no means to vindicate his judgment, but his conviction was that Longstreth right then and there decided that the thing to do was to kill Lawson. For Duane's part he wondered that Longstreth had not come to such a conclusion before. Not improbably the advent of his daughter had put Longstreth in conflict with himself.

Suddenly he threw off a somber cast of countenance, and he began to talk. He talked swiftly, persuasively, yet Duane imagined he was talking to smooth Lawson's passion for the moment. Lawson no more caught the fateful significance of a line crossed, a limit reached, a decree decided than if he had not been present. He was obsessed with himself. How, Duane wondered, had a man of his mind ever lived so long and gone so far among the exacting conditions of the Southwest? The answer was, perhaps, that Longstreth had guided him, upheld him, protected him. The coming of Ray Longstreth had been the entering-wedge of dissension.

"You're too impatient," concluded Longstreth. "You'll ruin any chance of happiness if you rush Ray. She might be won. If you told her who I am she'd hate you for ever. She might marry you to save me, but she'd hate you. That isn't the way. Wait. Play for time. Be different with her. Cut out your drinking. She despises that. Let's plan to sell out here—stock, ranch, property—and leave the country. Then you'd have a show with her."

"I told you we've got to stick," growled Lawson. "The gang won't stand for our going. It can't be done unless you want to sacrifice everything."

"You mean double-cross the men? Go without their knowing? Leave them here to face whatever comes?"

"I mean just that."

"I'm bad enough, but not that bad," returned Longstreth. "If I can't get the gang to let me off, I'll stay and face the music. All the same, Lawson, did it ever strike you that most of the deals the last few years have been *yours*?"

"Yes. If I hadn't rung them in there wouldn't have been any. You've had cold feet, and especially since this ranger has been here."

"Well, call it cold feet if you like. But I call it sense. We reached our limit long ago. We began by rustling a few cattle—at a time when rustling was laughed at. But as our greed grew so did our boldness. Then came the gang, the regular trips, the one thing and another till, before we knew it—before *I* knew it—we had shady deals, holdups, and *murders* on our record. Then we *had* to go on. Too late to turn back!"

"I reckon we've all said that. None of the gang wants to quit. They all think, and I think, we can't be touched. We may be blamed, but nothing can be proved. We're too strong."

"There's where you're dead wrong," rejoined Longstreth, emphatically. "I imagined that once, not long ago. I was bullheaded. Who would ever connect Granger Longstreth with a rustler gang? I've changed my mind. I've begun to think. I've reasoned out things, We're crooked, and we can't last. It's the nature of life, even here, for conditions to grow better. The wise deal for us would be to divide equally and leave the country, all of us."

"But you and I have all the stock—all the gain," protested Lawson.

"I'll split mine."

"I won't—that settles that," added Lawson, instantly.

Longstreth spread wide his hands as if it was useless to try to convince this man. Talking had not increased his calmness, and he now showed more than impatience. A dull glint gleamed deep in his eyes.

"Your stock and property will last a long time—do you lots of good when this ranger— "

"Bah!" hoarsely croaked Lawson. The ranger's name was a match applied to powder. "Haven't I told you he'd be dead soon—any time—same as Laramie is?"

"Yes, you mentioned the—the supposition," replied Longstreth, sarcastically. "I inquired, too, just how that very desired event was to be brought about."

"The gang will lay him out."

"Bah!" retorted Longstreth, in turn. He laughed contemptuously.

"Floyd, don't be a fool. You've been on the border for ten years. You've packed a gun and you've used it. You've been with rustlers when they killed their men. You've been present at many fights. But you never in all that time saw a man like this ranger. You haven't got sense enough to see him right if you had a chance. Neither have any of you. The only way to get rid of him is for the gang to draw on him, all at once. Then he's going to drop some of them."

"Longstreth, you say that like a man who wouldn't care much if he did drop some of them," declared Lawson; and now he was sarcastic.

"To tell you the truth, I wouldn't," returned the other bluntly. "I'm pretty sick of this mess."

Lawson cursed in amazement. His emotions were all out of proportion to his intelligence. He was not at all quick-witted. Duane had never seen a vainer or more arrogant man.

"Longstreth, I don't like your talk," he said.

"If you don't like the way I talk you know what you can do," replied Longstreth, quickly. He stood up then, cool and quiet, with flash of eyes and set of lips that told Duane he was dangerous.

"Well, after all, that's neither here nor there," went on Lawson, unconsciously cowed by the other. "The thing is, do I get the girl?"

"Not by any means except her consent."

"You'll not make her marry me?"

"No. No," replied Longstreth, his voice still cold, low-pitched.

"All right. Then I'll make her."

Evidently Longstreth understood the man before him so well that he wasted no more words. Duane knew what Lawson never dreamed of, and that was that Longstreth had a gun somewhere within reach and meant to use it. Then heavy footsteps sounded outside tramping upon the porch. Duane might have been mistaken, but he believe those footsteps saved Lawson's life.

"There they are," said Lawson, and he opened the door.

Five masked men entered. They all wore coats hiding any weapons. A big man with burly shoulders shook hands with Longstreth, and the others stood back.

The atmosphere of that room had changed. Lawson might have been a nonentity for all he counted. Longstreth was another man—a stranger to Duane. If he had entertained a hope of freeing himself from this band, of getting away to a safer country, he abandoned it at the very sight of these men. There was power here, and he was bound.

The big man spoke in low, hoarse whispers, and at this all the others gathered around him close to the table. There were evidently some signs of membership not plain to Duane. Then all the heads were bent over the table. Low voices spoke, queried, answered, argued. By straining his ears Duane caught a word here and there. They were planning, and they were brief. Duane gathered they were to have a rendezvous at or near Ord.

Then the big man, who evidently was the leader of the present convention, got up to depart. He went as swiftly as he had come, and was followed by his comrades. Longstreth prepared for a quiet smoke. Lawson seemed uncommunicative and unsociable. He smoked fiercely and drank continually. All at once he straightened up as if listening.

"What's that?" he called suddenly.

Duane's strained ears were pervaded by a slight rustling sound.

"Must be a rat," replied Longstreth.

The rustle became a rattle.

"Sounds like a rattlesnake to me," said Lawson.

Longstreth got up from the table and peered round the room.

Just at the instant Duane felt an almost inappreciable movement of the adobe wall which supported him. He could scarcely credit his senses. But the rattle inside Longstreth's room was mingling with little dull thuds of falling dirt. The adobe wall, merely dried mud, was crumbling. Duane distinctly felt a tremor pass through it. Then the blood gushed back to his heart.

"What in the hell!" exclaimed Longstreth.

"I smell dust," said Lawson, sharply.

That was the signal for Duane to drop down from his perch, yet despite his care he made a noise.

"Did you hear a step?" queried Longstreth.

No one answered. But a heavy piece of the adobe wall fell with a thud. Duane heard it crack, felt it shake.

"There's somebody between the walls!" thundered Longstreth.

Then a section of the wall fell inward with a crash. Duane began to squeeze his body through the narrow passage toward the patio.

"Hear him!" yelled Lawson. "This side!"

"No, he's going that way," yelled Longstreth.

The tramp of heavy boots lent Duane the strength of desperation. He was not shirking a fight, but to be cornered like a trapped coyote was another matter. He almost tore his clothes off in that passage. The dust nearly stifled him. When he burst into the patio it was not a single instant too soon. But one deep gasp of breath revived him and he was up, gun in hand, running for the outlet into the court. Thumping footsteps turned him back. While there was a chance to get away he did not want to fight. He thought he heard some one running into the patio from the other end. He stole along, and coming to a door, without any idea of where it might lead, he softly pushed it open a little way and slipped in.

20

A low cry greeted Duane. The room was light. He saw Ray Longstreth sitting on her bed in her dressing-gown. With a warning gesture to her to be silent he turned to close the door. It was a heavy door without bolt or bar, and when Duane had shut it he felt safe only for the moment. Then he gazed around the room. There was one window with blind closely drawn. He listened and seemed to hear footsteps retreating, dying away.

Then Duane turned to Miss Longstreth. She had slipped off the bed, half to her knees, and was holding out trembling hands. She was as white as the pillow on her bed. She was terribly frightened. Again with warning hand commanding silence, Duane stepped softly forward, meaning to reassure her.

"Oh!" she whispered, wildly; and Duane thought she was going to faint. When he got close and looked into her eyes he understood the strange, dark expression in them. She was terrified because she believed he meant to kill her, or do worse, probably worse. Duane realized he must have looked pretty hard and fierce bursting into her room with that big gun in hand.

The way she searched Duane's face with doubtful, fearful eyes hurt him.

"Listen. I didn't know this was your room. I came here to get away—to save my life. I was pursued. I was spying on—on your father and his men. They heard me, but did not see me. They don't know who was listening. They're after me now."

Her eyes changed from blank gulfs to dilating, shadowing, quickening windows of thought.

Then she stood up and faced Duane with the fire and intelligence of a woman in her eyes.

"Tell me now. You were spying on my father?"

Briefly Duane told her what had happened before he entered her room, not omitting a terse word as to the character of the men he had watched.

"My God! So it's that? I knew something was terribly wrong here—with him—with the place—the people. And right off I hated Floyd Lawson. Oh, it 'll kill me if—if—It's so much worse than I dreamed. What shall I do?"

The sound of soft steps somewhere near distracted Duane's attention, reminded him of her peril, and now, what counted more with him, made clear the probability of being discovered in her room.

"I'll have to get out of here," whispered Duane.

"Wait," she replied. "Didn't you say they were hunting for you?"

"They sure are," he returned, grimly.

"Oh, then you mustn't go. They might shoot you before you got away. Stay. If we hear them you can hide. I'll turn out the light. I'll meet them at the door. You can trust me. Wait till all quiets down, if we have to wait till morning. Then you can slip out."

"I oughtn't to stay. I don't want to—I won't," Duane replied, perplexed and stubborn.

"But you must. It's the only safe way. They won't come here."

"Suppose they should? It's an even chance Longstreth 'll search every room and corner in this old house. If they found me here I couldn't start a fight. You might be hurt. Then—the fact of my being here—"

Duane did not finish what he meant, but instead made a step toward the door. White of face and dark of eye, she took hold of him to detain him. She was as strong and supple as a panther. But she need not have been either resolute or strong, for the clasp of her hand was enough to make Duane weak.

"Up yet, Ray?" came Longstreth's clear voice, too strained, too eager to be natural.

"No. I'm in bed reading. Good night," instantly replied Miss Longstreth, so calmly and naturally that Duane marveled at the difference between man and woman. Then she motioned for Duane to hide in the closet. He slipped in, but the door would not close altogether.

"Are you alone?" went on Longstreth's penetrating voice.

"Yes," she replied. "Ruth went to bed."

The door swung inward with a swift scrape and jar. Longstreth half entered, haggard, flaming-eyed. Behind him Duane saw Lawson, and indistinctly another man.

Longstreth barred Lawson from entering, which action showed control as well as distrust. He wanted to see into the room. When he had glanced around he went out and closed the door.

Then what seemed a long interval ensued. The house grew silent once more. Duane could not see Miss Longstreth, but he heard her quick breathing. How long did she mean to let him stay hidden there? Hard and perilous as his life had been, this was a new kind of adventure. He had divined the strange softness of his feeling as something due to the magnetism of this beautiful woman. It hardly seemed possible that he, who had been outside the pale for so many years, could have fallen in love. Yet that must be the secret of his agitation.

Presently he pushed open the closet door and stepped forth. Miss Longstreth had her head lowered upon her arms and appeared to be in distress. At his touch she raised a quivering face.

"I think I can go now—safely," he whispered.

"Go then, if you must, but you may stay till you're safe," she replied.

"I—I couldn't thank you enough. It's been hard on me—this finding out—and you his daughter. I feel strange. I don't understand myself well. But I want you to know—if I were not an outlaw—a ranger—I'd lay my life at your feet."

"Oh! You have seen so—so little of me," she faltered.

"All the same it's true. And that makes me feel more the trouble my coming caused you."

"You will not fight my father?"

"Not if I can help it. I'm trying to get out of his way."

"But you spied upon him."

"I am a ranger, Miss Longstreth."

"And oh! I am a rustler's daughter," she cried. "That's so much more terrible than I'd suspected. It was tricky cattle deals I imagined he was engaged in. But only to-night I had strong suspicions aroused."

"How? Tell me."

"I overheard Floyd say that men were coming to-night to arrange a meeting for my father at a rendezvous near Ord. Father did not want to go. Floyd taunted him with a name."

"What name?" queried Duane.

"It was Cheseldine."

"*Cheseldine!* My God! Miss Longstreth, why did *you* tell me that?"

"What difference does that make?"

"Your father and Cheseldine are one and the same," whispered Duane, hoarsely.

"I gathered so much myself," she replied, miserably. "But Longstreth is father's real name."

Duane felt so stunned he could not speak at once. It was the girl's part in this tragedy that weakened him. The instant she betrayed the secret Duane realized perfectly that he did love her. The emotion was like a great flood.

"Miss Longstreth, all this seems so unbelievable," he whispered. "Cheseldine is the rustler chief I've come out here to get. He's only a name. Your father is the real man. I've sworn to get him. I'm bound by more than law or oaths. I can't break what binds me. And I must disgrace you—wreck your life! Why, Miss Longstreth, I believe I—I love you. It's all come in a rush. I'd die for you if I could. How fatal—terrible—this is! How things work out!"

She slipped to her knees, with her hands on his.

"You won't kill him?" she implored. "If you care for me—you won't kill him?"

"No. That I promise you."

With a low moan she dropped her head upon the bed.

Duane opened the door and stealthily stole out through the corridor to the court.

When Duane got out into the dark, where his hot face cooled in the wind, his relief equaled his other feelings.

The night was dark, windy, stormy, yet there was no rain. Duane hoped as soon as he got clear of the ranch to lose something of the pain he felt. But long after he had tramped out into the open there was a lump in his throat and an ache in his breast. All his thought centered around Ray Longstreth. What a woman she had turned out to be! He seemed to have a vague, hopeless hope that there might be, there must be, some way he could save her.

21

BEFORE going to sleep that night Duane had decided to go to Ord and try to find the rendezvous where Longstreth was to meet his men. These men Duane wanted even more than their leader. If Longstreth, or Cheseldine, was the brains of that gang, Poggin was the executor. It was Poggin who needed to be found and stopped. Poggin and his right-hand men! Duane experienced a strange, tigerish thrill. It was thought of Poggin more than thought of success for MacNelly's plan. Duane felt dubious over this emotion.

Next day he set out for Bradford. He was glad to get away from Fairdale for a while. But the hours and the miles in no wise changed the new pain in his heart. The only way he could forget Miss Longstreth was to let his mind dwell upon Poggin, and even this was not always effective.

He avoided Sanderson, and at the end of the day and a half he arrived at Bradford.

The night of the day before he reached Bradford, No. 6, the mail and express train going east, was held up by train-robbers, the Wells-Fargo messenger killed over his safe, the mail-clerk wounded, the bags carried away. The engine of No. 6 came into town minus even a tender, and engineer and fireman told conflicting stories. A posse of railroad men and citizens, led by a sheriff Duane suspected was crooked, was made up before the engine steamed back to pick up the rest of the train. Duane had the sudden inspiration that he had been cudgeling his mind to find; and, acting upon it, he mounted his horse again and left Bradford unobserved. As he rode out into the night, over a dark trail in the direction of Ord, he uttered a short, grim, sardonic laugh at the hope that he might be taken for a train-robber.

He rode at an easy trot most of the night, and when the black peak of Ord Mountain loomed up against the stars he halted, tied his horse, and slept until dawn. He had brought a small pack, and now he took his time cooking breakfast. When the sun was well up he saddled Bullet, and, leaving the trail where his tracks showed plain in the ground, he put his horse to the rocks and brush. He selected an exceedingly rough, roundabout, and difficult course to Ord, hid his tracks with the skill of a long-hunted fugitive, and arrived there with his horse winded and covered with lather. It added considerable to his arrival that the man Duane remembered as Fletcher and several others saw him come in the back way through the lots and jump a fence into the road.

Duane led Bullet up to the porch where Fletcher stood wiping his beard. He was hatless, vestless, and evidently had just enjoyed a morning drink.

"Howdy, Dodge," said Fletcher, laconically.

Duane replied, and the other man returned the greeting with interest.

"Jim, my hoss's done up. I want to hide him from any chance tourists as might happen to ride up curious-like."

"Haw! haw! haw!"

Duane gathered encouragement from that chorus of coarse laughter.

"Wal, if them tourists ain't too durned snooky the hoss 'll be safe in the 'dobe shack back of Bill's here. Feed thar, too, but you'll hev to rustle water."

Duane led Bullet to the place indicated, had care of his welfare, and left him there. Upon returning to the tavern porch Duane saw the group of men had been added to by others, some of whom he had seen before. Without comment Duane walked along the edge of the road, and wherever one of the tracks of his horse showed he carefully obliterated it. This procedure was attentively watched by Fletcher and his companions.

"Wal, Dodge," remarked Fletcher, as Duane returned, "thet's safer 'n prayin' fer rain."

Duane's reply was a remark as loquacious as Fletcher's, to the effect that a long, slow, monotonous ride was conducive to thirst. They all joined him, unmistakably friendly. But Knell was not there, and most assuredly not Poggin. Fletcher was no common outlaw, but, whatever his ability, it probably lay in execution of orders. Apparently at that time these men had nothing to do but drink and lounge around the tavern. Evidently they were poorly supplied with money, though Duane observed they could borrow a peso occasionally from the bartender. Duane set out to make himself agreeable and succeeded. There was card-playing for small stakes, idle jests of coarse nature, much bantering among the younger fellows, and occasionally a mild quarrel. All morning men came and went, until, all told, Duane calculated he had seen at least fifty. Toward the middle of the afternoon a young fellow burst into the saloon and yelled one word:

"Posse!"

From the scramble to get outdoors Duane judged that word and the ensuing action was rare in Ord.

"What the hell! muttered Fletcher, as he gazed down the road at a dark, compact bunch of horses and riders. "Fust time I ever seen thet in Ord! We're gettin' popular like them camps out of Valentine. Wish Phil was here or Poggy. Now all you gents keep quiet. I'll do the talkin'."

The posse entered the town, trotted up on dusty horses, and halted in a bunch before the tavern. The party consisted of about twenty men, all heavily armed, and evidently in charge of a clean-cut, lean-limbed cowboy. Duane experienced considerable satisfaction at the absence of the sheriff who he had understood was to lead the posse. Perhaps he was out in another direction with a different force.

"Hello, Jim Fletcher," called the cowboy.

"Howdy," replied Fletcher.

At his short, dry response and the way he strode leisurely out before the posse Duane found himself modifying his contempt for Fletcher. The outlaw was different now.

"Fletcher, we've tracked a man to all but three miles of this place. Tracks as plain as the nose on your face. Found his camp. Then he hit into the brush, an' we lost the trail. Didn't have no tracker with us. Think he went into the mountains. But we took a chance an' rid over the rest of the way, seein' Ord was so close. Anybody come in here late last night or early this mornin'?"

"Nope," replied Fletcher.

His response was what Duane had expected from his manner, and evidently the cowboy took it as a matter of course. He turned to the others of the posse, entering into a low consultation. Evidently there was difference of opinion, if not real dissension, in that posse.

"Didn't I tell ye this was a wild-goose chase, comin' way out here?" protested an old hawk-faced rancher. "Them hoss tracks we follored ain't like any of them we seen at the water-tank where the train was held up."

"I'm not so sure of that," replied the leader.

"Wal, Guthrie, I've follored tracks all my life—"

"But you couldn't keep to the trail this feller made in the brush."

"Gimme time, an' I could. Thet takes time. An' heah you go hell-bent fer election! But it's a wrong lead out this way. If you're right this road-agent, after he killed his pals, would hev rid back right through town. An' with them mail-bags! Supposin' they was greasers? Some greasers has sense, an' when it comes to thievin' they're shore cute."

"But we aint got any reason to believe this robber who murdered the greasers is a greaser himself. I tell you it was a slick job done by no ordinary sneak. Didn't you hear the facts? One greaser hopped the engine an' covered the engineer an' fireman. Another greaser kept flashin' his gun outside the train. The big man who shoved back the car-door an' did the killin'—he was the real gent, an' don't you forget it."

Some of the posse sided with the cowboy leader and some with the old cattleman. Finally the young leader disgustedly gathered up his bridle.

"Aw, hell! Thet sheriff shoved you off this trail. Mebbe he hed reason! Savvy thet? If I hed a bunch of cowboys with me—I tell you what—I'd take a chance an' clean up this hole!"

All the while Jim Fletcher stood quietly with his hands in his pockets.

"Guthrie, I'm shore treasurin' up your friendly talk," he said. The menace was in the tone, not the content of his speech.

"You can—an' be damned to you, Fletcher!" called Guthrie, as the horses started.

Fletcher, standing out alone before the others of his clan, watched the posse out of sight.

"Luck fer you-all thet Poggy wasn't here," he said, as they disappeared. Then with a thoughtful mien he strode up on the porch and led Duane away from the others into the bar-room. When he looked into Duane's face it was somehow an entirely changed scrutiny.

"Dodge, where'd you hide the stuff? I reckon I git in on this deal, seein' I staved off Guthrie."

Duane played his part. Here was his opportunity, and like a tiger after prey he seized it. First he coolly eyed the outlaw and then disclaimed any knowledge whatever of the train-robbery other than Fletcher had heard himself. Then at Fletcher's persistence and admiration and increasing show of friendliness he laughed occasionally and allowed himself to swell with pride, though still denying. Next he feigned a lack of consistent will-power and seemed to be wavering under Fletcher's persuasion and grew silent, then surly. Fletcher, evidently sure of ultimate victory, desisted for the time being; however, in his solicitous regard and close companionship for the rest of that day he betrayed the bent of his mind.

Later, when Duane started up announcing his intention to get his horse and make for camp out in the brush, Fletcher seemed grievously offended.

"Why don't you stay with me? I've got a comfortable 'dobe over here. Didn't I stick by you when Guthrie an' his bunch come up? Supposin' I hedn't showed down a cold hand to him? You'd be swingin' somewheres now. I tell you, Dodge, it ain't square."

"I'll square it. I pay my debts," replied Duane. "But I can't put up here all night. If I belonged to the gang it 'd be different."

"What gang?" asked Fletcher, bluntly.

"Why, Cheseldine's."

Fletcher's beard nodded as his jaw dropped.

Duane laughed. "I run into him the other day. Knowed him on sight. Sure, he's the king-pin rustler. When he seen me an' asked me what reason I had for bein' on earth or some such like—why, I up an' told him."

Fletcher appeared staggered.

"Who in all-fired hell air you talkin' about?"

"Didn't I tell you once? Cheseldine. He calls himself Longstreth over there."

All of Fletcher's face not covered by hair turned a dirty white.

"Cheseldine—Longstreth!" he whispered, hoarsely. "Gord Almighty! You braced the—" Then a remarkable transformation came over the outlaw. He gulped; he straightened his face; he controlled his agitation. But he could not send the healthy brown back to his face. Duane, watching this rude man, marveled at the change in him, the sudden checking movement, the proof of a wonderful fear and loyalty. It all meant Cheseldine, a master of men!

"*Who air you?*" queried Fletcher, in a queer, strained voice.

"You gave me a handle, didn't you? Dodge. Thet's as good as any. Shore it hits me hard. Jim, I've been pretty lonely for years, an' I'm gettin' in need of pals. Think it over, will you? See you *mañana*."

The outlaw watched Duane go off after his horse, watched him as he returned to the tavern, watched him ride out into the darkness—all without a word.

Duane left the town, threaded a quiet passage through cactus and mesquite to a spot he had marked before, and made ready for the night. His mind was so full that he found sleep aloof. Luck at last was playing his game. He sensed the first slow heave of a mighty crisis. The end, always haunting, had to be sternly blotted from thought. It was the approach that needed all his mind.

He passed the night there, and late in the morning, after watching trail and road from a ridge, he returned to Ord. If Jim Fletcher tried to disguise his surprise the effort was a failure. Certainly he had not expected to see Duane again. Duane allowed himself a little freedom with Fletcher, an attitude hitherto lacking.

That afternoon a horseman rode in from Bradford, an outlaw evidently well known and liked by his fellows, and Duane beard him say, before he could possibly have been told the train-robber was in Ord, that the loss of money in the holdup was slight. Like a flash Duane saw the luck of this report. He pretended not to have heard.

In the early twilight at an opportune moment he called Fletcher to him, and, linking his arm within the outlaw's, he drew him off in a stroll to a log bridge spanning a little gully. Here after gazing around, he took out a roll of bills, spread it out, split it equally, and without a word handed one half to Fletcher. With clumsy fingers Fletcher ran through the roll.

"Five hundred!" he exclaimed. "Dodge, thet's damn handsome of you, considerin' the job wasn't—"

"Considerin' nothin'," interrupted Duane. "I'm makin' no reference to a job here or there. You did me a good turn. I split my pile. If thet doesn't make us pards, good turns an' money ain't no use in this country."

Fletcher was won.

The two men spent much time together. Duane made up a short fictitious history about himself that satisfied the outlaw, only it drew forth a laughing jest upon Duane's modesty. For Fletcher did not hide his belief that this new partner was a man of achievements. Knell and Poggin, and then Cheseldine himself, would be persuaded of this fact, so Fletcher boasted. He had influence. He would use it. He thought he pulled a stroke with Knell. But nobody on earth, not even the boss, had any influence on Poggin. Poggin was concentrated ice part of the time; all the rest he was bursting hell. But Poggin loved a horse. He never loved anything else. He could be won with that black horse Bullet. Cheseldine was already won by Duane's monumental nerve; otherwise he would have killed Duane.

Little by little the next few days Duane learned the points he longed to know; and how indelibly they etched themselves in his memory! Cheseldine's hiding-place was on the far slope of Mount Ord, in a deep, high-walled valley. He always went there just before a contemplated job, where he met and planned with his lieutenants. Then while they executed he basked in the sunshine before one or another of the public places he owned. He was there in the Ord den now, getting ready to plan the biggest job yet. It was a bank-robbery; but where, Fletcher had not as yet been advised.

Then when Duane had pumped the now amenable outlaw of all details pertaining to the present he gathered data and facts and places covering a period of ten years Fletcher had been with Cheseldine. And herewith was unfolded a history so dark in its bloody régime, so incredible in its brazen daring, so appalling in its proof of the outlaw's sweep and grasp of the country from Pecos to Rio Grande, that Duane was stunned. Compared to this Cheseldine of the Big Bend, to this rancher, stock-buyer, cattle-speculator, property-holder, all the outlaws Duane had ever known sank into insignificance. The power of the man stunned Duane; the strange fidelity given him stunned Duane; the intricate inside working of his great system was equally stunning. But when Duane recovered from that the old terrible passion to kill consumed him, and it raged fiercely and it could not be checked. If that red-handed Poggin, if that cold-eyed, dead-faced Knell had only been at Ord! But they were not, and Duane with help of time got what he hoped was the upper hand of himself.

22

AGAIN inaction and suspense dragged at Duane's spirit. Like a leashed hound with a keen scent in his face Duane wanted to leap forth when he was bound. He almost fretted. Something called to him over the bold, wild brow of Mount Ord. But while Fletcher stayed in Ord waiting for Knell and Poggin, or for orders, Duane knew his game was again a waiting one.

But one day there were signs of the long quiet of Ord being broken. A messenger strange to Duane rode in on a secret mission that had to do with Fletcher. When he went away Fletcher became addicted to thoughtful moods and lonely walks. He seldom drank, and this in itself was a striking contrast to former behavior. The messenger came again. Whatever communication he brought, it had a remarkable effect upon the outlaw. Duane was present in the tavern when the fellow arrived, saw the few words whispered, but did not hear them. Fletcher turned white with anger or fear, perhaps both, and he cursed like a madman. The messenger, a lean, dark-faced, hard-riding fellow reminding Duane of the cowboy Guthrie, left the tavern without even a drink and rode away off to the west. This west mystified and fascinated Duane as much as the south beyond Mount Ord. Where were Knell and Poggin? Apparently they were not at present with the leader on the mountain. After the messenger left Fletcher grew silent and surly. He had presented a variety of moods to Duane's obser-vation, and this latest one was provocative of thought. Fletcher was dangerous.

It became clear now that the other outlaws of the camp feared him, kept out of his way. Duane let him alone, yet closely watched him.

Perhaps an hour after the messenger had left, not longer, Fletcher manifestly arrived at some decision, and he called for his horse. Then he went to his shack and returned. To Duane the outlaw looked in shape both to ride and to fight. He gave orders for the men in camp to keep close until he returned. Then he mounted.

"Come here, Dodge," he called.

Duane went up and laid a hand on the pommel of the saddle. Fletcher walked his horse, with Duane beside him, till they reached the log bridge, when he halted.

"Dodge, I'm in bad with Knell," he said. "An' it 'pears I'm the cause of friction between Knell an' Poggy. Knell never had any use fer me, but Poggy's been square, if not friendly. The boss has a big deal on, an' here it's been held up because of this scrap. He's waitin' over there on the mountain to give orders to Knell or Poggy, an' neither one's showin' up. I've got to stand in the breach, an' I ain't enjoyin' the prospects."

"What's the trouble about, Jim?" asked Duane.

"Reckon it's a little about you, Dodge," said Fletcher, dryly. "Knell hadn't any use fer you thet day. He ain't got no use fer a man onless he can rule him. Some of the boys here hev blabbed before I edged in with my say, an' there's hell to pay. Knell claims to know somethin' about you that'll make both the boss an' Poggy sick when he springs it. But he's keepin' quiet. Hard man to figger, thet Knell. Reckon you'd better go back to Bradford fer a day or so, then camp out near here till I come back."

"Why?"

"Wal, because there ain't any use fer you to git in bad, too. The gang will ride over here any day. If they're friendly I'll light a fire on the hill there, say three nights from to-night. If you don't see it thet night you hit the trail. I'll do what I can. Jim Fletcher sticks to his pals. So long, Dodge."

Then he rode away.

He left Duane in a quandary. This news was black. Things had been working out so well. Here was a setback. At the moment Duane did not know which way to turn, but certainly he had no idea of going back to Bradford. Friction between the two great lieutenants of Cheseldine! Open hostility between one of them and another of the chief's right-hand men! Among outlaws that sort of thing was deadly serious. Generally such matters were settled with guns. Duane gathered encouragement even from disaster. Perhaps the disintegration of Cheseldine's great band had already begun. But what did Knell know? Duane did not circle around the idea with doubts and hopes; if Knell knew anything it was that this stranger in Ord, this new partner of Fletcher's, was no less than Buck Duane.

Well, it was about time, thought Duane, that he made use of his name if it were to help him at all. That name had been MacNelly's hope. He had anchored all his scheme to Duane's fame. Duane was tempted to ride off after Fletcher and stay with him. This, however, would hardly be fair to an outlaw who had been fair to him. Duane concluded to await developments and when the gang rode in to Ord, probably from their various hiding-places, he would be there ready to be denounced by Knell. Duane could not see any other culmination of this series of events than a meeting between Knell and himself. If that terminated fatally for Knell there was all probability of Duane's being in no worse situation than he was now. If Poggin took up the quarrel! Here Duane accused himself again—tried in vain to revolt from a judgment that he was only reasoning out excuses to meet these outlaws.

Meanwhile, instead of waiting, why not hunt up Cheseldine in his mountain retreat? The thought no sooner struck Duane than he was hurrying for his horse.

He left Ord, ostensibly toward Bradford, but, once out of sight, he turned off the road, circled through the brush, and several miles south of town he struck a narrow grass-grown trail that Fletcher had told him led to Cheseldine's camp. The horse tracks along this trail were not less than a week old, and very likely much more. It would between low, brush-covered foothills, through arroyos and gullies lined with mesquite, cottonwood, and scrub-oak.

In an hour Duane struck the slope of Mount Ord, and as he climbed he got a view of the rolling, black-spotted country, partly desert, partly fertile, with long, bright lines of dry streambeds winding away to grow dim in the distance. He got among broken rocks and cliffs, and here the open, downward-rolling land disappeared, and he was hard put to it to find the trail. He lost it repeatedly and made slow progress. Fianlly he climbed into a region of all rock benches, rough here, smooth there, with only an occasional scrath of iron horseshoe to guide him. Many times he had to go ahead and then work to right or left till he found his way again. It was slow work; it took all day; and night found him half-way up the mountain. He halted at a little side-cañon with grass and water, and here he made camp. The night was clear and cool at that height, with a dark-blue sky and a streak of stars blinking across. With this day of action behind him he felt better satisfied than he had been for some time. Here, on this venture, he was answering to a call that had so often directed his movements, perhaps his life, and it was one that logic or intelligence could take little stock of. And on this night, lonely like the ones he used to spend in the Nueces gorge, and memorable of them because of a likeness to that old hiding-place, he felt the pressing return of old haunting things—the past so long ago, wild flights, dead faces—and the places of these were taken by one quiveringly alive, white, tragic, with its dark, intent, speaking eyes—Ray Longstreth's.

That last memory he yielded to until he slept.

In the morning, satisfied that he had left still fewer tracks than he had followed up this trail, he led his horse up to the head of the cañon, there a narrow crack in low cliffs, and with branches of cedar fenced him in. Then he went back and took up the trail on foot.

Without the horse he made better time and climbed through deep clefts, wide cañons, over ridges, up shelving slopes, along precipices—a long, hard climb— till he reached what he concluded was a divide. Going down was easier, though the farther he followed this dim and winding trail the wider the broken battlements of rock. Above him he saw the black fringe of the piñon and pine, and above that the bold peak, bare, yellow, like a desert butte. Once, through a wide gateway between great escarpments, he saw the lower country beyond the range, and beyond this, vast and clear as it lay in his sight, was the great river that made the Big Bend. He went down and down, wondering how a horse could follow that broken trail, believing there must be another better one somewhere into Cheseldine's hiding-place.

He rounded a jutting corner, where view had been shut off, and presently came out upon the rim of a high wall. Beneath, like a green gulf seen through blue haze, lay an amphitheater walled in on the two sides he could see. It lay perhaps a thousand feet below him; and, plain as all the other features of that wild environment, there shone out a big red stone or adobe cabin, white water shining away between great borders, and horses and cattle dotting the levels. It was a peaceful, beautiful scene. Duane could not help grinding his teeth at the thought of rustlers living there in quiet and ease.

Duane worked half-way down to the level, and, well hidden in a niche, he settled himself to watch both trail and valley. He made note of the position of the sun and saw that if anything developed or if he decided to descend any farther there was small likelihood of his getting back to his camp before dark. To try that after nightfall he imagined would be vain effort.

Then he bent his keen eyes downward. The cabin appeared to be a crude structure. Though large in size, it had, of course, been built by outlaws.

There was no garden, no cultivated field, no corral. Excepting for the rude pile of stones and logs plastered together with mud, the valley was as wild, probably, as on the day of discovery. Duane seemed to have been watching for a long time before he saw any sign of man, and this one apparently went to the stream for water and returned to the cabin.

The sun went down behind the wall, and shadows were born in the darker places of the valley. Duane began to want to get closer to that cabin. What had he taken this arduous climb for? He held back, however, trying to evolve further plans.

While he was pondering the shadows quickly gathered and darkened. If he was to go back to camp he must set out at once. Still he lingered. And suddenly his wide-roving eye caught sight of two horsemen riding up the valley. They must have entered at a point below, round the huge abutment of rock, beyond Duane's range of sight. Their horses were tired and stopped at the stream for a long drink.

Duane left his perch, took to the steep trail, and descended as fast as he could without making noise. It did not take him long to reach the valley floor. It was almost level, with deep grass, and here and there clumps of bushes. Twilight was already thick down there. Duane marked the location of the trail, and then began to slip like a shadow through the grass and from bush to bush. He saw a bright light before he made out the dark outline of the cabin. Then he heard voices, a merry whistle, a coarse song, and the clink of iron cooking-utensils. He smelled fragrant wood-smoke. He saw moving dark figures cross the light. Evidently there was a wide door, or else the fire was out in the open.

Duane swerved to the left, out of direct line with the light, and thus was able to see better. Then he advanced noiselessly but swiftly toward the back of the house. There were trees close to the wall. He would make no noise, and he could scarcely be seen—if only there was no watch-dog! But all his outlaw days he had taken risks with only his useless life at stake; now, with that changed, he advanced stealthy and bold as an Indian. He reached the cover of the trees, knew he was hidden in their shadows, for at few paces' distance he had been able to see only their tops. From there he slipped up to the house and felt along the wall with his hands.

He came to a little window where light shone through. He peeped in. He saw a room shrouded in shadows, a lamp turned low, a table, chairs. He saw an open door, with bright flare beyond, but could not see the fire. Voices came indistinctly. Without hesitation Duane stole farther along—all the way to the end of the cabin. Peeping round, he saw only the flare of light on bare ground. Retracing his cautious steps, he paused at the crack again, saw that no man was in the room, and then he went on round that end of the cabin. Fortune favored him. There were bushes, an old shed, a wood-pile, all the cover he needed at that corner. He did not even need to crawl.

Before he peered between the rough corner of wall and the bush growing close to it Duane paused a moment. This excitement was different from that he had always felt when pursued. It had no bitterness, no pain, no dread. There was as much danger here, perhaps more, yet it was not the same. Then he looked.

He saw a bright fire, a red-faced man bending over it, whistling, while he handled a steaming pot. Over him was a roofed shed built against the wall, with two open sides and two supporting posts. Duane's second glance, not so blinded by the sudden bright light, made out other men, three in the shadow, two in the flare, but with backs to him.

"It's a smoother trail by long odds, but ain't so short as this one right over the mountain," one outlaw was saying.

"What's eatin' you, Panhandle?" ejaculated another. "Blossom an' me rode from Faraway Springs, where Poggin is with some of the gang."

"Excuse me, Phil. Shore I didn't see you come in, an' Boldt never said nothing'."

"It took you a long time to get here, but I guess that's just as well," spoke up a smooth, suave voice with a ring in it.

Longstreth's voice—Cheseldine's voice!

Here they were—Cheseldine, Phil Knell, Blossom Kane, Panhandle Smith, Boldt—how well Duane remembered the names!—all here, the big men of Cheseldine's gang, except the biggest—Poggin. Duane had holed them, and his sensations of the moment deadened sight and sound of what was before him. He sank down, controlled himself, silenced a mounting exultation, then from a less-strained position he peered forth again.

The outlaws were waiting for supper. Their conversation might have been that of cowboys in camp, ranchers at a roundup. Duane listened with eager ears, waiting for the business talk that he felt would come. All the time he watched with the eyes of a wolf upon its quarry. Blossom Kane was the lean-limbed messenger who had so angered Fletcher. Boldt was a giant in stature, dark, bearded, silent. Panhandle Smith was the red-faced cook, merry, profane, a short, bow-legged man resembling many rustlers Duane had known, particularly Luke Stevens. And Knell, who sat there, tall, slim, like a boy in build, like a boy in years, with his pale, smooth, expressionless face and his cold, gray eyes. And Longstreth, who leaned against the wall, handsome, with his dark face and beard like an aristocrat, resembled many a rich Louisiana planter Duane had met. The sixth man sat so much in the shadow that he could not be plainly discerned, and though addressed, his name was not mentioned.

Panhandle Smith carried pots and pans into the cabin, and cheerfully called out: "If you gents air hungry fer grub, don't look fer me to feed you with a spoon."

The outlaws piled inside, made a great bustle and clatter as they sat to their meal. Like hungry men, they talked little.

Duane waited there awhile, then guardedly got up and crept round to the other side of the cabin. After he became used to the dark again he ventured to steal along the wall to the window and peeped in. The outlaws were in the first room and could not be seen.

Duane waited. The moments dragged endlessly. His heart pounded. Longstreth entered, turned up the light, and, taking a box of cigars from the table, he carried it out.

"Here, you fellows, go outside and smoke," he said. "Knell, come on in now. Let's get it over."

He returned, sat down, and lighted a cigar for himself. He put his booted feet on the table.

Duane saw that the room was comfortably, even luxuriously furnished. There must have been a good trail, he thought, else how could all that stuff have been packed in there. Most assuredly it could not have come over the trail he had traveled. Presently he heard the men go outside, and their voices became indistinct. Then Knell came in and seated himself without any of his chief's ease. He seemed preoccupied and, as always, cold.

"What's wrong, Knell? Why didn't you get here sooner?" queried Longstreth.

"Poggin, damn him! We're on the outs again."

"What for?"

"Aw, he needn't have got sore. He's breakin' a new hoss over there at Faraway, an you know him where a hoss's concerned. That kept him, I reckon, more than anythin'."

"What else? Get it out of your system so we can go on to the new job."

"Well, it begins back a ways. I don't know how long ago—weeks—a stranger rode into Ord an' got down easy-like as if he owned the place. He seemed familiar to me. But I wasn't sure. We looked him over, an' I left, tryin' to place him in my mind."

"What'd he look like?"

"Rangy, powerful man, white hair over his temples, still, hard face, eyes like knives. The way he packed his guns, the way he walked an' stood an' swung his right hand showed me what he was. You can't fool me on the gun-sharp. An' he had a grand horse, a big black."

"I've met your man," said Longstreth.

"No!" exclaimed Knell. It was wonderful to hear surprise expressed by this man that did not in the least show it in his strange physiognomy. Knell laughed a short, grim, hollow laugh. "Boss, this here big gent drifts into Ord again an' makes up to Jim Fletcher. Jim, you know, is easy led. He likes men. An' when a posse come along trailin' a blind lead, huntin' the wrong way for the man who held up No. 6, why, Jim—he up an' takes this stranger to be the fly road-agent an' cottons to him. Got money out of him sure. An' that's what stumps me more. What's this man's game? I happen to know, boss, that he couldn't have held up No. 6."

"How do you know?" demanded Longstreth.

"Because I did the job myself."

A dark and stormy passion clouded the chief's face.

"Damn you, Knell! You're incorrigible. You're unreliable. Another break like that queers you with me. Did you tell Poggin?"

"Yes. That's one reason we fell out. He raved. I thought he was goin' to kill me."

"Why did you tackle such a risky job without help or plan?"

"It offered, that's all. An' it was easy. But it was a mistake. I got the country an' the railroad hollerin' for nothin'. I just couldn't help it. You know what idleness means to one of us. You know also that this very life breeds fatality. It's wrong—that's why. I was born of good parents, an' I know what's right. We're wrong, an' we can't beat the end, that's all. An' for my part I don't care a damn when that comes."

"Fine wise talk from you, Knell," said Longstreth, scronfully. "Go on with your story."

"As I said, Jim cottons to the pretender, an' they get chummy. They're together all the time. You can gamble Jim told all he knew an' then some. A little liquor loosens his tongue. Several of the boys rode over from Ord, an' one of them went to Poggin an' says Jim Fletcher has a new man for the gang. Poggin, you know, is always ready for any new man. He says if one doesn't turn out good he can be shut off easy. He rather liked the way this new pard of Jim's was boosted. Jim an' Poggin always hit it up together. So until I got on the deal Jim's pard was already in the gang, withou Poggin or you ever seein' him. Then I got to figurin' hard. Just where had I ever seen that chap? As it turned out, I never had seen him, which accounts for my bein' doubtful. I'd never forget any man I'd seen. I dug up a lot of old papers from my kit an' went over them. Letters, pictures, clippin's, an' all that. I guess I had a pretty good notion what I was lookin' for an' who I wanted to make sure of. At last I found it. An' I knew my man. But I didn't spring it on Poggin. Oh no! I want to have some fun with him when the time comes. He'll be wilder than a trapped wolf. I sent Blossom over to Ord to get word from Jim, an' when he verified all this talk I sent Blossom again with a message calculated to make Jim hump. Poggin got sore, said he'd wait for Jim, an' I could come over here to see you about the new job. He'd meet me in Ord."

Knell had spoken hurriedly and low, now and then with passion. His pale eyes glinted like fire in ice, and now his voice fell to a whisper.

"Who do you think Fletcher's new man is?"

"Who?" demanded Longstreth.

"*Buck Duane!*"

Down came Longstreth's boots with a crash, then his body grew rigid.

"That Nueces outlaw? That two-shot ace-of-spades gunthrower who killed Bland, Alloway—?"

"An' Hardin." Knell whispered this last name with more feeling than the apparent circumstance demanded.

"Yes; and Hardin, the best one of the Rim Rock fellows—Buck Duane!"

Longstreth was so ghastly white now that his black mustache seemed outlined against chalk. He eyed his grim lieutenant. They understood each other without more words. It was enough that Buck Duane was there in the Big Bend. Longstreth rose presently and reached for a flask, from which he drank, then offered it to Knell. He waved it aside.

"Knell," began the chief, slowly, as he wiped his lips, "I gathered you have some grudge against this Buck Duane."

"Yes."

"Well, don't be a——fool now and do what Poggin or almost any of you men would—don't meet this Buck Duane. I've reason to believe he's a Texas Ranger now."

"The hell you say!" exclaimed Knell.

"Yes. Go to Ord and give Jim Fletcher a hunch. He'll get Poggin, and they'll fix even Buck Duane."

"All right. I'll do my best. But if I run into Duane—"

"Don't run into him!" Longstreth's voice fairly rang with the force of its passion and command. He wiped his face, drank again from the flask, sat down, resumed his smoking, and, drawing a paper from his vest pocket he began to study it.

"Well, I'm glad that's settled," he said, evidently referring to the Duane matter. "Now for the new job. This is October the eighteenth. On or before the twenty-fifth there will be a shipment of gold reach the Rancher's Bank of Val Verde. After you return to Ord give Poggin these orders. Keep the gang quiet. You, Poggin, Kane, Fletcher, Panhandle Smith, and Boldt to be in on the secret and the job. Nobody else. You'll leave Ord on the twenty-third, ride across country by the trail till you get within sight of Mercer. It's a hundred miles from Bradford to Val Verde—about the same from Ord. Time your travel to get you near Val Verde on the morning of the twenty-sixth. You won't have to more than trot your horses. At two o'clock in the afternoon, sharp, ride into town and up to the Rancher's Bank. Val Verde's a pretty big town. Never been any holdups there. Town feels safe. Make it a clean, fast, daylight job. That's all. Have you got the details?"

Knell did not even ask for the dates again.

"Suppose Poggin or me might be detained?" he asked

Longstreth bent a dark glance upon his lieutenant.

"You never can tell what'll come off," continued Knell. "I'll do my best."

"The minute you see Poggin tell him. A job on hand steadies him. And I say again—look to it that nothing happens. Either you or Poggin carry the job through. But I want both of you in it. Break for the hills, and when you get up in the rocks where you can hide your tracks head for Mount Ord. When all's quiet again I'll join you here. That's all. Call in the boys."

Like a swift shadow and as noiseless Duane stole across the level toward the dark wall of rock. Every nerve was a strung wire. For a little while his mind was cluttered and clogged with whirling thoughts, from which, like a flashing scroll, unrolled the long, baffling order of action. The game was now in his hands. He must cross Mount Ord at night. The feat was improbable, but it might be done. He must ride into Bradford, forty miles from the foothills before eight o'clock next morning. He must telegraph MacNelly to be in Val Verde on the twenty-fifth. He must ride back to Ord, to intercept Knell, face him, be denounced, kill him, and while the iron was hot strike hard to win Poggin's half-won interest as he had wholly won Fletcher's. Failing that last, he must let the outlaws alone to bide their time in Ord, to be free to ride on to their new job in Val Verde. In the mean time he must plan to arrest Longstreth. It was a magnificent outline, incredible, alluring, unfathomable in its nameless certainty. He felt like fate. He seemed to be the iron consequences falling upon these doomed outlaws.

Under the wall the shadows were black, only the tips of trees and crags showing, yet he went straight to the trail. It was merely a grayness between borders of black. He climbed and never stopped. It did not seem steep. His feet might have had eyes. He surmounted the wall, and, looking down into the ebony gulf pierced by one point of light, he lifted a menacing arm and shook it. Then he strode on and did not falter till he reached the huge shelving cliffs. Here he lost the trail; there was none; but he remembered the shapes, the points, the notches of rock above. Before he reached the ruins of splintered ramparts and jumbles of broken walls the moon topped the eastern slope of the mountain, and the mystifying blackness he had dreaded changed to magic silver light. It seemed as light as day, only soft, mellow, and the air held a transparent sheen. He ran up the bare ridges and down the smooth slopes, and, like a goat, jumped from rock to rock. In this light he knew his way and lost no time looking for a trail. He crossed the divide and then had all downhill before him. Swiftly he descended, almost always sure of his memory of the landmarks. He did not remember having studied them in the ascent, yet here they were, even in changed light, familiar to his sight. What he had once seen was pictured on his mind. And, true as a deer striking for home, he reached the cañon where he had left his horse.

Bullet was quickly and easily found. Duane threw on the saddle and pack, cinched them tight, and resumed his descent. The worst was now to come. Bare downward steps in rock, sliding, weathered slopes, narrow black gullies, a thousand openings in a maze of broken stone—these Duane had to descend in fast time, leading a giant of a horse. Bullet cracked the loose fragments, sent them rolling, slid on the scaly slopes, plunged down the steps, followed like a faithful dog at Duane's heels.

Hours passed as moments. Duane was equal to his great opportunity. But he could not quell that self in him which reached back over the lapse of lonely, searing years and found the boy in him. He who had been worse than dead was now grasping at the skirts of life—which meant victory, honor, happiness. Duane knew he was not just right in part of his mind. Small wonder that he was not insane, he thought! He tramped on downward, his marvelous faculty for covering rough ground and holding to the true course never before even in flight so keen and acute. Yet all the time a spirit was keeping step with him. Thought of Ray Longstreth as he had left her made him weak. But now, with the game clear to its end, with the trap to spring, with success strangely haunting him, Duane could not dispel memory of her. He saw her white face, with its sweet sad lips and the dark eyes so tender and tragic. And time and distance and risk and toil were nothing.

The moon sloped to the west. Shadows of trees and crags now crossed to the other side of him. The stars dimmed. Then he was out of the rocks, with the dim trail pale at his feet. Mounting Bullet, he made short work of the long slope and the foothills and the rolling land leading down to Ord. The little outlaw camp, with its shacks and cabins and row of houses, lay silent and dark under the paling moon. Duane passed by on the lower trail, headed into the road, and put Bullet to a gallop. He watched the dying moon, the waning stars, and the east. He had time to spare, so he saved the horse. Knell would be leaving the rendezvous about the time Duane turned back toward Ord. Between noon and sunset they would meet.

The night wore on. The moon sank behind low mountains in the west. The stars brightened for a while, then faded. Gray gloom enveloped the world, thickened, lay like smoke over the road. Then shade by shade it lightened, until through the transparent obscurity shone a dim light.

Duane reached Bradford before dawn. He dismounted some distance from the tracks, tied his horse, and then crossed over to the station. He heard the clicking of the telegraph instrument, and it thrilled him. An operator sat inside reading. When Duane tapped on the widow he looked up with startled glance, then went swiftly to unlook the door.

"Hello. Give me paper and pencil. Quick," whispered Duane.

With trembling hands the operator complied. Duane wrote out the message he had carefully composed.

"Send this—repeat it to make sure—then keep mum. I'll see you again. Good-by."

The operator stared, but did not speak a word.

Duane left as stealthily and swiftly as he had come. He walked his horse a couple miles back on the road and then rested him till break of day. The east began to redden, Duane turned grimly in the direction of Ord.

When Duane swung into the wide, grassy square on the outskirts of Ord he saw a bunch of saddled horses hitched in front of the tavern. He knew what that meant. Luck still favored him. If it would only hold! But he could ask no more. The rest was a matter of how greatly he could make his power felt. An open conflict against odds lay in the balance. That would be fatal to him, and to avoid it he had to trust to his name and a presence he must make terrible. He knew outlaws. He knew what qualities held them. He knew what to exaggerate.

There was not an outlaw in sight. The dusty horses had covered distance that morning. As Duane dismounted he heard loud, angry voices inside the tavern. He removed coat and vest, hung them over the pommel. He packed two guns, one belted high on the left hip, the other swinging low on the right side. He neither looked nor listened, but boldly pushed the door and stepped inside.

The big room was full of men, and every face pivoted toward him. Knell's pale face flashed into Duane's swift sight; then Boldt's, then Blossom Kane's, then Panhandle Smith's, then Fletcher's, then others that were familiar, and last that of Poggin. Though Duane had never seen Poggin or heard him described, he knew him. For he saw a face that was a record of great and evil deeds.

There was absolute silence. The outlaws were lined back of a long table upon which were papers, stacks of silver coin, a bundle of bills, and a huge gold-mounted gun.

"Are you gents lookin' for me?" asked Duane. He gave his voice all the ringing force and power of which he was capable. And he stepped back, free of anything, with the outlaws all before him.

Knell stood quivering, but his face might have been a mask. The other outlaws looked from him to Duane. Jim Fletcher flung up his hands.

"My Gawd, Dodge, what'd you bust in here fer?" he said, plaintively, and slowly stepped forward. His action was that of a man true to himself. He meant he had been sponsor for Duane and now he would stand by him.

"Back, Fletcher!" called Duane, and his voice made the outlaw jump.

"Hold on, Dodge, an' you-all, everybody," said Fletcher. "Let me talk, seein' I'm in wrong here."

His persuasions did not ease the strain.

"Go ahead. Talk," said Poggin.

Fletcher turned to Duane. "Pard, I'm takin' it on myself thet you meet enemies here when I swore you'd meet friends. It's my fault. I'll stand by you if you let me."

"No, Jim," replied Duane.

"But what'd you come fer without the signal?" bust out Fletcher, in distress. He saw nothing but catastrophe in this meeting.

"Jim, I ain't pressin' my company none. But when I'm wanted bad— "

Fletcher stopped him with a raised hand. Then he turned to Poggin with a rude dignity.

"Poggy, he's my pard, an' he's riled. I never told him a word thet'd make him sore. I only said Knell hadn't no more use fer him than fer me. Now, what you say goes in this gang. I never failed you in my life. Here's my pard. I vouch fer him. Will you stand fer me? There's goin' to be hell if you don't. An' us with a big job on hand!"

While Fletcher toiled over his slow, earnest persuasion Duane had his gaze riveted upon Poggin. There was something leonine about Poggin. He was tawny. He blazed. He seemed beautiful as fire was beautiful. But looked at closer, with glance seeing the physical man, instead of that thing which shone from him, he was of perfect build, with muscles that swelled and rippled, bulging his clothes, with the magnificent head and face of the cruel, fierce, tawny-eyed jaguar.

Looking at this strange Poggin, instinctively divining his abnormal and hideous power, Duane had for the first time in his life the inward quaking fear of a man. It was like a cold-tongued bell ringing within him and numbing his heart. The old instinctive firing of blood followed, but did not drive away that fear. He knew. He felt something here deeper than thought could go. And he hated Poggin.

That individual had been considering Fletcher's appeal.

"Jim, I ante up," he said, "an' if Phil doesn't raise us out with a big hand— why, he'll get called, an' your pard can set in the game."

Every eye shifted to Knell. He was dead white. He laughed, and any one hearing that laugh would have realized his intense anger equally with an assurance which made him master of the situation.

"Poggin, you're a gambler, you are—the ace-high, straight-flush hand of the Big Bend," he said, with stinging scorn. "I'll bet you my roll to a greaser peso that I can deal you a hand you'll be afraid to play."

"Phil, you're talkin' wild," growled Poggin, with both advice and menace in his tone.

"If there's anythin' you hate it's a man who pretends to be somebody else when he's not. Thet so?"

Poggin nodded in slow-gathering wrath.

"Well, Jim's new pard—this man Dodge—he's not who he seems. Oh-ho! He's a hell of a lot different. But *I* know him. An' when I spring his name on you, Poggin, you'll freeze to your gizzard. Do you get me? You'll freeze, an' your hand 'll be stiff when it ought to be lightnin'—All because you'll realize you've been standin' there five minutes—five minutes *alive* before him!"

If not hate, then assuredly great passion toward Poggin manifested itself in Knell's scornful, fiery address, in the shaking hand he thrust before Poggin's face. In the ensuing silent pause Knell's panting could be plainly heard. The other men were pale, watchful, cautiously edging either way to the wall, leaving the principals and Duane in the center of the room.

"Spring his name, then, you— " said Poggin, violently, with a curse.

Strangely Knell did not even look at the man he was about to denounce. He leaned toward Poggin, his hands, his body, his long head all somewhat expressive of what his face disguised.

"*Buck Duane!*" he yelled, suddenly.

The name did not make any great difference in Poggin. But Knell's passionate, swift utterance carried the suggestion that the name ought to bring Poggin to quick action. It was possible, too, that Knell's manner, the import of his denunciation, the meaning back of all his passion held Poggin bound more than the surprise. For the outlaw certainly was surprised, perhaps staggered at the idea that he, Poggin, had been about to stand sponsor with Fletcher for a famous outlaw hated and feared by all outlaws.

Knell waited a long moment, and then his face broke its cold immobility in an extraordinary expression of devilish glee. He had hounded the great Poggin into something that gave him vicious, monstrous joy.

"BUCK DUANE! Yes," he broke out, hotly. "The Nueces gunman! That two-shot, ace-of-spades lone wolf! You an' I—we've heard a thousand times of him—talked about him often. An' here he is *in front* of you! Poggin, you were backin' Fletcher's new pard, Buck Duane. An' he'd fooled you both but for me. But *I* know him. An' I know why he drifted in here. To flash a gun on Cheseldine—on you—on me! Bah! Don't tell me he wanted to join the gang. You know a gunman, for you're one yourself. Don't you always want to kill another man? An' don't you always want to meet a real man, not a four-flush? It's the madness of the gunman, an' I know it. Well, Duane faced you—called you! An' when I sprung his name, what ought you have done? What would the boss—anybody—have expected of Poggin? Did you throw your gun, swift, like you have so often? Naw; you froze. An' why? Because here's a man with the kind of nerve you'd love to have. Because he's great—meetin' us here alone. Because you know he's a wonder with a gun an' you love life. Because you an' I an' every damned man here had to take his front, each to himself. If we all drew we'd kill him. Sure! But who's goin' to lead? Who was goin' to be first? Who was goin' to make him draw? Not you, Poggin! You leave that for a lesser man—me—who've lived to see you a coward. It comes once to every gunman. You've met your match in Buck Duane. An', by God, I'm glad! Here's once I show you up!"

The hoarse, taunting voice failed. Knell stepped back from the comrade he hated. He was wet, shaking, haggard, but magnificent.

"Buck Duane, do you remember Hardin?" he asked, in scarcely audible voice.

"Yes," replied Duane, and a flash of insight made clear Knell's attitude.

"You met him—forced him to draw—killed him?"

"Yes."

"Hardin was the best pard I ever had."

His teeth clicked together tight, and his lips set in a thin line.

The room grew still. Even breathing ceased. The time for words had passed. In that long moment of suspense Knell's body gradually stiffened, and at last the quivering ceased. He crouched. His eyes had a soul-piercing fire.

Duane watched them. He waited. He caught the thought—the breaking of Knell's muscle-bound rigidity. Then he drew.

Through the smoke of his gun he saw two red spurts of flame. Knell's bullets thudded into the ceiling. He fell with a scream like a wild thing in agony.

Duane did not see Knell die. He watched Poggin. And Poggin, like a stricken and astounded man, looked down upon his prostrate comrade.

Fletcher ran at Duane with hands aloft.

"Hit the trail, you liar, or you'll hev to kill me!" he yelled.

With hands still up, he shouldered and bodied Duane out of the room.

Duane leaped on his horse, spurred, and plunged away.

23

DUANE returned to Fairdale and camped in the mesquite till the twenty-third of the month. The few days seemed endless. All he could think of was that the hour in which he must disgrace Ray Longstreth was slowly but inexorably coming. In that waiting time he learned what love was and also duty. When the day at last dawned he rode like one possessed down the rough slope, hurdling the stones and crashing through the brush, with a sound in his ears that was not all the rush of the wind. Something dragged at him.

Apparently one side of his mind was unalterably fixed, while the other was a hurrying conglomeration of flashes of thought, reception of sensations. He could not get calmness. By and by, almost involuntarily, he hurried faster on. Action seemed to make his state less oppressive; it eased the weight. But the farther he went on the harder it was to continue. Had he turned his back upon love, happiness, perhaps on life itself?

There seemed no use to go on farther until he was absolutely sure of himself. Duane received a clear warning thought that such work as seemed haunting and driving him could never be carried out in the mood under which he labored. He hung on to that thought. Several times he slowed up, then stopped, only to go on again. At length, as he mounted a low ridge, Fairdale lay bright and green before him not far away, and the sight was a conclusive check. There were mesquites on the ridge, and Duane sought the shade beneath them. It was the noon-hour, with hot, glary sun and no wind. Here Duane had to have out his fight. Duane was utterly unlike himself; he could not bring the old self back; he was not the same man he once had been. But he could understand why. It was because of Ray Longstreth. Temptation assailed him. To have her his wife! It was impossible. The thought was insidiously alluring. Duane pictured a home. He saw himself riding through the cotton and rice and cane, home to a stately old mansion, where long-eared hounds bayed him welcome, and a woman looked for him and met him with happy and beautiful smile. There might—there would be children. And something new, strange, confounding with its emotion, came to life deep in Duane's heart. There would be children! Ray their mother! The kind of life a lonely outcast always yearned for and never had! He saw it all, felt it all.

But beyond and above all other claims came Captain MacNelly's. It was then there was something cold and death-like in Duane's soul. For he knew, whatever happened, of one thing he was sure—he would have to kill either Longstreth or Lawson. Longstreth might be trapped into arrest; but Lawson had no sense, no control, no fear. He would snarl like a panther and go for his gun, and he would have to be killed. This, of all consummations, was the one to be calculated upon.

Duane came out of it all bitter and callous and sore—in the most fitting of moods to undertake a difficult and deadly enterprise. He had fallen upon his old strange, futile dreams, now rendered poignant by reason of love. He drove away those dreams. In their places came the images of the olive-skinned Longstreth with his sharp eyes, and the dark, evil-faced Lawson, and then returned tenfold more thrilling and sinister the old strange passion to meet Poggin.

It was about one o'clock when Duane rode into Fairdale. The streets for the most part were deserted. He went directly to find Morton and Zimmer. He found them at length, restless, somber, anxious, but unaware of the part he had played at Ord. They said Longstreth was home, too. It was possible that Longstreth had arrived home in ignorance.

Duane told them to be on hand in town with their men in case he might need them, and then with teeth locked he set off for Longstreth's ranch.

Duane stole through the bushes and trees, and when nearing the porch he heard loud, angry, familiar voices. Longstreth and Lawson were quarreling again. How Duane's lucky star guided him! He had no plan of action, but his brain was equal to a hundred lightning-swift evolutions. He meant to take any risk rather than kill Longstreth. Both of the men were out on the porch. Duane wormed his way to the edge of the shrubbery and crouched low to watch for his opportunity.

Longstreth looked haggard and thin. He was in his shirt-sleeves, and he had come out with a gun in his hand. This he laid on a table near the wall. He wore no belt.

Lawson was red, bloated, thick-lipped, all fiery and sweaty from drink, though sober on the moment, and he had the expression of a desperate man in his last stand. It was his last stand, though he was ignorant of that.

"What's your news? You needn't be afraid of my feelings," said Lawson.

"Ray confessed to an interest in this ranger," replied Longstreth.

Duane thought Lawson would choke. He was thick-necked anyway, and the rush of blood made him tear at the soft collar of his shirt. Duane awaited his chance, patient, cold, all his feelings shut in a vise.

"But *why* should your daughter meet this ranger?" demanded Lawson, harshly.

"She's in love with him, and he's in love with her."

Duane reveled in Lawson's condition. The statement might have had the force of a juggernaut. Was Longstreth sincere? What was his game?

Lawson, finding his voice, cursed Ray, cursed the ranger, then Longstreth.

"You damned selfish fool!" cried Longstreth, in deep bitter scorn. "All you think of is yourself—your loss of the girl. Think once of *me*—my home—my life!"

Then the connection subtly put out by Longstreth apparently dawned upon the other. Somehow through this girl her father and cousin were to be betrayed. Duane got that impression, though he could not tell how true it was. Certainly Lawson's jealousy was his paramount emotion.

"To hell with you!" burst out Lawson, incoherently. He was frenzied. "I'll have her, or nobody else will!"

"You never will," returned Longstreth, stridently. "So help me God I'd rather see her the ranger's wife than yours!"

While Lawson absorbed that shock Longstreth leaned toward him, all of hate and menace in his mien.

"Lawson, you made me what I am," continued Longstreth. "I backed you—shielded you. *You're* Cheseldine—if the truth is told! Now it's ended. I quit you. I'm done!"

Their gray passion-corded faces were still as stones.

"*Gentlemen!*" Duane called in far-reaching voice as he stepped out. "*You're both done!*"

They wheeled to confront Duane.

"Don't move! Not a muscle! Not a finger!" he warned.

Longstreth read what Lawson had not the mind to read. His face turned from gray to ashen.

"What d'ye mean?" yelled Lawson, fiercely, shrilly. It was not in him to obey a command, to see impending death.

All quivering and strung, yet with perfect control, Duane raised his left hand to turn back a lapel of his open vest. The silver star flashed brightly.

Lawson howled like a dog. With barbarous and insane fury, with sheer impotent folly, he swept a clawing hand for his gun. Duane's shot broke his action.

Before Lawson ever tottered, before he loosed the gun, Longstreth leaped behind him, clasped him with left arm, quick as lightning jerked the gun from both clutching fingers and sheath. Longstreth protected himself with the body of the dead man. Duane saw red flashes, puffs of smoke; he heard quick reports. Something stung his left arm. Then a blow like wind, light of sound yet shocking in impact, struck him, staggered him. The hot rend of lead followed the blow. Duane's heart seemed to explode, yet his mind kept extraordinarily clear and rapid.

Duane heard Longstreth work the action of Lawson's gun. He heard the hammer click, fall upon empty shells. Longstreth had used up all the loads in Lawson's gun. He cursed as a man cursed at defeat. Duane waited, cool and sure now. Longstreth tried to lift the dead man, to edge him closer toward the table where his own gun lay. But, considering the peril of exposing himself, he found the task beyond him. He bent peering at Duane under Lawson's arm, which flopped out from his side. Longstreth's eyes were the eyes of a man who meant to kill. There was never any mistaking the strange and terrible light of eyes like those. More than once Duane had a chance to aim at them, at the top of Longstreth's head, at a strip of his side.

Longstreth flung Lawson's body off. But even as it dropped, before Longstreth could leap, as he surely intended, for the gun, Duane covered him, called piercingly to him:

"Don't jump for the gun! Don't! I'll kill you! Sure as God I'll kill you!"

Longstreth stood perhaps ten feet from the table where his gun lay. Duane saw him calculating chances. He was game. He had the courage that forced Duane to respect him. Duane just saw him measure the distance to that gun. He was magnificent. He meant to do it. Duane would have to kill him.

"Longstreth, listen," cried Duane, swiftly. "The game's up. You're done. But think of your daughter! I'll spare your life—I'll try to get you freedom on one condition. For her sake! I've got you nailed—all the proofs. There lies Lawson. You're alone. I've Morton and men to my aid. Give up. Surrender. Consent to demands, and I'll spare you. Maybe I can persuade MacNelly to let you go free back to your old country. It's for Ray's sake! Her life, perhaps her happiness, can be saved! Hurry, man! Your answer!"

"Suppose I refuse?" he queried, with a dark and terrible earnestness.

"Then I'll kill you in your tracks! You can't move a hand! Your word or death! Hurry, Longstreth! Be a man! For her sake! Quick! Another second now—I'll kill you!"

"All right, Buck Duane, I give my word," he said, and deliberately walked to the chair and fell into it.

Longstreth looked strangely at the bloody blot on Duane's shoulder.

"There come the girls!" he suddenly exclaimed. "Can you help me drag Lawson inside? They mustn't see him.'

Duane was facing down the porch toward the court and corrals. Miss Longstreth and Ruth had come in sight, were swiftly approaching, evidently alarmed. The two men succeeded in drawing Lawson into the house before the girls saw him.

"Duane, you're not hard hit?" said Longstreth.

"Reckon not," replied Duane.

"I'm sorry. If only you could have told me sooner! Lawson, damn him! Always I've split over him!"

"But the last time, Longstreth."

"Yes, and I came near driving you to kill me, too. Duane, you talked me out of it. For Ray's sake! She'll be in here in a minute. This 'll be harder than facing a gun."

"Hard now. But I hope it 'll turn out all right."

"Duane, will you do me a favor?" he asked, and he seemed shamefaced.

"Sure."

"Let Ray and Ruth think Lawson shot you. He's dead. It can't matter. Duane, the old side of my life is coming back. It's been coming. It 'll be here just about when she enters this room. And, by God, I'd change places with Lawson if I could!"

"Glad you—said that, Longstreth," replied Duane. "And sure—Lawson plugged me. It's our secret."

Just then Ray and Ruth entered the room. Duane heard two low cries, so different in tone, and he saw two white faces. Ray came to his side, She lifted a shaking hand to point at the blood upon his breast. White and mute, she gazed from that to her father.

"Papa!" cried Ray, wringing her hands.

"Don't give way," he replied, huskily. "Both you girls will need your nerve. Duane isn't badly hurt. But Floyd is—is dead. Listen. Let me tell it quick. There's been a fight. It—it was Lawson—it was Lawson's gun that shot Duane. Duane let me off. In fact, Ray, he saved me. I'm to divide my property—return so far as possible what I've stolen—leave Texas at once with Duane, under arrest. He says maybe he can get MacNelly, the ranger captain, to let me go. For your sake!''

She stood there, realizing her deliverance, with the dark and tragic glory of her eyes passing from her father to Duane.

"You must rise above this," said Duane to her. "I expected this to ruin you. But your father is alive. He will live it down. I'm sure I can promise you he'll be free. Perhaps back there in Louisiana the dishonor will never be known. This country is far from your old home. And even in San Antonio and Austin a man's evil repute means little. Then the line between a rustler and a rancher is hard to draw in these wild border days. Rustling is stealing cattle, and I once heard a well-known rancher say that all rich cattlemen had done a little stealing. Your father drifted out here, and, like a good many others, he succeeded. It's perhaps just as well not to split hairs, to judge him by the law and morality of a civilized country. Some way or other he drifted in with bad men. Maybe a deal that was honest somehow tied his hands. This matter of land, water, a few stray head of stock had to be decided out of court. I'm sure in his case he never realized where he was drifting. Then one thing led to another, until he was face to face with dealing that took on crooked form. To protect himself he bound men to him. And so the gang developed. Many powerful gangs have developed that way out here. He could not control them. He became involved with them. And eventually their dealings became deliberately and boldly dishonest. That meant the inevitable spilling of blood sooner or later, and so he grew into the leader because he was the strongest. Whatever he is to be judged for, I think he could have been infinitely worse.''

24

On the morning of the twenty-sixth Duane rode into Bradford in time to catch the early train. His wounds did not seriously incapacitate him. Longstreth was with him. And Miss Longstreth and Ruth Herbert would not be left behind. They were all leaving Fairdale for ever. Longstreth had turned over the whole of his property to Morton, who was to divide it as he and his comrades believed just. Duane had left Fairdale with his party by night, passed through Sanderson in the early hours of dawn, and reached Bradford as he had planned.

That fateful morning found Duane outwardly calm, but inwardly he was in a tumult. He wanted to rush to Val Verde. Would Captain MacNelly be there with his rangers, as Duane had planned for them to be? Memory of that tawny Poggin returned with strange passion. Duane had borne hours and weeks and months of waiting, had endured the long hours of the outlaw, but now he had no patience. The whistle of the train made him leap.

It was a fast train, yet the ride seemed slow.

Duane, disliking to face Longstreth and the passengers in the car, changed his seat to one behind his prisoner. They had seldom spoken. Longstreth sat with bowed head, deep in thought. The girls sat in a seat near by and were pale but composed. Occasionally the train halted briefly at a station. The latter half of that ride Duane had observed a wagon-road running parallel with the railroad, sometimes right alongside, at others near or far away. When the train was about twenty miles from Val Verde Duane espied a dark group of horsemen trotting eastward. His blood beat like a hammer at his temples. The gang! He thought he recognized the tawny Poggin and felt a strange inward contraction. He thought he recognized the clean-cut Blossom Kane, the black-bearded giant Boldt, the red-faced Panhandle Smith, and Fletcher. There was another man strange to him. Was that Knell? No! it could not have been Knell.

Duane leaned over the seat and touched Longstreth on the shoulder.

"Look!" he whispered. Cheseldine was stiff. He had already seen.

The train flashed by; the outlaw gang receded out of range of sight.

"Did you notice Knell wasn't with them?" whispered Duane.

Duane did not speak to Longstreth again till the train stopped at Val Verde.

They got off the car, and the girls followed as naturally as ordinary travelers. The station was a good deal larger than that at Bradford, and there was considerable action and bustle incident to the arrival of the train.

Duane's sweeping gaze searched faces, rested upon a man who seemed familiar. This fellow's look, too, was that of one who knew Duane, but was waiting for a sign, a cue. Then Duane recognized him—MacNelly, clean-shaven. Without mustache he appeared different, younger.

When MacNelly saw that Duane intended to greet him, to meet him, he hurried forward. A keen light flashed from his eyes. He was glad, eager, yet suppressing himself, and the glances he sent back and forth from Duane to Longstreth were questioning, doubtful. Certainly Longstreth did not look the part of an outlaw.

"Duane! Lord, I'm glad to see you," was the Captain's greeting. Then at closer look into Duane's face his warmth fled—something he saw there checked his enthusiasm, or at least its utterance.

"MacNelly, shake hand with Cheseldine," said Duane, low-voiced.

The ranger captain stood dumb, motionless. But he saw Longstreth's instant action, and awkwardly he reached for the outstretched hand.

"Any of your men down here?" queried Duane, sharply.

"No. They're up-town."

"Come. MacNelly, you walk with him. We've ladies in the party. I'll come behind with them."

They set off up-town. Longstreth walked as if he were with friends on the way to dinner. The girls were mute. MacNelly walked like a man in a trance. There was not a word spoken in four blocks.

Presently Duane espied a stone building on a corner of the broad street. There was a big sign, "Rancher's Bank."

"There's the hotel," said MacNelly. "Some of my men are there. We've scattered around."

They crossed the street, went through office and lobby, and then Duane asked MacNelly to take them to a private room. Without a word the Captain complied. When they were all inside Duane closed the door, and, drawing a deep breath as if of relief, he faced them calmly.

"Miss Longstreth, you and Miss Ruth try to make yourselves comfortable now," he said. "And don't be distressed." Then he turned to his captain. "MacNelly, this girl is the daughter of the man I've brought to you, and this one is his niece."

Then Duane briefly related Longstreth's story, and, though he did not spare the rustler chief, he was generous.

"When I went after Longstreth," concluded Duane, "it was either to kill him or offer him freedom on conditions. So I chose the latter for his daughter's sake. He has already disposed of all his property. I believe he'll live up to the conditions. He's to leave Texas never to return. The name Cheseldine has been a mystery, and now it'll fade."

A few moments later Duane followed MacNelly to a large room, like a hall, and here were men reading and smoking. Duane knew them—rangers!

MacNelly beckoned to his men.

"Boys, here he is."

"How many men have you?" asked Duane.

"Fifteen."

MacNelly almost embraced Duane, would probably have done so but for the dark grimness that seemed to be coming over the man. Instead he glowed, he sputtered, he tried to talk, to wave his hands. He was beside himself. And his rangers crowded closer, eager, like hounds ready to run. They all talked at once, and the word most significant and frequent in their speech was "outlaws."

MacNelly clapped his fist in his hand.

"This'll make the adjutant sick with joy. Maybe we won't have it on the Governor! We'll show them about the ranger service. Duane! how'd you ever do it?"

"Now, Captain, not the half nor the quarter of this job's done. The gang's coming down the road. I saw them from the train. They'll ride into town on the dot—two-thirty.''

"How many?" asked MacNelly.

"Poggin, Blossom Kane, Panhandle Smith, Boldt, Jim Fletcher, and another man I don't know. These are the picked men of Cheseldine's gang. I'll bet they'll be the fastest, hardest bunch you rangers ever faced.''

"Poggin—that's the hard nut to crack! I've heard their records since I've been in Val Verde. Where's Knell? They say he's a boy, but hell and blazes!''

"Knell's dead.''

"Ah!'' exclaimed MacNelly, softly. Then he grew businesslike, cool, and of harder aspect. "Duane, it's your game to-day. I'm only a ranger under orders. We're all under your orders. We've absolute faith in you. Make your plan quick, so I can go around and post the boys who're not here.''

"You understand there's no sense in trying to arrest Poggin, Kane, and that lot?" queried Duane.

"No, I don't understand that,'' replied MacNelly, bluntly.

"It can't be done. The drop can't be got on such men. If you meet them they shoot, and mighty quick and straight. Poggin! That outlaw has no equal with a gun—unless— He's got to be killed quick. They'll all have to be killed. They're all bad, desperate, know no fear, are lightning in action.''

"Very well, Duane; then it's a fight. That'll be easier, perhaps. The boys are spoiling for a fight. Out with your plan, now.''

"Put one man at each end of this street, just at the edge of town. Let him hide there with a rifle to block the escape of any outlaw that we might fail to get. I had a good look at the bank building. It's well situated for our purpose. Put four men up in that room over the bank—four men, two at each open window. Let them hide till the game begins. They want to be there so in case these foxy outlaws get wise before they're down on the ground or inside the bank. The rest of your men put inside behind the counters, where they'll hide. Now go over to the bank, spring the thing on the bank officials, and don't let them shut up the bank. You want their aid. Let them make sure of their gold. But the clerks and cashier ought to be at their desks or window when Poggin rides up. He'll glance in before he gets down. They make no mistakes, these fellows. We must be slicker than they are, or lose. When you get the bank people wise, send your men over one by one. No hurry, no excitement, no unusual thing to attract notice in the bank.''

"All right. That's great. Tell me, where do you intend to wait?''

Duane heard MacNelly's question, and it struck him peculiarly. He had seemed to be planning and speaking mechanically. As he was confronted by the fact it nonplussed him somewhat, and he became thoughtful, with lowered head.

"Where'll you wait, Duane?'' insisted MacNelly, with keen eyes speculating.

"I'll wait in front—just inside the door," replied Duane, with an effort.

"Why?" demanded the Captain.

"Well," began Duane, slowly, "Poggin will get down first and start in. But the others won't be far behind. They'll not get swift till inside. The thing is— they *mustn't* get clear inside, because the instant they do they'll pull guns. That means death to somebody. If we can we want to stop them just at the door."

"But will you hide?" asked MacNelly.

"Hide!" The idea had not occurred to Duane.

"There's a wide-open doorway, a sort of round hall, a vestibule, with steps leading up to the bank. There's a door in the vestibule, too. It leads somewhere. We can put men in there. You can be there."

Duane was silent.

"See here, Duane," began MacNelly, nervously. "You sha'n't take any undue risk here. You'll hide with the rest of us?"

"No!" The word was wrenched from Duane.

MacNelly stared, and then a strange, comprehending light seemed to flit over his face.

"Duane, I can give you no orders to-day," he said, distinctly. "I'm only offering advice. Need you take any more risks? You've done a grand job for the service—already. You've paid me a thousand times for that pardon. You've redeemed yourself. The Governor, the adjutant-general—the whole state will rise up and honor you. The game's almost up. We'll kill these outlaws, or enough of them to break for ever their power. I say, as a ranger, need you take more risk than your captain?"

Still Duane remained silent. He was locked between two forces. And one, a tide that was bursting at its bounds, seemed about to overwhelm him. Finally that side of him, the retreating self, the weaker, found a voice.

"Captain, you want this job to be sure?" he asked.

"Certainly."

"I've told you the way. I alone know the kind of men to be met. Just *what* I'll do or *where* I'll be I can't say yet. In meetings like this the moment decides. But I'll be there!"

MacNelly spread wide his hands, looked helplessly at his curious and sympathetic rangers, and shook his head.

"Now you've done your work—laid the trap—is this strange move of yours going to be fair to Miss Longstreth?" asked MacNelly, in significant low voice.

Like a great tree chopped at the roots Duane vibrated to that. He looked up as if he had seen a ghost.

Mercilessly the ranger captain went on: "You can win her, Duane! Oh, you can't fool me. I was wise in a minute. Fight with us from cover—then go back to her. You will have served the Texas Rangers as no other man has. I'll accept your resignation. You'll be free, honored, happy. That girl loves you! I saw it in her eyes. She's—''

But Duane cut him short with a fierce gesture. He lunged up to his feet, and the rangers fell back. Dark, silent, grim as he had been, still there was a transformation singularly more sinister, stranger.

"Enough. I'm done," he said, somberly. "I've planned. Do we agree—or shall I meet Poggin and his gang alone?"

MacNelly cursed and again threw up his hands, this time in baffled chagrin. There was deep regret in his dark eyes as they rested upon Duane.

Duane was left alone.

Never had his mind been so quick, so clear, so wonderful in its understanding of what had heretofore been intricate and elusive impulses of his strange nature. His determination was to meet Poggin; meet him before any one else had a chance—Poggin first—and then the others! He was as unalterable in that decision as if on the instant of its acceptance he had become stone.

Why? Then came realization. He was not a ranger now. He cared nothing for the state. He had no thought of freeing the community of a dangerous outlaw, of ridding the country of an obstacle to its progress and prosperity. He wanted to kill Poggin. It was significant now that he forgot the other outlaws. He was the gunman, the gun-thrower, the gun-fighter, passionate and terrible. His father's blood, that dark and fierce strain, his mother's spirit, that strong and unquenchable spirit of the surviving pioneer—these had been in him; and the killings, one after another, the wild and haunted years, had made him, absolutely in spite of his will, the gunman. He realized it now, bitterly, hopelessly. The thing he had intelligence enough to hate he had become. At last he shuddered under the driving, ruthless, inhuman blood-lust of the gunman. Long ago he had seemed to seal in a tomb that horror of his kind—the need, in order to forget the haunting, sleepless presence of his last victim, to go out and kill another. But it was still there in his mind, and now it stalked out, worse, more powerful, magnified by its rest, augmented by the violent passions peculiar and inevitable to that strange, wild product of the Texas frontier—the gun-fighter. And those passions were so violent, so raw, so base, so much lower than what ought to have existed in a thinking man. Actual pride of his record! Actual vanity in his speed with a gun! Actual jealousy of any rival!

Duane could not believe it. But there he was, without a choice. What he had feared for years had become a monstrous reality. Respect for himself, blindness, a certain honor that he had clung to while in outlawry—all, like scales, seemed to fall away from him. He stood stripped bare, his soul naked—the soul of Cain. Always since the first brand had been forced and burned upon him he had been ruined. But now with conscience flayed to the quick, yet utterly powerless over this tiger instinct, he was lost. He said it. He admitted it. And at the utter abasement the soul he despised suddenly leaped and quivered with the thought of Ray Longstreth.

Then came agony. As he could not govern all the chances of this fatal meeting—as all his swift and deadly genius must be occupied with Poggin, perhaps in vain—as hard-shooting men whom he could not watch would be close behind, this almost certainly must be the end of Buck Duane. That did not matter. But he loved the girl. He wanted her. All her sweetness, her fire, and pleading returned to torture him.

At that moment the door opened, and Ray Longstreth entered.

"Duane," she said softly. "Captain MacNelly sent me to you."

"But you shouldn't have come," replied Duane.

"As soon as he told me I would have come whether he wished it or not. You left me—all of us—stunned. I had no time to thank you. Oh, I do—with all my soul. It was noble of you. Father is overcome. He didn't expect so much. And he'll be true. But, Duane, I was told to hurry, and here I'm selfishly using time."

"Go, then—and leave me. You mustn't unnerve me now, when there's a desperate game to finish."

"Need it be desperate?" she whispered, coming close to him.

"Yes; it can't be else."

MacNelly had sent her to weaken him; of that Duane was sure. And he felt that she had wanted to come. Her eyes were dark, strained, beautiful, and they shed a light upon Duane he had never seen before.

"You're going to take some mad risk," she said. "Let me persuade you not to. You said—you cared for me—and I—oh, Duane—don't you—know—?"

The low voice, deep, sweet as an old chord, faltered and broke and failed.

Duane sustained a sudden shock and an instant of paralyzed confusion of thought.

She moved, she swept out her hands, and the wonder of her eyes dimmed in a flood of tears.

"My God! You can't care for me?" he cried, hoarsely.

Then she met him, hands outstretched.

"But I do—I do!"

Swift as light Duane caught her and held her to his breast. He stood holding her tight, with the feel of her warm, throbbing breast and the clasp of her arms as flesh and blood realities to fight a terrible fear. He felt her, and for the moment the might of it was stronger than all the demons that possessed him. And he held her as if she had been his soul, his strength on earth, his hope of Heaven, against his lips.

The strife of doubt all passed. He found his sight again. And there rushed over him a tide of emotion unutterably sweet and full, strong like an intoxicating wine, deep as his nature, something glorious and terrible as the blaze of the sun to one long in darkness. He had become an outcast, a wanderer, a gunman, a victim of circumstances; he had lost and suffered worse than death in that loss; he had gone down the endless bloody trail, a killer of men, a fugitive whose mind slowly and inevitably closed to all except the instinct to survive and a black despair; and now, with this woman in his arms, her swelling breast against his, in this moment almost of resurrection, he bent under the storm of passion and joy possible only to him who had endured so much.

"Do you care—a little?" he whispered, unsteadily.

He bent over her, looking deep into the dark wet eyes.

She uttered a low laugh that was half sob, and her arms slipped up to his neck.

"A little! Oh, Duane—Duane—a great deal!"

Their lips met in their first kiss. The sweetness, the fire of her mouth seemed so new, so strange, so irresistible to Duane. His sore and hungry heart throbbed with thick and heavy beats. He felt the outcast's need of love. And he gave up to the enthralling moment. She met him half-way, returned kiss for kiss, clasp for clasp, her face scarlet, her eyes closed, till, her passion and strength spent, she fell back upon his shoulder.

Duane suddenly thought she was going to faint. He divined then that she had understood him, would have denied him nothing, not even her life, in that moment. But she was overcome, and he suffered a pang of regret at his unrestraint.

Presently she recovered, and she drew only the closer, and leaned upon him with her face upturned. He felt her hands on his, and they were soft, clinging, strong, like steel under velvet. He felt the rise and fall, the warmth of her breast. A tremor ran over him. He tried to draw back, and if he succeeded a little her form swayed with him, pressing closer. She held her face up, and he was compelled to look. It was wonderful now: white, yet glowing, with the red lips parted, and dark eyes alluring. But that was not all. There was passion, unquenchable spirit, woman's resolve deep and mighty.

"I love you, Duane!" she said. "For my sake don't go out to meet this outlaw face to face. It's something wild in you. Conquer it if you love me."

Duane became suddenly weak, and when he did take her into his arms again he scarcely had strength to lift her to a seat beside him. She seemed more than a dead weight. Her calmness had fled. She was throbbing, palpitating, quivering, with hot wet cheeks and arms that clung to him like vines. She lifted her mouth to his, whispering, "Kiss me!" She meant to change him, hold him.

Duane bent down, and her arms went round his neck and drew him close. With his lips on hers he seemed to float away. That kiss closed his eyes, and he could not lift his head. He sat motionless holding her, blind and helpless, wrapped in a sweet dark glory. She kissed him—one long endless kiss—or else a thousand times. Her lips, her wet cheeks, her hair, the softness, the fragrance of her, the tender clasp of her arms, the swell of her breast—all these seemed to inclose him.

Duane could not put her from him. He yielded to her lips and arms, watching her, involuntarily returning her caresses, sure now of her intent, fascinated by the sweetness of her, bewildered, almost lost. This was what it was to be loved by a woman. His years of outlawry had blotted out any boyish love he might have known. This was what he had to give up—all this wonder of her sweet person, this strange fire he feared yet loved, this mate his deep and tortured soul recognized. Never until that moment had he divined the meaning of a woman to a man. That meaning was physical inasmuch that he learned what beauty was, what marvel in the touch of quickening flesh; and it was spiritual in that he saw there might have been for him, under happier circumstances, a life of noble deeds lived for such a woman.

"Don't go! Don't go!" she cried, as he started violently.

"I must. Dear, good-by! Remember I loved you!"

He pulled her hands loose from his, stepped back.

"Ray, dearest—I believe—I'll come back!" he whispered.

These last words were falsehood.

He reached the door, gave her one last piercing glance, to fix for ever in memory that white face with its dark, staring, tragic eyes.

"Duane!"

He fled with that moan like thunder, death, hell in his ears.

To forget her, to get back his nerve, he forced into mind the image of Poggin—Poggin, the tawny-haired, the yellow-eyed, like a jaguar, with his rippling muscles. He brought back his sense of the outlaw's wonderful presence, his own unaccountable fear and hate. Yes, Poggin had sent the cold sickness of fear to his marrow. Why, since he hated life so? Poggin was his supreme test. And this abnormal and stupendous instinct, now deep as the very foundation of his life, demanded its wild and fatal issue. There was a horrible thrill in his sudden remembrance that Poggin likewise had been taunted in fear of him.

So the dark tide overwhelmed Duane, and when he left the room he was fierce, implacable, steeled to any outcome, quick like a panther, somber as death, in the thrall of his strange passion.

There was no excitement in the street. He crossed to the bank corner. A clock inside pointed the hour of two. He went through the door into the vestibule, looked around, passed up the steps into the bank. The clerks were at their desks, apparently busy. But they showed nervousness. The cashier paled at sight of Duane. There were men—the rangers—crouching down behind the low partition. All the windows had been removed from the iron grating before the desks. The safe was closed. There was no money in sight. A customer came in, spoke to the cashier, and was told to come tomorrow.

Duane returned to the door. He could see far down the street, out into the country. There he waited, and minutes were eternities. He saw no person near him; he heard no sound. He was insulated in his unnatural strain.

At a few minutes before half past two a dark, compact body of horsemen appeared far down, turning into the road. They came at a sharp trot—a group that would have attracted attention anywhere at any time. They came a little faster as they entered town; then faster still; now they were four blocks away, now three, now two. Duane backed down the middle of the vestibule, up the steps, and halted in the center of the wide doorway.

There seemed to be a rushing in his ears through which pierced sharp, ringing clip-clop of iron hoofs. He could see only the corner of the street. But suddenly into that shot lean-limbed dusty bay horses. There was a clattering of nervous hoofs pulled to a halt.

Duane saw the tawny Poggin speak to his companions. He dismounted quickly. They followed suit. They had the manner of ranchers about to conduct some business. No guns showed. Poggin started leisurely for the bank door, quickening step a little. The others, close together, came behind him. Blossom Kane had a bag in his left hand. Jim Fletcher was left at the curb, and he had already gathered up the bridles.

Poggin entered the vestibule first, with Kane on one side, Boldt on the other, a little in his rear.

As he strode in he saw Duane.

"Hell's Fire!" he cried.

Something inside Duane burst, piercing all of him with cold. Was it that fear?

"BUCK DUANE!" echoed Kane.

One instant Poggin looked up and Duane looked down.

Like a striking jaguar Poggin moved. Almost as quickly Duane threw his arm. The guns boomed almost together.

Duane felt a blow just before he pulled trigger. His thoughts came fast, like the strange dots before his eyes. His rising gun had loosened in his hand. Poggin had drawn quicker! A tearing agony encompassed his breast. He pulled—pulled—at random. Thunder of booming shots all about him! Red flashes, jets of smoke, shrill yells! He was sinking. The end; yes, the end! With fading sight he saw Kane go down, then Boldt. But supreme torture, bitterer than death, Poggin stood, mane like a lion's, back to the wall, bloody-faced, grand, with his guns spouting red!

All faded, darkened. The thunder deadened. Duane fell, seemed floating. There it drifted—Ray Longstreth's sweet face, white, with dark, tragic eyes, fading from his sight . . . fading . . . fading . . .

25

LIGHT shone before Duane's eyes—thick, strange light tht came and went. For a long time dull and booming sounds rushed by, filling all. It was a dream in which there was nothing; a drifting under a burden; darkness, light, sound, movement; and vague, obscure sense of time—time that was very long. There was fire—creeping, consuming fire. A dark cloud of flame enveloped him, rolled him away.

He saw then, dimly, a room that was strange, strange people moving about over him, with faint voices, far away, things in a dream. He saw again, clearly, and consciousness returned, still unreal, still strange, full of those vague and far-away things. Then he was not dead. He lay stiff, like a stone, with a weight ponderous as a mountain upon him and all his bound body racked in slow, dull-beating agony.

A woman's face hovered over him, white and tragic-eyed, like one of his old haunting phantoms, yet sweet and eloquent. Then a man's face bent over him, looked deep into his eyes, and seemed to whisper from a distance: "Duane—Duane! Ah, he knew me!"

After that there was another long interval of darkness. When the light came again, clearer this time, the same earnest-faced man bent over him. It was MacNelly. And with recognition the past flooded back.

Duane tried to speak. His lips were weak, and he could scarcely move them.

"Poggin!" he whispered. His first real conscious thought was for Poggin. Ruling passion—eternal instinct!

"Poggin is dead, Duane; shot to pieces," replied MacNelly, solemnly. "What a fight he made! He killed two of my men, wounded others. God! he was a tiger. He used up three guns before we downed him."

"Who—got—away?"

"Fletcher, the man with the horses. We downed all the others. Duane, the job's done—it's done! Why, man, you're—"

"What of—of—*her*?"

"Miss Longstreth has been almost constantly at your bedside. She helped the doctor. She watched your wounds. And, Duane, the other night, when you sank low—so low—I think it was her spirit that held yours back. Oh, she's a wonderful girl. Duane, she never gave up, never lost her nerve for a moment. Well, we're going to take you home, and she'll go with us. Colonel Longstreth left for

Louisiana right after the fight. I advised it. There was great excitement. It was best for him to leave.''

"Have I—a—chance—to recover?''

"Chance? Why, man," exclaimed the Captain, "you'll get well! You'll pack a sight of lead all your life. But you can stand that. Duane, the whole Southwest knows your story. You need never again be ashamed of the name Buck Duane. The brand outlaw is washed out. Texas believes you've been a secret ranger all the time. You're a hero. And now think of home, your mother, of this noble girl—of your future.''

The rangers took Duane home to Wellston.

A railroad had been built since Duane had gone into exile. Wellston had grown. A noisy crowd surrounded the station, but it stilled as Duane was carried from the train.

A sea of faces pressed close. Some were faces he remembered—schoolmates, friends, old neighbors. There was an upflinging of many hands. Duane was being welcomed home to the town from which he had fled. A deadness within him broke. This welcome hurt him somehow, quickened him; and through his cold being, his weary mind, passed a change. His sight dimmed.

Then there was a white house, his old home. How strange, yet how real! His heart beat fast. Had so many, many years passed? Familiar yet strange it was, and all seemed magnified.

They carried him in, these ranger comrades, and laid him down, and lifted his head upon pillows. The house was still, though full of people. Duane's gaze sought the open door.

Some one entered—a tall girl in white, with dark, wet eyes and a light upon her face. She was leading an old lady, gray-haired, austere-faced, somber and sad. His mother! She was feeble, but she walked erect. She was pale, shaking, yet maintained her dignity.

The some one in white uttered a low cry and knelt by Duane's bed. His mother flung wide her arms with a strange gesture.

"This man! They've not brought back my boy. This man's his father! Where is my son? My son—oh, my son!''

When Duane grew stronger it was a pleasure to lie by the west window and watch Uncle Jim whittle his stick and listen to his talk. The old man was broken now. He told many interesting things about people Duane had known—people who had grown up and married, failed, succeeded, gone away, and died. But it was hard to keep Uncle Jim off the subject of guns, outlaws, fights. He could not seem to divine how mention of these things hurt Duane. Uncle Jim was childish now, and he had a great pride in his nephew. He wanted to hear of all of Duane's exile. And if there was one thing more than another that pleased him it was to talk about the bullets which Duane carried in his body.

"Five bullets, ain't it?" he asked, for the hundredth time. "Five in that last scrap! By gum! And you had six before?"

"Yes, uncle," replied Duane.

"Five and six. That makes eleven. By gum! A man's a man, to carry all that lead, But, Buck, you could carry more. There's that nigger Edwards, right here in Wellston. He's got a ton of bullets in him. Doesn't seem to mind them none. And there's Cole Miller. I've seen him. Been a bad man in his day. They say he packs twenty-three bullets. But he's bigger than you—got more flesh . . . . Funny, wasn't it, Buck, about the doctor only bein' able to cut one bullet out of you—that one in your breastbone? It was a forty-one caliber, an unusual cartridge. I saw it, and I wanted it, but Miss Longstreth wouldn't part with it. Buck, there was a bullet left in one of Poggin's guns, and that bullet was the same kind as the one cut out of you. By gum! Boy, it'd have killed you if it'd stayed there."

"It would indeed, uncle," replied Duane, and the old, haunting, somber mood returned.

But Duane was not often at the mercy of childish old hero-worshiping Uncle Jim. Miss Longstreth was the only person who seemed to divine Duane's gloomy mood, and when she was with him she warded off all suggestion.

One afternoon, while she was there at the west window, a message came for him. They read it together.

You have saved the ranger service to the Lone Star State

MACNELLY.

Ray knelt beside him at the window, and he believed she meant to speak then of the thing they had shunned. Her face was still white, but sweeter now, warm with rich life beneath the marble; and her dark eyes were still intent, still haunted by shadows, but no longer tragic.

"I'm glad for MacNelly's sake as well as the state's," said Duane.

She made no reply to that and seemed to be thinking deeply. Duane shrank a little.

"The pain— Is it any worse to-day?" she asked, instantly.

"No; it's the same. It will always be the same. I'm full of lead, you know. But I don't mind a little pain."

"Then—it's the old mood—the fear?" she whispered. "Tell me."

"Yes. It haunts me. I'll be well soon—able to go out. Then that—that hell will come back!"

"No, no!" she said, with emotion.

"Some drunken cowboy, some fool with a gun, will hunt me out in every town, wherever I go," he went on, miserably. "Buck Duane! To kill Buck Duane!"

"Hush! Don't speak so. Listen. You remember that day in Val Verde, when I came to you—plead with you not to meet Poggin? Oh, that was a terrible hour for me. But it showed me the truth. I saw the struggle between your passion to kill and your love for me. I could have saved you then had I known what I know now. Now I understand that—that thing which haunts you. But you'll never have to draw again. You'll never have to kill another man, thank God!"

Like a drowning man he would have grasped at straws, but he could not voice his passionate query.

She put tender arms round his neck. "Because you'll have me with you always," she replied. "Because always I shall be between you and that—that terrible thing."

It seemed with the spoken thought absolute assurance of her power came to her. Duane realized instantly that he was in the arms of a stronger woman than she who had plead with him that fatal day.

"We'll—we'll be married and leave Texas," she said, softly, with the red blood rising rich and dark in her cheeks.

"Ray!"

"Yes we will, though you're laggard in asking me, sir."

"But, dear—suppose," he replied, huskily, "suppose there might be—be children—a boy. A boy with his father's blood!"

"I pray God there will be. I do not fear what you fear. But even so—he'll be half my blood."

Duane felt the storm rise and break in him. And his terror was that of joy quelling fear. The shining glory of love in this woman's eyes made him weak as a child. How could she love him—how could she so bravely face a future with him? Yet she held him in her arms, twining her hands round his neck, and pressing close to him. Her faith and love and beauty—these she meant to throw between him and all that terrible past. They were her power, and she meant to use them all. He dared not think of accepting her sacrifice.

"But Ray—you dear, noble girl—I'm poor. I have nothing. And I'm a cripple."

"Oh, you'll be well some day," she replied. "And listen. I have money. My mother left me well off. All she had was her father's—Do you understand? We'll take Uncle Jim and your mother. We'll go to Louisiana—to my old home. It's far from here. There's a plantation to work. There are horses and cattle—a great cypress forest to cut. Oh, you'll have much to do. You'll forget there. You'll learn to love my home. It's a beautiful old place. There are groves where the gray moss blows all day and the nightingales sing all night."

"My darling!" cried Duane, brokenly. "No, no, no!"

Yet he knew in his heart that he was yielding to her, that he could not resist her a moment longer. What was this madness of love?

"We'll be happy," she whispered. "Oh, I know. Come!—come!—come!"

Her eyes were closing, heavy-lidded, and she lifted sweet, tremulous, waiting lips.

With bursting heart Duane bent to them. Then he held her, close pressed to him, while with dim eyes he looked out over the line of low hills in the west, down where the sun was setting gold and red, down over the Nueces and the wild brakes of the Rio Grande which he was never to see again.

It was in this solemn and exalted moment that Duane accepted happiness and faced a new life, trusting this brave and tender woman to be stronger than the dark and fateful passion that had shadowed his past.

It would come back—that wind of flame, that madness to forget, that driving, relentless instinct for blood. It would come back with those pale, drifting, haunting faces and the accusing fading eyes, but all his life, always between them and him, rendering them powerless, would be the faith and love and beauty of this noble woman.

UNDER THE TONTO RIM

1

LUCY WATSON did not leave home without regrets. For a long time she gazed at the desert scenery through tear-blurred eyes. But this sadness seemed rather for the past—the home that had been, before the death of her mother and the elopement of her younger sister with a cowboy. This escapade of Clara's had been the last straw. Lucy had clung to the home in the hope she might save her sister from following in the footsteps of others of the family. Always she had felt keenly the stigma of being the daughter of a saloon-keeper. In her school days she had suffered under this opprobrium, and had conceived an ideal to help her rise above the circumstances of her position. Clara's defection had left her free. And now she was speeding away from the town where she had been born, with an ache in her heart, and yet a slowly dawning consciousness of relief, of hope, of thrill. By the time she reached Oglethorpe, where she was to take a branch-line train, she was able to address all her faculties to a realization of her adventures.

Lucy had graduated from high school and normal school with honors. Of the several opportunities open to her she had chosen one of welfare work among backwoods people. It was not exactly missionary work, as her employers belonged to a department of the state government. Her duty was to go among the poor families of the wilderness and help them to make better homes. The significance of these words had prompted Lucy to make her choice. Better homes! It had been her ideal to help make her own home better, and so long as her mother lived she had succeeded. The salary offered was small, but that did not cause her concern. The fact that she had the welfare department of the state behind her, and could use to reasonable extent funds for the betterment of these primitive people, was something of far greater importance. When she had accepted this position two remarks had been made to her, both of which had been thought-provoking. Mr. Sands, the head of the department, had said: "We would not trust every young woman with this work. It is a sort of state experiment. But we believe in the right hands it will be a great benefit to these uncultivated people of the backwoods. Tact, cleverness, and kindliness of heart will be factors in your success."

Lucy had derived gratification from this indirect compliment. The other remark had aroused only amusement. Mrs. Larabee, also connected with the welfare work, had remarked: "You are a good-looking young woman, Miss Watson. You will cause something of a stir among the young men at Cedar Ridge. I was there last summer. Such strapping young giants I never saw! I liked them, wild and uncouth as they were. I wouldn't be surprised if one of them married you."

Oglethorpe was a little way station in the desert. The branch-line train, consisting of two cars and the engine, stood waiting on a side track. Mexicans in huge sombreros and Indians with colored blankets stolidly watched Lucy carry her heavy bags from one train to the other. A young brakeman espied her and helped her aboard, not forgetting some bold and admiring glances. The coach was only partly filled with passengers, and those whom Lucy noticed bore the stamp of the range.

Soon the train started over an uneven and uphill roadbed. Lucy began to find pleasure in gazing out of the window. The flat bare desert had given place to hills, fresh with spring greens. The air had lost the tang of the cattle range. Occasionally Lucy espied a black tableland rising in the distance, and this she guessed was timbered mountain country, whither she was bound.

At noon the train arrived at its terminal stop, San Dimas, a hamlet of flat-roofed houses. Lucy was interested only in the stagecoach that left here for her destination, Cedar Ridge. The young brakeman again came to her assistance and carried her baggage. "Goin' up in the woods, hey?" he queried, curiously.

"Yes, I think they did say woods, backwoods," laughed Lucy. "I go to Cedar Ridge, and farther still."

"All alone—a pretty girl!" he exclaimed, gallantly. "For two cents I'd throw up my job an' go with you."

"Thank you. Do you think I need a—a protector?" replied Lucy.

"Among those bee hunters an' white-mule drinkers! I reckon you do, miss."

"I imagine they will not be any more dangerous than cowboys on the range—or brakemen on trains," replied Lucy, with a smile. "Anyway, I can take care of myself."

"I'll bet you can," he said, admiringly. "Good luck."

Lucy found herself the sole passenger in the stagecoach and soon bowling along a good road. The driver, a weather-beaten old man, appeared to have a grudge against his horses. Lucy wanted to climb out in front and sit beside him, so that she could see better and have opportunity to ask questions about the

country and the people. The driver's language, however, was hardly conducive to nearer acquaintance; therefore Lucy restrained her inquisitive desires and interested herself in the changing nature of the foliage and the occasional vista that opened up between the hills.

It seemed impossible not to wonder about what was going to happen to her; and the clinking of the harness on the horses, the rhythmic beat of their hoofs, and the roll of wheels all augmented her sense of the departure from an old and unsatisfying life toward a new one fraught with endless hopes, dreams, possibilities. Whatever was in store for her, the worthy motive of this work she had accepted would uphold her and keep her true to the ideal she had set for herself.

The only instructions given Lucy were that she was to go among the families living in the backwoods between Cedar Ridge and what was called the Rim Rock and to use her abilities to the best advantage in teaching them to have better homes. She had not been limited to any method or restricted in any sense or hampered by any church or society. She was to use her own judgment and report her progress. Something about this work appealed tremendously to Lucy. The responsibility weighed upon her, yet stimulated her instinct for conflict. She had been given a hint of what might be expected in the way of difficulties. Her success or failure would have much to do with future development of this state welfare work. Lucy appreciated just how much these isolated and poor families might gain or lose through her. Indeed, though beset by humility and doubt, she felt that a glorious opportunity had been presented to her, and she called upon all the courage and intelligence she could summon. There was little or nothing she could plan until she got among these people. But during that long ride through the lonely hills, up and ever upward into higher country, she labored at what she conceived to be the initial step toward success—to put into this work all her sympathy and heart.

Presently she plucked up spirit enough to address the stage driver.

"How far is it to Cedar Ridge?"

"Wal, some folks calkilate it's round twenty-five miles, then there's tothers say it's more," he drawled. "But I don't agree with nary of them."

"You would know, of course," said Lucy, appreciatingly. "How far do you call it?"

"Reckon aboot twenty miles as a crow flies an' shinnyin' round forty on this uphill road."

Lucy felt rather bewildered at this reply and did not risk incurring more confusion. She was sure of one thing, however, and it was that the road assuredly wound uphill. About the middle of the afternoon the stage reached the summit of what appeared rolling upland country, grassy in patches and brushy in others, and stretching away toward a bold black mountain level with a band of red rock shining in the sun. Lucy gazed westward across a wide depression, gray and

green, to a range of ragged peaks, notched and sharp, with shaggy slopes. How wild and different they seemed to her! Farther south the desert mountains were stark and ghastly, denuded rock surfaces that glared inhospitably down upon an observer. But these mountains seemed to call in wild abandon. They stirred something buoyant and thrilling in Lucy. Gradually she lost sight of both ranges as the road began to wind down somewhat, obstructing her view. Next to interest her were clearings in the brush, fields and fences and cabins, with a few cattle and horses. Hard as she peered, however, Lucy did not see any people.

The stage driver made fast time over this rolling country, and his horses trotted swingingly along, as if home and feed were not far off. For Lucy the day had been tiring; she had exhausted herself with unusual sensation. She closed her eyes to rest them and fell into a doze. Sooner or later the stage driver awoke her.

"Say, miss, there's Cedar Ridge, an' thet green hill above is what gives the town its name," he said. "It's a good ways off yit, but I reckon we'll pull in aboot dark."

Lucy's eyes opened upon a wonderful valley, just now colored by sunset haze. A cluster of cottages and houses nestled under a magnificent sloping ridge, billowy and soft with green foliage. The valley was pastoral and beautiful. This could not be the backwoods country into which she was going. Lucy gazed long with the most pleasing of impressions. Then her gaze shifted to the ridge from which the town derived its name. Far as she could see to east and west it extended, a wild black barrier to what hid beyond. It appeared to slope higher toward the east, where on the horizon it assumed the proportions of a mountain.

To Lucy's regret, the winding and ascending nature of the road again obscured distant views. Then the sun set; twilight appeared short; and soon darkness settled down. Lucy had never before felt mountain air, but she recognized it now. How cold and pure! Would the ride never end? She peered through the darkness, hoping to see lights of the village. At last they appeared, dim pin-points through the blackness. She heard the barking of dogs. The stage wheeled round a corner of trees, to enter a wide street, and at last to slow down before looming flat-topped houses, from which the yellow lights shone.

"Miss, anybody goin' to meet you?" queried the driver.

"No," replied Lucy.

"Wal, whar shall I set you down? Post office, store, or hotel?"

Lucy was about to answer his question when he enlightened her by drawling that she did not need to make any choice, because all three places mentioned were in the same house.

When the stage came to a halt Lucy saw a high porch upon which lounged the dark forms of men silhouetted against the yellow light of lamps. Despite the

lights, she could scarcely see to gather up her belongings. To her relief, the stage driver reached in for her grips.

"Hyar we air—Cedar Ridge—last stop—all out," he drawled.

Lucy stepped down hurriedly so that she could stay close to him. The darkness, and the strangeness of the place, with those silent men so close, made her heart beat a little quicker. She followed her escort up wide rickety steps, between two lines of men, some of whom leaned closer to peer at her, and into a large room, dimly lighted by a hanging lamp.

"Bill, hyar's a party fer you," announced the driver, setting down the baggage. "An', miss, I'll thank you fer ten dollars—stage fare."

Lucy stepped under the lamp so that she could see to find the money in her purse, and when she turned to pay the driver she espied a tall man standing with him.

"Madam, do you want supper an' bed?" he asked.

"Yes. I am Lucy Watson of Felix, and I shall want room and board, perhaps for a day or two, until I find out where I'm to go," replied Lucy.

He lighted a lamp and held it up so that he could see her face.

"Glad to help you any way I can," he said. "I'm acquainted in these parts. Come this way."

He led her into a hallway, and up a stairway, into a small room, where he placed the lamp upon a washstand. "I'll fetch your baggage up. Supper will be ready in a few minutes."

When he went out Lucy looked first to see if there was a key in the lock on the door. There was not, but she found a bolt, and laughed ruefully at the instant relief it afforded.

"I'm a brave welfare worker," she whispered to herself, scornfully. Then she gazed about the room. Besides the washstand before noted it contained a chair and a bed. The latter looked clean and inviting to Lucy. There would be need of the heavy roll of blankets at the foot. The cold air appeared to go right through Lucy. And the water in the pitcher was like ice. Before she had quite made herself ready to go downstairs she heard a bell ring, and then a great trampling of boots and a scraping of chairs on a bare floor.

"Those men coming in to supper!" she exclaimed. "Bee hunters and white-mule drinkers, that brakeman said! . . . Well, if I *have* to meet them I—I can stand it now, I guess."

The hall and stairway were so dark Lucy had to feel her way down to the door. She was guided by the loud voices and laughter in the dining room. Lucy could not help hesitating at the door. Neither her courage nor her pride could prevent the rise of unfamiliar emotions. She was a girl, alone, at the threshold of new life. Catching her breath, she opened the door.

The dining room was now brightly lighted and full of men sitting at the tables.

As Lucy entered, the hubbub of voices quieted and a sea of faces seemed to confront her. There was a small table vacant. Lucy seated herself in one of the two chairs. Her feeling of strangeness was not alleviated by the attention directed toward her. Fortunately, the proprietor approached at once, asking what she would have to eat. When she had given her order Lucy casually looked up and around the room. To her surprise and relief, none of the young men now appeared to be interested in her. They had lean hard faces and wore dark rough clothes. Lucy rather liked their appearance, and she found herself listening to the snatches of conversation.

"Jeff's rarin' to plow right off," said one. "Reckon it'll be plumb boggy," was the reply. And then others of them spoke. "My hoss piled me up this mawnin'," and, "Who air you goin' to take to the dance?" and, "Lefty March paid what he owed me an' I near dropped daid," and, "Did you-all hear about Edd Denmeade makin' up to Sadie agin, after she dished him once?" and, "Edd's shore crazy fer a wife. Wants a home, I reckon."

The talk of these young men was homely and crude. It held a dominant note of humor. Probably they were as fun-loving as the riders of the low country. Lucy had expected to be approached by some of them or at least to hear witticisms at her expense. But nothing of the kind happened. She was the only woman in the room, and she might not have been there at all, for any attention she received. Something of respect was forced from Lucy, yet, woman-like, she suffered a slight pique. Soon her supper came, and being hungry she attended to that.

After supper there was nothing for her to do but go to her room. It was cold and she quickly went to bed. For a while she lay there shivering between the cold sheets, but presently she grew warm and comfortable. The darkness appeared pitch-black. Distant voices penetrated from the lower part of the house, and through the open window came the sound of slow footsteps accompanied by clink of spurs. Then from somewhere far off sounded the bay of a hound and it was followed by the wild bark of a coyote. Both bay and bark struck lonesomely upon her spirit.

Lucy realized that actually to experience loneliness, to be really cut off from family and friends, was vastly different from the thought of it. She had deliberately severed all ties. She was alone in the world, with her way to make. A terrible blank sense of uncertainty assailed her. Independence was wholly desirable, but in its first stage it seemed hard. Lucy was not above tears, and she indulged in a luxury long unfamiliar to her. Then she cried herself to sleep.

When she awoke the sun was shining in upon her. The air was crisp and cold and bore a fragrance wild and sweet, new to Lucy. With the bright daylight all her courage returned, even to the point of exhilaration. She put on a woolen dress and heavier shoes. The cold air and water had greatly accelerated her toilet. When had her cheeks glowed as rosily as now? And for that matter, when had her hair been as rebellious? But she had no time now to brush it properly, even if her hands had not been numb. She hurried down to the dining room. A wood fire blazed and cracked in the stove, to Lucy's great satisfaction. The dining room was empty. Presently the kitchen door opened and a stout woman entered with pleasant greeting.

"Miss Watson, my husband said we might find somethin' we could do for you," she said, kindly.

"Yes indeed, you may be able to give me information I need," replied Lucy.

"I'll fetch your breakfast an' then you can tell me what you want to know."

The proprietor's wife introduced herself as Mrs. Lynn, and appeared to be a motherly person, kindly and full of curiosity. Lucy frankly explained the nature of the work she was about to undertake.

"I think it's a fine idea," responded Mrs. Lynn, emphatically. "If only the Denmeades an' the rest of them will have it."

"Will they be too proud or—or anything to give me a chance?" asked Lucy, anxiously.

"We're all plain folks up here, an' the backwoods families keep to themselves," she replied. "I don't know as I'd call them proud. They're ignorant enough, Lord knows. But they're just backwoods. Like ground-hogs, they stay in their holes."

On the moment the woman's husband came in from the street. He appeared to be a gaunt man, pallid, and evidently suffered from a lung complaint, for he had a hoarse cough.

"Bill, come here," called his wife. "Miss Watson has what I think a wonderful mission. If it will only work! . . . She's been hired by the state government to go among our people up here in the backwoods an' teach them things. She has explained to me a lot of things she will do. But in few words it means better homes for those poor people. What do you think about it?"

"Wal, first off I'd say she is a plucky an' fine little girl to take such a job," replied Mr. Lynn. "Then I'd say it's good of the state. But when it comes to what the Denmeades an' the Claypools will think about it I'm up a stump."

"Bill, it's such a splendid idea," said his wife, earnestly. "She can do much for the mothers an' children up there. We must help her to get a start."

"I reckon. Now let's see," returned her husband, ponderingly. "If our backwoods neighbors are only approached right they're fine an' hospitable. The women would welcome anyone who could help them. But the men ain't so easy. Miss Watson, though, bein' young an' nice-lookin', may be able to make a go of it. . . . If she can keep Edd Denmeade or one of them bee hunters from marryin' her!"

Here Lynn laughed good-humoredly and smiled knowingly at Lucy. Mrs. Lynn took the question more seriously.

"I was goin' to tell her that myself," she said. "But we mustn't give her the wrong impression about our neighbors. These backwoodsmen are not Bluebeards or Mormons, though they are strong on gettin' wives. They are a clean, hardy, pioneer people. Edd Denmeade, for instance now—he's a young man the like of which you won't see often. He's a queer fellow—a bee hunter, wonderful good to look at, wild like them woods he lives in, but a cleaner, finer boy I never knew. He loves his sisters. He gives his mother every dollar he earns, which, Lord Knows, isn't many. . . . Now, Miss Lucy, Edd like as not will grab you right up an' pack you off an' marry you. That would settle your welfare work."

"But, Mrs. Lynn," protested Lucy, laughing, "it takes two to make a bargain. I did not come up here to marry anyone. With all due respect to Mister Edd's manner of courting, I feel perfectly capable of taking care of myself. We can dismiss that."

"Don't you be too sure!" ejaculated Mrs. Lynn, bluntly. "It's better to be safe than sorry! . . . I ain't above tellin' you, though—if Edd Denmeade really fell in love with you—that'd be different. Edd has been tryin' to marry every single girl in the country. An' I don't believe he's been in love with any one of them. He's just woman hungry, as sometimes these backwoodsmen get. That speaks well for him bein' too clean an' fine to be like many others. An' as to that, Edd is only one of a lot of good boys."

"Thanks for telling me," replied Lucy, simply. "Of course I want to know all I can find out about these people. But just now what I need to know is how to get among them."

"Mary, I've been thinkin'," spoke up Mr. Lynn, "an' I've an idea. Suppose I call in the Rim Cabin school-teacher. He's in the post office now—just rode in. I reckon he's the one to help Miss Watson."

"Fetch him in pronto," replied Mrs. Lynn, with alacrity; and as her husband went out she continued: "It's Mr. Jenks, the school-teacher. First man teacher ever here. You see, the youngsters at Rim Cabin school never got much teachin', because whenever a schoolmarm did come one of the boys would up an' marry her. So they're tryin' a man. It's workin' out fine, I hear. Mr. Jenks is in this high, dry country for his health, same as my husband. I reckon he wasn't always a school-teacher. Anyway, he's a good Christian man, not young enough to have the girls makin' sheep eyes at him."

At this juncture Mr. Lynn returned with a slight, stoop-shouldered man whose thin serious face showed both suffering and benevolence. He was introduced to Lucy, who again, somewhat more elaborately, explained the reason for her presence in Cedar Ridge.

He made her a very gallant bow, and seated himself at the table, to bend keen kind blue eyes upon her.

"You are a courageous young woman," he said, "and if you are sincere these people will take you into their homes."

"No one could be more sincere," replied Lucy, with spirit. "I have absolutely no motive but to do good. I chose this out of a number of positions offered me. I wanted something different—and not easy."

"You have found it," he said. "The opportunity is here and it is big. There are a score or more of children who might as well belong to savages for all the civilization they get. No doctor when they are sick, no church, no amusement, no pretty things common to children, no books or toys—nothing except what little schooling I can give them. They have no school in winter, on account of weather. I've been here a month. There are twenty-seven pupils in my school, the eldest a boy of nineteen—a man, really—and the youngest a girl of four. They are like a lot of wild Hottentots. But I really think more of them than any children I ever taught. The problem is to win them."

"It must be a problem for an outsider," replied Lucy, seriously.

"I believe they will take more quickly to a girl," he went on. "At least the children and boys will. Your problem will be a different one from mine. I'll not dwell on it, lest I discourage you. What's more to the point, I can say as their teacher I've learned a good deal about their lives. At first this seemed a tragedy to me, but I am learning that a good many of our necessities are not really necessary, after all. These children and young people are really happy. They have few wants because they do not know what more civilized people have in their lives. It is not through sophistication that you will benefit them. To brighten their surroundings, change the primitive squalor, teach the children useful things—therein lies your opportunity."

"Can you advise me how to start—whom to approach first?" asked Lucy.

"Come with me," replied Mr. Jenks, earnestly. "I'm driving back to-day. I live at Johnson's—five miles down from the Rim Cabin, which, by the way, is the name of my school. I'll take you up to see Lee Denmeade. He lives some miles farther on, up in the woods under the Rim Rock. He's probably the most influential man among these backwoodsmen. I rather incline to the opinion that he will like your proposition."

"It's very good of you. Thank you," replied Lucy, gratefully. "I am ready now to go with you."

"I'll call for you in an hour," said Mr. Jenks, rising.

After he had gone out Lucy turned to Mrs. Lynn to ask: "I wonder—when he hinted about my problem and said he didn't want to discourage me—did he mean this—this marrying propensity you spoke of?"

"I reckon you hit it plumb," replied Mrs. Lynn, gravely, yet with a smile. "It's the only problem you have. You will be a blessin' to them overworked mothers an' a godsend to the children."

"Then—I can stand anything," rejoined Lucy, happily, and she ran upstairs to repack the grip she had opened. While her hands were busy her mind was preoccupied, now humorously and then thoughtfully, and again dreamily. She was indeed curious about these backwoods people—earnestly and sympathetically curious. It was impossible not to conjecture about this Edd Denmeade. She made a mental picture of him, not particularly flattering. Poor fellow! So all he wanted was a wife, any girl he could get. The thought afforded Lucy amusement, yet she felt pity for the lonesome fellow. "I hope to goodness he doesn't run after me!" soliloquized Lucy, suddenly aghast. "I certainly wouldn't marry a backwoodsman—or a cowboy. . . . Poor little foolish sister! I wonder how soon she'll find out her mistake. That Jim Middleton was no good. . . . I wish everybody wouldn't make me think of marriage. It'll be a long time until I want to—if ever."

Lucy sighed, dispelled her dreams, and finished her packing, after which she gazed out of the window.

It was considerably longer than an hour before Lucy found herself seated in an old buckboard beside Mr. Jenks, rattling along a dusty road behind the heels of two big shaggy horses.

But the brisk trot soon ended at the base of the steep ridge, up which the road zigzagged through a low-branched thick-foliaged forest, remarkable for its fragrance.

"What smells so sweet?" was one of Lucy's many questions.

"Cedar. Those gnarled trees with the gray sheafs of bark, hanging like ribbons, and the dense fine light-green foliage, are the cedars that give name to the ridge and village," replied Mr. Jenks. "They are an upland tree, an evergreen. I like them but not so well as this more graceful tree with the checkered bark. That's a juniper. See the lilac-colored berries. They grow ripe about every two years. And this huge round green bush with the smooth red-barked branches is manzanita. And that pale green plant with the spear-pointed leaves like a century plant—that's mescal. . . . But perhaps you would be more interested to hear about the people."

"Yes. But I love the outdoors and all that grows," replied Lucy, enthusiastically. "I've never had a chance to live in the country, let alone in the wilds."

"You may find it too wild, as I did at first," replied the teacher, in grim amusement. "I walk from Johnson's to the school—five miles. I used to see fresh bear tracks in mud or dust. I seldom see them now, as the bears have moved up higher. Almost every day I see deer and wild turkey. One night I was late leaving the cabin. It was moonlight. A big gray animal followed me halfway down to Johnson's. I didn't know what it was until next day, but anyhow my hair stood on end."

"And what was it?" queried Lucy.

"A mountain lion," replied Mr. Jenks, impressively.

"A lion?" echoed Lucy, incredulously. "I didn't know there were lions in this country."

"It was a panther, or cougar. But mountain lion is the proper name. I'll show you his skin. Lee Denmeade put his hounds on the track of the beast and killed it. He gave me the skin. . . . Oh, it'll be wild enough for you. After we get on top of the ridge you won't wonder that bears and lions live there."

Lucy, being an artful questioner and inspiring listener, led Mr. Jenks to talk about the people among whom she expected to dwell.

He told how some of his child pupils rode their little burros six and eight miles to school; how a slip of a boy came on horseback from his home twelve miles away; how sometimes they were frightened by wild animals and cattle. He told of the dance that was held at the schoolhouse once every week—how everyone for miles around attended—babies, children, young people, and grown-ups—and stayed from sundown to sunrise. All of which time the boys and girls danced! It was their one and only time to be together. Distance and hard work precluded the pleasure of company. Sometimes on a Sunday or a birthday one family would visit another. The girls spent what little leisure they had in sewing. The boys passed their spare time in hunting and fighting. Mr. Jenks said he had at first been dreadfully concerned at the frequent fights. But as these young backwoodsmen appeared to thrive on it, and seldom were any less friendly for all their bloody battles, he had begun to get used to it.

So interesting was the talk of the school-teacher that Lucy scarcely noted the tedious miles up the long ascent of the ridge, and was only reminded of distance when he informed her they were almost on top and would soon have a magnificent view. Despite his statement, however, Lucy was wholly unprepared for what suddenly burst upon her gaze from the summit.

"Oh—how glorious!" she cried.

It seemed she gazed down on an endless green slope of massed tree-tops, across a rolling basin black with forest, to a colossal wall of red rock, level and black fringed on top, but wildly broken along its face into gigantic cliffs, escarpments, points, and ledges, far as eye could see to east or west. How different from any other country Lucy had ever viewed! A strong sweet breath of pine assailed her nostrils. Almost she tasted it. In all the miles of green and black there was not a break. If homes of people existed there, they were lost in the immensity of the forest. An eagle soared far beneath her, with the sun shining on his wide-spread wings. A faint roar of running water floated up from the depths, and that was the only sound to disturb the great stillness. To one who had long been used to flat desert, the drab and yellow barrenness, how fertile and beautiful these miles and miles of rolling green! That wild grand wall of rock seemed to shut in the basin, to bar it from what lay beyond. Lastly the loneliness, the solitude, gripped Lucy's heart.

"We're on top of Cedar Ridge," the school-teacher was saying. "That mountain wall is called the Red Rim Rock. It's about thirty miles in a straight line. . . . We're looking down upon the homes of the backwoodsmen you've come to live among."

2

THE road down into this forest-land contrasted markedly with the ascent on the other side of the ridge; it was no longer steep and dusty; the soil was a sandy loam; the trees that shaded it were larger and more spreading. Birds, rabbits, and squirrels made their presence known.

Some ferns and mosses appeared on the edge of the woods, and pine trees were interspersed among the cedars. Mr. Jenks was nothing if not loquacious, and he varied his talk with snatches of natural history, bits of botany, and considerable of forestry. It appeared he had once been a forest ranger in one of the Northern states. Lucy had a natural thirst for knowledge, something that her situation in life had tended to develop.

They descended to a level and followed the road through pine thickets above which an occasional monarch of the forest reared itself commandingly. At length they abruptly drove out of the woods into the first clearing. Lucy's thought was—how hideous! It was a slash in the forest, a denuded square, with dead trees standing in the brown fields, a rickety fence of crooked poles surrounding a squat log cabin, with open door and dark window suggestive of vacancy.

"Family named Sprall once lived here," said Mr. Jenks. "Improvident sort of man. He has a large family, more or less addicted to white mule. They moved back in some canyon under the Rim."

"I've heard of this white mule," replied Lucy. "Of course it's a drink, and I gather that it kicks like a mule. But just what is it?"

"Just plain mooshine whisky without color. It looks like alcohol. It *is* alcohol. I once took a taste. Fire and brimstone! I nearly choked to death. . . . The people of this district make it to some extent. They raise a kind of cane from which they distill the liquor. But I'm bound to say that seldom indeed do I see a drunken man."

Beyond this deserted clearing the road tunneled into a denser forest where the pungent odor of pine thickly pervaded the atmosphere. The ground was a smooth mat of pine needles, only sparsely grown over with underbrush. Live-oak trees appeared, at first stunted, but gradually developing into rugged members of the forest. Noon found the travelers halted beside the first brook, a tiny trickling rill of clear water. Lucy was grateful for a cool drink. Mr. Jenks had been thoughtful to provide a lunch, of which they partook while sitting in the shade of an oak.

Here Lucy had opportunity to observe a small reddish-brown squirrel that was the sauciest little animal she had ever beheld. It occupied a branch above her and barked in no uncertain notes its displeasure and curiosity. Presently its chatter attracted a beautiful crested blue jay that flew close and uttered high-pitched notes, wild and fierce in their intensity.

"I hope the people here are not as antagonistic as this squirrel and bird," observed Lucy.

"A few of them are—like the Spralls, for instance," replied Mr. Jenks. "Well, we still have far to go. I call it five miles from here to Johnson's. You'll say it's five leagues."

If Lucy had not been eager and anxious to establish her position securely here in the region she would have reveled in the winding shady road through the green-canopied, sun-flecked forest. Along here it had a considerable sameness, that added to the distance. Lucy indeed found the so-called five miles almost interminable. About two o'clock Mr. Jenks drove into another clearing, somewhat less hideous than the first one, but still a crude, ragged, unpastoral kind of farm. A wide green field dotted by cows and horses was the only redeeming feature. Log corrals and pole fences led the eye to a large log cabin surrounded by shacks old and moldy-roofed, manifestly the first buildings erected.

"This is the Johnson place, where I live," said Mr. Jenks, with a smile. "That framework of boards, covered by a tent, is my humble domicile. Do you know, Miss Watson, I have actually grown to love sleeping out there? . . . This is Sunday, which means the Johnsons will all be home or all away visiting."

The school-teacher drove through an open gate in the log fence, and past a huge flat barn, dark and odorous of horses, to draw rein at the back of the cabin.

"I was wrong. Sam Johnson is home, at least. I don't know the boy with him," said Mr. Jenks, as he threw the reins and got down.

"I'd like to walk a little," rejoined Lucy.

"You'll probably walk, and climb, and besides ride horseback, before you're through to-day," replied Mr. Jenks, laughing, as he reached for his parcels on the seat.

"Oh, that'll be fine!" exclaimed Lucy, delighted. And naturally she gazed over at the young men sitting on the rude porch. They might have been two of the boys she had seen in the dining room at Cedar Ridge.

"Sam, she's a looker," drawled one of them, in a perfectly audible voice.

The other stood up, disclosing a tall, lithe form clad in blue jeans. He had a shock of tousled chestnut hair and a freckled face that on the moment bore a broad grin.

"Dog-gone me!" he ejaculated. "Teacher has fetched back a wife."

Lucy met the teacher's eyes. They were twinkling. She could not restrain a laugh, yet she felt a blush rise to her face.

"Sam flatters me, Miss Watson," said Mr. Jenks, in low voice. "But that illustrates."

"They must have this wife business on the brain," retorted Lucy, half nettled.

The teacher called to the young man, Sam, who approached leisurely, a young giant somewhere over twenty years of age, clean-eyed and smooth-faced.

"Howdy, teacher!" he drawled, but his light hazel eyes were fixed on Lucy.

"This is Sam Johnson," spoke up Mr. Jenks, turning to Lucy. "Sam, meet Miss Lucy Watson of Felix. She has come to sojourn awhile with us."

"Right glad to meet you," said Sam, somewhat shyly.

"Thank you, Mr. Johnson," replied Lucy.

"Sam, will you saddle two horses for us? I'm taking Miss Watson up to Denmeade's," interposed Mr. Jenks.

"Shore will, teacher," rejoined Sam, and moved away with sidelong glance at Lucy.

"Have you any riding clothes?" inquired Mr. Jenks, as if suddenly reminded of something important.

"Yes. I was careful not to forget outdoor things," replied Lucy.

"Good! I'll carry your grips to my tent, where you can change. Of course we'll have to leave your baggage here until we interview Denmeade. If all goes well it can be packed up to-night."

The interior of Mr. Jenks's abode was vastly more prepossessing than the exterior. It was such an attractive little place that Lucy decided she wanted one similar to it, for the summer at least. The furnishings included a comfortable-looking cot, a washstand with mirror above, a table, books, lamp, and pictures. Several skins, notably a long gray furry one she took to have belonged to the lion Mr. Jenks had mentioned, served as rugs for the rude board floor. A picture of a sweet, sad-looking woman occupied a prominent place. Lucy wondered if she was his wife.

It did not take her many minutes to get into her riding clothes. Fortunately they had seen a service which now appeared likely to serve her in good stead. At normal school Lucy had ridden horseback once a week, and felt that she was not altogether a tenderfoot. Finding her gauntlets, she had the forethought to pack her traveling suit, so that in case she remained at Denmeade's her baggage could be sent for. Then, with a last and not unsatisfied glance at herself in the mirror, she sallied forth from the tent, keen for this next stage of her adventure.

A glossy, spirited little bay pony stood there saddled and bridled, champing his bit. Another horse, dusty and shaggy, large in build and very bony, was haltered to the hitching rail near by. Mr. Jenks was lacing something on the saddle of the smaller horse. Sam Johnson lounged beside him and the other fellow had approached. He did not appear so tall or so lean as young Johnson.

Lucy felt uncertain how these backwoodsmen would take her rather trim and natty riding suit, but as she knew she looked well it gave her no great concern. She had made up her mind to win the liking of all these people, if possible.

"What a pretty pony!" she exclaimed. "Am I to ride him, Mr. Jenks?"

"Yes—if you can," returned the teacher, dubiously, as he looked up from his task. "I assure you he is no pony, but a very mettlesome mustang."

"Aw, teacher, Buster's as gentle as a lamb," protested Sam. Then, indicating his companion by a sweep of his long arm, he said, "Miss Lucy, this here is my cousin, Gerd Claypool."

Lucy had to give her hand to the brown-faced young man, for he had extended a great paw. She liked his face. It was rich and warm with healthy blood, and expressive of both eagerness and bashfulness. Lucy was not going to forget his remark, "Sam, she's a looker!" and she gazed as demurely as possible into his blue eyes. It took only one glance to convince her that he was of the type Mrs. Lynn had praised so heartily. Lucy also saw that he was quite overcome.

"Mettlesome mustang?" echoed Lucy, gazing from Mr. Jenks to Sam. "Does that mean anything terrible? I assure you I'm no cowgirl."

Sam's shrewd eyes sought her boots and then her gauntlets. "Wal, you're shore no stranger to a hoss. Buster isn't a bronc. He's never pitched with a girl yet. Talk to him some an' pat him as if you'd no idea a hoss could be mean."

Lucy did as she was bidden, successfully hiding her nervousness; and it appeared that Buster did not show any viciousness or fear. He had a keen, dark eye, somewhat fiery, but not at all fierce. As he was a small horse, Lucy mounted him easily, to her satisfaction.

"How's the length of your stirrups?" asked Mr. Jenks.

"Just right, I think," replied Lucy, standing up in them.

"Wal, I reckon they're a little long—I mean short," drawled Sam, approaching.

Lucy was quick to grasp the guile in this young gentleman of the woods. He was as clear as an inch of crystal water. She grasped just as quickly the fact that she was going to have a good deal of fun with these boys. Sam knew her stirrups were all right; what he wanted was a chance to come close to her while she was in the saddle. It was an old cowboy trick.

"Thanks, I'm very comfortable," she said, smiling at him.

Meanwhile Mr. Jenks had mounted and turned his horse toward the road.

"I never rode this nag," he said. "Come now, Miss Watson."

"Teacher, look out she doesn't run off from you," called Sam, as they started. His voice was full of mirth. "An', Miss Lucy, that's shore a regular hoss you're ridin'."

Lucy turned in the saddle. "I nearly forgot to thank you, Mr. Johnson. It is good of you to let me ride him."

She found Buster rather hard to hold in. Before she had followed Mr. Jenks many paces she heard Sam blurt out to his cousin, "Gerd, by golly! it's shore worth a lot to have Edd Denmeade see *that* girl ridin' my best hoss."

"Haw! Haw!" roared Gerd, and then made reply Lucy could not distinguish.

Presently she caught up with her guide and together they rode out through the corral.

"Mr. Jenks, did you hear what they said?" inquired Lucy.

"Indeed I did. They're full of the old Nick, those boys. I'd like to be in your boots, yet again I wouldn't."

"What did he mean by saying it was worth a lot to have Edd Denmeade see me riding his horse?"

"It was a compliment to you, especially his emphasis on the qualifying adjective before girl," replied the teacher, with a chuckle. "You see, Edd Demeade seems a superior sort of person to most of the boys. Really he is only forceful— a strong, simple, natural character. But the boys don't understand him. And the girls do still less. That is why I suspect some have refused to marry him. Sam now is tickled to have Edd see the very prettiest girl who ever came to Cedar Ridge ride up on his horse. Edd will be wild with jealousy."

"Goodness! I'm afraid most girl visitors here have been homely," replied Lucy.

"No, they haven't been, either," declared the teacher. "Now, Miss Watson, we have a mile or so of good sandy road before we cut off on the trails. Let's have a gallop. But be sure you don't do what Sam hinted—run off from me. You might get lost."

With that he urged his mount from walk to trot and from trot to gallop. Lucy's horse did not need urging; he bolted and shot down the road ahead of Mr. Jenks. Lucy was alarmed at first and found it hard to keep her feet in the stirrups. But soon she caught the swing of the mustang and then a wild impulse prompted her to let him run. How fast he sped on under the pines! His gait made the saddle seem like a rocking-chair. But she hauled hard on Buster, obedient to the resolve she had made—that she would restrain herself in all ways. Pulling him to a swinging canter, Lucy took stock of pleasant sensations. The rush through the pine-scented air was exhilarating; soon the exercise had her blood dancing all over her; low branches of pine tore at her hair; the turns of the winding road through the woods allured with their call of strange new scenes. Rabbits darted ahead of her, across the open, into the pine thickets. At length, some distance ahead she saw where the road forked, and here she brought Buster to a stand. She was tingling, pulsing with heated blood, and felt that she could have cried out with the joy of the moment.

Mr. Jenks came galloping up to halt beside her. "That was bully," he said. "Miss Watson, you need not be ashamed of your riding. . . . We take the left-hand road. That to the right goes on to my log-cabin school. I wish we had time to see it. A little way farther we strike a trail."

Soon after that Lucy was riding behind the teacher along a narrow trail that almost at once began to lead downhill. The forest grew denser and the shade became dark and cool. Rocks and ledges cropped out of the ground, and all about her appeared to tend toward a wilder and more rugged nature. The dreamy, drowsy hum which filled Lucy's ears swelled to a roar. It came from far down through the forest. It was running water and it thrilled Lucy. How sweet and welcome this verdant forest to eyes long used to desert glare!

The trail took a decided pitch, so that Lucy had to cling to the pommel of her saddle. It led down and down, into a ravine full of mellow roar, deep, murmuring, mystical, where the great trees shut out the sky. Only faint gleams of sunlight filtered down. They came to a rushing brook of amber water, brawling and foaming over rocks, tearing around huge mossy bowlders, and gleaming on down a wild defile, gloomy with its shadows.

The horses stopped to drink and then forded the brook, crashing on the rocks, plunging on to splash the water ahead. Lucy had a touch of that sweet cold water on her face. On the other side the trail turned up this beautiful glen, and followed the brook, winding in and out among bowlders that loomed high overhead. Ferns and flowers bordered the trail. Maples and birches grew thickly under the stately pines. Lucy became aware of another kind of tree, the most wonderful she had ever seen, huge-trunked, thick with drooping foliage, and lifting its proud height spear-shaped to the sky. Her guide informed her that this tree was a silver spruce, which name seemed singularly felicitous.

Again they forded the brook, to Lucy's mingled dismay and delight, and after that so many times that she forgot them and also her fears. The forest became a grand temple. Higher towered the forest patriarchs, two hundred feet and more above her head, mingling their foliage in a lacy canopy, like a green veil against the blue. She caught a glimpse of wild sleek gray creatures bounding as on rubber legs into the brush. Deer!

At last the trail led out of the fragrant glen and zig-zagged up a slope, to the dry forest of pines, and on and upward, farther and higher until Lucy felt she had ascended to the top of a mountain. She lost the mellow roar of the brook. The woodland changed its aspect, grew hot with dusty trail and thick with manzanita, above which the yellow-barked pines reached with great gnarled arms. Open places were now frequent. Once Lucy saw a red wall of rock so high above her that she gasped in astonishment. That was the Red Rim Rock, seemingly so close, though yet far away. Lucy became conscious of aches and pains. She shifted from side to side in the saddle, and favored this foot, then the other. Often she had to urge Buster on to catch up with her guide.

Suddenly she turned a corner of the brushy trail to ride out into a clearing. Bare brown earth, ghastly dead pines, like specters, seemed to lift her gaze, to where, sky-high, the red wall heaved, bold, strange, terrific, yet glorious with its zigzag face blazing in the hues of sunset, and its black-fringed crown wandering away as if to the ends of the earth.

Strangely then into her mind flashed a thought of this backwoods boy whose name had been on the lips of everyone she had met. Born under that colossal wall! All his life in this forest and rock solitude! Lucy could not help but wonder what manner of man he was. She resented an involuntary interest. The force of a personality had been thrust upon her. It was feminine intuition that caused her, unconsciously, to fortify herself by roused antagonism.

Mr. Jenks pointed to a little rough gray house, half log, half stones, that dominated the clearing. "Denmeade built it twenty-three years ago," said the teacher. "He and his wife walked up here, from no one knows where. They had a burro, a cow, a gun, and an ax, and some dogs. They homesteaded this section. He had five girls and four boys, all born in that little one-room hut. Edd is the oldest—he's twenty-two. Last year they built quite a fine log cabin, up in the woods beyond the fields. You can't see it from here."

The surroundings seemed fitting for such heroic people as these Denmeades.

"They may be backwoodsmen," declared Lucy, voicing her thought, "but I'd call them pioneers. Which is to say real Americans!"

"Miss Watson, I like that," replied the teacher, warmly. "You have gotten the significance. These people are great."

Over against that impulsive impression Lucy had the crudeness of the scene to oppose it. She was intelligent enough to accept crudeness as a part of pioneer life. It could not be otherwise. But she gazed over the slash cut in the forest, and found it lacking in anything she could admire. The Red Rim Rock and the encircling belt of mighty green were facts of nature. This space of bare ground with its ghastly dead trees, its ruined old hut, its uncouth shacks of boards and poles, its pigs rooting around, its utter lack of what constituted her idea of a farm, somehow did not seem to harmonize with the noble pioneer spirit. Lucy hesitated to make this impression permanent. She did not like the look of this place, but she was broad-minded enough to wait. She hoped she would not find these people lazy, shiftless, dirty, existing in squalid surroundings. Yet she feared that would be exactly what she would find.

The trail led along a patchwork fence of poles and sticks, here rotting away and there carelessly mended by the throwing of an untrimmed branch of tree.

At the corner of the huge field snuggled the rude shacks she had seen from afar, all the worse for nearer view. They rode between these and a round log corral, full of pigs of all sizes, and from which came an unbearable stench. Some of the hogs were stuck in the mud. Lucy saw some tiny baby pigs, almost pink, with funny little curly tails, and sight of these gave her unexpected pleasure. So she experienced two extremes of feeling in passing that point.

From there the trail led through an uncared-for orchard of peach trees, into a narrow lane cut in the woods. The pines had been left where they had fallen, and lay brown and seared in the tangle of green. This lane was full of stumps.

"You appreciate why we needed horses to get here, don't you?" inquired Mr. Jenks.

"Indeed I do!" replied Lucy.

"Denmeade said he'd never live in a place where wheels could go. I rather sympathize with that spirit, but it is not one of a progressive farmer. I dare say you will have it to combat."

The lane descended into a ravine, where clear water ran over stones that rang hollow under the hoofs of the horses. Lucy saw cows and calves, a very old sheep, woolly and dirty, and a wicked-looking steer with wide sharp horns. Lucy was glad to get safely past him. They rode up again, into a wider lane, at the end of which showed a long cabin, somewhat obscured by more peach trees. A column of blue smoke curled up against the background of red wall. A fence of split boards surrounded the cabin. A strip of woods on the right separated this lane from the bare field. Lucy could see light through the pine foliage. The brook meandered down a shallow ravine on this side; and on the other a deep gully yawned, so choked with dead trees and green foliage and red rocks that Lucy could not see the bottom. She heard, however, the fall of water.

A dog barked. Then rose a chorus of barks and bays, not in the least a friendly welcome. It increased to an uproar. Lucy began to be conscious of qualms when a loud sharp voice rang out. The uproar ceased.

"Hyar, you ornery dawgs, shet up!" the voice continued.

Then Lucy saw a tall man emerge from the peach trees and come to the gate. His garb was dark, his face also at that distance, and they gave a sinister effect.

"That's Denmeade," whispered Mr. Jenks. "We're lucky. Now, young lady, use your wits."

They rode on the few remaining rods, and reaching the rude hitching rail in front of the fence, they halted the horses. Mr. Jenks dismounted and greeted the big man at the gate.

"Howdy, teacher!" he replied, in a deep, pleasant drawl.

"Fine, thank you, Denmeade," returned Mr. Jenks, as he extended his hand over the fence. "I've brought a visitor to see you. This is Miss Lucy Watson of Felix."

Lucy essayed her most winning smile as she acknowledged the introduction.

"Glad to meet you, miss," responded Denmeade. "Get down an' come in."

Dismounting, Lucy approached the gate, to look up into a visage as rugged as the rock wall above. Denmeade was not old or gray, though his features showed the ravages of years. Lucy had no time to mark details. The man's eyes, gray and piercing as those of an eagle, caught and held her gaze.

"If you please, I'd like to talk to you alone before I go in," she said, appealingly.

Denmeade removed the huge battered black sombrero, and ran a brawny hand through his thick dark hair. The gray eyes twinkled and a smile changed the craggy nature of his face.

"Wal, seein' as Edd ain't hyar, I reckon I can risk it," he drawled.

Mr. Jenks suggested that they sit in the shade; and presently Lucy found herself seated on a stump, facing this curious backwoodsman. He seemed a more approachable person than she had pictured, yet there was something about him, strong, raw, fierce, like the wilds in which he lived. Lucy had worried about this coming interview; had schooled herself to a deliberate diplomacy. But she forgot worry and plan. The man's simplicity made her sincere.

"Mr. Denmeade, I want a job," she announced, bluntly.

It was good to see his astonishment and utter incredulity. Such a situation had never before happened in his life. He stared. His seamed visage worked into a wonderful grin.

"Wal, I reckon yore foolin'," he said, and he turned to Jenks. "Teacher, shore you've hatched some kind of a joke."

"No, Denmeade. Miss Watson is in earnest," replied the school-teacher.

"Indeed I am," added Lucy, trying to restrain her impulsiveness.

But Denmeade still could not take her seriously. "Wal, can you chop wood, carry water, pick beans, an' hop around lively—say fer a fellar like my Edd?"

"Yes, I could, but that is not the kind of a job I want," returned Lucy.

"Wal, there ain't no other kind of work up hyar fer a woman," he said, seriously.

"Yes, there is. . . . It's to make better homes for the children."

"Better homes! What you mean?" ejaculated Denmeade.

Briefly Lucy explained some of the ways the homes in the wilderness could be made happier for women and children. Denmeade was profoundly impressed.

"Wal now, young woman, I reckon it's good of you to think of them nice an' pretty ways fer our kids an' their mothers. But we're poor. We couldn't pay you, let alone fer them things they need so bad."

Lucy's heart throbbed with joy. She knew intuitively that she had struck the right chord in this old backwoodsman. Whereupon she produced her papers.

"It's a new thing, Mr. Denmeade," she said, earnestly. "State welfare work.

My salary and the expenses I incur are paid by the state. It's all here for you to read, and my references.''

Denmeade took her papers in his horny hands, and began to read with the laborious and intense application of one to whom reading was unfamiliar and difficult. He took long to go over the brief typed words, and longer over the personal letter from the superintendent of the state department that had engaged Lucy. Finally he absorbed the import.

"Welfare! State government! Dog-gone me!'' he ejaculated, almost bewildered. "Say, Jenks, what ails them fellars down thar?''

"Perhaps they have just waked up to the needs of this north country,'' replied the teacher.

"Shore them papers don't read like they had an ax to grind. Reckon it ain't no politics or some trick to make us pay taxes?''

"Denmeade, they read honest to me, and my advice, if you ask it, is to accept their help.''

"Humph! It shore took them a long time to build us a schoolhouse an' send us a teacher. Whar did they ever get this hyar welfare idee?''

"Mr. Denmeade,'' spoke up Lucy, "I had something to do with this idea. It really developed out of my offer to go into welfare work in a civilized district.''

"Wal, comin' from a girl like you, it ain't hard to accept,'' he declared, and he extended his great brown hand. His gray eyes flashed with a softened light.

Lucy placed her hand in his, and as he almost crushed it she was at considerable pains to keep from crying out. When he released it she felt that it was limp and numb.

"You—you mean it—it's all right?'' she stammered. "You'll let me stay— help me get started?''

"I shore will,'' he replied, forcefully. "You stay hyar with us as long as you want. I reckon, though, the other four families close by in this high country need you more'n us. Seth Miller's, Hank Claypool's, Ora Johnson's, an' Tom Sprall's.''

"Miss Watson, the Ora Johnson he means is a brother of the Sam Johnson you met,'' interposed Mr. Jenks.

Lucy was too happy to express her gratitude, and for a moment lost her dignity. Her incoherent thanks brought again the broad grin to Denmeade's face.

"Jenks, come to think about it, thar's angles to this hyar job Miss Lucy is aimin' at,'' he remarked, thoughtfully. "She can't do a lot for one family an' slight another. If she stays hyar with us she'll have to stay with the others.''

"Of course. That's what I expect to do,'' said Lucy.

"Wal, miss, I ain't given to brag, but I reckon you'll find it different after stayin' with us,'' rejoined Denmeade, shaking his shaggy head.

Plain it was for Lucy to see that Mr. Jenks agreed with him.

"In just what way?" queried Lucy.

"Lots of ways, but particular, say—Ora Johnson has an old cabin with one room. Countin' his wife, thar's eight in the family. All live in that one room! With one door an' no winder!"

Lucy had no ready reply for such an unexpected circumstance as this, and she gazed at Mr. Jenks in mute dismay.

"I have a tent I'll lend her," he said. "It can be erected on a frame with board floor. Very comfortable."

"Wal, I reckon that would do fer Johnson's. But how about Tom Sprall's? Thar's more in his outfit, an' only two cabins. But shore no room for her. An' the tent idee won't do—sartin not whar Bud Sprall goes rarin' around full of white mule. It wouldn't be safe."

"Denmeade, I had that very fear in mind," said Mr. Jenks, earnestly. "Miss Watson will have to avoid Sprall's."

"Shore, it'd ought to be done. But I'm reckonin' that'll raise hell. Tom is a mean cuss, an' his outfit of wimmen are jealous as coyote poison. They'll all have to know Miss Lucy is hyar helpin' everybody equal. They'll all want equal favors from the state. I ain't sayin' a word ag'in' Tom, but he's a rustler. An' thar's turrible bad blood between Bud Sprall an' my boy Edd."

"You see, Miss Watson, it's not going to be as rosy as we hoped," said Mr. Jenks, regretfully.

"I'm not afraid," replied Lucy, resolutely. "It never looked easy. I accept it, come what may. The Spralls shall not be slighted."

"Wal, you've settled it, an' thar ain't nothin' wrong with your nerve," replied Denmeade. "Come in now an' meet my folks. Teacher, you'll eat supper with us?"

"I'm sorry, Denmeade. I must hurry back and send Sam up with her baggage," returned Jenks, rising. "Good-by, Miss Watson. I wish you luck. Come down to school with the children. I'll see you surely at the dance Friday night."

"I'm very grateful to you, Mr. Jenks," replied Lucy. "You've helped me. I will want to see you soon. But I can't say that it will be at the dance."

"Shore she'll be thar, teacher," said Denmeade. "She can't stay hyar alone, an' if she wanted to, Edd wouldn't let her."

"Oh—indeed!" murmured Lucy, constrainedly, as Denmeade and the schoolteacher exchanged laughs. How irrepressibly this Edd bobbed up at every turn of conversation! Right then Lucy resolved that she would certainly not go to the dance. And she realized an undue curiosity in regard to this backwoods boy.

3

LUCY followed her escort into the yard and between the blossoming peach trees to the cabin. She saw now that it was a new structure built of flat-hewn logs, long and low, with a peaked roof of split shingles covering two separate square cabins and the wide space between them. This roof also extended far out to cover a porch the whole length of the building. Each cabin had a glass window, and the door, which Lucy could not see, must have faced the middle porch. The rude solid structure made a rather good impression.

A long-eared hound stood wagging his tail at the head of the porch steps. Lucy's roving eye took in other dogs asleep in sunny spots; several little puppies with ears so long they stumbled over them as they ran pell-mell to meet Denmeade; heavy rolls of canvas, no doubt blankets or bedding, were piled along the wall; saddles and saddle blankets were ranged in similar order on the opposite side; the cabin wall on the right was studded with pegs upon which hung kitchen utensils and tools; that on the left held deer and elk antlers used as racks for hats, guns, ropes. The wide space of porch between the two cabins evidently served as an out-door dining room, for a rude home-carpentered table and benches occupied the center.

At Denmeade's call a flock of children came trooping out of the door of the left cabin. They were big-eyed, dirty and ragged, and sturdy of build. A sallow, thin-faced little woman, in coarse dress and heavy shoes, followed them.

"Ma, this hyar is Miss Lucy Watson from Felix," announced Denmeade.

Mrs. Denmeade greeted Lucy cordially and simply, without show of curiosity or astonishment. Then Denmeade told her in his blunt speech what Lucy had come for. This information brought decided surprise and welcome to the woman's face. Lucy was quick to see what perhaps Denmeade had never known in his life. She added a few earnest words in her own behalf, calculated to strengthen Mrs. Denmeade's impression, and to say that when convenient they would talk over the work Lucy was to undertake.

"Reckon you're a new kind of teacher?" queried Mrs. Denmeade. "Sort of home-teacher?"

"Why yes, you could call me that," replied Lucy, smiling.

"Shore that'll please the kids," said Denmeade. "They sort of look up to a teacher. You see we've only had schoolteachers a few years. Edd went four years, Allie three, Dick an' Joe three, Mertie two, Mary an' Dan one. Liz an' Lize, the twins hyar, five years old—they haven't started yet.''

Whereupon the children were presented to Lucy, a situation rich in pleasure and interest for her. The twins were as like as two peas in a pod, chubby, rosey-cheeked little girls, fair-haired, with big eyes of gray like their father's. To Lucy's overtures they were shy, silent, yet fascinated. Dan was a dark-headed youngster, with eyes to match, dirty, mischievous, bold, and exceedingly responsive to Lucy. Mary, too, was dark, though lighter than Dan, older by a year or two, a thin overworked girl who under favorable conditions would be pretty. The several other children present were Claypools, visiting the Denmeades. When Lucy had greeted them all she was to meet Denmeade's older daughters Allie, a young woman, huge of build, with merry face, and Mertie, a girl of sixteen, quite beautiful in a wild-rose kind of way. She was the only one of the family who showed anything of color or neatness in her attire. Manifestly she wore her Sunday dress, a coarse print affair. Her sharp dark eyes seemed more concerned with Lucy's riding habit, the way she had arranged her hair and tied her scarf, than with Lucy's presence there.

Lucy was taken into the left-hand cabin, to meet the mother and sister of the Claypool children. They, too, were hard-featured, unprepossessing, and bore the unmistakable marks of hard labor in a hard country. All these impressions of Lucy's were hasty ones that she knew might pass entirely or change. Intense as was her interest, she could not stare at or study these people. She had to confess that they put her at her ease. There was not a suspicion of inhospitality, or, for that matter, except on the part of the children, the betrayal of anything unusual about this newcomer. Lucy was given one of the few home-made chairs, a rude triangular board affair that could be set two ways. And then the conversation which no doubt her advent had interrupted was resumed by the older women.

The twins began to manifest signs of being irresistibly drawn to Lucy. They were in the toils of a new experience. Lucy had been used to children, and had taken several months of kindergarten work, which was going to be of infinite value to her here. She listened to the conversation, which turned out to be homely gossip, differing only in content from gossip anywhere. And while doing so she had a chance to gaze casually round the room.

The walls were bare, of rough-hewn logs, with the chinks between plastered with clay. There was a window on each side. A huge rough stone fireplace occupied nearly all the west end of the cabin. In a left-hand corner, next to the fireplace, was a closet of boards reaching from floor to ceiling. This ceiling appeared to be of the same kind of shingling Lucy had observed on the roof. The floor was rough clapboard, like that of the porch outside. The two corners opposite the fireplace contained built-in beds, bulky with a quilted covering. There were no other articles of furniture, not even a table or lamp.

Lucy appreciated that this living room, despite its lack of comforts, might be far superior to the dark, clay-floored cabin rooms she had heard about. It was at least dry and light. But its bareness jarred on her. What did these people do with their leisure time, if they had any? The younger women talked of nothing save dances and boys; their elders interpolated their gossip with bits of news about the homely labors that spring had brought. Mary was the only one of the children whom Lucy could induce to talk; and she had, apparently, a limited range of subjects. School, the burro she rode, the puppies she played with, appeared to be in possession of her mind.

At length the Claypools announced that if they were to reach home by dark they must hurry.

"Come an' see us," invited the mother, addressing Lucy, and the grown daughter added: "'By. Reckon Edd'll be fetchin' you an' Mertie to the dance."

Lucy murmured something noncommittal in reply, and accompanied the women and children outside. They left the porch at the far end of the cabin, and went through a side gate out into the woods, where two horses and a burro were haltered to trees. Dogs, sheep, and chickens tagged at their heels. There was a rather open clearing under the pines, trodden bare, and covered with red and white chips of wood. Women and children talked all together, so that it was impossible for Lucy to distinguish much of what was said. She gathered, however, that Mrs. Denmeade told Mrs. Claypool something about Lucy's welfare work. Then mother and daughter, unmindful of their skirts, mounted the two horses.

The burro raised one long ear and cocked the other at the three Claypool youngsters. Mrs. Denmeade and Allie lifted them up on the back of the burro. It had a halter tied round its nose. The little boy, who could not have been more than four years old, had the foremost position astride the burro. He took up the halter. His sisters, aged, respectively, about three and two, rode behind him. The older girl got her arms round the boy, and the younger did likewise by her sister. Lucy was not only amazed and frightened for the youngsters, but also so amused she could scarcely contain herself.

"Aren't you afraid you'll fall off?" she asked, standing abreast of them.

"Naw!" said the boy. And the elder girl, with a sober smile at Lucy, added: "'Tain't nuthin' to fall off. But it's hard gettin' back on."

It required considerable beating and kicking on the part of the three to start the burro after the horses, but at last he decided to move, and trotted off.

"How far have they to go?" inquired Lucy, as she watched them disappear in the woods.

"Reckon five miles or so. They'll get home about dark," replied Mrs. Denmeade. "Now, girls, there's supper to get. An', Miss Watson, you're goin' to be more one of the family than company. Make yourself to home."

Mary attached herself to Lucy and led her around the corner of the cabin to see the puppies, while the twins toddled behind. Lucy wanted to know the names of the puppies and all about them. When Mary had exhausted this subject she led Lucy to see her especial playground, which was across the ravine in a sheltered spot redolent of pine needles. She showed Lucy a nook under a large manzanita where she played with pine cones and bits of Indian pottery, which she said she had found right there. Lucy had to see the spring, and the stone steps across the brook, and the big iron kettle and tub which were used in washing. Lucy looked in vain for an outhouse of any description. There was none, not even a chicken-coop. Mary said the chickens roosted in trees, like the wild turkeys, to keep from being eaten by beasts. Lucy inquired about these beasts, and further if there were snakes and bugs.

"Rattlers, trantulars, an' scorpions in summer. That's all that's bad," said Mary.

"Goodness! That's enough!" exclaimed Lucy.

"They won't hurt nobody," added the child, simply. Then she led Lucy across the clearing, where the twins tarried on an enterprise of their own, and down a trail into the deep gully. Here among the rocks and ferns, overshadowed by the pines and sycamores, they got away from the despoiled forest above. Lucy was glad to rest a little and listen to Mary's prattle. How wild and rugged this gully! Yet it was scarcely a stone's-throw from the cabin. The clear water babbled over smooth red stone and little falls and gravelly bars.

"It dries up in summer," said Mary, indicating the brook. "Sometimes the spring does, too. Then we all have to pack water from way down."

They came at length to a green bench that had been cleared of brush and small trees, yet, owing to the giant spreading pines above, did not long get direct rays of the sun. Rude boxes, some of them painted, were scattered around on little platforms of stones.

"Edd's beehives," said Mary, with grave importance. "We must be awful good. Edd doesn't mind if we behave."

"I'll be very careful, Mary. I don't want to get stung. Are they real wild bees?"

"Shore. But Edd tames them. Oh, Edd loves bees somethin' turrible," answered the child, solemnly. "Bees never sting him, even when he's choppin' a new bee tree."

"Why does Edd do that?" inquired Lucy.

"Didn't you ever, ever hear of Edd Denmeade's honey?" returned Mary, in great surprise. "Pa says it's the best in the world. Oh-umum! He'll shore give *you* some. Edd likes girls next to his bees. . . . He's a bee hunter. Pa says Edd's the best bee liner he ever seen."

"Bee liner! What's that, Mary?"

"Why, he watches for bees, an' when they come he lines them. Bees fly straight off, you know. He lines them to their hive in a tree. Then he chops it down. Always he saves the honey, an' sometimes he saves the bees."

The child added to the interest accumulating round the name of Edd Denmeade.

"Where is Edd now?" asked Lucy.

"He went to Winbrook with the pack burros," replied Mary. "That's up over the Rim an' far off, to the railroad. Edd's promised to take me there some day. Shore he ought to be back soon. I want him awful bad. Candy! Edd always fetches us candy. He'll come by Mertie's birthday. That's next Wednesday. He's fetchin' Mertie's new dress. Her first boughten one! She's sixteen. An' Edd's givin' it to her. Oh, he'll come shore, 'cause he loves Mertie."

"Of course he loves you, too?" queried Lucy, winningly.

"Ma says so. But Mertie's his favorite. She's so pretty. I wish I was," replied Mary, with childish pathos.

"You will be, Mary, when you are sixteen, if you are good and learn how to take care of yourself, and have beautiful thoughts," said Lucy.

"Ma told Mrs. Claypool you was a home-teacher. Are you goin' to teach me all that?"

"Yes, and more. Won't you like to learn how to make nice dresses?"

"Oh!" cried Mary, beamingly, and she burst into a babble of questions. Lucy answered. How simple! She had anticipated cudgeling her brains to satisfy these backwoods children. But Mary was already won. They remained in the gully until the sun sank, and then climbed out. Mary ran to confide her bursting news to the little twin sisters, and Lucy was left to herself for the time being. She walked down the lane, and across the strip of woodland to the open fields, and out where she could see.

Westward along the Rim vast capes jutted out, differing in shape and length, all ragged, sharp fringed, reaching darkly for the gold and purple glory of the sunset. Shafts and rays of light streamed from the rifts in the clouds, blazing upon the bold rock faces of the wall. Eastward the Rim zigzagged endlessly into pale cold purple. Southward a vast green hollow ran like a river of the sea, to empty, it seemed, into space. Beyond that rose dim spectral shapes of mountains, remote and detached. To the north the great wall shut out what might lie beyond.

How unscalable it looked to Lucy! Points of rim ran out, narrow, broken, sloping, apparently to sheer off into the void. But the distance was far and the light deceiving. Lucy knew a trail came down the ragged cape that loomed out over Denmeade's ranch. She had heard some one say Edd would come back that way with the pack-train. It seemed incredible for a man, let alone a burro. Just to gaze up at that steep of a thousand deceptive ridges, cracks, slants, and ascents was enough to rouse respect for these people who were conquering the rock-confined wilderness.

This lifting of Lucy's spirit gave pause to the growth of something akin to contempt that had unconsciously formed in her mind. After hearing and reading about these primitive inhabitants of the wild she had developed abstract conceptions of kindliness, sympathy, and close contact with them. They had been very noble sentiments. But she was going to find them hard to live up to. By analyzing her feelings she realized that she did not like the personal intimations. Her one motive was to help these people and in so doing help herself. She had come, however, with an unconscious sense of her personal aloofness, the height to which, of course, these common people could not aspire. Yet their very first and most natural reaction, no doubt, was to imagine a sentimental attachment between her and one of these backwoods boys.

From amusement Lucy passed to annoyance, and thence to concern. She had experienced her troubles with cowboys even in town, where there were ample avenues of escape. What would she encounter here? Would she find at the very outset a ridiculous obstacle to her success, to the fine record of welfare work she longed to establish?

One matter became a problem, no less because a faint accusing voice had begun to reach her conscience. She listened to it and strained at it until she heard something like doubt of her being big enough for this job. She humiliated herself. A wonderfully stabilizing though painful idea this was. After all, what excuse had she for superiority?

Standing there in the open fields, Lucy forgot the magnificent red wall and the gorgeous sunset-flushed panorama. She realized her vanity, that she had wounded it, that in all probability it would have to be killed before she could be wholly worthy of this work. Her humility, however, did not withstand the rush of resentment, eagerness, and confidence of her youth. Lucy stifled in its incipiency a thought vaguely hinting that she would have to suffer and grow before she really was what she dreamed she was.

Presently she heard the crack of hoofs on rock, and, turning, she espied two riders entering the corral at the end of the field. She decided they must be two more of the Denmeades, Dick and Joe, if she remembered rightly. They dismounted, threw their saddles, turned the horses loose. They appeared to be long, lean, rangy young men, wearing huge sombreros that made them look top-heavy. They whistled and whooped, creating sounds which clapped back in strange echo from the wall. It emphasized the stillness to Lucy. Such hilarity seemed out of place there. Lucy watched the tall figures stride out of sight up the lane toward the cabin.

"One thing sure," soliloquized Lucy, gravely, "I've got to realize I have myself to contend with up here. Myself! . . . It seems I don't know much about *me*."

She returned to the cabin, entering the yard by the side gate. Some of the hounds followed her, sniffing at her, not yet over their hostility. The Denmeades were collecting round the table on the porch. The mother espied Lucy and greeted her with a smile.

"Reckon we was about ready to put the hounds on your trail," she called, and when Lucy reached the table she added: "You set in this place. . . . Here's Dick an' Joe. You've only one more to see, an' that's Edd. Boys, meet Miss Lucy Watson of Felix."

Lucy smiled at the young men, waiting to sit down opposite her. Which was Dick and which Joe she could not tell yet. The younger was exceedingly tall and thin. The older, though tall and angular, too, appeared short by comparison. Both had smooth, still, shining faces, lean and brown, with intent clear eyes.

"Hod-do!" said the older boy to Lucy, as he took his seat across the table. He was nothing if not admiring.

"Joe, did you meet teacher Jenks?" asked Denmeade, from the head of the table.

"Yep. Saw him at Johnson's. He told us aboot Miss Watson. An' we passed Sam on the trail. He was packin' her baggage."

Before Allie and Mertie, who were carrying steaming dishes from the kitchen, had brought in all the supper, the Denmeades set about the business of eating.

"Help yourself, miss," said the father.

The table was too small for so many. They crowded close together. Lucy's seat was at one end of a bench, giving her the free use of her right hand. Mary sat on her left, happily conscious of the close proximity. The heads of the little girls and Dan just topped the level of the table. In fact, their mouths were about on a level with their tin plates. At first glance Lucy saw that the table was laden with food, with more still coming. Pans of smoking biscuits, pans of potatoes, pans of beans, pans of meat and gravy, and steaming tin cups of black coffee! Lucy noted the absence of milk, butter, sugar, green or canned vegetables. She was hungry and she filled her plate. And despite the coarseness of the food she ate heartily. Before she had finished, dusk had settled down around the cabin, and when the meal ended it was quite dark.

"I hear Sam's hoss," said Dick, as he rose, clinking his spurs. "Reckon I'll help him unpack."

Lucy sat down on the edge of the porch, peering out into the woods. The children clustered round her. Mrs. Denmeade and her older daughters were clearing off the supper table. A dim lamplight glimmered in the kitchen. Lucy was aware of the tall form of Dick Denmeade standing to one side. He had not yet spoken a word. Lucy addressed him once, but for all the answer she got he might as well have been deaf. He shifted one of his enormous boots across the other. In the dim light Lucy made out long spurs attached to them. Then Mrs.

Denmeade ordered the children off to bed. One by one they vanished. Mary's pale face gleamed wistfully and was gone.

It dawned on Lucy, presently, that the air was cold. It had changed markedly in an hour. Big white stars had appeared over the tips of the pines; the sky was dark blue. The blackness of the night shadows had lightened somewhat or else her eyes had become accustomed to it. Quiet settled over the cabin, broken only by low voices and sounds from the kitchen. It struck Lucy as sad and somber, this mantle of night descending upon the lonely cabin, yet never before had she felt such peace, such sweet solitude. By straining her ears she caught a dreamy murmur of the stream down in the gorge, and a low mourn of wind in the pines. Where were the coyotes, night hawks, whippoorwills, all the noisy creatures she had imagined lived in the wilderness?

Pound of hoofs and clink of spurs became audible in the lane, approaching the cabin. Lucy heard a laugh she recognized, and low voices, merry, subtle, almost hoarse whisperings. Then the gate creaked, and the musical clink of spurs advanced toward the porch. At last Lucy made out two dark forms. They approached, and one mounted the steps, while the other stopped before Lucy. She conceived an idea that this fellow could see in the dark.

"Wal, Miss Lucy, here's your bags without a scratch," said Sam Johnson's drawling voice. "Shore I bet you was worried. How'd you find my hoss Buster?"

"Just fine, thank you," replied Lucy. "Full of spirit and go. Yet he obeyed promptly. I never had a slip. Now were you not trying to frighten me a little— or was it Mr. Jenks?—telling me he was some kind of a mustang?"

"Honest, Buster's gentle with girls," protested Sam. "Shore he pitches when one of these long-legged Denmeades rake him. But don't you believe what anyone tells you."

"Very well, I won't. Buster is a dandy little horse."

"Wal, then, you're invited to ride him again," said Sam, with subtle inflection.

"Oh, thank you," replied Lucy. "I—I'll be pleased—if my work allows me any spare time."

"Howdy, Sam!" interposed Allie, from the kitchen door. "Who're you goin' to take to the dance?"

"Wal, I ain't shore, jest yet," he returned. "Reckon I know who I'd like to take."

"Sadie told me you asked her."

"Did she? . . . Sent her word. But she didn't send none back," protested Sam, lamely.

"Sam, take a hunch from me. Don't try to shenanegin out of it now," retorted Allie, and retreated into the kitchen.

Lucy was both relieved and amused at Allie's grasp of the situation. No doubt Sam had been approaching another invitation.

Denmeade's heavy footfall sounded on the porch, accompanied by the soft pad of a dog trotting. "That you, Sam? How's yore folks?"

"Tip top," replied Sam, shortly.

"Get down an' come in," drawled Denmeade as the other shuffled restlessly.

"Reckon I'll be goin'," said Sam. "I've a pack-hoff waitin'. . . . Evenin', Miss Lucy. Shore I hope to see you at the dance."

"I hardly think you will," replied Lucy. "Thank you for fetching my baggage."

Sam's tall form disappeared in the gloom. The gate creaked as if opened and shut with forceful haste. Almost directly followed the sound of hoofs going off into the darkness.

"Hey, Sam!" called Joe, coming out of the cabin, where he had carried Lucy's grips.

"He's gone," said his father, laconically.

"Gone! Why, the dinged galoot had somethin' of mine! Funny, him runnin' off. He shore was rarin' to get here. Never saw him make such good time on a trail. What riled him?"

"Wal, I have an idee," drawled Denmeade. "Allie give him a dig."

"I shore did," spoke up Allie, from the kitchen, where evidently she heard what was going on outside. "It's a shame the way he treats Sadie."

Lucy began to gather snatches of the complexity of life up here. After all, how like things at home! This girl Sadie had refused to marry Edd Denmeade. There was an intimation that she was attached to Sam Johnson. On his part, Sam had manifested a slight interest in a newcomer to the country.

Mrs. Denmeade came out of the kitchen carrying a lighted lamp, and she called Lucy to accompany her into the other cabin. She set the lamp on the high jutting shelf of the fireplace.

"You sleep in here with the children," she said, simply.

"Yes—that will be nice," rejoined Lucy, peering around. Dan was asleep on the floor in a corner, his bed a woolly sheep skin, his covering a rag quilt. Mary and the twins were fast asleep in one of the beds. Lucy stepped close to peer down at them. Liz and Lize lay at the foot, curly fair heads close together. Their faces had been washed and now shone sweet and wan in the lamplight. Their chubby hands were locked. Mary lay at the head of the bed, and her thin face bore a smile as if she were having pleasant dreams.

"Where—shall I wash?" asked Lucy, with diffidence.

"You'll find water, basin, towel out on the porch. . . . Good night. I reckon you're tired. Hope you sleep good."

Lucy bade her hostess good night and turned musingly to the opening of one of her grips. She could hear the low breathing of the sleepers. Somehow, to be there with them, under such circumstances, touched her deeply. It was for the sake of such as they that she had forsaken personal comfort and better opportunities. Despite a somewhat depressed spirit, Lucy could not regret her action. If only she won their love and taught them fine, clean, wholesome ways with which to meet their hard and unlovely futures! That would transform her sacrifice into a blessing.

The room was cold. A fire in the big stone fireplace would have been much to her liking. By the time she got ready for bed she was chilled through. Before blowing out the lamp she took a last look at the slumbering children. They seemed so still, so calm, so white and sweet. Lucy trembled for them, in a vague realization of life. Then, with some difficulty she opened one of the windows. Once in bed, she stretched out in aching relief. That long ride, especially on the horse, had cramped and chafed her. The bed was as cold and hard as ice. There were no sheets. The blankets under her did not do much to soften the feel of what she concluded was a mattress filled with corn husks. It rustled like corn husks, though it might have been coarse straw. The coverings were heavy rag quilts.

Nevertheless, Lucy had never before been so grateful for a bed. If this bed was good enough for those innocent and happy and unfortunate children, it was good enough for her. Unfortunate! She pondered. She would have to learn as much as she taught.

She heard heavy boots and the jangle of spurs on the porch, the unrolling of one of the canvas packs, faint voices from the kitchen, and then footsteps over her head in the attic. One of the boys spoke up there. Probably that was where they slept. Lucy now remembered seeing the ladder that led from the middle porch to a wide hole in the ceiling. She wondered where the rest of the Denmeades slept. No doubt she was robbing father and mother of their room and bed.

Gradually all sounds ceased, except the faint murmur of water and wind, out in the woods. Lucy grew warm and sleepy. Yet so novel and strange were her sensations that she fought off the drowsy spell. She was really there up in the backwoods. She could scarcely credit it. The blackness of the room, the silence, the unfamiliar fragrance of pine and wood smoke, were like unrealities of a dream. She lived over the whole journey and would not have changed any of it. Suddenly the stillness broke to a deep-ringing, long-drawn bay of a hound. It made her flesh creep. How it rang out the truth of her presence in the wild forest, in the hard bed of these lowly pioneers! The home that had failed her was gone forever. The one person she had loved most—her sister Clara—had failed her. And in the lonely darkness she wept, not as on the night before, childishly and unrestrainedly, but with sorrow for loss and gratefulness for the future that promised so much.

She would be happy to face the morrow, come what might. It could only bring another kind of strife, that in itself might be good for her soul. With such hope and a prayer that it would be so she fell asleep.

4

Lucy awakened in a half-conscious dream that she was in a place unfamiliar to her. Before she opened her eyes she smelled wood smoke. Then she saw that daylight had come and she was looking at her open window through which blue smoke and sunlight were pouring in. Bewildered, she gazed around this strange room—bare wood and clay walls—big stone fireplace—rude ceiling of poles and shingles. Where was she?

With a start she raised on her elbow. Then the effort that cost her, the sense of sore muscles, and the rustling of the corn-husk mattress brought flashing to memory her long ride of yesterday and the backwoods home of the Denmeades.

She was surprised, and somewhat mortified, to see that the children were up and gone. On the moment Lucy heard the patter of their feet outside on the porch and the ringing strokes of an ax on hard wood. Whereupon she essayed to hop out of bed. She managed it all right, but not without awkwardness and pain.

"Oh, I'm all crippled!" she cried, ruefully. "That ride! . . . And say, it's Greenland's icy mountains here."

The plain, substantial woolen garments that she had brought for cold weather were going to be welcome now. Lucy dressed in less time than ever before in her life. Then with soap, towel, comb, and brush she sallied out on the porch and round to the side of the cabin. The children were in the kitchen. An old man sat on a bench. He was thin, gray, with cadaverous cheeks, a pointed chin bristling with stubby beard.

"Good mawnin'," he said.

Lucy greeted him and asked where the water was.

"I jest fetched some," he said, pointing to a stand at the end of the porch. "Right pert this mawnin'. I reckon the frost won't do them peach blossoms no good."

Lucy indeed found the water pert. Her ablutions, owing to her impetuosity, turned out to be an ordeal. Evidently the old fellow had watched her with interest, for as she finished her hair and turned back he said with a huge grin, "Rosy cheeks!"

"Thanks," replied Lucy, brightly. "I'm Lucy Watson. I didn't meet you last night."

"Nope. But I seen you. I'm Lee's oldest brother. Thar's four of us brothers hyar in the woods. Uncle Bill the kids call me."

Upon her way back to the room she encountered the extremely tall young Denmeade who appeared too bashful to return her greeting. Lucy hurriedly put her things away and made her bed, then presented herself at the kitchen door, to apologize for being late.

"Reckoned you'd be tired, so I wouldn't let the children call you," replied Mrs. Denmeade. "Come an' eat."

They were having breakfast in the kitchen. Mary was the only one of the children to answer Lucy's greeting. Dan did not appear bashful, but his mouth was so full he could not speak. Mrs. Denmeade and Mertie were sitting at the table, while Allie stood beside the big stove. They did not seem stolid or matter-of-fact; they lacked expression of whatever they did feel. Lucy sat down to ham, eggs, biscuits, coffee. "Some of Edd's honey," indicated Mrs. Denmeade, with pride, as she placed a pan before her. Lucy was hungry. She enjoyed her breakfast, and as for the honey, she had never tasted anything so delicious, so wild and sweet of flavor.

After breakfast, Lucy was greatly interested in the brief preparations for school. Dan had to be forced away from the table. He was bareheaded and barefooted. Lucy went out to the gate with him and Mary. Dick was coming up the lane, leading two little gray lop-eared burros and a pony, all saddled. Dan climbed on one burro and Mary the other. Mertie came out carrying small tin buckets, one of which she handed to each of the children. Mary seemed reluctant to leave Lucy, but Dan rode off down the lane, mightily unconcerned. Mertie mounted the pony, and then had her brother hand up books and bucket. She smiled at Lucy. "You must get the boys to lend you a horse, so you can ride down to school with us," she said.

"That'll be fine," replied Lucy. "But the ride I had yesterday was enough for a while. I'm afraid I'm a tenderfoot."

Dick picked up a bucket and a rifle, and made ready to start.

"Do you walk to school?" queried Lucy, smiling.

"Yes'm. I like walkin'," he replied.

"Look at his legs," said Mertie. "Pa says Dick can outwalk any of them, even Edd."

"He does look as if he could take long steps," returned Lucy, laughing.

"Reckon it'd be nice if you could teach us at home," said Dick, shyly.

"Yes, it would, and I shall teach you a good deal," replied Lucy. "But I'm not a regular school-teacher."

Lucy watched them go down the lane after Dan and was unexpectedly stirred

at sight of the little procession. When she turned back up the path, Mrs. Denmeade met her.

"They're gone. It was fun to see the little burros," said Lucy. "How far do
they have to ride and why does Dick carry the gun?"

"It's five miles. Woods all the way. An' Dick doesn't pack that gun for fun.
There's bears an' cats. An' hydrophobia skunks. I'm afraid of them. But when
Dick's with the children I don't worry."

"What in the world are hydrophobia skunks?" queried Lucy.

"Nothin' but polecats with hydrophobia," replied the other. "Lee reckons
the skunks get bitten by coyotes that have hydrophobia. It makes the skunks
crazy. They come right for you. If you ever run across a pretty white-an'-black
cat with a bushy tail—you run!"

"I will indeed," declared Lucy. "An ordinary skunk is bad enough. But this
kind you tell of must be dreadful."

"Wal, Miss Lucy, this is wash-day for us," said Mrs. Denmeade. "An' we
never seem to have time enough to do all the work. But I want to help you get
started. Now if you'll tell me——"

"Mrs. Denmeade, don't you worry one minute," interrupted Lucy. "I'm here
to help you. And I shall lend a hand whenever I can. As for my work, all I want
is your permission to plan for what I think necessary—to buy things and make
things for the house."

"Reckon I'm glad to agree on anythin' you want," replied Mrs. Denmeade.
"Just call on me, an' Lee or the boys."

As they walked up the path to the cabin Lucy was telling Mrs. Denmeade
how it had been the decision of the welfare board to endeavor to teach the people
living in remote districts to make things that would further easier and better
living.

Denmeade, coming from the fields, apparently, met them and couldn't help
but hear something of what Lucy said. It brought the broad grin to his weath-
erbeaten face.

"Wife," he said, as he surveyed Lucy from head to foot, "this hyar city girl
has got sense. An' she looks like she might grow into a strappin' fine young
woman. 'To work with their hands,' she says. She's hit it plumb. That's all we
ever done in our lives. That's why we never learned new tricks. . . . All the
same, if Miss Lucy teaches us somethin', we can do the same for her."

"I certainly expect you to," said Lucy, gladly. "I'd like to learn to take care
of a horse, chop wood, and line bees."

Denmeade let out a hearty laugh.

"Wal, now, listen to her," he ejaculated. "Take care, young woman, an'
don't let my boy Edd hear you say you want to line bees. 'Cause if you do he'll

shore take you. An' say, mebbe hangin' to that long-legged boy when he's on a bee line, mebbe it ain't work!''

"All the same, I shall ask him to take Mertie and me sometime," declared Lucy.

"You couldn't hire Mertie to tramp up an' down these woods all day for anythin', let alone bees," replied Mrs. Denmeade, with scorn. "Mertie sews clothes for herself or me all day, an' shore she dances all night. But she's not like the rest of the Denmeades. I reckon Dick would be the best one to go with you an' Edd."

"Wal, how'd you like to help me an' Uncle Bill plow today?" asked Denmeade, quizzingly.

"Plow! Oh, that would be a little too much for me just yet!" laughed Lucy. "Why, that ride yesterday knocked me out! I'm stiff and sore this morning."

"Shore. That's no easy trail to anyone new to hosses," said Denmeade.

"Mr. Denmeade, I'd like to accept the loan of that tent the school-teacher offered," rejoined Lucy. "I think I could make myself very comfortable and I would not be depriving you and your wife of your room."

"Shore. Anythin' you like. Reckon the boys could make a tent tight enough to keep out bugs, snakes, dogs, wild cats, lions an' bears—an' mebbe hydrophobia skunks."

"Goodness! . . . Mr. Denmeade, you're teasing me," exclaimed Lucy.

"Wal, reckon I was," he replied. "Fact is, though, it ain't a bad idee. Summer is comin' an' the weather will soon get fine fer sleepin' outdoors. I seen the way Jenks had his tent fixed. Reckon me an' the boys can do it. But to-day we want to get through plowin' before the rain. . . . See them clouds comin' up out of the southwest? That means storm. Mebbe to-night or to-morrow or next day— but storm shore an' sartin."

"I hope Edd gets in before the rain," said Mrs. Denmeade. "Mertie would be sick if her new dress got spoiled."

"Ahuh! I reckon," returned Denmeade, gruffly. Then as Lucy mounted the steps to the porch he said to her, "You have the run of the place now, Miss Lucy, an' you can call on me or the boys any time."

"Who's the best carpenter?" queried Lucy.

"Wal, I reckon Dick is shore handy with tools," replied Denmeade. "An' he has time before an' after school. But tools is all-fired scarce about hyar."

"Can we buy them at Cedar Ridge?"

"Shore. An' I reckon some one will be ridin' down after the dance."

Lucy did not need to spend much more time looking around the cabins, inside or outside. The possessions of the Denmeades were so few that a glance had sufficed to enumerate them. Manifestly also their wants were few. But the comfort and health of a home did not depend upon how little was necessary.

The children of pioneers should have some of the conveniences of civilization. Lucy did not underestimate the problem on her hands.

She found that Mrs. Denmeade had removed from the closet whatever had been there, leaving it for Lucy's use. This enabled Lucy to unpack most of her belongings. When that was done she took pencil and pad and went outdoors to find a place to sit down and think and plan.

One of the old black hounds, a dignified and solemn dog, looked at Lucy as if he realized she should have company, and he went with her. How amused Lucy was to see the hound walk along with her, manifesting no evidence of friendliness other than his accompanying her.

Lucy crossed the strip of woods to the edge of the field, and then walked along under the pines toward the slope. Through the green and black of the forest she could see the looming red wall. At the end of the field she halted. Deep dark woodland merged upon the edge of the clearing. She sat down under a huge pine, from which position she could see out across the open.

"Oh, I'll never be able to concentrate on anything here!" murmured Lucy, thrilled with the wildness and splendor of the forest. Birds and squirrels were boisterous, as if rejoicing at the spring. The wind moaned through the tree-tops, a new sound to Lucy, stirring her blood. Most striking of all was the fragrance of pine. Lucy reveled a few moments in this sweet wild solitude, then made a valiant effort to put her mind on her work. At the very outset she made notes on her pad. The fact that expenditure of funds for the betterment of living conditions up here had been trusted to her common sense and discretion made Lucy extremely conscientious. She would purchase only what was absolutely necessary, and superintend the making of many useful things for the Denmeades. To this end she applied herself to the task of choosing the articles she must buy and those she must make.

It turned out to be a fascinating task, made easy by the course of manual training she had taken at normal school. Prominent among the articles selected to buy were tools and a sewing-machine. Tools meant the constructing of chairs, tables, closets, shelves, and many other household articles; a sewing-machine meant the making of sheets, pillows, towels, curtains, table-covers, and wearing apparel.

Lucy pictured in her mind what the inside of that cabin would look like in a couple of months. It filled her with joy for them and pride for herself. The expense would be little; the labor great. She had already convinced Denmeade that this welfare work was not charity; in the long run it must be for the good of the state.

Between such dreams and calculations Lucy mapped out the letters and orders she would write that afternoon. Then she would have to wait so long until the things arrived. Still, she reflected, a number of necessities could be obtained at the store in Cedar Ridge. She would persuade Denmeade to go or send some one at once.

At length Lucy discovered that without thinking about it she had changed her position several times to get out of the shade into the sun. The air had grown chill. Then she became aware of the moan of wind in the pines. How loud, mournful, strange! Clouds were scudding up from the southwest. They were still broken, but much heavier and darker than they had been in the early morning. They made great dark shadows sail along the rolling green crest of the forest. Gazing upward, Lucy was amazed to see that the clouds obscured the Rim at the high points. From up there drifted down a low, steady roar. Wind in the pines! It was a different sun from the sough in the near-by tree-tops. Birds and squirrels had ceased song and chatter.

Once more Lucy applied herself diligently to her task, and for a while forgot herself. The wind increased to a gale, intermittent, but steadily growing less broken. She heard it and thrilled, yet went on with her figuring. Suddenly a heavy crash somewhere in the woods close at hand thoroughly frightened her. No doubt a dead tree had blown over. Nervously Lucy gazed about her to see if there were other dead trees. She espied several and many bleached gnarled branches shaking in the wind. A great primeval forest like this seemed to be a dangerous place.

"I always imagined it would be wonderful to live like an Indian—wild in the woods," soliloquized Lucy. "But I guess it might be fearful on occasions."

She became prey then to conflicting impulses—one to run back to the cabin, the other to stay out in this roaring forest. For a moment the latter dominated her. She stepped out from under the pine into a glade and threw back her head. How the wind whipped her hair! The odor of pine was now so strong that it was not far from suffocating. Yet its sweetness seemed intoxicating. The cold air was exhilarating, in spite of its increasing chill. Against the background of blue sky and gray cloud the pine crests waved wildly and thin streams of brown pine needles flew before the gale.

Lucy's daring did not extend beyond a moment or so. Then the old black dog appeared, to eye her solemnly and trot off. She followed as fast as she could walk, sometimes breaking into a little run. Soon she was breathless and light-headed. Such little exertion to tire her! Lucy recollected that high altitudes affected some persons thus. Her heart pounded in her breast. It became absolutely imperative that she go slower, or give out completely. Even then, when she reached the cabin porch she was glad to sink upon it with a gasp.

The golden sunshine was gone. A gray mantle appeared to be creeping over the forest world. The roar of the wind now seemed behind and above the cabin. Presently Mrs. Denmeade, coming out for a pail of water, espied Lucy sitting there.

"Storm comin'," she said. "It'll blow for a while, then rain."

"Oh—I'm—so—out of—breath!" panted Lucy. "It was—wonderful, but—scared me. . . . The children! Will they stay at school?"

"Not much. They'll come home, rain or shine. Edd is goin' to catch it good. Dave Claypool just rode by an' stopped to tell me he met Edd up on the mountain."

"Met E—your son! When?"

"This mornin'. Dave was ridin' through. He lets his hosses range up there. Said he'd run across Edd about fifteen miles back down the Winbrook trail. Shore now Edd can drive a pack-train of burros. But they're loaded heavy, an' Edd will spare the burros before himself. I reckon he'll hit the Rim just about dark. An' if the storm breaks before then he'll have somethin' tough. Rain down here will be snow up there. But he'll come in to-night shore."

Her matter-of-factness over what seemed exceedingly serious and her confidence in the return of her son through gale and darkness awakened in Lucy a first appreciation of the elemental strength of these backwoods people. Lucy respected strength to endure above all virtues. How infinitely she herself had been found wanting! She hurried to her room, conscious that again this Edd Denmeade had been forced upon her attention.

Lucy got out her writing materials and set herself to the important task of the letters she had planned. At intervals she found her mind wandering, a thing not habitual with her. Yet the circumstances here were extenuating. And all the time she was aware of the gale. It swooped down the chimney with hollow roar. She was able to think and write consistently through the hours. The Denmeades ate whenever some of them came in hungry, a bad and labor-consuming habit, Lucy thought, which she would endeavor to break. She was glad, however, that there was no midday meal except Sundays. She grew cramped and cold from sitting so long on the uncomfortable chair, writing on her lap. But she accomplished the task of a dozen letters, and an enlarging and copying of her notes.

This accomplishment afforded her great satisfaction. Putting on a heavy coat, she went outside to walk off the chill in her blood. She found Mrs. Denmeade and Allie carrying the day's wash up from the brook down in the gully. Lucy promptly lent her assistance, and when she had made four trips, carrying a heavy burden, she was both out of breath and hot from the effort.

The gray mantle overhead had darkened. Only occasional rifts showed a glimpse of blue sky. The air was perceptibly damper. And the roar of wind now had no break.

Lucy rested a little, trying the while to win Liz and Lize to talk to her. They did not sidle away from her any longer, but had not yet reached the communicative stage.

Lucy was conscious of worry, of dread, and not until she saw Mary and Dan, with Mertie behind them, coming up the lane, did she realize the significance of her feelings. They were safe. And by the time they reached the gate the tall form of Dick came stalking into sight.

Manifestly for them the journey home through the forest under the threshing boughs of the trees, was merely an incident of school days. However, when Mertie heard from her mother that Edd had been seen back up on the Rim and would surely be caught in the storm, she gave vent to an excited concern. Not for her brother's safety and comfort, but for her birthday present of the new dress! Mrs. Denmeade petted and soothed her. "Don't worry, Mertie," she concluded. "Reckon you ought to know Edd. There's sacks of flour on them pack-burros. It ain't likely he'll see that flour spoiled, let along your new dress."

"But, ma!" protested Mertie, miserably, "Edd's only human! An' you know how terrible storms are up there."

"Wal, it was your fault Edd packed to Winbrook," retorted her mother. "He could of got the flour at Cedar Ridge, only one day's pack. But you had to have a city dress."

Mertie subsided into sullen restless silence and took no part in the preparations for supper. The children gravitated to Lucy, who essayed to play with them on the windy porch. The afternoon darkened. Presently the men returned from their labors, loud-voiced and cheery, smelling of horses and newly plowed earth. At the wash-bench they made much splashing.

"Wal, ma, we got the field plowed, an' now let her rain," announced Denmeade.

"Let her rain!" cried Mertie, shrilly, as if driven. "That's all anybody cares. Storm—rain—snow! For Edd to be caught out!"

"Aw, so thet's what ails you," returned her father. "Wal, don't you worry none about him."

During supper Denmeade again silenced his unhappy daughter, and though he drawled the reprimand in cool, easy words, there was a note in them that gave Lucy an idea of the iron nature of these backwoodsmen. This was the only instance so far in which the slightest discord or evidence of authority had appeared in the Denmeade family. To Lucy they seemed so tranquil, so set in their rugged simplicity.

After supper the gray twilight deepened and a misty rain blew in Lucy's face as she stood on the porch. Above the sound of the wind she heard a patter of rain on the roof.

"Reckon she'll bust directly," said Denmeade, as he passed Lucy, his arms full of wood. "I'm buildin' a fire fer you. It's shore goin' to storm."

By turning her ear to the north and attending keenly Lucy was able to distinguish between the two main sounds of the storm—the rush and gusty violence of the wind around the cabin, and the deep mighty roar of the gale up on the

Rim. She shivered with more than cold. At dark the fury of the storm burst. Torrents of rain fell, drowning all other sounds. Lucy was forced back against the wall, but the rain, driving under the porch roof in sheets, sent her indoors.

A bright log fire blazed and cracked in the open fireplace of the room she occupied. The children were sitting on the floor, talking, and such was the roar on the roof and the bellow down the chimney that Lucy could not hear a word they said. Evidently, however, something in the fire attracted them. Mary was looking at it, too, thoughtfully, even dreamily, her thin face and large eyes expressive of a childish hunger for something.

The hour seemed a restless, uncertain one for Lucy. How the storm raged and lashed! She had an almost irresistible desire to run out into it, a sensation at once overcome by abject fear. Even the porch, with its two open doors of lighted rooms, was as black as pitch. Lucy knew she could not have gone a rod from the cabin without being lost. The gale outside would howl and shriek accompaniments to the roar on the roof; now and then a gust of wind sent a volley of raindrops, thick as a stream, against the windowpanes. The red fire hissed with the water that dripped down the chimney. Lucy walked from window to window, from the fireplace to the door; she sat down to gaze with the children at the opalescent embers settling on the hearth; and she rose to pace the floor. Her thoughts were wholly dominated by the sensations of the storm. At last Lucy put on her long heavy coat and braved the porch. But this time she went to the back, where in the lee of the cabin she was out of the fury of wind and rain. There she stood against the wall, peering out into the blackness, feeling the whip of wind, the cold wet sting of flying hail.

It had grown colder. The rain was lessening in volume and some of it was freezing to sleet. While she cowered there the roar on the roof subsided, and gradually the strife of the elements around the cabin slowed and softened. Presently Lucy became aware of the terrific roar of the storm up on the Rim. It shook her heart. It seemed a continuous thunder and it roused in her unaccustomed feelings. How strange to realize that she both feared and loved the black wild roaring void out there!

She seemed thousands of miles from her home, from the desert where she had lived always, the hot glaring little city, with its sun-baked streets winter and summer, its throng of people, intent upon money-making, marrying, living. What a contrast they presented to these few hardy families of the mountains! Lucy wondered if a race of people, in their gregarious instincts, their despoliation and destruction of the wilderness, could not lose something great and beautiful. She felt it vaguely. How had men lived in the long ages before there were cities or settlements?

How was it possible for this Edd Denmeade to find his way home, in this ebony blackness, under the roaring and cracking pines, down over a two-thousand-foot mountain wall? The thing was incredible. Yet his father and his mother expected him as a matter of course. He had done it before. They trusted him. Even the vain Mertie, despite her fears and doubts, knew he would come. Then considering all this, what manner of man was Edd Denmeade? Lucy no longer repudiated her interest. In her heart there was a vague longing for she knew not what, but in this case she imagined it due to her disappointment at home, with Clara and her suitors, with the type of young men that had the good will of her father. They had received scant courtesy from Lucy. No understanding of sentiment stirred in Lucy. What could a boy of the backwoods be to her? But this wild-bee hunter was surely pretty much of a man, and Lucy was curious to see him.

She remained out on the porch until she was thoroughly cold and wet, and still longer, until she had convinced herself that she had a faint realization of what a storm was in this high timbered country. Then she went in.

All the family, including Uncle Bill, had assembled in her room. Denmeade, his brother, and Dick and Joe, were grouped near the fireplace. Denmeade knelt on one knee, in what Lucy later discovered was his characteristic resting position, his dark face in the light, his big black hat pushed back on his head. The others were sitting on the floor, backs to the wall, listening to what he was saying. The mother and Allie were seated, silent, on the children's bed. Mertie, crouched on one of the chairs, stared somberly into the fire. Mary was bent over, so she could catch the light on a book. The children played as before.

As Lucy went in, it was Mary who got up to offer her chair. Lucy, as she advanced to the blazing logs, was astonished to see how wet her coat had become. She held it to the fire, most gratefully conscious of the warmth. Then at the moment Joe interrupted his father's talk.

"I hear bells. Reckon some of the burros got in. Edd won't be far."

"Wal, he'll be with the pack outfit. Rustle out thar," replied his father.

While Denmeade replenished the fire the others stamped out, their spurs clanking. Mrs. Denmeade and Allie went into the kitchen. Mertie's apathy vanished and she rushed out into the darkness of the porch. Her voice pealed out, calling to Edd. Likewise the children responded to the home-coming of their brother.

Lucy felt happy for all of them. Hanging up her coat, she wiped the raindrops from her face and gave a touch here and there to her disheveled hair. Then she stood, back to the fire, palms turned to the genial heat, and, watching the door, she waited with sustained interest, with something of amusement, yet conscious of a vague unformed emotion.

Presently clamor of childish voices, pitched high above the deeper ones of men, and the thump of heavy boots, and jingle of spurs, moved across the porch to the door of the cabin. Lucy stepped aside into the shadow. Then the light of the fire streamed out of the door.

"In thar, all of you," boomed Denmeade. "Let Edd get to the fire."

It seemed to Lucy that a tall dark form emerged from the gloom into the light, and entered the door with the children and girls. For a moment there was a hubbub. The older members of the household came in, somewhat quieting the mêlée.

"Mertie, here's your present," said the newcomer. His voice seemed rather drawling and deep. Disengaging himself from clinging hands, he laid a large parcel, wrapped in a wet slicker, upon a vacant chair. Mertie let out a squeal, and pouncing upon the package, dropped to her knees and began to tear it open.

"Oh, Edd! . . . If you got it—wet!" she panted.

"No fear. It's wrapped in paper an' oilskin, under the slicker," he said. Then he drew another package from the inside of his huge fur-collared coat. "Liz! Lize! Danny!"

"*Candy!*" screamed the children in unison. And straightway pandemonium broke loose.

When the young man threw his wet sombrero on the floor near the hearth, and removed his rain-soaked coat, Lucy had a better chance to see what he looked like. Certainly his face was not handsome, but she could not say how much of its dark, haggard rawness was due to exposure. He did not change expression as he gazed down upon those whom he had made happy. But Lucy's keen sight and power to read divined the fact that he worshiped Mertie and loved the children. He untied a wet scarf from his neck and threw that beside his sombrero. All the older members of the family were silently gazing down upon the fortunate one. Mary seemed to be reveling in Mertie's excitement, yet, as she gazed up at Edd her large eyes questioned him.

"Mary, reckon I have somethin' for you in my pack," he said. "Wait till I warm my hands. I'm near froze."

With that he strode to the fire and knelt before it, one knee on the floor, in a posture Lucy had descried as characteristic of his father. Edd extended big, strong, capable-looking hands to the blaze. They were actually stiff and blue. Seen nearer, his face, with the firelight shining directly upon it, was an open one, lean, smooth, with prominent nose and large firm-lipped mouth and square chin. His eyes were larger than any of the other Denmeades', light in color, intent in gaze. Still, Lucy could not be certain she liked his face. It looked bruised, pinched, blackened. His hands, too, were grimy. Water dripped from him and ran in little streams over the hearth to sizzle on the hot ashes. He seemed to bring with him the breath of the open, cold and damp, the smell of the pines and burros, odorous, rank.

Gasps of delight emanated from those surrounding Mertie as she held up a white beribboned dress, and many were the mingled exclamations that followed. It was the mother who first recovered from the spell. Peering into the shadow, she at last espied Lucy.

"There you are," she said. "I was wonderin' if you was seein' the circus. . . . This is my oldest boy. Edd, meet Miss Lucy Watson from Felix. She's our home-teacher, come to live with us for a spell."

Lucy spoke from the shadow. Edd peered out of the firelight, as if locating her with difficulty. She did not see the slightest indication that he was surprised or interested. What had she expected from this much-talked-of wild-bee hunter?

"Can't see you, but hod-do just the same," he drawled.

Then Denmeade advanced to lean his tall form against the mantel.

"Dave rode down early—said he'd seen you, an' figgered you'd hit the Rim trail before the storm busted."

"Wind held us back all afternoon," replied the son. "An' some of the packs slipped. Reckon I'd made it shore but for that. The storm hit us just back from the Rim. I'll be doggoned if I didn't think we'd never get to where the trail starts down. Hard wind an' snow right in our faces. Shore was lucky to hit the trail down before it got plumb dark. I led my hoss an' held on to Jennie's tail. Honest I couldn't see an inch in front of my nose. I couldn't hear the bells. For a while I wasn't shore of anythin'. But when we got down out of the snow I reckoned we might get home. All the burros but Baldy made it. I didn't miss him till we got here. He might have slipped over the cliff on the narrow place. It shore was wet. Reckon, though, he'll come in. He was packin' my camp outfit."

"Edd, come an' eat, if you're hungry," called his mother from the kitchen.

"Nary a bite since sun-up. An' I'm a-rarin' to feed," he replied, and gathering up his smoking coat, scarf, and sombrero, he rose.

"Boy, did Blake buy yore honey?" queried his father, accompanying him toward the door.

"I reckon. Every bucket, an' I whooped it up to a dollar a gallon."

"Whew! Dog-gone me! Why, Edd, you'll make a bizness of your bee huntin'!" ejaculated Denmeade.

"Shore I will. I always meant to," asserted the son. "Pa, if I can find an' raise as much as five hundred gallons this summer I'll sell every pint of it."

"No!" Denmeade's exclamation was one of mingled doubt, amaze, and wondering appreciation of a fortune. They crossed the porch into the kitchen, from which Lucy heard them but indistinctly. Then Mrs. Denmeade appeared at the farther door.

"Lucy, take the candy away from the children an' put it where they can't reach it," she called. "Else they'll gorge themselves an' be sick."

Lucy approached this dubious task with infinite tact, kindliness, and persuasion. Liz and Lize were presently prevailed upon, but Dan was a different proposition. He would not listen to reason. When he found Lucy was firm he attempted to compromise, and, failing of that, he gave in ungraciously. Flouncing down on his sheepskin rug, he pulled the rag coverlet over him. Lucy could see his eyes glaring in the firelight.

"Danny, don't you undress when you go to bed?" asked Lucy, gently.

"Naw!" he growled.

"Don't you ever?" she went on.

"Not any more. The kids do, but not me."

"Why not you?" demanded Lucy. "It's not healthy to sleep in your clothes. Tell me, Danny. I'm your home-teacher, you know."

"Nobody ever said nuthin' to me," retorted the lad. "Pa an' Joe an' Dick sleep in their clothes. An' Edd—why, I've sleeped with him up in the loft when he never took off nuthin'. Went to bed right in his boots an' spurs."

"Oh, indeed!" murmured Lucy, constrainedly, somewhat taken aback. "Well, Danny, all the same it's not a healthy thing to do, and I shall teach you not to."

"Teacher, you'd make me sleep naked?" he protested. "Aw, it'd be cold in winter, an' I never have enough covers nohow."

"Danny, I shall make you nightclothes to sleep in. Nice soft warm woolly stuff."

"No long white thing like Mertie sleeps in," he asserted, belligerently.

"Any way you want. Shirt and pants, if you like," said Lucy.

"Then I can wear them all day, too," he rejoined with interest, and lay down.

Lucy turned her attention to the twins, very pleased to find them growing less shy with her.

"Tan we have some, too?" asked Lize, timidly.

"Have what, my dear?" queried Lucy, as she drew the children to her.

"Them Danny'll have to sleep in."

"Indeed you shall! Long white nightgowns, like the princess in the fairy story."

The twins had never heard of princesses or fairies, but they manifested the most human trait of children—love of stories. Lucy held them entranced while she undressed them and put them to bed. She was quick to realize her power over them. Her victory was assured.

Then Denmeade entered, carrying some sticks of wood.

"Reckon you can put them on, if you want to keep up the fire," he said. "Wal, you've put the kids to bed. Now, Miss Lucy, shore that will please ma."

When Mrs. Denmeade came in with towel and basin she appeared astounded to find the children undressed and in bed.

"You rascals never did it all by your lonesome," she averred. "Teacher has been takin' you in hand. But she forgot your dirty faces an' hands."

"Teacher telled us stories," whispered Liz, rapturously.

"Candy an' stories all at once!" exclaimed the mother as she wielded the towel. "Reckon that'll make bad dreams. . . . Stop wigglin'. Don't you ever want a clean face? . . . An' your teacher is tired an' needs sleep, too."

After Mrs. Denmeade had gone Lucy closed the door, catching as she did so a glimpse into the dimly lighted kitchen with its dark faces, and she dropped the bar in place, quite instinctively. The action made her wonder why she did it, for last night she had left the door unbarred. But tonight she had found the Denmeades walking in and out, as if she were not domiciled there. She did not put it beyond any one of them to burst unbidden in upon her at any hour. And she wished for the tent Mr. Jenks had offered. Yet, suppose she had been in a tent to-night, out there alone in the blackness, with a flimsy shelter overhead and a scant flooring under her feet! It actually gave her a tremor.

Lucy made no effort to hurry to bed. Drawing the chair closer to the dying fire, she toasted her hands and feet and legs that had felt like ice all evening. Outside, the wind moaned under the eaves, and from high on the Rim came that thrilling roar. Rain was pattering steadily on the roof, a most pleasant sound to desert ears. Heat Lucy knew in all its prolonged variations; but cold and rain and snow were strangers. She imagined she was going to love them.

Gradually as the fire died down to a pale red glow the room darkened. It seemed full of deep warm shadows, comforting Lucy, easing the strain under which she had unconsciously labored.

The event that had hung over the Denmeade home ever since she reached it had been consummated—the bee hunter had returned. Lucy had no idea what she had expected, but whatever it had been, it had not been realized. An agreeable disappointment dawned upon her. Edd Denmeade had not struck her as bold, or as a bully or a backwoods lout, foolish over girls. His indifference to her presence or appearance had struck her singularly. Her relief held a hint of pique.

"I think I had a poor opinion of him because everybody talked of him," she mused. "He fooled me."

But that could not account for her sensations now. Never before in her life had Lucy welcomed the firelit shadows, the seclusion of her room, to think about any young man. During school, too, she had imagined she had been falling in love. This feeling which grew strangely upon her now was vastly dissimilar from that mawkish sentiment. She could analyze nothing clearly. Edd Denmeade had impressed her profoundly, how or why or just what moment she could not tell. Had she been repelled or attracted? She fancied it was the former. She could be repelled by his raw, uncouth, barbarian presence, yet be fascinated by the man of him. That hurried return through the storm, down over the fearful trail, in a

Stygian blackness—a feat none the less heroic because it had been performed to please a shallow little peacock of a sister—that called to something deep in Lucy. She thought of her sister Clara, selfish, unloving, thoughtless of others. Lucy felt that she and Edd Denmeade had something in common—a sister going the wrong way!

She recalled his look as Mertie had frantically torn at the package. Serene, strong, somehow understanding! It flashed over Lucy, intuitively as much as from deduction, that Edd Denmeade knew his sister's weakness and loved her perhaps all the more because of it. That thrilled her, warmed her heart, as did her memory of his smile at the twins, Liz and Lize.

But all the rest was incomprehensible. Her pride, not of family, but of personal attainments and consciousness of her power to rise above her station, precluded any romantic thought of Edd Denmeade. He was a backwoodsman. She had come there to teach his people and their relatives and neighbors how to alleviate the squalor of their homes. The distance between her and them could not be bridged. So her interest and admiration must have been impersonal: it was the strange resentment which grew on her, the sense of being repelled by a hunter of the woods, that was personal and intimate.

Lucy crouched there before the fire till the red embers faded. The rain pattered steadily, the wind mourned, the wild night wore one. Forced thoughts, trying to solve riddles of her mind and heart, did not bring her tranquillity. At night her imagination and emotion were always more active. Lucy did not trust them. She fought the insidious drifting toward dreams, repelled it, and went to bed sure of herself.

5

On Mertie Denmeade's birthday several of her girl schoolmates rode up from the school with her. They were to stay overnight and go back to school next morning. Lucy could not help wondering where they were going to sleep.

Among these girls was Sadie Purdue, whom Lucy observed with attention. Sadie possessed but little charm, so far as Lucy could see. Her face and figure were common-place, not to be compared with Mertie's, and her complexion was pitted and coarse-fibered, well suited to her bold eyes and smug expression. Her shoulders were plump, her hands large, her feet clumsy. Lucy could not but wonder what Edd Denmeade saw in this girl. She reflected then that it was absurd for her to have assumptions or opinions, until she knew more of these people. Every one of these Jacks had their Jills. It seemed inconceivable for Lucy to pass critical judgment on this Sadie Purdue and not include her companions. Lucy found them colorless, civil, hardy girls, somewhat like Allie Denmeade. She was gravely astonished to find that she had an inexplicable antagonism toward Sadie. For that reason she went out of her way to engage Sadie in conversation.

The girl, as well as her companions, was exceedingly curious about Lucy's work. She asked numerous questions, the gist of which appeared to be a greedy interest in what they all were going to gain through Lucy's presence.

"We live 'way down near Cedar Ridge," she informed Lucy. "I stay with my cousin, Amy Claypool, while I'm goin' to school. This's my last term, thank goodness."

"What will you do then?" inquired Lucy. "Teach school?"

"Me teach? Laws no! I couldn't teach. Reckon a girl in this country has nothin' to do but marry when she leaves school. I've had offers, but I'm in no hurry."

"Do girls up here marry so young?" asked Lucy.

"From fifteen up. I'm sixteen, same as Mertie."

Lucy encouraged the girl to talk, which seemed to be very easy to do. Sadie was impressed by Lucy's interest, and besides that manifestly had motives of her own for establishing a repute. Lucy gathered that neither Sadie nor Mertie wanted to marry one of these bee-hunting, corn-raising, wood-chopping "jacks." They aspired to homes in Winbrook, or at least Cedar Ridge. But they were not averse to being courted and taken to dances.

"Trouble is, when a fellow keeps company with you, he ain't long satisfied with just courtin'," confided Sadie, giggling. "He wants to marry—wants a woman. Here's Edd, Mertie's brother. He took me to one dance an' spent a Sunday callin' on me. Asked me to marry him! . . . When he'd never even kissed me or put his arm round me!—The boob! I told him he hadn't learned much from his honey-bee huntin'."

Lucy found that remark a difficult one to answer, and she was at some pains to conceal her own reaction. Fortunately Sadie was rushed off by her several friends for the purpose of a joint attack upon Mertie, to make her display the birthday dress. It amused Lucy to see how Mertie refused and affected modesty, when underneath she was burning to reveal herself in the new dress. At last she allowed herself to be persuaded. "All right, but only you girls can see me."

They were in the room Lucy occupied. Mertie barred the door, saying: "I don't mind you, teacher. But you mustn't tell."

Whereupon, with utter lack of modesty, and obsessed by a strange frenzy, Mertie donned the dress, to create consternation and rapture among her friends.

By a lucky chance, which Lucy appreciated more than the others, the dress actually fitted the girl, and changed her wondrously. Many were the exclamations uttered, and one found lodgment in Lucy's memory. "Mertie," said Amy Claypool, soberly, "you an' Sadie call Edd a big boob. But I think he's grand."

Late in the afternoon Mrs. Denmeade and Allie began to spread the porch table with a birthday dinner for Mertie and her visitors. Several young men had ridden in, foremost of whom Lucy recognized as Sam Johnson. These young people arranged themselves around the porch and began what seemed to Lucy a remarkable exhibition of banter and absurdity.

The children dragged Lucy out on the porch, where Sam Johnson performed the office of introduction that Mertie neglected or omitted by choice. Gerd Claypool was a blue-eyed young giant with tawny hair, and Hal Miller was a lean, rangy cowboy type, solemn of face, droll of speech. These new visitors manifested enough interest in Lucy to convince her that it was not pleasing to Mertie and Sadie, so Lucy made excuses and left them to their peculiar fun. She played with the children, helped Mrs. Denmeade, and then sat in her room, the door and window of which were open. Part of the time Lucy was aware of the banter going on, but she did not become acutely interested until the Denmeade boys came on the scene.

"Wal, if here ain't the ole bee hunter, home early an' all shaved nice an' clean," drawled Sam Johnson.

"Mertie's birthday, Sam," replied Edd. "How are you all?"

"Jest a-rarin' to go," said Gerd Claypool.

"Edd, I reckon we'd like a lick of that honey pot of yours," added Hal Miller.

"I gave ma the last half-gallon for Mertie's party," replied Edd. "You might get some, if you don't hold back on your halter too long."

"What's become of all your honey?" queried Sam, with interest. "I remember you had a lot."

"Sold. An' I'm offered a dollar a gallon for all I can fetch to Winbrook."

Sam whistled. "Say, you ain't such a dog-gone fool as we thought, chasin' bees all the time."

"I'll make it a business," said Edd.

"Edd, it wouldn't be a bad idea for you to save some of your honey," interposed Sadie Purdue, slyly.

"What you mean?" asked Edd, bluntly.

"Girls like honey," she answered, in a tormenting tone no one could mistake.

"Reckon I savvy," returned Edd, with good humor. "But honey words an' honey ways with girls don't come natural to me, like with Sam."

His reply raised a howl of laughter at Sam's expense.

"Wal, I ain't noticin' that I ever go to any dances alone," rejoined Sam, sarcastically.

Lucy could see from the shadow of her room through the door most of the group of young people on the porch. Sam leaned behind Sadie, who sat by the porch rail. Gerd and Hal occupied seats on the canvas packs. The other girls sat on a bench. Dick was the only one of the Denmeade boys in sight. He appeared rather out of it, and stood in the background, silent, listening, with a rather pleasant smile on his keen face.

It was most interesting and instructive for Lucy to observe and hear these young people. What struck her most was the simple, unrestrained expression of what she divined as a primitive pleasure in tormenting. At the bottom of it was the unconscious satisfaction at another's pain. Sadie's expression was a teasing, joyful malignance. Manifestly she was reveling in the fun at the boys' expense. Mertie wore a bored look of superiority, as if she were tolerating the attentions of these young men for the moment. Amy Claypool's face, honest and comely, was wreathed in smiles. The boys near them wore lazy, bantering expressions, without selfish or unfriendly hint. But to the sensitive Lucy, used to the better educated, their talk seemed crude, almost brutal.

For a while the sole topic of conversation was the dance on Friday night. It expressed the wholesome and happy regard these youths and maidens held in the only recreation and social function that fell to their lot.. Personalities and banterings were forgotten for the moment; other wonderful dances were remembered; conjectures as to attendance, music, ice cream, were indulged in. Presently, however, when they had exhausted the more wholesome reactions to this dance subject they reverted to the inevitable banter.

"Say, Dick, have you found a girl tall enough to take to the dance—one you wouldn't have to stoop 'way over to reach?" drawled Sam Johnson.

Dick's youthful face turned ruddy. The attention suddenly and unexpectedly thrown upon him caused him intense embarrassment. The prominent bone in his throat worked up and down.

"Boy, yore handy with tools," interposed Hal. "Make a pair of stilts for that fat little sister of mine yore sweet on. She's four feet eight an' weighs one fifty. Reckon you'd make Sam an' Sadie look sick."

Other sallies, just as swift and laugh-provoking, gave the poor boy no time to recover, even if he had been able to retaliate. It was his sister Allie who came to the rescue from the door of the kitchen.

"Sadie, who're you goin' with?" she inquired, sweetly.

"Sam. He's the best dancer in this county," she announced.

"So it's settled then," rejoined Allie, casually. "When I asked him the other day who he was goin' with I kind of got a hunch it might not be you."

Sadie flashed a surprised and resentful look up at Sam. He took it, as well as the mirth roused by Allie's covert remark, with an equanimity that showed him rather diplomatic.

"Sadie, I told Allie you hadn't accepted my invite, which you hadn't," he said.

"Reckon it wasn't necessary," she retorted, in a tone that conveyed the impression of an understanding between them.

"Wal, Sadie," drawled Edd's slow, cool voice, "I reckon you'll find it necessary to hawg-tie Sam for dances—or *any other* kind of shindig."

This sly speech from Edd Denmeade gave Lucy an unexpected and delightful thrill. Almost she joined in the hilarity it stirred. Even the self-conscious Mertie burst into laughter. For a moment the tables had been turned; Sam was at a loss for a retort; and Sadie gave a fleeting glimpse of her cat-like nature under her smugness and pleasant assurance.

"Edd, have you asked any girl yet?" she inquired, sweetly.

"Nope. Not yet. I've been away, you know," he replied.

" 'Course you're goin'?"

"Never missed a dance yet, Sadie."

"It's gettin' late in the day, Edd," she went on, seriously. "You oughtn't go alone to dances, as you do sometimes. It's not fair to break in on boys who have partners. They just have to set out those dances. . . . Edd, you ought to be findin' you a regular girl."

Sadie's voice and face were as a transparent mask for the maliciousness of her soul.

"Shore, Edd," put in Sam, "an' you ought to hawg-tie her, too."

"Funny aboot Edd, ain't it?" interposed Gerd. "The way he can see in the woods. Say, he's got eyes! He can line a bee fer half a mile. But he can't line a girl."

"Nope, you're wrong, boy," replied Edd, with evident restraint. "Never had no trouble linin' a girl. But I haven't got the soft soap stuff you fellows use."

"Who are you goin' to ask to the dance?" insisted Sadie.

They nagged him, then, with this query, and with advice and suggestions, and with information that no matter what girl he asked he would find she had already accepted an invitation. It must have been their way of having fun. But to Lucy it seemed brutal. Almost she felt sorry for Edd Denmeade. It struck her that his friends and relatives must have some good reason for so unmercifully flaying him. For, despite the general bantering, they had made him the center and the butt of their peculiar way of enjoying themselves. The girl Sadie seemed the instigator of this emphasis thrown upon Edd, and Sam ably seconded her.

Amy Claypool, however, manifested a kindlier spirit, though apparently she did not realize the tirade was little short of a jealous brutality.

"Edd, I'd ask the new schoolmarm," she said, lowering her voice. "She's awful pretty an' nice. Not a bit stuck-up!"

Lucy heard this suggestion, and at once became a prey to amusement and dismay. Why could not the young people, and their elders, too, leave her out of all reckoning? Her pulse quickened with an excitation that displeased her. How her very ears seemed to burn!

Sadie Purdue burst into a peal of laughter. "Amy, you're crazy!" she exclaimed. "That city girl wouldn't go dancin' with a wild-bee hunter!"

This positive assertion did not produce any mirth. No doubt Sadie had no intention now of being funny. A red spot showed in her cheek. The sudden scrape of boots and clank of spurs attested to the fact that Edd Denmeade had leaped to his feet.

"Sadie Purdue, I reckon it's no disgrace to hunt bees," he said, sharply.

"Who said it was?" she retorted. "But I've been among town folks. You take my hunch an' don't ask her."

Edd stalked off the porch, coming into range of Lucy's sight when he got down into the yard. His stride seemed to be that of a man who was hurrying to get away from something unpleasant.

"Sadie, you shore don't know it all," said Amy, mildly. "If this home-schoolmarm wasn't a nice an' kind sort she'd not be up heah. Fun is fun, but you had no call to insult Edd."

"Insult nothin'," snapped Sadie. "I was only tryin' to save his feelin's."

"You never liked Edd an' you don't want anyone else to," returned Amy. "I know two girls who might have liked Edd but for you."

Lucy's heart warmed to this mild-voiced Amy Claypool. She did not make the least show of spirit. Sadie turned petulantly to Sam, and there was a moment of rather strained silence.

"Come an' get it, you birthday party," called Allie from the door.

That call relieved the situation, and merriment at once reclaimed the young people. Lucy was glad to see them dive for seats at the table. She was conscious of a strength and depth of interest quite out of proportion to what should have been natural to her. Still, she had elected to undertake a serious work among these mountaineers. How could she help but be interested in anything that pertained to them? But the wild-bee hunter! Quick as a flash then Lucy had an impulse she determined to satisfy. Would Edd Denmeade give these guests of his sister's the last bit of the honey upon which he set such store? Lucy felt that he ought not do so and would not, yet she contrarily hoped that he might. There appeared to her only one way to ascertain, and that was to walk by the table and see. Despite her determination, she hesitated. Then fortunately the problem was solved for her.

Allie, sailing out of the kitchen door, set a pan rather noisily upon the table. "There's the last of Edd's honey. Fight over it!"

The next few moments' observation afforded Lucy the satisfaction of seeing the birthday guests actually engaged according to Allie's suggestion. From that scene Lucy formed her impression of the deliciousness of wild-bee honey.

Lucy did not lay eyes upon Edd Denmeade until late the following morning, when, after the visitors and school children had ridden away, he presented himself before her where she played with the twins on the porch.

"Mornin'. Reckon I'd like a few words with you," he said.

"Why, gladly!" replied Lucy, as she sat up to gaze at him.

Edd was standing down in the yard, holding his sombrero in his hands and turning it edgewise round and round. On the moment he did not look at her. Seen now at close range, with all the stains of that terrible ride home removed from garb and face, he appeared vastly different. He was laboring with thought.

"Ma an' pa have been tellin' me about you, but I reckon I'm not satisfied."

"Yes? Is there anything I can tell you?" said Lucy, relieved. She had actually been afraid he would ask her to go to the dance.

"Shore. I want to know about this here work you're goin' to do."

Then he looked up to meet her eyes. Lucy had never met just such a glance. His eyes were so clear and gray that they seemed expressionless. Yet Lucy conceived a vivid impression of the honesty and simplicity of the soul from which they looked. Whereupon Lucy took the pains to explain quite at length the nature of the work she had undertaken among his people. He listened intently, standing motionless, watching her with a steady gaze that was disconcerting.

"Pa an' ma talked more about things you were goin' to get the state to buy for us," he said, reflectively. "I'm wonderin' if they don't take more to that."

"It would be only natural," responded Lucy, earnestly. "I must have time to show actual good, rather than gain."

"I reckon. Pa's sendin' me to Cedar Ridge, where I'm to post your letters an' buy all that outfit you want. I'm takin' three burros to pack. Reckon I'll put the sewin' machine on Jennie."

"Oh—a little burro to carry it—all alone!" exclaimed Lucy.

"Shore. Jennie packed the kitchen stove up that trail you come on. An' she packed a hundred an' fifty pounds of honey to Winbrook."

"Well, I'll say that Jennie is a wonderful little beast of burden," replied Lucy.

"Now—you aim to stay with us awhile, an' then go to Claypool's an' Johnson's an' Miller's an' Sprall's?"

"Yes, that is my plan, but no definite time is set. I have all the time there is, as I heard your Uncle Bill say."

"Wal, it's a bad idea. It won't do," he declared.

"How? Why?" queried Lucy, anxiously.

"First off, you're too young an' pretty," he said, wholly unconscious of the language of compliment.

"Oh!" returned Lucy, almost confused. "But, surely, Mr. Denmeade——"

"Nobody ever called me mister," he interrupted.

"Indeed! . . . I—well—surely my youth—and my good looks, as you are kind to call them, need not stand in my way?"

"Shore they will. If you were an old woman, or even middle-aged, it might do. But you're a girl."

"Yes, I am," rejoined Lucy, puzzled and amused. "I can't deny that."

Manifestly he regarded his bare statement as sufficient evidence on the point, whatever this was; for he went on to say that the several families would quarrel over her and it would all end in a row.

"Reckon no matter what pa said I'd never let you go to Sprall's," he concluded, simply.

"You! . . . May I ask what business it would be of yours?"

"Wal, somebody has to take these here things on his shoulders, an' I reckon most of them fall on me," he replied.

"I don't understand you," said Lucy, forcibly.

"Wal, somethin' wrong is always happenin' up here among us people. An' I reckon I'm the only one who sees it."

"Wrong! How could it be wrong for me to go to Sprall's?" protested Lucy. "From what I hear, they need me a great deal more than any family up here."

"Miss, I reckon you'd better not believe all you hear," he returned. "If you was to ride over to Sprall's you'd say they'd ought to be washed an' dressed, an' their cabin burned. But that's all you'd see unless you stayed a day or so."

"Oh! . . . Suppose I'd stay?" queried Lucy.

"You'd see that was long enough."

"But don't you understand I'm here to help poor families, no matter how dirty or ignorant or—or even wicked?" cried Lucy, poignantly.

"Shore I understand. An' I reckon it's your goodness of heart, an' of these people who sent you. But it won't do, maybe not for us, an' shore an' certain never for such as the Spralls."

"You must tell me why, if you expect me to pay the least attention to what you say," retorted Lucy, stubbornly.

"Shore I can't talk about the Sprall women to a girl like you," he protested. "If ma won't tell you, it's no job for me. But I reckon there's no need. You're not goin' to Sprall's."

Lucy was at a loss for words. His rare assertion did not seem to stir her anger so much as a conviction that for some reason or other she would not go to Sprall's.

"I've heard, since I've been here, that there was bad blood between you and Bud Sprall. It must have been your mother who said it," replied Lucy, slowly, trying to keep her temper.

"Nope. The bad blood is on Bud's side. Reckon if there'd been any on mine I'd have killed him long ago. . . . Now, miss, you're a city girl, but you ought to have a little sense. If I told you I couldn't let Mertie stay where Bud Sprall was—you'd understand that, I reckon."

"Yes. I am not quite so stupid as you seem to think," retorted Lucy.

"Wal, for the same reason I'd not let you go, either. . . . Now we're wastin' time talkin' about Sprall's. To come back to this here work of yours, I'm sorry I can't see it favorable like pa an' ma. But I just can't."

"I'm sorry, too," replied Lucy, soberly. "It'll be discouraging to have even one person against me. But why—why?"

"I reckon I can't figure that out so quick," he replied. "It's the way I feel. If you was goin' to live among us always I might feel different. But you won't last up here very long. An' suppose you do teach Liz an' Lize an' Danny a lot of things. They've got to grow up an' *live* here. They might be happier knowin' less. It's what they don't know that don't make any difference."

"You're terribly wrong, Edd Denmeade," replied Lucy with spirit.

"Ahuh! Wal, that's for you to prove," he returned, imperturbably. "I'll be goin' now. An' I reckon I'll fetch your outfit in about midday to-morrow."

Lucy stared after the tall figure as it stalked with a flapping of chaps keeping time with a clinking of spurs. Edd Denmeade was six feet tall, slender, yet not lean like his brothers. He was built like a narrow wedge, only his body and limbs were rounded, with small waist, small hips, all giving an impression of extraordinary suppleness and strength. Lucy had seen riders of the range whose form resembled this young bee hunter's. They had been, however, awkward on their feet, showing to best advantage when mounted on horseback. This Denmeade had a long, quick, springy stride.

When he had passed out of sight down the lane Lucy let the children play alone while she pondered over his thought-provoking words. She realized that he was right in a way, and that it might be possible to do these children more harm than good. But never if she could only impress them lastingly. The facts of the case were as plain as printed words to her. These backwoods people were many generations behind city people in their development.

In a fairly intelligent and broad way Lucy had grasped at the fundamentals of the question of the evolution of the human race. Not so many thousand years back all the human family, scattered widely over the globe, had lived nomad lives in the forests, governed by conditions of food and water. Farther back, their progenitors had been barbarians, and still more remotely they had been cave men, fighting the cave bear and the saber-toothed tiger. Lucy had seen pictures in a scientific book of the bones of these men and beasts. In ages back all the wandering tribes of men had to hunt to live, and their problems were few. Meat to eat, skins to wear, protection from beasts and ravaging bands of their own species! Yet, even so, through the long ages, these savages had progressed mentally and spiritually. Lucy saw that as a law of life.

These backwoods people were simply a little closer to the old order of primitive things than their more fortunate brethren of civilization. Even if they so willed with implacable tenacity they could not forever hold on to their crude and elemental lives. They could never evade the line of progress. Edd Denmeade's father was a backwoodsman; Edd himself was a bee hunter; his son would most likely be a forest ranger or lumberman, and his grandson perhaps become a farmer or a worker in the city.

Naturally this giant boy of the woods understood nothing of all this. Yet he had a quaint philosophy which Lucy felt she understood. In a sense the unthinking savage and the primitive white child were happier than any children of civilized peoples. In a way it might be a pity to rob them of their instincts, educate them out of a purely natural existence. But from the very dawn of life on the planet the advance of mind had been inevitable. Lucy was familiar with many writers who ascribed this fact to nature. Her personal conviction was that beyond and above nature was God.

If Edd Denmeade was not stupid and stubborn she believed that she could enlighten him. It might be interesting to teach him; yet, on the other hand, it might require more patience and kindliness than she possessed. Evidently he was the strongest factor among the young Denmeades, and perhaps among all these young people. Despite the unflattering hints which had fostered her first impression, she found that, after talking seriously with him, she had a better opinion of him than of any of the other young men she had met. In all fairness she was bound to admit this.

All the rest of the day and evening Lucy found the thoughts Edd had roused running in her mind, not wholly unsatisfying. Somehow he roused her combativeness, yet, viewed just as one of the Denmeades, she warmed to the problem of helping him. Moreover, the success of her venture with this family no doubt hinged mostly upon converting the elder son to her support. Perhaps she could find an avenue open to her through his love of Mertie and devotion to the children.

Next morning found Lucy more energetic and active mentally than she had been so far. She had rested; the problem she confronted had shifted to a matter of her own powers. Nevertheless, neither the children, nor helping Mrs. Denmeade, nor reading over some half-forgotten treatises relative to her work, interested her to the point of dismissing Edd Denmeade from mind. Lucy realized this, but refused to bother with any reflection upon it.

She was in her room just before the noon hour when she heard Uncle Bill stamp up on the porch and drawl out: "Say, Lee, hyar comes Edd drivin' the pack-burros."

Denmeade strode out to exclaim. "So soon! Wal, it do beat hell how that boy can rustle along with a pack-outfit."

"Heavy load, too. Jennie looks like a camel," replied Uncle Bill. "Reckon I'll lend a hand onpackin'."

Lucy quite unnecessarily wanted to run out to see the burros, a desire that she stifled. She heard the tinkle of their bells and the patter of their little hoofs as they came up to the porch.

"Wal, son, you must been a-rarin' to git home," drawled Denmeade.

"Nope. I just eased them along," replied Edd. "But I packed before sunup."

"Fetch all Miss Lucy's outfit?"

"Some of it had to be ordered. Sewin' machine an' a lot of dry goods. It'll be on the stage next week, an' I'll pack it then. Reckon I had about all I could pack to-day, anyhow."

"Say, Edd," called Allie's lusty voice from the kitchen, "who'd you go an' storm for the dance?"

"Reckon I haven't asked nobody yet," replied Edd, laconically.

"You goin' to stay home?" rejoined Allie, her large frame appearing in the kitchen doorway. Her round face expressed surprise and regret.

"Never stayed home yet, Allie, did I?"

"No. But, Edd, you mustn't go to any more dances alone," said his sister, solicitously. "It makes the boys mad, an' you've had fights enough."

"Wal, you didn't notice I got licked bad, did you?" he drawled.

Allie went back into the kitchen, where she talked volubly in the same strain to her mother.

"Edd, reckon we'd better carry this stuff in where Miss Lucy can keep the kids out of it, huh?" queried Denmeade.

"I shore say so. It cost a lot of money. I hope to goodness she makes out with it."

Lucy heard his quick step on the porch, then saw him, burdened with bundles and boxes, approaching her door. She rose to meet him.

"Howdy! I got back pronto," he said. "Pa thinks you'd better have this stuff under your eye. Where'll we stack it? Reckon it'll all make a pile."

"Just set light things on the beds, heavy ones on the floor. I'll look after them," replied Lucy. "Indeed you made splendid time. I'm very grateful. Now I shall be busy."

Sometime during the afternoon, when the curious members of the household had satisfied themselves with an exhaustive scrutiny of the many articles Lucy had in her room, and had gone about their work and play, Edd Denmeade presented himself at the door.

"Reckon I'd like to ask you somethin'," he said, rather breathlessly and low.

"Come in," replied Lucy, looking up from where she knelt among a disarray of articles she had bought.

"Will you go to the dance with me?" he asked.

Lucy hesitated. His shyness and anxiety manifestly clashed. But tremendous as must have been this issue for him, he had come out frankly with it.

"Oh, I'm sorry! Thank you, Edd, but I must decline," she replied. "You see what a mess I'm in here with all this stuff. I must straighten it out. To-morrow work begins."

He eyed her with something of a change in his expression or feeling, she could not tell what. "Reckon I savvied you'd say no. But I'm askin' if you mean that no for good. There's a dance every week, an' you can't help bein' asked. I'm givin' you a hunch. If any schoolmarm stayed away from dances, folks up here would believe she thought she was too good for us."

"Thank you. I understand," replied Lucy, impressed by his sincerity. "Most assuredly I don't think I'm too good to go to a dance here, and enjoy myself, too."

"Maybe, then—it's just me you reckon you'd not like to go with," he returned, with just a tinge of bitterness.

"Not at all," Lucy hastened to reply. "I'd go with you the same as with anyone. Why not?"

"Reckon I don't know any reason. But Sadie Purdue was pretty shore she did. . . . You wouldn't really be ashamed of me, then?"

"Of course not," replied Lucy, at her wits' end to meet this situation. "I heard you spoken of very highly by Mrs. Lynn at Cedar Ridge. And I can see how your parents regard you. At my home in Felix it was not the custom for a girl to go to a dance upon such slight acquaintance as ours. But I do not expect city customs up here in the woods."

"Reckon I like the way you talk," he said, his face lighting. "Shore it doesn't rile me all up. But that's no matter now. . . . Won't you please go with me?"

"No," answered Lucy, decidedly, a little nettled at his persistence, when she had been kind enough to explain.

"Shore I didn't ask any girl before you," he appealed, plaintively.

"That doesn't make any difference."

"But it means an awful lot to me," he went on, doggedly.

It would never do to change her mind after refusing him, so there seemed nothing left but to shake her head smilingly and say she was sorry. Then without a word he strode out and clanked off the porch. Lucy went on with the work at hand, becoming so interested that she forgot about him. Sometime later he again presented himself at her door. He was clean shaven; he had brushed his hair while wet, plastering it smooth and glossy to his fine-shaped head; he wore a light colored flannel shirt and a red tie; and new blue-jeans trousers. Lucy could not help seeing what a great improvement this made in his appearance.

"Reckon you haven't thought it over?" he queried, hopefully.

"What?" returned Lucy.

"About goin' to the dance?"

"I've been very busy with all this stuff, and haven't had time to think of anything else."

"Shore I never wanted any girl to go with me like I do you," he said. "Most because Sadie made fun of the idea."

This did not appear particularly flattering to Lucy. She wondered if the young man had really been in love with that smug-faced girl.

"Edd, it's not very nice of you to want me just to revenge yourself on Sadie," rejoined Lucy, severely.

"Reckon it's not all that," he replied hurriedly. "Sadie an' Sam an' most of them rake me over. It's got to be a sore point with me. An' here you bob up, the prettiest an' stylishest girl who ever came to Cedar Ridge. Think what a beat I'd have on them if I would take you. An' shore that's not sayin' a word about my own feelin's."

"Well, Edd, I must say you've made amends for your other speech," said Lucy, graciously. "All the same, I said no and I meant no."

"Miss Lucy, I swear I'd never asked you again if you'd said that for good. But you said as much as you'd go sometime. Shore if you're ever goin' to our dances why not this one, an' let me be the first to take you?"

He was earnest; he was pathetic; he was somehow most difficult to resist. Lucy felt that she had not been desired in this way before. To take her would be the great event in his life. For a moment she labored with vacillation. Then she reflected that if she yielded here it would surely lead to other obligations and very likely to sentiment. Thereupon she hardened her heart, and this time gave him a less kindly refusal. Edd dropped his head and went away.

Lucy spent another hour unpacking and arranging the numerous working materials that had been brought from Cedar Ridge. She heard Mrs. Denmeade and Allie preparing an early supper, so they could ride off to the dance before sunset. Lucy had finished her task for the afternoon and was waiting to be called to supper when again Edd appeared at the door.

"Will you go to the dance with me?" he asked, precisely as he had the first time. Yet there seemed some subtle change in both tone and look.

"Well, indeed you are perservering, if not some other things," she replied, really annoyed. "Can't you understand plain English? . . . I said no!"

"Shore I heard you the first time," he retorted. "But I reckoned, seein' it's so little for you to do, an' means so much to me, maybe you'd——"

"Why does it mean so much to you?" she interrupted.

"Cause if I can take you I'll show them this once, an' then I'll never go again," he replied.

It cost Lucy effort to turn away from his appealing face and again deny him, which she did curtly. He disappeared. Then Mrs. Denmeade called her to supper. Edd did not show himself during the meal.

"Edd's all het up over this dance," observed Mrs. Denmeade. "It's on account of Sadie's sharp tongue. Edd doesn't care a rap for her now an' never did care much, if my reckonin' is right. But she's mean."

"Laws! I hope Edd doesn't fetch that Sally Sprall," interposed Allie. "He said he was dog-goned minded to do it."

"That hussy!" ejaculated Mrs. Denmeade. "Edd wouldn't take her."

"Ma, he's awful set on havin' a girl this dance," responded Allie.

"I'll bet some day Edd gets a better girl than Sadie Purdue or any of her clan," declared the mother.

A little while later Lucy watched Mrs. Denmeade and Allie, with the children and Uncle Bill, ride off down the lane to disappear in the woods. Edd had not returned. Lucy concluded he had ridden off as had his brothers and their father. She really regretted that she had been obdurate. Coming to think about it, she did not like the idea of being alone in the cabin all night. Still, she could bar herself in and feel perfectly safe.

She walked on the porch, listening to the murmur of the stream and the barking of the squirrels. Then she watched the sun set in golden glory over the yellow-and-black cape of wall that jutted out toward the west. The day had been pleasantly warm and now growing cool. She drew a deep breath of the pine-laden air. This wild country was drawing her. A sense of gladness filled her at the thought that she could stay here indefinitely.

Her reflections were interrupted by the crack of iron-shod hoof on rock. Lucy gave a start. She did not want to be caught there alone. Peering through the foliage, she espied Edd striding up the lane, leading two saddled horses. She was immensely relieved, almost glad at sight of him, and then began to wonder what this meant.

"If he's not going to ask me again!" she soliloquized, and the paradox of her feeling on the moment was that she was both pleased and irritated at his persistence. "The nerve of him!"

Edd led the two horses into the yard and up to the porch. His stride was that of a man who would not easily be turned back. In spite of her control, Lucy felt a thrill.

"Reckon you thought I'd gone?" he queried as he faced her.

"No; I didn't think about you at all," returned Lucy, which speech was not literally true.

"Wal, you're goin' to the dance," he drawled, cool and easy, with a note in his voice she had never heard.

"Oh—indeed! I am?" she exclaimed, tartly.

"You shore are."

"I am not," flashed Lucy.

With a lunge he reached out his long arms and, wrapping them round her, he lifted her off the porch as easily as if she had been an empty sack. Lucy was so astounded that for an instant she could not move hand or foot. A knot seemed to form in her breast. She began to shake. Then awakening to this outrage, she began to struggle.

"How dare you? Let me down! Release me!" she cried.

"Nope. You're goin' to the dance," he said, in the same drawling tone with its peculiar inflection.

"You—you ruffian!" burst out Lucy, suddenly beside herself with rage. Frantically she struggled to free herself. This fierce energy only augmented her emotions. She tore at him, wrestled and writhed, and then in desperation fraught with sudden fear she began to beat him with her fists. At that he changed his hold on her until she seemed strung in iron bands. She could not move. It was a terrible moment, in which her head reeled. What did he mean to do with her?

"Reckon I'll have to hold you till you quit fightin'," he said. "Shore it'd never do to put up on Baldy now. He's a gentle hoss, but if you kicked around on him I reckon he might hurt you."

"Let—me—go!" gasped Lucy, hoarsely. "Are—you crazy?"

"Nope. Not even riled. But shore my patience is wearin' out."

"Patience! Why, you lout—you brute—you wild-bee hunter!" raved Lucy, and again she attempted to break his hold. How utterly powerless she was! He had the strength of a giant. A sudden panic assailed her fury.

"My God! You don't mean—to hurt me—harm me?" she panted.

"You dog-gone fool!" he ejaculated, as if utterly astounded.

"Oh! . . . Then what— do you mean?"

"I mean nothin' 'cept you're goin' to that dance," he declared, ruthlessly. "An' you're goin' if I have to hawgtie you. Savvy?"

Whereupon he lifted her and set her in the saddle of one of the horses, and threw her left foot over so that she was astride.

"No kickin' now! Baldy is watchin' out of the corner of his eye," said this wild-bee hunter.

The indignity of her position, astride a horse with her dress caught above her knees, was the last Lucy could endure.

"Please let— me down," she whispered. "I'll—go—with you."

"Wal, I'm shore glad you're goin' to show sense," he drawled, and with action markedly in contrast to his former ones he helped her dismount.

Lucy staggered back against the porch, so weak she could hardly stand. She stared at this young backwoodsman, whose bronzed face had paled slightly. He had bruised her arms and terrified her. Overcome by her sensations, she burst into tears.

"Aw, don't cry!" Edd expostulated. "I'm sorry I had to force you. . . . An' you don't want to go to a dance with red eyes an' nose."

If Lucy had not been so utterly shocked she could have laughed at his solicitude. Hopeless indeed was this backwoodsman. She strove to regain control over her feelings, and presently moved her hands from her face.

"Is there any place down there—to change—where a girl can dress?" she asked, huskily. "I can't ride horseback in this."

"Shore is," he said, gayly.

"Very well," returned Lucy. "I'll get a dress—and go with you."

She went to her room and, opening the closet, she selected the prettiest of the several dresses she had brought. This, with slippers, comb, and brush and mirror, she packed in a small grip. She seemed stunned, locked in a kind of maze. Kidnapped! Forced by a wild-bee hunter to go to a backwoods dance! Of all adventures possible to her, this one seemed the most incredible! Yet had she not been selfish, heartless? What right had she to come among such crude people and attempt to help them? This outrage would end her ambition.

Then hurriedly slipping into her riding clothes, Lucy took the bag and returned to the porch.

"Wal, now that's fine," said Edd, as he reached for the grip. He helped her mount and shortened the stirrups without speaking. Then he put a big hand on the pommel of her saddle and looked up at her.

"Shore now, if it'd been Sadie or any girl I know she'd have gone in an' barren the door," he said. "I just been thinkin' that over. Shore I didn't think you'd lie."

Lucy endeavored to avert her gaze. Her horror had not faded. But again the simplicity of this young man struck her.

"Do you want to back out now an' stay home?" he went on.

"You are making me go by force," she returned. "You said you'd 'hawg-tie' me, didn't you?"

"Wal, reckon I did," he replied. "But I was riled an' turrible set on takin' you. . . . Your havin' a chance to lock yourself in! Now you didn't do it an' I savvied you wouldn't."

Lucy made no reply. What was going on in the mind of this half-savage being? He fascinated while he repelled her. It would have been false to herself had she denied the fact that she felt him struggling with his instincts, unconsciously fighting himself, reaching out blindly. He was a living proof of the evolution of man toward higher things.

"Wal, reckon I'll let you off," he declared at length.

"Are you afraid I'll tell what a brute you were?" she flashed, sarcastically.

His lean face turned a dark red and his eyes grew piercing.

"Hell, no!" he ejaculated. "Shore I don't care what you tell. But I'd hate to have you think same as Sadie an' those girls."

"It doesn't matter what I think," she replied. "You'd never understand."

"Wal, I would, if you thought like them."

"Is it possible you could expect me to think anything but hard of you—after the way you treated me?" she demanded, with returning spirit.

"Hard? Reckon I don't mind that," he returned, ponderingly. "Anyway, I'll let you off, just because you wasn't tricky."

"No, you won't let me off," asserted Lucy. "I'm going to this dance . . . and you'll take the consequences!"

6

AT the corral gate Edd Denmeade swung his long length off his horse and held the gate open for Lucy to ride through.

"Wal, want to go fast or slow?" he asked, as he mounted again.

"Prisoners have no choice," retorted Lucy.

Evidently that remark effectually nipped in the bud any further desire for conversation. His gray eyes seemed to be piercing her, untroubled yet questioning. He put his horse to a trot. Lucy's mount, without urging, fell in behind. His easy gait proved to be most agreeable to her. He was a pacer, and Lucy recognized at once that he was the kind of a horse it was a great pleasure to ride. He appeared to be eager, spirited, yet required no constant watching and holding.

The trail led into the forest, a wide, dusty, winding path full of all kinds of tracks, one of which Lucy thought she recognized as Dick's. She had noticed his enormous feet. Patches of manzanita, clumps of live-oak, thickets of pine, bordered the trail. Above these towered the stately rugged-barked monarchs of the forest. The last of the afterglow of sunset flowed rosily on the clouds; through the green lacework of the trees gleamed the gold of the wandering wall far above her. Shadows were lying low in the ravines that headed away from the trail.

Presently this level bench of woodland ended and there was a sharp descent, down which the trail zigzagged by easy stages. Then again the forest appeared level. Lucy heard the dreamy hum of a waterfall. Here Edd took to a swinging lope, and Lucy's horse, as before, fell into the faster stride.

The forest grew darker and cooler. The trail wound in and out, always hiding what was beyond. Sometimes Edd's horse was out of sight. Lucy found herself in a strange contention of mind. Despite her anger and the absurdity of her being dragged virtually a prisoner to this dance, the novelty of the situation and the growing sensations of the ride seemed to be combining to make her enjoy them, whether she wanted to or not. That would be a humiliation she must not suffer. Yet no doubt the horse Baldy was the finest she had ever ridden. She had to fight herself to keep from loving him. Nor could she help but revel in this lonely, fragrant trail through the wild dales and glades. They rode out levels and down steps, and crossed rushing brooks; and it appeared that Edd kept going a little faster all the time. Yet he never looked back to see how she fared. No doubt he heard her horse.

Twilight turned the greens and browns to gray. In the denser parts of the forest Lucy could scarcely see the dim pale trail ahead. Suddenly she caught a glimpse of a fire. It disappeared as she loped along, and then reappeared. Then, all too soon, she thought, they rode into a clearing dominated by a large low building, half logs and half rough boards. A fire burned brightly under a huge pine near the edge of the clearing, and it was surrounded by noisy boys and girls. Horses were haltered to saplings all around. Wagons and queer-looking vehicles attested to the fact that a road led to this forest schoolhouse.

Edd halted at the rear of the building, and dismounting, he set Lucy's grip on the ground and turned to help her off. But Lucy ignored him and slipped quickly down. She was warm, throbbing from the brisk exertion of riding, and in spite of herself not wholly unresponsive to the adventure.

"Wal, we're shore here," drawled Edd, happily, no doubt keenly alive to the shouts of the young people around the fire. "You can dress in there."

He led her to a door at the back of the schoolhouse. Lucy mounted the high log steps to enter. The room was bare, a small addition built against the building. There was no one in it, a fact that relieved Lucy. A lighted lamp stood on a table. On one side was a built-in couch covered with dried pine boughs. Besides these articles of furniture there was a box to serve as a chair.

Lucy closed the door and hurriedly set about the business of dressing. She was not in any hurry to go out to meet Edd and the people at this dance; but she found it expedient to do so, owing to the cold. The bare room was like a barn. Once dressed, Lucy rather regretted bringing her best and most attractive gown. She had selected it hastily and in a moment of stress. Excitement and exertion had left her pale, with eyes darker than usual. She could not spare time on her hair, but it looked the better for that.

"If this mirror doesn't lie I never looked half so well," she murmured. "Now Mr. Edd Denmeade, wild-bee hunter and wild kidnapper, we'll see!"

Lucy's mood did not tolerate the maxims and restraints she had set for herself. On the moment she was ready to abandon her cherished ambition to succeed in welfare work. Gorillas and outlaws and bee hunters were a little beyond her ken. Edd Denmeade had laid hold of her in a savage manner, to which the dark-blue marks on her white arms could attest. Lucy did not stop to analyze her anger and the limits to which it might drive her. One thing at least was clear to her, and it was that she would use all a woman's guile and charm to make Edd Denmeade rue this night. At first she had intended to go straight to his father and mother and tell of the indignity that had been done her. But she had changed her mind during the ride, and now that she was dressed in her best her mood underwent further change. She had brought a light-blue silk scarf to go with her white gown, and throwing this round her bare shoulders she sallied forth. As she stepped down to the ground the bright blaze from the fire blinded her, yet she saw a tall dark form detach itself from the circle there and approach her.

"You shore dressed pronto," drawled Edd.

Lucy put her hand on his arm and walked beside him, perfectly aware of his long stare. He led her round the schoolhouse to a front entrance, where another crowd of boys and girls whispered and gaped.

"Our old fiddler's late," said her escort, "an' I reckon the gang is rarin' to dance."

Edd had to push himself through a crowd just inside the door, and he did it in a rather imperative way. Once through this line, Lucy saw a large bare board floor, then a large room lighted by many lamps, and many people sitting and standing around the walls. Edd was leading her across the room toward a corner where there were a stove and a table. Here was congregated another group, including women and children. Mrs. Denmeade and Allie came to meet them; and if Lucy had wanted any evidence of creating a sensation, she had it now.

"Wal, ma, here we are," drawled Edd, as coolly as if there were no strained situation. Perhaps for him there was none.

"For goodness' sake!" exclaimed his mother, in delight. "Lucy, I'm shore awful glad to see you here. You fooled us bad. That boy of mine is a fox."

Lucy's murmured reply did not include any of the epithets she might have laid upon Edd Denmeade. Allie appeared even more delighted to see her.

"Oh, it was good of you to come!" she whispered, taking Lucy's arm and squeezing it. "You look perfectly lovely. An' all the boys will die."

"I hope it'll not be so bad as that," laughed Lucy, softening unexpectedly. The warmth of her welcome and the extravagant praise of her appearance were

too much for her. Whatever she felt toward Edd Denmeade, she could not extend
to these simple, impulsive people. This was their social life, the one place they
gathered to have pleasure, and here they seemed very different. Lucy was at
once the cynosure of all eyes, and was surrounded by old and young alike. The
twins, Liz and Lize, after their first blank bewilderment as at an apparition in
white, clung to her with the might of conscious pride of possession. Denmeade
and Uncle Bill greeted her with wrinkled faces wreathed in smiles. Lucy met
Claypools, Millers, Johnsons, and numberless others whose names she could not
remember. Edd brought young men, all lean, rangy giants, whom she could not
have distinguished one from another. It dawned on Lucy that he wanted most
of the boys there to meet her and dance with her. Indeed, he showed no selfish
interest. But Lucy did not really look at Edd until Mrs. Denmeade, during an
opportune moment, whispered to her:

"Lucy, I reckon Edd's the proudest boy in the whole world. Pa said the same.
We never seen him this way before. He was never happy at our dances. But
you've done him good by comin', an' I'm thankin' you."

Whereupon Lucy forced herself to gaze upon the escort who had gone to such
an extreme to bring her to this dance. And she was to discern that, whatever his
misconduct toward her, he was now wearing his laurels with becoming modesty.
For Lucy could not blind herself to the fact that she was the star attraction of
this dance and that Edd had brought his rivals to a state of envy. Both circumstances pleased her. Seldom had she ever been the belle of a dance. Every young
man who met her begged the privilege of dancing with her. And as introductions
were quick and many she could not remember names. How she enjoyed seeing
Sam Johnson beg Edd for a dance with her! And Edd showed no rancor, no
remembrance of insults, but with a courtesy that would not have ill become one
in higher walks of life he gratified Sam. Lucy found the situation different from
what she had anticipated. To revenge herself upon Edd Denmeade she had
determined to be frigid to him and as sweet as she could make herself to every
other boy there, particularly Sam Johnson. Not yet did she repudiate that unworthy resolve, though something was working on her—the warmth of her
welcome—the pleasure she was giving—the honor she had unwittingly conferred
upon this crude woodsman, the simplicity with which he took his triumph.

It dawned upon Lucy that there was only one reason why she could not
thoroughly enjoy this dance, and it was because of what she called the brutal
circumstances of her coming. Why had she not been willing and glad to come?
Too late! The indignity had been perpetrated and she could not forget it. Nevertheless, she felt stir in her something besides the desire to shine and attract for
the sole purpose of making Edd Denmeade miserably jealous. It was an honest
realization that she could like these people and enjoy herself.

Commotion and stamping of feet and merry voices rose from the front of the schoolhouse. Lucy was informed that the music had arrived. She saw an old man proudly waving a violin and forging his way to the tiny platform. The children screeched and ran for him. Edd joined the group with whom Lucy was standing. Then a loud twang from the fiddler set everyone to expectancy. When he began to play the couples moved out upon the floor. Edd said no word, but he reached for Lucy.

"Wait. Let me watch a moment," she said. "I want to see how you dance."

"Wal, shore we're no great shucks at it, but we have fun."

Soon the floor was half full of wheeling, gliding couples, with more falling in line every moment. Their dancing had only one feature in common with what she understood about dancing, and that was they caught the rhythm of the old fiddler's several chords.

"Very well, Mr. Denmeade, I think I can catch the step," said Lucy.

As he took hold of her it was not possible to keep from stiffening somewhat and to hold back. Still, she was to ascertain that Edd showed no thought of holding her closely. How serious he was about this dancing! He was surprisingly easy on his feet. At first Lucy could not fall in with his way of dancing; gradually, however, she caught it, and after several rounds of the room she was keeping time with him. It required a great deal of effort and concentration for Lucy to live up to her repute as a dancer. Manifestly Edd Denmeade did not talk while he danced. In fact, none of the dancers talked. They were deadly serious about it, and the expressions on different faces highly amused Lucy. She could not see that dancing held any sentimental opportunities for these young people. It seemed to Lucy a bobbing, gyrating performance, solemnly enjoyed by boy and girl in markedly loose contact. Really they danced wholly with their own intent and energy. Lucy found Edd's arm as rugged and unyielding as the branch of an oak. At last the dance ended, to Lucy's relief.

"Shore you can dance!" exclaimed Edd, heartily. "Like a feather! If you hadn't leaned on my arm I'd not have known you was there. New kind of dancin' for me!"

Lucy did not deign to reply. He led her back to the corner, where he found her a seat beside his mother. "Shore I hope you dance them all down," he whispered. "Reckon I wouldn't be in Sam Johnson's boots for a lot."

"What did he mean?" inquired Lucy of his mother, after he had left them.

"Dancin' anyone down is to make him give up—tire him out," she replied. "An' that about Sam Johnson is funny. Sam is reckoned to be the best dancer in these parts. An' so is Sadie. Wal, as everybody seen right off, Sadie can't hold a candle to you. An' Sam is goin' to find it out."

"Some one will surely dance me down," replied Lucy, with a laugh. "I am out of practice."

It developed that the time between dances was long, and given over to much hilarity and promenading around. The children took advantage of this opportunity to romp over the floor. Lucy soon was surrounded again, so that she could not see very much of what was going on. Sam Johnson claimed her for the next dance. He struck Lucy as being something of a rural beau, quite taken with himself, and not above intimating that she would surely like dancing with him better than with a big-footed bee hunter.

As a matter of fact, when the fiddler started up again Lucy found Sam's boast to be true. He was a surprisingly good dancer and she enjoyed dancing with him. But it was not this that prompted her to be prodigal of her smiles, and to approach audacity, if not actual flirtation, to captivate Sam. She did not stop to question her motive. He and his girl Sadie had been largely responsible for Edd Denmeade's affront to her. Yet Lucy did not dream that she was championing Edd. She had been deeply roused. The primitive instincts of these young people were calling to the unknown in her.

Once in the whirling maze of flushed faces Lucy found herself looking right into Sadie Purdue's eyes. Lucy nodded smilingly. Her greeting was returned, but Sadie failed to hide her jealousy and resentment.

When that dance ended Lucy was besieged by the young men, and gradually she gave herself up to the novelty of the occasion. Now and then she saw Edd dancing or attending some one, but he did not approach her. Mrs. Denmeade apparently took great pride in Lucy's popularity. The children gradually drooped and were put to sleep in the corner back of the stove. Lucy had to take a peep at them, some dozen or more of curly-headed little boys and girls, and several babies, all worn out with excitement and now fast asleep.

Dance after dance followed, stealing the hours away. By midnight, when the intermission and supper were announced by Mr. Denmeade, it seemed to Lucy that she had allowed her impulsiveness and resentment to carry her away. Sam Johnson had more than lived up to the reputation Edd had given him. Only Lucy's tact saved him from utterly neglecting Sadie; and as it was he made a fool of himself. Mr. Jenks, the teacher, did not dance, and devoted himself to the older people. He had not found opportunity for more than a few words with Lucy, but several times she had caught him intently watching her, especially while she was with Sam. This, more than any other thing, made her reflect that perhaps she had already forgotten the ideal she had propounded to him. She suffered a moment of regret; then, when at the intermission Edd presented himself before her, cool and nonchalant, she could not help being rebellious.

"Wal, reckon I'll have to lick somebody before this night's over," he drawled as he led her across the room.

"Indeed! How interesting!" replied Lucy, icily.

"Shore will, unless somebody backs down on what he said. . . . Ma wants you to set with her at supper. Teacher Jenks has somethin' to say to you. Shore tickles me. . . . Why, Lucy Watson, you've made this night the wonderfulest of my life! I've had enough dancin' an' gettin' even an' crawlin' of these here corn-huskers to last forever."

Lucy was afraid that for her, too, something wonderful lurked under the commonplaces of this experience, but she could not confess that Edd Denmeade had created it. She felt how little she was to regret that he had surprised her by not living up to the status of boor and ruffian. Instead of this he had turned out to be something approaching a gentleman. He became an enigma to her. It must be that he had no conception of his rude seizure of her person, his utter disregard of her feelings. Yet here at the dance he had eliminated himself, content to see her whirled about by his cousins and friends, simply radiating with the pride of being her cavalier.

"Reckon I'll help feed this outfit," he said, leaving her in a seat between his mother and Mr. Jenks.

"Well, I'd hardly have known you," said the schoolteacher, with a smile and cordial greeting.

"Wal, I said the same," averred Mrs. Denmeade. "Shore she just looks lovely."

Lucy had the grace to blush her pleasure. "I declare this night will ruin my promise as a welfare worker. Too many compliments!"

"Not your promise, but your possibility," whispered Mr. Jenks, significantly. "Young lady, I intend to talk to you like a Dutch uncle."

"Indeed, I hope you do," replied Lucy, soberly. "Then I'll have something to tell you."

A corps of young men, among whom was Edd, passed round the room, distributing sandwiches and coffee, cake and ice cream. Soon the large hall-like place hummed with voices. Every seat along the walls was occupied. Around the entrance clustered a group of youths who had come without partners, and it was plain they felt their misfortune. Nevertheless, they had established some kind of rapport between themselves and other boys' partners. Lucy's keen susceptibilities grasped the fact that many of the girls welcomed this state of affairs.

Presently Mr. Jenks found opportunity to say, "You have created a havoc, Miss Lucy."

"Have I? Well, Mr. Jenks, I'm surely afraid that I wanted to," she confessed.

"I am not joking," he continued, more earnestly. "Indeed, I make all allowance for a girl's natural vanity and pleasure in being admired. You are 'shore good fer sore eyes,' as I heard one old codger say. You have stormed this schoolhouse crowd. If looks could kill, Sadie Purdue would have had you dead hours ago. They all say, 'Sam is gone!' . . . It would be funny—if it were anywhere else but up in this backwoods."

"Oh, have I forgotten myself?" exclaimed Lucy, aghast.

"Pray don't misunderstand," said Mr. Jenks, hastily. "I think you very modest and nice, considering the unusual situation. But you *have* forgotten your welfare work. Of course I don't see how you can avoid these dances. And that's the rub. Your popularity will make enemies among the girls and fights among the boys."

In self-defense Lucy related briefly and vividly how Edd Denmeade had seized her and held her powerless, threatening to tie her, until in her shame and fear she had consented to come to the dance.

"I'm not surprised," said Mr. Jenks, gravely. "These fellows are built that way, and Edd is really what they call him, a wild-bee hunter. I believe that implies almost an Indian's relationship to the woods. But you must not mistake Edd and do him injustice. It never dawned on him that violence would be a profanation to a girl such as you. . . . Could you honestly accuse him of the least boldness—you know what I mean?"

"No, I'm bound to confess that he handled me as if I were a boy or an old sack," replied Lucy, honestly.

"Well, then, try to understand him. It will not be easy. He's a savage. But savages are closer to nature than other men, and somehow the better for it. . . . What surprises me is that Edd has not made any fuss yet over Bud Sprall's attentions to you."

"Bud Sprall!" exclaimed Lucy, with a start of amaze. "Have I met him?"

"Wal, I reckon, as Edd would say," rejoined the teacher, amused at Lucy's consternation. "You have danced twice with Bud, and showed that you liked it."

"Oh, but I didn't know," wailed Lucy. "I didn't catch half the names. . . . Show him to me."

The school-teacher managed presently, in an unobtrusive manner, to indicate which one of Lucy's partners had been the disreputable Bud Sprall.

"That handsome young fellow!" she burst out, incredulously.

"Handsome, yes; Bud's good-looking enough and he can dance. But he is not just the fellow you can have dangling after you."

"I took him for one of the relations. There's so many. And I didn't see anything wrong with him except, come to think of it, he might have been drinking a little. But he was not the only one upon whom I detected drink."

"White mule! These boys will fetch a bottle to the dances. It's the one objectionable feature about their social family affairs. Naturally white mule kicks up fights."

"Oh, how unfortunate! How thoughtless of me not to *know* what I was doing!" cried Lucy.

"Don't be distressed," he returned, kindly. "No harm yet. But I advise you to avoid Bud hereafter."

"I'm sure I promised him another dance," said Lucy, in perplexity.

"Get out of it, then. And that's the worst of it. Bud will be sore and make trouble, unless you are very clever."

"Oh dear! How can I get out of a dance I've promised? . . . And that Sam Johnson! I *was* nice to him, deliberately. He's such a conceited fellow. I'm afraid I let him think he'd made a wonderful impression on me."

"Miss Watson, I have an inspiration," rejoined Mr. Jenks, animatedly. "Confide in Edd. Get him to help you out of your dilemma."

"Edd! How could I? Impossible!" replied Lucy, heatedly.

"Of course that's for you to say. But if you don't, and cannot extricate yourself, I imagine you will only get in deeper."

Lucy seeing Mrs. Denmeade approaching with friends, was unable to continue discussing the situation with Mr. Jenks. The parents of the children present were eager to talk to Lucy, and they asked innumerable questions. Before she realized the fleeting by of the supper hour the fiddler started one of his several tunes, and there followed a rush of dancers to the floor.

Edd did not exhibit any considerable alacrity in approaching her for this first number after the intermission.

"Want to dance this with me?" he queried, coolly.

"Isn't it customary?" replied Lucy as she glanced over the dancers to select some she knew.

"Shore. But if you don't *want* to dance with me I'd as lief not have you."

"Oh, really! . . . Would you expect me to be dying to dance with you?" retorted Lucy, with sarcasm.

"Nope. I'm not thinkin' about myself. But you think I am. My folks all reckon you're havin' the wonderfulest time. Wal, I hope so, but I've a hunch you're not. For I've been watchin' you. I saw you with Mr. Jenks."

"Really, it'd only be honest to confess that—that I'm enjoying myself—when I forget how I happened to come," said Lucy.

"So I reckoned. An' you can have this dance with anyone you want."

"But—you brought me here. Won't it look strange if you don't dance with me?" she queried, with concern.

"Wal, the strangest thing that ever happened in this schoolhouse was for a Denmeade's girl to dance with a Sprall," he returned, bitterly.

"Oh! I am not your girl. . . . And I had not the remotest idea I was dancing with Bud Sprall. I only just found out. Mr. Jenks told me."

"Say, you didn't know it was Bud Sprall you danced with twice?" he demanded, with piercing eyes of doubt.

"Absolutely no. I never caught his name," confessed Lucy.

"Wal, I'll be dog-goned! I wish everybody knew that. Shore I can tell my folks," he said, ponderingly.

"Edd, I'm afraid I promised him another dance—after supper," went on Lucy, nervously. She realized there was an undercurrent here, a force of antagonism quite beyond her. When his face turned white she was nearer the truth. Abruptly he wheeled to leave her, but Lucy was quick to catch his sleeve and drew him back. The dancers crowded them to the wall.

"Do not leave me alone," she said, swiftly. "Remember that I am a stranger here. You brought me against my will. I can hardly be blamed for dancing with Bud Sprall when I did not know who he was."

"Reckon that's all right," he replied, gazing down on her. "But you was sweet on Bud an' you've shore turned Sam Johnson's head."

Lucy strove valiantly to keep her temper and find her wits. She began to have an inkling why Mr. Jenks was so concerned over her predicament.

"Suppose I was? Didn't you deserve to be punished?" she queried.

"Reckon I don't savvy you," he rejoined, doubtfully. "Shore you strike me a little like Sadie Purdue."

"We are all women. Nevertheless, I don't consider that a compliment. But . . . you brought me here. I've made a mess of it. I was—well, never mind now. Only, it's your duty to help me not make it *worse*."

"Who's sayin' I wouldn't help you?" he queried.

"You started to leave me."

"Wal, you said you'd another dance with Bud."

"But I didn't know who he was. Now I do know. I won't dance with him. I don't want to. I'm very sorry I blundered. But he seemed nice and—and——"

"Bud has a way with girls," said Edd, simply. "Shore he's slicker than Sam."

"Will you take me home?" she asked, urgently.

"Shore. But I reckon that'd make worse talk. You'd better stay an' let me take care of you."

"I—I'll do what you want me to," replied Lucy, faintly.

"Wal, dance this with me. Then I'll hang around an' keep an eye on you. Keep out of that ring-around dance where they change partners all the time. When Bud or Sam comes up, you give me a look, an' I'll be there pronto. Shore all your dances are mine, an' I don't have to give any more to Bud or Sam."

"Thank you. I—I hope it turns out all right," replied Lucy.

While she danced her mind was active. She regretted her rash determination to make this crude backwoods youth jealous. He had certainly disappointed her in that regard. After awakening to the situation, first through her conversation with Mr. Jenks and later with Edd, she realized she had jeopardized her welfare work. No matter what affront she had suffered, she should not have been so silly, so reckless, so undeserving of the trust placed in her. Yet what provocation! Her nerves tingled at the thought.

When the dance ended Edd relinquished her to one of his cousins, and gradually Lucy lost her worry for the time being. The next dance was the ring-around, which Lucy refused to enter, remaining beside Mrs. Denmeade. Here she had opportunity to watch, and enjoyed it immensely. The dancing grew fast and furious. When the dancers formed in a ring and wheeled madly round the room, shrieking and laughing, they shook the schoolhouse till it rattled.

It developed that Edd Denmeade was more than a match for Bud Sprall when he presented himself for the dance Lucy had promised. But the interchange of cool speech struck Lucy keenly with its note of menace. Sprall's dark handsome face expressed a raw, sinister hate. Denmeade wore a laconic mask, transparent to any observer. The advantage was his. Finally Sprall turned to Lucy.

"I ain't blamin' you, for I know you want to dance with me," he said. "Reckon I'll not forget. Good night."

Sam Johnson was not so easy to dispose of. Manifestly he and Edd were friends, which fact made the clash devoid of rancor.

"Wal, Sam, see here," drawled Edd, finally. "You go an' fetch Sadie up. Reckon I'd like a dance with her. You've only had five dances with Miss Lucy. This here one will be six, if Sadie is willin' to trade off. So fetch her up."

"Edd, I haven't got Sadie for this dance," fumed Sam.

"Then you're out of luck. For I shore won't give up my partner."

Sam tramped away in high dudgeon. Lucy danced once round the room with Edd, and then joined the group outside eating ice cream beside the fire. Dawn was gray in the east. How dark the forest and mournful the wind! Lucy edged nearer the fire. She had become conscious of extreme fatigue, and longed for this unforgettable night to end.

Nevertheless, she danced until daylight. Her slippers were worn through. Her feet were dead. Never before in her life had Lucy expended such physical energy. She marveled at those girls who were reluctant to let the old fiddler off.

Lucy changed the white dress and slippers for her riding clothes. Though the morning was frosty, she did not feel the cold. How she could ever ride up to the Denmeade cabin she had no idea.

"Better get me on your horse before I drop," she told Edd.

He wanted her to remain there at the schoolhouse with the children and girls, who were not to go home until evening. Mrs. Denmeade and Mrs. Claypool were getting breakfast for those who stayed. Lucy, refusing, was persuaded to drink a cup of coffee. Then Edd put her up on Baldy. All around the clearing boys and girls were mounting horses, and some of the older folk were driving off in wagons. Gay good-bys were exchanged. Lucy rode into the woods with the Denmeades.

At first the saddle and motion seemed a relief after such incessant dancing. But Lucy soon discovered that her strength was almost spent. Only vaguely did she see the beauty of the forest in the clear, crisp, fragrant morning. She had no sense of the stirrups and she could not catch the swing of the horse. The Denmeades trotted and loped on the levels, and walked up the slopes. Lucy could not have endured any one kind of riding for very long. She barely managed to hang on until they reached home.

The sun was rising in rosy splendor over the eastern wall. Wild turkeys were gobbling from the ridge behind the cabin. The hounds rang out a chorus of bays and barks in welcome.

Lucy almost fell out of the saddle. Edd was there beside her, quick to lend a hand.

"Wal, I reckon it was a night for both of us," he said. "But shore I don't want another like it, unless what I pretended was really true."

Murmuring something in reply, Lucy limped to her room, and barring the door she struggled to remove her boots. They might as well have been full of thorns, considering the pangs they gave her.

"Oh—oh—what a—terrible night!" she gasped, falling on the bed, fully dressed. "Yet—I know I wouldn't have missed it—for worlds . . . Oh, I'm dead! I'll never wake up!'

7

It was midsummer. The mornings were pleasant, the days hot and still, the evenings sultry and purple, with massed clouds in the west.

The July rains had left the ridges and open patches and the edges of the clearings colorful and fragrant with flowers. Corn and cane and beans were green and wavy in the fields. A steady line of bees flew by the cabin porch, to and fro from hives to woods. And a drowsy murmuring hum made music down by the shady stream.

At sunrise the home of the Denmeades seemed to be a rendezvous for the frisky chipmunk and chattering red squirrel, for squalling blue jay and whistling hawk and cawing crow, and for the few wild singing birds of the locality. At noon the woods were locked in hot, drowsy stillness; the pine needles did not quiver; heat veils rose smokily from the glades. At evening a melancholy pervaded the wilderness.

One Saturday Lucy sat meditating in the tent that had long been her abode. It was situated out under the pines on the edge of the gully. The boys had built a platform of rough-hewn boards, and a framework of poles, over which the canvas had been stretched. The floor was high above the ground, so that Lucy had long lost the fear of snakes and tarantulas. Indeed this outdoor home had grown wonderfully dear to her. By day she heard the tiny patter of pine needles on the tent; at night the cool winds blew through, and in the moonlight shadows of swaying branches moved above her.

Lucy had problems on her mind. As far as the Denmeades were concerned, her welfare work had been successful beyond her dreams. The time was approaching when in all fairness she must go to another family. She would keenly regret leaving this place she had learned to love, yet she wanted to do as well by others as she had done by the Denmeades. When to go—that was part of the problem.

Another disturbing factor came in the shape of a letter from her sister Clara. It had shocked her and induced a regurgitation of almost forgotten emotions. The letter lay open in her lap. It must be reread and considered and decided upon—matters Lucy was deferring.

The last and perhaps most perplexing question concerned Edd Denmeade. Lucy had to go back in retrospect. The trouble between Edd and her dated back to the dance in May, the one which he had forced her to attend. Lucy had gone to other dances since then, but Edd had never attended another. She might in time have forgiven him for that exhibition of his primitiveness, but shortly afterward he had precipitated something which resulted in their utter estrangement. The bee hunter was the only one of the Denmeades who had not wondrously benefited by her work. He had lost by her presence. He had gone back farther. He exhibited signs of becoming a solitary wanderer in the woods most of the time, a violent and dangerous young man when he did mingle with people. Lucy had forced upon her the undoubted fact that she was the cause of this. No one else knew yet, not even Edd's mother. Lucy could not take unadulterated pride and joy in her success. She did not see how she could have avoided such a situation, yet regret haunted her. And now with decisions to make she vacillated over the important ones, and brought to mind the scene that had turned Edd Denmeade aside from the happier influences and tasks which she had imposed upon his family.

Shortly after that dance Edd had come up to her where she sat on the corral fence watching the boys roping and shoeing a horse.

"I reckon I'm goin' to ask you a question," he announced. Almost his tone was the cool drawling one habitual with him; here, however, there seemed something deep, inevitable behind his words.

"Goodness! Don't ask me to go to another dance," laughed Lucy.

"Reckon I'll never dance again, unless——" He broke off. "An' what I'm goin' to ask you I've asked other girls. Shore this is the last time."

"Well, what is it?" queried Lucy, suddenly perturbed.

"Will you marry me?"

Notwithstanding the fact that she was startled, Lucy burst into mirth. It must have been the opposite to what she felt, a nervousness expressing itself in laughter. But it appeared to be unfortunate.

"I—I beg pardon, Edd," she made haste to say. "Really I didn't mean to laugh at you. But you—you surprised me so. . . . You can't be serious."

"Reckon I don't know just what I am," he replied, grimly. "But I'm askin' you to marry me."

"Because you want a home and a woman? I heard your father say that."

"Shore. That's the way I've felt. Reckon this is more. I've told my folks an' relations I was askin' you. Wanted them to know."

"Edd, I cannot marry you," she replied, gravely.

"Why not?" he demanded. "You're here. You want to work for us. An' I reckon I could help you as much as you could me."

"That's true. You *could* help me a great deal. But I'm sorry I can't marry you."

"Reckon you're too good for a backwoodsman, a wild-bee hunter who's been jilted by other girls," he asserted, with a strange, deep utterance.

"No. You're wrong," declared Lucy, both touched and angered by his speech. "I don't think I'm too good. That dance you dragged me to cured me of my vanity."

"Wal, then, what's the reason?" he went on. "Ma says you're goin' to stay among us people for years. If that's so you'll *have* to marry one of us. I'm askin' you first."

"Edd, an honest girl could not marry a man she didn't love," replied Lucy. "Nor can a man be honest asking a girl whom *he* does not love."

"Shore I am honest. I'm no liar," he retorted. "I'm just plain man. I don't know much of people or books. But I know the woods, an' reckon I can learn what you want me to."

"I don't mean honest in that sense," rejoined Lucy. "I mean you don't love me."

"Love you! Are you like Sadie, who told around that I'd never kissed her?"

"No, I'm not like Sadie," answered Lucy, with rising temper.

"Wal, I'm askin' your pardon," he said. "Shore you're different from Sadie. . . . As for this love you girls talk about I don't know—I always felt a man should keep his hands an' his lips to himself until he had a wife."

"Edd, I respect you for that," replied Lucy, earnestly. "And understand you better. . . . But love is not kisses and all that."

"Wal, what is it, then?"

"It is something beautiful, spiritual as well as physical. It is a longing for the welfare, the happiness, the good of some one as well as the sweetness of desire. For a woman love means what Ruth said in the Bible. 'Whither thou goest, I will go. Thy people shall be my people, thy God my God.' . . . A man who loves a woman will do anything for her—sacrifice himself. The greater his sacrifice the greater his love. And last he ought to feel that he could not live without the object of his affections."

"Wal, I reckon I don't love you," replied Edd, pondering.

"Of course you don't. You're only thinking of yourself," rejoined Lucy.

"Reckon I can't help what I think. Who put all this in my head?"

"Edd, you haven't got anything in your head," retorted Lucy, unable to restrain her pique and scorn. "That's the trouble. You need education. All your people need education more than anything else."

"Wal, why don't you teach me same as you do Liz an' Lize?" he complained.

"You're a grown man!" ejaculated Lucy. "You want to marry me! And you talk like a child."

"Shore I could make you marry me—same as I made you go to the dance," he said, ruthlessly.

For an instant Lucy stared at him, too stunned to reply. The simplicity of his words and conviction was as monstrous as the idea they conveyed. How strange that, though a fury suddenly flamed up in her breast, she had a doubt of herself, a fear that he could do what he wanted to do with her!

"Make me marry you! Never!" she burst out, thickly.

"Shore I'd not care what you said," he replied.

Lucy's amaze and wrath knew no bounds. "You—you——" She choked, almost unable to express herself. "You savage! You couldn't even love yourself. You're——" She was utterly at a loss to find words. "Why, you're a fool— that's what you are! . . . If you mention marriage again I'll give up my work here and leave."

Then and then only did it seem to dawn upon him that there was something wrong with his mind. He gave Lucy a blank, dead stare, as if he saw something through her. The vitality and intensity withered out of his face. He dropped his head and left her.

That scene had been long weeks past. For days Edd had remained out in the woods, and when he returned there was a difference in him. None of the family, however, apparently attributed it to Lucy. But she knew. At first, such was her antagonism, she did not care what he did or what became of him; but gradually, as the weeks wore on and she had such wonderful success with her work, while he grew wilder and stranger, she began to pity instead of despising him. Poor backwoods boy! How could he help himself? He had been really superior to

most of his cousins and friends. Seldom did he do any work at home, except
with his bees. Rumor credited him with fights and brawls, and visits to the old
moonshiner who distilled the liquor called white mule. His mother worried
incessantly. His father passed from concern to grief. "Dog-gone me!" he ejaculated. "Edd's headed like them Sprall boys. An' who'd ever think it!"

Likewise, Lucy passed from pity to worry, and from that to a conscience-
stricken accusation. If for no other reason she was to blame because she had
come to Cedar Ridge. This fall of Edd's was taking the sweetness out of her
success. Could the teaching of a few children balance the ruin of their brother?
How impossible not to accuse herself of the change in him! She felt it every
time she saw him.

At last Lucy saw clearly that her duty consisted in a choice between giving
up her welfare work there and winning Edd Denmeade back to what he had been
before she came. Thought of abandoning that work would scarcely stay before
her consciousness, yet she forced herself to think of it. She had found a congenial,
uplifting vocation for herself. But it was one that she could give up, if it were
right to do so. There were other things she could find to do. Coming to think
of the change in the Denmeade household, the cleanliness and brightness, the
elimination of unsanitary habits, the saving of labor, the development of the
children's minds, she could not persuade herself that it would be otherwise than
cowardice for her to quit now.

"I must stay," soliloquized Lucy, at last seeing clearly. "If I quit now, all
my life I'd be bitter because I failed of the opportunity I prayed for. . . . Then,
if I stay I must save Edd Denmeade. . . . It would be welfare work of the noblest
kind. . . . What it costs me must not matter."

Lucy deliberately made the choice, for good or ill to herself, with her eyes
wide open and all her faculties alive to the nature of her task and the limits it
might demand. Her home life had inured her to sacrifice. That thought brought
her back to Clara and the letter which lay open in her lap. With a wrench of her
spirit she took it up and reread:

FELIX, *July 10*.

DEAREST LUCY

I came back from Mendino to find you gone. I deserved my
disappointment, because I've never written you. But, Lucy,
it wasn't because I'd forgotten. I was ashamed. I eloped with
Jim, as you know, because father had no use for him. Well,
if I had listened to you I'd not be miserable and alone now.
Jim turned out worse than anyone thought. He didn't even
marry me. I'm as much to blame for the whole business as he.

The most shameful thing for me, however, was to discover I didn't love him. I was just crazy.

Father shut the door in my face. I've been staying with an old schoolmate, Mamie Blaize, who has been kind. But, Lucy, I can't stay here. Felix will be no place for me, after they find out.

I went to the State Department who employ you. From them I got your address. The woman there was very nice. She spoke of your success, and that you had paved the way for extensive welfare work in other parts of the state. Lucy, I'm proud of you. It was always in you—to do good.

I'm not very well or very strong. Won't you please let me come out there and stay with you? I'll get well and I'll work my fingers to the bone for you. Let me show you I've had my bitter lesson. I need you, Lucy dear, for sometimes I grow reckless. I have horrible spells of blues. I'm afraid. And if you fail me I don't know what in the world I'll do. But you won't fail me. I seem to feel that deep inside me. It makes me realize what I lacked.

Send me money at once to come, and tell me what to do— how to get there. Please, Lucy, I beg you. I'm in the dust. To think after scorning your love and advice I'd come crawling on my knees to you! Judge what has happened to me by that. Hurry and write.

LOVE,
CLARA.

This letter saddened Lucy more because of its revival of memory of the beloved little sister than the news it contained. Lucy had never expected anything but catastrophe for Clara. It had come, and speedily. Clara had been away from Felix a year and a half. She was now nearly nineteen. This frank letter revealed a different girl.

Lucy reread it, pondered over what she confessed, wept over the ruin of her, yet rejoiced over the apparent birth of soul. Clara had never been one to beg. She had been a sentimental, headstrong girl and she could not be restrained. Lucy forgave her now, sorrowed for the pitiful end of her infatuation for the cowboy Jim Middleton, and with a rush of the old sisterly tenderness she turned to her table to answer that letter. Her response was impulsive, loving, complete, with never a word of reproach. She was accepting Clara's changed attitude toward life as an augury of hope for the future. It was never too late. Clara must reconstruct her life among new people, and if her disgrace became public she could never return to Felix. Better perhaps that Felix become only a memory!

Lucy concluded that letter with interesting bits of information about this wilderness country, the beauty of its forests, and the solitude of its backwoods homes. She did not include any remarks anent the stalwart young backwoodsmen or their susceptibilities to the charms of young girls. Even as she thought of this Lucy recalled Clara's piquant, pretty face, her graceful form, her saucy provocative ways. How would Edd Denmeade, and that fine quiet brother Joe, respond to the presence of the pretty sister? Lucy had to dispel misgivings. The die was cast. She would not fail the erring Clara. Inclosing a money order on her office, Lucy sealed the letter and stamped it with an air of finality and a feeling of relief and happiness. It had taken a calamity to drive Clara to her heart and protection.

"There!" she breathed low, almost with a sob. "That's done, and I'm glad. . . . Come to remember, that's the seond decision in regard to my problem. There was a third—when should I leave the Denmeades? . . . I can't leave just yet. I will stay. They have begged me to stay. . . . It cannot matter, just so long as I do my duty by these other families."

Then Lucy assuaged her conscience and derived a strange joy out of the decision she had made. Where might they lead her? The great forest arms of the wilderness seemed to be twining round her. She was responding to unknown influences. Her ideals were making pale and dim the dreams she had once cherished of her own personal future—a home—children—happiness. These were not for everyone. She sighed, and cast away such sentiment.

"Edd would say I'm bogged down in welfare work," she said. "Now to go out and begin all over again!"

It seemed significant that as she stepped out of her tent she espied Edd stalking up the lane toward the cabin. He had not been home for days and his ragged apparel showed contact with the woods. As Lucy halted by the gate to wait for him she felt her heart beat faster. Whatever sensations this wild-bee hunter roused, not one of them was commonplace.

"Good morning, Edd," said Lucy, cheerfully, as if that greeting had always been her way with him. "You're just the person I wanted to see. Where have you been so long?"

"Howdy!" he replied as he stopped before her. He gave her one of his piercing looks, but showed no surprise. He appeared thin, hard, hungry, and strained. He had not shaved for days, and his dark downy beard enhanced the strange wild atmosphere that seemed to cling round him. "I've been linin' new bees. Reckon it was high time I set to work. It's shore a fine year for bees. You see, there wasn't much rain. A rainy spring makes lots of yellow-jackets, an' them darn insects kill the wild bees an' steal their honey. This dry season keeps down the yellow-jackets. Reckon I'll have my best year findin' honey. Lined two trees to-day."

"When will you get the honey?" inquired Lucy.

"Not till after frost comes. October is best."

"Will you take me some day when you line bees and also when you get the honey?" asked Lucy, plunging headlong into her chosen task. She wanted to burn her bridges behind her. If she listened to caution and selfish doubts she could never keep to her decision. She expected her deliberate request to amaze Edd and cause him to show resentment or bitterness. But he exhibited neither.

"Shore will. Any time you say," he drawled, as he dragged his trailing rope to him and coiled it.

"I've news for you. I'm having my sister Clara come out to live with me," she announced.

"Shore that'll be good," he replied, with interest. "How old is she an' what's she like?"

"Clara is nearly nineteen. She's blond, very different from me. And very pretty."

"Wal, you're light-headed yourself, an' I reckon not so different."

"Edd, are you paying me a compliment?" she asked, archly.

"Nope. I just mean what I say. When'll your sister come?"

"If all goes well she'll arrive in Cedar Ridge on the stage Wednesday week. But some one must ride in to-morrow so my letter can catch Monday's stage."

"Give it to me. I'm ridin' to Cedar Ridge this afternoon."

"Edd, did you intend to go anyway?"

"Wal, reckon I didn't," he declared, honestly. "I've had about enough of town."

"You've been drinking and fighting?"

"Shore," he answered, simply, as if there were no disgrace attached to that.

"I don't want you to go to town with my letter unless you promise me you'll neither drink nor fight," she said, earnestly.

Edd laughed. "Say, you're takin' interest in me mighty late. What for?"

"Better late than never. I refuse to discuss my reasons. But will you promise?"

"Wal, yes, about the white mule. Sorry I can't promise about fightin'. I've too many enemies I've licked, an' if I happened to run into one of them, drunk or no drunk, they'd be a-rarin' to get at me."

"Then I'd rather you stayed away from Cedar Ridge."

"Wal, so would I. Honest, Lucy, I'm sort of sick. Don't know what it is. But to-day in the woods I began to feel a little like my old self. It's bee huntin' I need. To get away from people!"

"People will never hurt you, Edd. It's only that you will not like them. . . . Tell me, have you had trouble with Bud Sprall?"

"Nope. Funny, too. For Bud's been lookin' powerful hard for me. He never goes to town an' I never go to dances, so we haven't bucked into each other."

"What's this trouble between you and Bud? Doesn't it date back to that dance you took me to?"

"Wal, it's part because of somethin' he said about you at that dance. I'd have beat him half to death right there, only I didn't want to spoil your good time." He seemed apologizing to her for a softness that he regretted.

"About me!" exclaimed Lucy, in surprise. "What was it?"

"Reckon I'm not hankerin' to tell," he replied, reluctantly. "Shore I always blamed myself for lettin' it happen. But that night I was plumb locoed."

"Edd, if it is something you *can* tell me, do so at once," demanded Lucy.

"Wal, I can tell it easy enough," returned Edd, with a smile breaking the hardness of his grimy face. "Bud just bragged about peepin' through the cracks of the shed back of the schoolhouse. Swore he watched you undress."

"Oh—the sneak!" burst out Lucy, suddenly flaming.

"Wal, don't let the idea upset you," drawled Edd. "For Bud was a liar. He never saw you. He just hatched that up after you wouldn't give him the other dance."

"How do you know?" queried Lucy, in swift relief.

"Reckon I didn't know that night. But shore I found out afterward. I rode down to the schoolhouse an' looked. There wasn't a crack in that shed anywheres. Not a darn one! You can bet I was careful to make shore. Bud just lied, that's all. He's always been a liar. But I reckon I hold it as much against him as if he had seen you. . . . An' now there's more I'm sore about."

Lucy did not delve into her mind to ascertain why she had no impulse to nullify Edd's anger against Bud Sprall. The subject seemed natural to Edd, but it was embarrassing for her.

"How about my letter?" she asked, ignoring his last speech.

"Gerd's ridin' in to-day an' he'll go by here. Fetch me the letter an' I'll see he gets it."

Lucy ran back to her tent, and securing it she returned to hand it to Edd, with a word as to its importance.

"Shore. More trouble for us backwoods boys!" he ejaculated, amicably, as he grinned.

"Trouble! What do you mean?" she asked, though she knew perfectly well.

"Another pretty girl ridin' in," he rejoined, with a hint of pathos, "an' one that wouldn't an' couldn't care a darn for the likes of us."

"Edd, that is unkind," protested Lucy, uncertain how to meet such speeches of his. There seemed only one course to pursue and that called on all her courage.

"Reckon it is. I'm not as kind feelin' as I used to be."

"Indeed you're not," returned Lucy, hastily. "And I want to talk to you about that. Not now. Sometime when you're rested and cheerful. . . . Come here. I want to show you what I have done during this last absence of yours."

She led him across the open clearing and along a new-cut path into the woods. It ended abruptly on the edge of the gully. A board walk had been erected on poles, extending some yards out over the gully, to a point just above the spring. By means of a pulley and rope a bucket could be lowered into the spring and hauled up full of water, at very little expenditure of energy. Lucy demonstrated it with ease, showing the great saving of time and effort. Mrs. Denmeade and Allie had been compelled to make many trips a day to this spring, going down the steep trail and climbing back.

"Now what do you say to me? I thought that out and had your father and Uncle Bill put it up," declared Lucy, with pride.

Edd appeared to be either dumfounded or greatly impressed. He sat down rather abruptly, as if this last manifestation of Lucy's practical sense had taken something out of him.

"Simple as a b c," he ejaculated. "Why didn't pa or me—or somebody think of that long ago? I reckon ma an' Allie are ashamed of us."

His torn black sombrero fell to the ground, and as he wiped his moist face with a soiled scarf his head drooped. How tremendously he seemed to be struggling with a stolid mind! He resembled a man learning to think. Finally he looked up squarely at her.

"Reckon I'm about licked," he declared. "I've been dyin' hard—Miss Lucy Watson from Felix. But thick as I am I'm shore no darned fool. This here job to make fetchin' water easy for ma an' Allie is shore enough to make me kick myself. It makes me understand what you mean. I was against you. Every time I came home ma showed me somethin' new. Shore that livin' room, as they call it now, seemed no place for my boots an' spurs an' chaps—for *me*. But I couldn't help seein' a difference in ma an' Allie an' the kids. They began to look like that room, with its furniture an' curtains an' pictures an' rugs an' bright both day an' night. Reckon I can't tell you just how, but it felt so to me. Clean clothes, pretty things, must mean a lot to women an' kids. . . . An' so I'm comin' down off my hoss an' I'm thankin' you."

"Then you really believe I'm helping to make your people live better and happier?" asked Lucy, earnestly.

"It's hard for me to knuckle, but I do. I'm not blind. You've been a blessin' to us," he replied, with emotion.

"But—Edd," she began, hurriedly, "I—I haven't helped you."

"Me! . . . Wal, some fellows are beyond helpin'. I'm a savage. A big fool! . . . Only a wild-bee hunter!"

As his head drooped and his bitter reply ended Lucy divined the havoc that had been wrought by those hard words of hers, uttered long weeks before, in an anger she could not brook. He had taken them to heart. Lucy yearned to retract them, but that was impossible.

"Edd, judged by my standard for men, you were—what I called you," she said. "But I was unjust. I should have made allowance for you. I was hot-tempered. You insulted me. I should have slapped you good and hard."

"Wal, reckon I could have stood that," he replied. "You must have heard what Sadie an' other girls called me. An' *you* said it, too. Shore that was too much for me."

"If you'll promise not to—to talk the way you did then—never again, I'll forgive you," said Lucy, hesitatingly.

"Wal, don't worry, I'll shore never do it again. But I'm not askin' you to forgive me," he returned, bluntly, and rising, he stalked away toward the cabin.

Lucy realized that somehow she had been too impulsive, too hasty in her approach toward friendliness. Perhaps the old lofty superiority had unwittingly cropped out again. Nevertheless, something had been gained, if only her deeper insight into this wild-bee hunter. He was vastly ignorant of an infinite number of things Lucy knew so well. Somehow she had not accorded him a depth of emotion, a strength of individuality, the same that abided in her. Because he was a backwoodsman she had denied him an intimate personal sense of himself. She had not tried to enter into his way of looking at life or people or things. As far as he was concerned she had been a poor judge of humanity, a poor teacher. No easy task would it be to change him. Her reflection brought out the fact that the brief conversation with him had only added to her concern. His confession gratified her exceedingly. She had wanted more than she knew to have him see that she was helping his people to a better and happier life. How powerfully this motive of hers had seized hold of her heart! It had become a passion. He had called her a blessing to his family. That was sweet, moving praise for Lucy. No matter how he had been hurt in his crude sensitiveness, he surely was grateful to her. He was not wholly unapproachable. Only she must be tactful, clever, sincere. The last seemed the most important. Perhaps Edd Denmeade would see through tact and cleverness. Lucy pondered and revolved in mind the complexity of the situation. It must be made so that it was no longer complex. The solution did not dawn on her then, but she divined that she could learn more about him through his love of bees and the forest where he roamed.

Mary Denmeade espied Lucy sitting by the path to the spring, and, as always, she ran to her. The children could not get enough of Lucy's companionship. Through her their little world had widened wonderfully. Games and books, work and play, had already made incalculable differences. These backwoods children were as keen mentally as any children Lucy had been associated with in the city, and vastly easier to interest.

"Here you are," cried Mary, excitedly, her eyes wide. "Edd is scolding

Mertie. She's awful mad. So's ma. But ma is mad at Mertie and Mertie's mad at Edd.''

"Oh, I'm sorry, Mary. Perhaps I had better not go in yet," returned Lucy. "What's the trouble? Isn't it very strange for Edd to scold anyone, much less Mertie?''

"Strange? I don't know. He never scolds any of us *but* Mertie. Ma says it's because he loves her best. . . . Miss Lucy, Edd's not like he used to be. He stays away more an' when he does come home he's no time for us. Mertie said he was moony about you.''

"Was that what caused the trouble?" asked Lucy, quickly.

"Oh no. Mertie said that a long time ago. . . . I wasn't in the kitchen, but I peeped in and heard him say: 'Mert, you've been ridin' with Bud Sprall again.' An' Mertie said: 'I've no such thing. But it'd be no business of yours if I had.' An' Edd said: 'don't lie to me. Some one saw you.' Then Mertie had one of her bad spells. She raved an' cried. Ma took her part. Edd got hold of Mertie an' said he'd choke the truth out of her. He looked awful. Ma made him let Mertie go. An' Edd said: 'Wal, you stayed last night at Claypool's. Now what time did you get there after school?' Mertie said she couldn't remember. She had the reddest spots in her cheeks an' she couldn't look at Edd.''

"Mary, did you listen to all that?" asked Lucy, disapprovingly, as the child halted to catch her breath.

"I couldn't help hearing," went on Mary. "But I did peep in the door. But they didn't see me. Edd said: 'I had a hunch before, Mert Denmeade. An' yesterday when I was told by some one who seen you I just rode down to Claypool's, an' I found out you didn't get there till near dark. Took you three hours to ride from school to Amy's home! I asked Amy when she seen you last. She looked darn queer, but I made her tell. You went off down the road with Sadie Purdue.' Then ma pitched into Mertie so mad that I run.''

Lucy soothed the excited child and importuned her not to tell anyone else about the family quarrel and that perhaps it was not so much against Mertie as it looked. Mary shook her head dubiously, and presently, finding Lucy preoccupied, she gravitated toward the other children playing in the yard.

This was not the first time Lucy had been cognizant of an upset among the Denmeades owing to Mertie's peculiar ways of being happy. She had been the idol of the family, solely, no doubt, because of her prettiness. Lucy considered Mertie a vain little ignoramus with not enough character to be actually bad. Nevertheless, Lucy reflected, she might be as mistaken in Mertie as she had been in Edd. Of all the Denmeades, this second daughter was the easiest to influence because of her vanity. Lucy had won the girl's regard with a few compliments, a few hours of instruction in dressmaking, and perhaps that was why Lucy did not value it very highly. Still, for Edd's sake, and, more seriously considered,

for the girl's sake also, Lucy was now prepared to go to any pains to bring about
a happier relation between brother and sister. Perhaps, however, before she could
be accused of meddling in personal affairs she had better wait until her kind
offices were invited.

On her way back to her tent she heard the gate chain clank violently, and
upon turning she espied Edd stalking away, black as a thundercloud. Should she
let him go or halt him? Inspirations were not altogether rare with Lucy, but she
had one now that thrilled her. This was her opportunity. She called Edd. As he
did not appear to hear, she raised her voice. Then he wheeled to approach her.

"My, but you were tramping away fast and furiously!" said Lucy, amiably.

"Reckon I was. What you want?"

"Are you in any great hurry?"

"No, I can't say I am. Fact is I don't know where I'm goin'. But I'm a-rarin'
to go, just the same." His voice was strained with spent passion and his lean
face seemed working back to its intent, still expression.

"Come over in the shade and talk with me," said Lucy, and led him into the
pines to a nook overlooking the gully, where she often sat. Plain it was that Edd
followed her under compulsion. But this rather stimulated than inhibited Lucy.

"Don't go away angry," she began, and seating herself on the clean brown
pine mats, she clasped her knees and leaned back to look up at him.

"Reckon it's not with you," he rejoined, drawing his breath hard.

"Of course not. I know what's wrong. Mary heard you quarreling with Mertie.
She told me. . . . Now, Edd, I wouldn't for worlds meddle in your affairs. But
my job is as wide as your woods. It's hard for me to tell where to leave off. The
question is, if I can be good for Mertie, you want me to, don't you?"

"Wal, I shore do," he declared, forcibly. "More'n once I had a hunch to ask
you. But I—I just couldn't."

"You should have. I'm sorry I've been so—so offish. It's settled, then. Now
tell me what you think is wrong with Mertie."

"Reckon I don't think. I know," he replied, heavily. "Mertie is just plain
no good. All she thinks of is her face an' of somethin' to deck herself in so
she'll attract the boys. Any boy will do, though she sticks up her nose at most
of them, just the same. She's got one beau, Bert Hall, who lives in Cedar Ridge.
Bert is sweet on Mertie an' I know she likes him best of all the fellows who run
after her. Bert owns a ranch an' he's got a share in his father's sawmill. Course
he wants to marry Mertie an' Mertie wants to run wild. Dance an' ride! I reckon
Sadie Purdue hasn't helped her none. . . . Wal, this summer Mertie has taken
on airs. She says if she's old enough to be asked to dances an' to marry, she's
her own boss. Pa an' ma can't do nothin' with Mertie. I used to hold her down.
But shore—I've a hunch my time is past."

"Well?" queried Lucy, as he ended haltingly. "I understand. What about this Bud Sprall?"

"Mertie always liked that black-faced pup!" declared Edd, darkly. "She's been meetin' him on the sly. Not alone yet, but with Sadie, who's got the same kind of interest in Bud's pard, a hoss-wrangler who lives over Winbrook way. Mertie lied about it. . . . Wal, if I can't break it up one way I can another."

"You mean you'll go to Bud Sprall?" queried Lucy, instantly.

"I shore do," he said, tersely.

"You two will fight—perhaps spill blood," went on Lucy, intensely. "That might be worse than Mertie's affair with Bud, whatever it is. Edd, surely it is just a flirtation."

"Reckon I fooled myself with ideas like that," returned Edd, bluntly. "Boys an' girls up here do their flirtin' at dances. Straight out, Miss Lucy, this here sneakin' has a bad look. I know Sadie Purdue. She jilted me because I was too slow. Reckon she'd never have married me. Funny thing is she *never* would, even if she'd wanted to, because I found her out. Nobody but you knows that. Wal, Mertie is thick with Sadie. An' they're meetin' these boys. Reckon you know how it will end, unless we stop it. Bert's an easy-goin' boy. But Mertie could go too far. . . . You see, Miss Lucy, you haven't guessed yet just how— how thick many of us backwoods boys an' girls get. Not me! That's one reason why I'm a big boob. . . . An' I always hoped an' prayed I could keep Mertie different. Shore it goes kind of hard to see I'm failin'."

"Edd, you've failed yourself," asserted Lucy, ringingly. "You're on the down grade yourself. You've taken to the bottle and to fights. How can you expect to influence your sister to go straight if you're no good yourself?"

"By God! that shore's been—eatin' into me!" he ejaculated, huskily, and hid his somber face in his grimy hands.

"Oh, I'm glad you see it!" cried Lucy, putting a hand on his shoulder. "Edd, you must come back to your old self."

"Yes, I reckon I have to," he agreed. "If only it's not too late—for Mertie!"

"Let us hope and pray it is not," rejoined Lucy, earnestly. "I'm shocked at what you say, but yet I feel absolutely sure Mertie is still good. She's vain, she's wild. I know her kind. And, Edd, I promise to devote myself to Mertie. I must go to Felix for a week this fall. I'll talk about that to Mertie, hold it out to her. I'll take her with me. Oh, I know how to manage her. We'll marry her to Bert before she knows it."

"Wal, what ma said about you is shore true," he said, lifting his dark face stained with tears. "An' I'll make you a promise."

"Yes?" queried Lucy, encouragingly.

"I'll go back to my wild-bee huntin'."

Lucy divined the import of that strange promise and she rejoiced over it, happily proud for him and the Denmeades.

8

THE news that Lucy's sister was coming spread all over the immediate country. Lucy was hugely amused at the number of gallants who visited Denmeade's on Sunday and found transparent excuses to interview her. There was no use to try to avoid them on the issue that portended.

Lucy exhibited Clara's picture with conscious pride, and did not deem it necessary to explain that the likeness dated back several years. She was both delighted and concerned over the sensation it created. Of all the boys she had met there, Joe Denmeade appeared to be the quietest and nicest, the least given to dances, white mule, and girls. Lucy experienced one acute qualm of conscience before she approached Joe to ask him to meet her sister at Cedar Ridge. That qualm was born of a fear that Joe might meet his downfall in Clara. She silenced it with the resigned conviction that circumstances were beyond her. What a feeble little woman she was!

Sunday afternoon on the Denmeade porch found the usual visiting crowd largely augmented. Sam Johnson paid his first call for weeks, this time without Sadie. He seemed less debonair and obtrusive than had been his wont. Least of all did he question Lucy about the pretty sister, but he drank in all that was said. Lucy watched Sam closely as he looked at Clara's picture; and soberly she judged by his expression that, unless, as she devoutly hoped, Clara had changed, there would be some love-lorn gallants haunting the Denmeade homestead.

"When's she comin'?" queried Sam.

"I'll hear in to-morrow's mail. Wednesday or Saturday," replied Lucy.

"Reckon you're goin' in to meet her?"

"Indeed I am. Joe will drive me to town from the schoolhouse. Mr. Jenks has offered his buckboard."

"Joe! So he's the lucky cub?" snorted Sam. "Reckon you'd need a man."

Lucy's choice was news to all the listeners, including Joe himself, who, as usual, sat quietly in the background. She had shot him a quick glance, as if to convey they had an understanding. Whereupon Joe exhibited surprising quali-fications for the trust she had imposed upon him.

"Sam, you don't get the hunch," he drawled. "Miss Lucy's sister isn't a well girl. She's goin' to need *rest!*"

The crowd was quick to grasp Joe's import, and they laughed their glee and joined in an unmerciful bantering of the great backwoods flirt.

After supper, as Lucy sat on the steps of her tent, Joe approached her.

"Now, teacher, how'd you come to pick on me?" he asked, plaintively.

"Pick on you! Joe, you don't mean ——"

"Reckon I mean pick me *out,* as the lucky boy," he interrupted. "I'm just curious aboot it."

Lucy liked his face. It was so young and clean and brown, square-jawed, fine-lipped, with eyes of gray fire!

"Joe, I chose you because I think you will give my sister a better impression than any other boy here," replied Lucy, with deliberation.

"Aw, teacher!" he protested, as shyly as might have a girl. "Are you jokin' me? An' what you mean by this heah impression?"

"Joe, I ask you to keep what I tell you to yourself. Will you?"

"Why, shore!"

"My sister is not well and she's not happy. It would give her a bad impression to meet first thing a fellow like Sam or Gerd or Hal, who would get mushy on sight. Edd now would be too cold and strange. I ask you because I know you'll be just the same to Clara as you are to me. Won't you?"

"An' how's that, teacher?" he queried, with his frank smile.

"Why, Joe, you're just yourself!" answered Lucy, somewhat taken at a disadvantage.

"Never thought aboot bein' just like myself. But I'll try. I reckon you're not savvyin' what a big job you're givin' me. I mean pickin' me out to take you to town. If your sister comes on Saturday's stage every boy under the Rim will be there in Cedar Ridge. Reminds me of what I heard teacher Jenks say once. Some men are born great an' some have greatness thrust on them. Shore I'm goin' to be roped in that last outfit."

"I like you, Joe, and I want you to live up to what I think of you."

"Miss Lucy, are you shore aboot me bein' worth it?" he asked solemnly.

"Yes, I am. . . . To-morrow you stay till the mail comes for Mr. Jenks. He'll have mine. Then we'll know whether Clara is coming Wednesday or Saturday. I'd like you to borrow Edd's horse Baldy for Clara to ride up from the school-house. Any horse will do for me. We'll have to leave early."

"It'd be better. I can drive in from the schoolhouse in three hours. The stage arrives anywheres from eleven to four. I'm givin' you a hunch. We want to be *there* when it comes."

The following day when Joe rode home from school he brought Lucy's mail,

among which was the important letter from Clara—only a note, a few lines
hastily scrawled, full of a wild gratitude and relief, with the news that she would
arrive at Cedar Ridge on Saturday.

"It's settled, then, she's coming," mused Lucy, dreamily. "I don't believe
I was absolutely sure. Clara was never reliable. But now she'll come. There
seems some kind of fate in this. I wonder will she like my wild, lonesome
country."

Lucy had imagined the ensuing days might drag; she had reckoned falsely,
for they were singularly full of interest and work and thought. Edd had taken
to coming home early in the afternoons, serious and moody, yet intent on making
up for his indifference toward Lucy's activities with his family. He veered to
the opposite extreme. He would spend hours listening to Lucy with the children.
He was not above learning to cut animals and birds and figures out of paper, and
his clumsy attempts roused delight. Lucy had, in a way vastly puzzling to the
Denmeades, succeeded in winning Mertie to a great interest in manual training,
which she now shared with Mary. Edd wanted to know the why and wherefore
of everything. He lent Dick a hand in the carpentry work, of which Lucy invented
no end. And he showed a strange absorption at odd moments in the children's
fairy-story books. He was a child himself.

Naturally, during the late afternoon and early evening hours of the long summer
days he came much in contact with Lucy. She invited his co-operation in even
the slightest tasks. She was always asking his help, always inventing some reason
to include him in her little circle of work and play. She found time to ask him
about his bee hunting, which was the one subject that he would talk of indefinitely. Likewise she excited and stimulated an interest in reading. As he read
very slowly and laboriously, he liked best to listen to her, and profited most by
that, but Lucy always saw he was left to finish the passage himself.

At night when all was dark and still, when she lay wide-eyed and thoughtful
under the shadowy canvas, she would be confronted by an appalling realization.
Her sympathy, her friendliness, her smiles and charms, of which she had been
deliberately prodigal, her love for the children and her good influence on Mertie—
all these had begun to win back Edd Denmeade from the sordid path that had
threatened to lead to his ruin. He did not know how much of this was owing to
personal contact with her, but she knew. Edd was unconsciously drawn toward
a girl, in a way he had never before experienced. Lucy felt he had no thought
of sentiment, of desire, of the old obsession that he "must find himself a
woman." Edd had been stung to his soul by his realization of ignorance. She
had pitied him. She had begun to like him. Something of pride, something
elevating, attended her changing attitude toward him. What would it all lead to?
But there could be no turning back. Strangest of all was for her to feel the dawn
of a real happiness in this service.

Saturday morning arrived earlier for Lucy than any other she remembered. It came in the dark hour before dawn, when Joe called her to get up and make ready for the great ride to Cedar Ridge—to meet Clara. Lucy dressed by lamplight and had her breakfast in the dim, pale obscurity of daybreak. Mrs. Denmeade and Edd were the only others of the household who had arisen. Even the dogs and the chickens were asleep.

It was daylight when Lucy arrived at the corrals, where the boys had the horses saddled.

"I'd like to ride Baldy as far as we go horseback," said Lucy.

"Shore," replied Edd. "An' I reckon you'd better ride him back. For he knows you an' he might not like your sister. Horses have likes an' dislikes, same as people."

"Oh, I want Clara to have the pleasure of riding him."

"Shore she'll take a shine to him, an' then you'll be out of luck," drawled Edd as he held the corral gate open.

"Indeed, I hope she takes a shine to Baldy and everything here," declared Lucy, earnestly.

"Me an' Joe, too?" he grinned.

"Yes, both of you."

"Wal, I reckon it'll be Joe. . . . Good-by. We'll be lookin' for you all about sundown."

Joe rode into the trail, leading an extra horse, which would be needed upon the return; and he set off at a gait calculated to make time. Lucy followed, not forgetting to wave a gloved hand back at Edd; then she gave herself up to the compelling sensations of the hour and thoughts of the day.

There were scattered clouds in the sky, pale gray, pearly white where the light of dawn touched their eastern edges, and pink near the great bright flare above the Rim. The forest seemed asleep. The looming wall wandered away into the soft misty distance.

Joe did not take the schoolhouse trail, but the wilder and less traveled one toward Cedar Ridge. The woodland was dark, gray, cool. Birds and squirrels had awakened noisily to the business of the day. Deer and wild turkeys ran across the trail ahead of the horses. The freshness and fragrance of the forest struck upon Lucy as something new and sweet. Yet the wildness of it seemed an old familiar delight. Green and brown and gray enveloped her. There were parts of the trail where she had to ride her best, for Joe was making fast time, and others where she could look about her, and breathe freely, and try to realize that she had grown to love this wilderness solitude. Her grandfather had been a pioneer, and her mother had often spoken of how she would have preferred life in the country. Lucy imagined she had inherited instincts only of late cropping out. How would her sister react to this lonely land of trees and rocks? Lucy

hoped against hope. There was a healing strength in this country. If only Clara
had developed mind and soul enough to appreciate it!

Lucy well remembered the dark ravine, murmurous with its swift stream, and
the grand giant silver spruces, and the mossy rocks twice as high as her head,
and the gnarled roots under banks suggestive of homes for wild cats, and the
amber eddying pools, deep like wells, and the rushing rapids.

The climb out of this deep endlessly sloped canyon brought sight of sunrise,
a rose and gold burst of glory over the black-fringed Rim. Then a brisk trot
through a lighter and drier forest ended in the clearing of the Johnsons'.

Early as was the hour, the Johnsons were up, as was evidenced by curling
blue smoke, ringing stroke of ax, and the clatter of hoofs. Mr. Jenks, too, was
stirring, and soon espying Lucy, he hastened to come out to the fence.

"Mawnin', folks," he drawled, imitating the prevailing mode of speech.
"Miss Lucy, I shore forgot this was your great day. Reckon I'm out of luck,
for I'll not be here when you drive back. I'm going to visit Spralls', to see why
their children are absent so much from school."

"Mr. Jenks, will you please take note of these Spralls, so you can tell me
about them?" asked Lucy, eagerly. "I feel that I *must* go there, in spite of all
I hear."

"Yes, I'll get a fresh line on them," he replied. "And if that isn't enough
to keep you away I'll find other means."

"Oh, you are conspiring against me," cried Lucy, reproachfully.

"Yes, indeed. But listen, I've news for you," he went on as Joe led the
unsaddled horses inside the fence. "Your sister's coming has given me a wonderful idea. When she gets well, which of course she will do here very quickly,
why not let her take my school? Affairs at my home are such that I must return
there, at least for a time, and this would provide me with a most welcome
opportunity."

"I don't know," replied Lucy, doubtfully. "Clara had a good education. But
whether or not she could or would undertake such a work, I can't say. Still, it's
not a bad idea. I'll think it over, and wait awhile before I speak to her."

Mr. Jenks made light of Lucy's doubts, and argued so insistently that she
began to wonder if there were not other reasons why he wanted a vacation. She
had an intuitive feeling that he wanted to give up teaching, at least there, for
good. They conversed a few moments longer, until Joe drove up in the buckboard.
Then Mr. Jenks helped Lucy to mount the high seat beside Joe and bade them
a merry good-by.

Whatever the trail had been, the road was jarringly new to Lucy. There
developed ample reason for Joe's advice to "hang on to the pommel," by which
he must have meant anything to hold on to, including himself. The big team of
horses went like the wind, bowling over rocks, ruts, and roots as if they were

not there at all. Lucy was hard put to it to remain in her seat; in fact, she succeeded only part of the time.

"Say—Joe," cried Lucy, after a particularly sharp turn, which the buckboard rounded on two wheels, and Lucy frantically clung to Joe, "are you—a regular—driver?"

"Me? Say, I'm reckoned the best driver in this heah country," he declared.

"Heaven preserve me—from the worst," murmured Lucy.

"You picked me out, Miss Lucy, an' I shore mean to beat that outfit of boys in to Cedar Ridge," said Joe. "The whole darned caboodle of them will be there. Gerd an' Hal slept heah all night with Sam. An' they're already gone. Suppose the stage beats us to Cedar Ridge! . . . Say, Sam is up to anythin'."

"Drive as fast as you want, only don't upset me—or something awful!" returned Lucy, desperately.

On the long descent of the cedared ridge Joe held the big team to a trot. Lucy regained her breath and her composure. When at last they turned out of the brush into the main road of the little town Lucy was both thrilled and relieved.

"Wal, heah we are, an' we beat the stage," drawled Joe.

"You must be a wonderful driver, Joe, since we actually got here," averred Lucy. "But there'll be no need to drive that way going back—will there?"

"Reckon we want Clara to know she's had a ride, don't we?" he queried, coolly.

"Joe!"

"What'd you pick me out for? Reckon I've got to be different from that outfit. Look at the hosses. Whole string of them!"

"You mean the boys will waylay us?" queried Lucy, anxiously.

"Like as not they'd bust this heah buckboard if I left it long enough. Shore they'll expect to meet Clara an' have a chance to show off. But we'll fool them. When the stage comes you grab her. Go in to Mrs. Lynn's an' get some grub to pack with us. Don't eat in there. Sam'll be layin' for that. Hurry out an' we'll leave pronto, before the gang get their breath."

"But, Joe, why all this—this fear of the boys, and the rush?" queried Lucy.

"Reckon you know the boys. They'll be up to tricks. An' on my side, since you picked *me,* I want to have Clara first."

"Oh, I—see!" ejaculated Lucy. "Very well, Joe. I trust you, and we'll do your way."

They reached the post office, where Joe reined in the team. Lucy espied a porch full of long-legged big-sombreroed clean-shaven young men, whose faces flashed in the sun.

"Miss Lucy, I'll feed an' water the hosses," said Joe. "Reckon you need a little stretch after that nice easy ride."

"It'll be welcome," declared Lucy, getting down. "You keep an eye open for the stage while I run in to see Mrs. Lynn."

By going into the hotel entrance Lucy avoided the boys slowly gravitating toward her. Mrs. Lynn greeted her most cordially, and was equally curious and informative. Lucy took advantage of the moment, while she was chatting, to peep out of the window. The cavaliers of Cedar Ridge lounged on the porch, and stalked to and fro. One group in particular roused Lucy's amused suspicions. Sam Johnson was conferring most earnestly with several of his cronies, two of whom were Hal Miller and Gerd Claypool. They were not particularly amiable, to judge from their faces. A gesture of Sam's attracted Lucy's gaze toward two picturesque riders, lean and dark and striking. She recognized the handsome face and figure of one of them. Bud Sprall! The other was a taller lither man, with flashing red face and flaming hair of gold. Young, bold, sinister, dissipated as he appeared, the virility and physical beauty of him charmed Lucy's eye.

"Who is that man—there, with Bud Sprall?" queried Lucy, trying to appear casual.

Mrs. Lynn peeped out. "I was askin' my husband that very question. He didn't know the fellow's name. Pard of Bud's he said. Two of a kind! Some of the boys told him Bud was thick with cowboys of the Rim outfit. This one is new in Cedar Ridge."

Presently as Joe appeared driving the buckboard to a shady place under a cottonwood, some rode from the front of the post office. Through the window, which was open, Lucy caught amusing and significant remarks.

"Howdy, boys!" drawled Joe, in answer to a unity of greetings.

"What you-all doin' here with them work clothes on?" queried one.

"Joe, yore shore kinda young to tackle this hyar city proposition," said another.

"Wal, Joe, I reckon you can't drive that big team with your left hand," asserted a third, banteringly.

"Hey, Joe, I see you're a Denmeade all over," said another. "But take a hunch from Edd's old tricks."

These remarks and others in similar vein attested the dominant idea in the minds of these young countrymen—that a new girl was soon to appear upon the scene and that only one attitude was possible. She was to be seen, fought over humorously and otherwise, and to be won. It afforded Lucy much amusement, yet it was also thought-arresting.

She went out and climbed to a seat beside Joe, careful to appear very vivacious and smiling. The effect was to silence the bantering boys and to cause, on the part of Sam and several others, a gradual edging toward the buckboard. Lucy appeared not to notice the attention she was receiving and she quite bewildered

Joe with a flood of rather irrelevant talk. Then one of the boys shouted that the stage was coming.

That checked all fun-loving impulses in Lucy. Her heart gave a lift and began to pound against her side. Glimpses she caught of the dusty well-remembered stage, while many thoughts flashed through her mind. Would Clara come, after all? How much had she changed? Would she be as sweet and repentant and appealing as her letters had implied? What a situation would arise if she did not like this wilderness country! Then a thrilling, palpitating joy that Clara had at last yearned for her!

The stage wheeled round the corner of cottonwoods, and the old driver, with great gusto and awareness of his importance, hauled the sweaty horses to a halt in front of the post office.

Lucy leaped down and ran. There were four or five passengers, and a great store of bags, boxes, and bundles, all of which she saw rather indistinctly. But as she reached the stage she cleared her eyes of tears and gazed up expectantly, with a numbness encroaching upon her tingling nerves. Clara might not have come.

There was a hubbub of voices. Manifestly others of these passengers had friends or relatives waiting.

"Hello—Lucy!" cried a girl's excited, rather broken voice.

Lucy almost screamed her reply. Behind a heavy old woman, laboriously descending the stage steps, Lucy espied a slim, tall, veiled girl clad in an ultra-fashionable gown and hat the like of which had not been seen at Cedar Ridge. Lucy knew this was her sister, but she did not recognize her. As the girl stepped down to the ground she threw back her veil, disclosing a pale face, with big haunting blue eyes that seemed to strain at Lucy with hunger and sadness. Indeed it was Clara—vastly changed!

"Sister!" cried Lucy, with a sudden rush of tenderness. Clara met her embrace, mute and shaking. How strange and full that moment! Lucy was the first to think of the onlookers, and gently disengaging herself from clinging hands she burst out: "Oh, I—I didn't know you. I was afraid you'd not be in the stage. . . . I'm so glad I'm half silly. . . . Come, we'll go in the hotel a moment. . . . Don't mind all this crowd."

Thus Lucy, talking swiftly, with no idea of what she was saying, led Clara away; but she was acutely aware of the fierce clutch on her arm and the pearly whiteness of her sister's cheek. Lucy did not dare look at her yet.

The sitting room inside the hotel happened to be vacant. Clara did not seem to be able to do anything but cling mutely to Lucy.

"You poor dear! Are you *that* glad to see me?" murmured Lucy, holding her close.

"Glad!—My God!" whispered Clara, huskily. "You'll never—know how glad. For you've never—been without—friends, love, home, strength."

"Oh, Clara, don't—don't talk so!" cried Lucy, in distress. "Don't break down here. Outside there are a lot of young backwoods boys, curious to see you. We can't avoid that. They are nice, clean, fine chaps, but crazy over girls. . . . Don't cry. I'm so glad to see you I could cry myself. Brace up. We'll hurry away from here. There's a long ride in a buckboard and a short one on horseback. You'll love the horse you're to ride. His name is Baldy. You'll love the woods. I live in a tent, right in the pines."

This meeting had proved to be unexpectedly poignant. Lucy had prepared herself for a few moments of stress, but nothing like this. Clara seemed utterly changed, a stranger, a beautiful, frail, haunted-eyed young woman. Lucy was deeply shocked at the havoc in that face. It told her story. But strange as Clara seemed, she yet radiated something Lucy had never felt in the old days, and it was love of a sister. That quite overpowered Lucy's heart. It had come late, but not too late.

"Clara, I hope you're strong enough to go on to-day—to my home," said Lucy, gently.

"I'm not so weak as that," replied Clara, lifting her face from Lucy's shoulder. It was tear-stained and convulsive. "I was overcome. I—I never was sure—till I saw you."

"Sure of what?" asked Lucy.

"That you'd take me back."

"You can be sure of me forever. I can't tell you how happy it makes me to know you want to come. . . . Let us sit here a few moments. As soon as you rest a little and compose yourself we'll start. I've ordered a lunch which we'll eat as we ride along."

"Ought I not tell you—about my trouble—my disgrace—before we go?" asked Clara, very low.

"Why should you—now?" rejoined Lucy, in surprise.

"It might—make a difference."

"Oh no! You poor unhappy girl. Do you imagine anything could change me? Forget your troubles," returned Lucy, tenderly.

"I wanted to—at least when I met you after so long a separation. But those tall queer men outside. Such eyes they had! They must know about me."

"Only that you're my sister and coming to stay with me," said Lucy, hurriedly. "They've ridden into town to see you—meet you. Don't worry. They won't meet you. I have told only that you were ill."

Clara seemed passionately grateful for Lucy's thoughtfulness. She had little to say, however, yet listened strainingly to Lucy.

A little later, when they left the hotel, Clara had dropped the veil over her white face, and she clung closely to Lucy. Meanwhile Joe had driven up to the high porch, from which Lucy helped her sister into the buckboard.

"Clara, this is Joe Denmeade," said Lucy as she stepped in beside Clara.

Joe quaintly doffed his huge sombrero and spoke rather bashfully. Lucy was pleased to see his fine brown, frank face smile in the sunlight.

"Wal, reckon we're all heah," he said, briskly. "The stage driver gave me five valises—four big an' one small. They were tagged Clara Watson. I packed them in. An' if that's all the baggage we can be movin' along."

"That is all, thank you," returned Clara.

"Miss Lucy, did you fetch the lunch?" asked Joe, with his eye on the boys, who had nonchalantly sauntered closer to the buckboard.

"I have it, Joe. Drive away before— " whispered Lucy.

Sam Johnson, the foremost of the group, stepped forward to put a foot on the wheel of the buckboard. His manner was supremely casual. No actor could have done it better.

"Howdy, Joe! Good afternoon, Miss Lucy," he drawled, blandly.

Lucy replied pleasantly, and introduced him to Clara, and after they had exchanged greetings she added: "Sorry we've no time to chat. We must hurry home."

Sam made rather obtrusive efforts to pierce Clara's veil. Then he addressed Joe: "My hoss went lame comin' in, an' I reckon I'll ride out with you."

"Awful sorry, Sam," drawled Joe, "but I've got a load. Heah's Miss Clara's five valises, an' a pack of truck for ma."

"I won't mind ridin' in the back seat with the girls," rejoined Sam, in the most accommodating voice.

"Shore reckon you wouldn't," returned Joe, drily. "But this heah's Mr. Jenks's buckboard an' he asked me particular not to load heavy. So long, Sam."

Joe whipped the reins smartly and the team started so suddenly that Sam, who had been leaning from the porch with one foot on the wheel, was upset in a most ridiculous manner. The boys on the porch let out a howl of mirth. Lucy could not repress a smile.

"Serves him right," said Joe. "Sam's shore got a nerve. All the time with Sadie in town!"

"Joe! Did you see her?" asked Lucy, quickly.

"I shore did. She was across the road, peepin' out of Bell's door when Sam got that spill."

Lucy, relieved as well as amused at the quick start, turned to find Clara removing the veil. Her face was lightened by a smile. Slight as it was, it thrilled Lucy.

"Young men are—funny," she said, with a tinge of bitterness.

"Indeed they are," vouchsafed Lucy, heartily. "Well, we're free of that crowd. Joe, are they apt to ride after us?"

"Like as not," drawled Joe. "But the road is narrow. They shore can't pass us, an' all they'll get will be our dust."

"Suppose we eat lunch while we don't have to hold on," suggested Lucy. "Presently the road will be rough, and—to say the least, Joe drives."

"Let him drive as fast as he can," replied Clara, tensely. "Oh—the breeze feels so good! The air seems different."

"Clara, you'll find everything different up here. But I'm not going to say a word till you ask me. . . . Now, let's eat. We'll not get supper till dark or later. . . . Biscuits with jam. Chicken—and pie. Joe, I overheard one of those boys speak of your driving with one hand. So, surely you can drive and eat at the same time?"

"I reckon," rejoined Joe. "But see heah, Miss Lucy. Gerd Claypool said that, an' he shore didn't mean I'd be usin' my free hand to eat."

"Joe, do you think me so dense? Don't those boys ever think sense about girls?"

"Never that I reckoned. Edd used to be worse than any of them. But he's over it, I guess, since you came, Miss Lucy!"

Whereupon Clara's quick glance caught Lucy blushing, though she laughed merrily.

"Joe Denmeade! That is a doubtful compliment. . . . Come, you'd better begin to eat—this and this and this. . . . Clara, I get ravenously hungry up here. It's the wonderful air. I hope it will affect you that way."

Whereupon they fell to eating the ample lunch, during which time Lucy made merry. Nevertheless she took occasion now to observe Clara, unobtrusively, at opportune moments. Out in the clear bright sunlight Clara seemed indeed a pale frail flower. Always as a girl she had been pretty, but it would have been trivial to call her so now. Her face had strangely altered, and the only features remaining to stir her memory were the violet eyes and golden hair. They were the same in color, though Clara's eyes, that had once been audacious, merry, almost bold in their bright beauty, were now shadowed deeply with pain. Clara had been an unconscionable flirt; to-day no trace of pert provocativeness was manifest. Indeed, suffering, shock, whatever had been the calamity which was recorded there, had removed the callow coarseness of thoughtless adolescence, and had left a haunting, tragic charm. Lucy thought the transformation almost incredible. It resembled that birth of soul she had divined in Clara's letters. What had happened to her? Lucy shrank from the truth. Yet her heart swelled with wonder and ache for this sister whom she had left a wild girl and had found a woman.

By the time the lunch had vanished Joe was driving up the narrow zigzag road leading to the height of the cedared ridge. Here he ceased to look back down the road, as if no longer expecting the boys to catch up with him. But he lived up to his reputation as a driver.

"Reckon you froze them off," he said, at length. "Sam, anyhow. He'll shore never get over bein' dumped on the porch."

Lucy, talking at random, discovered that Clara was intensely interested in her welfare work in this backwoods community. Thus encouraged, Lucy began at the beginning and told the story of her progress in every detail possible, considering that Joe was there to hear every word. In fact, she talked the hours away and was amazed when Joe drove into the Johnson clearing.

"What a hideous place!" murmured Clara as she gazed around. "You don't live here?"

"No, indeed!" replied Lucy. "This is where Sam Johnson lives. We have a few miles to go on horseback. Clara, have you anything to ride in?"

"Yes; I have an old riding suit that I hate," said her sister.

"It doesn't matter how you feel about it," laughed Lucy. "Where's it packed? We can go into Mr. Jenks's tent while Joe tends to the horses."

Lucy conducted Clara to the teacher's lodgings, and then made some pretext to go outside. She wanted to think. She had not been natural. Almost fearing to look at Clara, yearning to share her burdens, hiding curiosity and sorrow in an uninterrupted flow of talk, Lucy had sought to spare her sister. What a situation! Clara the incorrigible, the merciless, the imperious, crawling on her knees! Lucy divined it was love Clara needed beyond all else. She had been horribly cheated. She had cheated herself. She had flouted sister, mother, home. Lucy began to grasp here the marvelous fact that what she had prayed for had come. Years before she had tried in girlish unformed strength to influence this wayward sister. When she gave up city life to come to the wilderness it had been with the settled high resolve to do for others what she had been forced to do for herself. The failure of her home life had been its sorrow, from which had sprung this passion to teach. She had prayed, worked, hoped, despaired, struggled. And lo! as if by some omniscient magic, Clara had been given back to her. Lucy choked over the poignancy of her emotion. She was humble. She marveled. She would never again be shaken in her faith in her ideals. How terrible to contemplate now her moments of weakness, when she might have given up!

Her absorption in thought and emotion was broken by Clara emerging from the tent.

"Lucy, here's all that's left of me," she said, whimsically.

It was not possible then for Lucy to say what she thought. Clara's remark about an old riding suit had been misleading. It was not new, but it was striking. Clara's slenderness and fragility were not manifest in this outdoor garb. If she was bewitching to Lucy, what would she be to these simple girlworshiping backwoodsmen?

When Joe came up with the horses, and saw Clara, there was no need for Lucy to imagine she exaggerated. The look in his eyes betrayed him. But if he had been struck as by lightning it was only for a moment. "Reckon I can pack one of the valises on my saddle, an' carry another," he said, practically. "Tomorrow I'll fetch a burro to pack home the rest. I'll put them in Mr. Jenks's tent."

"This is Baldy. Oh, he's a dear horse!" said Lucy. "Get up on him, so Clara. . . . Have you ridden lately?"

"Not so—very," replied Clara, with voice and face sharply altering. Then she mounted with a grace and ease which brought keenly home to Lucy the fact that Clara had eloped with a cowboy and had gone to live on a ranch south of Mendino. Clara had always been an incomparable rider.

Soon they were traveling down the road, Joe in the lead, Lucy and Clara side by side. For Lucy there was an unreality about the situation, a something almost like a remembered dream. Clara's reticence seemed rather to augment this feeling. Gradually there welled into Lucy's mind a happy assurance, tinged perhaps with sadness.

Once Clara remarked that it was new to her to ride in the shade. She began to show interest in the trees, and when they turned off on the trail into the forest she exclaimed, "Oh, how beautiful!"

Lucy was quick to observe that Clara managed Baldy perfectly, but she was not steady in the saddle. She showed unmistakable weakness. They rode on, silent, on and on, and then down into the deep green forest, so solemn and stately, murmurous with the hum of the stream. Clara subtly changed.

"If anything could be good for me, it would be this wild forest," she said.

"Don't say if, dear. It *will* be," responded Lucy.

"It makes me feel like going out of the cruel hateful light—that I have to face—down into cool sweet shadow. Where I can feel—and not be seen!"

At the fording of the rushing brook Clara halted her horse as if compelled to speak. "Lucy, to be with you here will be like heaven," she said, low and huskily. "I didn't think anything could make me really want to live. But *here!* . . . I'll never leave this beautiful, comforting woods. I could become a wild creature."

"I—I think I understand," replied Lucy, falteringly.

From the last crossing of the rocky brook Clara appeared perceptibly to tire. Lucy rode behind her. Halfway up the long benched slope Clara said, with a wan smile:

"I don't know—I'm pretty weak."

Lucy called a halt then, and Joe manifested a silent solicitude. He helped

Clara dismount and led her off the trail to a little glade carpeted with pine needles. Lucy sat down and made Clara lay her head in her lap. There did not seem to be anything to say. Clara lay with closed eyes, her white face and golden hair gleaming in the subdued forest light. Her forehead was wet. She held very tightly to Lucy's hand. Lucy was not unaware of the strange, rapt gaze Joe cast upon the slender form lying so prone. Several times he went back to the horses, and returned, restlessly. On the last of these occasions, as he reached Lucy's side Clara opened her eyes to see him. It was just an accident of meeting glances, yet to Lucy, in her tense mood, it seemed an unconscious searching, wondering.

"You think me—a poor weak creature—don't you?" asked Clara, smiling.

"No. I'm shore sorry you're sick," he replied, simply, and turned away.

Presently they all mounted again and resumed the journey up the slope. When they reached the level forest land above, Clara had to have a longer rest.

"What's that awful wall of rock?" she asked, indicating the towering Rim.

"Reckon that's the fence in our back yard," replied Joe.

"I couldn't very well jump that, could I?" murmured Clara.

Meanwhile the sun sank behind scattered creamy clouds that soon turned to rose and gold, and beams of light stretched along the wandering wall. Lucy thrilled to see how responsive Clara was to the wildness and beauty of the scene. Yet all she said was, "Let me live here."

"It'll be dark soon, and we've still far to go," returned Lucy, with concern.

"Oh, I can make it," replied Clara, rising. "I meant I'd just like to lie here— forever."

They resumed the ride. Twilight fell and then the forest duskiness enveloped them. The last stretch out of the woods and across the Denmeade clearing, up the lane, was ridden in the dark. Lucy leaped off and caught Clara as she reeled out of the saddle, and half carried her into the tent to the bed. The hounds were barking and baying; the children's voices rang out; heavy boots thumped on the cabin porch.

Lucy hastened to light her lamp. Joe set the valises inside the tent.

"Is she all right?" he asked, almost in a whisper.

"I'm—here," panted Clara, answering for herself, and the purport of her words was significant.

"She's worn out," said Lucy. "Joe, you've been very good. I'm glad I 'picked you,' as you called it."

"What'll I tell ma?" he asked.

"Just say Clara can't come in to supper. I'll come and fetch her something."

Joe tramped away in the darkness, his spurs jingling. Lucy closed the door, brightened the lamp, threw off gloves, hat, coat, and bustled round purposely finding things to do, so that the inevitable disclosure from Clara could be postponed. Lucy did not want to know any more.

"Come here—sit by me," said Clara, weakly.

Lucy complied, and felt a constriction in her throat. Clara clung to her. In the lamplight the dark eyes looked unnaturally big in the white face.

"I'm here," whispered Clara.

"Yes, thank Heaven, you are," asserted Lucy, softly.

"I must tell you—about——"

"Clara, you needn't tell me any more. But if you must, make it short."

"Thank you. . . . Lucy, you never saw Jim Middleton but once. You didn't know him. But what you heard was true. He's no good—nothing but a wild rodeo cowboy—a handsome devil. . . . I ran away with him believing in him—thinking I loved him. I was crazy. I might have—surely would have loved him—if he had been what I thought he was. . . . We went to a ranch, an awful hole, in the desert out of Mendino. The people were low trash. He told them we *were* married. He swore to me we *would* be married next day. I refused to stay and started off. He caught me, threatened me, frightened me. I was only a kid. . . . Next day we went to Mendino. There was no preacher nearer than Sanchez. We went there, and found he was out of town. Jim dragged me back to the ranch. There I learned a sheriff was looking for him. We had a terrible quarrel. . . . He was rough. He was not at all—what I thought. He drank—gambled. . . . Of course he meant to marry me. He wanted to do so in Felix. But I was afraid. We hurried away from there. But after . . . he didn't care—and I found I didn't love him. . . . To cut it short I ran away from him. I—couldn't go home. So I went to work at Kingston. I tried several jobs. They were all so hard—the last one too much for me. I went downhill. . . . Then——"

"Clara," interrupted Lucy, distraught by the husky voice, the torture of that face, the passion to confess what must have been almost impossible, "never mind any more. That's enough. . . . You poor girl! Indeed you were crazy! But, dear, I don't hold you guilty of anything but a terrible mistake. You thought you loved this Jim Middleton. You meant well. If he had been half a man you would have turned out all right. God knows, no one can judge you harshly for your error. It certainly does not matter to me, unless to make me love you more."

"But—sister—I must tell you," whispered Clara, faintly.

"You told enough. Forget that story. You're here with me. You're going to stay. You'll get well. In time this trouble will be as if it had never been!"

"But Lucy—my heart is broken—my life ruined," whispered Clara. "I begged to come to you—only for fear of worse."

"It's bad now, I know," replied Lucy, stubbornly. "But it's not as bad as it looks. I've learned that about life. I can take care of you, get back your health and spirit, let you share my work. Sister, there's no worse, whatever you meant by that. This wilderness, these backwoods people will change your whole outlook on life. I *know*, Clara. They have changed me.''

Mutely, with quivering lips and streaming eyes, Clara drew Lucy down to a close embrace.

9

''WAL, didn't you-all invite yourselves to pick beans?'' drawled Edd, coming out at the head of a procession of big and little Denmeades.

''Wal, we shore did aboot that,'' drawled Lucy, mimicking him. ''Don't you see I'm rigged out to chase beans, bears, or bees?''

''Which reminds me you haven't gone wild-bee huntin' yet,'' said he, reflectively.

''Humph! I'd have to invite myself again to that, also,'' declared Lucy.

''Honest, soon as the beans are picked I'll take you. An' I've lined a new tree. Must have a lot of honey.''

Mrs. Denmeade called out: ''Make him stick to that, Miss Lucy. He's shore awful stingy about takin' anyone bee huntin'.''

''Come, Clara,'' called Lucy, into the tent. ''We're farmers to-day. Fetch my gloves.''

When Clara appeared the children, Liz and Lize, made a rush for her and went romping along, one on each side of her, down the trail ahead of the procession. Lucy fell in beside Edd, and she was thinking, as she watched Clara adapting herself to the light steps of the youngsters, that the improvement in her sister was almost too good to be true. Yet the time since Clara had arrived at the Denmeades', measured by the sweetness and strength of emotion it had engendered, seemed very much longer than its actual duration of a few weeks.

''Wal, teacher, summer's about over,'' Edd was saying. ''An' soon the fall dances will begin.''

''Indeed? What a pity you can't go!'' exclaimed Lucy, tantalizingly.

''Why can't I?''

''Because you vowed you had enough after taking *me* that time.''

''Wal, reckon I did. But shore I could change my mind—same as you.''

''Am I changeable? . . . I was only teasing, Edd. I got a hunch that you're going to ask me again.''

''Correct. You're a smart scholar. How do you feel about goin'?''

"Shall I refuse, so you can indulge your—your wild-bee-hunter proclivities and pack me down on your horse?" queried Lucy, demurely.

"Sometimes I don't savvy you," he said, dubiously. "Reckon all girls have a little Sadie Purdue in them."

"Yes, they have, Edd, I'm ashamed to confess," replied Lucy, frankly. "I'd like to go with you. But of course that'll depend on Clara. To be sure, she's getting well, wonderful! It makes me happy. Still, she's far from strong enough for one of your dances."

"Joe asked her, an' she said she'd go if you went, too. I reckon she meant with me."

"Edd, you're learning from Sam Johnson."

"Nope, not me. I'd choke before I'd copy that honeybee."

"So Joe asked her? . . . Well!" murmured Lucy, thoughtfully.

"Reckon she likes him, Lucy."

"Oh, I hope—I know she does. But, Edd ——"

"Wal, I get your hunch," he interrupted. "You think maybe she oughtn't go with Joe because it'll only make him worse."

"Worse?" queried Lucy, turning to eye Edd.

"Yes, worse. But, Lucy, I reckon it couldn't be worse. Joe thinks of Clara by day an' dreams of her by night. He's been that way since the day she came to us."

"Edd, you're pretty sharp. I imagined no one but me had seen that. I'm sure Clara hasn't. . . . It's a problem, Edd. But I knew it'd come."

"Wal, you're shore good at problems. What're you goin' to do about this one?"

"What would *you* do?" Lucy countered.

"I'd let Joe take her to the dance. You can manage her. Why, your slightest wish is law to Clara. That shore makes me think heaps of her. Wal, she could dance a few, an' look on some. Then we'd come home early."

"Would you promise that?"

"I shore would."

"Well, Edd, I'll think it over. You know if we go to this dance we'll be inclined to go again—perhaps often."

"Not with Joe an' me. I reckon this one would do us for a spell."

"Oh, that is different! And why?"

"Wal, you forget how you drove them boys crazy. I reckon this time, with Clara, you'd break up the dance. I've a hunch once would be enough for a spell. But shore I'd like it. So would Joe."

"Edd, this little sister of mine has broken up more than one dance—and a cowboy dance at that. Why couldn't we go and have a nice time, dance a little, and leave early, without what you hinted?—Fights!"

"That'd be easy, if you an' Clara could behave," he drawled.

"Edd Denmeade!" cried Lucy.

"Wal, you know you played hob with the boys. Why can't you be honest? Shore, Lucy, I wouldn't want to go if you did that again."

"All right. I promise to behave if I go. I'll talk to Clara."

"Wal, suit yourself. But I reckon you know I'll never go to another dance unless I can take you."

"Never?" echoed Lucy.

"Yes, never," he retorted.

"Why, Edd? That's a strong statement."

"Reckon because every dance before that one I was made fun of, most when I took a girl. But when I had you they didn't dare. That shore was sweet."

"Thanks, Edd. Sometimes you say nice things."

So they talked as they walked along the cool, sandy, pine-mat bordered trail. It was quite a walk from the cabin to what the Denmeades called the High Field. This was a level piece of ground, perhaps fifty acres in area, irregular in shape, and surrounded by the green forest of cedar and pine.

Of all the slashes cut into the woodland, this appeared to Lucy the most hideous. It was not a well-cultivated piece of ground. These Denmeades were hunters, woodhewers, anything but farmers. Yet they were compelled to farm to raise food for themselves and grain for horses and hogs. Nevertheless, the hogs ran wild, subsisting most of the year upon roots, nuts, acorns, and what the backwoodsmen called mast.

A hundred or more dead trees stood scattered round over this clearing, cedars and pines and oaks, all naked and bleached and rotting on their stumps. They had been girdled by an ax, to keep the sap from rising, which eventually killed them. This was done to keep the shade of foliaged trees from dwarfing the crops. Corn and beans and sorghum required the sun.

It was the most primitive kind of farming. In fact, not many years had passed since Denmeade had used a plow hewn from the fork of an oak. High Field was fenced by poles and brush, which did not look very sure of keeping out the hogs. Right on the moment Danny and Dick were chasing hogs out of the field. Corn and weeds and yellow daisies, almost as large as sunflowers, flourished together, with the corn perhaps having a little advantage. The dogs were barking at some beast they had treed. Hawks and crows perched upon the topmost branches of the dead pines; woodpeckers hammered on the smooth white trunks; and the omnipresent jays and squirrels vied with each other in a contest calculated to destroy the peace of the morning.

Beyond the large patch of ground that had been planted in potatoes lay the three acres of beans, thick and brown in the sunlight. Beans furnished the most important article of food for the backwoods people. Meat, potatoes, flour, honey mostly in place of sugar, were essential and appreciated, but it was as Denmeade said, "We shore live on beans."

This triangle of three acres, then, represented something vastly important in their simple lives. They made the picking of beans a holiday, almost a gala occasion. Every one of the Denmeades was on hand, and Uncle Bill packed two big bags of lunch and a bucket of water. The only company present, considering that Lucy and Clara were not classified under this head, was Mertie's beau, young Bert Hall, a quiet boy whom all liked. Lucy regarded his presence there as a small triumph of her own. The frivolous Mertie really liked him, as anyone could plainly see. She had only been under the influence of Sadie Purdue. By a very simple expedient Lucy had counteracted and so far overcome this influence. She had devoted herself to Mertie; roused her pride through her vanity, subtly showed Bert's superiority to the other boys who ran after her, and lastly had suggested it would be nice to have Bert go with them to Felix. How important little things could become in this world of the Denmeades! It caused Lucy many pangs to reflect upon how often their lives went wrong for lack of a little guidance.

Manifestly Edd was the captain of this bean-picking regiment. He was conceded to be a great picker, and had a pride in his prowess second only to that of his lining of bees. Denmeade, the father, had two great gifts, according to repute—he could wield an ax as no other man in the country, and he was wonderful with his hunting hounds. Joe was the best one with horses, Dick with tools. Uncle Bill would plow when, according to him, all his relatives had been laid away in the fence corners. Thus they all excelled in some particular thing peculiarly important to their primitive lives.

"Wal, all hands get ready," called out Edd, cheerily. "Reckon we got to clean up this patch to-day. You girls an' the kids can pick here in the shade. We'll pack loads of beans to you. . . . Bert, seein' you're company, I'll let you off pickin' out there in the sun. You can set with the girls. But I'm recommendin' you set between Lucy an' Clara. Haw! Haw!"

So the work of picking beans began. The children made it a play, a game, a delight, over which they screamed and fought. Yet withal they showed proficiency and industry.

The men fetched huge bundles of beans on the vines, and deposited them on the ground under the shady oaks at the edge of the field. Mrs. Denmeade and Allie picked with nimble and skillful hands. The girls sat in a little circle, with Bert in attendance and the children monopolizing all the space and most of the beans. Bert, having deposited piles of beans in front of each member of the party, was careful to sit down between Lucy and Clara, an action that caused Mertie to pout and laugh.

The process of stripping beans appeared a simple one to Lucy, yet she saw at once where experience counted. She could not do so well even as Mary. It piqued her a little. After all, intelligence and reason were not factors that could at once bridge the gap between inexperience and dexterity.

As they sat there talking and laughing and working, Lucy's thought ran on in pleasant and acquiring trend. Above all, what brought her happiness in this hour was the presence of her sister. Clara had begun to mend physically, and that, with the lonely environment, the simplicity of the Denmeades, the strength of natural things, had unconsciously affected her spiritually. She loved the children. She was intensely interested in their little lives. She fell to this fun of bean picking with a pleasure that augured well for the blotting of trouble from her mind. Clara had begun to be conscious of the superficiality of many sides and points of life in civilized communities. Here in the backwoods life seemed an easier, happier, simpler thing.

From time to time Lucy stole a look out into the field at Edd, as he worked. He moved forward on his knees, keeping a sack pushed in front of him, and his hands flew. He was an engine of devastation to the rows of beans. She seldom heard his voice. When he finished a row he would get up, and gathering a huge bundle of vines he would carry them to where the women were picking. Dust and sweat had begrimed his face; his shirt was wet through. There seemed something tremendously rugged, vital, raw about his physical presence. He took this task seriously. Lucy wondered what was going on in his mind. Did things she had talked of or read to him revolve as he worked? There was a suggestion of the plodding nature of his thought, strangely in contrast with the wonderful physical energy of his work. She mused over the fact that she liked him as he was, yet was striving to teach him, change him, put him on the road to being a civilized man. Yet ——! Something vaguely regretful stirred deeply within her consciousness.

These more serious thoughts, however, only recurred at intervals; for the most part she was alive to the objective task of learning to pick beans, and to the conversation around her. Allie Denmeade was as incessant a talker as Joe was a listener; she had a shrewd wit and a sharp tongue. Mertie was charming under favorable influence and when she was receiving her meed of attention. Mrs. Denmeade had a dry geniality and a store of wilderness wisdom. Mary was the sweet dreaming one of the family.

Lucy had no idea that the noon hour had arrived until the dusty men stalked in from the field, hungry and thirsty, bringing with them an earthy atmosphere.

"Nineteen rows for me," declared Edd, "an' I'm spittin' cotton. . . . Where's the bucket? I'll fetch fresh water from the spring."

"Wal, ma, how'd you-all git along?" queried Denmeade, wiping his sweaty face.

"I disremember any better mawnin' for pickin'," she replied. "Bert has been fillin' the sacks. Reckon there's quite a few."

"Even dozen," exulted Bert.

"Good! We'll finish early. Edd shore is a cyclone for pickin' beans. . . . An' now, ma, spread out the grub. I'm a hungry old Jasper."

Uncle Bill carried forth the packs of food, which he had hidden from the children.

"It was a tolerable pickin', though I've seen better," he said. "The season's been dry an' thet's good for beans an' pickin'. . . . Wal, Lee, I'm noticin' Miss Lucy an' her sister have shore done themselves proud, fer tenderfeet."

Denmeade surveyed the respective piles of beans, one before Lucy, and a smaller one in front of Clara.

"Not so bad," he said, genially. "An' it shore is good to see you both settin' thar."

"Lee, tell their fortune with beans," suggested Mrs. Denmeade.

"I reckon I wouldn't risk that," he replied.

"Ma, you tell them. An' Bert's, too. It'll be fun. He's never been here to a bean pickin'," said Mertie.

"All the same, I had mine told once, down at Sadie's. Her old aunt told it," said Bert. "An' once is enough for me."

"A Mexican woman once told my fortune," interposed Clara, with a smile that was not all mirth. "It came true. And I—I don't want to know any more what's going to happen to me."

"Oh, I'm not afraid," called out Lucy. "Come, Mrs. Denmeade. Tell mine."

Whereupon Mrs. Denmeade, to the infinite delight of the children, selected some differently colored beans and pressed these into Lucy's palm. Then she intently studied Lucy's face, after which she struck the outstretched hand, causing some of the beans to roll off and others to change position and settle.

"Wal, you're goin' to find happiness takin' some one else's troubles on your shoulders," said Mrs. Denmeade, impressively. "Your past has been among many people who didn't care for you. Your future will be among a few who love you. . . . I see a journey—a secret—somethin' that'll never come out— two dark years with white ones followin'. A child! . . . A cabin! A happy wife!"

This conclusion was greeted with a merry shout from the children and girls. Lucy, in her amusement, wished to carry the thing as far as possible to please them all. It struck her that Clara's faint color had vanished. How a few words could pain her! Lucy had no faith in any kind of fortune telling; she hardly took Mrs. Denmeade seriously.

"Wonderful!" she ejaculated. "Do the beans tell what kind of a husband I get?"

"No," rejoined Mrs. Denmeade, "but I reckon he won't be a city man."

"How interesting! I think I'm rather glad. Clara, I'm to have a country man for a husband. These red and white beans have foretold my fate."

She became aware then that Edd had returned and, standing behind her, evidently had heard her concluding words. Quite absurdly the fact embarrassed Lucy. The gay remarks forthcoming from all around fell upon her somewhat unfelicitously.

"Wal, Lucy, I see ma an' Allie have worked an old trick on you," he drawled. "Shore I told you to look out for them."

"Oh—it was only fun!" exclaimed Lucy, relieved despite her common sense.

Mrs. Denmeade smiled enigmatically. She seemed to possess some slight touch of mysticism, crude and unconscious. Lucy dispelled any idea that there was connection between the red and white beans and Mrs. Denmeade's prophecies. For that reason she found herself fixing in mind the content of those statements regarding her past and future.

"Come set around, folks," called Uncle Bill, with gusto.

The lunch hour of the bean pickers was as merry as a picnic dinner. The Denmeades had rushed through the morning hours; now they had leisure to eat slowly and to talk and joke. Lucy enjoyed this pleasant interval. It had but one break, an instant toward the end, when she espied Joe Denmeade sitting as always quietly in the background, with eyes of worship fixed upon Clara's face. That troubled Lucy's conscience.

Lucy wore out her gloves and made blisters on her fingers, acquiring along with these accidents a proficiency in the art of picking beans. Clara wearied early in the afternoon, and went to sleep under a pine tree. Mertie and Bert finished their allotment of beans, and wandering along the edge of the forest, they seemed to become absorbed in each other. Mrs. Denmeade and Allie worked like beavers, and the children drifted to playing.

The men soon finished picking and sacking the beans. Then Edd and his brothers stalked off to fetch the pack-burros. Uncle Bill still found tasks to do, while Denmeade rested and talked to his wife. Lucy leaned comfortably against the oak, grateful for relief from work, and because of it, appreciating infinitely more the blessing of rest. She did not try very hard to resist a drowsy spell, out of which she was roused to attention by a remark of Denmeade to his wife.

"Wal, it'd shore make bad feelin' between the Denmeades an' Johnsons if Sam homesteaded on the mesa."

"Reckon it would, but he's goin' to do it," returned Mrs. Denmeade. "Mertie told me."

"Sadie Purdue's back of that," said Denmeade, meditatively.

"She's never forgive Edd. . . . It'd be too bad if Sam beat Edd out of that homestead."

"Don't worry, wife. Sam ain't agoin' to," returned her husband. "Edd located the mesa, found the only water. He's just been waitin' to get himself a woman."

"But Edd oughtn't to wait no longer," protested Mrs. Denmeade.

"Wal, I reckon," rejoined Denmeade, thoughtfully. "We'll begin cuttin' logs an' get ready to run up a cabin. It's bad enough for us to be on the outs with Spralls, let alone Johnsons. . . . I'm goin' to walk up to the mesa right now."

Suiting action to word, Denmeade started off. Lucy sat up and impulsively called. "Please take me with you, Mr. Denmeade. I—I'd like to walk a little."

"Come right along," he responded, heartily.

Lucy joined him and entered the woods, taking two steps to one of his long strides.

"I'm goin' up to a place we call the mesa," he was saying. "Edd has long set his heart on homesteadin' there. It ain't far, but uphill a little. Sam Johnson has been talkin' around. Shore there ain't no law hyar to prevent him stealin' Edd's homestead. An' I reckon there's bad blood enough. So I'm goin' to begin work right off. That'll throw Sam off the trail an' then we won't have no call to hurry."

Lucy was interested to ask questions until she became out of breath on a rather long and steep slope. Here she fell back and followed her guide, whose idea of distance, she averred, was vastly different from hers.

At last, however, they reached a level. Lucy looked up, to be stunned by the towering, overpowering bulk of the Rim, red and gold, with its black-fringed crown, bright and beautiful in the westering sun. She gazed backward, down over a grand sweep of forest, rolling and ridging away to the far-flung peaks. Her position here was much higher than on any point she had frequented, and closer to the magnificent Rim.

"There's two or three hundred acres of flat land hyar," said Denmeade, sweeping his hand back toward the dense forest. "Rich red soil. Enough water for two homesteads, even in dry spells. It's blue snow water, the best kind, comin' down from the Rim. Wal, I'm hopin' Dick or Joe will homestead hyar some day. It's the best farm land I know of."

"Why, Mr. Denmeade, it's all forest!" exclaimed Lucy.

"Shore. It'll have to be cleared. An' that's a heap of work."

"Goodness! It looks it. How do you go about making a farm out of a thick forest?"

"Wal, we'll cut logs first to run up a cabin," replied Denmeade. "Then we'll clear off timber an' brush, an' set fire to it, leavin' the stumps. They'll rot out in a few years. The big trees we kill an' leave standin'. . . . This hyar mesa is high an' dry, warm in winter an' cool in summer. It joins on to a big canyon where there's water an' grass for stock. An' it's the best place for bees in this country. I reckon Edd's pretty smart. He's shore goin' to do somethin' with his bee huntin'.''

They entered the level forest, and Lucy was at once charmed and fascinated. This woodland differed from any she had visited. It was level, open in glades, aisles, and dense in thickets and patches. A dry hot fragrance of pine and cedar and juniper seemed to wave up from the brown-carpeted earth. How easy and delightful the walking here! As they penetrated deep into the forest the pines grew so huge that they actually thrilled her. Then the other trees were as large in proportion. Some of the junipers were truly magnificent, six feet thick at the base, symmetrical and spreading, remarkable for their checker-board bark and lilac-hued berries. Under every one of these junipers the ground was a soft gray-green mat of tiny needles, fragrant, inviting rest. Under the pines Lucy kicked up furrows in the dry depths of brown needles, and these places even more called her to tarry. A wonderful sweet silence pervaded this mesa forest. No birds, no squirrels, no deer or turkeys! Yet Denmeade pointed out tracks in every dusty trail. "Reckon game's all down by the water," he explained. "There's a gully runs right through this mesa, dividin' it in half. Shore is a wild place. I'll show you where an old she bear jumped on me. She had cubs, an' a mother bear is bad.''

Lucy reveled in this exploration. The farther she followed Denmeade the more delighted she was with the wilderness and beauty, the color and fragrance of the forest.

"Oh, but it will be a shame to cut all these trees—and burn a hideous slash in this beautiful forest!"

"I reckon. Shore Edd says the same," replied Denmeade. "But we have to make homes. An' the forest, just like this, will surround the homesteads. We only cut an' clear land where there's water. A few acres slashed don't make much of a hole in this woods. . . . Look hyar. See between the pines, up there where the bluffs run down—it shows a break in the woods. That's the canyon I spoke of. It looks narrow an' short. Wal, it's wide an' long, an' it'll always be wild. It can't never be cut. An' there's many canyons like it, runnin' in under the Rim. . . . Miss Lucy, I come hyar twenty years ago. There's as many bear an' deer now as then. An' I reckon it'll be the same in twenty more years.''

"I'm glad," breathed Lucy, as if in relief. How strange for her to feel that she did not want the wilderness despoiled! Indeed, she was responding fully to inherited instincts.

Denmeade led her on under the vast pines and through glades the beauty of which swelled Lucy's heart, and finally to the edge of a gully. She looked down into a green, white, brown, golden chaos of tree trunks, foliage, bowlders, and cliffs, trailing vines and patches of yellow flowers, matted thickets of fallen timber—in all an exceedingly wild hollow cut deeply into the mesa. Lucy heard the babble and tinkle of water she could not see.

"Edd aims to have his cabin hyar," explained Denmeade. "I heard him say once he'd clear an acre hyar, leaving these big trees, an' the forest all around. The crop field he wants a little ways off. He'd keep his bees down in the gully, clearin' out some. . . . Now you rest yourself while I climb down to the water. It's shore been a dry season, an' last winter the snows was light. I reckon I can get a good line on how much water there'll be in dry seasons."

Denmeade clambered down a steep trail, leaving Lucy above. Though she stood amid deep forest, yet she could see the Rim in two directions, and the magnificent looming tower stood right above her. It marked the bold entrance of the canyon. In the other direction Lucy looked down a slant of green, darkly divided by the depression made by the gully, to the rolling forest below, that led the eye on and on to the dim purple ranges. A cry seemed to ring out of the remote past, appealing to Lucy's heart. It stung her mind to flashing, vivid thought. Her immediate ancestors had lived a few hundred years in villages, towns, cities; the early progenitors from which her people had sprung had lived thousands of years in the forested wilderness, barbarians, nomads. She felt it all so intensely. The giant seamy-barked pines, rough and rugged, were more than trees. They had constituted a roof for her race in ages past, and wood for fire. The fragrance, the strength of them, were in her blood. Likewise of the cedars, the junipers, the gray and white sycamores down in the gully, the maples and oaks, the patches of sumach, all that spread colorful protection around her. Deeper than sentiment, stronger than education, this passion claimed her for the moment.

"If I loved Edd Denmeade, how happy I could be in a home here!"

It did not seem to be the Lucy Watson she knew that whispered these involuntary words. They came from beyond reason, intelligence, consideration. They just flashed up out of instinct. She did not resent them, though she stood aghast at intimations beyond her control. How impossible was fulfillment of them! Yet she pondered why they had come. In vain! The loneliness, the solitude, the grand imminence of the Rim, the silent guarding pines, the eye-soothing softness of gray and green—these physical things dominated her and would not be denied.

"It is a *fact*," she whispered. "I *could* live here. . . . now and then. . . . I'd want books, letters, papers—to keep up with my idea of progress. . . . I'd want to go on with my welfare work. But these are nothing. *They* do not induce me to want to live in a log cabin. . . . I am amazed at myself; I don't know myself. I am not what I think I am!"

Lucy remained alone on the shady rim of the gorge for half an hour—surely a critical and portentous time in her realization of change. Yet, what seemed incredible to her was the fact that she would not have changed anything in the present. Perhaps she had given too much thought to herself. Vanity! Mertie Denmeade was not alone in this peculiar feminine trait. Lucy arraigned herself, and tried to persuade herself that she possessed something of worldliness. All to little purpose! She was happier than she had ever been in her life and that was all there was to it.

Denmeade led back across the mesa by a shorter route, and down the slope by an old trail. Lucy trudged along in his tracks, vastly less curious than on the way up. It had been another full day. Her hands attested to the labor of it. And as to her mind, the shadows of the past seemed dim, fading away.

As they again approached level forest Lucy caught glimpses of the yellow clearing. She heard the discordant bray of a burro, then the shrill peal of childish laughter. She emerged on the edge of the timber in time to see the packed burros filing away through the corn, and on top of the last two sat Liz and Lize, triumphantly riding on sacks of beans. Edd strode beside them. Mrs. Denmeade and Allie were plodding on ahead. Far down the edge of the field Mertie and Bert appeared hand in hand, sauntering away toward the trail for home. Something about them, perhaps those linked hands, stirred Lucy to a divination of how little other people mattered to them. She had been right in her surmise. Propinquity was all that had been needed.

Denmeade cut across the corn-field, while Lucy wended her way back along the edge of the woods to the pine tree where she had left Clara. Perhaps Clara, too, had gone with the others.

The day was over. Sunset was gilding the Rim. Crickets had begun to chirp. The air had perceptibly cooled. Crows were sailing across the clearing. Faint and sweet came the shouts of the children.

Then Lucy espied her sister sitting with her back against the pine. Joe Denmeade stood near, gazing down upon her. If either was talking, Lucy could not hear what was said; but she inclined to the thought that on the instant there was no speech. They did not hear her footsteps on the soft earth.

Without apparent cause Lucy experienced a thrill that closely approached shock. How utterly she, too, was at the mercy of her imagination! Clara and Joe together, in perfectly simple pose—what was there in that to stop Lucy's heart? Verily she was growing like the Denmeades. On the other hand, there seemed profound significance in Joe's gazing down upon Clara, as she sat there, with the last touch of the sun making a golden blaze of her hair. Joe had been hopelessly lost, from that first sight of Clara. It had seemed of no great moment. Lucy in her passionate devotion had thought only of her sister. But Lucy had a flash of revelation. This wilderness environment was marvelously strong. Lucy caught just a vague hint of its elemental power—the earth, its rugged beauty and vitality, its secret to unite and procreate, since the dawn of human life ages before. What little people knew! They were but moving atoms dominated by nature.

"Oh, here you are!" called Lucy, to start the pensive couple out of their trance. "I had the dandiest walk. Climb, I should say. . . . And what have you two been talking about all this time?"

"Joe came just this moment to tell me they were going home," replied Clara, looking up at Lucy.

"Teacher, I was aboot to say she was goin' to get well heah in the woods, an' that I'd heard her laugh to-day," he replied, in his slow speech.

"How strange!" murmured Clara, as if mocking a belief. She studied Joe with doubtful eyes, as if she refused to believe the truth manifested in him.

Lucy wisely saw nothing, said nothing, though she was stirred to speak.

"It has been a lovely day," she said as she turned away. "Come, we must go."

"Wait, Lucy," complained Clara. "I may be getting well, but I can't run."

"Make her hurry, Joe. It's late," replied Lucy, and she crossed the devastated bean-field to enter the rustling rows of corn. She did not look back. It was twilight when she arrived at the tent, and wearied with exertion and emotion, throbbing and burning, she threw herself on the bed to rest a few moments.

Clara came just as darkness fell. "Are you there, Lucy?" she asked, stumbling into the tent.

"Shore I'm heah," drawled Lucy.

"Why did you leave me alone—to walk back with that boy?" queried Clara, plaintively. "He's falling in love with me—the fool!"

"Oh, Clara, he'd be a fool if he wasn't," retorted Lucy.

"But it'll only make him wretched. And you—you must stop believing I'm worthy of love."

"Maybe Joe is like me," said Lucy, and this reply silenced her sister.

10

September came, with the first touches of frost on the foliage, the smoky haze hovering over the hollow, the melancholy notes of robins and wild canaries, the smell of forest fire in the air.

Edd did not remind Lucy that he had promised to take her bee hunting. This, like so many things in the past, piqued her; and the more she upbraided herself for that the less could she forget it. Finally she said to him one night at supper:

"Edd, I thought you were going to take me bee hunting."

"Shore. Whenever you say," replied Edd.

"Then I say to-morrow," returned Lucy.

A clamor from the children and an excited little cry from Clara attested to the eagerness of others to share Lucy's good fortune. She was curious to see if Mrs. Denmeade would approve of some one else accompanying them. Lucy had in mind that among the people with whom she had associated in Felix it would hardly have been the proper thing for her to go with Edd into the woods alone.

Edd laughed down the importunities of the children.

"Nope, kids; you wait till I'm ready to cut down a bee tree not far away," he said, to appease them. "I've got one located. . . . An' as for you, Miss Clara, I reckon you'd better not risk a long climb till you're stronger."

"Will you take me with the children?" asked Clara, witfully.

"Shore. Reckon I'll be glad to have you-all packin' buckets of honey," drawled Edd.

"Edd, I seen the other day that Miss Lucy's boots wasn't hobnailed," spoke up Denmeade. "Reckon you mustn't forget to put some nails in them for her. Else she might slip an' hurt herself."

"Wal, now you tax me, I'll just naturally have to hobnail her boots," returned Edd, drily. "But fact was I wanted to see her slide around some."

"Very sweet of you, Edd," interposed Lucy, in the same tone. "Couldn't you wait till winter and find me some ice?"

"Say, slidin' down a slope of grass an' pine needles will take the tenderfoot out of you," he retorted.

"Oh, then you think I need that?" she queried.

"Wal, I reckon you don't need no more," he said, quaintly.

"Is Edd complimenting me?" asked Lucy, appealing to Mrs. Denmeade. She nodded smilingly.

"Thanks. Very well, Edd. I shall fetch my boots for you to hobnail. And to-morrow you may have the pleasure of watching me slide."

After supper she watched him at work. He had an iron last, upside down, over which he slipped one of her boots. Then with hammer he pounded small-headed hobnails into the soles. He was so deft at it that Lucy inquired if he were a shoemaker.

"Reckon so. I used to tan leather an' make my own shoes. But I only do half-solin' now."

Presently he removed the boot from the last, and felt inside to find if any nails had come through.

"That one's jake," he said.

Lucy examined the sole to find two rows of hobnails neatly and symmetrically driven round the edge. Inside these rows were the initials of her name.

"Well, you're also an artist," she said. "I suppose you want to make it easy for anyone to know my boot tracks."

"Wal, I can't say as I'd like anyone trailin' you," he replied, with a deep grave look at her.

Lucy changed the subject. When she returned to her tent dusk had fallen and Clara was sitting in the doorway. Lucy threw the boots inside and sat down on the lower step to lean back against her sister. Often they had spent the gloaming hour this way. The cool melancholy night was settling down like a mantle over the forest land. Bells on the burros tinkled musically; a cow lowed in the distance; a night hawk whistled his strange piercing note.

"Lucy, I like Edd Denmeade," said Clara, presently.

"Goodness! Don't let him see it—or, poor fellow, he——"

"Please take me seriously," interrupted Clara. "I believed I'd always hate men. But to be honest with myself and you I find I can't. I like Mr. Denmeade and Uncle Bill—and the boys. Edd is a wonderful fellow. He's deep. He's so cool, drawly, kind. At first his backwoodsness, so to call it, offended me. But I soon saw that is his great attraction for me. As you know, I've gone with a lot of city boys, without ever thinking about what they *were*. . . . I wonder. City clothes and manners, nice smooth white hands, ought not be much in the make-up of a man. Edd's old jeans, his crude talk and ways, his big rough hands—they don't repel me any more. I don't quite understand, but I feel it. He's good for me, Lucy dear. Do you know what I mean?"

"Yes. And I'm glad. You've had a bitter blow. No wonder you think now what boys are. . . . As for me, I don't really know whether Edd has been good—or bad for me."

"Lucy!"

"Listen. I'll tell you something," went on Lucy, and she related the story of Edd's taking her to the dance.

"How funny! How——" exclaimed Clara, laughing—"how I don't know what! . . . Lucy, I just believe it tickles me. If he had been rude—you know, fresh, I mean—I'd have despised him. But the way you told it. Oh, I think it's rich! I believe I would have liked him better."

Lucy might have confessed that deep in her heart she had alone this very thing, herself, but the fact was not acceptable to her.

"Joe is the best of the Denmeades, and quite the nicest boy I ever knew," she said, earnestly. "What do you think of him, Clara?"

"It's dreadful of me, but I like to be with him," whispered Clara. "He's so—so sweet. That's the only word. But it does not fit him, either. He has the same strong qualities as Edd. . . . Lucy, that boy *rests* me. He soothes me. He makes me ashamed. . . . Tell me all about him.''

"Well, Joe's ears will burn," laughed Lucy, and then she began her estimate of Joe Denmeade. She was generous. But in concluding with the facts about him that had come under her observation and been told by his people, Lucy held rigidly to truth.

"All that!" murmured Clara, thoughtfully. "And I'm the only girl he *ever* looked at? . . . Poor Joe!"

Next morning there was a white frost. Lucy felt it and smelled it before she got up to peep out behind the curtain of the tent door. The sun had just tipped the great promontory, a pale blaze that made the frost on grass and logs shine like an encrustment of diamonds.

"Ooooo but it's cold!" exclaimed Lucy as she threw on her dressing gown. "Now I know why Edd insisted on installing this stove. Any old morning now I'd wake up frozen!"

"Come back to bed," advised Clara, sleepily.

"I'll start the fire, then slip back for a little. Oh, I wonder—will we have to give up living out here when winter comes?"

The stove was a wood-burning one, oval in shape, and flat on top, with a sheet-iron pipe running up through the roof of the tent. Lucy had thought it sort of a toy affair, despite Edd's assertion as to its utility. He had laid the pine needles and splinters and billets of wood, so that all Lucy had to do was to strike a match. She was not an adept at building fires, and expected this to go out. Instead it flared up, blazed, crackled, and roared. Fortunately Lucy recollected Edd's warning to have a care to turn the damper in the stovepipe.

"This stove is going to be a success. How good it feels!"

Then she noticed the neat pile of chips and billets of redwood stacked behind the stove, and a small box full of pine needles. Edd Denmeade was thoughtful. Lucy put a pan of water on the stove to heat, and slipped back into bed. Her hands and feet were like ice, matters that Clara was not too sleepy to note. Soon the tent room was cozy and warm. Lucy felt encouraged to think it might be possible for her and Clara to occupy this lodging all winter. Edd had averred the little stove would make them as snug as birds in a nest. To make sure, however, that they could live outdoors, he had suggested boarding the tent wall halfway up and shingling the roof.

"Sleepy-head!" called Lucy, shaking her sister.

"Ah-h! . . . I just never can wake up," replied Clara. "It's so good to sleep here. . . . I didn't sleep much down there in the desert."

"My dear, you've slept three-fourths of the time you've been here, day as

well as night. It's this mountain air. I was almost as bad. Well, good sleep is
better than wasted waking hours. Now I'm going to be heroic.''

By nine o'clock all trace of frost had vanished from grass and logs. Edd
presented himself at the tent. "Wal, I'm a-rarin' to go.''

"Yes, you are!" called Lucy, banteringly. "Here I've been ready these last
two hours.''

"City girl! You can't line bees till the sun gets warm.''

"Backwoods boy! Why not?''

"Bees don't work so early. You see, it's gettin' along towards fall.''

"I'll be right out. . . . Let's see—my gloves and knapsack. . . . Well, sister
mine, why do you stare at me?''

Clara was sitting at the little table, with speculative gaze fastened upon Lucy.
It made Lucy a little sensitive to her attire. This consisted of a slouch felt hat,
a red scarf round the neck of her brown blouse, corduroy riding trousers, and
high boots. On the moment Lucy was slipping on her gauntlets.

"Clara, it'll be a long hard tramp, up and down,'' declared Lucy, as if in
self-defense.

"You look great,'' rejoined Clara, with one of her sweet rare smiles. "I'm
not so sure about your welfare work, in that get-up. I think it's plain murder.''

Clara made an expressive gesture, to indicate Edd outside. Lucy was not quite
equal to a laugh. Sometimes this realistic sister of hers forced home a significance
that escaped her idealistic mind.

"If you only could go!'' sighed Lucy. "I—I think I need you as much as you
need me. . . . Don't forget *your* welfare work. Good-by.''

Edd carried a gun, a small black tin bucket, and a package which he gave to
Lucy to put in her knapsack.

"Ma reckoned you'd like somethin' to eat,'' he explained.

So they set off across the lane, through the strip of woods, and out into the
sorghum-field. Lucy experienced an unaccountable embarrassment. She felt like
a callow girl taking her first walk with a boy. She did not feel at all at her ease
in this riding garb, though the freedom of it had never been so manifest. She
was guilty of peering round to see if any of the Denmeades were in sight,
watching them cross the field. She could not see anyone, which fact helped a
little. Then she did not discover her usual fluency of speech. Finding herself
alone with this stalwart bee hunter, facing a long day in the wilderness, had
turned out to be something more than thrilling. Lucy essayed to throw off the
handicap.

"What's in your little black bucket?'' she inquired.

"Honey. I burn it to make a sweet strong scent in the woods. That shore
fetches the bees.''

"What's the gun for?"

"Wal, sometimes a bear smells the honey an' comes along. Bears love sweet stuff, most of all honey."

"Bears! In broad daylight?" ejaculated Lucy.

"Shore. One day not long ago I had four bears come for my honey. Didn't have no gun with me, so I slipped back an' hid. You should have seen the fun they had stickin' their noses an' paws in my bucket of honey. They stole it, too, an' took it off with them."

"You won't leave me alone?" queried Lucy, fearfully.

"Wal, if I have to I'll boost you up into a tree," drawled Edd.

"I wonder if this is going to be fun," pondered Lucy. Suddenly she remembered the proclivity for playing tricks natural to these backwoods boys. "Edd, promise me you will not try to scare me. No tricks! Promise me solemnly."

"Aw, I'm shore not mean, Lucy," he expostulated. "Fun is fun an' I ain't above little tricks. But honest, you can trust me."

"I beg your pardon. That about bears—and boosting me up into a tree— somehow flustered me a little."

Soon they crossed the clearing to the green wall of cedars and pines. Here Edd led into a narrow trail, with Lucy at his heels. His ordinary gait was something for her to contend with. At once the trail began to wind down over red earth and round the head of rocky gullies, choked with cedars, and downward under a deepening forest growth.

Lucy had never been on this trail, which she knew to be the one that led over the Rim. She thrilled at the thought of climbing to the loft summit of that black-fringed mountain mesa, but she was sure Edd would not put her to that ascent without a horse. The low hum which filled her ears grew into the roar of brawling brook.

"Bear track," said her guide, halting to point at a rounded depression in the dust of the trail. Lucy saw the imprint of huge toes. Her flesh contracted to a cold creeping sensation. "That old Jasper went along here last night. Reckon he's the bear that's been killin' our little pigs. Pa shore will be rarin' to chase him with the hounds."

"Edd! Is there any danger of our meeting this old Jasper, as you called him?" inquired Lucy.

"Reckon not much. Shore we might, though. I often run into bears. They're pretty tame. Hope we do meet him. I'd shore have some fun."

"Oh, would you? I don't believe it'd be very funny for *me*," declared Lucy.

"Wal, in case we do, you just mind what I say," concluded Edd.

Somehow his drawling confidence reassured her and she reverted again to the pleasurable sensations of the walk. The trail led down into a deep gorge, dense with trees large and small, and along a wildly bowlder-strewn stream bed, where the water roared unseen through its channel. Here towered the lofty silver spruces, so delicate of hue and graceful in outline. The sunlight filtered through the foliage. Everywhere Lucy gazed were evidences of the wildness of this forest, in timber and rocks and windfalls, in the huge masses of driftwood, in the precipitous banks of the stream, showing how the flood torrents tore and dug at their confines.

Lucy did not see a bird or squirrel, nor hear one. But as to the latter the roar of rushing water would have drowned any ordinary sound. Gradually the trail left the vicinity of the stream and began a slight ascent, winding among beds of giant bowlders covered with trailing vines. Lucy was particularly struck by the almost overpowering scent of the woodland. It appeared dominated by the fragrance of pine, but there was other beside that spicy tang. Through the woods ahead she caught glimpse of light and open sky. Then Edd halted her.

"I hear turkeys cluckin'," he whispered. "Hold my bucket, an' keep right close to me, so you can see. Walk Injun, now."

Lucy complied instinctively, and she was all eyes and ears. She could not, however, give undivided attention to the scene in front and at the same time proceed noiselessly. Edd walked slower and stooped lower as the trail led round a corner of thicket toward the open. Lucy saw a long narrow clearing, overgrown with small green cedars and patches of sumach shining red and gold in the sunlight. At the same instant she saw something move, a white-and-brown object flashing low down. Edd swiftly rose. The gun cracked so suddenly that Lucy was startled. Then followed a tremendous flapping of wings. Huge black-and-gray birds flew and sailed out of the clearing into the woods, crashing through the foliage. Next Lucy heard a loud threshing in the brush just in front, and a heavy thumping. Both sounds diminished in volume, then ceased.

"Wal, I reckon you'll have turkey for dinner to-morrow," said Edd, looking to his gun. "Did you see them before they flew?"

"I saw a flash. Oh, it went swiftly! Then you shot, and I saw them rise. What a roar! Did you kill one?" replied Lucy, excitedly.

"I shore did. It was a good shot. He was rarin' to get out of here," said Edd, as he walked forward through the patch of sumach.

Lucy followed him to the open place where lay a beautiful wild turkey, its shiny plumage all ruffled and disheveled, its wings wide, its gorgeous bronze-and-white tail spread like a huge fan. Lucy was astonished at the variety and harmony of the colors. This wild bird was as beautiful as a peacock.

"Gobbler, two years old," said Edd. "Just fine for eatin'. I'll hang him up in the shade an' get him on our way home. Shore it's risky, though because there's cats and lions around."

He carried the turkey into the edge of the woods, where Lucy heard him tramping around and breaking branches. When he emerged again he led her to the upper end of this clearing, meanwhile telling her that his father had years before cut the timber and tried to cultivate the ground. It had not been a successful venture. A tiny stream of water ran through the upper end, making smooth deep holes in the red clay. Edd pointed out deer and turkey tracks, with muddy water in them. He followed the stream to its source in a spring at the head of the clearing. A small shallow basin full of water, weeds, and moss lay open to the sun.

"Wal, here's where we start," announced Edd, enthusiastically. "Listen to the hum of bees."

The air seemed murmurous and melodious with the hum of innumerable bees. What a sweet, drowsy summer sound! Lucy gazed all around.

"Oh, I hear them! But where are they?" she cried.

"Wal, they're flyin' around, workin' in the tops of these pine saplings," replied Edd.

"Do they get honey up there?" queried Lucy, in amaze.

"They shore get somethin'," replied Edd. "If you go climbin' round pine trees an' get your hands all stuck up with pitch an' sap you'll think so, too. I reckon bees get somethin' in these pines to help make their wax. . . . Now look down along the edge of the water. You'll see bees lightin' an' flyin' up. I've watched them hundreds of times, but I never made shore whether they drank, or diluted their honey, or mixed their wax with water."

"Well! Who'd have thought honeybees so interesting? . . . Yes, I see some. Will they sting me?"

"Tame as flies," returned Edd, easily.

Trustingly Lucy got down on hands and knees, and then lay prone, with her face just above the water. Here, at distance of a foot, she could see the bees distinctly. At once she noted several varieties, some yellow and black, which she knew to be yellow-jackets, some fuzzy and brown like the tame honeybee, and a few larger, darker. As she leaned there these wilder bees flew away.

Edd knelt to one side and pointed at the bees. "The yellow ones are jackets, an' she shore hates them."

"She! Who's she?" queried Lucy.

"Wal, I call the wild bees she. Reckon because I've caught an' tamed queen bees. Shore that's some job."

"I remember now. You told me in rainy season the yellow-jackets fought and killed the wild bees and stole their honey. These yellow bees are the ones. . . . They're pretty, but they're mean-looking."

"Hold still," said Edd, suddenly. "There's a wild bee, the kind I'm goin' to line to-day. He lit by that little stone."

"I see him," whispered Lucy.

"Wal, now look close. Is he drinkin' or movin' his legs in the water? You see he's just at the edge. Look at his knees. See the little yellow balls? That's wax.''

"How funny!" said Lucy, laughing. "Why, his legs look deformed, burdened with those balls! Where does he carry his honey?"

"I never was shore, but I reckon in his mouth. Some bee hunters think the yellow balls are honey. I never did. It tastes like wax."

"It's beeswax. I know what that is. But where does the bee use it?"

"Shore you'll see that when I cut down a bee tree."

Apart from Lucy's great sympathy with the singular passion this wild-bee hunter had for his calling she was quite fascinated on her own account. It needed very little to stimulate Lucy's interest, especially in a problem or mystery, or something that required reason, study, perseverance to solve. She was getting acquainted with bees. The yellow-jackets were lively, aggressive, busybody little insects that manifestly wanted the place to themselves. The wild bees had a very industrious and earnest look. At the approach of yellow-jackets they rose and flew, to settle a little farther away. Lucy espied bees all along the edge of the water. The big one Edd had called her attention to flew away, and presently another took its place. Lucy wished for a magnifying glass, and told Edd that if they had one they could tell exactly what the bee was doing there.

"By George!" ejaculated Edd, in most solemn rapture. "Shore we could. I never thought of that. Wal, I never even heard of a glass that'd magnify. Where can we get one?"

"I'll fetch you one from Felix."

"Lucy, I reckon I don't want you to go, but I'd shore love to have that kind of a glass."

"Why don't you want me to go?" asked Lucy, gayly.

"It's hard to say. I've heard the folks talkin'. Ma thinks it grand for Mertie. But I'm not so shore. Reckon Mertie will have a grand time. You're awful good to take her. But won't she get her head full of notions about clothes an' city boys?"

"Edd, you're worrying a lot, aren't you?"

"Yes," he said, simply.

"Haven't you faith in me? I'm going to satisfy Mertie's passion for pretty things. Once in her life! And I'm going to see that Bert Hall goes with us."

Lucy raised on her elbows to mark the effect of this statement upon her companion. For once his stoicism was disrupted. He seemed thunderstruck. Then his dark face beamed and his gray eyes shone with the piercing light Lucy found hard to face.

"Wal!—Who in the world's ever goin' to make up to you for your goodness?"

"Edd, it's not goodness, exactly," returned Lucy, somewhat affected by his emotion. "It's not my welfare work, either. I guess I'll get more out of it than Mertie and Bert. Real happiness, you know."

"Shore. But I know what I think."

Lucy dropped back to study the bees. A number of the wild species had settled down right under her eyes. They were of different sizes and hues, and the very smallest carried the largest balls of wax on his knees. She strained her eyes to see perfectly, and was rewarded by sight of an almost imperceptible motion of both their heads and legs.

"Edd, I believe they drink and wet their wax. Both. At the same time."

"Wal, shore I've reckoned that often. Now get up an' watch me line a bee."

This brought Lucy to her feet with alacrity. Edd's voice sounded a note entirely at variance with his usual easy, cool, drawling nonchalance. About most things he was apparently indifferent. But anything pertaining to his beloved bee hunting touched him to the quick.

"Now, you stand behind me an' a little to one side," he directed. "An' we'll face toward that far point on the Rim. Eagle Rock we call it. Most of the bees here take a line over there."

Suddenly he pointed. "See that one."

Though Lucy strained her eyes, she saw nothing. The wide air seemed vacant.

"Don't look up so high," he said. "These bees start low. You've shore got to catch her right close. . . . There goes another."

"I'm afraid my eyes aren't good," complained Lucy, as she failed again.

"No. Keep on lookin'. You'll line her in a minute."

Just then Lucy caught sight of a tiny black object shooting over her head and darting with singularly level swift flight straight away. It did not appear to fly. It swept.

"Oh, Edd, I see one!. . . . He's gone."

"Shore. You've got to hang your eye on to her."

Lucy caught a glimpse of another speeding bee, lost it, and then sighted another. She held this one in view for what seemed an endless moment. Then having got the knack of following, she endeavored to concentrate all her powers of vision. Bee after bee she watched. They had a wonderful unvarying flight. Indeed, she likened them to bullets. But they were remarkably visible. No two bees left the waterhole together. There was a regularity about their appearance.

"Wal, you're doin' fine. You'll shore make a bee hunter," said Edd. "Now let's face west awhile."

Lucy found this direction unobstructed by green slope and red wall. It was all open sky. A line of bees sped off and Lucy could follow them until they seemed to merge into the air.

"Why do some bees go this way and some that other way?" she queried.

"She belongs to different bee trees. She knows the way home better than any other livin' creature. Can't you see that? Straight as a string! Reckon you never heard the old sayin', 'makin' a bee line for home.' "

"Oh, is that where that comes from?" ejaculated Lucy, amused. "I certainly appreciate what it means now."

"Now shift back to this other bee line," instructed Edd. "When you ketch another, follow her till you lose her, an' then tell me where that is. Mark the place."

Lucy made several attempts before she succeeded in placing the disappearance of a bee close to the tip of a tall pine on the distant ridge.

"Wal, that's linin' as good as ever Mertie or Allie," asserted Edd, evidently pleased, and he picked up his gun and bucket. "We're off."

"What do we do now?" queried Lucy.

"Can't you reckon it out?"

"Oh, I see! We've got the bee line. We follow it to that pine tree where I lost the last bee."

"Right an' exactly," drawled Edd.

"Oh—what fun! It's like a game. Then where do we go?"

"Wal, I can't say till we get there."

"We'll watch again. We'll sight more bees. We'll get their line. We'll follow it as far as we can see—mark the spot—and then go on," declared Lucy, excitedly.

"Lucy, your granddad might have been a wild-bee hunter," said Edd, with an approving smile.

"He might, only he wasn't," laughed Lucy. "You can't make any wild-bee hunter of me, Edd Denmeade."

"Shore, but you might make one of yourself," drawled Edd.

Lucy had no reply for that. Falling in behind him as he headed across the clearing, she pondered over his words. Had they been subtle, a worthy response to her rather blunt double meaning, or just his simplicity, so apt to hit the truth? She could not be sure, but she decided hereafter to think before she spoke.

Edd crossed the clearing and plunged into the forest. As he entered the timber Lucy saw him halt to point out a tree some distance ahead. This, of course, was how he marked a straight line. Lucy began to guess the difficulty of that and the strenuous nature of traveling in a straight line through dense and rugged forest. She had to scramble over logs and climb over windfalls; she had to creep through brush and under fallen trees; she had to wade into ferns as high as her head and tear aside vines that were as strong as ropes.

They reached the bank above the roaring brook. As Edd paused to choose a place to get down the steep declivity, Lucy had a moment to gaze about her. What a wild, dark, deep glen! The forest monarchs appeared to mat overhead and hide the sun. Bowlders and trees, brook and bank, all the wild jumble of rocks and drifts, and the tangle of vines and creepers, seemed on a grand scale. There was nothing small. The ruggedness of nature, of storm and flood, of fight to survive, manifested itself all around her.

"Wal, shore if you can't follow me you can squeal," shouted Edd, above the roar of the brook.

"Squeal! Me? Never in your life!" replied Lucy, with more force than elegance. "If I can't follow you, I can't, that's all. But I'll try."

"Reckon I didn't mean squeal as you took it," returned Edd, and without more ado he plunged in giant strides right down the bank.

Lucy plunged likewise, fully expecting to break her neck. Instead, however, she seemed to be taking seven-league-boot-steps in soft earth that slid with her. Once her hands touched. Then, ridiculously easily, she arrived at the bottom of the forty-foot embankment. Most amusing of all was the fact that Edd never even looked back. Certainly it was not discourtesy, for Edd was always thoughtful. He simply had no concern about her accomplishing this descent.

Crossing the brook had more qualms for Lucy, and when she saw Edd leap from one slippery rock to another she thought it was a good thing she had been put on her mettle. Edd reached the other side without wetting a foot. Lucy chose bowlders closer together, and by good judgment, added to luck, she got safely across, though not without wet boots.

Then Lucy climbed after Edd up a bank of roots that was as easy as a ladder, and thence on into the forest again. A thicket of pine saplings afforded welcome change. How subdued the light—how sweet the scent of pine! She threaded an easy way over smooth level mats of needles, brown as autumn leaves. Edd broke the dead branches and twigs as he passed, so that she did not have to stoop. On all sides the small saplings shut out the light and hid the large trees. Soon the hum of the brook died away. Footsteps on the soft needles gave forth no sound. Silent, shaded, lonely, this pine swale appealed strongly to Lucy. Soon it ended in a rough open ridge of cedar, oak, and occasional pine, where Edd's zigzag climb seemed steep and long. It ended in an open spot close to a tree Lucy recognized.

"I thought—we'd never—get here," panted Lucy.

"That was easy. Can you pick out where we stood down in the clearin'?"

Lucy gazed down the slope, across the green thicket and then the heavy timber marking the channel of the brook, on to the open strip bright with its red sumach.

"Yes, I see the water," she replied.

"Wal, turn your back to that an' look straight the other way an' you'll soon get our—bee line."

She had not stood many moments as directed before she caught the arrowy streak of bees, flying straight over the ridge. But owing to the background of green, instead of the sky that had served as background, she could not follow the bees very far.

"Here's where we make easy stages," remarked Edd, and started on.

Open ridge and hollow occupied the next swift hour. Lucy had enough to do to keep up with her guide. The travel, however, was not nearly as rough as that below, so that she managed without undue exertion. She had been walking and climbing every day, and felt that she was equal to a grueling task. She had misgivings, however, as to that endurance being sufficient for all Edd might require. Still, she had resolved to go her very limit, as a matter of pride. Mertie had confided to Lucy that the only time Sadie Purdue had ever gone bee hunting with Edd she had given out, and that, too, on a rather easy bee line. It would have to be a bad place and a long walk that would daunt Lucy this day.

Edd's easy stages proved to be short distances from mark to mark, at every one of which he took pleasure in having Lucy again catch the bee line.

"When are you going to burn the honey in your bucket?" asked Lucy, once, happening to remember what Edd had told her.

"I don't know. Maybe I won't have to," he replied. "If I lose the bee line, then I'll need to burn honey."

"It seems, if things keep on as they are, you'll lose only *me*," observed Lucy.

"Tired?"

"Not a bit. But if I had to keep this up all day I *might* get tired."

"We'll eat lunch under this bee tree."

"That's most welcome news. Not because I want the hunt to be short, at all! I'm having the time of my life. But I'm hungry."

"It's always good to be hungry when you're in the woods," he said.

"Why?" she asked.

"Because when you do get to camp or back home, near starved to death, everythin' tastes so good, an' you feel as if you never knew how good food is."

Lucy was beginning to appreciate what this philosophy might mean in more ways than applied to hunger. It was good to starve, to thirst, to resist, to endure.

The bee line led to the top of a slope, and a hollow deeper, rougher than any of the others, and much wider. Edd lined the bees across to the timber on the summit of the ridge beyond, but he was concerned because there appeared so little to mark the next stage. The pines on that side were uniform in size, shape, and color. There were no dead tops or branches.

"Now, this is easy if we go straight down an' up," said Edd. "But if we go round, head this hollow, I reckon I might lose our bee line."

"Why should we go round?" inquired Lucy.

"Because that'd be so much easier for you," he explained.

"Thanks. But did you hear me squeal?"

Edd let out a hearty laugh, something rare with him, and it was an acceptance that gratified Lucy. There upon he went straight down the slope. Lucy strode and trotted behind, finding it took little effort. All she had to do was to move fast to keep from falling. This mode of travel appeared to be exhilarating. At least something was exhilarating, perhaps the air. Lucy knew she was excited, buoyant. Her blood ran warm and quick. What an adventure! If only she could have felt sure of herself! Yet she did not admit to her consciousness where she felt uncertain. "I'll live this with all I have," she soliloquized, "for I might never go again."

The slope into this hollow was a delusion and a snare. From above it had appeared no denser than the others. It turned out to be a jungle of underbrush. Live oak, manzanita, buckbrush formed an almost impenetrable thicket on the southerly exposed side. Edd crashed through the oaks, walked on top of the stiff manzanita, and crawled under the buckbrush.

Water ran down the rocky gully at the bottom. How Lucy drank and bathed her hot face! Here Edd filled a canvas water bag he had carried in his pocket, and slung it over his shoulder.

"Shore was fun ridin' the manzanitas, wasn't it?" he queried.

"Edd, it's—all fun," she breathed. "Remember, if I fall by the wayside— I mean by the bee line—that my spirit was willing but my flesh was weak."

"Humph! Sometimes I don't know about you, Lucy Watson," he said, dubiously.

When Lucy imagined she deserved a compliment it seemed rather disillusioning to hear an ambiguous speech like that. Meekly she followed him in and out of the clumps of brush toward the slope. Her meekness, however, did not last very long. Edd had the most astonishing faculty for bringing out all that was worst in her. Then by the time she had gotten halfway through a grove of large-leaved oaks she had forgotten what had inflamed her spirit. Every strenuous section of this journey had its reward in an easy stretch, where beauty and color and wilderness took possession of her.

Edd zigzagged up this slope, and the turns were so abrupt that Lucy began for the first time to feel a strain. Edd saw it and paused every few moments to give her time to regain breath and strength. He did not encourage her to waste either in speech. This slope stood on end. The ridge proved to be a mountain. Lucy was compelled to dig heels and toes in the hard red earth, and often grasp a bush or branch, to keep from slipping back.

At last they surmounted the great timbered incline. Lucy fell on a pine mat, so out of breath that she gasped. She had an acute pain in her side. It afforded her some satisfaction to see Edd's heaving breast and his perspiring face.

"What're—you—panting about?" she asked, heroically sitting up.

"Reckon that pull is a good one to limber up on," he said.

"Oh-h-h! Are there—any worse pulls?"

"Shore I don't know. We might have to climb up over the Rim."

"Well," concluded Lucy, with resignation, "where's our bee line?"

"I got plumb off," confessed Edd, in humiliation, as if the error he had made was one of unforgivable proportions. "But, honest, sometimes it's impossible to go straight."

"I accept your apology, Edward," said Lucy, facetiously. "But it wasn't necessary. No human being—even a bee hunter—can pass through rocks, trees, hills, walls of brush, and piles of logs. . . . What'll we do now?"

"I'll walk along an' see if I can find her. If I don't we'll burn some honey. That'll take time, but it'll shore fetch her. You rest here."

Lucy could see the two clearings of the Denmeades nestling green and yellow in the rolling lap of the forest. How far she had traveled! She was proud of this achievement already. With her breath regained, and that pain gone from her side, she was not in the least the worse for her exertion. Indeed, she felt strong and eager to pursue the bee line to its end. Only by such effort as this could she see the wonderful country or learn something about the forest land. She was high up now, and yet the Rim still towered beyond and above, unscalable except for eagles. She was reveling in the joy of her sensations when Edd's step disrupted them.

"I found her. We wasn't so far off. Come now, if you're rested," he said.

"Edd, how far do bee lines usually run from where you find them?" asked Lucy.

"Sometimes miles. But I reckon most bee lines are short. Shore they seem long because you have to go up an' down, right over everythin'."

Rolling forest stretched away from the ridge-top, neither level nor hilly. Despite the heavy growth of pines the bee line seemed to penetrate the forest and still preserve its unwavering course. Lucy could see the bees flying down the aisles between the tree-tops, and she was unable to make certain that they curved in the least. Edd could line them only a short distance, owing to intervening trees. Progress here was necessarily slower, a fact that Lucy welcomed. Birds and squirrels and rabbits enlivened this open woodland; and presently when Edd pointed out a troop of sleek gray deer, wonderfully wild and graceful as they watched with long ears erect, Lucy experienced the keenest of thrills.

"Black-tails," said Edd, and he raised his gun.

"Oh—please don't kill one of them!" cried Lucy, appealingly.

"Shore I was only takin' aim at that buck. I could take him plumb center."

"Well, I'll take your word for it," rejoined Lucy. "How tame they are! . . . They're going. . . . Oh, there's a beautiful little fawn!"

She watched them bound out of sight, and then in her relief and pleasure to see them disappear safely she told Edd she was glad he was a bee hunter instead of a deer hunter.

"Wal, I'm not much on bees to-day," he acknowledged. "But that's natural, seein' I've a girl with me."

"You mean you do better alone?"

"I reckon."

"Are you sorry you brought me?"

"Sorry? Wal, I guess not. 'Course I love best to be alone in the woods. But havin' you is somethin' new. It's not *me,* but the woods an' the bees an' the work you're thinkin' about. You don't squeal an' you don't want to get mushy in every shady place."

Lucy, failing of an adequate response to this remarkable speech, called his attention to the bees; and Edd stalked on ahead, peering through the green aisles. The beautiful open forest was soon to end in a formidable rocky canyon, not more than half a mile wide, but very deep and rugged. Lucy stood on the verge and gazed, with her heart in her eyes. It was a stunning surprise. This deep gorge notched the Rim. Red and yellow crags, cliffs, ledges, and benches varied with green slopes, all steps down and down to the black depths. A murmur of running water soared upward. Beneath her sailed an eagle, brown of wing and back, white of head and tail, the first bald eagle Lucy had ever seen.

"Dog-gone!" ejaculated Edd. "Shore I was hopin' we'd find our bee tree on this side of Doubtful Canyon."

"Doubtful? Is that its name?"

"Yes, an' I reckon it's a Jasper."

"Edd, it may be doubtful, but it's grand," declared Lucy.

"You won't think it's grand if we undertake to cross."

"Then our bee tree is 'way over there some place," said Lucy, gazing at the blue depths, the black slopes, the yellow crags, the red cliffs. They would have looked close but for the dominating bulk of the Rim, rising above and beyond the canyon wall. All was green growth over there except the blank faces of the rocks. Ledges and benches, nooks and crannies, irresistibly beckoned for Lucy to explore.

"If! We're certainly going to cross, aren't we?" she queried, turning to Edd.

"Wal, if you say so, we'll try. But I reckon you can't make it."

"Suppose I *do* make it—can we go home an easier way?"

"Shore. I can find easy goin', downhill all the way," replied Edd.

"Well, then I propose we rest here and have our lunch. Then cross! Before we start, though, you might let me see you burn some honey. Just for fun."

This plan met with Edd's approval. Just below they found a huge flat ledge of rock, projecting out over the abyss. Part of it was shaded by a bushy pine, and here Edd spread the lunch. Then while Lucy sat down to eat he built a tiny fire out on the edge of the rock. Next he placed a goodly bit of honey on a stone close enough to the fire to make it smoke.

"Pretty soon we'll have some fun," he said.

"Wrong! We're having fun now. At least I am," retorted Lucy.

"Wal, then, I mean some more fun," he corrected.

Whereupon they fell with hearty appetites upon the ample lunch Mrs. Denmeade had provided. Edd presently said he heard bees whizz by. But a quarter of an hour elapsed before any bees actually began to drop down over the smoking honey. Then Edd poured some of the honey out on the rock. The bees circled and alighted. More came and none left. Lucy asked why they did not fly away.

"Makin' pigs of themselves," he said. "But soon as they get all they can hold they'll fly."

By the time the lunch was finished a swarm of bees of different sizes and hues had been attracted to the honey, and many were departing. As they came from different directions, so they left. Edd explained this to be owing to the fact that these bees belonged to different trees.

"Do all these wild bees live in trees?" she asked.

"All but the yellow-jackets. They have holes in the ground. I've seen where many holes had been dug out by bears. . . . Wal, we played hob with the lunch. An' now I reckon it's high time we begin our slide down this canyon."

"Slide? Can't we walk?"

"I reckon you'll see. It'll be a slidin' walk," averred Edd. "Shore I'm goin' to have all the fun I can, 'cause you'll shore never go anywheres with me again."

"My! How terrible this sliding walk must be! . . . But I might fool you, Edd. I've decided to go to the dance with you, an' let Clara go with Joe."

"Aw! That's nice of you," he replied, with frank gladness. His face lighted at some anticipation. "Joe will shore be proud."

He walked out upon the ledge to get his bucket, driving the bees away with his sombrero, and when he had secured it he took a last long look across the canyon. Lucy noticed what a picture he made, standing there, tall, round-limbed, supple, his youthful leonine face sharp against the sky. He belonged there. He fitted the surroundings. He was a development of forest and canyon wilderness. The crudeness once so objectionable to her was no longer manifest. Was it because of change and growth in him—or in her? Lucy fancied it was the latter. Edd had vastly improved, but not in the elemental quality from which had sprung his crudeness.

"She'll be right across there," he said, pointing with long arm. "I can line her halfway across. Reckon I see the tree now. It's an oak, sort of gray in color, standin' on a ledge. An' it's got a dead top an' one big crooked branch."

"Very well, I'll remember every word," warned Lucy.

"I'll go ahead, so when you come slidin' I can grab you," he said.

"See that you don't miss me," replied Lucy, as she started to follow him down off the ledge. At first the descent, though steep, was easy enough. Had

Edd zigzagged down she would have had no trouble at all. But he descended straight down over bare earth, rock slides, banks and benches, swerving only for trees and brush, and then taking care to get back again in alignment with whatever he had marked to guide him. Lucy could not go slowly, unless she sat down, which, despite an almost irresistible temptation, she scorned to do. Quite abruptly, without preparation, she found herself standing at the top of a wonderful green and brown slope dotted by pine trees and remarkable for its waved effect. It descended at an angle of forty-five degrees, an open forest standing almost on end! The green color was grass; the brown, pine needles. This place made Lucy's heart leap to her throat. An absolutely unaccountable and new species of fright assailed her. Never in her life before had she seen a slope like that or been attacked by such dread.

"Wal, here's where we slide," drawled Edd, gazing up at her. "Whatever you do, do it quick, an' keep in line with me."

Then he started down. His action here was very much different from any before. He descended sidewise, stepping, or rather running, on the edge of his boots, holding gun and bucket in his left hand, and reaching back with his right. His position corresponded with the slant of the slope. He slid more than he ran. His right hand often touched the ground behind him. He felt a furrow in grass and needles. Forty or fifty feet below he lodged on a bench. Then he straightened round to look up at Lucy.

"Wal, city girl?" he called, gayly. His voice was bantering, full of fun.

It lent Lucy recklessness. Through it she recovered from the queer locked sensation.

"All right, country boy, I'm coming," she replied, with bravado.

Then she launched herself, heedlessly attempting to imitate Edd's method of procedure. A few swift steps landed her upon the pine needles. Quick as lightning her feet flew up and she fell. Frantically she caught the ground with her hands and held on, stopped her momentum. Both breath and bravado had been jarred out of her.

"Wal, you've started comin', so come on," called Edd, never cracking a smile.

Lucy, holding on in most undignified manner, glared down upon him, making one last desperate effort to keep her equilibrium and her temper. If he had laughed or smiled, she might have trusted him more.

"Did you get me here on purpose?" she demanded, with magnificent disregard of reason.

"Shore. We're on our bee line. You couldn't be talked out of it," he replied.

"I mean on this terrible hill," she added, weakening.

"How'd I know she'd make a bee line over this hill?" he demanded.

Lucy, seeing that action, not talk, was imperative, got up, and ran downhill right at him. She forgot his method of descending, but executed a very good one of her own. She ran, she flew, she fell, right upon Edd. He caught her outstretched hands and kept her from upsetting.

"Heavens!" gasped Lucy. "Suppose you hadn't been here?"

"Wal, you'd have slid some," he said. "But, honest, you did that fine."

"It was an accident," confessed Lucy as she fearfully gazed below. The next stage, to a bench below, seemed still steeper, and the one below that made Lucy's head reel.

"I'm sorry I called you city girl," he said, contritely. "For you're shore game, an' quick on your feet. You hunt bees like you dance."

Lucy's misery was not alleviated by the compliment, because she knew she was a sham; nevertheless, she felt a weak little thrill. Maybe she could go on without killing herself.

"Don't hang on to me," added Edd, as again he started. "That's not the way. We'll both slip, an' if we do we'll go clear to the bottom, same as if this hill was snow. . . . When I make it down there you come, same as you got here."

"Ha! Ha!" laughed Lucy, wildly. "Don't worry, I'll come."

Edd made a splendid achievement of the next descent, and halted in favorable position to wait for Lucy. It encouraged her. Stifling her vacillations, she launched herself with light steps, leaning back, and depending on her gloved hand. She kept her feet most of the distance, but landed before Edd in a sliding posture. On the next attempt a couple of pine trees made descent easy for her. Below that were successive stages calculated to give her undue confidence.

"Wal, this is plumb bad," ejaculated Edd, gazing below and to right and left. "But we can't climb back. An' it's worse on each side. Reckon there's nothin' to do but slide."

And he did slide and fall and roll, and finally lodge against a tree.

"Hey! you can't do worse than that!" he shouted. "Come on. Don't wait an' think. . . . Come a-rarin'."

Lucy was in a strange state of suspended exhilaration and acute panic. She was both inhibited and driven. Actually she closed her eyes on the instant she jumped. Then she ran. Her objective was Edd and she had to look. She expected to plunge head over heels, yet she reached Edd upright, and earned another compliment. They went on with varying luck, but at least they made remarkable progress. The farther down this slope they proceeded the thicker lay the mats of pine needles and the scanter grew the patches of grass. Naturally the needles slipped and slid downward. Also, trees and brush grew scarce. Then to make the situation worse the descent took a sharper angle and the benches cropped out farther apart. At last they reached a point where Edd seemed at a loss. The slope just below was not only more precipitous and longer than any yet, but it ended in a jump-off, the extent of which Edd could not determine.

"Lucy, I've played hob gettin' you into this," he said, in remorse.

"It was my fault," returned Lucy, frightened by his gravity. "Go on. Let's get down—before I lose my nerve."

All the nerve she had left oozed out as she watched Edd slide to the landing place selected below. He never took a step. He sat down and slid like a streak. Lucy thought he was going over the precipice. But he dug heels into needles and ground, and stopped his flight in the nick of time.

"Not so bad as it looked," he shouted. How far below he was now! "Come on. It's safe if you let yourself slide straight. So you won't miss me!"

But Lucy did not obey. She realized how silly she was, but she simply could not deliberately sit down and slide. She essayed to do as she had done above. And her feet flew higher than her head. She alighted upon her back and began to shoot down. She turned clear over on her face. Dust and flying needles blinded her. Frantically she dug in with hands and feet, and rolled and slid to a halt.

When she cleared her sight she found she had gotten out of line with Edd. He was crawling along the precipice to intercept her. Lying prone on the slippery slope, she had to hold with all her might to keep from sliding. Edd's yells, added to all that had happened, terrified her, and she clung there instinctively. It seemed a frightful drop to where Edd knelt. She would miss him and slide over the precipice. Inch by inch she felt herself slip. She screamed. Edd's voice pierced her drumming ears.

". . . darn fool, you! Let go! Slide!"

Lucy let go because she could no longer hold on. Then she seemed to rush through air and flying needles and clouds of dust. Swifter she slid. Her sight blurred. Sky and trees grew indistinct. She slid from her back over on her face, and plunged down. A mass of débris seemed to collect on her as she plunged. Suddenly she collided with something and stopped with terrific shock. She felt Edd's clutch on her. But she could not see. Again she was moving, sliding, held back, pulled and dragged, and at last seemed to reach a halt. Breathless, stunned, blinded, burning as with fire, and choked with dust, Lucy wrestled to sit up.

"You shore slid," Edd was saying. "You knocked us over the ledge. But we're all right now. I'll go back for my gun."

Lucy's mouth was full of dirt and pine needles; her eyes of dust. She sputtered and gasped, and could not see until welcome tears washed her sight clear. Then she found she was at the foot of the terrible slope. Edd was crawling up to the bench above. Her hair and blouse and trousers, even her boots and pockets, were full of dust, pine needles, twigs, and dirt. Standing up, shaking and spent, she essayed to rid herself of all she had collected in that slide. Incredible to believe, she had not sustained even a bruise that she was aware of. Then Edd came slipping down, gun and bucket in hand. As he reached her he seemed to be laboring under some kind of tremendous strain.

"No—use!" he choked. "Shore—I can't—hold it."

"What, for goodness' sake?" burst out Lucy.

"If I—don't laugh—I'll bust," he replied, suddenly falling down.

"Pray don't do anything so—so vulgar as that last," said Lucy, attempting hauteur.

But sight of this imperturbable backwoods boy giving way to uncontrollable mirth affected Lucy peculiarly. Her resentment melted away. Something about Edd was infectious.

"I must have been funny," she conceded.

Edd appeared incapacitated for any verbal explanation of how laughter-provoking she had been; and Lucy at last broke her restraint and shared his hilarity.

An hour later Lucy perched upon a ledge high above the canyon, exhausted and ragged, triumphant and gay, gazing aloft at a gray old oak tree that had breasted the winds and lightnings for centuries. Part of it was dead and bleached, but a mighty limb spread from the fork, with branches bearing myriads of broad green leaves and clusters of acorns. On the under side of this huge limb was a knot hole encrusted with a yellow substance. Beeswax. It surrounded the hole and extended some distance along the under side, changing the gray color of the bark to yellow. A stream of bees passed in and out of that knot hole. Edd had followed his bee line straight to the bee tree.

"She's a hummer," he was saying as he walked to and fro, gazing upward with shining eyes. "Shore, it's an old bee tree. Reckon that whole limb is hollow an' full of honey. . . . Easy to cut an' let down without smashin'! I'll save maybe fifty gallons."

"Aren't you afraid of those bees?" asked Lucy, seeing how they swooped down and circled round Edd.

"Bees never sting me," he said.

Lucy assumed that if there was no danger for him there would be none for her; and desiring to see the bees at close range as they streamed in and out of the aperture, she arose and approached to where Edd stood.

Hardly had she raised her head to look up when a number of bees whizzed down round her face. In alarm Lucy struck at them with her gloves, which she carried in her hand.

"Don't hit at them!" shouted Edd in concern. "You'll make them mad."

But it was too late. Lucy had indeed incurred their wrath and she could not resist beating at them.

"Oh, they're after me! . . . Chase them away! . . . Edd! . . ." She screamed the last as she backed away, threshing frantically at several viciously persistent bees. Then as she backed against a log and lost her balance, one of the bees darted down to sting her on the nose. Lucy fell back over the log. The bee stayed on her nose until she pulled it off, not by any means without voicing a piercing protest. Then she bounded up and beat a hasty retreat to a safer zone. For a moment she ached with the burning sting. Then the humiliation of it roused her ire. The glimpse she had of Edd through the saplings caused her to suspect that he had again succumbed to shameless glee. Else why did he hide behind the bee tree?

Lucy was inclined to nurse her wrath as well as her nose. At any rate, she sat down to tenderly hold the injured member. It was swelling. She would have a huge, red, ugly nose. When Edd came to her at length, looking rather sheepish, Lucy glared at him.

"That horrid old bee stung me right on my nose," she burst out. "Just for that I'll not go to the dance."

"I have some salve I made. It'll take out the sting an' swellin'," he replied, kindly.

"Does it look very bad yet?"

"No one'd ever see it," he comforted.

"Oh, but it hurts. But if it doesn't disfigure me for life I guess I can stand it."

He gazed thoughtfully down upon her.

"You stuck to me better than any girl I ever took on a bee hunt. I'm shore goin' to tell everybody. Pa an' ma will be tickled. Now I'm askin' you. Reckonin' it all, aren't you glad you had that awful spill an' then got stung?"

"Well," replied Lucy, gazing up at him just as thoughtfully, "I'm not glad just this minute—but perhaps I will be later."

Two hours of leisurely travel down a gradual descent, through a trailless forest, brought Lucy and her guide back to the brook. Edd had been careful to choose open woodland and the easiest going possible. Sunset found them crossing the clearing. Lucy could just wag along, yet she could still look up with delight in the golden cloud pageant, and at the sun-fired front of the Rim.

"Edd, you forgot the turkey," said Lucy as they entered the lane.

"Nope. It was only out of our way, comin' back. After supper I'll jump a hoss an' ride after it."

"Well, Edd, thank you for—our bee hunt."

As she passed the yard she waved and called gayly to the Denmeades, hiding to the last the fact that she was utterly spent. Clara heard her and flung open the door of the tent glad-eyed and excited. Lucy staggered up into the tent and, closing the door, she made a long fall to the bed.

"Oh—Clara," she whispered, huskily, "I'm killed! I'm dead! . . . Walked, climbed, slid, and stung to death! . . . Yes, *stung!* Look at my poor nose! . . . We found a bee line, and went a thousand miles—up and down . . . . I stuck to that wild-bee hunter. I *did,* Clara. . . . . But, oh, it's done something to me! . . . What a glorious, glorious day!''

Clara leaned lovingly over her, and listened intently, and watched with sad, beautiful, wise eyes.

"Lucy dear," she said, gently, "you're in love with that wild-bee hunter.''

11

LATE in October Lucy returned from Felix, where she had stayed four weeks instead of two, as she originally intended. Her work had so interested the welfare board that they considered the experiment a success, and they brought her in contact with other workers whom they wanted to have the benefit of Lucy's experience. Thus she had found herself rather an important personage in that little circle.

Though the stage arrived at Cedar Ridge late in the afternoon, Lucy did not want to tarry there till next day. She had a strange, eager longing to get back to her sister and to the place she called home, the lonely homestead under the Rim. That had been the cause, she thought, of her restlessness while in the city.

Bert and Mertie, vastly important about the change in their lives, hurried to his home to reveal their secret, assuring Lucy that they would come out to the ranch next day. Lucy hired one of the few automobiles in Cedar Ridge, and in charge of a competent driver she arrived at Johnson's just before sunset. Sam's younger brother offered to ride up to Denmeade's with her, and pack her baggage. As there was no school session during late fall and winter, Mr. Jenks had left with the understanding that he would return in the spring.

Once on horseback again, Lucy began to feel free. How long she had been gone! What changes had come! These were exemplified in the transformation fall had wrought in the verdue along the trails. Only the great pines had not changed, yet their needle foliage had a tinge of brown. The fern leaves that had waved so beautifully green and graceful were now crisp and shriveled; the grape vines were yellow; the brown-eyed daisies were all gone; the sycamore trees were turning and the cottonwoods had parted with their beauty. Likewise had the walnut trees.

In places where Lucy could see the Rim she was astounded and delighted. She had carried away a picture of the colored walls, but now there was a blaze of gold, purple, cerise, scarlet, all the hues of fire. Frost had touched maples, aspens, oaks, with a magic wand. It seemed another and more beautiful forest land that she was entering. Up and down, everywhere along the trail, her horse waded through autumn leaves. The level branches of spruce and pine, that reached close to her, were littered with fallen leaves, wrinkled and dried. How different the sound of hoofs! Now they padded, rustled, when before they had crunched and cracked.

The melancholy days had come. As the sunset hues failed Lucy saw purple haze as thick as smoke filling the hollows. The aisles were deserted of life, sear and brown, shading into twilight. She rode down into the deep forest glen and up out of it before overtaken by night. How comforting the dusky halls of the woodland! Assuredly she was going to find out something about herself when she could think it out. Sam's little brother talked whenever the trail was steep and his horse lagged close to Lucy's. Homely bits of news, pertaining to his simple life, yet Lucy found them sweet.

The hunter's moon lighted the last mile of the ride up to the Denmeade clearing. Weird, moon-blanched, the great wall seemed to welcome her. What had come to her under its looming shadow? Black and silent the forest waved away to the dim boundaries. Lucy forgot her weariness. The baying of the hounds loosened the thrills that had been in abeyance, waiting for this moment when she rode up the lane. She peered for the white gleam of her canvas tent. Gone! Had Clara moved into the cabin? Then she made out that the tent wall had been boarded halfway up and the roof shingled. A light shone through the canvas. Lucy could scarcely wait to get her baggage from the boy and to tell him what to do.

Her voice stirred scrape of chair and flying footsteps inside the tent. The door swept open and Clara rushed out with a cry of welcome. Even in the poignant joy of the moment Lucy, as she folded Clara in a close embrace, missed the fragile slenderness that had characterized her sister's form. Then they were in the brightly lighted tent, where for a little the sweetness of reunion precluded all else.

"Let go of me, so I can see you," said Lucy, breaking away from her sister. "Oh, Clara!"

That was all she could say to this beautiful brown-faced radiant-eyed apparition.

"Yes, I'm well!" cried Clara. "Strong as a bear. Almost fat! I wondered what you'd think. . . . You see, your wilderness home and people have cured me. . . . More! Oh, sister, I'm afraid to say it—but I'm happy, too."

"Darling! Am I dreaming?" burst out Lucy, in a rapture. "What has happened? How have you done it? Who? . . . Why, I worried myself sick about you! Look at *me*! I'm thin, pale. And here you show yourself . . . Oh, Clara, you're just lovely! What have you been doing?"

"Simple as a b c, as Danny says," returned Clara. "When you left I just felt that I would get well and—and all right again—or I'd die trying. I took up your work, and I've done it. I worked every way they'd let me. I rode and climbed and walked every day with Joe. And eat? Oh, I've been a little pig!"

"Every day with Joe!" echoed Lucy, with eyes of love, hope, fear, doubt upon this strange sister. "Has *that* changed you so wonderfully?"

When had Lucy seen such a smile on Clara's face?

"Yes. But no more than taking up your work," she rejoined, with serious sweetness. "Joe cured my body. He got me out into the fields and the woods. I really wasn't so sick. I was weak, starved, spiritless. Then your work with the children, with all the Denmeades, showed me how life is worth living. I just woke up."

"I don't care who or what has done it," cried Lucy, embracing her again. "Bless Joe! . . . But, oh, Clara, if he was the way Edd said he was before I left—what is he now?"

"He loves me, yes," said Clara, with a dreaming smile.

Lucy's lips trembled shut on a query she feared to utter, and she endeavored to conceal her emotion by lifting her baggage to the bed.

"Well, that's no news," she said, lightly. "How's my wild-bee hunter?"

"I can't see any change," replied Clara, laughing. "You wrote me only twice, and him not at all."

"Him? Clara, did *he* expect to hear from me?" asked Lucy, facing about.

"I'm sure not, but he wanted to. Every night when he got home from his work—he's gathering honey now—he'd come to me and ask if I'd heard. I think he missed you and Mertie. He wondered how she'd get along in Felix."

"I ought to have written," said Lucy, as much to herself as to Clara. "But I found it hard. I *wanted* to. . . . I don't know where I stand. Perhaps now . . . Heigho! Well, as for Mertie, he needn't have worried about *her*."

"Lucy, I confess I'm curious myself," replied Clara.

"Mertie was just a crazy country girl who'd been badly influenced," went on Lucy. "She had good stuff in her, as I guessed, and she really cared for Bert. Mertie wanted something, she didn't know what. But I knew. And I gave it to her. I bought her everything she fancied and I took her everywhere. It did not seem possible to me that anyone could be so wildly happy as she was. And Bert? Goodness! It was good to see him. . . . They're married, and, I'm sure, settled for life."

"Married! Well, Lucy Watson, you *are* a worker. So that was why you took them to Felix?" replied Clara.

"Not at all. But it fell in with the natural order of things. Don't you breathe it. Mertie and Bert will be out here to-morrow to surprise the folks. They'll be glad. I wonder how Edd will take it."

"He'll be happy," mused Clara. "He loves that flipperty gibbet. . . . So they're married. It seems about all young people can do."

"Are you speaking for yourself, or for me, sister?" queried Lucy, teasingly.

"Not for myself, surely. . . . Lucy, I think I hear Allie calling us to supper."

The welcome accorded Lucy in that simple household was something even more satisfying than the meed of praise she had received at Felix. Edd Denmeade was not present. His father said he was out, camping on a long bee hunt. Lucy tried to ward off conviction that his absence was a relief. Yet she wanted to see him. The feelings were contrary.

Lucy parried the queries about Mertie by saying that she would be home to-morrow to answer for herself. The clamor of the children was subdued by the delivery of sundry presents from town. For that matter, Lucy did not forget any of the Denmeades. She had remembered what joy a gift brought to them, one and all. For Edd she had purchased a magnifying glass and a field glass, for use in his study of bees.

"Sis, what'd you bring me?" queried Clara, jealously, when they were back in the tent.

"Myself. Is that enough?" teased Lucy.

"Of course. . . . Lucy, you must have spent a lot of money," said Clara, seriously.

"I shore did. All I had except what you wrote for. I have that."

"It's very—good of you," replied Clara.

"What'd you need so much money for?" asked Lucy, frankly. "It surprised me."

"It's—— I—— Well, there's a woman in Kingston," said Clara, averting her face. "I owed her money. I hated to tell you before, hoping she'd wait till I could earn some. But she wrote me."

"How did she know you were here?" queried Lucy, in surprise.

"I wrote to her first—about it," returned Clara.

"You mustn't owe money to anyone," said Lucy, decidedly. "Send her a money order from Cedar Ridge. . . . Don't look like that, dear. I'm glad to help you. What's mine is yours. . . . You'll be pleased when I tell you my salary was raised and my work highly recommended. I had to teach several new welfare workers."

And Lucy talked on and on, trying to chase away that strange look from Clara's face, and also to talk herself into a forgetfulness of questioning surprise and vague misgivings. Not in a month could Clara recover wholly from the past! Lucy was unutterably grateful for a change far beyond her hopes.

"It was warm in Felix. Here it's cold," said Lucy, shivering closer to the little stove. "But the frost, the air feel so good."

"We had six inches of snow," replied Clara, importantly. "I just loved it.

Second snow I ever saw! But it melted off next day. . . . Edd and Joe fixed up our tent. Oh, when the wind howled and the snow seeped, it would have been great if you'd been here. I was a little afraid, all alone!''

"Snow already? Well, I missed it, didn't I? . . . Clara, let's stay out here all winter.''

"Oh, I hope we can. I don't see what else we can do—not till spring. . . . Lucy, I've news for you. Mr. Denmeade told me that both the Claypools and Johnsons had complained to him because he was *keeping* you here so long. They say you're partial to the Denmeades, and that if you don't go to them soon they'll report you. I hope it's not possible for them to hurt you.''

Lucy had expected to hear this very news. While in Felix she had anticipated it and prepared her employers for complaints of this nature.

"They can't hurt me, Clara,'' she rejoined, soberly. "I made this job and I can handle it to suit myself. But the Claypools and Johnsons are right. I *am* partial to the Denmeades, so far. I always meant to be fair and I shall try to be. Circumstances, however, make my duty harder than I thought it would be. Indeed, I was fortunate to come here first. I owe my success to that. Now I've got to face the music. We'll ride down to Claypool's and then to Johnson's, and arrange to go to them in the spring and summer. But we'll return here in the fall.''

"We! Must *I* go with you?'' exclaimed Clara.

"Must you? Why, Clara, of course you must go with me,'' declared Lucy, in amaze. "Whatever are you thinking of? How could I get along without you now?''

"I—I thought you might let me stay here,'' replied Clara, with confusion rare in her. "They have talked about it, and I'd hate to leave, to break into a strange family. Mr. Denmeade and Joe, the mother and children, all say they won't let you go. Edd says you'll *have* to go, and you will go because you're honest. . . . I'm selfish, Lucy. I hope you can do your welfare work from here. You could in all seasons but winter. We could ride horseback twice a day, even as far as Miller's. But if you can't see it that way, or let me stay here at least part of the time, of course I'll be glad to go, to work for you. I'm just a coward. These Denmeades have put something back in my heart. To live near that Sam Johnson would drive me wild. Mrs. Denmeade says the Spralls are bad, and Edd says you'll go there despite him or all of us. I met Bud Sprall one day when I was hunting squirrels with Joe. He was at the dance we went to in September. I caught him looking at me. And you should have seen him looking at me when I was with Joe. . . . Lucy, he couldn't have heard about me, could he?''

"I don't see how,'' declared Lucy, emphatically. "'Way up here in this wilderness? Impossible! I did not hear about you even in Felix. I met all our old friends. But no one even hinted of what you fear.''

Clara received this information with a stress of feeling disproportionate to its importance, Lucy thought, and she seemed singularly grateful for it.

"Lucy, there's bad blood between Edd and this Bud Sprall," went on Clara. "I've heard things not intended for my ears. You've got to hold in your wild-bee hunter or he'll kill Bud Sprall."

"Clara, I called Edd Denmeade my wild-bee hunter just for fun," protested Lucy. "I—I thought it would amuse you. But goodness! he's not mine! That's ridiculous! And I'm not responsible for his feuds. He hated Bud Sprall before I ever came here."

"That's perfectly true, Lucy, but the fact remains Edd *is* yours whether you want him or not. And you *can* keep him from killing this fellow."

"What have I got to do?" demanded Lucy, flippantly. "I suppose you'll suggest that I—I throw myself into Edd's arms to keep him from becoming a murderer."

"It'd be noble welfare work, wouldn't it? And you like the boy!"

"I don't like him as much as that," muttered Lucy, doggedly.

"Well then, you're as fickle as I used to be. For when you came back from the bee hunt with Edd last month you were in love. Or else I don't know that little old disease."

"Nonsense, Clara!" exclaimed Lucy, greatly irritated and perplexed with her sister. "I was out of my head. Excited, full of the joy of the outdoors. I might have been in love with the forest, the canyon, the wildness and beauty of this country. I am so still. But that's——"

"Edd Denmeade and this wilderness are one and the same," interrupted Clara. "But pray don't mind my arguments, dearest Lucy. Sometimes you seem my little sister, instead of me being yours. We always disagreed. I suppose we always shall. I don't think you will ever care to live in Felix again. I know I never shall. And we can't help the effect we have on these boys. . . . Something will come of it, that's all. . . . You're tired, and I've worried you. Let's go to bed."

Next day Lucy was too devoted to getting settled and taking up the threads of her work to face at once the serious self-scrutiny that was inevitable. She welcomed any excuse to postpone it. Besides, she was weary of introspection. She felt like a fluttering leaf attached to a shaking twig and soon to be at the mercy of the storm. Always something was going to happen, but so far as she could tell it had not happened yet. Clara was an enigma. Despite the marvelous improvement in her, Lucy could not dispel a vague dread. It was intuitive, and resembled the shadow of a sword over her head.

She had a frank talk with Denmeade about the Claypools and the Johnsons. The old backwoodsman was honest and fair in his attitude toward them, in his statement of how much more they needed Lucy now than his own family. She could not delay her service in their behalf longer than early spring. He believed that Lucy could allay their jealous anxieties by going to see them and to plan with them for her coming. At the conclusion of this interview with Denmeade Lucy carried away the rather disturbing impression that the Denmeades had made her presence there a sort of personal triumph. She was living with them. What she had taught them, the improvements she had installed for cleaner and happier living, had only elevated them in their own regard above their neighbors. It made a bad situation.

Late that afternoon Mertie and Bert arrived in their best Felix clothes, mysteriously radiant.

"Clara, look," said Lucy, peeping out of the tent. "I knew nothing in the world would keep Mertie from arriving in that dress. She has ridden horseback—from Johnsons's anyway."

"She looks nice. It's a pretty dress," replied Clara. "Bert, though—isn't he perfectly killing? Acts like a young lord. . . . Well, I hope they'll be happy."

"Let's not miss this. They can't keep it longer. Why, it shines from them!"

"Excuse me, Lucy. You go. I'll see them later," returned Clara.

Though Lucy went out at once, she was too late to be present when the young couple confessed. As Lucy entered the yard an uproar began on the porch. Mertie and Bert had timed their arrival for an hour when the whole family was at home. The parental blessing had certainly been received. Lucy halted a moment to peep through the thin foliaged peach trees. The children were screaming at the top of their lungs, yet that din could not quite drown the gay, happy, excited voices of the Denmeade women and the deep, hoarse tones of the men.

Lucy's eyes suddenly filled with tears and her heart throbbed with gladness. Only she knew just how responsible she had been for this happy event. Only she—and perhaps Edd—had known the narrow verge Mertie Denmeade had willfully trod. Therefore she tarried a little longer at the fence, patting the noses of the smoking horses.

When she did present herself to the family on the porch the wild excitement had subsided.

"Reckon the boys an' girls will storm Mertie to-morrow, shore," Denmeade was saying. "An' you want to make ready for a high old time."

Lucy mounted the porch to gaze about her, smiling, with pretended surprise.

"What's all the fun about?" she inquired.

"Wal now, Miss Lucy!" ejaculated Denmeade, rising and actually taking off his hat. Then he seized her hand in his big rough ones and beamed down on her, his brown grizzled face as rugged as the bark of a pine, yet expressive of the deepest feeling. "Wal now, you played hob!"

That was all he had time to say before the children enveloped Lucy, and Allie and Mrs. Denmeade for once manifested their womanly appreciation of her goodness to them. The boys were undemonstrative. Dick stood like a tall sapling outlined against the open sky. Joe sat in the background against the wall, quiet-eyed, intent. Edd had evidently just come home, for his ragged leather chaps and his jeans bore substance and odor of the woods. He stood behind Mertie, who sat on the edge of the table, pale with passion of her importance and the sensation she had created. She had her hands back of her, holding to Edd's. The bright silk dress contrasted strangely with the subdued colors around her. Bert stood, foot on a bench, elbow on his knee, gazing adoringly down upon his bride. His gaudy necktie matched her gown.

"Howdy, city girl!" drawled Edd, to Lucy. He gave her no other greeting. The deep gaze accompanying his words was embarrassing and baffling to Lucy. She laughed and retorted:

"Howdy, wild-bee hunter!"

Thereupon Mertie launched again into the wild and whirling recital that evidently Lucy's arrival had broken for the moment. When, presently, she paused for breath, Bert flicked the ashes off his cigarette and announced to Denmeade:

"Pa turned over the sawmill to me. Weddin' present!"

"Dog-gone me!" ejaculated Denmeade, vociferously. "If you ain't lucky—gettin' the mill an' Mert at one lick."

"Yep, my luck turned that day we had our bean pickin'," replied Bert, happily.

"Wal, to talk business, we've been runnin' up a log cabin for Joe's homestead, over on the mesa. 'Crost the gully from Edd's place. An' I'm wonderin' if you can saw an' deliver a lot of floor boards, door frames, an' such."

"I just can, you bet," declared the young man. "Give me your order. I'll deliver lumber at foot of the mesa trail in less than a week."

"Fine! You're a Jasper for rustlin'. Shore I expected to pack the lumber up on the burros. Long job, but Dick an' Joe can drive the pack while the rest of us work. Edd expects to be done cuttin' for honey soon. Then he can help. We'll have Joe's cabin done by the time snow flies."

"Get pencil an' paper so we can figure out just what lumber you want."

Father and son-in-law went into the kitchen, while Mertie broke into further elaboration of her romance. Lucy remained a few moments longer, fascinated by the rapt faces of the listening Denmeades, especially Edd. He seemed transfigured. Lucy suffered a twinge of remorse for having considered him a clod. How tremendously he had been affected by this happy settling of Mertie's affairs! More than once Lucy had heard it said that a Denmeade married was safe. Presently Lucy returned to her tent and unfinished tasks.

Supper was not ready until dusk, a fact which testified to the upsetting of the household. Then the lack of the usual bountiful meal was made up for by merriment. Lucy felt glad to free herself from an excitement that had begun to wear on her nerves. Moreover, she needed to be alone. As she passed Clara and Joe sitting on the porch steps she could just catch the gleam of their faces in the dim lamplight. Clara's pensive and sweet, and Joe's locked in its impassive youthful strength. Oh, boy and girl! thought Lucy with a pang. They could not help themselves. One called to the other. Clara's tragic girlhood was fading into a past that was gone. She had to live, to breathe, to move; and this wilderness called to primitive emotions.

As Lucy halted a moment to pay her usual silent tribute to the black Rim above and the stars of white fire, she heard the gate creak, and then a quick step and jingle of spurs.

"Wait!" called Edd, with a ring in his voice. He could see her in the dark when she could not see him. The word, the tone halted her, and she seemed conscious of sudden inward stilling. His tall form appeared, blacker than the darkness, loomed over her. Involuntarily Lucy took a backward step. Then Edd clasped her in his arms.

It was like the hug of a bear. Lucy's arms were pinned to her sides and she was drawn so close she could scarcely catch her breath. A terrible weakness assailed her. Not of anger, not of resentment! It was something else, strangely akin to a mingling of amaze and relief. Caught at last in her own toils!

"Oh—Edd!" she whispered, meaning to beg to be let go, but she never completed the appeal. Her arms moved instinctively upward, until stopped by the giant clasp that held her. What had she meant to do? How her mind whirled! He did not speak, and the moment seemed an age.

She felt the ripple of his muscles and the rough flannel of his shirt against her cheek. The scent of pine and honeybees and the woodland clung to his clothes. Lucy quivered on the brink of a tumultuous unknown.

Suddenly his arms uncoiled. Lucy swayed a little, not sure of her equilibrium.

"Shore I had to," he gasped, huskily. "Words don't come easy—for me. . . . God bless you for savin' Mertie!"

He plunged away into the blackness, his boots thumping, his spurs clinking. Lucy stood motionless, gazing into the gloom where he had vanished. Her heart seemed to take a great drop. Shivering, she went into the tent.

There she swiftly put a few knots of wood into the stove, set the damper, blew out the lamp, and hurriedly undressed for bed.

The darkness and the blankets were comforting. A faint crackle of burning wood broke the silence and tiny streaks of firelight played upon the tent walls.

"It was for Mertie he held me in his arms," whispered Lucy.

And she had taken it for herself. His gratitude had betrayed her. Lucy realized now that if her arms had been free she would have lifted them round his neck. She had not known what she was doing. But now she knew she loved him. Edd

Denmeade, backwoodsman, wild-bee hunter! She suffered no shame in that. Indeed there was a hidden voice deep within her ready to ring the truth. She had sought to save and she had lost herself.

Lucy lay wide-eyed long after Clara slept, nestled with an arm around her, as in childish days. The night wind moaned through the forest, mournful, wild, lonely, as if voicing the inscrutable cry in Lucy's soul.

She had no regrets. She had burned her bridges behind her. The visit to Felix had clarified in mind all the perplexing doubts and dreads about the past. She and Clara had not had the training, the love, and the home life happily. All her childhood she had suffered under the ban of position; all her girlhood had been poisoned by longings she could not attain, ignominies she could not avoid. She had grown to young womanhood terribly sensitive to the class distinctions so ruthlessly adhered to in all cultivated communities. She was old enough now to realize that true worth always was its own reward, and seldom failed of ultimate appreciation. But city life, multitudes of people, the social codes had all palled upon her. Never again could she live under their influence. Her victory over environment had come too late. The iron had entered Lucy's soul.

It was good to find herself at last. Every hour since her return to the Denmeades had been fraught with stirrings and promptings and misgivings now wholly clear to her. The wild-bee hunter, in his brotherly love, had hugged away her vanity and blindness. Poor groping Edd! It was what he was that had made her love him. Not what she wanted to make him! Yet the cold sensation of shock round her heart seemed to warm at the consciousness of his growth. Before her coming to the wilderness home of the Denmeades had he, or any of the children, ever thought of God? Lucy realized that the higher aspect of her work was missionary. Always she had been marked for sacrifice. In this hour of humility she delved out her acceptance.

Her sister slept on, with that little hand clinging close even in slumber. Lucy listened to her gentle breathing and felt the soft undulation of her breast. The mystery of life was slowly dawning upon Lucy. She had no wish to change what was, and the prayer she mutely voiced eliminated herself.

Outside the night wind rose, from mournful sough to weird roar. A hound bayed off in the forest. A mouse or ground squirrel rustled in the brush under the floor of the tent. The flicker of the fire died out. A frosty air blew in the window. These things were realities, strong in their importunity for peace and joy of living. It was only the ghosts of the past that haunted the black midnight hour.

12

DENMEADE'S prediction was verified. Before noon of the next day the younger members of the neighboring families began to ride in, nonchalant, casual, as if no unusual event had added significance to their visit. Then when another string headed in from the Cedar Ridge trail Denmeade exploded.

"Wal, you're goin' to be stormed," he said, warningly, to the bride and groom. "Shore it'll be a Jasper, too."

"For the land's sake!" exclaimed his good wife. "They'll eat us out of house an' home. An' us not ready!"

"Now, ma, I gave you a hunch yestiddy," replied Denmeade. "Reckon you can have dinner late. Mrs. Claypool will help you an' Allie."

"But that young outfit will drive me wild," protested Mrs. Denmeade.

"Never mind, ma. I'll take care of them," put in Edd. "Fact is I've a bee tree only half a mile from home. I've been savin' it. I'll rustle the whole caboodle up there an' make them pack honey back."

"Mertie will want to stay home, dressed all up," averred his mother.

"Wal, she can't. We'll shore pack her along, dress or no dress."

Early in the afternoon Edd presented himself before Lucy's tent and announced:

"Girls, we're packin' that spoony couple away from home for a spell. The women folks got to have elbow room to fix up a big dinner. Whole country goin' to storm Mert!"

Clara appeared at the door, eager and smiling. "Edd, this storm means a crowd coming to celebrate?"

"Shore. But a storm is an uninvited crowd. They raise hell. Between us, I'm tickled. I never thought Mertie would get a storm. She wasn't any too well liked. But Bert's the best boy in this country."

"*Maybe* he is," retorted Clara, archly. "I know a couple of boys left. . . . Edd, give us a hunch what to wear?"

"Old clothes," he grinned. "An' some kind of veil or net to keep from gettin' stung. Wild bees don't like a crowd. An' Sam Johnson thinks he's a bee tamer. This tree I'm goin' to cut is a hummer. Full of sassy bees. An' there's goin' to be some fun."

Lucy and Clara joined the formidable group of young people waiting in the yard, all armed with buckets. Lucy sensed an amiable happy spirit wholly devoid of the vexatious bantering common to most gatherings of these young people.

Marriage was the consummation of their hopes, dreams, endeavors. Every back-woods youth looked forward to a homestead and a wife.

Mertie assuredly wore the bright silk dress, and ribbons on her hair, and white stockings, and low shoes not meant for the woods. Bert, however, had donned blue-jeans overalls.

The merry party set out, with Edd in the lead, and the gay children, some dozen or more, bringing up the rear. Edd carried an ax over his shoulder and a huge assortment of different-sized buckets on his arm. He led out of the clearing, back of the cabin, into the pine woods so long a favorite haunt of Lucy's, and up the gradual slope. The necessities of travel through the forest strung the party mostly into single file. Lucy warmed to the occasion. It *was* happy. How good to be alive! The golden autumn sunlight, the flame of color in the trees, the fragrant brown aisles of the forest, the flocks of birds congregating for their annual pilgrimage south—all these seemed new and sweet to Lucy. They roused emotion that the streets and houses of the city could not reach. Bert might have been aware of the company present, but he showed no sign of it. He saw nothing except Mertie. Half the time he carried her, lifting her over patches of dust, logs, and rough ground. Only where the mats of pine needles offered clean and easy travel did he let her down, and then he still kept his arm round her. Mertie was no burden for his sturdy strength. He swung her easily up and down, as occasion suited him. Lucy was struck by his naturalness.

Mertie, however, could not forget herself. She posed. She accepted. She bestowed. She was the beginning and the end of this great day. Yet despite exercise of the ineradicable trait of her nature, the romance of her marriage, the fact of her being possessed, had changed her. She had awakened. She saw Bert now as he actually was, and she seemed reaping the heritage of a true woman's feelings.

Aside from these impressions Lucy received one that caused her to sigh. Clara reacted strangely to sight of Mertie and Bert. Lucy caught a glimpse of the mocking half-smile that Clara's face used to wear. No doubt this bride and groom procession through the woods, the open love-making, oblivious at least on Bert's part, brought back stinging memories to Clara.

Edd led the gay party out of the woods into a beautiful canyon, wide and uneven, green and gold with growths, dotted by huge gray rocks, and trees. A dry stream bed wound by stony steps up the canyon. Edd followed this bowlder-strewn road for a few hundred yards, then climbed to a wide bench. Maples and sycamores spread scattered patches of shade over this canyon glade. A riot of autumn colors almost stunned the eyesight. The thick grass was green, the heavy carpet of ferns brown.

"Wal, there she is," said Edd, pointing to a gnarled white-barked tree perhaps a hundred paces distant. "First sycamore I ever found bees in. It's hollow at the trunk where she goes in. I reckon she's a hummer. Now you-all hang back a ways while I look her over.''

Edd strode toward the sycamore, and his followers approached, mindful of his admonition. They got close enough, however, to see a swarm of bees passing to and fro from the dark hollow of the tree trunk. Edd's perfect sang-froid probably deceived the less experienced boys. He circled the sycamore, gazed up into the hollow, and made what appeared to be a thorough examination. Sam Johnson showed that he was holding back only through courtesy. The remarks of the boys behind him were not calculated to make him conservative. Sadie Purdue and Amy Claypool expressed diverse entreaties, the former asking him to cut down the bee tree and the latter begging him to keep away from it. Lucy had an idea that Amy knew something about bees.

Presently Edd returned from his survey and drew the "honey-bucket outfit," as he called them, back into the shade of a maple. Mertie draped herself and beautiful dress over a clean rock, as if she, instead of the bees, was the attraction. Lucy sensed one of the interesting undercurrents of backwoods life working in those young men. Edd's position was an enviable one, as far as bees were concerned. This was a bee day. Sam Johnson could not possibly have kept himself out of the foreground. There were several boys from Cedar Ridge, including Bert, who ran a close second to Sam. On the other hand, the boys who inhabited this high country, especially Gerd Claypool, appeared unusually prone to let the others have the stage. Joe Denmeade wore an inscrutable expression and had nothing to say. Edd was master of ceremonies, and as he stood before the boys, his ax over his shoulder, Lucy conceived a strong suspicion that he was too bland, too drawling, too kind to be absolutely honest. Edd was up to a trick. Lucy whispered her suspicions to Clara, and that worthy whispered back: "I'm wise. Why, a child could see through that *hombre!* But isn't he immense?''

"Sam, I reckon you ought to be the one to chop her down,'' Edd was saying, after a rather elaborate preamble. "Course it ought to fall to Bert, seein' he's the reason for this here storm party. But I reckon you know more about wild bees, an' you should be boss. Shore it'd be good if you an' Bert tackled the tree together.''

"I'll allow myself aboot three minutes' choppin' to fetch that sycamore,'' replied Sam. "But Bert can help if he likes.''

"Somebody gimme an ax,'' said Bert, prowling around. Dick Denmeade had the second ax, which he gladly turned over to Bert.

"Bert, I don't want you gettin' all stung up,'' protested Mertie.

"No bees would sting me to-day,'' replied Bert, grandly.

"Don't you fool yourself,'' she retorted.

"Aw, she's tame as home bees,'' interposed Edd. "Besides, there's been some heavy frost. Bees get loggy along late in the fall. Reckon nobody'll get stung. If she wakes up we can run.''

"I'm a-rarin' for that honey,'' declared Sam, jerking the ax from Edd. ''Come on, Bert. Start your honeymoon by bein' boss.''

That remark made a lion out of the bridegroom, while eliciting howls and giggles from his admirers. Sam strode toward the sycamore and Bert followed.

"Reckon we-all better scatter a little,'' said the wily Edd, and he punched Gerd Claypool in the ribs. Gerd, it appeared, was doubled up in noiseless contortions.

"Serve Sam just right,'' declared Sadie, ''for bein' so darn smart. He never chopped down a bee tree in his life.''

"Well, if I know anythin' eh'll never try another,'' added Amy. "Oh, Edd Denmeade, you're an awful liar. Sayin' wild bees won't sting!''

"Shore Sam wanted to cut her down. He asked me back home,'' declared Edd.

Some of the party stood their ground, notably Mertie, who rather liked the clean dry rock. Edd gravitated toward Lucy and Clara, presently leading them unobtrusively back toward some brush.

"Dog-gone!'' he whispered, chokingly, when he was out of earshot of the others. "Chance of my life! . . . Sam's cut a few bee trees in winter, when the bees were froze. . . . But, gee! these wild bees are mad as hornets. I got stung on the ear, just walkin' round. She's been worried by yellow-jackets. . . . Now there's goin' to be some fun. She'll be a hummer. . . . Girls, put on whatever you fetched along an' be ready to duck into this brush.''

"Edd, you're as bad as a cowboy,'' said Clara, producing a veil.

"Looks like great fun for us, but how about the bees?'' rejoined Lucy.

"There you go, sister. Always thinking about the under dog! . . . Edd, do you know, I can't see how anyone could help loving Lucy,'' retorted Clara, mischievously.

"Shore. I reckon nobody does,'' drawled Edd. "Wal, Sam's begun to larrup it into my sycamore. *Now watch!*''

Sam had sturdily attacked the tree, while the more cautious Bert had cut several boughs, evidently to thresh off bees. Scarcely had he reached the objective spot when Sam jerked up spasmodically as if kicked from behind.

"Beat 'em off!'' he yelled.

Then, as the valiant Bert dropped his ax, and began to thresh with the boughs, Sam redoubled his energies at the chopping. He might not have possessed much knowledge about wild bees, but he could certainly handle an ax. Quick and hard rang his blows. The sycamore was indeed rotten, for it sounded hollow and crackling, and long dusty strips fell aside.

Lucy stole a glance at Edd. He was manifestly in the grip of a frenzied glee.

Never before had Lucy seen him so. He was shaking all over; his face presented a wonderful study of features in convulsions; his big hands opened and shut. All at once he burst out in stentorian yell: "Wow! There she comes!"

Lucy flashed her glance back toward the axman, just in time to see a small black cloud, like smoke, puff out of the hollow of the tree and disintegrate into thin air. Sam let out a frantic yell, and dropping the ax he plunged directly toward his admiring comrades.

"You darn fool!" roared Edd. "Run the other way!"

But Sam, as if pursued by the furies, sprang, leaped, wrestled, hopped, flew, flapping his hands like wings and yelling hoarsely. Bert suddenly became as if possessed of a thousand devils, and he raced like a streak, waving his two green boughs over his head, till he plunged over a bank into the brush.

Some of the Cedar Ridge boys had approached a point within a hundred feet of the sycamore. Suddenly their howls of mirth changed to excited shouts, and they broke into a run. Unfortunately, they were not on the moment chivalrously mindful of the girls.

"Run for your lives!" screamed Amy Claypool.

Lucy found herself being rushed into the bushes by Edd, who had also dragged Clara. He was laughing so hard he could not speak. He fell down and rolled over. Clara had an attack of laughter that seemed half hysterical. "Look! Look!" she cried.

Lucy was more frightened than amused, but from the shelter of the bushes she peered forth, drawing aside her veil so she could see better. She was in time to see the bright silk dress that incased Mertie soaring across the ground like a spread-winged bird. Mertie was noted for her fleetness of foot. Sadie Purdue, owing to a rather short stout figure, could not run very well. Sam, by accident or design, had fled in her direction. It did not take a keen eye to see the whirling dotted circle of bees he brought with him. Some of them sped like bullets ahead of him to attack Sadie. Shrieking, she ran away from Sam as though he were a pestilence. She was the last to flee out of sight.

Presently Edd sat up, wet-faced and spent from the energy of his emotions.

"Reckon I've played hob—but dog-gone!—it was fun," he said. "Shore Sam's a bee hunter! I'll bet he'll look like he had measles. . . . Did you see Sadie gettin' stung? She was that smart. Haw! Haw! Haw!"

Joe came crawling to them through the bushes. For once his face was not quiet, intent. He showed his relationship to Edd.

"Say, Sam will be hoppin' mad," he said.

"He shore was hoppin' when last I seen him," replied Edd. "Wal, I reckon I'll have to finish the job. You girls stay right here, for a while, anyhow."

Whereupon Edd pulled a rude hood from his pocket and drew it over his head and tight under his chin. It was made of burlap and had two rounded pieces of window screen sewed in to serve as eyeholes. Then putting his gloves on he got up and tramped out toward the sycamore. Lucy left Clara with Bert, and slipped along under the bushes until she reached the end nearest the tree. Here she crouched to watch. She could see the bees swarm round Edd, apparently without disturbing him in the least. He picked up the ax, and with swift powerful strokes he soon chopped through on one side of the hollow place, so that the other side broke, letting the tree down with a splitting crash. After the dust cleared away Lucy saw him knocking the trunk apart. The swarm of bees spread higher and wider over his head. Lucy could hear the angry buzz. She felt sorry for them. How ruthless men were! The hive had been destroyed; the winter's food of the bees would be stolen.

"Hey, Joe!" called Edd. "Round up that outfit to pack honey back home. There's more here than we got buckets to hold. Tell them I'll fetch it part way, so they won't get stung no more."

Lucy caught glimpses of the members of the party collecting a goodly safe distance away, along the edge of the timber. Judging by gestures and the sound of excited voices coming faintly, Lucy concluded that the storm party was divided in its attitude toward Edd. Sadie Purdue evidently was in a tantrum, the brunt of which fell upon Sam. Amy's high sweet laugh pealed out. Presently the girls were seen entering the forest, no doubt on their way back to the cabin; the boys showed indications of standing by Edd, at least to the extent of waiting for him to collect the honey.

Lucy saw him filling the buckets. He used a small wooden spoon or spade with which he reamed the honey out of the hollow log. She was intensely eager to see this bee hive and Edd's work at close hand, but felt it wise to remain under cover. The screams of the girls who had been stung were a rather potent inhibition of curiosity.

The honey had a grayish-yellow cast and a deep amber color, from which Lucy deducted that one was the comb, the other the honey. When Edd had filled four buckets he took them up and proceeded to carry them toward the waiting boys. A number of bees kept him company. How grotesque he looked with that homemade hood over his head!

"Hey! you better lay low," he called to Lucy, seeing her peeping out of her brushy covert, "unless you want your pretty little pink nose stung!"

"Edd Denmeade, my nose isn't little—or pink!" protested Lucy.

"Wal, no matter; it shore will be pink if you don't watch out. Didn't you get stung on it once?"

Halfway between the bee tree and the boys Edd set the buckets down on a rock, and cutting some brush he covered them with it. Then he shouted:

"Pack these home, you storm-party honey suckers!"

Upon his return to the fallen sycamore he scraped up a bundle of dead grass

ZANE GREY

and sticks, and kindled a fire, then added green boughs to make a heavy smoke. Lucy saw him vigorously slap his back and his legs, from which action she surmised that he too was getting stung. Next with two leafy boughs he made an onslaught on the whirling shining mill-wheel of bees. He broke that wheel, and either killed or scattered most of the swarm. Then he proceeded to fill more buckets, which he carried away as before. Meanwhile Joe and Gerd Claypool had come for the first buckets.

Lucy crawled back through the bushes to where she had left Clara. She found her prone on the grass, her chin propped on her hands, musingly watching the proceedings.

"Funny how we are," she said. "It's a long time since I felt so good over anything. Sam and Sadie were immense. . . . Pride—and conceit, too—go before a fall!"

"You remember I was stung on the nose by one of these wild bees," replied Lucy. "It hurts terribly."

They remained in the shade and security of this covert until Edd had filled all his buckets.

"Hello, girls! Go back through the bushes to the bank, an' get down," he called. "Wait for us below."

Lucy and Clara scrambled away into the thicket and down into the stream bed, which they followed to the woods. Joe and Gerd and Dick came along laden with heavy buckets, and rather harassed by a few persistent bees.

"Keep away from us," cried Lucy. "I've been initiated into the wild-bee fraternity."

"But Clara hasn't," replied Joe.

"Young man, if you know when you're well off, you'll not lead any wild bees to me," warned Clara, gathering up her skirts ready to flee into the woods. She was smiling, yet earnest. How pretty she looked, her eyes flashing, her brown cheeks flushed, her blue veil flying round her golden hair! Lucy saw what Joe saw.

Next Edd came striding out of the willows, down into the gully. He carried four buckets, all manifestly laden. He had removed his hood, and his face was wet with sweat and wreathed in smiles.

"Run along ahead till she gets tired followin' me," he called to the girls.

They were not slow to act upon his advice, yet did not get so far ahead that they could not see the boys coming. The forest seemed so shady and cool after the hot sunny open.

"Why does Edd speak of bees as she?" queried Clara, curiously.

"He told me once he had captured and tamed queen bees, and after that always called bees she, whether collectively or individually. It is funny."

"He'll be making you queen bee of his hive some day," said Clara, tantalizingly.

"Oh, will he? It requires the consent of the queen, I imagine. . . . As to queen-bee hives, Joe's is being built, I hear."

Clara squeezed Lucy's arm and cringed close to her, as if to hide a shamed or happy face. "Oh, what will become of us? . . . When I don't *think,* I'm full of some new kind of joy. When I *remember,* I'm wretched."

"Clara, we are two babes lost in the woods," declared Lucy, half sadly. "But if you must think, do it intelligently. We could be worse off."

"I love it here," answered Clara, swiftly, with a flash of passion.

Then Edd's halloo halted them. Presently Lucy had opportunity to see wild honey fresh from the hive. The buckets were full of the yellow combs and amber honey, all massed together, in which numbers of bees had been drowned.

"Shore it's got to be strained," explained Edd.

"What'll become of the bees—those you didn't kill?" she inquired.

"Wal, now, I wish you hadn't asked that," complained Edd. "Shore you always hit at the sufferers. . . . Lucy, I hate to treat a bee tree like we did this one. But I can't capture an' tame the old swarms. They're too wild. I have to destroy them. Sometimes I burn them out. . . . She'll hang round that sycamore, an' starve to death or freeze. It's too bad. I reckon I'm no better than the yellow-jackets."

That bee-tree episode had taken the younger element of the storm party away from the Denmeade home for the greater part of the afternoon, a fact for which Mrs. Denmeade was devoutly thankful. She and Allie, with the kind assistance of the Claypool women, prepared on short notice an adequate feast for this formidable array of uninvited guests.

Lucy learned this, and much more, upon her arrival at the cabin. Mertie had torn the bright silk dress and was inconsolable. She did not seem to mind so much the sundry stings she had sustained. But Sadie Purdue almost disrupted the hilarious and joyful tone of the occasion. She had been severely stung on hands and arms and face. Sam Johnson, however, was the one who had suffered most. All the members of that expedition, except Lucy and Clara, had reason to vow vengeance upon Edd.

"Oh, wait, you wild hunter of bees! Wait till you're married!" was the reiterated threat.

"Shore I'm safe," drawled Edd. "No girl would ever throw herself away on me."

Sam took his punishment like a man, and made up for the ravings of his *fiancée.* She had the grace, presently, to get over her fury. And by supper-time, when Mertie was won back to a happy appreciation of the honor of having the largest storm party ever known in that country, the jarring notes were as if they had never been.

All the chair, bench, and porch space was necessary to seat this merry company. It was quite impossible for Lucy to keep track of what followed. But she had never seen the like of that dinner. Uproarious, even violent, it yet gave expression to the joy and significance of marriage in that wilderness.

White mule flowed freely, but in marked contrast with its effect at the dances, it added only to the mirth and the noise. After dinner the young people nearly tore the cabin down with their onslaughts upon the bride and groom, the former of whom they hugged and kissed, and the latter mauled. Dancing was not on this program. Then, evidently, for the young backwoodsmen present, it was a natural climax to fly from their felicitations of the bride to salutations to the possible brides-to-be in that gathering. They were like young bears.

Lucy and Clara fled to the security of their tent, and refused to come out. Certain it was that both of them were more than amused and frightened. Manifestly a storm party on a bride was regarded as an unexampled opportunity.

"Whew!" gasped Clara, with wide eyes on Lucy. "I thought cowboys were wild. But alongside these fellows they're tame."

"Deliver—me!" panted Lucy. "Almost it'd be—safer to be—in Mertie's boots!"

The celebration, however, turned out to be as short as it had been intense. Before dark the older people were riding down the lane, calling back their merry good-nights, and not long after the boys and girls followed. Soon the homestead of the Denmeades was as quiet as ever; and a little later, when Lucy peeped out, yard and cabin were shrouded in the blackness of the melancholy autumn night.

13

It was midwinter. Lucy's tent was cozy and warm, softly colored with its shaded lamplight, falling on bear rugs and bright blankets, on the many paper pictures. The Clara that sat there beside the little stove, occupied with needlework, was not the Clara who had arrived at Cedar Ridge one memorable day last summer. Lucy was having leisure for books.

The tent seemed to be full of the faint fragrance of juniper, and that came from the wood which the little stove burned so avidly. Lucy was wont to say that of all Clara's homestead accomplishments that of feeding wood to a fire was what she did best and liked most. "Maybe I'll have to *cho*' wood myself some day. I could do worse," was Clara's enigmatic reply.

Outside, the snow seeped down, rustling like the fall of leaves on dry grass, floating softly against the window. No mournful wail of wind broke the dead silence. The homestead of the Denmeades was locked in winter. Lucy and Clara had long since grown used to it. For a while they had suffered from cold, but that was owing to their susceptibility rather than severe weather. Denmeade's heavy bear rugs on the floor had added much to the comfort of the tent. The girls wore woolen sweaters and no longer noticed the cold. At ten o'clock they went to bed, enjoying to the utmost this most important factor of outdoor life. Night after night, for weeks, they had spent like this, reading, sewing, studying, writing, talking, and then sleeping.

The zero mornings had put them to the test. With the fire long dead, the cold was practically the same inside as outside. They had taken turn about kindling a fire, and the one whose morning it was to lie snug and warm in bed while the other slipped out into the icy air seldom failed to tease and crow.

When the tent was warm they got up and dressed, and made coffee or tea, and cooked some breakfast. No matter how deep the new-fallen snow, there was always a path shoveled from their tent to the cabin, Edd and Joe vying with each other to see who could beat the other at this task. Lucy's work now was confined to instructing the children, and Clara was studying hard to enable her to take Mr. Jenks's place as teacher of the school. The afternoons were usually sunny and clear. After a snowstorm the warm sun melted the snow away in a few days. But there were unexampled opportunities to tramp and romp and play in the snow, things in which the girls found much pleasure. They had been born and brought up in a snowless country, where the summers were torrid and the winters pleasant.

The Denmeades, however, might as well have been snowed in. Lucy marveled at this, and came to understand it as a feature of backwoods life. The men kept the fires burning and fed the stock, outside of which they had nothing, or thought they had nothing, to do. The women cooked, sewed, and washed, almost as actively as in summer. No visitors called any more on Sundays. They saw no outsiders. Once a week Dick or Joe would ride down to Johnson's for the mail, or for supplies that had been sent for. It seemed a lonely, peaceful, unproductive existence.

Edd, being the eldest of the Denmeade boys, had received the least schooling, a fact he keenly deplored, and through these winter days he laboriously pored over the books Lucy gave him. Joe was the keenest of the children, as well as the quietest, and he seconded Edd in this pursuit of knowledge.

Lucy and Clara had supper with the Denmeades, which they endeavored to serve before dark. Sometimes, when the meal was late, the light in the kitchen

was so dim they could hardly see to eat. After supper the children and young
people would make a rush into the other cabin where Denmeade kept a huge log
or stump burning in the open fireplace. Mertie was gone, and her absence seemed
a benefit. Allie and Joe were the thoughtful ones who helped Mrs. Denmeade.
Seldom was a lamp lighted until Edd stamped in to resort to his books.

Every time the door was opened the dogs would try to slip in, and always one
or more of them succeeded, and occupied a warm place in front of the fire. The
children played until put·to bed. Uncle Bill was not long in climbing to his bed
in the attic. Denmeade smoked his pipe and sat gazing at the blazing log. How
many hours of his life must have been spent so! Lucy and Clara always passed
part of the early evening hours in this living room. Seldom or never did they
have a moment alone with the boys. It was a family gathering, this after-supper
vigil in front of the big fire.

Denmeade typified the homesteader of that high altitude. Winter was a time
of waiting. Almost he was like a bear. Spring, summer, fall were his active
seasons. The snow, the sleet, the icy winds of winter shut him in.

Lucy counteracted this growing habit in the boys. She convinced them that
winter was the time to improve the mind and to learn something of what was
going on in the outside world. Her success in this she considered equal to any
of her achievements here. The old folks, of course, could not be changed; and
Lucy confined herself to the children. Many times she thought of how all over
the wild parts of the west, in high districts, children and young people were
wasting golden hours, with nothing to do but what their parents had done before
them. What a splendid work she would accomplish if she could make known
the benefits of home instruction! But it really did not seem like work. Thus the
winter days and nights passed.

The coming of spring was marked by Allie Denmeade's marriage to Gerd
Claypool. These young people, wise in their generation, invited everybody to
their wedding, which took place in Cedar Ridge. Lucy and Clara remained at
home with the children.

March brought surprisingly fine weather, the mornings and evenings cold, but
the middle of the day sunny and warm. Soon the wet red soil dried out. The
men, liberated from the confines of winter, were busy taking up the tasks that
had been interrupted by the first fall of snow. One of these was the completion
of Joe's cabin. Lucy, using a walk with the children as excuse, climbed the mesa
trail to see the men at work. Clara did not want to go. She was more studious
and complex than ever, yet seemed strangely, dreamily happy.

The mesa, with its open glades, its thickets of red manzanita, its clumps of
live oak, and giant junipers and lofty pines, manifested a difference hard to
define. Lucy thought it had to do with spring. The birds and squirrels and turkeys
voiced the joyfulness of the season.

Joe's homestead edifice was a two-cabin affair, similar to that of the Denmeades. Lucy particularly liked the clean, freshly cut pine and its fragrant odor. She urged Joe to build in several closets and to insist on windows, and kitchen shelves, and a number of improvements new to the cabin of the backwoodsman.

"Joe, are you going to live here alone?" queried Lucy.

"On an' off, while I prove up on my homesteadin' patent," he replied. "You see, I have to put in so many days here for three years before the government will give me the land."

His frank answer relieved Lucy, who had of late been subtly influenced by a strangeness, an aloofness, in Clara, which mood somehow she had attributed to Joe's infatuation for her. The boy had no pretense. His soul was as clear as his gray eyes. Lucy was compelled to believe that the erecting of this cabin was solely to forestall a threatened invasion of the mesa by other homesteaders.

On the way home Lucy stopped awhile at the beautiful site Edd had selected for his cabin. She found that thought of the place, during the fall and winter months, had somehow endeared it to her. Long communion with the secret affection of her heart had brought happiness with resignation. She knew where she stood; and daily she gathered strength to bear, to serve, to go on, to find a wonderful good in her ordeal.

The forest had wrought incalculable change in her. It was something she felt rush over her thrillingly when she approached the green wall of pines and entered it, as if going into her home. She thought more actively, she worked better, she developed more under its influence than in the city. This she knew to be because the old bitter social feud under which her youth had oppressed was not present here. Lucy was ashamed of that relief, but she could never change it.

As she was soon to go to the Claypools to take up her work there, Lucy knew it might be long before she had the strange, inexplicable joy of dreaming here in this spot of perfect solitude and wild beauty. So while the children played at keeping house among the bears and turkeys, she gazed around her and listened and felt. She was quite at the mercy of unknown forces and she had ceased to beat and bruise her heart against them, as might have a bird against the bars of its cage. Above all, there came to her the great simple fact of a harmony with this environment. She could not resist it and she ceased to try.

Mr. Jenks arrived at the Johnsons' in the latter part of March and attended the meeting of the school board. He wanted to turn over the teaching to Clara, but in case she did not accept the position he would be glad to remain another summer. Denmeade returned from that board meeting to place a proposition squarely before Clara. And in his own words it was this: "Reckon we don't want to change teachers so often. Every schoolmarm we've had just up an' married one of the boys. Wal, if you will agree to teach two years, whether you get married or not, we'll shore be glad to let you have the job.''

"I give my word," replied Clara, with a firmness Lucy knew was a guerdon that the promise would be kept.

What struck Lucy markedly on the moment was the fact that Clara did not disavow any possibility of marriage.

The deal was settled then and there, and later, when the girls had gone to the seclusion of their tent, Clara evinced a deep emotion.

"Lucy, I'll be independent now," she said. "I can pay my debt . . . I—I need money——''

"My dear, you don't owe *me* any money," interposed Lucy, "if that's what you mean."

Clara's reply was more evasive than frank, again rousing in Lucy the recurrence of a surprise and a vague dread. But she dismissed them from her consciousness.

"We'll have to settle another thing, too," said Lucy. "Once before you hinted you didn't want to go to Claypool's with me."

"I don't, but I'll go if you insist," rejoined Clara.

"If you will be happier here than with me, by all means stay," replied Lucy, in a hurt tone.

"Don't misunderstand, Lucy, darling," cried Clara, embracing her. "I'm used to this place—these Denmeades. It's like a sanctuary after——'' She broke off falteringly. "It will be hard enough for me to teach school, let alone live among strangers. . . . And aren't you coming back here in the fall?''

"I don't know. It depends," answered Lucy, dubiously. "Well, it's settled then. You will live here. I suppose you'll ride horseback to and fro from the schoolhouse. That would be fine."

"Yes. Joe or Dick will ride with me every day, so I'll never be alone."

Lucy turned away her face and busied herself with papers on her table.

"Clara, have you anything particular you want to tell me?''

"Why—no," came the constrained and low reply.

Lucy divined then that there was something Clara could not tell her, and it revived the old worry.

Edd Denmeade, alone of all the family, did not take kindly to Lucy's going to the Claypools. The others, knowing that Clara was to continue to live with them and that Lucy would probably come back in the fall, were glad to propitiate their neighbors at so little a loss.

"But, Edd, why do you disapprove?" Lucy demanded, when she waylaid him among his beehives. She did not want to lose her good influence over him. She wanted very much more from him than she dared to confess.

"I reckon I've a good many reasons," returned Edd.

"Oh, you have? Well, tell me just one," said Lucy.

"Wal, the Claypools live right on the trail from Sprall's to Cedar Ridge."

"Sprall's! . . . What of it?" demanded Lucy, nonplussed.

"Bud Sprall rides that trail."

"Suppose he does. How can it concern me?" rejoined Lucy, growing irritated.

"Wal, it concerns you more'n you think. Bud told in Cedar Ridge how he was layin' for you."

"I don't understand. What did he mean?"

"Lucy, that *hombre* isn't above ropin' you an' packin' you off up over the Rim, where he holds out with his red-faced cowboy pard."

"Nonsense! The day of the outlaw is past, Edd. I haven't the least fear of Bud Sprall. Indeed, so little that I intend some day to take up my work with the Spralls."

Wheeling from his work, he loomed over her, and fastening a brawny hand in her blouse he drew her close. His eyes flashed a steely fire.

"You're not goin' to do anythin' of the kind," he said, darkly.

"Who'll prevent me?" queried Lucy.

"If you go to Sprall's I'll pack you back if I have to tie you on a hoss."

"You—will?" Lucy's voice broke in her fury.

"Shore you bet I will. Reckon you haven't forgot that dance I made you go to. I wasn't mad then. Wal, I'm as mad as hell now."

"Why do you presume to interfere with my work?"

"Can you crawl in a hog-pen without gettin' dirty?" he demanded. "I reckon your work is somethin' fine an' good. I don't begrudge that to Sprall's. But you can't go there, unless just in daytime, an' then with somebody. . . . You think I'm jealous. Wal, I'm not. Ask pa an' ma about this Sprall idea of yours."

"But, Edd, weren't you somewhat like Bud Sprall once? Didn't you tell me I helped you? Might I not do the same for——"

Edd shoved her away with violence.

"Ahuh! So you want to work the same on Bud? . . . Wal, the day you make up to him as you did to me I'll go back to white mule. . . . An' I'll kill him!"

As he stalked away, grim and dark, Lucy shook off a cold clutch of fear and remorse, and ran after him.

"Edd! You must not talk so—so terribly!" she cried, appealingly. "You seem to accuse me of—of something. . . . Oh! that I haven't been fair to you!"

"Wal, have you, now?" he queried, glaring down at her.

"Indeed—I—I think so."

"Aw, you're lyin'. Maybe you're as deep as your sister. Shore I'd never deny you'd been an angel to my family. But you worked different on me. I was only a wild-bee hunter. You made me see what I was—made me hate my ignorance an' habits. You let me be with you, many an' many a time. You talked for hours an' read to me, an' worked with me, all the time with your sweet, sly girl ways.

An' I changed. I don't know how I changed, but it's so. You're like the queen of the bees. . . . All you told me love meant I've come to know. I'd do any an' all of those things you once said love meant. . . . But if you work the same on Bud Sprall you'll be worse than Sadie Purdue. She had sweet, purry cat ways, an' she liked to be smoothed. That was shore where Sadie didn't cheat.''

"Cheat! . . . Edd Denmeade, do you mean—you think I made you love me— just to save you from your drinking, fighting habits?'' queried Lucy, very low.

"No, I reckon I don't mean that. You just used your—yourself. Your smiles an' sweet laugh—your talk—your pretty white dresses—your hands—lettin' me see you—lettin' me be with you—keepin' me from other girls—workin' on me with yourself. . . . Now didn't you? Be honest.''

"Yes. You make me see it. I did,'' confessed Lucy, bravely. "I'm not sorry— for I—I——''

"Wal, you needn't figure me wrong,'' he interrupted. "I'm not sorry, either. Reckon for my family's sake I'm glad. Shore I have no hopes of ever bein' anythin' but a lonely wild-bee hunter. . . . But I couldn't stand your workin' that on Bud Sprall.''

"You misunderstood me, Edd,'' returned Lucy. "I couldn't have done what you imagined. Now I fear I can never do anything. . . . You have made me ashamed. Made me doubt myself.''

"Wal, I reckon that won't be so awful bad for you,'' he drawled, almost caustically, and left her.

This interview with Edd befell just before Lucy's time of departure to the Claypools, most inopportunely and distressingly for her. Edd had declared a great, and what he held a hopeless, love for her. Lucy suffered an exaltation embittered by doubt, distress, even terror. The sheer fact that he loved her was a tremendous shock. Not that she had not known of his affection, but that he had arisen out of his crudeness to her ideal of love! She could not overcome her pride in her power to uplift him. It was sweet, strange, sustaining, yet fraught with terrors for her. It forced her into a position where she must find out the truth and bigness of love herself. She could not trust this new elemental self, this transformation of Lucy Watson in the wilderness. She must have long lonely hours—days—nights to fight the problem. What terrified her was the memory of that beautiful mesa homestead and the thought of Edd Denmeade's love. Together they threatened to storm her heart.

Next morning Lucy was ready early for her departure. She had entirely over-looked what kind of an occasion it might be, but she soon discovered that it was not to be joyous. The children were pitiful in their grief. Lucy felt as if she had died. They were inconsolable. Mary was the only one of them who bade her good-by. Mrs. Denmeade said she was glad for the sake of the Claypools.

"Wal, Miss Lucy," said Denmeade, with his rugged grin, "reckon by the time you get through with the Claypools an' Johnsons you'll find us all gone to seed an' needin' you powerful bad."

"Then I'll be happy to come back," replied Lucy.

Clara, however, gave Lucy the most thought-provoking surprise of this leave-taking. Evidently she had cried before getting up, and afterward she was pale and silent. When Edd and Joe arrived with saddle horses and the burros, Lucy, after taking out her baggage to be packed, returned to find Clara had broken down. Lucy could not understand this sudden weakness. It was not like Clara. They had a most affecting scene, which left Lucy shaken and uncertain. But she had the sweet assurance of Clara's love and reliance upon her. For the rest her sister's emotion seemed a betrayal. Lucy felt that in Clara's clinging hands, her streaming hidden eyes, her incoherent words. But in the few moments of stress left her before departure she could neither comfort Clara nor find out any adequate reason for this collapse.

"Hey!" called Edd, for the third time. "Reckon the burros are rarin' to go, if you ain't."

Lucy left Clara face down on the bed. Before she closed the door she called back, softly: "Don't be afraid to trust me with your troubles. I'll share them. . . . Good-by."

Lucy had seen the Claypool clearing, but she had never been inside the cabins. There were two families and many children, all assembled to greet her. Allie and Gerd still lived there, pending the clearing of a new tract of forest near by. They took charge of Lucy and led her to the little hut that had been constructed for her use. It had been built of slabs fresh from the sawmill, and these boards, being the outside cut from logs, still retained the bark. The structure was crude, yet picturesque, and it pleased Lucy. The inside was the yellow hue of newly cut pine, and it smelled strongly of the woods. Lucy had to laugh. What a wonderful little playhouse that would have been—if she were still a little girl! It had one window, small, with a wooden shutter, a table, and a closet, a shelf, and a built-in box couch, full of fragrant spruce. A deer skin with the fur uppermost lay on the floor. In the corner nearest the door was a triangular-shaped shelf, three feet above the floor, and under it sat a bucket full of water and on it a basin and dipper and lamp.

Allie and Gerd were plainly proud of this lodging house for Lucy.

"It's pretty far from the cabins," concluded Gerd, "but there's a big bar for your door. Nothin' can get in."

"I am delighted with it," declared Lucy.

Edd and Joe drove the pack burros over to Lucy's new abode and carried her bags in. She noted that Edd was so tall he could not stand upright in her little room.

"Wal, I reckon Gerd shore didn't figure on your entertainin' me," drawled Edd, with a grin.

"It's pretty nice," said Joe, practically. "With your rugs an' pictures, an' the way you fix things up, it'll be Jake."

Edd lingered a moment longer than the others at the door, his big black sombrero turning round in his hands.

"Wal, Lucy, do I go get me some white mule an' hunt up Bud Sprall?" he queried, with all his cool, easy complexity.

Lucy felt the sting of blood in her cheeks. When she stepped toward him, as he stood outside and below, one foot on the threshold, his face was about on a level with hers. Lucy looked straight into his eyes.

"No, you don't, unless you want me to call you again what hurt you so once."

"An' what's that? I disremember."

"You know!" she retorted, not quite sure of herself.

"Wal, I reckon you won't need do that," he said, simply. "I was only foolin' you about the white mule. I wouldn't drink again, no matter what you did. An' I reckon I wouldn't pick a fight, like I used to."

Lucy had been subjected to a wide range of emotions through the last twenty-four hours, and she was not prepared for a statement like this. It wrought havoc in her breast. In swift impulse she bent forward and kissed Edd on the cheek. Then as swiftly she drew back, slammed the door, and stood there trembling. She heard him gasp, and the jingle of his spurs, as slowly he walked away.

"There! I've played hob at last!" whispered Lucy. "But I don't care. . . . Now, my wild-bee hunter, I wonder if you'll take that for a Sadie Purdue trick?"

14

CONGENIAL work with happy, eager, simple people made the days speed by so swiftly that Lucy could not keep track of them.

She let six weeks and more pass before she gave heed to the message Clara sent from the schoolhouse by the Claypool children. From other sources Lucy learned that Clara was the best teacher ever employed by the school board. She was making a success of it, from a standpoint of both good for the pupils and occupation for herself.

Joe Denmeade happened to ride by Claypool's one day, and he stopped to see Lucy. Even in the few weeks since she left the Denmeades there seemed to be marked improvement in Joe, yet in a way she could hardly define. Something about him rang so true and manly.

During Joe's short visit it chanced that all the Claypools gathered on the porch, and Gerd, lately come from Cedar Ridge, narrated with great gusto the gossip. It was received with the interest of lonely people who seldom had opportunities to hear about what was going on. Gerd's report of the latest escapade of one of the village belles well known to them all was received with unrestrained mirth. Such incident would have passed unmarked by Lucy had she not caught the expression that fleeted across Joe Denmeade's face. That was all the more marked because of the fact of Joe's usually serene, intent impassibility. Lucy conceived the certainty that this boy would suffer intensely if he ever learned of Clara's misfortune. It might not change his love, but it would surely kill something in him—the very something that appealed so irresistibly to Clara.

The moment was fraught with a regurgitation of Lucy's dread—the strange premonition that had haunted her—that out of the past must come reckoning. It remained with her more persistently than ever before, and was not readily shaken off.

Some days later, one Friday toward the end of May, Lucy rode down the schoolhouse trail to meet Clara and fetch her back to Claypool's to stay over Sunday. It had been planned for some time, and Lucy had looked forward to the meeting with both joy and apprehension.

This schoolhouse trail was new to her, and therefore one of manifold pleasure. It led through forest and glade, along a tiny brook, and on downhill toward the lower country.

Lucy was keen to catch all the woodland features that had become part of her existence, without which life in this wilderness would have lost most of its charm. Only a year had passed since first it had claimed her! The time measured in work, trial, change, seemed immeasurably longer. Yet Lucy could not say that she would have had it otherwise. Always she was putting off a fateful hour or day until she was ready to meet it. Her work had engrossed her. In a few weeks she had accomplished as much with the Claypools as she had been able to do for the Denmeades in months. She had learned her work. Soon she could go to the Johnsons. Then back to the Denmeades! To the higher and wilder forest land under the Rim! But she was honest enough to confess that there were other reasons for the joy. Lucy lingered along the trail until a meeting with the Claypool and Miller children told her that school was out. They were riding burros and ponies, in some cases two astride one beast, and they were having fun. Lucy was hailed with the familiarity of long-established regard, a shrill glad clamor that swelled her heart with its message.

"Hurry home, you rascals," admonished Lucy, as she rode back into the trail behind them. Then she urged her horse into a lope, and enjoyed the sweet forest scents fanning her face, and the moving by of bright-colored glades and shady green dells. In a short time she reached the clearing and the schoolhouse. She had not been there for a long time. Yet how well she remembered it!

At first glance she could not see any horses hitched about, but she heard one neigh. It turned out to be Baldy, and he was poking his nose over the bars of a small corral that had recently been erected in the shade of pines at the edge of the clearing. Lucy tied her horse near and then ran for the schoolhouse.

The door was open. Lucy rushed in, to espy Clara at the desk, evidently busy with her work.

"Howdy, little schoolmarm!" shouted Lucy.

Clara leaped up, suddenly radiant.

"Howdy yourself, you old backwoods Samaritan!" returned Clara, and ran to embrace her.

Then, after the first flush of this meeting, they both talked at once, without any particular attention to what the other was saying. But that wore off presently and they became rational.

"Where's Joe?" queried Lucy, desirous of coming at once to matters about which she had a dearth of news.

"He and Mr. Denmeade have gone to Winbrook to buy things for Joe's cabin."

"Are you riding the trails alone?" asked Lucy, quickly.

"I haven't yet," replied Clara, with a laugh. "Joe has taken good care of that. Edd rode down with me this morning. He went to Cedar Ridge to get the mail. Said he'd get back to ride up with us."

"You told him I was coming after you?"

"Shore did, an' reckon he looked silly," drawled Clara.

"Oh! Indeed? . . ." Lucy then made haste to change the subject. She had not set eyes upon Edd since the day she had shut her door in his face, after the audacious and irreparable kiss she had bestowed upon his cheek. She did not want to see him, either, and yet she did want to tremendously.

"Let's not wait for him," she said, hurriedly.

"What's wrong with *you?*" demanded Clara. "Edd seems quite out of his head these days. When I mention you he blushes. . . . Yes!"

"How funny—for that big bee hunter!" replied Lucy, essaying a casual laugh.

"Well, I've a hunch you're the one who should blush," said Clara, dryly.

"Clara, sometimes I don't know about you," observed Lucy, musingly, as she gazed thoughtfully at her sister.

"How many times have I heard you say that!" returned Clara, with a mingling of pathos and mirth. "Lucy, the fact is you *never* knew about me. You never had me figured. You were always so big yourself that you couldn't see the littleness of me.''

"Ahuh!'' drawled Lucy. Then more seriously she went on: "Clara, I'm not big. I've a big love for you, but that's about all.''

"Have it your own way. All the same, I'm going to tell you about myself. That's why I sent word by the children. You didn't seem very curious or anxious to see me.''

"Clara, I was only in fun. I don't want to—to know any more about you— unless it is you're happy—and have forgotten—your—your trouble,'' rejoined Lucy, soberly.

"That's just why I *must* tell you,'' said her sister, with swift resolution. "I *did* forget because I *was* happy. But my conscience won't let me be happy any longer until I tell you.''

Lucy's heart contracted. She felt a sensation of inward chill. Why had Clara's brown tan changed to pearly white? Her eyes had darkened unusually and were strained in unflinching courage. Yet full of fear!

"All right. Get it over, then,'' replied Lucy.

Notwithstanding Clara's resolve, it was evidently hard for her to speak. "Lucy, since—March the second—I've been—Joe Denmeade's wife,'' she whispered, huskily.

Lucy, braced for something utterly different and connected with Clara's past, suddenly succumbed to amaze. She sat down on one of the school benches.

"Good Heavens!'' she gasped, and then could only stare.

"Darling, don't be angry,'' implored Clara, and came to her and knelt beside her. Again Lucy felt those clinging, loving hands always so potent in their power.

"I'm not angry—yet,'' replied Lucy. "I'm just flabbergasted. I—I can't think. It's a terrible surprise. . . . Your second elopement!''

"Yes. And this made up for the—the other,'' murmured Clara.

"March the second? That was the day you took the long ride with Joe? Got back late. On a Saturday. You were exhausted, pale, excited. . . . I remember now. And you never told me!''

"Lucy, don't reproach me,'' protested Clara. "I meant to. Joe wanted to let you into our secret. But I couldn't. It's *hard* to tell you things.''

"Why? Can't I be trusted?''

"It's because you do trust so—so beautifully. It's because you are so—so good, so strong yourself. Before I did it I felt it would be easy. Afterwards I found out differently.''

"Well, too late now,'' said Lucy, sadly. "But how'd you do it? Where? Why?''

"We rode down to Gordon,'' replied Clara, hurriedly. "That's a little village below Cedar Ridge. We hired a man to drive us to Menlo. More than fifty miles. There we were married. . . . Came home the same way. It was a terrible trip. But for the excitement it'd have killed me.''

"March the second! You kept it secret all this time?''

"Yes. And want still to keep it, except from you.''

"Clara—I don't know what to say,'' rejoined Lucy, helplessly. "What on earth made you do it?''

"Joe! Joe!'' cried Clara, wildly. "Oh, let me tell you. Don't condemn me till you hear. . . . From the very first Joe Denmeade made love to me. You could never dream what's in that boy. He loved me. My refusals only made him worse. He waylaid me at every turn. He wrote me notes. He never let me forget for an hour that he worshipped me. . . . And it grew to be sweet. Sweet to my bitter heart! I was hungry for love. I wanted, needed the very thing he felt. I fought— oh, how I fought! The idea of being loved was beautiful, wonderful, saving. But to fall in love—myself—that seemed impossible, wicked. It mocked me. But I *did* fall in love. I woke up one morning to another world. . . . Then I was as weak as water.''

Lucy took the palpitating Clara in her arms and held her close. After all, she could not blame her sister. If no dark shadow loomed up out of the past, then it would be well. Then as the first flush of excitement began to fade Lucy's logical mind turned from cause to effect.

"Clara, you didn't tell Joe about your past,'' asserted Lucy, very low. She did not question. She affirmed. She knew. And when Clara's head drooped to her bosom, to hide her face there, Lucy had double assurance.

"I couldn't. I couldn't,'' said Clara, brokenly. "Between my fears and Joe's ridiculous faith in me, I couldn't. Time and time again—when he was making love to me—before I cared—I told him I was no good—selfish, callous little flirt! He would only laugh and make harder love to me. I tried to tell him about the cowboy beaus I'd had. He'd say the more I'd had, the luckier he was to win me. To him I was good, innocent, noble. An angel! He wouldn't listen to me. . . . Then when I fell in love with him it wasn't easy—the idea of telling. I quit trying until the night before the day we ran off to get married. Honestly I meant seriously to tell him. But I'd hardly gotten a word out when he grabbed me— and—and kissed me till I couldn't talk. . . . Then—I was sort—of carried away— the—the second time.''

She ended in a sobbing whisper. All was revealed in those last few words. Lucy could only pity and cherish.

"You poor child! I understand. I don't blame you. I'm glad. If you love him so well and he loves you so well—it must—it *shall* come out all right. . . . Don't cry, Clara. I'm not angry. I'm just stunned and—and frightened.''

Clara responded to kindness as to nothing else, and her passion of gratitude further strengthened Lucy's resolve to serve.

"Frightened! Yes, that's what I've become lately," she said. "Suppose Joe should find out—all about me. It's not probable, but it *might* happen. He would never forgive me. He's queer that way. He doesn't understand women. Edd Denmeade, now—he could. He'd stick to a girl—if—if—— But Joe wouldn't, I know. At that I can tell him *now*, if you say I must. But it's my last chance for happiness—for a home. I *hate* the thought that I'm not the angel he believes me. I know I could become anything in time—I love him so well. Always I remember that I wasn't wicked. I was only a fool."

"Dear, regrets are useless," replied Lucy, gravely. "Let's face the future. It seems to me you should tell Joe. After all, he hasn't so much to forgive. He's queer, I know——"

"But, Lucy," interrupted Clara, and she looked up with a strange, sad frankness, "there was a baby."

"My God!" cried Lucy, in horrified distress.

"Yes . . . a girl—my own. She was born in Kingston at the home of the woman with whom I lived—a Mrs. Gerald. She had no family. She ran a little restaurant for miners. No one else knew, except the doctor, who came from the next town, and he was a good old soul. In my weakness I told Mrs. Gerald my story—whom I'd run off with—all about it. She offered to adopt the baby if I'd help support it. So we arranged to do that."

"That was the debt you spoke of," replied Lucy, huskily. "Why you needed money often."

"Yes. And that's why I was in such a hurry to find work—to take up this teaching. . . . She had written me she would return the child or write to its— its father unless I kept my part of the bargain. I was so scared I couldn't sleep. . . . I was late in sending money, but I'm sure it's all right."

"You married Joe—with this—hanging over you?" queried Lucy, incredulously.

"I *told* you how that came about. I know what I felt. I suffered. But it all came about. It happened," answered Clara, as if driven to desperation.

"Only a miracle can keep Joe from learning it some day."

"Miracles sometimes happen. For instance, your giving me a home. And my love for this boy! . . . You can never understand how close I was to death or hell. . . . Kingston is a long way off. This is a wilderness. It might happen that God won't quite forget me."

"Oh, the pity of it!" wailed Lucy, wringing her hands. "Clara, how can you repudiate your own flesh and blood?"

"I had to," replied Clara, sadly. "But I've lived with the memory, and I've changed. . . . I'll meet Mrs. Gerald's demands, and some day I'll make other and happier arrangements."

"If you only hadn't married Joe! Why, oh, why didn't you come to me?" cried Lucy.

Clara offered no reply to that protest. She straightened up and turned away.

"I hear a horse," she said, rising to look at Lucy.

"Must be Edd," returned Lucy, nervously.

"Riding pretty fast for Edd. You know he never runs a horse unless there's a reason."

The sisters stood a moment facing each other. Perhaps their emotions presaged catastrophe. Outside the sound of rapid hoofbeats thudded to a sliding halt. Lucy was occupied with anticipation of being compelled to face Edd Denmeade. Less prepared than at any time since her sentimental impulse at Claypool's, she could not on such short notice master her feelings.

Nevertheless, under the strain of the moment she hurried toward the door, to make her hope that the arrival was not Edd a certainty.

Clara went to the window and looked out.

Lucy reached the threshold just as her keen ear caught the musical jingle of spurs. Then a step too quick and short for Edd! In another second a tall slim young man confronted her. He wore the flashy garb of a rider. Lucy wondered where she had seen that striking figure, the young, handsome, heated red face with its wicked blue eyes. He doffed a wide sombrero. When Lucy saw the blaze of his golden hair she recognized him as the individual once pointed out to her at Cedar Ridge. Comrade of Bud Sprall!

"Howdy, Luce! Reckon your kid sister is heah," he said, cooly.

Lucy's heart seemed to sink within her. Dread and anger leaped to take the place of softer emotions now vanishing.

"How dare you?" she demanded.

"Wal, I'm a darin' *hombre*," he drawled, taking a step closer. "An' I'm goin' in there to even up a little score with Clara."

"Who are you?" queried Lucy, wildly.

"None of your business. Get out of my way," he said, roughly.

Lucy blocked the door. Open opposition did much to stabilize the whirl of her head.

"You're not coming in," cried Lucy. "I warn you. Edd Denmeade's expected here any moment. It'll be bad for you if he finds you."

"Wal, I reckon Edd won't get heah pronto," rejoined this cowboy, impertinently. "I left my pard, Bud Sprall, down the trail. An' he's a-rarin' to stop Edd one way or another. Bud an' I have been layin' for this chance. Savvy, Luce?"

She gave him a stinging slap in the face—so hard a blow that even her open hand staggered him.

"Don't you believe it, Mr. Red-face," retorted Lucy, furiously. "It'd take more than you or Bud Sprall to stop Edd Denmeade."

"Wild cat, huh? All same Clara!" he ejaculated, with his hand going to his face. The wicked eyes flashed like blue fire. Then he lunged at her, and grasping her arm, in a single pull he swung her out of the doorway. Lucy nearly lost her balance. Recovering, she rushed back into the schoolhouse in time to see this stranger confront Clara. For Lucy it was a terrible thing to see her sister's face.

"Howdy, kid! Reckon you was lookin' for me," he said.

"*Jim Middleton!*" burst out Clara in queer, strangled voice. Then she slipped limply to the floor in a faint.

For Lucy uncertainty passed. She realized her sister's reckoning had come, like a lightning flash out of a clear sky, and it roused all the tigress in her. Running to Clara, she knelt at her side, to find her white and cold and unconscious. Then she rose to confront the intruder with a determination to get rid of him before Clara recovered consciousness.

"So you're Jim Middleton?" she queried, in passionate scorn. "If I had a gun I'd shoot you. If I had a whip I'd beat you as I would a dog. Get out of here. You shall not talk to my sister. She hates you. Nothing you can have to say will interest her."

"Wal, I'm not so shore," returned Middleton, without the coolness or nonchalance that before had characterized his speech. He looked considerably shaken. What contrasting gleams of passion—hate—wonder—love—changed the blue gaze he bent upon Clara's white face! "I've a letter she'll want to read."

"A letter! From Mrs. Gerald?" flashed Lucy, quivering all over as his hand went to his breast.

"Yes, if it's anythin' to you," retorted the cowboy, shaking a letter at her.

"Mrs. Gerald wants money?" Lucy went on.

"She shore does," he answered, resentfully.

"I suppose you're going to send it to her?"

"I am like hell!"

"Also I suppose you'll want to right the wrong you did Clara? You'll want to marry her truly?" demanded Lucy, with infinite sarcasm.

"You've got the wrong hunch, Luce," he replied, laughing coarsely. "I jest want to read her this letter. Shore I've been keepin' it secret these days for her to see first. Then I'll tell Joe Denmeade an' every other man in this woods."

"Haven't you made Clara suffer enough?" queried Lucy, trying to keep her voice steady and her wits working.

"She ran off from me. I reckon with another man."

"You're a liar! Oh, I'll make you pay for this!" cried Lucy, in desperation. Suddenly she saw him turn his head. Listening. He had not heard her outburst.

Then Lucy's strained hearing caught the welcome clatter of hoofs. Quick as a flash she snatched the letter out of Middleton's hands.

"Heah, give that back!" he shouted, fiercely.

Like a cat Lucy leaped over desks into another aisle, and then facing about, she thrust the letter into the bosom of her blouse. Middleton leaned forward, glaring in amaze and fury.

"I'll tear your clothes off," he shouted, low and hard.

"Jim Middleton, if you know when you're well off you'll get out of here and out of the country before these Denmeades learn what you've done," returned Lucy.

"An' I'll beat you good while I'm tearin' your clothes off," he declared as he crouched.

"Edd Denmeade will kill you!" whispered Lucy, beginning to weaken.

"Once more," he hissed, venomously, "give me that letter. . . . It's my proof about the baby!"

And on the instant a quick jangling step outside drew the blood from Lucy's heart. Middleton heard it and wheeled with muttered curse.

Edd Denmeade leaped over the threshold and seemed to fill the schoolroom with his presence. Blood flowed from his bare head, down his cheek. His eyes, like pale flames, swept from Lucy to Middleton, to the limp figure of the girl on the floor, and then back to Lucy. The thrill that flooded over her then seemed wave on wave of shock. He had been fighting. His clothes were in rags and wringing wet. He advanced slowly, with long strides, his piercing gaze shifting to Middleton.

"Howdy, cowboy! I met your pard, Bud Sprall, down the trail. Reckon you'd better go rake up what's left of him an' pack it out of here."

"The hell you say!" ejaculated Middleton, stepping to meet Edd halfway. He was slow, cautious, menacing, and somehow sure of himself. "Wal, I'd as lief meet one Denmeade as another. An' I've shore got somethin' to say."

"You can't talk to me," returned Edd, with measured coldness. "I don't know nothin' about you—cept you're a pard of Sprall's. That's enough. . . . Now go along with you pronto."

The red of Middleton's face had faded to a pale white except for the livid mark across his cheek. But to Lucy it seemed his emotion was a passionate excitement rather than fear. He swaggered closer to Edd.

"Say, you wild-bee hunter, you're goin' to heah somethin' aboot this Watson girl."

Edd took a slow easy step, then launched body and arm into pantherish agility. Lucy did not see the blow, but she heard it. Sharp and sudden, it felled Middleton to the floor half a dozen paces toward the stove. He fell so heavily that he shook the schoolhouse. For a moment he lay gasping while Edd stepped closer. Then he raised himself on his elbow and turned a distorted face, the nose of which appeared smashed flat. He looked a fiend inflamed with lust to murder. But cunningly as he turned away and began to labor to get to his feet, he did not deceive Lucy.

"Watch out, Edd! He has a gun!" she screamed.

Even then Middleton wheeled, wrenching the gun from his hip. Lucy saw its sweep as she saw Edd leap, and suddenly bereft of strength she slipped to the floor, back against a desk, eyes tight shut, senses paralyzed, waiting for the report she expected. But it did not come. Scrape of boots, clash of spurs, hard expulsions of breath, attested to another kind of fight.

She opened wide her eyes. Edd and Middleton each had two hands on the weapon, and were leaning back at arm's-length, pulling with all their might.

"I'm agonna bore you—you damn wild-bee hunter!" panted the cowboy, and then he bent to bite at Edd's hands. Edd gave him a tremendous kick that brought a bawl of pain and rage from Middleton.

Then began a terrific struggle for possession of the gun. Lucy crouched there, fascinated with horror. Yet how the hot nerves of her body tingled! She awoke to an awful attention, to a dim recollection of a fierce glory in man's prowess, in blood, in justice. Edd was the heavier and stronger. He kept the cowboy at arm's-length and swung him off his feet. But Middleton always came down like a cat. He was swung against the desks, demolishing them; then his spurred boots crashed over the teacher's table. They wrestled from there to the stove, knocking that down. A cloud of soot puffed down from the stovepipe. The cowboy ceased to waste breath in curses. His sinister expression changed to a panic-stricken fear for his own life. He was swung with violence against the wall. Yet he held on to the gun in a wild tenacity. They fought all around the room, smashing desk after desk. The time came when Middleton ceased to jerk at the gun, but put all a waning strength in efforts to hold it.

When they were on the other side of the room Lucy could not see them. What she heard was sufficient to keep her in convulsive suspense.

Suddenly out of the corner of her eye she saw Clara sit up and reel from side to side, and turn her white face toward the furiously struggling men.

"Clara—don't look!" cried Lucy, huskily, almost unable to speak. She moved to go to her sister, but she was spent with fright, and when Clara's purple eyes fixed in an appalling stare, she quite gave out. Then crash and thud and scrape, harder, swifter, and the whistle of men's breath moved back across the room into the field of her vision. Edd was dragging Middleton, flinging him. The fight was going to the implacable bee hunter.

"Let go, cowboy. I won't kill you!" thundered Edd.

Middleton's husky reply was incoherent. For a moment renewed strength seemed to come desperately, and closing in with Edd he wrestled with the frenzy of a madman.

Suddenly there burst out a muffled bellow of the gun. Edd seemed released from a tremendous strain. He staggered back toward Lucy. For a single soul-riving instant she watched, all faculties but sight shocked into suspension. Then Middleton swayed aside from Edd, both his hands pressed to his breast. He sank to his knees. Lucy's distended eyes saw blood gush out over his hands. Dragging her gaze up to his face, she recoiled in a fearful awe.

"She—she was—" he gasped, thickly, his changed eyes wavering, fixing down the room. Then he lurched over on his side and lay doubled up in a heap.

Edd's long arm spread out and his hand went low, to release the smoking gun, while he bent rigidly over the fallen man.

"It went—off," he panted. "I was only—tryin' to get it—away from him. . . . Lucy, you saw."

"Oh yes, I saw," cried Lucy. "It wasn't—your fault. He'd have killed you. . . . Is he—is he? ——"

Edd straightened up and drew a deep breath.

"Reckon he's about gone."

Then he came to help Lucy to her feet and to support her. "Wal, you need a little fresh air, an' I reckon some won't hurt me."

"But Clara! . . . Oh, she has fainted again!"

"No wonder. Shore she was lucky not to see the—the fight. That fellow was a devil compared to Bud Sprall."

"Oh! . . . Edd, you didn't kill him, too?" implored Lucy.

"Not quite. But he's bad used up," declared Edd as he half carried her across the threshold and lowered her to a seat on the steps. "Brace up now, city girl. Reckon this is your first real backwoods experience. . . . Wal, it might have been worse. . . . Now wouldn't you have had a fine time makin' Bud an' his pard better men? . . . There, you're comin' around. We need to do some tall figurin'. . . . But I reckon, far as I'm concerned, there's nothin' to worry over."

After a moment he let go of Lucy and rose from the step. "Lucy, what was it all about?" he queried, quietly.

She covered her face with her hands and a strong shudder shook her frame.

"Wal," he went on, very gently, "I heard that fellow ravin' as I come in. But all I understood was 'proof about the baby.' "

"That was enough to hear, don't you think?" replied Lucy, all at once recovering her composure. Out of the chaos of her conflicting emotions had arisen an inspiration.

"Reckon it was a good deal," he said, simply, and smiled down on her. "But you needn't tell me nothin' unless you want to. I always knew you'd had some trouble."

"Trouble!" sighed Lucy. Then averting her gaze she continued: "Edd, I ask you to keep my secret. . . . The baby he spoke of—was—is mine."

He did not reply at once, nor in any way she could see or hear express whatever feeling he might have had. Lucy, once the damnable falsehood had crossed her lips, was stricken as by a plague. When she had thrown that off there was a horrible remorse pounding at the gates of her heart. Her body seemed first to receive the brunt of the blow she had dealt herself.

"Wal, wal—so that's it," said Edd, in queer, broken voice. He paused a long moment, then went on, in more usual tone: "Shore I'll never tell. . . . I'm dog-gone sorry, Lucy. An' I'm not askin' questions. I reckon it doesn't make no difference to me. . . . Now let's think what's best to do. I'll have to send word from Johnson's about this fight. But I'm goin' to see you home first, unless you think you can get there all right."

"That depends on Clara. Come with me."

They went back into the schoolhouse to find Clara showing signs of returning consciousness.

"Please carry her outside," said Lucy.

As he lifted the girl in his arms Lucy's fearful gaze roved round the room. Amid the ruins of the crude furniture lay the inert form of Jim Middleton, face down, hands outstretched in a pool of blood. Though the sight sickened her, Lucy gazed until she had convinced herself that there was no life in the prostrate form. Then she hurried after Edd and reeled out into the sunlight and the sweet fresh air. Edd carried Clara to the shade of pines at the edge of the clearing.

"I'll go down to the brook," he said. "Reckon we don't want her seein' me all over blood."

Presently Clara's pale eyelids fluttered and unclosed, to reveal eyes with purple abysses, hard for Lucy to gaze into. She raised Clara's head in her arms.

"There, dear, you're all right again, aren't you?"

"Where is he?" whispered Clara.

"Edd's gone down to the brook to fetch some water. He's all right."

"I mean—him! . . . Ah, I saw!" went on Clara. "Edd killed him!"

"I fear so," said Lucy, hurriedly. "But it was an accident. Edd fought to get the gun. It went off. . . . Don't think of that. God has delivered you. I have the letter Mrs. Gerald wrote Middleton. He did not betray you. And now he's dead. . . . Edd knows nothing about your relation to this cowboy. See that you keep silent."

Edd returned at this juncture with a shining face, except for a wound over his temple; and he handed his wet scarf to Lucy.

"Wal, shore she's come to," he drawled, with all his old coolness. "That's good. . . . Now I'll saddle up her horse an' pretty soon she'll be able to ride home."

"I think she will," returned Lucy. "But what shall I say about—about this?"

"Say nothin'," he replied, tersely. "I'll do the talkin' when I get home.
. . . An', Lucy, on my way to Johnson's I'll take a look at my old friend Bud
Sprall. If he's alive, which I reckon he is, I'll tell him damn good an' short
what happened to his pard, an' that he'll get the same unless he moves out of
the country. These woods ain't big enough for us two."

"He might waylay you again as he did this time—and shoot you," said Lucy,
fearfully.

"Wal, waylayin' me once will be enough, I reckon. Bud had a bad name,
an' this sneaky trick on you girls will fix him. They'll run him out of the
country."

While Edd saddled Clara's horse Lucy walked her to and fro a little.

"Let's go. I can ride," averred Clara. "I'd rather fall off than stay here."

Edd helped her mount and walked beside her to where the trail entered the
clearing. Lucy caught up with them, full of misgiving, yet keen to get out of
sight of the schoolhouse.

"Go right home," said Edd. "I'll stop at Claypool's on my way up an' tell
them somethin'. Shore I won't be long. An' if you're not home I'll come a-
rarin' down the trail to meet you."

"Oh, Edd—be careful!" whispered Lucy. She hardly knew what she meant
and she could not look at him. Clara rode on into the leaf-bordered trail. Lucy
made haste to follow. Soon the golden light of the clearing no longer sent gleams
into the forest. They entered the green, silent sanctuary of the pines. Lucy felt
unutterable relief. How shaded, how protecting, how helpful the great trees!
They had the primitive influence of nature. They strengthened her under the
burden she had assumed. Whatever had been the wild prompting of her sacrifice,
she had no regret for herself, nor could she alter it.

Clara reeled in her saddle, clinging to the pommel; but as she rode on it
appeared she gathered strength, until Lucy came to believe she would finish out
the ride. And what a tragic ride that was! Clara never once looked back, never
spoke. The pearly pallor still showed under her tan. Lucy felt what was going
on in her sister's soul, and pitied her. Scorn for Clara's weakness, anger at her
duplicity, had no power against love. The reckoning had come and the worst
had befallen. Lucy experienced relief in the knowledge of this. Clara's future
must be her care. It was not right, but she would make it right; it was not safe,
yet she must insure its safety. And all at once she realized how she loved Edd
Denmeade, and that eventually she would have gone to him as naturally as a
bird to its mate. Then the green forest seemed to pierce her agony with a thousand
eyes.

15

AT the conclusion of that ride Clara collapsed and had to be carried into her tent, where she fell victim to hysteria and exhaustion. Lucy had her hands full attending to her sister and keeping the kindly Denmeades from hearing some of Clara's ravings.

Next day Clara was better, and on Sunday apparently herself again. To Lucy's amaze she announced she could and would go back to school next day.

"But, Clara—how *can* you, considering—" faltered Lucy.

"I know what you mean," replied her sister. "It'll be rather sickening, to say the least. Yet I'd prefer to be sick than have the awful feeling of dread I had before."

Nevertheless, Lucy would not hear of Clara's going to teach for at least a week. Amy Claypool would be glad to act as substitute teacher for a few days, or failing that, the pupils could be given a vacation. Clara did not readily yield this point, though at last she was prevailed upon. During these days Lucy avoided much contact with the Denmeades. It was not possible, however, not to hear something about what had happened.

Upon his return Edd had conducted himself precisely as before the tragedy, a circumstance that had subtle effect upon Lucy. By degrees this bee hunter had grown big in her sight, strong and natural in those qualities which to her mind constituted a man. From Joe she learned certain developments of the case. Bud Sprall, late on the day of the fight, had been carried to Johnson's, the nearest ranch, and there he lay severely injured. Middleton had not been removed until after the sheriff had viewed his remains on Saturday. Gossip from all quarters was rife, all of it decidedly favorable to Edd. The dead cowboy had not been well known at Cedar Ridge, and not at all by the name of Middleton.

On Monday Lucy returned to her work at Claypool's, leaving the situation unchanged so far as she was concerned. She and Edd had not mentioned the thing that naturally concerned them both so vitally; nor had Lucy confessed to Clara what she had taken upon herself. There would be need of that, perhaps, after the sheriff's investigation.

Lucy's work did not in this instance alleviate a heavy heart. Once more alone, away from the worry about Clara's health and the excitement of the Denmeades, she was assailed by grief. Clara's act, viewed in any light possible, seemed a sin, no less terrible because of unfortunate and mitigating circumstances. It was something that had been fostered long ago in the family. Lucy had expected it. She blamed the past, the lack of proper home training and ideals, the influence inevitable from her father's business.

After her work hours each day she would walk off into the deep forest, and there, hidden from any eyes, she would yield to the moods of the moment. They seemed as various as the aspects of her trouble. But whatever the mood happened to be, grief was its dominant note. Clara had gotten beyond her now. She was married, and settled, providing Joe Denmeade was as fine a boy as he seemed. But if Clara's true story became public property and Joe repudiated her, cast her off—then her future was hopeless. Lucy could not face this possibility. It quite baffled her.

Then there was something else quite as insupportable to face. Sooner or later she must take up the burden she had claimed as her own. It would be hard. It meant she must abandon her welfare work there among the people she had come to love. They needed her. She would have to go farther afield or take up some other kind of work. It was not conceivable that her sister's child could be left to the bringing up of strangers. That would only be shifting the responsibility of the weak Watson blood upon some one else. It did not make in the least for the ideal for which Lucy was ready to lay down her life.

Perhaps hardest of all was the blow to what now she recognized as her unconscious hopes of love, dreams of happy toil as a pioneer's wife. She knew now, when it was too late, what she could have been capable of for Edd Denmeade. She had found a fine big love for a man she had helped develop. She would rather have had such consciousness than to have met and loved a man superior in all ways to Edd. Somehow the struggle was the great thing. And yet she had loved Edd also because he was self-sufficient without her help. How she cared for him now, since the killing of one enemy and crippling of another, was hard for her to define. So that this phase of her grief was acute, poignant, ever-present, growing with the days.

She found out, presently, that going into the forest was a source of comfort. When there seemed no comfort she went to the lonely solitude of trees and brush, of green coverts and fragrant wild dells, and always she was soothed, sustained. She could not understand why, but it was so. She began to prolong the hours spent in the woods, under a looming canyon wall, or beside a densely foliaged gorge from which floated up the drowsy murmur of a stream. All that the wild forest land consisted of passed into her innermost being. She sensed that the very ground she trod was full of graves of races of human beings who had lived and fought there, suffered in their blindness and ignorance, loved and reared their young, and had grown old and died. No trace left! No more than autumn leaves! It seemed to be this lesson of nature that gradually came to her. Thereafter she went to the woods early in the mornings as well as the afternoons, and finally she had courage to go at night.

And it was at night she came to feel deepest. Darkness emphasized the mystery of the forest. Night birds and crickets, prowling coyotes with their haunting barks, the wind sad and low in the pines, the weird canopy of foliage overhead studded with stars of white fire—these taught her the littleness of her life and the tremendousness of the spirit from which she had sprung. She was part of the universe. The very fear she had of the blackness, the beasts, and the unknown told of her inheritance. She came at length to realize that this spell engendered by nature, if it could be grasped in its entirety and held, would make bearable all aches of heart and miseries of mind. Her contact with actual life covered twenty little years in a town, among many people; her instincts, the blood that beat at her temples, the longings of her bones, had been bred of a million years in the solitude and wild environment of the dim past. That was why the forest helped her.

A Saturday in June was the day set for an investigation of the fight that had resulted in the death of Jim Middleton. It would be an ordeal for which Lucy had endeavored to prepare herself.

But from what she heard and saw of the people interested she judged the day was to be rather a gala one. Certainly the Denmeades were not worried. Lucy did not see Edd, but Joe seemed more than usually cheerful, and evidently he had prevailed somewhat upon Clara. If she had any misgivings as to what might develop, she certainly did not show them. She rode by with Joe and the other Denmeades before Lucy was ready. Allie and Gerd dressed up for the occasion as if they were going to a dance. Lucy rode with them as far as Johnson's where she was invited to go the rest of the way in a car with Sam and other of the Johnsons. During this part of the ride Lucy had little chance to think or brood. The party was a merry one, and their attitude toward the occasion was manifested by a remark Sam finally made to Lucy:

"Say, cheer up. You're worryin' about this investigation. It won't amount to shucks. Everybody in the country is glad of what Edd did. Shore there won't be any court proceedings. This whole case would have been over long ago an' forgotten if Bud Sprall hadn't been too bad crippled to talk. Just you wait."

Lucy found some little grain of assurance in Sam's words, and bore up under her dread. Perhaps she worried too much, and felt too deeply, she thought. Sam drove as if he were going to a party, and the twenty miles or more seemed as nothing. Cedar Ridge was full of people, to judge from the horses, cars, and vehicles along each side of the main street. When Sam halted with a grand flourish before the hotel Lucy was thrilled to see Edd Denmeade step out from a motley crowd. He was looking for her, and he smiled as he met her glance. He read her mind.

"Howdy, Lucy! Reckon you needn't be scared. Shore it's all right," he said, pressing her hand as he helped her out. "Howdy, there, you Sam! Just saw Sadie an' she shore looks pert. Howdy, you-all!"

Lucy was conducted into the hotel parlor by the sheriff, who seemed very gallant and apologetic and most desirous of impressing her with the fact that this meeting was a pleasure to him.

The magistrate she met there appeared equally affable. He was a little man, with sharp blue eyes and ruddy shaven face, and he had only one arm.

"Wal, now, it was too bad to drag you away from the good work we're all a-hearin' aboot," he said.

"Judge," spoke up the sheriff, "we got Edd's story an' now all we want is this girl's. She see the fight over the gun."

"Set down, miss, an' pray don't look so white," said the magistrate, with a kindly smile. "We see no call to take this case to court. Jest answer a few questions an' we'll let you off. . . . You was the only one who see the fight between Edd an' thet cowboy?"

"Yes. My sister had fainted and lay on the floor," replied Lucy. "But just at the last of it I saw her sit up. And after, when I looked back, she had fainted again."

"Now we know thet Harv Sprall threw a gun on Edd——"

"Sprall!" interrupted Lucy. "You're mistaken. The other fellow was Bud Sprall and he wasn't in the schoolroom. Edd had the fight for the gun with——"

"Excuse me, miss," interrupted the judge in turn. "The dead cowboy was Harv Sprall, a cousin of Bud's. He wasn't well known in these parts, but we got a line on him from men over Winbrook way. . . . Now jest tell us what you saw."

Whereupon Lucy began with the blow Edd had delivered to the so-called Harv Sprall, and related hurriedly and fluently the details of the fight.

"Wal, thet'll be aboot all," said the judge, with his genial smile, as he bent over to begin writing. "I'm much obliged."

"All! May—I go—now?" faltered Lucy.

"Go. I should smile. I'm escortin' you out. Not thet we're not sorry to have you go," replied the sheriff, and forthwith he led her out to where the others were waiting on the porch.

Lucy came in for considerable attention from the surrounding crowd; and by reason of this and the solicitude of her friends she quickly regained her composure. Presently she was carried away to the house of friends of the Johnsons.

She wondered where Clara was, and Joe and Edd, but being swift to grasp the fact that the investigation had been trivial, she was happy to keep her curiosity to herself.

During the several hours she remained in town, however, she was destined to learn a good deal, and that by merely listening. The name Jim Middleton was mentioned as one of several names under which Harv Sprall had long carried on dealings not exactly within the law. He had been known to absent himself for long periods from the several places where he was supposed to work. If Bud Sprall had known anything about his cousin's affairs with Clara, he had kept his mouth shut. The investigation had turned a light on his own unsavory reputation, and what with one thing and another he was liable to be sent to state prison. The judge had made it known that he would give Sprall a chance to leave the country.

It seemed to be the universally accepted idea that the two Spralls had planned to waylay Edd or Joe Denmeade, and then surprise the young school-teacher or overtake her on the trail. Their plans had miscarried and they had gotten their just deserts; and that evidently closed the incident.

Lucy did not see Edd again on this occasion, and some one said he had ridden off alone toward home. Clara and Joe did not show inclination for company; and they too soon departed.

Before dark that night Lucy got back with the Claypools, too tired from riding, and weary with excitement and the necessity for keeping up appearances, to care about eating, or her usual walk after supper. She went to bed, and in the darkness and silence of her little hut she felt as alone as if she were lost in the forest. To-morrow would be Sunday. She would spend the whole day thinking over her problem and deciding how to meet it. If only the hours could be lengthened— time made to stand still!

That Sunday passed by and then another, leaving Lucy more at sea than ever. But she finished her work with the Claypools. July was to have been the time set for her to go to the Johnsons or the Millers. When the date arrived Lucy knew that she had no intention of going. Her own day of reckoning had come. Somehow she was glad in a sad kind of way.

The Denmeades welcomed her as one of the family, and their unstinted delight did not make her task any easier. They all had some characteristic remark to thrill and yet hurt her. Denmeade grinned and said: "Wal, I reckon you're back for good. It shore looks like a go between Joe an' your sister."

Meeting Clara was torturing. "Well, old mysterious, get it off your chest," said her sister, with a shrewd bright look. "Something's killing you. Is it me or Edd?"

"Goodness! Do I show my troubles as plainly as that?" replied Lucy, pathetically.

"You're white and almost thin," returned Clara, solicitously. "You ought to stay here and rest—ride around—go to school with me."

"Perhaps I do need a change. . . . And you, Clara—how are you? Have you found it hard to go down there—to be in that schoolroom every day?"

"Me? Oh, I'm fine. It bothered me some at first—especially that—that big stain on the floor. I couldn't scrub it out. So I took down a rug. I'm not so squeamish as I was. But I go late, and you bet I don't keep any of my scholars in after school hours."

"Don't you ever think of—of——" faltered Lucy, hardly knowing what she meant.

"Of course, you ninny," retorted Clara. "Am I a clod? I think too much. I have my fight. . . . But, Lucy, I'm happy. Every day I find more in Joe to love. I'm going to pull out and make a success of life. First I thought it was for Joe's sake—then yours. But I guess I've begun to think of myself a little."

"Have you heard from Mrs. Gerald?" queried Lucy, finally.

"Yes. As soon as she got my letter, evidently it was all right again. But she never mentioned writing to Jim."

"She would be glad to get rid of her charge—I imagine?" went on Lucy, casually.

"I've guessed that, myself," rejoined Clara, soberly. "It worries me some, yet I——"

She did not conclude her remark, and Lucy did not press the subject any further at the moment, though she knew this was the time to do it. But Lucy rather feared a scene with Clara and did not want it to occur during the waking hours of the Denmeades.

"Have you and Joe told your secret?" queried Lucy.

"Not yet," replied Clara, briefly.

"Where is Joe now?"

"He's working at his homestead. Has twenty acres planted, and more cleared. They're all helping him. Edd has taken a great interest in Joe's place since he lost interest in his own."

"Then Edd has given up work on his own farm. Since when?"

"I don't know. But it was lately. I heard his father talking about it. Edd's not the same since he—since that accident. Joe comes home here every night and he tells me how Edd's changed. Hasn't he been to see you, Lucy?"

"No."

"Of course Edd's down in the mouth about you. I don't think killing that cowboy worries him. I heard him say he was sorry he hadn't done for Bud Sprall, too, and that if he'd known the job those two put up on him there'd have been a different story to tell. . . . No. It's just that Edd's horribly in love with you."

"Poor—Edd, if it's so!" murmured Lucy. "But maybe you take too much for granted, just because Joe feels that way about you."

"Maybe," replied her sister, mockingly. "Edd will probably come home today with Joe, as he hasn't been here lately. Take the trouble to look at him and see what you think."

"Are you trying to awaken my sympathies?" queried Lucy, satirically.

"I wish to goodness I could," returned Clara, under her breath.

Lucy realized that she was not her old self, and this had affected Clara vexatiously, perhaps distressingly. Lucy strove against the bitterness and sorrow which in spite of her will influenced her thought and speech. She would not let another day go by without telling Clara what she had taken upon herself. That would be destroying her last bridge behind her; she could go forth free to meet new life somewhere else, knowing she had done the last faithful service to her family.

The Denmeade boys come home early, but Lucy did not see Edd until at supper, which, as usual, was eaten on the porch between the cabins. He did seem changed, and the difference was not physical. He was as big and brawny and brown as ever. Sight of him reopened a wound she thought had healed.

"Come down an' see my bees," he invited her after supper.

The time was near sunset and the green gully seemed full of murmuring of bees and stream and wind. Edd had added several new hives to his collection, all of which were sections of trees that he had sawed out and packed home.

"How'd you ever keep the bees in?" she asked, wonderingly.

"I stuffed the hole up an' then cut out the piece," he replied. "It can't be done with every bee tree, by a long shot."

For once he seemed not to be keen to talk about his beloved bees, nor, for that matter, about anything. He sat down ponderingly, as a man weighted by cares beyond his comprehension. But the stubborn strength of him was manifest. Lucy had at first to revert to the thought that the flying bees were harmless. With them humming round her, alighting on her, this association of safety did not come at once. She walked to and fro over the green grass and by the sturdy pines, trying to bring back a self that had gone forever. The sun sank behind purple silver-edged clouds, and the golden rim stood up to catch the last bright flare of dying day.

"Wal, you're leavin' us soon?" queried Edd, presently.

"Yes. How did you know?" replied Lucy, halting before him.

"Reckon I guessed it. . . . I'm awful sorry. We're shore goin' to miss you."

That was all. He did not put queries Lucy feared she could not answer. He showed no sign of thoughts that pried into her secret affairs. Somehow he gave Lucy the impression of a faithful animal which had been beaten. He was dumb. Yet she imagined his apparent stolidity came from her aloofness. Lucy, in her misery, essayed to talk commonplaces. But this failed, and she was forced to choose between falling on her knees before him and flying back to the tent. So she left him sitting there, and then from the bench above she spied down through the foliage upon him until dusk hid him from view.

Was she a traitor to the best in herself? Had she not betrayed this backwoods boy who had responded so nobly to every good impulse she had fostered in him? But blood ties were stronger than love. How terribly remorse flayed her! And doubts flew thick as leaves in a storm. Nevertheless, she could not weaken, could never depart in any degree from the course she had prescribed for herself. That was a dark hour. Her deepest emotions were augmented to passion. She was reaching a crisis, the effect of which she could not see.

Later the moon arose and blanched the lofty Rim and the surrounding forest. Black shadows of trees fell across the trail and lane. The air had a delicious mountain coolness, and the silence was impressive. Lucy drank it all in, passionately loath to make the move that must of its very momentum end these wilderness joys for her. But at last she dragged herself away from the moonlit, black-barred trail.

She found Clara and Joe sitting in lover-like proximity on the rustic bench near the tent. As she approached them she did not espy any sign of their embarrassment.

"Joe, I want to have a serious talk with Clara. Would you oblige me by letting me have her alone for a while?" said Lucy.

"If it's serious, why can't I hear it?" queried Joe.

"I can't discuss a purely family matter before you," returned Lucy. "I'm going away soon. And this matter concerns us—me—and things back home."

"Lucy, I belong to your family now," said Joe, as slowly he disengaged himself from Clara and stood up.

"So you do," replied Lucy, laboring to keep composed. "What of it?"

"I've a hunch you haven't figured us Denmeades," he rejoined, rather curtly, and strode away.

"What'd he mean?" asked Lucy, as she stared down at Clara, whose big eyes looked black in the moonlight.

"I'm pretty sure he meant the Denmeades are not fairweather friends," said Clara, thoughtfully. "He's been trying to pump me. Wants to know why you're here and going away—why you look so troubled. . . . I told him, and Edd, too, that I wasn't in your confidence. It's no lie. And here I've been scared stiff at the look of you."

"If you're not more than scared you're lucky. Come in the tent," said Lucy.

Inside, the light was a pale radiance, filtering through the canvas. Lucy shut the door and locked it, poignantly aware of Clara's lingering close to her. Her eyes seemed like great staring gulfs.

Lucy drew a deep breath and cast off the fetters that bound her.

"Clara, do you remember the day of the fight in the schoolhouse—that you were unconscious when Edd arrived?"

"Yes," whispered Clara.

"Then of course you could not have heard what Jim Middleton said. He was about to leap upon me to get the letter I had snatched. He threatened to tear my clothes off. Then he said it was his proof about the baby. . . . Edd ran into the schoolroom just in time to hear the last few words. . . . Later he said he'd heard—and he asked me—whose it was. I told him—mine!"

"Good—God!" cried Clara, faintly, and sat down upon the bed as if strength to stand had left her.

"I spoke impulsively, yet it was the same as if I had thought for hours," went on Lucy, hurriedly. "I never could have given you away . . . and I couldn't lie—by saying it—it was somebody's else."

"Lie! It's a—terrible lie!" burst out Clara, hoarsely. "It's horrible. . . . You've ruined your good name. . . . You've broken Edd's heart. *Now* I know what ails him. . . . But I won't stand for your taking my shame—my burden on your shoulders."

"The thing is done," declared Lucy, with finality.

"I won't—I won't!" flashed her sister, passionately. "What do you take me for? I've done enough."

"Yes, you have. And since you've shirked your responsibilities—cast off your own flesh and blood to be brought up by a greedy, callous woman—I intend to do what is right by that poor unfortunate child."

Her cutting words wrought Clara into a frenzy of grief, shame, rage, and despair. For a while she was beside herself, and Lucy let her rave, sometimes holding her forcibly from wrecking the tent and from crying out too loud. She even found a grain of consolation in Clara's breakdown. What manner of woman would her sister have been if she had not shown terrible agitation?

At length Clara became coherent and less violent, and she begged Lucy to abandon this idea. Lucy answered as gently and kindly as was possible for her under the circumstances, but she could not be changed. Clara was wildly importunate. Her conscience had stricken her as never before. She loved Lucy and could not bear this added catastrophe. Thus it was that Clara's weak though impassioned pleas and Lucy's efforts to be kind yet firm, to control her own temper, now at white heat, finally led to a terrible quarrel. Once before, as girls, they had quarreled bitterly over an escapade of Clara's. Now, as women, they clinched again in such passion as could only be born of blood ties, of years of sacrifice on the part of one, of realization of ignominy on the part of the other.

And the battle went to Lucy, gradually, because of the might of her will and right of her cause.

"You can't see what you've done," concluded Lucy, in spent passion. "You're like our father. Poor weak thing that you are, I can't blame you. It's in the family. . . . If only you'd had the sense and the honor to tell me the truth!—Before you married this clean simple-minded boy! Somehow we might have escaped the worst of it. But you *married* him, you selfish, callous little egotist! And now it's too late. Go on. Find what happiness you can. Be a good wife to this boy and let that make what little amends is possible for you. . . . I'll shoulder your disgrace. I'll be a mother to your child. I'll fight the taint in the Watson blood—the thing that made you what you are. To my mind your failure to make such fight yourself is the crime. I don't hold your love, your weakness against you. But you abandoned part of *yourself* to go abroad in the world to grow up as you did. To do the same thing over! . . . You are little, miserable, wicked. But you are my sister—all I have left to love. And I'll do what you cannot!"

Clara fell back upon the pillow, disheveled, white as death under the pale moonlit tent. Her nerveless hands loosened their clutch on her breast. She shrank as if burned, and her tragic eyes closed to hide her accuser.

"Oh, Lucy—Lucy!" she moaned. "God help me!"

16

Lucy walked alone in the dark lane, and two hours were but as moments. Upon her return to the tent she found Clara asleep. Lucy did not light the lamp or fully undress, so loath was she to awaken her sister. And exhausted herself, in a few moments she sank into slumber. Morning found her refreshed in strength and spirit.

She expected an ordeal almost as trying as the conflict of wills the night before—that she would have to face a cringing, miserable girl, wrung by remorse and shame. But Clara awoke in strange mood, proud, tragic-eyed, and aloof, reminding Lucy of their youthful days when her sister had been reproved for some misdemeanor. Lucy accepted this as a welcome surprise, and, deep in her own perturbation, she did not dwell seriously upon it. The great fact of her crisis crowded out aught else—she must leave the Denmeade ranch that day, and the wilderness home which was really the only home she had ever loved. Delay would be only a cruelty to herself. Still, the ordeal was past and she had consolation in her victory. At least she would not fail. This was her supreme and last debt to her family.

Never before had the forest been so enchanting as on that summer morning. She punished herself ruthlessly by going to the fragrant glade where she had learned her first lessons from the wilderness. Weeks had passed, yet every pine needle seemed in its place. Woodpeckers hammered on the dead trunks; sap suckers glided head downward round the brown-barked trees; woodland butterflies fluttered across the sunlit spaces; blue jays swooped screechingly from bough to bough; red squirrels tore scratchingly in chattering pursuit of one another. Crows and hawks and eagles sailed the sunny world between the forest tips and the lofty Rim. It was hot in the sun; cool in the shade. The scent of pine was overpoweringly sweet. A hot, drowsy summer breeze stirred through the foliage. And the golden aisle near Lucy's retreat seemed a stream for myriads of Edd's homing bees, humming by to the hives.

Lucy tried to convince herself that all forests possessed the same qualities as this one—that the beauty and charm and strength of it came from her eye and heart—that wherever she went to work she now could take this precious knowledge with her. Trees and creatures of the wild were ministers to a harmony with nature.

A forest was a thing of infinite mystery, of multiple detail, of immeasurable design. Trees, rocks, brush, brooks could not explain the home instinct engendered in the wild coverts, the shaded dells, the dark caverns, the lonely aisles, the magnificent archways. The green leaves of the trees brought the rain from the sea and created what they lived upon. The crystal springs under the mossy cliffs were born of thirsty foliage, of the pulse in the roots of the trees. These springs were the sources of rivers. They were the fountains of all life. If the forests perished, there would be left only desert, desolate and dead.

Lucy sat under her favorite pine, her back against the rough bark, and she could reach her hand out of the shade into the sun. She thought for what seemed a long time. Then she forgot herself in a moment of abandon. She kissed and smelled the fragrant bark; she crushed handfuls of the brown pine needles, pricking her fingers till they bled; she gathered the pine cones to her, soiling her hands with the hot pitch. And suddenly overcome by these physical sensations, she lifted face and arms to the green canopy above and uttered an inarticulate cry, poignant and wild.

Then a rustling in the brush startled her; and as if in answer to her cry Edd Denmeade strode out of the green wall of thicket, right upon her.

"Reckon you was callin' me," he said, in his cool, easy drawl.

"Oh-h! . . . You frightened me!" she exclaimed, staring up at him. He wore his bee-hunting garb, ragged from service and redolent of the woods. His brown brawny shoulder bulged through a rent. In one hand he carried a short-handled ax. His clean-shaven tanned face shone almost golden, and his clear gray eyes held a singular piercing softness. How tall and lithe and strong he looked! A wild-bee hunter! But that was only a name. Lucy would not have had him any different.

"Where'd you come from?" she asked, suddenly realizing the imminence of some question that dwarfed all other problems.

"Wal, I trailed you," he replied.

"You saw me come here? . . . You've been watching me?"

"Shore. I was standin' in that thicket of pines, peepin' through at you."

"Was that—nice of you—Edd?" she faltered.

"Reckon I don't know. All I wanted to find out was how you really felt about leavin' us all—an' my woods."   •

"Well, did you learn?" she asked, very low.

"I shore did."

"And what is it?"

"Wal, I reckon you feel pretty bad," he answered, simply. "First off I thought it was only your old trouble. But after a while I could see you hated to leave our woods. An' shore we're all part of the woods. If I hadn't seen that I'd never have let you know I was there watchin' you."

"Edd, I do hate to leave your woods—and all your folks—and you—more than I can tell," she said, sadly.

"Wal, then, what're you leavin' for?" he asked, bluntly.

"I must."

"Reckon that don't mean much to me. Why must you?"

"It won't do any good to talk about it. You wouldn't understand—and I'll be upset. Please don't ask me."

"But, Lucy, is it fair not to tell me anything?" he queried, ponderingly. "You know I love you like you told me a man does when he thinks of a girl before himself."

"Oh no—it isn't!" burst out Lucy, poignantly, suddenly, strangely overcome by his unexpected declaration.

"Wal, then, tell me all about it," he entreated.

Lucy stared hard at the clusters of fragrant pine needles she had gathered in her lap. Alarming symptoms in her breast gave her pause. She was not mistress of her emotions. She could be taken unawares. This boy had supreme power over her, if he knew how to employ it. Lucy struggled with a new and untried situation.

"Edd, I owe a duty to—to myself and to my family," she said, and tried bravely to look at him.

"An' to somebody else?" he demanded, with sudden passion. He dropped on his knees and reached for Lucy. His hands were like iron. They lifted her to her knees and drew her close. He was rough. His clasp hurt. But these things were nothing to the expression she caught in his eyes—a terrible flash that could mean only jealousy.

"Let me go!" she cried, wildly, trying to get away. Her gaze drooped. It seemed she had no anger. Her heart swelled as if bursting. Weakness of will and muscle attacked her.

"Be still an' listen," he ordered, shaking her. He need not have employed violence. "Reckon you've had your own way too much. . . . I lied to you about how I killed that cowboy."

"Oh, Edd—then it wasn't an accident?" cried Lucy, sinking limp against him. All force within her seemed to coalesce.

"It shore wasn't," he replied, grimly. "But I let you an' everybody think so. That damned skunk! He was tryin' his best to murder me. I had no gun. . . . I told him I wouldn't hurt him. . . . Then what'd he do? He was cunnin' as hell. He whispered things—hissed them at me like a snake—vile words about you— what you were. It was a trick. Shore he meant to surprise me—make me lose my nerve . . . so he could get the gun. An' all the time he pulled only the harder. He could feel I loved you. An' his trick near worked. But I seen through it— an' I turned the gun against him."

"Oh, my God! you killed him—intentionally!" exclaimed Lucy.

"Yes. An' it wasn't self-defense. I killed him because of what he called you."

"Me! . . . Oh, of course," cried Lucy, hysterically. A deadly sweetness of emotion was fast taking the remnant of her sense and strength. In another moment she would betray herself—her love, bursting at its dam—and what was infinitely worse, her sister.

"Lucy, it don't make no difference what that cowboy said—even if it was true," he went on, now huskily. "But—were you his wife or anybody's?"

"No!" flashed Lucy, passionately, and she spoke the truth in a fierce pride that had nothing to do with her situation, or the duty she had assumed.

"Aw—now!" he panted, and let go of her. Rising, he seemed to be throwing off an evil spell.

Lucy fell back against the pine tree, unable even to attempt to fly from him. Staring at Edd, she yet saw the green and blue canopy overhead, and the golden gleam of the great wall. Was that the summer wind thundering in her ears? How strangely Edd's grimness had fled! Then—there he was looming over her again— eager now, rapt with some overwhelming thought. He fell beside her, close, and took her hand in an action that was a caress.

"Lucy—will you let me talk—an' listen close?" he asked, in a tone she had never heard.

She could not see his face now and dared not move.

"Yes," she whispered, her head sinking a little, drooping away from his eyes.

"Wal, it all come to me like lightnin'," he began, in a swift, full voice, singularly rich. And he smoothed her hand as if to soothe a child. "I've saved up near a thousand dollars. Reckon it's not much, but it'll help us start. An' I can work at anythin'. Shore you must have a little money, too. . . . Wal, we'll get your baby an' then go far off some place where nobody knows you, same as when you come here. We'll work an' make a home for it. Ever since you told me I've been findin' out I was goin' to love your baby. . . . It'll be the same as if it was mine. We can come back here to live, after a few years. I'd hate never to come back. I've set my heart on that mesa homestead. . . . Wal, no one will ever know. I'll forget your—your trouble, an' so will you. I don't want to know any more than you've told me. I don't hold that against you. It might have happened to me. But for you it would have happened to my sister Mertie. . . . Life is a good deal like bee huntin'. You get stung a lot. But the honey is only the sweeter. . . . All this seems to have come round for the best, an' I'm not sorry, if only I can make you happy."

Lucy sat as if in a vise, shocked through and through with some tremendous current.

"Edd Denmeade," she whispered, "are you asking me—to—to marry you?"

"I'm more than askin', Lucy darlin'."

"After what I confessed?" she added, unbelievingly.

"Shore. But for that I'd never had the courage to ask again. . . . I've come to hope maybe you'll love me some day."

This moment seemed the climax of the strain under which Lucy had long kept up. It had the shocking power of complete surprise and unhoped-for rapture. It quite broke down her weakened reserve.

"I—love you *now*—you big—big——" she burst out, choking at the last, and blinded by tears she turned her face to Edd's and, kissing his cheek, she sank on his shoulder. But she was not so close to fainting that she failed to feel the effect of her declaration upon him. He gave a wild start, and for a second Lucy felt as if she were in the arms of a giant. Then he let go of her, and sat rigidly against the tree, supporting her head on his shoulder. She could hear the thump of his heart. Backwoodsman though he was, he divined that this was not the time to forget her surrender and her weakness. In the quiet of the succeeding moments Lucy came wholly into a realization of the splendor of her love.

It was late in the day when they returned to the clearing. Hours had flown on the wings of happiness and the thrill of plans. Lucy forgot the dark shadow. And not until they emerged from the forest to see Clara standing in the tent door, with intent gaze upon them, did Lucy remember the bitter drops in her cup.

Clara beckoned imperiously, with something in her look or action that struck

Lucy singularly. She let go of Edd's hand, which she had been holding almost unconsciously.

"Wal, I reckon your sharp-eyed sister is on to us," drawled Edd.

"It seems so. But, Edd—she'll be glad, I know."

"Shore. An' so will Joe an' all the Denmeades. It's a mighty good day for us."

"The good fortune is all on my side," whispered Lucy, as they approached the tent.

Clara stood on the threshold, holding the door wide. Her face had the pearly pallor and her eyes the purple blackness usual to them in moments of agitation. She did not seem a girl any longer. Her beauty was something to strike the heart.

"Lucy—come in—you and your gentleman friend," she said, her voice trembling with emotion. Yet there was a faint note of pride or mockery of self or of them in it.

"Wal, Clara, you may as well kiss me an' be done with it," drawled Edd, as he entered behind Lucy. "For you're goin' to be my sister two ways."

Clara's response was electrifying. Her face seemed to blaze with rapture and the swift kiss she gave Edd admitted of no doubt as to her acceptance of Edd's blunt speech. But she made no move to approach Lucy.

Joe Denmeade sat on the edge of the bed, white and spent. Sight of him caused Lucy's heart to leap to her throat.

"Howdy, Lucy!" he said, with a smile that was beautiful. "Is my brother Edd talkin' straight?"

"Yes, Joe, I'm going to be doubly your sister," she replied.

"I couldn't ask no more," he rejoined, with deep feeling.

There followed a moment of constraint. Lucy could not grasp the situation, but she felt its tensity. Then, trembling, she turned to face Clara.

"I have told Joe," said Clara as Lucy met her eyes.

Lucy received this blow fully, without preparation, and following hard on stress of feeling that had left her spent. Her intelligence was swift to accept the wondrous and almost incredible fact of Clara's regeneration, but her emotions seemed dead or locked in her breast. Mutely she stared at this beloved sister. She saw an incalculable change, if she saw clearly at all. She might have been dazed. In that endless moment there was a slow action of her own mind, but something she expressed wrought havoc in Clara. The glow, the rapture, the exaltation that so enhanced Clara's beauty, suddenly faded and died. Even her moment of supreme victory had been full of thought of self. But Lucy's agony transformed it.

"I—told him," burst out Clara, sobbing. "I couldn't *stand* it—any longer. I *wanted* him to know. . . . I could have gone on—living a lie—if you had not taken my—my shame. But that was too much. It killed something in me. . . .

So I told him I couldn't let you do it. I must do it myself. And I gave Joe up. . . . But, Lucy, he forgave me! . . . He will stand by me!''

"Oh, Joe—how splendid—of you!" gasped Lucy, and with the hard utterance her bound faculties seemed to loosen. She ran to Joe's side. "But how can you meet this—this terrible situation?"

Joe took her trembling hands in his.

"Why, Lucy, don't be upset!" he said. "It's not so bad. If Clara had told me long ago I reckon you'd both been saved a lot of heart-breakin'. . . . There's only one way. The preacher who married Clara an' me will keep our secret. An' he'll marry us again. We'll just leave out tellin' anybody that this—this cowboy forgot to marry Clara himself.''

"Yes—yes!" cried Lucy, wildly.

"Reckon thet's aboot all," continued Joe, with his rare smile. "Clara an' I will tell the folks, an' leave at once. . . . An' we'll come back with the baby!''

Here Edd Denmeade strode to a position before them, and though he seemed to be about to address Joe, he certainly looked at Lucy.

"Reckon you'd do well to have the parson meet you in Cedar Ridge an' marry you there," he said.

Lucy could have laughed had she not been fighting tears. "Edd, are you talking to Joe—or me?"

"Lucy, would you marry me at the same time?" he queried, hoarsely.

"I—I fear the crowd at Cedar Ridge. They'll storm us," faltered Clara.

"Shore we can fool them," returned Edd.

"All right. We've settled it all," said Joe, in a grave kind of happiness. "I'll go in an' tell the folks.''

"Wal, I'm goin' with you," rejoined Edd as Joe rose. They strode out together, and Edd's brawny arm went round his brother's shoulder. "Joe, I reckon it's as good one way as another. It's all in the family. The three of them'll be Denmeades.''

Lucy closed the tent door after them and turned to her sister. Clara's eyes were shining through tears.

"Aren't they good?" she murmured. " 'It's all in the family,' Edd said. Either he or Joe would have been happy to be father to my baby. . . . Oh, I did not appreciate them. I did not understand Joe—or you—or myself. . . . I did not know what love was. . . . Now I can atone for the past.''

At sunset Lucy escaped the hilarious Denmeades and slipped into the forest, to hide in an unfrequented glade. She had to be alone.

The profound transformations of the day were less baffling and incredible once she found herself in the loneliness and solitude of the forest. Life was real and earnest, beautiful and terrible, inexplicable as the blaze of the setting sun, so fiery golden on the rugged towering Rim. In the depths of the quiet woods she could understand something of simplicity. For her and Clara life had been throbbing and poignant. For the Denmeades life seemed like that of the trees and denizens of the forest.

The sun sank, the birds ceased their plaintive notes, and a dreaming silence pervaded the green world of foliage. Late bees hummed by. The drowsy summer heat began to cool.

Lucy's heart was full of reverent gratitude to whatever had wrought the change in Clara. Love, suffering, the influence of nature, all had combined to burn out the baneful selfish weakness that had made Clara a victim to circumstances. And these were only other names for God.

How inscrutably had things worked to this happy end! She tried to look backward and understand. But that seemed impossible. Yet she realized how stubbornly, miserably, she had clung to her ideal. If she had only known the reward!

The great solemn forest land was after all to be her home. She would go on with her work among these simple people, grateful that she would be received by them, happy that she could bring good to their lonely homes. The thing she had prayed most for had become a reality. If doubt ever assailed her again, it would be of short duration. She thought of the bee hunter. She would be his wife on the morrow!

Dusk mantled the forest. A faint night wind arose, mournful and sweet. Lucy threaded her way back toward the clearing. And the peace of the wilderness seemed to have permeated her soul. She was just one little atom in a vast world of struggling humans, like a little pine sapling lifting itself among millions of its kind toward the light. But that lifting was the great and the beautiful secret.

WYOMING

1

WHEN Martha Ann Dixon found herself on the open Nebraska road she realized with a shock that at last her innate propensity for running away from home had definitely materialized. She pinched herself. . . . It was true. She was here, and her face was turned to the West!

Her first yielding to this strange wanderlust had occurred at the age of five when she ran off from her aunt's home on the shore of Lake Michigan and was found strolling about in the woods as naked and unashamed as any little savage. The second excursion, a flight from school, had come somewhat later; and then there had followed other occasions not so vividly remembered.

But this one, in the last year of her teens, was vastly different. This adventure was the result of long planning and deliberation to make a dream come true, a dream of lovely roads and bright-colored hills, of dim horizons and purple ranges, and at last the longed-for goal—the West.

The rattle of a slowing Ford swerved Martha Ann off the road.

"Hello, kid. Want a lift?" called out a cheery voice. A red-headed, freckle-faced youth accommodated the speed of his car to her brisk stop.

"No, thanks," she replied, "I'd rather walk."

"Cripes! If youse ain't a girl! 'Scuse *me*," the driver ejaculated with a grin. "Come on. It ain't every day a dame gets a chance to ride with me."

"I'll leave that golden opportunity for someone more appreciative."

"Aw—awright. I jest thought mebbe you was tired. What you doin'?"

"Hitchhiking."

"Say, you ain't hitchin' on very well this mornin'."

"I'll hike every day till I'm tired."

"Where you goin'?"

605

"Wyoming!" exclaimed Martha Ann, belligerently. It was the first time she had spoken that magic word aloud.

"Whew! . . . Well, I'll be dogged!" the redhead exclaimed. Then with an incredulous glance at the diminutive figure on the highway he started up his ancient car and was soon lost in clouds of dust.

Martha Ann giggled softly to herself. So she finally had nerve enough to speak it! "Wyoming!" How sweet it sounded! What untold promise the world held! What did it matter that her destination was some unknown town in Wyoming— what difference did it make that she had only fifty dollars in her pocket which would have to last indefinitely?

She walked on happily. Spring was in the air. The fields were golden and the trees and fence rows showed freshly green; swamp blackbirds and meadowlarks sang melodiously from the roadside; a fragrance of burning leaves was carried on the soft breeze. From beyond where the white road disappeared over the horizon something beckoned imperiously.

To the girl it still seemed like a miracle that she should be here. Again she reviewed the events that had led her to this open road which she hoped would take her to Wyoming.

There had been sufficient money to put Martha Ann through high school. That had satisfied her mother, but Martha wanted to go on. Mrs. Dixon was making too many references to Martha Ann's chances of marriage. She argued that Martha at eighteen had grown into an attractive girl who could marry well. But Martha Ann had ideas of her own which had nothing at all to do with marriage.

She wanted to go to the university for a while, and then work, and above all to see something of the world. The world to her meant the West. A twofold reason accounted for Martha's obsession. As a child she had heard all about her grandmother's only brother, who had run away from home to seek his fortune in the West. And it had helped to make her a rabid reader of Western romances.

For thirty years Uncle Nick Bligh had not been heard from. But when Martha Ann was seventeen, her grandmother had received a letter from the missing brother, explaining that as he had failed to make his fortune he had never troubled himself to write. But age and poor health, together with a realization of the false pride that had motivated his silence, had prompted him at last to write for news of his family. The letter bore a postmark of Randall, Wyoming.

This communication from the long-lost uncle had fixed in Martha Ann's mind a secret and daring idea. She would go west to find Uncle Nick. That was incentive and excuse enough to crystallize what had been only a vague purpose.

Ways and means to attend the university and at the same time save money enough to start her trip kept Martha Ann wide-eyed for many long hours at night, as well as pensive by day. But she had solved the problem. She obtained work as an assistant in a dentist's office, and in addition to after classes she worked on Saturdays, Sunday mornings, and during all vacations.

. More than a year and a half of this intensive strain had told upon Martha Ann's mental and physical well-being. But nothing daunted her. As time went on her secret purpose grew more and more alluring. It satisfied her longing for happiness. But strange to discover, the busier she became the greater grew the masculine demands upon her leisure. To their persistent requests for dates she remained indifferent.

Martha Ann had long wondered about her attitude toward men. Perhaps, as her mother and some of her friends claimed, she was abnormal. But she could not willingly admit this charge, and from distress she passed to impatience and finally to disgust. Yet she liked boys. She admired young men who were making good in life. She could at times have great fun with them—in the earlier stages of friendship—and could by intense inward pressure wring some sort of romantic emotion out of her heart for them. But to her dismay, almost every friendship led to one of two sad conclusions—a proposal of marriage or a fumbling pass which disgusted her. Why couldn't they just be friends? As for those few bolder young men who attempted to be too free with their hands—Martha Ann despised them.

The time came when the strain of study and outside work, the importunities of her admirers and the constant nagging of her mother had changed Martha Ann, even in her own eyes. She wanted to get far away from the dirty, noisy, crowded city. Open spaces beckoned her. Into her dreams came more and more lovely green places, where flowers and birds abounded. From feeling stifled and weary she gradually sank into a state of real melancholy. The terrific burden on the slender shoulders had at last become too heavy; her flesh was not the equal of her spirit. Also, her mother, anxiously regarding Martha's future, was now urging her to marry young Bob Wirth; "who can take care of you nicely, so you won't have to worry about a little money or a new dress." But worry had become part of Martha's very existence—worry about school credits, about making her little earnings go a long way, about the dissatisfaction and nagging at home, about the pressing fact of the increasing demands of the young men. The proms, the formals, the movies, all had become stale and unprofitable to her. She longed for something to happen—something unforeseen and tremendous.

Finally the pressure had become too great. Even though she had not finished her semester at college she realized with the coming of spring that the time to leave had come. Martha Ann caught her breath as she recalled the day of her decision.

Deceiving her father had not hurt her conscience. He had never appeared to care whether Martha came or went, and outwardly at least he had evinced little interest in her pursuit of happiness. But to deceive her mother! That had hurt.

Suddenly faced with the enormity of what she was about to do, she was filled with remorse. Never in all her life had she told her mother a deliberate lie. She now thought to excuse herself on the basis that the glorious end justified almost any means. But a still, accusing voice kept calling at the gate of her consciousness. Lie to mother—who had always been so good, so faithful, so forgiving! It gave Martha Ann a painful twinge. But she had launched her canoe on the current of this great adventure. She could not turn back.

And yet, how simple and easy it all had been to accomplish! Martha Ann had calmly announced at dinner one evening that a girl friend at the university had asked her to drive with her to Omaha, and she wanted to go. Her father and brother made the usual perfunctory murmurs. Her mother, however, had anxiously asked how long she would be gone. Martha could give only a vague answer.

"Dear, you're sure you are going to Omaha?" asked Mrs. Dixon.

"Mother! . . . Yes, of course," she had replied hastily. At least that was no out-and-out falsehood!

"I was afraid you might be remembering your old madness to go out West," concluded Mrs. Dixon.

But Martha had been impatient, too, even with her mother. Why could she not understand how wonderful it would be to go out West? If Mrs. Dixon had ever had any adventurous desires of her own they had long ago become atrophied.

Every moment that Martha had had to herself in the apartment, she had spent getting her belongings into readiness. What to take and what to leave? How impossible to remember that she had to *carry* everything, and therefore the less she took the easier would be her burden! Finally she had decided on her brother's packsack! She was agreeably surprised to find that it held so much. Still she wondered how she could ever manage with anything so small.

As the day of departure had drawn nearer, her feeling of anticipation had become mixed with other emotions. What might not happen to her on the way! She elevated her chin and smiled oftener to reassure herself. Nevertheless there lurked the shadow of panic in her consciousness. Once while kneeling in the middle of her bedroom, trying to find place in her pack for a precious book, she had found herself murmuring aloud: "Oh dear Lord—I want to go so terribly. I must go . . . please don't let anything happen!" and the very next moment her hoydenish nature had asserted itself, and she had cried with Topsy-like simplicity: "Can't you heah me, God?"

At length Martha Ann had her packsack ready. It could hold no more. Besides a few infinitesimal underthings, it contained one pair of pajamas, two toothbrushes, soap, towel and wash cloth, comb and brush, two pairs of heavy woolen hose, three pairs of cotton socks, an emergency kit containing tape, mercurochrome, bandages, cotton, a bottle of disinfectant, a few threaded needles, a tiny pair of scissors, a fountain pen and some sheets of paper and stamped envelopes, and three clean shirts. She had pondered a long while on the possibility of ever having an occasion to dress up, and at last had put in her navy blue crepe with the flat pleats. This would fold easily and flat. In the end she had found room for her patent leather slippers and two pairs of silk stockings. Her short suede jacket, her hiking boots, and corduroy breeches she would carry in a box, ready to don when she started on the road.

Then had come, finally, the day of parting, the tears, the incoherent farewell, the precipitate flight to meet the mythical girl friend, the station and the train. She could scarcely clamber to the Pullman platform. Her eyes were so dim that she could not see the steps. A voice had whispered: "Running away! . . . Leaving home, mother, brother, Bob—all of them—forever!" It was the "forever" that had appalled Martha Ann.

And now, after a night on the sleeper, Martha Ann was on the road outside of Omaha, hitchhiking toward the next town.

She still felt self-conscious and queer in the soft corduroy riding breeches and high-topped boots that she had donned in the dressing room of the station. She had rolled her heavy woolen socks down over her hiking boots; and the sleeves of her white shirt over slim round arms that she hoped would soon get tanned.

As Martha Ann swung along the road her mind seemed both busy and absent. How good it was just to be alive and free on a morning like this! She had a heavenly sense of having been newly born. Would it not be wonderful to walk on like this forever? There was no need of hurry. Even the goal of Wyoming failed to seem so far away and unattainable.

For a while Martha Ann strode rhythmically along, her feet light, her heart dancing, her thoughts at peace. She stopped at the first gas station she came to on the road, where she was favored with amused glances and deluged with maps. A few cars passed her, and as one of them seemed about to stop, she waved it on. Martha wanted to prolong the enchantment of these first hours of freedom.

The sun rose high in the sky. It was beginning to get hot. After a time the road began to slope uphill, necessitating a change in her gait. Near the summit, a Ford coupé came puffing up behind her and stopped. A sandy-haired young man put his head out of the window.

"Hey, pigeon, where do you think you're flyin'?" he called, in a good-natured voice.

Long had Martha Ann schooled herself in the replies that would have to be made. Always it would be diplomatic to name the nearest town as her destination, which subterfuge would enable her to take her leave of any undesirable who might offer her a lift. Accordingly she named the first village she had read on the road map.

"Hop in. I'm going within half a mile of there."

Martha slid off the packsack, the weight of which she had not fully appreciated until relieved of it, and climbed into the car.

"Got relatives there?" inquired the driver, as he put the Ford into motion.

"Yes," replied Martha, warily.

"Where you from?"

"Chicago."

He whistled his surprise. "Hike all the way from there?"

"No. I came as far as Omaha by train," she replied, feeling that she liked this not overly curious driver. He glanced at her packsack.

"Nice army pack. That leather bottom keeps your stuff dry."

"Yes, Colonel Brinkerhoff gave it to my brother."

"That so," he said, and flashed a keen glance at her. Then he attended to the road ahead. The car was speeding between fields of winter grain and pastureland. Farmhouses stood among groves of trees rapidly turning green.

Suddenly he launched a query: "Do your folks know you're out here alone like this?"

"No," rejoined Martha Ann, caught unawares.

"Ahuh. Well, why don't they?"

"Why? . . . I—I suppose—because if I'd told them—I wouldn't be here," she replied, haltingly. It annoyed her to be quizzed but his directness had momentarily confused her.

"Does anyone know you're hitchhiking?"

"Yes, our family lawyer. I bound him to secrecy. He promised, provided I'd keep in touch with him. If I didn't he threatened to have the police on my trail."

"Not a bad idea. How old are you?"

"Nineteen."

"Humph! You look more like fifteen."

Martha Ann glared at him.

"Listen, kid," he said, ignoring her look of disdain, "you can't lie worth a hoot! Some girls are like that. Just where are you headed for?"

"I'm going to Randall, Wyoming, but I can't see where it's any concern of yours," retorted Martha.

"Good lord! . . . Say, do you know how far that is? To hitchhike?"

"I've a pretty good idea."

"And do you know you'll have to go through the Black Hills?"

"N—no-o, I didn't . . . Are they as awful as they sound?"

"You'll never come out alive. A few tourists motor through the Hills. But for the most part they're darned lonely and deserted. A refuge for fugitives and criminals. Believe me, kid, you'll get yours!"

"Gracious! . . . Oh, you're just trying to scare me."

"Not a chance! Look here. I belong to the armory. I know Colonel Brinkerhoff, whose packsack you're carrying. I'm going to take you to the armory with me while I wire the Colonel to find out if he really approves of this crazy hike you're on."

Martha Ann sat back stunned. What if this assertive young man were to make good his threat? What would her mother say? And do! Martha could see what a disgrace it would be to be sent home just when she had such a fine start. But she simply must not let this terrible thing happen.

"Wiring Colonel Brinkerhoff won't be any use now," she spoke up, her wit reasserting itself.

"Why won't it?"

"Because he isn't in Chicago now."

"Where is he?"

"Fishing in northern Canada."

"How do you know that?"

"Because he went with a friend of my uncle."

Plainly the sandy-haired young man was at a loss as far as proceeding along the line he had adopted was concerned.

"I'll bet you haven't any money?"

"Indeed I have."

"Enough to get home to Chicago?" he queried doubtfully.

"Yes. And then some."

"What on earth put this crazy idea in your head?"

That for Martha was waving a red flag of battle.

"Crazy! Sure I'm crazy. But it's to see the West. Why, I've never been away from home in my life. I've never seen any places but Chicago and Lake Michigan. This is my chance. I *must* go on. . . . Besides, I've never seen my uncle. I wrote him. . . . He—he's expecting me."

This last was far from the truth, but Martha Ann had become desperate.

"Uncle, uh? That's different. Still my duty to Brinkerhoff is to hold you till some of your people are communicated with."

"Hold me! How?" burst out Martha. If she ever got away from this armory person she would never accept another ride.

"Well, you can't jump out while we're doing forty-five," he declared, grimly. "I'll drive straight to the armory and hold you till Captain Stevens can be notified."

"Hold me—by force?" faltered Martha. She realized that he was in the right and it gave her a sense of guilt. What could she do? She must fall back upon feminine wiles, a procedure she usually scorned. Whereupon she made a frantic pretense of escaping from the car.

"Hold you? I should smile I will," he said, suiting his action to the word.

"If necessary, I'll hold on to you with one arm. But, heck, I'll bet you wouldn't make too much fuss."

Martha Ann resorted to tears, which were so near the surface that weeping was hardly any dissimulation.

"Say, I give up, young lady, I can't stand for bawling," he said irritably. "I'll let you go if you promise to watch your step. Don't get in cars where there's more than one man, and be sure you're never in *any* car after dark."

Martha promised eagerly.

"And look each driver over before you accept a ride?"

"Yes, sir," replied Martha, demurely.

"I've got a kid sister. And I'd have a fit if I caught her hitchhiking alone. But she has queer ideas, too. Girls are sure beyond understanding these days. . . .Well, here's where I turn off. And there's the village."

Martha got out and thanked him.

"Would you mind dropping me a post card—if you get by the Black Hills? I'll be sort of worried. My name's Arthur Anderson. And I live here."

"Mine's Martha Ann Dixon. I'll send you a card. Thank you—and good-by!"

She started down the road, and after a little turned to look back. The car was still there at the turn-off. And the young man was waving his cap. Martha went on, a considerably sobered and thoughtful girl.

In the village she stopped at a little hot-dog stand to rest and eat lunch. From there a farmer and two small boys gave her a lift that took her thirty-five miles to another crossroad settlement, where she decided to call it a day. And upon being directed to a tourist home, she found pleasant accommodations for the night.

The twittering and fluttering of birds in the vines outside Martha's window aroused her at five-thirty. She bounded up, eager and refreshed. Another day— the second! What would the day bring forth? How beautiful the rosy sunrise over the rolling eastern Nebraska hills! At breakfast she was informed that if she did not mind riding in a truck, she could accompany her host as far as the next town.

"Oh, fine! That will be fun," she exclaimed.

But that anticipated lift turned out to be all too short, and therefore not such fun after all. Halfway up a steep hill the engine stalled. The driver had to begin tinkering with obstinate machinery. Martha got out and began to walk.

The truck never caught up with her. After several cars had passed she accepted a ride with a merry family of five, who cheerfully made room for her, and welcomed her without curiosity. Martha liked this plain man and his fat spouse, and the dirty, bright-eyed children. It was noon when their village was reached. Martha had lunch and once more went on her way.

It occurred to her that she was now traveling through the Nebraska plains and that towns would be few and far between. Farms seemed to spread out. Anyway, there were fewer farmhouses. Cars passed her. She had learned by now that her solitary, unusual, little figure would not escape notice on the road. The afternoon sun grew hot. She rested, and hoped an acceptable lift soon would happen along. Then she started hiking again. She walked on and on, and in two hours' time not a single automobile passed in her direction. Then came a string of cars, so close together that Martha could not get a good look at their occupants. She found, presently, that when she was tired and impatient, as she grew to be by late afternoon, she was likely to forget the good advice she had been given, and to accept any ride that was offered. She began to wonder—was she being erratic, irresponsible? Was this unheard-of adventure for a girl of nineteen who looked fifteen a proof of an unstable character? She defended herself stoutly, but somehow the buoyant spirit of the morning had vanished.

A lengthy hill invited a long rest. When she resumed her hike and had surmounted the grade the sun was setting red and glorious in the west. The rolling plains began to disappear in the purple haze of the horizon. In this scene, still dominated by the habitations of man, Martha imagined she saw a semblance to the western range. And this thought so thrilled and delighted her that she forgot her hot tired feet and aching limbs, and trudged on, almost her old self once more.

From the height she looked down upon lonelier country, which the road bisected to the next town, now visible in the clear evening light some few miles ahead. Martha thought that she could still make it before it became pitch dark. Downhill was easy and the air had cooled. At the foot of the incline the road turned abruptly. A brook gleamed under a dark patch of woods that shaded the road and there was a bridge to cross. Below the bridge Martha saw a little fire and two rough-looking men, sitting beside it. Could they be tramps?

Martha realized that she had to pass them. With bated breath she quickened her steps. Twilight was stealing out of the woods. She might get by without attracting notice. But when one of the men called out, her heart leaped wildly.

"Bill, stop thet boy, an' see what he's got in thet bag."

Then Martha, who had been watching the two men beside the fire, was astounded to be confronted by a dark form that appeared to rise out of the earth. It belonged to a third man who evidently had been invisible against the background of the bridge.

"Hyar, sonny, what you totin' there?" he queried, in brisk good humor.

Martha Ann, suddenly rendered weak by terror, made an ineffectual attempt to elude the man. He caught her with so violent a jerk that she would have fallen but for his hold. She dropped the small parcel she carried in her hand.

"Oh!—let me—go!" she cried out, fearfully.

The man swung her around to the westering light and peered closely down upon her. Martha got an impression of a hard, coarse face and a pair of wolfish eyes. She tried to wrench free from the iron grip which was hurting her wrist.

"Hey, fellars, it ain't no boy. It's a girl. Purtier'n a pitcher," called the man to his associates.

"Haw! Haw! Wal, Bill, you know your weakness. But throw us the baggage," came the hoarse reply.

"Come hyar, little one, an' set—"

Martha struggled with what little strength she had left. A kind of paralysis had taken possession of her. It was a new and devastating numbness of will and flesh. All in a flash peril had leaped out of the dusk, and wit, nerve, energy deserted her to be replaced by a horrible sickening faintness.

"Hey, Bill, hyar's a car!" hurriedly called one of the men beside the fire.

Martha Ann heard the puff and then the vibration of a car. Its presence revived her, and she jerked herself free, calling loudly at the same time.

"Let that boy go," came a commanding voice from the car. Then the occupant stepped out to loom big and wide of shoulder before them. "What's the idea?"

"Aw, nuthin'. Jest havin' fun with the kid," returned the tramp surlily, as he backed away.

"Oh—n-no sir," quavered Martha Ann. "He meant to rob—me—and I don't know what—when he saw I was a girl!"

"*Girl!*" The newcomer moved like a swift shadow. Martha heard a sudden crash. The tramp appeared lifted as by a catapult to go tottering against the bank with a sickening impact.

"Beat it, you hoboes, or I'll come down there and mess you up," called Martha's rescuer. Then he turned to her.

"Are you really a girl?"

"Yes, sir . . . And sometimes I wish—I wasn't," replied Martha, picking up her parcel.

"Of course, you live along here somewhere?"

"No-o. My home's—far away."

"How'd you come to be caught on this lonely road?" he queried.

"I'm hitchhiking out West."

"Hitchhiking?" he exclaimed.

"It's a—a kind of sport. Sometimes I accept lifts—when I can—and hike between."

"Sport! I admire your nerve," he laughed. His voice had a pleasant depth, with an intonation that told Martha that he was quite different from the others she had met on this jaunt. She looked up. There was still light enough for her to discern the features of a young man in his early twenties. His eyes were intently on her face. They appeared to have a mocking look. Martha saw that again she was under suspicion, and the realization almost canceled the sweet warm sensation of gratitude and relief flooding over her.

"Thank you for saving me from I—I don't know what," she murmured, shyly. The strain of her struggle with the tramp, and the manner in which the stranger had accepted her explanation, or perhaps both together, had reacted strangely upon Martha Ann Dixon.

"Girls of today pay a price for the kick they try to get out of everything," he replied, enigmatically. "You look faint. Get in. I'll take you as far as Norfolk."

2

NOT for may minutes did the effect of panic wear off Martha Ann. It all had been so totally unexpected. She had never before realized what real fright was like. The rickety old car crept slowly along! She relaxed back in the seat, spent and nerveless, scarcely able to hold the packsack upon her lap.

But presently her usual buoyant spirit returned, and Martha Ann became acutely aware of the driver beside her. She realized that she must summon her wits to meet another quizzing. This young man, however, appeared completely oblivious of her presence. His silence condemned her. And before they had gone very far Martha began to find it unendurable.

"You don't live—in these parts?" she began, haltingly.

"How'd you guess that?"

Martha Ann, analyzing her sensations, could not very well tell him that he did not smell of horses, gas stations or harness oil.

"Where are you from?" she substituted.

His hesitation in replying to her question hinted to Martha that he might have considered her query unduly curious.

"I'm a hick from Missouri," he finally replied, with a light laugh tinged with bitterness.

"Yes, you are!" she exclaimed accusingly. "And I suppose your name is Hiram Perkins?"

"My name is Andrew Bonning," he returned, soberly, as if the admission had been forcibly extracted from him.

Martha Ann's best overtures failed to stimulate the conversation and at length she subsided into silence. She peered at him, however, out of the corner of her eye. He wore overalls that had seen very little service. She could make out a clean-cut profile. He was bare-headed and had dark hair, somewhat long and wavy. Martha Ann reluctantly had to admit that this strange rescuer who obviously disapproved of her was good-looking even in the dusk.

"Where are you going?"

"Wyoming."

"Humph. . . . Well, here's your next town," he spoke up, presently. "See the lights?"

"Oh, it must be a pretty big town," said Martha Ann, excitedly.

"You'll get another kick here."

"Kick?" she echoed, doubtfully.

"Yes, kick. Isn't that what you're after? Isn't that what all girls think of nowadays?"

Martha Ann had no reply, for his query edged with bitterness had thrown her back upon introspection. All at once she felt vexed, and because it seemed to be only with herself, she promptly chose to foist her feeling of annoyance upon this disturbing young man. After all, what did she care what he thought about her? Just the same that reflection did not wholly satisfy. The excitement of entering a new and larger town, however, precluded any hope of Martha's to deliver a telling retort. The main street was wide, paved, lined with automobiles, and bright with lights. Martha chose a modest-appearing hotel, and asked to be dropped at its entrance. The fact that he got out first to help her, and to lift out her packsack, struck Martha as significant. He moved with a careless grace which her sensitive observations scarcely associated with overalls.

"Thank you, Mr. Bonning, for—for everything," murmured Martha.

"You're welcome. I wish you better luck on the next lap of your hitchhike. . . . You forgot to tell me your name."

"I didn't forget. I was—"

As he lifted out her packsack he noticed the lettering Martha Ann had so carefully printed in indelible ink on the side of the pack. She had neglected to use punctuation.

"*Mad!*" he exclaimed. Then suddenly he smiled down upon her in a way that made Martha feel like a wayward little girl. Under the electric light she could now see him distinctly, and somehow, someway, that pale handsome face with its sad and piercing eyes seemed incomprehensibly to be her undoing. "Wyoming Mad? It suits you better than any real name. And as you are an unforgettable kid I'll remember you by that. I hope we don't meet again. Good-by."

He got into the car and drove off, leaving Martha Ann standing on the sidewalk, bag in hand, staring up the crowded street. Unforgettable kid? But not because she was pretty or sweet or nice—only because she was mad! Insulted and crestfallen, Martha Ann went into the hotel, engaged a room, and wearily proceeded to unpack and remove the stains of travel. Her left arm pained, and she discovered a bruise where the tramp had gripped her wrist. These were the only tangible proofs of her adventure with the bad men. What if Andrew Bonning had not happened to arrive at such an opportune moment? Martha Ann shivered. They might have murdered her and cast her into the dark stream. Then what of mother! Martha's spirit quailed for a little and her heart warmed again toward her rescuer. How wide-shouldered and powerful—what a blow he had struck for her! Then the next moment, remembering his veiled distrust of her, his spiteful designation of her as "Wyoming Mad," all of Martha Ann's more charitable feelings were forgotten. They would never meet again and she was gladder of that than he could possibly be.

Next morning bright and early Martha was on her way once more. Yesterday's events lay as far behind her as the distance over which she had come. The yellow road entranced her, ever new, ever offering the unknown adventures that were to come. In the broad daylight, so clear and fresh, between the green fields with their singing birds—how could she feel afraid? She stepped out with eager stride, with glad eyes toward the beckoning miles.

During the day that followed automobiles were plentiful. She could take her pick, and she had lifts aggregating a hundred miles or more before mid-afternoon. She likened this passing from car to car to the reading of a huge book which devoted just so much space to each individual. All rides were fascinating to Martha Ann, whether short or long, but she still preferred walking. During the afternoon there seemed to be a scarcity of cars on the road. She walked until she was glad to hear the hum of another motor.

A Cadillac roadster sped past. The occupant, a young man, looked back at her. As Martha continued walking, presently she saw the big car slow down and stop. When she caught up with it, the driver leaned out to say: "Hello, my beauty, wilt ride on my trusty steed?"

"Is it safe?" she queried.

"Is it safe! Lady, you appall me. I'm the original Sir Galahad. My middle name is Saint. Mothers leave their puling infants with me. Old ladies phone days ahead just to have me escort them to the village—"

"I believe I've read about you," interrupted Martha Ann. "You're too good to be true. I'd better walk."

"Aw, have a heart! I've got to drive all the way to Sidonia. Please don't mind my kidding. Really I'm mild under my bold exterior."

"All right," laughed Martha. "I'm only going a short distance and I'll take a chance on you."

"Get in. My name's George Proctor."

"Mine's Martha Ann Dixon."

They rode along in the warm sunshine, just two young people thrown idly together, and George's fluent talk of the lore of the Nebraska countryside found Martha a rapt listener. At length George explained that his business was insurance, and proceeded to quote numerous statistics for Martha's edification and profit.

"Whoever heard of a hitchhiker being killed?" she queried.

"Say, you're only one of a pioneer game. You might be the very first to get killed."

"If I had known you'd be saying such pessimistic things to me I wouldn't have accepted this ride."

"Hold everything, Beautiful. I'll make this an enjoyable ride for you."

"Well, speaking of hazards, if you're tired driving let me try."

"Do you drive? Great! I'm sure fed up with driving. It's all I ever do."

Whereupon Martha changed her seat for the one behind the wheel, and drove on, evidently to young Proctor's pleasure. It did not take long for Martha Ann to decide that his intentions were strictly honorable, and since Sidonia was on her way she would continue that far with him. At six o'clock they were within sight of Sidonia.

"My uncle runs the hotel here," said George "I'll introduce you. And— would you think me awfully cheeky if I ask you to have dinner with us?"

"N-no-o. . . . But I've just one dress—and it'll be fearfully wrinkled."

"Pshaw! Nobody dresses up for dinner in Sidonia."

It so happened that Martha did not think to relinquish the wheel, and as she drove up to an unpretentious hotel she was astounded to recognize a bystander as Andrew Bonning. Yielding a swift warm impulse she was about to nod gaily when a look in the young man's keen dark eyes sent a hot blush coursing over her cheeks. He inclined his head in recognition, a courtesy Martha did not answer, and which young Proctor did not see. He took her baggage and helped her out, talking gaily all the while. Anyone would have noticed his rapture, which all of a sudden seemed to incense Martha Ann. She knew for a certainty that Bonning had seen Proctor escort her into the hotel, where she confusedly prayed that the uncle-proprietor would be in charge. But he was out. George got her a room, carried her baggage up, and said at the door: "Doll up now, Beautiful, and knock Uncle's eye out at dinner!"

This young fellow was certainly courteous and wholesome. But something had cast a shadow over Martha Ann's spirit. She locked the door and slammed things around, taking out her vague feeling of uncertainty upon a completely innocent bystander.

"Andrew Bonning!" she soliloquized, wrathfully. "Didn't want to meet me again? . . . Doesn't approve of me? . . . What does he think I am, anyway?"

Her wrath and her pride, however, in no wise soothed the little ache this second unexpected meeting had engendered. Martha Ann bathed, pressed her one dress, and gazing in the mirror at the proud amber eyes and the golden hair, knew that she need not be ashamed of her looks. Would Bonning see her? Was he staying at this hotel? She went downstairs all a-quiver and still furious with herself. George met her, to introduce a kindly old man, whose twinkling blue eyes made much of Martha Ann. She knew at once that George had told him about her hitchhiking.

"Wal, Miss Marthy, young George tells me you're goin' to stop over with us for a night."

"Yes, I am."

"We'll take good care of you tonight, but you're liable to be scalped by Indians when you get to the Black Hills."

"Oh dear! Those dreadful Black Hills again!"

"Wal, mabbe you'll slip through. But you oughtn't to walk it. . . . Go right in to dinner, George. I'll be along pronto."

Fate was against Martha Ann. As they entered the dining room with George hanging on to her arm, whom should Martha see but Bonning at one of the tables. He wore the same rough garb, but it did not make him look like a laborer. As they passed he glanced up, and Martha knew as well as if he had spoken it that he thought she had flirted with this young Nebraskan and was getting her kick out of it. Martha Ann could have boxed his ears. She determined that she would make him notice her.

"Howdy, Hiram Perkins," she drawled, as she passed him. "Hope you heered from Mizzourie."

"Good evening, Wyoming Mad," he replied, rising with a bow.

Young Proctor wheeled in surprise, but did not speak until he had placed Martha Ann at a table and found a seat for himself.

"You spoke to that fellow. He called you 'Wyoming' something!"

"Yes. We met back at Norfolk. Just a little camaraderie of the road."

"Oh, I see. Gosh, it sort of took the starch out of me. . . . Well, I can sure recommend our fried chicken."

Martha Ann sat where she faced Bonning and had to meet his eyes. Suddenly the hot blood stole along her veins. If she did not read disappointment, as well as scorn in his dark gaze, then her reckoning was all wrong. At any rate, it had the same unaccountable effect that his first look had had upon her. Martha deigned not to notice him again and audaciously plied young Proctor with all the feminine wiles she could muster. She was actually flirting with eyes, lips, smiles and arch words when Bonning suddenly left his table and went out. The entrance of George's uncle saved Martha Ann at that blank juncture.

Nevertheless, she enjoyed her dinner, and later, when the old Nebraskan began to tell stories of his life on the frontier, Martha forgot all about Bonning. Once again in her room, however, packing the pretty dress, she remembered him, and she found herself thinking of that evening when a young man's strength had stood between her and a terrible fate. She divined that she would meet him tomorrow, or sometime on the road west, and the thought was both bitter and sweet. Before she went to sleep she had almost forgotten the young man's obvious disapproval in the anticipation of meeting him again on the open road.

At six next morning she bade good-by to the Proctors and started out again on her way northward. If her heart beat faster whenever she heard the hum of approaching cars she did not permit herself to turn around to identify the driver. But as car after car caught up with her and passed she confessed to herself that she had hoped Andrew Bonning might be driving one of them, and would give her another lift. Could he pass her by?

The freshness and fragrance of pastures, the green folds of the lonely hills, the lure of the road, and the warming sun—all seemed to have lost some of their delight for the runaway. Martha Ann marveled at this and wondered why the beautiful morning had not the zest of other days. She walked steadily along until nine o'clock. As the sun rose higher and higher she found the road narrowing and the farm houses growing more scattered.

She heard the sounds of wagon wheels and hoof beats behind her. As they drew nearer Martha looked back and observed an ancient wagon with a man perched on a high seat, and five small boys leaning over the side of the wagon box.

"Wal, sis, kin we give you a lift?" called the driver, as he halted the vehicle beside her.

"You surely can," replied Martha, gladly.

"Scramble up. Boys, make room thar for sis. . . . Air you goin' fur?"

"Wyoming."

"Ain't thinkin' of walkin' all thet way?"

"No indeed, not when I can meet such accommodating people as you."

"Wal, this ain't no gas wagon, but you're welcome. Hep yourself to some apples an' make yourself comfortable for three miles."

Munching juicy red apples and talking to these five lively farm boys was the most enjoyable experience Martha Ann had had so far on her journey. But it ended all too soon. Once more she was reduced to shank's mare.

In the ensuing hour only one car caught up with her. It was full and did not stop. The sun was beating down now with tropical intensity and her clothes were soaked with perspiration. She had not seen a farm house for hours. Worry followed soon upon fatigue and she began to wonder about how far it was to the next town. Fields after fields! They must run on forever. But after a time the fields gave way to rocky wasteland harboring only tall weeds.

Four o'clock found Martha Ann still trudging along the highway. A lump seemed fixed in her throat and often the landscape was blurred by the tears in her weary eyes. She kept saying that she did not mind the walk, endless though it seemed. Before she had started this wild-goose venture she had realized that there would be many, many miles of walking. It was the uncertainty of where she might find shelter and the approach of night that weighed her down with anxiety.

Martha Ann stumbled on over the mud-caked road and more than once came near falling. Both her heart and her feet seemed leaden. Suddenly the sound of a laboring motor caught her ear. She stood still and listened. She heard the sound again—the straining clatter of a car traversing the uncertain road. Soon it came in sight. Should she flag it? How could she stay on the road all night? Coyotes, snakes—probably more tramps! She waved frantically. The car halted, and Martha, running hurriedly to meet it, called out: "Please can you take me to the next town."

The occupants, a man and a woman, were Negroes. Martha swallowed her surprise. They evidently were as surprised as she. Martha studied the couple with penetrating eyes, but they looked honest and kind.

"Missy, if you-all don't mind ridin' with us yo's sho welcome," replied the woman, in a soft drawl.

"Thank you. I'm glad to come with you," said Martha, as she climbed in. "I didn't know it was so far to the next town."

"We are lost, too. I nevah did see so much land in all mah life with nuthin' on it."

"I didn't either," agreed Martha.

While the man drove his buxom spouse talked. They were from St. Louis, on the way west to find work and a home. Sundown found them still on the road, but by seven o'clock they had reached the outskirts of a town. At the town square Martha got out and thanked them, and bade them good luck and good-by. She stopped at a small restaurant for a light supper, and was directed to the only hotel in the valley. She went immediately to bed. To be tired out was the usual thing, but this night she felt forlorn and homesick for the first time. She could no longer keep home and mother out of her consciousness, because she had not sent either telegrams or letter, and she absolutely must not delay another day.

In the morning she was so stiff and sore that she could hardly get up. What would this new day bring forth? Always this was her waking thought. But this morning her sense of humor and the call of adventure did not come to the rescue of her drooping spirits. For the first time she was experiencing the pangs of the guilty conscience of a runaway.

Therefore the first thing she did upon going downstairs was to begin a letter to her mother. She discovered that the decision to write was one thing. What to write was something else again. In the end she found that she would have to continue with the falsehood with which she had started her journey. She wrote with tears blotting the page that when she and Alice McGinnis had arrived in Omaha, Alice's uncle had invited them to drive to the Black Hills with them. Of course she and Alice were wild to go. "And you know, mother darling, how I've always yearned to see the West, so don't scold—and forgive me for disobeying."

Posting that letter was a relief, yet it did not still her accusing conscience. How could she ever make amends for this untruth to her family, especially her mother? Her first innocent falsehood had enmeshed her in a situation which would require more and more lies and deception. Where would it all end?

Martha Ann had not been on the road ten minutes that morning before a touring car bearing an Illinois license plate passed with two middle-aged men in the front seat. They slowed down, smiled an invitation, then waved and went on. Soon after that a truck ground up a grade behind Martha and stopped at the crest of the hill.

"Whoa," sang out a deep booming voice. A little boy on the seat beside the driver reached down and with tiny hands made what Martha thought was a pretense of helping to stop the car.

"Hey, traveler, want a ride with my pardner an' me?" called the same deep voice.

Martha glanced up at a strange pair—the man in a blue shirt open at a bronzed throat, with a ruddy frank face and his left arm off at the elbow—the lad in diminutive overalls, looking like a wistful little elf.

"I'd like to ride very much if I won't crowd you," replied Martha.

"Plenty room," he boomed.

She hopped up onto the high seat beside the boy. He smiled at her and she smiled back. Then for a while they rattled along the road in silence. Martha thought of a hundred questions she wanted to ask.

After some time the driver started to talk. He came originally from Detroit and had lost his arm in the war. Upon arriving home from France he had learned from the doctors that he had lung trouble and would not live long unless he went west. He had come to Nebraska and in eight months he was a well man. Then he had gone in for farming and had been successful. Much of this good fortune, he said, was owing to the wonderful wife he had found out west.

"I've an older boy, too," he concluded with pardonable pride. "But I just couldn't get along without this young fellow here. He's my left-hand man."

At this sally both father and son laughed happily. Martha at last had run across one returned and disabled veteran of the war who had found himself. This broad open land seemed hospitable to strangers. Martha added to her growing list another reason to love the West.

They drove along chattering gaily until they let her off at a road that branched off to the south. Martha waved farewell to a gallant soldier and a lovable youngster.

"Well," soliloquized Martha Ann, "there's nothing to this hitchhiking but walking and riding, and meeting a lot of people I like . . . and a few I don't."

She thought of Andrew Bonning. He seemed to be fading into the past, the truth of which she recognized with a pang. How could she ever forget his gallant service in her behalf? But he had taken her for a common flirt. "Oh! it's just as well if I never meet him again," she sighed.

The country was growing more rugged. It swept away in series of desolate ridges where signs of civilization were becoming scarce. The trees were now taller and more numerous; the air had a finer, keener edge. It was invigorating. Martha Ann felt that she could walk on forever. Gradually with the exercise she found her stiffness was wearing away. She hoped to reach the next town late in the afternoon. If these towns were only not so far apart she would not have to be so much afraid of not getting a ride. As she swung along, her mind skipping from one thought to another, from home to the imagined ranch of her uncle, a Ford coupé came rolling up behind her and with a screeching of brakes stopped a few feet beyond her.

"How's chances, baby?" queried a young fellow from the driver's seat. He was alone and he had a sunburned, impudent face.

"Not so good," replied Martha Ann, shortly. He kept his car moving alongside of her as she walked.

"Long way to Barton," he said significantly, and stopped the Ford.

Nothing else in the way of words could have made such an impression on the weary wayfarer. She had found very little traffic on this road and she wanted so very much to get along with her journey. She stopped. He smiled at her in a knowing way, as if he were accustomed to being indulgent to a willful girl who was bound to capitulate in the end. When he opened the door her old confidence reasserted itself and she stepped in. She had done so despite an instant instinctive dislike for this overconfident young man. Perhaps her feeling derived mostly from the way he called her "baby." He started the car with one hand and passed his cigarette case with the other.

"Have one?"

"No, thanks."

"Don't you really smoke or are you being snooty?" His eyes were a little too close together and emitted curious glints as they ran over her slim person.

"I really don't like cigarettes. . . . How far are you going on this road?"

"A few miles more. Have to turn off to see a farmer. . . . Where are you bound for, babe?"

"Wyoming," she returned, curtly, hating the epithet he used so freely. She began to fear that she had made a blunder in accepting this young man's lift.

"Gee! That's too far for a dame to be going alone. Not in a hurry, are you, babe?"

"Indeed I am. In a very big hurry," declared Martha Ann sharply. Whether or not her reply penetrated his mind Martha could not tell. Certainly he seemed not to resent it.

"Ever been to an Indian pow-wow?"

"No-o."

"We're having a pow-wow and dance in Lagrange tonight. Why doncha come on and go with me. You'll have a swell time."

"I've relatives expecting me at Barton tonight."

"Tell that to your grandmother," he retorted with a grin. "You're one of these hitchhikers. They're all sports. I know."

"Well, this one isn't."

"C'mon, babe. Be a sport. You can phone from Lagrange. Say you got in late. I'll give you a real time."

"I'm sorry, but I couldn't think of it," rejoined Martha. She felt his eyes on her, as she watched the speedometer mounting higher.

" 'Smatter, babe? Afraid to speed a little?"

"I'm not afraid," she said scornfully. "I was just wondering if you were driving to a fire."

He laughed and laid a freckled hand upon Martha's knee. "Maybe you're afraid of me, babe?"

"Humph! Hardly," she returned. Then decisively, and very deliberately and firmly she removed his hand.

"You know, baby, I could go for you in a big way," he said, persuasively.

"I dare say. But it's not necessary. If you'll slow down I'll get out and walk."

"Aw, don't be like that. You just came. Am I such a bad guy?"

"Skip it!" ejaculated Martha Ann, in disgust. "I'm not your type."

"You're just trying to high-hat me."

"Stop this car and let me out!"

"But, gee whiz, girlie, we're nearly there."

By this time the Ford was careening along the road at the rate of a mile a minute. Martha grew frightened with the speed of the car, if not with the lout who was driving it. To be killed in a wreck—what a futile and tragic end to her dream! Why had she ever yielded to this mad escapade? She called sharply to be let out.

He lifted his foot from the accelerator and made a quick turn to the right down a grassy lane lined with trees that brushed against the car. The swerve of the car had thrown Martha off her balance and over against the driver. He let go of the wheel with one hand and seized her around the waist. Then he slowed down the car so that he would not drive off the rough lane into the brush. He tried to pull the girl to him.

"How dare you! Let me go—you rowdy!" cried Martha Ann, drawing back with all her might.

"Too late, babe!" He had the car barely moving now. "C'mon. Be nice to me. What're you afraid of?"

"Not a thing! Least of all—you!" panted Martha, struggling. "Let me go—let me out of this car—or I'll have you arrested."

"Say, cutie, where do you think you are? There's no sheriff near here."

"I have—relatives near enough—to see that plenty is done to you. . . . Let me out!"

He gave a derisive laugh. "Say, listen, dame, you're so far from a sheriff, or anybody, that it isn't even funny. No one will hear you if you do scream. But have a heart. Cut the upstage stuff. Am I as bad as all that?"

"Our tastes differ. I just don't happen to care for your type."

"Hell you say! I'll just have to change your mind. Anyway, I like my women wild."

With that he let go of the wheel and caught her to him. Martha had succeeded in wrenching almost free. For an instant she was fascinated by his small, scalloped, tobacco-stained teeth. She recognized for the first time in her life contact with a raw, bold elemental force. Then his thick mouth was moving toward her. All the other features faded before this animal ugliness. A terrible rage flashed hot and overpowering through her. What a miserable rotten bully! She sensed that there was no use to scream. She had better save her breath. She was utterly dependent upon her own resourcefulness and strength. The car bumped against a stump, and lurched along the bank side of the lane. She feared for a moment that it might overturn. He had been trying to get farther and farther off the main road. Martha knew that she could not afford to get any further away from the highway.

With one arm tight and contracting around her shoulder he suddenly pressed his other grimy hand over Martha's breast. She kicked out with all her might. One of her heavy hiking boots struck him on the shin. He let out a yell of pain, but continued to hold her tighter than ever with one arm while again he endeavored to steer with the other. He wanted to get her far along this lonely lane, out of sight and sound of the highway.

The savage kick Martha had administered to the driver of the Ford awakened her to her one chance. She knew her greatest strength was in her legs, so she lashed out again with both feet. At length she kicked herself free, and then doubling up, she shot both boots into the pit of his stomach. Yelling hoarsely he let go of the wheel. Swiftly Martha reached down, locked the ignition, and flung the key far out into the tall grass.

"You damn she-devil!" he screamed, his face contorted by anger and pain.

Then Martha's rage knew no bounds. If she had felt any fear before, it now vanished. With her back braced in the corner of the coupé and her feet up she continued to batter him—all over the front of his body—with swift, hard, savage kicks from her heavy boot. Twice he seized her flying feet, but could not hold them. He was not strong enough—Martha saw, savagely exultant. He could not force her. She could whip him any day. And she kicked him with a hard left to the stomach and a harder right in the nose. Blood spattered the interior of the car. But that only augmented her determination to maim him and even to kill him.

"Let up—you infernal wildcat," he bawled.

Martha Ann dropped her boots with a thump, and sat up to snatch at her bag. Then, opening the door, she plunged out. He had his hands to his nose. Blood was pouring through his fingers down his wrists, staining his shirt sleeves.

"Next time you—get fresh—" she panted, "pick some girl—your class and size—you big bully!"

She marched breathlessly back down the lane to the road—an outraged but a triumphant young woman. This elation lasted only for a few moments; then a reaction set in, and she began to tremble violently and to sob. She could no longer stand up. Staggering against a culvert she sat down, trying to dip her handkerchief into the water to wipe her face and hands with it. A car hummed close by. Could that bully be after her again? Oh, God, she could not find the strength for another battle. But the hum did not come from down the lane. A car hove in sight. She recognized it as the Illinois Buick that had passed her with the two pleasant-faced men. They bore down upon the culvert, and seeing her, halted.

"Hello—you again," called one.

"What's wrong, little girl?" queried the other quickly and got out.

The sound of a kindly voice in the terrible loneliness upset Martha still more. Her sobs increased. She could not answer the queries they put to her. They got a canteen and offered her water. At length she recovered enough to be coherent. "I accepted a lift—from a young man—in a Ford. . . . He drove—over sixty. . . . Turned off down—that lane there and attacked me. . . . Oh, he was beastly! . . . But I fought him off—left him there."

"Damned scoundrel!" rasped one of the men. "Biston, you look after her while I find this fellow."

He strode off and was gone for some time, during which the other gentleman tried to calm Martha, and to assure her that he and his companion, Mr. Madison, would be glad to have her ride with them to the next town.

Martha was in the car, in the back seat, and somewhat composed when Mr. Madison came striding back.

"Well, Miss—," he began cheerfully.

"Dixon," Martha supplied.

"I found your assailant and from his appearance I'm inclined to believe that the question Biston and I were pondering a while back—can that kid take care of herself—is very amply answered. But I gave him a little more punishment just for good measure."

3

ANDREW BONNING decided that there must be something amiss when James, the butler, disturbed his leisurely perusal of the Sunday *New York Times,* and informed him that his father wished to see him in the library.

"Well, it can't come any too soon for me," muttered Andrew, sensing a long-threatened ultimatum, no doubt brought to a climax by his brother Raymond's latest escapade. Thoughtfully he descended the stairway to the second floor, feeling the oppressive atmosphere of that house as never before.

As he expected, Raymond was already there, standing with the elegant non-chalance his handsome person never failed to radiate. His blond head was bent slightly as he scrutinized a bit of paper he held before him. Mr. Bonning sat at his desk, looking up with a cool air of finality.

"That's the last, Raymond," he was saying. "You are on your own now."

"Okay, Pater," replied Raymond, looking up from the check. "Thanks, of course. It's more than I'd hoped for. . . . And I'm to clear out."

"Your sister and I will take an apartment—where there will not be any room for you boys."

"Morning, Andy," said Raymond. "We're in for a ride. . . . So long to both of you." He strode out fluttering the check in a white hand.

"Dad, I guess I don't need to ask what you want," spoke up Andrew, with a short laugh.

"Will you sit down?" queried his father, courteously.

"No, thanks. And please make it short and sweet."

"It can't be anything else," rejoined the senior Bonning. "You doubtless are aware of how hard the latest Wall Street crash has hit me. I hoped to retrieve. But . . . well, I need not go into details. . . . Here is a check for you."

Andrew received it without glancing at the figures it bore. "Dad, I'm sorry," he said, haltingly. "At your age—it's tough. . . . With neither of us boys and help—and Gloria— "

"Your sister has her income," interrupted Mr. Bonning. "Fortunately she has not squandered the principal of the money your mother left her. And she will marry well. I can take care of myself in a modest way. But Raymond and you must now fare for yourselves."

"I gathered as much, Dad," returned Andrew, thoughtfully. He was still fond of his father, which fact seemed suddenly to erase all the misunderstandings and aloofness of the past few years.

"Andrew, I didn't trouble to bore Raymond with my opinions," went on Mr. Bonning, "but if you will permit me, I'd like to express my bitter disappointment in you."

"Dad, I've been under the impression that you had expressed that—more than once," rejoined Andrew, sadly. "But if it will relieve you—go ahead."

"You quit college before you were half through your sophomore year."

"Why not? I wasn't learning a damn thing," said Andrew impatiently.

"You couldn't make good even in football—where you had every requirement except guts," replied his father contemptuously. "Big, heavy, fast on your feet—you could have made a name for yourself!"

"Yeah! Like hell I could," retorted Andrew hotly. "Didn't I go out for the freshman team and scrub team for two years and rip the varsity line to ribbons? The coaches were hot for me, but Captain Higgins and the athletic directors played their favorites. I lost heart and finally lay down on the job."

"Yes, you sure did. But if you had stuck it out!"

"Dad, would it surprise you to learn that I regarded college as too much football, too many fast cars and too much money, instead of a place to study?"

"No, that wouldn't surprise me. You're an adept at excuses. . . . The fact is you failed to get a college training. Either physical or cultural. And lastly, you have failed in business."

"Dad, that last I admit," replied Andrew regretfully. "I've been a flop at each job you've got me. I tried hard. Honest to God, I tried! It wasn't that I'm exactly a dumbbell. I'm poor at figures. I can't stand a desk. Confinement strangles me somehow. . . . And, Dad, to come clean—I hate modern business methods."

"Thank you for being frank, at last," declared Mr. Bonning. "You might have saved us both considerable friction, not to say grief."

Andrew slowly tore the check in two pieces and laid them before his father.

"Dad, you need have no further concern about me."

"What!—you won't take it?"

"No."

"Why not?"

"Because you'll need it more than I. . . . And you've awakened me—to my shame. All the same I don't feel wholly to blame for my failure. The world is out of joint or maybe I just don't fit in. I haven't found anything I want to and can do. That's all. . . . Good-by, father."

Andrew stalked out of the library with head erect and resolute step, deaf to Mr. Bonning's call. On the landing above he encountered his sister Gloria, leaning over the rail. She wore a blue dressing gown.

"Andy!"

"Morning, Gloria! Why so intense and dramatic? You always were a trage-dienne, but just now you've got Duse tied to the mast. . . . Say, what an idea! Why don't you go into the movies, Gloria? What'd be better than— "

"I heard," she whispered, and drawing him into her room, closed the door. Then she asked gravely: "Dad has refused you the parental roof any longer?"

"It amounts to that, Sis, though I gathered this particular parental roof was lost to all of us."

"Andy, I'm not a damn bit sorry," she said fervently. "Ray is a rotter. And this break will make a man of you."

"Thanks, old thing. You give me hope. In fact, Gloria, you've been the only one who ever held out the slightest hope for me. I'll not forget that. Even Constance always thought me a flop."

"Yes, and she'll give you the gate when she hears this," declared Gloria significantly. "Andy, it gets my goat the way she strings you along."

"We're not engaged, Sis—and honestly, I don't think I care any more about her than she does about me. We've just been together since before I went to college."

"What'll you do, Andy!" she queried, her dark eyes studying him.

"Beat it!" he burst out, as if a sudden thought had possessed him.

"Where?"

"I don't know. Far away, though . . . where there's room—great open spaces—no business."

"West?" she flashed.

"Darling, you can't imagine me going abroad!"

"Andy, you should have taken Dad's check."

"Not me!"

"I'll stake you to five grand."

"You will not! . . . Thanks, old girl. I've still about twelve thousand of what mother left me. It's more than enough."

"Far West," mused the sister, with wondering eyes. "I've been to Yellow-

stone, Andy. Oh, Wyoming was marvelous! Go there. . . . Andy, you know
I have queer inspirations at long intervals.''

"Okay. It's Wyoming," replied Andrew, relieved that something had been
decided for him.

"It'll be the making of you," she went on. "Somehow, Andy, you never
could have made the grade here. New York has lost its kick for you."

"Kick! I hate that word," he declared irritably. "It seems to be the sole aim
of everybody nowadays."

"It is—for all of us anyway," she replied, somberly. "I suppose we can't
escape the present. It simply is. . . . I've tried every last thing under the sun—
except marriage—and I'd try that if I believed it'd be interesting enough."

Andrew bit his lip to restrain a sharp retort. Whatever Gloria's shortcomings,
in his opinion she was a thoroughbred and she had been loyal to him, and loyalty
loomed big in this hour.

"Draw the line somewhere, darling," he said lightly. "Marrying Ellerton,
or even Blackstone, for their money might not give you much of a kick, but it
would be safe."

"Andy, you're old-fashioned. And that's where you are wrong. The idea of
a twentieth-century girl marrying to be safe—settled—taken care of! Bunk! Who
wants to be safe?"

"Sis, I think *you* can take care of yourself at that," rejoined Andrew with a
laugh. "Well, I'll go pack up a few things before I change my mind."

"Do. If you weaken now you're sunk forever. Only don't beat it without
saying good-by to me."

Andrew plodded on upstairs to his room, obsessed with the resolve he had
impulsively made, conscious of sensations he had not experienced since boyhood.
He was twenty-four years old. And the thought that struck him so forcibly at
the moment was—why had this idea never come to him before? He flung himself
down on his bed to face the realization that the turning point in his life had
arrived. He had reached an indifferent stage in a futile existence where he
imagined nothing worth while could happen to him. But he realized now this
was because he had not made anything happen. Until the last six months he had
accepted his inability to do so with good nature and resignation. He was just a
misfit. Later had come discontent and chafing, leading to his present genuine
unhappiness. A few words from his sophisticated yet wise sister had changed
all this in a twinkling—had shaken him out of his doldrums. He found himself
suddenly facing a future that offered a chance and a challenge.

Yet in his heart he realized that he had not given the old life a fair break. The
great modern city was all right, for young people who had kept pace with the
times. Andrew was not speed-mad, drink-mad, pleasure-mad, money-mad, but

there was something lacking. He had not been willing to give the old life what it took to make the grade.

"But I can raise wheat," he replied to his accusations, "or be a garage mechanic, or a forest ranger . . . or something, by golly!"

What should be his first move? A definite, irrevocable one! First he'd telephone Constance. Sure of her reaction, and eager to have it over, he called her number. And while he waited he visualized her blonde head on her white pillow.

"Hello," came the answer presently, in the sleepy, rich, contented voice he knew so well.

"Good morning, Connie. This is Andy," he replied.

"Oh, it's you, big boy? What's the idea—calling me at this ungodly hour?" she pouted.

"News, Connie," he plunged in. "Dad has shot the works. I've been disinherited—turned out—on my own!"

"*Andy!* Don't be so dramatic! Are you kidding me?"

He assured her solemnly that it was only too true and that somehow he felt strangely glad. "You know, Connie, I've been a total loss in this burg."

Then followed a silence so long that Andrew had to restrain himself not to break it.

"Oh, Andy—what a rotten break! I'm so sorry, dear," she said finally, and that reply gave him the relief he sought.

"Sure you're sorry, Connie. But your heart isn't going to break?"

"My heart break? Andy, be yourself!"

"Darling, I'm being myself. . . . What I mean is that if you—if you considered our—our friendship. . . . Oh, hang it, Connie, if you want to hold me— "

"Dear old Andy! What a child you are!" came the answer accompanied by Constance's mellow laugh. "Listen. I never would have married you, and I thought you knew it. We were just good pals."

"I think I remember your telling me that before. But I wanted to play the game straight."

"Andy, darling, you're too fine, too simple, too square for this crazy town. . . . What will you do?"

"Beat it out West."

"Where?"

"Wild and wooly Wyoming."

"Wyoming? For the love of Mike! Wouldn't St. Louis be far enough?"

"Nix on the madding crowd, Connie."

"Darling, you're being a little mad yourself. That's what I always liked about you."

"Me for the tall timbers and the open range!"

"How you do rave! . . . At least you'll get a kick out of it. I'm envious!"

"Can that stuff, will you?" retorted Andrew. "And just get this straight. It's something Gloria sprung on me a moment ago." And Andrew told her exactly what Gloria had said. He heard Connie's low lazy laugh. Then she added: "Tell Gloria it's not so hot."

"Okay, I'll tell her. . . . Well, Connie, old dear, good-by."

"Good-by, Andy—and good luck!"

Slowly Andrew hung up the receiver, conscious of immeasurable relief and at the same time a vague sadness. His thoughts turned back to the many gay times he and Connie and Gloria had had together. He was turning his back upon those irresponsible times, but there would be no feeling of irreparable loss.

Andrew stood at the window for a moment, in a pensive mood. The street was empty, with that stillness which always meant the Sabbath. Beyond the corner house he could see Central Park, with the maples, the beeches and oaks beginning to show freshly green. Spring had come again. And suddenly the realization that soon he would be out where he could breathe, where he could see the sky and face the free wind, and feel the hot sun on his back and smell the earth, rushed over him with almost a suffocating necessity. By that fleeting sensation Andrew knew for almost the first time that what he was about to do was right for him.

Packing was the last act of severance, difficult and a little sad because he had to choose little out of abundance. He packed two large grips and a traveling bag. Only his favorite possessions were included. And to his amazement, when all the selections had been made and the job finished, that Sabbath day had almost come to an end. He changed to a light traveling suit and, calling a taxi, left the house without seeing his father or Gloria again. He would have said farewell to her if she had not been out.

Andrew went to the Manhattan Hotel, took a room, had dinner, and then crossed to Grand Central Station to engage a berth on the Twentieth-Century Limited for Monday morning. That done, he swung down Forty-second Street toward the theater district, conscious of a deep tranquil excitement in his breast. It was done. And he chose a Western movie as his swan song to life in New York.

The picture was a thriller, full of color and action, raucous with sound, and melodramatic in plot. The hero turned his profile too often to the camera and the heroine heaved her obvious breast too consciously. Andrew could not piece together any thread of story. Yet he sat there in the dark, reveling in the sweep of rangeland, the white-tipped peaks, and the racing of horses, the gun-throwing cowboys, the lean Indian riders. He had always experienced a secret pleasure in such pictures, and had kept his habit of going to see them to himself. Now he reveled in it. It happened that the location of this motion picture was near the Tetons of Wyoming. Andrew remained for the second showing of it, and left the theater as keen as any boy who had ever read of Deadwood Dick and Calamity Jane. Such pictures were made for his kind. Strutting actors had to be endured and the pretty stars tolerated because they had youth and charm, but their great undeniable fascination was in the picture quality, the action of horses and the violence of man, thrown upon a wild and picturesque background.

The next morning Andrew Bonning transferred his securities into cash, nine-tenths in bills of large denomination, which he placed in a little leather sack to wear under his shirt. That money had to go a long way. His ticket read second tourist to Omaha, Nebraska. He, who had never considered the value of a dollar before, now meant to make the most of a dime.

"See here, bozo. Thirty-five bucks is highway robbery for this antediluvian Ford," declared Bonning, as he shook the rattling old car with one powerful grasp of his hand.

The scene was a vacant lot far from the business center of Omaha. Andrew Bonning felt that he had put on a new character with the outfit of blue jeans he had purchased. Certainly it must have had some powerful transforming power, for never before that he could remember had he haggled over the price of any commodity.

"Cheapest Ford here, boss," replied the open-lot car distributor. "What you lookin' fer?"

"I want an old car that nobody can run. Something to tinker with," replied Andrew.

"I'll be doggoned!" ejaculated the garage man with a grin. "Reckon we ain't comin' to a deal. All my cars run slick as a whistle."

"Let's hear this Ford purr."

The eager salesman jumped in with alacrity, turned on the ignition and tried to start the car. But nothing happened. He rasped and pumped and pulled to no purpose. Red in the face he looked down at Andrew somewhat sheepishly.

"Stranger, did you jimmy the works?"

"How could I? You haven't turned your back on me. . . . Can't you start it?"

"'Pears not. Cold, I reckon. But I'll make her shoot in a minute."

Several minutes elapsed and the salesman had lost much of his confidence. In the dealer's chagrin Andrew recognized the psychological moment.

"If you throw in that old lap robe there I'll buy this pile of junk."

"How much?" queried the car owner, resignedly.

"Fifteen dollars."

"Take it," snorted the other, throwing up his hands. "But you're worse than Jesse James."

Andrew found himself in possession of a car. Leisurely he set about determining what was wrong with the engine. He had a knack for machinery. In less than ten minutes he discovered that the carburetor intake tube was choked with dirt.

"Hey, I found out what ailed her," he called to the car merchant.

"Ahuh? An' what was thet?"

"The locomotive ingredient failed to coincide with the perihelion," replied Andrew cheerfully.

"Aw, go-wan, you can't kid me," returned the other. "Bet you don't belong in them overalls."

"Nope. And you belong in Wall Street. Funny old world! . . . So long!"

On the way to the lodginghouse where Andrew had left his bags he stopped at a grocery store to buy some fruit and provisions. Soon he was on his way out of Omaha, his last stop being at a filling station on the outskirts of the city. Here he procured gas, oil and road maps. Then driving north on the highway, he realized that his new life had begun at last.

Something like a gray curtain had dropped in his consciousness to hide all of his past failures. He was alone, perfectly free, speeding along an open road into an unknown country. Fields, grazing cows, apple trees in bloom, flights of blackbirds, long strings of swallows on the telegraph wires were realities with which he came in close contact for the first time. Rush-lined ponds by the wayside where ducks paddled, wandering willow-bordered brooks, groves of oaks and elms, with other trees unfamiliar to him, met his eager eyes and brought back long-past summer visits in New England, and vague memories of an even remoter period.

Andrew's mood was one of quiet exultation. As he did not rush at the miles, neither did he inquire too avidly into this unfamiliar mood. He felt, however, as he visualized the ranges of the West, that he was undergoing a transformation. It was a transformation which he welcomed. He had pulled his stakes from the East and must transplant them somewhere in the West. But just how the change would take place did not concern Andrew greatly at this time: he was fascinated none the less by the initiation into the process through which he would be made over.

Toward noon he passed through a village that boasted flaring signs of gas stations at both entrance and exit. Somewhere, Andrew promised himself with satisfaction, he would be traveling beyond the smell of gasoline.

Andrew drove along at about twenty-five miles an hour. This snail's pace caused him to be hooted to the side of the road by other cars impatient to pass. One big flashy touring car honked at him impatiently, and as it got by a florid-faced driver in shirt sleeves, evidently a tourist, yelled something about junking a tin can.

"Drive on, mister," said Andrew, aloud. "You represent what I have turned my back on—speed, luxury, restlessness, idleness, high blood pressure—flesh-pots of Egypt.''

The hours passed by all too quickly for Andrew Bonning. Sunset caught him at the top of a hill, where he stopped to admire the scene. He drove on, presently, coasting down a winding hilly road, and at the bottom turned a curve under a wooded bank that accentuated the twilight.

Andrew caught sight of a camp fire, whose blaze disclosed two slouchy dark forms moving about it. His lights were not working so he moved slowly along the soft road. When about opposite the fire Andrew's sharp ears heard a cry. Then against the evening sky he saw a man and a boy silhouetted in violent action. Andrew stopped the car. He had come upon his first adventure.

"Let that boy go," shouted Andrew and jumped out of his car. Advancing upon the two he asked what the idea was. The man retreated, with a reply about only having fun.

"Oh—no sir," cried the youngster, in a voice that startled Andrew. "He meant to rob—me—and I don't know what—when he saw I was a girl!"

Andrew's exclamation of amazement was followed by a swift leap, a lunge and a blow, the power of which he had not calculated. Like a flung sack the man went over the bank out of sight. Andrew yelled for the tramp's comrades to make themselves scarce.

"Are you really a girl?" he queried, turning to the little figure in the middle of the road. Indeed, after peering down into a white oval face and great staring dark eyes he found that he need not have asked that question.

The girl admitted it and said she sometimes wished she were not. Andrew asked her a couple of pertinent questions, to learn that she did not belong thereabouts, and that she was a hitchhiker. As she stood there, looking up at him, Andrew Bonning found himself divided between two impressions—one of admiration and solicitation for a pretty slip of a girl who had been caught in a perilous predicament; the other a sudden bitter reminder of modern woman's wiles and the fact that even on a lonely Nebraska road at night he might expect to meet a girl who was only looking for a thrill. The second impression won out over the former. Andrew offered the girl a lift as far as Norfolk, and helping her in, resumed his seat at the wheel and went on.

He could see her dimly in the paling afterglow without appearing to notice her, and it was not easy to subdue his curiosity. She had slim brown hands, beautifully shaped, that clung nervously to the pack she held on her lap. He could feel that she wanted to speak to him, and finally she did, hazarding a remark that he evidently did not live in this section. Then, in the short interchange of conversation that followed, which he did not encourage because he resented his interest in a girl hiker, he was led to reveal his name. But she did not give hers, an omission Andrew added to her discredit. At last they arrived at Norfolk.

He called her attention to the fact and remarked her enthusiasm over the bright lights.

"You'll get another kick here," he replied, slowing down preparatory to a stop.

"Kick?" she echoed, turning those strange, luminous eyes upon him in doubt, not of the word, but of his intimation. Andrew could have sworn not only to her innocence, but to the fact that in the bright light he was gazing at the very prettiest girl he had ever seen in his life.

"Yes, kick," he replied curtly, annoyed with himself. Then he laughed. "Isn't that what you're after? Isn't that about all girls think of nowadays?"

She did not reply and seemed to have been affronted by his accusation.

"Please let me out here," she requested, pointing toward a modest looking hotel.

They stopped, and he stepped out to assist her. Then she said, hesitatingly: "Thank you, Mr. Bonning, for—for everything."

He replied that she was welcome and that he hoped she would have better luck on the next lap of her hike. . . . "You forgot to tell me your name."

"I didn't forget. I was— "

No doubt her faltering was due to Andrew's exposure of the letters M A D on the pack he lifted from the car, and at which he stared.

"Mad!" he spelled out, "Wyoming Mad?" with a laugh. "It suits you better than any name. And as you are an unforgettable kid I'll remember you by that. . . . I hope we don't meet again. Good-by."

She stood there at the curb, holding her bag, her sweet face uplifted, puzzled, shy, slowly awakening to his rudeness. Andrew flung himself into the car and drove away, conscious of several conflicting feelings. He halted on the next corner at a gas station to fill up. Then he continued on to another hotel further down the street, where he put up for the night.

Andrew ate a dinner less frugal than had been his intention. But he gave very little thought to his plan of travel. He was in a curious state of mind. After dinner he walked twice past the hotel where the hiking girl had stopped, and nearly succumbed to a desire to go in to inquire for her. Then he went to a motion picture theater and stood in front of it for a while hoping like a fool that she might come along. He went in but soon left. After that he walked to and fro in the town's little park, and at length returned to his hotel and room.

"Well, my first adventure is a puzzler," soliloquized Andrew while he undressed. He had to own up to having received a thrill from his rescue of the little hiker with the big eyes. He had been shocked to meet a girl, hardly sixteen years old, he calculated, alone on a country road after dark, confessedly engaged upon what he considered to be a mad prank. He had been alienated by a recurrent bitterness which fostered the thought that she could not be anything else but a wayward girl, on adventure bent. It was this thought that had accounted for his sudden rudeness.

"Unforgettable kid? Nuts!" he concluded, turning out the light. "The world was full of alluring, seductive, irresistible females. What chance had a man? Wyoming Mad? . . . If this isn't the queerest deal I ever had. Suppose I meet that girl again? It'll be funny. Ha! Ha! . . . I don't think! . . . That kid's just no good!" Then Andrew was amazed to hear an inward voice damn him for a sophisticated, suspicious and embittered Easterner who could not recognize innocence when he met it.

"My God!" muttered Andrew aghast. "What would Connie or Gloria say to that? That I'm 'Wyoming Mad' myself." But his derision was not convincing. In this new voice there appeared to be the nucleus of a revolt.

At daylight Andrew was behind the wheel of his Ford, and he started with a speed which indicated that he wanted to leave something far behind. Twenty-five or thirty miles an hour, however, was about the limit his old battered car could produce and soon cars began to pass him. To save his life he could not resist trying to get a look at their occupants. But that was seldom possible, unless he deliberately stared as the cars sped by. All day long, he reflected, a trim little figure, between lifts, was probably hiking along that road. Her eyes haunted him, not because of their size, he imagined, or their strange glow, or their color—because he had no idea of their color—but because of the wistful look they held. Had he misjudged her? Had he placed her in a class with all the neckers, flirts and thrill seekers, just because he had found her on a lonely road, waylaid by tramps? It did seem unjust, he had to admit. There was some unquenchable chivalry in Andrew Bonning which had often been the jest of his sportive acquaintances.

Andrew made no stop that day, except at a crossroad refueling station. Toward evening he had dinner at a little wayside hamlet, and then he drove on a few miles to camp in his car. All the next day engine trouble occupied his attention, and gave him enough tinkering to satisfy a long-felt want. It halted him, too, at Sidonia for a minor repair.

He was standing in front of the one hotel, watching the traffic and awaiting the dinner hour, when a car gingerly approached the curb.

The driver was the girl who had been causing him so much speculation. Her companion appeared to be a young local chap to whom this was an auspicious occasion. As Andrew recognized the hitchhiker, she simultaneously looked up to meet his gaze. Then a sudden light, a half-break of a smile, was blotted out in a crimson blush.

Andrew strode into the hotel, somehow glad that she had had the grace to blush. Caught with the goods, he thought scornfully! She had picked up this country bumpkin on the road and had ended a short or long, probably long, ride by driving his car, no doubt to allow him freer use of his arms. It made Andrew slightly sick, because that queer streak of chivalry in him had almost won a battle in her behalf. He wished she would appear in the dining room before he left. He wanted just one more look at her.

Andrew, however, had given up hope and had almost finished his meal when she did come in, escorted by the young fellow who was very overceremonious and obviously self-conscious. Andrew, considerably surprised at her appearance, could only stare.

She had changed the masculine hiking garb for a pretty blue dress that was exceedingly feminine. She had trim shapely legs and little feet on which were patent-leather slippers. Her dainty head, carried high, was bare. The wavy, golden hair caught and held the light. All this Andrew saw in a glance before her face transfixed him. Its opal hue, just hinting of tan, took on a little warmth and color. As she passed she spoke, impudently he thought.

"Howdy, Hiram Perkins. Hope you heerd from Mizzourie."

"Good evening, Wyoming Mad," he returned, rising and bowing.

Her escort seated her at a nearby table, and evidently was concerned by the exchange of greetings between her and Andrew. She made some casual explanation, with a deprecatory motion of her hand that seemed to satisfy her escort.

"Knows her stuff," muttered Andrew to himself, and then, drawing a deep breath, as a man about to undergo an ordeal, he looked deliberately at her. It was to find that she was already gazing fixedly at him. For a long moment their eyes held their gaze. Andrew had an odd thought—if those wonderful eyes had expressed the least softness, the least hint of yielding, he would not have been accountable for himself. All Andrew could detect, however, was pride and disdain. And he caught these impressions only as she averted her face.

Then he had his opportunity and he made the most of it. Pretty? Beautiful? Such terms did not do her justice. She was lovely. Engrossed with his scrutiny Andrew had not at once grasped one dismaying fact. She was flirting outrageously with her escort. She never deigned to give Andrew another glance. Again his vision of her became distorted, though her actions were merely those of a gay young girl having an enjoyable dinner with a newly made acquaintance. Andrew knew that, but his biased mind would not accept it. He imagined them in the shadowy park—nay—riding along a country road in the moonlight to some lonesome spot. He shook his head angrily. Suddenly Andrew found himself hating the girl.

Abruptly he arose, leaving his dessert untasted, and stalked out.

"One born every minute!" he muttered, and then in bitter conflict with his skepticism: "Connie, old girl, I guess you ruined the makings of a square fellow!"

He got his car, and after driving half the night, he stopped to watch the moon go down over the western horizon.

4

A WEEK later Andrew Bonning made camp outside a little Wyoming town called Split Rock. This was on the Old Oregon Trail which he had followed all the way from Torrington, on the Nebraska line.

Many places along the famous old trail of the trappers, explorers, Indian fighters and pioneers had interested him and almost persuaded him to stop for a spell. But satisfying as had been the rolling sagebrush prairie, Andrew had continued on his way in answer to a call he could not define. On clear mornings he could see the mountains white-toothed in the blue. And they lured him. The Platte River saw three of his camps before he left it at Alcova. He passed over the Rattlesnake Range, and as he drove into Split Rock one golden sunset he saw the Granite Mountains on his right and the Green Mountains on his left. And westward, a hundred miles more or less, stood the Continental Divide, dim yet rosy-white in the sunset, the great wall of the Rockies.

Andrew left his car in a thicket not far off the road, deciding to walk the half mile into Split Rock for the exercise. Satisfying himself that it could not readily be detected by passersby, he proceeded into the town to make some much needed purchases.

By this time Andrew had become accustomed to the Wyoming villages along the trail. Casper had been a fairly large place. The other towns from central to western Wyoming held little of interest for the wayfarer. Some of them appeared to be no more than the old wide streeted, board fronted frontier towns modernized principally by the gasoline stations of the present. He found that Split Rock leaned a little more toward the past.

Indeed, his observing eyes detected more cowboys than truck drivers or garage attendants. He listened to snatches of their conversation satisfying for the hundredth time his avid pleasure in things western. Deciding to make inquiries on the morrow about the range country hereabouts he returned to his car.

By this time it was quite dark. A wonderful light still glowed in the west, whence came a cold breeze, keen and penetrating, sweet with a tang of the mountain and the range. Andrew breathed deeply of it, and reveled in the lonesomeness of his surroundings. Every camp of late had been visited by coyotes to his growing delight. These wild prairie dogs could not bark and yelp and mourn and ki-yi too much for him. He even threw scraps of his meals to the stealthy prowlers.

He had collected a bundle of dry sticks and bits of sagebrush when a clip-clop of hoofs drew his attention. A rider was passing on the road. He halted opposite Andrew, lighted a cigarette, then rode on a little further, only to come back. It was evident that he was waiting for someone. Andrew had no mind to disclose his hiding place, so he sat down to watch and listen.

The rider appeared to be impatient. Andrew heard his spurs clinking. Evidently he smoked his cigarette half through, then lit another. His spirited horse would not stand still. And the night was so still, the air so clear that this rider's voice carried to Andrew's vibrant ears.

"You dawggone ornery hawse—cain't you stand on yore fo' feet?" drawled the rider. After another cigarette he appeared to start, to crouch and then to stare up the road toward the town. Andrew heard rapid footsteps approaching from that direction.

"Thet you, McCall?" queried the rider, in a sharp tone which carried far.

"Yes, it's me," came the answer.

"Git off the road over heah," commanded the rider, heading his horse toward the thicket that screened Andrew's car.

Rider and pedestrian met half way and continued as far as a large rock scarcely thirty feet from where Andrew crouched behind a clump of low sagebrush. There the two halted, and the unmounted one hunched himself up on the rock.

"Tex, I been lookin' fer you at my ranch," he said. "Jest happened to be in town today an' got your word."

"Wal, I shore would have rid down on you pronto, if you hadn't showed up tonight," retorted the rider, curtly. "Mac, I want some money."

"Hyar's all I got," returned the other hastily, and passed his hand up to the horseman. "You'll have to wait till I ship some more cattle."

"Ahuh! Always waitin'," growled the younger man. "I cain't see. How much you got heah?"

"Two-hundred-odd."

"Wal, I'll let you off on thet. But only fer a while. I reckon I'm not long fer this range. I got to pull oot, Mac, an' it's mostly yore cattle deals thet's chasin' me."

"Aw, Texas, thet ain't so. You was talked of before you ever forked a hoss fer me."

"Shore I was. But fer makin' love an' throwin' a gun—not fer burnin' yore brand on calves," snapped the cowboy, in a voice so cold and strange to Andrew that it sent shivers up his spine.

"Have it your own way, Tex. I don't want to argue with you. But I heerd

Sheriff Slade hang suspicion on you. Right before half a dozen cattlemen, one of which was Jeff Little, who you rode fer once.''

"Ahuh. An' what did Jeff say?''

"He got a little het up at Slade. Said you was a wild one all right, but straight as a string, an' thet Slade hadn't savvied thet you was from the old Texas breed.''

"Damn thet four-flush of a sheriff!'' cursed the cowboy. "He's not so above a slick deal himself. I know. . . . Reckon I'm liable to take a shot at him one of these heah nights.''

"Tex, you'll kill somebody yet,'' declared McCall, anxiously.

"Shouldn't wonder. All you gotta do, Mac, is to make damn good an' shore it ain't you. . . . When do I git the rest of the dough?''

"Reckon pronto. . . . Tex, I got a new deal on.''

"Ahuh. Wal, spring it on me.''

"There's an old geezer named Nick Bligh just drove in a thousand head of cows, a sprinklin' of yearlings, an' a lot of calves. Hails from Randall, somewhere near the Montana line. This rancher hasn't no outfit at all—jest a middle-aged man to help him handle thet stock. Why, before the snow flies there'll be a couple hundred unbranded calves bawlin' around.''

"Humph. How come this Nick Bligh hasn't got no punchers?''

"There can be only one reason fer thet, if he's a Westerner. No money.''

"Wal, thet's no reason why a cowboy worth a damn wouldn't ride fer him. I've done it. All depends on the rancher.''

"Tex, thet gives me an idee. Suppose you go ride fer this Bligh—''

"Ump-umm, Mac. I don't mind brandin' a few mavericks. Thet's legitimate. An' even when a cattleman knows the mavericks ain't his—he brands them anyhow. All ranchers have done thet—gettin' their start. But what you propose would be stealin'.''

"If you're set on splittin' hairs over it—hell, yes!'' replied McCall, testily.

"I'll go in on the deal—burnin' your brand on stray calves.''

"But, Tex, there ain't much money in thet for me or you,'' continued the other persuasively. "On the other hand, two hundred calves would fetch between forty an' fifty dollars a head next year.''

"Mac, thet's most like old-time rustlin',''expostulated the cowboy.

"Look hyar, puncher. You oughta know thet there's plenty of rustlin' goin' on on Wyomin' ranges right now.''

"Shore. But what's a few haid of stock to a cattleman who owns ten thousand? Mac, safety lies in small numbers. You aim to hire me to be crooked. An' I'll be damned if I'll fall for it.''

Silence ensued after the puncher's forceful speech. Andrew scarcely breathed in the intensity of his interest and the peril he risked in being discovered. The cowboy struck a match for his cigarette. By its light Andrew saw a youthful reckless face, singularly handsome, almost as red as his flaming hair.

"Tex, I don't trust Smoky Reed over much," at length replied McCall.

"Wal, Smoky is on the level. If you want him to snake oot all the calves thet poor devil owns he'll do it. Smoky told me he'd lost out with the K-Bar ootfit an' was goin' to ride fer the Three Flags. I reckon he won't last much longer heah, no more'n me."

"Will you make Smoky an offer fer me?"

"Wal, I'll carry any word you say. But get this, McCall, *I* won't have nothin' to do with Smoky's work."

"Thet's all right, Tex. Don't get het up."

"This Bligh deal ain't so good. I'm advisin' you, Mac. If you go whale bang at it you may lose oot. Shore, I've got you figgered. If it come to a showdown you'd lay it on to a couple range-marked punchers."

"Tex, I wouldn't give no one away."

"Aw, the hell's fire you wouldn't," retorted the cowboy shortly. "To save yore own skin you'd do thet an' more. But so far as I'm concerned I can look oot fer myself. I was thinkin' of Smoky."

"Safest way," continued McCall as if he had not heard Texas, "is to drive cow an' calf into rough brush or timber, or a rocky draw—kill the cow, then brand the calf an' fetch it out. Coyotes an' buzzards would make short work of the carcass. An' there ain't one chance in a thousand of Bligh missin' his cows until the job's all done."

"Aw, it's safe enough, but it just sticks in my craw, McCall," rejoined the cowboy in disgust.

"Thet ain't the point. Will you put Smoky wise to this deal?"

"Shore, I'll do thet. An' I'll do my part. But before you bust into this, Mac, listen to me. I never heahed of this Nick Bligh. Most likely he's a pore cattleman, drove west, an' makin' a stand. But s'pose this all happened. S'pose aboot the time you got yore deal half done, say, thet a pardner with money enough to buy more stock an' hire some real cowboys—s' pose he'd show up?"

"Ha! Tex, miracles like thet don't happen in these cattle times."

"Hell they don't! Anythin' can happen, man. Where's yore sense? I ain't carin' a damn, 'cept for the old geezer Bligh. But I'm jest tellin' you."

"Reckon you're losin' your nerve, Tex, or figgerin' overcareful."

"Shore, if thet's the way you get me. . . . Where's this Bligh feller located?"

"Down across the Sweetwater River," replied McCall eagerly. "He's bought or leased the old Boseman ranch, on the south bank of the river, halfway between the Antelope Hills an' the Green Mountains. Damn fine range, when the grass is good. An' this spring it's comin' strong."

"Ahuh. I know thet ranch," mused Texas. "Looked at it with a longin' eye myself, more'n once. But it'd take some dough to make good there."

"Thet's not our concern. For your an' Smoky's information put this under your hat. There are three outfits on thet big range south of the Sweetwater. The Cross Bar, owned by Cheney Brothers, the Triangle X, run by Hale Smith, an' the Wyomin' Cattle Association, runnin' the W.C. They all work up into the foothills of the Green Mountains, an' anyone ridin' in there must have sharp eyes. Savvy?"

"Shore, I savvy. Slade is in thet Wyomin' Cattle Association," returned Texas, thoughtfully.

"Yes, but not very deep. Slade's in more'n one deal jest for a blind." McCall slid down off the rock. "Reckon thet's about all fer tonight."

"Wal, it'll last me a spell, Mac," drawled the cowboy. "Don't overlook my hunch. So long."

With a wave of his hand the cowboy loped his horse over to the road, and taking the direction away from town, soon disappeared in the darkness. McCall watched him out of sight and stood listening to the dying clip-clop of hoofs.

"By Gawd, thet Texas puncher will spill the beans fer me yet—if I don't fix him," he muttered, and then with a snap of his fingers strode away toward the town.

When he, too, had gone Andrew arose to stretch his cramped legs. His face was wet with sweat and his heart was thumping. He had to laugh at his first introduction to a western drama that was not in any sense fictitious.

"Well, Andy, what do you know about this?" he asked himself. "By golly, I like that redheaded cowpuncher. I'll bet he's the goods. But McCall is that same little old proposition one meets the world around, I guess. And Bligh, just the old fall guy who's to be fleeced. Now I wonder where do I come in?"

Andrew almost forgot that he was cold and hungry. After some deliberation he built a fire, deciding that if the cowboy or McCall should happen back there—which was wholly unlikely—he could allay suspicion by claiming he had just arrived. To be thrown upon his own resources had become an increasing joy to Andrew, but so far he did not exactly shine as a cook. He burned both the ham and the potatoes, and let the coffee boil over. Nevertheless he ate what he had cooked with a relish.

This night he decided not to sleep in the car. He had added a couple of blankets to the old lap robe, and he made his bed on the ground beside the fire. Then he gathered all the available firewood in the near vicinity, and removing only his shoes he prepared to make a night of it.

All the same, slumber soon gripped Andrew and held him tight for half the night. Awakening stiff with cold, he got up to renew the fire. Despite his discomfort, the traveler decided that life in the open had its good points. Andrew had known camp life, but only in a luxurious way. As he sat beside the little fire warming his hands and feet, he knew that he had become a part of this land of the purple sage.

The sky was a deep dark blue, studded with innumerable stars. Black rocks stood up bold and sharp above the brush. There was not a sound except the faint rustling of leaves in the night wind.

On and off, he was up like this during the remainder of the night, until the blackness yielded to gray, when he fell soundly asleep for a couple of hours. He drove into town with the sunrise. While eating breakfast at a lunch counter frequented by dusty-booted men, refueling his car at the service station, stocking a goodly supply of food at a grocery, buying a very fine secondhand cowboy outfit at a merchandise store, Andrew asked the cheerful and casual questions of the tenderfoot. Having thus acquired a lot of general information, he was about to leave town when he happened to think that he had not inquired the way to the Sweetwater River and Nick Bligh's ranch.

He leaned out of his car to accost a Westerner who happened along at that moment. He was a man of about sixty years of age, gray and weather-beaten. His boots and garb gave ample evidence of considerable contact with the soil.

"Excuse me, sir," said Andrew. "Can you direct me to the Sweetwater River?"

"Good morning, young man," the Westerner replied, as he halted. "Straight ahead about thirty miles out."

"Thanks. And how to get to Nick Bligh's ranch?"

Andrew became aware of keen blue eyes fixed upon him.

"You know Nick?"

"Sorry to say I don't, but I'd like to," replied Andrew heartily.

"Selling hardware, life insurance, lightning rods—or bootleg whiskey?" queried the old man dryly.

"No. Just trying to sell myself."

"Job, eh?"

"Yes, I want a job."

"Who told you to hit Nick Bligh?"

"I happened to hear that he'd lately come to this range with cattle and no cowboys. So I thought he might want one."

"Wal, son, I happen to know Nick wants cowboys. But he's hard up at present. Looking for big wages?"

"I'll work for my board," declared Andrew eagerly.

"Where you from?"

"East."

"Reckoned that. But East means anywhere from the Missouri to the Atlantic."

"All right, call it Missouri. I don't want to advertise I'm a dude."

"I reckon Nick will be glad to talk to you. . . . Don't cross the river. Take the road left and drive onto his place. You can't miss it, as there's only one. If Nick's not home, wait."

"Much obliged. I'll do that," rejoined Andrew heartily.

The Westerner turned to resume his walk, almost bumping into a tall man wearing a wide sombrero.

"Morning, Slade," he said shortly and passed on.

"Howdy, Nick," drawled the other. Then he approached Andrew and gave him a searching look from keen yellow eyes. Andrew was quick to see the glint of a silver shield half concealed under the man's vest. He was without a coat. His face was sallow and he wore a long drooping mustache. Andrew's pulse quickened a few beats when he realized that he was facing Sheriff Slade.

"Stranger hereabouts?" he queried.

"You bet I am," responded Andrew pleasantly enough.

"Salesman?"

"Nope. Just a tin-Lizzie tramp looking for a job."

"Was that what you was askin' Nick Bligh?"

"Who?"

"Wal, the man you was jest talkin' to," returned the sheriff tersely.

"Oh—him! Was *that* Nick Bligh?"

"Air you shore you didn't know thet?"

"Say, mister, I just arrived here this A.M. I was merely asking the gentleman about work on ranches."

"I see you're loaded up with a cowpuncher's junk. Wonder what you got hid under all this. . . . Get out!"

"Sheriff, eh?" rejoined Andrew lightly as he slid out of the seat. "Delighted to meet you."

Slade searched the car thoroughly, during which performance a little crowd collected. Andrew pretended a show of resentment.

"I'm a stranger, out of work, driving west—and get held up for doing nothing," he complained to the bystanders resentfully.

Slade continued his search in silence. Finally he closed the car door and spoke: "*Quien sabe?* You can never tell who's packin' liquor."

"No offense," returned Andrew cheerily. "I appreciate what the West is up against. . . . Why, Officer Slade, even *you* might be a bootlegger!" And Andrew gave the sheriff a cool stare, mitigated by a smile.

"Don't get fresh, young feller," replied Slade gruffly, annoyed by the laughter among the bystanders. "Be on your way an' keep goin'."

Andrew got back into his car. "Most western towns welcome travelers and prospective settlers. What's the matter with this burg?"

"Wal, we Wyomin' folks air partic'lar about our brands," drawled the sheriff.

"But not so particular about whose calf you slap them on," retorted Andrew, and stepped on the throttle. "Tosh!" he ejaculated. "This will never do. I must learn to keep my mouth shut and my temper down. But wouldn't I have liked to sock that yellow-eyed hypocrite!"

Once out of town he slowed to the speed he liked best, which was in fact merely crawling along. All the way across Wyoming he had feasted his eyes upon the increasingly fascinating vistas. What he could not get enough of was the far-flung leagues of open rangeland. Along here, however, he was shut in by low mountains to the north, and some few miles to the south by a higher, rougher range.

For the time being Andrew shelved some of the aspects of his latest adventure, content to return to them again after he had reached the ranch on the Sweetwater. Why, he wondered, had Nick Bligh not revealed his identity?

At the end of two hours of somewhat rough going, he passed the limits of the Granite Range. From there the rolling plains to the north appeared endless. He saw a winding line of trees which probably marked the river course. Cattle in considerable number in the aggregate, but scattered so far and wide over the rangeland that they seemed very few, could be seen grazing. Once he spied a lone horseman topping a ridge, and the sight gave Andrew an inexplicable thrill.

The black patches on the green, so few and far between, he had come to recognize as ranch houses. By his uncertain calculation a dozen miles or more separated the closest of the ranches. And gradually these distances widened, as the ranches decreased in number, until the hour came when he could not see a single house.

At length he approached the river on a long gradual down grade. When he arrived at the point where the highway crossed a bridge, and an apology for a road branched to the south, it was the big moment in that day's drive.

The Sweetwater River was a delight to the eye, as it must have been a boon to the immense range that it traversed. It wound away between wooded banks, now flowing in shallow ripples over gravel bars, and now in long deep reaches, and again spread into several channels around willow-bordered islands. Coyotes stood on the opposite bank to watch Andrew; jack rabbits abounded, and wild ducks skittered off the shoals to wing in rapid flight up the river.

Andrew's view to the south was obstructed owing to the foothills of the Green Mountains which encroached upon the river bottom lands.

After gazing long at the superb view, the traveler turned into the branch road, with the feeling that he was leaving his bridges behind him, if not burning them. The road kept to the river bank, and was of such a nature that he had to attend to careful driving instead of indulging his desire for enjoying the scenery. In due time he arrived at the point where the foothills trooped down to the stream. He drove along their base until he had passed the last one. Here two scenic spots met his delighted gaze—the first, a grove of cottonwoods just bursting into bright green, and the other, a high, isolated knoll from which he was certain one could get a commanding view of the country. Andrew did not make any choice. He would possess them both; and he drove down into the grove of cottonwoods.

A wide-spreading giant of a tree invited rest. Grassy plots and sandy places alternated through the grove down to the high weeds and yellow daisies, and the wall of willows.

"Immense!" ejaculated Andrew with a tremendous sigh. He did not know exactly what he meant by immense, but the feeling was profound. Lifting out the boxes of food, Andrew selected crackers and sardines and a can of peaches for his lunch. This was faring sumptuously. He had a canteen full of fresh water, but he decided to go down to the river. Finding a cattle track he followed it out of the grove, through the breast-high sunflowers and the willows, down to where the river murmured and gurgled over a gravelly bar. Andrew waded in, and scooped up water with his cupped hands. It was sweet and cold. He wondered where it came from and tried to picture its rocky source.

He retraced his steps, stripping leaves and a few of the yellow daisies on the way. Andrew put the boxes back in the car and then headed for the knoll.

As he had been deceived before by distance and elevation, so he was again in this instance. The knoll proved not very close to the road and considerably higher than he had imagined it to be. As he climbed, the necessity for taking the easiest way worked him round to the north slope, so that when he surmounted the knoll he faced the range keenly expectant but completely unprepared for what greeted his view.

"My Lord!" he gasped, amazed at the vivid coloring and infinite grandeur of the view.

The vast panorama spreading fan-shaped before him, with the green-bordered shining river turning to the right, and the rugged slopes of the mountain range on the left, formed a gateway to what appeared to be a purple abyss, and leading to a blue-based, white-peaked barrier in the far distance.

"Aw, have a heart, Wyoming!" cried Andrew. "What are you giving me? . . . Are you real—or is this just one of my dreams?"

He stood there gazing his fill. This was his first unlimited view. The sweep of prairie land, hills and valleys, mountain ranges in the distance—these had become scenes of growing frequency and increasing impressiveness during the last few days of travel. But the scene unfolding before him here dwarfed anything that he had yet seen.

"No, this is no mirage. This is real. . . . And oh, boy, this is the one spot in all the world I've been looking for," he exclaimed.

Westward he followed the black and green river bottom and the shining water to the north of a low range of symmetrical knolls, marked Antelope Hills on his map. Then miles or more beyond he sighted the ranch that must be Nick Bligh's. Indeed, there was no other ranch visible south of the Sweetwater. Its location seemed all satisfying to the traveler. The river went on and on, growing dimmer, becoming a mere thread, to vanish in a blue haze out of which the Rocky Mountains rose, first obscure and like low masses of clouds, and then clear blue, to rise up and up in magnificent reaches to pierce the sky with their snow-white peaks. That was the Continental Divide, the backbone of the West, the end of the Great Plains, the wall of iron, set so formidably on the earth with its jagged teeth in the heavens.

The Antelope Hills blocked the center of the gateway to the south. They shone white and gray and pink in the sunlight. Some were crowned with a fringe of black; others showed black clefts deep down between the domes; still others appeared craggy and rough, with belts of timber at their bases.

But it was the spreading of the fanlike range southward that drew and held Andrew Bonning's gaze. He felt dwarfed. How cramped he had been all his life! New York City would hardly have been a visible dot down in the center of that purple immensity. Poor, struggling, plodding, suffocating millions of men—of toilers—if they could only have found themselves there! Andrew felt a singular uplift of spirits. His instinct had been true. Its source and its meaning still remained inscrutable, but he realized that in following it he had found an unknown heritage.

So engrossed had Andrew been that he had forgotten the field glasses he had carried up the hill with him. These he now remembered and focused upon that mysterious gulf of purple.

What had been wavy lines and pale spots and dim shadows and blank reaches, veiled in differing degrees of the purple hue of distance, resolved themselves into endless rolling ridges like atolls in a smooth sea, and vast areas of flat land, bare and desolate, and wide green valleys, with here and there the tiny dots of ranches leagues apart.

The Easterner descended the knoll with giant strides. He had never, that he could remember, heard the singing of his heart as at that moment. Whatever had brought about the accident of his arrival here, he would bless all his life long. His failures now seemed like successive steps to a new life. He divined that any labors he undertook on this range would be labors of love, and they could not fail. He was profoundly grateful now to his own past inability to fit into an office or to sell bonds or to play the market; to the criticism, the misunderstanding, the bitter defeats and his father's financial fall that had sent him to Wyoming.

Andrew Bonning drove up to Bligh's ranch in this almost reverent mood, which perhaps cast a sort of glamour over the low-walled, mud-roofed rambling cabin, and especially to a large structure on the river bank—a cabin, deserted, with gaping windows, bleached gray logs and crumbling, yellow chimney. He had no time for more than this first glance because the old man whom he had interviewed in town suddenly appeared from behind the nearer cabin.

"You beat me here, Mr. Bligh," said Andrew smilingly.

"Yes, I saw your car as I passed the cottonwoods. How'd you know me?" His blue eyes were twinkling and kindly. Andrew read in them liking for his fellow man. Yet the bronzed thin face, wrinkled like withered parchment, attested to a life of struggle and trial.

"I heard that Sheriff Slade call your name. . . . What do you know? He held me up, searched my car for contraband—the yellow-eyed goofer! I didn't take much to him, Mr. Bligh."

"Did he find any?" inquired the rancher. Andrew saw more in the penetrating eyes than the casual query testified.

"He did not. It made me sore—that digging into my gear. And I made a crack that I'm afraid was pretty foolish. It made the crowd laugh, anyway."

"Yeah? What'd you say to Slade?"

"I told him he might be a bootlegger himself, for all *I* knew."

"Wal! You said that to Slade? Young man, you should bridle your tongue. . . . But get down and come in."

"Say, that's a new one on me," declared Andrew. " 'Get down and come in!' Range greeting, eh?"

"Yes. Motors will never take the place of horses on the range."

"Thanks, Mr. Bligh. But before I get out—or down—please give me some hope that I can land a job with you. I climbed a hill back there to get a look at the country. I'm just plain crazy about it. I'll simply have to get a job here. I can do any kind of work. . . . And, well, Mr. Bligh, I'm the man you need."

"I like your enthusiasm. What's your name?"

"Andrew Bonning."

"Where from?"

"I told you—the East. Some day I'll tell you more about myself. It ought to be enough now to say I come to you clean and straight." And Andrew met the keen scrutiny of those usually mild blue eyes with a level open glance.

"Bonning, we cattlemen often hire men without names or homes or pasts. What counts here is, what you *are* —what you can *do.*"

"Well, in that case all a fellow can do is to ask for a chance to prove himself."

"It amounts to that."

"Will you give me a chance, Mr. Bligh?"

"I reckon I will, on conditions."

"What are they?"

"You offered to work for your keep, didn't you?"

"Yes, sir. I'll be glad to. You see, I bought a secondhand cowboy outfit."

"No cattleman could miss seein' all them trappin's, son. . . . My condition is this—that you work for your board until I can afford to pay you real wages—provided we get along together."

"Okay. Suits me and I'm much obliged. I'll do my level best to please you—and I'm darned sure I can help you."

"Can you ride?"

"Yes."

"Throw a rope?"

"No."

"Or a gun?"

"No, but I'm a good rifle shot."

"Cook?"

"No, I thought I could. But eating my own cooking for two weeks has changed my mind."

"Good at figures?"

"Lord, no! I couldn't add up a columun of figures ten times and get less than ten different sums."

"Neither can I. But we won't have much figuring to do. . . . Bonning, I like your looks and I like your talk. One more question and it's a deal."

"Okay. Spring that one on me."

"Have you got guts?"

"Guts!" echoed Andrew.

"Nerve, in an Easterner's way of puttin' it. I got robbed of most of my cattle up north. Had a ranch on the Belle Fourche River, near Aladdin. Made up my mind to pull up stakes an' try a new range. Like this one fine. But today I learned there's some cattle stealing here, same as everywhere on the Wyomin' ranges."

"Who told you, Mr. Bligh?"

"Cattleman named McCall. Agreeable chap. Went out of his way to scrape acquaintance with me. An' I verified that news. Got laughed at for my pains. One old rancher said to me, 'Rustlin'? Hell, yes, enough left to make the cattle business healthy. When rustlin' peters out in Wyomin' thet'll be the end of the cattleman!' "

"Well, that's a point of view to make one think!"

"Wal, it needn't worry you. But when I put it up to you I'm makin' it plain. If you're white-livered or softhearted, not to say yellow, you just won't do. I've only one man on the ranch. Happened to run across him on the Belle Fourche. He's from Arizona, has seen a lot of range life, crippled—which is why he finds it hard to get jobs—but he's a real man. Married, by the way, to a nice little woman who sure can keep house. I never had a woman about my ranch before. An' eatin' my own sourdough biscuits nearly killed me. . . . Wal, his name is

Jim Fenner, an' if you make a good runnin' mate for him, I reckon my stock will increase.''

"I'm only a tenderfoot," replied Andrew, discouraged in spite of his ardor. Bligh had a set, hard look around his mouth.

"I don't need to be told that. In a way it's in your favor. The thing is—will you learn this hard game of the range—fight for my interests—an' stick to me? It might lead to your good fortune. An' I'm puttin' it strong because I want you to declare yourself strong.''

"I do, Mr. Bligh," replied Andrew ringingly, as he took the proffered hand. "I see it as tough, steady work—and no lark. It's a chance that will make a man of me. I'll do my damndest!''

5

MARTHA ANN responded quickly to the cheery and kindly interest of the two travelers who had come upon her in the road, just after the ugly episode with the bully in the Ford. They were on a fishing trip to northern Nebraska.

They did not again refer to the distressing incident, and their keen sense of humor and lively knack of relating their own experiences soon restored Martha Ann to her old self.

They drove at a steady pace all the rest of the day, stopping only for a light supper, and at half past eight they arrived at the small town of Colfax. The men were camping along the way, so they left Martha at the inn, promising to call for her in the morning.

Soon after daylight the three were off again. At Benton, where they arrived in time for lunch, the gentlemen had to take a branch road, leading north. They were sorry that Martha Ann could not proceed further with them. She bade them good-by regretfully, promising to send them a post card when she had safely reached her destination.

Martha Ann faced the road alone once more, on foot, and somewhat forlornly. It seemed a long time since she had hiked even a short distance. All the old apprehensions trooped back into her mind. But when she saw great dark ridges rising above the horizon, and apparently not so very far away, she began to recapture her old adventurous spirit. These were the Black Hills. They thrilled her and also frightened her. Had she not been warned that she would never get through these lonesome hills alive?

A man and woman in a Packard stopped alongside the runaway girl, and the latter asked her if she would like a ride. Martha Ann smiled gratefully, and as the driver reached back and opened the door, she got into the back seat. They introduced themselves as Mr. and Mrs. Corbett of Chicago. In replying Martha gave her name, but neglected to add her address.

"Bet you are headed for Hollywood," chuckled Mr. Corbett.

When she told them that Wyoming, not Hollywood, was her destination, the man said: "If I really thought you were a movie-struck kid, I'd turn you over to the authorities and have you sent home."

Martha Ann realized that this very thing could easily be done. She could not prove that she was over eighteen. She earnestly explained that she was on her way to visit an uncle in Wyoming, and that she was hiking for the fun of it and to save money.

"All right, young lady, I'll take your word for it," replied Mr. Corbett. "I'm in the show business myself, but I am glad you're not another girl who wants to be a star."

They reached the next town in time for an early dinner, and then Martha accompanied them to a movie. It featured Tom Mix and his horse, Tony, in a Western. It was a romantic story which left the Chicago girl a trifle sad. How utterly impossible for anything like this picture to happen to her! The only romance so far on this long, long journey had been Andrew Bonning's rescue of her from the clutches of a tramp. The memory of that occasion still warmed her heart. But his rude relegation of her to the ranks of a type of girl she despised had removed any possibility of romance from the episode. Where could he be now? Long ago he had passed by her on the road, perhaps too indifferent even to offer her a lift.

Since the Corbetts were remaining in this town to have extensive repairs made on the car, Martha left next morning on foot.

The air was cold, with a decided sharpness which the young traveler attributed to the altitude. Before noon she had received three uneventful rides, which brought her up into the wooded hills. Passing the beautiful hotel at the Springs, Martha Ann longed to spend a few days there. The tourists lounging around on the verandas seemed so carefree and happy. She wondered if any of them had to work for a living or had ever worried about anything in life.

She walked on to a roadside inn, where she had lunch, and then took again to the white ribbon of road through the black forest of firs. The fragrance of these trees made her short of breath and lightheaded with exhilaration. Except for an occasional car, the road was deserted. No hikers! No campers! Suddenly Martha heard a rustling in the brush, and saw a deer walk into an open glade to stand with long ears erect and watch her warily. How wild and beautiful appeared this creature of the forests—the only one she had ever seen in her whole life. She had a great desire to wander off the road, to mount up the steep slope where the tall dark fir trees shot up straight and spear pointed. She sat down on a rock to watch the trout in a clear pool. Shafts of golden sunlight pierced through the foliage, and a breeze sighed through the trees above her head. As she sat there in the sweet silence the hum of a motor broke in upon her meditations. She heard it almost with regret. And as she rose to resume her hike she determined that some day, far out in the wilds of Wyoming, she would find perfect loneliness where neither motor nor man would interrupt her thoughts.

A huge touring car caught up with her and stopped. She heard a terrier dog barking furiously and childish voices crying out: "Ride with us. Daddy says to ask you."

Martha turned to face a welcoming family, father and mother in the front seat, and a boy, a girl and a dog in the back.

They were so friendly, so eager to have her join them, that Martha could not refuse. When she got in between the children, however, she found them suddenly shy.

"How do you like the Black Hills?" inquired the smiling lady in front.

"Oh, I love them!" exclaimed Martha. "And I had been so scared. People back along the road predicted all sorts of terrible things."

"Nonsense! There's no one to hurt you. We come here often. . . . Tell us, where are you from and where are you going? We arrived at the inn just as you were leaving. A girl hitchhiker! We are dying of curiosity."

"My name is Martha Ann Dixon. I live in Chicago, and am on my way to Wyoming to visit an uncle."

"What part of Wyoming?"

"Randall."

"Don't know it. Must be far. . . . Have you hiked all this way from Chicago?"

"Oh, no. I took a train to Omaha."

"I see. Why didn't you hike all the way?"

"Guess I didn't want to meet anyone who might know me!"

"Naughty child!" interposed the lady. "Do you go to school?"

"Yes, to the university."

"Wonder what your professors would say—to see their star student wandering through the Black Hills?" queried the man, with a smile to his wife, as if they both were familiar with the college and its teachers.

The car climbed higher. The air grew thin and cold. Martha experienced a faint giddiness. When she caught sight of patches of snow along the road, she found herself agreeing with the children when they clamored to get out of the car. They climbed still higher, until they could look out and down over the green slopes to the variegated mosaic of farmlands far below. The driver halted the car by the side of a huge snowdrift, announcing that the radiator was boiling and that they had better stop to let it cool.

Martha marveled at the lovely white snow bank on one side of the road and on the other, wild flowers and green things growing down to a wall of fir trees. From where she sat the eye was led down to the gray and green earth far below.

"No wonder you come here often," sighed Martha.

Shortly afterward the family had to go off the road to a camp where their children were going later in the summer. They told Martha to proceed up to the lodge, where they advised her to take the bus to Rapid City.

She walked the all too short mile up to the lodge, which she expected to find on a mountaintop, but it stood near the edge of a beautiful little lake, under a lofty tower of gray, snow-patched rock. After a short wait on the cool porch of the lodge she found the bus was ready to start. By the time the bus had reached Rapid City night had fallen, and Martha was glad to find a comfortable hotel where she had supper and went promptly to bed.

Before starting out the next morning, she went into the office of the Chamber of Commerce, and of the three smiling occupants she asked collectively: "What is the best and quickest way to get to Belle Fourche?"

"Straight from here to Deadwood and then to Spearfish," replied one of the attendants, spreading a map on the counter. "Where you hail from?"

"Chicago."

Many questions followed which Martha answered good-naturedly and frankly. And when they learned that she actually was on her way to Wyoming, they had several sound suggestions to offer.

"Young lady," said one of the men, "let me fix your packsack so it will be easier for you. I am an old-timer with packsacks. And yours is on wrong."

"I'll be eternally grateful," replied Martha slipping off her pack. He went into an adjoining room and returned with straps, buckles and tools. Then he proceeded to alter the straps on the packsack, and to add more. The other two men kept offering suggestions, and between them all they managed to get it to suit them, whereupon they tried it on their visitor.

"I'll choke. Straps all too high," protested Martha.

"No, you just imagine that. Doesn't it feel easier—lighter?"

"I believe it does, at that."

"Are you going to try to make Deadwood tonight?"

"I'll try, you can bet. I'm falling behind my schedule."

"Perhaps I can help you out. There's a gentleman I know, and will vouch for, who intends driving to Deadwood today. May I call him up?"

Martha consented gratefully, and was promised her lift over the phone. She sat down to wait, thinking how many kind and nice people there really were. Presently two men came in, and Martha recognized them as people she had seen up at the lodge the day before. They greeted her in the friendly manner which she had come to expect as typical of the West. After being introduced one of the strangers said, "Well, Miss, let's go." They carried Martha's baggage out, and making her comfortable in the back seat, alone, they drove off.

"I'd like to ask a couple of questions, Miss," said the one who was not driving.

"A couple? That'll be easy. I usually have to answer a hundred. And I have a lot of stock answers."

"Did your parents give you permission to take this long trip alone?"

"No, indeed," Martha confessed.

"You don't need to answer this one: Have you a gun with you?"

"Oh, n-no."

"Or any kind of weapon?"

"I guess I haven't anything you could call a weapon. Except my little embroidery scissors."

Martha's questioner gave his companion a dig in the ribs. "Hear that, Jim Dawson?"

"Sure, I heard. . . . We're a couple of daffy brave firemen, believe you me."

Then they both laughed loud and long. Finally the first speaker turned to Martha again: "Miss, this probably doesn't seem funny to you. But it struck *us* as funny. We're on a little trip in the hills. We bought two shotguns, a revolver, a hatchet, a billy, and two ferocious butcher knives. Each of us weighs around one hundred and eighty pounds. . . . And here we meet up with a wisp of a girl, pretty enough to be a movie queen, hiking the highways alone, her only weapon of defense a pair of embroidery scissors! . . . Can you beat it?"

"Oh, I forgot to mention my hiking boots," said Martha demurely.

The general laugh made them all good friends and that ride seemed to Martha to be one of the best of the whole trip. At Deadwood they insisted on taking her to dinner and letting the hotel people see that she had friends. Moreover next morning early they sent up word to her room that they had engaged a ride for her with a nice old couple driving on into Wyoming. The welcome news expedited Martha's ablutions and dressing. The farther west she got, the more she was beginning to dread the lonely hikes.

In the lobby she was approached by an elderly couple, plain, substantial people whom she trusted on sight. The man might have been a retired country merchant, and his wife appeared to be a motherly soul. She had, Martha thought, rather a sad, sweet face.

They explained that they had been instructed to introduce themselves and offer her a ride as far as Randall.

"It's just lovely of you both," replied Martha feelingly. "I'm a lucky girl."

Not a word about hitchhiking, parents, running away! They had breakfast together and while Mr. Jones went to the garage to get his car Martha helped his wife get together a lunch for the day.

Soon they were off in the bright keen morning, with the dark hills of Wyoming looming on the horizon. That ride almost spoiled Martha Ann forever for hiking. The car was comfortable, the old man drove leisurely and his wife appeared to consider it her duty to entertain their guest. That night when they stopped at an auto camp, Mrs. Jones hardly let Martha out of her sight. She even came into Martha's cottage and tucked her in bed, something that both embarrassed and touched the young hitchhiker deeply.

"You must have a young girl of your own," suggested Martha shyly.

"We were never blessed with a child, my dear."

Before they left the camp next morning Martha came upon her friends in earnest conversation. Her presence ended it so abruptly that she surmised that she must have been the subject of it. And again at noon, when they had lunch along the roadside and Martha stretched her legs by walking to and fro, the earnest talk between the man and his wife appeared to be resumed. She became sure of it when that night at Aladdin, where they stopped, Martha heard Mr. Jones agree to something his wife evidently had been urging most earnestly. "But don't ask her till mornin'," she heard him warn.

All this greatly excited Martha Ann's curiosity. She wondered if she had better get up very early and leave for Randall without bidding these people good-by. She could not understand what urged her to do such a thing, but she refused to consider it as ungrateful. At breakfast next morning, after Mr. Jones had gone out to look after the car, Martha realized that the moment had come.

"My dear, I want to talk seriously to you," said Mrs. Jones, placing a gentle hand on Martha's. "Please listen and don't be offended. I am a childless old woman, but I have known hundreds of girls. I have been a teacher, a worker in our church. John and I did not believe the story your last two traveling companions told us. I know that this hitchhike of yours is more than a lark. You are running away from home. Some misunderstanding has driven you from your relatives. You are a spirited, wild little thing, but I am sure that you are innocent. And you are singularly lovable. Everyone you meet will be drawn to you. But this very attractiveness, this independence of spirit only add to your very great danger on this reckless adventure of yours. Now John has consented to let me ask you this: Will you come with us? We are visiting relatives on a ranch, and then will go on west, stopping where and when we like, on the way to California. Come with us, Martha. And if you ever can learn to love us as we love you, and if it can be arranged with your relatives, then we will adopt you as our own."

Martha Ann's surprising reaction to this proposition was to burst into sudden tears. "Oh, I-I'm such a big b-baby," cried Martha, fighting to recover her composure. "It makes me—so—so angry that people take me for a g-good girl, when I'm really such a bad. . . . I lied to Mother! And she's the dearest mother in all—the world. She'll never forgive me. . . . But how can I ever thank you and Mr. Jones for your kindness to me? You have paid me a beautiful compliment, Mrs. Jones. I wish I could be your daughter, too. I know I'd love you. . . . But I've got to go on with this foolish adventure—and God only knows what will become of me."

Martha was in Randall at last! In the excitement of reaching her destination she forgot everything else, even to thank the farmer who helped her on the last lap.

It was about eleven o'clock in the morning. Having breakfasted very early Martha elected to eat lunch. After eating, she sallied forth to ask a few questions. The first person she interrogated was not acquainted with Nick Bligh. Martha reflected that a garage man or store keeper would be certain to know of her uncle. A boy at the service station told her to ask at Toller's store where every rancher for miles around the country dealt. A moment later, Martha Ann stepped into the emporium and asked for Mr. Toller. She was directed to a little, lean, gray man at the back of the store.

"Mr. Toller, do you know Nicholas Bligh?" she asked.

"Wal, I reckon I do, Miss," returned the merchant, eying the strange girl up and down with friendly interest.

"I'm his niece—Martha Ann Dixon—from Chicago. And I've come to visit him. I want to be directed to his ranch."

"Wal, wal, if thet jest ain't too bad!" ejaculated Mr. Toller. "Nick never knowed you was comin', thet I'll swear."

"No. I-I wanted to surprise him," faltered Martha Ann, her heart sinking like a leaden weight in her breast.

"Wal, Miss Dixon, your uncle left his ranch on the Belle Fourche several months ago. Jest as soon as the snow thawed. Drove his cattle south an' west to a new range!"

"Gone! Oh, why did he leave his ranch?" cried Martha Ann on the verge of tears.

"Wal, bad luck one way at' t' other. Nick was no hand to keep cowboys an' his stock got lost, mired in quicksand, an' stole till he got mad an' pulled up stakes. Reckon it was a good move."

"Where did he go?" asked Martha Ann.

"Down on the Sweetwater—the best damn range in Wyomin'," replied Mr. Toller. "He left his address. Split Rock is the Post Office."

"How—far?"

"Matter of three hundred odd miles, I reckon, Miss."

"So far!" Martha almost wailed. To travel three hundred miles in this rough country had taken her days, since she had had to hike part of the way. It was too discouraging! Martha had been having such good fortune of late that she was unprepared for such a blow as this.

"Yes, pretty far, an' roundabout. But outside of a couple of short runs, like from here to Beulah, travel is all on state highways. Can be drove in a day— if you want to hire a car."

"I've been hiking—and getting rides—when I could."

"Miss, you can't hike any more. Not safe. You'd be caught out all night."

"But I'll have to walk. I've no money—to hire a car," faltered Martha, tears of disappointment trembling in her eyes.

"Then you'll have to beg a ride, Miss Dixon. Perhaps I—"

"Thank you," mumbled Martha, and fearful of breaking down before Mr. Toller and the clerks, she hastily left the store. What in the world could she do? Of course she could only go on as she had come thus far, but the distance was so great and her disappointment so keen that for the moment she simply could not face the problem. Blinded by tears Martha made slow progress to a bench at a filling station, and there she sat down, feeling very sorry for herself. She had just about decided to go back to Toller's store when a young man came running up to her.

"Miss Dixon, Mr. Toller sent me," he explained. "He's got a ride for you clear through to Split Rock. You're pretty lucky, ma'am. Hurry, and let me take your pack."

Martha, murmuring incoherently, slipped the straps of her pack, and trotted after the boy. He led her back to Toller's store in front of which stood a long, low car, covered with dust and mud. It was a powerful car, and the engine was running smoothly.

"This Bligh's niece?" inquired a tanned individual, in the driver's seat, of Mr. Toller who stood near.

"Yes. Miss Dixon, we've found you a ride. Meet Mr. Lee Todd. He'll land you in Split Rock tonight by ten or eleven."

"Oh, Mr. Toller—Mr. Todd—" But Martha could say no more than that. The girl's hesitation was taken by both men as speechless gratitude.

"Glad to meet you, Miss. I know Nick Bligh. Salt of the earth. . . . Do you mind travelin' fast?"

Martha shook her head.

"I've got to be in Lauder by mornin'. Glad to take you—if you've got nerve."

"That's my—middle name," cried Martha huskily.

"Get in beside me. Put her bags in back. . . . So long, Sol. See you next week."

The car roared and lurched, drowning Mr. Toller's good-by. Martha waved to him and the sympathetic youngster. Then the stores, the service station, flashed by and Martha Ann realized that she was in for the ride of her life.

"Never talk while I'm drivin'!" said Mr. Todd, shouting to make himself heard above the roar of his car.

Martha sank back in the seat and closed her eyes. She did not care how fast he drove. The faster the better! She had been a silly child to give way to her disappointment and homesickness. All the way, everything always had ended well. More than good fortune had watched over her. Prayers that she had never been too weary or discouraged to remember had been answered. Martha just laid her head back and rested for a long while.

At length, when her weakness had passed, she opened her eyes to see the landscape speeding past. The gray road split the rolling plain for miles and miles ahead. But there were hills in the distance, and beyond them low dark ranges of mountains. There were few green fields and the patches of trees and farm houses appeared even scarcer than in Nebraska. Before Martha had realized it they were beyond Beulah, out on the Custer Battlefield Highway. Sundance, Carlisle, Moorcroft were passed in succession, so quickly that Martha imagined the towns to be close together. At Moorcroft the driver crossed the Belle Fourche River and struck off the main highway for Newcastle. He drove too fast for Martha to see either country or towns with any satisfaction. At Newcastle Mr. Todd stopped at a gas station.

"Gas, oil, water," he ordered, as he stepped out. "We'll have a couple of minutes here, Miss Dixon. Get out an' stretch. I'll fetch some sandwiches an' pie."

Martha Ann took advantage of the stop to get a little exercise. She wanted to ask questions, as well as walk, but as she could not do both she chose the latter. Mr. Todd soon returned carrying two paper bags which he deposited in the front seat. Martha hurried back to the car.

"How are you ridin'?" he grinned.

"Fine. You're the most satisfactory man who has given me a lift on the whole trip west."

"Thanks. Here's some grub, an' milk, too. Pile in, an' we'll hit the pike. Lusk is our next stop. About seventy-odd miles. We'll do it in an hour or so. At Lusk we'll hit the Yellowstone Highway, an' then we will really step on her."

"Seems to me you've been doing fairly well," laughed Martha. "I can't see the scenery."

"Wal, you'll not miss much along here. Too wide an' bare. But it gets pretty out along the Sweetwater."

"What will you have for lunch?" asked Martha peeping into the bags.

"I had a little bite an' a big drink. I'll smoke if you don't object."

"No, indeed. I don't mind!''

"Wal, I kinda took you to be one who didn't smoke," he replied, offering his box of cigarettes.

"I don't.''

"Good. There's a few old-fashioned girls left. Say good-by to Newcastle.''

Martha found it quite a novelty to eat lunch flying along at a mile a minute. She did not know anything about racing cars or drivers, but she had confidence in this bronzed Westerner. She had liked Mr. Toller, too. Uncle Nick had been thirty years and more in the West, and surely he would have become genuinely western. Musing thus Martha slowly ate her lunch. They passed through Clifton, through which Todd drove slowly enough for her to see the post office. After Clifton came Mule Creek, Hatcreek and then Lusk.

From Lusk the towns on the highway became more numerous, and prosperous looking. And at Douglas they crossed the North Platte River, one of the famous streams of the West, according to Todd. Martha had glimpses of it here and there, as they raced on west, and the wide reaches of sand, the grazing cattle, the green bottom lands of willow and cottonwood, delighted her eyes.

Sweeps of country beyond the river caused Martha more than once to exclaim with rapture. They seemed to promise mysterious and marvelous things to come. Perhaps her uncle's new range land lay in that direction.

At dusk they rolled into Casper, which the city girl found to her surprise to be quite a large place. A wide street, bright with electric lights was crowded with cars, and the sidewalks were thronged with evening shoppers. She kept her seat in the car and ate the remainder of the lunch while Mr. Todd attended to his affairs.

She had more than her reward. A slim wide-sombreroed young man, with mischief written all over his smooth dark face, clinked up to the car and addressed her:

"Howdy, kid, how'd you like to step out tonight?" he inquired with a smile.

"I'd love it," replied Martha, rising to the occasion. It would take a good deal to affront her on this wonderful day.

"Was thet broad-shouldered driver your pop?''

"He was, and he is never so happy as when he is beating up cowboys.''

"By glory, he looked it," rejoined the youth sheepishly. "Then we're up again it, sweetheart. Unless you can give him the slip. What say?''

"Can't be done, Lancelot. I've tried that all too often.''

"Lancelot? Who's thet guy?" inquired the cowboy doubtfully.

"Lancelot was a swell guy in the middle ages. Wonderful lover, according to history.''

"Say, are you razzin' me?''

Martha laughed merrily. "Run along, cowboy. I'm afraid you're no Lochinvar. And here comes pop."

Mr. Todd arrived just in time to witness the rather precipitate departure of the cowboy.

"What was that puncher hangin' around you for?"

"I think he wanted to take me out. Called me 'sweetheart.' I don't think our eastern boys have anything on your Westerners for being fast workers. I told that boy you were my pop and made a specialty of beating up cowboys. It worked splendidly."

The rancher appeared to enjoy Martha's joke. "Doggone me! I wish I *was* your pop. . . . Wal, we'll let 'em eat our dust from here on."

"What road do we take out of Casper?"

"The Old Oregon Trail—one of the first an' greatest roads thet opened up the West. Sorry it's night."

"When will we get to Split Rock?" asked Martha eagerly.

"Wal, if we don't chuck a shoe or somethin' I'd say about ten o'clock."

They were off, beyond the red and white lights into the black open. The night air was cold. Martha's jacket afforded but slight protection—at least on her windward shoulder. The car droned like a giant wasp. The runaway slid down a little way in the seat and fell asleep. She awoke with a start, out of a dream in which she had been struggling with tramps. Mr. Todd was shaking her arm.

"Wal, you was dead to the world," he said. "You shore had a fine nap. We made it in good time. This is your town an' here's your lodgin' house. I've stopped here. Nice woman runs it, good grub an' clean beds. The automobile has sure changed the West."

He carried her bags in, engaged her room, and told the proprietress who she was and directed her to take good care of Martha.

"Remember me to your uncle, Miss. An' now good luck an' good-by."

"Mr. Todd, it was the swiftest—and happiest—ride I ever had! I just can't thank you enough. Good-by."

6

MARTHA ANN was awakened the following morning by a bold baritone voice singing "La Paloma." Evidently the singer was below in the yard at the back of the inn. The sun was already high in the sky. Surprised that she had slept so late, she hopped out of bed, quickly, to find that the air was cold. It was quiet except for the slightly nasal rendition of "La Paloma" in the yard below.

"Smoky, you shore cain't sing," drawled a very slow accusing voice, rich with a southern twang. "No more'n you can make love."

"Ahuh. I reckon all I'm good for is to fork a hoss an' hawg-tie a steer," replied another voice, of quite different timber.

"Wal, you play a pretty good game of draw, among some strange punchers."

"All right, Texas Jack. You win. I shore got— "

"Hey, you lean, hungry lookin' *hombres*," interrupted a highpitched feminine voice. "Maw says to come an' get it."

Rapid footsteps, accompanied by a clinking sound, attested to the importance of this call to breakfast. Martha was at a loss, for a moment, to name the musical, metallic clink. "Spurs, of course," she said, presently. "Cowboys! Golly, this is Wyoming!" Then she gave a tiny squeal as she dipped her hands into the basin of cold Wyoming water.

Martha became conscious of a tendency to delay going downstairs. This was the first time she could remember ever being tardy for breakfast. Notwithstanding her joy and eagerness, and her curiosity, she would just as lief not meet those cowboys, especially the one with the drawl, who evidently considered himself a Lothario.

At length, however, she was packed and ready, without any further excuse to linger. Picking up her pack, she proceeded down the stairs. There was no one in the front room, which appeared to be the office. Martha deposited her luggage in a chair and walked down the hall to the dining room, the location of which was not hard to place. As she entered the room she almost tripped over the foot of someone whom she had not seen.

"Look where you're goin', kid," complained a hard voice. "I got a bunion."

"You've got more, sir—and that is—a pair of enormous feet," retorted Martha, looking up from the huge dusty boots into the lean sharp face of a blond cowboy. He froze with sudden amazement.

"Smoky, you shore air clumsy," drawled a voice Martha recognized. "Let the lady pass."

A long arm shot out and dragged the stunned Smoky from in front of the door. Then Martha saw the second cowboy, and if sight of him did not petrify her in her tracks it was not because he was not the wildest and most magnificent human she had ever seen.

"Good mornin', Miss Dixon," said Mrs. Glemm, the proprietress, and she rescued Martha and led her to a small table near a window. "Hope you rested right well."

"I slept like a log. Don't believe I'd ever have awakened but for some terrible singing in the garden."

The dining room was small and Martha's high young voice carried well. From the hall came a sound of stamping boots and then a "Haw! Haw! Haw!"

"Meet my daughter, Nellie," continued Mrs. Glemm, as a buxom pleasant-faced girl entered the room. "This is Miss Dixon, daughter, who's come out West to visit an uncle. . . . Now, Miss, Nellie will get you a nice breakfast, an' I'm at your service."

"Can you hire someone to drive me out to my Uncle's—Nicholas Bligh?" asked Martha Ann eagerly.

"Yes, indeedie. We'll have a car all ready."

Martha enjoyed a western breakfast, as well as a chat with the Glemm girl. She had nice brown eyes and rosy cheeks. The city girl asked casual questions about the weather, the town, the cattle business, the movies, what kind of social life they had in Split Rock, to all of which she received very full and cheerful answers. Evidently Split Rock was an up-and-coming place.

After finishing breakfast and paying her bill, Martha Ann was informed that her car and driver were waiting. Mrs. Glemm carried her packsack out to a dilapidated Ford, the driver of which, a nice young boy, jumped out to assist.

"Sim, did you find out where Mr. Bligh's ranch is?"

"No, ma'am. He's new hereabouts. But Sam Johnson will know."

"Don't forget to have Sam fill up. . . . Good-by, Miss. Hope you stay long an' have a fine visit. But you never will go back—east—not with them eyes of your'n."

The boy drove down a wide street, where red signs and garish fronts were conspicuous by their absence. Horses, vehicles, cars, dust and men were everywhere in evidence. Martha saw that Split Rock was a small place, but exciting. A halt was made at a service station.

"Sam, fill this bus up, an' tell me where to find Nicholas Bligh," said the young driver.

"Don't know, Sim, but I do know who does. Rustle down to Jed Price. He'll tell you."

No sooner had the boy left than from the little glass-windowed office stepped a lithe, tall young man. The instant Martha espied him she recognized him, and realized that he had been waiting there to waylay her. Her second glance, as he leisurely approached the car, appraised him more closely. His shapely feet were encased in high-top, decorated boots, much the worse for wear, and his spurs dragged in the gravel. He wore jeans, also stained and old, and above his narrow hips was a belt shiny with brass shells. A yellow scarf hung full and loose from his neck. He had a red face, clean as a baby's, eyes of intense, vivid blue, and hair as red as a flame. It stood up like a mane. In his hand he carried a huge old sombrero of a tan color.

"Mawnin', Miss Dixon," he drawled, with a smile that no girl, much less a western-struck maiden like Martha, could have found anything but agreeable.

"Good morning," she replied, a little coolly. It would never do to encourage this cowboy. But Martha wanted to.

"I shore hope thet clumsy cowpuncher didn't hurt you when he kicked you over heah at Glemm's."

"No, I guess I'm the one who did the kicking."

He leaned in at the window on the driver's side, and ringed the brim of his sombrero with strong brown fingers. His piercing eyes took Martha in from head to boots, and back again. But she liked his look, though it verged upon the audacious.

"Hitchhiker, I reckon, an' all alone. Doggone, but I like a girl who ain't afraid."

"What's there to be afraid of in Wyoming?"

"Wal, a lot, Miss. Tough lot of cowpunchers aboot heah."

"Indeed! I've only seen—two that I know of."

He never blinked one of those speculative eyes of his. "You shore need an escort, wherever you're goin'."

"Isn't this young man trustworthy?"

"Aw, Sim is fine. But he's only a kid. You need a man."

"Yes? I'm afraid I'll have to take the risk. I've no money to waste."

"Shore, I wouldn't take no money from a lady."

"You are very kind, indeed. But I think I'll dispense with an escort. What *can* there be to be afraid of?"

"Wal, ootside of tough punchers, there's Injuns, hawse thieves, bootleggers, hijackers, a big stiff of a sheriff who thinks he's a lady killer—to name a few reasons why you shouldn't go alone."

"Oh, what a formidable list! How can I tell, Mr. Texas, that you don't belong to one of those classifications?"

"My Gawd, lady, do I look it?" he protested.

"No. You look very innocuous—not to say innocent."

"What's thet inno-yus?" he inquired, with his dazzling smile. "An' how'd you know I'm Texas Haynes?"

"I didn't. I only heard the prefix. You, of course, read *my* name on the ledger in the hotel?"

"Shore did, Miss Martha. Hope you ain't offended. You see only once in a life-time does a girl like you roll into this town."

"Is that a compliment?" asked Martha, archly.

"Wal, if you want it straight, no girl so purty ever did— "

"That'll do, thanks. It's a compliment."

He stared at her coolly.

"You don't get me. I'll bet you've been scared, bothered, insulted on yore long hitchhike? Haven't you?"

"Yes, I'm sorry to say."

"But by no Texan. . . . Miss Martha, the cowboy from Texas who'd insult a girl ain't been born yet," he drawled with a slow, almost passionate, pride.

"That's something splendid to know. But aren't cowboys from Wyoming just as—as chivalrous?"

"I'll leave thet for you to find oot. An' you're liable to pronto if you don't let me go along with you."

"I'll risk it."

"Where air you haided for?"

"I don't know exactly. My uncle lives on the Sweetwater. The driver has gone to find out."

"Miss Dixon, if you don't reckon me too nosy, what's yore uncle's name?" queried Haynes. His flashing blue eyes seemed shadowed with his swift change of thought.

"It is Nicholas Bligh."

"*Bligh!*" echoed the cowboy. He stepped back from the car to make her a gallant bow. "I've heahed of Nick Bligh, a new cattleman in these parts. Sorry I cain't tell you I've rode for him. . . . Good day, Miss Dixon."

He put on his huge sombrero and strode across the street, a superb figure, and graceful save for the slightly bowed legs. He did not look back. Martha Ann, watching him, pondered over the sudden slight change in his demeanor and expression upon hearing her uncle's name.

Then the young man delegated to drive Martha came running back and jumped into the car. "Found out, Miss. Aw, easy! An' not so fur. Take us mebbe three hours. We turn off at Sweetwater bridge. Only ranch down river, so we can't miss it."

"That's fine news. Is it safe?"

"Safe? You mean this Ford?"

"No, the road. That redheaded cowboy scared me."

"Tex Haynes? The son of a gun! What'd he tell you?"

Martha repeated in full the dire list of calamities which Haynes had vowed would imperil her.

"I'll bet he wanted to drive you."

"Not exactly. He wanted to go along."

"Ahuh. Thet *hombre* will be hittin' yore uncle for a job. I'll give you a hunch, Miss, but you mustn't squeal on me. Tell yore uncle not to hire Tex."

"Thank you. And why?"

"Aw, Tex is gittin' a bad name. He's crippled a couple of cowboys. Been in jail for fightin'. But it's not thet. There are hints out about him. I don't know what they are. Darn shame, too. Tex is a wonder puncher. Wins all the rodeos at Cheyenne. An' you can't help likin' him.''

Martha feared that all her driver had succeeded in doing was to increase her interest in Texas Haynes. Her insurgent mind always veered to the underdog. Moreover, he had not looked down upon her scornfully because she was a hitchhiker.

"Who is Smoky?'' asked the Chicago girl, as they drove out of town.

"Smoky Reed? He's a sure 'nough bad egg of a cowpuncher. Sweet on Nell Glemm. An' Nell is loony over Tex. Smoky lost his job, I heerd. An' Tex ain't had a job for ages. He could get one, though. Any cattleman would be glad to have Tex.''

"Tell me all about this country. Range, you Westerners call it. Oh, I can't see a thing but these scaly hills.''

"Sorta shet in here, for a spell, Miss. But you jest wait till we come to the Sweetwater.''

"I'm waiting. . . . You didn't tell me your name.''

"Sim Glemm. Sim is nickname for Simpson. I'm Mrs. Glemm's nephew.''

Martha Ann loosed the battery of her inquisitive mind, and as there was nothing pretty or unusual to look at in the scenery, she plied her loquacious driver with question after question. Driving the two hours required to reach a point where they could see the river she came into possession of a vast store of Wyoming lore, concerning the history, people and gossip, some of which she accepted with a grain of salt. Sim had the kind of narrative mind that always tried and usually succeeded in amplifying the truth.

But when they drove around a curve that brought them out from the shelter of a drab range which like a wall had hidden the view to the south and west, Martha Ann sat up with eyes wide open.

"Here's the river,'' pointed the lad. "Shines like a ribbon, don't it? Good fishin' along here, too. An' see the green willows winding down from thet blue range. It ain't the sky you're lookin' at, Miss, but Wyomin' range land. See them round pink an' red things standin' up? Row of little mountains called the Antelope Hills. Yore uncle's ranch is right under them. An' shore you're missin' them white saw teeth way yonder. . . . Way high, Miss. Them's the snow-tipped Rockies. . . . *Now* what do you say about Wyomin'?''

"Wonderful!'' cried Martha.

"I'll tell the world,'' sang out the western youth proudly.

During the descent toward the river and bridge Martha Ann soon lost the far-flung view which had made her imagine that she was looking through colored glasses that magnified and glorified everything she saw. Across the Sweetwater, however, she had an unobstructed vision for leagues and leagues. There was nothing over there—nothing but endless land of many hues dominated by a hazy purple, countless acres of level land, rolling ridges, dark valleys, on and on to the shimmering horizon. She felt that to understand this amazing country, to appreciate it, she must begin with separate parts, first those that lay close at hand and intimate, and by studying them, graduate one day to some semblance of grasp of the vast infinitude that lay beyond.

The river came first. It was indeed a bright ribbon, and in places, several ribbons, flowing between islands of sand and green cotton-woods. But it struck her that there was very little water for so wide a river bottom. From bank to bank the bed was wide. In times of flood the Sweetwater must be truly awe inspiring. The verdant banks and islands, the sparkling white and amber water, presented a vivid contrast to the somber range of grass and sage. Martha Ann gave this lonely river its proper place in the scene as the life and vitality of that magnificent range.

"But I don't see a single living creature!" she burst out.

"Say, Miss Tenderfoot, you oughta fetched a spyglass," replied the driver. "See them tiny little specks yonder?"

"Ye-es, I guess so."

"Cattle," he said, with finality. Cattle were the aim and end of this vast country.

Sim turned off the road to the left just before reaching the bridge, and Martha Ann soon lost sight of all the open country. The bumpy road necessitated slow driving along the river bank. Groves of cottonwoods and patches of willow filled the river bottom.

"See thet tree down thar?" queried her guide, pointing to a huge round-foliaged cottonwood, with wide-spreading branches. "My dad has helped hang rustlers on thet tree."

"Oh, how dreadful! . . . What are rustlers?"

"Fellers who rustle cattle."

"How do they rustle them? Make noises to frighten them?"

"Whoopee!" roared Sim, and then gave way to mirth.

"I dare say I'm very much a tenderfoot. But how can I learn if I am not told?"

"You're gonna be a circus for the cowpunchers. But come to think of it you'll have the best of them right off pronto."

"That's good news, anyway. How will I?"

" 'Cause you're so durn pretty thet they won't dare—not even Tex Haynes—to torment you an' play tricks."

"I fail to see why my—why that will protect me?"

"Shucks! You jest wait."

"I'll wait patiently, young man. But tell me, what does 'rustle' really mean?"

"Rustle means to rustle off with cattle. To *steal* them. Calves, cows, yearlin's, two-year olds, all kinds of cattle. An' there are rustlers workin' yet on this range.

Only two-bit stuff, sure. But my dad says there always has been rustlers in Wyomin' an' always will be.''

'' 'Two-bit stuff.' What's that?''

''Two bits is twenty-five cents.''

A long stretch of better road put a different face on the last lap of the approach to Bligh's Ranch. The land to the left began to slope gradually upward toward the beautiful bare colored hills. And suddenly Martha Ann became conscious of a nearer view of the grand panorama which had so enraptured her more than twenty miles back. Here it was clearer, closer, more eye filling and breath taking. But the near approach to the ranch drew and held the young girl's gaze. She saw a long low squat building without a vestige of green about it, and beyond it stood sheds and pens and fences, all sadly in need of repair. And then as the car advanced farther she caught view of a gray old log cabin, picturesque in its isolation and ruin, situated on the river bank, facing the west.

Martha's mounting excitement left her with a sudden constriction of her throat. She swallowed hard and found breathing oppressive. If she had been mad with yearning for Wyoming, with the sacrifices this trip had cost, she now realized how true her instinct had been. The solitude of the scene drew her, the wildness of the view called to something deep and instinctive within her, the beauty made her soul ache with sadness.

But she must not give way to her emotions now that she was here, or present herself to Uncle Nick as a maudlin, sentimental girl. The driver was babbling on, but Martha could not attend to him. She saw a colt sticking a curious lean head over a fence, she saw two busy little puppies that could scarcely waddle, then a big yellow-haired, fierce-eyed dog. Suddenly she realized that the car had come to a stop.

''Hi! Anybody home?'' yelled the driver, with the lusty voice of youth.

''Don't shout. I-I'll go in.''

''Nix. Not with thet yaller dawg eyin' us.''

Trepidation vied in Martha's breast with a bursting joyous expectancy as she espied a man, little and lean and gray, fit habitant for that dwelling, come ambling around a corner of the house. When he aimed a gentle kick at the yellow dog she saw that he was bow-legged. But all Westerners had legs more or less bowed. Already she had the door of the car open, and now she leaped out to run up to the little man.

''Uncle Nick—I'm—your niece—come to—'' she cried, and failing of voice threw her arms around him and quickly kissed his cheek.

''For the land's sakes!'' he ejaculated mildly, as he gently released himself. ''Lass, I'm plumb sorry, but I jest don't happen to be yore Uncle Nick.''

''Oh-h! . . . Ex-cuse me. You must think I'm crazy. . . . But I never saw him,'' burst out the fair visitor, adding confusion to her agitation.

"Hey Nick, come a-runnin'," yelled the little man.

The door opened to reveal a tall man, gray-haired, weather-beaten of face standing in the doorway. The instant his astonished blue eyes saw the girl he ejaculated: "Martha Dixon!"

"Yes," cried Martha, running to him. "Martha Ann. . . . Your niece."

A swift change from amazement to unmistakable gladness, and the quick embrace, relieved the girl, not only of her strength, but of the overwhelming dread that had consumed her. Uncle Nick resembled her grandmother. He had kind keen blue eyes that were filling with tears.

"My niece? Bless your heart! Child, I'm plumb buffaloed. . . . Who's with you? How'd you come? What—"

"I'm alone. Walked a lot of the way. Begged rides—to save my money. . . . And here I am—to stay."

"Martha, did you run away from home?"

"So did you, Uncle Nick. . . . I—I wanted to help you."

He held her in his arms a little closer and bent his lined face close to hers.

"I never expected to see any of my kin again," he said, with a voice that trembled. "Much less havin' Martha Dixon's daughter run away from home on my account."

"It wasn't, Uncle—all on your account. I was crazy to see the West."

"You must have been. Never heard of such a thing. Trampin' alone an' stealin' rides! Jim, what do you think of thet?"

"Wal, Nick, I reckon I'm loco," grinned the little man.

"Come in, Martha. You can tell us all about it," said her uncle. "Jim, fetch in her packs."

"Oh, I mustn't forget to pay Sim," cried Martha, running back to the car.

"I'm tellin' you, Miss. It won't be very long till you're gettin' all the free rides you want," said Sim, pocketing his fee.

Martha's uncle led her into the house, apologizing for his humble abode, which he had not expected to be graced by such a fair guest. Martha's quick survey was much at variance with her preconceived idea of the interior of this rude house. She saw a fairly large room, consisting of roughly plastered walls covered with skins and Indian ornaments, guns lying across the horns of a deer head over the open fireplace, a wooden floor, bare except for a couple of Indian rugs, table and oil lamp, an old rocker and a couch. There was only one window, which was large enough to let in the western light.

"Come in, Mrs. Fenner. See who's here," called Bligh through an open door.

"I been lookin'," replied a feminine voice, and a little woman hopped in like a bird. She had the brightest of dark eyes shining out from a small face, pleasant despite the havoc wrought by a hard, lonely life.

"Mrs. Fenner, this is my niece, Martha Ann Dixon," said Bligh proudly. "Martha, meet Jim's wife."

Greetings had scarcely been exchanged before Martha had taken a liking for this little western woman. Then Jim came in with Martha's bags.

"Set down, Martha, an' make yourself to home," invited Bligh, as he placed the rocker for her. "Mrs. Fenner, I reckon this room will have to be Martha's."

"Oh, I couldn't take your living room," protested the girl.

"Wal, you'll have to, 'cause it's our only one. It's got to be fixed up, too. What'll we need, Mrs. Fenner?"

"Washstand, mirror, bureau, some pegs to hang clothes on, some more rugs on the floor an' a curtain for the window," replied Mrs. Fenner practically.

"Reckon we can find all but the bureau. We'll get thet in town. We'll rustle things pronto. . . . Martha, tell us how in the world you ever got here, alone, an' in them togs."

Whereupon Martha, inspired as well as excited by her glad-eyed, wondering audience, related the pleasantest part of her hitchhiking experience.

"An' nothin' else happened?" ejaculated her uncle.

"Not much. Tramps tried to rob me and a couple of young men got fresh. But altogether my trip was uneventful."

"Nick, it was them eyes," spoke up Jim Fenner solemnly.

"No—the good Lord!" added Mrs. Fenner.

"Wal, she's here, an' I say the day of miracles isn't past. . . . Come, we'll rustle what we can find to make her comfortable."

"But, Uncle, the driver told me that to rustle means to steal," remonstrated Martha. "Please don't rustle all those things for me."

They laughed and departed in great excitement, plainly bewildered by her unexpected arrival, but undoubtedly happy over it. And that was what made Martha's heart sing. She began to unpack her luggage, but the unpacking, owing to frequent interruptions, took a long time. At last between the four of them they had the living room most satisfactorily furnished.

"Wal, thet's fine," declared Bligh, viewing the result of their labors. "I'll send Jim or Andrew into town tomorrow for what else we can think of. . . . Mrs. Fenner, will you fix some lunch for us? Are you hungry, lass?"

"I'll say I am!" cried Martha.

"Wal, it does my eyes good to see you," replied her uncle, taking her hand. "You look so much like your mother that at first I thought she had come. . . . Child, I don't know what to say to you."

"Don't scold, Uncle," she pleaded. "I just had to come."

"You ran off?"

"Yes. I lied to Mother. That hurts terribly. It seems so much worse now."

"Have you written her?"

"Once. I told her I was with a girl friend, whose uncle wanted to take us to the Black Hills."

"Your mother will have to know."

"Yes—but—but there's no hurry. . . . Oh, what can I say to her?"

"Martha, is this a visit you are paying me?"

"A long one—perhaps forever," replied Martha Ann, as she looked away.

"What has hurt you, lass?"

"Oh, everything."

"An unhappy love affair?" he asked, with a grave smile.

"No. I'm sick of boys and men who keep pestering me. . . . Then I grew to hate the city—the noise, dirt, rush—and being poor. I worked while I went to college—paid my own way—saved a little to come west. . . . Uncle, I didn't realize till I got to the Black Hills what it was I really wanted and needed. It was change, freedom, loneliness. To be thrown on my own!"

"How old are you, Martha?"

"Nineteen last February."

"You look younger. . . . Now, my dear, I'm curious to know how a slip of a college girl aims to help a poor old cattleman?"

"Uncle Nick, wait till you get acquainted with this modern college girl! I shall help you in a thousand ways. . . . Tell me, Uncle, just how are you situated?"

"Wal, I've picked up considerable in health out here. It's higher country. As for worldly wealth, lass, I have mighty little. Got here with the last thousand head of cattle I saved back at Belle Fourche. I should tell you thet before I left there I corresponded with a cattleman whose range is on the Sweetwater. An' he induced me to come in on a deal with him—which I'm sorry to say Jim Fenner doesn't like."

"What kind of deal?" queried Martha Ann.

"I was to furnish stock an' he would run them with his, savin' me the expense of an outfit."

"On what basis?"

"Equal shares. But when I got out here he bucked. I expected an equal share of his stock, but he claims I was only to get a share of my own thet he'd raise an' market."

"How much stock has this man?"

"Wal, some less than mine."

"I think he drove a sharp bargain."

"So do I. Anyway, he now refuses to reconsider the deal. Says he has my agreement in black an' white. An' if I don't agree he'll take the deal to court."

"What's his name?"

"McCall. What's more, he claims thet he has a lien on this homestead. A homesteader named Boseman settled here, but never proved up on his claim.

Abandoned the farm, which was homesteaded by other cowmen, who in turn never got a patent on it.''

''Did you lay out any more for it?''

''Only on improvements.''

''How much?''

''I don't know. Not much yet.''

''Then if you have to get off you won't.stand to lose much?''

''No. But I've taken a shine to the place. Spring water has some mineral quality. Good for me. I'd like to stay.''

''Then you bet we'll stay,'' declared Martha Ann.

Uncle Nick clapped his hands. ''Once in a long while I have a hunch. . . . I just had one.''

''What is it, Uncle?'' asked Martha smilingly.

''You've changed my luck.''

''Why, of course. What do you think I hitchhiked out here for?''

''I reckon the Lord sent you. Come to think of it, Martha, I believe he's rememberin' my years of toil an' defeat on the ranges. He has sent me help. This man Jim Fenner is an Arizonian. He threw in with me, not in hope of profit, but because he an' his wife liked me. They've had a hard time since Jim got crippled an' couldn't do a regular cowboy's work. Then a handy man came along—works for his board. Now you come with a modern college girl's ideas on cattle raisin'!''

''Uncle, I'm going to run outdoors where I can yell!''

Martha Ann did run. She ran so fast that she could scarcely see where she was going. Pell-mell she ran around a corner of the barn only to bump so violently into a man that she sat down with a thud. Her hat fell off and her hair cascaded down over her eyes. She put both hands flat on the ground in order to raise herself when the person with whom she had collided uttered a strange exclamation.

''Do you occupy all the land on this range?'' inquired Martha flippantly.

She shook the hair out of her eyes to see a tall, wide-shouldered young man in blue jeans. His face was familiar. She saw a sudden cloud of red tinge his brown cheek. His gray gaze seemed to bore right through her.

''*You!*'' he burst out.

''Who else did you think I am?''

''Wyoming Mad!'' And he threw up his hands.

Then Martha Ann recognized him. He was changed somehow, thinner, sun blistered yet he was the one real hero of her hitch-hike, the rescuer who had so rudely disapproved of her, and whom she could never forget—Andrew Bonning.

''You!'' she exclaimed weakly, and she would have crawled into a hole had there been one near to hide her blush.

"Howdy, little kick hunter. . . . Who else do you think I am?"

"Here—in Wyoming—on Uncle Nick's ranch?"

"Sure. Don't you see me?"

"You're the new hired man—the handy man—who works for his board?"

"The very same, Wyoming Mad," returned Bonning, with a bow.

Martha Ann leaped in front of him. "Then—you're fired!" she cried.

7

ANDREW BONNING leaned back against the corral gate a victim of emotions that were compounded of surprise, annoyance, amusement and reluctant admiration. So this independent young hitchhiker who had haunted him for the past few weeks had turned up again under even more complex and bewildering circumstances. He might have expected her to bob up any day.

"Yeah? So I'm fired?" he queried slowly.

"You bet you are," she snapped.

"Who's firing me?"

"I am."

Andrew studied the girl. She was certainly angry, as well as surprised. Her face was pale and her eyes were blazing. She had the strangest, most beautiful eyes he had ever seen in a woman, and though he remembered them, this nearer view under the bright sun seemed to render null his former impression. They flared upon him with a clear amber light. She had red lips, just now set determinedly.

"Who are you?" asked Andrew.

"I'm Martha Ann Dixon. Mr. Bligh is my uncle. And I've come west to help him run his ranch."

A laugh interrupted Andrew's gravity. "Miss Martha Ann Dixon," he said. "That accounts for the M A D. . . . Well, we seem fated to meet each other. I'm sorry. . . . Do you mean to run Bligh's ranch, or to run off the hired men who don't fall for you at the drop of a hat?"

"Mr. Bonning, all I mean is that I wouldn't have you on this ranch," she blazed.

"I see. Well, if I were to consider only myself, I wouldn't want to stay. But it just happens that Mr. Bligh needs me."

"No more than any other hand, I'm sure."

"Indeed he does—more than *any* man you might find."

"Oh. You certainly have a poor opinion of yourself."

"If I had, it evidently could not be as poor as yours of me. May I inquire why my presence on this ranch is so obnoxious to you?"

"If you were on the level you wouldn't ask."

"That's the last thing I'm not, Miss Dixon," he returned, coldly. "And if you're not throwing a bluff with your pretty pride, your outraged dignity, you'll explain why you say I'm not on the level."

"You're not—because you—you insulted me."

"I did nothing of the sort," declared Andrew flatly.

"You did! I was terribly indebted to you when you rescued me from those tramps. But you spoiled it by—by taking me for a common—for something I'm not."

"Miss Dixon, that wild stunt of yours, hiking the roads alone, hunting for kicks, ready and willing to be picked up by anyone, laid you open to—"

"I wasn't hunting for kicks," she interrupted almost in tears. "I wasn't ready and willing to be picked up by anybody—"

"Now *you're* not being on the level," he returned, with obvious sarcasm in his voice. His anger was struggling with a deeper emotion.

"I *am* on the level, but I don't care to prove it to you," she retorted, her face flaming red. "I simply don't care what you think. I did, but not any more. . . . For all I know you might be a confidence man, a rustler—anything but a Missouri farm hand."

"I might be, but I'm not. It doesn't matter in the least to you, or to anyone out here, what or who I am. I'm honest, and I chose to offer my services free to your uncle because I needed a home and he needed an honest hired man. That's all. And you're sore at me because I saw through you."

"You didn't see through me."

"Wyoming Mad, you'll understand me better if I say that you're not very convincing."

She grew white even to her bright red lips.

"Andrew Bonning, you thought me a wild, wayward girl, didn't you?" she queried furiously.

"What else *could* I think?" he retorted.

"You called me 'an unforgettable kid,' didn't you?"

"I'm afraid you are."

"*Why* am I?"

"You are rather pretty and distinctly original," he answered in a way that made what he said sound almost uncomplimentary.

"But sailing under false colors?"

"I certainly wouldn't call you true blue. You strike me as the chameleon type,

Miss Dixon. You change your color—or your line—to suit the individual you want to impress.''

"You think I flirted with that boy who took me to dinner?''

"I saw you. And you impressed me as a fast little worker—especially with hicks like him.''

"You think—I'm even—worse?'' she faltered, in a suffocated little voice.

"I'm ashamed to confess that I did. I let my imagination run riot—and pictured you with him in the park, or in his car.''

"Oh, you're like all the rest of the beastly men,'' she cried, with renewed fury. "You've a one-track mind when it comes to women. What kind of sister could you have, or girl friends? . . . Isn't there *any* man who can understand a girl's longings to be free—to have adventures—to find herself—to be let alone? Oh, what a rotten world! I thought I'd escape from all *that*—way out here in Wyoming.''

"So did I, Miss Dixon,'' he returned, stung to a bitterness that overcame his surprise.

"Well, you can go to blazes!'' she concluded, with finality, as she turned away.

"Thank you. After firing me you consign me to blazes. You certainly have a nice, gentle, sweet disposition,'' he replied, following her around the barn. "Here's your uncle now. I'll tell him.''

It was evident that Miss Dixon wanted to escape this encounter.

"Hello, here you are,'' called out Bligh, intercepting them. "Have you scraped an acquaintance? . . . Martha, this is Andrew—''

"Uncle, we've met before, to my sorrow,'' interposed the girl icily.

"Eh? What? Wal now?''

"Mr. Bligh, we have met, back in Nebraska somewhere,'' said Andrew hurriedly. "I did her some trifling service. But I offended her because I disapproved of a young girl hiking alone along the highway—picking up men to ride with. I'm sorry. But I think it's a pretty reckless stunt even for these modern days. I had no right to criticize her. And for that I apologize. The harm is done, however . . . and in fact she won't have me on the ranch.''

"Uncle, I fired him,'' cried Martha. "I hope you agree with me!''

"Fired him! . . . Why, lass, what're you talkin' about? Of course I wouldn't keep any man—but be reasonable. I agree with Andrew that your hike out here was a pretty wild thing to do. The Lord must have watched over you, Martha. . . . An' as for Andrew's leavin'—I'd hate to see him go. Cowboys are hard customers for me to handle, Martha. They drink an' leave the ranch. Now Andrew is steady. He's different, lass. He'll fit in here. Jim Fenner particularly likes him. Can't we fix up your quarrel somehow?''

"No, Uncle. But if Mr. Bonning is so valuable to you I withdraw my objection," replied the girl, and walked away with her head proudly erect.

"Wal, Andrew, this day is one of surprises," said the rancher. "Strange you two should meet on the road an' then meet again out here. She seems a mighty fiery little lass. . . . Which of you is to blame for this?"

"I am," replied Andrew, emphatically. "I reproved her pretty harshly for this hiking stunt. It was none of my business."

"Reckon you've been pretty hard on the lass. She's only a spirited filly. Like her mother and grandmother before her. . . . Fine old family—the Campbells. Poor now, an' perhaps thet's one reason why Martha ran off. I ran off thirty years ago. . . . How about you?"

"Well, I ran off from something, that's sure. Probably my own morbid self."

"It will all come right. But not soon. The Campbells don't forgive easily. . . . Thet was funny about her firin' you. Wal, she withdrew her objection. I hope thet'll be the end of it."

Andrew had his doubts about that. As he walked away toward his quarters he found that his unreasonable temper had cooled, and that he was now in a state close to self-reproach. He had answered the girl's pertinent queries coolly and to her discredit. Any young woman with a grain of spirit would have resented what he had said and would have defended herself. She had done more. Then remembering what she had declaimed so passionately, he felt deeply ashamed, and suddenly he was horrified by the thought that it was quite possible that he had completely misjudged her. How scathingly she had denounced all men! It made him feel decidedly uncomfortable. She was perfectly right. But what else could she expect from men? It seemed to Andrew that she had almost invited approach. Of all the escapades that had ever come under his notice, of all the crazy stunts that he could conceive, this hiking alone by a stunningly pretty girl through the West was the most audacious and questionable. She seemed clever, intelligent, refined. Bligh vouched for her good blood. All the more reason to suspect her! This twentieth-century restlessness and thoughtlessness, this boldness so typical of the age, this urge for thrills she could not satisfy at home, this wanderlust of the past combined with this modern obsession to meet and captivate strange men—these all must be at the bottom of Martha Ann Dixon's flight from a good home. It was a pity. Old Bligh would never be able to see through this clever little minx.

"But she can't fool me," he reassured himself. "Not a chance! She knows her stuff. She has my sister and Connie tied to the mast. For they played the game openly and aboveboard."

Having delivered this ultimatum to his smarting conscience, Andrew stamped into the old cabin where he had elected to make his abode. It was getting to mean a great deal to him—this ancient abandoned cabin. The initials cut on the logs and the charcoal drawings of brands on the stone fireplace, the accumulation of years of range dust on the rafters, the friendly mice and squirrels that had at first regarded his presence as an intrusion, the bleached antlers over the mantle, the old couch of boughs in one corner, the black smoke stains on the chimney, the holes in the roof that he had not yet mended—these things and everything about the big room held for him the atmosphere of bygone frontier days.

Andrew worked at odd times on making the cabin more habitable. Before the snow came he would have it snug and dry and comfortable. Just now there was nothing but his blankets and his bags and saddle. He pictured himself during the winter, on dark nights when the blizzard was howling, sitting beside an open fire, watching the red embers, and reveling in his solitude. His favorite place during this summer weather was out on the porch that faced the river and the magnificent reach of purple and gold stretching to the Rockies.

This porch spoke as eloquently as the big room of what had happened there. It certainly needed a good many repairs. Andrew decided, however, that the bullet holes in the posts and cabin wall, made during a rustler-cowboy war in early days, should not be removed for any repairs. The slope of the land toward the river caused the floor of the porch to stand high off the ground. The wide steps leading down had rotted away until they were now unsafe.

Andrew flung himself into one of the old crude chairs, and threw his sombrero aside. His brow and hair were moist. No matter how hot it was in the sun, the shade was always cool. Bligh's cattle grazed along the river banks and down in the bottom lands. Soon they would work up into the draws of the hills; and then the real riding for Andrew would begin. There were horses out on the grassy slope.

All at once it struck Andrew that a rift had come into his new and pleasant way of life. He did not need to puzzle it out. That amber-eyed girl! He thought he had dismissed her and the disturbing thoughts she had aroused with a scornful finality. And here she was back!

"What a sweet, pretty kid!" he mused regretfully. "She will put this range on the blink. . . . Damn it, I like her! Maybe she didn't hand it to me! Eyes and lips! Never will I forget those eyes. . . . If that girl was only straight I'd—I'd—fall for her like a ton of bricks."

Andrew admitted this startling possibility. He realized, too, that he was in a strangely receptive and unusual condition of mind. He had severed old ties. He had traveled far and every league, it seemed, had eased his pain and bitterness. This great open range land had expanded his soul. Now this new self seemed in conflict with the old.

While Andrew was in the midst of these introspective self-confessions, the little Arizonian, Jim Fenner, limped into the cabin.

"Where are you, Andrew?"

"Come out here, Jim."

"Bligh wants some goods trucked from town. Will you drive me in? I'm leery of thet truck. She bucked on me last time."

"Jim, I can make her run if anybody can."

"Wal, I'd like to see you take to hosses thet way. But we haven't a decent nag in the outfit."

"What'd a good horse cost, Jim?"

"Around fifty. An' thet reminds me. I heerd the little cyclone who jest blew in askin' about hosses. Andrew, we haven't one thet's safe for her. An' Bligh can't afford to buy one."

"Is he pretty hard up, Jim?" queried Andrew thoughtfully.

"Hard up ain't tellin' it. But I'm glad this niece came. She'll put new life in us, Andrew."

"Life? If that were only all!"

"Say, I was in the barn when you an' Martha had thet set-to," confided the Arizonian.

"Yeah? . . . Then you heard me get fired?"

"Wal, I reckon, an' told to go to blazes. . . . Andrew, you an' me took to each other right off. We're goin' to get along. Mebbe thet doesn't give me license to be too curious. All the same I'll risk it. . . . Wasn't you an' Martha kinda gone on each other—before you landed out west?"

"No. I never met her until one night on the road. I came on her in the hands of a tramp, so I slugged him. We met once after that."

"An' what happened then?"

"Nothing. We had very few words until this meeting. Then we had plenty, believe me."

"I savvied thet you had sort of a pore opinion of her an' it riled her."

"Yes."

"How pore an opinion, Bonnin'?"

Andrew shook his head as if reluctant to interrogate himself. "Pretty poor, I'm afraid, Jim."

"Wal, you know these eastern youngsters. An' I reckon they're a wild outfit these days. It shore was a turrible thing for thet kid to run off from home an' come out here alone."

Andrew nodded gloomily.

"But she's honest, Andrew."

"Honest?" echoed Andrew, quickly.

"Straight, I mean. No matter how wild thet kid's been she is decent. *Sabe, Señor?*"

The curt assertion of the Arizonian annoyed Andrew as much as the hint of his own lack of chivalry.

"Jim, I'm sure I didn't think—"

"Wal, I'm glad you didn't," interrupted Jim bluntly. "My hunch came from my wife, Sue. She never made a mistake about figgerin' a girl. She cottoned pronto to this pore little runaway. An' so did I. An' Bligh, why she'll make a new man out of him. I'm tellin' you, Andrew, 'cause I want you on our side of the fence."

"Thanks, Jim . . . Lordy, I'm not such a poor fish. . . . And see here, old-timer, I've got something to tell you. It has weighed on my mind."

"Wal, go ahaid an' shoot," replied the Arizonian, leaning back against a post to fix Andrew with his penetrating eyes.

"Listen. The night I reached town I camped out in the brush," began Andrew swiftly. "Walked in to buy some grub. It was dark when I got back to camp. You couldn't see my car from the road. I was about to make a fire when a horseman came along from the open country. Then a man on foot from town. They met—came off the road—near where I had crouched down. Briefly, the rider was a cowboy called Texas something. The other was a cattleman. He owed the cowboy money for branding calves with his brand. The man's name was McCall. He told Texas about Bligh's recent arrival on the range—that Bligh had driven in so much stock, an' he wanted Texas to begin what I grasped to be wholesale stealing. Texas refused. He agreed to brand calves as before. Also to carry a message for McCall to another cowboy, named Smoky Reed, who was to clean out Bligh. . . . I heard all the conversation distinctly. When Texas rode away McCall made a crack that showed he feared the cowboy."

"Wal, you don't say?" mused Jim thoughtfully.

"I forgot to include some pertinent remarks about Sheriff Slade. He must get a rake-off from bootleggers and Texas knows it. Next morning when I was about to start out here that sheriff searched my car. Quite a crowd collected, and I told Slade to his face that for all I knew he might be a bootlegger himself."

"Andy, you'll do," returned Jim dryly. And Andrew gathered that a compliment greater than he could estimate had been paid him. "Wal, I oughta have a smoke. . . . Say, why didn't you tell Bligh about this deal?"

"I meant to. But he seemed already to be bearing a pretty heavy burden. I didn't want to add to it."

"You figgered correct. It'd never do to tell the boss right now. You an' me have got to handle this deal."

"Jim, that tickles me," responded Andrew eagerly. "Do you know I had a fool notion I'd like to work it out alone. Absurd, of course, but it sure got into me."

"Wal, you an' me together can handle it at present. I don't know about later."

"How'd you suggest we handle it, Jim?"

"We'll ketch those cowpunchers red-handed."

"Then what?"

"I reckon beatin' the rustlin' out of them would be a good idee. Of course we used to string up rustlers in the old days. Jail is about all they get now, an' thet not for long."

"Humph! That Texas cowboy wouldn't take a beating. He'd shoot, Jim. Struck me as a tough proposition."

"Wal, if it comes to shootin' you'd be in serious."

"I'm okay with a rifle."

"Good, so long as you ain't in close quarters."

"You'll have to coach me, Jim. . . . What'd you mean when you said you didn't know how to handle the deal later?"

"Wal, Andy, if Bligh loses a lot of his cattle or if McCall gyps him, an' I reckon both is liable to happen, it'll take a long time to build up again. I'd hate to fail on this range. So I'd persuade Bligh to keep on. He's gettin' along in years an' a crownin' disappointment would go hard."

"But Jim, how can disaster be averted?"

"It cain't. Thet's the hell of this cattle business. Good grass, good water at times are no better than a bad drought. Because all the calves will be stole. It's not easy to trace stolen calves. You jest can't unless you ketch the brander with his runnin' iron."

"You believe there's a paying ranch business to be developed here?"

"Payin'? Hell, there's twenty per cent at least."

"How'd you go about developing this ranch to clear such a big percentage of profit?"

"Wal, son, you gotta have some coin. Cattle are way down now. You can buy cheap. If Bligh could restock, say with a mixed herd of two thousand haid, an' get some Arizona punchers to ride this range, why he'd double his money when prices went up."

"That's the rub, then? Bligh is without means to restock. . . . Couldn't he borrow?"

"The banks jest ain't lendin' money without big securities."

"Why hire Arizona cowboys?"

"Wal, to be shore, they ain't any better than Wyomin' punchers. But they'd be on the prod. They'd be like a pack of hounds. Playin' one outfit agin a rival one used to be an old trick of mine. I've been foreman on some great ranches. Bucked the Hash Knife outfit once. An' I still carry some of their lead."

"What was the Hash Knife outfit?"

"Hardest ridin', drinkin', shootin', an' sometimes hardest stealin' outfit in Arizona."

"You'll have to tell me all about it some day. . . . Well, Jim, then it's lack of capital that handicaps our boss—and that stands between us and a swell job?"

"It is, Andy. But what's the use to smoke our pipes? We're all broke, an' the best we can hope for is to make a bare livin' for Bligh an' ourselves. Andy, we wouldn't have any jobs at all if we asked wages."

"Jim! Are you working for your board, the same as I am?"

"Shore am, an' satisfied, too. I tell you, son, I don't mind for myself, but it sticks in my craw thet I can't give Sue the pretty things women like."

"Jim, wait a minute," said Andrew, acting upon an impulse. He ran inside to return with his wallet which he got out of his grip. "I've got a little money—and I'm going to lend you some, Jim."

"Hell, no!"

"Yes, I am. It worries me, all this dough. There—two hundred bucks. I'd lose it in town. I've got a little left, Jim. I want to buy some lumber and tools and odd things to fix up my place here."

The Arizonian fingered the crisp bills while his eyes shed a warm light on Andrew.

"Son, you don't know me."

"I'll gamble on you, anyhow."

Jim folded the greenbacks and stowed them carefully in an inside vest pocket.

"Wal, all my life I've found two kinds of men. One kind makes you want to keep on fightin' an' hopin'. . . . Let's go in to dinner. I heerd the bell."

"I'll wait and get mine in town," replied Andrew hastily. "When will you be ready?"

"Pronto. You see if you can start thet truck."

"Okay."

Half an hour later Andrew drove the truck over in front of the house and honked the horn. Jim and his wife came out beaming, to be followed by Bligh and his niece. Andrew had only to see her again to realize why he had shirked dinner when he was hungry. Martha had changed her gray blouse to a white shirt, and she had done something to her hair. It was fluffy and shone like spun gold.

"All aboard," sang out Andrew. "Mrs. Fenner, hadn't you better come with Jim? I won't guarantee his sobriety."

"Wal, *I* will," declared Jim, as he climbed in.

Whereupon Andrew reacted to a sudden impulse. "Miss Dixon, there's room for you. Won't you come? You'll get a kick out of my driving."

"I'd do anything under the sun for a kick, Mr. Bonning, as you know—except ride with you," she replied coldly.

"Wal, Sue, you'd better wait up for us," said Jim.

"I haven't done thet for years, but I shall tonight," returned his wife, with an air of happy mystery.

"Mr. Bligh, what can I fetch you?" inquired Andrew casually.

"Jim has the list."

"Don't you dare forget *mine*," spoke up Martha saucily. "Go to a dry-goods store and ask the price of what I want. It's all carefully written out. If the price comes to more than fifteen dollars cut out the articles checked off. Can you remember all those instructions?"

"Andrew, you heerd them, so you can jar my memory."

"If we forget or lose the list we'll buy lollipops, gum, candy, some movie magazines and a victrola with a dozen jazz records," replied Andrew facetiously.

Martha Dixon did not join in the laugh that followed, but fixed Andrew with unfathomable eyes. She might either have hated or loved him, to judge by the look she gave him.

"Mr. Bonning will be surprised to see that I can make my own clothes," said the girl.

Andrew spent a strenuous and absorbing afternoon in town. What with Jim's supplies and the bulky nature of his own purchases, they had a good load by the time they were ready to start back. Leaving after supper, they gave several hours to the return drive, but Jim made the trip seem short by the resumption of his coaching of the tenderfoot. Andrew let all the Arizonian told him sink in. If there were any range subjects Jim did not touch upon Andrew could not imagine them.

"I shore liked both the hosses you bought," Jim said on one occasion. "Thet bay had good points, an' the pinto is a purty dogie. I reckon he'll make trouble for you at the ranch, an' I ain't sayin' how. . . . Hosses are most important on the range. Now when you're ridin' to an' fro practice with your rope. You don't do so bad. But practice. Rope everythin'. An' shoot at every jack rabbit an' coyote you see. Learn to see trails an' tracks on the ground. By studyin' your own hoss tracks an' others at the ranch, fresh or old, you can judge other tracks out on the range. For instance, you see your fresh track. You study it. An' then one made earlier. You see what has happened to it—a little dust blown in or water, or mebbe another track over it. You know just when they was made, an' if you make pictures of them in your mind soon you'll get the hang of a tracker. Don't miss nothin', Andrew. Use yore eyes. You've got field glasses. Use them when you're undecided or too far away from somethin'. When you're lookin' for strange riders keep out of sight. In the brush or timber, behind ridges an' back from canyon rims. If you're ridin' in the open do it bold, as if you saw nothin'. When the cattle get up in the foothills—an' thet'll be any day soon— you can ride out at daybreak, find a hidin' place an' watch. I'll be with you part of the time, an' I'll tell you how to look an' what you see. But shore you'll be alone a good deal. An' it'll happen when you're alone. These two-bit rustlers of McCall's will be slick an' keep to cover. But often they'll drive a cow an' calf from the open into rough goin'. You listen for a gun shot an' look for smoke. An' when you sneak up on one of them draw down on him with your rifle. Order him to throw up his hands an' turn his back. Then disarm him an' march him to the boss.''

Andrew was up with the dawn. How many years had he slept away the beautiful hours from the break of day to the burst of the sunrise! The soft mist above the river, the winging of ducks across the bars, the obscurity of the range yielding to a sudden magic brightness, the ghosts of mountains growing clear—these new facets of the morning held him absorbed. Then came the change from gray to rose and at last the glory of the lord of day.

He unloaded the truck and packed his purchases inside the old cabin. He discovered a fondness for tools, as well as hands unskilled in their use except when it came to tinkering with automobiles.

Mornings and evenings thereafter he labored at the pleasant task of rendering his new abode dry and warm and less bare to his gaze. But he had made no luxurious purchases. A hard, primitive simplicity seemed to be Andrew's goal.

As he ate with Jim in the kitchen and was absent from the house except at meal hours, he saw little of Martha Ann Dixon. Nevertheless she seemed omnipresent. She filled the lives of her uncle and this Arizona couple. They had suddenly awakened to something joyous. Andrew watched her from afar and sometimes, to his discomfiture, he was caught in the act. Yet he wondered how she could have caught him had she not also been taking cognizance of him. He had to listen to Jim's talk of her interest in horses, in the ranch, in everything and everyone but Andrew Bonning. On Sunday more visitors called on Bligh than during the entire preceding time since he had arrived on the Sweetwater. Some of these were cowboys, spick-and-span in their Sunday best, with boots as shiny as their hair. Andrew regarded them with a vague uneasiness.

Late one afternoon Andrew was riding in from the range, and coming to a wide shallow valley he espied a saddled but riderless horse galloping up the opposite slope toward the ranch. The distance was too great for him to recognize the horse, which disappeared before he could bring his field glasses into use.

Andrew rode rapidly down into the draw, and had not proceeded far along one of the banks when he saw a bright object on the sand. Urging on his horse, he plunged down into the dry stream bed to verify his fears. He came upon Martha Dixon sitting on the sand, her face white and drawn with pain, her hands trembling endeavoring to unlace one of her boots. Andrew leaped off his mount to rush to her side.

"Miss Dixon, you've had a spill?" he queried anxiously.

"Yeah," she replied, without looking up.

"I saw your horse galloping home. . . . Did he buck you off?"

"The old bag of bones tripped in the sand."

"I hope you're not badly hurt," continued Andrew solicitously. "There's blood on your cheek."

"That's rouge. . . . I hate to ask you, Mr. Bonning—but please ride to the house and send Jim or Uncle."

"Nonsense. Take all that time while you're suffering? Let me see. You appear to have sprained an ankle." Andrew knelt down to place his hands gently on the boot she had half unlaced.

"Thank you—never mind," she said, pulling her foot away. "I can get it off. You go for help."

"But I can help you, Miss Dixon," he said, looking up into a frowning face lighted by pain darkened eyes.

"I don't want you to."

"But it's only common courtesy."

"I'd lie here and die before I'd let you help me," she said, turning her face away. He could not help noticing, before she did so, that her lips were trembling.

"So I see. All the same I shall not allow you to sacrifice yourself. . . . Take your hands away." He pulled them free and unlaced the rest of her boot and despite his care in removing it, he hurt her.

"Oh-h! You brute. . . . Great, big, strong, he-man stuff, eh?"

"Your ankle is swollen. I advise you not to try to walk on it."

"Mr. Bonning, you seem to know all about the shape of people's ankles—"

"I have been in college athletics," he replied stiffly.

Struggling to her feet she tried to take a step with the injured member, but faltered. With a moan she sank to the sandy floor of the draw.

"You stubborn little fool. I told you," he burst out, sorry for her, but angrier still.

"Go get—somebody," she said faintly.

"I'll do nothing of the kind. I'm going to pack you up to the house."

"You will not!"

"Watch me!" Whereupon he led his horse beside a low bank from which he could easily step astride the saddle. Then he returned to the girl.

"Don't you dare touch me," she flared.

"Martha Dixon, you ought to get a real kick out of this," he replied with a grim laugh.

"*You* really are a brute, aren't you?"

In spite of her struggles, he picked her up bodily. She kicked out with her feet, but suddenly subsided with a scream.

"Serves you right. Lie still!" And he shook her slightly. "Anyone would think you imagine I *want* to take you in my arms. Well, let me set your silly little mind at ease. I don't.''

"You don't because *you* imagine I'd want you to—that I planned all this," she retorted.

"I never allow my imagination to run riot," he replied coldly, and approaching his horse, cautioned him with stern words, then stepped astride. "I forgot your boot. Oh well, I can come back for that later. There. Are you comfortable?''

"I have never been so wretched—in a man's arms," she answered, avoiding his eyes.

"You don't need to remind me that it is no uncommon experience." He held her in front of him with his left arm around her and her head against his shoulder. He had his right arm under her knees, and managed also with his right hand to hold the bridle. He gazed down at the pale face against his arm, aware of its loveliness and its danger. She was watching him with a look no man could have interpreted. But it was a look that made him tremble. Her eyes were the clearest amber, large, luminous, the color of a tawny pansy or a topaz. But it was the look in them rather than their beauty that moved Andrew. In times past he had found himself susceptible to feminine charms. He recognized the symptoms now, in magnified form and he determined that he would not permit it to happen again.

"I hate—you," she panted.

"That's all too obvious," he replied, inclining his head. "And it puzzles me. It seems to be my misfortune to keep receiving you—and getting no thanks for my pains. If you ran true to form you would be employing the moment—to your peculiar satisfaction.''

"You are simply horrid.''

"Why? Because I tell you the truth? Martha Dixon, you certainly are the prettiest creature the sun ever shone on. And it infuriates me that one so sweet, so fresh, so young, so intelligent, so much of a joy to people like your uncle, and Jim and Sue, should be such a cheat to them—and to everyone.''

"I'm not—a cheat," she cried.

"Yes, you are, if not a brazen little hussy. Didn't I see you come down the street driving that boy's car? Didn't I see you at dinner, all dolled up, flirting shamelessly with him?''

"Yes, you—did. But I did it because you expected it of me. If you were half as smart as you think you are—you'd have known why I was doing it. You had hurt my feelings. I was mad. . . . I played up to your opinion of me . . . and I was just fool enough to want to make you jealous.''

"Good Lord! You switch your line to suit the occasion. Martha, you have no finesse. You just trust everything to your looks. Well, you've cause. But you can't get me with such sugar.''

"I don't want you," she cried struggling to pull herself erect.

"I meant string me, darling," he rejoined mockingly.

"Miss Dixon to you, if you don't mind."

"And what were you to the young fellow at the hotel?"

"Just a 'sweetie,' of course, if it's any of your business."

"Bah! You're as bad as Connie—worse, for she was only a gold digger. You run away from home—from a nice mother. You want to get out where no one will know who you are or care what you do. And you pick up a saphead like that—drive his car so he can put his arms round you—doll up for him, a mere stranger—eat with him—go out with him—let him kiss you—let him—"

"That's enough of that," she commanded hotly. "No one can talk to me like that! Whoever your Connie was I'll bet she handed you exactly what you deserved."

"Plumb center," he returned. "I'm sorry that I spoke that way. I have no right to ask you, but . . . did you go with him that night?"

"No!"

"Did you let him kiss you?"

"No!"

"Martha, I think you're a little liar," he said softly. "Just to prove it, I'll bet even *I* can kiss you and get away with it."

Fired by a sudden rash impulse he bent his face close over hers. He had not really meant to carry out his threat. But once under the spell of her dilating eyes, and the sweet red lips so close to his he found it impossible to refrain. He pressed his lips to hers in a kiss that started in defiance of her and scorn of himself, but which lingered in ecstasy. Sharply he drew erect, astonished by his act, ashamed of having given way to his real feelings when he had meant only scorn.

"I'll kill—you!" she whispered huskily.

" 'Hell hath no fury . . . ' Martha, that was coming to you. But don't get me wrong. . . . Well, here we are in sight of the house. Your uncle sees us. And there's your horse tied to the fence."

"Jim! Sue! Rustle out here," shouted Bligh, as Andrew halted. "My Gawd, boy, don't say she's bad hurt."

"She had a spill. Sprained her ankle. But she'll go to the dance next week. . . . Here. Easy now. She's a pretty hefty little armful."

As Andrew handed her down to eager arms he had a last look at her white strained face and great eyes, dark with emotion, as she turned her eyes away from his. They haunted him all the way back to the draw where he returned to fetch her boot.

8

TRAINING for college football had been mild compared to the strenuous exactions of Andrew's ranch work.

Digging post holes, building fences, repairing barns and corrals, piping water down from the hills, and innumerable odd jobs fell to Andrew's lot aside from the work on his cabin. There were hours in the saddle and an occasional trip to town in the truck or car. His labors began at dawn and ended long after dark.

For the past few weeks his portion had been blistered hands, sunburned face and aching muscles. He thinned down to one hundred and seventy pounds, which was considerably less than the weight his football coaches had allowed him. Steady hard toil with his hands was something entirely new to Andrew. In the first stages sheer physical discomfort, then actual pain and fatigue that dragged him to bed heavy as a log, could not be denied. In spite of the unaccustomed toil he remained cheerful and to all outward appearances indifferent to the hardships.

But it was the actual range-riding, all day and every day under the hot sun, or facing dust or hail or rain, that put him to the crucial test. A stock saddle was a new contrivance to him; and to keep on riding when he wanted to rest was surely the hardest physical ordeal that he had ever met. When hot midsummer arrived Andrew had to hunt the cattle up in the foothills. Sometimes Jim rode with him, and they would lie out over night in the cedars, or out under the stars. That first week of torture in the saddle sweated and bled all the softness and the indolence, and most of the morbidity, out of Andrew Bonning. He had welcomed the trial; never for a single moment had he quit. From the very first he had sensed something vastly healing in this elemental contact, in this driving of spirit and flesh. He just kept on without thinking much about it, realizing that some distant day he would be made over.

In due time Andrew grew hard and strong and enduring. The day came when he awoke to the fact that joy in action and labor had imperceptibly come to him. Happiness still held aloof; often a strange melancholy lay on his spirit like a mantle; and sometimes his old bitter, mocking self returned, though less and less often. Martha Dixon could still rouse that almost forgotten self in many baffling and humiliating ways. When he was out on the range, where he could not see her as she puttered around, planting flowers, feeding the stock that she had adopted as pets, riding the horses, doing everything imaginable—even to standing like a statue to watch the sunset—then he seemed free of his old somber self. Also it had no place in a man's mind while out in the open. There were the elemental things for man to combat, the inherited instinct for action without introspection. Martha Dixon did not belong in the West any more than he, and he doubted her complete assimilation. Yet she appeared the gayest, happiest girl he had ever seen. On Sundays the cowboys rode in, more and more each Sabbath. Andrew had to admit that she had handled the situation in a different fashion than he had anticipated.

Andrew knew the West had claimed him. Still he had not faced that realization yet. It was too good to be true. He had expected to find work, to wander from place to place until he was settled, but to fit in as he had, to love the open, the solitude, and particularly the man's game of wrenching home and competence from wild nature—this had been a revelation to him. And in it he was going to become completely absorbed.

This range had once supported millions of buffalo. It could never be cultivated, except along the waterways and around the spring holes. It would support cattle and horses, in which he calculated man would always find use and profit. There would never be any radical change in the level reaches, in the rolling ridges, the black and gray foothills, the vast purple hollow of sage and grass, in the white-tipped barrier of the mountains. What inexplicable comfort he derived from this assurance!

"Andy, where was you ridin' yestiddy?" queried the Arizonian one morning.

"South. Along the foothills to Stone Tank."

"No wonder I didn't run acrost you. Reckon you seen some of our stock?"

"Yes, a good many. Branded three calves. Cows getting wild. Saw a lot of Triangle X and Cross Bar stock."

"See any riders?"

"No, and I didn't pick up any tracks."

"Wal, I had better luck, or wuss, accordin' to how we take it. I rode west along the river, haided the creek thet runs in about ten miles down, an' then struck for the west end of the Antelope Hills. Must have rid nigh unto thirty miles. Rough and brushy in the draws. Lots of water an' grass. Reckon I seen two thousand haid of cattle. Located three daid cows by watchin' the buzzards. Thet's our best bet, Andy. You gotta have sharp eyes, though."

"Dead cows?" repeated Andrew. "Dead from what?"

"Lead slugs, son. What'd you expect? I cut one bullet out. Forty-five, I reckon. Gave it to the boss. He hit the roof. He's touchy these days, with McCall pressin' him."

"Jim, then—it's begun?"

"Begun! Why, cowboy, it's been goin' on for weeks. I'll bet we've lost a hundred calves. An' thet means the same number of cows."

"Two hundred head!" cried Andrew, shocked by the Arizonian's estimate.

"Wal, it's a hell of a big country. Our stock is scattered all over, same as thet of the other outfits. We couldn't keep track of them if we had a dozen riders. I found where some slick hombre had buried the ashes of his brandin' fire. Trailed him half a mile, then lost the tracks. I've a hunch he tied up those calves in the brush an' drove them away after dark."

"Where would he drive them?"

"Ask me an easy one. Across the river, mebbe, or around in some canyon where there were cows wearin' the brand he was burnin' or possibly to some far part of the range. We're helpless unless we can ketch him at it. An' then if there's more'n one rustler operatin' . . . Aw, hell, it ain't no cinch, as I heerd Martha say."

"Jim, locate me out there. Give me a landmark," said Andrew eagerly.

"Wal, jest make for the west end of the Antelope Hills. Anywhere up them draws. I reckon on the south side we'll have our eyes opened. But thet's purty far. You'll have to lay out all night."

"I'll be glad to! Will you come?"

"Can't today. Mebbe I'll meet you out there tomorrow. Keep yore eyes peeled, Bonnin'. You want to see these *hombres* first an' hold 'em up. Otherwise—wal, you mightn't come back. Two cowpunchers was shot last spring, an' one's still missin'. Blamed on bandits. But I'm doubtful of thet. You look sharp. I hadn't ought to let you go alone, but the boss needs me here."

"Don't worry, Jim, I'll be careful," replied Andrew, and turning toward the kitchen he saw Martha Dixon standing in the doorway. Something about her eyes told him she had heard what Jim had said. It pleased Andrew. Her wonderful eyes had fooled him often, but he felt certain that he saw in them now a fleeting look of apprehension.

"Morning. Is Mrs. Sue here? I could use a little grub," said Andrew, briskly, as he moved closer to the girl.

"She's house-cleaning."

Andrew noted then that Martha's sleeves were rolled high over slender round arms. Her hands were white with flour. She wore a colored gingham apron which did not entirely conceal her shapeliness. A golden tan had now replaced the sunburn of her face. Her golden hair waved rebelliously. He could not look at her saucy mouth without remembering the kiss he had stolen, and which had left him ashamed and troubled.

"What are you doing?" he queried brusquely.

"Mixing dough."

"Dough tell?" he said with a grin.

"Can't you ever come near me without saying something mean?"

"Martha Dixon, you get me wrong. You always do. . . . I was surprised, of course, to see flour on your hands. But I didn't mean to be mean. I was even trying to be funny. It flashed over me what a distractingly pretty little wife you'll make some cowboy—*maybe*.''

"Indeed!" she retorted mockingly. But a blush mantled her neck and cheek.

"Would you be good enough to fix me up some sandwiches?" he asked.

"Certainly," she answered, and went into the kitchen.

Andrew stepped inside and sat down. Martha paid no attention to him, and he watched her in silence, sure of only one thing—that she was decidedly pleasing to look at. He made up his mind then and there never to say another mean thing to her. Presently she turned to hand him a small package wrapped in brown paper.

"Thank you," he said, rising, and made as if to go. But he did not. "How's your ankle?"

"Most well."

"Well enough to dance—at the rodeo?"

"Oh, yes." She seemed detached, and the absence of her usual spirit and excitement impressed Andrew acutely. Yet he admitted his inconsistency. It was certainly ridiculous of him to disapprove of her, doubt her, insult her, and then feel peevish because she did not act as though she enjoyed being in his presence.

"If I go, will you dance with me?" he found himself asking, outwardly cool and nonchalant, but inwardly uncertain and fearful.

"Do you dance?" she inquired, as though in great surprise.

"Of course I do."

"I rather imagined that you would think dancing immoral."

"Do you take me for a prissy reformer?"

"I take you for a mid-Victorian."

"Well, that's better than being a modern lounge lizard. . . . You haven't said you would dance with me?"

"No."

"Oh, all right. . . . I asked you—anyhow," he replied lamely, and went out. His unpremeditated friendly overture had been rebuffed. It made him smart. Still for some occult reason beyond his ken he was glad that he had unbent as far as he had. When he came out of the corral with his horse a few minutes later he glanced back at the house and felt sure that he saw her peeping from behind the window curtain. That was a queer thing for her to do when she despised him so cordially. He ruminated over it. Perhaps she was just curious about his trip—from which he might not return! That prompted him to shout to Jim, who had come out with Bligh.

"Hey, Jim, I'll be back tomorrow night sure—unless something unexpected happens."

At the moment he had a juvenile impulse to stay out another night, just to frighten Martha Dixon. However, he doubted that she would even notice that he was away. He mounted and rode away toward the west.

He took the river trail, a hard-packed cattle thoroughfare that wound through the cottonwoods and out into the open. Andrew had long since learned to know his horse, and liked him better every day. He was a bay with white spots and bars. Andrew changed the cowboy name of Slats to Zebra. It had required a little time for him to find out that Zebra was fast, tireless, spirited yet tractable under a gentle hand, and that he was what the former owner had called a single-footer.

As he rode along, thoughts of the girl, and her strange attraction for him, gradually gave place to more tangible things—his horse, the river, the fragrance of sage, the long swelling slope up to the Antelope Hills, and the vigilant search for moving objects. Rabbits, coyotes, deer crossed his vision. For Andrew, in a ride like this, the absorbing fascination of it and his intense eagerness to practice what he had learned from the Arizonian, seemed to make the hours fly. Always the sense of bigness, of openness came first, then the tremendous force of the range as a thing to be conquered. This horse, this range, this wildness was a job; and always before he had been a failure. Now he was on his mettle, and he must win.

By mid-afternoon Andrew had reached the foothills at the west end of the range. Down between them opening wide and choked with rocks and cedars, ran draws that were almost as deep as canyons. They were dry as dust and hot, despite the breeze from the heights. Far up these draws water remained in pockets in the rocky stream beds. Cattle trails threaded the maze of narrow deer trails zig-zagging through the brush up the slopes. White bleached grass stood knee high in the aisles and glades, while under the shade of the trees, the grass was still green. The air was fragrant, a tangy mixture of dry sage, dry cedars and the hot earth.

Andrew penetrated to a grassy glade where a thin ribbon of water ran down a shallow gully, forming shallow pools here and there. He unsaddled and hobbled his horse, hung his canteen and food on a branch and, rifle in hand, took to the trails.

It occurred to him that he was proceeding with almost ridiculous caution. But since that was the order he had given himself he kept to it, peering, listening, smelling, sensing—using all of the faculties he had learned to use. Whenever he came to a patch of sand or bare earth, or a dusty length of trail, he searched for tracks. And old tracks, which he had learned to know on sight, did not interest him. Fresh signs of cattle did, however, and soon he heard rustlings in the brush, the bawling of calves and the lowing of cows. As the afternoon was very quiet he sat down often to listen, rifle in hand. The several horse tracks he found were old and had been made by unshod animals.

From time to time he arose to steal on up the draw, which became wilder and rougher as he progressed. It surprised him to find how wild the cattle were. He would come upon a group standing on guard like listening deer, and as soon as they espied him they would gallop off, crashing through the brush. And presently it occurred to him that if there were any cattle thieves working this canyon they surely would be forewarned and be able to slip away. A better plan might be to hide at the entrance to one of these wide draws and wait.

Zebra was quietly grazing, yet scented or heard him. For he threw up his fine head to look. Andrew approached him with keen appreciation of what a horse could be to a man in the open. He ought to have a dog, too. Twilight was stealing into the glade and the air was turning cold. An abundance of firewood, however, assured him that he could make a comfortable night of it. First he cut some armloads of cedar boughs for a bed; then he collected a store of dead wood and started a fire. By this time darkness had set in. With his rifle at hand, and his saddle blankets for a seat, he sat down and opened the package of food Martha Dixon had put up for him. He had tied it up in his slicker. Opening it, he was more than surprised to discover its generous contents. Where had his eyes been while that girl had packed this food for him? Where? He shook his head dubiously: "I'm skating on thin ice. Character in a woman has nothing to do with what a man falls for," he muttered. "Well! I'll be jiggered!"

Evidently Martha had taken him for a dude tourist. He had asked for sandwiches. In addition, she had supplied cake, pie, cheese and lastly, wrapped in a small packet which he nearly missed, a single lump of sugar. Sugar! She might as well have included apple sauce or caviar. Sweets to the sweet!

This discovery, however, did not keep Andrew from enjoying his supper. When he had finished eating he drew his saddle up for a back rest, and made himself comfortable before the fire.

As he sat there, watching the glow of the embers and the last ruddy flames, it was hard for him to realize that only a few months ago, all of this would have been impossible. The night was black, the sky overcast, the silence oppressive. After a while the wild ki-yiing of a coyote accentuated the loneliness of the wilderness. This little scene of a lone rider and his horse, a campfire in the hills had been enacted there many, many times for years on end. The Indian, the padre, the *courriere des bois*, the trapper, the explorer, the gold digger, the frontiersman, the soldier, the hunter, the pioneer, the cattleman, the cowboy, the rustler and bandit and outlaw—all of these alone, and with their kind, had sat by a campfire in the wilderness. That lonely scene had been epochal in the history of the West.

As he sat there watching the embers, he knew that he had never been meant for the crowd, for work in an office, for gambling in business deals with men. Peace hovered somewhere near him.

He lay down to sleep with one blanket underneath, the other over him, his feet to the replenished fire, and his head pillowed on his saddle. He lay down expecting to stay awake for hours only to find his eyelids grow heavy, his body grow still, his thoughts fade. When he awakened, chilled to the marrow, the fire was dead. He rebuilt it, warmed his hands and feet and his back, then went to sleep again. Gray cold dawn saw him stirring.

Leading his horse, he walked down to the open slope and then kept to the edge of the cedars along the base of the hills. He passed several draws where cattle were grazing.

Sunrise was lost to Andrew because he had gotten around to the western side of the hills. But the glory and color now were spreading across the vast prairie leading to the mountains. Something to be conquered—this range land! That was how it affected Andrew. To endure it, to fight it, to live by it—what a man's game!

Coming to another canyon with rugged slopes, he entered it far enough to hide his horse in a thicket, and then continued on foot. First he spent hours high up on a bank watching the gray slope down to the river. During this vigil he counted more than a hundred cattle, near and far. Then he went down to explore the canyon. The sight of lowing cows with full milk bags, dripping udders, and no calves filled him with deep anger. Manifestly here was the work of Smoky Reed or one of his henchmen. When Andrew came upon the remains of a little branding fire, he felt of the ashes, but they were cold. Between this point and the head of the draw he found three more such signs. Allowing for the very small amount of the actual acreage he could cover, he estimated that the brander of calves had done well there. But what he did with the calves was a question. Ranchers had spring and fall roundups when each collected all stock wearing his brand. The game puzzled Andrew and roused him thoroughly. He saw but few of Bligh's cattle, and did not find a single dead cow nor a horse track.

The day passed swiftly. Night overtook him before he got back to where he had left his horse. He made camp and relished what was left of his dry sandwiches, leaving one for the next day. What would Jim Fenner and Bligh think of his absence? They would be worried. What would Martha Dixon think? Andrew regretted his impulse, in so far as she had been the cause of it. He slept more warmly that night.

At break of day he rode into the wide entrance of the largest draw he had yet encountered. It actually was the opening of a valley leading up into the hills. Cattle dotted the landscape.

Andrew decided that he ought to watch that gateway during the early morning hours. Returning to a patch of cedars half a mile back along the way he had come, he halted Zebra in a well-screened shady spot. Then he took his field glasses and rifle and set out on foot.

By the time he had reached the wide draw again the slopes, the range land and mountains had lost their gray mantle to take the color of the sunrise. For his hiding place he selected an outcropping of rocks on the slope nearest his horse, and taking up his position there he swept with his glasses the ten miles of sage slope between the hills and the river. Halfway down the slope he picked up two moving objects.

"Horsemen, by Judas!" he muttered excitedly.

With his naked eye Andrew could scarcely discern the riders. But through the field glasses he watched them approaching at a brisk trot. It was to be expected that he would see cowboys at any time or anywhere on that range. Most of them would be going about their work honestly, which meant that any one of them was innocent until proved guilty. Branding of calves went on daily. And he could not assume that all the calves belonged to Bligh. Not a tenth of them! McCall's hired rustlers, however, were concentrating on Bligh's stock simply because there was little risk for them. He had to come upon one of them branding a calf the mother of which wore the N.B. brand. It was a ticklish job, and he revolved slowly in his mind all of Jim's words of advice.

Meanwhile the riders came on, making straight for the wide canyon entrance. Since both rode horses that camouflaged well against the sage brush, he could not make certain that he would be able to recognize them.

As he watched them through the glasses, he saw the horsemen halt at the edge of the scattered thickets and carefully survey the range between the hills and the river, and on to the north. One of them removed his sombrero, revealing a brightly shining head of flaming red hair and a red face, which could belong only to the cowboy Texas. The other rider wore a black sombrero which hid his face. All that could be noted as distinctive about him was a striped gray and black shirt, plainly visible through the glasses.

After a brief discussion they separated, the rider in the striped shirt taking the left side of the valley, and Texas proceeding to the right. He was the last to disappear. Andrew could hear the cracking of dead branches and the ring of metal on stone. Presently all was quiet again.

"Well, they're here," said Andrew to himself, feeling his pulse beating high. "Smoky Reed's the one in the striped shirt, I'll gamble. It's not likely that Texas would take up with another cowboy. . . . They're both crooked. And now what?"

He answered his own query with immediate action, gaining a higher level without risk of being seen. He slung the field glasses over his shoulder, and moved on, ears alert and eyes roving. Presently he came to the place where the nearest rider had entered the canyon. He quickly picked up the fresh hoof tracks, and started to trail them, conscious of a thrill he had never before felt in his life.

He was on the track of a crooked cowboy whom he meant to brand as an outlaw on that range.

He followed the tracks for half an hour before he realized that he was moving too slowly. Becoming bolder he quickened his pace. Before long he heard a distant crash of brush, and the bellow of a cow. But he could not locate either sound. Cattle trooped down the draw but they were mostly steers and yearlings. Andrew crouched behind some brush while they passed. Then he went on. The valley was no longer silent, and that emboldened him. Nevertheless he did not advance without being sure of cover. This needful caution grew more difficult to act upon as he advanced. The open places increased, and the cedars and thickets correspondingly afforded less protection. From before came the sound of water splashing somewhere near over stones.

Suddenly the whip-like crack of a gun rang out. The surprise of it shocked Andrew. Cold sweat exuded from his face. Then he realized that he should have expected it. Reed's method was to drive the mother of a calf into a thicket or rocky recess, kill her, and then brand the calf.

Andrew stole forward as noiselessly as he could, soon learning that stiff cowboys' boots were poor adjuncts for a stalk of this nature. Presently across an open patch of grass and beyond some cedars there rose a thin column of blue smoke. Andrew knew that he must hurry if he were going to catch the rustler redhanded, yet he doubted the wisdom of crossing that open place. So he made a detour and then could no longer locate the smoke. He listened. Far across the canyon he could see dust rising, and could hear faint thudding sounds. Texas must be busy over there. On this side there was now comparative silence. The movement of excited cattle did not mean much to Andrew at the moment. But his nostrils were assailed by a pungent odor of burning hair.

He came to a clump of cedars and scrub oaks. All at once against the background of barred light he caught sight of something moving. It was crossing a small sunlit aperture in the foliage. A patch of striped gray and black! At the sight Andrew's nerves grew tense. He felt that he had been heard, but he had no idea if he had yet been seen. An impulse to shoot flashed over him, difficult to restrain in the heat of that moment.

The next instant dead cedar branches close to his head exploded to scatter their fragments almost in his face. The heavy report of a gun followed. Andrew gasped, and actually ducked when he realized that he had been shot at and narrowly missed by a bullet. Angrily he leveled his Winchester and fired into the midst of the cedar brush where he had seen the gray and black object. The high-powered projectile crashed through the branches and ricocheted off some rocks. The thump of hoofs, the plunging of a horse, either tied or under a strong hand, gave Andrew another location for a target. He sent a bullet spatting through the thicket, and working the lever of the rifle as fast as he could, he shot three more times. Sound of the bullets hitting and glancing afforded him considerable satisfaction. Then he waited with rifle cocked.

Rustlings and crashings, apparently both close at hand and far away, stealthy footsteps and heavy hoof beats—these all confused Andrew, and added to his rage. His determination to close with the man who had tried to kill him caused him to make a precipitate move from behind the tree that had screened him.

He felt something like the snap of a whip above his temple, then a tearing pain, followed by a stunning blow that knocked him against the tree. He sank to his knees. Realizing that he had been hit and aware of hot blood pouring down his cheek, he still knew that he was conscious, that he had the will and the strength to kill his assailant. He waited for him to appear. But the wall of gray-green thicket did not split to emit a man. Instead a rapid crunch of boots, a clink of spur on iron stirrup, a crash in the brush and the pounding clip-clop of hoofs, told Andrew that the cowboy he had been stalking was on his way out of there.

"Thinks he—got me," grunted Andrew, sinking to a seat. "Maybe he has. Look at the damn blood!"

He took off his sombrero to find that the bullet had gone through the band. It took courage for Andrew to run his forefinger into the wound from which the blood was streaming. For a moment he thought it was all up with Andrew Bonning. Then he found the shallow groove above his ear.

"Close shave, but I'm still kicking," he muttered grimly. "Smoky Reed, if I ever get my hands on you—good night!"

He folded his scarf and bound the wound tightly. While he was attending to his wound he heard another horse rapidly passing his position over to the right. That would be Texas making himself scarce. Listening until the sounds had ceased, Andrew got up to wipe his bloody hands on the cedar foliage. Then he pushed through the thicket to the open patch of ground from which the rustler had shot at him. A little fire of dead cedar sticks still was burning brightly. A running-iron, still smoking and smelling of scorched hair, lay on the ground. But the calf had disappeared. Andrew's search beyond the opening in the thicket was rewarded by finding a dead cow with the brand N.B. on her flank.

"Well, I can prove Bligh's cow was killed, his calf branded, and that I was shot . . . but no more. . . . I'll have to look Smoky Reed up, and see if I can make him give himself away."

Andrew went back for the branding iron, and after cooling it in a pool of water, he hurried down the canyon. At the entrance his search with the field glasses for riders proved unavailing. Soon thereafter he returned to the spot where he had tied Zebra, mounted his horse and headed ranchward. The sick giddiness had left him, and except for a dull throbbing pain, he did not seem to suffer any great inconvenience from his recent experience. As he rode slowly along, the determination to discover his would-be murderer vied in Andrew's

Bligh's household were to eat together. During supper Andrew began to feel that his status with Martha Dixon had changed somewhat. She was a disturbing presence at any time, but now that she seemed no longer angry with him, he could see complications ahead.

After supper Jim found him on the front porch of his cabin.

"What's on your mind, son?"

"Martha Ann Dixon," replied Andrew, truthfully.

"Wal, thet's fine an' shore sarves you right. But I mean about this deal you had in the hills. You didn't tell Bligh an' me all of it."

"No. I thought I'd better not. But I'll tell you, Jim." And Andrew recounted the entire adventure in detail, and ended the account with his own deductions.

"Wal, whoever thet cowpuncher was, he shore figgered he'd done for you. An' if you can face him sudden-like, surprise him, he'll give himself away, if he recognizes you."

"Jim, that is my angle. I *know* it's Smoky Reed."

"Ahuh. But no proof except the striped shirt. There might be two cowboys wearin' thet brand. Anyway, it's a good clue, thet an' the brandin' iron. What you goin' to do if you identify him?"

"Old-timer, I'll incapacitate that cowboy for some time to come."

"Sounds good—thet word, but I don't savvy it. . . . Andy, whoever this *hombre* is, he'll be with his outfit. They'll be mean. They'll kid the pants off you. Razz you in front of the girls. Cowboys are death on tenderfeet. You'll have to take a crack at ridin' somethin' in the rodeo. An' thet'll give them a chance to humiliate you still more. But it'll give you a chance, too—to get sore."

"Don't need it, Jim. I'm sore now—at any outfit that Mr. Striped Shirt rides for."

"You'll have to fight them all."

"Okay."

"Andy, was you skeered out there in the hills—when you heerd thet bullet?"

"I'll say I was. Scared stiff," declared Andrew, with a short laugh.

"Are you goin' to be thet way when you meet this outfit at the rodeo?" asked Jim curiously.

"Will they be packing guns?"

"No. Thet ain't allowed at rodeos."

"Then I'll simply be delighted."

"Humph! I don't figger you, son. It shore ain't no cinch to buck up agin an outfit of mean cowpunchers."

"Jim, out here on the range, on a horse, or alone in the hills I'm not of much account," returned Andrew. "But flat on my feet—facing a bunch of unarmed men—well, that's different. I may say I've often held my own in a husky crowd. Ha!''

"Ahuh. You have? Wal, I ain't never seen a puncher yet who could pitch a hundred pound sack of oats around like you can. I'm gonna be there when you meet up with thet outfit. I'll get a man to take my place here for a couple of days. But don't tell the boss.''

On the following day Andrew felt very little the worse for his creased skull, and ten days later he dispensed with the bandage over his temple. If anyone had been particularly interested in the young man's movements these several days, they would have discovered something unusual for a ranch. He had filled a small burlap bag with sand and had hung it up about face high from a rafter in the barn. Then he put on his buckskin riding gloves and proceeded to punch that bag. When he hit the bag it gave forth a sodden sound.

"Not so bad!" he muttered, at the end of his last workout, which was on the morning Bligh asked him to drive the car to town.

Martha was the last to come out of the house. That was one of her failings, Andrew had long ago observed. She just could not be on time. But when she appeared she looked bewitching in a trim blue dress she had made herself. Her shapely legs were bare, except for socks rolled down over flat-heeled shoes. She had apparently given up wearing hats. Andrew turned away his eyes. This young lady was getting surprisingly on his nerves.

"Please, may I drive?" she asked, leaning over the car door on Andrew's side. He might have refused the spoken solicitation, but the man did not live who could have denied the appealing look in those amber eyes.

"Why—er—certainly," stammered Andrew, hastily sliding over to the right side of the front seat.

Martha threw her little bag upon the seat and got in, and as she manipulated the gears with deft hands, her eyes on the dashboard, she said in a most casual way: "When I ride with a handsome young man I always like to drive.''

"Yeah, so I've noticed," Andrew retorted, and looked across the range to the hills. Her remark hinted at the old enmity. But the look in her eyes when she had asked permission to drive remained with him. He pondered over the lovely expression in those amber eyes. Had it been nothing but youthful, thrilling eagerness to drive the car? Any expression in them was bewildering. They were dangerous eyes because they appeared to any poor, asinine, masculine clod to say infinitely more than she obviously meant. Their exquisite light, their strange color, their indescribable loveliness were simply facts of nature, and therefore false. He had seen them blaze with scorn and that had been something to remember. They had been true then. But how much of their play and change and charm had been intended, for instance, that evening when she flirted so outra-

geously with the callow youth at the hotel? The recollection of that occasion
seemed crude and raw to him. As Jim would say, "it stuck in his craw." But
nature could make a woman a flirt when she was absolutely innocent and unconscious of it. Then he groaned inwardly at the realization that he was developing an excuse like this for everything that Martha Ann Dixon had done. All
the same the idea persisted, and another formed, haunting and ruthless—an
attempt to imagine how perfectly glorious her marvelous eyes would be if motivated by real, unselfish love.

Martha drove all the way to Split Rock without exchanging another word with
Andrew. In town, the moment they stopped, the Glemm girls and their friends
claimed her and drove off with her in their car to the rodeo. Andrew felt relieved.
If it were not for the serious business he had in mind he would have gone back
to the ranch. Bligh learned that McCall had gone to Casper. A few minutes later
they took to the road again with Andrew at the wheel.

The run from the ranch to Split Rock had been short, but this one to Casper
seemed endless, although he gave the old engine all it could stand. They arrived
about dark. Andrew did not remember very much about Casper. It appeared to
be a big town and the main street blazoned a welcome to visitors. They went
to two hotels before they could find lodgings. The town was full of visitors,
tourists, cowboys, ranchers, with two girls to every man.

The hotel to which Bligh had taken Sue and Andrew appeared to be a second-
class place, full of noisy cowboys. That suited the Easterner, and immediately
he was on the *qui vive*. Bligh took Sue in to supper while Bonning changed his
rough garb. When he came downstairs the lobby and lunchroom were crowded
with a noisy, jostling, smoking, haranguing lot of cowboys. All were youthful
and some had been drinking, though Andrew could not help liking them.

After supper he sat down beside a plain, weather-beaten little cattleman and
made himself agreeable.

"Stranger hereabouts?" queried the cattleman casually.

"Yes, I suppose I am, though I've been west a while."

"Easterner, I see."

"I was. My name is Bonning."

"I'm Jeff Little. Reckon you're here for the rodeo, same as everybody."

"Sure am. Never saw one before. Just what is a rodeo, anyhow?"

"Cowboy circus. Thet's about all. Casper puts on a good show. But nothin'
compared to Cheyenne or Kalispel. Some professionals here, though."

"What are professionals?"

"Cowboys an' girls who make their livin' out of rodeos. Trick riders. There's
some home talent here, though, thet can make any riders go some. I've a couple
in my own outfit."

"Interesting. Where's your range, Mr. Little?"

"Down on the Platte River, south of the Pathfinder Reservation. I run the Double X."

"How is the cattle business right now?"

"Perkin' up. I'm runnin' about forty thousand head, an' am not sellin' this year. Thet's a hunch."

"Forty thousand. You must employ many cowboys?"

"Only two outfits now, but they're good. I don't keep poor riders. Reckon one time or another I've hired every puncher in middle Wyomin'."

"Ever hire a redheaded cowboy called Texas something?"

"Shore have, an' ain't likely to forget him. Likable lad, finest of horsemen, wonder with a rope, but unreliable, if you know what I mean. Proud, wild, Texas breed. Never heard his last name. He's here, by the way. Saw him today. Great fellow for the girls."

"Aren't they all pretty much the same?" inquired Andrew, with a laugh. "Let's see. There's another cowboy I heard mentioned over at Split Rock. Smoky—somethin'."

"Reed. I know him. He rode for me once—about a day," returned the cattleman, with a brevity that was significant to Andrew.

"Thanks. I think I'll go out and look them over," said Bonning, rising.

"So you like Wyomin'?"

"Crazy about it!"

"Any idea of ranchin'?" queried the older man shrewdly.

"Well, the idea has occurred to me."

"Buy cattle before fall then. In a year you'll double your money."

Andrew strolled thoughtfully out into the street. He was revolving in his mind the fact that out here in the West everything gravitated to him. Back east they had passed him by. If he were going to get into the cattle business this appeared to be the time. He walked down his side of the gaily thronged street and up on the other. One busy place halted him and that was a brilliantly lighted corner store where ice cream, sodas and other refreshments were served. It was being patronized so briskly by young people that he could not get waited on. Then he went into a moving-picture theater where there was standing room only. Tiring of the picture, he left and went back to the hotel to bed. He was honest enough with himself to admit that he felt disappointed at not having seen Martha Dixon. A melancholy and absurd regret was plaguing his spirit, though he knew that if he had not been a fed-up and morbid Easterner, he might have been having a jolly time with that girl.

In the morning Andrew donned his cowboy duds, except the chaps, and sallied forth to what he had a feeling would be a memorable day. He devoted a few hours to listening and watching on the street and in the stores and hotels. More than one bantering cowboy made his ears tingle, not by some tart or crude words of ridicule, but because he seemed unable to hide the tenderfoot in him. This, however, was more than compensated for by the decidedly roguish and flattering glances which he received from several pretty girls. The town was full of them. In all the store windows were placards advertising the rodeo dance. Andrew kept a keen eye open for three persons—Martha Dixon, Texas and Smoky Reed.

On the street, in the hotel lobby or at the lunch counter, everywhere that he encountered cowboys he met with the prevailing good-natured western raillery, offensive only in a few instances. He started early for the fair grounds, where the rodeo was to be held.

A short time afterward, he found himself inside the high fence, free of the noisy crowd and gibing cowboys, holding in his hand a ticket that permitted him to enter any or all contests. The preliminaries were being run off before a half-filled grandstand, and Andrew thought he would get the agony over quickly. At a window to which some one directed him, he made application and presently found himself outside the circular fence bounding the race track. Things were happening right then, but he was told to do this and that, and before he realized it he was climbing into a little pen. To his horror the beast therein was not a horse but a ferocious-looking long-horned steer of a species unfamiliar to Andrew. There was a rope around its body, evidently for the rider to clutch.

"Get set, cowboy," called the guard curtly. "Fork him!"

Andrew dropped down to straddle the steer, grasped the rope with his hands, squeezed the huge body with his legs and held on desperately. The door slid back, the wild buffalo, or whatever the beast was, bawled and plunged out.

A tremendous force broke Andrew's leg hold and flung his feet high in the air. But he held on to the rope to descend with a sickening thud upon the back of the animal. Up he was flung again, like a feather. The spectators roared with glee, and Andrew was sure that they were looking at him. Down and up, down and up, while the infuriated beast ran faster than any horse Andrew had ever ridden. It bounded like a monstrous jack rabbit, all the way down the oval enclosure, to wheel and plunge back again, at every leap flinging Andrew aloft. He long had ceased to come down astride the steer. At last Andrew's tenacious hold broke and he soared aloft for the last time and then crashed to the turf. The fall jarred his teeth to the roots, but he did not appear to be killed or maimed. To his astonishment the audience gave him unstinted applause. Bonning limped off vowing that his ambitions to be a rodeo star had been completely squelched. At the gate he encountered Jim, who drew him inside.

"How'd you like thet?" queried the Arizonian mildly.

"Man alive! Never again!" panted Andrew, feeling to see if any of his bones were whole.

"Bust anythin'?"

"I guess not."

"Wal, you needn't look so flustered. You rode thet steer better'n any puncher I ever seen. Fact! An' the crowd cheered you."

"Quit your kidding, Jim."

"Honest. It was funny—the way you rode in, standin' on your haid. But it ain't the way you ride thet counts. It's stickin' on. I'll bet you win a prize."

"No!"

"Wal, anyway, Martha Ann is up in the grandstand with a bunch of girls. You should have heerd them squeal."

"Okay, Jim. You're an encouraging chap," declared Andrew, plainly pleased. "I'd like to take another whack at somethin'."

"Wal, we'll see. Come along here, Andy. I've located a striped shirt an' it's on Smoky Reed."

He felt his arm swell tight under his companion's guiding hand. "Yeah," he said, glancing at the dark, impassive profile of the Arizonian.

"Lot of punchers over here, waitin' for their turns an' watchin'," explained Jim. "Some of them been lookin' on red likker too. I reckon you won't have no trouble gettin' a rise out of Reed, unless he recognizes you. In thet case you'll know him, an' you can brace him pronto. But if he doesn't know you, then you'll have to get a rise out of him. . . . There he is. Tall puncher, freckled, tow-haided, wearin' the striped shirt. Strut up an' down before him an' the outfit he's with. I'll hang back an' watch."

Andrew saw a long shed, open in front, facing the arena and directly next to the circular fence. Horses and cowboys were much in evidence, to men standing mostly in little groups, smoking, talking, laughing. There was a fairly wide aisle between the benches and the fence.

When he got a close view of the four cowboys Jim had pointed out, Andrew strode toward them. As he did so he felt for his buckskin gloves, to find that he had not removed them from his hands. There was no redheaded cowboy in the quartet. The nearest to him was a mature man, stocky in build, with a round paunch protruding above his belt. The next two were lean, hard-faced youths, and the fourth was the cowboy Jim had described. He appeared to be muscular, but not heavy. His eyes were blue and bold of expression, gleaming from under bushy brows. He had a sallow freckled face somewhat flushed from drink. When Andrew saw the striped gray and black shirt his heart leaped, and he was certain that he recognized it. But recalling Jim's instructions, he got himself well in hand, and walked past the four men, looking squarely at them. Then he wheeled and came back, this time giving Reed the benefit of a searching glance.

The cowboy stared at him, but did not wink an eye. If he had associated Andrew in the slightest with the man he had deliberately tried to kill and had left for dead or wounded, he would not have been able to conceal some slight start that would have given him away.

Nevertheless Andrew felt doggedly sure that he had his man cornered. He was absolutely certain of McCall's offer, of Texas' promise to arrange the rustling deal, and of the fact that the two had ridden into the canyon out in the Antelope Hills.

"Hey, puncher, was you the *hombre* who jest forked thet steer?" called one of the four.

"Yes, if it's any of your damned business," retorted Andrew. "Trying to kid me, huh?"

"Not at all. You did fine—fer a Yankee tenderfoot."

Andrew glared at the speaker, who was the short stout one of the four. His retort focused the attention of the others upon Andrew, and evidently they at once discovered the aptness of their comrade's epithet. Bonning proceeded to strut and swagger up and down before them. And they began to make remarks. The tenderfoot pretended to take no heed, but his sharp ears took in everything. Meanwhile, with his object nearly attained, he used his eyes to further good advantage. There was an open space between the grandstand and the shed where the men were standing. Spectators could look right down upon it. To the right stood a refreshment booth before which a crowd was lined up. People were straggling in through the gates. Jim, within ear shot, leaned over the fence watching the preliminary exercises on the rodeo track.

"Shore he's a Yankee," drawled the spokesman of the quartet.

"Pretty snooty," said another.

"Lady killer, I'd say. Swell Stetson, fancy-top boots, buckskin gloves, an' all."

"Swelled-up tenderfoot," snorted Reed, loud enough for cowboys of other groups to hear. Laughs were immediately forthcoming. Plenty of fun seemed imminent. Only Andrew knew just how much fun there was going to be. Perhaps Jim, standing now back to the fence, had an inkling. A flood of range banter eddied around Andrew's ears. He gave no sign that he heard, and went on strutting to and fro.

"Look at that mail-order cowboy!"

"Ump-umm. He's a dude-ranch tourist."

"Where'd he git thet outfit?"

"Hey, pretty boy, stop obstructin' the landscape," called Reed derisively. "Reckon you're thet dude tenderfoot who drives the little hitchhikin' queen around."

"Are your remarks addressed to me?" Andrew queried, wheeling. He did not raise his voice, but there was a note in it that stopped the conversation and directed everyone's attention upon him. A moment of surprised silence ensued. The tenderfoot's sudden change of front gave the cowboys pause.

"Shore they was," replied the older man cheerily. "We was jest pokin' fun."

"Fun, hell! If you didn't insult me, you sure insulted a lady!"

"Aw wal, take it thet way if you like," returned the other, plainly nettled.

"That's how I do take it," snapped Andrew. "Certainly I'm a tenderfoot. An Easterner new to the range. I'm not used to cowboy humor. But I know the difference between fun and insult. And I demand an apology!"

"Haw! Haw!"

"Say, dude, shet your loud mouth."

Andrew poked a finger in the face of the eldest of the four.

"One at a time, will you?" he cried. "You seem to be half human. Answer me this. If an eastern tenderfoot called an outfit of Westerners like you—called them some choice names and invited them to swallow it or fight—what would happen?"

"Wal, I'm afeared the tenderfoot would git mauled jest to beat hell, an' swallow a lot of dust in the process."

"All right, then, listen. You're a bunch of dirty pack rats! Four lousy cow-punchers! Coyotes, skunks, and all the rest of the range vermin put together. And probably rustlers besides."

"Stranger, we're shore gittin' an earful," retorted the eldest, sharply, red as a beet in the face.

"Do the three of you know the company you keep?" demanded Andrew, scornfully indicating the astounded Smoky Reed, whose slow mind seemed to be assimilating a startling thought.

"Keepin' company at rodeos doesn't mean ridin' pards, stranger," parried the other harshly, as the blood left his face.

"Then the three of you are only vermin, but this striped-shirt *hombre* is a coward in the bargain. Now you gentlemen of the range are invited to step out, one at a time. Let me see the western stuff you're made of."

"Wal, it'll only take one of us, you rantin' dude," yelped the stout man, and he lunged out.

Andrew swung a savage right uppercut to the pit of that prominent abdomen. A deep bass sound rumbled out. The victim doubled up and his round face grew distorted, with eyes bulging, and mouth open sucking at air that would not go in. He sank down to his knees convulsively clutching his paunch.

Swiftly Bonning leaped forward to swing a snakelike left to the gaping mouth of the next cowboy and a right to the breadbasket of the third. Down like tenpins they crashed.

"Step out, Smoky, you polecat, and get yours," shouted Andrew, and snatching at the striped shirt, he gave the cowboy a powerful pull which propelled him out from under the shed into the open space below the grandstand. Excited yells drew the spectators on that side of the grandstand to the rail.

"Lay off me, you bruiser! I'm on to you," harshly rasped out Reed.

Bonning threw his sombrero aside, and pointed to the angry red bullet mark over his temple.

"See that, Reed! You did that! *You* shot me! From behind a bush like the coward you are!"

The cowboy turned livid and snatched at a gun that was not on him.

"You dirty low-down calf rustler!" yelled Andrew, in a voice he meant to carry into the stand. "This is no gun-slinging scrap." Then he charged the cowboy, beat down his defense, slugged him with lefts and rights, knocked him down and dragged him up, and then backing him against the fence landed terrific blows on the already bloody face, and would soon have knocked him out completely but for the interference of some shocked bystanders.

"Hyar, let up!" roared a rough voice, and its owner seized the angry Easterner by the shoulders. Like a top he spun round to strike the man before he could see him clearly. The would-be peacemaker fell his length in the dust.

"Did you sock me?" he bawled, in strident rage, as he labored to his feet, one hand at his bleeding nose.

"No—but I will if you lay hands on me again," panted Andrew.

"You're thet tenderfoot puncher of Bligh's. You're arrested. Assault an' battery . . . resistin' an officer!"

Then Andrew recognized the man as Sheriff Slade.

"Okay. Suits me fine, provided you arrest Reed too."

"Who?"

"Smoky Reed, the cowboy I was punishing when you interrupted me."

That battered cowboy manifestly had taken advantage of the moment to slink away into the crowd. Slade, however, did not make any apparent attempt to locate him.

"Stick out your hands," ordered Slade, producing handcuffs.

"I'll go with you," replied Andrew quickly, as the crowd surged closer.

"Stick 'em out, I tell you."

"No!"

Jim Fenner interposed his person on the scene, confronting the sheriff with cold narrowed eyes and hard lips.

"Slade, cut the grandstand play," said the Arizonian sharply. "I'll be responsible for this lad."

"Who the hell air you?" demanded Slade.

"I left my cyard at the gate," rejoined Jim, significantly. "If you're keen about seein' it, we'll stop as we go out."

"By Gawd, you strangers air gittin' altogether too cussed fresh. . . . Come on."

Between them they led Andrew out of the press of spectators. As he passed the grandstand he looked up to see a line of girls leaning over the rail, and in the center stood Martha Dixon, white as a flower, with telltale eyes upon him.

9

Two incidents, the bold overtures of a cowboy named Reed and the arrest of Andrew Bonning, spoiled what would have been a perfectly marvelous day for Martha Ann.

That very morning on the way to the rodeo Martha had received a letter from her mother, not only forgiving her for the mad escapade to which she had confessed, but also enclosing a check to defray her expenses home. Martha had arrived in Casper with her new friends, excited and happy. The crude overture of a cowboy whom the Glemm girls knew had disturbed her, because the man had evidently heard of her hitchhiking, and had assumed that to be sufficient license to make an advance which had to be squelched in no uncertain words. Then Andrew's spectacular riding of the steer, ludicrous as it was, had won her unwilling admiration. These had been forgotten, however, in the excitement of the rodeo, the magnificent horses and the daring trick riders, until Andrew's fight and arrest had broken up the show for Martha Ann.

It chanced that she had been a witness to both. Nellie Glemm, leaving her seat to meet some friends coming up the steps, had halted with them to look over the rail. Something evidently had happened below. People were leaving their seats. At the moment there was nothing going on the track. Suddenly Nellie had turned to beckon her sister, Martha and the two other girls.

"There's Smoky Reed now," said the Glemm girl, pointing. "Cal Brice, and the Hazelett boys. . . . Making fun of the young man who drove you to town. Bligh's hired hand, isn't he?"

"Yes. That's Andrew . . . his name is Andrew Bonning," returned Martha Ann.

"I've seen him before," said one of the girls.

"Handsome fellow," added Nellie.

"Say, look at him parade! That Brice outfit won't do a thing to him."

"Girls. He's just showing off—for their benefit," Martha had hastily interposed. "Andrew isn't the least conceited."

"This is going to be fun," replied Nellie. "I'll say he has his nerve with him. That's a bad outfit."

The ensuing harangue and fight, the interception by the sheriff and Andrew's arrest had quite robbed Martha Ann of any further enjoyment in the rodeo.

"Looks like your big boy picked a fight with Smoky's outfit," declared Nellie Glemm, meaningly, after they had returned to town to their hotel.

"He's not mine," replied Martha Ann, hastily feeling her cheeks grow hot.

"Well, he sure made hash out of Smoky. And wasn't it rich when he hit Cal Brice in the breadbasket?"

"Will they keep him—in jail?" queried Martha nervously.

"They sure will, if he can't pay his fine."

"Jim Fenner went with him. I hope they have enough money."

Martha Ann felt on pins and needles. She was at a loss how to escape from these spirited Western girls, all so friendly and eager for her enjoyment, without giving them further reason to think that she was interested in Andrew. Still she simply had to find out if he had been released. The idea of his being kept in jail over night was intolerable. The terrific beating she had seen him administer to Reed had made her forget completely the latter's insulting words. She could not explain her swift championship of Andrew, her unholy delight at the sight of the vulgar cowboy bully standing helpless before Andrew's amazing onslaught, and lastly her unreasonable alarm over his arrest. These varying emotions left her heart in something of a fluster. For long she had accused herself in the comforting darkness of her room of thinking too much about Andrew Bonning, a confession she had easily scorned in the light of day.

The entrance of Mr. Bligh, with Jim and Sue, delivered Martha Ann from the turmoil of her thoughts.

"Howdy, niece, we been huntin' you," said her uncle. "Have you had a nice day? You sure looked excited."

"Oh Uncle Nick! . . . Yes, I-I've had a nice day—pretty nice," cried Martha, and checked her impulsiveness.

"You girls stayin' here?"

"Yes. We have rooms all in a row. . . . The girls are taking me to the rodeo dance tonight. Uncle, you've heard of course about Andrew?"

"Yes. We just come from the jail."

"Isn't he—out?" faltered Martha.

"Lass, thet bloomin' Slade locked Andy up an' slapped a fine of a hundred dollars on him," declared Jim, without his usual dry humor. "Andy said he had the money, but couldn't get at it. Don't know what he meant. So I rustled out to find the boss."

"Martha, think of it!" exclaimed Bligh, mournfully. "Jim an' Sue an' I altogether can't dig up enough to get Andrew out."

"I can," retorted Martha gladly, tearing open her handbag. "Came this morning from Mother. Can you cash it?"

"Sure right here. You endorse the check," he said, and led Martha to the desk. Jim and Sue followed.

Martha Ann found herself writing in a scribble that bore little resemblance to her usual neat, firm handwriting.

"Damned outrage!" ejaculated her uncle as he received the check. "Hundred dollar fine for nothin' but a fist fight."

"Wal, Andy socked Sheriff Slade," interposed Jim. "It's all over town. Casper don't 'pear to like Slade much."

"Never mind, Uncle. It was worth a hundred dollars—even if the money was sent to fetch me home. Now I can't ever go!"

"Andy will pay it back. But if you'll be leavin' us, I hope he doesn't pay you for a long time."

"I'm not leaving you, Uncle," replied Martha warmly.

"Lass, did you see thet scrap?" queried Jim, curiously.

"Indeed I did. Lordy! I was scared at first—and then tickled pink."

"Andy had somethin' up his sleeve, didn't he?"

"He did, Jim. It looked as if he deliberately picked a fight with those cowboys. The fellow he beat so terribly was Smoky Reed. The Glemm girls know him. He was introduced to me right after we got here. And he got fresh immediately."

The Arizonian studied Martha Ann with shrewd penetrating eyes that seemed to read her thoughts.

"Wal, I reckon thet was what Andrew was so het-up about," he drawled.

Something suddenly struck Martha Ann that seemed surprise and pain and bliss all together. "Jim—d-did Andrew know?"

"I reckon so, lass."

"Beat that lout—for my sake?"

"Shore. What else?"

"But how'd he find out?"

"I heard Reed speak light of you to Andy."

Bligh returned with the cash, which he forced into Jim's hands. "Rustle an' get Andrew out."

"Jim, don't tell Andrew—" called Martha, but Jim already had got out of hearing.

"Lass, are you havin' supper with us?" asked Bligh.

"I'm not hungry," replied Martha, trying to appear composed. "Besides I've got to fix my dress for the dance."

"Tell me, how'd this Smoky Reed insult you?" demanded Bligh.

"It was at the Glemm's. He boards there. I met him and several other cowboys. Reed had had a drink or two. He followed me out to the car, hanging on to my arm. 'Baby,' he said, 'you're such a swell little hiker, suppose you step out with me tonight?' I declined and got into the car. He didn't take the hint. 'I'm the neckin'est *hombre* on this range. Don't you want some of my brand?' Here Nellie Glemm broke in. 'Shut up, Smoky. You're half lit. If you haven't any manners, at least try to be decent.' Reed drew back on the curb and said: 'Aw hell, she's lookin' for it, ain't she?' ''

"Martha, I'd hoped that hikin' stunt of yours wouldn't become common gossip," returned Bligh regretfully.

"Uncle, I'm afraid it was a mistake," replied Martha Ann, her lip trembling. "But I had to come. And there was no other way. . . . I don't care what vile-minded people think."

"Don't be distressed, child. Jim says Andrew's takin' it up so fierce will end cowboy talk, anyway."

Martha Ann made some excuse to the girls and fled to her room. When she had locked the door against intrusion, she went to the mirror and stood there gazing at her face. And as she looked, she felt that a false shell fell away from her. That afternoon the blazing stunning truth had burst upon Martha with Jim Fenner's revelation. Until now she had been pretending to be in love with Andrew Bonning. Now she realized that she was hopelessly, terribly, passionately in love with him.

"In love with *him?* . . . With Andrew Bonning? With a man who thinks me a flirt, a loose woman, a hussy! . . . My God, if this isn't the limit!" Her eyes filled with rebellious tears. She began walking up and down in the tiny room, beating her fist into the palm of her other hand. There came a knock on the door which shocked her into an appreciation of the time and place.

"Who's there?"

"Just me," called Nellie Glemm gayly. "You've got one hour to dress. Doll up for us, Martha. You'll drive Wyoming mad tonight."

"Do my—damnedest," replied Martha Ann, trying to sound gay, too. Wyoming mad! The words stung her to battle. Quickly she undressed and washed and tried to brush her hair into staid waves. Then she put on her stockings and blue slippers, and at last the flimsy blue gown with its simple relief of color.

It was a new and demure Martha Ann Dixon whose amber eyes met her gaze in the mirror. Where had vanished all her golden tan? Her face was the hue of marble. But rouge changed that, so far as lips and cheeks were concerned. Only what to do with her eyes! It seemed to Martha that all the old mischievous and deceiving lights had gone. What she saw now no pride could hide. Now her eyes were transparent windows of amber through which love shone, unashamed. And she suddenly realized with a kind of wonder that never in her life had she looked so well. Would Andrew come to the dance? Would he see her and think her pretty? And chide herself as she might, it made no difference; she gloried in the thought.

That thought might have been short-lived, to judge from warning memory, had not happy voices in the hall and the pounding of impatient hands upon the door, given Martha Ann the glad assurance that she would not be alone any more till the dance was over.

She opened the door, to be swooped down upon and swept away downstairs, lighthearted once more as her natural response to the gaiety and the bright colors and movement of young people reasserted itself with vivid pleasure. The lobby of the hotel was filled with many young men and girls, with all of whom the Glemm girls desired to make Martha acquainted. They were all wholesome red-cheeked girls, and clean-cut tanned boys, none of the latter appearing to have the earmarks of cowboys. They escorted Martha a couple of blocks down the main street, and up a wide stairway of a large building to the top floor. Here they had to run a gauntlet to get into the hall.

It was a big bare place, decorated with bunting and every manner of rodeo paraphernalia that Martha had seen this eventful day. The shiny floor was vacant at the moment, except along the sides where young people sat or stood in gay conversation. At the far end of the hall there was a wide stage on which the musicians sat tuning their instruments. Arched doorways on one side led out upon a porch. Martha's quick eyes took in all these details, also the obvious fact that the young men far outnumbered the girls.

Once inside Martha met many more young people including some cowboys. She did not catch many names. These Westerners were a democratic, free and easy people, not at all strong on formality. She liked their simplicity and sincerity. She had to admit, too, that she had been stared at more at a university formal than here. She had quickened to the promise of an enjoyable evening—until she suddenly found herself gazing about the hall, searching for someone who was not there.

"Martha here's Texas," whispered Nellie Glemm. "You remember the cowboy who wanted to drive you out to the ranch? Well, it's he. Such a handsome boy! He's a gentleman, too! Too bad he's so wild."

Martha looked up easily recognizing the red-haired cowboy.

"Howdy, Nell. I shore am glad to see you-all," he drawled.

"Howdy, yourself," replied the Glemm girl pleasantly, and turned to Martha. "Let me introduce one of our real cowboys, Texas Haynes. . . . Tex, meet Miss Martha Ann Dixon."

Texas made her a graceful bow and his flashing blue eyes took her in admiringly.

"Evenin', Miss. We've met before but not reg'lar," he drawled.

"Good evening, Mr. Texas Haynes," returned Martha Ann smiling. "I seem to remember something about you."

"Wal, my red hair, I reckon. Doggone it, I don't see why I cain't be towhaided, or somethin' else."

"No. I was not alluding to your hair."

"Did you ever dance with a cowboy?" he asked.

"Not yet."

"Will you let me be the first?"

"Certainly, if you ask me!"

"Thank you. I'm askin' you for the openin' dance, an' if I don't step all over yore feet, mebbe I'll make bold to ask for another."

"I don't know about two dances," replied Martha, dubiously. "I'll ask Nellie. Your last name is Haynes isn't it?"

"Wal, I don't use it very often," replied Texas with a smile. "Fact is, Miss Martha, I kinda forget it myself."

"Oh, I see."

"I don't care much aboot Tex fer a handle, but I'd like you to call me Jack."

"You do things rather quickly in Wyoming, don't you?"

"Shore, an' I gotta be quick now. Let's dance before them other buckaroos horn in heah."

He led her out and somewhat diffidently put his arm around her. Martha needed only that and his touch to decide that he was quite all right, and that she need not have been on her guard against this cowboy. He held her lightly and at a distance. He took his dancing very seriously and did almost no talking. According to Martha's standard he was a very poor dancer. At the conclusion of this first number he led her back to her party. There was something quaint and charming and deferential about him.

"Gosh, thet was the swellest dance I ever had," he said gratefully, as his dark blue eyes gazed admiringly down on her. "Last summer I was up at Cody where the dude ranches are. An' I met an eastern girl who rode an' danced with me—when she couldn't get nobody else. I shore fell for her powerful hard. But I'm tellin' you, ma'am, as a looker an' as a dancer she wasn't in the same corral with you."

"I see you have kissed the blarney stone, Mr. Jack," returned Martha with a laugh.

"Nope. I'm no kissin' bug. Don't brand me with these other punchers, Miss Dixon," he said curtly. "I was jest tryin' to tell you how proud an' happy you made me by dancin' with me."

"Thank you. That is a lovely compliment," she replied, quick to sense a fiery pride in him. "It will be something to remember my first cowboy dance by."

"Wal, thet makes me bold—"

"Hello, you two. How'd you get along?" interposed Nellie Glemm, with her frank eyes upon them.

"Powerful swell for me, Nell. I'm hankerin' turrible to ask—"

"For another dance? The nerve of you, Tex."

"Nellie, I'd be glad to give him another if you say it's all right," interposed Martha hastily. From what she had seen of couples on the floor, Texas Jack would be more than acceptable as a dance partner.

"You lucky cowboy! All right, let's see. As for me, I'm dolin' out these treats pretty stingily, believe me," replied Nellie, consulting a card. "You can have the sixth from this."

"*Gracias, Señorita,* I shore will dance at yore weddin'," he drawled, with the bow that became him so well. "Don't forget, Miss," he said turning to Martha. "I'll do better next time."

He made way for other aspirants to Martha's hand. From then on she met and danced with five young Westerners, all of whom were more accustomed to dancing, and four of whom added to her growing pleasure of the evening. The fifth, however, a tall, dark-faced young man, reminded her that all dances could not be so innocently enjoyed.

"You are holding me too tight," she said, the instant she took to the floor with the tall stranger. He laughed and eased the clasp of his arm, and during the round of the hall he acquainted her with the fact that he had run over from Cody to see the rodeo.

"You did not strike me as being western," replied Martha, and presently when she again felt a slight tightening of his arm she said she was tired and wanted to stop.

"Have a heart, honey," he remonstrated. "What's this line you're giving me?"

Martha left him standing at the entrance to the dressing room. She had recourse to her vanity case, and only when the music ceased did she return to the hall. Nellie's party was not in sight at the moment. And before Martha had gone very far, she was intercepted by Texas Jack.

"Wal, heah I am," he said, happily. "I watched you dance with thet last *hombre* an' I cain't say I liked it."

"Neither can I, Mr. Texas. But I got rid of him as quickly as I could," she replied, smiling up at him.

"I seen he tried to hug you an' you shied," he said tersely. "He jest don't belong heah, Miss Martha. An' if he tried to get fresh. . . . Did he?"

"He didn't try. He just did."

"Wal, I'll look him up after I dance this one with you."

"What for?" asked Martha quickly, suddenly alive to his cool drawl and the blue threat in his eyes.

"Where I come from Miss Martha, thet sort of thing ain't imposed on girls."

"That would be Texas, of course. And why is Texas so different from the forty-seven other states?"

They were stopped in the middle of their promenade by someone.

"Pardon me," said a pleasant deep voice Martha recognized with a start. She looked up into the face of Andrew Bonning. He wore a dark suit which detracted from his muscular build and gave him an air of distinction. It clarified something that had often puzzled Martha. She quickly looked down, anxious that her eyes should not give away her love for him. "Good evening, Miss Dixon. I was detained. I hope I am not too late for a dance."

"I—I'm afraid you are," replied Martha, in evident confusion.

Bonning shifted his dark gaze to her escort.

"Hello, Texas," he said familiarly.

"Stranger, you got the best of me," replied the cowboy.

"I have, at that. But I hope you'll give me this dance without my having to explain."

"Explainin' what?" queried Texas, bluntly.

"How I've got the best of you."

"Say who'n—who air you?"

"Andrew Bonning. I ride for Bligh."

"Ahuh. I heahed yore handle somewheres," drawled the cowboy, his expression changing almost imperceptibly. "Air you the fellar who pulled the sluggin' trick oot heah at the rodeo?"

"Yes."

"Wal, thet ain't givin' you any the best of me. I'm no pard of Cal Brice or Smoky Reed."

"No, but if I were to remind you of the night you met McCall some weeks ago?"

"McCall!" repeated the cowboy, turning slightly pale.

"Yes, McCall. Do you recollect?"

"I cain't say that I do, Bonnin'," rejoined Texas guardedly, feeling his way. Martha Ann sensed something in him that made her shiver. Andrew, too, was strangely quite another person, cold, sarcastic of speech, piercing of eye.

"Texas, you don't strike me as a liar."

"Air you callin' me one?"

"Not yet. I'm just reminding you."

"What of?"

"The night you rode nearly into Split Rock. And met a man on foot. McCall. Does that help you to remember?"

"Wal, I reckon it does."

"Then you'll be sport enough to let me have your dance with Miss Dixon?"

"Bonnin', I don't know aboot bein' a sport. But I'll oblige you jest 'cause I don't want to call yore bluff heah—an' embarrass this lady any more. Savvy?"

"Good. You can call it some other time and place."

Texas turned to Martha with a somber and troubled look on his face.

"Miss Dixon, I shore hate to give up this dance."

"Then why should you?" asked Martha, finding her voice. *"I'm* sure I don't want you to."

"Wal, yore N.B. rider has insinuated somethin' agin my good name, an' I don't want to call him heah before you. . . . Adios."

He stalked away, his red head held high, and left the hall. Martha Ann watched him depart, as if his going had spoiled some of the happiness of the evening.

"Martha, that was the only way I could stop it."

"Stop—what?" He seemed laboring under a strain, his brow clouded, his eyes bent sternly upon her. It was what he so obviously was thinking that liberated her. In another moment she could again be flippant, but right now he was too close to her, too overpoweringly the man who had captured her heart whether she liked it or not.

"Your carrying on with him."

"Yes? Please explain what you mean by carrying on, will you?"

"I just won't allow you to flirt with *that* cowboy, anyway."

"You won't?" she queried with deadly sweetness, while her spirit leaped at his assumption of authority. "I'll flirt and carry on, and—and . . . with anyone I like, Andrew Bonning."

"Smoky Reed was the cowboy who shot me. And Texas Jack was with him at the time."

"Oh!" cried Martha, suddenly weak with all the blood rushing back to her heart. "Smoky Reed! . . . But Texas said he wasn't a friend of . . . Andrew, you don't mean to say—you don't think that he was a partner to that attempt on your life."

"I don't claim so much. But he was with Reed. I saw him."

"That nice, soft-spoken, old-fashioned boy! . . . Andrew, I simply don't believe you. It was just a mean trick to get his dance."

"Good heavens! I didn't want to dance with you. But I suppose I'll have to for appearances' sake. That Glemm outfit is watching us."

"You needn't trouble yourself. What do I care about appearances?"

"Come," he said as the music rose seductively, and he whirled her away.

She felt as stiff in body as she was pliable of mind. He would take for granted that she—she hated him for what he was thinking. But she suddenly realized that he was the most wonderful dancer she had ever known. The surprise of it dwarfed her other feelings, and it drew from her a mechanical response. Her uncle's hired man! With her mind suddenly averted from herself, from her shame and humiliation, Martha Ann had not glided half round the hall with him before she was sure she had penetrated his masquerade. Missouri farm hand, indeed! The strong yet light clasp with which he held her, the perfect timing of his steps and their intricacy, the flying grace of the swing he gave her on the reverse—

these told the well-schooled Martha Ann that he was to the manner born. It explained so many of the acts that sat rather incongruously upon a rough-clad, heavy-booted cowboy. He was no cowboy, no garage mechanic, nothing that he pretended to be. Tonight he had the grace and cut of a college athlete.

"Put one over on us, didn't you, Mr. Andrew Bonning?" she said, unable to keep silent longer.

"Yes—and I'm reaping the whirlwind," he replied bitterly.

"Ne'er-do-well, blasé society man, wanderlusting realist, swell fugitive from the law—or what?" she queried mockingly.

"Outcast, Martha Ann."

She quivered in his arms and left off that tack. She gave up to the sheer sensual joy of the dance, and if it had lasted longer she knew she would have swooned. But before she had betrayed her true feelings the music ended.

"Let's get a breath of fresh air," he said, and led her out through one of the arches to the porch. The moon was shining brightly. Couples were leaning over the wooden railing.

"May I smoke?" he asked, without offering her his cigarettes, an omission which she noted.

"Yes."

"Found these among my store clothes—relic of my past."

Martha Ann tried to be her old audacious self, the hitchhiker whom no road or man could daunt. What she wanted to appear to Andrew was what she really believed herself at heart to be. But wit, flippancy, flirtation would not come, any more than the play of eyes and smiles which she once had lavished upon the country youth back there on the journey west.

"You dance beautifully. With whom did you study ballet?"

"I've had ten thousand teachers."

"Starry Eyes, I have been kidded by experts. Actresses, heiresses, adventuresses. You didn't learn to dance like that in the night clubs."

"Nor did you—in Missouri," she retorted.

He laughed as he flicked the ash from his cigarette. He seemed entirely natural tonight. There was nothing forced, moody, or brooding about him.

"I wonder what Connie would say to that."

"Who is Connie?"

"A girl I once thought I loved—but didn't."

"Did she love you?"

"Martha Ann, I have not thanked you for getting me out of jail," he said, ignoring her query. "It was good of you. I'd have had to stay in that dirty hole all night."

"Now all of us are broke."

"No, not quite. I have a little left and will pay you when we get home."

"I have something to thank you for too," she replied softly, her face downcast. "But I can't understand why you did it."

"What?"

"Beat up that cowboy Reed."

"I had it in for him anyhow, Martha Ann. But I could have killed him for the crack he made about you. Just as well brother Slade dragged me off him."

"Did Jim tell you Reed insulted me this morning, at the Glemms'?"

"No, he didn't."

"Funny—these western folk."

"Aren't they? When I told the magistrate that I'd been shot at by a rustler— no other than the cowboy Smoky Reed, he wanted to know if I'd caught him with the goods on. I admitted that I had not. Then he said I'd better be careful how I shot off my chin about rustling around here. And the sheriff searched me again for bootleg whiskey."

"We're Easterners—tenderfeet."

Then they fell silent. Martha Ann chafed under the fallaciousness of her position. Why did he not do one of two things—make some advance that accorded with his shallow conception of her—or tell her what a damned idiot he had been to judge her from appearances? How she would have reveled in an affront! But he was too much a gentleman to respond to what he imagined she was inviting; and too stupid to see that a girl could defy certain conventions, could long for her own freedom to court adventure, and still be a decent person. She turned from the rail as the music started up again. He threw his cigarette away.

"It's a pity, isn't it, Martha Ann?" he asked, his somber eyes on her face.

"Yes. . . . I wonder if you can possibly mean what I mean?"

"Not a chance. Come, my dear, I have monopolized you long enough."

They went in. The dancers were whirling out from all sides. Martha Ann hoped that Andrew would take her again into their midst, and betrayed her wishes with a shy, uplifted glance.

"Martha Ann, you are too lovely a girl and too wonderful a dancer to waste yourself on me," he said.

"Fiddlesticks! You don't think me lovely or wonderful or—or anything but—" She could not conclude the passionate speech, but she showed him very plainly the silent wrath in her eyes.

"Don't deceive yourself about that. The genus homo is a queer duck. In this judgment of Paris I hand you—"

"A lemon," she interrupted with a wild little laugh. How cheerfully he could cut her to the quick! How miserably she longed for his respect! They were strangers—as far apart as the poles—he a mid-Victorian and she a waif of the highway. "I would suggest that you don't interfere the next time you see me with Tex. . . . So long!"

If she expected a protest, it was not forthcoming. He conducted her to the little group waiting for her, and with an easy courtesy that made Martha feel almost like a rowdy he thanked her for the dance and bade her good night. Nellie Glemm's face expressed a curiosity which she did not voice. But it was easy to see that she and her friends would have liked to meet Andrew Bonning.

The rest of the dance was a nightmare to Martha Ann. She did not know or care with whom she danced. She would have welcomed Texas Jack or even Smoky Reed, if dancing with either of them could have brought Andrew back. She railed at herself for having played up to his idea of her. There it was; the evening had been spoiled. All seemed tasteless dust and bitter ashes in her mouth.

In the wee small hours she returned to the hotel and crept into bed, her feet dead and her heart numb and her brain the abode of conflicting tides of thought, and proceeded to cry herself to sleep.

10

ONE late afternoon, a week after the rodeo, Martha Ann caught sight of Jim Fenner approaching her favorite seat under a shady tree on the river bank. It had been a painful period of suspense for Martha, first on account of her own uncertain and baffling state of mind, and secondly owing to her uncle's increasing troubles.

Jim limped across the road and, favoring his crippled leg, placed himself beside her on the grass. The August day had been hot. His lean face, like a bronzed mask, gave no indication of his feelings, but there was a shadow in his hazel-flecked eyes.

"Lookin' fer Andy?" he asked, as he swept the purple slope toward the hills.

"Jim, I like you very much," she replied. "But if you don't leave off this Andy stuff I'm off you for life. How many times have I told you that I come here because of the view, so open and beautiful, because I can see the river wind away, and all the range and the mountains beyond?"

"Wal, shore. It's a grand view. Most as fine as some in Arizony. But no scenery is worth much without some life to go with it."

"I see horses, cattle, sometimes a rider, rabbits, wild ducks, eagles, and once I saw an airplane. What more do you want?"

"Wal, I kinda hoped you might be watchin' for Andy," replied the Arizonian simply. "You see it's this way, Martha. The comin' of you two young folks bucked us all up. Bligh was failin' in more than stock raisin'. An' me an' Sue, never havin' had a youngster, an' always yearnin' for one, sort of got a new lease on life. Natural-like we're powerful interested in you. Both of you so young an' live an' full of fire. Don't hold it against us, lass. We're growin' old an' all alone.''

"Forgive me, Jim. I'm sorry,'' replied Martha, a little hand going impulsively to his. "I am a cross, spiteful, ungrateful cat. I don't deserve your interest and kindness. . . . But you don't seem old to me, Jim.''

"Wal, I'm ten years older'n Bligh, an' he's nigh on to sixty.''

"I wouldn't have believed it,'' replied Martha Ann, with a sigh. "Have you got bad news, Jim?''

"I reckon so, lass. We went to town, hopin' to fix up the deal with McCall. But he's a mean *hombre*. Appealin' to the Wyomin' Cattlemen's Association didn't get us nowhere. An' Cheney Brothers wouldn't lend us two bits. Money is still tight an' stock has jest begun to move. McCall insisted on stickin' to the original deal, which we know now ain't to be thought of. I started to tell him thet in Arizony his deals would look mighty shady, but your uncle shet me up. Jest as wal, fer McCall got redheaded. We laid the deal before a magistrate. An' it's up to Bligh to decide to go in with McCall or stand trial.''

"What did you advise, Jim?''

"I'd stand trial. This feller McCall ain't a big cattleman. An' he ain't any too wal thought of. In the meantime we might get somethin' on him.''

"But if we don't?''

"Wal, we lose, thet's all.''

"Does it mean ruin for uncle?''

"Yes, so far as runnin' cattle is concerned. I doubt thet he could ever get another start, at his age, an' without capital. It's a good farm, though, an' we can live off it.''

"That's a grain of comfort. Oh, let's hope it is not as bad as you fear.''

"Martha, what air you goin' to do?''

"Me?'' queried Martha, with a start.

"Yes. Air you goin' to stick by yore uncle? Me an' Sue have wondered a lot about you. Pretty, smart girl like you—thet could do most anythin'—an' shore marry a million if you was thet sort—comin' to this lonesome range. But you've seemed so happy—till jest lately—layin' yore hands on all kinds of work. An' so crazy about horses an' the outdoors. We jest kinda figgered thet this sort of life was intended for you. What do you suppose brought the pioneers out West? It was thet, Martha—thet spread of prairie an' valley an' hill an' mountain all open an' free to the eye. Wal, thet pioneer stuff is in you if you only knew it.''

"Oh, Jim, do you really think so?'' murmured the girl, deeply moved.

"Shore I do. Lemme see them little hands of yores.''

Martha Ann stretched forth the small brown members for his inspection, smiling at his earnestness as he stroked them and turned them palms upward.

"Prettier to me than when they was so white an' soft. . . . Wal, work is good for anybody. All the same, lass, I wouldn't like to see you chop wood, plow the field, an' clean out the stable. Andy said thet same thing one day."

"Goodness gracious! How kind of him! . . . Neither would I. But honest, Jim, I like to bake, to sew, to milk the cows, although I hated housework at home."

"Wal, you gotta do some tall figger'n', my lass. It's only fair to tell you thet we may go from bad to wuss here. Sue an' me will stay by yore uncle. I put thet up to Andy an' he cussed me proper fer hintin' thet he might want to quit jest 'cause the goin' has got hard."

"He did? . . . That was good of him," she murmured.

"Andy can't see the bad side of it," continued Jim. "He says we'll lick hell out of McCall an' his range riders. Somethin' will turn up. Wal, Bonnin' is young an' full of hope—an' shore in love."

"In love? I don't believe it. He's too—too—" protested Martha.

"These boys air all crazy about you."

"I hadn't noticed it, Jim. . . . Are you sure you haven't been eating some of that Arizona loco weed you told me about?"

"Hosses an' cattle eat loco, my child. I may be smokin' my pipe at thet. But I reckon Andrew Bonnin' is as deep in love with you, lass, as a man ever falls."

"Jim!"

"Wal, you needn't bark at me like thet. . . . An' go red—an' then white—as you air now. You know it, don't you?"

"No," whispered Martha, averting her face.

"Haven't boys an' men, too, been fallin' in love with you, ever since you put on long dresses?"

"No."

"Ain't thet Texas Jack cowboy who rode out here Sunday—ain't *he* in love with you?"

"Cowboy-taffy," replied Martha Ann tremulously, striving against the rising tide within her breast.

"Ridic'lous, lass. Thet's yore own word. I've heerd it often. Ridic'lous! . . . I don't know about you, girl. You're a deep youngster. You're honest as daylight, mostly. But I can't figger you, in this partic'lar. I'm afraid you're—"

"Jim Fenner, if *you* side with my parents, my relatives—and a lot of old fogies—and An-Andrew Bonning—I-I'll never speak to you again," cried Martha Ann, the tears coming into her eyes.

"All right. Thet settles thet," said Fenner placatingly. "From now on I'm

takin' you on yore word. I'm on yore side, Martha. An' thet means Sue, too.
If we two old Westerners can't understand, we shore can trust an' sympathize
an' love. I reckon it ain't been so easy fer you back home, or anywheres. You
ought to have been a boy. An' instead you're the sweetest girl thet ever was
born to vex men. It's tough, honey. When a girl can't lift her eyes or smile
without some fool feller thinkin' she wants him to grab her—wal, thet's shore
tough."

"It's just exactly what happens, Jim," she replied brokenly. "It was that way
at home. . . . And it's almost as bad here."

"Martha, did Andrew do thet?"

"No, not he."

"Wal, thet's somethin' to his credit. I can't see Andrew makin' game of a
girl."

"Bah! He'd be no different from any of them—if he believed he was the *only*
one."

"Are you shore, lass?"

"Well, no. But I've met boys like that. Boys who want a girl all to themselves—and hate her if she looks at someone else. I was fed up on all of them."

"Listen, Martha. You've got Andy figgered wrong," continued Jim earnestly.
"He ain't what he lets on to be. An' at thet I don't savvy what he is pretendin'.
Sue says she always feels funny when he sets a chair fer her, or stands up when
she comes in—things like thet thet women notice. But he *is* somebody."

"At the rodeo they called him a prize fighter," said Martha with a queer little
laugh.

"Wal, he shore was a whirlwind. I ain't got over tinglin' over thet fight yet.
. . . No, Andrew Bonnin' ain't no common sort. Whatever druv *him* out here
it wasn't anythin' crooked. All my life I've dealt with men who have things to
hide. Andy hasn't anythin'. But he's awful sad an' quiet."

"Some woman," ventured Martha Ann, with a twinge of jealousy.

"Some girl! . . . Martha, when you first come here Andy was pretty hard on
you. I called him fer it, an' he's never mentioned it again. I reckon he still thinks
the same about your hikin' out here alone. I didn't use to blame Andy. I used
to think myself thet thet was the foolest stunt any girl ever tried. But I see it
different now. The rest of us air wrong. Thet idee was natural an' innocent,
'cause it was *you*."

Martha Ann laid her head against Jim's shoulder. "Jim, you'd have made a
swell Daddy," she sighed.

"Not too late yet, by jingo! . . . But don't upset me, lass. I'm in turrible
earnest. I feel like—like one of them wise fellars who settles the fates of nations.
. . . No matter how Andy disapproved of you—or what he thought you was—

it still didn't keep him from fallin' in love with you. An' grow wuss an' wuss as time goes on."

"What makes—you think—he—he—?"

"Wal, Sue seen it first. An' believe me, Martha, thet woman never is wrong. . . . An' after I was put wise I watched Andy an' I've seen a hundred proofs of it."

"Give me just one, I dare you," said the girl, color mounting in her cheeks.

"Wal, let me see. It's darn hard to pick jest one out. . . . Do you remember the day yore hoss piled you up on the sand down here?"

"Yes."

"I didn't know what it all was about till afterward. But when Andrew went back for your boot I happened to be ridin' along the bank an' I seen him get off an' pick somethin' up, an' set down on the sand to hold the thing in his hand, an' look mighty fond at it. I swear it looked thet way to me. Course it was most dusk an' I'm a sentimental old cuss. But he sat there like a Navajo watchin' the sunset. Somethin' pathetic an' lonely about the way he looked off over the range. So I didn't call. Later I asked him where he'd been, an' then he told me about goin' after yore lost boot. . . . Now, lass, is thet convincin'?"

"Not at all! You certainly have an imagination, Jim. . . . Tell me something else."

"Wal, the way he beat up Smoky Reed," ventured Fenner.

"No. He meant to do that anyhow."

"The rodeo dance, then. He never seen any other girl but you—let alone danced with one. An' the girls was certainly layin' fer him. A blind man could have seen thet."

"It might be taken as testimony," she replied ponderingly. "But it would never convince me. You lose, Jim, unless you have a better one—out of those hundred proofs." And she drew back from his shoulder to regard him demurely.

"Wal, he shore watches fer you all the time, an' you couldn't pop yore head up anywhere on this blasted range but he'd see it."

"Masculine curiosity and his obsession to boss some woman. No more," proclaimed Martha.

"Sue says it's somethin' she can *feel* in Andy, whenever you come near."

"But *I* don't feel it."

"Then you're jest not flesh an' blood. . . . Martha, I tell you I know he's fallen for you. An' I shore feel low-down to double cross him this way. But I gotta do it. 'Cause you might up an' do somethin' jest fer spite. So I'll tell you. Andy carries a little round picture of you in a frame. I seen him lookin' at somethin', an' when I come into camp he slipped it back pronto in his breast pocket. After supper he went to washin' in the creek, an' I sneaked to his clothes an' fished thet picture out of his shirt pocket. It shore was a sweet picture."

"Oh! the—the. . . . I missed that picture on the day we went to the rodeo. I drove. . . . He had my bag in his lap. It dropped out or he sneaked it."

"Wal, is thet any proof?"

"Jim, that's very strange indeed—*if* he took it and kept it and looked at it—just to see what a bad girl looks like. . . . Still I couldn't be sure."

"Do you want to be shore?" he demanded suddenly, as if he now had her at his mercy.

"Jim! . . . You—I—Oh, yes!" she cried, and her composure seemed about to leave her.

"I seen him kiss thet little picture," cried Jim triumphantly.

"You're lying, Jim Fenner! . . . He didn't—he couldn't. Not Andrew."

"I swear to Gawd I seen him."

"You're cruel, Jim. You've tormented me for weeks. But today you're a positive fiend."

"Ain't you glad I told you?" he asked chuckling.

"Go away!"

"Shore, I'll mosey along," he replied, getting up stiffly. "But you haven't tole me yet if you'll stay here with yore uncle an' see it through."

"I shall see it through, Jim," she replied simply.

"Wal, if thet ain't fine. I reckoned you would. You can go home on a visit some day—or have yore folks visit you. It'll all turn out right in the end."

"Go away!" cried Martha Ann. "Or I'll—I'll kiss you!"

"Wal, as I don't want thet big gazabo to lambaste me one I reckon I'd better make tracks."

Martha Ann leaned back against the tree. She would stay and see it through! Both sadness and rapture pervaded her soul. By what strange steps had she finally found her niche in life. Tomorrow she would ride and ride, far away and up the purple slope, to some lonely spot where only the wilderness could witness her joy.

The sun was sinking gold and red behind the Rockies. The river traced its winding, green-bordered course out to fade in the ruddy haze of the range. Great clouds of rose and pearl piled to the zenith, stately and serene. Like a sea, the sagebrush rolled and heaved as far as the scalloped hills.

No living creature crossed Martha Ann's vision. How lonely were the vast spaces! They had been like that forever or, remembering her geology, for the millions of years since the icecap of the north had receded. What was there here so restful to her soul, so like some place she had known before she was even born? The peace that was in her heart had something to do, too, with what Jim had told her about a man's strange behavior with a misplaced locket.

At that moment a lone horseman appeared, far out in the sage, a black spot becoming gradually perceptible of movement. He gave life to the scene. All it needed! But it gave infinitely more to Martha Ann, who pressed her hands tightly to her bosom, and watched and watched with slowly dimming eyes.

It was toward noon of the following day, and for hours Martha Ann had been alternately trotting and walking her horse up the endless purple slope. She had never before dared to ride so far alone. But this day she knew that she had to find solitude. How easy to think things out in the saddle, riding alone over the range, with the wind whipping in her face, the sun bright and warm, the loneliness calling!

She was heading for the Antelope Hills and they now loomed close. She would wait, she would hold herself in, she would postpone this battle between her two selves until she had found an ideal spot where no other woman creature had ever poured out her innermost heart before.

Soon she was riding among a grove of trees. It was dry and sweet there among these scattered trees where the sage mingled with silver grass and golden flowers. When she looked back down the long slope she was thrilled by the splendor of the descent, sloping to the distant thread of the river and the dot that was the ranch.

At last she felt that she could ride no longer. She had come upon a kind of bowl of silver grass, surrounded by straggling trees, a lonely, isolated glade, hidden from all eyes except those of the eagles, and shining there, peaceful and tranquil, an altar for her abnegation. For she would never rise from this lonely vigil the same wild, intolerant, proud and selfish girl.

Martha tied her horse in the fringe of trees, and chose a lowspreading one under which to rest. A thick fragrant brown carpet of tiny needles covered the ground. Her tree was some species of pine. She gathered a lapful of the little spears, and let them run through her cupped hands.

She found herself loath to give up feeling, seeing, smelling this lonesome covert for the thoughts that she knew she had to straighten out. She had her first intimation of how wonderful it would be never to think at all. Only to use her senses! Perhaps it was that inherited instinct that had lured her to Wyoming. Who could understand who had never felt that enchantment?

And presently Martha Ann lay back on the bed of pine needles and let her thoughts roam. "So he stole my picture! . . . Darling!—Oh, if you *do* love me—how terribly I shall make you suffer before I prove that I'm not what you believe I am. . . . And if you *don't* I shall—be what you believe I . . . Oh, no! no!—I shall only die!"

A sudden sound interrupted the girl's bittersweet reverie. It was a sound which at first she could not define. Alarmed, Martha sat up trembling. The thumping sound grew louder. Hoofs! Her horse had broken away. No, the pounding came from the opposite side of the little amphitheater. Crashings among the trees preceded the shrill bawl of a calf. A cow stumbled through an opening between the trees and behind it galloped a calf. Then something yellow and snaky shot from behind the green, to loop round the calf and jerk it off its feet. In the next instant a horse appeared whose rider was bending low to escape the branches. He pulled his horse back on its haunches and leaped off, to throw the calf down and kneel upon it.

Martha Ann crouched there, her terror of the unknown changing to the terror of an act whose significance she vaguely guessed. When the rider arose to toss his sombrero aside and wipe his sweaty face, he exposed a flaming mop of red hair. But Martha had recognized the lithe form of Texas Jack even before he revealed the telltale hair.

"Bawl an' be damned, you ornery little cuss. You're a maverick now. An' you git oot of heah." He picked up a rock to fling it at the cow. She lowered her head and threatened him, but another rock, well directed, struck her with a resounding thump. Martha Ann's wide eyes glimpsed the N.B. brand on the flank of the cow. The distracted beast went as far as the edge of the open and continued to bawl.

Texas broke some dead branches off the nearest tree. These he placed on the ground near the calf. He struck a match and started a fire. Picking up his sombrero he fanned the fire until it roared. Then he slipped something from under the flap of his saddle—a thin curved tool. Martha had seen its like—a running iron, Jim had called it—a thing to burn brands on stock. Texas placed an end of the iron in the fire and began again to fan the flames with his hat. They roared as if blown by a bellows.

Suddenly he bent down, and seizing the iron he ran to the calf, and knelt to apply it to its trembling red flank. The calf bawled lustily. Martha heard a sizzle, another and another. She saw smoke arise, and then she smelled burning hair. The smell of it sickened her.

But nausea, fright, and all her other feelings yielded precedence to righteous wrath. Texas Jack was branding her uncle's calf. He was a thief—a rustler. She had caught him red-handed in the very act.

Quickly Martha Ann rose to brush aside the branches that had screened her and to step into the open.

Texas heard her step and his flaming head shot up like that of a frightened deer. Suddenly he wheeled and whipped out a gun in one single action. At any other time, Martha might have recoiled from his fierce face, but now she kept right on, indifferent to his menacing posture, and to the gun held low and level.

"Wal, fer Gawd's sake!" he burst out, astounded and visibly relieved.

Martha Ann kept on until the bound calf lay at her feet. On its flank had been branded a double X, the lines of which shone raw and bright in its hide.

"McCall's brand!" she ejaculated in amazement, and then she faced the cowboy. "Texas Jack, you have burned McCall's brand on one of my uncle's calves."

"Caught with the goods," replied Texas, and flipping up his gun he caught it by the butt, to return it to his belt. He seemed cool, laconic, devil-may-care, but the paleness that had not disappeared, and the quivering pinpoints in his blue eyes, told Martha that he was not altogether invulnerable.

"You calf thief, you paid rustler, you low-down thieving cowboy," she blazed, with eyes before which he quailed. "You ride for one man and steal for another. You come to my uncle's house. You eat and drink there, accepting his hospitality, and my friendship. . . . Oh, you despicable vermin. You coward, liar, cheat! . . . You brag of being a Texan—you wouldn't insult a girl—bah! You're worse than Smoky Reed. At least he doesn't sail under false colors."

"Martha, doggone it, I'm not so low-down as all thet," he expostulated, his face now scarlet, his eyes shamed and appealing. "You're a tenderfoot. You jest cain't savvy the West. All cattlemen brand mavericks, when they happen on them. It ain't exactly stealin'."

"A maverick is a calf without a mother," flashed Martha. "There's this calf's mother. And she's got an N.B. brand on her."

"Wal, if you split hairs over it—I reckon I'm a rustler," he said, and kneeling beside the calf he released it. Then, when it had scrambled up to bawl and run he sat down in the grass. He took out a little tobacco pouch, and rolled himself a cigarette with steady fingers.

"Texas, I'm simply shocked. I'm terribly disappointed. Only last Sunday you told me you loved me."

"Wal, I did an' I do. What's thet got to do with this job? I swear to Gawd it was my last—this deal with McCall. But I was in it before I ever seen you. He owes me money. He even threatens to give me away. I had to go on with it, thet's all."

"But, Texas, if you're a rustler you just can't make honest love to a decent girl," declared Martha.

"Shore it was honest love, I was goin' to ask you to marry me."

"Oh! To think I—liked you—and I might even have fallen in love with you!"

"Wal, you didn't act much like it," growled Texas, and took a long pull on his cigarette. "An' don't roast me no more. I cain't stand it from you."

"Have you no shame? Can you sit there and make excuses for this piece of crooked work? Deliberately ruining my uncle, who's old and poor! Oh, you're a fine Texan."

"Say, my little spitfire, I'll clap a hand over yore pretty trap in a minnit, if you don't shet it. If I wasn't a gentleman an' a Texan, I'd do what Smoky would do, or any other free-lance rider on this range."

"And what is that?"

"I'd pack you off in the hills an' keep you there," he replied with sullen passion.

"Texas, you couldn't do a cowardly thing like that!" she returned hurriedly, not so sure as she pretended to be. The cowboy looked like a man at bay.

"No, I couldn't do that. An' you can bet yore sweet little self thet it's only because I am a Texan. An' what'n hell air you doin' way oot heah? Suppose it'd been Smoky, dozen *hombres* I could name, you damn little fool! Haven't you got no sense at all? You gallivant oot west alone in a pair of short pants an' now you come ridin' into the foothills all by yoreself."

"I'm not afraid."

"No, I seen thet. But you're too brainless—too damned innocent an' trustin'. If you keep this heah sort of thing up, Martha Dixon, you'll meet with outrage from someone who'll think you're askin' fer it!"

She gazed at him with mute lips, surprised by his passion.

"Thet's all. Somebody had to tell you. Why didn't yore friend Bonnin' tell you?"

"Why should he?"

"Wal, why doesn't he make you stay home? If he's so doggone stuck on you as the girls say?"

"He's not. . . . And he couldn't make me do anything."

"It's too damned bad somebody cain't. You oughta fall for some lucky dawg an' stop this heartbreakin' game. . . . Wal, you caught me with the goods. Now what're you gonna do aboot it?"

"Texas, what'll you do if I tell?" she asked earnestly.

"Wal, I'll try to collect some money from McCall, an' vamoose oot of the country onless someone tries to stop me, which wouldn't be so healthy for him!"

"If I promise not to betray you will you promise never to steal again?"

Texas rose to his feet, with the blood of shame again flooding his face. It receded, leaving him pale. His eyes held a piercing blue intensity.

"Martha, thet's a big order, as you see it," he said. "I reckon I never appreciated jest what kind of a girl you air. I'm askin' you to overlook my love-makin' which wasn't so honest as I swore it was. But I'd never laid a hand on you. . . . If you don't squeal on me I'll promise to go straight."

"It's a bargain, Texas. Here's my hand," she returned gravely, and held it out to him.

"Wal, I had a close shave," he drawled with his old smile, as he pressed her hand. "Come, fine yore hawse. Smoky Reed is workin' round in thet next draw, an' if he seen us I'd have to kill him."

"Perhaps you had better ride home with me, or part way," she suggested, nervously.

"Go ahaid. I'll trail along an' keep you in sight."

Breathless and exultant Martha Ann ran to untie her horse, and after tightening the cinches she mounted and rode down the slope.

For once in her life she had done something worth while. One good deed, at least, might result from her mad Wyoming adventure. Martha placed reforming a wild cowboy above saving some of her uncle's stock. And somehow she felt certain that this footloose and reckless Texan would keep his word. If he did not keep it from any innate reversion to what was right, he would because of that queer honor held by Texans in regard to women. Martha Ann was proud of herself. She could confide in Jim Fenner, at least. But she would not tell her uncle. And as for Andrew Bonning, he would not believe it even if she did confess. The thought galled her. At the same time she knew it was true—she had caught Texas Jack red-handed and she had brought the perplexing and dangerous situation to a clever and happy close.

Looking back over her shoulder she saw Texas half a mile behind, sitting sidewise in his saddle, a figure of a rider that fitted the wild environment. After she had traveled several miles further, to drop into the trail, the exuberance of her feeling wore away, and she came down out of the clouds. It astonished her a little to realize that the revelation that Texas Jack was a rustler had not destroyed her liking for him. He still seemed to be a thoroughly likeable chap. She did not see any reason why she should not loiter on the trail until Texas caught up with her. Accordingly, she held her horse to a walk, which he did not like on the homeward trip; and was presently chagrined to observe that Texas also had slowed his gait to accommodate hers. He was showing consideration on her behalf, and suddenly Martha realized just what Texas meant by this holding back, when it certainly would have been so much more interesting for them to proceed down the trail together. Texas was keeping her in sight as a matter of protection, and avoiding the ride with her, because in the event that his status as a cowboy might be revealed, such association would reflect upon her good name.

"Amazing! I can't escape that even out on this uninhabited desert," exclaimed Martha Ann disgustedly, all her old antagonism welling up. She felt here, as in everything, that she knew her own motives, her integrity, the truth about herself; and for anything else that could be thought by curious, narrow people she did not concern herself in the least.

She halted her horse, and while waiting for Texas Jack to catch up, she gazed down upon the ranch. Those gray houses appeared lost in any immensity of green. It was a lonely place. She tried to picture it with snow everywhere, white and desolate. But the thought pleased rather than otherwise. Winter would be a time to read and study and sew and learn to cook; and perhaps go home some Christmas time. Across the white-barred, green-bordered river the range spread far as the eye could see, endlessly rolling, unrelieved by a break of any kind.

A clatter of hoofs distracted the girl's thoughts as Texas came loping up to come to a stop beside her.

"Wal, what's it all aboot?" he asked, eying her keenly.

"I got tired loafing along alone," she replied with a smile. "Let's have a little run down this wide stretch."

"Martha, I reckon you oughta be moseyin' on by yoreself," he drawled.

"Don't you want to ride with me?" she demanded.

"Doggone! Girls air queer. . . . I reckon I'll ride as far as the creek with you."

Martha urged her horse into a canter, but when Texas' bay lined up beside her that gait did not suit either horses or riders. They broke into a gallop and then into a run. Martha awoke to something she had heretofore never experienced—the thrill of riding at break-neck speed, the sting of the wind in her face, the blur of sage whirling past, the unexcelled joy of violent action.

The race was won by Martha, a victory no less delightful because she knew Texas had let her win, and she sat her horse breathless and tingling, with smarting skin and flying hair.

"Oh, that was glorious! I never—dared go—so fast before," she panted.

"Wal, you don't fork thet hawse so porely at that," drawled the cowboy. "Shore you cain't help lookin' beautiful, but I'm not figgerin' looks. Reckon you got strong laigs an' thet's what it takes to ride. You set a little too stiff. You wanta be easy in the saddle. Ketch the swing of yore hawse with yore body. An' squeeze with yore knees. . . . It wouldn't take long fer me to make a rodeo rider oot of you."

"Please—please do," pleaded Martha Ann.

Texas sat up with a start and his expression of genuine pleasure vanished. "Wal, I reckon thet'll be aboot all," he said. "Look who's comin'."

Martha whirled in her saddle, all her delight suddenly ended. Halfway across the sandy draw she saw a black horse trotting toward her. The rider was Andrew.

"It might be a good idee fer me to vamoose," suggested Texas.

"Why?"

"Wal, if my eyes ain't pore, Bonnin' is seein' red. I can always tell the way a fellar sets his saddle."

"Suppose he is?"

"Shore it was fer yore sake, Martha," he replied coolly. "The man doesn't live who can scare me."

"Stay then. Andrew Bonning has no claim on me. I can ride with whom I choose."

Andrew blocked the narrow trail, so that they had to halt their horses or turn aside into bad going. They were at the place in the dry creek bottom where Martha had once been thrown.

"Hello, Andrew," called Martha gaily. But her spontaneity did not ring sincere. How white his face was! And his eyes gazed upon her with a dark, scornful look of passionate conviction.

"Howdy, Bonnin'! Fine day fer ridin'," drawled Texas, nonchalantly, as he leisurely rolled a cigarette.

Andrew did not give the cowboy so much as a glance or a nod. He fixed eyes upon Martha that suddenly she felt to be filled with accusation and with terrible disappointment. They were desperately hard to meet.

"So you've done it," he spoke coldly, bitterly.

"Done what?" she demanded, a hot blush burning her cheek. His look, his query aroused the red flag of her ready anger. But there was some quality in his tone, of disillusionment, or pain, or bitter conviction, that enraged Martha more than his interference.

"You met this cowboy out on the range."

"Certainly I did. Anyone could see that."

"You had a date with him."

"No, I didn't. It was purely accident. I . . . But see here, Andrew, this is none of your business. I'm free, white and over eighteen. I can meet whom I want to. You have no claim on me. I told Texas that."

"You would," he replied, darkly. "No, indeed, I haven't any claim on you. But I happen to be the only one who dares oppose you, Martha Dixon. You ran away from your mother, father, brother—if you have them. You can easily fool these two doting old men back home—who worship you. There's no one left but me to try to save you from making a complete fool of yourself."

"Oh, fiddlesticks! The old stuff! Andrew Bonning, I'm *not* making a fool of myself!" she cried hotly.

"I hope I'm not too late," he retorted, with a look that made Martha quail inwardly.

"Maybe you are. But it's none of your damned business," she burst out.

"I've made it my business," he said deliberately.

"Is that so? Well, try to remember where I told you to go once before."

"Girl, if you are absolutely shameless yourself, can't you have some regard for your uncle?"

"Regard? You know that I love him dearly. What do you mean—regard?"

"An old-fashioned virtue in disrepute with modern girls. Honor. Something due Bligh because he has given you a home. He is a newcomer here on this range. He needs to make friends. It will not do him any good to have his niece gossiped about. To have open scandal about her rendezvous in the hills with a dissolute cowboy."

"Andrew, you don't know what you are talking about," replied Martha Ann, beginning to feel her spirits flag.

"Nothing to you! Good Lord! What a cold-blooded, self centered, kick-hunting little proposition you are!"

"I've done—nothing that I'm ashamed of," faltered Martha Ann.

"Could you ever feel shame?"

"Yes, I could."

"About what? For what?"

"That a supposedly decent man like you—could make me out the—the rotten little hussy—"

"I didn't make you out rotten," he interrupted, a dark flush spreading over his stern, pale face. "Some other time I'll tell you what I think about you. Suffice it now to say that you are a reckless girl who isn't helping an uncle who is very much in need of help—as this cowboy knows!"

"Oh! And you have constituted yourself the valiant knight to rescue me?" she exclaimed satirically.

"Only today Jim Fenner said you'd make bad blood out here—and spill it, too, if you were not stopped."

"Jim! Did Jim—say that?" gasped Martha, stung to the quick.

"Yes. And it was Jim who sent me out to look for you. I, like an idiot, thought you were riding the ranch trails."

"I rode too far, perhaps, this time—to—to— Oh, never mind," cried Martha tragically. "You couldn't understand. Let me pass. I want to go home."

"Very well, go on home. I'll settle this with your friend here," rejoined Andrew grimly, and dismounted to lead his horse out of the trail.

"Texas will come with me," spoke up Martha hurriedly. She did not like Andrew's look or the cowboy's cool silence. She dared not leave them alone.

"Wal, Bonnin', a lady's word is law with me," drawled Texas.

"Just the same you don't go," snapped Bonning, and seized the cowboy's bridle.

"I'm liable to run you down. Let go them reins. Don't you know any better than to grab—"

"Stop, Andrew," cried Martha Ann fearfully, as the cowboy's horse reared. "Texas will stay. So will I. . . . But have a heart—and get it over with."

"Texas, pile off and face me like a man, if you're not too much of a coward," commanded Andrew.

"Say, tenderfoot, I wouldn't be scared of a million Easterners," drawled Texas with a smile, and he leisurely slipped out of his saddle.

"Listen then. This reckless girl is not on the level. Do you get me? She doesn't care a rap for you or me or for anybody. All she thinks of is getting kicks out of everything. She will vamp some poor sucker just to watch him wriggle. And believe me, cowboy, it doesn't make a damn bit of difference *how far* she has gone with you. Do you understand?"

"I'm listenin' powerful hard, Bonnin', an' I'm gettin' mighty riled," replied the cowboy.

"All the better. I intend to rile you, one way or another. . . . You're supposed to be a square shooter, Texas, at least, so they say. Everybody likes you, especially the girls. I like you myself. You're a clean, fine good-looking cowboy. I'd sure want you for a partner, if that were possible. Well, considering all this, do you think you're living up to your reputation—do you think it is honorable of you—and *fair* to this girl—to meet her way out on the lonely range?"

"No, doggone it, I don't," declared the Texan, as if moved by Andrew's eloquence.

"You made love to Martha last Sunday, and before that. I saw you."

"Bonnin', I ask you, what in hell would any cowboy do? Or any man?"

"Dubious flattery, cowboy, if you get what I mean," snapped Andrew. "I see that you have made quite some headway with the little lady."

"Bonnin', you talk too fast an' too deep fer me," declared Texas angrily. "Let's get down to callin' cyards."

"I told Martha that you were with Smoky Reed when he shot me."

"Hell you say! Who else did you tell?"

"I didn't repeat that about you. But I told Sheriff Slade and the magistrate at Casper who shot me. They wanted to know if I could prove it. Well, I couldn't. And they advised me not to make cracks about Westerners, unless I could prove them. I'm going on my own after this."

"Ahuh. An' what's all this heah talk got to do with me?"

"You were with Reed. I saw you—recognized you through my field glasses. You separated, and you took the far side of the canyon. Do you imagine I thought you were hunting birds' nests?"

The same fierce wolfish look that Texas had exhibited to Martha when he had wheeled upon her with his gun now settled on his lean face. Blue flames darted from his eyes.

"Not on your life," went on Andrew accusingly. "You were up there for precisely the same reason as Smoky Reed."

"Naw, I wasn't."

"You lie, Texas. I *know*, I tell you. I heard you make the deal with McCall. You refused to kill cows—like Reed is doing—and you stuck to your idea of maverick branding. But that is the bunk, Texas. You know it is. You stick to your method, because in case you are held up on suspicion you can use that maverick alibi."

"Bonnin', cut yore talk mighty short. You'll say somethin' in a minnit."

"You're damn right I will," cried Andrew. "You're a rustler!"

Out leaped Texas' blue six-shooter, to be thrust almost against Andrew's abdomen. Martha screamed.

"You cain't call me thet," rasped the cowboy. "Girl, mind yore hawse, an' keep oot of this!"

"The hell I can't. I do call you rustler, damn you! What do I care for your gun? You can't murder me in cold blood before the eyes of this girl. But I'd call you even if she weren't here. And that's what I mean. If you made a date with Martha Dixon—all the time when you knew that it couldn't be honorable love-making because you *are* a rustler—well, you're a disgrace to the Texas you seem so proud of, you're a low-down yellow thief whose aim is to ruin this girl's old uncle."

"Bonnin', if it wasn't fer her I'd shoot yore laig off."

"I don't doubt it. And that would simply prove what you are. Why, you poor ignorant cowhand, if you had any real manhood in you you'd fight for her, instead of betraying her and her family."

"I been comin' to thet. But you gab so much I cain't get a word in. Now gimme a chance. You hot-haided tenderfoot! You're wuss'n a Mexican fer bein' jealous. All because you ketch Martha with me! How the hell do you know what come off? As a matter of fact we had no date. She ketched me red-handed brandin' the Double X on a calf. An' she shore called me proper. Then she made me swear I'd never rustle another calf. An' by Gawd, I'll keep thet promise if it's the last thing I ever do. . . . Now you come along, like a baby cyclone, to insult as good an' sweet an' innocent a girl as ever breathed. Too innocent an' fun-lovin' fer you fed-up eastern highbrows. She had to run out west to get understood. An' thet to me makes it wuss fer you than my bein' a rustler."

"Rot! You do it well, Texas. But too late," snarled Andrew, his face blanched. "Drop your gun, if you're not too much of a coward. But if you are, then I'll have to fight you your own way. I've a gun on my saddle."

"Fairest thing you've said yet," replied the cowboy. Then he unbuckled his gun belt and hung it over the pommel of his saddle.

Martha Ann came out of her trance and got off her horse, almost falling, to run between belligerents, who were now glaring at each other.

"Andrew . . . Texas!" she cried imploringly. "Don't fight. It's so—so silly of both of you. All for nothing. Please, for my sake—Andy—"

He put her firmly aside. "Get out of my way, Wyoming Mad," he said with his bitter smile. "This is where your kick-hunting has led to. Now watch and see what I do to your cute cowboy."

"Oh, Texas—you give in. *He* is hopeless. Oh, I beg of you!"

"Hell, lady, what am I up again?" shouted Texas furiously. "Between the two of you I'm aboot nutty. I cain't stand around an' let him pound me the way he did Smoky."

He, too, thrust Martha to one side, not too gently, and when she recovered her balance they had plunged at each other like two infuriated bulls. Their first onset took them completely off the trail. The distracted girl stood riveted to the spot. If she had not been tongue-tied she would have screamed for Texas to whip Andrew within an inch of his life. But she knew that he could not do it. What she dreaded was the possibility of a fight with guns after this one with fists was settled. Andrew would punish the cowboy terribly and that portended a disastrous end for the duel.

It developed that Texas was a far tougher proposition than Smoky Reed. He was as tall as Andrew, as agile and supple, almost as heavy, and what he lacked in skill he made up for in ferocity. He resembled a redheaded whirlwind, swinging, striking, feinting. Many vicious blows were struck. It appeared that Andrew received almost as many as he gave. Blood flowed down both furious faces. In the midst of a lunge Andrew tripped in the sand. Texas, swinging hard, struck him alongside the head, a blow that sent Andrew flat on his back. Like a cat he leaped up just as Texas reached him, meaning to throw himself down upon him. Bonning met the charge by knocking Texas down. Nimbly the cowboy was up and at it again, bleeding, snorting, cursing. They fought all over the place, plowing up the sand.

In the end, the battle went against Texas. He could not cope with his antagonist, who appeared to release more vigor as the fight progressed. Again the cowboy went down. When he got to his feet, more slowly this time warily countering and backing away, Andrew yelled: "Stand up and fight, you range Romeo!"

"Wal, I ain't—no dancin' tenderfoot!" panted Texas, and suddenly he dove to catch Andrew by the legs and trip him up.

They rolled over and over in the sand. Then Martha saw where the cowboy had made a blunder. Andrew made no effort to rise again. With marvelous ease and swiftness he moved over the ground, breaking Texas' hold, but never letting him go, battering him on head and body. Texas evidently saw his mistake and endeavored to get up, but it was too late. He was being made a toy in the hands of a giant. Martha understood it when she saw Andrew tackle the half-rising cowboy, almost to bury him in the sand. A little more of these football tactics, a few more thumping blows, and Texas lay still, while Andrew got up to brush his clothes, and wipe his bleeding face with a handkerchief.

"Come—take a look—at your rustler friend," called Andrew gruffly.

Martha Ann left the trail, gathering strength as she went, until she reached Texas, who lay, a battered spectacle such as she had never seen.

"Help—me—sit up," he asked faintly.

Martha Ann assisted him to gain a sitting posture, and half supported him.

"Oh, Texas, he has hurt you—terribly," cried Martha, distressed at the sight of the sagging head. Texas' hair and face appeared a mass of sand and blood.

"I—reckon," whispered the cowboy.

"Fetch some water, Andrew," commanded Martha.

"Doggone! What kinda—avalanche struck—around heah?"

"Never mind, Texas. I'll never—never forgive him," sobbed Martha.

Andrew fetched a canteen and, unscrewing the top, poured water on his scarf, which he handed to Martha.

"Tex, you were okay—while you stayed on your feet," said Andrew, breathing heavily. "But you shouldn't have mixed it with me on the ground!"

Martha Ann gave him a fleeting hateful look. "You big bully!" She wiped the blood and sand off the cowboy's face, and her action disclosed sundry bruises and a bleeding nose.

"Wal, I feel kinda shaky, but I can hold a gun. Come on, Bonnin'. Mebbe this won't be—so easy fer you."

Martha fell on her knees beside him. "Don't—don't fight with guns! That would be awful. Texas! he whipped you—but didn't get off easy." Then she turned to clasp Andrew's knees.

"Let go. Don't do that," cried Andrew harshly.

But she would not let go. She clung to him. "Andrew—Andrew—don't make it any worse! . . . I was to blame. I—I must be just—no good. But I hated you so—for being—so—so wrong about me. . . . For God's sake—give in!"

Andrew gazed down upon her, his face working.

"Bonnin'," spoke up Texas, reaching for Andrew. "If you don't show yellow—I will."

"That's for me to do. I apologize. . . . Texas, you're a good sport. I must be the mad one. . . . Martha, get up," said Andrew huskily, and stooped to help her to her feet.

11

SEPTEMBER came with its frosty mornings, its hot hazy days and cool nights, painting the gold and scarlet hues of autumn on the Sweetwater Range.

The willows and cottonwoods along the river stood in colorful contrast with the dark-pooled, white-rippled wandering watercourse. And tiny bits of scarlet shone like fires amid the purple monotony of the plain. Flocks of wild ducks, flying from the north, heralding an early winter, alighted on the wide, still reaches.

Since Andrew's encounter with the rustling cowboy out in the hills, Bligh had refused to allow him to ride alone. Accordingly, Fenner accompanied Andrew on his scouting trips, of which they made several each week, sometimes camping out overnight. It did not take long for the old Arizonian to size up the situation. They never got within miles of any cowboys who were not minding their own business. As far as the Antelope Hills were concerned, the Cross Bar, Triangle X and the Wyoming Cattlemen's Association had set a date in early October for the fall roundup. The smaller outfits, of which Bligh's was the smallest, necessarily had to wait for that event. McCall's Double X cattle had ranged, or been driven two days' ride around on the south side of the hills.

But Jim and Andrew came upon an increasing number of branding fires, many of which must have been built by perfectly honest cowmen in the pursuit of their work. It was impossible to tell anything about them. On a few occasions, however, they had happened upon cowboys burning brands. These men had complaints of their own. They were losing cows and calves, as they had always lost them, but not in numbers that warranted any procedure such as Bligh's men were engaged in. This was the feature that made the case all but hopeless. What could two riders, one of them crippled and the other inexperienced, do in a big country where they could not find half the N.B. cattle in a month of searching? Nevertheless, up in the canyons, in the rough thickets and rocky fastnesses which they did get into, they came upon enough dead cows to make them sick and furious. These days the sky was black with buzzards and there was no choice of canyons over which the birds of prey hovered.

"Too slick fer us," said Jim one day, as he and Andrew rode the homeward trail. "They must have a lookout with a pair of glasses. He spots us long before we get near the canyons. He tips them off an' they ride somewhere else."

"How much are we losing, Jim?" queried Andrew, gloomily. He used the plural pronoun unconsciously, identifying himself with Bligh and his old stockman.

"Wal, thet's impossible to say. I hate to figger on it. But at least a few calves an' cows a day. Cows daid an' calves branded. Say two hundred dollars' loss every day. An' thet's low."

Andrew cursed through clenched teeth. Between McCall and these rustlers, Bligh would be ruined before the snow fell. There did not appear to be any redress. It was ridiculous to call on the law when Bligh's two riders could not prove anything except the presence of dead cows.

"What's to be done?" queried Andrew.

"Wal, if the worst comes, we'll go to farmin'," replied Fenner, with a sigh.

"Will you tell Bligh?"

"Let's hold off a while yet, Andy. We might ketch this *hombre* Reed, an' if we do we'll make it so damned hot for him thet he'll quit. An' he's runnin' this two-bit rustlin'."

"Will we hale him into court?"

"Hell, no! Thet'd do no good an' jest cost the boss more money. We'll try some old time Arizony medicine on thet *hombre*."

"Jim, let's camp out for a week, hiding all the time. Leave the ranch after dark, so they can't spot us on the way up."

"Not a bad idee. I'll figger it over."

When they rode up out of the river bottom, to pass the corrals and the barn, Jim who was ahead, reined in his mount.

"Look there, Andy," he said, pointing toward Andrew's cabin on the bank. "You shore ain't makin' any hay with Martha Ann these days!"

Andrew did not need to look, but he did. It was Sunday afternoon, and he knew what to expect. One reason why he rode on Sundays as well as on week days was to avoid seeing Martha with her admirers. On this occasion, she was evidently playing tag around his cabin with several boys. Three cars were parked in front of the ranch house. Andrew heard a shriek of gay laughter.

"Andy, damn if I wouldn't do somethin'," said the old Arizonian, doggedly.

"What about, Jim?"

"Wal, if I was you, I'd either fall in with this outfit of youngsters an' play their game, or I'd bust it up."

Andrew dismounted without a reply, and set to unsaddling his horse. For the day, at least, he had been free of the state of mind engendered by Martha Ann Dixon. It came back now. He walked slowly toward his cabin, to find the spacious front porch occupied by Martha and her friends, among whom were Nellie Glemm and her brother Tom, a girl named Bradshaw, whom he had met before, two young fellows whose faces were familiar, and Texas Jack Haynes.

"Hello, Andrew," called Martha, waving. "We've been dancing and picnicking on your front porch. Hope you don't mind!"

"Evening, Martha, and everybody. You're quite welcome, if you don't mind my ablutions."

"Andrew, you're gettin' to be the ridin'est cowpuncher," said Nellie Glemm. "Any old day and Sunday, too. You're missin' a lot, Mister."

"I dare say I am," replied Andrew slowly. He was dog tired, and the bewitching excited face of Martha, the glad light in her amber eyes, and the smile that she seemed to have for everybody but him kept smoldering in him a jealousy against which he was powerless. He removed the grime of his long hot ride, and went inside to change his shirt, while the young people kept on with their games.

Presently Martha Ann called through the doorway: "Are you presentable, cowboy? May I come in?"

"I'd hardly shock *you*. Come along," he replied.

She stood framed in the doorway, a perfect picture of joyous youth and beauty. Slowly she entered, and as she did so it seemed to Andrew that she lost something of her radiance.

"Andrew, please don't mind my taking possession of your cabin," she said. "There are some nice old people calling on Uncle. We were being rather noisy, so I brought my company over here."

"Why should I mind, Martha?" he asked.

"I thought—because Texas is here," she replied hurriedly. "Nellie brought him out. I've seen him, of course, since—since. . . . He seems to want to be friendly, Andrew. Will you meet him halfway?"

"For your sake?" asked Andrew quickly.

"Be yourself," she retorted, flushing. "Not for mine—or yours. But for *his.*"

"Oh, I see. Still on the reform job?"

"Andrew, you'd make an angel curse," she answered, glaring at him. "Forget it. Go out and break some more of his ribs."

"Gosh! Did I mess him up that bad? I'm sorry."

But Martha was hurrying out the front door, evidently on her way to the ranch house. Andrew presented himself on the porch and made himself agreeable. They were pleasant, wholesome young people, and excepting Texas, a little shy in his presence, yet obviously eager to know him better. When the supper bell rang they ran pellmell for the house, leaving him and Texas to follow.

"Jack, I hope you didn't come out to hold me to my word," said Andrew with a smile.

"What aboot?"

"That gun fight we damned near had."

"Aw, I thought better of thet, Bonnin'," drawled Texas. "It'd been oot on' oot murder. I'd had to beat it, leavin' Martha with a wuss name than she's already got."

"Very considerate of you, cowboy," replied Andrew coldly.

"Not at all. An' don't git sore. These range folks have nothin' to do but talk aboot each other. An' the women don't savvy Martha. Why, I heahed they reckoned she was thick with Smoky Reed, an' thet was why you licked him."

"It wasn't. But that's just as well," said Andrew curtly.

"Wal, I don't know. If this panther-eyed kid would behave herself I reckon thet turrible beatin' you gave Smoky would keep other fellars kinda shy. But Martha does the damnedest things anyone ever heahed of."

"What has she done now?" asked Andrew with a groan.

"Wal, it do beat hell. What do you call them night duds girls wear nowadays? Paji-bers, somethin' like."

"Pajamas. Eastern girls wear them during the day now. They're all the rage for the seashore or for lounging about. Bright colors, very pretty, and modest, too, believe me, compared to former styles."

"Ahuh. Wal, I don't give a damn aboot thet. This heah is Wyomin'. An' when Martha rode Jem Hart's pinto down Main Street the other day when it was crowded—in them flimsy paja-mas—wal, no circus could have beat thet.''

''Good Lord!'' gasped Andrew.

''She didn't even know Jem. Piled on to his hawse in front of the Glemms', an' jest rode off. She damn near got throwed, too. Thet was what jarred me. I gave Martha fits aboot it, called her good an' plenty. She swore she meant to ride oot of town, instead of down Main Street. You know Glemm's is at the end of town. But the blasted pinto run off with her.''

''How on earth did she come to wear pajamas?'' asked Andrew, helplessly.

''Wal, the Glemms had a party an' Martha stayed there all night. They slept late next mawnin' an' when the girls got up, then it happened. The wust of it, for Martha anyhow, was when Jem Hart reckoned thet stunt entitled him to get free with Martha.''

''Get free? My God!—What the devil did she do?''

''I didn't see it, wuss luck. But the girls told me thet she slapped Jem so hard he lost his hat. Later I called Jem all I could think of, which was wrong of me, seein' we was in a crowded drug store. 'Cause he yelped murder. He'd had a couple of sodas with a kick in them. 'Ahuh, I'm on to you, Tex. Want to hawg all the pettin' to yoreself!' . . . Wal, course I socked him one. He busted a showcase, which cost me fifty bucks. An' now Jem, same as Smoky, is hell-rattlin' agin me an' Martha.''

''It can't be helped,'' said Andrew, as if to himself.

''Nope. I reckon it cain't till some *hombre* kidnaps thet kid, breaks her an' marries her. An' even then I ain't so damned shore.''

''Original idea, to say the least,'' laughed Andrew. ''Speaking of breaking—Martha hinted I'd broken a rib for you, Texas. I hope that isn't true.''

''It shore was. Busted two ribs. I was laid up fer a week. Doggone, I don't savvy why I ain't gunnin' fer you, Bonnin'. Thet girl has worked a turrible change in me. I kinda like you, dammit.''

''Texas, that girl, as you call her, plays hell with *all* men.''

''Shore, but only 'cause she's so infernal sweet. Them eyes! My Gawd, did she ever look at you when she was mad? Thet's wuss fer me than when she's just full of the old Nick. . . . Bonnin', you oughta know you cain't touch thet kid with a ten-foot pole.''

''I don't know about that,'' replied Bonning shortly. ''Texas, I like you, too, in spite of myself. But please don't try to kid me.''

Texas threw up his hands. ''Wal, they're yellin' fer us to come an' get it,'' he drawled. ''Let's eat even if we air in love.''

Something about the cowboy's frank and open friendliness shamed Andrew. His first, almost irresistible impulse had been to rush off, forgo his supper, and as he had done many times before, sulk moodily on his porch or out under the stars. But for once he was able to overcome his moodiness and went in to supper. With Texas' example before him, he drove himself to a gaiety and spontaneity of which he had never believed himself capable. His unusual attitude drew from Martha Ann a look of amazement, and then of grateful and pleased attention. Her obvious pleasure spurred Andrew on. After supper he invited them all over to his cabin, and as the night was cool he started a roaring fire in the big open fireplace, around which the company sat in a circle with no other light save the ruddy blaze. They popped corn, and passed from merry badinage to storytelling.

It may not have added to Andrew's enjoyment that when his turn came he was well aware of Texas' close proximity to Martha Ann, and that the cowboy had his arm round her in the shadow. But so well did Bonning have his emotions under control that he did not even appear to notice.

He told a story of a famous football game, during which in reality he had sat on the side lines, but which he now related as if he had actually participated. The bitterness of the memory of his failure in college coupled with the prescience of a deeper failure here in the West lent his tale a vital and compelling interest which held his little audience spellbound. Once, at least, he was aware that he was holding the interest of the amber-eyed girl from Chicago.

"Doggone!" ejaculated Texas, the only one to break the silence. "Now I savvy why Bonnin' is like a mud turtle full of chain lightnin'."

Only Martha failed to join in the laugh that followed Texas' remark, as her thoughtful eyes were fixed upon the narrator.

Another week went by. Andrew rode the range four days, spent one day in town, and the weekend at the ranch. Looking backward on the Sunday night after the young people had gone, it seemed the hardest week of all since his arrival in Wyoming. The longest, fiercest riding had piled evidence upon evidence without the necessary proofs. In town there had been rumors that he was an upstart Easterner bent upon undermining the good name of certain Wyoming cowmen. Might seemed to be right on that range. Bligh could not pay his bills and Andrew was faced with the problem of a definite decision as to his future action.

On this late Sunday night as he sat smoking before the dying embers of his fire, and watched them glow and fade, two indisputable facts stood out from that eventful day and night in town, and the previous unforgettable weekend at the ranch. Both had to do with Martha Ann. The whole world seemed to revolve around her now.

He realized beyond further doubt that he was caught in the toils of her charm for better or worse, surely the latter. He had watched her for hours on end, when she had not even been aware of his presence. She had improved during her sojourn in Wyoming. Her face now had a clear golden glow, her eyes a wondrous luster, her cheeks a wild-rose flush, her lips an alluring sweetness. But her physical loveliness was only a small part of her charm. It was intangible, impossible to define. He thought of her smile, of her whimsical laugh, of her quaint gestures, and the little graces peculiar only to her. He thought of her sincere interest in all her uncle's troubles; and her voice, her words, and the touch of her hands. He thought of her friendliness. He could not deny the evidence of his eyes and ears. She liked everybody. People, just so long as they did not oppose or criticize her, were tremendously interesting to her. Martha Ann gave unstintingly of her time, her self, her friendliness, her liking to anybody who happened along. She could not go on an errand in town, to the post office, anywhere, without scraping acquaintance with someone. She was attracted by anything and everybody that she saw. She was quick to take the side of anyone maligned, especially if that person was not present.

This gracious side of Martha Ann proved itself to Andrew without her knowledge. But when she knew that he was present, then it seemed that she went out of her way to show the other side of her nature. If possible, she added something to the coquetry with which she had subjugated the youth back at the hotel in Nebraska. At the last dance in town she had been the gayest, wildest creature of a madcap group of girls whom she had inspired. She had verged dangerously close upon the immodest. He had been the miserable witness of her gay, roguish, seductive and resisting struggle with Texas, during which, in the end, she had been soundly kissed on the cheek and neck. She ran to be pursued. She denied only to be more desired. She played a game, with that side of her nature, which to Andrew could have only one interpretation.

And it was beginning to interfere with Andrew's work, peace of mind, happiness, hope for the future and his waking and sleeping hours. This he confessed to the dying embers of his fire, as the autumn wind moaned under the eaves of his cabin. It did not make any difference what Martha Dixon was, how many good and bad sides she had, what she did—he was lost, his future as well as his past. His failures in the East had only been steppingstones, but a failure here would be the end of Andrew Bonning. And without Martha Ann, life would not be worth living. That was the decision he made during his lonely vigil that cold, windy autumn night.

The next day Jim took Andrew off on a long ride to the headwaters of a creek, where in deep, dark pools under golden-leaved trees they fished for trout. Fishing was a passion with the old Arizonian, all the more so because of the little opportunity to indulge in it. They found few signs of N.B. cattle, but they had a day that gave the younger man a chance to forget his troubles. The streams, the silence of the lonely hills, the hard ride and the hard fare, the contact with nature that had awakened in him an endurance he had never suspected—these all contributed to a peace of mind which he had not felt for days.

On the way home Jim Fenner rode beside Andrew a long while in silence.

"Son, what's most important just now?" he queried, at last.

"With whom?"

"Wal, with Bligh, me an' Sue, an' you?"

"I hardly know, Jim. The cattle problem, I should say, because it's our living."

"No, it's thet girl."

"Girl!" echoed Andrew in surprise.

"Shore. Martha. She's upset us plumb bad. Thet ain't nothin' agin Martha. She's just like a young filly, feelin' her oats. I reckon Gawd Almighty is to blame fer it. It gets me, Andy. You know what the Bible says about a woman: 'Turrible as any army approachin' with banners!' . . . Wal, it is plumb so. I can remember the feelin's I had when I courted Sue over forty years ago. She was only eighteen. An' had a flock of beaus. . . . But to git back to Martha—"

"What are you driving at?" demanded Andrew gruffly.

"Wal, I want to give you a hunch."

"Thanks, old-timer. But judging what it might be from your eloquent preamble, I don't believe I want it."

"Son, thet girl really cares fer you," replied Fenner imperturbably.

"What girl?"

"Martha Ann!"

"Nonsense!"

"She does. I'm shore of it."

"You're loco."

"She watches you when you don't know it. I've seen her. Sue's seen her. We've seen her turn away from the window with the wistfulest look in her eyes."

"Yes. She's got the eyes, old-timer," interposed Andrew. "They'd fool any man, even more—er—an old jackass of a romancer like you."

"All right. I ain't tellin' you any more thet I seen. But take my hunch. She cares for you some way or other."

"You're crazy as a hyena. She hates me because I saw through her from the very first. Because I wouldn't fall for her."

"You was in idgit fer not fallin'. You had a chance to win thet girl. You have one yet, if you don't stay bull haided. What do you care how many fellers air after her—or what she's let them do?"

"What do I care?" repeated Andrew thoughtfully.

"She's wuth carin' fer, an' she needs carin' fer," replied Jim. "If you was half the man I thought you was, you'd take the bull by the horns, an' when you get back to the ranch tonight, you'd go right up to her and tell her how you feel."

It was dark when they reached the ranch. Andrew built a fire on his hearth before he washed up for supper. Then as a man plunging toward a precipice, he made for the house. Jim was eating alone in the kitchen, waited upon by Sue. Andrew did not do justice to the good supper, and did not respond to Jim's or Sue's efforts at conversation. Just when he was ready to rise from the table, Martha's fresh young voice could be heard singing in another room, and Jim kicked him in the leg. Andrew got up, stamped out, and going round to Martha's door, he rapped.

"That you, Uncle?" she replied.

"No."

"Jim?"

"No."

"Oh, it's Texas," cried a tantalizing, laughing voice. "Come in."

"It's Andrew."

"Excuse *me*. What do *you* want?"

"You."

"Indeed. How amazing!"

"Come out here," ordered Andrew.

After an interval the door opened, sending a broad beam of lamplight into the darkness, and exposing Martha, dressed in a pair of brightly flowered pajamas.

"Where are you?" she called.

"Shut the door."

She did so, leaving the step in darkness.

"Say, who was your personal slave this time last—"

He cut her short with one of his swift moves. As he caught her up in his arms, she cried out in protest. He set out for his cabin, carrying her as if she were an infant in his arms.

"Oh-h! Andrew! Put me down!"

He gazed down at the disheveled head in the crook of his elbow, at the big staring eyes, black in the starlight.

"Let me go!" she cried, suddenly beginning to struggle frantically. But when he tightened his arms about her she could scarcely move. Suddenly she ceased and relaxed, limp as an empty sack. "Andrew—what do—you mean?" she faltered.

He made no reply and when he looked down at her again her eyelids hid her eyes. He felt her warm body quivering in his arms. The softness of her, the warmth and fragrance, the appalling sweetness of her worked upon him so powerfully that when he entered his cabin, he dropped his burden on his bunk, and breathing heavily, backed away.

She lay there while he went to the grate to kick the smoldering sticks and put on some fresh ones. After a moment he got his breath back. The blaze brightened, lighting up the room. Martha sat up in a daze, her face white, her eyes large and strange in the firelight.

"Andrew! . . . What in the world has got into you? What are you doing with me?"

He stepped over to look down upon her.

"What do you think?" he demanded, leaning down.

"You look so—so terrible . . . I know I deserve . . . but you wouldn't—"

"No, I wouldn't—whatever it is you fear," he interrupted her. "I suppose you think I might treat you as you deserve. I wish to God I were beast enough to maul you good and plenty. To teach you that at last you had fallen into the hands of one guy who wasn't nothing but wax in your hands! . . . But I'm not. I'm—"

Then he stopped, unable to continue. The sight of her white, frightened face robbed him of his anger; checked him with the sudden thought that he might have completely misjudged this girl. He stepped back to the fire, kicked the sticks again, then paced to and fro with long, nervous strides, until he had recovered the stern purpose which had driven him to fetch her to his cabin.

"Martha, will you marry me?" he asked.

"Marry you?" she repeated incredulously, staring at him as if she were dreaming.

"Yes. That is why I so unceremoniously packed you over here . . . to ask you to be my wife!"

"Your—wife!" She seemed to undergo a sudden transformation. "Why are you asking me to—to—?"

"I don't blame you for asking that question. It does seem absurd, after my attitude toward you . . . but listen, Martha. I have just lately found myself. I think I must have fallen in love with you that very first night on the road, when I rescued you from the tramps. But I didn't know it. All I thought I knew was what a beautiful, unforgettable, wayward child you were. And because I had been hurt back east, by my own people, by life, by a woman I fancied I loved, I was intolerant and suspicious of your hitchhiking. And out here that feeling increased all the time, while I have grown so jealous that I was about ready to commit murder. While you were slaying these cowboys with your eyes—and your wiles—well, I fell too. And I have fallen for good and all, Martha. My rudeness to you, my indifference, have been simply because I was so desperately hurt by your flirtations that I could not be myself. Jealousy is a terrible thing. But it brought me to a realization of what was wrong. I have known for some time, dear, that I loved you. And it has taken such possession of me that I can think of nothing but that I adore you, I know now what a wonderful person you really are, and I want to marry you."

"Andrew Bonning! You love me like that?" she whispered.

"Yes. But words are futile. Won't you marry me, my darling? . . . Let me prove—"

She moved as if to lift her arms up to him. But then something like a sudden shadow chased the glory from her eyes. Andrew felt all love and hope and bliss trembling in the balance. He saw the quickening of intelligence over emotion—the cold reasoning that inhibited her.

"You ask me to marry you, believing me a hitchhiking, wild girl, tramping the road in order to meet men—to have adventures—to get kicks?" she queried, low and tense, her anger gathering like a sudden summer storm.

"Please don't think of that any more," entreated Andrew hastily, feeling the ground slip from under him. "Forget what I thought. I will forget it, too."

"Never. And if you are on the level, Andrew Bonning, you will tell me the truth. No man could change so completely or so suddenly."

"I would not lie to you," he said.

"You had nothing but contempt for that hitchhiking venture of mine, didn't you?" she demanded passionately.

"Yes."

"You believed I made it only to get out alone—away from home—from parents and friends—out where I could answer to some wild instinct to be free, to meet strange boys and men—who would never see me again and with whom I could be natural—to flirt, to get a kick out of life, and all the rest of the modern stuff you hate so strangely?"

"Yes, I am afraid I did," he replied, huskily.

"You think it still?"

"Martha, there has not been anything to change it."

"You thought I was a liar, a cheat, a rotten little hussy?"

"Not the last, Martha, I swear it. Just a crazy unthinking kid. You don't know yourself. You've two sides, dear."

"Don't hedge, Andrew. . . . I *know* what you thought. You made it perfectly plain to me. But I'm going to make you confess it . . . to face me with it. You believed me just no good, didn't you?"

"On the contrary I believed there was a great deal of good in you," he parried.

"Well, then—a bad girl?"

"Hardly bad. Wayward, perhaps heedless—"

"I know what you thought then, and what you think still," she interrupted, rising with white face from the bunk.

Andrew reached for her hands, but she put them behind her back.

"You're making it damned hard," he said. "Since you force me—I confess that I thought you had been pretty wild—and yet I hoped you hadn't. You'll have to allow for the thoughts of a man who had been an idler and a failure, which I was when you met me first, an Easterner, fresh from the disillusionment of my sister and my fiancée, who have a free and easy view on life. That side of me took you for the necking, lap-sitting type. But deep in me, at variance with all I had known and experienced, there was a conflicting still small voice, weak enough and pitiful, God knows, that tried to convince me that you were the innocent and gallant girl I love.''

"Andrew Bonning, I—I wouldn't marry you if you were the last man on earth," she blazed.

"If you really mean that, then you might have said so at once and spared me this."

"Did you ever spare me? Have you ever spared me any of your scorn and contempt?" she demanded, standing closer to him, with white, angry face uplifted to meet his gaze. "Andrew Bonning, I ran away from home to escape the very things of which you have accused me. I had been driven to sheer disgust by young men who wanted me, by marriage or otherwise. And college men like you had fed me up so sickeningly on love—their kind of love. What did they care for my fears, my needs? . . . So I ran away. Do you imagine if I had wanted *that* kind of kick, I would have had to hitchhike the highways with farmer boys, garage mechanics, traveling men, tourists and what not? No, I wanted to get away from all such rottenness, and with one single exception, I did escape it. I liked most all the boys and men who gave me lifts. I liked *you*, first off, until you froze me with your damned superiority. And that night at the hotel I flirted with a perfectly nice boy just to show you, to play up to your idea of me. To satisfy your morbid distrust of modern girls! And out here I have done that— and more—and worse, for the same and identical reason. Do you imagine I had no pride? I would have died before letting you see my shame, my humiliation. I let those boys hold my hand and clasp my waist—I even let Texas Jack kiss me—I endured contacts repugnant to me for no reason but to foster your vile suspicions. Did I get a kick out of *that?* I'll say I did! But you would never have known if you had not proposed to me tonight. Your offer of marriage squares you with me. It is the best any man can do for a woman. I suspect that you hoped, perhaps, to reform me. But there is nothing to reform, as you shall see from now on. I thank you, Andrew, but I must decline the honor."

"Martha! You're being rather hard on me! How could I . . . Don't go! Please!"

"No!" she almost screamed, running across the floor.

"You must care a little—or you—"

"No!" she cried from the doorway.

"Darling!" he beseeched.

"No!" came mockingly from the blackness outside. She was gone. Andrew sank down on the bunk she had so shortly vacated. The lovely scent of her still was in the room. The wind moaned under the eaves. The dead leaves on the cottonwood rustled on the roof. And the shadows deepened in the cabin. A familiar specter stalked out of the gloom. It was the stark, gaunt, ghost of another failure. Only this time it was life itself that had failed him.

12

WITH the coming of morning, after a few hours of sleep, the new savage spirit that had been lately born in Andrew reasserted itself. This spirit was based on pride. He had humbled himself to tell Martha of his love for her. Now he would put that love forever aside and he would give himself wholly to saving the fortunes of Bligh.

In order to forget he had to have ceaseless, exhausting action in the open, privation to undergo and problems to solve, something to fight physically and alone. With horse and meager fare, Andrew took to the hills.

Boldly he rode into cow camps at the eastern end of the hills where no N.B. stock had yet ranged, and made known his errand.

"You ridin' fer this newcomer, Bligh?" asked an old cattleman.

"Yes."

"I don't see no runnin' iron on your saddle."

"We haven't branded a calf this summer."

"How come?"

"My partner is a cripple and I'm a tenderfoot. There are riders who get to our stock first."

"Ahuh. I see you air packin' guns," returned the other, with a speculative glint in his eye, taking Andrew in from head to foot.

"Yes. And if I catch any cowman burning brands on Bligh's cattle, I'm going to use a gun."

"You the feller who licked Cal Brice an' his outfit at the rodeo?"

"I'm that fellow."

"Is it true that you blamed Reed fer shootin' at you an' licked him fer thet?"

"It is. And here's his trademark on my scalp," returned Andrew, exposing the long red welt.

"Close shave, youngster. What makes you think Reed shot you?"

"I don't think it. I know."

"Wal, thet's short an' sweet. Git down an' come in. Grub is aboot cooked."

Half a dozen cowboys stood and sat around the campfire. A chuck wagon stood nearby. Horses grazed along the grassy flat.

"Boy, this hyar is Bligh's one rider—no old-timer as you can see," announced the cattleman. "Wyomin' hasn't done so well by him, an' some of us ought to be ashamed. He's the feller who busted Cal Brice's outfit. Partic'lar sore at Smoky Reed fer shootin' at him. He's lookin' fer Smoky or any other rider who's appropriatin' N.B. cattle."

They were civil, but not friendly. Andrew ate with them, absorbed considerable from this first contact with a range outfit. The older man evidently was the boss, and owner of the K Bar stock.

"Thanks. I'll be rolling along," said Andrew, when he had finished his meal.

"Packin' light," said his host. "You're welcome to a bed with us."

"No, thank you. I'll be hittin' the hay out here some place," replied Andrew as he mounted.

"Hope you don't mind me bein' curious?"

"Not at all."

"Is your crippled pardner a cowman?"

"Old-timer from Arizona."

"Wal, he'll learn the ropes hyar pronto. An' what you want to learn, youngster, is not to take this cattle stealin' too much to heart. So long as the range ain't fenced there'll be some stock missin'. All the cattlemen have the same thing to deal with. An' they just don't notice it."

"But in Bligh's case it can't be overlooked. He's a poor man. He had only a small herd to begin with, and because he can't afford enough cowboys to watch the stock these rustlers are taking advantage of it."

"Thet's different. Tell Bligh to throw in with some other cattleman."

"He can't because he made a deal of that nature with McCall. Then he changed his mind, which made McCall sore. He's taking the case to court."

"McCall? Runs the Double X. Wal, if I was Bligh, I'd buy or trade off."

"I'll tell him. So long."

Several of the cowboys waved. When Andrew had ridden a short distance, one of them called after him. "Work the big draws on the south."

That seemed like a reasonable and friendly gesture. Andrew rode on until sunset overtook him. Then he made camp beside a rocky stream. For half the night he was awake, alternately freezing and replenishing his fire. The still cold, the lonely hills, the white, watching stars calmed his spirit, but were not conducive to sleep. Next day, from daylight until dark, he rode the slopes and draws with which he and Jim had become familiar. The third day took him to the south side of the hills where cattle were more numerous. He saw several riders in the distance but did not come up with them. Late in the day while sitting beside his

little campfire he heard the thud of hoofs. Soon a horseman rode up. It was Jim
Fenner.

"Howdy, Andrew," he said, as he laboriously dismounted. "Been trackin'
you since noon."

"Anything wrong at the ranch?" asked Andrew quickly.

"No more'n usual. Bligh jest mopes around. Martha moons on yore porch.
An' Sue keeps agoin. . . . Run across anythin'?"

"I met the K Bar outfit. The boss was pretty decent," replied Andrew, and
related the circumstance of their meeting.

"Wal, he's right. I tell you, Andy, nobody can see our side of it. We're jest
too small potatoes."

"So I've gathered lately. Jim, if I'm ever to be a rancher, is this good
training?"

"Best in the world, son. But how'n hell you'll ever make a rancher by stickin'
to Bligh, I can't see. We're gonna be awful poor pronto."

Andrew bent over the fire to rake the red embers. "Jim, I had it out with
Martha. I packed her over to my cabin and asked her to marry me. She gave
me the damnedest acing any fellow ever got."

"What fer?"

"For once believing she was no good."

"Wal, you desarved thet," replied the Arizonian bluntly.

"So it appears," rejoined Andrew. "She declined the honor."

"Ahuh. Wal, she's crazy about you jest the same."

"You crazy old fool!" burst out Andrew derisively.

"Shore, I'm old, anyhow. An' I feel it tonight. . . . Say, would you like some
dried beef broiled over them coals, some biscuits an' coffee an' a piece of cake?"

"Jim, my spirit cries 'No!' But my flesh is awful weak."

"Wal, it's a way of the flesh. When I seen you hadn't fetched any camp tools
I reckoned I'd better hit yore trail."

"How did you find it out?"

"I didn't. Martha did thet. An' she told me."

"Yeah? . . . What'd she say?"

"Wal, she says, 'Andrew has run away empty-handed from home just to get
a kick and because he likes to sulk. I hope he starves to death!' "

"Kindly little soul!" said Andrew with a mirthless laugh. Yet his sore heart
warmed even to the sarcastic remembrance. She, too, had been terribly hurt.

"But Martha wrapped up the cake. Andy, I've discovered something pretty
damned cute about thet kid."

"Only *some*thing?" scoffed Andrew.

"Her bark is wuss than her bite. . . . Wal, let's eat. Kick up yore fire. An'
fetch some water while I open this pack."

A cheery crackling blaze, a hot meal and a companion drove away Andrew's melancholy thoughts. Fenner, however, did not appear to be in a talkative mood, and soon after the chores were finished he spread his blanket in the thick grass and rolled up in it without even removing his boots. Andrew paced to and fro under the stars. He was not ready yet to talk to Jim and Bligh about a new ranching venture, but he had pretty well made up his mind that he would make them a proposition sooner or later.

Clouds drifted over the sky, and an unusual mildness in the night air presaged a change of weather. The range needed rain. Many of the valleys that ran up into the hills were as dry as bone dust. Cattle had begun to work down toward the river, along which they would range during the winter.

A fine misty rain set in, sending Andrew back to camp. He dragged saddle, blankets and slicker under a thick bushy cedar, and made his bed there. The coyotes were unusually noisy. He lay snug in his covert and listened. The damp wind blew under the cedar across his face, and drops of rain filtered through and pattered down on him. The thin, high cadence of the insects seemed to carry a knell of passing autumn. The snow would soon sweep down this draw and winds would howl through the cedars.

Andrew got snatches of slumber during the night, and happened to be asleep when dawn broke. Jim called him. The morning was raw, dull and cloudy, with a light rain still falling.

"Rustle a fire, son, while I fetch in the hosses," said Jim. "You can strip a lot of bark from under the dry side of the cedars. Never hard to build fires in cedar country. I reckon a cedar is the range man's favorite tree, leastways in high country."

They rode out of the protected draw into the teeth of wind and sleet that were disagreeable to face. The range looked dreary and gray. For ten miles along the south slope cattle were few and far between. They worked two draws together, and then coming to a wide valley they separated, Andrew riding across to the east side. This evidently must be one of the big draws the K Bar cowboy had told him to investigate. It was unfamiliar to him, being farther to the east than he had ridden until this time. Grass was good in patches, water was running down the gulch, and there was a plentiful sprinkling of cattle of various brands. The N.B. mark appeared conspicuous by its absence.

Andrew rode through cedar groves and thickets of oak, across grassy parks and over rocky areas, up to where the alley narrowed to a canyon box, and travel became rough. He turned back presently and took to Jim's side. Farther down he met a considerable movement of cattle that evidently had been run that day. Fringes of thickets alternated with meadows. Andrew saw some steers running, and then he heard a distant shout. He galloped across a flat and worked through a wooded stretch to emerge into a small park. His quick eye spotted riderless horses, and then two men on foot, close together in a proximity that excited his suspicions. A thin column of smoke rising near the men confirmed Andrew's surmise. At last Jim had rounded up Reed or one of his thieving partners.

They were just outside the rocky timbered cape that jutted out from the north slope. Andrew soon reached them and leaped off his horse. Jim was holding a gun on a man who stood with his hands above his head. Near the smoking fire lay a bound calf, still panting desperately. The rustler had evidently been disturbed in the initial part of his branding procedure, for only one mark was visible upon the red hide of the calf.

"Andy, there was two of them," said Jim. "The other was ridin' a calf down when I busted out of the brush. He rode off. . . . Take this feller's gun."

Andrew located the butt of a weapon protruding from under the man's belt. It had been hidden by his coat.

"Cut thet calf loose, an' tie this *hombre's* hands behind his back," ordered Jim.

This order Andrew performed under pressure of excitement that made him clumsy, but he got the job done speedily.

"Rustler, walk ahead of me," curtly commanded Fenner. "I'm gonna introduce you to an old-time Arizony way of treatin' cattle thieves."

Andrew followed them, leading his horse, considerably disturbed by Jim's threat. The Arizonian had a flinty look. He kept punching his gun into the back of the rustler who shrank visibly at each thrust. Jim halted under the largest tree along that wall of timber.

"Bonnin', take yore rope off yore saddle, drop the noose over this gent's head, an' toss the other end over thet branch there."

"My God! Are you going to hang him?" cried Andrew incredulously.

"Shore I am. Rustle now."

"But Jim! You can't be serious. . . . Give the poor devil a good hiding, then let him go."

"Ahuh. To go right back stealin' our stock? Not much! There's two daid cows of ours in thet brush. I seen one, an' I heerd two shots. I'm gonna put a stop to this rustlin' once and fer all."

"To *hang* him! . . . Jim, that's taking the law into our own hands! We'd go up for manslaughter, if not murder. But even if we could get away with it—I couldn't be a party to such—such—"

"You blasted tenderfoot!" yelled Fenner, so fiercely that Andrew stood shocked. "Pitch me yore rope."

Andrew made haste to comply. The man turned deathly pale. He was not young. His haggard face had a bluish cast under the paling skin. He had thin, tobacco-stained lips, a beaked nose, and hard, glinting eyes. Jim made him turn his back, and sheathing the gun, in a twinkling he had done what he had ordered

Andrew to do. Then he strode round in front of the rustler and picking up the end of the rope he hauled it taut over the branch.

"If you want to talk, do it pronto," shouted Fenner in a threatening voice.

"I'm a poor man," replied the rustler hoarsely. "Been driven to steal. An' my cattle gets stole, too. Stringin' me up fer—"

"Who's backin' you?"

"Backin' me? Nobody. What d'ye mean?"

"You been hired to rustle?"

"No, sir. I won't hide behind thet. I done my—"

"You lyin' *hombre!* Up you go!"

Fenner hauled on the lasso. The man let out a strangled cry. His head stretched with the knot of the noose biting into his leathery neck. When he had been drawn up until his toes just supported his body Fenner held him there a moment, then slowly relaxed the rope. The man sagged back flat-footed, his mouth gaping, his eyes starting from their sockets.

"How'd you like thet?" demanded Jim.

"Fer—Gawd's—sake!" gasped the rustler. "Let me—off—"

"Who hired you to do this dirty work?"

"Nobody. I—mean—"

"Wal, mebbe I can help you remember," interrupted the Arizonian, and with a heave he drew the man higher still, until his shaking limbs appeared to stretch. Jim held him in that position until the man's tongue stuck out, his eyes rolled until only the whites showed and his face turned purple.

"Jim, let him down!" yelled Andrew frantically, charging in to snatch the rope from Fenner's hands. Andrew again let Jim's victim down. He fell to the ground, and was choking when Andrew tore the noose free. The hissing intake of his breath assured Andrew that the man still was able to breathe.

"Spoiled my necktie party," growled Fenner.

"You bloodthirsty Arizonian!" cried Andrew, almost beside himself. "I've a mind to bat you a couple."

The rustler sat up, sweating freely, and rubbing his neck with unsteady hands. Color began to creep back into his ghastly face.

"Boss," he said huskily, "you're on the wrong scent. Nobody's hirin' me. I been stealin' a few calves on my own hook. My name's Hall Pickens."

"Where you live?"

"My homestead is about twenty miles east, in Spring Canyon."

"You a homesteader?"

"Yes. Been hyar four years. Jest proved up on my property."

"You married?"

"Sure. An' got two kids. I've had a tough row to hoe."

"You swear nobody hired you?"

"I'm tellin' you honest."

"Who was the rider with you?"

"I ain't tellin'," replied Pickens.

"Happen to know a cowpuncher named Smoky Reed?"

"Don't recall thet name."

"All right. I could put you in jail fer this day's work. But if you'll agree to lay off N.B. stock from now on, I'll let you off."

"I'll agree to anythin'," returned Pickens gratefully.

"My name's Fenner. An' this is Andy Bonnin'. We ride fer Nick Bligh. He runs the N.B. Have you seen many cattle wearin' thet brand?"

"Good many steer, but mighty few cows."

"Have you been wise to another outfit workin' this cow-killin' game?"

"I been suspicious of some fellers from the Platte River country."

"Humph! None from the Sweetwater?"

"No. Course I know the Cross Bar an' the Wyomin' outfits across the Hills."

"Andy, toss his gun out there in the grass. . . . Pickens, you beat it. An' take a hunch from an old-timer. Fer the sake of yore wife an' kids quit the cow-killin' game."

The homesteader hastened to snatch up his gun and run for his horse. He was soon out of sight.

"You didn't really mean to hang him?" queried Andrew.

"No. I wanted to throw a scare into him an' make him confess he was ridin' fer McCall. But we was barkin' up the wrong tree."

"You had me scared stiff."

"Wal, I've seen many a rustler kick at the air, Andy. . . . I felt kinda sorry fer this *hombre*. Pore as Job's turkey. Did you see his feet? Had a boot on one an' a shoe on the other, both full of holes."

"He looked pretty seedy."

"Reckon you an' me will be scarecrows, too, like him, before long. . . . Andy, let's go home."

"Home!" echoed Andrew, startled.

"Shore. It ain't sense fer us to waste no more time hopin' to ketch Smoky Reed in the act. Probably he's quit fer a spell. Anyway they got about all of our young stock, that's a shore bet."

"When will we know for certain what we have left?"

"After the roundup."

"I hate to quit, Jim."

"We ain't quittin'. We're gonna tackle this game from some other angle. An' I'm damned if I can figger what."

"Okay. Back to the ranch," cried Andrew.

In a sense it seemed to him that Jim's ultimatum was a surrendering to evil forces which they were not strong enough to combat. He gave in only to experience and wisdom. After four hard days and nights with little to eat and no shelter, and the long ride in the face of rain and sleet, wet to the skin, Andrew could not help conjuring up supper at Sue's table, and the comfort of his own open fireplace. Taken all together, his labors at the ranch and his rides in the open during these months had pretty well acquainted him with the life of a cowman. The never-finished manual tasks, the sun and wind and dust, the long rides when the saddle burned, the hours of loneliness, and cold nights sleeping out and the sting of sleet in his face—these physical tests had been welcomed by Andrew, and met, he believed, without discredit to himself. He found in them absolute refuge from the complexes that had tormented him back in the East.

When he rode out of the canyon after Jim, with the hard ice-bitted wind at his back, he hugged something glad and strengthening to his heart. He would make good in the West.

The moment Andrew faced ranchward it all flooded back—the love he had determined to forget—only more tumultuous and demanding after these four harsh days of oblivion. If he had been alone he would have thrown back his head to laugh his scorn to the winds. If the mere thought of seeing Martha again could make his blood surge so madly, how desperately he must love the girl! Just at the thought of seeing her! How could he ever put such a love behind him?

Andrew rode for a long time with his head down, insensible to the wet and cold. And as he rode home he no longer doubted the strength and depth of his love for Martha Ann Dixon. How tragic that the realization had come too late, that she would never be able to forgive or forget his first mistaken estimate of her character. He was paying for that jealousy-inspired conclusion now—and would continue to pay. Yet Andrew was grateful to the fate that had sent him to Wyoming, though he railed at the bitter thought of finding his salvation in exultant, all-satisfying toil of body only to lose it in the scorn of the girl he loved.

Down off the high slopes Andrew and Jim rode into clearing weather. The gray cloud that hung over the hills did not extend to the river bottom. The sun came out to turn the water and the autumn foliage into silver and gold.

"Jim, do you ever take any stock in dreams?" asked Andrew, riding up to a position beside his comrade.

"No, son, I quit dreamin' long ago. Do you still believe in 'em?"

"No, but I can tell you a dream I had."

"Fire away."

"It was about Bligh's ranch. I dreamed we threw in two thousand head of cattle, best of stock, carefully selected for building a big herd and a successful cattle business. A bunch of fine horses from Colorado. You picked out four Arizona cowmen, the best you knew, steady, sober fellows, neither too young nor too old, to handle the stock. You brought in some Mexican farm hands. We built new barns, new corrals, new pens, fenced the pastures, pumped water for irrigation, planted whatever the soil will grow and all the acreage will stand, bought a tractor and truck, a new car—''

"By gorry, when you dream, you shore dream yourself dizzy," declared Jim heartily, as Andrew paused for breath.

"Chickens, pigs—did I include horses? A brace of good hunting dogs, a fine collie or shepherd, shotguns and rifles, saddles, bridles, chaps, spurs—and, oh hell! a lot more stuff!" Out of the corner of his eye Andrew saw the old range man turn to gaze at him, as though he were beginning to doubt his sanity.

"Oh, hell! Shore. An' you forgot a weddin' ring fer Martha."

Andrew landed out of the clouds with a jar.

"No, Jim. I sure didn't dream that," he replied soberly.

"Wal, if you had, I'd said thet was somethin' mighty fine. . . . Andy, I hope you ain't goin' dotty."

"Do I talk dotty?"

"Sorta. You started wal, but you've growed kinda wild. Yore face is red, too. I oughtn't have let you lay out four nights alone. Andrew, have you got a fever?"

"I guess so, come to think of it."

"Wal, you've ketched cold. Thet sudden change from dry to wet is bad. Sue will have to doctor you up a bit."

"Jim, it's not that kind of a fever."

"What kind then?" asked Fenner anxiously. "Is yore haid burnin'?"

"I'm afraid so."

"An' do you ache?"

"Fierce!"

"Hell! You're gonna be sick. Does thet ache ketch you all over?"

"No. Only in one place. . . . But, Jim, tell me, did that pipe dream I had seem far-fetched and impossible to you?"

"Shore, fer us, wuss luck. If we had a little money, though, it wouldn't be, by thunder! Bligh has a thousand acres—wal, he has if McCall doesn't force him off—finest kind of land thet'll raise most anythin'. Andy, we could develop a great ranch, the prettiest one in Wyomin' an' a plumb good money maker. . . . Aw hell! After all, dreams only make you sad."

"Jim, this one will come true. I know it!"

"Huh?" grunted Jim stupidly.

"I have been kidding you, old-timer," cried Andrew joyfully, finding it impossible to react calmly to the thing he had disclosed. "It has been a dream, ever since I got here. And now it's coming true!"

"Andy! You're out of yore haid!"

"No, Jim. I've figured it all out. I've got the cash. I've got enough for all the things I enumerated. And then some left to run things for a couple of years. . . . Lord, I don't see how I kept it from you so long!"

"You got the cash!" yelped Jim.

"Bet your life I have."

"Whar?"

"Under my cabin. Buried deep. Safe."

"Honest, Andy?"

"Absolutely. On my honor, Jim."

"Gawd Almighty! Andy, I always was leery about you. Don't say you're a bank robber or a politician!"

"Not on your life!"

"Whar did you git it?"

"My mother left me an inheritance, Jim."

"An' you're gonna stake Bligh?"

"Bligh and I will be partners."

"An' me?"

"You'll run the ranch. Foreman isn't a good enough job for you. You'll be superintendent!"

Fenner's face worked. He had halted his horse to confront Andrew. The sun had set and dusk was shadowing the trail.

"So thet—was it!" he finally ejaculated weakly, and nodded his lean old head as if to an invisible interrogator.

"What was?"

"All the time—thet was it!"

"Jim, you're the loco one now."

"Andy, somethin' kept me up," replied the Arizonian in a low voice. "I never seen a more hopeless deal than Bligh's. But I never gave up—not since you an' Martha came. I reckoned mebbe it was her sweetness, her gay bossin' me around an' never lettin' me be false to the hope an' youth of her—an' yore comin'—somethin' about you thet I could never figger."

"Whatever it was, I'm glad."

"Andy, the same thing thet called Martha out here called you," averred Fenner solemnly. "An' we old folks have been waitin'. . . . It'll make a new man of Bligh. Sue will be happy an' thet wonderful girl—thet Martha. . . . Aw! she's gonna break her heart now, an' crawl to you on her knees."

"That's where you're wrong," laughed Andrew. "Jim, you're not to tell

Bligh or Sue till we have it all worked out. And the whole deal must be kept absolutely secret from Martha.''

"Aw! to keep such good news!''

"Tough, yes. But I demand it. Let her be curious when the cattle and horses drift in. You will buy her the swellest pony in Wyoming. And saddle, and bridle to match. Get me, Jim?''

"I git you. An', by thunder! that Aladdin geezer never had nothin' on you, Andy. . . . I agree. I swear by you. I'll be dumb. But don't expect me to look down in the mouth while I'm doin' it.''

"Look any way you like. It'll be all the more mysterious. . . . Well, here we are at the barn,'' said Andrew, dismounting with cramped and stiff limbs. "I'm damn near frozen. . . . After supper you come over to my cabin. We'll go over all the plans and settle everything.''

After unsaddling and looking to his horse Andrew went with Jim to the kitchen. By this time it was dark, and the yellow lights from the windows of the house were shining a cheery welcome. Jim went in and Andrew followed.

"For the land's sake!'' exclaimed Sue. "Of all the bedraggled, dirty-faced punchers I ever seen, you two are the worst.''

Andrew bent over the hot stove to warm his red cold hands. The light, the warmth, the steaming kettle and coffee pot, the supper table already set, the familiar fragrance and comfort—these struck Andrew with a stunning realization of how little it took to make a man humble and grateful.

"Andy has had an orful drill, Sue. I had to track him. Whar's the boss an' Martha?''

"Bligh is not so well,'' replied Sue, and then turned to call Martha.

As she opened the door to enter, Andrew felt a lift of his heart. Had only five days elapsed since he had seen her? A glamorous light appeared to surround her lovely face and golden head. Her eyes showed the marks of weeping, but that did not account for the subtle change Andrew felt. She went to Jim, where he sat beside the stove, and put a hand on his shoulder.

"Howdy,'' she said, including both in the greeting. Then she took cognizance of their grimy state, and laughed. "Have you been mining coal? You look it!''

"Lass, I've tracked gophers an' badgers in my day, but fer a shore-enough ground hawg Andy takes the cake,'' drawled Jim.

"How come?'' she inquired quickly, and her eyes, dark in that light, swept from Jim to Andrew.

"Martha, what have you been crying about?'' asked Andrew.

"Uncle Nick,'' she replied forlornly.

"Is he ill?''

"He has worried himself sick over this McCall deal.''

"Anything developed?''

"McCall is going to force Uncle off the ranch."

"Well! That is bad news. Has he gone to court?"

"Not yet, Uncle says."

Andrew filled a lard pail with hot water from the kettle. "I'll run over and clean up. Don't let Jim eat all the grub," he said as he went out. While Andrew strode across to his cabin, and set about starting a fire his thoughts dwelt on the change in Martha Ann's attitude toward him. Her civility came as a surprise. His return could have meant nothing to her. Probably days ago she had relegated him to the long list of the undesired and discarded. Still there had been something—that same old unsatisfied look. He was glowing still with the delight her loveliness had inspired. He made haste to shave and change. The thrill of the new ranch project already had faded. Had he been nursing that dream, and divulged it to Fenner, solely for Martha Dixon?

Soberly Andrew went out into the dark, empty, windy hall of the night. He found himself strangely happy. There was no reason why he should feel at all hopeful as far as Martha was concerned. Had she not passionately scorned him? Had she not declared that she would not marry him if he were the last man on earth? Had he not accepted this decree? Certainly he had not blamed her. Whence, then, this longing to see her, to be in the same room with her? Would she be glad of his return—that he had come back safely? Would she think him brave, strong, courageous to venture forth to run down the rustlers? Jim would lose no time telling that story. Could he ever be a hero in her sight? Had she realized that she had driven him into the wilds where, like a wounded creature, he could hide and lick his wounds? Had she thought of him at all? In that short walk to the kitchen a hundred longing, questioning thoughts besieged him—to see her again, to hear her, to watch the play of her features for that sweet smile, to catch the light of her eyes. And at the very door he hesitated for fear that she would read him as an open page and laugh him to scorn.

Boldly he went in. Martha Ann was alone in the kitchen.

"Oh, I'm sorry to be so late. Where's Jim?"

"He went out to help Sue. I've kept your supper hot."

"Thank you," said Andrew, and sat down, feeling betrayed again. He did not look up while she placed his supper before him. She brushed against his shoulder and once her hand touched his. How easy it would be to jump up from the table and clasp her in his arms. What an idiot a man could be!

"You don't act hungry," she said presently.

"I am, though," he replied hastily, and fell to.

"Jim told us."

"What?" he mumbled.

"About your catching the rustler red-handed, then letting him off because he had a wife and babies. You would!"

"Yeah. But Jim had as much to do with it as I did."

"Andrew, it was very wrong of you to run off alone, without food or bedding," she went on severely. "Uncle was worried. And Sue scolded Jim roundly just now, as if poor Jim were to blame for your wild-goose chase."

"Ha! Wild-goose chase?"

"Yes! You rode off in a huff, like a little boy who hoped to get hurt, perhaps killed, just to make his—mother feel sorry."

"I had suffered a slight—disappointment," returned Andrew, raising his eyes. She stood by the table gazing down upon him with what seemed to be genuine disapproval.

"But suppose you had?" she retorted, flushing. "That is no reason for you to distress Sue, worry Uncle—and—"

"You?"

"Yes, me. . . . I—I suppose I hate you, Andrew. But that didn't keep me from worrying. . . . Once a young fellow shot himself on my account. . . . Oh, it was horrible." There was now a mischievous glint in Martha Ann's eyes.

"What for?" asked Andrew, fully aware that she was improvising as she went.

"Because I—I wouldn't give him a kiss."

"Did he kill himself?"

"No. But that wasn't his fault. And I felt almost as bad as if he had."

"My sympathy is all with him."

"Don't try to make fun of me, Andrew," she rejoined with asperity. "You're no callow youth. You've had real women sweethearts—"

"I had one and she was—all that's modern rolled into one."

"Connie. I'd like to meet her sometime. . . . But, Andrew, just because I— I do not love you—and do hate you—and wouldn't marry you—don't do such a foolish thing like this again. You aren't the type for heroics or for dramatizing yourself! Just to make me sorry! You've probably gotten over your—disappointment already!"

"That's what you think!"

"Now I ask you, Andrew," she expostulated. "If you go play-acting this way, with ruin staring us all in the face, running off to starve and be shot at— won't life around this ranch simply be impossible?"

"I'll say it will."

"Then please stop taking such risks."

"May I presume to inquire if you wish me to avoid risks?" he queried satirically.

"Yes, you may presume," she flared, and the flush on her face decidedly deepened.

"But why? I cannot conceive of a girl with your peculiar tendencies—"

Just then Jim and Sue entered the room to end an exchange that once more was headed for danger.

13

ANDREW BONNING had tackled a man's job—sawing wood. He had a notion to recommend to all college football coaches the unlimited possibilities in a bucksaw as an infallible test of an athlete's stamina. The huge pile of driftwood that Andrew had snaked up from the river bottom showed little inroad for all his labors. It seemed to require hours to reduce one hardwood log to firewood.

As an occasional relief from this back-breaking labor, Andrew packed the sawn billets into his cabin. The long room was too big and the north wall did not keep out the wind. So he decided to stack wood solidly all the way across and up to the roof. This would serve a double purpose, first as a wind break, and secondly to furnish an ample supply of firewood for the winter season soon to come. Already he had learned to love a ruddy blaze in the open fireplace. What that would mean on bitter nights, when the gale howled along the eaves, he could well imagine. He must have a comfortable chair, a bright lamp, and plenty to read. He did not choose to spend all of his leisure hours in moodily staring into the embers.

Several times he had caught glimpses of Martha passing to and fro, on errands too obvious to deceive him, and the last time he had discreetly withdrawn into the cabin. When he went out again, he found her tugging at the bucksaw. She was wearing dungarees, top boots and a white blouse, and with her hair flying, she made a most distracting picture. He watched her, surprised to see that she was strong enough to pull the saw through the hardwood log. The extreme effort she had to put forth showed in the clench of her little brown hands, and the strain and bind of the slender figure. As she tired, the saw moved more slowly.

"Damn!" she ejaculated, giving up, quite out of breath.

"Vain oblations, Martha. You will never make a pioneer woman," said Andrew.

"Who are you to talk?" she replied. "You've been at it for two whole days, yet I can't see that you have accomplished very much."

"Take a look inside."

She did so, only to return and say: "Well, I guess you *have* worked. . . . Looks as if you meant to stay all winter."

"All my life, Martha, if I am big enough to deserve it."

She sat down upon a log and watched him for a while. There plainly was something on her mind.

"Andrew, what has got into Uncle Nick and Jim and Sue the last few days?"

He took care not to meet her questioning eyes and kept on sawing. "Well, it must be the contagion of my indomitable spirit. My nature not to give up. My unquenchable hope. My unabatable faith."

"Honest injun, Andy? Are you really like that?" she asked, momentarily deceived.

"I wish to God I were."

"But Uncle is really much better. He's being almost cheerful. And as for Jim and Sue—they're certainly up to something. I hear them whispering, laughing. Sue is packing a grip for Jim. He's going some place. I asked him, but he put on an innocent air of surprise. What's come over them?"

"Come to think of it, I have noticed a tendency to cheerfulness," replied Andrew, resting an elbow on his saw.

"Tendency, my hat! They're happy now, and they weren't a week ago. . . . Andrew, this scarcely applies to you; I can see *you* are still feeling your customary grumpy self."

"Me? Oh, sure. I can't be any other way."

"I could forgive Jim and Sue, but never you," she said darkly.

"Forgive? What on earth for?"

"I don't know. But if there was any tiny little hope for us—and *you* knew about it and kept it from me I—I'd hate you even more than I already do."

"There is always hope for good people."

"Good people don't need hope. It's bad people, like me—and you."

Andrew shook his head and went on sawing. Martha would find out sooner or later. He sawed through the log. Martha picked up the blocks and carried it into the cabin. She remained a considerable while. Upon her return she said: "That's really a lovely big room. If you fixed it up, it'd be simply darling."

"I like it the way it is now."

"But it's so bare. You ought to clean it, stain the logs, hang curtains instead of bony old horns, put in some nice solid furniture and rugs. Oh, I could make it cosy and warm and bright."

"I dare say you could—for some girl. But unfortunately for me there is no girl. I'll make out somehow with my pet squirrels."

"You might send for Connie," she said mischievously, but as he ignored her remark she went on: "Are the squirrels really pets?"

"Yes. They run over my bed."

"Excuse me! I'll bet you have mice and snakes, too. Primitive stuff! You are a kind of a cave man, at that, aren't you Andrew?"

"I believe I reacted to some such instinct once with you. . . . Once was enough."

"Why?"

Andrew declined to answer. The girl was an enigma. Nevertheless, how much better this mood of hers than one of indifference or of hostility! He would not distrust her again, be she as infinitely various as the winds. He was beginning to have another and most disturbing suspicion, and it was that this mood of hers was a sincere one.

"Are you going to work all day?" she asked petulantly.

"Certainly I am."

"But you don't get paid for it. . . . I should think you'd want to loaf a little."

"Work is my one salvation."

"Oh! you confess then to being a sinner? . . . Gives me a kind of sisterly regard for you."

"Martha, I never knew what work really was until I got out West. It's great," he said, and spread out his big, strong, brown hands for her to see.

"What kind of work did you do after leaving college?" she asked curiously.

"I tried office work."

"I'll bet you were no shining success."

"Certainly I was a complete failure."

"I worked in an office for almost two years, and went to the university besides," she said casually.

"Indeed? Tell me about it."

"You'd be interested only in the formals, and the boys who were chasing me for dates between times. And there were hardly enough kicks in that to intrigue you."

"Kicks! I wonder where I heard that expression before?"

"This conversation is getting nowhere fast," she said, getting up. "You just saw wood and say nothing—at least nothing intelligent."

Andrew rested on his saw and ventured to look at her.

"Martha, why all this preamble?"

"Andrew, will you drive me into town?" she asked.

"Can't you go with Jim and Sue?"

"Uncle is going with them. They'll have the car full. Besides, I can't stand Jim's driving."

"Take my car. I guess it'll hold together for another trip."

"You won't drive me, even when I ask you as a favor?"

"But I have so much work to do. The ranch ought not be left completely alone. And—"

"Please, Andrew?"

"Well, all right, if you insist."

"Thanks," she cried eagerly. "The Earnshaw girls are giving a party tonight and I'd like to go. They're nice. . . . Will you take me, Andrew?"

Taken quite by surprise, he dropped the bucksaw, and while stooping to recover it he asked: "Why do you ask me—when you've a dozen admirers who would jump at the chance?"

"They've overdone the jumping, Andy," she returned, averting her eyes. "Same as I overdid—my fun. . . . I don't see why you and I can't be friends. Platonic friends, you know."

"There is no such thing as Platonic friendship. . . . Besides you are forgetting that you hate me."

"I—I don't exactly hate you now, Andrew. Of course, I don't love you—but—"

"Listen. Will you please stop harping on that? I *know* you don't love me. You told me. And once was enough."

"All right. All right, But, will you take me?" she pleaded, coming close to him.

"Very well, Martha, I'll be glad to escort you if you really want me to. When do you wish to go into town?"

"Right away," she said, glad-eyed and eager again. "Andrew, you're really awfully nice. You're so dependable. I was rather afraid to ask you. I wish you—you—that you could look on me as a—a sister. Then it'd be so—so nice to have a—a brother to ask favors of, without his wanting to marry me or something for my pains."

"Well, Martha Ann, even though I can't qualify as a brother, I can try to be agreeable."

"Oh, Andy, I'm truly sorry I can't love you the way you want me to," she said, and her voice sounded sad. Then she stopped. "There I go again. I'm the limit! But it's all the fault of you men. You never seem satisfied just to be friends. . . . I'll rustle and get ready while you get out of those overalls. I've a new dress, a lovely blue. Bought the goods and made it myself. Out of the money you paid me back! . . . But I'll have to shop a little today. You can pick me up at Glemms' before supper. I don't want to stay there. You can take me to that Mexican café where they have such delicious fried chicken. Then we'll go to the movies—there's a Western—and after that I can dress for the party. Is that all right?"

"I am entirely at your disposal," he replied, with an exaggerated bow.

"Still you're not smiling. Won't you get even a little kick out of it, Andy?"

"I suppose I will. Another jealous kick under the slats."

"Andrew Bonning, if you love me—as you swear you do—and if you are *with* me you ought to make an effort to be happy whatever I am, do, feel or say," she announced regally, with her head held high.

"My back's too stiff, or I'd get down and kiss your feet," he retorted. "I'm sure you're razzing me. . . . The funny thing, Martha, is that I shall be glad to be with you—whatever you are, do, feel or say." She saw that he was quite in earnest.

"Funny?" she asked with a doubtful smile, and suddenly reached out and gently touched his arm. "I love it when you're being funny." Then she ran toward the house, calling: "Rustle now. Get out your old bus."

As it turned out, if either Martha or Andrew had had expectations of anything romantic taking place on the ride into town, they were disappointed. For the rancher, at the last minute, elected to ride with them, which meant that what was to have been a twosome laden with all sorts of possibilities became a sedate threesome.

Not improbably this bore upon the young lady's mind, for after a while she stopped babbling and fell pensive.

"Andrew, let me drive," she begged after they had gone a short distance. And once seated at the wheel she sped up the ancient car until Mr. Bligh first cautioned and then importuned her to slow down. As for the vehicle's owner, he did not care how fast she drove; if they skidded over the bank into the river or wrapped the machine around a tree, at least he would be with her. To such a sad pass had love reduced him!

"I'll get out at the Glemms'," said Martha Ann, as they entered town. The car drew up in front of the Glemms' and she gathered up a large parcel, her bag and hat, and received her jacket from Andrew. As she stepped down, she gave him one of those quick nods of her head which were always so disconcerting. "You'll come for me about five?" she asked as seriously as if it were of very great importance to her.

"Okay. Unless I get pinched by my friend Slade," replied Andrew.

"If you have to punish another of my admirers, won't you please wait till tomorrow?" taunted Martha Ann.

"Miss Dixon, if I *have* to lick someone, it will be the first person wearing pants that I see with you," he retorted.

"Andrew, you and Martha seem to be speaking to each other, at least," remarked Bligh, drily.

"Yes. It's encouraging. . . . Where shall I drop you, boss?"

"Wal, I want to see Jim before I look up anybody, especially McCall. . . . Jim has got me all haywire with his hints and hunches."

"Me, too. Has he given you any facts?"

"No, except that he is goin' to Arizona in the hopes of raisin' money for me. I didn't take him too seriously at first. But I can see that he's got somethin' up his sleeve."

"I'll say he has. Trust him, Mr. Bligh. And no matter what McCall has up *his* sleeve, you discount it. I want to be with you today when you meet him."

They went up one side of the street and down the other, at length locating Fenner on the outskirts of town near the stockyards. He was talking to a Westerner named Stanley, whom Andrew knew by sight. Stanley was proprietor of a shady poolroom and rooming quarters for cowboys. He also ran a feed store and livery stable in connection with a large corral.

"Fenner, I can have the pick of them hosses hyar in ten days," Stanley was saying, as Bonning followed Bligh out of the car.

"Jim, are you hoss-tradin'?" queried Bligh with a laugh. "Give me a minute. Then I'll run along an' you can—"

"Hell!" ejaculated Fenner, looking with sharp eyes beyond Bligh. "McCall! An' it's a safe bet he's run you down."

Andrew wheeled to see Sheriff Slade and a short wide-shouldered, large-headed man get out of a car. Andrew would not have recognized in the smug, coarse features the McCall he had spied upon that memorable night of his arrival in this town.

"Howdy, Bligh. Was on my way out to your ranch when someone said you had come in," spoke up McCall sharply.

"How'd do," returned the rancher curtly, and nodded to the sheriff. "Just as well, I was on my way to see you."

"Good. We'll settle this deal pronto," said McCall, his light steely eyes glinting. "Come into Stan's place here, where we can be alone."

"Right here will do. An' I'm not talkin' any more business without a witness on my side. Fenner's my foreman, an' this is Andrew Bonnin'."

"All right," snarled McCall. "Are you goin' to settle?"

"Not on the terms you stated."

"There ain't any other terms."

"Then we're stuck," replied Bligh stubbornly, spreading his hands.

At this juncture Andrew heard a jingling, slow step behind him and felt a slap on the back. Texas Jack had evidently come out of the poolroom to join the group. The cowboy had been drinking, yet he appeared quite sober, but ugly. Face and hair flamed red.

"Howdy, all. I reckon I'll jest have to butt in," he drawled in his cool, slow way. But his usual geniality had given place to a reckless insolence. His piercing, blue eyes fell upon Slade and McCall with unmistakable intent.

"Hyar, puncher, watch yore step or I'll run you in," blusteringly interposed Slade.

"Sheriff, you cain't arrest me for insistin' on my money. Mac owes me plenty an' I'm askin' fer it now. Heah's witnesses."

Andrew could see in a flash that a startling revelation was about to ensue which could mean a change in the fortunes of everyone present. Texas had chosen an opportune moment for himself as well as for Bligh. Fenner's nudge alerted Andrew. McCall eyed the cowboy with exasperation.

"I don't owe you any money, Tex."

"The hell you don't!" shouted the cowboy, moving in a little. He was slow and easy. Slade regarded him uncertainly, but the little rancher manifestly had no doubts about his mastery of the situation.

"Bligh, never mind this drunken puncher. He's looked on redeye till he's red all over. Once more I tax you. Will you settle with me?"

"No. Do your damnedest, McCall," replied Bligh, trembling with anger.

Andrew concluded that it was time to put in his oar, which he imagined might be something of a surprise to the greedy little bargain driver.

"McCall, would you settle for cash?" he interposed calmly.

"I reckon I would. But what's the sense of talkin' cash? Bligh hasn't got two-bits, an' you're only a windy tenderfoot."

Andrew stepped forward and slapped the rancher's face so hard that his head jerked back and his hat fell off.

"Take it slow, McCall," cut in Andrew swiftly. "Don't call names and don't jump to conclusions. I am Bligh's partner."

McCall stepped back, an angry tide of color flooding his face.

"Slade, arrest this feller," he shouted.

"Don't do anything so foolish," cried Andrew in disgust. "Slade won't arrest me, because I won't stand for it again. He may be your paid henchman, but he's not a complete fool."

The sheriff, who had made a threatening gesture, suddenly checked it when he saw a lightning-swift movement on the part of Andrew. He might have guessed that, before he could get his gun half out, he would be knocked down by a fist whose devastating weight he already had witnessed.

Fenner eased himself into the foreground. "McCall, fer a Westerner, you strike me as shore dumb. You're in a corner."

"You calf-rustlin' Texan!" exploded McCall furiously. "Have you gone an' framed me?"

"Wal, not yet. But I ain't so damned patient, either," drawled the cowboy.

McCall stared at Texas for a moment and then turned to Bonning. "Bonnin', I'll settle with Bligh fer one thousand dollars," he declared.

"You're a highway robber!"

"How much will you pay?" fumed the cattleman.

"Not a plugged dime. What's more, Mister McCall, you won't burn another Double X brand on one single calf of ours."

That seemed to be like waving a red flag in the face of a bull. Andrew had seen his advantage and meant to push it.

"Mister Easterner, the Double X outfit is mine. An' thet insinuation comes from this thievin' cowpuncher. To hide his own crooked tracks!"

"You're a liar, McCall," returned Bonning coldly. Several cowboys had collected in front of the poolroom during the altercation. A Mexican and a cattleman had lounged out of the feed store. All these spectators added strength to Bligh's cause. "You know you're a liar. But I can prove it."

"Slade, stop this damned rantin'," cried the irate cattleman.

"Stop it yoreself. It's directed at you," replied the sheriff testily.

"I won't stay hyar an' listen any longer. This Bonnin' has framed somethin' with his low-down redheaded puncher pard."

McCall waved his arm in passionate finality, and lurched into a stride that would take him away from the scene.

"Mac, better stick it out," warned Stanley.

Andrew leaped to grasp McCall's coat and spin the cattleman around. "Not so fast, McCall. You started this, and you'll see it through," he declared firmly.

"Slade, do you hear this fresh tenderfoot threatenin' me?" shouted McCall.

"Sure I'm threatening you. You stand your ground or you'll measure your length on it, and damn pronto."

Slade interposed a hand. "I'm advisin' you to hold yore hosses, Mac," he said hurriedly. "You're on the track of business, not a fight. An' I'm tellin' you, if this slugger nails you one, you'll think a mule had kicked you."

"Lost your nerve, hey, sheriff?" queried McCall in furious scorn. "Bluffed by a redheaded cowpuncher! *He's* the one you're 'fraid of. But neither he nor his pard can bluff me. . . . Now, Bonnin', I'm damn good an' fed up. I'll take a thousand dollars or take over Bligh's property."

"You'll take a stiff pole in your ugly snoot if you don't cool off. Who the hell do you think you are? . . . McCall, you don't represent this Wyoming community or the law. You can't scare me. I've got plenty on you."

"So you been hintin'! Wal, spit it out!"

"All right," replied Andrew rapidly, as he glanced around. "Stanley, get this, and you fellows also. . . . McCall, one night late in May, you went on foot out of this town. You met a mounted cowboy on the road, and the two of you left the road to talk without being seen. But you were seen. You leaned against a big rock and the cowboy sat his horse close by you. Somebody saw you, and what's more—heard you."

"Aw, hell! What you givin' me? Some cock an' bull stuff?" ejaculated McCall, angrily. But it was noticeable that the red of his face had faded.

"Somebody heard every damned word you and that cowboy uttered," continued Andrew. "And *I'm* that somebody. I had driven my car off the road behind a thicket. I saw you coming. There was something sneaky about the way you left the road. So I crouched down behind some bushes, not five good steps

from you both and I listened. I heard every word of that plot. Now how'd you
like to have me tell what you and the cowboy plotted to do in a courtroom?''

"Mistook your man, Bonnin'," replied McCall hoarsely.

"I heard your name. McCall. I saw your face when the cowboy lighted his
cigarette. I recognize you now.''

"Jest a frame-up to save Bligh," the cattleman muttered. But he was looking
down.

"No, it's not a frame-up. And if you don't want that story told in court, you
lay off Bligh."

"Bonnin', I ain't hankerin' fer lawsuits or gossip no more'n you. I deny thet
I was the man you seen. But such talk won't do me no good. I'm willin' to call
the deal off."

"Okay, it's off. We'll meet over at the hotel and draw up a little paper to that
effect."

"My word is good," growled McCall. He had perceptibly weakened and
grown restless toward the end of the interview.

Texas Jack flipped away his cigarette and elbowed Andrew aside to confront
the cattleman.

"Mac, yore word ain't wuth a damn!" he drawled. "I been layin' back heah
listenin'. An' now I say thet'll be aboot all the fixin' you fellers will do. Yore
deal with Bligh is off. But with me you can bet yore sweet life it's on!"

The insolent, cool-voiced cowboy manifestly had the power to infuriate
McCall.

"You're responsible for this holdup," he fumed.

"Ump-umm. I ain't responsible fer nothin' nor nobody but myself. Air you
gonna fork over my dough?"

"What you aimin' at—blackmail?"

"I ain't above aimin' at you, if you press me, Mac. Come across, you dirty
crook!"

"You never rode fer me, Texas Jack. I don't owe you anythin'. You been
drinkin'. Your head's muddled."

"Mac, you overlook what kind of a man you're up agin. I'm wise now.
You're a hawg, a two-bit greedy cattleman who hires grubline cowpunchers to
do this dirty work. . . . What're you gonna do aboot all thet Bligh stock we
ironed yore Double X on?"

McCall jerked up as if a galvanized current had coursed up his frame.

"Puncher, I told you I'd have none of your rustlin' deals," he shouted stridently, his thick neck bulging purple. "If you put my brand on Bligh's stock,
you did it on your own hook, by Gawd!"

"An' you deny you was the man Bonnin' saw meet me thet night?" queried
the Texan. "You deny he heahed you make *me* thet proposition? I was thet

cowboy. I agreed to brand mavericks fer you. I took yore message to a cowboy who'd agree to kill Bligh's cows an' slap yore brand on his calves. . . . An' we played yore dirty game. All fer nothin'?''

"You're lyin', Texas. You can't palm your thievin' off on me."

"McCall, you're wuss'n a thief."

"I'll blow your laig off—you lyin' redheaded calf rustler," roared McCall, his right hand going significantly to his hip.

The cowboy's brown hand flashed down and out. Andrew saw the barrel of a gun stuck against McCall's prominent abdomen.

"Don't move!" His voice was cold.

But McCall did move. It might have been mere nervous contraction or a further action to draw. He quivered. His crooked arm straightened. Then came a muffled report. Texas leaped back to cover Slade.

"My—Gawd! He's—bored me!" gasped McCall, his working visage distorting. As his big hands came around to clasp his abdomen, a gun clattered to the ground.

"Gentlemen, I call on you all," said Texas swiftly, "you are witness that he tried to throw his gun on me."

"Yes, we all seen thet, cowboy," replied Jim Fenner.

McCall sagged with blood pouring out between his fat spread fingers. Stanley put an arm around him.

"Help me get him inside. Somebody run for a doctor."

But Stanley had to support the wounded man alone. The other bystanders seemed waiting in horror-stricken immobility for Texas to shoot the sheriff. Certainly that individual seemed to express the same fear himself.

"Slade, thet's exactly what you'll get if you don't lay off me, now an' forever," said Texas, his voice cold and hard. "You represent the law, an' I'd respect thet if you wasn't as low-down as McCall yoreself. You was in with him. Smoky gave you both away. An' you're a bootlegger besides. We can prove it. Figger on thet when you spill yore case agin me."

He backed the sheriff up to the car that McCall had been driving.

"Get in an' make tracks," ordered Texas.

Slade half fell backwards into the car, and floundering over the wheel made haste to drive away.

Texas watched him out of sight. "Bligh, pick up thet gun, an' turn it in as evidence," he said, sheathing his own weapon.

"Good God, boy, you've played hob!" ejaculated Andrew, coming out of his trance.

"Wal, it was aboot time."

Andrew and Fenner followed the cowboy to where he had his horse haltered.

Texas mounted, and began to roll a cigarette. His fingers were steady. The pallor of his face and the magnificent blue blaze of his eyes had not changed.

"You fellers will have better luck now," he said. "Make shore you git them Double X calves back."

"How many, Tex?" asked Jim huskily.

"Aboot a hundred, mebbe more, I reckon. All on this side of the river, anyway." He gathered up his bridle and looked down upon Andrew with a ghost of his old smile. "Say so long to my lost sweetie fer me!"

Spurring his spirited bay he galloped out beyond the corrals, and headed for the open range.

"Same ole Texas breed," muttered Fenner, as if to himself, wrenching his gaze from the fast disappearing horseman.

"Well," exclaimed Andrew, fighting for a full breath, "how sudden it all was!"

They joined Bligh, and the other shocked spectators of the shooting, in the wide areaway of the feed store. McCall lay on the slanted planking. His pallid, clammy face and closed eyes, his low rattling gasps suggested a speedy, tragic end.

"About gone," said Stanley, rising from his knees. "I reckoned he wouldn't need no doctor."

"What can be done?" queried Bligh.

"Nothin' fer him."

"Isn't there someone to notify?"

"Slade was his only particular friend thet I know of," responded Stanley. "He shore vamoosed quick. Damn close shave for him, I'd say."

"Let's go up town an' see what Slade's figgerin' on," suggested Jim.

They proceeded to the hotel and made inquiries. No one there had heard of the shooting. Nor had it been reported anywhere around town. Finally they went to the sheriff's office.

"Howdy men, has McCall cashed?" Slade queried as they stalked in.

"Reckon so by now. He was goin' fast when we left," replied Fenner.

"Bullheaded fool! I told him not to rile thet cowpuncher. He brought it all on himself."

"Slade, we was witnesses, an' we'd like to know what will be expected of us?"

"Nothin' much thet I can see. Soon as McCall croaks I'll phone the report in to the Caspar authorities."

"Ahuh. An' may we ask what yore report will be?"

Slade leaned back in his chair. "As I see it, McCall an' Texas had some dealin's. McCall evidently would not pay money owed. They clashed, an' McCall went fer his gun first. But he was beat to it. Thet's my report, gentlemen. I'll advise against tryin' to catch the cowboy. It couldn't be done. An' I don't see any sense in repeatin' the peculiar circumstances. Do you understand?''

"We shore do, an' agree," replied Fenner. "But here's a stumper. What're we gonna do about them Bligh calves thet Texas an' Smoky Reed stole?"

"It'll be roundup time in two weeks. By then this will be blowed over. I'll probably have to settle up McCall's affairs, as I had dealin's with him. An' I'll see you get all the Double X stock on this side of the Sweetwater."

Without more ado the three marched out of the sheriff's office. Once around the corner, they halted to face each other.

"What do you know about that?" queried Andrew.

"You could knock me over with a feather," added Bligh.

"Plain as print. Our law-abidin' sheriff is scared stiff," snorted Fenner.

"Jim, our luck has changed. Mr. Bligh, the worst is over," said Andrew feelingly.

"It does seem so. We haven't lost everythin' an' we can begin anew. . . . Jim, you won't need to go off on that mysterious errand."

"Wal, I'm started now, an' I'll jest keep agoin'," replied Jim cheerfully. "See you both later today. I've gotta talk hosses."

"I forget what I wanted to ask you," said Bligh ponderingly, and then as the Arizonian limped away he added: "Never saw Fenner like this before."

"Boss, as soon as I recover from the shock Texas gave us I'll be feeling sort of flighty myself," replied Andrew.

They separated, and Andrew went into a range supply store.

"I want to order a saddle," he said to the proprietor. "It must be a Mexican saddle with silver trimmings, bridle and spurs to match."

"They'll have to come from El Paso. Cost you plenty."

"How long will it take to get them here?"

"Inside of two weeks."

"Okay. I'll pay a deposit. Here are the specifications."

Andrew went out of the store conscious of the strangest emotion—a melancholy gladness following hard on the terrible excitement he had just labored under. He was on his way back to the hotel when he ran into Martha Ann. She was carrying an armful of bundles. Above the armload her flushed face, piquant and sweet, beamed upon him.

"Hello. I've blown my last red cent. . . . Andrew, you're pale! What's happened?"

"Let me pack that truck for you," he replied as he relieved her of most of the load. "Which way are we going?"

"Glemms. . . . Why do you look so?" she returned very quietly.

"I've had a little shock. It'll be bad for you, too, I fear. Brace yourself a little, Wyoming Mad."

"Uncle!" she cried.

"No. He's okay. It's just—bad news."

"You?"

"Well! If it were? I wouldn't expect you to look like—"

"Andrew, tell me," she insisted.

"Texas Jack shot McCall," replied Andrew. "We met him over here, and during the argument Texas bobbed up from somewhere. To be brief, he took the argument out of our mouths. McCall owed him money. Texas wanted it. They fell into hot talk, believe me. Slade, the sheriff, was with McCall. Then I saw my chance and butted in. I told McCall what I had on him, and that we would not give him a dime. Apparently I scared him, bluffed him. He withdrew his claim on your uncle, and—"

"Oh, Andrew, how perfectly splendid of you!" interrupted Martha Ann. "But this shooting—tell me quick."

"Well, Texas went after McCall again. This time it looked bad. Texas asked McCall what he was going to do about the Bligh calves he had put the Double X brand on. That precipitated hell. McCall accused Texas of putting up a rustling proposition to him, in fact, tried to lay the guilt on Texas when it was his own. Texas called *him* the thief. McCall, the idiot, tried to draw his gun. Then Texas bored him."

"Is—McCall—dead?"

"By now he is, surely."

"Oh, how dreadful! . . . Did Slade arrest Texas?"

"He did not. I thought for a few moments he'd get it, too. I was so paralyzed I couldn't open my lips to beg Texas not to kill him. But that cowboy was cool and calm as Christmas. He told Slade the plain facts and that he'd get the same if he didn't lay off. Then Texas ordered Slade uptown, and took to his horse and the range."

"He got away?" queried Martha happily.

"I'll say he did. But before he went he gave me a message—"

She turned to catch his arm. Her face was pale and her eyes dilated.

"Andy! You're—implicated? . . . You will be held?" she whispered.

"No, my dear. Don't rush at conclusions," he quickly replied. "It was self-defense. McCall tried to draw. Texas shot him. That's all there was to it. Slade has reasons of his own for not pressing the case. Your uncle is free. He'll get his stock back. It has been a pretty strenuous day for us, but also very rewarding."

"Oh, I—I can well understand. . . . Wait for me—please," she replied, and taking her parcels from him, she hurried into the Glemms' home.

While Andrew waited, he reviewed the girl's reaction to the news. All he succeeded in settling was the absurdity of his own hope. Naturally she would be disturbed for Texas' sake and for her uncle's, but that did not necessarily imply any intimate concern for the cowboy—or for him. Presently Martha came out, still white, with eyes dark with emotion.

"Take me somewhere," she pleaded.

"A ride? No, the movies would be better."

"Yes."

He observed that she clung to the sleeve of his coat and walked close to him, as they headed back to town. For the hundredth time that sense of her simple trust and her wistful youthfulness rushed over Andrew, rousing anew the longing to protect.

"Tell me, Martha. Do you care—very much—for Texas Jack?" he asked earnestly.

"Care? What do you mean?"

"Do you love him?"

"Andrew! Don't be ridiculous. I liked Texas. Who wouldn't like him?"

"Then why do you take this thing so hard?"

"He killed that McCall for our sakes. For mine!"

"Martha, you're being ridiculous now. Please be reasonable. It was an old grudge."

"You be reasonable, too! Texas was a rustler. I caught him in the act. That day, you remember? I promised I'd never betray him if he'd let that be the last time he stole. He gave me his word, and he kept it. I know. . . . One day not long ago I told him how McCall was hounding uncle, and was going to ruin us. . . . Andrew, what do you think that wild Texan said to me?"

"I've no idea, but I'll bet it was something original," replied Andrew.

"He took his cigarette out of his mouth and smiled at me, and in his lazy southern drawl he said: 'Sweetie, look heah. I'm gonna pic a fight with McCall an' shoot the gizzard oot of him!' . . . Those were his exact words. I'll never forget."

"Well! What did you say to that, Martha?"

"I coaxed and scolded. But it was no use. Finally he said: 'Listen, honey. You don't savvy us western *hombres* yet. If you was in love with me, or if there was any hope you ever might be, I'd let McCall off an' go straight. But you don't, darlin'. An' so it's all day with thet graspin' rustler!' "

"Ah! I see through it now," cried Andrew. "Tex could have bluffed McCall. But he forced the issue. Lordy! The crazy loyal, sacrificing idiot! He never thought that his act would make you unhappy. . . . Martha, he sent you a message by me."

"What?"

" 'Say so long to my sweetie for me!' "

" 'So long'? . . . Good-by forever! That's what he meant. It hurts me a little,

Andrew. . . . He was in love with me and I laughed at him.'' She halted in the center of the sidewalk, to gaze up with tear-wet, tragic eyes at Andrew.

"Come on, dear. Don't cry right here in the middle of the street. Be a good sport, Martha Ann, and try to be on the level, too. You never tried too hard to keep the men from loving you—now did you?''

"I never tried to make but *one* love me,'' she answered resentfully, turning aside.

"Martha, all women are loved at least once in their lives by one man. Some women are loved by more than one, and some by many. That is your case, Martha. It is because you are beautiful and because you are lovely. You look at a poor sap once—and presto! He is lost. It is nothing you feel or really want.''

"Oh, so you have changed your mind about me?'' she asked. "I'm not really a flirt, then?''

"I told you before that I had misjudged you.''

Inside the theater, after they had found seats in the dimly lighted place, Martha slipped her hand to Andrew's sleeve, and down to touch his wrist with the lightest of fingers, and on and on, until she had her hand in his. It was a cold little hand, and it was trembling. Andrew simply held it and pressed it warmly. If in these childish moods, when she seemed to need father, brother or friend, he would do his best, silently, without making any more blunders. She sat through the whole picture without speaking. When they reached the street, once more the colored lights were blazing along the sidewalk.

"Andrew, I don't want to go to that party tonight,'' she said.

"I dare say it wouldn't be much fun, considering.''

"Please take me to that Mexican café. After supper we'll go home with Sue and Uncle.''

The October days came, Indian summer days, hazy, purple, melancholy. A hush lay over the land. Nature seemed quiescent, waiting. Wild ducks lingered on the river; the willow leaves fell yellow and sear, to carpet the ground.

It was Andrew's favorite season. Often during his work he would pause to gaze down the gold-bordered river, out to the gray-bleached range, and on to the white-mantled peaks. And he would realize that the time and place suited him, that loneliness and solitude had claimed him for their own. His range-riding had, for the time being, been abandoned; and his work consisted of the various tasks around the ranch and his cabin that he could lay a hand to.

Andrew missed Jim. The Old Arizonian rang true as steel; still in his kindly and persistent mania to throw Andrew and Martha into each other's arms he had kept open a wound that would not heal. A few days after Jim had gone, the long-conceived plan of becoming a rancher and Bligh's partner had begun to lose its zest. All that was left was the satisfaction that the old man had been saved, and therefore that Martha Ann would be happy, too.

That last trip to town had supplied the final revelation that had quieted all his doubts about Martha. He had been wrong about her; and the truth was devastating. Probably Martha Ann had not the slightest idea there had ever been a battle for her soul. But Andrew knew it; and he would have liked to communicate his infinite gladness to this girl's mother. Martha had been deeply involved in her problem to get away, to be free from something like a deadening lichen on her heart, to discover the lure of new places, new faces, to yield to the unsatisfied longing for adventure, to seek and to find she knew not what. But Andrew understood it now, to his sorrow. Without a friend or protector this valiant young woman had set out alone on the highways, trusting in her belief in people, in life, in the future. Freed of her passionate intent to hurt as she had been hurt she had reverted to the gay, wistful, fun-loving, whimsical and curious girl that he in his cynicism and jealousy had failed to understand.

For days after Texas Jack's coup, which had made him an outlaw and had saved Martha's uncle, she was somber-eyed and unhappy, as if she might have been partly responsible for bloodshed and ruin, even though out of that good had come for her. But the spell passed. She was too young to be permanently affected by an act of violence that she had not witnessed. In a short time she was her happy self again. Life was good and she lived it to the full. She had found something she had risked so much to seek. She worked, she played, she sang, she was the life of the ranch. She rode often, but never far from home. She did not go to town, though she was sought and importuned by her friends there. On Sundays the place was overrun by the young people with whom she had become so popular. Her erstwhile severest critic, Andrew, however, could find nothing amiss with her deportment.

As for Andrew, during those pleasant Indian summer days, he found that his old cynicism was gone, and he thanked God for it. It had been love that had burned it to ashes, even though a love that appeared to be unrequited. Nevertheless his gratitude to her was infinite. In the East Andrew's sister and sweetheart had been thorns in his flesh. He had wanted them to be different from their class. They were independent, imperious, demanding, making playthings of men and never to be wholly won. They were victims of the age. But Martha Ann represented another type of womanhood, one that Andrew had not believed existed. There might be—there must be—many, many girls like Martha. He was glad to have found this new American girl, even though, for his own happiness, he had found her too late. Andrew had loved his mother, his sister, many girls, all that was feminine. And though he had lost his one chance of perfect happiness, he had gained the knowledge that girls actually existed who, like Martha, could be free and unspoiled and altogether lovely.

14

"FOR the land's sake!"

Sue's familiar exclamation, that always indicated a real reason for excitement, came trenchantly to Martha Ann's ears.

"Now, Sue, what's come off?" she called.

"Martha, if things don't stop comin' off around here, I'll go plain loco."

"Let me join you in loco land!" cried Martha gleefully, and ran from her room.

Sue had gone out of the kitchen leaving the door open. Martha discovered her in the yard, arms akimbo, gazing spellbound at a boy and a horse. The former did not appear to be anyone so unusual as to cause Sue to react so violently. Martha shifted her gaze to the horse.

"Oh!" she cried out, her eyes lighting up in admiration.

The horse was mottled buckskin with long black mane and tail, a graceful body, racing limbs and a most beautiful spirited head. There was a halter around his neck which he did not seem to like at all. The boy held it in one hand while with the other he brushed the glossy arched neck.

"Prettiest bit of hossflesh I've seen in ten years," said Sue fervently. "Like the mustangs we used to see in Arizona. Navajo ponies, black as coal, with white manes an' tails. Or Piute pintos with moon eyes! . . . Say, boy, what's the idear fetchin' him heah?"

The lad appeared to be about sixteen, a tanned, ragged youngster whose face was familiar. He smiled at Sue, but did not answer her.

"Whose horse? Why did you bring him here?" cried Martha Ann. "Oh, he's adorable! . . . Whom does he belong to? Where'd he come from?"

"Wind River Valley. Colorado sire. Them Colorado folks breed the bloodinest hosses in the West," replied the lad enthusiastically.

"He's the most beautiful pony in the whole world. Oh Sue, I never dreamed of such a horse. I'll buy him if I have to pawn all my jewelry. Boy, is he for sale?"

"I reckon not. You see he couldn't have been bought at all 'cept the girl who rode him died, an' her folks couldn't bear to see him around."

"But who owns him now? . . . Sue, I'll have him—if I have to—marry his owner."

"What's his name?" asked the more practical Sue.

"Buckskin."

"Who owns him?" almost shrieked Martha Ann.

"Wal, accordin' to my boss, Stanley, he was bought fer another girl," replied the boy.

"Who? What's he doing out here? Some one of those town girls showing him off—to make me miserable!"

"Name is Martha Ann Dixon."

"Me!" called Martha faintly, and sat down on the kitchen bench.

"For the land's sake! . . . Some of thet Jim Fenner's work. Martha, he was shore actin' queer before he left. . . . Boy, who sent him?"

"My boss, Mr. Stanley."

"An' how come?"

"Wal, all I know is thet Jim Fenner picked Buckskin out of a thousand haid an' sent him by cowboys with some other hosses. Buck arrived yestiddy, an' the saddle this mawnin'. So my boss sent me right out. Buck shore hated bein' led out by an old Ford, but he acted decent. He's shore a dandy pony."

"For—*me?*" gasped Martha, rising with bells ringing in her ears. "Boy, if this is a joke—I'll murder you."

"Fact, Miss. Look heah, yore name's on the tag." He stepped to the car nearby and lifting out a large package wrapped in brown paper he deposited it on the ground before Martha. "There."

"It's my name, all right," cried Martha incredulously. "Oh, dear, I *am* going loco, too. . . . But, Sue, I always believed in fairies. I never stopped playing with dolls. . . . I never grew up. This is a dream and I'm Alice in Wonderland."

"Lass, it 'pears to be true thet Jim sent the mustang an' this package," said Sue. "He's made some kind of a deal or trade. Mebbe gone deep in debt. You was always wantin' a nice hoss so bad. Wal, he's shore done it up brown. . . . Boy, help me open this pack."

Timidly Martha Ann took the halter, and then recalling Jim's advice never to be afraid of a horse she drew closer to Buckskin, her heart in her throat, and put a slow gentle hand on his neck. He threw up his head spiritedly and his fine dark eyes seemed to say: "Well, who are you? And what are you going to do about me?"

He pranced a little, until Martha drew him down, and he trembled under her hands, and finally surrendered to her soft voice and caressing fingers. When at length he rubbed his nose against her, then Martha gave way completely to her rapture. "Oh, you darling horse! Oh, you Buckskin! I adore you!"

"For the land's sake!" ejaculated Sue for the third time. "Martha, look heah! There's been a holdup, or a fire. This is all Mexican stuff, an' the finest ever."

"Oh, Lordy! What is it all?" asked Martha Ann, and gaped helplessly at what appeared to be a pile of shiny black, silver ornamented leather.

"Double-cinch saddle with tapadoros, bridle, spurs. All silvermounted. An' two Mexican saddle blankets.''

"Simply gorgeous! . . . But, Sue—''

"Shore. I'm stumped. Must have cost a lot of money. Finest of Mexican stuff. Been used some, which makes it all the better.''

"Where'd he get the money?'' faltered Martha Ann.

"Gawd only knows!''

Just then Andrew came striding across the road, his dark eyes alight, a smile on his usually stern face.

"What's doing? . . . Glory! What a pony! . . . And black saddle, bridle. . . . Martha, have you gone back to one of your old tricks?''

"Andrew, don't make fun of me *now*,'' she wailed. "Is it true? Do you see what I see?''

"Well, I see a wonderful little mustang and the swellest saddle and trappins I ever laid my eyes on.''

"Where did Jim get them?''

"Let's look. . . . Saddle marked Yaeger, El Paso. Yaeger? He's the most famous saddle maker in the West. . . . So Jim sent these? Well, I'll say that's fine. Martha, I'm tickled for you.'' His dark eyes shed a warm light upon her and his voice was rich with pleasure.

She tried to transfix him with accusing eyes, though at that moment she would have forgiven her worst enemy. "Andrew, did you lend Jim the money?''

"Me! . . . Absolutely not, child! . . . But don't distress yourself with where Jim got these gifts. Be happy with them.''

"Happy, when we are so hard up!''

"Martha, to me this seems like a sign of better days to come. Let's take it that way. . . . Go change to your riding togs. I'll saddle the mustang for you.''

Martha rushed to her room in a state bordering between tears and rapture. "He was *glad!*'' she whispered, as her hands flung things about. "I have never seen him look so glad.'' And the hot blood flooded her cheeks.

When she emerged from the house presently, Buckskin stood there saddled and bridled, with a bit of the bright saddle blanket showing. For anyone who loved a horse he was perfect.

"Don't stand staring. A horse is for riding,'' cried Andrew. "I wonder if he'll give you the flying mount. . . . Well, I'm a son of a gun! Martha, he's kneeling for you.''

To Martha's amazement and glee, Buckskin bent a knee and let her step into the saddle.

"A horse that'll do that will never pitch. Put him through his paces, Martha.''

She rode off into the grassy open pasture. The rest was pure enchantment.

That night, as usual, after dark Martha Ann slipped out of her room, careful not to let Sue or her uncle hear her. A cold wind blew off the range, and she needed her warm coat. The stars were all out, though there was no moon. Keen-eyed and vigilant she crossed the open to the river bank, and glided along the rim in the shadow of the trees. A pale gleam of water shone out of the darkness. The few remaining dead leaves whispered. Wild dogs of the range, as she called the coyotes, were making the welkin ring. For several nights she had been keeping this stealthy vigil, but tonight there seemed a subtle difference, and it must have had to do with the happiness Jim Fenner's gift had given her. That glorious ride had left her spent, rapturous. She was too happy, too strangely happy. For days and days Andrew had slowly drawn away, aloof, stern of lip, sad of eye, a lonely young man, a victim of his own pride, and of his firm decision, that if there were to be any change in the impasse between them, she would have to make the first move.

Martha stole like a stalking Indian under the tree whose branches brushed Andrew's cabin. Unseen, making no more sound than a cat, she glided to the wall and felt for the little peephole she had poked through a chink between the logs. The peephole had been made in the tenant's absence. Martha's heart always beat high during this act, her blood raced and her mind whirled between fear and delight. But before undertaking this nightly spying, she had been careful to ascertain just about when she might expect him to be sitting before his fire. So far she had succumbed to this temptation without suffering any embarrassment for her temerity. But trepidation always attended the moment that she glued her eye to the little peephole. More than once she had doubted the propriety of what she was doing, but—as she certainly meant to marry Andrew eventually it would not matter so terribly—. But that was always as far as she got and she always was hard put to it to stifle a giggle.

Andrew on this occasion sat in his accustomed place, in the light of the fire, his head bowed, his somber, piercing eyes upon the fire. How handsome, how chastened he looked! That bitter cynical line had left his lips. He was greatly mellowed. His face in this unguarded moment seemed infinitely sad. Martha Ann was jealous of the fire. What did he see in those flickering flames? Did the face of that vile Connie shine there, or the fair faces of other women he had known? But Andrew's eyes did not see the fire or the past. Had she but known, it was her own lovely face that he was seeing in those flames.

Martha tore herself away and silently walked through the frosty grass, back to the line of trees, and so across the open to the house and her room. She did not light either her fire or her lamp this night. She did not want to see her face. She knew that she was caught in her own toils. Undressing, she murmured her prayers and hastily got into bed to lie there with wide open eyes. And over again she repeated the same nightly refrain.

Andrew loved her. He was breaking his heart over her. The wrong he had done her in his judgment long had been atoned for. She knew beyond any passionate denial, any scornful needs of her pride and vanity, that he now knew her to be true. He had wanted to marry her believing her untrue to what he held the best in womanhood. And she had hated him for it. She had told him the truth, and from that very moment had recognized her real self.

The shame, the smart, the indignation he had caused her had eased away, as night after night she had witnessed his silently endured pain. But still she had not been satisfied. She wanted proof, proof of his misery, of his yearning, of his love. It had been unutterably sweet, this nightly vigil, this intimacy with him in his unguarded hours. The thing had taken a terrible hold on her. She had reproached herself, fought with her conscience, only to go back the next night to watch him brood over his lonely fire.

Martha Ann this last night was certain that she was being a spiteful, revengeful little cat. But she would have her due. And a voice whispered to her conscience, the greater his reward must be. That thought recurring oftener in these days, always filled Martha Ann with shame. She was lost as deeply as Andrew, though she would not face it. She would not have had his courage. The thing which consumed her now, and always denied the still, small voice, or froze the warm sweet tide, was the needful all-satisfying proof of Andrew's worship of her, of his will to renounce what his heart was not ready to renounce. She had to go on. She must watch him again and again, though she flayed herself, she must see more and more how he wanted her. And when the time came when she saw that he would have reached the end of his endurance—then—then—then.

"Then!" Martha whispered into her pillow. That night, as on every other night since she had begun this last mad prank, obeying this imperious need to look upon the forlorn face of the man she loved, she cried herself to sleep.

About noon on the following day Martha Ann was coming from the corral, which she had already visited three times to feel and pat and talk to Buckskin, when she saw a great cloud of dust up along the river road. She halted, nonplused. It could not be a storm for there was no wind. Then a low thunder of trampling hoofs and the bawling of a herd of cattle smote her ears.

"Of all things! Look what's coming," she cried, and mounted like a squirrel to the top bar of the corral fence. There she perched in the thrilled expectation of her first sight of a great range herd after the fall roundup. "Uncle Nick! Sue! Oh, Andy, where are you?"

Bligh heard her and ran out into the road, where he threw up his hands in excitement, and stood for a moment as if transfixed. Martha's shout was drowned in the oncoming uproar. Bligh ran to take refuge in the doorway of the house. Sue appeared from the kitchen to peer about as one bewildered. When she located the moving wall of dust she turned frantically as if to warn Martha. She ran to Bligh, and he pointed to where Martha was sitting astride the high corral fence.

The forefront of that herd appeared to be a mass of red and white cattle, of legs and horns moving through the rolling dust. It was not a stampede, as Martha had imagined, but the steady drive of a great herd, rendered frightful by the roar and bawl, and the cloud of yellow dust that swept onward with them. Like a cataract the left flank spilled over the river bank, the center came on squarely across the wide space comprising road and pasture, and the right, split by the house, sheered off across the range. Soon all the space between the house and Andrew's cabin was filled with bawling moving cattle. There were hundreds, thousands, Martha thought, steers and cows and yearlings and calves, a great herd on its way to the range.

It enveloped the ranch buildings and swallowed them up in the yellow dust pall, and rolled on past Martha Ann, leaving her excited and a little frightened, and choked and blinded by the dust. She kept her seat on the high fence, coughing, fanning herself with her handkerchief. The herd swept on and began to spread out over the range. The dust cloud blew away.

Then Martha Ann espied an odd, high-boarded wagon, drawn by two teams, and flanking the chuck wagon were five dusty riders on dusty tired horses. They dismounted before the house. The wagon stopped. The five men lined up before Mr. Bligh and shook hands. They talked. Bligh made gestures unusual for him. Sue ran in one door and out the other, wringing her apron, like one completely confused. Then Martha was startled to see four of the men turn to look in her direction, and then stalk toward her.

"Good heavens! What can these cowboys want?" she asked herself. "Where's Andrew? . . . Oh, well, let 'em come!"

Something about their leisurely arrogant bowlegged gait roused Martha's ire. They walked as if they knew that she could not help finding them irresistible. In fact they were, only she did not want them to know how she felt. As they approached she observed that they were older than the cowboys she had been accustomed to, a matured, rough, hard-bitten quartet. Moreover, they were dustgrimed from long riding. The one on the left was the tallest cowboy Martha had ever seen. He fairly towered over his companions and his sombrero was so huge that it made him look top-heavy. The one on the right was the shortest and oddest-looking cowboy that had ever come into Martha's view. He was so bowlegged that he never could have stopped a pig in a lane!

The pint-sized cowboy removed his sombrero with a sweep, to disclose a round red face, with black streaks of dust and sweat running down it, and the boldest, merriest, most mischievous eyes Martha Ann had ever looked into.

"Mawnin'," he said. "Air you Miss Martha Ann Dixon?"

"I guess I am," replied Martha dubiously.

"Mister Bligh said fer us to interduce ourselves to you," went on the cowboy pompously. "Thet tall member of us Four Musketeers is Tully Sloane."

The tallest cowboy promptly bared his head which was almost minus hair and shone like a polished nut. His face was thin and weathered, like Cordovan leather. He was so tall that his face was on a level with her knee. Martha liked his smile, but did not trust it. He had very clear, gray eyes that appeared to twinkle as he looked up at her.

"Howdy, Miss. I shore am glad to meet you," he drawled, and stuck out a hand as wide as a board.

"Thank you. I return the compliment," replied Martha, and gave over her hand to have it squeezed until she could have screamed.

"An' this hyar is our lady killer an' sport, Cash Tanner," went on the spokesman. And he indicated a handsome florid-faced man of at least forty years, large of frame, with a huge bow-shaped mustache and big ox-like brown eyes under bushy eyebrows.

"Miss Dixon, how do you do," replied this worthy in a deep, cavernous voice. "Don't pay no attention to Bandy. When you get to know me, wal—"

"An', lady, this heah is Sylvester Hay. He's shy—a gurl dodger from Montana," interrupted the short one, this time indicating a slim, superbly built cowboy, the youngest of the four, fair-haired and blue-eyed, with smooth unlined face just now betraying considerable embarrassment. He appeared to choke over his acknowledgment of the introduction. Martha Ann murmured her pleasure.

"An' I'm Bandy Wheelock," concluded the little man, grandiloquently, transfixing her with his merry, impudent eyes.

"Welcome to the ranch! How'do. And now what am I supposed to do?" said Martha Ann, divided between a desire to glare at him and to shout with mirth.

"Wal, fust off we gotta get acquainted," declared Bandy.

"That will be—lovely," replied Martha.

"Lady, air you free?" inquired the deep-voiced one.

"Free! I hope so. What do you mean?"

"Fancy-free an' unattached. 'Cause if you air—"

"Miss Dixon, I ain't pertickler," interposed Tully Sloane. "An' I'm gettin' my bid in pronto fer the dance thet's goin' to be give us soon."

"Thank you. I'll consider your invitation," rejoined Martha gravely.

"Wal, he was correct," said Bandy critically, running his bold gaze over Martha and back to her face. "She's the doggonedest, purtiest gurl I ever see."

Martha Ann blushed. This was being a little too sincere.

"May I inquire who has been flattering me?"

"Why, Jim, of course."

"Jim? Jim who?"

"Who else but Jim Fenner? He shore had us all het-up over you, Miss Martha."

"Jim Fenner! Do you know him?" cried Martha.

"Wal, I should sniggle we do."

"Where is he?"

"He come with us. Didn't you see him?"

"Where you from?" she asked weakly.

"Arizony. All of us 'cept Syl used to ride fer Jim, when he was foreman of the Hash Knife. But when thet outfit got shot up we scattered. Shore is a happy reunion fer us old timers."

"*Arizona!*" gasped Martha. "And this—cattle herd?"

"Wal, lady, we regret to state thet this stock ain't from Arizony. Jim picked 'em up down on the Medicine Bow, meanwhiles sendin' fer us to come pronto. We didn't let no dust collect."

"To come pronto?"

"Shore."

"To meet Jim?"

"Wal, Jim is shore some cow wrastler, but he couldn't drive twenty-two hundred haid of cattle alone."

"You drove them here?"

"Lady, them eyes of yorn don't look as if they could ever miss nothin'."

A light began to dawn in Martha Ann's bewildered brain. But for a moment her vocal powers were not equal to her curiosity. With a hand trying to steady her thumping heart she gazed down upon the four, from Bandy to Tully and back again. They stood at ease, warmly regarding her, already in their opinion personally and intimately known to her and happy because of it. Strong odors of dust and toil emanated from their soiled, shiny-leathered persons. The three older men packed guns in their belts.

"Whose cattle—are these?" Martha asked haltingly.

"Our new boss's, of course."

"*Boss!* Jim, you mean?"

"No. Jim's only foreman."

A loud halloo came from the house. Martha looked up to see Jim, her uncle and Sue, standing near the kitchen door. Jim was waving a gloved hand. Something about him seemed charged with importance. His lean brown face shone and his eyes were flashing.

"Lass, how you like our new ootfit?" he called.

Martha Ann leaped off the corral fence and ran over to the house.

"Jim! . . . Jim! . . ." she squealed, almost beside herself with joy. She hugged and kissed him. "Oh! but I'm—glad to see—you!" she panted. "But, what have you—put over—on me?"

"On us, Martha dear," interposed Bligh with strong feeling. He was pale and somewhat agitated. "All a surprise. I never dreamed this was what Jim left for."

"I told you that old fox had an idee," chimed in Sue. She was crying.

Martha Ann gripped the old Arizonian's vest with tight little hands. She shook him. "You've done it now! You deceiving, adorable wretch! . . . Are you a magician or a rustler? . . . Jim, is this herd ours?"

"Shore is, lass," he replied proudly.

"How did you get it?"

"Bought every darn hoof. Fer cash an' cheap. Shore is a bargain."

"Where did you get the money?"

"Andrew Bonnin'. He's gone in pardnership with yore uncle."

"An—drew?" faltered Martha Ann.

"I reckoned Andy would tell you. He wanted to surprise you. But I figgered he couldn't keep it from you."

"He—did. . . . Jim, where did he—get so much money?"

"Wal, he had it."

"All the time—since he's been here?"

"So he says. Lord knows, he's got me buffaloed. Sue swears he's a millionaire jest masqueradin' oot heah."

"So that's where my Buckskin came from?" whispered Martha Ann. "My Mexican saddle—my—"

"Lass, Andy made me promise not to give him away. But I can't lie to you. . . . There he comes now. Pitch into him, Martha."

Andrew came strolling leisurely from his cabin, his hands in his pockets, apparently quite cool and unconcerned over all the hubbub. Martha Ann knew that her eyes were dim with tears, but that could hardly account for a magnified vision of an Andrew Bonning whom she could not face just then.

"Folks, little Martha Ann'd better fade out of the picture—for a spell," she cried, and fled.

15

"Darling Mother," wrote Martha Ann, "since you have forgiven your naughty child I will be dutiful and truthful and tell you all that has happened to her in these last wonderful days.

"I wrote you about receiving the money, that I wasn't so happy, and couldn't think of coming home yet awhile. I hope I thanked you. Anyway I bought the sweetest dress and underthings with that railroad fare. But first I paid my hero's fine and got him out of jail, and then he paid me back.

"If you still love me and if you want me excruciatingly I will come home for the holidays—and bring *him*. You are all going to go loco—dippy, I mean, over my Andrew, and the girls who used to be so catty to me will be green with jealousy, and my old beaus won't ever again try to kiss me at the foot of the stairs in the hall—not after they see Andrew. To see him is enough. You don't have to be told that he was an end on one of the big college football teams.

"Mother, I'm so happy that I'm crying like a baby right now. And you know I never was the weepy kind. Uncle was just about ruined. What with cattle thieves (Oh, Honey, I caught one of them myself, and I *reformed* him, and he— but that's another story) and in a crazy deal uncle made with a rancher here, he lost nearly everything. I was ready to die. Uncle was down in the depths, like Father got when the bills used to come in. Then something strange happened. Jim Fenner, our man—he's an old Arizonian—left mysteriously for parts unknown, supposedly to try to raise money to save Uncle. Sue, that's Jim's wife and the dearest soul, suddenly perked up, and so did Uncle. Andrew, however, slowly and surely sank to the depths of despair. That was my doing, and had absolutely nothing to do with the ranch problem.

"I began to think that little Martha Ann had been so blue—so love-sick— yes, *love-sick,* herself that she would never be able to understand what was going on. I began to do a tall lot of cogitating. But for once I was on the wrong track.

"One day a boy came along with the most wonderful pony, and the most gorgeous silver-mounted Mexican saddle, bridle, etc. for *me*. I was dazed, then enraptured, then scared. Jim was fond of me, and I feared the old fellow had turned rustler or bank robber just to get me what I had yearned for so long.

"Then on another day along came a great herd of cattle, almost running over our house. They chased me to the top of the corral fence, where I nearly strangled with dust. When the herd passed, four cowpunchers appeared to face me up on my perch. Mother, they were the most thrilling, the toughest, the fiercest, the most enchanting, the funniest human beings I ever saw. At first they had me buffaloed (that means stampeded), and I'm afraid I was sort of upstage. They turned out to be old cronies of Jim Fenner's, when he rode the wild range in Arizona, and they had come with Jim, and had driven that great herd of cattle here for Uncle Nick.

"I was dumbfounded. I was thunderstruck—I was scared stiff. I couldn't understand it. Then Jim showed up to whoop at me. I tumbled off the fence and rushed to him. It all came out then. Jim had really bought the herd and sent for his cowboys—all for Uncle Nick! Andrew had supplied the money—thousands of dollars—and he and Jim had hatched the deal to surprise Uncle Nick and me. They darn near killed me of heart failure.

"Now, Mother, here's where we dig in, and try to get serious.

"I met Andrew Bonning on the night of May 13th at 7:35 on a lonely road. Some tramps had waylaid your not so dutiful daughter and one of them had collared me. I didn't have time to let out a squawk when up comes a Ford, out jumps Big Boy, and wham! that tramp must be falling yet. Well, it was 7:36 when I looked up at my savior and that moment was curtains for Martha Ann. I fell terribly in love with him right on the spot. But I didn't know it then.

"He gave me a lift. He took me for a wild little jayhawker, crazy to hitchhike the lonely roads to get kicks out of meeting men. Oh, Mother! I was sunk—and so mad that I saw red. He dropped me at the next town, and I know he hoped he'd never see me again. But I was crazy to meet him. Well, I did. Worse luck! I was picked up by a nice kid, was having a perfectly lovely time driving his car into a town, when all of a sudden I saw my rescuer. Oh, Mother! His eyes looked daggers at me. They said as plain as print that I had vamped this callow youth. I had a funny feeling around my heart. We met in the dining room. I don't know why I was so—so flip. But he infuriated me. He looked so disappointed in me. Well, for once in my life I flirted. I can understand now why girls like that line. But it was the only time I can remember that I ever tried deliberately, and I did it to prove to that big handsome prude that I was exactly what he took me to be. All the same, that night I cried myself to sleep.

"I went on my way. I had a wonderful time during all the rest of my hike, except for one horrible experience out of which I kicked myself—literally kicked myself free—the dirty bully—and which right there taught me the error of my innocent hitchhiking ways, and why Andrew was so absolutely right. This is hard to say, Mother honey, and I say it here for the first time, because I'll have to be on the level and say it to Andrew too. There are some things a girl simply cannot do. Spirit and virtue and religion and training—and *nerve* are not enough to see a girl through situations that she should never have gotten into. All this new woman, modern-century stuff is the bunk. Women cannot be as free as men. A girl is restricted—that is, a good girl—by her sex. She has a responsibility a boy does not have. She is the mother of the race, and if the race is to progress instead of retrogress, she has to hold herself more sacred than men do.

"How's that, Muth, for little Martha?

"Well, imagine! When I got to Randall at last, I found that Uncle Nick had moved way out into western Wyoming. I forgot to tell you that Andrew nicknamed me Wyoming Mad. I hated it—and very consistently ended by loving it. The blow nearly killed Martha. But I went on, and had the marvelous luck to get to Uncle Nick's ranch on the Sweetwater in less than two days, without hiking a step.

"Now brace yourself, old dear. Listen! I've already told you about Uncle Nick and the ranch. But not this. I hadn't been there an hour when I ran around a corner of the barn and plump into—Andrew Bonning. Right into his arms, in fact!

"He had become Uncle's hired man, working for his board. No accident! Not chance! It was fate, Mother, and it sure floored me. From that moment on we were at dagger's points. Then came a day when a horse pitched me off and I sprained my ankle. Andrew found me. He was kind, sorry, worried—insisted on helping me. But I was nasty—I didn't want him to carry me in his arms. But he did, and during that ride he kissed me. . . . Oh, dear! It was then that I found out I loved him madly. And that was where I started to backslide. I didn't want *him* to find it out. Things went on happening. I met young people; nice folk, wholesome Western girls, and some bad cowboys. They all took to me, especially the bad ones. Andrew came to the first dance I attended. That night I saw that he was no Missouri garage hand, as he had tried to palm himself off. He looked what he really is, and he danced my poor heart right out of my bosom. It has never come back.

"You couldn't expect your child to be anywhere without starting trouble. (Mother, I really ought to be married. I'm a menace to society.) It happened. Andrew caught me riding home with the cowboy cattle thief I told you I reformed. They were like a couple of gamecocks. Did they fight over me? Did they? They did. Andrew gave Texas Jack a terrible whipping. And then I had to go on my knees to Andrew to keep him from fighting the cowboy with guns. Another time at a rodeo (that's a cowboy circus) Andrew beat up four cowboys at one time because one of them had insulted me. Also he punched the sheriff on the beezer. Oh, Sir Galahad never had anything on my darling! This was when Andrew got arrested and I had to pay his fine.

"I flirted some more, Mother. I let the boys hold my hand, and once I let Texas Jack kiss me. If I had known then what I know now, I'd have let him hug me, too. All this when Andrew was in sight! To torture him! Because I knew by then how much he cared for me. All the same, Mother, despite my mad temptation to bring that proud boy to his knees, I did not lose my head over the other boys.

"At last my hour came. One night after supper Andrew called me out—and he—well, never mind what, except that he told me in as beautiful and manly and humble a way as any girl could ask, that he loved me, that despite disapproving of me he worshipped me, and he begged me to marry him.

"How I ever kept myself out of his arms, I have no idea. But I was a demon. I made him confess that he had thought me a vamp, a flirt, a necker, a—oh, almost everything that was bad—that he still thought so and would marry me in spite of it. To reform me! I told him honestly what I was and am. Poor

Andrew, that was a tough night for him. I thanked him for the honor and said I wouldn't marry him if he were the last man on earth. Like some royal lady I stalked away. But when I got in bed in the dark I thought I would die.

"That ended my play with the young fellows, and it was a relief, believe me. Since Andrew found out his blunder he has gradually gone downhill. I had my revenge. Little-souled as it seems of me it was sweet. Because, oh, how he had hurt me! And oh, how I loved him! I watched him. I gloated over his misery. I saw his heart breaking inch by inch. And all this while I worked, played, sang, made merry—I was a perfect angel. Mother, there is a sadistic streak in all women.

"Then came the unexpected—the thing that devastated me—that makes this letter to you possible—that bends the knees and bows the head of little Martha Ann. Andrew sent me that adorable pony—that magnificent saddle. But I was supposed never to know that they came from him. Only Jim could not keep the secret. Ah! but that old boy is a matchmaker!

"That was sweet of Andrew. But the noble thing, the great deed was for him to save uncle Nick and back him in a cattle deal that in this country is far from being a sure success. Jim and Sue imagine Andrew is a millionaire in disguise. I don't. I take him to be a boy of fine family, who came west for much the same reason as I. He had told me he had a little money. He never said how much, and of course I never dreamed that it was enough to save us and start us anew. Evidently it was.

"That's my tale, Martha Dixon, as uncle Nick calls you. The sequel is on the knees of the gods. I have yet to crawl to Andrew, to confess I loved him all the time—that when I swore I hated him I was a liar. Telling him will give me the greatest kick of all my life. This letter is my preparation.

"It would serve me right if he scorned me. I have a cold, sick feeling at the bottom of my heart when I think of it. But he, too, has found himself in this wonderful country. He could not change. He would not hate. He can only love.

"And so I dare to hope. I pray I do not hope in vain. You may be assured, dearest, best, most loving, long-suffering Mother, of your unworthy daughter's happiness—and through that the promise that she will be worthy. I will write again as soon as my fate is decided. But lest you distress yourself anew I give you my word here that I shall come home with Andrew for Christmas.

                                                         Martha Ann

"P.S. I think I'll steal unawares upon Andrew, when he is brooding before his fire, and slip in quietly and up behind him. Maybe I will plump right down in his lap. (I'll be pretty weak in the knees by then.) Maybe I won't have to, because if he is any good on earth he'll grab me.

M. A."

The night was dark and cool, with stars obscured, and a misty rain beating out of the north. Out there the open range gloomed like a vast windy hall, from whence came the bawling of cattle and the wailing of coyotes.

Martha Ann ran with light feet and lighter heart. Her hour had struck. It had been propelled by the long letter to her mother, and precipitated by Uncle Nick's startling news that Andrew thought he would go to California for a while. Never would Andrew Bonning leave for California without Martha Ann! She meant to make sure of that tonight.

A flickering light shone out of his window upon the bare boughs of the trees.

Martha Ann felt eager, cool, brave, happy to capitulate at last. But when she saw Andrew through the tiny aperture between the logs, all but her love deserted her. He was dozing in his chair, and with the mask off, his face appeared terrifyingly tragic and sorrowful. She had gone too far. Always too little or too much—she knew no happy medium! Was it too late? She must not lose another moment.

She drew back trembling. The cloak dropped from her head. She felt the cool rain drops upon her burning face.

Like a shadow she crept up onto the porch and tiptoed to the door. It was slightly ajar. She stood there, fighting for breath, in the grip of a strong sweet happiness that slowly replaced her terror. Her fingers shook when she flipped them inside the door. She opened it a little and glided in. The room was in shadow except for a ruddy circle before the forgotten fire. She smelled the pungent wood smoke. Andrew's dark head showed above the back of his chair. He stirred.

That broke the strain under which Martha Ann had labored. A shuddering gladness engulfed her. She had not lacked courage or strength, but she had not bargained for a failure of her heart, her breath, her thought, her sight.

She crept to the chair, laid a supporting hold upon it. She moved around beside him. Into his half-closed eyes came some change of perception, as if he were dreaming a dream. Martha Ann slid over the arm of the chair upon his lap, and as he started violently, she put an arm around his neck and hid her face from him. She felt him touch her, lightly, then with a hungry convulsive clasp.

"My God! . . . This is no dream," he cried hoarsely.

"No—Andy. . . . You wouldn't think so—if you'd had to do it," she replied quickly.

"Martha Ann!"

"Yes. I hope you were not dreaming of Connie."

"What? . . . Oh, you would! . . . Martha, you have come to thank me. Please don't! Don't!'' he begged.

"I haven't come for anything of the sort,'' she retorted.

He plied her with incoherent queries, all the time trying to raise her to the arm of the chair. But Martha Ann clung to him all the tighter.

"Listen, tenderfoot. Don't ask questions.''

"Good Heavens! Are you mad? Wyoming Mad! . . . What does this last mad prank mean?''

"What does this—mean?'' and she kissed him on the cheek. He sank back. All his rigidity left him. His hands fell limp to the arms of the chair. She felt a vast heave of his broad breast and she heard a thumping there.

"Martha, have you no heart—no conscience? . . . After all, are you only—''

She stopped that question with her lips.

"Andy, every time you try to question me I'll do that. . . . I have anticipated all your questions. I will answer them.''

She felt safe now. He could not see her face. She slipped her other arm around his neck.

"First. No, I have not come to torment you. Yes, I am terribly sorry I could not do this long before. No, I would not lie to you to gain the whole world. . . . Did I want a little revenge? I did. To my shame I confess it. I did—''

"For mercy's sake! Martha, do you love—''

"There! . . . I—I warned you,'' she went on shakily. The fire of his eyes—the response to her kiss had wrought their transformation in her. But she would see it through. "Yes. I do—love you! . . . Since thirty-six minutes after seven, on May thirteenth, I have loved you. First unwittingly. Then hopelessly. Then furiously. Then angrily. Then horribly. . . . And now, deathlessly, with all my heart and soul!''

"Oh, amber-eyes, my darling! . . . Are you just a wraith? Are you just that golden phantom I've been chasing—and trying to clasp—only to fail and fall and weep—''

"Again!'' she interrupted, to close her eyes and find his lips. "Oh! . . . I begin to doubt you. . . . All you want are kisses. . . . No, Andy, I am flesh and blood. Yours. . . . Yes, I—I will marry you. And be the happiest, luckiest girl. . . . Yes, I deserved your censure for my hitchhiking madness. It was a wild, desperate, perilous stunt. But I am glad, glad, glad. For it took me to you.''

"Wyoming Mad! You *do* love me after all—you *will* marry me?'' he cried rapturously.

"Once more! . . . I might just as well keep my lips close to yours!''

"When?'' he whispered.

"When what?''

"When will you marry me?"

"Andy, this *is* the last. . . . Oh, but I'm a little liar! How I have yearned to kiss you—to have you hold me like this! Don't imagine that you suffered alone, Andrew Bonning. That Connie dame. . . . When? When will I—oh, tomorrow—or next day—or next week—any day—if you do not put it off too long—and promise to take me home for Christmas—and never misjudge me again for being Wyoming Mad!"